# THE COMPLETE NOVELS
## AND
# SELECTED TALES OF
# NATHANIEL HAWTHORNE

# THE COMPLETE NOVELS

## AND

## SELECTED TALES OF

# NATHANIEL HAWTHORNE

EDITED, WITH AN INTRODUCTION, BY
NORMAN HOLMES PEARSON

## THE MODERN LIBRARY

### NEW YORK

MODERN LIBRARY EDITION, 1937

# CONTENTS

## From *THE SNOW IMAGE*

# INTRODUCTION

### *by*

### Norman Holmes Pearson

Although a century has now passed since Hawthorne's *Twice-Told Tales* first appeared before the American public, not even the changes of taste that have swept so many of his contemporaries from the affections of the people have done much to alter the admiration with which he has been read. A great deal of what flowered in New England now seems faded with the passing of time, despite the rare quality which it possessed and the extraordinary enthusiasm with which it was tended. But the pure beauty of Hawthorne's style and his deep perception of human nature have spread beyond the small region where he lived and over the years which separate his time from our own.

There was no truer child of the religious mood and the cultural heritage of New England. Most of Hawthorne's life was spent uneventfully there. He was born in the seaport town of Salem in 1804, and died sixty years later during a short journey from his Concord home. As an older man, his tales and most of his novels written, he spent some seven years in England and in Italy; but this late taste of cosmopolitanism came when he no longer needed it, or, at least, when he had already established both his approach to life and his manner of writing. He substituted the consulate at Liverpool for the custom house at Salem, the lichen of an English cathedral for the mosses of the Concord manse. The scene was altered, but he learned little that was new. This is not to say that Hawthorne knew all things about man and nature from his limited New England experience, but certain fundamentals he understood profoundly, and this understanding was expressed with a keener sense of the beauty of words and the cadence of language than any American had hitherto achieved. In Hawthorne, America had for the first time a writer of fiction for whom no apology was needed.

His life passed without much excitement. He did not, like Dana, round Cape Horn, the great jib flying to leeward and the fury of the waves breaking over the bow. He did not, like Melville, wander through the fragrant valley of the Typees with Fayaway, olive-skinned and flowergirdled, on his arm. He did not even stride the barren moors with dour Carlyle at Craigenputtock, as Emerson, his Concord neighbor, had. But as a boy he roamed the crooked streets of Salem, or, heels-up, lay outstretched upon the floor at home, reading Spenser and Bunyan and Milton, reading them again and again. He learned of the share his ancestors had had in the panic that seized Salem Village, when, near the close of the seventeenth century, witches had worried the minds of the villagers and pricked them into terror. He heard the old wife's tale of a curse hurled by the husband of a witch at grim Judge Hathorne. And he dreamed of the great inheritance of land that should have been his family's had deeds and titles been preserved.

The Hawthorne family was old, but it was not rich. Hawthorne's father had been a sea-captain and had died at Surinam. The log-book of one voyage of his father's ship *Herald,* from Boston to Madeira and the Indies, he owned when a child, and the report of the fight with a French privateer, in which the British *Cornwallis* was rescued, fascinated him. But his mind was more often ashore. For economy's sake, his widowed mother with her two daughters and her son left Salem for a time to live with her brother in Maine. There the boy went wandering through the woods about Sebago Lake with his uncle's dog, Watch, gunning for partridges and fishing for fat trout. "It was there," he said, "I first got my cursed habits of solitude." And later at Bowdoin College he still liked most of all to watch logs tumbling down the Androscoggin or to go bat-fowling in the summer twilight. Longfellow was in his class, but the two saw little of each other. It was not until years after, when Longfellow was an established author and Hawthorne was determined to be one, that they became in any sense friends. Longfellow was too elegant; and Hawthorne, when he took part in the life of the college, turned to the group which risked a fine to meet secretly at Ward's Tavern, or cut chapel, or gathered together for a little friendly gambling. He made friends, like Bridge, who later paid for the publication of the *Twice-Told Tales,* and Pierce, who as President gave him the Liverpool consulship; but usually Hawthorne remained aloof, preferring then, as throughout his life, to observe rather than to participate. He read enormously from the library of his college society, good novels by Scott and "that damned ranting stuff" of Neal and others' which he relished so much. At various times, with two or three other students, he donated to the library a set of Johnson, Percy's *Reliques,* a complete Swift and other volumes.

Even in childhood, Hawthorne had toyed with the idea of writing, and as he grew older an ambition to devote himself to literature was strengthened. Once his college life was ended he returned to Salem, where for over a decade he did little more than write. *Fanshawe,* published in 1828, was the first result, and although no one would call it a good novel, a great many in their zeal have made it out to be a much worse story of adventure than it is. It is full of Neal's damned rant and Scott's "racing and chasing o'er Cannobie Lee," which he used as a motto to one of his chapters. The setting is autobiographical though the events are not; and Hawthorne, not yet deep enough in the past to write *The Gray Champion,* nor mature enough to mold characters outside his own experience, seems to have derived more profit from Bowdoin in retrospect than in residence.

Hawthorne was always his own best critic; though he had paid for the publication of *Fanshawe* he withdrew it from circulation and tossed it to the flames. But he kept on writing. When in 1837 his next volume, the *Twice-Told Tales,* appeared, the toneless and awkward style of *Fanshawe* had been refined into a melodious and graceful delicacy. That Hawthorne should have turned from the writing of novels to a shorter form is not strange, for though he was not destitute, he still had to sell in order to live; and in an age when only the newspaper, the magazine and the annual flourished vigorously enough to support a native literature, a writer could not choose his form. It was thrust upon him, and Hawthorne, early in his career, wrote to an editor, "I have complied with your wishes in regard to brevity." Yet if ever a nation's failure to patronize its own literary figures ultimately resulted in some good it has been in America; for it is to this neglect we owe whatever we have contributed to the development of the short story. Thus Hawthorne kept his attention on the type of writing which he could sell and his eyes open for material to write about.

Not much is known about Hawthorne's life in the years immediately after college, and they have come, with his own romantic and somewhat self-conscious help, to be veiled in an air of mystery as pervading as that of his own tales. At times he travelled through New England; once westward even as far as Detroit. He was alert for detail to be jotted down in journals. "Think nothing too trifling to write down, so it be in the smallest degree characteristic. You will be surprised to find on reperusing your journal what an importance and graphic power these little particulars assume." This was the advice he wrote to a friend bound on a voyage to Africa; this was advice he followed himself on his cruise along Lake Champlain. Throughout the tales, and even later in his novels, these entries from his journals reappear. In *The Great Stone Face, The Great Carbuncle, Ethan Brand,* here and there, as though thrown in as ballast to keep his romanticism from floating away, these descriptive bits of realism can be found. Seated on a Berkshire stoop, Hawthorne chatted one evening with a filthy, one-armed soap-maker. " 'My study is man,' said he. And looking at me 'I do not know your name,' said he, 'but there is something of the hawk-eye about you too.' " Evenings at home in Salem, Hawthorne walked past the rich, white-pillared doors of homes he might have entered, sitting down beside the toll-gatherer, as the tin peddlers, the pickle manufacturers and the young girls strolled across the bridge or hurried by. He listened to the legends of the past from old women crouched all day over the kitchen fire, clicking their knitting-needles, or taking a turn at the spit; and in sending some of his earliest tales to a publisher in 1829 he wrote: "You will see that one of the stories is founded upon the superstitions of this part of the country. I do not know that such an attempt has hitherto been made, but, as I have thrown away much time in listening to such traditions, I could not help trying to put them into some shape. The tale is certainly rather wild and grotesque, but the outlines of many not less so might be picked up hereabouts."

What the life about him could not give, he got from books. In an

election sermon of the Puritans he grew to know the terror of the Black
Man better; from older histories like Cotton Mather's and newer ones
like Peter's *General History of Connecticut*; in English *Annual Registers*
and *State Trials*; in the newspapers and court-records of New England
he steeped himself until his intimacy with the past was worthy of a professional historian. Here his hereditary affiliation and childhood fascination coincided with the interest of a young and self-conscious nation and
a general literary fashion made popular by Walter Scott.

What Scott did not give him, however, and what he owed to his New
England heritage, was a sense of the depth and complexity of man's inner
life. The Puritan instinct, however it may have been expressed, was one
of honest and sober introspection. It penetrated the sham of man's exterior to his more animal nature beneath. It knew that man's heart is
better to be trusted than his lips, and this duplicity it attempted to lay
bare. All nature lay like an emblem-book spread open; each movement
had its own divine significance. The rush of wind, the roll of thunder,
the gentle springtime sun, equally showed the steady hand of God. Inextricably connected, divinely interwoven, was man with man and man
with nature. By Hawthorne's time the theology of Calvinism, which
armed the Puritan instinct, had largely disappeared. Hawthorne was no
Calvinist—he was not even a church-goer—but the Puritan instinct was
still his.

What his heritage made natural his early reading of Spenser, Bunyan
and Milton made literary. He saw the characters he wrote about in moral
chiaroscuro, and like Spenser's knights and Bunyan's brown-clad Puritans his figures moved in spiritual shadows. He sensed an intimacy of nature with the action of his tales. In Milton's epic of *Paradise Lost* the
heavens groaned at the fall of the angels, and in Hawthorne's tale of
Goodman Brown the winds whispered in sorrow the young man's loss of
Faith. Because Hawthorne believed in no theology, his knowledge of the
complexity of man's inner life was psychologically similar, in its literary
applications, to what he might have learned today. All this he made a
part of his story-telling, and it is from this sense of the total nexus of
things that the atmospheric intensity and the unity of tone result.

Until *The Scarlet Letter* appeared in 1850, he published nothing but
tales and essays. With these he was increasingly dissatisfied. "They
have," he wrote, "the pale tint of flowers that blossomed in too retired
a shade." Part essay, part tale, his stories centered in some mood or
incident. They recalled some episode in history, or probed some individual
problem of the soul. As the taste of the age demanded and the nature of
the author approved, they bore their lessons, but rather as though a
new Deucalion had cast moral tracts over his shoulder and found them
grown into literature. Yet Hawthorne's material for such tales was limited, and his increasing interest in psychological relationships demanded
larger form. "In the humblest event I resolved at least to achieve a novel
that should evolve some deep lesson and should possess physical substance enough to stand alone."

Meanwhile he experimented in living. Partly because at last he wanted a share in common life, mostly because he wanted an income large enough to marry on, he went to work as a surveyor in the custom house at Boston. There on long winter days he paced the icy decks of salt-ships and coal-vessels, or fled the freezing north winds by climbing down into dirty little cabins to warm himself beside red-hot stoves. His mind was too entangled in weights and measures, his emotions too concerned with love, to leave much energy for the creation of fiction, though he did manage a hack job or two to fill his pocket-book. He turned hopefully from Long Wharf to the fields of Brook Farm in an effort, as he first put it, to escape "all the fopperies and flummeries which have their origin in a false state of society;" and there, frocked in blue woolen, shod in heavy cow-hide boots, he passionately attacked a heap of manure. Reality stifled his hope. "It is my opinion, dearest," he wrote to his fiancée, "that a man's soul may be buried and perish under a dung-heap or in a furrow of the field, just as well as under a pile of money. . . . The real Me was never an associate of the community." Hawthorne wanted security much more than he cared what kind of society gave it to him, but he failed to find it in the transcendental socialism of Brook Farm. This hope gone, he cast his native prudence to the winds, married and went to live in Concord. In the old manse where Emerson had written *Nature* and a line of preachers had filled the attic with manuscripts of sermons, Hawthorne continued their didactic tradition. There by the gnarled apple-trees and sluggish stream lapsing through the meadow behind the house most of *Mosses from an Old Manse* was written. He lived here for four years, but, as his family increased, the old necessity for security urged him on, and for the following two years he was employed in the custom house at Salem. When this period was cut short, the bitter experiences of which he told in his introduction to *The Scarlet Letter*, he wrote at last his novel.

It made him famous. No novel so fine had appeared in America, and few so fine have appeared since. From a seventeenth-century New England punishment, an earlier mention of which he made in *Endicott and the Red Cross*, he drew a symbol of the diverse and protracted effects of sin. The great beauty of *The Scarlet Letter* as a literary achievement lies in its flexible unity within a strictly patterned complexity; the speculation within the characters' own minds gives the novel an inner as well as an outer action. The spiritual enrichment of Hester, the decay of Dimmesdale, the wizening of Chillingworth are each intensified by the development of the others' natures. The moral of the story lies in Hester's rebuke to Dimmesdale as they meet in the silence of the woods: "Thou wast not bold!—thou wast not true!" Chillingworth's revenge was not in itself the wrong; it was his hidden persecution of Dimmesdale and his relentless pursuit of a single aim, twisting his nature and warping his soul, which wrought evil in him. Because Dimmesdale confused his own conscience, rather than because he sinned, his body wasted away as though in sympathy with his soul. Not even Hester, whom nature forced into the open, was herself quite honest; had she been, the scarlet letter would have dropped of itself from her breast. Silently she permitted the revenge of Chillingworth, wittingly she perceived Dimmesdale's torture. For each of the characters, retribution was possible only where the sin was committed; and the flight which Hester and the minister planned would have brought no escape from the mind. This understanding was at the core of Chillingworth's outraged cry when Dimmesdale at last confessed. This was the reason Hester returned to live out her life near Boston. "The breach which guilt has once made into the human soul is never, in this mortal state, repaired," said Hawthorne; yet he understood the bitter kind of knowledge and sympathy, the enrichment of the soul this breach, by all the flooding in of experience, can bring. The moral paradox which Milton presented in *Paradise Lost* made Hester, like a Puritan Eve, a foreshadow of a new age for women. This new age, when knowledge should bring woman a deeper and a richer character, was in the future, as were the realizations of all of Hawthorne's reforms; but Hester had gone one step, and her Pearl, when grief matured the child into sympathetic understanding, went still further. In her the sin was expiated and the reward approached. Even Dimmesdale's ministry was deepened through his ill-earned sympathy. A similar knowledge of the evil of the world had come to Goodman Brown, but Hawthorne had himself matured since Brown had fled his fellow men.

Hawthorne's next two novels followed quickly. *The House of the Seven Gables* appeared in 1851 and *The Blithedale Romance* in the following year. With these he abandoned the directly historical, and made more and more use of his observation and his own experience. The general method, however, was not much altered. In *The House of the Seven Gables*, the great gray mansion brooding over the scene, he portrayed the tenacity of evil, the disintegration of a class, and the enlivening effect of the introduction of common and normal life through the sunny Phoebe and Holgrave, the daguerreotypist. The material was family history: the witch's husband's curse and the lost land grant. In *The Blithedale Romance* he used his experience at Brook Farm, patterning it with his study of individual types, and probing into the general movement of reform. Most of all he concerned himself with the character of Zenobia, who possessed something of the quality of the new woman in whom he was so interested, and who, like certain blue-stockings of his own day, felt herself possessed of much more than was actually there. Intellectually she was further advanced than Hester; morally she had left her heart behind, and her sympathy for those about her had gone with it. Hollingsworth was Hawthorne's study of the social reformer, a man whose goal was worthy enough, but who, in burying himself completely in one concern to the exclusion of his spiritual growth, had withdrawn into an isolation as barren as that of Ethan Brand, of Rappaccini, or even of Chillingworth. Hollingsworth ought, Hawthorne observed, "to have commenced his investigation of the subject by perpetrating some huge sin in his proper person, and examining the condition of his higher instinct afterwards."

In 1853 Hawthorne was appointed United States Consul at Liverpool, and the pressure of his duties there kept him from publishing anything new, though he filled the pages of his journals with minute observations of all he saw while in England and later during a year and a half in Italy. Finally, in 1860, *The Marble Faun* appeared. Here in an Italian mist, among a group of expatriate American artists who hoped to find Beauty wrapped in a Roman toga, Hawthorne's thrice-told tale of the moral growth of man was written once more. The carefree, faun-like Donatello and the dove-like Hilda were slowly transformed to maturity through the stain of sin. With Donatello it was through crime committed, and with Hilda through crime observed. Something fresh and innocent was lost to each, but life had grown so sadly serious, as Hawthorne knew, that there was no longer any place for such as they had been.

The themes of Hawthorne's works occur and recur. The reading of them is the pleasure of meeting an old friend slightly changed; giving not the excitement of a new acquaintanceship, but rather a touch of something fresh to what is known well. The familiarity by which one recognizes the spirit of Wakefield in the character of Ethan Brand, which draws Phoebe and Hilda together, binds all of Hawthorne's work into a single study of man's life. For with the deeper signficance which lies behind each tale and each novel, except *Fanshawe*, the characters not merely become figures in particular plots, but reflect and set off others in the total expression of what might be called Hawthorne's moral study of humanity. Thus in the larger, somewhat accidental synthesis of the body of his writing there is something of a repetition of the function and the more conscious beauty of the symbolism which integrates the individual works. Hawthorne's use of symbols is like Wagner's use of *leitmotif* to recall what has come before, and to bring the mind a greater consciousness than the ear alone can comprehend. The effect of this device is like that of T. S. Eliot's borrowed lines from the past, which not only have their direct and proper part in the progress of the poem but bring in allusive parallel the scenes from which originally they came. Symbolism is like a curl of wind that lifts three leaves to play, or for a moment bends a flower aside. Nothing essentially there is changed, but things are seen in new dimensions and new beauty. Touched by one of Hawthorne's symbols, thought spreads outward farther and farther until it embraces the whole book, then recedes to concentrate once more upon the particular object, before the eye goes on. The perplexed gesture with which Donatello tosses the little worm from the tower at Monte Beni reënacts all of *The Marble Faun*, yet it is the matter of but a sentence or two. The spirit of Zenobia is in her flower, the punishment of Hester in her letter, the innocence of Hilda in her doves. And in establishing the relationship between the idea and the fact, each reader becomes his own author.

Hawthorne's writing is not designed for broken or rapid reading; nor, certainly, is any style which depends upon the evocation of atmosphere and a unity of impression. It was for this reason that Hawthorne never permitted any of his novels to be serialized in magazines; and to one begging editor he wrote: "In all my stories, I think, there is one idea running through them like an iron rod, and to which all other ideas are referred and subordinate; and this circumstance gives the narrative a character of monotony; which, possibly, may strengthen the impression which it makes, if read off at once, but would become intolerably wearisome, if dragged slowly before the reader, through a term of weeks or months." Hawthorne depended on this rod-like structure to give body and direction to the air of unreality which hung like a mist over his stories and colored the romantic form in which he wrote. To a contemporary and very minor poet who asked Hawthorne's opinion of his manuscript poem, the novelist replied: "In a story like this, it is allowable, and highly advisable (as you yourself have felt) to have as much mist and glorified fog as possible diffused about on all sides, but still there should be a distinct pathway to tread upon—a clue that the reader shall confide in, as being firmly fastened somewhere. People will not advance far into a poem, unless they know—or, at least, begin to know, or fancy they are about knowing—something of the matter in hand."

As with the old story-teller of one of his earliest and least important tales, Hawthorne's "groundplots, seldom within the widest scope of probability, were filled up with homely and natural incidents, the gradual accretions of a long course of years, and fiction hid its grotesque extravagances in this garb of truth. . . . " These incidents, as he said of certain passages in The House of the Seven Gables, "ought to be finished with the minuteness of a Dutch picture." Thus in his account of the scene in which Clifford peers down from behind his curtained window at the inconsequential life in the street below, or in his brutally vivid relation of the grim night when Zenobia's drowned body is found by the river-bank, Hawthorne's dexterity in descriptive prose can be observed. Except that a scene like the first is integrally blended into the structure and background of the whole, it has the completeness of one of his essays.

Hawthorne complained in his preface to The Marble Fawn that America lacked the antique detail necessary to a writer like himself. "Romance and poetry, ivy, lichens, and wall-flowers, need ruin to make them grow." Yet it is the obtrusion of these details in The Marble Faun which makes it at times resemble a fictionalized guide-book, and its very absence in the American scene led him to substitute for concrete background the highly developed mental metaphor. To this substitution, perhaps, is owed the excellence of such a chapter as "Clifford's Chamber" in The House of the Seven Gables, with its extended description of Hepzibah's hesitation, or so intricately developed and Jamesian a passage as that in which the probings of Chillingworth into Dimmesdale's mind are described:

Then, after long search into the minister's dim interior, and turning over many precious materials, in the shape of high aspirations for the welfare of his race, warm love of souls, pure sentiments, natural piety, strengthened by thought and study, and illuminated by revelation—all of which invaluable gold was perhaps no better than rubbish to the seeker—he would turn back discouraged, and begin his quest towards another point. He groped along as stealthily, with as cautious a tread, and as wary an outlook, as a thief entering a chamber where a man lies only half asleep—or, it may be, broad awake— with purpose to steal the very treasure which this man guards as the apple of his eye. In spite of his premeditated carefulness, the floor would now and then creak; his garments would rustle; the shadow of his presence, in a forbidden proximity, would be thrown across his victim. In other words, Mr. Dimmesdale, whose sensibility of nerve often produced the effect of spiritual intuition, would become vaguely aware that something inimical to his peace had thrust itself into relation with him. But old Roger Chillingworth, too, had perceptions that were almost intuitive; and when the minister threw his startled eyes towards him, there the physician sat; his kind, watchful, sympathizing, but never intrusive friend.

Hawthorne's chief problem throughout his writing was, in his words, to provide "a neutral ground where the Actual and the Imaginary might meet." It was not easy. "The fact is," he said, "in writing a romance, a man is always—or always ought to be—careening on the utmost verge of a precipitous absurdity, and the skill lies in coming as close as possible, without actually tumbling over."

These are times that try literary men's souls as well as their styles. Now that certain nineteenth-century writers are being revived and relished for their premonitions of a new political order, somewhat as Virgil kept his respectability during the Middle Ages by his supposed forecast of Christianity, criticism is relearning a respect for the didactic in art. Literature may serve as well as merely satisfy. At least it may do one or the other, and yet be art. Even the moral tag which used to be thought of as a tin can tied to a dog's tail will be seen again in time to have its own, though limited, artistic function. It is more fittingly the jewel towards which the design of a circlet is traced; it is the truth towards which the story points. Hawthorne's concern with the problems of life was not political, and not always directly social. But his writing did contain social implications: clear the world of Ethan Brands, of Rappaccinis, of Lady Eleanores; make the new Pilgrim's progress better; mature the Hildas; regenerate man, and society will itself in turn be regenerate. Was the lesson wrong? Do we know? The beauty is still there! Human experience is so diverse that a man can be estimated only by the depth with which he understands what chance has thrown his way. Hawthorne might have led other lives, might have written many things. Literature is not made up of what men might have written, but what they wrote. Understanding this fact, one is ready to read Hawthorne.

Yale University
New Haven, Conn.

# FANSHAWE

>>>

*The publishers will be pleased to send, upon request, an illustrated folder setting forth the purpose and scope of* THE MODERN LIBRARY, *and listing each volume in the series. Every reader of books will find titles he has been looking for, handsomely printed, in unabridged editions, and at an unusually low price.*

>>>>>>>>>>>>>>>>>>>>>>>>>>>>>>>>>>>>>>>>>>>>>>>>>

# FANSHAWE

## CHAPTER I

"Our court shall be a little Academe."—SHAKESPEARE.

IN an ancient though not very populous settlement, in a retired corner of one of the New England States, arise the walls of a seminary of learning, which, for the convenience of a name, shall be entitled "Harley College." This institution, though the number of its years is inconsiderable compared with the hoar antiquity of its European sisters, is not without some claims to reverence on the score of age; for an almost countless multitude of rivals, by many of which its reputation has been eclipsed, have sprung up since its foundation. At no time, indeed, during an existence of nearly a century, has it acquired a very extensive fame; and circumstances, which need not be particularized, have, of late years, involved it in a deeper obscurity. There are now few candidates for the degrees that the college is authorized to bestow. On two of its annual "Commencement Days," there has been a total deficiency of baccalaureates; and the lawyers and divines, on whom doctorates in their respective professions are gratuitously inflicted, are not accustomed to consider the distinction as an honor. Yet the sons of this seminary have always maintained their full share of reputation, in whatever paths of life they trod. Few of them, perhaps, have been deep and finished scholars; but the college has supplied —what the emergencies of the country demanded—a set of men more useful in its present state, and whose deficiency in theoretical knowledge has not been found to imply a want of practical ability.

The local situation of the college, so far secluded from the sight and sound of the busy world, is peculiarly favorable to the moral, if not to the literary, habits of its students; and this advantage probably caused the founders to overlook the inconveniences that were inseparably connected with it. The humble edifices rear themselves almost at the farthest extremity of a narrow vale, which, winding through a long extent of hill-country, is wellnigh as inaccessible, except at one point, as the Happy Valley of Abyssinia. A stream, that farther on becomes a considerable river, takes its rise at a short distance above the college, and affords, along its wood-fringed banks, many shady retreats, where even study is pleasant, and idleness delicious. The neighborhood of the institution is not quite a solitude, though the few habitations scarcely constitute a village. These consist principally of farm-houses, of rather an ancient date (for the settlement is much older than the college), and of a little inn,

3

which even in that secluded spot does not fail of a moderate support. Other dwellings are scattered up and down the valley; but the difficulties of the soil will long avert the evils of a too dense population. The character of the inhabitants does not seem—as there was, perhaps, room to anticipate—to be in any degree influenced by the atmosphere of Harley College. They are a set of rough and hardy yeomen, much inferior, as respects refinement, to the corresponding classes in most other parts of our country. This is the more remarkable, as there is scarcely a family in the vicinity that has not provided, for at least one of its sons, the advantages of a "liberal education."

Having thus described the present state of Harley College, we must proceed to speak of it as it existed about eighty years since, when its foundation was recent, and its prospects flattering. At the head of the institution, at this period, was a learned and Orthodox divine, whose fame was in all the churches. He was the author of several works which evinced much erudition and depth of research; and the public, perhaps, thought the more highly of his abilities from a singularity in the purposes to which he applied them, that added much to the curiosity of his labors, though little to their usefulness. But, however fanciful might be his private pursuits, Dr. Melmoth, it was universally allowed, was diligent and successful in the arts of instruction. The young men of his charge prospered beneath his eye, and regarded him with an affection that was strengthened by the little foibles which occasionally excited their ridicule. The president was assisted in the discharge of his duties by two inferior officers, chosen from the alumni of the college, who, while they imparted to others the knowledge they had already imbibed, pursued the study of divinity under the direction of their principal. Under such auspices the institution grew and flourished. Having at that time but two rivals in the country (neither of them within a considerable distance), it became the general resort of the youth of the Province in which it was situated. For several years in succession, its students amounted to nearly fifty,—a number which, relatively to the circumstances of the country, was very considerable.

From the exterior of the collegians, an accurate observer might pretty safely judge how long they had been inmates of those classic walls. The brown cheeks and the rustic dress of some would inform him that they had but recently left the plough to labor in a not less toilsome field; the grave look, and the intermingling of garments of a more classic cut, would distinguish those who had begun to acquire the polish of their new residence; and the air of superiority, the paler cheek, the less robust form, the spectacles of green, and the dress, in general of threadbare black, would designate the highest class, who were understood to have acquired nearly all the science their Alma Mater could bestow, and to be on the point of assuming their stations in the world. There were, it is true, exceptions to this general description. A few young men had found their way hither from the distant seaports; and these were the models of fashion to their rustic companions, over whom they asserted a superiority in exterior accomplishments, which the fresh though unpolished intellect of the sons of the forest denied them in their literary competitions. A third class, differing widely from both the former, consisted of a few young descendants of the aborigines, to whom an impracticable philanthropy was endeavoring to impart the benefits of civilization.

If this institution did not offer all the advantages of elder and prouder seminaries, its deficiencies were compensated to its students by the inculcation of regular habits, and of a deep and awful sense of religion, which seldom deserted them in their course through life. The mild and gentle rule of Dr. Melmoth, like that of a father over his children, was more destructive to vice than a sterner sway; and though youth is never without its follies, they have seldom been more harmless than they were here. The students, indeed, ignorant of their own bliss, sometimes wished to hasten the time of their entrance on the business of life; but they found, in after-years, that many of their happiest remembrances, many of the scenes which they would with least reluctance live over again, referred to the seat of their early studies. The exceptions to this remark were chiefly those whose vices had drawn down, even from that paternal government, a weighty retribution.

Dr. Melmoth, at the time when he is to be introduced to the reader, had borne the matrimonial yoke (and in his case it was no light burden) nearly twenty years. The blessing of children, however, had been denied him,—a circumstance which he was accustomed to consider as one of the sorest trials that checkered his pathway; for he was a man of a kind and affectionate heart, that was continually seeking objects to rest itself upon. He was inclined to believe, also, that a common offspring would have exerted a meliorating influence on the temper of Mrs. Melmoth, the character of whose domestic government often compelled him to call to mind such portions of the wisdom of antiquity as relate to the proper endurance of the shrewishness of woman. But domestic comforts, as well as comforts of every other kind, have their drawbacks; and, so long as the balance is on the side of happiness, a wise man will not murmur. Such was the opinion of Dr. Melmoth; and with a little aid from philosophy, and more from religion, he journeyed on contentedly through life. When the storm was loud by the parlor hearth, he had always a sure and quiet retreat in his study; and there, in his deep though not always useful labors, he soon forgot whatever of disagreeable nature pertained to his situation. This small and dark apartment was the only portion of the house to which, since one firmly repelled invasion, Mrs. Melmoth's omnipotence did not extend. Here (to reverse the words of Queen Elizabeth) there was "but one master and no mistress"; and that man has little right to complain who possesses so much as one corner in the world where he may be happy or miserable, as best suits him. In his study, then, the doctor was accustomed to spend most of the hours that were unoccupied by the duties of his station. The flight of time was here as swift as the wind, and noiseless as the snow-flake; and it was a sure proof of real happiness that night often came upon the student before he knew it was midday.

Dr. Melmoth was wearing towards age (having lived nearly sixty years), when he was called upon to assume a character to which he had as yet been a stranger. He had possessed in his youth a very dear friend, with whom his education had associated him, and who in his early manhood had been his chief intimate. Circumstances, however, had separated them for nearly thirty years, half of which had been spent by his friend, who was engaged in mercantile pursuits, in a foreign country. The doctor had, nevertheless, retained a warm interest in the welfare of his old associate, though the different nature of their thoughts and occupations had prevented them from corresponding. After a silence of so long continuance, therefore, he was surprised by the receipt of a letter from his friend, containing a request of a most unexpected nature.

Mr. Langton had married rather late in life; and his wedded bliss had been but of short continuance. Certain misfortunes in trade, when he was a Benedict of three years' standing, had deprived him of a large portion of his property, and compelled him, in order to save the remainder, to leave his own country for what he hoped would be but a brief residence in another. But, though he was successful in the immediate objects of his voyage, circumstances occurred to lengthen his stay far beyond the period which he had assigned to it. It was difficult so to arrange his extensive concerns that they could be safely trusted to the management of others; and, when this was effected, there was another not less powerful obstacle to his return. His affairs, under his own inspection, were so prosperous, and his gains so considerable, that, in the words of the old ballad, "He set his heart to gather gold"; and to this absorbing passion he sacrificed his domestic happiness. The death of his wife, about four years after his departure, undoubtedly contributed to give him a sort of dread of returning, which it required a strong effort to overcome. The welfare of his only child he knew would be little affected by this event; for she was under the protection of his sister, of whose tenderness he was well assured. But, after a few more years, this sister, also, was taken away by death; and then the father felt that duty imperatively called upon him to return. He realized, on a sudden, how much of life he had thrown away in the acquisition of what is only valuable as it contributes to the happiness of life, and how short a time was left him for life's true enjoyments. Still, however, his mercantile habits were too deeply seated to allow him to hazard his present prosperity by any hasty measures; nor was Mr. Langton, though capable of strong affections, naturally liable to manifest them violently. It was probable, therefore, that many months might yet elapse before he would again tread the shores of his native country.

But the distant relative, in whose family, since the death of her aunt, Ellen Langton had remained, had been long at variance with her father, and had unwillingly assumed the office of her protector. Mr. Langton's request, therefore, to Dr. Melmoth, was, that his ancient friend (one of the few friends that time had left him) would be as a father to his daughter till he could himself relieve him of the charge.

The doctor, after perusing the epistle of his friend, lost no time in laying it before Mrs. Melmoth, though this was, in truth, one of the very few occasions on which he had determined that his will should be absolute law. The lady was quick to perceive the firmness of his purpose, and would not (even had she been particularly averse to the proposed measure) hazard her usual authority by a fruitless opposition. But, by long disuse, she had lost the power of consenting graciously to any wish of her husband's.

"I see your heart is set upon this matter," she observed; "and, in truth, I fear we cannot decently refuse Mr. Langton's request. I see little good of such a friend, doctor, who never lets one know he is alive till he has a favor to ask."

"Nay; but I have received much good at his hand," replied Dr. Melmoth; "and, if he asked more of me, it should be done with a willing heart. I remember in my youth, when my worldly goods were few and ill managed (I was a bachelor, then, dearest Sarah, with none to look after my household), how many times I have been beholden to him. And see— in his letter he speaks of presents, of the produce of the country, which he has sent both to you and me."

"If the girl were country-bred," continued the lady, "we might give her house-room, and no harm done. Nay, she might even be a help to me; for Esther, our maid-servant, leaves us at the month's end. But I warrant, she knows as little of household matters as you do yourself, doctor."

"My friend's sister was well grounded in the *re familiari*," answered her husband; "and doubtless she hath imparted somewhat of her skill to this damsel. Besides, the child is of tender years, and will profit much by your instruction and mine."

"The child is eighteen years of age, doctor," observed Mrs. Melmoth, "and she has cause to be thankful that she will have better instruction than yours."

This was a proposition that Dr. Melmoth did not choose to dispute; though he perhaps thought that his long and successful experience in the education of the other sex might make him an able coadjutor to his wife in the care of Ellen Langton. He determined to journey in person to the seaport where his young charge resided, leaving the concerns of Harley College to the direction of the two tutors. Mrs. Melmoth, who, indeed, anticipated with pleasure the arrival of a new subject to her authority, threw no difficulties in the way of his intention. To do her justice, her preparations for his journey, and the minute instructions with which she favored him, were such as only a woman's true affection could have suggested. The traveller met with no incidents important to this tale; and, after an absence of about a fortnight, he and Ellen Langton alighted from their steeds (for on horseback had the journey been performed) in safety at his own door.

If pen could give an adequate idea of Ellen Langton's loveliness, it would achieve what pencil (the pencils, at least, of the colonial artists who attempted it) never could; for, though the dark eyes might be painted, the pure and pleasant thoughts that peeped through them could only be seen and felt. But descriptions of beauty are never satisfactory. It must, therefore, be left to the imagination of the reader to conceive of something not more than mortal, nor, indeed, quite the perfection of mortality, but charming men the more, because they felt, that, lovely as she was, she was of like nature to themselves.

From the time that Ellen entered Dr. Melmoth's habitation, the sunny days seemed brighter and the cloudy ones less gloomy, than he had ever before known them. He naturally delighted in children; and Ellen, though her years approached to womanhood, had yet much of the gayety and simple happiness, because the innocence, of a child. She consequently became the very blessing of his life,—the rich recreation that he promised himself for hours of literary toil. On one occasion, indeed, he even made her his companion in the sacred retreat of his study, with the purpose of entering upon a course of instruction in the learned languages. This measure, however, he found inexpedient to repeat; for Ellen, having discovered an old romance among his heavy folios, contrived, by the charm of her sweet voice, to engage his attention therein till all more important concerns were forgotten.

With Mrs. Melmoth, Ellen was not, of course, so great a favorite as with her husband; for women cannot, so readily as men, bestow upon the offspring of others those affections that nature intended for their own; and the doctor's extraordinary partiality was anything rather than a pledge of his wife's. But Ellen differed so far from the idea she had previously formed of her, as a daughter of one of the principal merchants, who were then, as now, like nobles in the land, that the stock of dislike which Mrs. Melmoth had provided was found to be totally inapplicable. The young stranger strove so hard, too (and undoubtedly it was a pleasant labor), to win her love, that she was successful to a degree of which the lady herself was not, perhaps, aware. It was soon seen that her education had not been neglected in those points which Mrs. Melmoth deemed most important. The nicer departments of cookery, after sufficient proof of her skill, were committed to her care; and the doctor's table was now covered with delicacies, simple indeed, but as tempting on account of their intrinsic excellence as of the small white hands that made them. By such arts as these,—which in her were no arts, but the dictates of an affectionate disposition,—by making herself useful where it was possible, and agreeable on all occasions, Ellen gained the love of everyone within the sphere of her influence.

But the maiden's conquests were not confined to the members of Dr. Melmoth's family. She had numerous admirers among those whose situation compelled them to stand afar off, and gaze upon her loveliness, as if she were a star, whose brightness they saw, but whose warmth they could not feel. These were the young men of Harley College, whose chief opportunities of beholding Ellen were upon the Sabbaths, when she worshipped with them in the little chapel, which served the purposes of a church to all the families of the vicinity. There was, about this period (and the fact was undoubtedly attributable to Ellen's influence), a general and very evident decline in the scholarship of the college, especially in regard to the severer studies. The intellectual powers of the young men seemed to be directed chiefly to the construction of Latin and Greek verse, many copies of which, with a characteristic and classic gallantry, were strewn in the path where Ellen Langton was accustomed to walk. They, however, produced no perceptible effect; nor were the aspirations of another ambitious youth, who celebrated her perfections in Hebrew, attended with their merited success.

But there was one young man, to whom circumstances, independent of his personal advantages, afforded a superior opportunity of gaining Ellen's favor. He was nearly related to Dr. Melmoth, on which account he received his education at Harley College, rather than at one of the English universities, to the expenses of which his fortune would have been adequate. This connection entitled him to a frequent and familiar access to the domestic hearth of the dignitary,—an advantage of which, since Ellen Langton became a member of the family, he very constantly availed himself.

Edward Walcott was certainly much superior, in most of the particulars of which a lady takes cognizance, to those of his fellow-students who had come under Ellen's notice. He was tall; and the natural grace of his manners had been improved (an advantage which few of his associates could boast) by early intercourse with polished society. His features, also, were handsome, and promised to be manly and dignified when they should cease to be youthful. His character as a scholar was more than respectable, though many youthful follies, sometimes, perhaps, approaching near to vices, were laid to his charge. But his occasional derelictions from discipline were not such as to create any very serious apprehensions respecting his future welfare; nor were they greater than, perhaps, might be expected from a young man who possessed a considerable command of money, and who was, besides, the fine gentleman of the little community of which he was a member,—a character which generally leads its possessor into follies that he would otherwise have avoided.

With this youth Ellen Langton became familiar, and even intimate; for he was her only companion, of an age suited to her own, and the difference of sex did not occur to her as an objection. He was her constant companion on all necessary and allowable occasions, and drew upon himself, in consequence, the envy of the college.

## CHAPTER II

"Why, all delights are vain, but that most vain,
   Which, with pain purchased, doth inherit pain:
      As painfully to pore upon a book
         To seek the light of truth, while truth, the while,
      Doth falsely blind the eyesight of his look."

                                        SHAKESPEARE.

ON one of the afternoons which afforded to the students a relaxation from their usual labors, Ellen was attended by her cavalier in a little excursion over the rough bridle-roads that led from her new residence. She was an experienced equestrian,—a necessary accomplishment at that period, when vehicles of every kind were rare. It was now the latter end of spring; but the season had hitherto been backward, with only a few warm and pleasant days. The present afternoon, however, was a delicious mingling of spring and summer, forming in their union an atmosphere so mild and pure, that to breathe was almost a positive happiness. There was a little alternation of cloud across the brow of heaven, but only so much as to render the sunshine more delightful.

The path of the young travellers lay sometimes among tall and thick standing trees, and sometimes over naked and desolate hills, whence man had taken the natural vegetation, and then left the soil to its barrenness. Indeed, there is little inducement to a cultivator to labor among the huge stones which there peep forth from the earth, seeming to form a continued ledge for several miles. A singular contrast to this unfavored tract of country is seen in the narrow but luxuriant, though sometimes swampy, strip of interval, on both sides of the stream, that, as has been noticed, flows down the valley. The light and buoyant spirits of Edward Walcott and Ellen rose higher as they rode on; and their way was enlivened, wherever its roughness did not forbid, by their conversation and pleasant laughter. But at length Ellen drew her bridle, as they emerged from a thick portion of the forest, just at the foot of a steep hill.

"We must have ridden far," she observed,—"farther than I thought. It will be near sunset before we can reach home."

"There are still several hours of daylight," replied Edward Walcott; "and we will not turn back without ascending this hill. The prospect from the summit is beautiful, and will be particularly so now, in this rich sunlight. Come, Ellen,—one light touch of the whip,—your pony is as fresh as when we started."

On reaching the summit of the hill, and looking back in the direction in which they had come, they could see the little stream, peeping forth many times to the daylight, and then shrinking back into the shade. Farther on, it became broad and deep, though rendered incapable of navigation, in this part of its course, by the occasional interruption of rapids.

"There are hidden wonders of rock and precipice and cave, in that dark forest," said Edward, pointing to the space between them and the river. "If it were earlier in the day, I should love to lead you there. Shall we try the adventure now, Ellen?"

"Oh no!" she replied. "Let us delay no longer. I fear I must even now abide a rebuke from Mrs. Melmoth, which I have surely deserved. But who is this, who rides on so slowly before us?"

She pointed to a horseman, whom they had not before observed. He was descending the hill; but, as his steed seemed to have chosen his own pace, he made a very inconsiderable progress.

"Oh, do you not know him? But it is scarcely possible you should," exclaimed her companion. "We must do him the good office, Ellen, of stopping his progress, or he will find himself at the village, a dozen miles farther on, before he resumes his consciousness."

"Has he then lost his senses?" inquired Miss Langton.

"Not so, Ellen,—if much learning has not made him mad," replied Edward Walcott. "He is a deep scholar and a noble fellow; but I fear we shall follow him to his grave erelong. Dr. Melmoth has sent him to ride in pursuit of his health. He will never overtake it, however, at this pace."

As he spoke, they had approached close to the subject of their conversation; and Ellen had a moment's space for observation before he started from the abstraction in which he was plunged. The result of her scrutiny was favorable, yet very painful.

The stranger could scarcely have attained his twentieth year, and was possessed of a face and form such as Nature bestows on none but her favorites. There was a nobleness on his high forehead, which time would have deepened into majesty; and all his features were formed with a strength and boldness, of which the paleness, produced by study and confinement, could not deprive them. The expression of his countenance was not a melancholy one: on the contrary, it was proud and high, perhaps triumphant, like one who was a ruler in a world of his own, and independent of the beings that surrounded him. But a blight, of which his thin pale cheek, and the brightness of his eye, were alike proofs, seemed to have come over him ere his maturity.

The scholar's attention was now aroused by the hoof-tramps at his side; and, starting, he fixed his eyes on Ellen, whose young and lovely countenance was full of the interest he had excited. A deep blush immediately suffused his cheek, proving how well the glow of health would have become it. There was nothing awkward, however, in his manner; and, soon recovering his self-possession, he bowed to her, and would have ridden on.

"Your ride is unusually long to-day, Fanshawe," observed Edward Walcott. "When may we look for your return?"

The young man again blushed, but answered, with a smile that had a beautiful effect upon his countenance, "I was not, at the moment, aware in which direction my horse's head was turned. I have to thank you for arresting me in a journey which was likely to prove much longer than I intended."

The party had now turned their horses, and were about to resume their ride in a homeward direction; but Edward perceived that Fanshawe, having lost the excitement of intense thought, now looked weary and dispirited.

"Here is a cottage close at hand," he observed. " We have ridden far, and stand in need of refreshment. Ellen, shall we alight?"

She saw the benevolent motive of his proposal, and did not hesitate to comply with it. But, as they paused at the cottage door, she could not but observe that its exterior promised few of the comforts which they required. Time and neglect seemed to have conspired for its ruin; and, but for a thin curl of smoke from its clay chimney, they could not have believed it to be inhabited. A considerable tract of land in the vicinity of the cottage had evidently been, at some former period, under cultivation, but was now overrun by bushes and dwarf pines, among which many huge gray rocks, ineradicable by human art, endeavored to conceal themselves. About half an acre of ground was occupied by the young blades of Indian-corn, at which a half-starved cow gazed wistfully over the mouldering log-fence. These were the only agricultural tokens. Edward Walcott, nevertheless, drew the latch of the cottage door, after knocking loudly but in vain.

The apartment which was thus opened to their view was quite as wretched as its exterior had given them reason to anticipate. Poverty was there, with all its necessary and unnecessary concomitants. The intruders would have retired had not the hope of affording relief detained them.

The occupants of the small and squalid apartment were two women, both of them elderly, and, from the resemblance of their features, appearing to be sisters. The expression of their countenances, however, was very different. One, evidently the younger, was seated on the farther side of the large hearth, opposite to the door at which the party stood. She had the sallow look of long and wasting illness; and there was an unsteadiness of expression about her eyes, that immediately struck the observer. Yet her face was mild and gentle, therein contrasting widely with that of her companion.

The other woman was bending over a small fire of decayed branches, the flame of which was very disproportionate to the smoke, scarcely producing heat sufficient for the preparation of a scanty portion of food. Her profile only was visible to the strangers, though, from a slight motion of her eye, they perceived that she was aware of their presence. Her features were pinched and spare, and wore a look of sullen discontent, for which the evident wretchedness of her situation afforded a sufficient reason. This female, notwithstanding her years, and the habitual fretfulness (that is more wearing than time), was apparently healthy and robust, with a dry, leathery complexion. A short space elapsed before she thought proper to turn her face towards her visitors; and she then regarded them with a lowering eye, without speaking, or rising from her chair.

"We entered," Edward Walcott began to say, "in the hope"— But he paused, on perceiving that the sick woman had risen from her seat, and with slow and tottering footsteps was drawing near to him. She took his hand in both her own; and, though he shuddered at the touch of age and disease, he did not attempt to withdraw it. She then perused all his features, with an expression, at first of eager and hopeful anxiety, which faded by degrees into disappointment. Then, turning from him, she gazed into Fanshawe's countenance with the like eagerness, but with the same result. Lastly, tottering back to her chair, she hid her face and wept bitterly. The strangers, though they knew not the cause of her grief, were deeply affected; and Ellen approached the mourner with words of comfort, which, more from their tone than their meaning, produced a transient effect.

"Do you bring news of him?" she inquired, raising her head. "Will he return to me? Shall I see him before I die?" Ellen knew not what to answer; and, ere she could attempt it, the other female prevented her.

"Sister Butler is wandering in her mind," she said, "and speaks of one she will never behold again. The sight of strangers disturbs her, and you see we have nothing here to offer you."

The manner of the woman was ungracious; but her words were true. They saw that their presence could do nothing towards the alleviation of the misery they witnessed; and they felt that mere curiosity would not authorize a longer intrusion. So soon, therefore, as they had relieved, according to their power, the poverty that seemed to be the least evil of this cottage, they emerged into the open air.

The breath of heaven felt sweet to them, and removed a part of the weight from their young hearts, which were saddened by the sight of so much wretchedness. Perceiving a pure and bright little fountain at a short distance from the cottage, they approached it, and, using the bark of a birch-tree as a cup, partook of its cool waters. They then pursued their homeward ride with such diligence, that, just as the sun was setting, they came in sight of the humble wooden edifice which was dignified with the name of Harley College. A golden ray rested upon the spire of the little chapel, the bell of which sent its tinkling murmur down the valley to summon the wanderers to evening prayers.

Fanshawe returned to his chamber that night, and lighted his lamp as he had been wont to do. The books were around him which had hitherto been to him like those fabled volumes of Magic, from which the reader could not turn away his eye till death were the consequence of his studies. But there were unaccustomed thoughts in his bosom now; and to these, leaning his head on one of the unopened volumes, he resigned himself.

He called up in review the years, that, even at his early age, he had spent in solitary study, in conversation with the dead, while he had scorned to mingle with the living world, or to be actuated by any of its motives. He asked himself to what purpose was all this destructive labor, and where was the happiness of superior knowledge. He had climbed but a few steps of a ladder that reached to infinity: he had thrown away his life in discovering, that, after a thousand such lives, he should still know comparatively nothing. He even looked forward with dread—though once the thought had been dear to him—to the eternity of improvement that lay before him. It seemed now a weary way, without a resting-place and without a termination; and at that moment he would have preferred the dreamless sleep of the brutes that perish to man's proudest attribute,—of immortality.

Fanshawe had hitherto deemed himself unconnected with the world, unconcerned in its feelings, and uninfluenced by it in any of his pursuits. In this respect he probably deceived himself. If his inmost heart could have been laid open, there would have been discovered that dream of undying fame, which, dream as it is, is more powerful than a thousand realities. But, at any rate, he had seemed, to others and to himself, a solitary being, upon whom the hopes and fears of ordinary men were ineffectual.

But now he felt the first thrilling of one of the many ties, that, so long as we breathe the common air, (and who shall say how much longer?) unite us to our kind. The sound of a soft, sweet voice, the glance of a gentle eye, had wrought a change upon him; and in his ardent mind a few hours had done the work of many. Almost in spite of himself, the new sensation was inexpressibly delightful. The recollection of his ruined health, of his habits (so much at variance with those of the world),—all the difficulties that reason suggested, were inadequate to check the exulting tide of hope and joy.

### CHAPTER III

"And let the aspiring youth beware of love,—
Of the smooth glance beware; for 't is too late
When on his heart the torrent softness pours;
Then wisdom prostrate lies, and fading fame
Dissolves in air away."

THOMSON.

A FEW months passed over the heads of Ellen Langton and her admirers, unproductive of events, that, separately, were of sufficient importance to be related. The summer was now drawing to a close; and Dr. Melmoth had received information that his friend's arrangements were nearly completed, and that by the next home-bound ship he hoped to return to his native country. The arrival of that ship was daily expected.

During the time that had elapsed since his first meeting with Ellen, there had been a change, yet not a very remarkable one, in Fanshawe's habits. He was still the same solitary being, so far as regarded his own sex; and he still confined himself as sedulously to his chamber, except for one hour—the sunset hour—of every day. At that period, unless prevented by the inclemency of the weather, he was accustomed to tread a path that wound along the banks of the stream. He had discovered that this was the most frequent scene of Ellen's walks; and this it was that drew him thither.

Their intercourse was at first extremely slight,—a bow on the one side, a smile on the other, and a passing word from both; and then the student hurried back to his solitude. But, in course of time, opportunities occurred for more extended conversation; so that, at the period with which this chapter is concerned, Fanshawe was, almost as constantly as Edward Walcott himself, the companion of Ellen's walks.

His passion had strengthened more than proportionably to the time that had elapsed since it was conceived; but the first glow and excitement which attended it had now vanished. He had reasoned calmly with himself, and rendered evident to his own mind the almost utter hopelessness of success. He had also made his resolution strong, that he would not even endeavor to win Ellen's love, the result of which, for a thousand reasons, could not be happiness. Firm in this determination, and confident of his power to adhere to it; feeling, also, that time and absence could not cure his own passion, and having no desire for such a cure,—he saw no reason for breaking off the intercourse that was established between Ellen and himself. It was remarkable, that, notwithstanding the desperate nature of his love, that, or something connected with it, seemed to have a beneficial effect upon his health. There was now a slight tinge of color in his cheek, and a less consuming brightness in his eye. Could it be that hope, unknown to himself, was yet alive in his breast; that a sense of the possibility of earthly happiness was redeeming him from the grave?

Had the character of Ellen Langton's mind been different, there might, perhaps, have been danger to her from an intercourse of this nature with such a being as Fanshawe; for he was distinguished by many of those asperities around which a woman's affection will often cling. But she was formed to walk in the calm and quiet paths of life, and to pluck the flowers of happiness from the wayside where they grow. Singularity of character, therefore, was not calculated to win her love. She undoubtedly felt an interest in the solitary student, and perceiving, with no great exercise of vanity, that her society drew him from the destructive intensity of his studies, she perhaps felt it a duty to exert her influence. But it did not occur to her that her influence had been sufficiently strong to change the whole current of his thoughts and feelings.

Ellen and her two lovers (for both, though perhaps not equally, deserved that epithet) had met, as usual, at the close of a sweet summer day, and were standing by the side of the stream, just where it swept into a deep pool. The current, undermining the bank, had formed a recess, which, according to Edward Walcott, afforded at that moment a hiding-place to a trout of noble size.

"Now would I give the world," he exclaimed with great interest, "for a hook and line, a fish-spear, or any piscatorial instrument of death! Look, Ellen, you can see the waving of his tail from beneath the bank!"

"If you had the means of taking him, I should save him from your cruelty, thus," said Ellen, dropping a pebble into the water, just over the fish. "There! he has darted down the stream. How many pleasant caves and recesses there must be under these banks, where he may be happy! May there not be happiness in the life of a fish?" she added, turning with a smile to Fanshawe.

"There may," he replied, "so long as he lives quietly in the caves and recesses of which you speak. Yes, there may be happiness, though such as few would envy; but, then, the hook and line"—

"Which, there is reason to apprehend, will shortly destroy the happiness of our friend the trout," interrupted Edward, pointing down the stream. "There is an angler on his way toward us, who will intercept him."

"He seems to care little for the sport, to judge by the pace at which he walks," said Ellen.

"But he sees, now, that we are observing him, and is willing to prove that he knows something of the art," replied Edward Walcott. "I should think him well acquainted with the stream; for, hastily as he walks, he has tried every pool and ripple where a fish usually hides. But that point will be decided when he reaches yonder old bare oak-tree."

"And how is the old tree to decide the question?" inquired Fanshawe. "It is a species of evidence of which I have never before heard."

"The stream has worn a hollow under its roots," answered Edward,— "a most delicate retreat for a trout. Now, a stranger would not discover the spot; or, if he did, the probable result of a cast would be the loss of hook and line,—an accident that has occurred to me more than once. If, therefore, this angler takes a fish from thence, it follows that he knows the stream."

They observed the fisher, accordingly, as he kept his way up the bank. He did not pause when he reached the old leafless oak, that formed with its roots an obstruction very common in American streams; but, throwing his line with involuntary skill as he passed, he not only escaped the various entanglements but drew forth a fine large fish.

"There, Ellen, he has captivated your *protégé*, the trout, or, at least, one very like him in size," observed Edward. "It is singular," he added, gazing earnestly at the man.

"Why is it singular?" inquired Ellen Langton. "This person, perhaps, resides in the neighborhood, and may have fished often in the stream."

"Do but look at him, Ellen, and judge whether his life can have been spent in this lonely valley," he replied. "The glow of many a hotter sun than ours has darkened his brow; and his step and air have something foreign in them, like what we see in sailors who have lived more in other countries than in their own. Is it not so, Ellen? for your education in a seaport must have given you skill in these matters. But come, let us approach nearer."

They walked towards the angler, accordingly, who still remained under the oak, apparently engaged in arranging his fishing-tackle. As the party drew nigh, he raised his head, and threw one quick, scrutinizing glance towards them, disclosing, on his part, a set of bold and rather coarse features, weather-beaten, but indicating the age of the owner to be not above thirty. In person he surpassed the middle size, was well set, and evidently strong and active.

"Do you meet with much success, sir?" inquired Edward Walcott, when within a convenient distance for conversation.

"I have taken but one fish," replied the angler, in an accent which his hearers could scarcely determine to be foreign, or the contrary. "I am a stranger to the stream, and have doubtless passed over many a likely place for sport."

"You have an angler's eye, sir," rejoined Edward. "I observed that you made your casts as if you had often trod these banks, and I could scarcely have guided you better myself."

"Yes, I have learned the art, and I love to practise it," replied the man. "But will not the young lady try her skill?" he continued, casting a bold eye on Ellen. "The fish will love to be drawn out by such white hands as those."

Ellen shrank back, though almost imperceptibly, from the free bearing of the man. It seemed meant for courtesy; but its effect was excessively disagreeable. Edward Walcott, who perceived and coincided in Ellen's feelings, replied to the stranger's proposal.

"The young lady will not put the gallantry of the fish to the proof, sir," he said, "and she will therefore have no occasion for your own."

"I shall take leave to hear my answer from the young lady's own mouth," answered the stranger, haughtily. "If you will step this way, Miss Langton" (here he interrupted himself),—"if you will cast the line by yonder sunken log, I think you will meet with success."

Thus saying, the angler offered his rod and line to Ellen. She at first drew back, then hesitated, but finally held out her hand to receive them. In thus complying with the stranger's request, she was actuated by a desire to keep the peace; which, as her notice of Edward Walcott's crimsoned cheek and flashing eye assured her, was considerably endangered. The angler led the way to the spot which he had pointed out, which, though not at such a distance from Ellen's companions but that words in a common tone could be distinguished, was out of the range of a lowered voice.

Edward Walcott and the student remained by the oak: the former biting his lip with vexation; the latter, whose abstraction always vanished where Ellen was concerned, regarding her and the stranger with fixed and silent attention. The young men could at first hear the words that the angler addressed to Ellen. They related to the mode of managing the rod; and she made one or two casts under his direction. At length, however, as if to offer his assistance, the man advanced close to her side, and seemed to speak, but in so low a tone, that the sense of what he uttered was lost before it reached the oak. But its effect upon Ellen was immediate and very obvious. Her eyes flashed; and an indignant blush rose high on her cheek, giving to her beauty a haughty brightness, of which the gentleness of her disposition in general deprived it. The next moment, however, she seemed to recollect herself, and, restoring the angling-rod to its owner, she turned away calmly, and approached her companions.

"The evening breeze grows chill; and mine is a dress for a summer day," she observed. "Let us walk homeward."

"Miss Langton, is it the evening breeze alone that sends you homeward?" inquired Edward.

At this moment the angler, who had resumed, and seemed to be intent upon his occupation, drew a fish from the pool, which he had pointed out to Ellen.

"I told the young lady," he exclaimed, "that, if she would listen to me a moment longer, she would be repaid for her trouble; and here is the proof of my words."

"Come, let us hasten towards home," cried Ellen, eagerly; and she took Edward Walcott's arm, with a freedom that, at another time, would have enchanted him. He at first seemed inclined to resist her wishes, but complied, after exchanging, unperceived by Ellen, a glance with the stranger, the meaning of which the latter appeared perfectly to understand. Fanshawe also attended her. Their walk towards Dr. Melmoth's dwelling was almost a silent one; and the few words that passed between them did not relate to the adventure which occupied the thoughts of each. On arriving at the house, Ellen's attendants took leave of her, and retired.

Edward Walcott, eluding Fanshawe's observation with little difficulty, hastened back to the old oak-tree. From the intelligence with which the stranger had received his meaning glance, the young man had supposed that he would here await his return. But the banks of the stream, upward and downward, so far as his eye could reach, were solitary. He could see only his own image in the water, where it swept into a silent depth; and could hear only its ripple, where stones and sunken trees impeded its course. The object of his search might, indeed, have found concealment among the tufts of alders, or in the forest that was near at hand; but thither it was in vain to pursue him. The angler had apparently set little store by the fruits of his assumed occupation; for the last fish that he had taken lay, yet alive, on the bank, gasping for the element to which Edward was sufficiently compassionate to restore him. After watching him as he glided down the stream, making feeble efforts to resist its current, the youth turned away, and sauntered slowly towards the college.

Ellen Langton, on her return from her walk, found Dr. Melmoth's little parlor unoccupied; that gentleman being deeply engaged in his study, and his lady busied in her domestic affairs. The evening, notwithstanding Ellen's remark concerning the chillness of the breeze, was almost sultry; and the windows of the apartment were thrown open. At one of these, which looked into the garden, she seated herself, listening, almost unconsciously, to the monotonous music of a thousand insects, varied occasionally by the voice of a whippoorwill, who, as the day departed, was just commencing his song. A dusky tint, as yet almost imperceptible, was beginning to settle on the surrounding objects, except where they were opposed to the purple and golden clouds, which the vanished sun had made the brief inheritors of a portion of his brightness. In these gorgeous vapors, Ellen's fancy, in the interval of other thoughts, pictured a fairy-land, and longed for wings to visit it.

But as the clouds lost their brilliancy, and assumed first a dull purple, and then a sullen gray tint, Ellen's thoughts recurred to the adventure of the angler, which her imagination was inclined to invest with an undue singularity. It was, however, sufficiently unaccountable that an entire stranger should venture to demand of her a private audience; and she assigned, in turn, a thousand motives for such a request, none of which were in any degree satisfactory. Her most prevailing thought, though she could not justify it to her reason, inclined her to believe that the angler was a messenger from her father. But wherefore he should deem it necessary to communicate any intelligence that he might possess only by means of a private interview, and without the knowledge of her friends, was a mystery she could not solve. In this view of the matter, however, she half regretted that her instinctive delicacy had impelled her so suddenly to break off their conference, admitting, in the secrecy of her own mind, that, if an opportunity were again to occur, it might not again be shunned. As if that unuttered thought had power to conjure up its object, she now became aware of a form standing in the garden, at a short distance from the window where she sat. The dusk had deepened, during Ellen's abstraction, to such a degree, that the man's features were not perfectly distinguishable; but the maiden was not long in doubt of his identity, for he approached, and spoke in the same low tone in which he had addressed her when they stood by the stream.

"Do you still refuse my request, when its object is but your own good, and that of one who should be most dear to you?" he asked.

Ellen's first impulse had been to cry out for assistance; her second was to fly: but, rejecting both these measures, she determined to remain, endeavoring to persuade herself that she was safe. The quivering of her voice, however, when she attempted to reply, betrayed her apprehensions.

"I cannot listen to such a request from a stranger," she said. "If you bring news from—from my father, why is it not told to Dr. Melmoth?"

"Because what I have to say is for your ear alone," was the reply; "and if you would avoid misfortune now, and sorrow hereafter, you will not refuse to hear me."

"And does it concern my father?" asked Ellen, eagerly.

"It does—most deeply," answered the stranger.

She meditated a moment, and then replied, "I will not refuse, I will hear—but speak quickly."

"We are in danger of interruption in this place, and that would be fatal to my errand," said the stranger. "I will await you in the garden."

With these words, and giving her no opportunity for reply, he drew back; and his form faded from her eyes. This precipitate retreat from

a. ment was the most probable method that he could have adopted of
g. .ing his end. He had awakened the strongest interest in Ellen's mind;
a. he calculated justly in supposing that she would consent to an inter-
w upon his own terms.

Dr. Melmoth had followed his own fancies in the mode of laying out
s garden; and, in consequence, the plan that had undoubtedly existed
. his mind was utterly incomprehensible to every one but himself. It was
n intermixture of kitchen and flower garden, a labyrinth of winding
paths, bordered by hedges, and impeded by shrubbery. Many of the original trees of the forest were still flourishing among the exotics which the
doctor had transplanted thither. It was not without a sensation of fear,
stronger than she had ever before experienced, that Ellen Langton found
herself in this artificial wilderness, and in the presence of the mysterious
stranger. The dusky light deepened the lines of his dark, strong features;
and Ellen fancied that his countenance wore a wilder and a fiercer look
than when she had met him by the stream. He perceived her agitation,
and addressed her in the softest tone of which his voice was capable.

"Compose yourself," he said; "you have nothing to fear from me. But
we are in open view from the house, where we now stand; and discovery
would not be without danger to both of us."

"No eye can see us here," said Ellen, trembling at the truth of her own
observation, when they stood beneath a gnarled, low-branched pine,
which Dr. Melmoth's ideas of beauty had caused him to retain in his
garden. "Speak quickly; for I dare follow you no farther."

The spot was indeed sufficiently solitary; and the stranger delayed no
longer to explain his errand.

"Your father," he began,—"do you not love him? Would you do aught
for his welfare?"

"Everything that a father could ask I would do," exclaimed Ellen,
eagerly. "Where is my father? and when shall I meet him?"

"It must depend upon yourself, whether you shall meet him in a few
days or never."

"Never!" repeated Ellen. "Is he ill? Is he in danger?"

"He is in danger," replied the man, "but not from illness. Your father
is a ruined man. Of all his friends, but one remains to him. That friend
has travelled far to prove if his daughter has a daughter's affection."

"And what is to be the proof?" asked Ellen, with more calmness than
the stranger had anticipated; for she possessed a large fund of plain
sense, which revolted against the mystery of these proceedings. Such a
course, too, seemed discordant with her father's character, whose strong
mind and almost cold heart were little likely to demand, or even to pardon, the romance of affection.

"This letter will explain," was the reply to Ellen's question. "You will
see that it is in your father's hand; and that may gain your confidence,
though I am doubted."

She received the letter; and many of her suspicions of the stranger's
truth were vanquished by the apparent openness of his manner. He was

preparing to speak further, but paused, for a footstep was now heard, approaching from the lower part of the garden. From their situation,—at some distance from the path, and in the shade of the tree,—they had a fair chance of eluding discovery from any unsuspecting passenger; and, when Ellen saw that the intruder was Fanshawe, she hoped that his usual abstraction would assist their concealment.

But, as the student advanced along the path, his air was not that of one whose deep inward thoughts withdrew his attention from all outward objects. He rather resembled the hunter, on the watch for his game; and, while he was yet at a distance from Ellen, a wandering gust of wind waved her white garment, and betrayed her.

"It is as I feared," said Fanshawe to himself. He then drew nigh, and addressed Ellen with a calm authority that became him well, notwithstanding that his years scarcely exceeded her own. "Miss Langton," he inquired, "what do you here at such an hour, and with such a companion?"

Ellen was sufficiently displeased at what she deemed the unauthorized intrusion of Fanshawe in her affairs; but his imposing manner and her own confusion prevented her from replying.

"Permit me to lead you to the house," he continued, in the words of a request, but in the tone of a command. "The dew hangs dank and heavy on these branches; and a longer stay would be more dangerous than you are aware."

Ellen would fain have resisted; but though the tears hung as heavy on her eyelashes, between shame and anger, as the dew upon the leaves, she felt compelled to accept the arm that he offered her. But the stranger, who, since Fanshawe's approach, had remained a little apart, now advanced.

"You speak as one in authority, young man," he said. "Have you the means of compelling obedience? Does your power extend to men? Or do you rule only over simple girls? Miss Langton is under my protection, and, till you can bend me to your will, she shall remain so."

Fanshawe turned calmly, and fixed his eyes on the stranger. "Retire, sir," was all he said.

Ellen almost shuddered, as if there were a mysterious and unearthly power in Fanshawe's voice; for she saw that the stranger endeavored in vain, borne down by the influence of a superior mind, to maintain the boldness of look and bearing that seemed natural to him. He at first made a step forward, then muttered a few half-audible words; but, quailing at length beneath the young man's bright and steady eye, he turned and slowly withdrew.

Fanshawe remained silent a moment after his opponent had departed; and, when he next spoke, it was in a tone of depression. Ellen observed, also, that his countenance had lost its look of pride and authority; and he seemed faint and exhausted. The occasion that called forth his energies had passed; and they had left him.

"Forgive me, Miss Langton," he said almost humbly, "if my eagerness to serve you has led me too far. There is evil in this stranger, more than your pure mind can conceive. I know not what has been his errand; but let me entreat you to put confidence in those to whose care your father has intrusted you. Or if I—or—or Edward Walcott— But I have no right to advise you; and your own calm thoughts will guide you best."

He said no more; and, as Ellen did not reply, they reached the house, and parted in silence.

## CHAPTER IV

"The seeds by nature planted
Take a deep root in the soil, and though for a time
The trenchant share and tearing harrow may
Sweep all appearance of them from the surface,
Yet with the first warm rains of spring they'll shoot,
And with their rankness smother the good grain.
Heaven grant, it mayn't be so with him."

RICHES.

THE scene of this tale must now be changed to the little inn, which at that period, as at the present, was situated in the vicinity of Harley College. The site of the modern establishment is the same with that of the ancient; but everything of the latter that had been built by hands has gone to decay and been removed, and only the earth beneath and around it remains the same. The modern building, a house of two stories, after a lapse of twenty years, is yet unfinished. On this account, it has retained the appellation of the "New Inn," though, like many who have frequented it, it has grown old ere its maturity. Its dingy whiteness, and its apparent superfluity of windows (many of them being closed with rough boards), give it somewhat of a dreary look, especially in a wet day.

The ancient inn was a house, of which the eaves approached within about seven feet of the ground; while the roof, sloping gradually upward formed an angle at several times that height. It was a comfortable and pleasant abode to the weary traveller, both in summer and winter; for the frost never ventured within the sphere of its huge hearths; and it was protected from the heat of the sultry season by three large elms that swept the roof with their long branches, and seemed to create a breeze where there was not one. The device upon the sign, suspended from one of these trees, was a hand holding a long-necked bottle, and was much more appropriate than the present unmeaning representation of a black eagle. But it is necessary to speak rather more at length of the landlord than of the house over which he presided.

Hugh Crombie was one for whom most of the wise men, who considered the course of his early years, had predicted the gallows as an end before he should arrive at middle age. That these prophets of ill had been deceived was evident from the fact that the doomed man had now passed the fortieth year, and was in more prosperous circumstances than most of those who had wagged their tongues against him. Yet the failure of their forebodings was more remarkable than their fulfilment would have been.

He had been distinguished, almost from his earliest infancy, by those precocious accomplishments, which, because they consist in an imitation of the vices and follies of maturity, render a boy the favorite plaything of men. He seemed to have received from nature the convivial talents, which, whether natural or acquired, are a most dangerous possession; and, before his twelfth year, he was the welcome associate of all the idle and dissipated of his neighborhood, and especially of those who haunted the tavern of which he had now become the landlord. Under this course of education, Hugh Crombie grew to youth and manhood; and the lovers of good words could only say in his favor, that he was a greater enemy to himself than to any one else, and that, if he should reform, few would have a better chance of prosperity than he.

The former clause of this modicum of praise (if praise it may be termed) was indisputable; but it may be doubted, whether, under any circumstances where his success depended on his own exertions, Hugh would have made his way well through the world. He was one of those unfortunate persons, who, instead of being perfect in any single art or occupation, are superficial in many, and who are supposed to possess a larger share of talent than other men, because it consists of numerous scraps, instead of a single mass. He was partially acquainted with most of the manual arts that gave bread to others; but not one of them, nor all of them, would give bread to him. By some fatality, the only two of his multifarious accomplishments in which his excellence was generally conceded were both calculated to keep him poor rather than to make him rich. He was a musician and a poet.

There are yet remaining in that portion of the country many ballads and songs,—set to their own peculiar tunes,—the authorship of which is attributed to him. In general, his productions were upon subjects of local and temporary interest, and would consequently require a bulk of explanatory notes to render them interesting or intelligible to the world at large. A considerable proportion of the remainder are Anacreontics; though, in their construction, Hugh Crombie imitated neither the Teian nor any other bard. These latter have generally a coarseness and sensuality intolerable to minds even of no very fastidious delicacy. But there are two or three simple little songs, into which a feeling and a natural pathos have found their way, that still retain their influence over the heart. These, after two or three centuries, may perhaps be precious to the collectors of our early poetry. At any rate, Hugh Crombie's effusions, tavern-haunter and vagrant though he was, have gained a continuance of fame (confined, indeed, to a narrow section of the country), which many who called themselves poets then, and would have scorned such a brother, have failed to equal.

During the long winter evenings, when the farmers were idle round their hearths, Hugh was a courted guest; for none could while away the hours more skilfully than he. The winter, therefore, was his season of prosperity; in which respect he differed from the butterflies and useless insects, to which he otherwise bore a resemblance. During the cold months, a very desirable alteration for the better appeared in his outward man. His cheeks were plump and sanguine; his eyes bright and cheerful; and the tip of his nose glowed with a Bardolphian fire,—a flame, indeed, which Hugh was so far a vestal as to supply with its necessary fuel at all seasons of the year. But, as the spring advanced, he assumed a lean and sallow look, wilting and fading in the sunshine that brought life and joy to every animal and vegetable except himself. His winter patrons eyed him with an austere regard; and some even practised upon him the modern and fashionable courtesy of the "cut direct."

Yet, after all, there was good, or something that Nature intended to be so, in the poor outcast,—some lovely flowers, the sweeter even for the weeds that choked them. An instance of this was his affection for an aged father, whose whole support was the broken reed,—his son. Notwithstanding his own necessities, Hugh contrived to provide food and raiment for the old man: how, it would be difficult to say, and perhaps as well not to inquire. He also exhibited traits of sensitiveness to neglect and insult, and of gratitude for favors; both of which feelings a course of life like his is usually quick to eradicate.

At length the restraint—for such his father had ever been—upon Hugh Crombie's conduct was removed by death; and then the wise men and the old began to shake their heads; and they who took pleasure in the follies, vices, and misfortunes of their fellow-creatures, looked for a speedy gratification. They were disappointed, however; for Hugh had apparently determined, that, whatever might be his catastrophe, he would meet it among strangers, rather than at home. Shortly after his father's death, he disappeared altogether from the vicinity; and his name became, in the course of years, an unusual sound, where once the lack of other topics of interest had given it a considerable degree of notoriety. Sometimes, however, when the winter blast was loud round the lonely farm-house, its inmates remembered him who had so often chased away the gloom of such an hour, and, though with little expectation of its fulfilment, expressed a wish to behold him again.

Yet that wish, formed, perhaps, because it appeared so desperate, was finally destined to be gratified. One summer evening, about two years previous to the period of this tale, a man of sober and staid deportment, mounted upon a white horse, arrived at the Hand and Bottle, to which some civil or military meeting had chanced, that day, to draw most of the inhabitants of the vicinity. The stranger was well though plainly dressed, and anywhere but in a retired country town would have attracted no particular attention; but here, where a traveller was not of every-day occurrence, he was soon surrounded by a little crowd, who, when his eye was averted, seized the opportunity diligently to peruse his person. He was rather a thick-set man, but with no superfluous flesh; his hair was of iron-gray; he had a few wrinkles; his face was so deeply sunburnt, that, excepting a half-smothered glow on the tip of his nose, a dusky yellow was the only apparent hue. As the people gazed, it was observed that the elderly men, and the men of substance, gat themselves silently to their steeds, and hied homeward with an unusual degree of haste; till at length the inn was deserted, except by a few wretched objects to whom it was a constant resort. These, instead of retreating, drew closer to the traveller, peeping anxiously into his face, and asking, ever and anon, a question, in order to discover the tone of his voice. At length, with one consent, and as if the recognition had at once burst upon them, they hailed their old boon-companion, Hugh Crombie, and, leading him into the inn, did him the honor to partake of a cup of welcome at his expense.

But, though Hugh readily acknowledged the not very reputable acquaintances who alone acknowledged him, they speedily discovered that he was an altered man. He partook with great moderation of the liquor for which he was to pay; he declined all their flattering entreaties for one of his old songs; and finally, being urged to engage in a game at all-fours, he calmly observed, almost in the words of an old clergyman on a like occasion, that his principles forbade a profane appeal to the decision by lot.

On the next Sabbath Hugh Crombie made his appearance at public worship in the chapel of Harley College; and here his outward demeanor was exceptionally serious and devout,—a praise which, on that particular occasion, could be bestowed on few besides. From these favorable symptoms, the old established prejudices against him began to waver; and as he seemed not to need, and to have no intention to ask, the assistance of any one, he was soon generally acknowledged by the rich as well as by the poor. His account of his past life, and of his intentions for the future, was brief, but not unsatisfactory. He said that, since his departure, he had been a seafaring man, and that, having acquired sufficient property to render him easy in the decline of his days, he had returned to live and die in the town of his nativity.

There was one person, and the one whom Hugh was most interested to please, who seemed perfectly satisfied of the verity of his reformation. This was the landlady of the inn, whom, at his departure, he had left a gay, and, even at thirty-five, a rather pretty wife, and whom, on his return, he found a widow of fifty, fat, yellow, wrinkled, and a zealous member of the church. She, like others, had, at first, cast a cold eye on the wanderer; but it shortly became evident to close observers, that a change was at work in the pious matron's sentiments respecting her old acquaintance. She was now careful to give him his morning dram from her own peculiar bottle, to fill his pipe from her private box of Virginia, and to mix for him the sleeping-cup in which her late husband had delighted. Of all these courtesies Hugh Crombie did partake with a wise and cautious moderation, that, while it proved them to be welcome, expressed his fear of trespassing on her kindness. For the sake of brevity, it shall suffice to say, that, about six weeks after Hugh's return, a writing appeared on one of the elm-trees in front of the tavern (where, as the place of greatest resort, such notices were usually displayed) setting forth that marriage was intended between Hugh Crombie and the Widow Sarah Hutchins. And the ceremony, which made Hugh a landholder, a house-holder, and a substantial man, in due time took place.

As a landlord, his general conduct was very praiseworthy. He was moderate in his charges, and attentive to his guests; he allowed no gross and evident disorders in his house, and practised none himself; he was kind and charitable to such as needed food and lodging, and had not wherewithal to pay,—for with these his experience had doubtless given him a fellow-feeling. He was also sufficiently attentative to his wife; though it must be acknowledged that the religious zeal which had had a considerable influence in gaining her affections grew, by no moderate degrees, less fervent. It was whispered, too, that the new landlord could, when time, place, and company were to his mind, upraise a song as merrily, and drink a glass as jollily, as in the days of yore. These were the weightiest charges that could now be brought against him; and wise men thought, that, whatever might have been the evil of his past life, he had returned with a desire (which years of vice, if they do not sometimes produce, do not always destroy) of being honest, if opportunity should offer; and Hugh had certainly a fair one.

On the afternoon previous to the events related in the last chapter, the personage whose introduction to the reader has occupied so large a space was seated under one of the elms in front of his dwelling. The bench which now sustained him, and on which were carved the names of many former occupants, was Hugh Crombie's favorite lounging-place, unless when his attentions were required by his guests. No demand had that day been made upon the hospitality of the Hand and Bottle; and the landlord was just then murmuring at the unfrequency of employment. The slenderness of his profits, indeed, were no part of his concern; for the Widow Hutchin's chief income was drawn from her farm, nor was Hugh ever miserly inclined. But his education and habits had made him delight in the atmosphere of the inn, and in the society of those who frequented it; and of this species of enjoyment his present situation certainly did not afford an overplus.

Yet had Hugh Crombie an enviable appearance of indolence and ease, as he sat under the old tree, polluting the sweet air with his pipe, and taking occasional draughts from a brown jug that stood near at hand. The basis of the potation contained in this vessel was harsh old cider, from the widow's own orchard; but its coldness and acidity were rendered innocuous by a due proportion of yet older brandy. The result of this mixture was extremely felicitous, pleasant to the taste, and producing a tingling sensation on the coats of the stomach, uncommonly delectable to so old a toper as Hugh.

The landlord cast his eye, ever and anon, along the road that led down the valley in the direction of the village; and at last, when the sun was wearing westward, he discovered the approach of a horseman. He immediately replenished his pipe, took a long draught from the brown jug, summoned the ragged youth who officiated in most of the subordinate departments of the inn, and who was now to act as hostler, and then prepared himself for confabulation with his guest.

"He comes from the sea-coast," said Hugh to himself, as the traveller emerged into open view on the level road. "He is two days in advance of the post, with its news of a fortnight old. Pray Heaven he prove communicative!" Then, as the stranger drew nigher, "One would judge that his dark face had seen as hot a sun as mine. He has felt the burning breeze of the Indies, East and West, I warrant him. Ah, I see we shall send away the evening merrily! Not a penny shall come out of his purse, —that is, if his tongue runs glibly. Just the man I was praying for— Now may the Devil take me if he is!" interrupted Hugh, in accents of alarm, and starting from his seat. He composed his countenance, however, with the power that long habit and necessity had given him over his emotions, and again settled himself quietly on the bench.

The traveller, coming on at a moderate pace, alighted, and gave his horse to the ragged hostler. He then advanced towards the door near which Hugh was seated, whose agitation was manifested by no perceptible sign, except by the shorter and more frequent puffs with which he plied his pipe. Their eyes did not meet till just as the stranger was about to enter, when he started apparently with a surprise and alarm similar to those of Hugh Crombie. He recovered himself, however, sufficiently to return the nod of recognition with which he was favored, and immediately entered the house, the landlord following.

"This way, if you please, sir," said Hugh. "You will find this apartment cool and retired."

He ushered his guest into a small room the windows of which were darkened by the creeping plants that clustered round them. Entering, and closing the door, the two gazed at each other a little space without speaking. The traveller first broke silence.

"Then this is your living self, Hugh Crombie?" he said. The landlord extended his hand as a practical reply to the question. The stranger took it, though with no especial appearance of cordiality.

"Ay, this seems to be flesh and blood," he said, in the tone of one who would willingly have found it otherwise. "And how happens this, friend Hugh? I little thought to meet you again in this life. When I last heard from you, your prayers were said, and you were bound for a better world."

"There would have been small danger of your meeting me there," observed the landlord, dryly.

"It is an unquestionable truth, Hugh," replied the traveller. "For which reason I regret that your voyage was delayed."

"Nay, that is a hard word to bestow on your old comrade," said Hugh Crombie. "The world is wide enough for both of us; and why should you wish me out of it?"

"Wide as it is," rejoined the stranger, "we have stumbled against each other,—to the pleasure of neither of us, if I may judge from your countenance. Methinks I am not a welcome guest at Hugh Crombie's inn."

"Your welcome must depend on the cause of your coming, and the length of your stay," replied the landlord.

"And what if I come to settle down among these quiet hills where I was born?" inquired the other. "What if I, too, am weary of the life we have led,—or afraid, perhaps, that it will come to too speedy an end? Shall I have your good word, Hugh, to set me up in an honest way of life? Or will you make me a partner in your trade, since you know my qualifications? A pretty pair of publicans should we be; and the quart pot would have little rest between us."

"It may be as well to replenish it now," observed Hugh, stepping to the door of the room, and giving orders accordingly. "A meeting between old friends should never be dry. But for the partnership, it is a matter in which you must excuse me. Heaven knows I find it hard enough to be honest, with no tempter but the Devil and my own thoughts; and, if I have you also to contend with, there is little hope of me."

"Nay, that is true. Your good resolutions were always like cobwebs, and your evil habits like five-inch cables," replied the traveller. "I am to understand, then, that you refuse my offer?"

"Not only that; but, if you have chosen this valley as your place of rest, Dame Crombie and I must look through the world for another. But hush! here comes the wine."

The hostler, in the performance of another part of his duty, now appeared, bearing a measure of the liquor that Hugh had ordered. The wine of that period, owing to the comparative lowness of the duties, was of more moderate price than in the mother-country, and of purer and better quality than at the present day.

"The stuff is well chosen, Hugh," observed the guest, after a draught large enough to authorize an opinion. "You have most of the requisites for your present station; and I should be sorry to draw you from it. I trust there will be no need."

"Yet you have a purpose in your journey hither," observed his comrade.

"Yes; and you would fain be informed of it," replied the traveller. He arose, and walked once or twice across the room; then, seeming to have taken his resolution, he paused, and fixed his eye steadfastly on Hugh Crombie. "I could wish, my old acquaintance," he said, "that your lot had been cast anywhere rather than here. Yet, if you choose it, you may do me a good office, and one that shall meet with a good reward. Can I trust you?"

"My secrecy, you can," answered the host, "but nothing further. I know the nature of your plans, and whither they would lead me, too well to engage in them. To say the truth, since it concerns not me, I have little desire to hear your secret."

"And I as little to tell it, I do assure you," rejoined the guest. "I have always loved to manage my affairs myself, and to keep them to myself. It is a good rule; but it must sometimes be broken. And now, Hugh, how is it that you have become possessed of this comfortable dwelling and of these pleasant fields?"

"By my marriage with the Widow Sarah Hutchins," replied Hugh Crombie, staring at a question which seemed to have little reference to the present topic of conversation.

"It is a most excellent method of becoming a man of substance," continued the traveller; "attended with little trouble, and honest withal."

"Why, as to the trouble," said the landlord, "it follows such a bargain, instead of going before it. And for honesty,—I do not recollect that I have gained a penny more honestly these twenty years."

"I can swear to that," observed his comrade. "Well, mine host, I entirely approve of your doings, and, moreover, have resolved to prosper after the same fashion myself."

"If that be the commodity you seek," replied Hugh Crombie, "you will find none here to your mind. We have widows in plenty, it is true; but most of them have children, and few have houses and lands. But now to be serious,—and there has been something serious in your eye all this while,—what is your purpose in coming hither? You are not safe here. Your name has had a wider spread than mine, and, if discovered, it will go hard with you."

"But who would know me now?" asked the guest.

"Few, few indeed!" replied the landlord, gazing at the dark features of his companion, where hardship, peril, and dissipation had each left their traces. "No, you are not like the slender boy of fifteen, who stood on the hill by moonlight to take a last look at his father's cottage. There were tears in your eyes then; and, as often as I remember them, I repent that I did not turn you back, instead of leading you on."

"Tears, were there? Well, there have been few enough since," said his comrade, pressing his eyelids firmly together, as if even then tempted to give way to the weakness that he scorned. "And, for turning me back, Hugh, it was beyond your power. I had taken my resolution, and you did but show me the way to execute it."

"You have not inquired after those you left behind," observed Hugh Crombie.

"No—no; nor will I have aught of them," exclaimed the traveller, starting from his seat, and pacing rapidly across the room. "My father, I know, is dead, and I have forgiven him. My mother—what could I hear of her but misery? I will hear nothing."

"You must have passed the cottage as you rode hitherward," said Hugh. "How could you forbear to enter?"

"I did not see it," he replied. "I closed my eyes and turned away my head."

"Oh, if I had had a mother, a loving mother! if there had been one being in the world that loved me, or cared for me, I should not have become an utter castaway," exclaimed Hugh Crombie.

The landlord's pathos, like all pathos that flows from the winecup, was sufficiently ridiculous; and his companion, who had already overcome his own brief feelings of sorrow and remorse, now laughed aloud.

"Come, come, mine host of the Hand and Bottle," he cried in his usual hard, sarcastic tone; "be a man as much as in you lies. You had always a foolish trick of repentance; but, as I remember, it was commonly of a morning, before you had swallowed your first dram. And now, Hugh, fill the quart pot again, and we will to business."

When the landlord had complied with the wishes of his guest, the latter resumed in a lower tone than that of his ordinary conversation,—

"There is a young lady lately become a resident hereabouts. Perhaps you can guess her name; for you have a quick apprehension in these matters."

"A young lady?" repeated Hugh Crombie. "And what is your concern with her? Do you mean Ellen Langton, daughter of the old merchant Langton, whom you have some cause to remember?"

"I do remember him; but he is where he will speedily be forgotten," answered the traveller. "And this girl,—I know your eye has been upon her, Hugh,—describe her to me."

"Describe her!" exclaimed Hugh with much animation. "It is impossible in prose; but you shall have her very picture in a verse of one of my own songs."

"Nay, mine host, I beseech you to spare me. This is no time for quavering," said the guest. "However, I am proud of your approbation, my old friend; for this young lady do I intend to take to wife. What think you of the plan?"

Hugh Crombie gazed into his companion's face for the space of a moment, in silence. There was nothing in its expression that looked like a jest. It still retained the same hard, cold look, that, except when Hugh had alluded to his home and family, it had worn through their whole conversation.

"On my word, comrade!" he at length replied, "my advice is, that you give over your application to the quart pot, and refresh your brain by a short nap. And yet your eye is cool and steady. What is the meaning of this?"

"Listen, and you shall know," said the guest. "The old man, her father, is in his grave."

"Not a bloody grave, I trust," interrupted the landlord, starting, and looking fearfully into his comrade's face.

"No, a watery one," he replied calmly. "You see, Hugh, I am a better man than you took me for. The old man's blood is not on my head, though my wrongs are on his. Now listen: he had no heir but this only daughter; and to her, and to the man she marries, all his wealth will belong. She shall marry me. Think you her father will rest easy in the ocean, Hugh Crombie, when I am his son-in-law?"

"No, he will rise up to prevent it, if need be," answered the landlord. "But the dead need not interpose to frustrate so wild a scheme."

"I understand you," said his comrade. "You are of opinion that the young lady's consent may not be so soon won as asked. Fear not for that, mine host. I have a winning way with me, when opportunity serves; and it shall serve with Ellen Langton. I will have no rivals in my wooing."

"Your intention, if I take it rightly, is to get this poor girl into your power, and then to force her into a marriage," said Hugh Crombie.

"It is; and I think I possess the means of doing it," replied his comrade. "But methinks, friend Hugh, my enterprise has not your good wishes."

"No; and I pray you to give it over," said Hugh Crombie, very earnestly. "The girl is young, lovely, and as good as she is fair. I cannot aid in her ruin. Nay, more: I must prevent it."

"Prevent it!" exclaimed the traveller, with a darkening countenance. "Think twice before you stir in this matter, I advise you. Ruin, do you say? Does a girl call it ruin to be made an honest wedded wife? No, no, mine host! nor does a widow either, else have you much to answer for."

"I gave the Widow Hutchins fair play, at least, which is more than poor Ellen is like to get," observed the landlord. "My old comrade, will you not give up this scheme?"

"My old comrade, I will not give up this scheme," returned the other, composedly. "Why, Hugh, what has come over you since we last met? Have we not done twenty worse deeds of a morning, and laughed over them at night?"

"He is right there," said Hugh Crombie, in a meditative tone. "Of a certainty, my conscience has grown unreasonably tender within the last two years. This one small sin, if I were to aid in it, would add but a trifle to the sum of mine. But then the poor girl!"

His companion overheard him thus communing with himself, and having had much former experience of his infirmity of purpose, doubted not that he should bend him to his will. In fact, his arguments were so effectual, that Hugh at length, though reluctantly, promised his coöperation. It was necessary that their motions should be speedy; for on the second day thereafter, the arrival of the post would bring intelligence of the shipwreck by which Mr. Langton had perished.

"And after the deed is done," said the landlord, "I beseech you never to cross my path again. There have been more wicked thoughts in my head within the last hour than for the whole two years that I have been an honest man."

"What a saint art thou become, Hugh!" said his comrade. "But fear not that we shall meet again. When I leave this valley, it will be to enter it no more."

"And there is little danger that any other who has known me will chance upon me here," observed Hugh Crombie. "Our trade was unfavorable to length of days, and I suppose most of our old comrades have arrived at the end of theirs."

"One whom you knew well is nearer to you than you think," answered the traveller; "for I did not travel hitherward entirely alone."

CHAPTER V

"A naughty night to swim in."—SHAKESPEARE.

THE evening of the day succeeding the adventure of the angler was dark and tempestuous. The rain descended almost in a continuous sheet; and occasional powerful gusts of wind drove it hard against the northeastern windows of Hugh Crombie's inn. But at least one apartment of the interior presented a scene of comfort and of apparent enjoyment, the more delightful from its contrast with the elemental fury that raged without. A fire, which the chillness of the evening, though a summer one, made necessary, was burning brightly on the hearth; and in front was placed a small round table, sustaining wine and glasses. One of the guests for whom these preparations had been made was Edward Walcott; the other was a shy, awkward young man, distinguished, by the union of classic and rural dress, as having but lately become a student of Harley College. He seemed little at his ease, probably from a consciousness that he was on forbidden ground, and that the wine, of which he nevertheless swallowed a larger share than his companion, was an unlawful draught.

In the catalogue of crimes provided against by the laws of Harley College, that of tavern-haunting was one of the principal. The secluded situation of the seminary, indeed, gave its scholars but a very limited choice of vices; and this was, therefore, the usual channel by which the wildness of youth discharged itself. Edward Walcott, though naturally temperate, had been not an unfrequent offender in this respect, for which a superfluity both of time and money might plead some excuse. But, since his acquaintance with Ellen Langton, he had rarely entered Hugh Crombie's doors; and an interruption in that acquaintance was the cause of his present appearance there.

Edward's jealous pride had been considerably touched on Ellen's compliance with the request of the angler. He had, by degrees, imperceptible perhaps to himself, assumed the right of feeling displeased with her conduct; and she had, as imperceptibly, accustomed herself to consider what would be his wishes, and to act accordingly. He would, indeed, in no contingency have ventured an open remonstrance; and such a proceeding would have been attended by a result the reverse of what he desired. But there existed between them a silent compact (acknowledged perhaps by neither, but felt by both), according to which they had regulated the latter part of their intercourse. Their lips had yet spoken no word of love; but some of love's rights and privileges had been assumed on the one side, and at least not disallowed on the other.

Edward's penetration had been sufficiently quick to discover that there was a mystery about the angler, that there must have been a cause for the blush that rose so proudly on Ellen's cheek; and his Quixotism had been not a little mortified, because she did not immediately appeal to his protection. He had, however, paid his usual visit the next day at Dr. Melmoth's, expecting that, by a smile of more than common brightness, she would make amends to his wounded feelings; such having been her usual mode of reparation in the few instances of disagreement that had occurred between them. But he was disappointed. He found her cold, silent, and abstracted, inattentive when he spoke, and indisposed to speak herself. Her eye was sedulously averted from his; and the casual meeting of their glances only proved that there were feelings in her bosom which he did not share. He was unable to account for this change in her deportment; and, added to his previous conceptions of his wrongs, it produced an effect upon his rather hasty temper, that might have manifested itself violently, but for the presence of Mrs. Melmoth. He took his leave in very evident displeasure; but, just as he closed the door, he noticed an expression in Ellen's countenance, that, had they been alone, and had not he been quite so proud, would have drawn him down to her feet. Their eyes met, when, suddenly, there was a gush of tears into those of Ellen; and a deep sadness, almost despair, spread itself over her features. He paused a moment, and then went his way, equally unable to account for her coldness, or for her grief. He was well aware, however, that his situation in respect to her was unaccountably changed,—a conviction so disagreeable, that, but for a hope that is latent even in the despair of youthful hearts, he would have been sorely tempted to shoot himself.

The gloom of his thoughts—a mood of mind the more intolerable to him, because so unusual—had driven him to Hugh Crombie's inn in search of artificial excitement. But even the wine had no attractions; and his first glass stood now almost untouched before him, while he gazed in heavy thought into the glowing embers of the fire. His companion perceived his melancholy, and essayed to dispel it by a choice of such topics of conversation as he conceived would be most agreeable.

"There is a lady in the house," he observed. "I caught a glimpse of her in the passage as we came in. Did you see her, Edward?"

"A lady!" repeated Edward, carelessly. "What know you of ladies? No, I did not see her; but I will venture to say that it was Dame Crombie's self, and no other."

"Well, perhaps it might," said the other, doubtingly. "Her head was turned from me, and she was gone like a shadow."

"Dame Crombie is no shadow, and never vanishes like one," resumed Edward. "You have mistaken the slipshod servant-girl for a lady."

"Ay; but she had a white hand, a small white hand," said the student, piqued at Edward's contemptuous opinion of his powers of observation; "as white as Ellen Langton's." He paused; for the lover was offended by the profanity of the comparison, as was made evident by the blood that rushed to his brow.

"We will appeal to the landlord," said Edward, recovering his equanimity, and turning to Hugh, who just then entered the room. "Who is this angel, mine host, that has taken up her abode in the Hand and Bottle?"

Hugh cast a quick glance from one to another before he answered, "I keep no angels here, gentlemen. Dame Crombie would make the house anything but heaven for them and me."

"And yet Glover has seen a vision in the passageway,—a lady with a small white hand."

"Ah, I understand! A slight mistake of the young gentleman's," said Hugh, with the air of one who could perfectly account for the mystery. "Our passageway is dark; or perhaps the light had dazzled his eyes. It was the Widow Fowler's daughter, that came to borrow a pipe of tobacco for her mother. By the same token, she put it into her own sweet mouth, and puffed as she went along."

"But the white hand," said Glover, only half convinced.

"Nay, I know not," answered Hugh. "But her hand was at least as white as her face: that I can swear. Well, gentlemen, I trust you find everything in my house to your satisfaction. When the fire needs renewing, or the wine runs low, be pleased to tap on the table. I shall appear with the speed of a sunbeam."

After the departure of the landlord, the conversation of the young men amounted to little more than monosyllables. Edward Walcott was wrapped in his own contemplations; and his companion was in a half-slumberous state, from which he started every quarter of an hour, at the chiming of the clock that stood in a corner. The fire died gradually away; the lamps began to burn dim; and Glover, rousing himself from one of his periodical slumbers, was about to propose a return to their chambers. He was prevented, however, by the approach of footsteps along the passageway; and Hugh Crombie, opening the door, ushered a person into the room, and retired.

The new-comer was Fanshawe. The water that poured plentifully from his cloak evinced that he had but just arrived at the inn; but, whatever was his object, he seemed not to have attained it in meeting with the young men. He paused near the door, as if meditating whether to retire.

"My intrusion is altogether owing to a mistake, either of the landlord's or mine," he said. "I came hither to seek another person; but, as I could not mention his name, my inquiries were rather vague."

"I thank Heaven for the chance that sent you to us," replied Edward, rousing himself. "Glover is wretched company; and a duller evening have I never spent. We will renew our fire and our wine, and you must sit down with us. And for the man you seek," he continued in a whisper, "he left the inn within a half-hour after we encountered him. I inquired of Hugh Crombie last night."

Fanshawe did not express his doubts of the correctness of the information on which Edward seemed to rely. Laying aside his cloak, he accepted his invitation to make one of the party, and sat down by the fireside.

The aspect of the evening now gradually changed. A strange wild glee spread from one to another of the party, which, much to the surprise of his companions, began with and was communicated from, Fanshawe. He seemed to overflow with conceptions inimitably ludicrous, but so singular, that, till his hearers had imbibed a portion of his own spirit, they could only wonder at, instead of enjoying them. His applications to the wine were very unfrequent; yet his conversation was such as one might expect from a bottle of champagne endowed by a fairy with the gift of speech. The secret of this strange mirth lay in the troubled state of his spirits, which, like the vexed ocean at midnight (if the simile be not too magnificent), tossed forth a mysterious brightness. The undefined apprehensions that had drawn him to the inn still distracted his mind; but, mixed with them, there was a sort of joy not easily to be described. By degrees, and by the assistance of the wine, the inspiration spread, each one contributing such a quantity, and such quality of wit and whim, as was proportioned to his genius; but each one, and all, displaying a greater share of both than they had ever been suspected of possessing.

At length, however, there was a pause,—the deep pause of flagging spirits, that always follows mirth and wine. No one would have believed, on beholding the pensive faces, and hearing the involuntary sighs of the party, that from these, but a moment before, had arisen so loud and wild a laugh. During this interval Edward Walcott (who was the poet of his class) volunteered the following song, which, from its want of polish, and from its application to his present feelings, might charitably be taken for an extemporaneous production:—

> The wine is bright, the wine is bright;
>     And gay the drinkers be:
> Of all that drain the bowl to-night,
>     Most jollily drain we.
> Oh, could one search the weary earth,—
>     The earth from sea to sea,—
> He'd turn and mingle in our mirth;
>     For we're the merriest three.
>
> Yet there are cares, oh, heavy cares!
>     We know that they are nigh:
> When forth each lonely drinker fares,
>     Mark then his altered eye.
> Care comes upon us when the jest
>     And frantic laughter die;
> And care will watch the parting guest—
>     Oh late, then let us fly!

Hugh Crombie, whose early love of song and minstrelsy was still alive, had entered the room at the sound of Edward's voice, in sufficient time to accompany the second stanza on the violin. He now, with the air of one who was entitled to judge in these matters, expressed his opinion of the performance.

"Really, Master Walcott, I was not prepared for this," he said in the tone of condescending praise that a great man uses to his inferior when he chooses to overwhelm him with excess of joy. "Very well, indeed, young gentleman! Some of the lines, it is true, seem to have been dragged in by the head and shoulders; but I could scarcely have done much better myself at your age. With practice, and with such instruction as I might afford you, I should have little doubt of your becoming a distinguished poet. A great defect in your seminary, gentlemen,—the want of due cultivation in this heavenly art."

"Perhaps, sir," said Edward, with much gravity, "you might yourself be prevailed upon to accept the professorship of poetry?"

"Why, such an offer would require consideration," replied the landlord. "Professor Hugh Crombie of Harley College: it has a good sound, assuredly. But I am a public man, Master Walcott; and the public would be loath to spare me from my present office."

"Will Professor Crombie favor us with a specimen of his productions?" inquired Edward.

"Ahem, I shall be happy to gratify you, young gentleman," answered Hugh. "It is seldom, in this rude country, Master Walcott, that we meet with kindred genius; and the opportunity should never be thrown away."

Thus saying, he took a heavy draught of the liquor by which he was usually inspired, and the praises of which were the prevailing subject of his song; then, after much hemming, thrumming, and prelusion, and with many queer gestures and gesticulations, he began to effuse a lyric in the following fashion:—

> I've been a jolly drinker this five-and-twenty year,
> And still a jolly drinker, my friends, you see me here:
> I sing the joys of drinking; bear a chorus, every man,
> With pint pot and quart pot and clattering of can.

The sense of the professor's first stanza was not in exact proportion to the sound; but, being executed with great spirit, it attracted universal applause. This Hugh appropriated with a condescending bow and smile; and, making a signal for silence, he went on,—

> King Solomon of old, boys (a jolly king was he),—

But here he was interrupted by a clapping of hands, that seemed a continuance of the applause bestowed on his former stanza. Hugh Crombie, who, as is the custom of many great performers, usually sang with his eyes shut, now opened them, intending gently to rebuke his auditors for their unseasonable expression of delight. He immediately perceived, however, that the fault was to be attributed to neither of the three young men; and, following the direction of their eyes, he saw near the door, in the dim background of the apartment, a figure in a cloak. The hat was flapped forward, the cloak muffled round the lower part of the face; and only the eyes were visible.

The party gazed a moment in silence, and then rushed *en masse* upon the intruder, the landlord bringing up the rear, and sounding a charge upon his fiddle. But, as they drew nigh, the black cloak began to assume a familiar look; the hat, also, was an old acquaintance; and, these being removed, from beneath them shone forth the reverend face and form of Dr. Melmoth.

The president, in his quality of clergyman, had, late in the preceding afternoon, been called to visit an aged female who was supposed to be at the point of death. Her habitation was at the distance of several miles from Harley College; so that it was nightfall before Dr. Melmoth stood at her bedside. His stay had been lengthened beyond his anticipation, on account of the frame of mind in which he found the dying woman; and, after essaying to impart the comforts of religion to her disturbed intellect, he had waited for the abatement of the storm that had arisen while he was thus engaged. As the evening advanced, however, the rain poured down in undiminished cataracts; and the doctor, trusting to the prudence and sure-footedness of his steed, had at length set forth on his return. The darkness of the night, and the roughness of the road, might have appalled him, even had his horsemanship and his courage been more considerable than they were; but by the special protection of Providence, as he reasonably supposed (for he was a good man, and on a good errand), he arrived safely as far as Hugh Crombie's inn. Dr. Melmoth had no intention of making a stay there; but, as the road passed within a very short distance, he saw lights in the windows, and heard the sound of song and revelry. It immediately occurred to him, that these midnight rioters were, probably, some of the young men of his charge; and he was impelled, by a sense of duty, to enter and disperse them. Directed by the voices, he found his way, with some difficulty, to the apartment, just as Hugh concluded his first stanza; and, amidst the subsequent applause, his entrance had been unperceived.

There was a silence of a moment's continuance after the discovery of Dr. Melmoth, during which he attempted to clothe his round, good-natured face in a look of awful dignity. But, in spite of himself, there was a little twisting of the corners of his mouth, and a smothered gleam in his eye.

"This has, apparently, been a very merry meeting, young gentlemen," he at length said; "but I fear my presence has cast a damp upon it."

"Oh yes! your reverence's cloak is wet enough to cast a damp upon anything," exclaimed Hugh Crombie, assuming a look of tender anxiety. "The young gentlemen are affrighted for your valuable life. Fear deprives them of utterance: permit me to relieve you of these dangerous garments."

"Trouble not yourself, honest man," replied the doctor, who was one of the most gullible of mortals. "I trust I am in no danger; my dwelling being near at hand. But for these young men"—

"Would your reverence but honor my Sunday suit,—the gray broadcloth coat, and the black velvet smallclothes, that have covered my unworthy legs but once? Dame Crombie shall have them ready in a moment," continued Hugh, beginning to divest the doctor of his garments.

"I pray you to appease your anxiety," cried Dr. Melmoth, retaining a firm hold on such parts of his dress as yet remained to him. "Fear not for my health. I will but speak a word to those misguided youth, and be gone."

"Misguided youth, did your reverence say?" echoed Hugh, in a tone of utter astonishment. "Never were they better guided than when they entered my poor house. Oh, had your reverence but seen them, when I heard their cries, and rushed forth to their assistance. Dripping with wet were they, like three drowned men at the resurrec— Ahem!" interrupted Hugh, recollecting that the comparison he meditated might not suit the doctor's ideas of propriety.

"But why were they abroad on such a night?" inquired the president.

"Ah! doctor, you little know the love these good young gentlemen bear for you," replied the landlord. "Your absence, your long absence, had alarmed them; and they rushed forth through the rain and darkness to seek you."

"And was this indeed so?" asked the doctor, in a softened tone, and casting a tender and grateful look upon the three students. They, it is but justice to mention, had simultaneously made a step forward in order to contradict the egregious falsehoods of which Hugh's fancy was so fertile; but he assumed an expression of such ludicrous entreaty, that it was irresistible.

"But methinks their anxiety was not of long continuance," observed Dr. Melmoth, looking at the wine, and remembering the song that his entrance had interrupted.

"Ah! your reverence disapproves of the wine, I see," answered Hugh Crombie. "I did but offer them a drop to keep the life in their poor young hearts. My dame advised strong waters; 'But, Dame Crombie,' says I, 'would ye corrupt their youth?' And in my zeal for their good, doctor, I was delighting them, just at your entrance, with a pious little melody of my own against the sin of drunkenness."

"Truly, I remember something of the kind," observed Dr. Melmoth. "And, as I think, it seemed to meet with good acceptance."

"Ay, that it did!" said the landlord. "Will it please your reverence to hear it?—

> King Solomon of old, boys (a wise man I'm thinking),
> Has warned you to beware of the horrid vice of drinking—

But why talk I of drinking, foolish man that I am! And all this time, doctor, you have not sipped a drop of my wine. Now I entreat your reverence, as you value your health and the peace and quiet of these youth."

Dr. Melmoth drank a glass of wine, with the benevolent intention of allaying the anxiety of Hugh Crombie and the students. He then prepared to depart; for a strong wind had partially dispersed the clouds, and occasioned an interval in the cataract of rain. There was, perhaps, a little suspicion yet remaining in the good man's mind respecting the truth of the landlord's story: at least, it was his evident intention to see the students fairly out of the inn before he quitted it himself. They therefore proceeded along the passageway in a body. The lamp that Hugh Crombie held but dimly enlightened them; and the number and contiguity of the doors caused Dr. Melmoth to lay his hand upon the wrong one.

"Not there, not there, doctor! It is Dame Crombie's bedchamber," shouted Hugh, most energetically. "Now Beelzebub defend me!" he muttered to himself, perceiving that his exclamation had been a moment too late.

"Heavens! what do I see?" ejaculated Dr. Melmoth, lifting his hands, and starting back from the entrance of the room. The three students pressed forward; Mrs. Crombie and the servant-girl had been drawn to the spot by the sound of Hugh's voice; and all their wondering eyes were fixed on poor Ellen Langton.

The apartment in the midst of which she stood was dimly lighted by a solitary candle at the farther extremity; but Ellen was exposed to the glare of the three lamps, held by Hugh, his wife, and the servant-girl. Their combined rays seemed to form a focus exactly at the point where they reached her; and the beholders, had any been sufficiently calm, might have watched her features in their agitated workings and frequent change of expression, as perfectly as by the broad light of day. Terror had at first blanched her as white as a lily, or as a marble statue, which for a moment she resembled, as she stood motionless in the centre of the room. Shame next bore away; and her blushing countenance, covered by her slender white fingers, might fantastically be compared to a variegated rose with its alternate stripes of white and red. The next instant, a sense of her pure and innocent intentions gave her strength and courage; and her attitude and look had now something of pride and dignity. These, however, in their turn, gave way; for Edward Walcott pressed forward, and attempted to address her.

"Ellen, Ellen!" he said, in an agitated and quivering whisper; but what was to follow cannot be known; for his emotion checked his utterance. His tone and look, however, again overcame Ellen Langton, and she burst into tears. Fanshawe advanced, and took Edward's arm. "She has been deceived," he whispered. "She is innocent: you are unworthy of her if you doubt it."

"Why do you interfere, sir?" demanded Edward, whose passions, thoroughly excited, would willingly have wreaked themselves on any one. "What right have you to speak of her innocence? Perhaps," he continued, an undefined and ridiculous suspicion arising in his mind,—"perhaps you are acquainted with her intentions. Perhaps you are the deceiver."

Fanshawe's temper was not naturally of the meekest character; and having had a thousand bitter feelings of his own to overcome, before he could attempt to console Edward, this rude repulse had almost aroused him to fierceness. But his pride, of which a more moderate degree would have had a less peaceable effect, came to his assistance; and he turned calmly and contemptuously away.

Ellen, in the mean time, had been restored to some degree of composure. To this effect, a feeling of pique against Edward Walcott had contributed. She had distinguished his voice in the neighboring apartment, had heard his mirth and wild laughter, without being aware of the state of feeling that produced them. She had supposed that the terms on which they parted in the morning (which had been very grievous to herself) would have produced a corresponding sadness in him. But while she sat in loneliness and in tears, her bosom distracted by a thousand anxieties and sorrows, of many of which Edward was the object, his reckless gayety had seemed to prove the slight regard in which he held her. After the first outbreak of emotion, therefore, she called up her pride (of which, on proper occasions, she had a reasonable share), and sustained his upbraiding glance with a passive composure, which women have more readily at command than men.

Dr. Melmoth's surprise had during this time kept him silent and inactive. He gazed alternately from one to another of those who stood around him, as if to seek some explanation of so strange an event. But the faces of all were as perplexed as his own; even Hugh Crombie had assumed a look of speechless wonder,—speechless, because his imagination, prolific as it was, could not supply a plausible falsehood.

"Ellen, dearest child," at length said the doctor, "what is the meaning of this?"

Ellen endeavored to reply; but, as her composure was merely external, she was unable to render her words audible. Fanshawe spoke in a low voice to Dr. Melmoth, who appeared grateful for his advice.

"True, it will be the better way," he replied. "My wits are utterly confounded, or I should not have remained thus long. Come, my dear child," he continued, advancing to Ellen, and taking her hand, "let us return home, and defer the explanation till the morrow. There, there: only dry your eyes, and we will say no more about it."

"And that will be your wisest way, old gentleman," muttered Hugh Crombie.

Ellen at first exhibited but little desire, or, rather, an evident reluctance, to accompany her guardian. She hung back, while her glance passed almost imperceptibly over the faces that gazed so eagerly at her; but the one she sought was not visible among them. She had no alternative, and suffered herself to be led from the inn.

Edward Walcott alone remained behind, the most wretched being (at least such was his own opinion) that breathed the vital air. He felt a sinking and sickness of the heart, and alternately a feverish frenzy, neither of which his short and cloudless existence had heretofore occasioned him to experience. He was jealous of, he knew not whom, and he knew not what. He was ungenerous enough to believe that Ellen—his pure and lovely Ellen—had degraded herself; though from what motive, or by whose agency, he could not conjecture. When Dr. Melmoth had taken her in charge, Edward returned to the apartment where he had spent the evening. The wine was still upon the table; and, in the desperate hope of stupefying his faculties, he unwisely swallowed huge successive draughts. The effect of his imprudence was not long in manifesting itself; though insensibility, which at another time would have been the result, did not now follow. Acting upon his previous agitation, the wine seemed to set his blood in a flame; and, for the time being, he was a perfect madman.

A phrenologist would probably have found the organ of destructiveness in strong development, just then, upon Edward's cranium; for he certainly manifested an impulse to break and destroy whatever chanced to be within his reach. He commenced his operations by upsetting the table, and breaking the bottles and glasses. Then, seizing a tall heavy chair in each hand, he hurled them with prodigious force,—one through the window, and the other against a large looking-glass, the most valuable artical of furniture in Hugh Crombie's inn. The crash and clatter of these outrageous proceedings soon brought the master, mistress, and maid-servant to the scene of action; but the two latter, at the first sight of Edward's wild demeanor and gleaming eyes, retreated with all imaginable expedition. Hugh chose a position behind the door, from whence, protruding his head, he endeavored to mollify his inebriated guest. His interference, however, had nearly been productive of most unfortunate consequences; for a massive andiron, with round brazen head, whizzed past him, within a hair's-breadth of his ear.

"I might as safely take my chance in a battle," exclaimed Hugh, withdrawing his head, and speaking to a man who stood in the passageway. "A little twist of his hand to the left would have served my turn as well as if I stood in the path of a forty-two pound ball. And here comes another broadside," he added, as some other article of furniture rattled against the door.

"Let us return his fire, Hugh," said the person whom he addressed, composedly lifting the andiron. "He is in want of ammunition: let us send him back his own."

The sound of this man's voice produced a most singular effect upon Edward. The moment before, his actions had been those of a raving maniac; but, when the words struck his ear, he paused, put his hand to his forehead, seemed to recollect himself, and finally advanced with a firm and steady step. His countenance was dark and angry, but no longer wild.

"I have found you, villain!" he said to the angler. "It is you who have done this."

"And, having done it, the wrath of a boy—his drunken wrath—will not induce me to deny it," replied the other, scornfully.

"The boy will require a man's satisfaction," returned Edward, "and that speedily."

"Will you take it now?" inquired the angler, with a cool, derisive smile, and almost in a whisper. At the same time he produced a brace of pistols, and held them towards the young man.

"Willingly," answered Edward, taking one of the weapons. "Choose your distance."

The angler stepped back a pace; but before their deadly intentions, so suddenly conceived, could be executed, Hugh Crombie interposed himself between them.

"Do you take my best parlor for the cabin of the Black Andrew, where a pistol-shot was a nightly pastime?" he inquired of his comrade. "And you, Master Edward, with what sort of a face will you walk into the chapel to morning prayers, after putting a ball through this man's head, or receiving one through your own? Though, in this last case, you will be past praying for, or praying either."

"Stand aside: I will take the risk. Make way, or I will put the ball through your own head," exclaimed Edward, fiercely: for the interval of rationality that circumstances had produced was again giving way to intoxication.

"You see how it is," said Hugh to his companion, unheard by Edward. "You shall take a shot at me, sooner than at the poor lad in his present state. You have done him harm enough already, and intend him more. I propose," he continued aloud, and with a peculiar glance towards the angler, "that this affair be decided to-morrow, at nine o'clock, under the old oak, on the bank of the stream. In the mean time, I will take charge of these popguns, for fear of accidents."

"Well, mine host, be it as you wish," said his comrade. "A shot more or less is of little consequence to me." He accordingly delivered his weapon to Hugh Crombie and walked carelessly away.

"Come, Master Walcott, the enemy has retreated. Victoria! And now, I see, the sooner I get you to your chamber, the better," added he aside; for the wine was at last beginning to produce its legitimate effect, in stupefying the young man's mental and bodily faculties.

Hugh Crombie's assistance, though not, perhaps, quite indispensable, was certainly very convenient to our unfortunate hero, in the course of the short walk that brought him to his chamber. When arrived there, and in bed, he was soon locked in a sleep scarcely less deep than that of death.

The weather, during the last hour, had appeared to be on the point of changing: indeed, there were, every few minutes, most rapid changes. A strong breeze sometimes drove the clouds from the brow of heaven, so as to disclose a few of the stars; but, immediately after, the darkness would again become Egyptian, and the rain rush like a torrent from the sky.

## CHAPTER VI

"About her neck a packet-mail
Fraught with advice, some fresh, some stale,
Of men that walked when they were dead."

HUDIBRAS.

SCARCELY a word had passed between Dr. Melmoth and Ellen Langton, on their way home; for, though the former was aware that his duty towards his ward would compel him to inquire into the motives of her conduct, the tenderness of his heart prompted him to defer the scrutiny to the latest moment. The same tenderness induced him to connive at Ellen's stealing secretly up to her chamber, unseen by Mrs. Melmoth; to render which measure practicable, he opened the house-door very softly, and stood before his half-sleeping spouse (who waited his arrival in the parlor) without any previous notice. This act of the doctor's benevolence was not destitute of heroism; for he was well assured that, should the affair come to the lady's knowledge through any other channel, her vengeance would descend not less heavily on him for concealing, than on Ellen for perpetrating, the elopement. That she had, thus far, no suspicion of the fact, was evident from her composure, as well as from the reply to a question, which, with more than his usual art, her husband put to her respecting the non-appearance of his ward. Mrs. Melmoth answered, that Ellen had complained of indisposition, and after drinking, by her prescription, a large cup of herb-tea, had retired to her chamber early in the evening. Thankful that all was yet safe, the doctor laid his head upon his pillow; but, late as was the hour, his many anxious thoughts long drove sleep from his eyelids.

The diminution in the quantity of his natural rest did not, however, prevent Dr. Melmoth from rising at his usual hour, which at all seasons of the year was an early one. He found, on descending to the parlor, that breakfast was nearly in readiness; for the lady of the house (and, as a corollary, her servant-girl) was not accustomed to await the rising of the sun in order to commence her domestic labors. Ellen Langton, however, who had heretofore assimilated her habits to those of the family, was this morning invisible,—a circumstance imputed by Mrs. Melmoth to her indisposition of the preceding evening, and by the doctor, to mortification on account of her elopement and its discovery.

"I think I will step into Ellen's bedchamber," said Mrs. Melmoth, "and inquire how she feels herself. The morning is delightful after the storm, and the air will do her good."

"Had we not better proceed with our breakfast? If the poor child is sleeping, it were a pity to disturb her," observed the doctor; for, besides his sympathy with Ellen's feelings, he was reluctant, as if he were the guilty one, to meet her face.

"Well, be it so. And now sit down, doctor; for the hot cakes are cooling fast. I suppose you will say they are not so good as those Ellen made yesterday morning. I know not how you will bear to part with her, though the thing must soon be."

"It will be a sore trial, doubtless," replied Dr. Melmoth,—"like tearing away a branch that is grafted on an old tree. And yet there will be a satisfaction in delivering her safe into her father's hands."

"A satisfaction for which you may thank me, doctor," observed the lady. "If there had been none but you to look after the poor thing's doings, she would have been enticed away long ere this, for the sake of her money."

Dr. Melmoth's prudence could scarcely restrain a smile at the thought that an elopement, as he had reason to believe, had been plotted, and partly carried into execution, while Ellen was under the sole care of his lady, and had been frustrated only by his own despised agency. He was not accustomed, however,—nor was this an eligible occasion,—to dispute any of Mrs. Melmoth's claims to superior wisdom.

The breakfast proceeded in silence, or, at least, without any conversation material to the tale. At its conclusion, Mrs. Melmoth was again meditating on the propriety of entering Ellen's chamber; but she was now prevented by an incident that always excited much interest both in herself and her husband.

This was the entrance of the servant, bearing the letters and newspaper, with which, once a fortnight, the mail-carrier journeyed up the valley. Dr. Melmoth's situation at the head of a respectable seminary, and his character as a scholar, had procured him an extensive correspondence among the learned men of his own country; and he had even exchanged epistles with one or two of the most distinguished dissenting clergymen of Great Britain. But, unless when some fond mother enclosed a one-pound note to defray the private expenses of her son at college, it was frequently the case that the packets addressed to the doctor were the sole contents of the mail-bag. In the present instance, his letters were very numerous, and, to judge from the one he chanced first to open, of an unconscionable length. While he was engaged in their perusal, Mrs. Melmoth amused herself with the newspaper,—a little sheet of about twelve inches square, which had but one rival in the country. Commencing with the title, she labored on through advertisements old and new, through poetry lamentably deficient in rhythm and rhymes, through essays, the ideas of which had been trite since the first week of the creation, till she finally arrived at the department that, a fortnight before, had contained the latest news from all quarters. Making such remarks upon these items as to her seemed good, the dame's notice was at length attracted by an article which her sudden exclamation proved to possess uncommon interest. Casting her eye hastily over it, she immediately began to read aloud to her husband; but he, deeply engaged in a long and learned letter, instead of listening to what she wished to communicate, exerted his own lungs in opposition to hers, as is the custom of abstracted men when disturbed. The result was as follows:—

"A brig just arrived in the outer harbor," began Mrs. Melmoth, "reports, that on the morning of the 25th ult."—Here the doctor broke in, "Wherefore I am compelled to differ from your exposition of the said passage, for those reasons, of the which I have given you a taste; provided"—The lady's voice was now almost audible, "ship bottom upward, discovered by the name on her stern to be the Ellen of"—"and in the same opinion are Hooker, Cotton, and divers learned divines of a later date."

The doctor's lungs were deep and strong, and victory seemed to incline toward him; but Mrs. Melmoth now made use of a tone whose peculiar shrillness, as long experience had taught her husband, augured a mood of mind not to be trifled with.

"On my word, doctor," she exclaimed, "this is most unfeeling and unchristian conduct! Here am I endeavoring to inform you of the death of an old friend, and you continue as deaf as a post."

Dr. Melmoth, who had heard the sound, without receiving the sense, of these words, now laid aside the letter in despair, and submissively requested to be informed of her pleasure.

"There, read for yourself" she replied, handing him the paper, and pointing to the passage containing the important intelligence,—"read, and then finish your letter, if you have a mind."

He took the paper, unable to conjecture how the dame could be so much interested in any part of its contents; but, before he had read many words, he grew pale as death. "Good Heavens! what is this?" he exclaimed. He then read on, "being the vessel wherein that eminent son of New England, John Langton, Esq., had taken passage for his native country, after an absence of many years."

"Our poor Ellen, his orphan child!" said Dr. Melmoth, dropping the paper. "How shall we break the intelligence to her? Alas! her share of the affliction causes me to forget my own."

"It is a heavy misfortune, doubtless; and Ellen will grieve as a daughter should," replied Mrs. Melmoth, speaking with the good sense of which she had a competent share. "But she has never known her father; and her sorrow must arise from a sense of duty, more than from strong affection. I will go and inform her of her loss. It is late, and I wonder if she be still asleep."

"Be cautious, dearest wife," said the doctor. "Ellen has strong feelings, and a sudden shock might be dangerous."

"I think I may be trusted, Dr. Melmoth," replied the lady, who had a high opinion of her own abilities as a comforter, and was not averse to exercise them.

Her husband, after her departure, sat listlessly turning over the letters that yet remained unopened, feeling little curiosity, after such melancholy intelligence, respecting their contents. But, by the handwriting of the direction on one of them, his attention was gradually arrested, till he found himself gazing earnestly on those strong, firm, regular characters. They were perfectly familiar to his eye; but from what hand they came, he could not conjecture. Suddenly, however, the truth burst upon him; and after noticing the date, and reading a few lines, he rushed hastily in pursuit of his wife.

He had arrived at the top of his speed and at the middle of the staircase, when his course was arrested by the lady whom he sought, who came, with a velocity equal to his own, in an opposite direction. The consequence was a concussion between the two meeting masses, by which Mrs. Melmoth was seated securely on the stairs; while the doctor was only preserved from precipitation to the bottom by clinging desperately to the balustrade. As soon as the pair discovered that they had sustained no material injury by their contact, they began eagerly to explain the cause of their mutual haste, without those reproaches, which, on the lady's part, would at another time have followed such an accident.

"You have not told her the bad news, I trust?" cried Dr. Melmoth, after each had communicated his and her intelligence, without obtaining audience of the other.

"Would you have me tell it to the bare walls?" inquired the lady in her shrillest tone. "Have I not just informed you that she has gone, fled, eloped? Her chamber is empty; and her bed has not been occupied."

"Gone!" repeated the doctor. "And, when her father comes to demand his daughter of me, what answer shall I make?"

"Now, Heaven defend us from the visits of the dead and drowned!" cried Mrs. Melmoth. "This is a serious affair, doctor, but not, I trust, sufficient to raise a ghost."

"Mr. Langton is yet no ghost," answered he; "though this event will go near to make him one. He was fortunately prevented, after he had made every preparation, from taking passage in the vessel that was lost."

"And where is he now?" she inquired.

"He is in New England. Perhaps he is at this moment on his way to us," replied her husband. "His letter is dated nearly a fortnight back; and he expresses an intention of being with us in a few days."

"Well, I thank Heaven for his safety," said Mrs. Melmoth. "But truly the poor gentleman could not have chosen a better time to be drowned, nor a worse one to come to life, than this. What we shall do, doctor, I know not; but had you locked the doors, and fastened the windows, as I advised, the misfortune could not have happened."

"Why, the whole country would have flouted us!" answered the doctor. "Is there a door in all the Province that is barred or bolted, night or day? Nevertheless, it might have been advisable last night, had it occurred to me."

"And why at that time more than at all times?" she inquired. "We had surely no reason to fear this event."

Dr. Melmoth was silent; for his worldly wisdom was sufficient to deter him from giving his lady the opportunity, which she would not fail to use to the utmost, of laying the blame of the elopement at his door. He now proceeded, with a heavy heart, to Ellen's chamber, to satisfy himself with his own eyes of the state of affairs. It was deserted too truly; and the wild-flowers with which it was the maiden's custom daily to decorate her premises were drooping, as if in sorrow for her who had placed them there. Mrs. Melmoth, on this second visit, discovered on the table a note addressed to her husband, and containing a few words of gratitude from Ellen, but no explanation of her mysterious flight. The doctor gazed long on the tiny letters, which had evidently been traced with a trembling hand, and blotted with many tears.

"There is a mystery in this,—a mystery that I cannot fathom," he said. "And now I would I knew what measures it would be proper to take."

"Get you on horseback, Dr. Melmoth, and proceed as speedily as may be down the valley to the town," said the dame, the influence of whose firmer mind was sometimes, as in the present case, most beneficially exerted over his own. "You must not spare for trouble, no, nor for danger. Now—Oh, if I were a man!"—

"Oh, that you were!" murmured the doctor, in a perfectly inaudible voice. "Well—and when I reach the town, what then?"

"As I am a Christian woman, my patience cannot endure you!" exclaimed Mrs. Melmoth. "Oh, I love to see a man with the spirit of a man! but you"— And she turned away in utter scorn.

"But, dearest wife," remonstrated the husband, who was really at a loss how to proceed, and anxious for her advice, "your worldly experience is greater than mine, and I desire to profit by it. What should be my next measure after arriving at the town?"

Mrs. Melmoth was appeased by the submission with which the doctor asked her counsel; though, if the truth must be told, she heartily despised him for needing it. She condescended, however, to instruct him in the proper method of pursuing the runaway maiden, and directed him, before his departure, to put strict inquiries to Hugh Crombie respecting any stranger who might lately have visited his inn. That there would be wisdom in this, Dr. Melmoth had his own reasons for believing; and still, without imparting them to his lady, he proceeded to do as he had been bid.

The veracious landlord acknowledged that a stranger had spent a night and day at his inn, and was missing that morning; but he utterly denied all acquaintance with his character, or privity to his purposes. Had Mrs. Melmoth, instead of her husband, conducted the examination, the result might have been different. As the case was, the doctor returned to his dwelling but little wiser than he went forth; and, ordering his steed to be saddled, he began a journey of which he knew not what would be the end.

In the mean time, the intelligence of Ellen's disappearance circulated rapidly, and soon sent forth hunters more fit to follow the chase than Dr. Melmoth.

## CHAPTER VII

"There was racing and chasing o'er Cannobie Lee."

WALTER SCOTT.

WHEN Edward Walcott awoke the next morning from his deep slumber, his first consciousness was of a heavy weight upon his mind, the cause of which he was unable immediately to recollect. One by one, however, by means of the association of ideas, the events of the preceding night came back to his memory; though those of latest occurrence were dim as dreams. But one circumstance was only too well remembered,—the discovery of Ellen Langton. By a strong effort he next attained to an uncertain recollection of a scene of madness and violence, followed, as he at first thought, by a duel. A little further reflection, however, informed him that this event was yet among the things of futurity; but he could by no means recall the appointed time or place. As he had not the slightest intention (praiseworthy and prudent as it would unquestionably have been) to give up the chance of avenging Ellen's wrongs and his own, he immediately arose, and began to dress, meaning to learn from Hugh Crombie those particulars which his own memory had not retained. His chief apprehension was, that the appointed time had already elapsed; for the early sunbeams of a glorious morning were now peeping into his chamber.

More than once, during the progress of dressing, he was inclined to believe that the duel had actually taken place, and been fatal to him, and that he was now in those regions to which, his conscience told him, such an event would be likely to send him. This idea resulted from his bodily sensations, which were in the highest degree uncomfortable. He was tormented by a raging thirst, that seemed to have absorbed all the moisture of his throat and stomach; and, in his present agitation, a cup of icy water would have been his first wish, had all the treasures of earth and sea been at his command. His head, too, throbbed almost to bursting; and the whirl of his brain at every movement promised little accuracy in the aim of his pistol, when he should meet the angler. These feelings, together with the deep degradation of his mind, made him resolve that no circumstances should again draw him into an excess of wine. In the mean time, his head was, perhaps, still too much confused to allow him fully to realize his unpleasant situation.

Before Edward was prepared to leave his chamber, the door was opened by one of the college bed-makers, who, perceiving that he was nearly dressed, entered, and began to set the apartment in order. There were two of these officials pertaining to Harley College; each of them being (and, for obvious reasons, this was an indispensable qualification) a model of perfect ugliness in her own way. One was a tall, raw-boned, huge-jointed, double-fisted giantess, admirably fitted to sustain the part of Glumdalia, in the tragedy of "Tom Thumb." Her features were as excellent as her form, appearing to have been rough-hewn with a broadaxe, and left unpolished. The other was a short, squat figure, about two thirds the height, and three times the circumference, of ordinary females. Her hair was gray, her complexion of a deep yellow; and her most remarkable feature was a short snub nose, just discernible amid the broad immensity of her face. This latter lady was she who now entered Edward's chamber. Notwithstanding her deficiency in personal attractions, she was rather a favorite of the students, being good-natured, anxious for their comfort, and, when duly encouraged, very communicative. Edward perceived, as soon as she appeared, that she only waited his assistance in order to disburden herself of some extraordinary information; and, more from compassion than curiosity, he began to question her.

"Well, Dolly, what news this morning?"

"Why, let me see,—oh, yes! It had almost slipped my memory," replied the bed-maker. "Poor Widow Butler died last night, after her long sickness. Poor woman! I remember her forty years ago, or so,—as rosy a lass as you could set eyes on."

"Ah! has she gone?" said Edward, recollecting the sick woman of the cottage which he had entered with Ellen and Fanshawe. "Was she not out of her right mind, Dolly?"

"Yes, this seven years," she answered. "They say she came to her senses a bit, when Dr. Melmoth visited her yesterday, but was raving mad when she died. Ah, that son of hers!—if he is yet alive. Well, well!"

"She had a son, then?" inquired Edward.

"Yes, such as he was. The Lord preserve me from such a one!" said Dolly. "It was thought he went off with Hugh Crombie, that keeps the tavern now. That was fifteen years ago."

"And have they heard nothing of him since?" asked Edward.

"Nothing good,—nothing good," said the bed-maker. "Stories did travel up the valley now and then; but for five years there has been no word of him. They say Merchant Langton, Ellen's father, met him in foreign parts, and would have made a man of him; but there was too much of the wicked one in him for that. Well, poor woman! I wonder who'll preach her funeral sermon."

"Dr. Melmoth, probably," observed the student.

"No, no! The doctor will never finish his journey in time. And who knows but his own funeral will be the end of it," said Dolly, with a sagacious shake of her head.

"Dr. Melmoth gone a journey!" repeated Edward. "What do you mean? For what purpose?"

"For a good purpose enough, I may say," replied she. "To search out Miss Ellen, that was run away with last night."

"In the Devil's name, woman, of what are you speaking?" shouted Edward, seizing the affrighted bed-maker forcibly by the arm.

Poor Dolly had chosen this circuitous method of communicating her intelligence, because she was well aware that, if she first told of Ellen's flight, she should find no ear for her account of the Widow Butler's death. She had not calculated, however, that the news would produce so violent an effect upon her auditor; and her voice faltered as she recounted what she knew of the affair. She had hardly concluded, before Edward—who, as she proceeded, had been making hasty preparations—rushed from his chamber, and took the way towards Hugh Crombie's inn. He had no difficulty in finding the landlord, who had already occupied his accustomed seat, and was smoking his accustomed pipe, under the elm-tree.

"Well, Master Walcott, you have come to take a stomach-reliever this morning, I suppose," said Hugh, taking the pipe from his mouth. "What shall it be?—a bumper of wine with an egg? or a glass of smooth, old, oily brandy, such as Dame Crombie and I keep for our own drinking? Come, that will do it, I know."

"No, no! neither," replied Edward, shuddering involuntarily at the bare mention of wine and strong drink. "You know well, Hugh Crombie, the errand on which I come."

"Well, perhaps I do," said the landlord. "You come to order me to saddle my best horse. You are for a ride, this fine morning."

"True; and I must learn of you in what direction to turn my horse's head," replied Edward Walcott.

"I understand you," said Hugh, nodding and smiling. "And now, Master Edward, I really have taken a strong liking to you; and, if you please to hearken to it, you shall have some of my best advice."

"Speak," said the young man, expecting to be told in what direction to pursue the chase.

"I advise you, then," continued Hugh Crombie, in a tone in which some real feeling mingled with assumed carelessness,—"I advise you to forget that you have ever known this girl, that she has ever existed; for she is as much lost to you as if she never had been born, or as if the grave had covered her. Come, come, man, toss off a quart of my old wine, and keep up a merry heart. This has been my way in many a heavier sorrow than ever you have felt: and you see I am alive and merry yet." But Hugh's merriment had failed him just as he was making his boast of it; for Edward saw a tear in the corner of his eye.

"Forget her? Never, never!" said the student, while his heart sank within him at the hopelessness of pursuit which Hugh's words implied. "I will follow her to the ends of the earth."

"Then so much the worse for you and for my poor nag, on whose back you shall be in three minutes," rejoined the landlord. "I have spoken to you as I would to my own son, if I had such an incumbrance.—Here, you ragamuffin; saddle the gray, and lead him round to the door."

"The gray? I will ride the black," said Edward. "I know your best horse as well as you do yourself, Hugh."

"There is no black horse in my stable. I have parted with him to an old comrade of mine," answered the landlord, with a wink of acknowledgment to what he saw were Edward's suspicions. "The gray is a stout nag, and will carry you a round pace, though not so fast as to bring you up with them you seek. I reserved him for you, and put Mr. Fanshawe off with the old white, on which I travelled hitherward a year or two since."

"Fanshawe! Has he, then, the start of me?" asked Edward.

"He rode off about twenty minutes ago," replied Hugh; "but you will overtake him within ten miles, at farthest. But, if mortal man could recover the girl, that fellow would do it, even if he had no better nag than a broomstick, like the witches of old times."

"Did he obtain any information from you as to the course?" inquired the student.

"I could give him only this much," said Hugh, pointing down the road in the direction of the town. "My old comrade trusts no man further than is needful, and I ask no unnecessary questions."

The hostler now led up to the door the horse which Edward was to ride. The young man mounted with all expedition; but, as he was about to apply the spurs, his thirst, which the bed-maker's intelligence had caused him to forget, returned most powerfully upon him.

"For Heaven's sake, Hugh, a mug of your sharpest cider; and let it be a large one!" he exclaimed. "My tongue rattles in my mouth like"—

"Like the bones in a dice-box," said the landlord, finishing the comparison, and hastening to obey Edward's directions. Indeed, he rather exceeded them, by mingling with the juice of the apple a gill of his old brandy, which his own experience told him would at that time have a most desirable effect upon the young man's internal system.

"It is powerful stuff, mine host; and I feel like a new man already," observed Edward, after draining the mug to the bottom.

"He is a fine lad, and sits his horse most gallantly," said Hugh Crombie to himself as the student rode off. "I heartily wish him success. I wish to Heaven my conscience had suffered me to betray the plot before it was too late. Well, well, a man must keep his mite of honesty."

The morning was now one of the most bright and glorious that ever shone for mortals; and, under other circumstances, Edward's bosom would have been as light, and his spirit would have sung as cheerfully, as one of the many birds that warbled around him. The raindrops of the preceding night hung like glittering diamonds on every leaf of every tree, shaken, and rendered more brilliant, by occasional sighs of wind, that removed from the traveller the superfluous heat of an unclouded sun. In spite of the adventure, so mysterious and vexatious, in which he was engaged, Edward's elastic spirit (assisted, perhaps, by the brandy he had unwittingly swallowed) rose higher as he rode on; and he soon found himself endeavoring to accommodate the tune of one of Hugh Crombie's ballads to the motion of the horse. Nor did this reviving cheerfulness argue anything against his unwavering faith, and pure and fervent love for Ellen Langton. A sorrowful and repining disposition is not the necessary accompaniment of a "leal and loving heart"; and Edward's spirits were cheered, not by forgetfulness, but by hope, which would not permit him to doubt of the ultimate success of his pursuit. The uncertainty itself, and the probable danger of the expedition, were not without their charm to a youthful and adventurous spirit. In fact, Edward would not have been altogether satisfied to recover the errant damsel, without first doing battle in her behalf.

He had proceeded but a few miles before he came in sight of Fanshawe, who had been accommodated by the landlord with a horse much inferior to his own. The speed to which he had been put had almost exhausted the poor animal, whose best pace was now but little beyond a walk. Edward drew his bridle as he came up with Fanshawe.

"I have been anxious to apologize," he said to him, "for the hasty and unjust expressions of which I made use last evening. May I hope that, in consideration of my mental distraction and the causes of it, you will forget what has passed?"

"I had already forgotten it," replied Fanshawe, freely offering his hand. "I saw your disturbed state of feeling, and it would have been unjust both to you and to myself to remember the errors it occasioned."

"A wild expedition this," observed Edward, after shaking warmly the offered hand. "Unless we obtain some further information at the town, we shall hardly know which way to continue the pursuit."

"We can scarcely fail, I think, of lighting upon some trace of them," said Fanshawe. "Their flight must have commenced after the storm subsided, which would give them but a few hours the start of us. May I beg," he continued, noticing the superior condition of his rival's horse, "that you will not attempt to accommodate your pace to mine?"

Edward bowed, and rode on, wondering at the change which a few months had wrought in Fanshawe's character. On this occasion, especially, the energy of his mind had communicated itself to his frame. The color was strong and high in his cheek; and his whole appearance was that of a gallant and manly youth, whom a lady might love, or a foe might fear. Edward had not been so slow as his mistress in discovering the student's affection; and he could not but acknowledge in his heart that he was a rival not to be despised, and might yet be a successful one, if, by his means, Ellen Langton were restored to her friends. This consideration caused him to spur forward with increased ardor; but all his speed could not divest him of the idea that Fanshawe would finally overtake him, and attain the object of their mutual pursuit. There was certainly no apparent ground for this imagination; for every step of his horse increased the advantage which Edward had gained, and he soon lost sight of his rival.

Shortly after overtaking Fanshawe, the young man passed the lonely cottage formerly the residence of the Widow Butler, who now lay dead within. He was at first inclined to alight, and make inquiries respecting the fugitives; for he observed through the windows the faces of several persons, whom curiosity, or some better feeling, had led to the house of mourning. Recollecting, however, that this portion of the road must have been passed by the angler and Ellen at too early an hour to attract notice, he forbore to waste time by a fruitless delay.

Edward proceeded on his journey, meeting with no other noticeable event, till, arriving at the summit of a hill, he beheld, a few hundred yards

before him, the Rev. Dr. Melmoth. The worthy president was toiling onward at a rate unexampled in the history either of himself or his steed;
the excellence of the latter consisting in sure-footedness rather than rapidity. The rider looked round, seemingly in some apprehension at the
sound of hoof-tramps behind him, but was unable to conceal his satisfaction on recognizing Edward Walcott.

In the whole course of his life, Dr. Melmoth had never been placed in
circumstances so embarrassing as the present. He was altogether a child
in the ways of the world, having spent his youth and early manhood in
abstracted study, and his maturity in the solitude of these hills. The expedition, therefore, on which fate had now thrust him, was an entire dev-
iation from the quiet pathway of all his former years; and he felt like one
who sets forth over the broad ocean without chart or compass. The affair
would undoubtedly have been perplexing to a man of far more experience
than he; but the doctor pictured to himself a thousand difficulties and
dangers, which, except in his imagination, had no existence. The perturbation of his spirit had compelled him, more than once since his departure,
to regret that he had not invited Mrs. Melmoth to a share in the adventure; this being an occasion where her firmness, decision, and confident
sagacity—which made her a sort of domestic hedgehog—would have been
peculiarly appropriate. In the absence of such a counsellor, even Edward
Walcott—young as he was, and indiscreet as the doctor thought him—
was a substitute not to be despised; and it was singular and rather ludicrous to observe how the gray-haired man unconsciously became as a
child to the beardless youth. He addressed Edward with an assumption of
dignity, through which his pleasure at the meeting was very obvious.

"Young gentleman, this is not well," he said. "By what authority have
you absented yourself from the walls of Alma Mater during term-time?"

"I conceived that it was unnecessary to ask leave at such a conjuncture,
and when the head of the institution was himself in the saddle," replied
Edward.

"It was a fault, it was a fault," said Dr. Melmoth, shaking his head;
"but, in consideration of the motive, I may pass it over. And now, my
dear Edward, I advise that we continue our journey together, as your
youth and inexperience will stand in need of the wisdom of my gray head.
Nay, I pray you lay not the lash to your steed. You have ridden fast and
far; and a slower pace is requisite for a season."

And, in order to keep up with his young companion, the doctor smote
his own gray nag; which unhappy beast, wondering what strange con-
catenation of events had procured him such treatment, endeavored to
obey his master's wishes. Edward had sufficient compassion for Dr. Melmoth (especially as his own horse now exhibited signs of weariness) to
moderate his pace to one attainable by the former.

"Alas, youth! these are strange times," observed the president, "when
a doctor of divinity and an under-graduate set forth, like a knight-errant
and his squire, in search of a stray damsel. Methinks I am an epitome of
the church militant, or a new species of polemical divinity. Pray Heaven,

however, there be no encounter in store for us; for I utterly forgot to provide myself with weapons."

"I took some thought for that matter, reverend knight," replied Edward, whose imagination was highly tickled by Dr. Melmoth's chivalrous comparison.

"Ay, I see that you have girded on a sword," said the divine. "But wherewith shall I defend myself, my hand being empty, except of this golden headed staff, the gift of Mr. Langton?"

"One of these, if you will accept it," answered Edward, exhibiting a brace of pistols, "will serve to begin the conflict, before you join the battle hand to hand."

"Nay, I shall find little safety in meddling with that deadly instrument, since I know not accurately from which end proceeds the bullet," said Dr. Melmoth. "But were it not better, seeing we are so well provided with artillery, to betake ourselves, in the event of an encounter, to some stone-wall or other place of strength?"

"If I may presume to advise," said the squire, "you, as being most valiant and experienced, should ride forward, lance in hand (your long staff serving for a lance), while I annoy the enemy from afar."

"Like Teucer behind the shield of Ajax," interrupted Dr. Melmoth, "or David with his stone and sling. No, no, young man! I have left unfinished in my study a learned treatise, important not only to the present age, but to posterity, for whose sakes I must take heed to my safety.—But, lo! who ride yonder?" he exclaimed, in manifest alarm, pointing to some horsemen upon the brow of a hill at a short distance before them.

"Fear not, gallant leader," said Edward Walcott, who had already discovered the objects of the doctor's terror. "They are men of peace, as we shall shortly see. The foremost is somewhere near your own years, and rides like a grave, substantial citizen,—though what he does here, I know not. Behind come two servants, men likewise of sober age and pacific appearance."

"Truly your eyes are better than mine own. Of a verity, you are in the right," acquiesced Dr. Melmoth, recovering his usual quantum of intrepidity. "We will ride forward courageously, as those who, in a just cause, fear neither death nor bonds."

The reverend knight-errant and his squire, at the time of discovering the three horsemen, were within a very short distance of the town, which was, however, concealed from their view by the hill that the strangers were descending. The road from Harley College, through almost its whole extent, had been rough and wild, and the country thin of population; but now, standing frequent, amid fertile fields on each side of the way, were neat little cottages, from which groups of white-headed children rushed forth to gaze upon the travellers. The three strangers, as well as the doctor and Edward, were surrounded, as they approached each other, by a crowd of this kind, plying their little bare legs most pertinaciously in order to keep pace with the horses.

As Edward gained a nearer view of the foremost rider, his grave aspect and stately demeanor struck him with involuntary respect. There were deep lines of thought across his brow; and his calm yet bright gray eye betokened a steadfast soul. There was also an air of conscious importance, even in the manner in which the stranger sat his horse, which a man's good opinion of himself, unassisted by the concurrence of the world in general, seldom bestows. The two servants rode at a respectable distance in the rear; and the heavy portmanteaus at their backs intimated that the party had journeyed from afar. Dr. Melmoth endeavored to assume the dignity that became him as the head of Harley College; and with a gentle stroke of his staff upon his wearied steed and a grave nod to the principal stranger, was about to commence the ascent of the hill at the foot of which they were. The gentleman, however, made a halt.

"Dr. Melmoth, am I so fortunate as to meet you?" he exclaimed in accents expressive of as much surprise and pleasure as were consistent with his staid demeanor. "Have you, then, forgotten your old friend?"

"Mr. Langton! Can it be?" said the doctor, after looking him in the face a moment. "Yes, it is my old friend indeed: welcome, welcome! though you come at an unfortunate time."

"What say you? How is my child? Ellen, I trust, is well?" cried Mr. Langton, a father's anxiety overcoming the coldness and reserve that were natural to him, or that long habit had made a second nature.

"She is well in health. She was so, at least, last night," replied Dr. Melmoth unable to meet the eye of his friend. "But—but I have been a careless shepherd; and the lamb has strayed from the fold while I slept."

Edward Walcott, who was a deeply interested observer of this scene, had anticipated that a burst of passionate grief would follow the disclosure. He was, however, altogether mistaken. There was a momentary convulsion of Mr. Langton's strong features, as quick to come and go as a flash of lightning; and then his countenance was as composed—though, perhaps, a little sterner—as before. He seemed about to inquire into the particulars of what so nearly concerned him, but changed his purpose on observing the crowd of children, who, with one or two of their parents, were endeavoring to catch the words that passed between the doctor and himself.

"I will turn back with you to the village," he said in a steady voice; "and at your leisure I shall desire to hear the particulars of this unfortunate affair."

He wheeled his horse accordingly, and, side by side with Dr. Melmoth, began to ascend the hill. On reaching the summit, the little country town lay before them, presenting a cheerful and busy spectacle. It consisted of one long, regular street, extending parallel to, and at a short distance from, the river; which here, enlarged by a junction with another stream, became navigable, not indeed for vessels of burden, but for rafts of lumber and boats of considerable size. The houses, with peaked roofs and jutting stories, stood at wide intervals along the street; and the commercial character of the place was manifested by the shop door and windows that occupied the front of almost every dwelling. One or two mansions, however, surrounded by trees, and standing back at a haughty distance from the road, were evidently the abodes of the aristocracy of the village. It was not difficult to distinguish the owners of these—self-important personages, with canes and well-powdered periwigs—among the crowd of meaner men who bestowed their attention upon Dr. Melmoth and his friend as they rode by. The town being the nearest mart of a large extent of back country, there were many rough farmers and woodsmen, to whom the cavalcade was an object of curiosity and admiration. The former feeling, indeed, was general throughout the village. The shop-keepers left their customers, and looked forth from the doors; the female portion of the community thrust their heads from the windows; and the people in the street formed a lane through which, with all eyes concentrated upon them, the party rode onward to the tavern. The general aptitude that pervades the populace of a small country town to meddle with affairs not legitimately concerning them was increased, on this occasion, by the sudden return of Mr. Langton after passing through the village. Many conjectures were afloat respecting the cause of this retrograde movement; and, by degrees, something like the truth, though much distorted, spread generally among the crowd, communicated, probably, from Mr. Langton's servants. Edward Walcott, incensed at the uncourteous curiosity of which he, as well as his companions, was the object, felt a frequent impulse (though, fortunately for himself, resisted) to make use of his riding-switch in clearing a passage.

On arriving at the tavern, Dr. Melmoth recounted to his friend the little he knew beyond the bare fact of Ellen's disappearance. Had Edward Walcott been called to their conference, he might, by disclosing the adventure of the angler, have thrown a portion of light upon the affair; but, since his first introduction, the cold and stately merchant had honored him with no sort of notice.

Edward, on his part, was not well pleased at the sudden appearance of Ellen's father, and was little inclined to coöperate in any measures that he might adopt for her recovery. It was his wish to pursue the chase on his own responsibility, and as his own wisdom dictated: he chose to be an independent ally, rather than a subordinate assistant. But, as a step preliminary to his proceedings of every other kind, he found it absolutely necessary, having journeyed far, and fasting, to call upon the landlord for a supply of food. The viands that were set before him were homely but abundant; nor were Edward's griefs and perplexities so absorbing as to overcome the appetite of youth and health.

Dr. Melmoth and Mr. Langton, after a short private conversation, had summoned the landlord, in the hope of obtaining some clew to the development of the mystery. But no young lady, nor any stranger answering to the description the doctor had received from Hugh Crombie (which was indeed a false one), had been seen to pass through the village since daybreak. Here, therefore, the friends were entirely at a loss in what direction to continue the pursuit. The village was the focus of several roads, di-verging to widely distant portions of the country; and which of these the fugitives had taken, it was impossible to determine. One point, however, might be considered certain,—that the village was the first stage of their flight; for it commanded the only outlet from the valley, except a rugged path among the hills, utterly impassable by horse. In this dilemma, ex-presses were sent by each of the different roads; and poor Ellen's impru-dence—the tale nowise decreasing as it rolled along—became known to a wide extent of country. Having thus done everything in his power to re-cover his daughter, the merchant exhibited a composure which Dr. Mel-moth admired, but could not equal. His own mind, however, was in a far more comfortable state than when the responsibility of the pursuit had rested upon himself.

Edward Walcott, in the mean time, had employed but a very few mo-ments in satisfying his hunger; after which his active intellect alternately formed and relinquished a thousand plans for the recovery of Ellen. Fan-shawe's observation, that her flight must have commenced after the sub-siding of the storm, recurred to him. On inquiry, he was informed that the violence of the rain had continued, with a few momentary intermissions, till near daylight. The fugitives must, therefore, have passed through the village long after its inhabitants were abroad; and how, without the gift of invisibility, they had contrived to elude notice, Edward could not con-ceive.

"Fifty years ago," thought Edward, "my sweet Ellen would have been deemed a witch for this trackless journey. Truly, I could wish I were a wizard, that I might bestride a broomstick, and follow her."

While the young man, involved in these perplexing thoughts, looked forth from the open window of the apartment, his attention was drawn to an individual evidently of a different, though not of a higher, class than the countrymen among whom he stood. Edward now recollected that he had noticed his rough dark face among the most earnest of those who had watched the arrival of the party. He had then taken him for one of the boatmen, of whom there were many in the village, and who had much of a sailor-like dress and appearance. A second and more attentive observa-tion, however, convinced Edward that this man's life had not been spent upon fresh water; and, had any stronger evidence than the nameless marks which the ocean impresses upon its sons been necessary, it would have been found in his mode of locomotion. While Edward was observing him, he beat slowly up to one of Mr. Langton's servants who was standing near the door of the inn. He seemed to question the man with affected carelessness; but his countenance was dark and perplexed when he turned to mingle again with the crowd. Edward lost no time in ascertaining from the servant the nature of his inquiries. They had related to the elopement of Mr. Langton's daughter, which was, indeed, the prevailing, if not the sole, subject of conversation in the village.

The grounds for supposing that this man was in any way connected with the angler were, perhaps, very slight; yet, in the perplexity of the whole affair, they induced Edward to resolve to get at the heart of his mystery. To attain this end, he took the most direct method,—by applying to the man himself.

He had now retired apart from the throng and bustle of the village, and was seated upon a condemned boat, that was drawn up to rot upon the banks of the river. His arms were folded, and his hat drawn over his brows. The lower part of his face, which alone was visible, evinced gloom and depression, as did also the deep sighs, which, because he thought no one was near him, he did not attempt to restrain.

"Friend, I must speak with you," said Edward Walcott, laying his hand upon his shoulder, after contemplating the man a moment, himself unseen.

He started at once from his abstraction and his seat, apparently expecting violence, and prepared to resist it; but, perceiving the youthful and solitary intruder upon his privacy, he composed his features with much quickness.

"What would you with me?" he asked.

"They tarry long,—or you have kept a careless watch," said Edward, speaking at a venture.

For a moment, there seemed a probability of obtaining such a reply to this observation as the youth had intended to elicit. If any trust could be put in the language of the stranger's countenance, a set of words different from those to which he subsequently gave utterance had risen to his lips. But he seemed naturally slow of speech; and this defect was now, as is frequently the case, advantageous in giving him space for reflection.

"Look you, youngster: crack no jokes on me," he at length said, contemptuously. "Away! back whence you came, or"— And he slightly waved a small rattan that he held in his right hand.

Edward's eyes sparkled, and his color rose. "You must change this tone, fellow, and that speedily," he observed. "I order you to lower your hand, and answer the questions that I shall put to you."

The man gazed dubiously at him, but finally adopted a more conciliatory mode of speech.

"Well, master; and what is your business with me?" he inquired. "I am a boatman out of employ. Any commands in my line?"

"Pshaw! I know you, my good friend, and you cannot deceive me," replied Edward Walcott. "We are private here," he continued, looking around. "I have no desire or intention to do you harm; and, if you act according to my directions, you shall have no cause to repent it."

"And what if I refuse to put myself under your orders?" inquired the man. "You are but a young captain for such an old hulk as mine."

"The ill consequences of a refusal would all be on your own side," replied Edward. "I shall, in that case, deliver you up to justice: if I have not the means of capturing you myself," he continued, observing the seaman's eye to wander rather scornfully over his youthful and slender figure, "there are hundreds within call whom it will be in vain to resist. Besides, it requires little strength to use this," he added, laying his hand on a pistol.

"If that were all, I could suit you there, my lad," muttered the stranger. He continued aloud, "Well, what is your will with me? D——d un-genteel treatment this! But put your questions; and, to oblige you, I may answer them,—if so be that I know anything of the matter."

"You will do wisely," observed the young man. "And now to business. What reason have you to suppose that the persons for whom you watch are not already beyond the village?"

The seaman paused long before he answered, and gazed earnestly at Edward, apparently endeavoring to ascertain from his countenance the amount of his knowledge. This he probably overrated, but, nevertheless, hazarded a falsehood.

"I doubt not they passed before midnight," he said. "I warrant you they are many a league towards the sea-coast ere this."

"You have kept watch, then, since midnight?" asked Edward.

"Ay, that have I! And a dark and rough one it was," answered the stranger.

"And you are certain that, if they passed at all, it must have been before that hour?"

"I kept my walk across the road till the village was all astir," said the seaman. "They could not have missed me. So, you see, your best way is to give chase; for they have a long start of you, and you have no time to lose."

"Your information is sufficient, my good friend," said Edward, with a smile. "I have reason to know that they did not commence their flight before midnight. You have made it evident that they have not passed since: ergo, they have not passed at all,—an indisputable syllogism. And now will I retrace my footsteps."

"Stay, young man," said the stranger, placing himself full in Edward's way as he was about to hasten to the inn. "You have drawn me in to betray my comrade; but, before you leave this place, you must answer a question or two of mine. Do you mean to take the law with you? or will you right your wrongs, if you have any, with your own right hand?"

"It is my intention to take the latter method. But, if I choose the former, what then?" demanded Edward.

"Nay, nothing: only you or I might not have gone hence alive," replied the stranger. "But as you say he shall have fair play"—

"On my word, friend," interrupted the young man, "I fear your intelligence has come too late to do either good or harm. Look towards the inn: my companions are getting to horse, and, my life on it, they know whither to ride."

So saying, he hastened away, followed by the stranger. It was indeed evident that news of some kind or other had reached the village. The people were gathered in groups, conversing eagerly; and the pale cheeks, uplifted eyebrows, and outspread hands of some of the female sex filled Edward's mind with undefined but intolerable apprehensions. He forced his way to Dr. Melmoth, who had just mounted, and, seizing his bridle, peremptorily demanded if he knew aught of Ellen Langton.

### CHAPTER VIII

"Full many a miserable year hath passed:
    She knows him as one dead, or worse than dead:
    And many a change her varied life hath known;
    But her heart none."                                MATURIN.

SINCE her interview with the angler, which was interrupted by the appearance of Fanshawe, Ellen Langton's hitherto calm and peaceful mind had been in a state of insufferable doubt and dismay. She was imperatively called upon—at least, she so conceived—to break through the rules which nature and education impose upon her sex, to quit the protection of those whose desire for her welfare was true and strong, and to trust herself, for what purpose she scarcely knew, to a stranger, from whom the instinctive purity of her mind would involuntarily have shrunk, under whatever circumstances she had met him. The letter which she had received from the hands of the angler had seemed to her inexperience to prove beyond a doubt that the bearer was the friend of her father, and authorized by him, if her duty and affection were stronger than her fears, to guide her to his retreat. The letter spoke vaguely of losses and misfortunes, and of a necessity for concealment on her father's part, and secrecy on hers; and, to the credit of Ellen's not very romantic understanding, it must be acknowledged that the mystery of the plot had nearly prevented its success. She did not, indeed, doubt that the letter was from her father's hand; for every line and stroke, and even many of its phrases, were familiar to her. Her apprehension was, that his misfortunes, of what nature soever they were, had affected his intellect, and that, under such an influence, he had commanded her to take a step which nothing less than such a command could justify. Ellen did not, however, remain long in this opinion; for when she reperused the letter, and considered the firm, regular characters, and the style,—calm and cold, even in requesting such a sacrifice,—she felt that there was nothing like insanity here. In fine, she came gradually to the belief that there were strong reasons, though incomprehensible by her, for the secrecy that her father had enjoined.

Having arrived at this conviction, her decision lay plain before her. Her affection for Mr. Langton was not, indeed,—nor was it possible,—so strong as that she would have felt for a parent who had watched over her from her infancy. Neither was the conception she had unavoidably formed of his character such as to promise that in him she would find an equivalent for all she must sacrifice. On the contrary, her gentle nature and loving heart, which otherwise would have rejoiced in a new object of affection, now shrank with something like dread from the idea of meeting her father,—stately, cold, and stern as she could not but imagine him. A sense of duty was therefore Ellen's only support in resolving to tread the dark path that lay before her.

Had there been any person of her own sex in whom Ellen felt confidence, there is little doubt that she would so far have disobeyed her father's letter as to communicate its contents, and take counsel as to her proceedings. But Mrs. Melmoth was the only female—excepting, indeed, the maid-servant—to whom it was possible to make the communication; and, though Ellen at first thought of such a step, her timidity, and her knowledge of the lady's character, did not permit her to venture upon it. She next reviewed her acquaintances of the other sex; and Dr. Melmoth first presented himself, as in every respect but one, an unexceptionable confidant. But the single exception was equivalent to many. The maiden, with the highest opinion of the doctor's learning and talents, had sufficient penetration to know, that, in the ways of the world, she was herself the better skilled of the two. For a moment she thought of Edward Walcott; but he was light and wild, and, which her delicacy made an insurmountable objection, there was an untold love between them. Her thoughts finally centred on Fanshawe. In his judgment, young and inexperienced though he was, she would have placed a firm trust; and his zeal, from whatever cause it arose, she could not doubt.

If, in the short time allowed her for reflection, an opportunity had occurred for consulting him, she would, in all probability, have taken advantage of it. But the terms on which they had parted the preceding evening had afforded him no reason to hope for her confidence; and he felt that there were others who had a better right to it than himself. He did not, therefore, throw himself in her way; and poor Ellen was consequently left without an adviser.

The determination that resulted from her own unassisted wisdom has been seen. When discovered by Dr. Melmoth at Hugh Crombie's inn, she was wholly prepared for flight, and, but for the intervention of the storm, would, ere then, have been far away.

The firmness of resolve that had impelled a timid maiden upon such a step was not likely to be broken by one defeat; and Ellen, accordingly, confident that the stranger would make a second attempt, determined that no effort on her part should be wanting to its success. On reaching her chamber, therefore, instead of retiring to rest (of which, from her sleepless thoughts of the preceding night, she stood greatly in need), she sat watching for the abatement of the storm. Her meditations were now calmer than at any time since her first meeting with the angler. She felt as if her fate was decided. The stain had fallen upon her reputation: she was no longer the same pure being in the opinion of those whose approbation she most valued.

One obstacle to her flight—and, to a woman's mind, a móst powerful one—had thus been removed. Dark and intricate as was the way, it was easier now to proceed than to pause; and her desperate and forlorn situation gave her a strength which hitherto she had not felt.

At every cessation in the torrent of rain that beat against the house, Ellen flew to the window, expecting to see the stranger form beneath it. But the clouds would again thicken, and the storm recommence with its former violence; and she began to fear that the approach of morning would compel her to meet the now dreaded face of Dr. Melmoth. At length, however, a strong and steady wind, supplying the place of the fitful gusts of the preceding part of the night, broke and scattered the clouds from the broad expanse of the sky. The moon, commencing her late voyage not long before the sun, was now visible, setting forth like a lonely ship from the dark line of the horizon, and touching at many a little silver cloud the islands of that aerial deep. Ellen felt that now the time was come; and, with a calmness wonderful to herself, she prepared for her final departure.

She had not long to wait ere she saw, between the vacancies of the trees, the angler advancing along the shady avenue that led to the principal entrance of Dr. Melmoth's dwelling. He had no need to summon her either by word or signal; for she had descended, emerged from the door, and stood before him, while he was yet at some distance from the house.

"You have watched well," he observed in a low, strange tone. "As saith the Scripture, 'Many daughters have done virtuously; but thou excellest them all.'"

He took her arm; and they hastened down the avenue. Then, leaving Hugh Crombie's inn on their right, they found its master in a spot so shaded that the moonbeams could not enlighten it. He held by the bridle two horses, one of which the angler assisted Ellen to mount. Then, turning to the landlord he pressed a purse into his hand; but Hugh drew back, and it fell to the ground.

"No! this would not have tempted me; nor will it reward me," he said. "If you have gold to spare, there are some that need it more than I."

"I understand you, mine host. I shall take thought for them; and enough will remain for you and me," replied his comrade. "I have seen the day when such a purse would not have slipped between your fingers. Well, be it so. And now, Hugh, my old friend, a shake of your hand; for we are seeing our last of each other."

"Pray Heaven it be so! though I wish you no ill," said the landlord, giving his hand.

He then seemed about to approach Ellen, who had been unable to distinguish the words of this brief conversation; but his comrade prevented him. "There is no time to lose," he observed. "The moon is growing pale already, and we should have been many a mile beyond the valley ere this." He mounted as he spoke; and, guiding Ellen's rein till they reached the road, they dashed away.

It was now that she felt herself completely in his power; and with that consciousness there came a sudden change of feeling, and an altered view of her conduct. A thousand reasons forced themselves upon her mind, seeming to prove that she had been deceived; while the motives, so powerful with her but a moment before, had either vanished from her memory or lost all their efficacy. Her companion, who gazed searchingly into her face, where the moonlight, coming down between the pines, allowed him to read its expression, probably discerned somewhat of the state of her thoughts.

"Do you repent so soon?" he inquired. "We have a weary way before us. Faint not ere we have well entered upon it."

"I have left dear friends behind me, and am going I know not whither," replied Ellen, tremblingly.

"You have a faithful guide," he observed, turning away his head, and speaking in the tone of one who endeavors to smother a laugh.

Ellen had no heart to continue the conversation; and they rode on in silence, and through a wild and gloomy scene. The wind roared heavily through the forest, and the trees shed their raindrops upon the travellers. The road, at all times, rough, was now broken into deep gullies, through which streams went murmuring down to mingle with the river. The pale moonlight combined with the gray of the morning to give a ghastly and unsubstantial appearance to every object.

The difficulties of the road had been so much increased by the storm, that the purple eastern clouds gave notice of the near approach of the sun just as the travellers reached the little lonesome cottage which Ellen remembered to have visited several months before. On arriving opposite to it, her companion checked his horse, and gazed with a wild earnestness at the wretched habitation. Then, stifling a groan that would not altogether be repressed, he was about to pass on; but at that moment the cottage-door opened, and a woman, whose sour, unpleasant countenance Ellen recognized, came hastily forth. She seemed not to heed the travellers; but the angler, his voice thrilling and quivering with indescribable emotion, addressed her.

"Woman, whither do you go?" he inquired.

She started, but, after a momentary pause, replied, "There is one within at the point of death. She struggles fearfully; and I cannot endure to watch alone by her bedside. If you are Christians, come in with me."

Ellen's companion leaped hastily from his horse, assisted her also to dismount, and followed the woman into the cottage, having first thrown the bridles of the horses carelessly over the branch of a tree. Ellen trembled at the awful scene she would be compelled to witness; but, when death was so near at hand, it was more terrible to stand alone in the dim morning light than even to watch the parting of soul and body. She therefore entered the cottage.

Her guide, his face muffled in his cloak, had taken his stand at a distance from the death-bed, in a part of the room which neither the increasing daylight nor the dim rays of a solitary lamp had yet enlightened. At

Ellen's entrance, the dying woman lay still, and apparently calm, except that a plaintive, half-articulate sound occasionally wandered through her lips.

"Hush! For mercy's sake, silence!" whispered the other woman to the strangers. "There is good hope now that she will die a peaceable death; but, if she is disturbed, the boldest of us will not dare to stand by her bedside."

The whisper by which her sister endeavored to preserve quiet perhaps reached the ears of the dying female; for she now raised herself in bed, slowly, but with a strength superior to what her situation promised. Her face was ghastly and wild, from long illness, approaching death, and disturbed intellect; and a disembodied spirit could scarcely be a more fearful object than one whose soul was just struggling forth. Her sister, approaching with the soft and stealing step appropriate to the chamber of sickness and death, attempted to replace the covering around her, and to compose her again upon the pillow. "Lie down and sleep, sister," she said; "and, when the day breaks, I will waken you. Methinks your breath comes freer already. A little more slumber, and to-morrow you will be well."

"My illness is gone: I am well," said the dying woman, gasping for breath. "I wander where the fresh breeze comes sweetly over my face; but a close and stifled air has choked my lungs."

"Yet a little while, and you will no longer draw your breath in pain," observed her sister, again replacing the bedclothes, which she continued to throw off.

"My husband is with me," murmured the widow. "He walks by my side, and speaks to me as in old times; but his words come faintly on my ear. Cheer me and comfort me, my husband; for there is a terror in those dim, motionless eyes, and in that shadowy voice."

As she spoke thus, she seemed to gaze upon some object that stood by her bedside; and the eyes of those who witnessed this scene could not but follow the direction of hers. They observed that the dying woman's own shadow was marked upon the wall, receiving a tremulous motion from the fitful rays of the lamp, and from her own convulsive efforts. "My husband stands gazing on me," she said again; "but my son,—where is he? And, as I ask, the father turns away his face. Where is our son? For his sake, I have longed to come to this land of rest. For him I have sorrowed many years. Will he not comfort me now?"

At these words the stranger made a few hasty steps towards the bed; but, ere he reached it, he conquered the impulse that drew him thither, and, shrouding his face more deeply in his cloak, returned to his former position. The dying woman, in the mean time, had thrown herself back upon the bed; and her sobbing and wailing, imaginary as was their cause, were inexpressibly affecting.

"Take me back to earth," she said; "for its griefs have followed me hither."

The stranger advanced, and, seizing the lamp, knelt down by the bed-side, throwing the light full upon his pale and convulsed features.

"Mother, here is your son!" he exclaimed.

At that unforgotten voice, the darkness burst away at once from her soul. She arose in bed, her eyes and her whole countenance beaming with joy, and threw her arms about his neck. A multitude of words seemed struggling for utterance; but they gave place to a low moaning sound, and then to the silence of death. The one moment of happiness, that recompensed years of sorrow, had been her last. Her son laid the lifeless form upon the pillow, and gazed with fixed eyes on his mother's face.

As he looked, the expression of enthusiastic joy that parting life had left upon the features faded gradually away; and the countenance, though no longer wild, assumed the sadness which it had worn through a long course of grief and pain. On beholding this natural consequence of death, the thought, perhaps, occurred to him, that her soul, no longer dependent on the imperfect means of intercourse possessed by mortals, had communed with his own, and become acquainted with all its guilt and misery. He started from the bedside, and covered his face with his hands, as if to hide it from those dead eyes.

Such a scene as has been described could not but have a powerful effect upon any one who retained aught of humanity; and the grief of the son, whose natural feelings had been blunted, but not destroyed, by an evil life, was much more violent than his outward demeanor would have expressed. But his deep repentance for the misery he had brought upon his parent did not produce in him a resolution to do wrong no more. The sudden consciousness of accumulated guilt made him desperate. He felt as if no one had thenceforth a claim to justice or compassion at his hands, when his neglect and cruelty had poisoned his mother's life, and hastened her death. Thus it was that the Devil wrought with him to his own destruction, reversing the salutary effect which his mother would have died exultingly to produce upon his mind. He now turned to Ellen Langton with a demeanor singularly calm and composed.

"We must resume our journey," he said, in his usual tone of voice. "The sun is on the point of rising, though but little light finds its way into this hovel."

Ellen's previous suspicions as to the character of her companion had now become certainty so far as to convince her that she was in the power of a lawless and guilty man; though what fate he intended for her she was unable to conjecture. An open opposition to his will, however, could not be ventured upon; especially as she discovered, on looking round the apartment, that, with the exception of the corpse, they were alone.

"Will you not attend your mother's funeral?" she asked, trembling, and conscious that he would discover her fears.

"The dead must bury their dead," he replied. "I have brought my mother to her grave,—and what can a son do more? This purse, however, will serve to lay her in the earth, and leave something for the old hag.

Whither is she gone?" interrupted he, casting a glance round the room in search of the old woman. "Nay, then, we must speedily to horse. I know her of old."

Thus saying, he threw the purse upon the table, and, without trusting himself to look again towards the dead, conducted Ellen out of the cottage. The first rays of the sun at that moment gilded the tallest trees of the forest.

On looking towards the spot where the horses had stood, Ellen thought that Providence, in answer to her prayers, had taken care for her deliverance. They were no longer there,—a circumstance easily accounted for by the haste with which the bridles had been thrown over the branch of the tree. Her companion, however, imputed it to another cause.

"The hag! She would sell her own flesh and blood by weight and measure," he muttered to himself. "This is some plot of hers, I know well."

He put his hand to his forehead for a moment's space, seeming to reflect on the course most advisable to be pursued. Ellen, perhaps unwisely, interposed.

"Would it not be well to return?" she asked, timidly. "There is now no hope of escaping; but I might yet reach home undiscovered."

"Return!" repeated her guide, with a look and smile from which she turned away her face. "Have you forgotten your father and his misfortunes? No, no, sweet Ellen: it is too late for such thoughts as these."

He took her hand, and led her towards the forest, in the rear of the cottage. She would fain have resisted; but they were all alone, and the attempt must have been both fruitless and dangerous. She therefore trod with him a path so devious, so faintly traced, and so overgrown with bushes and young trees, that only a most accurate acquaintance in his early days could have enabled her guide to retain it. To him, however, it seemed so perfectly familiar, that he was not once compelled to pause, though the numerous windings soon deprived Ellen of all knowledge of the situation of the cottage. They descended a steep hill, and, proceeding parallel to the river,—as Ellen judged by its rushing sound,—at length found themselves at what proved to be the termination of their walk.

Ellen now recollected a remark of Edward Walcott's respecting the wild and rude scenery through which the river here kept its way; and, in less agitating circumstances, her pleasure and admiration would have been great. They stood beneath a precipice, so high that the loftiest pinetops (and many of them seemed to soar to heaven) scarcely surmounted it. This line of rock has a considerable extent, at unequal heights, and with many interruptions, along the course of the river; and it seems probable that, at some former period, it was the boundary of the waters, though they are now confined within far less ambitious limits. The inferior portion of the crag, beneath which Ellen and her guide were standing, varies so far from the perpendicular as not to be inaccessible by a careful footstep. But only one person has been known to attempt the ascent of the superior half, and only one the descent; yet, steep as is the height, trees and bushes of various kinds have clung to the rock, wherever their roots could gain the slightest hold; thus seeming to prefer the scanty and difficult nourishment of the cliff to a more luxurious life in the rich interval that extends from its base to the river. But, whether or no these hardy vegetables have voluntarily chosen their rude resting-place, the cliff is indebted to them for much of the beauty that tempers its sublimity. When the eye is pained and wearied by the bold nakedness of the rock, it rests with pleasure on the cheerful foliage of the birch, or upon the darker ·green of the funereal pine. Just at the termination of the accessible portion of the crag, these trees are so numerous, and their foliage so dense, that they completely shroud from view a considerable excavation, formed, probably, hundreds of years since, by the fall of a portion of the rock. The detached fragment still lies at a little distance from the base, gray and moss-grown, but corresponding, in its general outline, to the cavity from which it was rent.

But the most singular and beautiful object in all this scene is a tiny fount of crystal water, that gushes forth from the high, smooth forehead of the cliff. Its perpendicular descent is of many feet; after which it finds its way, with a sweet diminutive murmur, to the level ground.

It is not easy to conceive whence the barren rock procures even the small supply of water that is necessary to the existence of this stream; it is as unaccountable as the gush of gentle feeling which sometimes proceeds from the hardest heart: but there it continues to flow and fall, undiminished and unincreased. The stream is so slender, that the gentlest breeze suffices to disturb its descent, and to scatter its pure sweet waters over the face of the cliff. But in that deep forest there is seldom a breath of wind; so that, plashing continually upon one spot, the fount has worn its own little channel of white sand, by which it finds its way to the river. Alas that the Naiades have lost their old authority! for what a deity of tiny loveliness must once have presided here!

Ellen's companion paused not to gaze either upon the loveliness or the sublimity of this scene, but, assisting her where it was requisite, began the steep and difficult ascent of the lower part of the cliff. The maiden's ingenuity in vain endeavored to assign reasons for this movement; but when they reached the tuft of trees, which, as has been noticed, grew at the ultimate point where mortal footstep might safely tread, she perceived through their thick branches the recess in the rock. Here they entered; and her guide pointed to a mossy seat, in the formation of which, to judge from its regularity, art had probably a share.

"Here you may remain in safety," he observed, "till I obtain the means of proceeding. In this spot you need fear no intruder; but it will be dangerous to venture beyond its bounds."

The meaning glance that accompanied these words intimated to poor Ellen, that, in warning her against danger, he alluded to the vengeance with which he would visit any attempt to escape. To leave her thus alone, trusting to the influence of such a threat, was a bold, yet a necessary and by no means a hopeless measure. On Ellen it produced the desired effect; and she sat in the cave as motionless, for a time, as if she had herself been a part of the rock. In other circumstances this shady recess would have been a delightful retreat during the sultry warmth of a summer's day. The dewy coolness of the rock kept the air always fresh and the sunbeams never thrust themselves so as to dissipate the mellow twilight through the green trees with which the chamber was curtained. Ellen's sleeplessness and agitation for many preceding hours had perhaps deadened her feelings; for she now felt a sort of indifference creeping upon her, an inability to realize the evils of her situation, at the same time that she was perfect-ly aware of them all. This torpor of mind increased, till her eyelids began to grow heavy and the cave and trees to swim before her sight. In a few moments more she would probably have been in dreamless slumber; but, rousing herself by a strong effort, she looked round the narrow limits of the cave in search of objects to excite her worn-out mind.

She now perceived, wherever the smooth rock afforded place for them, the initials, or the full-length names of former visitants of the cave. What wanderer on mountain-tops or in deep solitudes has not felt the influence of these records of humanity, telling him, when such a conviction is sooth-ing to his heart, that he is not alone in the world? It was singular, that, when her own mysterious situation had almost lost its power to engage her thoughts, Ellen perused these barren memorials with a certain degree of interest. She went on repeating them aloud, and starting at the sound of her own voice, till at length, as one name passed through her lips, she paused, and then, leaning her forehead against the letters, burst into tears. It was the name of Edward Walcott; and it struck upon her heart, arousing her to a full sense of her present misfortunes and dangers, and, more painful still, of her past happiness. Her tears had, however, a sooth-ing, and at the same time a strengthening effect upon her mind; for, when their gush was over, she raised her head, and began to meditate on the means of escape. She wondered at the species of fascination that had kept her, as if chained to the rock, so long, when there was, in reality, nothing to bar her pathway. She determined, late as it was, to attempt her own de-liverance, and for that purpose began slowly and cautiously to emerge from the cave.

Peeping out from among the trees, she looked and listened with most painful anxiety to discover if any living thing were in that seeming soli-tude, or if any sound disturbed the heavy stillness. But she saw only Na-ture in her wildest forms, and heard only the plash and murmur (almost inaudible, because continual) of the little waterfall, and the quick, short throbbing of her own heart, against which she pressed her hand as if to hush it. Gathering courage, therefore, she began to descend; and, starting often at the loose stones that even her light footstep displaced and sent rattling down, she at length reached the base of the crag in safety. She then made a few steps in the direction, as nearly as she could judge, by which she arrived at the spot, but paused, with a sudden revulsion of the blood to her heart, as her guide emerged from behind a projecting part of the rock. He approached her deliberately, an ironical smile writhing his features into a most disagreeable expression; while in his eyes there was something that seemed a wild, fierce joy. By a species of sophistry, of which oppressors often make use, he had brought himself to believe that he was now the injured one, and that Ellen, by her distrust of him, had fairly subjected herself to whatever evil it consisted with his will and power to inflict upon her. Her only restraining influence over him, the consciousness, in his own mind, that he possessed her confidence, was now done away. Ellen, as well as her enemy, felt that this was the case. She knew not what to dread; but she was well aware that danger was at hand, and that, in the deep wilderness, there was none to help her, except that Being with whose inscrutable purposes it might consist to allow the wicked to triumph for a season, and the innocent to be brought low.

"Are you so soon weary of this quiet retreat?" demanded her guide, continuing to wear the same sneering smile. "Or has your anxiety for your father induced you to set forth alone in quest of the afflicted old man?"

"Oh, if I were but with him!" exclaimed Ellen. "But this place is lonely and fearful; and I cannot endure to remain here."

"Lonely, is it, sweet Ellen?" he rejoined; "am I not with you? Yes, it is lonely,—lonely as guilt could wish. Cry aloud, Ellen, and spare not. Shriek, and see if there be any among these rocks and woods to hearken to you!"

"There is, there is One," exclaimed Ellen, shuddering, and affrighted at the fearful meaning of his countenance. "He is here! He is there!" And she pointed to heaven.

"It may be so, dearest," he replied. "But if there be an Ear that hears, and an Eye that sees all the evil of the earth, yet the Arm is slow to avenge. Else why do I stand before you a living man?"

"His vengeance may be delayed for a time, but not forever," she answered, gathering a desperate courage from the extremity of her fear.

"You say true, lovely Ellen; and I have done enough, erenow, to insure its heaviest weight. There is a pass, when evil deeds can add nothing to guilt, nor good ones take anything from it."

"Think of your mother,—of her sorrow through life, and perhaps even after death," Ellen began to say. But, as she spoke these words, the expression of his face was changed, becoming suddenly so dark and fiend-like, that she clasped her hands, and fell on her knees before him.

"I have thought of my mother," he replied, speaking very low, and putting his face close to hers. "I remember the neglect, the wrong, the lingering and miserable death, that she received at my hands. By what claim can either man or woman henceforth expect mercy from me? If God will help you, be it so; but by those words you have turned my heart to stone."

At this period of their conversation, when Ellen's peril seemed most imminent, the attention of both was attracted by a fragment of rock, which, falling from the summit of the crag, struck very near them. Ellen started from her knees, and, with her false guide, gazed eagerly upward,—he in the fear of interruption, she in the hope of deliverance.

## CHAPTER IX

"At length, he cries, behold the fated spring!
Yon rugged cliff conceals the fountain blest,
Dark rocks its crystal source o'ershadowing."

PSYCHE.

THE tale now returns to Fanshawe, who, as will be recollected, after being overtaken by Edward Walcott, was left with little apparent prospect of aiding in the deliverance of Ellen Langton.

It would be difficult to analyze the feelings with which the student pursued the chase, or to decide whether he was influenced and animated by the same hopes of successful love that cheered his rival. That he was conscious of such hopes, there is little reason to suppose; for the most powerful minds are not always the best acquainted with their own feelings. Had Fanshawe, moreover, acknowledged to himself the possibility of gaining Ellen's affections, his generosity would have induced him to refrain from her society before it was too late. He had read her character with accuracy, and had seen how fit she was to love, and to be loved, by a man who could find his happiness in the common occupations of the world; and Fanshawe never deceived himself so far as to suppose that this would be the case with him. Indeed, he often wondered at the passion with which Ellen's simple loveliness of mind and person had inspired him, and which seemed to be founded on the principle of contrariety, rather than of sympathy. It was the yearning of a soul, formed by Nature in a peculiar mould, for communion with those to whom it bore a resemblance, yet of whom it was not. But there was no reason to suppose that Ellen, who differed from the multitude only as being purer and better, would cast away her affections on the one, of all who surrounded her, least fitted to make her happy. Thus Fanshawe reasoned with himself, and of this he believed that he was convinced. Yet ever and anon he found himself involved in a dream of bliss, of which Ellen was to be the giver and the sharer. Then would he rouse himself, and press upon his mind the chilling consciousness that it was and could be but a dream. There was also another feeling, apparently discordant with those which have been enumerated. It was a longing for rest, for his old retirement, that came at intervals so powerfully upon him, as he rode on, that his heart sickened of the active exertion on which fate had thrust him.

After being overtaken by Edward Walcott, Fanshawe continued his journey with as much speed as was attainable by his wearied horse, but at a pace infinitely too slow for his earnest thoughts. These had carried him far away, leaving him only such a consciousness of his present situation as to make diligent use of the spur, when a horse's tread at no great distance struck upon his ear. He looked forward and behind; but, though a considerable extent of the narrow, rocky, and grass-grown road was visible, he was the only traveller there. Yet again he heard the sound, which, he now discovered, proceeded from among the trees that lined the roadside. Alighting, he entered the forest, with the intention, if the steed proved to be disengaged, and superior to his own, of appropriating him to his own use. He soon gained a view of the object he sought; but the animal rendered a closer acquaintance unattainable, by immediately taking to his heels. Fanshawe had, however, made a most interesting discovery; for the horse was accoutred with a side-saddle; and who but Ellen Langton could have been his rider? At this conclusion, though his perplexity was thereby in no degree diminished, the student immediately arrived. Returning to the road, and perceiving on the summit of the hill a cottage, which he recognized as the one he had entered with Ellen and Edward Walcott, he determined there to make inquiry respecting the objects of his pursuit.

On reaching the door of the poverty-stricken dwelling, he saw that it was not now so desolate of inmates as on his previous visit. In the single inhabitable apartment were several elderly women, clad evidently in their well-worn and well-saved Sunday clothes, and all wearing a deep grievous expression of countenance. Fanshawe was not long in deciding that death was within the cottage, and that these aged females were of the class who love the house of mourning, because to them it is a house of feasting. It is a fact, disgusting and lamentable, that the disposition which Heaven, for the best of purposes, has implanted in the female breast—to watch by the sick and comfort the afflicted—frequently becomes depraved into an odious love of scenes of pain and death and sorrow. Such women are like the Ghouls of the Arabian Tales, whose feasting was among tombstones and upon dead carcasses.

(It is sometimes, though less frequently, the case, that this disposition to make a "joy of grief" extends to individuals of the other sex. But in us it is even less excusable and more disgusting, because it is our nature to shun the sick and afflicted; and, unless restrained by principles other than we bring into the world with us, men might follow the example of many animals in destroying the infirm of their own species. Indeed, instances of this nature might be adduced among savage nations.) Sometimes, however, from an original *lusus naturæ*, or from the influence of circumstances, a man becomes a haunter of death-beds, a tormentor of afflicted hearts, and a follower of funerals. Such an abomination now appeared before Fanshawe, and beckoned him into the cottage. He was considerably beyond the middle age, rather corpulent, with a broad, fat, tallow-complexioned countenance. The student obeyed his silent call, and entered the room, through the open door of which he had been gazing.

He now beheld, stretched out upon the bed where she had so lately lain in life, though dying, the yet uncoffined corpse of the aged woman, whose death has been described. How frightful it seemed!—that fixed countenance of ashy paleness, amid its decorations of muslin and fine linen, as if a bride were decked for the marriage-chamber, as if death were a bridegroom, and the coffin a bridal bed. Alas that the vanity of dress should extend even to the grave!

The female who, as being the near and only relative of the deceased, was supposed to stand in need of comfort, was surrounded by five or six of her own sex. These continually poured into her ear the stale, trite maxims which, where consolation is actually required, add torture insupportable to the wounded heart. Their present object, however, conducted herself with all due decorum, holding her handkerchief to her tearless eyes, and answering with very grievous groans to the words of her comforters. Who could have imagined that there was joy in her heart, because, since her sister's death, there was but one remaining obstacle between herself and the sole property of that wretched cottage?

While Fanshawe stood silently observing this scene, a low, monotonous voice was uttering some words in his ear, of the meaning of which his mind did not immediately take note. He turned, and saw that the speaker was the person who had invited him to enter.

"What is your pleasure with me, sir?" demanded the student.

"I make bold to ask," replied the man, "whether you would choose to partake of some creature comfort, before joining in prayer with the family and friends of our deceased sister?" As he spoke, he pointed to a table, on which was a moderate-sized stone jug and two or three broken glasses; for then, as now, there were few occasions of joy or grief on which ardent spirits were not considered indispensable, to heighten the one or to alleviate the other.

"I stand in no need of refreshment," answered Fanshawe; "and it is not my intention to pray at present."

"I pray your pardon, reverend sir," rejoined the other; "but your face is pale, and you look wearied. A drop from yonder vessel is needful to recruit the outward man. And for the prayer, the sisters will expect it; and their souls are longing for the outpouring of the Spirit. I was intending to open my own mouth with such words as are given to my poor ignorance, but"—

Fanshawe was here about to interrupt this address, which proceeded on the supposition, arising from his black dress and thoughtful countenance, that he was a clergyman. But one of the females now approached him, and intimated that the sister of the deceased was desirous of the benefit of his conversation. He would have returned a negative to this request, but, looking towards the afflicted woman, he saw her withdraw her handkerchief from her eyes, and cast a brief but penetrating and most intelligent glance upon him. He immediately expressed his readiness to offer such consolation as might be in his power.

"And in the mean time," observed the lay-preacher, "I will give the sisters to expect a word of prayer and exhortation, either from you or from myself."

These words were lost upon the supposed clergyman, who was already at the side of the mourner. The females withdrew out of ear-shot to give place to a more legitimate comforter than themselves.

"What know you respecting my purpose?" inquired Fanshawe, bending towards her.

The woman gave a groan—the usual result of all efforts at consolation—for the edification of the company, and then replied in a whisper, which reached only the ear for which it was intended. "I know whom you come to seek: I can direct you to them. Speak low, for God's sake!" she continued, observing that Fanshawe was about to utter an exclamation. She then resumed her groans with greater zeal than before.

"Where—where are they?" asked the student, in a whisper which all his efforts could scarcely keep below his breath. "I adjure you to tell me."

"And, if I should, how am I like to be bettered by it?" inquired the old woman, her speech still preceded and followed by a groan.

"O God! The *auri sacra fames!*" thought Fanshawe with a sickening heart, looking at the motionless corpse upon the bed, and then at the wretched being, whom the course of nature, in comparatively a moment of time, would reduce to the same condition.

He whispered again, however, putting his purse into the hag's hand. "Take this. Make your own terms when they are discovered. Only tell me where I must seek them—and speedily, or it may be too late."

"I am a poor woman, and am afflicted," said she, taking the purse, unseen by any who were in the room. "It is little that worldly goods can do for me, and not long can I enjoy them." And here she was delivered of a louder and a more heartfelt groan than ever. She then continued: "Follow the path behind the cottage, that leads to the river-side. Walk along the foot of the rock, and search for them near the water-spout. Keep a slow pace till you are out of sight," she added, as the student started to his feet.

The guests of the cottage did not attempt to oppose Fanshawe's progress, when they saw him take the path towards the forest, imagining, probably, that he was retiring for the purpose of secret prayer. But the old woman laughed behind the handkerchief with which she veiled her face.

"Take heed to your steps, boy," she muttered; "for they are leading you whence you will not return. Death, too, for the slayer. Be it so."

Fanshawe, in the mean while, contrived to discover, and for a while to retain, the narrow and winding path that led to the river-side. But it was originally no more than a track, by which the cattle belonging to the cottage went down to their watering-place, and by these four-footed passengers it had long been deserted. The fern-bushes, therefore, had grown over it; and in several places trees of considerable size had shot up in the midst. These difficulties could scarcely have been surmounted by the utmost caution; and as Fanshawe's thoughts were too deeply fixed upon the end to pay a due regard to the means, he soon became desperately bewildered both as to the locality of the river and of the cottage. Had he known, however, in which direction to seek the latter, he would not, probably, have turned back; not that he was infected by any chivalrous desire to finish the adventure alone, but because he would expect little assistance from those he had left there. Yet he could not but wonder—though he had not in his first eagerness taken notice of it—at the anxiety of the old woman that he should proceed singly, and without the knowledge of her guests, on the search. He nevertheless continued to wander on,— pausing often to listen for the rush of the river, and then starting forward with fresh rapidity, to rid himself of the sting of his own thoughts, which became painfully intense when undisturbed by bodily motion. His way was now frequently interrupted by rocks, that thrust their huge gray heads from the ground, compelling him to turn aside, and thus depriving him, fortunately, perhaps, of all remaining idea of the direction he had intended to pursue.

Thus he went on, his head turned back, and taking little heed to his footsteps, when, perceiving that he trod upon a smooth, level rock, he looked forward, and found himself almost on the utmost verge of a precipice.

After the throbbing of the heart that followed this narrow escape had subsided, he stood gazing down where the sunbeams slept so pleasantly at the roots of the tall old trees, with whose highest tops he was upon a level. Suddenly he seemed to hear voices—one well-remembered voice— ascending from beneath; and, approaching to the edge of the cliff, he saw at its base the two whom he sought.

He saw and interpreted Ellen's look and attitude of entreaty, though the words with which she sought to soften the ruthless heart of her guide became inaudible ere they reached the height where Fanshawe stood. He felt that Heaven had sent him thither, at the moment of her utmost need, to be the preserver of all that was dear to him; and he paused only to consider the mode in which her deliverance was to be effected. Life he would have laid down willingly, exultingly: his only care was, that the sacrifice should not be in vain.

At length, when Ellen fell upon her knees, he lifted a small fragment of rock, and threw it down the cliff. It struck so near the pair, that it immediately drew the attention of both.

When the betrayer, at the instant in which he had almost defied the power of the Omnipotent to bring help to Ellen, became aware of Fanshawe's presence, his hardihood failed him for a time, and his knees actually tottered beneath him. There was something awful, to his apprehension, in the slight form that stood so far above him, like a being from another sphere, looking down upon his wickedness. But his half-superstitious dread endured only a moment's space; and then, mustering the courage that in a thousand dangers had not deserted him, he prepared to revenge the intrusion by which Fanshawe had a second time interrupted his designs.

"By Heaven, I will cast him down at her feet!" he muttered through his closed teeth. "There shall be no form nor likeness of man left in him. Then let him rise up, if he is able, and defend her."

Thus resolving, and overlooking all hazard in his eager hatred and desire for vengeance, he began a desperate attempt to ascend the cliff. The space which only had hitherto been deemed accessible was quickly passed; and in a moment more he was half-way up the precipice, clinging to trees, shrubs, and projecting portions of the rock, and escaping through hazards which seemed to menace inevitable destruction.

Fanshawe, as he watched his upward progress, deemed that every step would be his last; but when he perceived that more than half, and apparently the most difficult part, of the ascent was surmounted, his opinion changed. His courage, however, did not fail him as the moment of need drew nigh. His spirits rose buoyantly; his limbs seemed to grow firm and strong; and he stood on the edge of the precipice, prepared for the death-struggle which would follow the success of his enemy's attempt.

But that attempt was not successful. When within a few feet of the summit, the adventurer grasped at a twig too slenderly rooted to sustain his weight. It gave way in his hand, and he fell backward down the precipice. His head struck against the less perpendicular part of the rock, whence the body rolled heavily down to the detached fragment, of which mention has heretofore been made. There was no life left in him. With all the passions of hell alive in his heart, he had met the fate that he intended for Fanshawe.

The student paused not then to shudder at the sudden and awful overthrow of his enemy; for he saw that Ellen lay motionless at the foot of the cliff. She had indeed fainted at the moment she became aware of her deliverer's presence; and no stronger proof could she have given of her firm reliance upon his protection.

Fanshawe was not deterred by the danger, of which he had just received so fearful an evidence, from attempting to descend to her assistance; and, whether owing to his advantage in lightness of frame, or to superior caution, he arrived safely at the base of the precipice.

He lifted the motionless form of Ellen in his arms, and, resting her head against his shoulder, gazed on her cheek of lily paleness with a joy, a triumph, that rose almost to madness. It contained no mixture of hope; it had no reference to the future: it was the perfect bliss of a moment,— an insulated point of happiness. He bent over her, and pressed a kiss— the first, and he knew it would be the last—on her pale lips; then, bearing her to the fountain, he sprinkled its waters profusely over her face, neck, and bosom. She at length opened her eyes, slowly and heavily; but her mind was evidently wandering, till Fanshawe spoke.

"Fear not, Ellen: you are safe," he said.

At the sound of his voice, her arm, which was thrown over his shoulder, involuntarily tightened its embrace, telling him, by that mute motion, with how firm a trust she confided in him. But, as a fuller sense of her situation returned, she raised herself to her feet, though still retaining the support of his arm. It was singular, that, although her insensibility had commenced before the fall of her guide, she turned away her eyes, as if instinctively, from the spot where the mangled body lay; nor did she inquire of Fanshawe the manner of her deliverance.

"Let us begone from this place," she said in faint, low accents, and with an inward shudder.

They walked along the precipice. seeking some passage by which they might gain its summit, and at length arrived at that by which Ellen and her guide had descended. Chance—for neither Ellen nor Fanshawe could have discovered the path—led them, after but little wandering, to the cottage. A messenger was sent forward to the town to inform Dr. Melmoth of the recovery of his ward; and the intelligence thus received had interrupted Edward Walcott's conversation with the seaman.

It would have been impossible, in the mangled remains of Ellen's guide, to discover the son of the Widow Butler, except from the evidence of her sister, who became, by his death, the sole inheritrix of the cottage. The history of this evil and unfortunate man must be comprised within very narrow limits. A harsh father, and his own untamable disposition, had driven him from home in his boyhood; and chance had made him the temporary companion of Hugh Crombie. After two years of wandering, when in a foreign country and in circumstances of utmost need, he attracted the notice of Mr. Langton. The merchant took his young countryman under his protection, afforded him advantages of education, and, as his capacity was above mediocrity, gradually trusted him in many affairs of importance. During this period, there was no evidence of dishonesty on his part. On the contrary, he manifested a zeal for Mr. Langton's interest, and a respect for his person, that proved his strong sense of the benefits he had received. But he unfortunately fell into certain youthful indiscretions, which, if not entirely pardonable, might have been palliated by many considerations that would have occurred to a merciful man. Mr. Langton's justice, however, was seldom tempered by mercy; and, on this occasion, he shut the door of repentance against his erring *protégé*, and left him in a situation not less desperate than that from which he had relieved him. The goodness and the nobleness, of which his heart was not destitute, turned, from that time, wholly to evil; and he became irrecoverably ruined and irreclaimably depraved. His wandering life had led him, shortly before the period of this tale, to his native country. Here the erroneous intelligence of Mr. Langton's death had reached him, and suggested the scheme, which circumstances seemed to render practicable, but the fatal termination of which has been related.

The body was buried where it had fallen, close by the huge, gray, moss-grown fragment of rock,—a monument on which centuries can work little change. The eighty years that have elapsed since the death of the widow's son have, however, been sufficient to obliterate an inscription, which some one was at the pains to cut in the smooth surface of the stone. Traces of letters are still discernible; but the writer's many efforts could never discover a connected meaning. The grave, also, is overgrown with fern-bushes, and sunk to a level with the surrounding soil. But the legend, though my version of it may be forgotten, will long be traditionary in that lonely spot, and give to the rock and the precipice and the fountain an interest thrilling to the bosom of the romantic wanderer.

## CHAPTER X

"Sitting then in shelter shady,
To observe and mark his mone
Suddenly I saw a lady
Hasting to him all alone,
Clad in maiden-white and green,
Whom I judged the Forest Queen."
THE WOODMAN'S BEAR.

DURING several weeks succeeding her danger and deliverance, Ellen Langton was confined to her chamber by illness, resulting from the agitation she had endured. Her father embraced the earliest opportunity to express his deep gratitude to Fanshawe for the inestimable service he had rendered, and to intimate a desire to requite it to the utmost of his power. He had understood that the student's circumstances were not prosperous, and, with the feeling of one who was habituated to give and receive a *quid pro quo*, he would have rejoiced to share his abundance with the deliverer of his daughter. But Fanshawe's flushed brow and haughty eye, when he perceived the thought that was stirring in Mr. Langton's mind, sufficiently proved to the discerning merchant that money was not, in the present instance, a circulating medium. His penetration, in fact, very soon informed him of the motives by which the young man had been actuated in risking his life for Ellen Langton; but he made no allusion to the subject, concealing his intentions, if any he had, in his own bosom.

During Ellen's illness, Edward Walcott had manifested the deepest anxiety respecting her: he had wandered around and within the house, like a restless ghost, informing himself of the slightest fluctuation in her health, and thereby graduating his happiness or misery. He was at length informed that her convalescence had so far progressed, that, on the succeeding day, she would venture below. From that time Edward's visits to Dr. Melmoth's mansion were relinquished. His cheek grew pale and his eye lost its merry light; but he resolutely kept himself a banished man. Multifarious were the conjectures to which this course of conduct gave rise; but Ellen understood and approved his motives. The maiden must have been far more blind than ever woman was in such a matter, if the late events had not convinced her of Fanshawe's devoted attachment; and she saw that Edward Walcott, feeling the superior, the irresistible strength of his rival's claim, had retired from the field. Fanshawe, however, discovered no intention to pursue his advantage. He paid her no voluntary visit, and even declined an invitation to tea, with which Mrs. Melmoth, after extensive preparations, had favored him. He seemed to have resumed all the habits of seclusion by which he was distinguished previous to his acquaintance with Ellen, except that he still took his sunset walk on the banks of the stream.

On one of these occasions, he stayed his footsteps by the old leafless oak which had witnessed Ellen's first meeting with the angler. Here he mused upon the circumstances that had resulted from that event, and upon the rights and privileges (for he was well aware of them all) which those circumstances had given him. Perhaps the loveliness of the scene and the recollections connected with it, perhaps the warm and mellow sunset, perhaps a temporary weakness in himself, had softened his feelings, and shaken the firmness of his resolution, to leave Ellen to be happy with his rival. His strong affections rose up against his reason, whispering that bliss—on earth and in heaven, through time and eternity—might yet be his lot with her. It is impossible to conceive of the flood of momentary joy which the bare admission of such a possibility sent through his frame; and, just when the tide was highest in his heart, a soft little hand was laid upon his own, and, starting, he beheld Ellen at his side.

Her illness, since the commencement of which Fanshawe had not seen her, had wrought a considerable, but not a disadvantageous, change in her appearance. She was paler and thinner; her countenance was more intellectual, more spiritual; and a spirit did the student almost deem her, appearing so suddenly in that solitude. There was a quick vibration of the delicate blood in her cheek, yet never brightening to the glow of perfect health; a tear was glittering on each of her long, dark eyelashes; and there was a gentle tremor through all her frame, which compelled her, for a little space, to support herself against the oak. Fanshawe's first impulse was to address her in words of rapturous delight; but he checked himself, and attempted—vainly indeed—to clothe his voice in tones of calm courtesy. His remark merely expressed pleasure at her restoration to health; and Ellen's low and indistinct reply had as little relation to the feelings that agitated her.

"Yet I fear," continued Fanshawe, recovering a degree of composure, and desirous of assigning a motive (which he felt was not the true one) for Ellen's agitation,—"I fear that your walk has extended too far for your strength."

"It would have borne me farther with such a motive," she replied, still trembling,—"to express my gratitude to my preserver."

"It was needless, Ellen, it was needless; for the deed brought with it its own reward," exclaimed Fanshawe, with a vehemence that he could not repress. "It was dangerous, for"—

Here he interrupted himself, and turned his face away.

"And wherefore was it dangerous?" inquired Ellen, laying her hand gently on his arm; for he seemed about to leave her.

"Because you have a tender and generous heart, and I a weak one," he replied.

"Not so," answered she, with animation. "Yours is a heart full of strength and nobleness; and if it have a weakness"—

"You know well that it has, Ellen,—one that has swallowed up all its strength," said Fanshawe. "Was it wise, then, to tempt it thus, when, if it yield, the result must be your own misery?"

Ellen did not affect to misunderstand his meaning. On the contrary, with a noble frankness, she answered to what was implied rather than expressed.

"Do me not this wrong," she said, blushing, yet earnestly. "Can it be misery? Will it not be happiness to form the tie that shall connect you to the world? to be your guide—a humble one, it is true, but the one of your choice—to the quiet paths from which your proud and lonely thoughts have estranged you? Oh, I know that there will be happiness in such a lot, from these and a thousand other sources!"

The animation with which Ellen spoke, and, at the same time, a sense of the singular course to which her gratitude had impelled her, caused her beauty to grow brighter and more enchanting with every word. And when, as she concluded, she extended her hand to Fanshawe, to refuse it was like turning from an angel, who would have guided him to heaven. But, had he been capable of making the woman he loved a sacrifice to her own generosity, that act would have rendered him unworthy of her. Yet the struggle was a severe one ere he could reply.

"You have spoken generously and nobly, Ellen," he said. "I have no way to prove that I deserve your generosity, but by refusing to take advantage of it. Even if your heart were yet untouched, if no being more happily constituted than myself had made an impression there, even then, I trust, a selfish passion would not be stronger than my integrity. But now"— He would have proceeded; but the firmness which had hitherto sustained him gave way. He turned aside to hide the tears which all the pride of his nature could not restrain, and which, instead of relieving, added to his anguish. At length he resumed, "No, Ellen, we must part now and forever. Your life will be long and happy. Mine will be short, but not altogether wretched, nor shorter than if we had never met. When you hear that I am in my grave, do not imagine that you have hastened me thither. Think that you scattered bright dreams around my pathway, —an ideal happiness, that you would have sacrificed your own to realize."

He ceased; and Ellen felt that his determination was unalterable. She could not speak; but, taking his hand, she pressed it to her lips, and they saw each other no more. Mr. Langton and his daughter shortly after returned to the seaport, which, for several succeeding years, was their residence.

After Ellen's departure, Fanshawe returned to his studies with the *melancholy* same absorbing ardor that had formerly characterized him. His face was *student* as seldom seen among the young and gay; the pure breeze and the blessed sunshine as seldom refreshed his pale and·weary brow; and his lamp burned as constantly from the first shade of evening till the gray morning light began to dim its beams. Nor did he, as weak men will, treasure up his love in a hidden chamber of his breast. He was in reality the thoughtful and earnest student that he seemed. He had exerted the whole might of his spirit over itself, and he was a conqueror. Perhaps, indeed, a summer breeze of sad and gentle thoughts would sometimes visit him; but, in these brief memories of his love, he did not wish that it should be revived, or mourn over its event.

There were many who felt an interest in Fanshawe; but the influence of none could prevail upon him to lay aside the habits, mental and physical, by which he was bringing himself to the grave. His passage thither was consequently rapid, terminating just as he reached his twentieth year. His fellow-students erected to his memory a monument of rough-hewn granite, with a white marble slab for the inscription. This was borrowed from the grave of Nathanael Mather, whom, in his almost insane eagerness for knowledge, and in his early death, Fanshawe resembled.

THE ASHES OF A HARD STUDENT
AND A GOOD SCHOLAR.

Many tears were shed over his grave; but the thoughtful and the wise, though turf never covered a nobler heart, could not lament that it was so soon at rest. He left a world for which he was unfit; and we trust, that, among the innumerable stars of heaven, there is one where he has found happiness.

Of the other personages of this tale,—Hugh Crombie, being exposed to no strong temptations, lived and died an honest man. Concerning Dr. Melmoth it is unnecessary here to speak. The reader, if he have any curiosity upon the subject, is referred to his Life, which, together with several sermons and other productions of the doctor, was published by his successor in the presidency of Harley College, about the year 1768.

It was not till four years after Fanshawe's death, that Edward Walcott was united to Ellen Langton. Their future lives were uncommonly happy. Ellen's gentle, almost imperceptible, but powerful influence drew her husband away from the passions and pursuits that would have interfered with domestic felicity; and he never regretted the worldly distinction of which she thus deprived him. Theirs was a long life of calm and quiet bliss; and what matters it, that, except in these pages, they have left no name behind them?

# THE SCARLET LETTER

## Preface to the Second Edition

Much to the author's surprise, and (if he may say so without additional offence) considerably to his amusement, he finds that his sketch of official life, introductory to The Scarlet Letter, has created an unprecedented excitement in the respectable community immediately around him. It could hardly have been more violent, indeed, had he burned down the Custom House, and quenched its last smoking ember in the blood of a certain venerable personage, against whom he is supposed to cherish a peculiar malevolence. As the public disapprobation would weigh very heavily on him, were he conscious of deserving it, the author begs leave to say that he has carefully read over the introductory pages, with a purpose to alter or expunge whatever might be found amiss, and to make the best reparation in his power for the atrocities of which he has been adjudged guilty. But it appears to him, that the only remarkable features of the sketch are its frank and genuine good-humor, and the general accuracy with which he has conveyed his sincere impressions of the characters therein described. As to enmity, or ill-feeling of any kind, personal or political, he utterly disclaims such motives. The sketch might, perhaps, have been wholly omitted, without loss to the public, or detriment to the book; but, having undertaken to write it, he conceives that it could not have been done in a better or a kindlier spirit, nor, so far as his abilities availed, with a livelier effect of truth.

The author is constrained, therefore, to republish his introductory sketch without the change of a word.

Salem, *March* 30, 1850.

# THE SCARLET LETTER

## THE CUSTOM HOUSE

### INTRODUCTORY TO "THE SCARLET LETTER"

IT is a little remarkable, that—though disinclined to talk overmuch of myself and my affairs at the fireside, and to my personal friends—an autobiographical impulse should twice in my life have taken possession of me, in addressing the public. The first time was three or four years since, when I favored the reader—inexcusably, and for no earthly reason, that either the indulgent reader or the intrusive author could imagine—with a description of my way of life in the deep quietude of an Old Manse. And now—because, beyond my deserts, I was happy enough to find a listener or two on the former occasion—I again seize the public by the button, and talk of my three years' experience in a Custom House. The example of the famous "P. P., Clerk of this Parish," was never more faithfully followed. The truth seems to be, however, that, when he casts his leaves forth upon the wind, the author addresses, not the many who will fling aside his volume, or never take it up, but the few who will understand him, better than most of his schoolmates or lifemates. Some authors, indeed, do far more than this, and indulge themselves in such confidential depths of revelation as could fittingly be addressed, only and exclusively, to the one heart and mind of perfect sympathy; as if the printed book, thrown at large on the wide world, were certain to find out the divided segment of the writer's own nature, and complete his circle of existence by bringing him into communion with it. It is scarcely decorous, however, to speak all, even where we speak impersonally. But, as thoughts are frozen and utterance benumbed, unless the speaker stand in some true relation with his audience, it may be pardonable to imagine that a friend, a kind and apprehensive, though not the closest friend, is listening to our talk; and then, a native reserve being thawed by this genial consciousness, we may prate of the circumstances that lie around us, and even of ourself, but still keep the inmost Me behind its veil. To this extent, and within these limits, an author, methinks, may be autobiographical, without violating either the reader's rights or his own.

It will be seen likewise, that this Custom House sketch has a certain propriety, of a kind always recognized in literature, as explaining how a large portion of the following pages came into my possession, and as offering proofs of the authenticity of a narrative therein contained. This, in fact,—a desire to put myself in my true position as editor, or very little more, of the most prolix among the tales that make up my volume,—this, and no other is my true reason for assuming a personal relation with the public. In accomplishing the main purpose, it has appeared allowable, by a few extra touches, to give a faint representation of a mode of life not heretofore described, together with some of the characters that move in it, among whom the author happened to make one.

In my native town of Salem, at the head of what, half a century ago, in the days of old King Derby, was a bustling wharf,—but which is now burdened with decayed wooden warehouses, and exhibits few or no symptoms of commercial life; except, perhaps, a bark or brig, half-way down its melancholy length, discharging hides; or, nearer at hand, a Nova Scotia schooner, pitching out her cargo of firewood,—at the head, I say, of this dilapidated wharf, which the tide often overflows, and along which, at the base and in the rear of the row of buildings, the track of many languid years is seen in a border of unthrifty grass,—here, with a view from its front windows adown this not very enlivening prospect, and thence across the harbor, stands a spacious edifice of brick. From the loftiest point of its roof, during precisely three and a half hours of each forenoon, floats or droops, in breeze or calm, the banner of the republic; but with the thirteen stripes turned vertically, instead of horizontally, and thus indicating that a civil, and not a military post of Uncle Sam's government is here established. Its front is ornamented with a portico of half a dozen wooden pillars, supporting a balcony, beneath which a flight of wide granite steps descends towards the street. Over the entrance hovers an enormous specimen of the American eagle, with outspread wings, a shield before her breast, and, if I recollect aright, a bunch of intermingled thunderbolts and barbed arrows in each claw. With the customary infirmity of temper that characterizes this unhappy fowl, she appears, by the fierceness of her beak and eye, and the general truculency of her attitude, to threaten mischief to the inoffensive community; and especially to warn all citizens, careful of their safety, against intruding on the premises which she overshadows with her wings. Nevertheless, vixenly as she looks, many people are seeking, at this very moment, to shelter themselves under the wing of the federal eagle; imagining, I presume, that her bosom has all the softness and snugness of an eider-down pillow. But she has no great tenderness, even in her best of moods, and, sooner or later,—oftener soon than late,—is apt to fling off her nestlings, with a scratch of her claw, a dab of her beak, or a rankling wound from her barbed arrows.

The pavement round about the above-described edifice—which we may as well name at once as the Custom House of the port—has grass enough growing in its chinks to show that it has not, of late days, been worn by any multitudinous resort of business. In some months of the year, however, there often chances a forenoon when affairs move onward with a livelier tread. Such occasions might remind the elderly citizen of that period before the last war with England, when Salem was a port by itself; not scorned, as she is now, by her own merchants and ship-owners, who permit her wharves to crumble to ruin, while their ventures go to swell, needlessly and imperceptibly, the mighty flood of commerce at New York or Boston. On some such morning, when three or four vessels happen to have arrived at once,—usually from Africa or South America, —or to be on the verge of their departure thitherward, there is a sound of frequent feet, passing briskly up and down the granite steps. Here, before his own wife has greeted him, you may greet the sea-flushed shipmaster, just in port, with his vessel's papers under his arm, in a tarnished tin box. Here, too, comes his owner, cheerful or sombre, gracious or in the sulks, accordingly as his scheme of the now accomplished voyage has been realized in merchandise that will readily be turned to gold, or has buried him under a bulk of incommodities, such as nobody will care to rid him of. Here, likewise,—the germ of the wrinkle-browed, grizzly-bearded, careworn merchant,—we have the smart young clerk, who gets the taste of traffic as a wolf-cub does of blood, and already sends adventures in his master's ships, when he had better be sailing mimic-boats upon a millpond. Another figure in the scene is the outward-bound sailor in quest of a protection; or the recently arrived one, pale and feeble, seeking a passport to the hospital. Nor must we forget the captains of the rusty little schooners that bring firewood from the British provinces; a rough-looking set of tarpaulins, without the alertness of the Yankee aspect, but contributing an item of no slight importance to our decaying trade.

Cluster all these individuals together, as they sometimes were, with other miscellaneous ones to diversify the group, and, for the time being, it made the Custom House a stirring scene. More frequently, however, on ascending the steps, you would discern—in the entry, if it were summer time, or in their appropriate rooms, if wintry or inclement weather—a row of venerable figures, sitting in old-fashioned chairs, which were tipped on their hind legs back against the wall. Oftentimes they were asleep, but occasionally might be heard talking together, in voices between speech and a snore, and with that lack of energy that distinguishes the occupants of almshouses, and all other human beings who depend for subsistence on charity, on monopolized labor, or anything else, but their own independent exertions. These old gentlemen—seated, like Matthew, at the receipt of customs, but not very liable to be summoned thence, like him, for apostolic errands—were Custom House officers.

Furthermore, on the left hand as you enter the front door, is a certain room or office, about fifteen feet square, and of a lofty height; with two of its arched windows commanding a view of the aforesaid dilapidated wharf, and the third looking across a narrow lane, and along a portion of Derby Street. All three give glimpses of the shops of grocers, blockmakers, slop-sellers, and ship-chandlers; around the doors of which are generally to be seen, laughing and gossiping, clusters of old salts, and such other wharf-rats as haunt the Wapping of a seaport. The room itself is cobwebbed, and dingy with old paint; its floor is strewn with gray sand, in a fashion that has elsewhere fallen into long disuse; and it is easy to conclude, from the general slovenliness of the place, that this is a sanctuary into which womankind, with her tools of magic, the broom and mop, has very infrequent access. In the way of furniture, there is a stove with a voluminous funnel; an old pine desk, with a three-legged stool beside it; two or three wooden-bottom chairs, exceedingly decrepit and infirm; and —not to forget the library—on some shelves, a score or two of volumes of the Acts of Congress, and a bulky Digest of the Revenue Laws. A tin pipe ascends through the ceiling, and forms a medium of vocal communication with other parts of the edifice. And here, some six months ago,—pacing from corner to corner, or lounging on the long-legged stool, with his elbow on the desk, and his eyes wandering up and down the columns of the morning newspaper,—you might have recognized, honored reader, the same individual who welcomed you into his cheery little study, where the sunshine glimmered so pleasantly through the willow branches, on the western side of the Old Manse. But now, should you go thither to seek him, you would inquire in vain for the Locofoco Surveyor. The besom of reform has swept him out of office; and a worthier successor wears his dignity, and pockets his emoluments.

This old town of Salem—my native place, though I have dwelt much away from it, both in boyhood and maturer years—possesses, or did possess, a hold on my affections, the force of which I have never realized during my seasons of actual residence here. Indeed, so far as its physical aspect is concerned, with its flat, unvaried surface, covered chiefly with wooden houses, few or none of which pretend to architectural beauty,— its irregularity, which is neither picturesque nor quaint, but only tame,— its long and lazy street lounging wearisomely through the whole extent of the peninsula, with Gallows Hill and New Guinea at one end, and a view of the almshouse at the other,—such being the features of my native town, it would be quite as reasonable to form a sentimental attachment to a disarranged checker-board. And yet, though invariably happiest elsewhere, there is within me a feeling for old Salem, which, in lack of a better phrase, I must be content to call affection. The sentiment is probably assignable to the deep and aged roots which my family has struck into the soil. It is now nearly two centuries and a quarter since the original Briton, the earliest emigrant of my name, made his appearance in the wild and forest-bordered settlement, which has since become a city. And here his descendants have been born and died, and have mingled their earthly substance with the soil, until no small portion of it must necessarily be akin to the mortal frame wherewith, for a little while, I walk the streets. In part, therefore, the attachment which I speak of is the mere sensuous sympathy of dust for dust. Few of my countrymen can know what it is; nor, as frequent transportation is perhaps better for the stock, need they consider it desirable to know.

But the sentiment has likewise its moral quality. The figure of that first ancestor, invested by family tradition with a dim and dusky grandeur, was present to my boyish imagination, as far back as I can remember. It still haunts me, and induces a sort of home-feeling with the past, which I scarcely claim in reference to the present phase of the town. I seem to have a stronger claim to a residence here on account of his grave, bearded, sabled-cloaked and steeple-crowned progenitor,—who came so early, with his Bible and his sword, and trode the unworn street with such a stately port, and made so large a figure, as a man of war and peace,—a stronger claim than for myself, whose name is seldom heard and my face hardly known. He was a soldier, legislator, judge; he was a ruler in the Church; he had all the Puritanic traits, both good and evil. He was likewise a bitter persecutor, as witness the Quakers, who have remembered him in their histories, and relate an incident of his hard severity towards a woman of their sect, which will last longer, it is to be feared, than any record of his better deeds, although these were many. His son, too, inherited the persecuting spirit, and made himself so conspicuous in the matyrdom of the witches, that their blood may fairly be said to have left a stain upon him. So deep a stain, indeed, that his old dry bones, in the Charter Street burial-ground, must still retain it, if they have not crumbled utterly to dust! I know not whether these ancestors of mine bethought themselves to repent, and ask pardon of Heaven for their cruelties; or whether they are now groaning under the heavy consequences of them, in another state of being. At all events, I, the present writer, as their representative, hereby take shame upon myself for their sakes, and pray that any curse incurred by them—as I have heard, and as the dreary and unprosperous condition of the race, for many a long year back, would argue to exist— may be now and henceforth removed.

Doubtless, however, either of these stern and black-browed Puritans would have thought it quite a sufficient retribution for his sins, that, after so long a lapse of years, the old trunk of the family tree, with so much venerable moss upon it, should have borne, as its topmost bough, an idler like myself. No aim, that I have ever cherished, would they recognize as laudable; no success of mine—if my life, beyond its domestic scope, had ever been brightened by success—would they deem otherwise than worthless, if not positively disgraceful. "What is he?" murmurs one gray shadow of my forefathers to the other. "A writer of story-books! What kind of a business in life,—what mode of glorifying God, or being serviceable to mankind in his day and generation,—may that be? Why, the degenerate fellow might as well have been a fiddler!" Such are the compliments bandied between my great-grandsires and myself, across the gulf of time! And yet, let them scorn me as they will, strong traits of their nature have intertwined themselves with mine.

Planted deep, in the town's earliest infancy and childhood, by these two earnest and energetic men, the race has ever since subsisted here; always, too, in respectability; never, so far as I have known, disgraced by a single unworthy member; but seldom or never, on the other hand, after the first two generations, performing any memorable deed, or so much as putting forward a claim to public notice. Gradually, they have sunk almost out of sight; as old houses, here and there about the streets, get covered half-way to the eaves by the accumulation of new soil. From father to son, for above a hundred years, they followed the sea; a gray-headed shipmaster, in each generation, retiring from the quarter-deck to the homestead, while a boy of fourteen took the hereditary place before the mast, confronting the salt spray and the gale, which had blustered against his sire and grandsire. The boy, also, in due time, passed from the forecastle to the cabin, spent a tempestuous manhood, and returned from his world-wanderings, to grow old, and die, and mingle his dust with the natal earth. This long connection of a family with one spot, as its place of birth and burial, creates a kindred between the human being and the locality, quite independent of any charm in the scenery or moral circumstances that surround him. It is not love, but instinct. The new inhabitant —who came himself from a foreign land, or whose father or grandfather came—has little claim to be called a Salemite; he has no conception of the oyster-like tenacity with which an old settler, over whom his third century is creeping, clings to the spot where his successive generations have been imbedded. It is no matter that the place is joyless for him; that he is weary of the old wooden houses, the mud and dust, the dead level of site and sentiment, the chill east wind, and the chillest of social atmospheres,—all these, and whatever faults besides he may see or imagine, are nothing to the purpose. The spell survives, and just as powerfully as if the natal spot were an earthly paradise. So has it been in my case. I felt it almost as a destiny to make Salem my home; so that the mould of features and cast of character which had all along been familiar here,— ever, as one representative of the race lay down in his grave, another assuming, as it were, his sentry-march along the main street,—might still in my little day be seen and recognized in the old town. Nevertheless, this very sentiment is an evidence that the connection, which has become an unhealthy one, should at last be severed. Human nature will not flourish, any more than a potato, if it be planted and replanted, for too long a series of generations, in the same worn-out soil. My children have had other birthplaces, and, so far as their fortunes may be within my control, shall strike their roots into unaccustomed earth.

On emerging from the Old Manse, it was chiefly this strange, indolent, unjoyous attachment for my native town, that brought me to fill a place in Uncle Sam's brick edifice, when I might as well, or better, have gone somewhere else. My doom was on me. It was not the first time, nor the second, that I had gone away,—as it seemed, permanently,—but yet returned, like the bad half-penny; or as if Salem were for me the inevitable centre of the universe. So, one fine morning, I ascended the flight of granite steps, with the President's commission in my pocket, and was introduced to the corps of gentlemen who were to aid me in my weighty responsibility, as chief executive officer of the Custom House.

I doubt greatly—or, rather, I do not doubt at all—whether any public functionary of the United States, either in the civil or military line, has ever had such a patriarchal body of veterans under his orders as myself. The whereabouts of the Oldest Inhabitant was at once settled, when I looked at them. For upwards of twenty years before this epoch, the independent position of the Collector had kept the Salem Custom House out of the whirlpool of political vicissitude, which makes the tenure of office generally so fragile. A soldier,—New England's most distinguished soldier,—he stood firmly on the pedestal of his gallant services; and, himself secure in the wise liberality of the successive administrations through which he had held office, he had been the safety of his subordinates in many an hour of danger and heartquake. General Miller was radically conservative; a man over whose kindly nature habit had no slight influence; attaching himself strongly to familiar faces, and with difficulty moved to change, even when change might have brought unquestionable improvement. Thus, on taking charge of my department, I found few but aged men. They were ancient sea-captains, for the most part, who, after being tost on every sea, and standing up sturdily against life's tempestuous blast, had finally drifted into this quiet nook; where, with little to disturb them, except the periodical terrors of a presidential election, they one and all acquired a new lease of existence. Though by no means less liable than their fellow-men to age and infirmity, they had evidently some talisman or other that kept death at bay. Two or three of their number, as I was assured, being gouty and rheumatic, or perhaps bedridden, never dreamed of making their appearance at the Custom House during a large part of the year; but, after a torpid winter, would creep out into the warm sunshine of May or June, go lazily about what they termed duty, and, at their own leisure and convenience, betake themselves to bed again. I must plead guilty to the charge of abbreviating the official breath of more than one of these venerable servants of the republic. They were allowed, on my representation, to rest from their arduous labors, and soon afterwards— as if their sole principle of life had been zeal for their country's service, as I verily believe it was—withdrew to a better world. It is a pious consolation to me, that, through my interference, a sufficient space was allowed them for repentance of the evil and corrupt practices into which, as a matter of course, every Custom House officer must be supposed to fall. Neither the front nor the back entrance of the Custom House opens on the road to Paradise.

The greater part of my officers were Whigs. It was well for their venerable brotherhood that the new Surveyor was not a politician, and though a faithful Democrat in principle, neither received nor held his office with any reference to political services. Had it been otherwise,—had an active politician been put into this influential post, to assume the easy task of making head against a Whig Collector, whose infirmities withheld him from the personal administration of his office,—hardly a man of the old corps would have drawn the breath of official life, within a month after the exterminating angel had come up the Custom House steps. According to the received code in such matters, it would have been nothing short of duty, in a politician, to bring every one of those white heads under the axe of the guillotine. It was plain enough to discern that the old fellows dreaded some such discourtesy at my hands. It pained, and at the same time amused me, to behold the terrors that attended my advent; to see a furrowed cheek, weather-beaten by half a century of storm, turn ashy pale at the glance of so harmless an individual as myself; to detect, as one or another addressed me, the tremor of a voice, which, in long-past days, had been wont to bellow through a speaking-trumpet hoarsely enough to frighten Boreas himself to silence. They knew, these excellent old persons, that, by all established rule,—and, as regarded some of them, weighed by their own lack of efficiency for business,—they ought to have given place to younger men, more orthodox in politics, and altogether fitter than themselves to serve our common Uncle. I knew it too, but could never quite find in my heart to act upon the knowledge. Much and deservedly to my own discredit, therefore, and considerably to the detriment of my official conscience, they continued, during my incumbency, to creep about the wharves, and loiter up and down the Custom House steps. They spent a good deal of time, also, asleep in their accustomed corners, with their chairs tilted back against the wall; awaking, however, once or twice in a forenoon, to bore one another with the several thousandth repetition of old sea-stories, and mouldy jokes, that had grown to be passwords and countersigns among them.

The discovery was soon made, I imagine, that the new Surveyor had no great harm in him. So, with lightsome hearts, and the happy consciousness of being usefully employed,—in their own behalf, at least, if not for our beloved country,—these good old gentlemen went through the various formalities of office. Sagaciously, under their spectacles, did they peep into the holds of vessels! Mighty was their fuss about little matters, and marvellous, sometimes, the obtuseness that allowed greater ones to slip between their fingers! Whenever such a mischance occurred,—when a wagon-load of valuable merchandise had been smuggled ashore, at noonday, perhaps, and directly beneath their unsuspicious noses,—nothing could exceed the vigilance and alacrity with which they proceeded to lock, and double-lock, and secure with tape and sealing-wax, all the avenues of the delinquent vessel. Instead of a reprimand for their previous negligence, the case seemed rather to require an eulogium of their praiseworthy caution, after the mischief had happened; a grateful recognition of the promptitude of their zeal, the moment that there was no longer any remedy.

Unless people are more than commonly disagreeable, it is my foolish habit to contract a kindness for them. The better part of my companion's character, if it have a better part, is that which usually comes uppermost in my regard, and forms the type whereby I recognize the man. As most of these old Custom House officers had good traits, and as my position in reference to them, being paternal and protective, was favorable to the growth of friendly sentiments, I soon grew to like them all. It was pleasant, in the summer forenoons,—when the fervent heat, that almost liquefied the rest of the human family, merely communicated a genial warmth to their half-torpid systems,—it was pleasant to hear them chatting in the back entry, a row of them all tipped against the wall, as usual; while the frozen witticisms of past generations were thawed out, and came bubbling with laughter from their lips. Externally, the jollity of aged men has much in common with the mirth of children; the intellect, any more than a deep sense of humor, has little to do with the matter; it is, with both, a gleam that plays upon the surface, and imparts a sunny and cheery aspect alike to the green branch, and gray, mouldering trunk. In one case, however, it is real sunshine; in the other, it more resembles the phosphorescent glow of decaying wood.

It would be sad injustice, the reader must understand, to represent all my excellent old friends as in their dotage. In the first place, my coadjutors were not invariably old; there were men among them in their strength and prime, of marked ability and energy, and altogether superior to the sluggish and dependent mode of life on which their evil stars had cast them. Then, moreover, the white locks of age were sometimes found to be the thatch of an intellectual tenement in good repair. But, as respects the majority of my corps of veterans, there will be no wrong done, if I characterize them generally as a set of wearisome old souls, who had gathered nothing worth preservation from their varied experience of life. They seemed to have flung away all the golden grain of practical wisdom, which they had enjoyed so many opportunities of harvesting, and most carefully to have stored their memories with the husks. They spoke with far more interest and unction of their morning's breakfast, or yesterday's, to-day's, or to-morrow's dinner, than of the shipwreck of forty or fifty years ago, and all the world's wonders which they had witnessed with their youthful eyes.

The father of the Custom House—the patriarch, not only of this little squad of officials, but, I am bold to say, of the respectable body of tide-waiters all over the United States—was a certain permanent Inspector. He might truly be termed a legitimate son of the revenue system, dyed in the wool, or, rather, born in the purple; since his sire, a Revolutionary colonel, and formerly collector of the port, had created an office for him, and appointed him to fill it, at a period of the early ages which few living men can now remember. This Inspector, when I first knew him, was a man of fourscore years, or thereabouts, and certainly one of the most wonderful specimens of wintergreen that you would be likely to discover in a lifetime's search. With his florid cheek, his compact figure, smartly arrayed in a bright-buttoned blue coat, his brisk and vigorous step, and his hale and hearty aspect, altogether he seemed—not young, indeed— but a kind of new contrivance of Mother Nature in the shape of man, whom age and infirmity had no business to touch. His voice and laugh, which perpetually reëchoed through the Custom House, had nothing of the tremulous quaver and cackle of an old man's utterance; they came strutting out of his lungs, like the crow of a cock, or the blast of a clarion. Looking at him merely as an animal,—and there was very little else to look at,—he was a most satisfactory object, from the thorough healthfulness and wholesomeness of his system, and his capacity, at that extreme age, to enjoy all, or nearly all, the delights which he had ever aimed at, or conceived of. The careless security of his life in the Custom House, on a regular income, and with but slight and infrequent apprehensions of removal, had no doubt contributed to make time pass lightly over him. The original and more potent causes, however, lay in the rare perfection of his animal nature, the moderate proportion of intellect, and the very trifling admixture of moral and spiritual ingredients; these latter qualities, indeed, being in barely enough measure to keep the old gentleman from walking on all-fours. He possessed no power of thought, no depth of feeling, no troublesome sensibilities; nothing, in short, but a few commonplace instincts, which, aided by the cheerful temper that grew inevitably out of his physical well-being, did duty very respectably, and to general acceptance, in lieu of a heart. He had been the husband of three wives, all long since dead; the father of twenty children, most of whom, at every age of childhood or maturity, had likewise returned to dust. Here, one would suppose, might have been sorrow enough to imbue the sunniest disposition, through and through, with a sable tinge. Not so with our old Inspector! One brief sigh sufficed to carry off the entire burden of these dismal reminiscences. The next moment, he was as ready for sport as any unbreeched infant; far readier than the Collector's junior clerk, who, at nineteen years, was much the elder and graver man of the two.

I used to watch and study this patriarchal personage with, I think, livelier curiosity, than any other form of humanity there presented to my notice. He was, in truth, a rare phenomenon; so perfect, in one point of view; so shallow, so delusive, so impalpable, such an absolute nonenity, in every other. My conclusion was that he had no soul, no heart, no mind; nothing, as I have already said, but instincts; and yet, withal, so cunningly had the few materials of his character been put together, that there was no painful perception of deficiency, but, on my part, an entire contentment with what I found in him. It might be difficult—and it was so—to conceive how he should exist hereafter, so earthly and sensuous did he seem; but surely his existence here, admitting that it was to terminate with his last breath, had been not unkindly given; with no higher moral responsibilities than the beasts of the field, but with a larger scope of enjoyment than theirs, and with all their blessed immunity from the dreariness and duskiness of age.

One point, in which he had vastly the advantage over his four-footed brethren, was his ability to recollect the good dinners which it had made no small portion of the happiness of his life to eat. His gourmandism was a highly agreeable trait; and to hear him talk of roast meat was as appetizing as a pickle or an oyster. As he possessed no higher attribute, and neither sacrificed nor vitiated any spiritual endowment by devoting all his energies and ingenuities to subserve the delight and profit of his maw, it always pleased and satisfied me to hear him expatiate on fish, poultry, and butcher's meat, and the most eligible methods of preparing them for the table. His reminiscences of good cheer, however ancient the date of the actual banquet, seemed to bring the savor of pig or turkey under one's very nostrils. There were flavors on his palate, that had lingered there not less than sixty or seventy years, and were still apparently as fresh as that of the mutton-chop which he had just devoured for his breakfast. I have heard him smack his lips over dinners, every guest at which, except himself, had long been food for worms. It was marvellous to observe how the ghosts of bygone meals were continually rising up before him; not in anger or retribution, but as if grateful for his former appreciation and seeking to reduplicate an endless series of enjoyment, at once shadowy and sensual. A tenderloin of beef, a hindquarter of veal, a sparerib of pork, a particular chicken, or a remarkably praiseworthy turkey, which had perhaps adorned his board in the days of the elder Adams, would be remembered; while all the subsequent experience of our race, and all the events that brightened or darkened his individual career, had gone over him with as little permanent effect as the passing breeze. The chief tragic event of the old man's life, so far as I could judge, was his mishap with a certain goose which lived and died some twenty or forty years ago; a goose of most promising figure, but which, at table, proved so inveterately tough that the carving-knife would make no impression on its carcass, and it could only be divided with an axe and handsaw.

But it is time to quit this sketch; on which, however, I should be glad to dwell at considerably more length, because, of all men whom I have ever known, this individual was fittest to be a Custom House officer. Most persons, owing to causes which I may not have space to hint at, suffer moral detriment from this peculiar mode of life. The old Inspector was incapable of it, and, were he to continue in office to the end of time, would be just as good as he was then, and sit down to dinner with just as good an appetite.

There is one likeness, without which my gallery of Custom House portraits would be strangely incomplete; but which my comparatively few opportunities for observation enable me to sketch only in the merest outline. It is that of the Collector, our gallant old General, who, after his brilliant military service, subsequently to which he had ruled over a wild Western territory, had come hither, twenty years before, to spend the decline of his varied and honorable life. The brave soldier had already numbered, nearly or quite, his threescore years and ten, and was pursuing the remainder of his earthly march, burdened with infirmities which even the martial music of his own spirit-stirring recollections could do little towards lightening. The step was palsied now that had been foremost in the charge. It was only with the assistance of a servant and by leaning his hand heavily on the iron balustrade, that he could slowly and painfully ascend the Custom House steps, and, with a toilsome progress across the floor, attain his customary chair beside the fireplace. There he used to sit, gazing with a somewhat dim serenity of aspect at the figures that came and went; amid the rustle of papers, the administering of oaths, the discussion of business, and the casual talk of the office; all which sounds and circumstances seemed but indistinctly to impress his senses, and hardly to make their way into his inner sphere of contemplation. His countenance, in this repose, was mild and kindly. If his notice was sought, an expression of courtesy and interest gleamed out upon his features; proving that there was light within him, and that it was only the outward medium of the intellectual lamp that obstructed the rays in their passage.

The closer you penetrated to the substance of his mind, the sounder it appeared. When no longer called upon to speak, or listen, either of which operations cost him an evident effort, his face would briefly subside into its former not uncheerful quietude. It was not painful to behold this look; for, though dim, it had not the imbecility of decaying age. The framework of his nature, originally strong and massive, was not yet crumbled into ruin.

To observe and define his character, however, under such disadvantages, was as difficult a task as to trace out and build up anew, in imagination, an old fortress, like Ticonderoga, from a view of its gray and broken ruins. Here and there, perchance, the walls may remain almost complete, but elsewhere may be only a shapeless mound, cumbrous with its very strength, and overgrown, through long years of peace and neglect, with grass and alien weeds.

Nevertheless, looking at the old warrior with affection,—for, slight as was the communication between us, my feeling towards him, like that of all bipeds and quadrupeds who knew him, might not improperly be termed so,—I could discern the main points of his portrait. It was marked with the noble and heroic qualities which showed it to be not by a mere accident, but of good right, that he had won a distinguished name. His spirit could never, I conceive, have been characterized by an uneasy activity; it must, at any period of his life, have required an impulse to set him in motion; but, once stirred up, with obstacles to overcome, and an adequate object to be attained, it was not in the man to give out or fail. The heat that had formerly pervaded his nature, and which was not yet extinct, was never of the kind that flashes and flickers in a blaze; but, rather, a deep, red glow, as of iron in a furnace. Weight, solidity, firmness; this was the expression of his repose, even in such decay as had crept untimely over him, at the period of which I speak. But I could imagine, even then, that under some excitement which should go deeply into his consciousness,—roused by a trumpet-peal loud enough to awaken all his energies that were not dead, but only slumbering,—he was yet capable of flinging off his infirmities like a sick man's gown, dropping the staff of age to seize a battle-sword, and starting up once more a warrior. And, in so intense a moment, his demeanor would have still been calm. Such an exhibition, however, was but to be pictured in fancy; not to be anticipated, nor desired. What I saw in him—as evidently as the indestructible ramparts of Old Ticonderoga already cited as the most appropriate simile—were the features of stubborn and ponderous endurance, which might well have amounted to obstinacy in his earlier days; of integrity, that, like most of his other endowments, lay in a somewhat heavy mass, and was just as unmalleable and unmanageable as a ton of iron ore; and of benevolence, which, fiercely as he led the bayonets on at Chippewa or Fort Erie, I take to be of quite as genuine a stamp as what actuates any or all the polemical philanthropists of the age. He had slain men with his own hand for aught I know,—certainly they had fallen, like blades of grass at the sweep of the scythe, before the charge to which his spirit imparted its triumphant energy; but, be that as it might, there was never in his heart so much cruelty as would have brushed the down off a butterfly's wing. I have not known the man, to whose innate kindliness I would more confidently make an appeal.

Many characteristics—and those, too, which contribute not the least forcibly to impart resemblance in a sketch—must have vanished, or been obscured, before I met the General. All merely graceful attributes are usually the most evanescent; nor does Nature adorn the human ruin with blossoms of new beauty that have their roots and proper nutriment only in the chinks and crevices of decay, as she sows wallflowers over the ruined fortress of Ticonderoga. Still, even in respect of grace and beauty, there were points well worth noting. A ray of humor, now and then, would make its way through the veil of dim obstruction, and glimmer pleasantly upon our faces. A trait of native elegance, seldom seen in the masculine character after childhood or early youth, was shown in the General's fondness for the sight and fragrance of flowers. An old soldier might be supposed to prize only the bloody laurel on his brow; but here was one who seemed to have a young girl's appreciation of the floral tribe.

There, beside the fireplace, the brave old General used to sit; while the Surveyor—though seldom, when it could be avoided, taking upon himself the difficult task of engaging him in conversation—was fond of standing at a distance, and watching his quiet and almost slumberous countenance. He seemed away from us, although we saw him but a few yards off; remote, though we passed close beside his chair; unattainable, though we might have stretched forth our hands and touched his own. It might be that he lived a more real life within his thoughts than amid the unappropriate environment of the Collector's office. The evolutions of the parade; the tumult of the battle; the flourish of old, heroic music, heard thirty years before,—such scenes and sounds, perhaps, were all alive before his intellectual sense. Meanwhile, the merchants and shipmasters, the spruce clerks and uncouth sailors, entered and departed; the bustle of this commercial and Custom House life kept up its little murmur round about him; and neither with the men nor their affairs did the General appear to sustain the most distant relation. He was as much out of place as an old sword—now rusty, but which had flashed once in the battle's front, and showed still a bright gleam along its blade—would have been, among the inkstands, paper-folders, and mahogany rulers, on the Deputy Collector's desk.

There was one thing that much aided me in renewing and re-creating the stalwart soldier of the Niagara frontier,—the man of true and simple energy. It was the recollection of those memorable words of his,—"I'll try, Sir!"—spoken on the very verge of a desperate and heroic enterprise, and breathing the soul and spirit of New England hardihood, comprehending all perils, and encountering all. If, in our country, valor were rewarded by heraldic honor, this phrase—which it seems so easy to speak, but which only he, with such a task of danger and glory before him, has ever spoken—would be the best and fittest of all mottoes for the General's shield of arms.

It contributes greatly towards a man's moral and intellectual health, to be brought into habits of companionship with individuals unlike himself, who care little for his pursuits, and whose sphere and abilities he must go out of himself to appreciate. The accidents of my life have often afforded me this advantage, but never with more fulness and variety than during my continuance in office. There was one man, especially, the observation of whose character gave me a new idea of talent. His gifts were emphatically those of a man of business; prompt, acute, clear-minded; with an eye that saw through all perplexities, and a faculty of arrangement that made them vanish, as by the waving of an enchanter's wand. Bred up from boyhood in the Custom House, it was his proper field of activity; and the many intricacies of business, so harassing to the interloper, presented themselves before him with the regularity of a perfectly comprehended system. In my contemplation, he stood as the ideal of his class. He was, indeed, the Custom House in himself, or, at all events, the mainspring that kept its variously revolving wheels in motion; for, in an institution like this, where its officers are appointed to subserve their own profit and convenience, and seldom with a leading reference to their fitness for the duty to be performed, they must perforce seek elsewhere the dexterity which is not in them. Thus, by an inevitable necessity, as a magnet attracts steel-filings, so did our man of business draw to himself the difficulties which everybody met with. With an easy condescension, and kind forbearance towards our stupidity,—which, to his order of mind, must have seemed little short of crime,—would he forthwith, by the merest touch of his finger, make the incomprehensible as clear as daylight. The merchants valued him not less than we, his esoteric friends. His integrity was perfect: it was a law of nature with him, rather than a choice or a principle; nor can it be otherwise than the main condition of an intellect so remarkably clear and accurate as his, to be honest and regular in the administration of affairs. A stain on his conscience, as to anything that came within the range of his vocation, would trouble such a man very much in the same way, though to a far greater degree, than an error in the balance of an account, or an ink-blot on the fair page of a book of record. Here, in a word,—and it is a rare instance in my life,—I had met with a person thoroughly adapted to the situation which he held.

Such were some of the people with whom I now found myself connected. I took it in good part, at the hands of Providence, that I was thrown into a position so little akin to my past habits, and set myself seriously to gather from it whatever profit was to be had. After my fellowship of toil and impracticable schemes with the dreamy brethren of Brook Farm; after living for three years within the subtile influence of an intellect like Emerson's; after those wild, free days on the Assabeth, indulging fantastic speculations, beside our fire of fallen boughs, with Ellery Channing; after talking with Thoreau about pine-trees and Indian relics, in his hermitage at Walden; after growing fastidious by sympathy with the classic refinement of Hillard's culture; after becoming imbued with poetic sentiment at Longfellow's hearth-stone,—it was time, at length, that I should exercise other faculties of my nature, and nourish myself with food for which I had hitherto had little appetite. Even the old Inspector was desirable, as a change of diet, to a man who had known Alcott. I look upon it as an evidence, in some measure, of a system naturally well balanced, and lacking no essential part of a thorough organization, that, with such associates to remember, I could mingle at once with men of altogether different qualities, and never murmur at the change.

Literature, its exertions and objects, were now of little moment in my regard. I cared not, at this period, for books; they were apart from me. Nature,—except it were human nature,—the nature that is developed in earth and sky, was, in one sense, hidden from me; and all the imaginative delight, wherewith it had been spiritualized, passed away out of my mind. A gift, a faculty if it had not departed, was suspended and inanimate within me. There would have been something sad, unutterably dreary, in all this, had I not been conscious that it lay at my own option to recall whatever was valuable in the past. It might be true, indeed, that this was a life which could not with impunity be lived too long; else, it might have made me permanently other than I had been without transforming me into any shape which it would be worth my while to take. But I never considered it as other than a transitory life. There was always a prophetic instinct, a low whisper in my ear, that, within no long period, and whenever a new change of custom should be essential to my good, a change would come.

Meanwhile, there I was, a Surveyor of the Revenue, and, so far as I have been able to understand, as good a Surveyor as need be. A man of thought, fancy, and sensibility (had he ten times the Surveyor's proportion of those qualities) may, at any time, be a man of affairs, if he will only choose to give himself the trouble. My fellow-officers, and the merchants and sea-captains with whom my official duties brought me into any manner of connection, viewed me in no other light, and probably knew me in no other character. None of them, I presume, had ever read a page of my inditing, or would have cared a fig the more for me if they had read them all; nor would it have mended the matter, in the least, had those same unprofitable pages been written with a pen like that of Burns or of Chaucer, each of whom was a Custom House officer in his day, as well as I. It is a good lesson—though it may often be a hard one—for a man who has dreamed of literary fame, and of making for himself a rank among the world's dignitaries by such means, to step aside out of the narrow circle in which his claims are recognized, and to find how utterly devoid of significance, beyond that circle, is all that he achieves, and all he aims at. I know not that I especially needed the lesson, either in the way of warning or rebuke; but, at any rate, I learned it thoroughly: nor, it gives me pleasure to reflect, did the truth, as it came home to my perception, ever cost me a pang, or require to be thrown off in a sigh. In the way of literary talk, it is true, the Naval Officer—an excellent fellow, who came into office with me and went out only a little later—would often engage me in a discussion about one or the other of his favorite topics, Napoleon or Shakespeare. The Collector's junior clerk, too,—a young gentleman who, it was whispered, occasionally covered a sheet of Uncle Sam's letter-paper with what (at the distance of a few yards) looked very much like poetry,—used now and then to speak to me of books, as matters with which I might possibly be conversant. This was my all of lettered intercourse; and it was quite sufficient for my necessities.

No longer seeking nor caring that my name should be blazoned abroad on title-pages, I smiled to think that it had now another kind of vogue. The Custom House marker imprinted it, with a stencil and black paint, on pepper-bags, and baskets of anatto, and cigar-boxes, and bales of all kinds of dutiable merchandise, in testimony that these commodities had paid the impost, and gone regularly through the office. Borne on such queer vehicle of fame, a knowledge of my existence, so far as a name conveys it, was carried where it had never been before, and, I hope, will never go again.

But the past was not dead. Once in a great while, the thoughts, that had seemed so vital and so active, yet had been put to rest so quietly, revived again. One of the most remarkable occasions, when the habit of bygone days awoke in me, was that which brings it within the law of literary propriety to offer the public the sketch which I am now writing.

In the second story of the Custom House there is a large room, in which the brick-work and naked rafters have never been covered with panelling and plaster. The edifice—originally projected on a scale adapt-ed to the old commercial enterprise of the port, and with an idea of subsequent prosperity destined never to be realized—contains far more space than its occupants know what to do with. This airy hall, therefore, over the Collector's apartments, remains unfinished to this day, and, in spite of the aged cobwebs that festoon its dusky beams, appears still to await the labor of the carpenter and mason. At one end of the room, in a recess, were a number of barrels, piled one upon another, containing bundles of official documents. Large quantities of similar rubbish lay lumbering the floor. It was sorrowful to think how many days and weeks and months and years of toil had been wasted on these musty papers, which were now only an encumbrance on earth, and were hidden away in this forgotten corner, never more to be glanced at by human eyes. But, then, what reams of other manuscripts—filled not with the dulness of official formalities, but with the thought of inventive brains and the rich effusion of deep hearts—had gone equally to oblivion; and that, moreover, without serving a purpose in their day, as these heaped-up papers had, and—saddest of all—without purchasing for their writers the comfortable livelihood which the clerks of the Custom House had gained by these worthless scratchings of the pen! Yet not altogether worthless, perhaps, as materials of local history. Here, no doubt, statistics of the former commerce of Salem might be discovered, and memorials of her princely merchants,—

old King Derby,—old Billy Gray,—old Simon Forrester,—and many another magnate in his day; whose powdered head, however, was scarcely in the tomb, before his mountain pile of wealth began to dwindle. The founders of the greater part of the families which now compose the aristocracy of Salem might here be traced, from the petty and obscure beginnings of their traffic, at periods generally much posterior to the Revolution, upward to what their children look upon as long-established rank.

Prior to the Revolution, there is a dearth of records; the earlier documents and archives of the Custom House having, probably, been carried off to Halifax, when all the King's officials accompanied the British army in its flight from Boston. It has often been a matter of regret with me; for, going back, perhaps, to the days of the Protectorate, those papers must have contained many references to forgotten or remembered men, and to antique customs, which would have affected me with the same pleasure as when I used to pick up Indian arrow-heads in the field near the Old Manse.

But one idle and rainy day, it was my fortune to make a discovery of some little interest. Poking and burrowing into the heaped-up rubbish in the corner; unfolding one and another document, and reading the names of vessels that had long ago foundered at sea or rotted at the wharves, and those of merchants never heard of now on 'Change, nor very readily decipherable on their mossy tombstones; glancing at such matters with the saddened, weary, half-reluctant interest which we bestow on the corpse of dead activity,—and exerting my fancy, sluggish with little use, to raise up from dry bones an image of the old town's brighter aspect, when India was a new region, and only Salem knew the way thither;—I chanced to lay my hand on a small package, carefully done up in a piece of ancient yellow parchment. This envelope had the air of an official record of some period long past, when clerks engrossed their stiff and formal chirography on more substantial materials than at present. There was something about it that quickened an instinctive curiosity, and made me undo the faded red tape, that tied up the package, with the sense that a treasure would here be brought to light. Unbending the rigid folds of the parchment cover I found it to be a commission, under the hand and seal of Governor Shirley, in favor of one Jonathan Pue, as Surveyor of his Majesty's Customs for the port of Salem, in the Province of Massachusetts Bay. I remembered to have read (probably in Felt's Annals) a notice of the decease of Mr. Surveyor Pue, about fourscore years ago; and likewise, in a newspaper of recent times, an account of the digging up of his remains in the little graveyard of St. Peter's Church, during the renewal of that edifice. Nothing, if I rightly call to mind, was left of my respected predecessor, save an imperfect skeleton, and some fragments of apparel, and a wig of majestic frizzle; which, unlike the head that it once adorned, was in very satisfactory preservation. But, on examining the papers which the parchment commission served to envelop, I found more traces of Mr. Pue's mental part, and the internal operations of his head, that the frizzled wig had contained of the venerable skull itself.

They were documents, in short, not official, but of a private nature, or, at least, written in his private capacity, and apparently with his own hand. I could account for their being included in the heap of Custom House lumber only by the fact that Mr. Pue's death had happened suddenly; and that these papers, which he probably kept in his official desk, had never come to the knowledge of his heirs, or were supposed to relate to the business of the revenue. On the transfer of the archives to Halifax, this package, proving to be of no public concern, was left behind and had remained ever since unopened.

The ancient Surveyor—being little molested, I suppose, at that early day, with business pertaining to his office—seems to have devoted some of his many leisure hours to researches as a local antiquarian, and other inquisitions of a similar nature. These supplied material for petty activity to a mind that would otherwise have been eaten up with rust. A portion of his facts, by the by, did me good service in the preparation of the article entitled "MAIN STREET," included in the third volume of this edition. The remainder may perhaps be applied to purposes equally valuable hereafter; or not impossibly may be worked up, so far as they go, into a regular history of Salem, should my veneration for the natal soil ever impel me to so pious a task. Meanwhile, they shall be at the command of any gentleman, inclined, and competent, to take the unprofitable labor off my hands. As a final disposition, I contemplate depositing them with the Essex Historical Society.

But the object that most drew my attention, in the mysterious package, was a certain affair of fine red cloth, much worn and faded. There were traces about it of gold embroidery, which, however, was greatly frayed and defaced; so that none, or very little, of the glitter was left. It had been wrought, as was easy to perceive, with wonderful skill of needlework; and the stitch (as I am assured by ladies conversant with such mysteries) gives evidence of a now forgotten art, not to be recovered even by the process of picking out the threads. This rag of scarlet cloth,—for time and wear and a sacrilegious moth had reduced it to little other than a rag,—on careful examination, assumed the shape of a letter. It was the capital letter A. By an accurate measurement, each limb proved to be precisely three inches and a quarter in length. It had been intended, there could be no doubt, as an ornamental article of dress; but how it was to be worn, or what rank, honor, and dignity, in by-past times, were signified by it, was a riddle which (so evanescent are the fashions of the world in these particulars) I saw little hope of solving. And yet it strangely interested me. My eyes fastened themselves upon the old scarlet letter, and would not be turned aside. Certainly, there was some deep meaning in it, most worthy of interpretation, and which, as it were, streamed forth from the mystic symbol, subtly communicating itself to my sensibilities, but evading the analysis of my mind.

While thus perplexed,—and cogitating, among other hypotheses, whether the letter might not have been one of those decorations which the white men used to contrive, in order to take the eyes of Indians,—I happened to place it on my breast. It seemed to me,—the reader may smile, but must not doubt my word,—it seemed to me, then, that I experienced a sensation not altogether physical, yet almost so, as of burning heat; and as if the letter were not of red cloth, but red-hot iron. I shuddered, and involuntarily let it fall upon the floor.

In the absorbing contemplation of the scarlet letter, I had hitherto neglected to examine a small roll of dingy paper, around which it had been twisted. This I now opened, and had the satisfaction to find, recorded by the old Surveyor's pen, a reasonably complete explanation of the whole affair. There were several foolscap sheets containing many particulars respecting the life and conversation of one Hester Prynne, who appeared to have been rather a noteworthy personage in the view of our ancestors. She had flourished during the period between the early days of Massachusetts and the close of the seventeenth century. Aged persons, alive in the time of Mr. Surveyor Pue, and from whose oral testimony he had made up his narrative, remembered her, in their youth, as a very old, but not decrepit woman, of a stately and solemn aspect. It had been her habit, from an almost immemorial date, to go about the country as a kind of voluntary nurse, and doing whatever miscellaneous good she might; taking upon herself, likewise, to give advice in all matters, especially those of the heart; by which means, as a person of such propensities inevitably must, she gained from many people the reverence due to an angel, but I should imagine, was looked upon by others as an intruder and a nuisance. Prying further into the manuscript, I found the record of other doings and sufferings of this singular woman, for most of which the reader is referred to the story entitled "THE SCARLET LETTER"; and it should be borne carefully in mind, that the main facts of that story are authorized and authenticated by the document of Mr. Surveyor Pue. The original papers, together with the scarlet letter itself,—a most curious relic,—are still in my possession, and shall be freely exhibited to whomsoever, induced by the great interest of the narrative, may desire a sight of them. I must not be understood as affirming, that, in the dressing up of the tale, and imagining the motives and modes of passion that influenced the characters who figure in it, I have invariably confined myself within the limits of the old Surveyer's half a dozen sheets of foolscap. On the contrary, I have allowed myself, as to such points, nearly or altogether as much license as if the facts had been entirely of my own invention. What I contend for is the authenticity of the outline.

This incident recalled my mind, in some degree, to its old track. There seemed to be here the groundwork of a tale. It impressed me as if the ancient Surveyor, in his garb of a hundred years gone by, and wearing his immortal wig,—which was buried with him, but did not perish in the grave,—had met me in the deserted chamber of the Custom House. In his port was the dignity of one who had borne his Majesty's commission, and who was therefore illuminated by a ray of the splendor that shone so dazzlingly about the throne. How unlike, alas! the hang-dog look of a republican official, who, as the servant of the people, feels himself less than the least, and below the lowest, of his masters. With his own ghostly hand, the obscurely seen but majestic figure had imparted to me the scarlet symbol, and the little roll of explanatory manuscript. With his own ghostly voice he had exhorted me, on the sacred consideration of my filial duty and reverence towards him,—who might reasonably regard himself as my official ancestor,—to bring his mouldy and moth-eaten lucubrations before the public. "Do this," said the ghost of Mr. Surveyor Pue, emphatically nodding the head that looked so imposing within its memorable wig,—"do this, and the profit shall be all your own! You will shortly need it; for it is not in your days as it was in mine, when a man's office was a life-lease, and oftentimes an heirloom. But, I charge you, in this matter of old Mistress Prynne, give to your predecessor's memory the credit which will be rightfully due!" And I said to the ghost of Mr. Surveyor Pue, "I will!"

On Hester Prynne's story, therefore, I bestowed much thought. It was the subject of my meditations for many an hour, while pacing to and fro across my room, or traversing, with a hundred-fold repetition, the long extent from the front-door of the Custom House to the side-entrance, and back again. Great were the weariness and annoyance of the old Inspector and the Weighers and Gaugers, whose slumbers were disturbed by the unmercifully lengthened tramp of my passing and returning footsteps. Remembering their own former habits, they used to say that the Surveyor was walking the quarter-deck. They probably fancied that my sole object—and, indeed, the sole object for which a sane man could ever put himself into voluntary motion—was, to get an appetite for dinner. And to say the truth, an appetite, sharpened by the east wind that generally blew along the passage, was the only valuable result of so much indefatigable exercise. So little adapted is the atmosphere of a Custom House to the delicate harvest of fancy and sensibility, that, had I remained there through ten Presidencies yet to come, I doubt whether the tale of "The Scarlet Letter" would ever have been brought before the public eye. My imagination was a tarnished mirror. It would not reflect, or only with miserable dimness, the figures with which I did my best to people it. The characters of the narrative would not be warmed and rendered malleable by any heat that I could kindle at my intellectual forge. They would take neither the glow of passion nor the tenderness of sentiment, but retained all the rigidity of dead corpses, and stared me in the face with a fixed and ghastly grin of contemptuous defiance. "What have you to do with us?" that expression seemed to say. "The little power you might once have possessed over the tribe of unrealities is gone! You have bartered it for a pittance of the public gold. Go, then, and earn your wages!" In short, the almost torpid creatures of my own fancy twitted me with imbecility, and not without fair occasion.

It was not merely during the three hours and a half which Uncle Sam claimed as his share of my daily life, that this wretched numbness held possession of me. It went with me on my sea-shore walks, and rambles into the country, whenever—which was seldom and reluctantly—I bestirred myself to seek that invigorating charm of Nature, which used to give me such freshness and activity of thought, the moment that I stepped across the threshold of the Old Manse. The same torpor, as regarded the capacity for intellectual effort, accompanied me home, and weighed upon me in the chamber which I most absurdly termed my study. Nor did it quit me, when, late at night, I sat in the deserted parlor, lighted only by the glimmering coal-fire and the moon, striving to picture forth imaginary scenes, which, the next day, might flow out on the brightening page in many-hued description.

If the imaginative faculty refused to act at such an hour, it might well be deemed a hopeless case. Moonlight, in a familiar room, falling so white upon the carpet, and showing all its figures so distinctly,—making every object so minutely visible, yet so unlike a morning or noontide visibility, —is a medium the most suitable for a romance-writer to get acquainted with his illusive guests. There is the little domestic scenery of the well-known apartment; the chairs with each its separate individuality; the centre-table, sustaining a work-basket, a volume or two, and an extinguished lamp; the sofa; the bookcase; the picture on the wall,—all these details, so completely seen, are so spiritualized by the unusual light, that they seem to lose their actual substance, and become things of intellect. Nothing is too small or too trifling to undergo this change, and acquire dignity thereby. A child's shoe; the doll, seated in her little wicker carriage; the hobby-horse,—whatever, in a word, has been used or played with, during the day, is now invested with a quality of strangeness and remoteness, though still almost as vividly present as by daylight. Thus, therefore, the floor of our familiar room has become a neutral territory, somewhere between the real world and fairy-land, where the Actual and the Imaginary may meet, and each imbue itself with the nature of the other. Ghosts might enter here, without affrighting us. It would be too much in keeping with the scene to excite surprise, were we to look about us and discover a form beloved, but gone hence, now sitting quietly in a streak of this magic moonshine, with an aspect that would make us doubt whether it had returned from afar, or had never once stirred from our fireside.

The somewhat dim coal-fire has an essential influence in producing the effect which I would describe. It throws its unobtrusive tinge throughout the room, with a faint ruddiness upon the walls and ceiling, and a reflected gleam from the polish of the furniture. This warmer light mingles itself with the cold spirituality of the moonbeams, and communicates, as it were, a heart and sensibilities of human tenderness to the forms which fancy summons up. It converts them from snow-images into men and women. Glancing at the looking-glass, we behold—deep within its haunted verge—the smouldering glow of the half-extinguished anthracite, the white moonbeams on the floor, and a repetition of all the gleam and shadow of the picture, with one remove further from the actual, and nearer to the imaginative. Then, at such an hour, and with this scene before him, if a man, sitting all alone, cannot dream strange things, and make them look like truth, he need never try to write romances.

But, for myself, during the whole of my Custom House experience, moonlight and sunshine, and the glow of firelight, were just alike in my regard; and neither of them was of one whit more avail than the twinkle of a tallow-candle. An entire class of susceptibilities, and a gift connected with them,—of no great richness or value, but the best I had,—was gone from me.

It is my belief, however, that, had I attempted a different order of composition, my faculties would not have been found so pointless and inefficacious. I might, for instance, have contented myself with writing out the narratives of a veteran shipmaster, one of the Inspectors, whom I should be most ungrateful not to mention, since scarcely a day passed that he did not stir me to laughter and admiration by his marvellous gifts as a story-teller. Could I have preserved the picturesque force of his style, and the humorous coloring which nature taught him how to throw over his descriptions, the result, I honestly believe, would have been something new in literature. Or I might readily have found a more serious task. It was a folly, with the materiality of this daily life pressing so intrusively upon me, to attempt to fling myself back into another age; or to insist on creating the semblance of a world out of airy matter, when, at every moment, the impalpable beauty of my soap-bubble was broken by the rude contact of some actual circumstance. The wiser effort would have been to diffuse thought and imagination through the opaque substance of to-day, and thus to make it a bright transparency; to spiritualize the burden that began to weigh so heavily; to seek, resolutely, the true and indestructible value that lay hidden in the petty and wearisome incidents, and ordinary characters, with which I was now conversant. The fault was mine. The page of life that was spread out before me seemed dull and commonplace, only because I had not fathomed its deeper import. A better book than I shall ever write was there; leaf after leaf presenting itself to me, just as it was written out by the reality of the flitting hour, and vanishing as fast as written, only because my brain wanted the insight and my hand the cunning to transcribe it. At some future day, it may be, I shall remember a few scattered fragments and broken paragraphs, and write them down, and find the letters turn to gold upon the page.

These perceptions have come too late. At the instant, I was only conscious that what would have been a pleasure once was now a hopeless toil. There was no occasion to make much moan about this state of affairs. I had ceased to be a writer of tolerably poor tales and essays, and had become a tolerably good Surveyor of the Customs. That was all. But, nevertheless, it is anything but agreeable to be haunted by a suspicion that one's intellect is dwindling away; or exhaling, without your consciousness, like ether out of a phial; so that, at every glance, you find a smaller and less volatile residuum. Of the fact there could be no doubt; and, examining myself and others, I was led to conclusions, in reference to the effect of public office on the character, not very favorable to the mode of life in question. In some other form, perhaps, I may hereafter develop these effects. Suffice it here to say, that a Custom House officer, of long continuance, can hardly be a very praiseworthy or respectable personage, for many reasons; one of them, the tenure by which he holds his situation, and another, the very nature of his business, which—though, I trust, an honest one—is of such a sort that he does not share in the united effort of mankind.

An effect—which I believe to be observable, more or less, in every individual who has occupied the position—is, that, while he leans on the mighty arm of the Republic, his own proper strength departs from him. He loses, in an extent proportioned to the weakness or force of his original nature, the capability of self-support. If he possess an unusual share of native energy, or the enervating magic of place do not operate too long upon him, his forfeited powers may be redeemable. The ejected officer—fortunate in the unkindly shove that sends him forth betimes to struggle amid a struggling world—may return to himself, and become all that he has ever been. But this seldom happens. He usually keeps his ground just long enough for his own ruin, and is then thrust out, with sinews all unstrung, to totter along the difficult foot-path of life as he best may. Conscious of his own infirmity,—that his tempered steel and elasticity are lost,—he forever afterwards looks wistfully about him in quest of support external to himself. His pervading and continual hope—a hallucination which, in the face of all discouragement, and making light of impossibilities, haunts him while he lives, and, I fancy, like the convulsive throes of the cholera, torments him for a brief space after death—is that finally, and in no long time, by some happy coincidence of circumstances, he shall be restored to office. This faith, more than anything else, steals the pith and availability out of whatever enterprise he may dream of undertaking. Why should he toil and moil, and be at so much trouble to pick himself up out of the mud, when, in a little while hence, the strong arm of his Uncle will raise and support him? Why should he work for his living here, or go to dig gold in California, when he is so soon to be made happy, at monthly intervals, with a little pile of glittering coin out of his Uncle's pocket? It is sadly curious to observe how slight a taste of office suffices to infect a poor fellow with this singular disease. Uncle Sam's gold—meaning no disrespect to the worthy old gentleman—has, in this respect, a quality of enchantment like that of the Devil's wages. Whoever touches it should look well to himself, or he may find the bargain to go hard against him, involving, if not his soul, yet many of its better attributes; its sturdy force, its courage and constancy, its truth, its self-reliance, and all that gives the emphasis to manly character.

Here was a fine prospect in the distance! Not that the Surveyor brought the lesson home to himself, or admitted that he could be so utterly undone, either by continuance in office or ejectment. Yet my reflections were not the most comfortable. I began to grow melancholy and restless; continually prying into my mind, to discover which of its poor properties were gone, and what degree of detriment had already accrued to the remainder. I endeavored to calculate how much longer I could stay in the Custom House, and yet go forth a man. To confess the truth, it was my greatest apprehension,—as it would never be a measure of policy to turn out so quiet an individual as myself, and it being hardly in the nature of a public officer to resign,—it was my chief trouble, therefore, that I was likely to grow gray and decrepit in the Surveyorship, and become much such another animal as the old Inspector. Might it not, in the tedious lapse of official life that lay before me, finally be with me as it was with this venerable friend,—to make the dinner-hour the nucleus of the day, and to spend the rest of it, as an old dog spends it, asleep in the sunshine or in the shade? A dreary look-forward this, for a man who felt it to be the best definition of happiness to live throughout the whole range of his faculties and sensibilities! But, all this while, I was giving myself very unnecessary alarm. Providence had meditated better things for me than I could possibly imagine for myself.

A remarkable event of the third year of my Surveyorship—to adopt the tone of "P. P."—was the election of General Taylor to the Presidency. It is essential, in order to a complete estimate of the advantages of official life, to view the incumbent at the incoming of a hostile administration. His position is then one of the most singularly irksome, and, in every contingency, disagreeable, that a wretched mortal can possibly occupy; with seldom an alternative of good, on either hand, although what presents itself to him as the worst event may very probably be the best. But it is a strange experience, to a man of pride and sensibility, to know that his interests are within the control of individuals who neither love nor understand him, and by whom, since one or the other must needs happen, he would rather be injured than obliged. Strange, too, for one who has kept his calmness throughout the contest, to observe the blood thirstiness that is developed in the hour of triumph, and to be conscious that he is himself among its objects! There are few uglier traits of human nature than this tendency—which I now witnessed in men no worse than their neighbors—to grow cruel, merely because they possessed the power of inflicting harm. If the guillotine, as applied to office holders, were a literal fact instead of one of the most apt of metaphors, it is my sincere belief that the active members of the victorious party were sufficiently excited to have chopped off all our heads, and have thanked Heaven for the opportunity! It appears to me—who have been a calm and curious observer, as well in victory as defeat—that this fierce and bitter spirit of malice and revenge has never distinguished the many triumphs of my own party as it now did that of the Whigs. The Democrats take the offices, as a general rule, because they need them, and because the practice of many years has made it the law of political warfare, which, unless a different system be proclaimed, it were weakness and cowardice to murmur at. But the long habit of victory has made them generous. They know how to spare, when they see occasion; and when they strike, the axe may be sharp, indeed, but its edge is seldom poisoned with ill-will; nor is it their custom ignominiously to kick the head which they have just struck off.

In short, unpleasant as was my predicament, at best, I saw much reason to congratulate myself that I was on the losing side, rather than the triumphant one. If, heretofore, I had been none of the warmest of partisans, I began now, at this season of peril and adversity, to be pretty acutely sensible with which party my predilections lay; nor was it without something like regret and shame, that, according to a reasonable calculation of chances, I saw my own prospect of retaining office to be better than those of my Democratic brethren. But who can see an inch into futurity beyond his nose? My own head was the first that fell!

The moment when a man's head drops off is seldom or never, I am inclined to think, precisely the most agreeable of his life. Nevertheless, like the greater part of our misfortunes, even so serious a contingency brings its remedy and consolation with it, if the sufferer will but make the best, rather than the worst, of the accident which has befallen him. In my particular case, the consolatory topics were close at hand, and, indeed, had suggested themselves to my meditations a considerable time before it was requisite to use them. In view of my previous weariness of office, and vague thoughts of resignation, my fortune somewhat resembled that of a person who should entertain an idea of committing suicide, and, although beyond his hopes, meet with the good hap to be murdered. In the Custom House, as before in the Old Manse, I had spent three years; a term long enough to rest a weary brain; long enough to break off old intellectual habits and make room for new ones; long enough, and too long, to have lived in an unnatural state, doing what was really of no advantage nor delight to any human being, and withholding myself from toil that would, at least, have stilled an unquiet impulse in me. Then, moreover, as regarded his unceremonious ejectment, the late Surveyor was not altogether ill-pleased to be recognized by the Whigs as an enemy; since his inactivity in political affairs—his tendency to roam, at will, in that broad and quiet field where all mankind may meet, rather than confine himself to those narrow paths where brethren of the same household must diverge from one another—had sometimes made it questionable with his brother Democrats whether he was a friend. Now, after he had won the crown of martyrdom (though with no longer a head to wear it on), the point might be looked upon as settled. Finally, little heroic as he was, it seemed more decorous to be overthrown in the downfall of the party with which he had been content to stand, than to remain a forlorn survivor, when so many worthier men were falling; and, at last, after subsisting for four years on the mercy of a hostile administration, to be compelled then to define his position anew, and claim the yet more humiliating mercy of a friendly one.

Meanwhile the press had taken up my affair, and kept me, for a week or two, careering through the public prints, in my decapitated state, like Irving's Headless Horseman; ghastly and grim, and longing to be buried, as a politically dead man ought. So much for my figurative self. The real human being, all this time with his head safely on his shoulders, had brought himself to the comfortable conclusion that everything was for the best; and, making an investment in ink, paper, and steel-pens, had opened his long-disused writing-desk, and was again a literary man.

Now it was that the lucubrations of my ancient predecessor, Mr. Surveyor Pue, came into play. Rusty through long idleness, some little space was requisite before my intellectual machinery could be brought to work upon the tale, with an effect in any degree satisfactory. Even yet, though my thoughts were ultimately much absorbed in the task, it wears, to my eye a stern and sombre aspect; too much ungladdened by genial sunshine; too little revealed by the tender and familiar influences which soften almost every scene of nature and real life, and, undoubtedly, should soften every picture of them. This uncaptivating effect is perhaps due to the period of hardly accomplished revolution, and still seething turmoil, in which the story shaped itself. It is no indication, however, of a lack of cheerfulness in the writer's mind; for he was happier, while straying through the gloom of these sunless fantasies, than at any time since he had quitted the Old Manse. Some of the briefer articles, which contribute to make up the volume, have likewise been written since my involuntary withdrawal from the toils and honors of public life, and the remainder are gleaned from annuals and magazines of such antique date that they have gone round the circle, and come back to novelty again.[1] Keeping up the metaphor of the political guillotine, the whole may be considered as the POSTHUMOUS PAPERS OF A DECAPITATED SURVEYOR; and the sketch which I am now bringing to a close, if too autobiographical for a modest person to publish in his lifetime, will readily be excused in a gentleman who writes from beyond the grave. Peace be with all the world! My blessing on my friends! My forgiveness to my enemies! For I am in the realm of quiet!

The life of the Custom House lies like a dream behind me. The old Inspector,—who, by the by, I regret to say, was overthrown and killed by a horse, some time ago; else he would certainly have lived forever,—he, and all those other venerable personages who sat with him at the receipt of custom, are but shadows in my view; white-headed and wrinkled images, which my fancy used to sport with, and has now flung aside forever. The merchants,—Pingree, Phillips, Shepard, Upton, Kimball, Bertram, Hunt,—these, and many other names, which had such a classic familiarity for my ear six months ago,—these men of traffic, who seemed to occupy so important a position in the world,—how little time has it required to disconnect me from them all, not merely in act, but recollection! It is with an effort that I recall the figures and appellations of these few. Soon, likewise, my old native town will loom upon me through the haze of memory, a mist brooding over and around it; as if it were no

[1] At the time of writing this article, the author intended to publish, along with *The Scarlet Letter*, several shorter tales and sketches. These it has been thought advisable to defer.

portion of the real earth, but an overgrown village in cloud-land, with only imaginary inhabitants to people its wooden houses, and walk its homely lanes, and the unpicturesque prolixity of its main street. Henceforth it ceases to be a reality of my life. I am a citizen of somewhere else. My good townspeople will not much regret me; for—though it has been as dear an object as any, in my literary efforts, to be of some importance in their eyes, and to win myself a pleasant memory in this abode and burial-place of so many of my forefathers—*there* has never been, for me, the genial atmosphere which a literary man requires, in order to ripen the best harvest of his mind. I shall do better amongst other faces; and these familiar ones, it need hardly be said, will do just as well without me.

It may be, however,—oh, transporting and triumphant thought!— that the great-grandchildren of the present race may sometimes think kindly of the scribbler of bygone days, when the antiquary of days to come, among the sites memorable in the town's history, shall point out the locality of THE TOWN PUMP!

# THE SCARLET LETTER

## I

### THE PRISON-DOOR

A THRONG of bearded men, in sad-colored garments, and gray, steeple-crowned hats, intermixed with women, some wearing hoods and others bareheaded, was assembled in front of a wooden edifice, the door of which was heavily timbered with oak, and studded with iron spikes.

The founders of a new colony, whatever Utopia of human virtue and happiness they might originally project, have invariably recognized it among their earliest practical necessities to allot a portion of the virgin soil as a cemetery, and another portion as the site of a prison. In accordance with this rule, it may safely be assumed that the forefathers of Boston had built the first prison-house somewhere in the vicinity of Cornhill, almost as seasonably as they marked out the first burial-ground, on Isaac Johnson's lot, and round about his grave, which subsequently became the nucleus of all the congregated sepulchres in the old churchyard of King's Chapel. Certain it is, that, some fifteen or twenty years after the settlement of the town, the wooden jail was already marked with weather-stains and other indications of age, which gave a yet darker aspect to its beetle-browed and gloomy front. The rust on the ponderous iron-work of its oaken door looked more antique than anything else in the New World. Like all that pertains to crime, it seemed never to have known a youthful era. Before this ugly edifice, and between it and the wheel-track of the street, was a grass-plot, much overgrown with burdock, pigweed, apple-peru, and such unsightly vegetation, which evidently found something congenial in the soil that had so early borne the black flower of civilized society, a prison. But, on óne side of the portal, and rooted almost at the threshold, was a wild rose-bush, covered, in this month of June, with its delicate gems, which might be imagined to offer their fragrance and fragile beauty to the prisoner as he went in, and to the condemned criminal as he came forth to his doom, in token that the deep heart of Nature could pity and be kind to him.

This rose-bush, by a strange chance, has been kept alive in history; but whether it had merely survived out of the stern old wilderness, so long after the fall of the gigantic pines and oaks that originally overshadowed it,—or whether, as there is fair authority for believing, it had sprung up under the footsteps of the sainted Anne Hutchinson, as she entered the prison-door,—we shall not take upon us to determine. Finding it so directly on the threshold of our narrative, which is now about to issue from that inauspicious portal, we could hardly do otherwise than pluck one of its flowers, and present it to the reader. It may serve, let us hope, to symbolize some sweet moral blossom, that may be found along the track, or relieve the darkening close of a tale of human frailty and sorrow.

## II

## THE MARKET-PLACE

THE grass-plot before the jail, in Prison Lane, on a certain summer morning, not less than two centuries ago, was occupied by a pretty large number of the inhabitants of Boston, all with their eyes intently fastened on the iron-clamped oaken door. Amongst any other population, or at a later period in the history of New England, the grim rigidity that petrified the bearded physiognomies of these good people would have augured some awful business in hand. It could have betokened nothing short of the anticipated execution of some noted culprit, on whom the sentence of a legal tribunal had been confirmed the verdict of public sentiment. But, in that early severity of the Puritan character, an inference of this kind could not so indubitably be drawn. It might be that a sluggish bond-servant, or an undutiful child, whom his parents had given over to the civil authority, was to be corrected at the whipping-post. It might be, that an Antinomian, a Quaker, or other heterodox religionist was to be scourged out of the town, or an idle and vagrant Indian, whom the white man's firewater had made riotous about the streets, was to be driven with stripes into the shadow of the forest. It might be, too, that a witch, like old Mistress Hibbins, the bitter-tempered widow of the magistrate, was to die upon the gallows. In either case, there was very much the same solemnity of demeanor on the part of the spectators; as befitted a people amongst whom religion and law were almost identical, and in whose character both were so thoroughly interfused, that the mildest and the severest acts of public discipline were alike made venerable and awful. Meagre, indeed, and cold was the sympathy that a transgressor might look for from such by-standers, at the scaffold. On the other hand, a penalty, which, in our days, would infer a degree of mocking infamy and ridicule, might then be invested with almost as stern a dignity as the punishment of death itself.

It was a circumstance to be noted, on the summer morning when our story begins its course, that the women, of whom there were several in the crowd, appeared to take a peculiar interest in whatever penal infliction might be expected to ensue. The age had not so much refinement, that any sense of impropriety restrained the wearers of petticoat and farthingale from stepping forth into the public ways, and wedging their not unsubstantial persons, if occasion were, into the throng nearest to the scaffold at an execution. Morally, as well as materially, there was a coarser fibre in those wives and maidens of old English birth and breeding, than in their fair descendants, separated from them by a series of six or seven generations; for, throughout that chain of ancestry, every sucessive mother has transmitted to her child a fainter bloom, a more delicate and briefer beauty, and a slighter physical frame, if not a character of less force and solidity, than her own. The women who were now standing about the prison-door stood within less than half a century of the period when the man-like Elizabeth had been the not altogether unsuitable representative of the sex. They were her countrywomen; and the beef and ale of their native land, with a moral diet not a whit more refined, entered largely into their composition. The bright morning sun, therefore, shone on broad shoulders and well-developed busts, and on round and ruddy cheeks, that had ripened in the far-off island, and had hardly yet grown paler or thinner in the atmosphere of New England. There was, moreover, a boldness and rotundity of speech among these matrons, as most of them seemed to be, that would startle us at the present day, whether in respect to its purport or its volume of tone.

"Goodwives," said a hard-featured dame of fifty, "I'll tell ye a piece of my mind. It would be greatly for the public behoof, if we women, being of mature age and church-members in good repute, should have the handling of such malefactresses as this Hester Prynne. What think ye, gossips? If the hussy stood up for judgment before us five, that are now here in a knot together, would she come off with such a sentence as the worshipful magistrates have awarded? Marry, I trow not!"

"People say," said another, "that the Reverend Master Dimmesdale, her godly pastor, takes it very grievously to heart that such a scandal should have come upon his congregation."

"The magistrates are God-fearing gentlemen, but merciful overmuch, —that is a truth," added a third autumnal matron. "At the very least, they should have put the brand of a hot iron on Hester Prynne's forehead. Madam Hester would have winced at that, I warrant me. But she, —the haughty baggage,—little will she care what they put upon the bodice of her gown! Why, look you, she may cover it with a brooch, or such like heathenish adornment, and so walk the streets as brave as ever!"

"Ah, but," interposed, more softly, a young wife, holding a child by the hand, "let her cover the mark as she will, the pang of it will be always in her heart."

"What do we talk of marks and brands, whether on the bodice of her gown, or the flesh of her forehead?" cried another female, the ugliest as well as the most pitiless of these self-constituted judges. "This woman has brought shame upon us all, and ought to die. Is there not law for it? Truly, there is, both in the Scripture and the statute-book. Then let the magistrates, who have made it of no effect, thank themselves if their own wives and daughters go astray!"

"Mercy on us, goodwife," exclaimed a man in the crowd, "is there no virtue in woman, save what springs from a wholesome fear of the gallows? That is the hardest word yet! Hush, now gossips! for the lock is turning in the prison-door, and here comes Mistress Prynne herself."

The door of the jail being flung open from within, there appeared, in the first place, like a black shadow emerging into sunshine, the grim and grisly presence of the town-beadle, with a sword by his side, and his staff of office in his hand. This personage prefigured and represented in his aspect the whole dismal severity of the Puritanic code of law, which it was his business to administer in its final and closest application to the offender. Stretching forth the official staff in his left hand, he laid his right upon the shoulder of a young woman, whom he thus drew forward; until, on the threshold of the prison-door, she repelled him, by an action marked with natural dignity and force of character, and stepped into the open air, as if by her own free will. She bore in her arms a child, a baby of some three months old, who winked and turned aside its little face from the too vivid light of day; because its existence, heretofore, had brought it acquainted only with the gray twilight of a dungeon, or other darksome apartment of the prison.

When the young woman—the mother of this child—stood fully revealed before the crowd, it seemed to be her first impulse to clasp the infant closely to her bosom; not so much by an impulse of motherly affection, as that she might thereby conceal a certain token, which was wrought or fastened into her dress. In a moment, however, wisely judging that one token of her shame would but poorly serve to hide another, she took the baby on her arm, and, with a burning blush, and yet a haughty smile, and a glance that would not be abashed, looked around at her townspeople and neighbors. On the breast of her gown, in fine red cloth, surrounded with an elaborate embroidery and fantastic flourishes of gold-thread, appeared the letter A. It was so artistically done, and with so much fertility and gorgeous luxuriance of fancy, that it had all the effect of a last and fitting decoration to the apparel which she wore; and which was of a splendor in accordance with the taste of the age, but greatly beyond what was allowed by the sumptuary regulations of the colony.

The young woman was tall, with a figure of perfect elegance on a large scale. She had dark and abundant hair, so glossy that it threw off the sunshine with a gleam, and a face which, besides being beautiful from regularity of feature and richness of complexion, had the impressiveness belonging to a marked brow and deep black eyes. She was lady-like, too, after the manner of the feminine gentility of those days; characterized by a certain state and dignity, rather than by the delicate, evanescent, and indescribable grace, which is now recognized as its indication. And never had Hester Prynne appeared more lady-like, in the antique interpretation of the term, than as she issued from the prison. Those who had before known her, and had expected to behold her dimmed and obscured by a disastrous cloud, were astonished, and even startled, to perceive how her beauty shone out, and made a halo of the misfortune and ignominy in which she was enveloped. It may be true, that, to a sensitive observer, there was something exquisitely painful in it. Her attire, which, indeed, she had wrought for the occasion, in prison, and had modelled much after her own fancy, seemed to express the attitude of her spirit, the desperate recklessness of her mood, by its wild and picturesque peculiarity. But the point which drew all eyes, and, as it were, transfigured the wearer,—so that both men and women, who had been familiarly acquainted with Hester Prynne, were now impressed as if they beheld her for the first time,—was that SCARLET LETTER, so fantastically embroidered and illuminated upon her bosom. It had the effect of a spell, taking her out of the ordinary relations with humanity, and enclosing her in a sphere by herself.

"She hath good skill at her needle, that's certain," remarked one of her female spectators; "but did ever a woman, before this brazen huzzy, contrive such a way of showing it! Why, gossips, what is it but to laugh in the faces of our godly magistrates, and make a pride out of what they, worthy gentlemen, meant for a punishment?"

"It were well," muttered the most iron-visaged of the old dames, "if we stripped Madam Hester's rich gown off her dainty shoulders; and as for the red letter, which she hath stitched so curiously, I'll bestow a rag of mine own rheumatic flannel, to make a fitter one!"

"Oh, peace, neighbors, peace!" whispered their youngest companion; "do not let her hear you! Not a stitch in that embroidered letter, but she has felt it in her heart."

The grim beadle now made a gesture with his staff.

"Make way, good people, make way, in the King's name!" cried he. "Open a passage; and, I promise ye, Mistress Prynne shall be set where man, woman, and child may have a fair sight of her brave apparel, from this time till an hour past meridian. A blessing on the righteous Colony of the Massachusetts, where iniquity is dragged out into the sunshine! Come along, Madam Hester, and show your scarlet letter in the market-place!"

A lane was forthwith opened through the crowd of spectators. Preceded by the beadle, and attended by an irregular procession of stern-browed men and unkindly visaged women, Hester Prynne set forth towards the place appointed for her punishment. A crowd of eager and curious school-boys, understanding little of the matter in hand, except that it gave them a half-holiday, ran before her progress, turning their heads continually to stare into her face, and at the winking baby in her arms, and at the ignominious letter on her breast. It was no great distance, in those days, from the prison-door to the market-place. Measured by the prisoner's experience, however, it might be reckoned a journey of some length; for, haughty as her demeanor was, she perchance underwent an agony from every footstep of those that thronged to see her, as if her heart had been flung into the street for them all to spurn and trample upon. In our nature, however, there is a provision, alike marvellous and merciful, that the sufferer should never know the intensity of what he endures by its present torture, but chiefly by the pang that rankles after it. With almost a serene deportment, therefore, Hester Prynne passed through this portion of her ordeal, and came to a sort of scaffold, at the western extremity of the market-place. It stood nearly beneath the eaves of Boston's earliest church, and appeared to be a fixture there.

In fact, this scaffold constituted a portion of a penal machine, which now, for two or three generations past, has been merely historical and traditionary among us, but was held, in the old time, to be as effectual an agent, in the promotion of good citizenship, as ever was the guillotine among the terrorists of France. It was, in short, the platform of the pillory; and above it rose the framework of that instrument of discipline, so fashioned as to confine the human head in its tight grasp, and thus holding it up to the public gaze. The very ideal of ignominy was embodied and made manifest in this contrivance of wood and iron. There can be no outrage, methinks, against our common nature,—whatever be the delinquencies of the individual,—no outrage more flagrant than to forbid the culprit to hide his face for shame; as it was the essence of this punishment to do. In Hester Prynne's instance, however, as not unfrequently in other cases, her sentence bore, that she should stand a certain time upon the platform, but without undergoing that gripe about the neck and confinement of the head, the proneness to which was the most devilish characteristic of this ugly engine. Knowing well her part, she ascended a flight of wooden steps, and was thus displayed to the surrounding multitude, at about the height of a man's shoulders above the street.

Had there been a Papist among the crowd of Puritans, he might have seen in this beautiful woman, so picturesque in her attire and mien, and with the infant at her bosom, an object to remind him of the image of Divine Maternity, which so many illustrious painters have vied with one another to represent; something which should remind him, indeed, but only by contrast, of that sacred image of sinless motherhood, whose infant was to redeem the world. Here, there was the taint of deepest sin in the most sacred quality of human life, working such effect, that the world was only the darker for this woman's beauty, and the more lost for the infant that she had borne.

The scene was not without a mixture of awe, such as must always invest the spectacle of guilt and shame in a fellow-creature, before society shall have grown corrupt enough to smile, instead of shuddering, at it. The witnesses of Hester Prynne's disgrace had not yet passed beyond their simplicity. They were stern enough to look upon her death, had that been the sentence, without a murmur at its severity, but had none of the heartlessness of another social state, which would find only a theme for jest in an exhibition like the present. Even had there been a disposition to turn the matter into ridicule, it must have been repressed and overpowered by the solemn presence of men no less dignified than the Governor, and several of his counsellors, a judge, a general and the ministers of the town; all of whom sat or stood in a balcony of the meeting-house, looking down upon the platform. When such personages could constitute a part of the spectacle, without risking the majesty or reverence of rank and office, it was safely to be inferred that the infliction of a legal sentence would have an earnest and effectual meaning. Accordingly, the crowd was sombre and grave. The unhappy culprit sustained herself as best a woman might, under the heavy weight of a thousand unrelenting eyes, all fastened upon her, and concentrated at her bosom. It was almost intolerable to be borne. Of an impulsive and passionate nature, she had fortified herself to encounter the stings and venomous stabs of public contumely, wreaking itself in every variety of insult; but there was a quality so much more terrible in the solemn mood of the popular mind, that she longed rather to behold all those rigid countenances contorted with scornful merriment, and herself the object. Had a roar of laughter burst from the multitude,— each man, each woman, each little shrill-voiced child, contributing their individual parts,—Hester Prynne might have repaid them all with a bitter and disdainful smile. But, under the leaden infliction which it was her doom to endure, she felt, at moments, as if she must needs shriek out with the full power of her lungs, and cast herself from the scaffold down upon the ground, or else go mad at once.

Yet there were intervals when the whole scene, in which she was the most conspicuous object, seemed to vanish from her eyes, or, at least, glimmered indistinctly before them, like a mass of imperfectly shaped and spectral images. Her mind, and especially her memory, was preternaturally active, and kept bringing up other scenes than this roughly hewn street of a little town, on the edge of the Western wilderness; other faces than were lowering upon her from beneath the brims of those steeple-crowned hats. Reminiscences the most trifling and immaterial, passages of infancy and school-days, sports, childish quarrels, and the little domestic traits of her maiden years, came swarming back upon her, intermingled with recollections of whatever was gravest in her subsequent life; one picture precisely as vivid as another; as if all were of similar importance, or all alike a play. Possibly, it was an instinctive device of her spirit, to relieve itself, by the exhibition of these phantasmagoric forms, from the cruel weight and hardness of the reality.

Be that as it might, the scaffold of the pillory was a point of view that revealed to Hester Prynne the entire track along which she had been treading since her happy infancy. Standing on that miserable eminence, she saw again her native village, in Old England, and her paternal home; a decayed house of gray stone, with a poverty-stricken aspect, but retaining a half-obliterated shield of arms over the portal, in token of antique gentility. She saw her father's face, with its bald brow, and reverend white beard, that flowed over the old-fashioned Elizabethan ruff; her mother's, too, with the look of heedful and anxious love which it always wore in her remembrance, and which, even since her death, had so often laid the impediment of a gentle remonstrance in her daughter's pathway.

She saw her own face, glowing with girlish beauty, and illuminating all the interior of the dusky mirror in which she had been wont to gaze at it. There she beheld another countenance, of a man well stricken in years, a pale, thin, scholar-like visage, with eyes dim and bleared by the lamplight that had served them to pore over many ponderous books. Yet those same bleared optics had a strange, penetrating power, when it was their owner's purpose to read the human soul. This figure of the study and the cloister, as Hester Prynne's womanly fancy failed not to recall, was slightly deformed, with the left shoulder a trifle higher than the right. Next rose before her, in memory's picture-gallery, the intricate and narrow thoroughfares, the tall, gray houses, the huge cathedrals, and the public edifices, ancient in date and quaint in architecture, of a Continental city; where a new life had awaited her, still in connection with the misshapen scholar; a new life, but feeding itself on time-worn materials, like a tuft of green moss on a crumbling wall. Lastly, in lieu of these shifting scenes, came back the rude market-place of the Puritan settlement, with all the townspeople assembled and levelling their stern regards at Hester Prynne,—. yes, at herself,—who stood on the scaffold of the pillory, an infant on her arm, and the letter A, in scarlet, fantastically embroidered with gold-thread, upon her bosom!

Could it be true? She clutched the child so fiercely to her breast, that it sent forth a cry; she turned her eyes downward at the scarlet letter, and even touched it with her finger, to assure herself that the infant and the shame were real. Yes!—these were her realities,—all else had vanished!

### III

### THE RECOGNITION

FROM this intense consciousness of being the object of severe and universal observation, the wearer of the scarlet letter was at length relieved, by discerning, on the outskirts of the crowd, a figure which irresistibly took possession of her thoughts. An Indian, in his native garb, was standing there; but the red men were not so infrequent visitors of the English settlements, that one of them would have attracted any notice from Hester Prynne at such a time; much less would he have excluded all other objects and ideals from her mind. By the Indian's side, and evidently sustaining a companionship with him, stood a white man, clad in a strange disarray of civilized and savage costume.

He was small in stature, with a furrowed visage, which, as yet, could hardly be termed aged. There was a remarkable intelligence in his features, as of a person who had so cultivated his mental part that it could not fail to mould the physical to itself, and become manifest by unmistakable tokens. Although, by a seemingly careless arrangement of his heterogeneous garb, he had endeavored to conceal or abate the peculiarity, it was sufficiently evident to Hester Prynne that one of this man's shoulders rose higher than the other. Again, at the first instant of perceiving that thin visage, and the slight deformity of the figure, she pressed her infant to her bosom with so convulsive a force that the poor babe uttered another cry of pain. But the mother did not seem to hear it.

At his arrival in the market-place, and some time before she saw him, the stranger had bent his eyes on Hester Prynne. It was carelessly, at first, like a man chiefly accustomed to look inward, and to whom external matters are of little value and import, unless they bear relation to something within his mind. Very soon, however, his look became keen and penetrative. A writhing horror twisted itself across his features, like a snake gliding swiftly over them, and making one little pause, with all its wreathed intervolutions in open sight. His face darkened with some powerful emotion, which, nevertheless, he so instantaneously controlled by an effort of his will, that, save at a single moment, its expression might have passed for calmness. After a brief space, the convulsion grew almost imperceptible, and finally subsided into the depths of his nature. When he found the eyes of Hester Prynne fastened on his own, and saw that she appeared to recognize him, he slowly and calmly raised his finger, made a gesture with it in the air, and laid it on his lips.

Then, touching the shoulder of a townsman who stood next to him, he addressed him, in a formal and courteous manner.

"I pray you, good Sir," said he, "who is this woman?—and wherefore is she here set up to public shame?"

"You must needs be a stranger in this region, friend," answered the townsman, looking curiously at the questioner and his savage companion, "else you would surely have heard of Mistress Hester Prynne, and her evil doings. She hath raised a great scandal, I promise you, in godly Master Dimmesdale's church."

"You say truly," replied the other. "I am a stranger, and have been a wanderer, sorely against my will. I have met with grievous mishaps by sea and land, and have been long held in bonds among the heathen-folk, to the southward; and am now brought hither by this Indian to be redeemed out of my captivity. Will it please you, therefore, to tell me of Hester Prynne's,—have I her name rightly?—of this woman's offences, and what has brought her to yonder scaffold?"

"Truly, friend; and methinks it must gladden your heart, after your troubles and sojourn in the wilderness," said the townsman, "to find yourself, at length, in a land where iniquity is searched out, and punished in the sight of rulers and people, as here in our godly New England. Yonder woman, Sir, you must know, was the wife of a certain learned man, English by birth, but who had long dwelt in Amsterdam, whence, some good time agone, he was minded to cross over and cast in his lot with us of the Massachusetts. To this purpose, he sent his wife before him, remaining himself to look after some necessary affairs. Marry, good Sir, in some two years, or less, that the woman has been a dweller here in Boston, no tidings have come of this learned gentleman, Master Prynne; and his young wife, look you, being left to her own misguidance"—

"Ah!—aha!—I conceive you," said the stranger with a bitter smile. "So learned a man as you speak of should have learned this too in his books. And who, by your favor, Sir, may be the father of yonder babe— it is some three or four months old, I should judge—which Mistress Prynne is holding in her arms?"

"Of a truth, friend, that matter remaineth a riddle; and the Daniel who shall expound it is yet a-wanting," answered the townsman. "Madam Hester absolutely refuseth to speak, and the magistrates have laid their heads together in vain. Peradventure the guilty one stands looking on at this sad spectacle, unknown of man, and forgetting that God sees him."

"The learned man," observed the stranger, with another smile, "should come himself, to look into the mystery."

"It behooves him well, if he be still in life," responded the townsman. "Now, good Sir, our Massachusetts magistracy, bethinking themselves that this woman is youthful and fair, and doubtless was strongly tempted to her fall,—and that, moreover, as is most likely, her husband may be at the bottom of the sea,—they have not been bold to put in force the extremity of our righteous law against her. The penalty thereof is death. But in their great mercy and tenderness of heart, they have doomed Mistress Prynne to stand only a space of three hours on the platform of the pillory, and then and thereafter, for the remainder of her natural life, to wear a mark of shame upon her bosom."

"A wise sentence!" remarked the stranger, gravely bowing his head. "Thus she will be a living sermon against sin, until the ignominious letter be engraved upon her tombstone. It irks me, nevertheless, that the partner of her iniquity should not, at least, stand on the scaffold by her side. But he will be known!—he will be known!—he will be known!"

He bowed courteously to the communicative townsman, and, whispering a few words to his Indian attendant, they both made their way through the crowd.

While this passed, Hester Prynne had been standing on her pedestal, still with a fixed gaze towards the stranger; so fixed a gaze, that, at moments of intense absorption, all other objects in the visible world seemed to vanish, leaving only him and her. Such an interview, perhaps, would have been more terrible than even to meet him as she now did, with the hot, mid-day sun burning down upon her face, and lighting up its shame; with the scarlet token of infamy on her breast; with the sin-born infant in her arms; with a whole people, drawn forth, as to a festival, staring at the features that should have been seen only in the quiet gleam of the fireside, in the happy shadow of a home, or beneath a matronly veil, at church. Dreadful as it was, she was conscious of a shelter in the presence of these thousand witnesses. It was better to stand thus, with so many betwixt him and her, than to greet him, face to face, they two alone. She fled for refuge, as it were, to the public exposure, and dreaded the moment when its protection should be withdrawn from her. Involved in these thoughts, she scarcely heard a voice behind her, until it had repeated her name more than once, in a loud and solemn tone, audible to the whole multitude.

"Hearken unto me, Hester Prynne!" said the voice.

It has already been noticed, that directly over the platform on which Hester Prynne stood was a kind of balcony, or open gallery, appended to the meeting-house. It was the place whence proclamations were wont to be made, amidst an assemblage of the magistracy, with all the ceremonial that attended such public observances in those days. Here, to witness the scene which we are describing, sat Governor Bellingham himself, with four sergeants about his chair, bearing halberds, as a guard of honor. He wore a dark feather in his hat, a border of embroidery on his cloak, and a black velvet tunic beneath; a gentleman advanced in years, with a hard experience written in his wrinkles. He was not ill fitted to be the head and representative of a community, which owed its origin and progress, and its present state of development, not to the impulses of youth, but to the stern and tempered energies of manhood, and the sombre sagacity of age; accomplishing so much, precisely because it imagined and hoped so little. The other eminent characters, by whom the chief ruler was surrounded, were distinguished by a dignity of mien, belonging to a period when the forms of authority were felt to possess the sacredness of Divine institutions. They were, doubtless, good men, just, and sage. But, out of the whole human family, it would not have been easy to select the same number of wise and virtuous persons, who should be less capable of sitting in judgment on an erring woman's heart, and disentangling its mesh of good and evil, than the sages of rigid aspect towards whom Hester Prynne now turned her face. She seemed conscious, indeed, that whatever sympathy she might expect lay in the larger and warmer heart of the multitude; for, as she lifted her eyes towards the balcony, the unhappy woman grew pale and trembled.

The voice which had called her attention was that of the reverend and famous John Wilson, the eldest clergyman of Boston, a great scholar, like most of his contemporaries in the profession, and withal a man of kind and genial spirit. This last attribute, however, had been less carefully developed than his intellectual gifts, and was, in truth, rather a matter of shame than self-congratulation with him. There he stood, with a border of grizzled locks beneath his skull-cap; while his gray eyes, accustomed to the shaded light of his study, were winking, like those of Hester's infant, in the unadulterated sunshine. He looked like the darkly engraved portraits which we see prefixed to old volume of sermons; and had no more right than one of those portraits would have to step forth, as he now did, and meddle with a question of human guilt, passion, and anguish.

"Hester Prynne," said the clergyman, "I have striven with my young brother here, under whose preaching of the word you have been privileged to sit,"—here Mr. Wilson laid his hand on the shoulder of a pale young man beside him,—"I have sought, I say, to persuade this godly youth, that he should deal with you, here in the face of Heaven and before these wise and upright rulers, and in hearing of all the people, as touching the vileness and blackness of your sin. Knowing your natural temper better than I, he could the better judge what arguments to use, whether of tenderness or terror, such as might prevail over your hardness and obstinacy; insomuch that you should no longer hide the name of him who tempted you to this grievous fall. But he opposes to me (with a young man's oversoftness, albeit wise beyond his years) that it were wronging the very nature of woman to force her to lay open her heart's secrets in such broad daylight, and in presence of so great a multitude. Truly, as I sought to convince him, the shame lay in the commission of the sin, and not in the showing of it forth. What say you to it, once again, Brother Dimmesdale? Must it be thou, or I, that shall deal with this poor sinner's soul?"

There was a murmur among the dignified and reverend occupants of the balcony; and Governor Bellingham gave expression to its purport, speaking in an authoritative voice, although tempered with respect towards the youthful clergyman whom he addressed.

"Good Master Dimmesdale," said he, "the responsibility of this woman's soul lies greatly with you. It behooves you, therefore, to exhort her to repentance, and to confession, as a proof and consequence thereof."

The directness of this appeal drew the eyes of the whole crowd upon the Reverend Mr. Dimmesdale; a young clergyman, who had come from one of the great English universities, bringing all the learning of the age into our wild forest-land. His eloquence and religious fervor had already given the earnest of high eminence in his profession. He was a person of very striking aspect, with a white, lofty, and impending brow, large, brown, melancholy eyes, and a mouth which, unless when he forcibly compressed it, was apt to be tremulous, expressing both nervous sensibility and a vast power of self-restraint. Notwithstanding his high native gifts and scholar-like attainments, there was an air about this young minister,—an apprehensive, a startled, a half-frightened look,—as of a being who felt himself quite astray and at a loss in the pathway of human existence, and could only be at ease in some seclusion of his own. Therefore, so far as his duties would permit, he trod in the shadowy by-paths, and thus kept himself simple and childlike; coming forth, when occasion was, with a freshness, and fragrance, and dewy purity of thought, which, as many people said, affected them like the speech of an angel.

Such was the young man whom the Reverend Mr. Wilson and the Governor had introduced so openly to the public notice, bidding him speak, in the hearing of all men, to that mystery of a woman's soul, so sacred even in its pollution. The trying nature of his position drove the blood from his cheek, and made his lips tremulous.

"Speak to the woman, my brother," said Mr. Wilson. "It is of moment to her soul, and therefore, as the worshipful Governor says, momentous to thine own, in whose charge hers is. Exhort her to confess the truth!"

The Reverend Mr. Dimmesdale bent his head, in silent prayer, as it seemed, and then came forward.

"Hester Prynne," said he, leaning over the balcony and looking down steadfastly into her eyes, "thou hearest what this good man says, and seest the accountability under which I labor. If thou feelest it to be for thy soul's peace, and that thy earthly punishment will thereby be made more effectual to salvation, I charge thee to speak out the name of thy fellow-sinner and fellow-sufferer! Be not silent from any mistaken pity and tenderness for him; for, believe me, Hester, though he were to step down from a high place, and stand there beside thee, on thy pedestal of shame, yet better were it so, than to hide a guilty heart through life. What can thy silence do for him, except it tempt him—yea, compel him, as it were—to add hypocrisy to sin? Heaven hath granted thee an open ignominy, that thereby thou mayest work out an open triumph over the evil within thee, and the sorrow without. Take heed how thou deniest to him —who, perchance, hath not the courage to grasp it for himself—the bitter, but wholesome, cup that is now presented to thy lips!"

The young pastor's voice was tremulously sweet, rich, deep, and broken. The feeling that it so evidently manifested, rather than the direct purport of the words, caused it to vibrate within all hearts, and brought the listeners into one accord of sympathy. Even the poor baby, at Hester's bosom, was affected by the same influence; for it directed its hitherto vacant gaze towards Mr. Dimmesdale, and held up its little arms, with a half-pleased, half-plaintive murmur. So powerful seemed the minister's appeal that the people could not believe but that Hester Prynne would speak out the guilty name; or else that the guilty one himself, in whatever high or lowly place he stood, would be drawn forth by an inward and inevitable necessity, and compelled to ascend the scaffold.

Hester shook her head.

"Woman, transgress not beyond the limits of Heaven's mercy!" cried the Reverend Mr. Wilson, more harshly than before. "That little babe hath been gifted with a voice, to second and confirm the counsel which thou hast heard. Speak out the name! That, and thy repentance, may avail to take the scarlet letter off thy breast."

"Never!" replied Hester Prynne, looking, not at Mr. Wilson, but into the deep and troubled eyes of the younger clergyman. "It is too deeply branded. Ye cannot take it off. And would that I might endure his agony, as well as mine!"

"Speak, woman!" said another voice, coldly and sternly, proceeding from the crowd about the scaffold. "Speak; and give your child a father!"

"I will not speak!" answered Hester, turning pale as death, but responding to this voice, which she too surely recognized. "And my child must seek a heavenly Father; she shall never know an earthly one!"

"She will not speak!" murmured Mr. Dimmesdale, who, leaning over the balcony, with his hand upon his heart, had awaited the result of his appeal. He now drew back, with a long respiration. "Wondrous strength and generosity of a woman's heart! She will not speak!"

Discerning the impracticable state of the poor culprit's mind, the elder clergyman, who had carefully prepared himself for the occasion, addressed to the multitude a discourse on sin, in all its branches, but with continual reference to the ignominious letter. So forcibly did he dwell upon this symbol, for the hour or more during which his periods were rolling over the people's heads, that it assumed new terrors in their imagination, and seemed to derive its scarlet hue from the flames of the infernal pit. Hester Prynne, meanwhile, kept her place upon the pedestal of shame, with glazed eyes, and an air of weary indifference. She had borne, that morning, all that nature could endure; and as her temperament was not of the order that escapes from too intense suffering by a swoon, her spirit could only shelter itself beneath a stony crust of insensibility, while the faculties of animal life remained entire. In this state, the voice of the preacher thundered remorselessly, but unavailingly, upon her ears. The infant, during the latter portion of her ordeal, pierced the air with its wailings and screams; she strove to hush it, mechanically, but seemed scarcely to sympathize with its trouble. With the same hard demeanor, she was led back to prison, and vanished from the public gaze within its iron-clamped portal. It was whispered, by those who peered after her, that the scarlet letter threw a lurid gleam along the dark passage-way of the interior.

## IV

### THE INTERVIEW

AFTER her return to the prison, Hester Prynne was found to be in a state of nervous excitement that demanded constant watchfulness lest she should perpetrate violence on herself, or do some half-frenzied mischief to the poor babe. As night approached, it proving impossible to quell her insubordination by rebuke or threats of punishment, Master Brackett, the jailer, thought fit to introduce a physician. He described him as a man of skill in all Christian modes of physical science, and likewise familiar with whatever the savage people could teach, in respect to medicinal herbs and roots that grew in the forest. To say the truth, there was much need of professional assistance, not merely for Hester herself, but still more urgently for the child; who, drawing its sustenance from the maternal bosom, seemed to have drank in with it all the turmoil, the anguish and despair, which pervaded the mother's system. It now writhed in convulsions of pain, and was a forcible type in its little frame, of the moral agony which Hester Prynne had borne throughout the day.

Closely following the jailer into the dismal apartment appeared that individual, of singular aspect, whose presence in the crowd had been of such deep interest to the wearer of the scarlet letter. He was lodged in the prison, not as suspected of any offence, but as the most convenient and suitable mode of disposing of him, until the magistrates should have conferred with the Indian sagamores respecting his ransom. His name was announced as Roger Chillingworth. The jailer, after ushering him into the room, remained a moment, marvelling at the comparative quiet that followed his entrance; for Hester Prynne had immediately become as still as death, although the child continued to moan.

"Prithee, friend, leave me alone with my patient," said the practitioner. "Trust me, good jailer, you shall briefly have peace in your house; and, I promise you, Mistress Prynne shall hereafter be more amenable to just authority than you may have found her heretofore."

"Nay, if your worship can accomplish that," answered Master Brackett, "I shall own you for a man of skill indeed! Verily, the woman hath been like a possessed one; and there lacks little, that I should take in hand to drive Satan out of her with stripes."

The stranger had entered the room with the characteristic quietude of the profession to which he announced himself as belonging. Nor did his demeanor change, when the withdrawal of the prison-keeper left him face to face with the woman, whose absorbed notice of him, in the crowd, had intimated so close a relation between himself and her. His first care was given to the child; whose cries, indeed, as she lay writhing on the trundle-bed, made it of peremptory necessity to postpone all other business to the task of soothing her. He examined the infant carefully, and then proceeded to unclasp a leathern case, which he took from beneath his dress. It appeared to contain medical preparations, one of which he mingled with a cup of water.

"My old studies in alchemy," observed he, "and my sojourn, for above a year past, among a people well versed in the kindly properties of simples, have made a better physician of me than many that claim the medical degree. Here, woman! The child is yours,—she is none of mine,—neither will she recognize my voice or aspect as a father's. Administer this draught, therefore, with thine own hand."

Hester repelled the offered medicine, at the same time gazing with strongly marked apprehension into his face.

"Wouldst thou avenge thyself on the innocent babe?" whispered she.

"Foolish woman!" responded the physician, half coldly, half soothingly. "What should ail me, to harm this misbegotten and miserable babe? The medicine is potent for good; and were it my child,—yea, mine own, as well as thine!—I could do no better for it."

As she still hesitated, being, in fact, in no reasonable state of mind, he took the infant in his arms, and himself administered the draught. It soon proved its efficacy, and redeemed the leech's pledge. The moans of the little patient subsided; its convulsive tossings gradually ceased; and, in a few moments, as is the custom of young children after relief from pain, it sank into a profound and dewy slumber. The physician, as he had a fair right to be termed, next bestowed his attention on the mother. With calm and intent scrutiny, he felt her pulse, looked into her eyes,—a gaze that made her heart shrink and shudder, because so familiar, and yet so strange and cold,—and, finally, satisfied with his investigation, proceeded to mingle another draught.

"I know not Lethe nor Nepenthe," remarked he; "but I have learned many new secrets in the wilderness, and here is one of them,—a recipe that an Indian taught me, in requital of some lessons of my own, that were as old as Paracelsus. Drink it! It may be less soothing than a sinless conscience. That I cannot give thee. But it will calm the swell and heaving of thy passion, like oil thrown on the waves of a tempestuous sea."

He presented the cup to Hester, who received it with a slow, earnest look into his face; not precisely a look of fear, yet full of doubt and questioning, as to what his purposes might be. She looked also at her slumbering child.

"I have thought of death," said she,—"have wished for it,—would even have prayed for it, were it fit that such as I should pray for anything. Yet, if death be in this cup, I bid thee think again, ere thou beholdest me quaff it. See! It is even now at my lips."

"Drink, then," replied he, still with the same cold composure. "Dost thou know me so little, Hester Prynne? Are my purposes wont to be so shallow? Even if I imagine a scheme of vengeance, what could I do better for my object than to let thee live,—than to give thee medicines against all harm and peril of life,—so that this burning shame may still blaze upon thy bosom?" As he spoke, he laid his long forefinger on the scarlet letter, which forthwith seemed to scorch into Hester's breast, as if it had been red-hot. He noticed her involuntary gesture, and smiled. "Live, therefore, and bear about thy doom with thee, in the eyes of men and women,—in the eyes of him whom thou didst call thy husband,—in the eyes of yonder child! And, that thou mayest live, take off this draught."

Without further expostulation or delay, Hester Prynne drained the cup, and, at the motion of the man of skill, seated herself on the bed where the child was sleeping; while he drew the only chair which the room afforded, and took his own seat beside her. She could not but tremble at these preparations; for she felt that—having now done all that humanity, or principle, or, if so it were, a refined cruelty, impelled him to do, for the relief of physical suffering—he was next to treat with her as the man whom she had most deeply and irreparably injured.

"Hester," said he, "I ask not wherefore, nor how, thou hast fallen into the pit, or say, rather, thou hast ascended to the pedestal of infamy, on which I found thee. The reason is not far to seek. It was my folly, and thy weakness. I,—a man of thought,—the book-worm of great libraries,—a man already in decay, having given my best years to feed the hungry dream of knowledge,—what had I to do with youth and beauty like thine own! Misshapen from my birth-hour, how could I delude myself with the idea that intellectual gifts might veil physical deformity in a young girl's fantasy! Men call me wise. If sages were ever wise in their own behoof, I might have foreseen all this. I might have known that, as I came out of the vast and dismal forest, and entered this settlement of Christian men, the very first object to meet my eyes would be thyself, Hester Prynne, standing up, a statue of ignominy, before the people. Nay, from the moment when we came down the old church steps together, a married pair, I might have beheld the bale-fire of that scarlet letter blazing at the end of our path!"

"Thou knowest," said Hester,—for, depressed as she was, she could not endure this last quiet stab at the token of her shame,—"thou knowest that I was frank with thee. I felt no love, nor feigned any."

"True," replied he. "It was my folly! I have said it. But, up to that epoch of my life, I had lived in vain. The world had been so cheerless! My heart was a habitation large enough for many guests, but lonely and chill, and without a household fire. I longed to kindle one! It seemed not so wild a dream,—old as I was, and sombre as I was, and misshapen as I was,—that the simple bliss, which is scattered far and wide, for all mankind to gather up, might yet be mine. And so, Hester, I drew thee into my heart, into its innermost chamber, and sought to warm thee by the warmth which thy presence made there!"

"I have greatly wronged thee," murmured Hester.

"We have wronged each other," answered he. "Mine was the first wrong, when I betrayed thy budding youth into a false and unnatural relation with my decay. Therefore, as a man who has not thought and philosophized in vain, I seek no vengeance, plot no evil against thee. Between thee and me, the scale hangs fairly balanced. But, Hester, the man lives who has wronged us both! Who is he?"

"Ask me not!" replied Hester Prynne, looking firmly into his face. "That thou shalt never know!"

"Never, sayest thou?" rejoined he, with a smile of dark and self-relying intelligence. "Never know him! Believe me, Hester, there are few things, —whether in the outward world, or, to a certain depth, in the invisible sphere of thought,—few things hidden from the man who devotes himself earnestly and unreservedly to the solution of a mystery. Thou mayest cover up thy secret from the prying multitude. Thou mayest conceal it, too, from the ministers and magistrates, even as thou didst this day, when they sought to wrench the name out of thy heart, and give thee a partner on thy pedestal. But, as for me, I come to the inquest with other senses than they possess. I shall seek this man, as I have sought truth in books; as I have sought gold in alchemy. There is a sympathy that will make me conscious of him. I shall see him tremble. I shall feel myself shudder, suddenly and unawares. Sooner or later, he must needs be mine!"

The eyes of the wrinkled scholar glowed so intensely upon her, that Hester Prynne clasped her hands over her heart, dreading lest he should read the secret there at once.

"Thou wilt not reveal his name? Not the less he is mine," resumed he, with a look of confidence, as if destiny were at one with him. "He bears no letter of infamy wrought into his garment, as thou dost; but I shall read it on his heart. Yet fear not for him! Think not that I shall interfere with Heaven's own method of retribution, or, to my own loss, betray him to the gripe of human law. Neither do thou imagine that I shall contrive aught against his life; no, nor against his fame, if, as I judge, he be a man of fair repute. Let him live! Let him hide himself in outward honor, if he may! Not the less he shall be mine!"

"Thy acts are like mercy," said Hester, bewildered and appalled. "But thy words interpret thee as a terror!"

"One thing, thou that wast my wife, I would enjoin upon thee," continued the scholar. "Thou hast kept the secret of thy paramour. Keep, likewise, mine! There are none in this land that know me. Breathe not, to any human soul, that thou didst ever call me husband! Here, on this wild outskirt of the earth, I shall pitch my tent; for, elsewhere a wanderer, and isolated from human interests, I find here a woman, a man, a child, amongst whom and myself there exist the closest ligaments. No matter whether of love or hate; no matter whether of right or wrong! Thou and thine, Hester Prynne, belong to me. My home is where thou art, and where he is. But betray me not!"

"Wherefore dost thou desire it?" inquired Hester, shrinking, she hardly knew why, from this secret bond. "Why not announce thyself openly, and cast me off at once?"

"It may be," he replied, "because I will not encounter the dishonor that besmirches the husband of a faithless woman. It may be for other reasons. Enough, it is my purpose to live and die unknown. Let, therefore, thy husband be to the world as one already dead, and of whom no tidings shall ever come. Recognize me not, by word, by sign, by look! Breathe not the secret, above all, to the man thou wottest of. Shouldst thou fail me in this, beware! His fame, his position, his life, will be in my hands. Beware!"

"I will keep thy secret, as I have his," said Hester.

"Swear it!" rejoined he.

And she took the oath.

"And now, Mistress Prynne," said old Roger Chillingworth, as he was hereafter to be named, "I leave thee alone; alone with thy infant, and the scarlet letter! How is it, Hester? Doth thy sentence bind thee to wear the token in thy sleep? Art thou not afraid of nightmares and hideous dreams?"

"Why dost thou smile so at me?" inquired Hester, troubled at the expression of his eyes. "Art thou like the Black Man that haunts the forest round about us? Hast thou enticed me into a bond that will prove the ruin of my soul?"

"Not thy soul," he answered, with another smile, "No, not thine!"

V

## HESTER AT HER NEEDLE

HESTER PRYNNE'S term of confinement was now at an end. Her prison-door was thrown open, and she came forth into the sunshine, which, falling on all alike, seemed, to her sick and morbid heart, as if meant for no other purpose than to reveal the scarlet letter on her breast. Perhaps there was a more real torture in her first unattended footsteps from the threshold of the prison, than even in the procession and spectacle that have been described, where she was made the common infamy, at which all mankind was summoned to point its finger. Then, she was supported by an unnatural tension of the nerves, and by all the combative energy of her character, which enabled her to convert the scene into a kind of lurid triumph. It was, moreover, a separate and insulated event, to occur but once in her lifetime, and to meet which, therefore, reckless of economy, she might call up the vital strength that would have sufficed for many quiet years. The very law that condemned her—a giant of stern features, but with vigor to support, as well as to annihilate, in his iron arm—had held her up, through the terrible ordeal of her ignominy. But now, with this unattended walk from her prison-door, began the daily custom; and she must either sustain and carry it forward by the ordinary resources of her nature, or sink beneath it. She could no longer borrow from the future to help her through the present grief. To-morrow would bring its own trial with it; so would the next day, and so would the next; each its own trial, and yet the very same that was now so unutterably grievous to be borne. The days of the far-off future would toil onward, still with the same burden for her to take up, and bear along with her, but never to fling down; for the accumulating days, and added years, would pile up their misery upon the heap of shame. Throughout them all, giving up her individuality, she would become the general symbol at which the preacher and moralist might point, and in which they might vivify and embody their images of woman's frailty and sinful passion. Thus the young and pure would be taught to look at her, with the scarlet letter flaming on her breast,—at her, the child of honorable parents,—at her, the mother of a babe, that would hereafter be a woman,—at her, who had once been innocent,—as the figure, the body, the reality of sin. And over her grave, the infamy that she must carry thither would be her only monument.

It may seem marvellous, that, with the world before her,—kept by no restrictive clause of her condemnation within the limits of the Puritan settlement, so remote and so obscure,—free to return to her birthplace, or to any other European land, and there hide her character and identity under a new exterior, as completely as if emerging into another state of being,—and having also the passes of the dark, inscrutable forest open to her, where the wildness of her nature might assimilate itself with a people

whose customs and life were alien from the law that had condemned her,
—it may seem marvellous that this woman should still call that place her
home, where, and where only, she must needs be the type of shame. But
there is a fatality, a feeling so irresistible and inevitable that it has the
force of doom, which almost invariably compels human beings to linger
around and haunt, ghostlike, the spot where some great and marked
event has given the color to their lifetime; and still the more irresistibly,
the darker the tinge that saddens it. Her sin, her ignominy, were the roots
which she had struck into the soil. It was as if a new birth, with stronger
assimilations than the first, had converted the forest-land, still so uncongenial to every other pilgrim and wanderer, into Hester Prynne's wild and
dreary, but life-long home. All other scenes of earth—even that village of
rural England, where happy infancy and stainless maidenhood seemed
yet to be in her mother's keeping, like garments put off long ago—were
foreign to her, in comparison. The chain that bound her here was of iron
links, and galling to her inmost soul, but could never be broken.

It might be, too,—doubtless it was so, although she hid the secret from
herself, and grew pale whenever it struggled out of her heart, like a serpent from its hole,—it might be that another feeling kept her within the
scene and pathway that had been so fatal. There dwelt, there trode the
feet of one with whom she deemed herself connected in a union, that, unrecognized on earth, would bring them together before the bar of final
judgment, and make that their marriage-altar, for a joint futurity of endless retribution. Over and over again, the tempter of souls had thrust this
idea upon Hester's contemplation, and laughed at the passionate and desperate joy with which she seized, and then strove to cast it from her. She
barely looked the idea in the face, and hastened to bar it in its dungeon.
What she compelled herself to believe—what, finally, she reasoned upon,
as her motive for continuing a resident of New England—was half a
truth, and half a self-delusion. Here, she said to herself, had been the
scene of her guilt, and here should be the scene of her earthly punishment; and so, perchance, the torture of her daily shame would at length
purge her soul, and work out another purity than that which she had lost;
more saint-like, because the result of martyrdom.

Hester Prynne, therefore, did not flee. On the outskirts of the town,
within the verge of the peninsula, but not in close vicinity to any other
habitation, there was a small thatched cottage. It had been built by an
earlier settler, and abandoned, because the soil about it was too sterile for
cultivation, while its comparative remoteness put it out of the sphere of
that social activity which already marked the habits of the emigrants. It
stood on the shore, looking across a basin of the sea at the forest-covered
hills, towards the west. A clump of scrubby trees, such as alone grew on
the penisula, did not so much conceal the cottage from view, as seem to
denote that here was some object which would fain have been, or at least
ought to be, concealed. In this little, lonesome dwelling, with some slender
means that she possessed, and by the license of the magistrates, who still
kept an inquisitorial watch over her, Hester established herself, with her

infant child. A mystic shadow of suspicion immediately attached itself to the spot. Children, too young to comprehend wherefore this woman should be shut out from the sphere of human charities, would creep nigh enough to behold her plying her needle at the cottage-window, or standing at the doorway, or laboring in her little garden, or coming forth along the pathway that led townward; and discerning the scarlet letter on her breast, would scamper off with a strange, contagious fear.

Lonely as was Hester's situation, and without a friend on earth who dared to show himself, she, however, incurred no risk of want. She possessed an art that sufficed, even in a land that afforded comparatively little scope for its exercise, to supply food for her thriving infant and herself. It was the art—then, as now, almost the only one within a woman's grasp—of needlework. She bore on her breast, in the curiously embroidered letter, a specimen of her delicate and imaginative skill, of which the dames of a court might gladly have availed themselves, to add the richer and more spiritual adornment of human ingenuity to their fabrics of silk and gold. Here, indeed, in the sable simplicity that generally characterized the Puritanic modes of dress, there might be an infrequent call for the finer productions of her handiwork. Yet the taste of the age, demanding whatever was elaborate in compositions of this kind, did not fail to extend its influence over our stern progenitors who had cast behind them so many fashions which it might seem harder to dispense with. Public ceremonies, such as ordinations, the installation of magistrates, and all that could give majesty to the forms in which a new government manifested itself to the people, were, as a matter of policy, marked by a stately and well-conducted ceremonial, and a sombre, but yet a studied magnificence. Deep ruffs, painfully wrought bands, and gorgeously embroidered gloves, were all deemed necessary to the official state of men assuming the reins of power; and were readily allowed to individuals dignified by rank or wealth, even while sumptuary laws forbade these and similar extravagances to the plebeian order. In the array of funerals, too,—whether for the apparel of the dead body, or to typify, by manifold emblematic devices of sable cloth and snowy lawn, the sorrow of the survivors,—there was a frequent and characteristic demand for such labor as Hester Prynne could supply. Baby-linen—for babies then wore robes of state—afforded still another possibility of toil and emolument.

By degrees, nor very slowly, her handiwork became what would now be termed the fashion. Whether from commiseration for a woman of so miserable a destiny; or from the morbid curiosity that gives a fictitious value even to common or worthless things; or by whatever other intangible circumstance was then, as now sufficient to bestow, on some persons, what others might seek in vain; or because Hester really filled a gap which must otherwise have remained vacant; it is certain that she had ready and fairly requited employment for as many hours as she saw fit to occupy with her needle. Vanity, it may be, chose to mortify itself, by putting on, for ceremonials of pomp and state, the garments that had been wrought by her sinful hands. Her needlework was seen on the ruff of the Governor;

military men wore it on their scarfs, and the minister on his band; it decked the baby's little cap; it was shut up to be mildewed and moulder away, in the coffins of the dead. But it is not recorded that, in a single instance, her skill was called in aid to embroider the white veil which was to cover the pure blushes of a bride. The exception indicated the ever-relentless rigor with which society frowned upon her sin.

Hester sought not to acquire anything beyond a subsistence, of the plainest and most ascetic description, for herself, and a simple abundance for her child. Her own dress was of the coarsest materials and the most sombre hue; with only that one ornament,—the scarlet letter,—which it was her doom to wear. The child's attire, on the other hand, was distinguished by a fanciful, or, we might rather say, a fantastic ingenuity, which served, indeed to heighten the airy charm that early began to develop itself in the little girl, but which appeared to have also a deeper meaning. We may speak further of it hereafter. Except for that small expenditure in the decoration of her infant, Hester bestowed all her superfluous means in charity, on wretches less miserable than herself, and who not unfrequently insulted the hand that fed them. Much of the time, which she might readily have applied to the better efforts of her art, she employed in making coarse garments for the poor. It is probable that there was an idea of penance in this mode of occupation, and that she offered up a real sacrifice of enjoyment, in devoting so many hours to such rude handiwork. She had in her nature a rich, voluptuous, Oriental characteristic,—a taste for the gorgeously beautiful, which, save in the exquisite productions of her needle, found nothing else, in all the possibilities of her life, to exercise itself upon. Women derive a pleasure, incomprehensible to the other sex, from the delicate toil of the needle. To Hester Prynne it might have been a mode of expressing, and therefore soothing, the passion of her life. Like all other joys, she rejected it as sin. This morbid meddling of conscience with an immaterial matter betokened, it is to be feared, no genuine and steadfast penitence, but something doubtful, something that might be deeply wrong, beneath.

In this manner, Hester Prynne came to have a part to perform in the world. With her native energy of character, and rare capacity, it could not entirely cast her off, although it had set a mark upon her, more intolerable to a woman's heart than that which branded the brow of Cain. In all her intercourse with society, however, there was nothing that made her feel as if she belonged to it. Every gesture, every word, and even the silence of those with whom she came in contact, implied, and ofter expressed, that she was banished, and as much alone as if she inhabited another sphere, or communicated with the common nature by other organs and senses than the rest of human kind. She stood apart from moral interests, yet close beside them, like a ghost that revisits the familiar fireside, and can no longer make itself seen or felt; no more smile with the household joy, nor mourn with the kindred sorrow; or, should it succeed in manifesting its forbidden sympathy, awakening only terror and horrible repugnance. These emotions, in fact, and its bitterest scorn besides, seemed to be the sole portion that she retained in the universal heart. It was not an age of delicacy; and her position, although she understood it well, and was in little danger of forgetting it, was often brought before her vivid self-perception, like a new anguish, by the rudest touch upon the tenderest spot. The poor, as we have already said, whom she sought out to be the objects of her bounty, often reviled the hand that was stretched forth to succor them. Dames of elevated rank, likewise, whose doors she entered in the way of her occupation, were accustomed to distil drops of bitterness into her heart, sometimes through that alchemy of quiet malice, by which women can concoct a subtle poison from ordinary trifles; and sometimes, also, by a coarser expression, that fell upon the sufferer's defenceless breast like a rough blow upon an ulcerated wound. Hester had schooled herself long and well; she never responded to these attacks, save by a flush of crimson that rose irrepressibly over her pale cheek, and again subsided into the depths of her bosom. She was patient,—a martyr, indeed,—but she forbore to pray for her enemies; lest, in spite of her forgiving aspirations, the words of the blessing should stubbornly twist themselves into a curse.

Continually, and in a thousand other ways, did she feel the innumerable throbs of anguish that had been so cunningly contrived for her by the undying, the ever-active sentence of the Puritan tribunal. Clergymen paused in the street to address words of exhortation, that brought a crowd, with its mingled grin and frown, around the poor, sinful woman. If she entered a church, trusting to share the Sabbath smile of the Universal Father, it was often her mishap to find herself the text of the discourse. She grew to have a dread of children; for they had imbibed from their parents a vague idea of something horrible in this dreary woman, gliding silently through the town, with never any companion but one only child. Therefore, first allowing her to pass, they pursued her at a distance with shrill cries, and the utterance of a word that had no distinct purport to their own minds, but was none the less terrible to her, as proceeding from lips that babbled it unconsciously. It seemed to argue so wide a diffusion of her shame, that all nature knew of it; it could have caused her no deeper pang, had the leaves of the trees whispered the dark story among themselves,—had the summer breeze murmured about it,—had the wintry blast shrieked it aloud! Another peculiar torture was felt in the gaze of a new eye. When strangers looked curiously at the scarlet letter,—and none ever failed to do so,—they branded it afresh into Hester's soul; so that oftentimes, she could scarcely refrain, yet always did refrain, from covering the symbol with her hand. But then, again, an accustomed eye had likewise its own anguish to inflict. Its cool stare of familiarity was intolerable. From first to last, in short, Hester Prynne had always this dreadful agony in feeling a human eye upon the token; the spot never grew callous; it seemed, on the contrary, to grow more sensitive with daily torture.

But sometimes, once in many days, or perchance in many months, she felt an eye—a human eye—upon the ignominious brand, that seemed to give a momentary relief, as if half of her agony were shared. The next instant, back it all rushed again, with still a deeper throb of pain; for, in that brief interval, she had sinned anew. Had Hester sinned alone?

Her imagination was somewhat affected, and, had she been of a softer moral and intellectual fibre, would have been still more so, by the strange and solitary anguish of her life. Walking to and fro, with those lonely footsteps, in the little world with which she was outwardly connected, it now and then appeared to Hester,—if altogether fancy, it was nevertheless too potent to be resisted,—she felt or fancied, then, that the scarlet letter had endowed her with a new sense. She shuddered to believe, yet could not help believing, that it gave her a sympathetic knowledge of the hidden sin in other hearts. She was terror-stricken by the revelations that were thus made. What were they? Could they be other than the insidious whispers of the bad angel, who would fain have persuaded the struggling woman, as yet only half his victim, that the outward guise of purity was but a lie, and that, if truth were everywhere to be shown, a scarlet letter would blaze forth on many a bosom besides Hester Prynne's? Or, must she receive those intimations—so obscure, yet so distinct—as truth? In all her miserable experience, there was nothing else so awful and so loathsome as this sense. It perplexed, as well as shocked her, by the irreverent inopportuneness of the occasions that brought it into vivid action. Sometimes the red infamy upon her breast would give a sympathetic throb, as she passed near a venerable minister or magistrate, the model of piety and justice, to whom that age of antique reverence looked up, as to a mortal man in fellowship with angels. "What evil thing is at hand?" would Hester say to herself. Lifting her reluctant eyes, there would be nothing human within the scope of view, save the form of this earthly saint! Again, a mystic sisterhood would contumaciously assert itself, as she met the sanctified frown of some matron, who, according to the rumor of all tongues, had kept cold snow within her bosom throughout life. That unsunned snow in the matron's bosom, and the burning shame on Hester Prynne's,—what had the two in common? Or, once more, the electric thrill would give her warning,—"Behold, Hester, here is a companion!" —and, looking up, she would detect the eyes of a young maiden glancing at the scarlet letter, shyly and aside, and quickly averted with a faint, chill crimson in her cheeks; as if her purity were somewhat sullied by that momentary glance. O Fiend, whose talisman was that fatal symbol, wouldst thou leave nothing, whether in youth or age, for this poor sinner to revere?—such loss of faith is ever one of the saddest results of sin. Be it accepted as a proof that all was not corrupt in this poor victim of her own frailty, and man's hard law, that Hester Prynne yet struggled to believe that no fellow-mortal was guilty like herself.

The vulgar, who, in those dreary old times, were always contributing a grotesque horror to what interested their imaginations, had a story about the scarlet letter which we might readily work up into a terrific legend. They averred, that the symbol was not mere scarlet cloth, tinged in an earthly dye-pot, but was red-hot with infernal fire, and could be seen glowing all alight, whenever Hester Prynne walked abroad in the night-time. And we must needs say, it seared Hester's bosom so deeply, that perhaps there was more truth in the rumor than our modern incredulity may be inclined to admit.

## VI

### PEARL

WE have as yet hardly spoken of the infant; that little creature, whose innocent life had sprung, by the inscrutable decree of Providence, a lovely and immortal flower, out of the rank luxuriance of a guilty passion. How strange it seemed to the sad woman, as she watched the growth, and the beauty that became every day more brilliant, and the intelligence that threw its quivering sunshine over the tiny features of this child! Her Pearl!—For so had Hester called her; not as a name expressive of her aspect, which had nothing of the calm, white, unimpassioned lustre that would be indicated by the comparison. But she named the infant "Pearl," as being of great price,—purchased with all she had,—her mother's only treasure! How strange, indeed! Man had marked this woman's sin by a scarlet letter, which had such potent and disastrous efficacy that no human sympathy could reach her, save it were sinful like herself. God, as a direct consequence of the sin which man thus punished, had given her a lovely child, whose place was on that same dishonored bosom, to connect her parent for ever with the race and descent of mortals, and to be finally a blessed soul in heaven! Yet these thoughts affected Hester Prynne less with hope than apprehension. She knew that her deed had been evil; she could have no faith, therefore, that its result would be good. Day after day, she looked fearfully into the child's expanding nature, ever dreading to detect some dark and wild peculiarity, that should correspond with the guiltiness to which she owed her being.

Certainly, there was no physical defect. By its perfect shape, its vigor, and its natural dexterity in the use of all its untried limbs, the infant was worthy to have been brought forth in Eden; worthy to have been left there, to be the plaything of the angels, after the world's first parents were driven out. The child had a native grace which does not invariably coexist with faultless beauty; its attire, however simple, always impressed the beholder as if it were the very garb that precisely became it best. But little Pearl was not clad in rustic weeds. Her mother, with a morbid purpose, that may be better understood hereafter, had bought the richest tissues that could be procured, and allowed her imaginative faculty its full play in the arrangement and decoration of the dresses which the child wore, before the public eye. So magnificent was the small figure, when thus arrayed, and such was the splendor of Pearl's own proper beauty, shining through the gorgeous robes which might have extinguished a paler loveliness, that there was an absolute circle of radiance around her, on the darksome cottage floor. And yet a russet gown, torn and soiled with the child's rude play, made a picture of her just as perfect. Pearl's aspect was imbued with a spell of infinite variety; in this one child there were many children, comprehending the full scope between the wild-flower prettiness of a peasant-baby, and the pomp, in little, of an infant princess. Throughout all, however, there was a trait of passion, a certain depth of hue, which she never lost; and if, in any of her changes, she had grown fainter or paler, she would have ceased to be herself,—it would have been no longer Pearl.

This outward mutability indicated, and did not more than fairly express, the various properties of her inner life. Her nature appeared to possess depth, too, as well as variety; but—or else Hester's fears deceived her—it lacked reference and adaptation to the world into which she was born. The child could not be made amenable to rules. In giving her existence, a great law had been broken; and the result was a being whose elements were perhaps beautiful and brilliant, but all in disorder; or with an order peculiar to themselves, amidst which the point of variety and arrangement was difficult or impossible to be discovered. Hester could only account for the child's character—and even then most vaguely and imperfectly—by recalling what she herself had been, during that momentous period while Pearl was imbibing her soul from the spiritual world, and her bodily frame from its material of earth. The mother's impassioned state had been the medium through which were transmitted to the unborn infant the rays of its moral life; and, however white and clear originally, they had taken the deep stains of crimson and gold, the fiery lustre, the black shadow, and the untempered light of the intervening substance. Above all, the warfare of Hester's spirit, at that epoch, was perpetuated in Pearl. She could recognize her wild, desperate, defiant mood, the flightiness of her temper, and even some of the very cloud-shapes of gloom and despondency that had brooded in her heart. They were now illuminated by the morning radiance of a young child's disposition, but later in the day of earthly existence might be prolific of the storm and whirlwind.

The discipline of the family, in those days, was of a far more rigid kind than now. The frown, the harsh rebuke, the frequent application of the rod, enjoined by Scriptural authority, were used, not merely in the way of punishment for actual offences, but as a wholesome regimen for the growth and promotion of all childish virtues. Hester Prynne, nevertheless, the lonely mother of this one child, ran little risk of erring on the side of undue severity. Mindful, however of her own errors and misfortunes, she early sought to impose a tender, but strict control over the infant immortality that was committed to her charge. But the task was beyond her skill. After testing both smiles and frowns, and proving that neither mode of treatment possessed any calculable influence, Hester was ultimately compelled to stand aside, and permit the child to be swayed by her own impulses. Physical compulsion or restraint was effectual, of course, while it lasted. As to any other kind of discipline, whether addressed to her mind or heart, little Pearl might or might not be within its reach, in accordance with the caprice that ruled the moment. Her mother, while Pearl was yet an infant, grew acquainted with a certain peculiar look, that warned her when it would be labor thrown away to insist, persuade, or plead. It was a look so intelligent, yet inexplicable, so perverse, sometimes so malicious, but generally accompanied by a wild flow of spirits, that Hester could not help questioning, at such moments, whether Pearl were a human child. She seemed rather an airy sprite, which, after playing its fantastic sports for a little while upon the cottage floor, would flit away with a mocking smile. Whenever that look appeared in her wild, bright, deeply-black eyes, it invested her with a strange remoteness and intangibility; it was as if she were hovering in the air and might vanish, like a glimmering light that comes we know not whence, and goes we know not whither. Beholding it, Hester was constrained to rush towards the child,—to pursue the little elf in the flight which she invariably began,—to snatch her to her bosom, with a close pressure and earnest kisses,—not so much from overflowing love, as to assure herself that Pearl was flesh and blood, and not utterly delusive. But Pearl's laugh, when she was caught, though full of merriment and music, made her mother more doubtful than before.

Heart-smitten at this bewildering and baffling spell, that so often came between herself and her sole treasure, whom she had bought so dear, and who was all her world, Hester sometimes burst into passionate tears. Then, perhaps,—for there was no foreseeing how it might affect her,— Pearl would frown, and clench her little fist, and harden her small features into a stern, unsympathizing look of discontent. Not seldom, she would laugh anew, and louder than before, like a thing incapable and unintelligent of human sorrow. Or—but this more rarely happened—she would be convulsed with a rage of grief, and sob out her love for her mother in broken words, and seem intent on proving that she had a heart, by breaking it. Yet Hester was hardly safe in confiding herself to that gusty tenderness; it passed as suddenly as it came. Brooding over all these matters, the mother felt like one who has evoked a spirit, but, by some irregularity in the process of conjuration, has failed to win the master-word that should control this new and incomprehensible intelligence. Her only real comfort was when the child lay in the placidity of sleep. Then she was sure of her, and tasted hours of quiet, delicious happiness; until—perhaps with that perverse expression glimmering from beneath her opening lids—little Pearl awoke!

How soon—with what strange rapidity, indeed!—did Pearl arrive at an age that was capable of social intercourse, beyond the mother's everready smile and nonsense-words! And then what a happiness would it have been could Hester Prynne have heard her clear, bird-like voice mingling with the uproar of other childish voices, and have distinguished and unravelled her own darling's tones, amid all the entangled outcry of a group of sportive children! But this could never be. Pearl was a born outcast of the infantile world. An imp of evil, emblem and product of sin, she had no right among christened infants. Nothing was more remarkable than the instinct, as it seemed, with which the child comprehended her loneliness; the destiny that had drawn an inviolable circle round about her; the whole peculiarity, in short, of her position in respect to other children. Never, since her release from prison, had Hester met the public gaze without her. In all her walks about the town, Pearl, too, was there; first as the babe in arms, and afterwards as the little girl, small companion of her mother, holding a forefinger with her whole grasp, and tripping along at the rate of three or four footsteps to one of Hester's. She saw the children of the settlement, on the grassy margin of the street, or at the domestic thresholds, disporting themselves in such grim fashion as the Puritanic nurture would permit; playing at going to church, perchance; or at scourging Quakers; or taking scalps in a sham-fight with the Indians; or scaring one another with freaks of imitative witchcraft. Pearl saw, and gazed intently, but never sought to make acquaintance. If spoken to, she would not speak again. If the children gathered about her, as they sometimes did, Pearl would grow positively terrible in her puny wrath, snatching up stones to fling at them, with shrill, incoherent exclamations, that made her mother tremble because they had so much the sound of a witch's anathemas in some unknown tongue.

The truth was, that the little Puritans, being of the most intolerant brood that ever lived, had got a vague idea of something outlandish, unearthly, or at variance with ordinary fashions, in the mother and child; and therefore scorned them in their hearts, and not unfrequently reviled them with their tongues. Pearl felt the sentiment, and requited it with the bitterest hatred that can be supposed to rankle in a childish bosom. These outbreaks of a fierce temper had a kind of value, and even comfort, for her mother; because there was at least an intelligible earnestness in the mood, instead of the fitful caprice that so often thwarted her in the child's manifestations. It appalled her, nevertheless, to discern here, again, a shadowy reflection of the evil that had existed in herself. All this enmity and passion had Pearl inherited, by inalienable right, out of Hester's heart. Mother and daughter stood together in the same circle of seclusion from human society; and in the nature of the child seemed to be perpetuated those unquiet elements that had distracted Hester Prynne before Pearl's birth, but had since begun to be soothed away by the softening influences of maternity.

At home, within and around her mother's cottage, Pearl wanted not a wide and various circle of acquaintance. The spell of life went forth from her ever-creative spirit, and communicated itself to a thousand objects, as a torch kindles a flame wherever it may be applied. The unlikeliest materials—a stick, a bunch of rags, a flower—were the puppets, of Pearl's witchcraft, and, without undergoing any outward change, became spiritually adapted to whatever drama occupied the stage of her inner world. Her one baby-voice served a multitude of imaginary personages, old and young, to talk withal. The pine-trees, aged, black, and solemn, and flinging groans and other melancholy utterances on the breeze, needed little transformation to figure as Puritan elders; the ugliest weeds of the garden were their children, whom Pearl smote down and uprooted, most unmercifully. It was wonderful, the vast variety of forms into which she threw her intellect, with no continuity, indeed, but darting up and dancing, always in a state of preternatural activity,—soon sinking down, as if exhausted by so rapid and feverish a tide of life,—and succeeded by other shapes of a similar wild energy. It was like nothing so much as the phantasmagoric play of the northern lights. In the mere exercise of the fancy, however, and the sportiveness of a growing mind, there might be little more than was observable in other children of bright faculties; except as Pearl, in the dearth of human playmates, was thrown more upon the visionary throng which she created. The singularity lay in the hostile feelings with which the child regarded all these offspring of her own heart and mind. She never created a friend, but seemed always to be sowing broadcast the dragon's teeth, whence sprung a harvest of armed enemies, against whom she rushed to battle. It was inexpressibly sad—then what depth of sorrow to a mother, who felt in her own heart the cause!—to observe, in one so young, this constant recognition of an adverse world, and so fierce a training of the energies that were to make good her cause in the contest that must ensue.

Gazing at Pearl, Hester Prynne often dropped her work upon her knees, and cried out with an agony which she would fain have hidden, but which made utterance for itself, betwixt speech and a groan,—"O Father in Heaven,—if Thou art still my Father,—what is this being which I have brought into the world!" And Pearl, overhearing the ejaculation, or aware, through some more subtile channel, of those throbs of anguish, would turn her vivid and beautiful little face upon her mother, smile with sprite-like intelligence, and resume her play.

One peculiarity of the child's deportment remains yet to be told. The very first thing which she had noticed in her life was—what?—not the mother's smile, responding to it, as other babies do, by that faint, embryo smile of the little mouth, remembered so doubtfully afterwards, and with such fond discussion whether it were indeed a smile. By no means! But that first object of which Pearl seemed to become aware was—shall we say it?—the scarlet letter on Hester's bosom! One day, as her mother stooped over the cradle, the infant's eyes had been caught by the glimmering of the gold embroidery about the letter; and, putting up her little hand, she grasped at it, smiling not doubtfully, but with a decided gleam, that gave her face the look of a much older child. Then, gasping for breath, did Hester Prynne clutch the fatal token, instinctively endeavoring to tear it away; so infinite was the torture inflicted by the intelligent touch of Pearl's baby-hand. Again, as if her mother's agonized gesture were meant only to make sport for her, did little Pearl look into her eyes, and smile! From that epoch, except when the child was asleep, Hester had never felt a moment's safety; not a moment's calm enjoyment of her. Weeks, it is true, would sometimes elapse, during which Pearl's gaze might never once be fixed upon the scarlet letter; but then, again, it would come at unawares, like the stroke of sudden death, and always with that peculiar smile, and odd expression of the eyes.

Once, this freakish, elfish cast came into the child's eyes, while Hester was looking at her own image in them, as mothers are fond of doing; and, suddenly,—for women in solitude, and with troubled hearts, are pestered with unaccountable delusions,—she fancied that she beheld, not her own miniature portrait, but another face, in the small black mirror of Pearl's eye. It was a face, fiend-like, full of smiling malice, yet bearing the semblance of features that she had known full well, though seldom with a smile, and never with malice in them. It was as if an evil spirit possessed the child, and had just then peeped forth in mockery. Many a time afterwards had Hester been tortured, though less vividly, by the same illusion.

In the afternoon of a certain summer's day, after Pearl grew big enough to run about, she amused herself with gathering handfuls of wildflowers, and flinging them, one by one, at her mother's bosom; dancing up and down, like a little elf, whenever she hit the scarlet letter. Hester's first motion had been to cover her bosom with her clasped hands. But, whether from pride or resignation, or a feeling that her penance might best be wrought out by this unutterable pain, she resisted the impulse, and sat erect, pale as death, looking sadly into little Pearl's wild eyes. Still came the battery of flowers, almost invariably hitting the mark, and covering the mother's breast with hurts for which she could find no balm in this world, nor knew how to seek it in another. At last, her shot being all expended, the child stood still and gazed at Hester, with that little, laughing image of a fiend peeping out—or, whether it peeped or no, her mother so imagined it—from the unsearchable abyss of her black eyes.

"Child, what art thou?" cried the mother.

"Oh, I am your little Pearl!" answered the child.

But, while she said it, Pearl laughed, and began to dance up and down, with the humorsome gesticulation of a little imp, whose next freak might be to fly up the chimney.

"Art thou my child, in very truth?" asked Hester.

Nor did she put the question altogether idly, but, for the moment, with a portion of genuine earnestness; for, such was Pearl's wonderful intelligence, that her mother half doubted whether she were not acquainted with the secret spell of her existence, and might not now reveal herself.

"Yes; I am little Pearl!" repeated the child, continuing her antics.

"Thou art not my child! Thou art no Pearl of mine!" said the mother, half playfully; for it was often the case that a sportive impulse came over her, in the midst of her deepest suffering. "Tell me, then, what thou art, and who sent thee hither."

"Tell me, mother!" said the child, seriously, coming up to Hester, and pressing herself close to her knees. "Do thou tell me!"

"Thy Heavenly Father sent thee!" answered Hester Prynne.

But she said it with a hesitation that did not escape the acuteness of the child. Whether moved only by her ordinary freakishness, or because an evil spirit prompted her, she put up her small forefinger, and touched the scarlet letter.

"He did not send me!" cried she, positively. "I have no Heavenly Father!"

"Hush, Pearl, hush! Thou must not talk so!" answered the mother, suppressing a groan. "He sent us all into this world. He sent even me, thy mother. Then, much more, thee! Or, if not, thou strange and elfish child, whence didst thou come?"

"Tell me! Tell me!" repeated Pearl, no longer seriously, but laughing, and capering about the floor. "It is thou that must tell me!"

But Hester could not resolve the query, being herself in a dismal labyrinth of doubt. She remembered—betwixt a smile and a shudder—the talk of the neighboring townspeople; who, seeking vainly elsewhere for the child's paternity, and observing some of her odd attributes, had given out that poor little Pearl was a demon offspring; such as, ever since old Catholic times, had occasionally been seen on earth, through the agency of their mother's sin, and to promote some foul and wicked purpose. Luther, according to the scandal of his monkish enemies, was a brat of that hellish breed; nor was Pearl the only child to whom this inauspicious origin was assigned, among the New England Puritans.

## VII

### The Governor's Hall

HESTER PRYNNE went, one day, to the mansion of Governor Bellingham, with a pair of gloves, which she had fringed and embroidered to his order, and which were to be worn on some great occasion of state; for, though the chances of a popular election had caused this former ruler to descend a step or two from the highest rank, he still held an honorable and influential place among the colonial magistracy.

Another and far more important reason than the delivery of a pair of embroidered gloves impelled Hester, at this time, to seek an interview with a personage of so much power and activity in the affairs of the settlement. It had reached her ears, that there was a design on the part of some of the leading inhabitants, cherishing the more rigid order of principles in religion and government, to deprive her of her child. On the supposition that Pearl, as already hinted, was of demon origin, these good people not unreasonably argued that a Christian interest in the mother's soul required them to remove such a stumbling-block from her path. If the child, on the other hand, were really capable of moral and religious growth, and possessed the elements of ultimate salvation, then, surely, it would enjoy all the fairer prospect of these advantages by being transferred to wiser and better guardianship than Hester Prynne's. Among those who promoted the design, Governor Bellingham was said to be one of the most busy. It may appear singular, and indeed not a little ludicrous, that an affair of this kind, which, in later days, would have been referred to no higher jurisdiction than that of the selectmen of the town, should then have been a question publicly discussed, and on which statesmen of eminence took sides. At that epoch of pristine simplicity, however, matters of even slighter public interest, and of far less intrinsic weight, than the welfare of Hester and her child, were strangely mixed up with the deliberations of legislators and acts of state. The period was hardly, if at all, earlier than that of our story, when a dispute concerning the right of property in a pig not only caused a fierce and bitter contest in the legislative body of the colony, but resulted in an important modification of the framework itself of the legislature.

Full of concern, therefore,—but so conscious of her own right that it seemed scarcely an unequal match between the public, on the one side, and a lonely woman, backed by the sympathies of nature, on the other,— Hester Prynne set forth from her solitary cottage. Little Pearl, of course, was her companion. She was now of an age to run lightly along by her mother's side, and, constantly in motion, from morn till sunset, could have accomplished a much longer journey than that before her. Often, nevertheless, more from caprice than necessity, she demanded to be taken up in arms; but was soon as imperious to be set down again, and frisked onward before Hester on the grassy pathway, with many a harmless trip and tumble. We have spoken of Pearl's rich and luxuriant beauty; a beauty that shone with deep and vivid tints; a bright complexion, eyes possessing intensity both of depth and glow, and hair already of a deep, glossy brown, and which, in after years, would be nearly akin to black. There was fire in her and throughout her; she seemed the unpremeditated offshoot of a passionate moment. Her mother, in contriving the child's garb, had allowed the gorgeous tendencies of her imagination their full play; arraying her in a crimson velvet tunic, of a peculiar cut, abundantly embroidered with fantasies and flourishes of gold-thread. So much strength of coloring, which must have given a wan and pallid aspect to cheeks of a fainter bloom, was admirably adapted to Pearl's beauty, and made her the very brightest little jet of flame that ever danced upon the earth.

But it was a remarkable attribute of this garb, and, indeed, of the child's whole appearance, that it irresistibly and inevitably reminded the •beholder of the token which Hester Prynne was doomed to wear upon her bosom. It was the scarlet letter in another form; the scarlet letter endowed with life! The mother herself—as if the red ignominy were so deeply scorched into her brain that all her conceptions assumed its form

—had carefully wrought out the similitude; lavishing many hours of morbid ingenuity, to create an analogy between the object of her affection and the emblem of her guilt and torture. But, in truth, Pearl was the one, as well as the other; and only in consequence of that identity had Hester contrived so perfectly to represent the scarlet letter in her appearance.

As the two wayfarers came within the precincts of the town, the children of the Puritans looked up from their play,—or what passed for play with those sombre little urchins,—and spake gravely one to another:—

"Behold, verily, there is the woman of the scarlet letter; and, of a truth, moreover, there is the likeness of the scarlet letter running along by her side! Come, therefore, and let us fling mud at them!"

But Pearl, who was a dauntless child, after frowning, stamping her foot, and shaking her little hand with a variety of threatening gestures, suddenly made a rush at the knot of her enemies, and put them all to flight. She resembled, in her fierce pursuit of them, an infant pestilence,— the scarlet fever, or some such half-fledged angel of judgment,—whose mission was to punish the sins of the rising generation. She screamed and shouted, too, with a terrific volume of sound, which, doubtless, caused the hearts of the fugitives to quake within them. The victory accomplished, Pearl returned quietly to her mother, and looked up, smiling, into her face.

Without further adventure, they reached the dwelling of Governor Bellingham. This was a large wooden house, built in a fashion of which there are specimens still extant in the streets of our older towns; now moss-grown, crumbling to decay, and melancholy at heart with the many sorrowful or joyful occurrences, remembered or forgotten, that have happened, and passed away, within their dusky chambers. Then, however, there was the freshness of the passing year on its exterior, and the cheerfulness, gleaming forth from the sunny windows, of a human habitation, into which death had never entered. It had, indeed, a very cheery aspect; the walls being overspread with a kind of stucco, in which fragments of broken glass were plentifully intermixed; so that, when the sunshine fell aslant-wise over the front of the edifice, it glittered and sparkled as if diamonds had been flung against it by the double handful. The brilliancy might have befitted Aladdin's palace, rather than the mansion of a grave old Puritan ruler. It was further decorated with strange and seemingly cabalistic figures and diagrams, suitable to the quaint taste of the age, which had been drawn in the stucco when newly laid on, and had now grown hard and durable, for the admiration of after times.

Pearl, looking at this bright wonder of a house, began to caper and dance, and imperatively required that the whole breadth of sunshine should be stripped off its front, and given her to play with.

"No, my little Pearl!" said her mother. "Thou must gather thine own sunshine. I have none to give thee!"

They approached the door; which was of an arched form, and flanked on each side by a narrow tower or projection of the edifice, in both of which were lattice-windows, with wooden shutters to close over them at need. Lifting the iron hammer that hung at the portal, Hester Prynne gave a summons, which was answered by one of the Governor's bond-servants; a free-born Englishman, but now a seven years' slave. During that term he was to be the property of his master, and as much a commodity of bargain and sale as an ox, or a joint-stool. The serf wore the blue coat, which was the customary garb of serving-men of that period, and long before, in the old hereditary halls of England.

"Is the worshipful Governor Bellingham within?" inquired Hester.

"Yea, forsooth," replied the bond-servant, staring with wide-open eyes at the scarlet letter, which, being a new-comer in the country, he had never before seen. "Yea, his honorable worship is within. But he hath a godly minister or two with him, and likewise a leech. Ye may not see his worship now."

"Nevertheless, I will enter," replied Hester Prynne, and the bond-servant, perhaps judging from the decision of her air, and the glittering symbol in her bosom, that she was a great lady in the land, offered no opposition.

So the mother and little Pearl were admitted into the hall of entrance. With many variations, suggested by the nature of his building-materials, diversity of climate, and a different mode of social life, Governor Bellingham had planned his new habitation after the residences of gentlemen of fair estate in his native land. Here, then, was a wide and reasonably lofty hall, extending through the whole depth of the house, and forming a medium of general communication, more or less directly, with all the other apartments. At one extremity, this spacious room was lighted by the windows of the two towers, which formed a small recess on either side of the portal. At the other end, though partly muffled by a curtain, it was more powerfully illuminated by one of those embowed hall-windows which we read of in old books, and which was provided with a deep and cushioned seat. Here, on the cushion, lay a folio tome, probably of the Chronicles of England, or other such substantial literature; even as, in our own days, we scatter gilded volumes on the centre-table, to be turned over by the casual guest. The furniture of the hall consisted of some ponderous chairs, the backs of which were elaborately carved with wreaths of oaken flowers; and likewise a table in the same taste; the whole being of the Elizabethan age, or perhaps earlier, and heirlooms, transferred hither from the Governor's paternal home. On the table—in token that the sentiment of old English hospitality had not been left behind—stood a large pewter tankard, at the bottom of which, had Hester or Pearl peeped into it, they might have seen the frothy remnant of a recent draught of ale.

On the wall hung a row of portraits, representing the forefathers of the Bellingham lineage, some with armor on their breasts, and others with stately ruffs and robes of peace. All were characterized by the sternness and severity which old portraits so invariably put on; as if they were the ghosts, rather than the pictures, of departed worthies, and were gazing with harsh and intolerant criticism at the pursuits and enjoyments of living men.

At about the centre of the oaken panels, that lined the hall, was suspended a suit of mail, not, like the pictures, an ancestral relic, but of the most modern date; for it had been manufactured by a skilful armorer in London, the same year in which Governor Bellingham came over to New England. There was a steel headpiece, a cuirass, a gorget, and greaves, with a pair of gauntlets and a sword hanging beneath; all, and especially the helmet and breastplate, so highly burnished as to glow with white radiance, and scatter an illumination everywhere about upon the floor. This bright panoply was not meant for mere idle show, but had been worn by the Governor on many a solemn muster and training field, and had glittered, moreover, at the head of a regiment in the Pequod war. For, though bred a lawyer, and accustomed to speak of Bacon, Coke, Noye, and Finch as his professional associates, the exigencies of this new country had transformed Governor Bellingham into a soldier as well as a statesman and ruler.

Little Pearl—who was as greatly pleased with the gleaming armor as she had been with the glittering frontispiece of the house—spent some time looking into the polished mirror of the breastplate.

"Mother," cried she, "I see you here. Look! Look!"

Hester looked, by way of humoring the child; and she saw that, owing to the peculiar effect of this convex mirror, the scarlet letter was represented in exaggerated and gigantic proportions, so as to be greatly the most prominent feature of her appearance. In truth, she seemed absolutely hidden behind it. Pearl pointed upward, also, at a similar picture in the headpiece; smiling at her mother, with the elfish intelligence that was so familiar an expression on her small physiognomy. That look of naughty merriment was likewise reflected in the mirror, with so much breadth and intensity of effect, that it made Hester Prynne feel as if it could not be the image of her own child, but of an imp who was seeking to mould itself into Pearl's shape.

"Come along, Pearl," said she, drawing her away. "Come and look into this fair garden. It may be we shall see flowers there; more beautiful ones than we find in the woods."

Pearl, accordingly, ran to the bow-window, at the farther end of the hall, and looked along the vista of a garden-walk, carpeted with closely shaven grass, and bordered with some rude and immature attempt at shrubbery. But the proprietor appeared already to have relinquished, as hopeless, the effort to perpetuate on this side of the Atlantic, in a hard soil and amid the close struggle for subsistence, the native English taste for ornamental gardening. Cabbages grew in plain sight; and a pumpkin-vine, rooted at some distance, had run across the intervening space, and deposited one of its gigantic products directly beneath the hall-window; as if to warn the Governor that this great lump of vegetable gold was as rich an ornament as New England earth would offer him. There were a few rose-bushes, however, and a number of apple-trees, probably the descendants of those planted by the Reverend Mr. Blackstone, the first settler of the peninsula; that half-mythological personage, who rides through our early annals, seated on the back of a bull.

Pearl, seeing the rose-bushes, began to cry for a red rose, and would not be pacified.

"Hush, child, hush!" said her mother, earnestly. "Do not cry, dear little Pearl! I hear voices in the garden. The Governor is coming, and gentlemen along with him!"

In fact, adown the vista of the garden avenue a number of persons were seen approaching towards the house. Pearl, in utter scorn of her mother's attempt to quiet her, gave an eldritch scream, and then became silent; not from any notion of obedience, but because the quick and mobile curiosity of her disposition was excited by the appearance of these new personages.

## VIII

### THE ELF-CHILD AND THE MINISTER

GOVERNOR BELLINGHAM, in a loose gown and easy cap,—such as elderly gentlemen loved to endue themselves with, in their domestic privacy,— walked foremost, and appeared to be showing off his estate, and expatiating on his projected improvements. The wide circumference of an elaborate ruff, beneath his gray beard, in the antiquated fashion of King James's reign, caused his head to look not a little like that of John the Baptist in a charger. The impression made by his aspect, so rigid and severe, and frost-bitten with more than autumnal age, was hardly in keeping with the appliances of worldly enjoyment wherewith he had evidently done his utmost to surround himself. But it is an error to suppose that our grave forefathers—though accustomed to speak and think of human existence as a state merely of trial and warfare, and though unfeignedly prepared to sacrifice goods and life at the behest of duty—made it a matter of conscience to reject such means of comfort, or even luxury, as lay fairly within their grasp. This creed was never taught, for instance, by the venerable pastor, John Wilson, whose beard, white as a snow-drift, was seen over Governor Bellingham's shoulder; while its wearer suggested that pears and peaches might yet be naturalized in the New England climate, and that purple grapes might possibly be compelled to flourish, against the sunny garden-wall. The old clergyman, nurtured at the rich bosom of the English Church, had a long-established and legitimate taste for all good and comfortable things; and however stern he might show himself in the pulpit, or in his public reproof of such transgressions as that of Hester Prynne, still, the genial benevolence of his private life had won him warmer affection than was accorded to any of his professional contemporaries.

Behind the Governor and Mr. Wilson came two other guests: one the Reverend Arthur Dimmesdale, whom the reader may remember as having taken a brief and reluctant part in the scene of Hester Prynne's disgrace; and, in close companionship with him, old Roger Chillingworth, a person of great skill in physic, who, for two or three years past, had been settled in the town. It was understood that this learned man was the physician as well as friend of the young minister, whose health had severely suffered, of late, by his too unreserved self-sacrifice to the labors and duties of the pastoral relation.

The Governor, in advance of his visitors, ascended one or two steps, and, throwing open the leaves of the great hall-window, found himself close to little Pearl. The shadow of the curtain fell on Hester Prynne, and partially concealed her.

"What have we here?" said Governor Bellingham, looking with surprise at the scarlet little figure before him. "I profess, I have never seen the like, since my days of vanity, in old King James's time, when I was wont to esteem it a high favor to be admitted to a court mask! There used to be a swarm of these small apparitions, in holiday time; and we called them children of the Lord of Misrule. But how gat such a guest into my hall?"

"Ay, indeed!" cried good old Mr. Wilson. "What little bird of scarlet plumage may this be? Methinks I have seen just such figures, when the sun has been shining through a richly painted window, and tracing out the golden and crimson images across the floor. But that was in the old land. Prithee, young one, who art thou, and what has ailed thy mother to bedizen thee in this strange fashion? Art thou a Christian child,—ha? Dost know thy catechism? Or art thou one of those naughty elfs or fairies, whom we thought to have left behind us, with other relics of Papistry, in merry old England?"

"I am mother's child," answered the scarlet vision, "and my name is Pearl!"

"Pearl?—Ruby, rather!—or Coral!—or Red Rose, at the very least, judging from thy hue!" responded the old minister, putting forth his hand in a vain attempt to pat little Pearl on the cheek. "But where is this mother of thine? Ah! I see," he added; and, turning to Governor Bellingham, whispered, "This is the salfsame child of whom we have held speech together; and behold here the unhappy woman, Hester Prynne, her mother!"

"Sayest thou so?" cried the Governor. "Nay, we might have judged that such a child's mother must needs be a scarlet woman, and a worthy type of her of Babylon! But she comes at a good time; and we will look 'nto this matter forthwith."

Governor Bellingham stepped through the window into the hall, followed by his three guests.

"Hester Prynne," said he, fixing his naturally stern regard on the wearer of the scarlet letter, "there hath been much question concerning thee, of late. The point hath been weightily discussed, whether we, that are of authority and influence, do well discharge our consciences by trusting an immortal soul, such as there is in yonder child, to the guidance of one who hath stumbled and fallen, amid the pitfalls of this world. Speak thou, the child's own mother! Were it not, thinkest thou, for thy little one's temporal and eternal welfare that she be taken out of thy charge, and clad soberly, and disciplined strictly, and instructed in the truths of heaven and earth? What canst thou do for the child, in this kind?"

"I can teach my little Pearl what I have learned from this!" answered Hester Prynne, laying her finger on the red token.

"Woman, it is thy badge of shame!" replied the stern magistrate. "It is because of the stain which that letter indicates, that we would transfer thy child to other hands."

"Nevertheless," said the mother, calmly, though growing more pale, "this badge hath taught me—it daily teaches me—it is teaching me at this moment—lessons whereof my child may be the wiser and better, albeit they can profit nothing to myself."

"We will judge warily," said Bellingham, "and look well what we are about to do. Good Master Wilson, I pray you, examine this Pearl—since that is her name,—and see whether she hath had such Christian nurture as befits a child of her age."

The old minister seated himself in an arm-chair, and made an effort to draw Pearl betwixt his knees. But the child, unaccustomed to the touch of familiarity of any but her mother, escaped through the open window, and stood on the upper step looking like a wild tropical bird, of rich plumage, ready to take flight into the upper air. Mr. Wilson, not a little astonished at this outbreak,—for he was a grandfatherly sort of personage, and usually a vast favorite with children,—essayed, however, to proceed with the examination.

"Pearl," said he, with great solemnity, "thou must take heed to instruction, that so, in due season, thou mayest wear in thy bosom the pearl of great price. Canst thou tell me, my child, who made thee?"

Now Pearl knew well enough who made her; for Hester Prynne, the daughter of a pious home, very soon after her talk with the child about her Heavenly Father, had begun to inform her of those truths which the human spirit, at whatever stage of immaturity, imbibes with such eager interest. Pearl, therefore, so large were the attainments of her three years' lifetime, could have borne a fair examination in the New England Primer, or the first column of the Westminster Catechisms, although unacquainted with the outward form of either of those celebrated works. But that perversity which all children have more or less of, and of which little Pearl had a tenfold portion, now, at the most inopportune moment, took thorough possession of her, and closed her lips, or impelled her to speak words amiss. After putting her finger in her mouth, with many ungracious refusals to answer good Mr. Wilson's questions, the child finally announced that she had not been made at all, but had been plucked by her mother off the bush of wild roses that grew by the prison-door.

This fantasy was probably suggested by the near proximity of the Governor's red roses, as Pearl stood outside of the window; together with her recollection of the prison rose-bush, which she had passed in coming hither.

Old Roger Chillingworth, with a smile on his face, whispered something in the young clergyman's ear. Hester Prynne looked at the man of skill, and even then, with her fate hanging in the balance, was startled to perceive what a change had come over his features,—how much uglier they were,—how his dark complexion seemed to have grown duskier, and his figure more misshapen,—since the days when she had familiarly known him. She met his eyes for an instant, but was immediately constrained to give all her attention to the scene now going forward.

"This is awful!" cried the Governor, slowly recovering from the astonishment into which Pearl's response had thrown him. "Here is a child of three years old, and she cannot tell who made her! Without question, she is equally in the dark as to her soul, its present depravity, and future destiny! Methinks, gentlemen, we need inquire no further."

Hester caught hold of Pearl, and drew her forcibly into her arms, confronting the old Puritan magistrate with almost a fierce expression. Alone in the world, cast off by it, and with this sole treasure to keep her heart alive, she felt that she possessed indefeasible rights against the world, and was ready to defend them to the death.

"God gave me the child!" cried she. "He gave her in requital of all things else, which ye had taken from me. She is my happiness!—she is my torture, none the less! Pearl keeps me here in life! Pearl punishes me too! See ye not, she is the scarlet letter, only capable of being loved, and so endowed with a million-fold the power of retribution for my sin? Ye shall not take her! I will die first!"

"My poor woman," said the not unkind old minister, "the child shall be well cared for!—far better than thou canst do it."

"God gave her into my keeping," repeated Hester Prynne, raising her voice almost to a shriek. "I will not give her up!"—And here, by a sudden impulse, she turned to the young clergyman, Mr. Dimmesdale, at whom, up to this moment, she had seemed hardly so much as once to direct her eyes.—"Speak thou for me!" cried she. "Thou wast my pastor, and hadst charge of my soul, and knowest me better than these men can. I will not lose the child! Speak for me! Thou knowest,—for thou hast sympathies which these men lack!—thou knowest what is in my heart, and what are a mother's rights, and how much the stronger they are, when that mother has but her child and the scarlet letter! Look thou to it! I will not lose the child! Look to it!"

At this wild and singular appeal, which indicated that Hester Prynne's situation had provoked her to little less than madness, the young minister at once came forward, pale, and holding his hand over his heart, as was his custom whenever his peculiarly nervous temperament was thrown into agitation. He looked now more careworn and emaciated than as we described him at the scene of Hester's public ignominy; and whether it were his failing health, or whatever the cause might be, his large dark eyes had a world of pain in their troubled and melancholy depth.

"There is truth in what she says," began the minister, with a voice sweet, tremulous, but powerful, insomuch that the hall reëchoed, and the hollow armor rang with it,—"truth in what Hester says, and in the feeling which inspires her! God gave her the child, and gave her, too, an instinctive knowledge of its nature and requirements,—both seemingly so peculiar,—which no other mortal being can possess. And, moreover, is there not a quality of awful sacredness in the relation between this mother and this child?"

"Ay!—how is that, good Master Dimmesdale?" interrupted the Governor. "Make that plain, I pray you!"

"It must be even so," resumed the minister. "For, if we deem it otherwise, do we not thereby say that the Heavenly Father, the Creator of all flesh, hath lightly recognized a deed of sin, and made of no account the distinction between unhallowed lust and holy love? This child of its father's guilt and its mother's shame hath come from the hand of God, to work in many ways upon her heart, who pleads so earnestly, and with such bitterness of spirit, the right to keep her. It was meant for a blessing, for the one blessing of her life! It was meant, doubtless, as the mother herself hath told us, for a retribution too; a torture to be felt at many an unthought-of moment; a pang, a sting, an ever-recurring agony, in the midst of a troubled joy! Hath she not expressed this thought in the garb of the poor child, so forcibly reminding us of that red symbol which sears her bosom?"

"Well said, again!" cried good Mr. Wilson. "I feared the woman had no better thought than to make a mountebank of her child!"

"Oh, not so!—not so!" continued Mr. Dimmesdale. "She recognizes, believe me, the solemn miracle which God hath wrought, in the existence of that child. And may she feel, too,—what, methinks, is the very truth, —that this boon was meant, above all things else, to keep the mother's soul alive, and to preserve her from blacker depths of sin into which Satan might else have sought to plunge her! Therefore it is good for this poor, sinful woman that she hath an infant immortality, a being capable of eternal joy or sorrow, confided to her care,—to be trained up by her to righteousness,—to remind her, at every moment, of her fall,—but yet to teach her, as it were by the Creator's sacred pledge, that, if she bring the child to heaven, the child also will bring its parent thither! Herein is the sinful mother happier than the sinful father. For Hester Prynne's sake, then, and no less for the poor child's sake, let us leave them as Providence hath seen fit to place them!"

"You speak, my friend, with a strange earnestness," said old Roger Chillingworth, smiling at him.

"And there is a weighty import in what my young brother hath spoken," added the Reverend Mr. Wilson. "What say you, worshipful Master Bellingham? Hath he not pleaded well for the poor woman?"

"Indeed hath he," answered the magistrate, "and hath adduced such arguments, that we will even leave the matter as it now stands; so long, at least, as there shall be no further scandal in the woman. Care must be had, nevertheless, to put the child to due and stated examination in the catechism, at thy hands or Master Dimmesdale's. Moreover, at a proper season, the tithing-men must take heed that she go both to school and to meeting."

The young minister, on ceasing to speak, had withdrawn a few steps from the group, and stood with his face partially concealed in the heavy folds of the window-curtains; while the shadow of his figure, which the sunlight cast upon the floor, was tremulous with the vehemence of his appeal. Pearl, that wild and flighty little elf, stole softly towards him, and taking his hand in the grasp of both her own, laid her cheek against it; a caress so tender, and withal so unobtrusive, that her mother, who was looking on, asked herself,—"Is that my Pearl?" Yet she knew that there was love in the child's heart, although it mostly revealed itself in passion, and hardly twice in her lifetime had been softened by such gentleness as now. The minister,—for, save the long-sought regards of woman, nothing is sweeter than these marks of childish preference, accorded spontaneously by a spiritual instinct, and therefore seeming to imply in us something truly worthy to be loved,—the minister looked round, laid his hand on the child's head, hesitated an instant, and then kissed her brow. Little Pearl's unwonted mood of sentiment lasted no longer; she laughed, and went capering down the hall, so airily, that old Mr. Wilson raised a question whether even her tiptoes touched the floor.

"The little baggage hath witchcraft in her, I profess," said he to Mr. Dimmesdale. "She needs no old woman's broomstick to fly withal!"

"A strange child!" remarked old Roger Chillingworth. "It is easy to see the mother's part in her. Would it be beyond a philosopher's research, think ye, gentlemen, to analyze that child's nature, and, from its make and mould, to give a shrewd guess at the father?"

"Nay; it would be sinful, in such a question, to follow the clew of profane philosophy," said Mr. Wilson. "Better to fast and pray upon it; and still better, it may be, to leave the mystery as we find it, unless Providence reveal it of its own accord. Thereby, every good Christian man hath a title to show a father's kindness towards the poor, deserted babe."

The affair being so satisfactorily concluded, Hester Prynne, with Pearl, departed from the house. As they descended the steps, it is averred that the lattice of a chamber-window was thrown open, and forth into the sunny day was trust the face of Mistress Hibbins, Governor Bellingham's bitter-tempered sister, and the same who, a few years later, was executed as a witch.

"Hist, hist!" said she, while her ill-omened physiognomy seemed to cast a shadow over the cheerful newness of the house. "Wilt thou go with us to-night? There will be a merry company in the forest; and I wellnigh promised the Black Man that comely Hester Prynne should make one."

"Make my excuse to him, so please you!" answered Hester, with a triumphant smile. "I must tarry at home, and keep watch over my little Pearl. Had they taken her from me, I would willingly have gone with thee into the forest, and signed my name in the Black Man's book too, and that with mine own blood!"

"We shall have thee there anon!" said the witchlady, frowning, as she drew back her head.

But here—if we suppose this interview betwixt Mistress Hibbins and Hester Prynne to be authentic, and not a parable—was already an illustration of the young minister's argument against sundering the relation of a fallen mother to the offspring of her frailty. Even thus early had the child saved her from Satan's snare.

## IX

### THE LEECH

UNDER the appellation of Roger Chillingworth, the reader will remember, was hidden another name, which its former wearer had resolved should never more be spoken. It has been related how, in the crowd that witnessed Hester Prynne's ignominious exposure, stood a man, elderly, travel-worn, who, just emerging from the perilous wilderness, beheld the woman, in whom he hoped to find embodied the warmth and cheerfulness of home, set up as a type of sin before the people. Her matronly fame was trodden under all men's feet. Infamy was babbling around her in the public market-place. For her kindred, should the tidings ever reach them, and for the companions of her unspotted life, there remained nothing but the contagion of her dishonor,—which would not fail to be distributed in strict accordance and proportion with the intimacy and sacredness of their previous relationship. Then why—since the choice was with himself —should the individual, whose connection with the fallen woman had been the most intimate and sacred of them all, come forward to vindicate his claim to an inheritance so little desirable? He resolved not to be pilloried beside her on her pedestal of shame. Unknown to all but Hester Prynne, and possessing the lock and key of her silence, he chose to withdraw his name from the roll of mankind, and, as regarded his former ties and interests, to vanish out of life as completely as if he indeed lay at the bottom of the ocean, whither rumor had long ago consigned him. This purpose once effected, new interests would immediately spring up, and likewise a new purpose; dark, it is true, if not guilty, but of force enough to engage the full strength of his faculties.

In pursuance of this resolve, he took up his residence in the Puritan town, as Roger Chillingworth, without other introduction than the learning and intelligence of which he possessed more than a common measure. As his studies, at a previous period of his life, had made him extensively acquainted with the medical science of the day, it was as a physician that he presented himself, and as such was cordially received. Skilful men, of the medical and chirurgical profession, were of rare occurrence in the colony. They seldom, it would appear, partook of the religious zeal that brought other emigrants across the Atlantic. In their researches into the human frame, it may be that the higher and more subtile faculties of such men were materialized, and that they lost the spiritual view of existence amid the intricacies of that wondrous mechanism, which seemed to involve art enough to comprise all of life within itself. At all events, the health of the good town of Boston, so far as medicine had aught to do with it, had hitherto lain in the guardianship of an aged deacon and apothecary, whose piety and godly deportment were stronger testimonials in his favor than any that he could have produced in the shape of a diploma. The only surgeon was one who combined the occasional exercise of that noble art with the daily and habitual flourish of a razor. To such a professional body Roger Chillingworth was a brilliant acquisition. He soon manifested his familiarity with the ponderous and imposing machinery of antique physic; in which every remedy contained a multitude of far-fetched and heterogeneous ingredients, as elaborately compounded as if the proposed result had been the Elixir of Life. In his Indian captivity, moreover, he had gained much knowledge of the properties of native herbs and roots; nor did he conceal from his patients, that these simple medicines, Nature's boon to the untutored savage, had quite as large a share of his own confidence as the European pharmacopœia, which so many learned doctors had spent centuries in elaborating.

This learned stranger was exemplary, as regarded, at least, the outward forms of a religious life, and, early after his arrival, had chosen for his spiritual guide the Reverend Mr. Dimmesdale. The young divine, whose scholar-like renown still lived in Oxford, was considered by his more fervent admirers as little less than a heaven-ordained apostle, destined, should he live and labor for the ordinary term of life, to do as great deeds for the now feeble New England Church as the early Fathers had achieved for the infancy of the Christian faith. About this period, however, the health of Mr. Dimmesdale had evidently begun to fail. By those best acquainted with his habits, the paleness of the young minister's cheek was accounted for by his too earnest devotion to study, his scrupulous fulfilment of parochial duty, and, more than all, by the fasts and vigils of which he made a frequent practice, in order to keep the grossness of this earthly state from clogging and obscuring his spiritual lamp. Some declared, that, if Mr. Dimmesdale were really going to die, it was cause enough, that the world was not worthy to be any longer trodden by his feet. He himself, on the other hand, with characteristic humility, avowed his belief, that, if Providence should see fit to remove him, it would be because of his own unworthiness to perform its humblest mission here on earth. With all this difference of opinion as to the cause of his decline, there could be no question of the fact. His form grew emaciated; his voice, though still rich and sweet, had a certain melancholy prophecy of decay in it; he was often observed, on any slight alarm or other sudden accident, to put his hand over his heart, with first a flush and then a paleness, indicative of pain.

Such was the young clergyman's condition, and so imminent the prospect that his dawning light would be extinguished, all untimely, when Roger Chillingworth made his advent to the town. His first entry on the scene, few people could tell whence, dropping down, as it were, out of the sky, or starting from the nether earth, had an aspect of mystery, which was easily heightened to the miraculous. He was now known to be a man of skill; it was observed that he gathered herbs, and the blossoms of wildflowers, and dug up roots, and plucked off twigs from the forest-trees, like one acquainted with hidden virtues in what was valueless to common eyes. He was heard to speak of Sir Kenelm Digby, and other famous men, —whose scientific attainments were esteemed hardly less than supernatural,—as having been his correspondents or associates. Why, with such rank in the learned world, had he come hither? What could he, whose sphere was in great cities, be seeking in the wilderness? In answer to this query, a rumor gained ground,—and, however absurd, was entertained by some very sensible people,—that Heaven had wrought an absolute miracle, by transporting an eminent Doctor of Physic, from a German university, bodily through the air, and setting him down at the door of Mr. Dimmesdale's study! Individuals of wiser faith, indeed, who knew that Heaven promotes its purposes without aiming at the stage-effect of what is called miraculous interposition, were inclined to see a providential hand in Roger Chillingworth's so opportune arrival.

The idea was countenanced by the strong interest which the physician ever manifested in the young clergyman; he attached himself to him as a parishioner, and sought to win a friendly regard and confidence from his naturally reserved sensibility. He expressed great alarm at his pastor's state of health, but was anxious to attempt the cure, and, if early undertaken, seemed not despondent of a favorable result. The elders, the deacons, the motherly dames, and the young and fair maidens, of Mr. Dimmesdale's flock, were alike importunate that he should make trial of the physician's frankly offered skill. Mr. Dimmesdale gently repelled their entreaties.

"I need no medicine," said he.

But how could the young minister say so, when, with every successive Sabbath, his cheek was paler and thinner, and his voice more tremulous than before,—when it had now become a constant habit, rather than a casual gesture, to press his hand over his heart? Was he weary of his labors? Did he wish to die? These questions were solemnly propounded to Mr. Dimmesdale by the elder ministers of Boston and the deacons of his church, who, to use their own phrase, "dealt with him" on the sin of rejecting the aid which Providence so manifestly held out. He listened in silence, and finally promised to confer with the physician.

"Were it God's will," said the Reverend Mr. Dimmesdale, when, in fulfilment of this pledge, he requested old Roger Chillingworth's professional advice, "I could be well content that my labors, and my sorrows, and my sins, and my pains, should shortly end with me, and what is earthly of them be buried in my grave, and the spiritual go with me to my eternal state, rather than that you should put your skill to the proof in my behalf."

"Ah," replied Roger Chillingworth, with that quietness which, whether imposed or natural, marked all his deportment, "it is thus that a young clergyman is apt to speak. Youthful men, not having taken a deep root, give up their hold of life so easily! And saintly men, who walk with God on earth, would fain be away, to walk with him on the golden pavements of the New Jerusalem."

"Nay," rejoined the young minister, putting his hand to his heart, with a flush of pain flitting over his brow, "were I worthier to walk there, I could be better content to toil here."

"Good men ever interpret themselves too meanly," said the physician.

In this manner, the mysterious old Roger Chillingworth became the medical adviser of the Reverend Mr. Dimmesdale. As not only the disease interested the physician, but he was strongly moved to look into the character and qualities of the patient, these two men, so different in age, came gradually to spend much time together. For the sake of the minister's health, and to enable the leech to gather plants with healing balm in them, they took long walks on the sea-shore, or in the forest; mingling various talk with the plash and murmur of the waves, and the solemn wind-anthem among the tree-tops. Often, likewise, one was the guest of the other, in his place of study and retirement. There was a fascination for the minister in the company of the man of science, in whom he recognized an intellectual cultivation of no moderate depth or scope; together with a range and freedom of ideas that he would have vainly looked for among the members of his own profession. In truth, he was startled, if not shocked, to find this attribute in the physician. Mr. Dimmesdale was a true priest, a true religionist, with the reverential sentiment largely developed, and an order of mind that impelled itself powerfully along the track of a creed, and wore its passage continually deeper with the lapse of time. In no state of society would he have been what is called a man of liberal views; it would always be essential to his peace to feel the pressure of a faith about him, supporting, while it confined him within its iron framework. Not the less, however, though with a tremulous enjoyment, did he feel the occasional relief of looking at the universe through the medium of another kind of intellect than those with which he habitually held converse. It was as if a window were thrown open, admitting a freer atmosphere into the close and stifled study, where his life was wasting itself away, amid lamplight, or obstructed day-beams, and the musty fragrance, be it sensual or moral, that exhales from books. But the air was too fresh and chill to be long breathed with comfort. So the minister, and the physician with him, withdrew again within the limits of what their church defined as orthodox.

Thus Roger Chillingworth scrutinized his patient carefully, both as he saw him in his ordinary life, keeping an accustomed pathway in the range of thoughts familiar to him, and as he appeared when thrown amidst other moral scenery, the novelty of which might call out something new to the surface of his character. He deemed it essential, it would seem, to know the man, before attempting to do him good. Wherever there is a heart and an intellect, the diseases of the physical frame are tinged with the peculiarities of these. In Arthur Dimmesdale, thought and imagination were so active, and sensibility so intense, that the bodily infirmity would be likely to have its groundwork there. So Roger Chillingworth— the man of skill, the kind and friendly physician—strove to go deep into his patient's bosom, delving among his principles, prying into his recollections, and probing everything with a cautious touch, like a treasure-seeker in a dark cavern. Few secrets can escape an investigator, who has opportunity and license to undertake such a quest, and skill to follow it up. A man burdened with a secret should especially avoid the intimacy of his physician. If the latter possess native sagacity, and a nameless something more,—let us call it intuition; if he show no intrusive egotism, nor disagreeably prominent characteristics of his own; if he have the power, which must be born with him, to bring his mind into such affinity with his patient's, that this last shall unawares have spoken what he imagines himself only to have thought; if such revelations be received without tumult, and acknowledged not so often by an uttered sympathy as by silence, an inarticulate breath, and here and there a word, to indicate that all is understood; if to these qualifications of a confidant be joined the advantages afforded by his recognized character as a physician,—then, at some inevitable moment, will the soul of the sufferer be dissolved, and flow forth in a dark, but transparent stream, bringing all its mysteries into the daylight.

Roger Chillingworth possessed all, or most, of the attributes above enumerated. Nevertheless, time went on; a kind of intimacy, as we have said, grew up between these two cultivated minds, which had as wide a field as the whole sphere of human thought and study, to meet upon; they discussed every topic of ethics and religion, of public affairs and private character; they talked much, on both sides, of matters that seemed personal to themselves; and yet no secret, such as the physician fancied must exist there, ever stole out of the minister's consciousness into his companion's ear. The latter had his suspicions, indeed, that even the nature of Mr. Dimmesdale's bodily disease had never fairly been revealed to him. It was a strange reserve!

After a time, at a hint from Roger Chillingworth, the friends of Mr. Dimmesdale effected an arrangement by which the two were lodged in the same house; so that every ebb and flow of the minister's life-tide might pass under the eye of his anxious and attached physician. There was much joy throughout the town when this greatly desirable object was attained. It was held to be the best possible measure for the young clergyman's welfare; unless, indeed, as often urged by such as felt authorized to do so, he had selected some one of the many blooming damsels, spiritually devoted to him, to become his devoted wife. This latter step, however, there was no present prospect that Arthur Dimmesdale would be prevailed upon to take; he rejected all suggestions of the kind, as if priestly celibacy were one of his articles of church-discipline. Doomed by his own choice, therefore, as Mr. Dimmesdale so evidently was, to eat his unsavory morsel always at another's board, and endure the life-long chill which must be his lot who seeks to warm himself only at another's fireside, it truly seemed that this sagacious, experienced, benevolent old physician, with his concord of paternal and reverential love for the young pastor, was the very man of all mankind to be constantly within reach of his voice.

The new abode of the two friends was with a pious widow, of good social rank, who dwelt in a house covering pretty nearly the site on which the venerable structure of King's Chapel has since been built. It had the graveyard, originally Isaac Johnson's homefield, on one side, and so well adapted to call up serious reflections, suited to their respective employments, in both minister and man of physic. The motherly care of the good widow assigned to Mr. Dimmesdale a front apartment, with a sunny exposure, and heavy window-curtains, to create a noontide shadow, when desirable. The walls were hung round with tapestry, said to be from the Gobelin looms, and at all events, representing the Scriptural story of David and Bathsheba, and Nathan the Prophet, in colors still unfaded, but which made the fair woman of the scene almost as grimly picturesque as the woe-denouncing seer. Here, the pale clergyman piled up his library, rich with parchment-bound folios of the Fathers, and the lore of Rabbis, and monkish erudition, of which the Protestant divines, even while they vilified and decried that class of writers, were yet constrained often to avail themselves. On the other side of the house, old Roger Chillingworth arranged his study and laboratory; not such as a modern man of science would reckon even tolerably complete, but provided with a distilling apparatus, and the means of compounding drugs and chemicals, which the practised alchemist knew well how to turn to purpose. With such commodiousness of situation, these two learned persons sat themselves down, each in his own domain, yet familiarly passing from one apartment to the other, and bestowing a mutual and not incurious inspection into one another's business.

And the Reverend Arthur Dimmesdale's best discerning friends, as we have intimated, very reasonably imagined that the hand of Providence had done all this, for the purpose—besought in so many public, and domestic, and secret prayers—of restoring the young minister to health. But —it must now be said—another portion of the community had latterly begun to take its own view of the relation betwixt Mr. Dimmesdale and the mysterious old physician. When an uninstructed multitude attempts to see with its eyes, it is exceedingly apt to be deceived. When, however, it forms its judgment, as it usually does, on the intuitions of its great and warm heart, the conclusions thus attained are often so profound and so unerring, as to possess the character of truths supernaturally revealed. The people, in the case of which we speak, could justify its prejudice against Roger Chillingworth by no fact or argument worthy of serious refutation. There was an aged handicraftsman, it is true, who had been a citizen of London at the period of Sir Thomas Overbury's murder, now some thirty years agone; he testified to having seen the physician, under some other name, which the narrator of the story had now forgotten, in company with Doctor Forman, the famous old conjurer, who was implicated in the affair of Overbury. Two or three individuals hinted, that the man of skill, during his Indian captivity, had enlarged his medical attainments by joining in the incantations of the savage priests; who were universally acknowledged to be powerful enchanters, often performing seemingly miraculous cures by their skill in the black art. A large number—and many of these were persons of such sober sense and practical observation that their opinions would have been valuable in other matters—affirmed that Roger Chillingworth's aspect had undergone a remarkable change while he had dwelt in town, and especially since his abode with Mr. Dimmesdale. At first his expression had been calm, meditative, scholar-like. Now, there was something ugly and evil in his face, which they had not previously noticed, and which grew still the more obvious to sight the oftener they looked upon him. According to the vulgar idea, the fire in his laboratory had been brought from the lower regions, and was fed with infernal fuel; and so, as might be expected, his visage was getting sooty with the smoke.

To sum up the matter, it grew to be a widely diffused opinion, that the Reverend Arthur Dimmesdale, like many other personages of especial sanctity, in all ages of the Christian world, was haunted either by Satan himself, or Satan's emissary, in the guise of old Roger Chillingworth. This diabolical agent had the Divine permission, for a season, to burrow into the clergyman's intimacy, and plot against his soul. No sensible man, it was confessed, could doubt on which side the victory would turn. The people looked, with an unshaken hope, to see the minister come forth out of the conflict transfigured with the glory which he would unquestionably win. Meanwhile, nevertheless, it was sad to think of the perchance mortal agony through which he must struggle towards his triumph.

Alas! to judge from the gloom and terror in the depths of the poor minister's eyes, the battle was a sore one, and the victory anything but secure.

## X

### THE LEECH AND HIS PATIENT

OLD Roger Chillingworth, throughout life, had been calm in temperament, kindly, though not of warm affections, but ever, and in all his relations with the world, a pure and upright man. He had begun an investigation, as he imagined, with the severe and equal integrity of a judge, desirous only of truth, even as if the question involved no more than the air-drawn lines and figures of a geometrical problem, instead of human passions, and wrongs inflicted on himself. But, as he proceeded, a terrible fascination, a kind of fierce, though still calm, necessity seized the old man within its gripe, and never set him free again until he had done all its bidding. He now dug into the poor clergyman's heart, like a miner searching for gold; or, rather, like a sexton delving into a grave, possibly in quest of a jewel that had been buried on the dead man's bosom, but likely to find nothing save mortality and corruption. Alas for his own soul, if these were what he sought!

Sometimes a light glimmered out of the physician's eyes, burning blue and ominous, like the reflection of a furnace, or, let us say, like one of those gleams of ghastly fire that darted from Bunyan's awful doorway in the hill-side, and quivered on the pilgrim's face. The soil where this dark miner was working had perchance shown indications that encouraged him.

"This man," said he, at one such moment, to himself, "pure as they deem him,—all spiritual as he seems,—hath inherited a strong animal nature from his father or his mother. Let us dig a little further in the direction of this vein!"

Then, after long search into the minister's dim interior, and turning over many precious materials, in the shape of high aspirations for the welfare of his race, warm love of souls, pure sentiments, natural piety, strengthened by thought and study, and illuminated by revelation,—all of which invaluable gold was perhaps no better than rubbish to the seeker,—he would turn back discouraged, and begin his quest towards another point. He groped along as stealthily, with as cautious a tread, and as wary an outlook, as a thief entering a chamber where a man lies only half asleep,—or, it may be, broad awake,—with purpose to steal the very treasure which this man guards as the apple of his eye. In spite of his premeditated carefulness, the floor would now and then creak; his garments would rustle; the shadow of his presence, in a forbidden proximity, would be thrown across his victim. In other words, Mr. Dimmesdale, whose sensibility of nerve often produced the effect of spiritual intuition, would become vaguely aware that something inimical to his peace had thrust itself into relation with him. But old Roger Chillingworth, too, had perceptions that were almost intuitive; and when the minister threw his startled eyes towards him, there the physician sat; his kind, watchful, sympathizing, but never intrusive friend.

Yet Mr. Dimmesdale would perhaps have seen this individual's character more perfectly, if a certain morbidness, to which sick hearts are liable, had not rendered him suspicious of all mankind. Trusting no man as his friend, he could not recognize his enemy when the latter actually appeared. He therefore still kept up a familiar intercourse with him, daily receiving the old physician in his study; or visiting the laboratory, and, for recreation's sake, watching the processes by which weeds were converted into drugs of potency.

One day, leaning his forehead on his hand, and his elbow on the sill of the open window, that looked towards the graveyard, he talked with Roger Chillingworth, while the old man was examining a bundle of unsightly plants.

"Where," asked he, with a look askance at them,—for it was the clergyman's peculiarity that he seldom, nowadays, looked straightforth at any object, whether human or inanimate,—"where, my kind doctor, did you gather those herbs, with such a dark, flabby leaf?"

"Even in the graveyard here at hand," answered the physician continuing his employment. "They are new to me. I found them growing on a grave, which bore no tombstone, nor other memorial of the dead man, save these ugly weeds, that have taken upon themselves to keep him in remembrance. They grew out of his heart, and typify, it may be, some hideous secret that was buried with him, and which he had done better to confess during his lifetime."

"Perchance," said Mr. Dimmesdale, "he earnestly desired it, but could not."

"And wherefore?" rejoined the physician. "Wherefore not; since all the powers of nature call so earnestly for the confession of sin, that these black weeds have sprung up out of a buried heart, to make manifest an unspoken crime?"

"That, good Sir, is but a fantasy of yours," replied the minister. "There can be, if I forebode aright, no power, short of the Divine mercy, to disclose, whether by uttered words, or by type or emblem, the secrets that may be buried with a human heart. The heart, making itself guilty of such secrets, must perforce hold them, until the day when all hidden things shall be revealed. Nor have I so read or interpreted Holy Writ, as to understand that the disclosure of human thoughts and deeds, then to be made, is intended as a part of the retribution. That, surely, were a shallow view of it. No; these revelations, unless I greatly err, are meant merely to promote the intellectual satisfaction of all intelligent beings, who will stand waiting, on that day, to see the dark problem of this life made plain. A knowledge of men's hearts will be needful to the completest solution of that problem. And I conceive, moreover, that the hearts holding such miserable secrets as you speak of will yield them up, at that last day, not with reluctance, but with a joy unutterable."

"Then why not reveal them here?" asked Roger Chillingworth, glancing quietly aside at the minister. "Why should not the guilty ones sooner avail themselves of this unutterable solace?"

"They mostly do," said the clergyman, griping hard at his breast as if afflicted with an importunate throb of pain. "Many, many a poor soul hath given its confidence to me, not only on the death-bed, but while strong in life, and fair in reputation. And ever, after such an outpouring, oh, what a relief have I witnessed in those sinful brethren! even as in one who at last draws free air, after long stifling with his own polluted breath. How can it be otherwise? Why should a wretched man, guilty, we will say, of murder, prefer to keep the dead corpse buried in his own heart, rather than fling it forth at once, and let the universe take care of it!"

"Yet some men bury their secrets thus," observed the calm physician.

"True; there are such men," answered Mr. Dimmesdale. "But, not to suggest more obvious reasons, it may be that they are kept silent by the very constitution of their nature. Or,—can we not suppose it?—guilty as they may be, retaining, nevertheless, a zeal for God's glory and man's welfare, they shrink from displaying themselves black and filthy in the view of men; because, thenceforward, no good can be achieved by them; no evil of the past be redeemed by better service. So, to their own unutterable torment, they go about among their fellow-creatures, looking pure as new-fallen snow while their hearts are all speckled and spotted with iniquity of which they cannot rid themselves."

"These men deceive themselves," said Roger Chillingworth, with somewhat more emphasis than usual, and making a slight gesture with his forefinger. "They fear to take up the shame that rightfully belongs to them. Their love for man, their zeal for God's service,—these holy impulses may or may not coexist in their hearts with the evil inmates to which their guilt has unbarred the door, and which must needs propagate a hellish breed within them. But, if they seek to glorify God, let them not lift heavenward their unclean hands! If they would serve their fellowmen, let them do it by making manifest the power and reality of conscience, in constraining them to penitential self-abasement! Wouldst thou have me to believe, O wise and pious friend, that a false show can be better—can be more for God's glory, or man's welfare—than God's own truth? Trust me, such men deceive themselves!"

"It may be so," said the young clergyman, indifferently, as waiving a discussion that he considered irrelevant or unreasonable. He had a ready faculty, indeed, of escaping from any topic that agitated his too sensitive and nervous temperament. "But, now, I would ask of my well-skilled physician, whether, in good sooth, he deems me to have profited by his kindly care of this weak frame of mine?"

Before Roger Chillingworth could answer, they heard the clear, wild laughter of a young child's voice, proceeding from the adjacent burial-ground. Looking instinctively from the open window,—for it was summer-time,—the minister beheld Hester Prynne and little Pearl passing along the footpath that traversed the enclosure. Pearl looked as beautiful as the day, but was in one of those moods of perverse merriment which, whenever they occurred, seemed to remove her entirely out of the sphere of sympathy or human contact. She now skipped irreverently from one grave to another; until, coming to the broad, flat, armorial tombstone of a departed worthy,—perhaps of Isaac Johnson himself,—she began to dance upon it. In reply to her mother's command and entreaty that she would behave more decorously, little Pearl paused to gather the prickly burrs from a tall burdock which grew beside the tomb. Taking a handful of these, she arranged them along the lines of the scarlet letter that decorated the maternal bosom, to which the burrs, as their nature was, tenaciously adhered. Hester did not pluck them off.

Roger Chillingworth had by this time approached the window, and smiled grimly down.

"There is no law, nor reverence for authority, no regard for human ordinances or opinions, right or wrong, mixed up with that child's composition," remarked he, as much to himself as to his companion. "I saw her, the other day, bespatter the Governor himself with water, at the cattle-trough in Spring Lane. What, in Heaven's name, is she? Is the imp altogether evil? Hath she affections? Hath she any discoverable principle of being?"

"None,—save the freedom of a broken law," answered Mr. Dimmesdale, in a quiet way, as if he had been discussing the point within himself. "Whether capable of good, I know not."

The child probably overhead their voices; for, looking up to the window, with a bright, but naughty smile of mirth and intelligence, she threw one of the prickly burrs at the Reverend Mr. Dimmesdale. The sensitive clergyman shrunk, with nervous dread, from the light missile. Detecting his emotion, Pearl clapped her little hands in the most extravagant ecstasy. Hester Prynne, likewise, had involuntarily looked up; and all these four persons, old and young, regarded one another in silence, till the child laughed aloud; and shouted,—"Come away, mother! Come away, or yonder old Black Man will catch you! He hath got hold of the minister already. Come away, mother, or he will catch you! But he cannot catch little Pearl!"

So she drew her mother away, skipping, dancing, and frisking fantastically, among the hillocks of the dead people, like a creature that had nothing in common with a bygone and buried generation, nor owned herself akin to it. It was as if she had been made afresh, out of new elements, and must perforce be permitted to live her own life, and be a law unto herself, without her eccentricities being reckoned to her for a crime.

"There goes a woman," resumed Roger Chillingworth, after a pause, "who, be her demerits what they may, hath none of that mystery of hidden sinfulness which you deem so grievous to be borne. Is Hester Prynne the less miserable, think you, for that scarlet letter on her breast?"

"I do verily believe it," answered the clergyman. "Nevertheless I cannot answer for her. There was a look of pain in her face, which I would gladly have been spared the sight of. But still, methinks, it must needs be better for the sufferer to be free to show his pain, as this poor woman Hester is, than to cover it all up in his heart."

There was another pause; and the physician began anew to examine and arrange the plants which he had gathered.

"You inquired of me, a little time agone," said he, at length, "my judgment as touching your health."

"I did," answered the clergyman, "and would gladly learn it. Speak frankly, I pray you, be it for life or death."

"Freely, then, and plainly," said the physician, still busy with his plants, but keeping a wary eye on Mr. Dimmesdale, "the disorder is a strange one; not so much in itself, nor as outwardly manifested,—in so far, at least, as the symptoms have been laid open to my observation. Looking daily at you, my good Sir, and watching the tokens of your aspect, now for months gone by, I should deem you a man sore sick, it may be, yet not so sick but that an instructed and watchful physician might well hope to cure you. But—I know not what to say—the disease is what I seem to know, yet know it not."

"You speak in riddles, learned Sir," said the pale minister, glancing aside out of the window.

"Then to speak more plainly," continued the physician, "and I crave pardon, Sir,—should it seem to require pardon,—for this needful plainness of my speech. Let me ask,—as your friend,—as one having charge, under Providence, of your life and physical well-being,—hath all the operation of this disorder been fairly laid open and recounted to me?"

"How can you question it?" asked the minister. "Surely, it were child's play to call in a physician, and then hide the sore!"

"You would tell me, then, that I know all?" said Roger Chillingworth, deliberately, and fixing an eye, bright with intense and concentrated intelligence, on the minister's face. "Be it so! But, again! He to whom only the outward and physical evil is laid open, knoweth, oftentimes, but half the evil which he is called upon to cure. A bodily disease, which we look upon as whole and entire within itself, may, after all, be but a symptom of some ailment in the spiritual part. Your pardon, once again, good Sir, if my speech give the shadow of offence. You, Sir, of all men whom I have known, are he whose body is the closest conjoined, and imbued, and identified, so to speak, with the spirit whereof it is the instrument."

"Then I need ask no further," said the clergyman, somewhat hastily rising from his chair. "You deal not, I take it, in medicine for the soul!"

"Thus, a sickness," continued Roger Chillingworth, going on, in an unaltered tone, without heeding the interruption,—but standing up, and confronting the emaciated and white-cheeked minister, with his low, dark, and misshapen figure,—"a sickness, a sore place, if we may so call it, in your spirit, hath immediately its appropriate manifestation in your bodily frame. Would you, therefore, that your physician heal the bodily evil? How may this be, unless you first lay open to him the wound or trouble in your soul?"

"No!—not to thee!—not to an earthly physician!" cried Mr. Dimmesdale, passionately, and turning his eyes, full and bright, and with a kind of fierceness, on old Roger Chillingworth. "Not to thee! But, if it be the soul's disease, then do I commit myself to the one Physician of the soul! He, if it stand with his good pleasure, can cure; or he can kill! Let him do with me as, in his justice and wisdom, he shall see good. But who art thou, that meddlest in this matter?—that dares thrust himself between the sufferer and his God?"

With a frantic gesture he rushed out of the room.

"It is as well to have made this step," said Roger Chillingworth to himself, looking after the minister with a grave smile. "There is nothing lost. We shall be friends again anon. But see, now, how passion takes hold upon this man, and hurrieth him out of himself! As with one passion, so with another! He hath done a wild thing erenow, this pious Master Dimmesdale, in the hot passion of his heart!"

It proved not difficult to reëstablish the intimacy of the two companions, on the same footing and in the same degree as heretofore. The young clergyman, after a few hours of privacy, was sensible that the disorder of his nerves had hurried him into an unseemly outbreak of temper, which there had been nothing to the physician's words to excuse or paliate. He marvelled, indeed, at the violence with which he had thrust back the kind old man, when merely proffering the advice which it was his duty to bestow, and which the minister himself had expressly sought. With these remorseful feelings, he lost no time in making the amplest apologies, and besought his friend still to continue the care, which, if not successful in restoring him to health, had, in all probability, been the means of prolonging his feeble existence to that hour. Roger Chillingworth readily assented, and went on with his medical supervision of the minister; doing his best for him, in all good faith, but always quitting the patient's apartment, at the close of a professional interview, with a mysterious and puzzled smile upon his lips. This expression was invisible in Mr. Dimmesdale's presence, but grew strongly evident as the physician crossed the threshold.

"A rare case!" he muttered. "I must needs look deeper into it. A strange sympathy betwixt soul and body! Were it only for the art's sake, I must search this matter to the bottom!"

It came to pass, not long after the scene above recorded, that the Reverend Mr. Dimmesdale, at noonday, and entirely unawares, fell into a deep, deep slumber, sitting in his chair, with a large black-letter volume open before him on the table. It must have been a work of vast ability in the somniferous school of literature. The profound depth of the minister's repose was the more remarkable, inasmuch as he was one of those persons whose sleep, ordinarily, is as light, as fitful, and as easily scared away, as a small bird hopping on a twig. To such an unwonted remoteness, however, had his spirit now withdrawn into itself, that he stirred not in his chair when old Roger Chillingworth, without any extraordinary precaution, came into the room. The physician advanced directly in front of his patient, laid his hand upon his bosom, and thrust aside the vestment that, hitherto, had always covered it even from the professional eye.

Then, indeed, Mr. Dimmesdale shuddered, and slightly stirred.

After a brief pause, the physician turned away.

But with what a wild look of wonder, joy, and horror! With what a ghastly rapture, as it were, too mighty to be expressed only by the eye and features, and therefore bursting forth through the whole ugliness of his figure, and making itself even riotously manifest by the extravagant gestures with which he threw up his arms towards the ceiling, and stamped his foot upon the floor! Had a man seen old Roger Chillingworth, at that moment of his ecstasy, he would have had no need to ask how Satan comports himself when a precious human soul is lost to heaven, and won into his kingdom.

But what distinguished the physician's ecstasy from Satan's was the trait of wonder in it!

## XI

### THE INTERIOR OF A HEART

AFTER the incident last described, the intercourse between the clergyman and the physician, though externally the same, was really of another character than it had previously been. The intellect of Roger Chillingworth had now a sufficiently plain path before it. It was not, indeed, precisely that which he had laid out for himself to tread. Calm, gentle, passionless, as he appeared, there was yet, we fear, a quiet depth of malice, hitherto latent, but active now, in this unfortunate old man, which led him to imagine a more intimate revenge than any mortal had ever wreaked upon an enemy. To make himself the one trusted friend, to whom should be confided all the fear, the remorse, the agony, the ineffectual repentance, the backward rush of sinful thoughts, expelled in vain! All that guilty sorrow, hidden from the world, whose great heart would have pitied and forgiven, to be revealed to him, the Pitiless, to him, the Unforgiving! All that dark treasure to be lavished on the very man, to whom nothing else could so adequately pay the debt of vengeance!

The clergyman's shy and sensitive reserve had balked this scheme. Roger Chillingworth, however, was inclined to be hardly, if at all, less satisfied with the aspect of affairs, which Providence—using the avenger and his victim for its own purposes, and, perchance, pardoning where it seemed most to punish—had substituted for his black devices. A revelation, he could almost say, had been granted to him. It mattered little, for his object, whether celestial, or from what other region. By its aid, in all the subsequent relations betwixt him and Mr. Dimmesdale, not merely the external presence, but the very inmost soul, of the latter, seemed to be brought out before his eyes, so that he could see and comprehend its every movement. He became, thenceforth, not a spectator only, but a chief actor, in the poor minister's interior world. He could play upon him as he chose. Would he arouse him with a throb of agony? The victim was forever on the rack; it needed only to know the spring that controlled the engine; and the physician knew it well! Would he startle him with sudden fear? As at the waving of a magician's wand, uprose a grisly phantom,—uprose a thousand phantoms,—in many shapes, of death, or more awful shame, all flocking round about the clergyman, and pointing with their fingers at his breast!

All this was accomplished with a subtlety so perfect that the minister, though he had constantly a dim perception of some evil influence watching over him, could never gain a knowledge of its actual nature. True, he looked doubtfully, fearfully,—even, at times, with horror and the bitterness of hatred,—at the deformed figure of the old physician. His gestures, his gait, his grizzled beard, his slightest and most indifferent acts, the very fashion of his garments, were odious in the clergyman's sight; a token implicitly to be relied on, of a deeper antipathy in the breast of the latter than he was willing to acknowledge to himself. For, as it was impossible to assign a reason for such distrust and abhorrence, so Mr. Dimmesdale, conscious that the poison of one morbid spot was infecting his heart's entire substance, attributed all his presentiments to no other cause. He took himself to task for his bad sympathies in reference to Roger Chillingworth, disregarded the lesson that he should have drawn from them, and did his best to root them out. Unable to accomplish this, he nevertheless, as a matter of principle, continued his habits of social familiarity with the old man, and thus gave him constant opportunities for perfecting the purpose to which—poor, forlorn creature that he was, and more wretched than his victim—the avenger had devoted himself.

While thus suffering under bodily disease, and gnawed and tortured by some black trouble of the soul, and given over to the machinations of his deadliest enemy, the Reverend Mr. Dimmesdale had achieved a brilliant popularity in his sacred office. He won it, indeed, in great part, by his sorrows. His intellectual gifts, his moral perceptions, his power of experiencing and communicating emotion, were kept in a state of preternatural activity by the prick and anguish of his daily life. His fame, though still on its upward slope, already overshadowed the soberer reputations of his fellow-clergymen, eminent as several of them were. There were scholars among them, who had spent more years in acquiring abstruse lore, connected with the divine profession, than Mr. Dimmesdale had lived; and who might well, therefore, be more profoundly versed in such solid and valuable attainments than their youthful brother. There were men, too, of a sturdier texture of mind than his, and endowed with a far greater share of shrewd, hard, iron, or granite understanding; which, duly mingled with a fair proportion of doctrinal ingredient, constitutes a highly respectable, efficacious, and unamiable variety of the clerical species.

There were others, again, true saintly fathers, whose faculties had been elaborated by weary toil among their books, and by patient thought, and etherealized, moreover, by spiritual communications with the better world, into which their purity of life had almost introduced these holy personages, with their garments of mortality still clinging to them. All that they lacked was the gift that descended upon the chosen disciples at Pentecost, in tongues of flames; symbolizing, it would seem, not the power of speech in foreign and unknown languages, but that of addressing the whole human brotherhood in the heart's native language. These fathers, otherwise so apostolic, lacked Heaven's last and rarest attestation of their office, the Tongue of Flame. They would have vainly sought —had they ever dreamed of seeking—to express the highest truths through the humblest medium of familiar words and images. Their voices came down, afar and indistinctly, from the upper heights where they habitually dwelt.

Not improbably, it was to this latter class of men that Mr. Dimmesdale, by many of his traits of character, naturally belonged. To the high mountain-peaks of faith and sanctity he would have climbed, had not the tendency been thwarted by the burden, whatever it might be, of crime or anguish, beneath which it was his doom to totter. It kept him down, on a level with the lowest; him, the man of ethereal attributes, whose voice the angels might else have listened to and answered! But this very burden it was that gave him sympathies so intimate with the sinful brotherhood of mankind, so that his heart vibrated in unison with theirs, and received their pain into itself, and sent its own throb of pain through a thousand other hearts, in gushes of sad, persuasive eloquence. Oftenest persuasive, but sometimes terrible! The people knew not the power that moved them thus. They deemed the young clergyman a miracle of holiness. They fancied him the mouth-piece of Heaven's messages of wisdom, and rebuke, and love. In their eyes, the very ground on which he trod was sanctified. The virgins of his church grew pale around him, victims of a passion so imbued with religious sentiment that they imagined it to be all religion, and brought it openly, in their white bosoms, as their most acceptable sacrifice before the altar. The aged members of his flock, beholding Mr. Dimmesdale's frame so feeble, while they were themselves so rugged in their infirmity, believed that he would go heavenward before them, and enjoined it upon their children, that their old bones should be buried close to their young pastor's holy grave. And, all this time, perchance, when poor Mr. Dimmesdale was thinking of his grave, he questioned with himself whether the grass would ever grow on it, because an accursed thing must there be buried!

It is inconceivable, the agony with which this public veneration tortured him! It was his genuine impulse to adore the truth, and to reckon all things shadowlike, and utterly devoid of weight or value, that had not its divine essence as the life within their life. Then, what was he?—a substance?—or the dimmest of all shadows? He longed to speak out, from his own pulpit, at the full height of his voice, and tell the people what he was.

"I, whom you behold in these black garments of the priesthood,—I, who ascend the sacred desk, and turn my pale face heavenward, taking upon myself to hold communion, in your behalf, with the Most High Omniscience,—I, in whose daily life you discern the sancity of Enoch,—I, whose footsteps, as you suppose, leave a gleam along my earthly track, whereby the pilgrims that shall come after me may be guided to the regions of the blest,—I, who have laid the hand of baptism upon your children,—I, who have breathed the parting prayer over your dying friends, to whom the Amen sounded faintly from a world which they had quitted, —I, your pastor, whom you so reverence and trust, am utterly a pollution and a lie!"

More than once, Mr. Dimmesdale had gone into the pulpit, with a purpose never to come down its steps until he should have spoken words like the above. More than once, he had cleared his throat, and drawn in the long, deep, and tremulous breath, which, when sent forth again, would come burdened with the black secret of his soul. More than once—nay, more than a hundred times—he had actually spoken! Spoken! But how? He had told his hearers that he was altogether vile, a viler companion of the vilest, the worst of sinners, an abomination, a thing of unimaginable iniquity; and that the only wonder was that they did not see his wretched body shrivelled up before their eyes, by the burning wrath of the Almighty! Could there be plainer speech than this? Would not the people start up in their seats, by a simultaneous impulse, and tear him down out of the pulpit, which he defiled? Not so, indeed! They heard it all, and did but reverence him the more. They little guessed what deadly purport lurked in those self-condemning words. "The godly youth!" said they among themselves. "The saint on earth! Alas, if he discern such sinfulness in his own white soul, what horrid spectacle would he behold in thine or mine!" The minister well knew—subtle, but remorseful hypocrite that he was!—the light in which his vague confession would be viewed. He had striven to put a cheat upon himself by making the avowel of a guilty conscience, but had gained only one other sin, and a self-acknowledged shame, without the momentary relief of being self-deceived. He had spoken the very truth, and transformed it into the veriest falsehood. And yet, by the constitution of his nature, he loved the truth, and loathed the lie, as few men ever did. Therefore, above all things else, he loathed his miserable self!

His inward trouble drove him to practices more in accordance with the old, corrupted faith of Rome, than with the better light of the church in which he had been born and bred. In Mr. Dimmesdale's secret closet, under lock and key, there was a bloody scourge. Oftentimes, this Protestant and Puritan divine had plied it on his own shoulders; laughing bitterly at himself the while, and smiting so much the more pitilessly because of that bitter laugh. It was his custom, too, as it has been that of many other pious Puritans, to fast,—not, however, like them, in order to purify the body and render it the fitter medium of celestial illumination, but rigorously, and until his knees trembled beneath him, as an act of penance.

He kept vigils, likewise, night after night, sometimes in utter darkness; sometimes with a glimmering lamp; and sometimes, viewing his own face in a looking-glass, by the most powerful light which he could throw upon it. He thus typified the constant introspection wherewith he tortured, but could not purify, himself. In these lengthened vigils, his brain often reeled, and visions seemed to flit before him; perhaps seen doubtfully, and by a faint light of their own, in the remote dimness of the chamber, or more vividly, and close beside him, within the looking-glass. Now it was a herd of diabolic shapes, that grinned and mocked at the pale minister, and beckoned him away with them; now a group of shining angels, who flew upward heavily, as sorrow-laden, but grew more ethereal as they rose. Now came the dead friends of his youth, and his white-bearded father, with a saint-like frown, and his mother, turning her face away as she passed by. Ghost of a mother,—thinnest fantasy of a mother,—methinks she might yet have thrown a pitying glance towards her son! And now, through the chamber which these spectral thoughts had made so ghastly, glided Hester Prynne, leading along little Pearl, in her scarlet garb, and pointing her forefinger, first at the scarlet letter on her bosom, and then at the clergyman's own breast.

None of these visions ever quite deluded him. At any moment, by an effort of his will, he could discern substances through their misty lack of substance, and convince himself that they were not solid in their nature, like yonder table of carved oak, or that big, square, leathern-bound and brazen-clasped volume of divinity. But, for all that, they were, in one sense, the truest and most substantial things which the poor minister now dealt with. It is the unspeakable misery of a life so false as his, that it steals the pith and substance out of whatever realities there are around us, and which were meant by Heaven to be the spirit's joy and nutriment. To the untrue man, the whole universe is false,—it is impalpable,—it shrinks to nothing within his grasp. And he himself, in so far as he shows himself in a false light, becomes a shadow, or, indeed, ceases to exist. The only truth that continued to give Mr. Dimmesdale a real existence on this earth was the anguish in his inmost soul, and the undissembled expression of it in his aspect. Had he once found power to smile, and wear a face of gayety, there would have been no such man!

On one of those ugly nights, which we have faintly hinted at, but forborne to picture forth, the minister started from his chair. A new thought had struck him. There might be a moment's peace in it. Attiring himself with as much care as if it had been for public worship, and precisely in the same manner, he stole softly down the staircase, undid the door, and issued forth.

## XII

### THE MINISTER'S VIGIL

WALKING in the shadow of a dream, as it were, and perhaps actually under the influence of a species of somnambulism, Mr. Dimmesdale reached the spot where, now so long since, Hester Prynne had lived through her first hours of public ignominy. The same platform or scaffold, black and weather-stained with the storm or sunshine of seven long years, and footworn, too, with the tread of many culprits who had since ascended it, remained standing beneath the balcony of the meeting-house. The minister went up the steps.

It was an obscure night of early May. An unvaried pall of cloud muffled the whole expanse of sky from zenith to horizon. If the same multitude which had stood as eye-witnesses while Hester Prynne sustained her punishment could now have been summoned forth, they would have discerned no face above the platform, nor hardly the outline of a human shape, in the dark gray of the midnight. But the town was all asleep. There was no peril of discovery. The minister might stand there, if it so pleased him, until morning should redden in the east, without other risk than that the dank and chill night-air would creep into his frame, and stiffen his joints with rheumatism, and clog his throat with catarrh and cough; thereby defrauding the expectant audience of to-morrow's prayer and sermon. No eye could see him, save that ever-wakeful one which had seen him in his closet, wielding the bloody scourge. Why, then, had he come hither? Was it but the mockery of penitence? A mockery, indeed, but in which his soul trifled with itself! A mockery at which angels blushed and wept, while fiends rejoiced, with jeering laughter! He had been driven hither by the impulse of that Remorse which dogged him everywhere, and whose own sister and closely linked companion was that Cowardice which invariably drew him back, with her tremulous gripe, just when the other impulse had hurried him to the verge of a disclosure. Poor, miserable man! what right had infirmity like his to burden itself with crime? Crime is for the iron-nerved, who have their choice either to endure it, or, if it press too hard, to exert their fierce and savage strength for a good purpose, and fling it off at once! This feeble and most sensitive of spirits could do neither, yet continually did one thing or another, which intertwined, in the same inextricable knot, the agony of heaven-defying guilt and vain repentance.

And thus, while standing on the scaffold, in this vain show of expiation, Mr. Dimmesdale was overcome with a great horror of mind, as if the universe were gazing at a scarlet token on his naked breast, right over his heart. On that spot, in very truth, there was, and there had long been, the gnawing and poisonous tooth of bodily pain. Without any effort of his will, or power to restrain himself, he shrieked aloud; an outcry that went pealing through the night, and was beaten back from one house to another, and reverberated from the hills in the background; as if a company of devils, detecting so much misery and terror in it, had made a plaything of the sound, and were bandying it to and fro.

"It is done!" muttered the minister, covering his face with his hands. "The whole town will awake, and hurry forth, and find me here!"

But it was not so. The shriek had perhaps sounded with a far greater power, to his own startled ears, than it actually possessed. The town did not awake; or, if it did, the drowsy slumberers mistook the cry either for something frightful in a dream, or for the noise of witches; whose voices, at that period, were often heard to pass over the settlements or lonely cottages, as they rode with Satan through the air. The clergyman, therefore, hearing no symptoms of disturbance, uncovered his eyes and looked about him. At one of the chamber-windows of Governor Bellingham's mansion, which stood at some distance, on the line of another street, he beheld the appearance of the old magistrate himself, with a lamp in his hand, a white nightcap on his head, and a long white gown enveloping his figure. He looked like a ghost, evoked unseasonably from the grave. The cry had evidently startled him. At another window of the same house, moreover, appeared old Mistress Hibbins, the Governor's sister, also with a lamp, which, even thus far off, revealed the expression of her sour and discontented face. She thrust forth her head from the lattice, and looked anxiously upward. Beyond the shadow of a doubt, this venerable witchlady had heard Mr. Dimmesdale's outcry, and interpreted it, with its multitudinous echoes and reverberations, as the clamor of the fiends and night-hags, with whom she was well known to make excursions into the forest.

Detecting the gleam of Governor Bellingham's lamp, the old lady quickly extinguished her own, and vanished. Possibly, she went up among the clouds. The minister saw nothing further of her motions. The magistrate, after a wary observation of the darkness,—into which, nevertheless, he could see but little further than he might into a mill-stone,—retired from the window.

The minister grew comparatively calm. His eyes, however, were soon greeted by a little, glimmering light, which, at first a long way off, was approaching up the street. It threw a gleam of recognition on here a post, and there a garden-fence, and here a latticed window-pane, and there a pump, with its full trough of water, and here, again, an arched door of oak, with an iron knocker, and a rough log for the doorstep. The Reverend Mr. Dimmesdale noted all these minute particulars, even while firmly convinced that the doom of his existence was stealing onward, in the footsteps which he now heard; and that the gleam of the lantern would fall upon him, in a few moments more, and reveal his long-hidden secret. As the light drew nearer, he behld, within its illuminated circle, his brother clergyman,—or, to speak more accurately, his professional father, as well as highly valued friend,—the Reverend Mr. Wilson; who, as Mr. Dimmesdale now conjectured, had been praying at the bedside of some dying man. And so he had. The good old minister came freshly from the death-chamber of Governor Winthrop, who had passed from earth to heaven within that very hour. And now, surrounded, like the saint-like personages of olden times, with a radiant halo, that glorified him amid this gloomy night of sin,—as if the departed Governor had left him an inheritance of his glory, or as if he had caught upon himself the distant shine of the celestial city, while looking thitherward to see the triumphal pilgrim pass within its gates,—now, in short, good Father Wilson was moving homeward, aiding his footsteps with a lighted lantern! The glimmer of this luminary suggested the above conceits to Mr. Dimmesdale, who smiled,—nay, almost laughed at them,—and then wondered if he were going mad.

As the Reverend Mr. Wilson passed beside the scaffold, closely muffling his Geneva cloak about him with one arm, and holding the lantern before his breast with the other, the minister could hardly restrain himself from speaking.

"A good evening to you, venerable Father Wilson! Come up hither, I pray you, and pass a pleasant hour with me!"

Good heavens! Had Mr. Dimmesdale actually spoken? For one instant, he believed that these words had passed his lips. But they were uttered only with his imagination. The venerable Father Wilson continued to step slowly onward, looking carefully at the muddy pathway before his feet, and never once turning his head towards the guilty platform. When the light of the glimmering lantern had faded quite away, the minister discovered, by the faintness which came over him, that the last few moments had been a crisis of terrible anxiety; although his mind had made an involuntary effort to relieve itself by a kind of lurid playfulness.

Shortly afterwards, the like grisly sense of the humorous again stole in among the solemn phantoms of his thought. He felt his limbs growing stiff with the unaccustomed chilliness of the night, and doubted whether he should be able to descend the steps of the scaffold. Morning would break, and find him there. The neighborhood would begin to rouse itself. The earliest riser, coming forth in the dim twilight, would perceive a vaguely defined figure aloft on the place of shame; and, half crazed betwixt alarm and curiosity, would go, knocking from door to door, summoning all the people to behold the ghost—as he needs must think it—of some defunct transgressor. A dusky tumult would flap its wings from one house to another. Then—the morning light still waxing stronger—old patriarchs would rise up in great haste, each in his flannel gown, and matronly dames, without pausing to put off their night-gear. The whole tribe of decorous personages, who had never heretofore been seen with a single hair of their heads awry, would start into public view, with the disorder of a nightmare in their aspects. Old Governor Bellingham would come grimly forth, with his King James's ruff fastened askew; and Mistress Hibbins, with some twigs of the forest clinging to her skirts, and looking sourer than ever, as having hardly got a wink of sleep after her night ride; and good Father Wilson, too, after spending half the night, at a death-bed, and liking ill to be disturbed, thus early, out of his dreams about the glorified saints. Hither, likewise, would come the elders and deacons of Mr. Dimmesdale's church, and the young virgins who so idolized their minister, and had made a shrine for him in their white bosoms; which now, by the by, in their hurry and confusion, they would scantly have given themselves time to cover with their kerchiefs. All people, in a word, would come stumbling over their thresholds, and turning up their amazed and horror-stricken visages around the scaffold. Whom would they discern there, with the red eastern light upon his brow? Whom, but the Reverend Arthur Dimmesdale, half frozen to death, overwhelmed with shame, and standing where Hester Prynne had stood!

Carried away by the grotesque horror of this picture, the minister, unawares, and to his own infinite alarm, burst into a great peal of laughter. It was immediately responded to by a light, airy, childish laugh, in which, with a thrill of the heart,—but he knew not whether of exquisite pain, or pleasure as acute,—he recognized the tones of little Pearl.

"Pearl! Little Pearl!" cried he after a moment's pause; then, suppressing his voice,—"Hester! Hester Prynne! Are you there?"

"Yes; it is Hester Prynne!" she replied, in a tone of surprise; and the minister heard her footsteps approaching from the sidewalk, along which she had been passing. "It is I, and my little Pearl."

"Whence come you, Hester!" asked the minister. "What sent you hither?"

"I have been watching at a death-bed," answered Hester Prynne,—"at Governor Winthrop's death-bed, and have taken his measure for a robe, and am now going homeward to my dwelling."

"Come up hither, Hester, thou and little Pearl," said the Reverend Mr. Dimmesdale. "Ye have both been here before, but I was not with you. Come up hither once again, and we will stand all three together!"

She silently ascended the steps, and stood on the platform, holding little Pearl by the hand. The minister felt for the child's other hand, and took it. The moment that he did so, there came what seemed a tumultuous rush of new life, other life than his own, pouring like a torrent into his heart, and hurrying through all his veins, as if the mother and the child were communicating their vital warmth to his half-torpid system. The three formed an electric chain.

"Minister!" whispered little Pearl.

"What wouldst thou say, child?" asked Mr. Dimmesdale.

"Wilt thou stand here with mother and me, tomorrow noontide?" inquired Pearl.

"Nay; not so, my little Pearl," answered the minister; for with the new energy of the moment, all the dread of public exposure, that had so long been the anguish of his life, had returned upon him; and he was already trembling at the conjunction in which—with a strange joy, nevertheless —he now found himself. "Not so, my child. I shall, indeed, stand with thy mother and thee, one other day, but not to-morrow."

Pearl laughed, and attempted to pull away her hand. But the minister held it fast.

"A moment longer, my child!" said he.

"But wilt thou promise," asked Pearl, "to take my hand and mother's hand, to-morrow noontide?"

"Not then, Pearl," said the minister, "but another time."

"And what other time?" persisted the child.

"At the great judgment day," whispered the minister,—and, strangely enough, the sense that he was a professional teacher of the truth impelled him to answer the child so. "Then, and there, before the judgment-seat, thy mother, and thou, and I must stand together. But the daylight of this world shall not see our meeting!"

Pearl laughed again.

But before Mr. Dimmesdale had done speaking, a light gleamed far and wide over all the muffled sky. It was doubtless caused by one of those meteors, which the night-watcher may so often observe, burning out to waste, in the vacant regions of the atmosphere. So powerful was its radiance, that it thoroughly illuminated the dense medium of cloud betwixt the sky and earth. The great vault brightened, like the dome of an immense lamp. It showed the familiar scene of the street, with the distinctness of mid-day, but also with the awfulness that is always imparted to familiar objects by an unaccustomed light. The wooden houses, with their jutting stories and quaint gable-peaks; the doorsteps and thresholds, with the early grass springing up about them; the garden-plots, black with freshly-turned earth; the wheel-track, little worn, and, even in the market-place, margined with green on either side,—all were visible, but with a singularity of aspect that seemed to give another moral interpretation to the things of this world than they had ever borne before. And there stood the minister, with his hand over his heart; and Hester Prynne, with the embroidered letter glimmering on her bosom; and little Pearl, herself a symbol, and the connecting link between those two. They stood in the noon of that strange and solemn splendor, as if it were the light that is to reveal all secrets, and the daybreak that shall unite all who belong to one another.

There was witchcraft in little Pearl's eyes, and her face, as she glanced upward at the minister, wore that naughty smile which made its expression frequently so elfish. She withdrew her hand from Mr. Dimmesdale's, and pointed across the street. But he clasped both his hands over his breast, and cast his eyes towards the zenith.

Nothing was more common, in those days, than to interpret all meteoric appearances, and other natural phenomena, that occurred with less regularity than the rise and set of sun and moon, as so many revelations from a supernatural source. Thus, a blazing spear, a sword of flame, a bow, or a sheaf of arrows, seen in the midnight sky, prefigured Indian warfare. Pestilence was known to have been foreboded by a shower of crimson light. We doubt whether any marked event, for good or evil, ever befell

New England, from its settlement down to Revolutionary times, of which the inhabitants had not been previously warned by some spectacle of this nature. Not seldom, it had been seen by multitudes. Oftener, however, its credibility rested on the faith of some lonely eye-witness, who beheld the wonder through the colored, magnifying, and distorting medium of his imagination, and shaped it more distinctly in his after-thought. It was, indeed, a majestic idea, that the destiny of nations should be revealed, in these awful hieroglyphics, on the cope of heaven. A scroll so wide might not be deemed too expansive for Providence to write a people's doom upon. The belief was a favorite one with our forefathers, as betokening that their infant commonwealth was under a celestial guardianship of peculiar intimacy and strictness. But what shall we say, when an individual discovers a revelation addressed to himself alone, on the same vast sheet of record! In such a case, it could only be the symptom of a highly disordered mental state, when a man, rendered morbidly self-contemplative by long, intense, and secret pain, had extended his egotism over the whole expanse of nature, until the firmament itself should appear no more than a fitting page for his soul's history and fate!

We impute it, therefore, solely to the disease in his own eye and heart, that the minister, looking upward to the zenith, beheld there the appearance of an immense letter,—the letter A,—marked out in lines of dull red light. Not but the meteor may have shown itself at that point, burning duskily through a veil of cloud; but with no such shape as his guilty imagination gave it; or, at least, with so little definiteness, that another's guilt might have seen another symbol in it.

There was a singular circumstance that characterized Mr. Dimmesdale's psychological state at this moment. All the time that he gazed upward to the zenith, he was, nevertheless, perfectly aware that little Pearl was pointing her finger towards old Roger Chillingworth, who stood at no great distance from the scaffold. The minister appeared to see him, with the same glance that discerned the miraculous letter. To his features, as to all other objects, the meteoric light imparted a new expression; or it might well be that the physician was not careful then, as at all other times, to hide the malevolence with which he looked upon his victim. Certainly, if the meteor kindled up the sky, and disclosed the earth, with an awfulness that admonished Hester Prynne and the clergyman of the day of judgment, then might Roger Chillingworth have passed with them for the arch-fiend, standing there with a smile and scowl to claim his own. So vivid was the expression, or so intense the minister's perception of it, that it seemed still to remain painted on the darkness, after the meteor had vanished, with an effect as if the street and all things else were at once annihilated.

"Who is that man, Hester?" gasped Mr. Dimmesdale, overcome with terror. "I shiver at him! Dost thou know the man? I hate him, Hester!"

She remembered her oath, and was silent.

"I tell thee, my soul shivers at him!" muttered the minister again.

"Who is he? Who is he? Canst thou do nothing for me? I have a nameless horror of the man!"

"Minister," said little Pearl, "I can tell thee who he is!"

"Quickly, then, child!" said the minister, bending his ear close to her lips. "Quickly!—and as low as thou canst whisper."

Pearl mumbled something into his ear, that sounded, indeed, like human language, but was only such gibberish as children may be heard amusing themselves with, by the hour together. At all events, if it involved any secret information in regard to old Roger Chillingworth, it was in a tongue unknown to the erudite clergyman, and did but increase the bewilderment of his mind. The elfish child then laughed aloud.

"Dost thou mock me now?" said the minister.

"Thou wast not bold!—thou wast not true!"—answered the child. "Thou wouldst not promise to take my hand, and mother's hand, to-morrow noontide!"

"Worthy Sir," answered the physician, who had now advanced to the foot of the platform. "Pious Master Dimmesdale, can this be you? Well, well, indeed! We men of study, whose heads are in our books, have need to be straitly looked after! We dream in our waking moments, and walk in our sleep. Come, good Sir, and my dear friend, I pray you, let me lead you home!"

"How knewest thou that I was here?" asked the minister, fearfully.

"Verily, and in good faith," answered Roger Chillingworth, "I knew nothing of the matter. I had spent the better part of the night at the bedside of the worshipful Governor Winthrop, doing what my poor skill might to give him ease. He going home to a better world, I, likewise, was on my way homeward, when this strange light shone out. Come with me, I beseech you, Reverend Sir; else you will be poorly able to do Sabbath duty to-morrow. Aha! see now, how they trouble the brain,—these books!—these books! You should study less, good Sir, and take a little pastime; or these night whimseys will grow upon you."

"I will go home with you," said Mr. Dimmesdale.

With a chill despondency, like one awaking, all nerveless, from an ugly dream, he yielded himself to the physician, and was led away.

The next day, however, being the Sabbath, he preached a discourse which was held to be the richest and most powerful, and the most replete with heavenly influences, that had ever proceeded from his lips. Souls, it is said more souls than one, were brought to the truth by the efficacy of that sermon, and vowed within themselves to cherish a holy gratitude towards Mr. Dimmesdale throughout the long hereafter. But, as he came down the pulpit steps, the gray-bearded sexton met him, holding up a black glove, which the minister recognized as his own.

"It was found," said the sexton, "this morning, on the scaffold where evil-doers are set up to public shame. Satan dropped it there, I take it, intending a scurrilous jest against your reverence. But, indeed, he was blind and foolish, as he ever and always is. A pure hand needs no glove to cover it!"

"Thank you, my good friend," said the minister, gravely, but startled at heart; for so confused was his remembrance, that he had almost brought himself to look at the events of the past night as visionary. "Yes, it seems to be my glove, indeed!"

"And, since Satan saw fit to steal it, your reverence must needs handle him without gloves, henceforward," remarked the old sexton, grimly smiling. "But did your reverence hear of the portent that was seen last night? —a great red letter in the sky,—the letter A, which we interpret to stand for Angel. For, as our good Governor Winthrop was made an angel this past night, it was doubtless held fit that there should be some notice thereof!"

"No," answered the minister, "I had not heard of it."

## XIII

### ANOTHER VIEW OF HESTER

IN her late singular interview with Mr. Dimmesdale, Hester Prynne was shocked at the condition to which she found the clergyman reduced. His nerve seemed absolutely destroyed. His moral force was abased into more than childish weakness. It grovelled helpless on the ground, even while his intellectual faculties retained their pristine strength, or had perhaps acquired a morbid energy, which disease only could have given them. With her knowledge of a train of circumstances hidden from all others, she could readily infer that, besides the legitimate action of his own conscience, a terrible machinery had been brought to bear, and was still operating, on Mr. Dimmesdale's well-being and repose. Knowing what this poor, fallen man had once been, her whole soul was moved by the shuddering terror with which he had appealed to her,—the outcast woman,— for support against his instinctively discovered enemy. She decided, moreover, that he had a right to her utmost aid. Little accustomed, in her long seclusion from society, to measure her ideas of right and wrong by any standard external to herself, Hester saw—or seemed to see—that there lay a responsibility upon her, in reference to the clergyman, which she owed to no other, nor to the whole world besides. The links that united her to the rest of human kind—links of flowers, or silk, or gold, or whatever the material—had all been broken. Here was the iron link of mutual crime, which neither he nor she could break. Like all other ties, it brought along with it its obligations.

Hester Prynne did not now occupy precisely the same position in which we beheld her during the earlier periods of her ignominy. Years had come and gone. Pearl was now seven years old. Her mother, with the scarlet letter on her breast, glittering in its fantastic embroidery, had long been a familiar object to the townspeople. As is apt to be the case when a person stands out in any prominence before the community, and, at the same time, interferes neither with public nor individual interests and convenience, a species of general regard had ultimately grown up in reference to Hester Prynne. It is to the credit of human nature, that, except where its selfishness is brought into play, it loves more readily than it hates. Hatred, by a gradual and quiet process, will even be transformed to love, unless the change be impeded by a continually new irritation of the original feeling of hostility. In this matter of Hester Prynne, there was neither irritation nor irksomeness. She never battled with the public, but submitted, uncomplainingly, to its worst usage; she made no claim upon it, in requital for what she suffered; she did not weigh upon its sympathies. Then, also, the blameless purity of her life during all these years in which she had been set apart to infamy, was reckoned largely in her favor. With nothing now to lose, in the sight of mankind, and with no hope, and seemingly no wish, of gaining anything, it could only be a genuine regard for virtue that had brought back the poor wanderer to its paths.

It was perceived, too, that while Hester never put forward even the humblest title to share in the world's privileges,—further than to breathe the common air, and earn daily bread for little Pearl and herself by the faithful labor of her hands,—she was quick to acknowledge her sisterhood with the race of man, whenever benefits were to be conferred. None so ready as she to give of her little substance to every demand of poverty; even though the bitter-hearted pauper threw back a gibe in requital of the food brought regularly to his door, or the garments wrought for him by the fingers that could have embroidered a monarch's robe. None so self-devoted as Hester, when pestilence stalked through the town. In all seasons of calamity, indeed, whether general or of individuals, the outcast of society at once found her place. She came, not as a guest, but as a rightful inmate, into the household that was darkened by trouble; as if its gloomy twilight were a medium in which she was entitled to hold intercourse with her fellow-creatures. There glimmered the embroidered letter, with comfort in its unearthly ray. Elsewhere the token of sin, it was the taper of the sick-chamber. It had even thrown its gleam, in the sufferer's hard extremity, across the verge of time. It had shown him where to set his foot, while the light of earth was fast becoming dim, and ere the light of futurity could reach him. In such emergencies, Hester's nature showed itself warm and rich; a well-spring of human tenderness, unfailing to every real demand, and inexhaustible by the largest. Her breast, with its badge of shame, was but the softer pillow for the head that needed one. She was self-ordained a Sister of Mercy; or, we may rather say, the world's heavy hand had so ordained her, when neither the world nor she looked forward to this result. The letter was the symbol of her calling. Such helpfulness was found in her,—so much power to do, and power to sympathize,—that many people refused to interpret the scarlet A by its original signification. They said that it meant Able; so strong was Hester Prynne, with a woman's strength.

It was only the darkened house that could contain her. When sunshine came again, she was not there. Her shadow had faded across the threshold. The helpful inmate had departed, without one backward glance to gather up the meed of gratitude, if any were in the hearts of those whom she had served so zealously. Meeting them in the street, she never raised her head to receive their greeting. If they were resolute to accost her, she laid her finger on the scarlet letter, and passed on. This might be pride, but was so like humility, that it produced all the softening influence of the latter quality on the public mind. The public is despotic in its temper; it is capable of denying common justice, when too strenuously demanded as a right; but quite as frequently it awards more than justice, when the appeal is made, as despots love to have it made, entirely to its generosity. Interpreting Hester Prynne's deportment as an appeal of this nature, society was inclined to show its former victim a more benign countenance than she cared to be favored with, or, perchance, than she deserved.

The rulers, and the wise and learned men of the community, were longer in acknowledging the influence of Hester's good qualities than the people. The prejudices which they shared in common with the latter were fortified in themselves by an iron framework of reasoning, that made it a far tougher labor to expel them. Day by day, nevertheless, their sour and rigid wrinkles were relaxing into something which, in the due course of years, might grow to be an expression of almost benevolence. Thus it was with the men of rank, on whom their eminent position imposed the guardianship of the public morals. Individuals in private life, meanwhile, had quite forgiven Hester Prynne for her frailty; nay, more, they had begun to look upon the scarlet letter as the token, not of that one sin, for which she had borne so long and dreary a penance, but of her many good deeds since. "Do you see that woman with the embroidered badge?" they would say to strangers. "It is our Hester,—the town's own Hester, who is so kind to the poor, so helpful to the sick, so comfortable to the afflicted!" Then, it is true, the propensity of human nature to tell the very worst of itself, when embodied in the person of another, would constrain them to whisper the black scandal of bygone years. It was none the less a fact, however, that, in the eyes of the very men who spoke thus, the scarlet letter had the effect of the cross on a nun's bosom. It imparted to the wearer a kind of sacredness, which enabled her to walk securely amid all peril. Had she fallen among thieves, it would have kept her safe. It was reported, and believed by many, that an Indian had drawn his arrow against the badge, and that the missile struck it, but fell harmless to the ground.

The effect of the symbol—or, rather, of the position in respect to society that was indicated by it—on the mind of Hester Prynne herself, was powerful and peculiar. All the light and graceful foliage of her character had been withered up by this red-hot brand, and had long ago fallen away, leaving a bare and harsh outline, which might have been repulsive, had she possessed friends or companions to be repelled by it. Even the attractiveness of her person had undergone a similar change. It might be partly owing to the studied austerity of her dress, and partly to the lack of demonstration in her manners. It was a sad transformation, too, that her rich and luxuriant hair had either been cut off, or was so completely hidden by a cap, that not a shining lock of it ever once gushed into the sunshine. It was due in part to all these causes, but still more to something else, that there seemed to be no longer anything in Hester's face for Love to dwell upon; nothing in Hester's form, though majestic and statue-like, that Passion would ever dream of clasping in its embrace; nothing in Hester's bosom, to make it ever again the pillow of Affection. Some attribute had departed from her, the permanence of which had been essential to keep her a woman. Such is frequently the fate, and such the stern development, of the feminine character and person, when the woman has encountered, and lived through, an experience of peculiar severity. If she be all tenderness, she will die. If she survive, the tenderness will either be crushed out of her, or—and the outward semblance is the same—crushed so deeply into her heart that it can never show itself more. The latter is perhaps the truest theory. She who has once been woman, and ceased to be so, might at any moment become a woman again if there were only the magic touch to effect the transfiguration. We shall see whether Hester Prynne were ever afterwards so touched, and so transfigured.

Much of the marble coldness of Hester's impression was to be attributed to the circumstance, that her life had turned, in a great measure, from passion and feeling, to thought. Standing alone in the world,—alone, as to any dependence on society, and with little Pearl to be guided and protected,—alone, and hopeless of retrieving her position, even had she not scorned to consider it desirable,—she cast away the fragments of a broken chain. The world's law was no law for her mind. It was an age in which the human intellect, newly emancipated, had taken a more active and a wider range than for many centuries before. Men of the sword had overthrown nobles and kings. Men bolder than these had overthrown and rearranged—not actually, but within the sphere of theory, which was their most real abode—the whole system of ancient prejudice, wherewith was linked much of  ancient principle. Hester Prynne imbibed this spirit. She assumed a freedom of speculation, then common enough on the other side of the Atlantic, but which our forefathers, had they known it, would have held to be a deadlier crime than that stigmatized by the scarlet letter. In her lonesome cottage, by the sea-shore, thoughts visited her, such as dared to enter no other dwelling in New England; shadowy guests, that would have been as perilous as demons to their entertainer, could they have been seen so much as knocking at her door.

It is remarkable that persons who speculate the most boldly often conform with the most perfect quietude to the external regulations of society. The thought suffices them, without investing itself in the flesh and blood of action. So it seemed to be with Hester. Yet, had little Pearl never come to her from the spiritual world, it might have been far otherwise. Then, she might have come down to us in history, hand in hand with Anne Hutchinson, as the foundress of a religious sect. She might, in one of her phases, have been a prophetess. She might, and not improbably would, have suffered death from the stern tribunals of the period, for attempting to undermine the foundations of the Puritan establishment. But, in the education of her child, the mother's enthusiasm of thought had something to wreak itself upon. Providence, in the person of this little girl, had assigned to Hester's charge the germ and blossom of womanhood, to be cherished and developed amid a host of difficulties. Everything was against her. The world was hostile. The child's own nature had something wrong in it, which continually betokened that she had been born amiss,— the effluence of her mother's lawless passion,—and often impelled Hester to ask, in bitterness of heart, whether it were for ill or good that the poor little creature had been born at all.

Indeed, the same dark question often rose into her mind, with reference to the whole race of womanhood. Was existence worth accepting, even to the happiest among them? As concerned her own individual existence, she had long ago decided in the negative, and dismissed the point as settled. A tendency to speculation, though it may keep woman quiet, as it does man, yet makes her sad. She discerns, it may be, such a hopeless task before her. As a first step, the whole system of society is to be torn down, and built up anew. Then, the very nature of the opposite sex, or its long hereditary habit, which has become like nature, is to be essentially modified, before woman can be allowed to assume what seems a fair and suitable position. Finally, all other difficulties being obviated, woman cannot take advantage of these preliminary reforms, until she herself shall have undergone a still mightier change; in which, perhaps, the ethereal essence, wherein she has her truest life, will be found to have evaporated. A woman never overcomes these problems by any exercise of thought. They are not to be solved, or only in one way. If her heart chance to come uppermost, they vanish. Thus, Hester Prynne, whose heart had lost its regular and healthy throb, wandered without a clew in the dark labyrinth of mind: now turned aside by an insurmountable precipice; now starting back from a deep chasm. There was wild and ghastly scenery all around her, and a home and comfort nowhere. At times, a fearful doubt strove to possess her soul, whether it were not better to send Pearl at once ,to heaven, and go herself to such futurity as Eternal Justice should provide.

The scarlet letter had not done its office.

Now, however, her interview with the Reverend Mr. Dimmesdale, on the night of his vigil, had given her a new theme of reflection, and held up to her an object that appeared worthy of any exertion and sacrifice for its attainment. She had witnessed the intense misery beneath which the minister struggled, or, to speak more accurately, had ceased to struggle. She saw that he stood on the verge of lunacy, if he had not already stepped across it. It was impossible to doubt, that, whatever painful efficacy there might be in the secret sting of remorse, a deadlier venom had been infused into it by the hand that proffered relief. A secret enemy had been continually by his side, under the semblance of a friend and helper, and had availed himself of the opportunities thus afforded for tampering with the delicate springs of Mr. Dimmesdale's nature. Hester could not but ask herself, whether there had not originally been a defect of truth, courage, and loyalty, on her own part, in allowing the minister to be thrown into a position where so much evil was to be foreboded, and nothing auspicious to be hoped. Her only justification lay in the fact, that she had been able to discern no method of rescuing him from a blacker ruin than had overwhelmed herself, except by acquiescing in Roger Chillingworth's scheme of disguise. Under that impulse, she had made her choice, and had chosen, as it now appeared, the more wretched alternative of the two. She determined to redeem her error, so far as it might yet be possible. Strengthened by years of hard and solemn trial, she felt herself no longer so inadequate to cope with Roger Chillingworth as on that night, abased by sin, and half maddened by the ignominy, that was still new, when they had talked together in the prison-chamber. She had climbed her way, since then, to a higher point. The old man, on the other hand, had brought himself nearer to her level, or perhaps below it, by the revenge which he had stooped for.

In fine, Hester Prynne resolved to meet her former husband, and do what might be in her power for the rescue of the victim on whom he had so evidently set his gripe. The occasion was not long to seek. One afternoon, walking with Pearl in a retired part of the peninsula, she beheld the old physician, with a basket on one arm, and a staff in the other hand, stooping along the ground, in quest of roots and herbs to concoct his medicines withal.

## XIV

### HESTER AND THE PHYSICIAN

HESTER bade little Pearl run down to the margin of the water, and play with the shells and tangled seaweed, until she should have talked awhile with yonder gatherer of herbs. So the child flew away like a bird, and, making bare her small white feet, went pattering along the moist margin of the sea. Here and there she came to a full stop, and peeped curiously into a pool, left by the retiring tide as a mirror for Pearl to see her face in. Forth peeped at her, out of the pool, with dark, glistening curls around her head, and an elf-smile in her eyes, the image of a little maid, whom Pearl, having no other playmate, invited to take her hand, and run a race with her. But the visionary little maid, on her part, beckoned likewise, as if to say,—"This is a better place! Come thou into the pool!" And Pearl, stepping in, mid-leg deep, beheld her own white feet at the bottom; while, out of a still lower depth, came the gleam of a kind of fragmentary smile, floating to and fro in the agitated water.

Meanwhile her mother had accosted the physician.

"I would speak a word with you," said she,—"a word that concerns us much."

"Aha! and is it Mistress Hester that has a word for old Roger Chillingworth?" answered he, raising himself from his stooping posture. "With all my heart! Why, Mistress, I hear good tidings of you on all hands! No longer ago than yester-eve, a magistrate, a wise and godly man, was discoursing of your affairs, Mistress Hester, and whispered me that there had been question concerning you in the council. It was debated whether or no, with safety to the common weal, yonder scarlet letter might be taken off your bosom. On my life, Hester, I made my entreaty to the worshipful magistrate that it might be done forthwith!"

"It lies not in the pleasure of the magistrates to take off this badge," calmly replied Hester. "Were I worthy to be quit of it, it would fall away of its own nature, or be transformed into something that should speak a different purport."

"Nay, then, wear it, if it suit you better," rejoined he. "A woman must needs follow her own fancy, touching the adornment of her person. The letter is gayly embroidered, and shows right bravely on your bosom!"

All this while, Hester had been looking steadily at the old man, and was shocked, as well as wonder-smitten, to discern what a change had been wrought upon him within the past seven years. It was not so much that he had grown older; for though the traces of advancing life were visible, he wore his age well, and seemed to retain a wiry vigor and alertness. But the former aspect of an intellectual and studious man, calm and quiet, which was what she best remembered in him, had altogether vanished, and been succeeded by an eager, searching, almost fierce, yet carefully guarded look. It seemed to be his wish and purpose to mask this expression with a smile; but the latter played him false, and flickered over his visage so derisively, that the spectator could see his blackness all the better for it. Ever and anon, too, there came a glare of red light out of his eyes; as if the old man's soul were on fire, and kept on smouldering duskily within his breast, until, by some casual puff of passion, it was blown into a momentary flame. This he repressed, as speedily as possible, and strove to look as if nothing of the kind had happened.

In a word, old Roger Chillingworth was a striking evidence of man's faculty of transforming himself into a devil, if he will only, for a reasonable space of time, undertake a devil's office. This unhappy person had effected such a transformation, by devoting himself, for seven years, to the constant analysis of a heart full of torture, and deriving his enjoyment thence, and adding fuel to those fiery tortures which he analyzed and gloated over.

The scarlet letter burned on Hester Prynne's bosom. Here was another ruin, the responsibility of which came partly home to her.

"What see you in my face," asked the physician, "that you look at it so earnestly?"

"Something that would make me weep, if there were any tears bitter enough for it," answered she. "But let it pass! It is of yonder miserable man that I would speak."

"And what of him?" cried Roger Chillingworth, eagerly, as if he loved the topic, and were glad of an opportunity to discuss it with the only person of whom he could make a confidant. "Not to hide the truth, Mistress Hester, my thoughts happen just now to be busy with the gentleman. So speak freely, and I will make answer."

"When we last spake together," said Hester, "now seven years ago, it was your pleasure to extort a promise of secrecy, as touching the former relation betwixt yourself and me. As the life and good fame of yonder man were in your hands, there seemed no choice to me, save to be silent, in accordance with your behest. Yet it was not without heavy misgivings that I thus bound myself; for, having cast off all duty towards other human beings, there remained a duty towards him; and something whispered me that I was betraying it, in pledging myself to keep your counsel. Since that day, no man is so near to him as you. You tread behind his every footstep. You are beside him, sleeping and waking. You search his thoughts. You burrow and rankle in his heart! Your clutch is on his life, and you cause him to die daily a living death; and still he knows you not. In permitting this, I have surely acted a false part by the only man to whom the power was left me to be true!"

"What choice had you?" asked Roger Chillingworth. "My finger, pointed at this man, would have hurled him from his pulpit into a dungeon,—thence, peradventure, to the gallows!"

"It had been better so!" said Hester Prynne.

"What evil have I done the man?" asked Roger Chillingworth again. "I tell thee, Hester Prynne, the richest fee that ever physician earned from monarch could not have bought such care as I have wasted on this miserable priest! But for my aid, his life would have burned away in torments, within the first two years after the perpetration of his crime and thine. For, Hester, his spirit lacked the strength that could have borne up, as thine has, beneath a burden like thy scarlet letter. Oh, I could reveal a goodly secret! But enough! What art can do, I have exhausted on him. That he now breathes, and creeps about on earth, is owing all to me!"

"Better he had died at once!" said Hester Prynne.

"Yea, woman, thou sayest truly!" cried old Roger Chillingworth, letting the lurid fire of his heart blaze out before her eyes. "Better had he died at once! Never did mortal suffer what this man has suffered. And all, all, in the sight of his worst enemy! He has been conscious of me. He has felt an influence dwelling always upon him like a curse. He knew, by some spiritual sense,—for the Creator never made another being so sensitive as this,—he knew that no friendly hand was pulling at his heart-strings, and that an eye was looking curiously into him, which sought only evil, and found it. But he knew not that the eye and hand were mine! With the superstition common to his brotherhood, he fancied himself given over to a fiend, to be tortured with frightful dreams, and desperate thoughts, the sting of remorse, and despair of pardon; as a foretaste of what awaits him beyond the grave. But it was the constant shadow of my presence!—the closest propinquity of the man whom he had most vilely wronged!—and who had grown to exist only by this perpetual poison of the direst revenge! Yea, indeed!—he did not err!—there was a fiend at his elbow! A mortal man, with once a human heart, has become a fiend for his especial torment!"

The unfortunate physician, while uttering these words, lifted his hands with a look of horror, as if he had beheld some frightful shape, which he could not recognize, usurping the place of his own image in a glass. It was one of those moments—which sometimes occur only at the interval of years—when a man's moral aspect is faithfully revealed to his mind's eye. Not improbably, he had never before viewed himself as he did now.

"Hast thou not tortured him enough?" said Hester, noticing the old man's look. "Has he not paid thee all?"

"No!—no! He has but increased the debt!" answered the physician; and as he proceeded, his manner lost its fiercer characteristics, and subsided into gloom. "Dost thou remember me, Hester, as I was nine years agone? Even then, I was in the autumn of my days, nor was it the early autumn. But all my life had been made up of earnest, studious, thoughtful, quiet years, bestowed faithfully for the increase of mine own knowledge, and faithfully, too, though this latter object was but casual to the other,—faithfully for the advancement of human welfare. No life had been more peaceful and innocent than mine; few lives so rich with benefits conferred. Dost thou remember me? Was I not, though you might deem me cold, nevertheless a man thoughtful for others, craving little for himself,—kind, true, just, and of constant, if not warm affections? Was I not all this?"

"All this, and more," said Hester.

"And what am I now?" demanded he, looking into her face, and permitting the whole evil within him to be written on his features. "I have already told thee what I am! A fiend! Who made me so?"

"It was myself!" cried Hester, shuddering. "It was I, not less than he. Why hast thou not avenged thyself on me?"

"I have left thee to the scarlet letter," replied Roger Chillingworth. "If that have not avenged me, I can do no more!"

He laid his finger on it, with a smile.

"It has avenged thee!" answered Hester Prynne.

"I judged no less," said the physician. "And now, what wouldst thou with me touching this man?"

"I must reveal the secret," answered Hester, firmly. "He must discern thee in thy true character. What may be the result, I know not. But this long debt of confidence, due from me to him, whose bane and ruin I have been, shall at length be paid. So far as concerns the overthrow or preservation of his fair fame and his earthly state, and perchance his life, he is in thy hands. Nor do I,—whom the scarlet letter has disciplined to truth, though it be the truth of red-hot iron, entering into the soul,—nor do I

perceive such advantage in his living any longer a life of ghastly emptiness, that I shall stoop to implore thy mercy. Do with him as thou wilt!
There is no good for him,—no good for me,—no good for thee! There is
no good for little Pearl! There is no path to guide us out of this dismal
maze!"

"Woman, I could wellnigh pity thee!" said Roger Chillingworth, unable to restrain a thrill of admiration too; for there was a quality almost
majestic in the despair which she expressed. "Thou hadst great elements.
Peradventure, hadst thou met earlier with a better love than mine, this
evil had not been. I pity thee, for the good that has been wasted in thy
nature!"

"And I thee," answered Hester Prynne, "for the hatred that has transformed a wise and just man to a fiend! Wilt thou yet purge it out of thee,
and be once more human? If not for his sake, then doubly for thine own!
Forgive, and leave his further retribution to the Power that claims it! I
said, but now, that there could be no good event for him, or thee, or me,
who are here wandering together in this gloomy maze of evil, and stumbling, at every step, over the guilt wherewith we have strewn our path. It is
not so! There might be good for thee, and thee alone, since thou hast been
deeply wronged, and hast it at thy will to pardon. Wilt thou give up that
only privilege? Wilt thou reject that priceless benefit?"

"Peace, Hester, peace!" replied the old man, with gloomy sternness.
"It is not granted me to pardon. I have no such power as thou tellest me
of. My old faith, long forgotten, comes back to me, and explains all that
we do, and all we suffer. By thy first step awry thou didst plant the germ
of evil; but since that moment, it has all been a dark necessity. Ye that
have wronged me are not sinful, save in a kind of typical illusion; neither
am I fiend-like, who have snatched a fiend's office from his hands. It is
our fate. Let the black flower blossom as it may! Now go thy ways, and
deal as thou wilt with yonder man."

He waved his hand, and betook himself again to his employment of
gathering herbs.

## XV

## HESTER AND PEARL

So Roger Chillingworth—a deformed old figure, with a face that haunted
men's memories longer than they liked—took leave of Hester Prynne, and
went stooping away along the earth. He gathered here and there an herb,
or grubbed up a root, and put it into the basket on his arm. His gray beard
almost touched thè ground, as he crept onward. Hester gazed after him a
little while, looking with a half-fantastic curiosity to see whether the ten-

der grass of early spring would not be blighted beneath him, and show the wavering track of his footsteps, sere and brown, across its cheerful verdure. She wondered what sort of herbs they were, which the old man was so sedulous to gather. Would not the earth, quickened to an evil purpose by the sympathy of his eye, greet him with poisonous shrubs, of species hitherto unknown, that would start up under his fingers? Or might it suffice him that every wholesome growth should be converted into something deleterious and malignant at his touch? Did the sun, which shone so brightly everywhere else, really fall upon him? Or was there, as it rather seemed, a circle of ominous shadow moving along with his deformity, whichever way he turned himself? And whither was he now going? Would he not suddenly sink into the earth, leaving a barren and blasted spot, where, in due course of time, would be seen deadly nightshade, dogwood, henbane, and whatever else of vegetable wickedness the climate could produce, all flourishing with hideous luxuriance? Or would he spread bat's wings and flee away, looking so much the uglier the higher he rose towards heaven?

"Be it sin or no," said Hester Prynne, bitterly, as she still gazed after him, "I hate the man!"

She upbraided herself for the sentiment, but could not overcome or lessen it. Attempting to do so, she thought of those long-past days, in a distant land, when he used to emerge at eventide from the seclusion of his study, and sit down in the firelight of their home, and in the light of her nuptial smile. He needed to bask himself in that smile, he said, in order that the chill of so many lonely hours among his books might be taken off the scholar's heart. Such scenes had once appeared not otherwise than happy; but now, as viewed through the dismal medium of her subsequent life, they classed themselves among her ugliest remembrances. She marvelled how such scenes could have been! She marvelled how she could ever have been wrought upon to marry him! She deemed it her crime most to be repented of that she had ever endured, and reciprocated, the lukewarm grasp of his hand, and had suffered the smile of her lips and eyes to mingle and melt into his own. And it seemed a fouler offence committed by Roger Chillingworth, than any which had since been done him, that, in the time when her heart knew no better, he had persuaded her to fancy herself happy by his side.

"Yes, I hate him!" repeated Hester, more bitterly than before. "He betrayed me! He has done me worse wrong than I did him!"

Let men tremble to win the hand of woman, unless they win along with it the utmost passion of her heart! Else it may be their miserable fortune, as it was Roger Chillingworth's, when some mightier touch than their own may have awakened all her sensibilities, to be reproached even for the calm content, the marble image of happiness, which they will have imposed upon her as the warm reality. But Hester ought long ago to have done with this injustice. What did it betoken? Had seven long years, under the torture of the scarlet letter, inflicted so much of misery, and wrought out no repentance?

The emotions of that brief space, while she stood gazing after the crooked figure of old Roger Chillingworth, threw a dark light on Hester's state of mind, revealing much that she might not otherwise have acknowledged to herself.

He being gone, she summoned back her child.

"Pearl! Little Pearl! Where are you?"

Pearl, whose activity of spirit never flagged, had been at no loss for amusement while her mother talked with the old gatherer of herbs. At first, as already told, she had flirted fancifully with her own image in a pool of water, beckoning the phantom forth, and—as it declined to venture—seeking a passage for herself into its sphere of impalpable earth and unattainable sky. Soon finding, however, that either she or the image was unreal, she turned elsewhere for better pastime. She made little boats out of birch-bark, and freighted them with snail-shells, and sent out more ventures on the mighty deep than any merchant in New England; but the larger part of them foundered near the shore. She seized a live horse-shoe by the tail, and made prize of several five-fingers, and laid out a jelly-fish to melt in the warm sun. Then she took up the white foam, that streaked the line of the advancing tide, and threw it upon the breeze, scampering after it, with winged footsteps, to catch the great snow-flakes ere they fell. Perceiving a flock of beach-birds, that fed and fluttered along the shore, the naughty child picked up her apron full of pebbles, and, creeping from rock to rock after these small sea-fowl, displayed remarkable dexterity in pelting them. One little gray bird, with a white breast, Pearl was almost sure, had been hit by a pebble, and fluttered away with a broken wing. But then the elf-child sighed, and gave up her sport; because it grieved her to have done harm to a little being that was as wild as the sea-breeze, or as wild as Pearl herself.

Her final employment was to gather sea-weed, of various kinds, and make herself a scarf, or mantle, and a head-dress, and thus assume the aspect of a little mermaid. She inherited her mother's gift for devising drapery and costume. As the last touch to her mermaid's garb, Pearl took some eel-grass, and imitated, as best she could, on her own bosom, the decoration with which she was so familiar on her mother's. A letter,—the letter A,—but freshly green, instead of scarlet! The child bent her chin upon her breast, and contemplated this device with strange interest; even as if the one only thing for which she had been sent into the world was to make out its hidden import.

"I wonder if mother will ask me what it means!" thought Pearl.

Just then, she heard her mother's voice, and flitting along as lightly as one of the little sea-birds, appeared before Hester Prynne, dancing, laughing, and pointing her finger to the ornament upon her bosom.

"My little Pearl," said Hester, after a moment's silence, "the green letter, and on thy childish bosom, has no purport. But dost thou know, my child, what this letter means which thy mother is doomed to wear?"

"Yes, mother," said the child. "It is the great letter A. Thou hast taught me in the horn-book."

Hester looked steadily into her little face; but, though there was that singular expression which she had so often remarked in her black eyes, she could not satisfy herself whether Pearl really attached any meaning to the symbol. She felt a morbid desire to ascertain the point.

"Dost thou know, child, wherefore thy mother wears this letter?"

"Truly do I!" answered Pearl, looking brightly into her mother's face. "It is for the same reason that the minister keeps his hand over his heart!"

"And what reason is that?" asked Hester, half smiling at the absurd incongruity of the child's observation; but, on second thoughts, turning pale. "What has the letter to do with any heart, save mine?"

"Nay, mother, I have told all I know," said Pearl, more seriously than she was wont to speak. "Ask yonder old man whom thou hast been talking with! It may be he can tell. But in good earnest now, mother dear, what does this scarlet letter mean?—and why dost thou wear it on thy bosom?—and why does the minister keep his hand over his heart?"

She took her mother's hand in both her own, and gazed into her eyes with an earnestness that was seldom seen in her wild and capricious character. The thought occurred to Hester that the child might really be seeking to approach her with childlike confidence, and doing what she could, and as intelligently as she knew how, to establish a meeting-point of sympathy. It showed Pearl in an unwonted aspect. Heretofore, the mother, while loving her child with the intensity of a sole affection, had schooled herself to hope for little other return than the waywardness of an April breeze; which spends its time in airy sport, and has its gusts of inexplicable passion, and is petulant in its best of moods, and chills oftener than caresses you, when you take it to your bosom; in requital of which misdemeanors, it will sometimes, of its own vague purpose, kiss your cheek with a kind of doubtful tenderness, and play gently with your hair, and then be gone about its other idle business, leaving a dreamy pleasure at your heart. And this, moreover, was a mother's estimate of the child's disposition. Any other observer might have seen few but unamiable traits, and have given them a far darker coloring. But now the idea came strongly into Hester's mind, that Pearl, with her remarkable precocity and acuteness, might already have approached the age when she could be made a friend, and intrusted with as much of her mother's sorrows as could be imparted, without irreverence either to the parent or the child. In the little chaos of Pearl's character there might be seen emerging—and could have been, from the very first—the steadfast principles of an unflinching courage,—an uncontrollable will,—a sturdy pride, which might be disciplined into self-respect,—and a bitter scorn of many things, which, when examined, might be found to have the taint of falsehood in them. She possessed affections, too, though hitherto acrid and disagreeable, as are the richest flavors of unripe fruit. With all these sterling attributes, thought Hester, the evil which she inherited from her mother must be great indeed, if a noble woman do not grow out of this elfish child.

Pearl's inevitable tendency to hover about the enigma of the scarlet letter seemed an innate quality of her being. From the earliest epoch of her conscious life, she had entered upon this as her appointed mission. Hester had often fancied that Providence had a design of justice and retribution, in endowing the child with this marked propensity; but never, until now, had she bethought herself to ask, whether, linked with that design, there might not likewise be a purpose of mercy and beneficence. If little Pearl were entertained with faith and trust, as a spirit messenger no less than an earthly child, might it not be her errand to soothe away the sorrow that lay cold in her mother's heart, and converted it into a tomb?—and to help her to overcome the passion, once so wild, and even yet neither dead nor asleep, but only imprisoned within the same tomb-like heart?

Such were some of the thoughts that now stirred in Hester's mind, with as much vivacity of impression as if they had actually been whispered into her ear. And there was little Pearl, all this while holding her mother's hand in both her own, and turning her face upward, while she put these searching questions, once, and again, and still a third time.

"What does the letter mean, mother?—and why dost thou wear it?—and why does the minister keep his hand over his heart?"

"What shall I say?" thought Hester to herself. "No! If this be the price of the child's sympathy, I cannot pay it."

Then she spoke aloud.

"Silly Pearl," said she, "what questions are these? There are many things in this world that a child must not ask about. What know I of the minister's heart? And as for the scarlet letter, I wear it for the sake of its gold-thread."

In all the seven bygone years, Hester Prynne had never before been false to the symbol on her bosom. It may be that it was the talisman of a stern and severe, but yet a guardian spirit, who now forsook her; as recognizing that, in spite of his strict watch over her heart, some new evil had crept into it, or some old one had never been expelled. As for little Pearl, the earnestness soon passed out of her face.

But the child did not see fit to let the matter drop. Two or three times, as her mother and she went homeward, and as often at supper-time, and while Hester was putting her to bed, and once after she seemed to be fairly asleep, Pearl looked up, with mischief gleaming in her black eyes.

"Mother," said she, "what does the scarlet letter mean?"

And the next morning, the first indication the child gave of being awake was by popping up her head from the pillow, and making that other inquiry, which she had so unaccountably connected with her investigations about the scarlet letter,—

"Mother!—Mother!—Why does the minister keep his hand over his heart?"

"Hold thy tongue, naughty child!" answered her mother, with an asperity that she had never permitted to herself before. "Do not tease me, else I shall shut thee into the dark closet!"

## XVI

## A FOREST WALK

HESTER PRYNNE remained constant in her resolve to make known to Mr. Dimmesdale, at whatever risk of present pain or ulterior consequences, the true character of the man who had crept into his intimacy. For several days, however, she vainly sought an opportunity of addressing him in some of the meditative walks which she knew him to be in the habit of taking, along the shores of the peninsula, or on the wooded hills of the neighboring country. There would have been no scandal, indeed, nor peril to the holy whiteness of the clergyman's good fame, had she visited him in his own study, where many a penitent, ere now, had confessed sins of perhaps as deep a dye as the one betoken by the scarlet letter. But, partly that she dreaded the secret or undisguised interference of old Roger Chillingworth, and partly that her conscious heart imputed suspicion where none could have been felt, and partly that both the minister and she would need the whole wide world to breathe in, while they talked together,—for all these reasons, Hester never thought of meeting him in any narrower privacy than beneath the open sky.

At last, while attending in a sick-chamber, whither the Reverend Mr. Dimmesdale had been summoned to make a prayer, she learnt that he had gone, the day before, to visit the Apostle Eliot, among his Indian converts. He would probably return, by a certain hour, in the afternoon of the morrow. Betimes, therefore, the next day, Hester took little Pearl,—who was necessarily the companion of all her mother's expeditions, however inconvenient her presence,—and set forth.

The road, after the two wayfarers had crossed from the peninsula to the mainland, was no other than a footpath. It straggled onward into the mystery of the primeval forest. This hemmed it in so narrowly, and stood so black and dense on either side, and disclosed such imperfect glimpses of the sky above, that, to Hester's mind, it imaged not amiss the moral wilderness in which she had so long been wandering. The day was chill and sombre. Overhead was a gray expanse of cloud, slightly stirred, however, by a breeze; so that a gleam of flickering sunshine might now and then be seen at its solitary play along the path. This flitting cheerfulness was always at the farther extremity of some long vista through the forest. The sportive sunlight—feebly sportive, at best, in the predominant pensiveness of the day and scene—withdrew itself as they came nigh, and left the spots where it had danced the drearier, because they had hoped to find them bright.

"Mother," said little Pearl, "the sunshine does not love you. It runs away and hides itself, because it is afraid of something on your bosom. Now see! There it is, playing, a good way off. Stand you here, and let me run and catch it. I am but a child. It will not flee from me, for I wear nothing on my bosom yet!"

"Nor ever will, my child, I hope," said Hester.

"And why not, mother?" asked Pearl, stopping short, just at the beginning of her race. "Will not it come of its own accord, when I am a woman grown?"

"Run away, child," answered her mother, "and catch the sunshine! It will soon be gone."

Pearl set forth, at a great pace, and, as Hester smiled to perceive, did actually catch the sunshine, and stood laughing in the midst of it, all brightened by its splendor, and scintillating with the vivacity excited by rapid motion. The light lingered about the lonely child, as if glad of such a playmate, until her mother had drawn almost nigh enough to step into the magic circle too.

"It will go now," said Pearl, shaking her head.

"See!" answered Hester, smiling. "Now I can stretch out my hand, and grasp some of it."

As she attempted to do so, the sunshine vanished; or, to judge from the bright expression that was dancing on Pearl's features, her mother could have fancied that the child had absorbed it into herself, and would give it forth again, with a gleam about her path, as they should plunge into some gloomier shade. There was no other attribute that so much impressed her with a sense of new and untransmitted vigor in Pearl's nature, as this never-failing vivacity of spirits; she had not the disease of sadness, which almost all children, in these latter days, inherit, with the scrofula, from the troubles of their ancestors. Perhaps this too was a disease, and but the reflex of the wild energy with which Hester had fought against her sorrows before Pearl's birth. It was certainly a doubtful charm, imparting a hard, metallic lustre to the child's character. She wanted—what some people want throughout life—a grief that should deeply touch her, and thus humanize and make her capable of sympathy. But there was time enough yet for little Pearl.

"Come, my child!" said Hester, looking about her from the spot where Pearl had stood still in the sunshine. "We will sit down a little way within the wood, and rest ourselves."

"I am not aweary, mother," replied the little girl. "But you may sit down, if you will tell me a story meanwhile."

"A story, child!" said Hester. "And about what?"

"Oh, a story about the Black Man," answered Pearl, taking hold of her mother's gown, and looking up, half earnestly, half mischievously, into her face. "How he haunts this forest, and carries a book with him,—a big, heavy book, with iron clasps; and how this ugly Black Man offers his book and an iron pen to everybody that meets him here among the trees; and they are to write their names with their own blood. And then he sets his mark on their bosoms! Didst thou ever meet the Black Man, mother?"

"And who told you this story, Pearl?" asked her mother, recognizing a common superstition of the period.

"It was the old dame in the chimney-corner, at the house where you watched last night," said the child. "But she fancied me asleep while she was talking of it. She said that a thousand and a thousand people had met him here, and had written in his book, and have his mark on them. And that ugly-tempered lady, old Mistress Hibbins, was one. And, mother, the old dame said that this scarlet letter was the Black Man's mark on thee, and that it glows like a red flame when thou meetest him at midnight, here in the dark wood. Is it true, mother? And dost thou go to meet him in the night-time?"

"Didst thou ever awake, and find thy mother gone?" asked Hester.

"Not that I remember," said the child. "If thou fearest to leave me in our cottage, thou mightest take me along with thee. I would very gladly go! But mother, tell me now! Is there such a Black Man? And didst thou ever meet him? And is this his mark?"

"Wilt thou let me be at peace, if I once tell thee?" asked her mother.

"Yes, if thou tellest me all," answered Pearl.

"Once in my life I met the Black Man!" said her mother. "This scarlet letter is his mark!"

Thus conversing, they entered sufficiently deep into the wood to secure themselves from the observation of any casual passenger along the forest track. Here they sat down on a luxuriant heap of moss, which, at some epoch of the preceding century, had been a gigantic pine, with its roots and trunk in the darksome shade, and its head aloft in the upper atmosphere. It was a little dell where they had seated themselves, with a leaf-strewn bank rising gently on either side, and a brook flowing through the midst, over a bed of fallen and drowned leaves. The trees impending over it had flung down great branches, from time to time, which choked up the current and compelled it to form eddies and black depths at some points; while, in its swifter and livelier passages, there appeared a chan-nelway of pebbles, and brown sparkling sand. Letting the eyes follow along the course of the stream, they could catch the reflected light from its water, at some short distance within the forest, but soon lost all traces of it amid the bewilderment of tree-trunks and underbrush, and here and there a huge rock covered over with gray lichens. All these giant trees and bowlders of granite seemed intent on making a mystery of the course of this small brook; fearing, perhaps, that, with its never-ceasing loquacity, it should whisper tales out of the heart of the old forest whence it flowed, or mirror its revelations on the smooth surface of a pool. Continually, indeed, as it stole onward, the streamlet kept up a babble, kind, quiet, soothing, but melancholy, like the voice of a young child that was spending its infancy without playfulness, and knew not how to be merry among sad acquaintance and events of sombre hue.

"O brook! O foolish and tiresome little brook!" cried Pearl, after listening awhile to its talk. "Why art thou so sad? Pluck up a spirit, and do not be all the time sighing and murmuring!"

But the brook, in the course of its little lifetime among the forest-trees, had gone through so solemn an experience that it could not help talking about it, and seemed to have nothing else to say. Pearl resembled the brook, inasmuch as the current of her life gushed from a well-spring as mysterious, and had flowed through scenes shadowed as heavily with gloom. But, unlike the little stream, she danced and sparkled, and prattled airily along her course.

"What does this sad little brook say, mother?" inquired she.

"If thou hadst a sorrow of thine own, the brook might tell thee of it," answered her mother, "even as it is telling me of mine! But now, Pearl, I hear a footstep along the path, and the noise of one putting aside the branches. I would have thee betake thyself to play, and leave me to speak with him that comes yonder."

"Is it the Black Man?" asked Pearl.

"Wilt thou go and play, child?" repeated her mother. "But do not stray far into the wood. And take heed that thou come at my first call."

"Yes, mother," answered Pearl. "But if it be the Black Man, wilt thou not let me stay a moment, and look at him, with his big book under his arm?"

"Go, silly child!" said her mother, impatiently. "It is no Black Man! Thou canst see him now, through the trees. It is the minister!"

"And so it is!" said the child. "And, mother, he has his hand over his heart! Is it because, when the minister wrote his name in the book, the Black Man set his mark in that place? But why does he not wear it outside his bosom, as thou dost, mother?"

"Go now, child, and thou shalt tease me as thou wilt another time," cried Hester Prynne. "But do not stray far. Keep where thou canst hear the babble of the brook."

The child went singing away, following up the current of the brook, and striving to mingle a more lightsome cadence with its melancholy voice. But the little stream would not be comforted, and still kept telling its unintelligible secret of some very mournful mystery that had happened—or making a prophetic lamentation about something that was yet to happen—within the verge of the dismal forest. So Pearl, who had enough of shadow in her own little life, chose to break off all acquaintance with this repining brook. She set herself, therefore, to gathering violets and wood-anemones, and some scarlet columbines that she found growing in the crevices of a high rock.

When her elf-child had departed, Hester Prynne made a step or two towards the track that led through the forest, but still remained under the deep shadow of the trees. She beheld the minister advancing along the path, entirely alone, and leaning on a staff which he had cut by the wayside. He looked haggard and feeble, and betrayed a nerveless despondency in his air, which had never so remarkably characterized him in his walks about the settlement, nor in any other situation where he deemed himself liable to notice. Here it was wofully visible, in the intense seclusion of the forest, which, of itself, would have been a heavy trial to the spirits. There was a listlessness in his gait; as if he saw no reason for taking one step farther, nor felt any desire to do so, but would have been glad, could he be glad of anything, to fling himself down at the root of the nearest tree, and lie there passive, for evermore. The leaves might bestrew him, and the soil gradually accumulate and form a little hillock over his frame, no matter whether there were life in it or no. Death was too definite an object to be wished for or avoided.

To Hester's eye, the Reverend Mr. Dimmesdale exhibited no symptom of positive and vivacious suffering, except that, as little Pearl had remarked, he kept his hand over his heart.

## XVII

### THE PASTOR AND HIS PARISHIONER

SLOWLY as the minister walked, he had almost gone by, before Hester Prynne could gather voice enough to attract his observation. At length, she succeeded.

"Arthur Dimmesdale!" she said, faintly at first; then louder, but hoarsely. "Arthur Dimmesdale!"

"Who speaks?" answered the minister.

Gathering himself quickly up, he stood more erect, like a man taken by surprise in a mood to which he was reluctant to have witnesses. Throwing his eyes anxiously in the direction of the voice, he indistinctly beheld a form under the trees, clad in garments so sombre, and so little relieved from the gray twilight into which the clouded sky and the heavy foliage had darkened the noontide, that he knew not whether it were a woman or a shadow. It may be, that his pathway through life was haunted thus, by a spectre that had stolen out from among his thoughts.

He made a step nigher, and discovered the scarlet letter.

"Hester! Hester Prynne!" said he. "Is it thou? Art thou in life?"

"Even so!" she answered. "In such life as has been mine these seven years past! And thou, Arthur Dimmesdale, dost thou yet live?"

It was no wonder that they thus questioned one another's actual and bodily existence, and even doubted of their own. So strangely did they meet, in the dim wood, that it was like the first encounter, in the world beyond the grave, of two spirits who had been intimately connected in their former life, but now stood coldly shuddering, in mutual dread; as not yet familiar with their state, nor wonted to the companionship of disembodied beings. Each a ghost, and awe-stricken at the other ghost! They were awe-stricken likewise at themselves; because the crisis flung back to them their consciousness, and revealed to each heart its history and experience, as life never does, except at such breathless epochs. The soul beheld its features in the mirror of the passing moment. It was with fear, and tremulously, and, as it were, by a slow, reluctant necessity, that Arthur Dimmesdale put forth his hand, chill as death, and touched the chill hand of Hester Prynne. The grasp, cold as it was, took away what was dreariest in the interview. They now felt themselves, at least, inhabitants of the same sphere.

Without a word more spoken,—neither he nor she assuming the guidance, but with an unexpressed consent,—they glided back into the shadow of the woods, whence Hester had emerged, and sat down on the heap of moss where she and Pearl had before been sitting. When they found voice to speak, it was, at first, only to utter remarks and inquiries such as any two acquaintance might have made, about the gloomy sky, the threatening storm, and, next, the health of each. Thus they went onward, not boldly, but step by step, into the themes that were brooding deepest in their hearts. So long estranged by fate and circumstances, they needed something slight and casual to run before, and throw open the doors of intercourse, so that their real thoughts might be led across the threshold.

After a while, the minister fixed his eyes on Hester Prynne's.

"Hester," said he, "hast thou found peace?"

She smiled drearily, looking down upon her bosom.

"Hast thou?" she asked.

"None!—nothing but despair!" he answered. "What else could I look for, being what I am, and leading such a life as mine? Were I an atheist, —a man devoid of conscience,—a wretch with coarse and brutal instincts, —I might have found peace, long ere now. Nay, I never should have lost it! But, as matters stand with my soul, whatever of good capacity there originally was in me, all of God's gifts that were the choicest have become the ministers of spiritual torment. Hester, I am most miserable!"

"The people reverence thee," said Hester. "And surely thou workest good among them! Doth this bring thee no comfort?"

"More misery, Hester!—only the more misery!" answered the clergyman, with a bitter smile. "As concerns the good which I may appear to do, I have no faith in it. It must needs be a delusion. What can a ruined soul, like mine, effect towards the redemption of other souls?—or a polluted soul towards their purification? And as for the people's reverence, would that it were turned to scorn and hatred! Canst thou deem it, Hester, a consolation, that I must stand up in my pulpit, and meet so many eyes turned upward to my face, as if the light of heaven were beaming from it!—must see my flock hungry for the truth, and listening to my words as if a tongue of Pentecost were speaking!—and then look inward, and discern the black reality of what they idolize? I have laughed, in bitterness and agony of heart, at the contrast between what I seem and what I am! And Satan laughs at it!"

"You wrong yourself in this," said Hester, gently. "You have deeply and sorely repented. Your sin is left behind you, in the days long past.

Your present life is not less holy, in very truth, than it seems in people's eyes. Is there no reality in the penitence thus sealed and witnessed by good works? And wherefore should it not bring you peace?"

"No, Hester, no!" replied the clergyman. "There is no substance in it! It is cold and dead, and can do nothing for me! Of penance, I have had enough! Of penitence, there has been none! Else, I should long ago have thrown off these garments of mock holiness, and have shown myself to mankind as they will see me at the judgment-seat. Happy are you, Hester, that wear the scarlet letter openly upon your bosom! Mine burns in secret! Thou little knowest what a relief it is, after the torment of a seven years' cheat, to look into an eye that recognizes me for what I am! Had I one friend—or were it my worst enemy!—to whom, when sickened with the praises of all other men, I could daily betake myself, and be known as the vilest of all sinners, methinks my soul might keep itself alive thereby. Even thus much of truth would save me! But, now, it is all falsehood!—all emptiness!—all death!"

Hester Prynne looked into his face, but hesitated to speak. Yet, uttering his long-restrained emotions so vehemently as he did, his words here offered her the very point of circumstances in which to interpose what she came to say. She conquered her fears, and spoke.

"Such a friend as thou hast even now wished for," said she, "with whom to weep over thy sin, thou hast in me, the partner of it!"—Again she hesitated, but brought out the words with an effort.—"Thou hast long had such an enemy, and dwellest with him, under the same roof!"

The minister started to his feet, gasping for breath, and clutching at his heart, as if he would have torn it out of his bosom.

"Ha! What sayest thou!" cried he. "An enemy! And under mine own roof! What mean you?"

Hester Prynne was now fully sensible of the deep injury for which she was responsible to this unhappy man, in permitting him to lie for so many years, or, indeed, for a single moment, at the mercy of one whose purposes could not be other than malevolent. The very contiguity of his enemy, beneath whatever mask the latter might conceal himself, was enough to disturb the magnetic sphere of a being so sensitive as Arthur Dimmesdale. There had been a period when Hester was less alive to this consideration; or, perhaps, in the misanthropy of her own trouble, she left the minister to bear what she might picture to herself as a more tolerable doom. But of late, since the night of his vigil, all her sympathies towards him had been both softened and invigorated. She now read his heart more accurately. She doubted not, that the continual presence of Roger Chillingworth,—the secret poison of his malignity, infecting all the air about him,—and his authorized interference, as a physician, with the minister's physical and spiritual infirmities,—that these bad opportunities had been turned to a cruel purpose. By means of them, the sufferer's conscience had been kept in an irritated state, the tendency of which was, not to cure by wholesome pain, but to disorganize and corrupt his spiritual being. Its result, on earth, could hardly fail to be insanity, and hereafter, that eternal alienation from the Good and True, of which madness is perhaps the earthly type.

Such was the ruin to which she had brought the man, once,—nay, why should we not speak it?—still so passionately loved! Hester felt that the sacrifice of the clergyman's good name, and death itself, as she had already told Roger Chillingworth, would have been infinitely preferable to the alternative which she had taken upon herself to choose. And now, rather than have had this grievous wrong to confess, she would gladly have lain down on the forest-leaves, and died, there, at Arthur Dimmesdale's feet.

"O Arthur," cried she, "forgive me! In all things else, I have striven to be true! Truth was the one virtue which I might have held fast, and did hold fast, through all extremity; save when thy good,—thy life,—thy fame,—were put in question! Then I consented to a deception. But a lie is never good, even though death threaten on the other side! Dost thou not see what I would say? That old man!—the physician!—he whom they call Roger Chillingworth!—he was my husband!"

The minister looked at her for an instant, with all that violence of passion, which—intermixed, in more shapes than one, with his higher, purer, softer qualities—was, in fact, the portion of him which the Devil claimed, and through which he sought to win the rest. Never was there a blacker or a fiercer frown than Hester now encountered. For the brief space that it lasted, it was a dark transfiguration. But his character had been so much enfeebled by suffering, that even its lower energies were incapable of more than a temporary struggle. He sank down on the ground, and buried his face in his hands.

"I might have known it," murmured he. "I did know it! Was not the secret told me, in the natural recoil of my heart, at the first sight of him, and as often as I have seen him since? Why did I not understand? O Hester Prynne, thou little, little knowest all the horror of this thing! And the shame!—the indelicacy!—the horrible ugliness of this exposure of a sick and guilty heart to the very eye that would gloat over it! Woman, woman, thou art accountable for this! I cannot forgive thee!"

"Thou shalt forgive me!" cried Hester, flinging herself on the fallen leaves beside him. "Let God punish! Thou shalt forgive!"

With sudden and desperate tenderness, she threw her arms around him, and pressed his head against her bosom; little caring though his cheek rested on the scarlet letter. He would have released himself, but strove in vain to do so. Hester would not set him free, lest he should look her sternly in the face. All the world had frowned on her,—for seven long years had it frowned upon this lonely woman,—and still she bore it all, nor ever once turned away her firm, sad eyes. Heaven, likewise, had frowned upon her, and she had not died. But the frown of this pale, weak, sinful, and sorrow-stricken man was what Hester could not bear and live!

"Wilt thou yet forgive me!" she repeated, over and over again. "Wilt thou not frown? Wilt thou forgive?"

"I do forgive you, Hester," replied the minister, at length, with a deep utterance, out of an abyss of sadness, but no anger. "I freely forgive you now. May God forgive us both! We are not, Hester, the worst sinners in the world. There is one worse than even the polluted priest! That old man's revenge has been blacker than my sin. He has violated, in cold blood, the sanctity of a human heart. Thou and I, Hester, never did so!"

"Never, never!" whispered she. "What we did had a consecration of its own. We felt it so! We said so to each other! Hast thou forgotten it?"

"Hush, Hester!" said Arthur Dimmesdale, rising from the ground. "No; I have not forgotten!"

They sat down again, side by side, and hand clasped in hand, on the mossy trunk of the fallen tree. Life had never brought them a gloomier hour; it was the point whither their pathway had so long been tending, and darkening ever, as it stole along; and yet it enclosed a charm that made them linger upon it, and claim another, and another, and, after all, another moment. The forest was obscure around them, and creaked with a blast that was passing through it. The boughs were tossing heavily above their heads; while one solemn old tree groaned dolefully to another, as if telling the sad story of the pair that sat beneath, or constrained to forebode evil to come.

And yet they lingered. How dreary looked the forest-track that led backward to the settlement, where Hester Prynne must take up again the burden of her ignominy, and the minister the hollow mockery of his good name! So they lingered an instant longer. No golden light had ever been so precious as the gloom of this dark forest. Here, seen only by his eyes, the scarlet letter need not burn into the bosom of the fallen woman! Here, seen only by her eyes, Arthur Dimmesdale, false to God and man, might be, for one moment, true!

He started at a thought that suddenly occurred to him.

"Hester," cried he, "here is a new horror! Roger Chillingworth knows your purpose to reveal his true character. Will he continue, then, to keep our secret? What will now be the course of his revenge?"

"There is a strange secrecy in his nature," replied Hester, thoughtfully; "and it has grown upon him by the hidden practices of his revenge. I deem it not likely that he will betray the secret. He will doubtless seek other means of satiating his dark passion."

"And I!—how am I to live longer, breathing the same air with this deadly enemy?" exclaimed Arthur Dimmesdale, shrinking within himself, and pressing his hand nervously against his heart,—a gesture that had grown involuntary with him. "Think for me, Hester! Thou art strong. Resolve for me!"

"Thou must dwell no longer with this man," said Hester, slowly and firmly. "Thy heart must be no longer under his evil eye!"

"It were far worse than death!" replied the minister. "But how to avoid it? What choice remains to me? Shall I lie down again on these withered leaves, where I cast myself when thou didst tell me what he was? Must I sink down there, and die at once?"

"Alas, what a ruin has befallen thee!" said Hester, with the tears gushing into her eyes. "Wilt thou die for very weakness? There is no other cause!"

"The judgment of God is on me," answered the conscience-stricken priest. "It is too mighty for me to struggle with!"

"Heaven would show mercy," rejoined Hester, "hadst thou but the strength to take advantage of it."

"Be thou strong for me!" answered he. "Advise me what to do."

"Is the world, then, so narrow?" exclaimed Hester Prynne, fixing her deep eyes on the minister's, and instinctively exercising a magnetic power over a spirit so shattered and subdued that it could hardly hold itself erect. "Doth the universe lie within the compass of yonder town, which only a little time ago was but a leaf-strewn desert, as lonely as this around us? Whither leads yonder forest-track? Backward to the settlement, thou sayest! Yes; but onward, too. Deeper it goes, and deeper, into the wilderness, less plainly to be seen at every step, until, some few miles hence, the yellow leaves will show no vestige of the white man's tread. There thou art free! So brief a journey would bring thee from a world where thou hast been most wretched, to one where thou mayest still be happy! Is there not shade enough in all this boundless forest to hide thy heart from the gaze of Roger Chillingworth?"

"Yes, Hester; but only under the fallen leaves!" replied the minister, with a sad smile.

"Then there is the broad pathway of the sea!" continued Hester. "It brought thee hither. If thou so choose, it will bear thee back again. In our native land, whether in some remote rural village or in vast London, —or, surely, in Germany, in France, in pleasant Italy,—thou wouldst be beyond his power and knowledge! And what hast thou to do with all these iron men, and their opinions? They have kept thy better part in bondage too long already!"

"It cannot be!" answered the minister, listening as if he were called upon to realize a dream. "I am powerless to go! Wretched and sinful as I am, I have had no other thought than to drag on my earthly existence in the sphere where Providence hath placed me. Lost as my own soul is, I would still do what I may for other human souls! I dare not quit my post, though an unfaithful sentinel, whose sure reward is death and dishonor, when his dreary watch shall come to an end!"

"Thou art crushed under this seven years' weight of misery," replied Hester, fervently resolved to buoy him up with her own energy. "But thou shalt leave it all behind thee! It shall not cumber thy steps, as thou treadest along the forest-path; neither shalt thou freight the ship with it, if thou prefer to cross the sea. Leave this wreck and ruin here where it hath happened. Meddle no more with it! Begin all anew! Hast thou exhausted possibility in the failure of this one trial? Not so! The future is yet full of trial and success. There is happiness to be enjoyed! There is good to be done! Exchange this false life of thine for a true one. Be, if thy spirit summon thee to such a mission, the teacher and apostle of the red men. Or,—as is more thy nature,—be a scholar and a sage among the wisest and most renowned of the cultivated world. Preach! Write! Act! Do anything, save to lie down and die! Give up this name of Arthur Dimmesdale, and make thyself another, and a high one, such as thou canst wear without fear or shame. Why shouldst thou tarry so much as one other day in the torments that have so gnawed into thy life!— that have made thee feeble to will and to do!—that will leave thee powerless even to repent! Up, and away!"

"O Hester!" cried Arthur Dimmesdale, in whose eyes a fitful light, kindled by her enthusiasm, flashed up and died away, "thou tellest of running a race to a man whose knees are tottering beneath him! I must die here! There is not the strength or courage left me to venture into the wide, strange, difficult world, alone!"

It was the last expression of the despondency of a broken spirit. He lacked energy to grasp the better fortune that seemed within his reach.

He repeated the word.

"Alone, Hester!"

"Thou shalt not go alone!" answered she, in a deep whisper.

Then, all was spoken!

## XVIII

### A FLOOD OF SUNSHINE

ARTHUR DIMMESDALE gazed into Hester's face with a look in which hope and joy shone out, indeed, but with fear betwixt them, and a kind of horror at her boldness, who had spoken what he vaguely hinted at but dared not speak.

But Hester Prynne, with a mind of native courage and activity, and for so long a period not merely estranged, but outlawed, from society, had habituated herself to such latitude of speculation as was altogether foreign to the clergyman. She had wandered, without rule or guidance, in a moral wilderness; as vast, as intricate and shadowy, as the untamed forest, amid the gloom of which they were now holding a colloquy that was to decide their fate. Her intellect and heart had their home, as it were, in desert places, where she roamed as freely as the wild Indian in his woods. For years past she had looked from this estranged point of view at human institutions, and whatever priests or legislators had established; criticising all with hardly more reverence than the Indian would feel for the clerical band, the judicial robe, the pillory, the gallows, the fireside, or the church. The tendency of her fate and fortunes had been to set her free. The scarlet letter was her passport into regions where other women dared not tread. Shame, Despair, Solitude! These had been her teachers,—stern and wild ones,—and they had made her strong, but taught her much amiss.

The minister, on the other hand, had never gone through an experience calculated to lead him beyond the scope of generally received laws; although, in a single instance, he had so fearfully transgressed one of the most sacred of them. But this had been a sin of passion, not of principle, nor even purpose. Since that wretched epoch, he had watched, with morbid zeal and minuteness, not his acts,—for those it was easy to arrange,—but each breath of emotion, and his every thought. At the head of the social system, as the clergymen of that day stood, he was only the more trammelled by its regulations, its principles, and even its prejudices. As a priest, the framework of his order inevitably hemmed him in. As a man who had once sinned, but who kept his conscience all alive and painfully sensitive by the fretting of an unhealed wound, he might have been supposed safer within the line of virtue than if he had never sinned at all.

Thus, we seem to see that, as regarded Hester Prynne, the whole seven years of outlaw and ignominy had been little other than a preparation for this very hour. But Arthur Dimmesdale! Were such a man once more to fall, what plea could be urged in extenuation of his crime? None; unless it avail him somewhat, that he was broken down by long and exquisite suffering; that his mind was darkened and confused by the very remorse which harrowed it; that between fleeing as an avowed criminal, and remaining as a hypocrite, conscience might find it hard to strike the balance; that it was human to avoid the peril of death and infamy, and the inscrutable machinations of an enemy; that, finally, to this poor pilgrim, on his dreary and desert path, faint, sick, miserable, there appeared a glimpse of human affection and sympathy, a new life, and a true one, in exchange for the heavy doom which he was now expiating. And be the stern and sad truth spoken, that the breach which guilt has once made into the human soul is never, in this mortal state, repaired. It may be watched and guarded; so that the enemy shall not force his way again into the citadel, and might even, in his subsequent assaults, select some other avenue, in preference to that where he had formerly succeeded. But there is still the ruined wall, and, near it, the stealthy tread of the foe that would win over again his unforgotten triumph.

The struggle, if it were one, need not be described. Let it suffice, that the clergyman resolved to flee, and not alone.

"If, in all these past seven years," thought he, "I could recall one instant of peace or hope, I would yet endure for the sake of that earnest of Heaven's mercy. But now,—since I am irrevocably doomed,—wherefore should I not snatch the solace allowed to the condemned culprit before his execution? Or, if this be the path to a better life, as Hester would persuade me, I surely give up no fairer prospect by pursuing it! Neither can I any longer live without her companionship; so powerful is she to sustain,—so tender to soothe! O Thou to whom I dare not lift mine eyes, wilt Thou yet pardon me!"

"Thou wilt go!" said Hester, calmly, as he met her glance.

The decision once made, a glow of strange enjoyment threw its flickering brightness over the trouble of his breast. It was the exhilarating effect—upon a prisoner just escaped from the dungeon of his own heart—of breathing the wild, free atmosphere of an·unredeemed, unchristianized, lawless region. His spirit rose, as it were, with a bound, and attained a nearer prospect of the sky, than throughout all the misery which had kept him grovelling on the earth. Of a deeply religious temperament, there was inevitably a tinge of the devotional in his mood.

"Do I feel joy again?" cried he, wondering at himself. "Methought the germ of it was dead in me! O Hester, thou art my better angel! I seem to have flung myself—sick, sin-stained, and sorrow-blackened—down upon these forest-leaves, and to have risen up all made anew, and with new powers to glorify Him that hath been merciful! This is already the better life! Why did we not find it sooner?"

"Let us not look back," answered Hester Prynne. "The past is gone! Wherefore should we linger upon it now? See! With this symbol, I undo it all, and make it as it had never been!"

So speaking, she undid the clasp that fastened the scarlet letter, and, taking it from her bosom, threw it to a distance among the withered leaves. The mystic token alighted on the hither verge of the stream. With a hand's-breadth farther flight it would have fallen into the water, and have given the little brook another woe to carry onward, besides the unintelligible tale which it still kept murmuring about. But there lay the embroidered letter, glittering like a lost jewel, which some ill-fated wanderer might pick up, and thenceforth be haunted by strange phantoms of guilt, sinkings of the heart, and unaccountable misfortune.

The stigma gone, Hester heaved a long, deep sigh, in which the burden of shame and anguish departed from her spirit. Oh exquisite relief! She had not known the weight, until she felt the freedom! By another impulse, she took off the formal cap that confined her hair; and down it fell upon her shoulders, dark and rich, with at once a shadow and a light in its abundance, and imparting the charm of softness to her features. There played around her mouth, and beamed out of her eyes, a radiant and tender smile, that seemed gushing from the very heart of womanhood. A crimson flush was glowing on her cheek, that had been long so pale. Her sex, her youth, and the whole richness of her beauty, came back from what men call the irrevocable past, and clustered themselves, with her maiden hope, and a happiness before unknown, within the magic circle of this hour. And, as if the gloom of the earth and sky had been but the effluence of these two mortal hearts, it vanished with their sorrow. All at once, as with a sudden smile of heaven, forth burst the sunshine, pouring a very flood into the obscure forest, gladdening each green leaf, transmuting the yellow fallen ones to gold, and gleaming adown the gray trunks of the solemn trees. The objects that had made a shadow hitherto, embodied the brightness now. The course of the little brook might be traced by its merry gleam afar into the wood's heart of mystery, which had become a mystery of joy.

Such was the sympathy of Nature—that wild, heathen Nature of the forest, never subjugated by human law, nor illumined by higher truth—with the bliss of these two spirits! Love, whether newly born, or aroused from a death-like slumber, must always create a sunshine, filling the heart so full of radiance, that it overflows upon the outward world. Had the forest still kept its gloom, it would have been bright in Hester's eyes, and bright in Arthur Dimmesdale's!

Hester looked at him with the thrill of another joy.

"Thou must know Pearl!" said she. "Our little Pearl! Thou hast seen her,—yes, I know it!—but thou wilt see her now with other eyes. She is a strange child! I hardly comprehend her! But thou wilt love her dearly, as I do, and wilt advise me how to deal with her."

"Dost thou think the child will be glad to know me?" asked the minister, somewhat uneasily. "I have long shrunk from children, because they often show a distrust,—a backwardness to be familiar with me. I have even been afraid of little Pearl!"

"Ah, that was sad!" answered the mother. "But she will love thee dearly, and thou her. She is not far off. I will call her! Pearl! Pearl!"

"I see the child," observed the minister. "Yonder she is, standing in a streak of sunshine, a good way off, on the other side of the brook. So thou thinkest the child will love me?"

Hester smiled, and again called to Pearl, who was visible, at some distance, as the minister had described her, like a bright-apparelled vision, in a sunbeam, which fell down upon her through an arch of boughs. The ray quivered to and fro, making her figure dim or distinct,—now like a real child, now like a child's spirit,—as the splendor went and came again. She heard her mother's voice, and approached slowly through the forest.

Pearl had not found the hour pass wearisomely, while her mother sat talking with the clergyman. The great black forest—stern as it showed itself to those who brought the guilt and troubles of the world into its bosom—became the playmate of the lonely infant, as well as it knew how. Sombre as it was, it put on the kindest of its moods to welcome her. It offered her the partridge-berries, the growth of the preceding autumn, but ripening only in the spring, and now red as drops of blood upon the withered leaves. These Pearl gathered, and was pleased with their wild flavor. The small denizens of the wilderness hardly took pains to move out of her path. A partridge, indeed, with a brood of ten behind her, ran forward threateningly, but soon repented of her fierceness, and clucked to her young ones not to be afraid. A pigeon, alone on a low branch, allowed Pearl to come beneath, and uttered a sound as much of greeting as alarm. A squirrel, from the lofty depths of his domestic tree, chattered either in anger or merriment,—for a squirrel is such a choleric and humorous little personage, that it is hard to distinguish between his moods,—so he chattered at the child, and flung down a nut upon her head. It was a last year's nut, and already gnawed by his sharp tooth. A fox, startled from his sleep by her light footstep on the leaves, looked inquisitively at Pearl, as doubting whether it were better to steal off, or renew his nap on the same spot.

A wolf, it is said,—but here the tale has surely lapsed into the improbable,—came up, and smelt of Pearl's robe, and offered his savage head to be patted by her hand. The truth seems to be, however, that the mother-forest, and these wild things which it nourished, all recognized a kindred wildness in the human child.

And she was gentler here than in the grassy-margined streets of the settlement, or in her mother's cottage. The flowers appeared to know it; and one and another whispered as she passed, "Adorn thyself with me, thou beautiful child, adorn thyself with me!"—and, to please them, Pearl gathered the violets, and anemones, and columbines, and some twigs of the freshest green, which the old trees held down before her eyes. With these she decorated her hair, and her young waist, and became a nymph-child, or an infant dryad, or whatever else was in closest sympathy with the antique wood. In such guise had Pearl adorned herself, when she heard her mother's voice, and came slowly back.

Slowly; for she saw the clergyman.

## XIX

### THE CHILD AT THE BROOK-SIDE

"Thou wilt love her dearly," repeated Hester Prynne, as she and the minister sat watching little Pearl. "Dost thou not think her beautiful? And see with what natural skill she has made those simple flowers adorn her! Had she gathered pearls, and diamonds, and rubies, in the wood, they could not have become her better. She is a splendid child! But I know whose brow she has!"

"Dost thou know, Hester," said Arthur Dimmesdale, with an unquiet smile, "that this dear child, tripping about always at thy side, hath caused me many an alarm? Methought—O Hester, what a thought is that, and how terrible to dread it!—that my own features were partly repeated in her face, and so strikingly that the world might see them! But she is mostly thine!"

"No, no! Not mostly!" answered the mother, with a tender smile. "A little longer, and thou needest not to be afraid to trace whose child she is. But how strangely beautiful she looks, with those wild-flowers in her hair! It is as if one of the fairies, whom we left in our dear old England, had decked her out to meet us."

It was with a feeling which neither of them had ever before experienced that they sat and watched Pearl's slow advance. In her was visible the tie that united them. She had been offered to the world, these seven years past, as the living hieroglyphic, in which was revealed the secret they so

darkly sought to hide,—all written in this symbol,—all plainly manifest,
—had there been a prophet or magician skilled to read the character of
flame! And Pearl was the oneness of their being. Be the foregone evil
what it might, how could they doubt that their earthly lives and future
destinies were conjoined, when they beheld at once the material union,
and the spiritual idea, in whom they met, and were to dwell immortally
together? Thoughts like these—and perhaps other thoughts, which they
did not acknowledge or define—threw an awe about the child as she came
onward.

"Let her see nothing strange—no passion nor eagerness—in thy way of
accosting her," whispered Hester. "Our Pearl is a fitful and fantastic
little elf, sometimes. Especially she is seldom tolerant of emotion, when
she does not fully comprehend the why and wherefore. But the child hath
strong affections! She loves me, and will love thee!"

"Thou canst not think," said the minister, glancing aside at Hester
Prynne, "how my heart dreads this interview, and yearns for it! But, in
truth, as I already told thee, children are not readily won to be familiar
with me. They will not climb my knee, nor prattle in my ear, nor answer
to my smile; but stand apart, and eye me strangely. Even little babes,
when I take them in my arms, weep bitterly. Yet Pearl, twice in her little
lifetime, hath been kind to me! The first time,—thou knowest it well!
The last was when thou ledst her with thee to the house of yonder stern
old Governor."

"And thou didst plead so bravely in her behalf and mine!" answered
the mother. "I remember it; and so shall little Pearl. Fear nothing! She
may be strange and shy at first, but will soon learn to love thee!"

By this time Pearl had reached the margin of the brook, and stood on
the farther side, gazing silently at Hester and the clergyman, who still sat
together on the mossy tree-trunk, waiting to receive her. Just where she
had paused, the brook chanced to form a pool, so smooth and quiet that
it reflected a perfect image of her little figure, with all the brilliant picturesqueness of her beauty, in its adornment of flowers and wreathed foliage,
but more refined and spiritualized than the reality. This image, so nearly
identical with the living Pearl, seemed to communicate somewhat of its
own shadowy and intangible quality to the child herself. It was strange,
the way in which Pearl stood, looking so steadfastly at them through the
dim medium of the forest-gloom; herself, meanwhile, all glorified with a
ray of sunshine that was attracted thitherward as by a certain sympathy.
In the brook beneath stood another child,—another and the same,—with
likewise its ray of golden light. Hester felt herself, in some indistinct and
tantalizing manner, estranged from Pearl; as if the child, in her lonely
ramble through the forest, had strayed out of the sphere in which she and
her mother dwelt together, and was now vainly seeking to return to it.

There was both truth and error in the impression; the child and mother
were estranged, but through Hester's fault, not Pearl's. Since the latter
rambled from her side, another inmate had been admitted within the
circle of the mother's feelings, and so modified the aspect of them all, that

Pearl, the returning wanderer, could not find her wonted place, and hardly knew where she was.

"I have a strange fancy," observed the sensitive minister, "that this brook is the boundary between two worlds, and that thou canst never meet thy Pearl again. Or is she an elfish spirit, who, as the legends of our childhood taught us, is forbidden to cross a running stream? Pray hasten her; for this delay has already imparted a tremor to my nerves."

"Come, dearest child!" said Hester, encouragingly, and stretching out both her arms. "How slow thou art! When hast thou been so sluggish before now? Here is a friend of mine, who must be thy friend also. Thou wilt have twice as much love, henceforward, as thy mother alone could give thee! Leap across the brook, and come to us. Thou canst leap like a young deer!"

Pearl, without responding in any manner to these honey-sweet expressions, remained on the other side of the brook. Now she fixed her bright, wild eyes on her mother, now on the minister, and now included them both in the same glance; as if to detect and explain to herself the relation which they bore to one another. For some unaccountable reason, as Arthur Dimmesdale felt the child's eyes upon him, his hand—with that gesture so habitual as to have become involuntary—stole over his heart. At length, assuming a singular air of authority, Pearl stretched out her hand, with the small forefinger extended, and pointing evidently towards her mother's breast. And beneath, in the mirror of the brook, there was the flower-girdled and sunny image of little Pearl, pointing her small forefinger too.

"Thou strange child, why dost thou not come to me?" exclaimed Hester.

Pearl still pointed with her forefinger; and a frown gathered on her brow; the more impressive from the childish, the almost baby-like aspect of the features that conveyed it. As her mother still kept beckoning to her, and arraying her face in a holiday suit of unaccustomed smiles, the child stamped her foot with a yet more imperious look and gesture. In the brook, again, was the fantastic beauty of the image, with its reflected frown, its pointed finger, and imperious gesture, giving emphasis to the aspect of little Pearl.

"Hasten, Pearl; or I shall be angry with thee!" cried Hester Prynne, who, however inured to such behavior on the elf-child's part at other seasons, was naturally anxious for a more seemly deportment now. "Leap across the brook, naughty child, and run hither! Else I must come to thee!"

But Pearl, not a whit startled at her mother's threats any more than mollified by her entreaties, now suddenly burst into a fit of passion, gesticulating violently and throwing her small figure into the most extravagant contortions. She accompanied this wild outbreak with piercing shrieks, which the woods reverberated on all sides; so that, alone as she was in her childish and unreasonable wrath, it seemed as if a hidden multitude were lending her their sympathy and encouragement. Seen in the brook, once more, was the shadowy wrath of Pearl's image, crowned and girdled with flowers, but stamping its foot, wildly gesticulating, and, in the midst of all, still pointing its small forefinger at Hester's bosom!

"I see what ails the child," whispered Hester to the clergyman, and turning pale in spite of a strong effort to conceal her trouble and annoyance. "Children will not abide any, the slightest, change in the accustomed aspect of things that are daily before their eyes. Pearl misses something which she has always seen me wear!"

"I pray you," answered the minister, "if thou hast any means of pacifying the child, do it forthwith! Save it were the cankered wrath of an old witch, like Mistress Hibbins," added he, attempting to smile, "I know nothing that I would not sooner encounter than this passion in a child. In Pearl's young beauty, as in the wrinkled witch, it has a preternatural effect. Pacify her, if thou lovest me!"

Hester turned again towards Pearl, with a crimson blush upon her cheek, a conscious glance aside at the clergyman, and then a heavy sigh; while, even before she had time to speak, the blush yielded to a deadly pallor.

"Pearl," said she, sadly, "look down at thy feet! There!—before thee! —on the hither side of the brook!"

The child turned her eyes to the point indicated; and there lay the scarlet letter, so close upon the margin of the stream, that the gold embroidery was reflected in it.

"Bring it hither!" said Hester.

"Come thou and take it up!" answered Pearl.

"Was ever such a child!" observed Hester, aside to the minister. "Oh, I have much to tell thee about her! But, in very truth, she is right as regards this hateful token. I must bear its torture yet a little longer,—only a few days longer,—until we shall have left this region and look back hither as to a land which we have dreamed of. The forest cannot hide it! The mid-ocean shall take it from my hand, and swallow it up forever!"

With these words, she advanced to the margin of the brook, took up the scarlet letter, and fastened it again into her bosom. Hopefully, but a moment ago, as Hester had spoken of drowning it in the deep sea, there was a sense of inevitable doom upon her, as she thus received back this deadly symbol from the hand of fate. She had flung it into infinite space! —she had drawn an hour's free breath!—and here again was the scarlet misery, glittering on the old spot! So it ever is, whether thus typified or no, that an evil deed invests itself with the character of doom. Hester next gathered up the heavy tresses of her hair, and confined them beneath her cap. As if there were a withering spell in the sad letter, her beauty, the warmth and richness of her womanhood, departed, like fading sunshine; and a gray shadow seemed to fall across her.

When the dreary change was wrought, she extended her hand to Pearl.

"Dost thou know thy mother now, child?" asked she, reproachfully, but with a subdued tone. "Wilt thou come across the brook, and own thy mother, now that she has her shame upon her,—now that she is sad?"

"Yes; now I will!" answered the child, bounding across the brook, and clasping Hester in her arms. "Now thou art my mother indeed! And I am thy little Pearl!"

In a mood of tenderness that was not unusual with her, she drew down her mother's head, and kissed her brow and both her cheeks. But then— by a kind of necessity that always impelled this child to alloy whatever comfort she might chance to give with a throb of anguish—Pearl put up her mouth, and kissed the scarlet letter too!

"That was not kind!" said Hester. "When thou hast shown me a little love, thou mockest me!"

"Why doth the minister sit yonder?" asked Pearl.

"He waits to welcome thee," replied her mother. "Come thou, and en- treat his blessing! He loves thee, my little Pearl, and loves thy mother too. Wilt thou not love him? Come! he longs to greet thee!"

"Doth he love us?" said Pearl, looking up, with acute intelligence, into her mother's face. "Will he go back with us, hand in hand, we three to- gether, into the town?"

"Not now, my dear child," answered Hester. "But in days to come, he will walk hand in hand with us. We will have a home and fireside of our own; and thou shalt sit upon his knee; and he will teach thee many things, and love thee dearly. Thou wilt love him; wilt thou not?"

"And will he always keep his hand over his heart?" inquired Pearl.

"Foolish child, what a question is that!" exclaimed her mother. "Come and ask his blessing!"

But, whether influenced by the jealousy that seems instinctive with every petted child towards a dangerous rival, or from whatever caprice of her freakish nature, Pearl would show no favor to the clergyman. It was only by an exertion of force that her mother brought her up to him, hang- ing back, and manifesting her reluctance by odd grimaces; of which, ever since her babyhood, she had possessed a singular variety, and could trans- form her mobile physiognomy into a series of different aspects, with a new mischief in them, each and all. The minister—painfully embarrassed, but hoping that a kiss might prove a talisman to admit him into the child's kindlier regards—bent forward, and impressed one on her brow. Here- upon, Pearl broke away from her mother, and, running to the brook, stooped over it, and bathed her forehead, until the unwelcome kiss was quite washed off, and diffused through a long lapse of the gliding water. She then remained apart, silently watching Hester and the clergyman; while they talked together, and made such arrangements as were sug- gested by their new position, and the purposes soon to be fulfilled.

And now this fateful interview had come to a close. The dell was to be left a solitude among its dark, old trees, which, with their multitudinous tongues, would whisper long of what had passed there, and no mortal be the wiser. And the melancholy brook would add this other tale to the mys- tery with which its little heart was already overburdened, and whereof it still kept up a murmuring babble, with not a whit more cheerfulness of tone than for ages heretofore.

## XX

### THE MINISTER IN A MAZE

As the minister departed, in advance of Hester Prynne and little Pearl, he threw a backward glance, half expecting that he should discover only some faintly traced features or outline of the mother and the child slowly fading into the twilight of the woods. So great a vicissitude in his life could not at once be received as real. But there was Hester, clad in her gray robe, still standing beside the tree-trunk, which some blast had over-thrown a long antiquity ago, and which time had ever since been covering with moss, so that these two fated ones, with earth's heaviest burden on them, might there sit down together, and find a single hour's rest and so-lace. And there was Pearl, too, lightly dancing from the margin of the brook,—now that the intrusive third person was gone,—and taking her old place by her mother's side. So the minister had not fallen asleep and dreamed!

In order to free his mind from this indistinctness and duplicity of im-pression, which vexed it with a strange disquietude, he recalled and more thoroughly defined the plans which Hester and himself had sketched for their departure. It had been determined between them that the Old World, with its crowds and cities, offered them a more eligible shelter and concealment than the wilds of New England, or all America, with its al-ternatives of an Indian wigwam, or the few settlements of Europeans, scattered thinly along the seaboard. Not to speak of the clergyman's health, so inadequate to sustain the hardships of a forest life, his native gifts, his culture, and his entire development would secure him a home only in the midst of civilization and refinement; the higher the state, the more delicately adapted to it the man. In furtherance of this choice, it so happened that a ship lay in the harbor; one of those questionable cruis-ers, fréquent at that day, which, without being absolutely outlaws of the deep, yet roamed over its surface with a remarkable irresponsibility of character. This vessel had recently arrived from the Spanish Main, and, within three days' time, would sail for Bristol. Hester Prynne—whose vocation, as a self-enlisted Sister of Charity, had brought her acquainted with the captain and crew—could take upon herself to secure the passage of two individuals and a child, with all the secrecy which circumstances rendered more than desirable.

The minister had inquired of Hester, with no little interest, the pre-cise time at which the vessel might be expected to depart. It would prob-ably be on the fourth day from the present. "That is most fortunate!" he had then said to himself. Now, why the Reverend Mr. Dimmesdale con-sidered it so very fortunate, we hesitate to reveal. Nevertheless,—to hold nothing back from the reader,—it was because, on the third day from the present, he was to preach the Election Sermon; and as such an occasion formed an honorable epoch in the life of a New England clergyman, he could not have chanced upon a more suitable mode and time of terminating his professional career. "At least, they shall say of me," thought this exemplary man, "that I leave no public duty unperformed, nor ill performed!" Sad, indeed, that an introspection so profound and acute as this poor minister's should be so miserably deceived! We have had, and may still have, worse things to tell of him; but none, we apprehend, so pitiably weak; no evidence, at once so slight and irrefragable, of a subtle disease, that had long since begun to eat into the real substance of his character. No man, for any considerable period, can wear one face to himself, and another to the multitude, without finally getting bewildered as to which may be the true.

The excitement of Mr. Dimmesdale's feelings, as he returned from his interview with Hester, lent him unaccustomed physical energy, and hurried him townward at a rapid pace. The pathway among the woods seemed wilder, more uncouth with its rude natural obstacles, and less trodden by the foot of man, than he remembered it on his outward journey. But he leaped across the plashy places, thrust himself through the clinging underbrush, climbed the ascent, plunged into the hollow, and overcame, in short, all the difficulties of the track, with an unweariable activity that astonished him. He could not but recall how feebly, and with what frequent pauses for breath, he had toiled over the same ground, only two days before. As he drew near the town, he took an impression of change from the series of familiar objects that presented themselves. It seemed not yesterday, not one, nor two, but many days, or even years ago, since he had quitted them. There, indeed, was each former trace of the street, as he remembered it, and all the peculiarities of the houses, with the due multitude of gable-peaks, and a weathercock at every point where his memory suggested one. Not the less, however, came this importunately obtrusive sense of change. The same was true as regarded the acquaintances whom he met, and all the well-known shapes of human life, about the little town. They looked neither older nor younger now; the beards of the aged were no whiter, nor could the creeping babe of yesterday walk on his feet to-day; it was impossible to describe in what respect they differed from the individuals on whom he had so recently bestowed a parting glance; and yet the minister's deepest sense seemed to inform him of their mutability. A similar impression struck him most remarkably, as he passed under the walls of his own church. The edifice had so very strange, and yet so familiar, an aspect, that Mr. Dimmesdale's mind vibrated between two ideas; either that he had seen it only in a dream hitherto, or that he was merely dreaming about it now.

This phenomenon, in the various shapes which it assumed, indicated no external change, but so sudden and important a change in the spectator of the familiar scene, that the intervening space of a single day had operated on his consciousness like the lapse of years. The minister's own will, and Hester's will, and the fate that grew between them, had wrought this transformation. It was the same town as heretofore; but the same minister returned not from the forest. He might have said to the friends who greeted him,—"I am not the man for whom you take me! I left him yonder in the forest, withdrawn into a secret dell, by a mossy tree-trunk, and near a melancholy brook! Go seek your minister, and see if his emaciated figure, his thin cheek, his white, heavy, pain-wrinkled brow, be not flung down there, like a cast-off garment!" His friends, no doubt, would still have insisted with him,—"Thou art thyself the man!"—but the error would have been their own, not his.

Before Mr. Dimmesdale reached home, his inner man gave him other evidences of a revolution in the sphere of thought and feeling. In truth, nothing short of a total change of dynasty and moral code, in that interior kingdom, was adequate to account for the impulses now communicated to the unfortunate and startled minister. At every step he was incited to do some strange, wild, wicked thing or other, with a sense that it would be at once involuntary and intentional; in spite of himself, yet growing out of a profounder self than that which opposed the impulse. For instance, he met one of his own deacons. The good old man addressed him with the paternal affection and patriarchal privilege, which his venerable age, his upright and holy character, and his station in the Church, entitled him to use; and, conjoined with this, the deep, almost worshipping respect, which the minister's professional and private claims alike demanded. Never was there a more beautiful example of how the majesty of age and wisdom may comport with the obeisance and respect enjoined upon it, as from a lower social rank, and inferior order of endowment, towards a higher. Now, during a conversation of some two or three moments between the Reverend Mr. Dimmesdale and this excellent and hoary-bearded deacon, it was only by the most careful self-control that the former could refrain from uttering certain blasphemous suggestions that rose into his mind, respecting the communion supper. He absolutely trembled and turned pale as ashes, lest his tongue should wag itself, in utterance of these horrible matters, and plead his own consent for so doing, without his having fairly given it. And, even with this terror in his heart, he could hardly avoid laughing, to imagine how the sanctified old patriarchial deacon would have been petrified by his minister's impiety!

Again, another incident of the same nature. Hurrying along the street, the Reverend Mr. Dimmesdale encountered the eldest female member of his church; a most pious and exemplary old dame; poor, widowed, lonely, and with a heart as full of reminiscences about her dead husband and children, and her dead friends of long ago, as a burial-ground is full of storied gravestones. Yet all this, which would else have been such heavy sorrow, was made almost a solemn joy to her devout old soul, by religious consolations and the truths of Scripture, wherewith she had fed herself continually for more than thirty years. And, since Mr. Dimmesdale had taken her in charge, the good grandam's chief earthly comfort—which, unless it had been likewise a heavenly comfort, could have been none at all—was to meet her pastor, whether casually, or of set purpose, and be refreshed with a word of warm, fragrant, heaven-breathing Gospel truth, from his beloved lips, into her dulled, but rapturously attentive ear. But, on this occasion, up to the moment of putting his lips to the old woman's ear, Mr. Dimmesdale, as the great enemy of souls would have it, could recall no text of Scripture, nor aught else, except a brief, pithy, and, as it then appeared to him, unanswerable argument against the immortality of the human soul. The instilment thereof into her mind would probably have caused this aged sister to drop down dead at once, as by the effect of an intensely poisonous infusion. What he really did whisper, the minister could never afterwards recollect. There was, perhaps, a fortunate disorder in his utterance, which failed to impart any distinct idea to the good widow's comprehension, or which Providence interpreted after a method of its own. Assuredly, as the minister looked back, he beheld an expression of divine gratitude and ecstasy that seemed like the shine of the celestial city on her face, so wrinkled and ashy pale.

Again a third instance. After parting from the old church-member, he met the youngest sister of them all. It was a maiden newly won—and won by the Reverend Mr. Dimmesdale's own sermon, on the Sabbath after his vigil—to barter the transitory pleasures of the world for the heavenly hope, that was to assume brighter substance as life grew dark around her, and which would gild the utter gloom with final glory. She was fair and pure as a lily that had bloomed in Paradise. The minister knew well that he was himself enshrined within the stainless sancity of her heart, which hung its snowy curtains about his image, imparting to religion the warmth of love, and to love a religious purity. Satan, that afternoon, had surely led the poor young girl away from her mother's side, and thrown her into the pathway of this sorely tempted, or—shall we not rather say?—this lost and desperate man. As she drew nigh, the arch-fiend whispered him to condense into small compass and drop into her tender bosom a germ of evil that would be sure to blossom darkly soon, and bear black fruit betimes. Such was his sense of power over this virgin soul, trusting him as she did, that the minister felt potent to blight all the field of innocence with but one wicked look, and develop all its opposite with but a word. So—with a mightier struggle than he had yet sustained—he held his Geneva cloak before his face, and hurried onward, making no sign of recognition, and leaving the young sister to digest his rudeness as she might. She ransacked her conscience,—which was full of harmless little matters, like her pocket or her work-bag,—and took herself to task, poor thing! for a thousand imaginary faults; and went about her household duties with swollen eyelids the next morning.

Before the minister had time to celebrate his victory over this last temptation, he was conscious of another impulse, more ludicrous, and almost as horrible. It was,—we blush to tell it,—it was to stop short in the road, and teach some very wicked words to a knot of little Puritan children who were playing there, and had but just begun to talk. Denying himself this freak, as unworthy of his cloth, he met a drunken seaman, one of the ship's crew from the Spanish Main. And, here, since he had so valiantly forborne all other wickedness, poor Mr. Dimmesdale longed, at least, to shake hands with the tarry blackguard, and recreate himself with a few improper jests, such as dissolute sailors so abound with, and a volley of good, round, solid, satisfactory, and heaven-defying oaths! It was not so much a better principle as partly his natural good taste, and still more his buckramed habit of clerical decorum, that carried him safely through the latter crisis.

"What is it that haunts and tempts me thus?" cried the minister to himself, at length, pausing in the street, and striking his hand against his forehead. "Am I mad? or am I given over utterly to the fiend? Did I make a contract with him in the forest, and sign it with my blood? And does he now summon me to its fulfilment, by suggesting the performance of every wickedness which his most foul imagination can conceive?"

At the moment when the Reverend Mr. Dimmesdale thus communed with himself, and struck his forehead with his hand, old Mistress Hibbins, the reputed witch-lady, is said to have been passing by. She made a very grand appearance; having on a high head-dress, a rich gown of velvet, and a ruff done up with the famous yellow starch, of which Ann Turner, her especial friend, had taught her the secret, before this last good lady had been hanged for Sir Thomas Overbury's murder. Whether the witch had read the minister's thoughts or no, she came to a full stop, looked shrewdly into his face, smiled craftily, and—though little given to converse with clergymen—began a conversation.

"So, reverend Sir, you have made a visit into the forest," observed the witch-lady, nodding her high head-dress at him. "The next time, I pray you to allow me only a fair warning, and I shall be proud to bear you company. Without taking overmuch upon myself, my good word will go far towards gaining any strange gentleman a fair reception from yonder potentate you wot of!"

"I profess, madam," answered the clergyman, with a grave obeisance, such as the lady's rank demanded, and his own good-breeding made imperative,—"I profess, on my conscience and character, that I am utterly bewildered as touching the purport of your words! I went not into the forest to seek a potentate; neither do I, at any future time, design a visit thither, with a view to gaining the favor of such a personage. My one sufficient object was to greet that pious friend of mine, the Apostle Eliot, and rejoice with him over the many precious souls he hath won from heathendom!"

"Ha, ha, ha!" cackled the old witch-lady, still nodding her high head-dress at the minister. "Well, well, we must needs talk thus in the daytime! You carry it off like an old hand! But at midnight, and in the forest, we shall have other talk together!"

She passed on with her aged stateliness, but often turning back her head and smiling at him, like one willing to recognize a secret intimacy of connection.

"Have I then sold myself," thought the minister, "to the fiend whom, if men say true, this yellow-starched and velveted old hag has chosen for her prince and master!"

The wretched minister! He had made a bargain very like it! Tempted by a dream of happiness, he had yielded himself, with deliberate choice, as he had never done before, to what he knew was deadly sin. And the infectious poison of that sin had been thus rapidly diffused throughout his moral system. It had stupefied all blessed impulses, and awakened into vivid life the whole brotherhood of bad ones. Scorn, bitterness, unprovoked malignity, gratuitous desire of ill, ridicule of whatever was good and holy, all awoke, to tempt, even while they frightened him. And his encounter with old Mistress Hibbins, if it were a real incident, did but show his sympathy and fellowship with wicked mortals, and the world of perverted spirits.

He had, by this time, reached his dwelling, on the edge of the burial-ground, and, hastening up the stairs, took refuge in his study. The minister was glad to have reached this shelter, without first betraying himself to the world by any of those strange and wicked eccentricities to which he had been continually impelled while passing through the streets. He entered the accustomed room, and looked around him on its books, its windows, its fireplace, and the tapestried comfort of the walls, with the same perception of strangeness that had haunted him throughout his walk from the forest-dell into the town, and thitherward. Here he had studied and written; here, gone through fast and vigil, and come forth half alive; here, striven to pray; here, borne a hundred thousand agonies! There was the Bible, in its rich old Hebrew, with Moses and the Prophets speaking to him, and God's voice through all! There, on the table, with the inky pen beside it, was an unfinished sermon, with a sentence broken in the midst, where his thoughts had ceased to gush out upon the page, two days before. He knew that it was himself, the thin and white-cheeked minister, who had done and suffered these things, and written thus far into the Election Sermon! But he seemed to stand apart, and eye this former self with scornful, pitying, but half-envious curiosity. That self was gone. Another man had returned out of the forest; a wiser one; with a knowledge of hidden mysteries which the simplicity of the former never could have reached. A bitter kind of knowledge that!

While occupied with these reflections, a knock came at the door of the study, and the minister said, "Come in!"—not wholly devoid of an idea that he might behold an evil spirit. And so he did! It was old Roger Chillingworth that entered. The minister stood, white and speechless, with one hand on the Hebrew Scriptures, and the other spread upon his breast.

"Welcome home, reverend Sir," said the physician. "And how found you that godly man, the Apostle Eliot? But methinks, dear Sir, you look pale; as if the travel through the wilderness had been too sore for you. Will not my aid be requisite to put you in heart and strength to preach your Election Sermon?"

"Nay, I think not so," rejoined the Reverend Mr. Dimmesdale. "My journey, and the sight of the holy Apostle yonder, and the free air which I have breathed, have done me good, after so long confinement in my study. I think to need no more of your drugs, my kind physician, good though they be, and administered by a friendly hand."

All this time, Roger Chillingworth was looking at the minister with the grave and intent regard of a physician towards his patient. But, in spite of this outward show, the latter was almost convinced of the old man's knowledge, or, at least, his confident suspicion, with respect to his own interview with Hester Prynne. The physician knew then, that, in the minister's regard, he was no longer a trusted friend, but his bitterest enemy. So much being known, it would appear natural that a part of it should be expressed. It is singular, however, how long a time often passes before words embody things; and with what security two persons, who choose to avoid a certain subject, may approach its very verge, and retire without disturbing it. Thus, the minister felt no apprehension that Roger Chillingworth would touch, in express words, upon the real position which they sustained towards one another. Yet did the physician, in his dark way, creep frightfully near the secret.

"Were it not better," said he, "that you use my poor skill to-night? Verily, dear Sir, we must take pains to make you strong and vigorous for this occasion of the Election discourse. The people look for great things from you; apprehending that another year may come about, and find their pastor gone."

"Yea, to another world," replied the minister, with pious resignation. "Heaven grant it be a better one; for, in good sooth, I hardly think to tarry with my flock through the flitting seasons of another year! But, touching your medicine, kind Sir, in my present frame of body, I need it not."

"I joy to hear it," answered the physician. "It may be that my remedies, so long administered in vain, begin now to take due effect. Happy man were I, and well deserving of New England's gratitude, could I achieve this cure!"

"I thank you from my heart, most watchful friend," said the Reverend Mr. Dimmesdale, with a solemn smile. "I thank you, and can but requite your good deeds with my prayers."

"A good man's prayers are golden recompense!" rejoined old Roger Chillingworth, as he took his leave. "Yea, they are the current gold coin of the New Jerusalem, with the King's own mint-mark on them!"

Left alone, the minister summoned a servant of the house, and requested food, which, being set before him, he ate with ravenous appetite. Then, flinging the already written pages of the Election Sermon into the fire, he forthwith began another, which he wrote with such an impulsive flow of thought and emotion, that he fancied himself inspired; and only wondered that Heaven should see fit to transmit the grand and solemn music of its oracles through so foul an organ-pipe as he. However, leaving that mystery to solve itself, or go unsolved forever, he drove his task onward, with earnest haste and ecstasy. Thus the night fled away, as if it were a winged steed, and he careering on it; morning came, and peeped, blushing, through the curtains; and at last sunrise threw a golden beam into the study and laid it right across the minister's bedazzled eyes. There he was, with the pen still between his fingers, and a vast, immeasurable tract of written space behind him!

## XXI

### The New England Holiday

Betimes in the morning of the day on which the new Governor was to receive his office at the hands of the people, Hester Prynne and little Pearl came into the market-place. It was already thronged with the craftsmen and other plebeian inhabitants of the town, in considerable numbers; among whom, likewise, were many rough figures, whose attire of deer-skins marked them as belonging to some of the forest settlements, which surrounded the little metropolis of the colony.

On this public holiday, as on all other occasions, for seven years past, Hester was clad in a garment of coarse gray cloth. Not more by its hue than by some indescribable peculiarity in its fashion, it had the effect of making her fade personally out of sight and outline; while, again, the scarlet letter brought her back from this twilight indistinctness, and revealed her under the moral aspect of its own illumination. Her face, so long familiar to the townspeople, showed the marble quietude which they were accustomed to behold there. It was like a mask; or, rather, like the frozen calmness of a dead woman's features; owing this dreary resemblance to the fact that Hester was actually dead, in respect to any claim of sympathy, and had departed out of the world, with which she still seemed to mingle.

It might be, on this one day, that there was an expression unseen before, nor, indeed, vivid enough to be detected, now; unless some preternaturally gifted observer should have first read the heart, and have afterwards sought a corresponding development in the countenance and mien. Such a spiritual seer might have conceived, that, after sustaining the gaze of the multitude through seven miserable years as a necessity, a penance, and something which it was a stern religion to endure, she now, for one last time more, encountered it freely and voluntarily, in order to convert what had so long been agony into a kind of triumph. "Look your last on the scarlet letter and its wearer!"—the people's victim and life-long bond-slave, as they fancied her, might say to them. "Yet a little while, and she will be beyond your reach! A few hours longer, and the deep mysterious ocean will quench and hide forever the symbol which ye have caused to burn upon her bosom!" Nor were it an inconsistency too improbable to be assigned to human nature, should we suppose a feeling of regret in Hester's mind, at the moment when she was about to win her freedom from the pain which had been thus deeply incorporated with her being. Might there not be an irresistible desire to quaff a last, long, breathless draught of the cup of wormwood and aloes, with which nearly all her years of womanhood had been perpetually flavored? The wine of life, henceforth to be presented to her lips, must be indeed rich, delicious, and exhilarating, in its chased and golden beaker; or else leave an inevitable and weary languor, after the lees of bitterness wherewith she had been drugged, as with a cordial of intensest potency.

Pearl was decked out with airy gayety. It would have been impossible to guess that this bright and sunny apparition owed its existence to the shape of gloomy gray; or that a fancy, at once so gorgeous and so delicate as must have been requisite to contrive the child's apparel, was the same that had achieved a task perhaps more difficult, in imparting so distinct a peculiarity to Hester's simple robe. The dress, so proper was it to little Pearl, seemed an effluence, or inevitable development and outward manifestation of her character, no more to be separated from her than the many-hued brilliancy from a butterfly's wing, or the painted glory from the leaf of a bright flower. As with these, so with the child; her garb was all of one idea with her nature. On this eventful day, moreover, there was a certain singular inquietude and excitement in her mood, resembling nothing so much as the shimmer of a diamond, that sparkles and flashes with the varied throbbings of the breast on which it is displayed. Children have always a sympathy in the agitations of those connected with them; always, especially, a sense of any trouble or impending revolution, of whatever kind, in domestic circumstances; and therefore Pearl, who was the gem on her mother's unquiet bosom, betrayed, by the very dance of her spirits, the emotions which none could detect in the marble passiveness of Hester's brow.

This effervescence made her flit with a bird-like movement, rather than walk by her mother's side. She broke continually into shouts of a wild, inarticulate, and sometimes piercing music. When they reached the market-place, she became still more restless, on perceiving the stir and bustle that enlivened the spot; for it was usually more like the broad and lonesome green before a village meeting-house, than the centre of a town's business.

"Why, what is this, mother?" cried she. "Wherefore have all the people left their work to-day? Is it a play-day for the whole world? See, there is the blacksmith! He has washed his sooty face, and put on his Sabbath-day clothes, and looks as if he would gladly be merry, if any kind body would only teach him how! And there is Master Brackett, the old jailer, nodding and smiling at me. Why does he do so, mother?"

"He remembers thee a little babe, my child," answered Hester.

"He should not nod and smile at me, for all that,—the black, grim, ugly-eyed old man!" said Pearl. "He may nod at thee, if he will; for thou art clad in gray, and wearest the scarlet letter. But see, mother, how many faces of strange people, and Indians among them, and sailors! What have they all come to do, here in the market-place?"

"They wait to see the procession pass," said Hester. "For the Governor and the magistrates are to go by, and the ministers, and all the great people and good people, with the music and the soldiers marching before them."

"And will the minister be there?" asked Pearl. "And will he hold out both his hands to me, as when thou ledst me to him from the brook-side?"

"He will be there, child," answered her mother. "But he will not greet thee to-day; nor must thou greet him."

"What a strange, sad man is he!" said the child, as if speaking partly to herself. "In the dark night-time he calls us to him, and holds thy hand and mine, as when we stood with him on the scaffold yonder. And in the deep forest, where only the old trees can hear, and the strip of sky see it, he talks with thee, sitting on a heap of moss! And he kisses my forehead, too, so that the little brook would hardly wash it off! But here, in the sunny day, and among all the people, he knows us not; nor must we know him! A strange, sad man is he, with his hand always over his heart!"

"Be quiet, Pearl! Thou understandest not these things," said her mother. "Think not now of the minister, but look about thee, and see how cheery is everybody's face to-day. The children have come from their schools, and the grown people from their workshops and their fields, on purpose to be happy. For, to-day, a new man is beginning to rule over them; and so—as has been the custom of mankind ever since a nation was first gathered—they make merry and rejoice; as if a good and golden year were at length to pass over the poor old world!"

It was as Hester said, in regard to the unwonted jollity that brightened the faces of the people. Into this festal season of the year—as it already was, and continued to be during the greater part of two centuries—the Puritans compressed whatever mirth and public joy they deemed allowable to human infirmity; thereby so far dispelling the customary cloud, that, for the space of a single holiday, they appeared scarcely more grave than most other communities at a period of general affliction.

But we perhaps exaggerate the gray or sable tinge, which undoubtedly characterized the mood and manners of the age. The persons now in the market-place of Boston had not been born to an inheritance of Puritanic gloom. They were native Englishmen, whose fathers had lived in the sunny richness of the Elizabethan epoch; a time when the life of England, viewed as one great mass, would appear to have been as stately, magnificent, and joyous, as the world has ever witnessed. Had they followed their hereditary taste, the New England settlers would have illustrated all events of public importance by bonfires, banquets, pageantries and processions. Nor would it have been impracticable, in the observance of majestic ceremonies, to combine mirthful recreation with solemnity, and give, as it were, a grotesque and brilliant embroidery to the great robe of state, which a nation, at such festivals, puts on. There was some shadow of an attempt of this kind in the mode of celebrating the day on which the political year of the colony commenced. The dim reflection of a remembered splendor, a colorless and manifold diluted repetition of what they had beheld in proud old London,—we will not say at a royal coronation, but at a Lord Mayor's show,—might be traced in the customs which our forefathers instituted, with reference to the annual installation of magistrates. The fathers and founders of the commonwealth—the statesman, the priest, and the soldier—deemed it a duty then to assume the outward state and majesty, which, in accordance with antique style, was looked upon as the proper garb of public or social eminence. All came forth, to move in procession before the people's eye, and thus impart a needed dignity to the simple framework of a government so newly constructed.

Then, too, the people were countenanced, if not encouraged, in relaxing the severe and close application to their various modes of rugged industry, which, at all other times, seemed of the same piece and material with their religion. Here, it is true, were none of the appliances which popular merriment would so readily have found in the England of Elizabeth's time, or that of James; no rude shows of a theatrical kind; no minstrel, with his harp and legendary ballad, nor glee-man, with an ape dancing to his music; no juggler, with his tricks of mimic witchcraft; no Merry Andrew, to stir up the multitude with jests, perhaps hundreds of years old, but still effective, by their appeals to the very broadest sources of mirthful sympathy. All such professors of the several branches of jocularity would have been sternly repressed, not only by the rigid discipline of law, but by the general sentiment which gives law its vitality. Not the less, however, the great, honest face of the people smiled, grimly, perhaps, but widely too. Nor were sports wanting, such as the colonists had witnessed, and shared in, long ago, at the country fairs and on the village-greens of England; and which it was thought well to keep alive on this new soil, for the sake of the courage and manliness that were essential in them. Wrestling-matches, in the different fashions of Cornwall and Devonshire, were seen here and there about the market-place; in one corner there was a friendly bout at quarterstaff; and—what attracted most interest of all—on the platform of the pillory, already so noted in our pages, two masters of defence were commencing an exhibition with the buckler and broadsword. But, much to the disappointment of the crowd, this latter business was broken off by the interposition of the town beadle, who had no idea of permitting the majesty of the law to be violated by such an abuse of one of its consecrated places.

It may not be too much to affirm, on the whole (the people being then in the first stages of joyless deportment, and the offspring of sires who had known how to be merry, in their day), that they would compare favorably, in point of holiday keeping, with their descendants, even at so long an interval as ourselves. Their immediate posterity, the generation next to the early emigrants, wore the blackest shade of Puritanism, and so darkened the national visage with it, that all the subsequent years have not sufficed to clear it up. We have yet to learn again the forgotten art of gayety.

The picture of human life in the market-place, though its general tint was the sad gray, brown, or black of the English emigrants, was yet enlivened by some diversity of hue. A party of Indians—in their savage finery of curiously embroidered deer-skin robes, wampum-belts, red and yellow ochre, and feathers, and armed with the bow and arrow and stone-headed spear—stood apart, with countenances of inflexible gravity, beyond what even the Puritan aspect could attain. Nor, wild as were these painted barbarians, were they the wildest feature of the scene. This distinction could more justly be claimed by some mariners,—a part of the crew of the vessel from the Spanish Main,—who had come ashore to see the humors of Election Day. They were rough-looking desperadoes, with sun-blackened faces, and an immensity of beard; their wide, short trousers were confined about the waist by belts, often clasped with a rough plate of gold, and sustaining always a long knife, and, in some instances, a sword. From beneath their broad-brimmed hats of palm-leaf gleamed eyes which, even in good-nature and merriment, had a kind of animal ferocity. They transgressed, without fear or scruple, the rules of behavior that were binding on all others; smoking tobacco under the beadle's very nose, although each whiff would have cost a townsman a shilling; and quaffing, at their pleasure, draughts of wine or aqua-vitæ from pocket-flasks, which they freely tendered to the gaping crowd around them. It remarkably characterized the incomplete morality of the age, rigid as we call it, that a license was allowed the seafaring class, not merely for their freaks on shore, but for far more desperate deeds on their proper element. The sailor of that day would go near to be arraigned as a pirate in our own. There could be little doubt, for instance, that this very ship's crew, though no unfavorable specimens of the nautical brotherhood, had been guilty, as we should phrase it, of depredations on the Spanish commerce, such as would have perilled all their necks in a modern court of justice.

But the sea, in those old times, heaved, swelled, and foamed, very much at its own will, or subject only to the tempestuous wind, with hardly any attempts at regulation by human law. The buccaneer on the wave might relinquish his calling, and become at once, if he chose, a man of probity and piety on land; nor, even in the full career of his reckless life, was he regarded as a personage with whom it was disreputable to traffic, or casually associate. Thus, the Puritan elders, in their black cloaks, starched bands, and steeple-crowned hats, smiled not unbenignantly at the clamor and rude deportment of these jolly seafaring men; and it excited neither surprise nor animadversion when so reputable a citizen as old Roger Chillingworth, the physician, was seen to enter the market-place, in close and familiar talk with the commander of the questionable vessel.

The latter was by far the most showy and gallant figure, so far as apparel went, anywhere to be seen among the multitude. He wore a profusion of ribbons on his garment, and gold-lace on his hat, which was also encircled by a gold chain, and surmounted with a feather. There was a sword at his side, and a sword-cut on his forehead, which, by the arrangement of his hair, he seemed anxious rather to display than hide. A landsman could hardly have worn this garb and shown this face, and worn and shown them both with such a galliard air, without undergoing stern question before a magistrate, and probably incurring fine or imprisonment, or perhaps an exhibition in the stocks. As regarded the shipmaster, however, all was looked upon as pertaining to the character, as to a fish his glistening scales.

After parting from the physician, the commander of the Bristol ship strolled idly through the market-place; until happening to approach the spot where Hester Prynne was standing, he appeared to recognize, and did not hesitate to address her. As was usually the case wherever Hester stood, a small vacant area—a sort of magic circle—had formed itself about her, into which, though the people were elbowing one another at a little distance, none ventured, or felt disposed, to intrude. It was a forcible type of the moral solitude in which the scarlet letter enveloped its fated wearer; partly by her own reserve, and partly by the instinctive, though no longer so unkindly, withdrawal of her fellow-creatures. Now, if never before, it answered a good purpose, by enabling Hester and the seaman to speak together without risk of being overheard; and so changed was Hester Prynne's repute before the public, that the matron in town most eminent for rigid morality could not have held such intercourse with less result of scandal than herself.

"So, mistress," said the mariner, "I must bid the steward make ready one more berth than you bargained for! No fear of scurvy or ship-fever this voyage! What with the ship's surgeon and this other doctor, our only danger will be from drug or pill; more by token, as there is a lot of apothecary's stuff aboard, which I traded for with a Spanish vessel."

"What mean you?" inquired Hester, startled more than she permitted to appear. "Have you another passenger?"

"Why, know you not," cried the shipmaster, "that this physician here —Chillingworth, he calls himself—is minded to try my cabin-fare with you? Ay, ay, you must have known it; for he tells me he is of your party, and a close friend to the gentleman you spoke of,—he that is in peril from these sour old Puritan rulers!"

"They know each other well, indeed," replied Hester, with a mien of calmness, though in the utmost consternation. "They have long dwelt together."

Nothing further passed between the mariner and Hester Prynne. But, at that instant, she beheld old Roger Chillingworth himself, standing in the remotest corner of the market-place, and smiling on her; a smile which—across the wide and bustling square, and through all the talk and laughter, and various thoughts, moods, and interests of the crowd—conveyed secret and fearful meaning.

## XXII

### THE PROCESSION

BEFORE Hester Prynne could call together her thoughts, and consider what was practicable to be done in this new and startling aspect of affairs, the sound of military music was heard approaching along a contiguous street. It denoted the advance of the procession of magistrates and citizens, on its way towards the meeting-house; where, in compliance with a custom thus early established, and ever since observed, the Reverend Mr. Dimmesdale was to deliver an Election Sermon.

Soon the head of the procession showed itself, with a slow and stately march, turning a corner and making its way across the market-place. First came the music. It comprised a variety of instruments, perhaps imperfectly adapted to one another, and played with no great skill; but yet attaining the great object for which the harmony of drum and clarion addresses itself to the multitude,—that of imparting a higher and more heroic air to the scene of life that passes before the eye. Little Pearl at first clapped her hands, but then lost, for an instant, the restless agitation that had kept her in a continual effervescence throughout the morning; she gazed silently and seemed to be borne upward, like a floating sea-bird, on the long heaves and swells of sound. But she was brought back to her former mood by the shimmer of the sunshine on the weapons and bright armor of the military company, which followed after the music, and formed the honorary escort of the procession. This body of soldiery —which still sustains a corporate existence, and marches down from past ages with an ancient and honorable fame—was composed of no mercenary materials. Its ranks were filled with gentlemen, who felt the stirrings of martial impulse, and sought to establish a kind of College of Arms, where as in an association of Knights Templars, they might learn the science, and, so far as peaceful exercise would teach them, the practices of war. The high estimation then placed upon the military character might be seen in the lofty port of each individual member of the company. Some of them, indeed, by their services in the Low Countries and on other fields of warfare, had fairly won their title to assume the name and pomp of soldiership. The entire array, moreover, clad in burnished steel, and with plumage nodding over their bright morions, had a brilliancy of effect which no modern display can aspire to equal.

And yet the men of civil eminence, who came immediately behind the military escort, were better worth a thoughtful observer's eye. Even in outward demeanor, they showed a stamp of majesty that made the warrior's haughty stride look vulgar, if not absurd. It was an age when what we call talent had far less consideration than now, but the massive materials which produce stability and dignity of character a great deal more. The people possessed, by hereditary right, the quality of reverence;

which, in their descendants, if it survive at all, exists in smaller proportion, and with a vastly diminished force, in the selection and estimate of public men. The change may be for good or evil, and is partly, perhaps, for both. In that old day, the English settler on these rude shores, having left king, nobles, and all degrees of awful rank behind, while still the faculty and necessity of reverence were strong in him, bestowed it on the white hair and venerable brow of age; on long-tried integrity; on solid wisdom and sad-colored experience; on endowments of that grave and weighty order which gives the idea of permanence, and comes under the general definition of respectability. These primitive statesmen, therefore,—Bradstreet, Endicott, Dudley, Bellingham, and their compeers,—who were elevated to power by the early choice of the people, seem to have been not often brilliant, but distinguished by a ponderous sobriety, rather than activity of intellect. They had fortitude and self-reliance, and, in time of difficulty or peril, stood up for the welfare of the state like a line of cliffs against a tempestuous tide. The traits of character here indicated were well represented in the square cast of countenance and large physical development of the new colonial magistrates. So far as a demeanor of natural authority was concerned, the mother country need not have been ashamed to see these foremost men of an actual democracy adopted into the House of Peers, or made the Privy Council of the sovereign.

Next in order to the magistrates came the young and eminently distinguished divine, from whose lips the religious discourse of the anniversary was expected. His was the profession, at that era, in which intellectual ability displayed itself far more than in political life; for—leaving a higher motive out of the question—it offered inducements powerful enough, in the almost worshipping respect of the community, to win the most aspiring ambition into its service. Even political power—as in the case of Increase Mather—was within the grasp of a successful priest.

It was the observation of those who beheld him now that never, since Mr. Dimmesdale first set his foot on the New England shore, had he exhibited such energy as was seen in the gait and air with which he kept his pace in the procession. There was no feebleness of step, as at other times; his frame was not bent; nor did his hand rest ominously upon his heart. Yet, if the clergyman were rightly viewed, his strength seemed not of the body. It might be spiritual, and imparted to him by angelic ministrations. It might be the exhilaration of that potent cordial which is distilled only in the furnace glow of earnest and long-continued thought. Or, perchance, his sensitive temperament was invigorated by the loud and piercing music, that swelled heavenward, and uplifted him on its ascending wave. Nevertheless, so abstracted was his look, it might be questioned whether Mr. Dimmesdale even heard the music. There was his body, moving onward, and with an unaccustomed force. But where was his mind? Far and deep in its own region, busying itself, with preternatural activity, to marshal a procession of stately thoughts that were soon to issue thence; and so he saw nothing, heard nothing, knew nothing, of what was around him; but the spiritual element took up the feeble frame, and carried it along, unconscious of the burden, and converting it to spirit like itself. Men of uncommon intellect, who have grown morbid, possess this occasional power of mighty effort, into which they throw the life of many days, and then are lifeless for as many more.

Hester Prynne, gazing steadfastly at the clergyman, felt a dreary influence come over her, but wherefore or whence she knew not; unless that he seemed so remote from her own sphere, and utterly beyond her reach. One glance of recognition, she had imagined, must needs pass between them. She thought of the dim forest, with its little dell of solitude, and love, and anguish, and the mossy tree-trunk, where, sitting hand in hand, they had mingled their sad and passionate talk with the melancholy murmur of the brook. How deeply had they known each other then! And was this the man? She hardly knew him now! He, moving proudly past, enveloped, as it were, in the rich music, with the procession of majestic and venerable fathers; he, so unattainable in his worldly position, and still more so in that far vista of his unsympathizing thoughts, through which she now beheld him! Her spirit sank with the idea that all must have been a delusion, and that, vividly as she had dreamed it, there could be no real bond betwixt the clergyman and herself. And thus much of woman was there in Hester, that she could scarcely forgive him,—least of all now, when the heavy footstep of their approaching Fate might be heard, nearer, nearer, nearer!—for being able so completely to withdraw himself from their mutual world; while she groped darkly, and stretched forth her cold hands, and found him not.

Pearl either saw and responded to her mother's feelings, or herself felt the remoteness and intangibility that had fallen around the minister. While the procession passed, the child was uneasy, fluttering up and down, like a bird on the point of taking flight. When the whole had gone by, she looked up into Hester's face.

"Mother," said she, "was that the same minister that kissed me by the brook?"

"Hold thy peace, dear little Pearl!" whispered her mother. "We must not always talk in the market-place of what happens to us in the forest."

"I could not be sure that it was he; so strange he looked," continued the child. "Else I would have run to him, and bid him kiss me now, before all the people; even as he did yonder among the dark old trees. What would the minister have said, mother? Would he have clapped his hand over his heart, and scowled on me, and bid me be gone?"

"What should he say, Pearl," answered Hester, "save that it was no time to kiss, and that kisses are not to be given in the market-place? Well for thee, foolish child, that thou didst not speak to him!"

Another shade of the same sentiment, in reference to Mr. Dimmesdale, was expressed by a person whose eccentricities—or insanity, as we should term it—led her to do what few of the townspeople would have ventured on; to begin a conversation with the wearer of the scarlet letter, in public. It was Mistress Hibbins, who, arrayed in great magnificence, with a triple ruff, a broidered stomacher, a gown of rich velvet, and a gold-headed cane, had come forth to see the procession. As this ancient lady had the renown (which subsequently cost her no less a price than her life) of being a principal actor in all the works of necromancy that were continually going forward, the crowd gave way before her, and seemed to fear the touch of her garment, as if it carried the plague among its gorgeous folds. Seen in conjunction with Hester Prynne,—kindly as so many now felt towards the latter,—the dread inspired by Mistress Hibbins was doubled, and caused a general movement from that part of the market-place in which the two women stood.

"Now, what mortal imagination could conceive it!" whispered the old lady, confidentially, to Hester. "Yonder divine man! That saint on earth, as the people uphold him to be, and as—I must needs say—he really looks! Who, now, that saw him pass in the procession, would think how little while it is since he went forth out of his study,—chewing a Hebrew text of Scripture in his mouth, I warrant,—to take an airing in the forest! Aha! we know what that means, Hester Prynne! But, truly, forsooth, I find it hard to believe him the same man. Many a church-member saw I, walking behind the music, that has danced in the same measure with me, when Somebody was fiddler, and, it might be, an Indian powwow or a Lapland wizard changing hands with us! That is but a trifle, when a woman knows the world. But this minister! Couldst thou surely tell, Hester, whether he was the same man that encountered thee on the forest-path?"

"Madam, I know not of what you speak," answered Hester Prynne, feeling Mistress Hibbins to be of infirm mind; yet strangely startled and awe-stricken by the confidence with which she affirmed a personal connection between so many persons (herself among them) and the Evil One. "It is not for me to talk lightly of a learned and pious minister of the Word, like the Reverend Mr. Dimmesdale!"

"Fie, woman, fie!" cried the old lady, shaking her finger at Hester. "Dost thou think I have been to the forest so many times, and have yet no skill to judge who else has been there? Yea; though no leaf of the wild garlands, which they wore while they danced be left in their hair! I know thee, Hester; for I behold the token. We may all see it in the sunshine; and it glows like a red flame in the dark. Thou wearest it openly; so there need be no question about that. But this minister! Let me tell thee, in thine ear! When the Black Man sees one of his own servants, signed and sealed, so shy of owning to the bond as is the Reverend Mr. Dimmesdale, he hath a way of ordering matters so that the mark shall be disclosed in open daylight to the eyes of all the world! What is it that the minister seeks to hide, with his hand always over his heart? Ha, Hester Prynne!"

"What is it, good Mistress Hibbins?" eagerly asked little Pearl. "Hast thou seen it?"

"No matter, darling!" responded Mistress Hibbins, making Pearl a profound reverence. "Thou thyself wilt see it, one time or another. They say, child, thou art of the lineage of the Prince of the Air! Wilt thou ride

with me, some fine night, to see thy father? Then thou shalt know wherefore the minister keeps his hand over his heart!"

Laughing so shrilly that all the market-place could hear her, the weird
old gentlewoman took her departure.

By this time the preliminary prayer had been offered in the meeting-
house, and the accents of the Reverend Mr. Dimmesdale were heard commencing his discourse. An irresistible feeling kept Hester near the spot.
As the sacred edifice was too much thronged to admit another auditor, she
took up her position close beside the scaffold of the pillory. It was in sufficient proximity to bring the whole sermon to her ears, in the shape of an
indistinct, but varied, murmur and flow of the minister's very peculiar
voice.

This vocal organ was in itself a rich endowment; insomuch that a listener, comprehending nothing of the language in which the preacher
spoke, might still have been swayed to and fro by the mere tone and cadence. Like all other music, it breathed passion and pathos, and emotions
high or tender, in a tongue native to the human heart, wherever educated.
Muffled as the sound was by its passage through the church-walls, Hester
Prynne listened with such intentness, and sympathized so intimately, that
the sermon had throughout a meaning for her, entirely apart from its indistinguishable words. These, perhaps, if more distinctly heard, might
have been only a grosser medium, and have clogged the spiritual sense.
Now she caught the low undertone, as of the wind sinking down to repose
itself; then ascended with it, as it rose through progressive gradations of
sweetness and power, until its volume seemed to envelop her with an atmosphere of awe and solemn grandeur. And yet, majestic as the voice
sometimes became, there was forever in it an essential character of plain-
tiveness. A loud or low expression of anguish,—the whisper, or the shriek,
as it might be conceived, of suffering humanity, that touched a sensibility
in every bosom! At times this deep strain of pathos was all that could be
heard, and scarcely heard, sighing amid a desolate silence. But even when
the minister's voice grew high and commanding,—when it gushed irrepressibly upward,—when it assumed its utmost breadth and power, so
overfilling the church as to burst its way through the solid walls and diffuse itself in the open air,—still, if the auditor listened intently, and for
the purpose, he could detect the same cry of pain. What was it? The complaint of a human heart, sorrow-laden, perchance guilty, telling its secret,
whether of guilt or sorrow, to the great heart of mankind; beseeching its
sympathy or forgiveness,—at every moment,—in each accent,—and never
in vain! It was this profound and continual undertone that gave the
clergyman his most appropriate power.

During all this time, Hester stood, statue-like, at the foot of the scaffold. If the minister's voice had not kept her there, there would nevertheless have been an inevitable magnetism in that spot, whence she dated the
first hour of her life of ignominy. There was a sense within her,—too ill-
defined to be made a thought, but weighing heavily on her mind,—that

her whole orb of life, both before and after, was connected with this spot, as with the one point that gave it unity.

Little Pearl, meanwhile, had quitted her mother's side, and was playing at her own will about the market-place. She made the sombre crowd cheerful by her erratic and glistening ray; even as a bird of bright plumage illuminates a whole tree of dusky foliage by darting to and fro, half seen and half concealed amid the twilight of the clustering leaves. She had an undulating, but, oftentimes, a sharp and irregular movement. It indicated the restless vivacity of her spirit, which to-day was doubly indefatigable in its tiptoe dance, because it was played upon and vibrated with her mother's disquietude. Whenever Pearl saw anything to excite her ever-active and wandering curiosity, she flew thitherward, and, as we might say, seized upon that man or thing as her own property, so far as she desired it; but without yielding the minutest degree of control over her motions in requital. The Puritans looked on, and, if they smiled, were none the less inclined to pronounce the child a demon offspring, from the indescribable charm of beauty and eccentricity that shone through her little figure, and sparkled with its activity. She ran and looked the wild Indian in the face; and he grew conscious of a nature wilder than his own. Thence, with native audacity, but still with a reserve as characteristic, she flew into the midst of a group of mariners, the swarthy-cheeked wild men of the ocean, as the Indians were of the land; and they gazed wonderingly and admiringly at Pearl, as if a flake of the sea-foam had taken the shape of a little maid, and were gifted with a soul of the sea-fire, that flashes beneath the prow in the night-time.

One of these seafaring men—the shipmaster, indeed, who had spoken to Hester Prynne—was so smitten with Pearl's aspect, that he attempted to lay hands upon her, with purpose to snatch a kiss. Finding it as impossible to touch her as to catch a humming-bird in the air, he took from his hat the gold chain that was twisted about it, and threw it to the child. Pearl immediately twined it around her neck and waist, with such happy skill, that, once seen there, it became a part of her, and it was difficult to imagine her without it.

"Thy mother is yonder woman with the scarlet letter," said the seaman. "Wilt thou carry her a message from me?"

"If the message pleases me, I will," answered Pearl.

"Then tell her," rejoined he, "that I spake again with the black-a-visaged, hump-shouldered old doctor, and he engages to bring his friend, the gentleman she wots of, aboard with him. So let thy mother take no thought, save for herself and thee. Wilt thou tell her this, thou witch-baby?"

"Mistress Hibbins says my father is the Prince of the Air!" cried Pearl, with a naughty smile. "If thou callest me that ill name, I shall tell him of thee, and he will chase thy ship with a tempest!"

Pursuing a zigzag course across the market-place, the child returned to her mother, and communicated what the mariner had said. Hester's strong, calm, steadfastly enduring spirit almost sank, at last, on beholding this dark and grim countenance of an inevitable doom, which—at the moment when a passage seemed to open for the minister and herself out of their labyrinth of misery—showed itself, with an unrelenting smile, right in the midst of their path.

With her mind harassed by the terrible perplexity in which the shipmaster's intelligence involved her, she was also subjected to another trial. There were many people present, from the country round about, who had often heard of the scarlet letter, and to whom it had been made terrific by a hundred false or exaggerated rumors, but who had never beheld it with their own bodily eyes. These, after exhausting other modes of amusement, now thronged about Hester Prynne with rude and boorish intrusiveness. Unscrupulous as it was, however, it could not bring them nearer than a circuit of several yards. At that distance they accordingly stood, fixed there by the centrifugal force of the repugnanace which the mystic symbol inspired. The whole gang of sailors, likewise, observing the press of spectators, and learning the purport of the scarlet letter, came and thrust their sunburnt and desperado-looking faces into the ring. Even the Indians were affected by a sort of cold shadow of the white man's curiosity, and, gliding through the crowd, fastened their snake-like black eyes on Hester's bosom; conceiving, perhaps, that the wearer of this brilliantly embroidered badge must needs be a personage of high dignity among her people. Lastly, the inhabitants of the town (their own interest in this worn-out subject languidly reviving itself, by sympathy with what they saw others feel) lounged idly to the same quarter, and tormented Hester Prynne, perhaps more than all the rest, with their cool, well-acquainted gaze at her familiar shame. Hester saw and recognized the self-same faces of that group of matrons, who had awaited her forthcoming from the prison-door, seven years ago; all save one, the youngest and only compassionate among them, whose burial-robe she had since made. At the final hour, when she was so soon to fling aside the burning letter, it had strangely become the centre of more remark and excitement, and was thus made to sear her breast more painfully than at any time since the first day she put it on.

While Hester stood in that magic circle of ignominy, where the cunning cruelty of her sentence seemed to have fixed her forever, the admirable preacher was looking down from the sacred pulpit upon an audience whose very inmost spirits had yielded to his control. The sainted minister in the church! The woman of the scarlet letter in the market-place! What imagination would have been irreverent enough to surmise that the same scorching stigma was on them both!

## XXIII

### THE REVELATION OF THE SCARLET LETTER

THE eloquent voice, on which the souls of the listening audience had been borne aloft as on the swelling waves of the sea, at length came to a pause. There was a momentary silence, profound as what should follow the utterance of oracles. Then ensued a murmur and half-hushed tumult; as if the auditors, released from the high spell that had transported them into the region of another's mind, were returning into themselves, with all their awe and wonder still heavy on them. In a moment more, the crowd began to gush forth from the doors of the church. Now that there was an end, they needed other breath, more fit to support the gross and earthly life into which they relapsed, than that atmosphere which the preacher had converted into words of flame, and had burdened with the rich fragrance of his thought.

In the open air their rapture broke into speech. The street and the market-place absolutely babbled, from side to side, with applauses of the minister. His hearers could not rest until they had told one another of what each knew better than he could tell or hear. According to their united testimony, never had man spoken in so wise, so high, and so holy a spirit, as he that spake this day; nor had inspiration ever breathed through mortal lips more evidently than it did through his. Its influence could be seen, as it were, descending upon him, and possessing him, and continually lifting him out of the written discourse that lay before him, and filling him with ideas that must have been as marvellous to himself as to his audience. His subject, it appeared, had been the relation between the Deity and the communities of mankind, with a special reference to the New England which they were here planting in the wilderness. And, as he drew towards the close, a spirit as of prophecy had come upon him, constraining him to its purpose as mightily as the old prophets of Israel were constrained; only with this difference, that, whereas the Jewish seers had denounced judgments and ruin on their country, it was his mission to foretell a high and glorious destiny for the newly gathered people of the Lord. But, throughout it all, and through the whole discourse, there had been a certain deep, sad undertone of pathos, which could not be interpreted otherwise than as the natural regret of one soon to pass away. Yes; their minister whom they so loved—and who so loved them all, that he could not depart heavenward without a sigh—had the foreboding of untimely death upon him, and would soon leave them in their tears! This idea of his transitory stay on earth gave the last emphasis to the effect which the preacher had produced; it was as if an angel, in his passage to the skies, had shaken his bright wings over the people for an instant,—at once a shadow and a splendor,—and had shed down a shower of golden truths upon them.

Thus, there had come to the Reverend Mr. Dimmesdale—as to most men, in their various spheres, though seldom recognized until they see it far behind them—an epoch of life more brilliant and full of triumph than any previous one, or than any which could hereafter be. He stood, at this moment, on the very proudest eminence of superiority, to which the gifts of intellect, rich lore, prevailing eloquence, and a reputation of whitest sanctity, could exalt a clergyman in New England's earliest days, when the professional character was of itself a lofty pedestal. Such was the position which the minister occupied, as he bowed his head forward on the cushions of the pulpit, at the close of his Election Sermon. Meanwhile Hester Prynne was standing beside the scaffold of the pillory, with the scarlet letter still burning on her breast!

Now was heard again the clangor of music, and the measured tramp of the military escort, issuing from the church-door. The procession was to be marshalled thence to the town-hall, where a solemn banquet would complete the ceremonies of the day.

Once more, therefore, the train of venerable and majestic fathers was seen moving through a broad pathway of the people, who drew back reverently, on either side, as the Governor and magistrates, the old and wise men, the holy ministers, and all that were eminent and renowned, advanced into the midst of them. When they were fairly in the market-place, their presence was greeted by a shout. This—though doubtless it might acquire additional force and volume from the childlike loyalty which the age awarded to its rulers—was felt to be an irrepressible outburst of enthusiasm kindled in the auditors by that high strain of eloquence which was yet reverberating in their ears. Each felt the impulse in himself, and, in the same breath, caught it from his neighbor. Within the church, it had hardly been kept down; beneath the sky, it pealed upward to the zenith. There were human beings enough, and enough of highly wrought and symphonious feeling, to produce that more impressive sound than the organ tones of the blast, or the thunder, or the roar of the sea; even that mighty swell of many voices, blended into one great voice by the universal impulse which makes likewise one vast heart out of the many. Never, from the soil of New England, had gone up such a shout! Never, on New England soil, had stood the man honored by his mortal brethren as the preacher!

How fared it with him then? Were there not the brilliant particles of a halo in the air about his head? So etherealized by spirit as he was, and so apotheosized by worshipping admirers, did his footsteps, in the procession, really tread upon the dust of earth?

As the ranks of military men and civil fathers moved onward, all eyes were turned towards the point where the minister was seen to approach among them. The shout died into a murmur, as one portion of the crowd after another obtained a glimpse of him. How feeble and pale he looked, amid all his triumph! The energy—or say, rather, the inspiration which had held him up until he should have delivered the sacred message that brought its own strength along with it from Heaven—was withdrawn, now that it had so faithfully performed its office. The glow, which they

had just before beheld burning on his cheek, was extinguished, like a flame
that sinks down hopelessly among the late-decaying embers. It seemed
hardly the face of a man alive, with such a deathlike hue; it was hardly a
man with life in him that tottered on his path so nervelessly, yet tottered,
and did not fall!

One of his clerical brethren,—it was the venerable John Wilson,—observing the state in which Mr. Dimmesdale was left by the retiring wave
of intellect and sensibility, stepped forward hastily to offer his support.
The minister tremulously, but decidedly, repelled the old man's arm. He
still walked onward, if that movement could be so described, which rather
resembled the wavering effort of an infant with its mother's arms in view,
outstretched to tempt him forward. And now, almost imperceptible as
were the latter steps of his progress, he had come opposite the well-remembered and weather-darkened scaffold, where, long since, with all that
dreary lapse of time between, Hester Prynne had encountered the world's
ignominious stare. There stood Hester, holding little Pearl by the hand!
And there was the scarlet letter on her breast! The minister here made a
pause, although the music still played the stately and rejoicing march to
which the procession moved. It summoned him onward,—onward to the
festival!—but here he made a pause.

Bellingham, for the last few moments, had kept an anxious eye upon
him. He now left his own place in the procession, and advanced to give assistance, judging, from Mr. Dimmesdale's aspect, that he must otherwise
inevitably fall. But there was something in the latter's expression that
warned back the magistrate, although a man not readily obeying the
vague intimations that pass from one spirit to another. The crowd, meanwhile, looked on with awe and wonder. This earthly faintness was, in their
view, only another phase of the minister's celestial strength; nor would
it have seemed a miracle too high to be wrought for one so holy, had he
ascended before their eyes, waxing dimmer and brighter, and fading at
last into the light of heaven.

He turned towards the scaffold, and stretched forth his arms.

"Hester," said he, "come hither! Come, my little Pearl!"

It was a ghastly look with which he regarded them; but there was
something at once tender and strangely triumphant in it. The child, with
the bird-like motion which was one of her characteristics, flew to him,
and clasped her arms about his knees. Hester Prynne—slowly, as if impelled by inevitable fate, and against her strongest will—likewise drew
near, but paused before she reached him. At this instant, old Roger Chillingworth thrust himself through the crowd,—or, perhaps, so dark, disturbed, and evil, was his look, he rose up out of some nether region,—to
snatch back his victim from what he sought to do! Be that as it might,
the old man rushed forward, and caught the minister by the arm.

"Madman, hold! what is your purpose?" whispered he. "Wave back
that woman! Cast off this child! All shall be well! Do not blacken your
fame, and perish in dishonor! I can yet save you! Would you bring infamy on your sacred profession?"

"Ha, tempter! Methinks thou art too late!" answered the minister, encountering his eye, fearfully, but firmly. "Thy power is not what it was! With God's help, I shall escape thee now!"

He again extended his hand to the woman of the scarlet letter.

"Hester Prynne," cried he, with a piercing earnestness, "in the name of Him, so terrible and so merciful, who gives me grace, at this last moment, to do what—for my own heavy sin and miserable agony—I withheld myself from doing seven years ago, come hither now, and twine thy strength about me! Thy strength, Hester; but let it be guided by the will which God hath granted me! This wretched and wronged old man is opposing it with all his might! with all his own might, and the fiend's! Come, Hester, come! Support me up yonder scaffold!"

The crowd was in a tumult. The men of rank and dignity, who stood more immediately around the clergyman, were so taken by surprise, and so perplexed as to the purport of what they saw,—unable to receive the explanation which most readily presented itself, or to imagine any other,—that they remained silent and inactive spectators of the judgment which Providence seemed about to work. They beheld the minister, leaning on Hester's shoulder, and supported by her arm around him, approach the scaffold, and ascend its steps; while still the little hand of the sin-born child was clasped in his. Old Roger Chillingworth followed, as one intimately connected with the drama of guilt and sorrow in which they had all been actors, and well entitled, therefore, to be present at its closing scene.

"Hadst thou sought the whole earth over," said he, looking darkly at the clergyman, "there was no one place so secret,—no high place nor lowly place, where thou couldst have escaped me,—save on this very scaffold!"

"Thanks be to Him who hath led me hither!" answered the minister.

Yet he trembled, and turned to Hester with an expression of doubt and anxiety in his eyes, not the less evidently betrayed, that there was a feeble smile upon his lips.

"Is not this better," murmured he, "than what we dreamed of in the forest?"

"I know not! I know not!" she hurriedly replied. "Better? Yea; so we may both die, and little Pearl die with us!"

"For thee and Pearl, be it as God shall order," said the minister; "and God is merciful! Let me now do the will which He hath made plain before my sight. For, Hester, I am a dying man. So let me make haste to take my shame upon me!"

Partly supported by Hester Prynne, and holding one hand of little Pearl's, the Reverend Mr. Dimmesdale turned to the dignified and venerable rulers; to the holy ministers, who were his brethren; to the people, whose great heart was thoroughly appalled, yet overflowing with tearful sympathy, as knowing that some deep life-matter—which, if full of sin, was full of anguish and repentance likewise—was now to be laid open to them. The sun, but little past its meridian, shone down upon the clergyman, and gave a distinctness to his figure, as he stood out from all the earth, to put in his plea of guilty at the bar of Eternal Justice.

"People of New England!" cried he, with a voice that rose over them, high, solemn, and majestic,—yet had always a tremor through it, and sometimes a shriek, struggling up out of a fathomless depth of remorse and woe,—"ye, that have loved me!—ye, that have deemed me holy!—behold me here, the one sinner of the world! A last!—at last!—I stand upon the spot where, seven years since, I should have stood; here, with this woman, whose arm, more than the little strength wherewith I have crept hitherward, sustains me, at this dreadful moment, from grovelling down upon my face! Lo, the scarlet letter which Hester wears! Ye have all shuddered at it! Wherever her walk hath been,—wherever, so miserably burdened, she may have hoped to find repose,—it hath cast a lurid gleam of awe and horrible repugnance round about her. But there stood one in the midst of you, at whose brand of sin and infamy ye have not shuddered!"

It seemed, at this point, as if the minister must leave the remainder of his secret undisclosed. But he fought back the bodily weakness,—and, still more, the faintness of heart,—that was striving for the mastery with him. He threw off all assistance, and stepped passionately forward a pace before the woman and the child.

"It was on him!" he continued, with a kind of fierceness,—so determined was he to speak out the whole. "God's eye beheld it! The angels were forever pointing at it! The Devil knew it well, and fretted it continually with the touch of his burning finger! But he hid it cunningly from men, and walked among you with the mien of a spirit, mournful, because so pure in a sinful world!—and sad, because he missed his heavenly kindred! Now, at the death-hour, he stands up before you! He bids you look again at Hester's scarlet letter! He tells you, that, with all its mysterious horror, it is but the shadow of what he bears on his own breast, and that even this, his own red stigma, is no more than the type of what has seared his inmost heart! Stand any here that question God's judgment on a sinner? Behold! Behold a dreadful witness of it!"

With a convulsive motion, he tore away the ministerial band from before his breast. It was revealed! But it were irreverent to describe that revelation. For an instant, the gaze of the horror-stricken multitude was concentred on the ghastly miracle; while the minister stood, with a flush of triumph in his face, as one who, in the crisis of acutest pain, had won a victory. Then, down he sank upon the scaffold! Hester partly raised him, and supported his head against her bosom. Old Roger Chillingworth knelt down beside him, with a blank, dull countenance, out of which the life seemed to have departed.

"Thou hast escaped me!" he repeated more than once. "Thou hast escaped me!"

"May God forgive thee!" said the minister. "Thou, too, hast deeply sinned!"

He withdrew his dying eyes from the old man, and fixed them on the woman and the child.

"My little Pearl," said he, feebly,—and there was a sweet and gentle smile over his face, as of a spirit sinking into deep repose; nay, now that the burden was removed, it seemed almost as if he would be sportive with the child,—"dear little Pearl, wilt thou kiss me now? Thou wouldst not, yonder, in the forest! But now thou wilt?"

Pearl kissed his lips. A spell was broken. The great scene of grief in which the wild infant bore a part, had developed all her sympathies; and as her tears fell upon her father's cheek, they were the pledge that she would grow up amid human joy and sorrow, nor forever do battle with the world, but be a woman in it. Towards her mother, too, Pearl's errand as a messenger of anguish was all fulfilled.

"Hester," said the clergyman, "farewell!"

"Shall we not meet again?" whispered she, bending her face down close to his. "Shall we not spend our immortal life together? Surely, surely, we have ransomed one another, with all this woe! Thou lookest far into eternity, with those bright dying eyes! Then tell me what thou seest?"

"Hush, Hester, hush!" said he, with tremulous solemnity. "The law we broke!—the sin here so awfully revealed!—let these alone be in thy thoughts! I fear! I fear! It may be that, when we forgot our God,—when we violated our reverence each for the other's soul,—it was thenceforth vain to hope that we could meet hereafter, in an everlasting and pure reunion. God knows; and He is merciful! He hath proved his mercy, most of all, in my afflictions. By giving me this burning torture to bear upon my breast! By sending yonder dark and terrible old man, to keep the torture always at red-heat! By bringing me hither, to die this death of triumphant ignominy before the people! Had either of these agonies been wanting, I had been lost forever! Praised be his name! His will be done! Farewell!"

That final word came forth with the minister's expiring breath. The multitude, silent till then, broke out in a strange, deep voice of awe and wonder, which could not as yet find utterance, save in this murmur that rol'ed so heavily after the departed spirit.

## XXIV

### CONCLUSION

AFTER many days, when time sufficed for the people to arrange their thoughts in reference to the foregoing scene, there was more than one account of what had been witnessed on the scaffold.

Most of the spectators testified to having seen, on the breast of the unhappy minister, a SCARLET LETTER—the very semblance of that worn by Hester Prynne—imprinted in the flesh. As regarded its origin, there were various explanations, all of which must necessarily have been conjectural. Some affirmed that the Reverend Mr. Dimmesdale, on the very day when Hester Prynne first wore her ignominious badge, had begun a course of penance,—which he afterwards, in so many futile methods, followed out, —by inflicting a hideous torture on himself. Others contended that the stigma had not been produced until a long time subsequent, when old Roger Chillingworth, being a potent necromancer, had caused it to appear, through the agency of magic and poisonous drugs. Others, again,— and those best able to appreciate the minister's peculiar sensibility, and the wonderful operation of his spirit upon the body,—whispered their belief, that the awful symbol was the effect of the ever-active tooth of remorse, gnawing from the inmost heart outwardly, and at last manifesting Heaven's dreadful judgment by the visible presence of the letter. The reader may choose among these theories. We have thrown all the light we could acquire upon the portent, and would gladly, now that it has done its office, erase its deep print out of our own brain, where long meditation has fixed it in very undesirable distinctness.

It is singular, nevertheless, that certain persons, who were spectators of the whole scene, and professed never once to have removed their eyes from the Reverend Mr. Dimmesdale, denied that there was any mark whatever on his breast, more than on a new-born infant's. Neither, by their report, had his dying words acknowledged, nor even remotely implied, any, the slightest connection, on his part, with the guilt for which Hester Prynne had so long worn the scarlet letter. According to these highly respectable witnesses, the minister, conscious that he was dying,— conscious, also, that the reverence of the multitude placed him already among saints and angels,—had desired, by yielding up his breath in the arms of that fallen woman, to express to the world how utterly nugatory is the choicest of man's own righteousness. After exhausting life in his efforts for mankind's spiritual good, he had made the manner of his death a parable, in order to impress on his admirers the mighty and mournful lesson, that, in the view of Infinite Purity, we are sinners all alike. It was to teach them, that the holiest among us has but attained so far above his fellows as to discern more clearly the Mercy which looks down, and repudiate more utterly the phantom of human merit, which would look aspiringly upward. Without disputing a truth so momentous, we must be allowed to consider this version of Mr. Dimmesdale's story as only an instance of that stubborn fidelity with which a man's friends—and especially a clergyman's—will sometimes uphold his character, when proofs, clear as the mid-day sunshine on the scarlet letter, establish him a false and sin-stained creature of the dust.

The authority which we have chiefly followed,—a manuscript of old date, drawn up from the verbal testimony of individuals, some of whom had known Hester Prynne, while others had heard the tale from contemporary witnesses,—fully confirms the view taken in the foregoing pages. Among many morals which press upon us from the poor minister's miserable experience, we put only this into a sentence: "Be true! Be true! Be true! Show freely to the world, if not your worst, yet some trait whereby the worst may be inferred!"

Nothing was more remarkable than the change which took place, almost immediately after Mr. Dimmesdale's death, in the appearance and demeanor of the old man known as Roger Chillingworth. All his strength and energy—all his vital and intellectual force—seemed at once to desert him; insomuch that he positively withered up, shrivelled away, and almost vanished from mortal sight, like an uprooted weed that lies wilting in the sun. This unhappy man had made the very principle of his life to consist in the pursuit and systematic exercise of revenge; and when, by its completest triumph and consummation, that evil principle was left with no further material to support it, when, in short, there was no more Devil's work on earth for him to do, it only remained for the unhumanized mortal to betake himself whither his Master would find him tasks enough, and pay him his wages duly. But to all these shadowy beings, so long our near acquaintances,—as well Roger Chillingworth as his companions,—we would fain be merciful. It is a curious subject of observation and inquiry, whether hatred and love be not the same thing at bottom. Each, in its utmost development, supposes a high degree of intimacy and heart-knowledge; each renders one individual dependent for the food of his affections and spiritual life upon another; each leaves the passionate lover, or the no less passionate hater, forlorn and desolate by the withdrawal of his subject. Philosophically considered, therefore, the two passions seem essentially the same, except that one happens to be seen in a celestial radiance, and the other in a dusky and lurid glow. In the spiritual world, the old physician and the minister—mutual victims as they have been—may, unawares, have found their earthly stock of hatred and antipathy transmuted into golden love.

Leaving this discussion apart, we have a matter of business to communicate to the reader. At old Roger Chillingworth's decease (which took place within the year), and by his last will and testament, of which Governor Bellingham and the Reverend Mr. Wilson were executors, he bequeathed a very considerable amount of property, both here and in England, to little Pearl, the daughter of Hester Prynne.

So Pearl—the elf-child,—the demon offspring, as some people, up to that epoch, persisted in considering her,—became the richest heiress of her day, in the New World. Not improbably, this circumstance wrought a very material change in the public estimation; and, had the mother and child remained here, little Pearl, at a marriageable period of life, might have mingled her wild blood with the lineage of the devoutest Puritan among them all. But, in no long time after the physician's death, the wearer of the scarlet letter disappeared, and Pearl along with her. For many years, though a vague report would now and then find its way across the sea,—like a shapeless piece of drift-wood tost ashore, with the initials of a name upon it,—yet no tidings of them unquestionably authentic were received. The story of the scarlet letter grew into a legend. Its spell, however, was still potent, and kept the scaffold awful where the poor minister had died, and likewise the cottage by the seashore, where Hester Prynne had dwelt. Near this latter spot, one afternoon, some children were at play, when they beheld a tall woman, in a gray robe, approach the cottage-door. In all those years it had never once been opened; but either she unlocked it, or the decaying wood and iron yielded to her hand, or she glided shadowlike through these impediments,—and, at all events, went in.

On the threshold she paused,—turned partly round,—for, perchance, the idea of entering all alone, and all so changed, the home of so intense a former life, was more dreary and desolate than even she could bear. But her hesitation was only for an instant, though long enough to display a scarlet letter on her breast.

And Hester Prynne had returned, and taken up her long-forsaken shame! But where was little Pearl? If still alive, she must now have been in the flush and bloom of early womanhood. None knew—nor ever learned, with the fulness of perfect certainty—whether the elf-child had gone thus untimely to a maiden grave, or whether her wild, rich nature had been softened and subdued, and made capable of a woman's gentle happiness. But, through the remainder of Hester's life, there were indications that the recluse of the scarlet letter was the object of love and interest with some inhabitant of another land. Letters came, with armorial seals upon them, though of bearings unknown to English heraldry. In the cottage there were articles of comfort and luxury such as Hester never cared to use, but which only wealth could have purchased, and affection have imagined for her. There were trifles, too, little ornaments, beautiful tokens of a continual remembrance, that must have been wrought by delicate fingers, at the impulse of a fond heart. And, once, Hester was seen embroidering a baby-garment, with such a lavish richness of golden fancy as would have raised a public tumult, had any infant, thus apparelled, been shown to our sober-hued community.

In fine, the gossips of that day believed,—and Mr. Surveyor Pue, who made investigations a century later, believed,—and one of his recent successors in office, moreover, faithfully believes,—that Pearl was not only alive, but married, and happy, and mindful of her mother, and that she would most joyfully have entertained that sad and lonely mother at her fireside.

But there was a more real life for Hester Prynne here, in New England, than in that unknown region where Pearl had found a home. Here had been her sin; here, her sorrow; and here was yet to be her penitence. She had returned, therefore, and resumed,—of her own free will, for not the sternest magistrate of that iron period would have imposed it,—resumed the symbol of which we have related so dark a tale. Never afterwards did it quit her bosom. But, in the lapse of the toilsome, thoughtful, and self-devoted years that made up Hester's life, the scarlet letter ceased to be a stigma which attracted the world's scorn and bitterness, and became a type of something to be sorrowed over, and looked upon with awe, yet with reverence too. And, as Hester Prynne had no selfish ends, nor lived in any measure for her own profit and enjoyment, people brought all their sorrows and perplexities, and besought her counsel, as one who had herself gone through a mighty trouble. Women, more especially,—in the continually recurring trials of wounded, wasted, wronged, misplaced, or erring and sinful passion,—or with the dreary burden of a heart unyielded, because unvalued and unsought,—came to Hester's cottage, demanding why they were so wretched, and what the remedy! Hester comforted and counselled them as best she might. She assured them, too, of her firm belief, that, at some brighter period, when the world should have grown ripe for it, in Heaven's own time, a new truth would be revealed, in order to establish the whole relation between man and woman on a surer ground of mutual happiness. Earlier in life, Hester had vainly imagined that she herself might be the destined prophetess, but had long since recognized the impossibility that any mission of divine and mysterious truth should be confided to a woman stained with sin, bowed down with shame, or even burdened with a life-long sorrow. The angel and apostle of the coming revelation must be a woman indeed, but lofty, pure, and beautiful; and wise, moreover, not through dusky grief, but the ethereal medium of joy; and showing how sacred love should make us happy, by the truest test of a life successful to such an end!

So said Hester Prynne, and glanced her sad eyes downward at the scarlet letter. And, after many, many years a new grave was delved, near an old and sunken one, in that burial-ground beside which King's Chapel has since been built. It was near that old and sunken grave, yet with a space between, as if the dust of the two sleepers had no right to mingle. Yet one tombstone served for both. All around, there were monuments carved with armorial bearings; and on this simple slab of slate—as the curious investigator may still discern, and perplex himself with the purport—there appeared the semblance of an engraved escutcheon. It bore a device, a herald's wording of which might serve for a motto and brief description of our now concluded legend; so sombre is it, and relieved only by one ever-glowing point of light gloomier than the shadow:—

"On a field, sable, the letter A, gules."

THE

# HOUSE OF THE SEVEN GABLES

A ROMANCE

WHEN a writer calls his work a Romance, it need hardly be observed that he wishes to claim a certain latitude, both as to its fashion and material, which he would not have felt himself entitled to assume had he professed to be writing a Novel. The latter form of composition is presumed to aim at a very minute fidelity, not merely to the possible, but to the probable and ordinary course of man's experience. The former—while, as a work of art, it must rigidly subject itself to laws, and while it sins unpardonably so far as it may swerve aside from the truth of the human heart—has fairly a right to present that truth under circumstances, to a great extent, of the writer's own choosing or creation. If he think fit, also, he may so manage his atmospherical medium as to bring out or mellow the lights and deepen and enrich the shadows of the picture. He will be wise, no doubt, to make a very moderate use of the privileges here stated, and, especially, to mingle the Marvellous rather as a slight, delicate, and evanescent flavor, than as any portion of the actual substance of the dish offered to the public. He can hardly be said, however, to commit a literary crime even if he disregard this caution.

In the present work, the author has proposed to himself—but with what success, fortunately, it is not for him to judge—to keep undeviatingly within his immunities. The point of view in which this tale comes under the Romantic definition lies in the attempt to connect a bygone time with the very present that is flitting away from us. It is a legend prolonging itself, from an epoch now gray in the distance, down into our own broad daylight, and bringing along with it some of its legendary mist, which the reader, according to his pleasure, may either disregard, or allow it to float almost imperceptibly about the characters and events for the sake of a picturesque effect. The narrative, it may be, is woven of so humble a texture as to require this advantage, and, at the same time, to render it the more difficult of attainment.

Many writers lay very great stress upon some definite moral purpose, at which they profess to aim their works. Not to be deficient in this particular, the author has provided himself with a moral,—the truth, namely, that the wrong-doing of one generation lives into the successive ones, and, divesting itself of every temporary advantage, becomes a pure and uncontrollable mischief; and he would feel it a singular gratification if this romance might effectually convince mankind—or, indeed, any one man—of the folly of tumbling down an avalanche of ill-gotten gold, or real estate, on the heads of an unfortunate posterity, thereby to maim and crush them, until the accumulated mass shall be scattered abroad in its original atoms. In good faith, however, he is not sufficiently imaginative to flatter himself with the slightest hope of this kind. When romances do really teach anything, or produce any effective operation, it is usually through a far more subtile process than the ostensible one. The author has considered it hardly worth his while, therefore, relentlessly to impale the story with its moral as with an iron rod,—or, rather, as by sticking a pin through a butterfly,—thus at once depriving it of life, and causing it to stiffen in an ungainly and unnatural attitude. A high truth, indeed, fairly, finely, and skilfully wrought out, brightening at every step, and crowning the final development of a work of fiction, may add an artistic glory, but is never any truer, and seldom any more evident, at the last page than at the first.

The reader may perhaps choose to assign an actual locality to the imaginary events of this narrative. If permitted by the historical connection, —which, though slight, was essential to his plan,—the author would very willingly have avoided anything of this nature. Not to speak of other objections, it exposes the romance to an inflexible and exceedingly dangerous species of criticism, by bringing his fancy-pictures almost into positive contact with the realities of the moment. It has been no part of his object, however, to describe local manners, nor in any way to meddle with the characteristics of a community for whom he cherishes a proper respect and a natural regard. He trusts not to be considered as unpardonably offending by laying out a street that infringes upon nobody's private rights, and appropriating a lot of land which had no visible owner, and building a house of materials long in use for constructing castles in the air. The personages of the tale—though they give themselves out to be of ancient stability and considerable prominence—are really of the author's own making, or, at all events, of his own mixing; their virtues can shed no lustre, nor their defects redound, in the remotest degree, to the discredit of the venerable town of which they profess to be inhabitants. He would be glad, therefore, if—especially in the quarter to which he alludes—the book may be read strictly as a Romance, having a great deal more to do with the clouds overhead than with any portion of the actual soil of the County of Essex.

LENOX, January 27, 1851.

# HOUSE OF THE SEVEN GABLES

## I

### THE OLD PYNCHEON FAMILY

HALF-WAY down a by-street of one of our New England towns stands a rusty wooden house, with seven acutely peaked gables, facing towards various points of the compass, and a huge, clustered chimney in the midst. The street is Pyncheon Street; the house is the old Pyncheon House; and an elm-tree, of wide circumference, rooted before the door, is familiar to every town-born child by the title of the Pyncheon Elm. On my occasional visits to the town aforesaid, I seldom failed to turn down Pyncheon Street, for the sake of passing through the shadow of these two antiquities,—the great elm-tree and the weather-beaten edifice.

The aspect of the venerable mansion has always affected me like a human countenance, bearing the traces not merely of outward storm and sunshine, but expressive, also, of the long lapse of mortal life, and accompanying vicissitudes that have passed within. Were these to be worthily recounted, they would form a narrative of no small interest and instruction, and possessing, moreover, a certain remarkable unity, which might almost seem the result of artistic arrangement. But the story would include a chain of events extending over the better part of two centuries, and, written out with reasonable amplitude, would fill a bigger folio volume, or a longer series of duodecimos, than could prudently be appropriated to the annals of all New England during a similar period. It consequently becomes imperative to make short work with most of the traditionary lore of which the old Pyncheon House, otherwise known as the House of the Seven Gables, has been the theme. With a brief sketch, therefore, of the circumstances amid which the foundation of the house was laid, and a rapid glimpse at its quaint exterior, as it grew black in the prevalent east wind,—pointing, too, here and there, at some spot of more verdant mossiness on its roof and walls,—we shall commence the real action of our tale at an epoch not very remote from the present day. Still, there will be a connection with the long past—a reference to forgotten events and personages, and to manners, feelings, and opinions, almost or wholly obsolete—which, if adequately translated to the reader, would serve to illustrate how much of old material goes to make up the freshest novelty of human life. Hence, too, might be drawn a weighty lesson from the little-regarded truth, that the act of the passing generation is the germ which may and must produce good or evil fruit in a far-distant time; that, together with the seed of the merely temporary crop, which mortals term expediency, they inevitably sow the acorns of a more enduring growth, which may darkly overshadow their posterity.

The House of the Seven Gables, antique as it now looks, was not the first habitation erected by civilized man on precisely the same spot of ground. Pyncheon Street formerly bore the humbler appellation of Maule's Lane, from the name of the original occupant of the soil, before whose cottage-door it was a cow-path. A natural spring of soft and pleasant water—a rare treasure on the sea-girt peninsula, where the Puritan settlement was made—had early induced Matthew Maule to build a hut, shaggy with thatch, at this point, although somewhat too remote from what was then the centre of the village. In the growth of the town, however, after some thirty or forty years, the site covered by this rude hovel had become exceedingly desirable in the eyes of a prominent and powerful personage, who asserted plausible claims to the proprietorship of this, and a large adjacent tract of land, on the strength of a grant from the legislature. Colonel Pyncheon, the claimant, as we gather from whatever traits of him are preserved, was characterized by an iron energy of purpose. Matthew Maule, on the other hand, though an obscure man, was stubborn in the defence of what he considered his right; and, for several years, he succeeded in protecting the acre or two of earth, which, with his own toil, he had hewn out of the primeval forest, to be his garden-ground and homestead. No written record of this dispute is known to be in existence. Our acquaintance with the whole subject is derived chiefly from tradition. It would be bold, therefore, and possibly unjust, to venture a decisive opinion as to its merits; although it appears to have been at least a matter of doubt, whether Colonel Pyncheon's claim were not unduly stretched, in order to make it cover the small metes and bounds of Matthew Maule. What greatly strengthens such a suspicion is the fact that this controversy between two ill-matched antagonists—at a period, moreover, laud it as we may, when personal influence had far more weight than now—remained for years undecided, and came to a close only with the death of the party occupying the disputed soil. The mode of his death, too, affects the mind differently, in our day, from what it did a century and a half ago. It was a death that blasted with strange horror the humble name of the dweller in the cottage, and made it seem almost a religious act to drive the plough over the little area of his habitation, and obliterate his place and memory from among men.

Old Matthew Maule, in a word, was executed for the crime of witchcraft. He was one of the martyrs to that terrible delusion, which should teach us, among its other morals, that the influential classes, and those who take upon themselves to be leaders of the people, are fully liable to all the passionate error that has ever characterized the maddest mob. Clergymen, judges, statesmen,—the wisest, calmest, holiest persons of their day,—stood in the inner circle round about the gallows, loudest to applaud the work of blood, latest to confess themselves miserably deceived. If any one part of their proceedings can be said to deserve less blame than another, it was the singular indiscrimination with which they persecuted, not merely the poor and aged, as in former judicial massacres, but people of all ranks; their own equals, brethren, and wives. Amid the disorder of such various ruin, it is not strange that a man of inconsiderable note, like Maule, should have trodden the martyr's path to the hill of execution almost unremarked in the throng of his fellow-sufferers. But, in after days, when the frenzy of that hideous epoch had subsided, it was remembered how loudly Colonel Pyncheon had joined in the general cry, to purge the land from witchcraft; nor did it fail to be whispered, that there was an individious acrimony in the zeal with which he had sought the condemnation of Matthew Maule. It was well known that the victim had recognized the bitterness of personal enmity in his persecutor's conduct towards him, and that he declared himself hunted to death for his spoil. At the moment of execution—with the halter about his neck, and while Colonel Pyncheon sat on horseback, grimly gazing at the scene— Maule had addressed him from the scaffold, and uttered a prophecy, of which history, as well as fireside tradition, has preserved the very words. "God," said the dying man, pointing his finger, with a ghastly look, at the undismayed countenance of his enemy,—"God will give him blood to drink!"

After the reputed wizard's death, his humble homestead had fallen an easy spoil into Colonel Pyncheon's grasp. When it was understood, however, that the Colonel intended to erect a family mansion—spacious, ponderously framed of oaken timber, and calculated to endure for many generations of his posterity—over the spot first covered by the log-built hut of Matthew Maule, there was much shaking of the head among the village gossips. Without absolutely expressing a doubt whether the stalwart Puritan had acted as a man of conscience and integrity throughout the proceedings which have been sketched, they, nevertheless, hinted that he was about to build his house over an unquiet grave. His home would include the home of the dead and buried wizard, and would thus afford the ghost of the latter a kind of privilege to haunt its new apartments, and the chambers into which future bridegrooms were to lead their brides, and where children of the Pyncheon blood were to be born. The terror and ugliness of Maule's crime, and the wretchedness of his punishment, would darken the freshly plastered walls, and infect them early with the scent of an old and melancholy house. Why, then,—while so much of the soil around him was bestrewn with the virgin forest-leaves,—why should Colonel Pyncheon prefer a site that had already been accurst?

But the Puritan soldier and magistrate was not a man to be turned aside from his well-considered scheme, either by dread of the wizard's ghost, or by flimsy sentimentalities of any kind, however specious. Had he been told of a bad air, it might have moved him somewhat; but he was ready to encounter an evil spirit on his own ground. Endowed with common-sense, as massive and hard as blocks of granite, fastened together by stern rigidity of purpose, as with iron clamps, he followed out his original design, probably without so much as imagining an objection to it. On the score of delicacy, or any scrupulousness which a finer sensibility might have taught him, the Colonel, like most of his breed and generation, was impenetrable. He, therefore, dug his cellar, and laid the deep foundations of his mansion, on the square of earth whence Matthew Maule, forty years before, had first swept away the fallen leaves. It was a curious, and, as some people thought, an ominous fact, that, very soon after the workmen began their operations, the spring of water, above mentioned, entirely lost the deliciousness of its pristine quality. Whether its sources were disturbed by the depth of the new cellar, or whatever subtler cause might lurk at the bottom, it is certain that the water of Maule's Well, as it continued to be called, grew hard and brackish. Even such we find it now; and any old woman of the neighborhood will certify that it is productive of intestinal mischief to those who quench their thirst there.

The reader may deem it singular that the head carpenter of the new edifice was no other than the son of the very man from whose dead gripe the property of the soil had been wrested. Not improbably he was the best workman of his time; or, perhaps, the Colonel thought it expedient, or was impelled by some better feeling, thus openly to cast aside all animosity against the race of his fallen antagonist. Nor was it out of keeping with the general coarseness and matter-of-fact character of the age, that the son should be willing to earn an honest penny, or, rather, a weighty amount of sterling pounds, from the purse of his father's deadly enemy. At all events, Thomas Maule became the architect of the House of the Seven Gables, and performed his duty so faithfully that the timber framework fastened by his hands still holds together.

Thus the great house was built. Familiar as it stands in the writer's recollection,—for it has been an object of curiosity with him from boyhood, both as a specimen of the best and stateliest architecture of a long-past epoch, and as the scene of events more full of human interest, perhaps, than those of a gray feudal castle,—familiar as it stands, in its rusty old age, it is therefore only the more difficult to imagine the bright novelty with which it first caught the sunshine. The impression of its actual state, at this distance of a hundred and sixty years, darkens inevitably through the picture which we would fain give of its appearance on the morning when the Puritan magnate bade all the town to be his guests. A ceremony of consecration, festive as well as religious, was now to be performed. A prayer and discourse from the Rev. Mr. Higginson, and the outpouring of a psalm from the general throat of the community, was to be made acceptable to the grosser sense by ale, cider, wine, and brandy, in copious effusion, and, as some authorities aver, by an ox, roasted whole, or at least, by the weight and substance of an ox, in more manageable joints and sirloins. The carcass of a deer, shot within twenty miles, had supplied material for the vast circumference of a pasty. A codfish of sixty pounds, caught in the bay, had been dissolved into the rich liquid of a chowder. The chimney of the new house, in short, belching forth its kitchen-smoke, impregnated the whole air with the scent of meats, fowls, and fishes, spicily concocted with odoriferous herbs, and onions in abundance. The mere smell of such festivity, making its way to everybody's nostrils, was at once an invitation and an appetite.

Maule's Lane, or Pyncheon Street, as it were now more decorous to call it, was thronged, at the appointed hour, as with a congregation on its way to church. All, as they approached, looked upward at the imposing edifice, which was henceforth to assume its rank among the habitations of mankind. There it rose, a little withdrawn from the line of the street, but in pride, not modesty. Its whole visible exterior was ornamented with quaint figures, conceived in the grotesqueness of a Gothic fancy, and drawn or stamped in the glittering plaster, composed of lime, pebbles, and bits of glass, with which the woodwork of the walls was overspread. On every side the seven gables pointed sharply towards the sky, and presented the aspect of a whole sisterhood of edifices, breathing through the spiracles of one great chimney. The many lattices, with their small, diamond-shaped panes, admitted the sunlight into hall and chamber, while, nevertheless, the second story, projecting far over the base, and itself retiring beneath the third, threw a shadowy and thoughtful gloom into the lower rooms. Carved globes of wood were affixed under the jutting stories. Little spiral rods of iron beautified each of the seven peaks. On the triangular portion of the gable, that fronted next the street, was a dial, put up that very morning, and on which the sun was still marking the passage of the first bright hour in a history that was not destined to be all so bright. All around were scattered shavings, chips, shingles, and broken halves of bricks; these, together with the lately turned earth, on which the grass had not begun to grow, contributed to the impression of strangeness and novelty proper to a house that had yet its place to make among men's daily interests.

The principal entrance, which had almost the breadth of a church-door, was in the angle between the two front gables, and was covered by an open porch, with benches beneath its shelter. Under this arched doorway, scraping their feet on the unworn threshold, now trod the clergymen, the elders, the magistrates, the deacons, and whatever of aristocracy there was in town or county. Thither, too, thronged the plebeian classes as freely as their betters, and in larger number. Just within the entrance, however, stood two serving-men, pointing some of the guests to the neighborhood of the kitchen, and ushering others into the statelier rooms,—hospitable alike to all, but still with a scrutinizing regard to the high or low degree of each. Velvet garments, sombre but rich, stiffly plaited ruffs and bands, embroidered gloves, venerable beards, the mien and countenance of authority, made it easy to distinguish the gentleman of worship, at that period, from the tradesman, with his plodding air, or the laborer, in his leathern jerkin, stealing awe-stricken into the house which he had perhaps helped to build.

One inauspicious circumstance there was, which awakened a hardly concealed displeasure in the breasts of a few of the more punctilious visitors. The founder of this stately mansion—a gentleman noted for the square and ponderous courtesy of his demeanor—ought surely to have stood in his own hall, and to have offered the first welcome to so many eminent personages as here presented themselves in honor of his solemn festival. He was as yet invisible; the most favored of the guests had not beheld him. This sluggishness on Colonel Pyncheon's part became still more unaccountable, when the second dignitary of the province made his appearance, and found no more ceremonious a reception. The lieutenant-governor, although his visit was one of the anticipated glories of the day, had alighted from his horse, and assisted his lady from her side-saddle, and crossed the Colonel's threshold, without other greeting than that of the principal domestic.

This person—a gray-headed man, of quiet and most respectful deportment—found it necessary to explain that his master still remained in his study, or private apartment; on entering which, an hour before, he had expressed a wish on no account to be disturbed.

"Do not you see, fellow," said the high-sheriff of the county, taking the servant aside, "that this is no less a man than the lieutenant-governor? Summon Colonel Pyncheon at once! I know that he received letters from England this morning; and, in the perusal and consideration of them, an hour may have passed away without his noticing it. But he will be ill-pleased, I judge, if you suffer him to neglect the courtesy due to one of our chief rulers, and who may be said to represent King William, in the absence of the governor himself. Call your master instantly!"

"Nay, please your worship," answered the man, in much perplexity, but with a backwardness that strikingly indicated the hard and severe character of Colonel Pyncheon's domestic rule; "my master's orders were exceeding strict; and, as your worship knows, he permits of no discretion in the obedience of those who owe him service. Let who list open yonder door; I dare not, though the governor's own voice should bid me do it!"

"Pooh, pooh, master high-sheriff!" cried the lieutenant-governor, who had overheard the foregoing discussion, and felt himself high enough in station to play a little with his dignity. "I will take the matter into my own hands. It is time that the good Colonel came forth to greet his friends; else we shall be apt to suspect that he has taken a sip too much of his Canary wine, in his extreme deliberation which cask it were best to broach in honor of the day! But since he is so much behindhand, I will give him a remembrancer myself!"

Accordingly, with such a tramp of his ponderous riding-boots as might of itself have been audible in the remotest of the seven gables, he advanced to the door, which the servant pointed out, and made its new panels reëcho with a loud, free knock. Then, looking round, with a smile, to the spectators, he awaited a response. As none came, however, he knocked again, but with the same unsatisfactory result as at first. And now, being a trifle choleric in his temperament, the lieutenant-governor uplifted the heavy hilt of his sword, wherewith he so beat and banged upon the door, that, as some of the by-standers whispered, the racket might have disturbed the dead. Be that as it might, it seemed to produce no awakening effect on Colonel Pyncheon. When the sound subsided, the silence through the house was deep, dreary, and oppressive, notwithstanding that the tongues of many of the guests had already been loosened by a surreptitious cup or two of wine or spirits.

"Strange, forsooth!—very strange!" cried the lieutenant-governor, whose smile was changed to a frown. "But seeing that our host sets us the good example of forgetting ceremony, I shall likewise throw it aside, and make free to intrude on his privacy!"

He tried the door, which yielded to his hand, and was flung wide open by a sudden gust of wind that passed, as with a loud sigh, from the outermost portal through all the passages and apartments of the new house. It rustled the silken garments of the ladies, and waved the long curls of the gentlemen's wigs, and shook the window-hangings and the curtains of the bedchambers; causing everywhere a singular stir, which yet was more like a hush. A shadow of awe and half-fearful anticipation—nobody knew wherefore, nor of what—had all at once fallen over the company.

They thronged, however, to the now open door, pressing the lieutenant-governor, in the eagerness of their curiosity, into the room in advance of them. At the first glimpse they beheld nothing extraordinary: a handsomely furnished room, of moderate size, somewhat darkened by curtains; books arranged on shelves; a large map on the wall, and likewise a portrait of Colonel Pyncheon, beneath which sat the original Colonel himself, in an oaken elbow-chair, with a pen in his hand. Letters, parchments, and blank sheets of paper were on the table before him. He appeared to gaze at the curious crowd, in front of which stood the lieutenant-governor; and there was a frown on his dark and massive countenance, as if sternly resentful of the boldness that had impelled them into his private retirement.

A little boy—the Colonel's grandchild, and the only human being that ever dared to be familiar with him—now made his way among the guests, and ran towards the seated figure; then pausing half-way, he began to shriek with terror. The company, tremulous as the leaves of a tree, when all are shaking together, drew nearer, and perceived that there was an unnatural distortion in the fixedness of Colonel Pyncheon's stare; that there was blood on his ruff, and that his hoary beard was saturated with it. It was too late to give assistance. The iron-hearted Puritan, the relentless persecutor, the grasping and strong-willed man, was dead! Dead, in his new house! There is a tradition, only worth alluding to as lending a tinge of superstitious awe to a scene perhaps gloomy enough without it, that a voice spoke loudly among the guests, the tones of which were like those of old Matthew Maule, the executed wizard,—"God hath given him blood to drink!"

Thus early had that one guest,—the only guest who is certain, at one time or another, to find his way into every human dwelling,—thus early had Death stepped across the threshold of the House of the Seven Gables!

Colonel Pyncheon's sudden and mysterious end made a vast deal of noise in its day. There were many rumors, some of which have vaguely drifted down to the present time, how that appearances indicated violence; that there were the marks of fingers on his throat, and the print of a bloody hand on his plaited ruff; and that his peaked beard was dishevelled, as if it had been fiercely clutched and pulled. It was averred, likewise, that the lattice window, near the Colonel's chair, was open; and that, only a few minutes before the fatal occurrence, the figure of a man had been seen clambering over the garden-fence, in the rear of the house. But it were folly to lay any stress on stories of this kind, which are sure to spring up around such an event as that now related, and which, as in the present case, sometimes prolong themselves for ages afterwards, like the toadstools that indicate where the fallen and buried trunk of a tree has long since mouldered into the earth. For our own part, we allow them just as little credence as to that other fable of the skeleton hand which the lieutenant-governor was said to have seen at the Colonel's throat, but which vanished away, as he advanced farther into the room. Certain it is, however, that there was a great consultation and dispute of doctors over the dead body. One—John Swinnerton by name—who appears to have been a man of eminence, upheld it, if we have rightly understood his terms of art, to be a case of apoplexy. His professional brethren, each for himself, adopted various hypotheses, more or less plausible, but all dressed out in a perplexing mystery of phrase, which, if it do not show a bewilderment of mind in these erudite physicians, certainly causes it in the unlearned peruser of their opinions. The coroner's jury sat upon the corpse, and, like sensible men, returned an unassailable verdict of "Sudden Death!"

It is indeed difficult to imagine that there could have been a serious suspicion of murder, or the slightest grounds for implicating any particular individual as the perpetrator. The rank, wealth, and eminent character of the deceased must have insured the strictest scrutiny into every ambiguous circumstance. As none such is on record, it is safe to assume that none existed. Tradition,—which sometimes brings down truth that history has let slip, but is oftener the wild babble of the time, such as was formerly spoken at the fireside and now congeals in newspapers,—tradition is responsible for all contrary averments. In Colonel Pyncheon's funeral sermon, which was printed, and is still extant, the Rev. Mr. Higginson enumerates, among the many felicities of his distinguished parishioner's earthly career, the happy seasonableness of his death. His duties all performed,—the highest prosperity attained,—his race and future generations fixed on a stable basis, and with a stately roof to shelter them, for centuries to come,—what other upward step remained for this good man to take, save the final step from earth to the golden gate of heaven! The pious clergyman surely would not have uttered words like these had he in the least suspected that the Colonel had been thrust into the other world with the clutch of violence upon his throat.

The family of Colonel Pyncheon, at the epoch of his death, seemed destined to as fortunate a permanence as can anywise consist with the inherent instability of human affairs. It might fairly be anticipated that the progress of time would rather increase and ripen their prosperity, than wear away and destroy it. For, not only had his son and heir come into immediate enjoyment of a rich estate, but there was a claim through an Indian deed, confirmed by a subsequent grant of the General Court, to a vast and as yet unexplored and unmeasured tract of Eastern lands. These possessions—for as such they might almost certainly be reckoned—comprised the greater part of what is now known as Waldo County, in the State of Maine, and were more extensive than many a dukedom, or even a reigning prince's territory, on European soil. When the pathless forest that still covered this wild principality should give place—as it inevitably must, though perhaps not till ages hence—to the golden fertility of human culture, it would be the source of incalculable wealth to the Pyncheon blood. Had the Colonel survived only a few weeks longer, it is probable that his great political influence, and powerful connections at home and abroad, would have consummated all that was necessary to render the claim available. But, in spite of good Mr. Higginson's congratulatory eloquence, this appeared to be the one thing which Colonel Pyncheon, provident and sagacious as he was, had allowed to go to at loose ends. So far as the prospective territory was concerned, he unquestionably died too soon. His son lacked not merely the father's eminent position, but the talent and force of character to achieve it: he could, therefore, effect nothing by dint of political interest; and the bare justice or legality of the claim was not so apparent, after the Colonel's decease, as it had been pronounced in his lifetime. Some connecting link had slipped out of the evidence, and could not anywhere be found.

Efforts, it is true, were made by the Pyncheons, not only then, but at various periods for nearly a hundred years afterwards, to obtain what they stubbornly persisted in deeming their right. But, in course of time, the territory was partly re-granted to more favored individuals, and partly cleared and occupied by actual settlers. These last, if they ever heard of the Pyncheon title, would have laughed at the idea of any man's asserting a right—on the strength of mouldy parchments, signed with the faded autographs of governors and legislators long dead and forgotten—to the lands which they or their fathers had wrested from the wild hand of nature by their own sturdy toil. This impalpable claim, therefore, resulted in nothing more solid than to cherish, from generation to generation, an absurd delusion of family importance, which all along characterized the Pyncheons. It caused the poorest member of the race to feel as if he inherited a kind of nobility, and might yet come into the possession of princely wealth to support it. In the better specimens of the breed, this peculiarity threw an ideal grace over the hard material of human life, without stealing away any truly valuable quality. In the baser sort, its effect was to increase the liability to sluggishness and dependence, and induce the victim of a shadowy hope to remit all self-effort, while awaiting the realization of his dreams. Years and years after their claim had passed out of the public memory, the Pyncheons were accustomed to consult the Colonel's ancient map, which had been projected while Waldo County was still an unbroken wilderness. Where the old land-surveyor had put down woods, lakes, and rivers, they marked out the cleared spaces, and dotted the villages and towns, and calculated the progressively increasing value of the territory, as if there were yet a prospect of its ultimately forming a princedom for themselves.

In almost every generation, nevertheless, there happened to be some one descendant of the family gifted with a portion of the hard, keen sense, and practical energy, that had so remarkably distinguished the original founder. His character, indeed, might be traced all the way down, as distinctly as if the Colonel himself, a little diluted, had been gifted with a sort of intermittent immortality on earth. At two or three epochs, when the fortunes of the family were low, this representative of hereditary qualities had made his appearance, and caused the traditionary gossips of the town to whisper among themselves, "Here is the old Pyncheon come again! Now the Seven Gables will be new-shingled!" From father to son, they clung to the ancestral house with singular tenacity of home attachment. For various reasons, however, and from impressions often too vaguely founded to be put on paper, the writer cherishes the belief that many, if not most, of the successive proprietors of this estate were troubled with doubts as to their moral right to hold it. Of their legal tenure there could be no question; but old Matthew Maule, it is to be feared, trode downward from his own age to a far later one, planting a heavy footstep, all the way, on the conscience of a Pyncheon. If so, we are left to dispose of the awful query, whether each inheritor of the property—conscious of wrong, and failing to rectify it—did not commit anew the great guilt of his ancestor, and incur all its original responsibilities. And supposing such to be the case, would it not be a far truer mode of expression to say of the Pyncheon family, that they inherited a great misfortune, than the reverse?

We have already hinted that it is not our purpose to trace down the history of the Pyncheon family, in its unbroken connection with the House of the Seven Gables; nor to show, as in a magic picture, how the rustiness and infirmity of age gathered over the venerable house itself. As regards its interior life, a large, dim looking-glass used to hang in one of the rooms, and was fabled to contain within its depths all the shapes that had ever been reflected there,—the old Colonel himself, and his many descendants, some in the garb of antique babyhood, and others in the bloom of feminine beauty or manly prime, or saddened with the wrinkles of frosty age. Had we the secret of that mirror, we would gladly sit down before it, and transfer its revelations to our page. But there was a story, for which it is difficult to conceive any foundation, that the posterity of Matthew Maule had some connection with the mystery of the looking-glass, and that, by what appears to have been a sort of mesmeric process, they could make its inner region all alive with the departed Pyncheons; not as they had shown themselves to the world nor in their better and happier hours, but as doing over again some deed of sin, or in the crisis of life's bitterest sorrow. The popular imagination, indeed, long kept itself busy with the affair of the old Puritan Pyncheon and the wizard Maule; the curse, which the latter flung from his scaffold, was remembered, with the very important addition, that it had become a part of the Pyncheon inheritance. If one of the family did but gurgle in his throat, a bystander would be likely enough to whisper, between jest and earnest, "He has Maule's blood to drink!" The sudden death of a Pyncheon, about a hundred years ago, with circumstances very similar to what have been related of the Colonel's exit, was held as giving additional probability to the received opinion on this topic. It was considered, moreover, an ugly and ominous circumstance, that Colonel Pyncheon's picture—in obedience, it was said, to a provision of his will—remained affixed to the wall of the room in which he died. Those stern, immitigable features seemed to symbolize an evil influence, and so darkly to mingle the shadow of their presence with the sunshine of the passing hour, that no good thoughts or purposes could ever spring up and blossom there. To the thoughtful mind there will be no tinge of superstition in what we figuratively express, by affirming that the ghost of a dead progenitor—perhaps as a portion of his own punishment —is often doomed to become the Evil Genius of his family.

The Pyncheons, in brief, lived along, for the better part of two centuries, with perhaps less of outward vicissitude than has attended most other New England families during the same period of time. Possessing very distinctive traits of their own, they nevertheless took the general characteristics of the little community in which they dwelt; a town noted for its frugal, discreet, well-ordered, and home-loving inhabitants, as well as for the somewhat confined scope of its sympathies; but in which, be it said, there are odder individuals and, now and then, stranger occurrences, than one meets with almost anywhere else. During the Revolution, the Pyncheon of that epoch, adopting the royal side, became a refugee; but repented, and made his reappearance, just at the point of time to preserve the House of the Seven Gables from confiscation. For the last seventy years the most noted event in the Pyncheon annals had been likewise the heaviest calamity that ever befell the race; no less than the violent death—for so it was adjudged—of one member of the family by the criminal act of another. Certain circumstances attending this fatal occurrence had brought the deed irresistibly home to a nephew of the deceased Pyncheon. The young man was tried and convicted of the crime; but either the cirumstantial nature of the evidence, and possibly some lurking doubt in the breast of the executive, or, lastly,—an argument of greater weight in a republic than it could have been under a monarchy,—the high respectability and political influence of the criminal's connections, had availed to mitigate his doom from death to perpetual imprisonment. This sad affair had chanced about thirty years before the action of our story commences. Latterly, there were rumors (which few believed, and only one or two felt greatly interested in) that this long-buried man was likely, for some reason or other, to be summoned forth from his living tomb.

It is essential to say a few words respecting the victim of this now almost forgotten murder. He was an old bachelor, and possessed of great wealth, in addition to the house and real estate which constituted what remained of the ancient Pyncheon property. Being of an eccentric and melancholy turn of mind, and greatly given to rummaging old records and hearkening to old traditions, he had brought himself, it is averred, to the conclusion that Matthew Maule, the wizard, had been foully wronged out of his homestead, if not out of his life. Such being the case, and he, the old bachelor, in possession of the ill-gotten spoil,—with the black stain of blood sunken deep into it, and still to be scented by conscientious nostrils,—the question occurred, whether it were not imperative upon him, even at this late hour, to make restitution to Maule's posterity. To a man living so much in the past, and so little in the present, as the secluded and antiquarian old bachelor, a century and a half seemed not so vast a period as to obviate the propriety of substituting right for wrong. It was the belief of those who knew him best, that he would positively have taken the very singular step of giving up the House of the Seven Gables to the representative of Matthew Maule, but for the unspeakable tumult which a suspicion of the old gentleman's project awakened among his Pyncheon relatives. Their exertions had the effect of suspending his purpose; but it was feared that he would perform, after death, by the operation of his last will, what he had so hardly been prevented from doing in his proper lifetime. But there is no one thing which men so rarely do, whatever the provocation or inducement, as to bequeath patrimonial property away from their own blood. They may love other individuals far better than their relatives,—they may even cherish dislike, or positive hatred, to the latter; but yet, in view of death, the strong prejudice of propinquity revives, and impels the testator to send down his estate in the line marked out by custom so immemorial that it looks like nature. In all the Pyncheons, this feeling had the energy of disease. It was too powerful for the conscientious scruples of the old bachelor; at whose death, accordingly, the mansion-house, together with most of his other riches passed into the possession of his next legal representative.

This was a nephew, the cousin of the miserable young man who had been convicted of the uncle's murder. The new heir, up to the period of his accession, was reckoned rather a dissipated youth, but had at once reformed, and made himself an exceedingly respectable member of society. In fact, he showed more of the Pyncheon quality, and had won higher eminence in the world than any of his race since the time of the original Puritan. Applying himself in earlier manhood to the study of the law, and having a natural tendency towards office, he had attained, many years ago, to a judicial situation in some inferior court, which gave him for life the very desirable and imposing title of judge. Later, he had engaged in politics, and served a part of two terms in Congress, besides making a considerable figure in both branches of the State legislature. Judge Pyncheon was unquestionably an honor to his race. He had built himself a country-seat within a few miles of his native town, and there spent such portions of his time as could be spared from public service in the display of every grace and virtue—as a newspaper phrased it, on the eve of an election—befitting the Christian, the good citizen, the horticulturist, and the gentleman.

There were few of the Pyncheons left to sun themselves in the glow of the Judge's prosperity. In respect to natural increase, the breed had not thriven; it appeared rather to be dying out. The only members of the family known to be extant were, first, the Judge himself, and a single surviving son, who was now travelling in Europe; next, the thirty years' prisoner, already alluded to, and a sister of the latter, who occupied, in an extremely retired manner, the House of the Seven Gables, in which she had a life-estate by the will of the old bachelor. She was understood to be wretchedly poor, and seemed to make it her choice to remain so; inasmuch as her affluent cousin, the Judge, had repeatedly offered her all the comforts of life, either in the old mansion or his own modern residence. The last and youngest Pyncheon was a little country-girl of seventeen, the daughter of another of the Judge's cousins, who had married a young woman of no family or property, and died early and in poor circumstances. His widow had recently taken another husband.

As for Matthew Maule's posterity, it was supposed now to be extinct. For a very long period after the witchcraft delusion, however, the Maules had continued to inhabit the town where their progenitor had suffered so unjust a death. To all appearance, they were a quiet, honest, well-meaning race of people, cherishing no malice against individuals or the public for the wrong which had been done them; or if, at their own fireside, they transmitted, from father to child, any hostile recollection of the wizard's fate and their lost patrimony, it was never acted upon, nor openly expressed. Nor would it have been singular had they ceased to remember that the House of the Seven Gables was resting its heavy framework on a foundation that was rightfully their own. There is something so massive, stable, and almost irresistibly imposing in the exterior presentment of established rank and great possessions, that their very existence seems to give them a right to exist; at least, so excellent a counterfeit of right, that few poor and humble men have moral force enough to question it, even in their secret minds. Such is the case now, after so many ancient prejudices have been overthrown; and it was far more so in ante-Revolutionary days, when the aristocracy could venture to be proud, and the low were content to be abased. Thus the Maules, at all events, kept their resentments within their own breasts. They were generally poverty-stricken; always plebeian and obscure; working with unsuccessful diligence at handicrafts; laboring on the wharves, or following the sea, as sailors before the mast; living here and there about the town, in hired tenements, and coming finally to the almshouse as the natural home of their old age. At last, after creeping as it were, for such a length of time, along the utmost verge of the opaque puddle of obscurity, they had taken that downright plunge, which, sooner or later, is the destiny of all families, whether princely or plebeian. For thirty years past, neither town-record, nor gravestone, nor the directory, nor the knowledge or memory of man, bore any trace of Matthew Maule's descendants. His blood might possibly exist elsewhere; here, where its lowly current could be traced so far back, it had ceased to keep an onward course.

So long as any of the race were to be found, they had been marked out from other men—not strikingly, nor as with a sharp line, but with an effect that was felt rather than spoken of—by an hereditary character of reserve. Their companions, or those who endeavored to become such, grew conscious of a circle round about the Maules, within the sanctity or the spell of which, in spite of an exterior of sufficient frankness and good-fellowship, it was impossible for any man to step. It was this indefinable peculiarity, perhaps, that, by insulating them from human aid, kept them always so unfortunate in life. It certainly operated to prolong in their case, and to confirm to them as their only inheritance, those feelings of repugnance and superstitious terror with which the people of the town, even after awakening from their frenzy, continued to regard the memory of the reputed witches. The mantle, or rather the ragged cloak, of old Matthew Maule, had fallen upon his children. They were half believed to inherit mysterious attributes; the family eye was said to possess strange power. Among other good-for-nothing properties and privileges, one was especially assigned them,—that of exercising an influence over people's dreams. The Pyncheons, if all stories were true, haughtily as they bore themselves in the noonday streets of their native town, were no better than bond-servants to these plebeian Maules, on entering the topsy-turvy commonwealth of sleep. Modern psychology, it may be, will endeavor to reduce these alleged necromancies within a system, instead of rejecting them as altogether fabulous.

A descriptive paragraph or two, treating of the seven-gabled mansion in its more recent aspect, will bring this preliminary chapter to a close. The street in which it upreared its venerable peaks has long ceased to be a fashionable quarter of the town; so that, though the old edifice was sur-rounded by habitations of modern date, they were mostly small, built entirely of wood, and typical of the most plodding uniformity of common life. Doubtless, however, the whole story of human existence may be lat-ent in each of them, but with no picturesqueness, externally, that can attract the imagination or sympathy to seek it there. But as for the old structure of our story, its white-oak frame, and its boards, shingles, and crumbling plaster, and even the huge, clustered chimney in the midst, seemed to constitute only the least and meanest part of its reality. So much of mankind's varied experience had passed there,—so much had been suffered, and something, too, enjoyed,—that the very timbers were oozy, as with the moisture of a heart. It was itself like a great human heart, with a life of its own, and full of rich and sombre reminiscences.

The deep projection of the second story gave the house such a medita-tive look, that you could not pass it without the idea that it had secrets to keep, and an eventful history to moralize upon. In front, just on the edge of the unpaved sidewalk, grew the Pyncheon Elm, which, in reference to such trees as one usually meets with, might well be termed gigantic. It had been planted by a great-grandson of the first Pyncheon, and, though now fourscore years of age, or perhaps nearer a hundred, was still in its strong and broad maturity, throwing its shadow from side to side of the street, overtopping the seven gables, and sweeping the whole black roof with its pendent foliage. It gave beauty to the old edifice, and seemed to make it a part of nature. The street having been widened about forty years ago, the front gable was now precisely on a line with it. On either side extended a ruinous wooden fence of open lattice-work, through which could be seen a grassy yard, and, especially in the angles of the building, an enormous fertility of burdocks, with leaves, it is hardly an exaggeration to say, two or three feet long. Behind the house there appeared to be a garden, which undoubtedly had once been extensive, but was now infringed upon by other enclosures, or shut in by habitations and outbuildings that stood on another street. It would be an omission, trifling, indeed, but unpardonable, were we to forget the green moss that had long since gathered over the projections of the windows, and on the slopes of the roof; nor must we fail to direct the reader's eye to a crop, not of weeds, but flower-shrubs, which were growing aloft in the air, not a great way from the chimney, in the nook between two of the gables. They were called Alice's Posies. The tradition was, that a certain Alice Pyncheon had flung up the seeds, in sport, and that the dust of the street and the decay of the roof gradually formed a kind of soil for them, out of which they grew, when Alice had long been in her grave. However the flowers might have come there, it was both sad and sweet to observe how Nature adopted to herself this desolate, decaying, gusty, rusty old house of the Pyncheon family; and how the ever-returning summer did her best to gladden it with tender beauty, and grew melancholy in the effort.

There is one other feature, very essential to be noticed, but which, we greatly fear, may damage any picturesque and romantic impression which we have been willing to throw over our sketch of this respectable edifice. In the front gable, under the impending brow of the second story, and contiguous to the street, was a shop-door, divided horizontally in the midst, and with a window for its upper segment, such as is often seen in dwellings of a somewhat ancient date. This same shop-door had been a subject of no slight mortification to the present occupant of the august Pyncheon House, as well as to some of her predecessors. The matter is disagreeably delicate to handle; but, since the reader must needs be let into the secret, he will please to understand, that, about a century ago, the head of the Pyncheons found himself involved in serious financial difficulties. The fellow (gentleman, as he styled himself) can hardly have been other than a spurious interloper; for, instead of seeking office from the king or the royal governor, or urging his hereditary claim to Eastern lands, he bethought himself of no better avenue to wealth than by cutting a shop-door through the side of his ancestral residence. It was the custom of the time, indeed, for merchants to store their goods and transact business in their own dwellings. But there was something pitifully small in this old Pyncheon's mode of setting about his commercial operations; it was whispered, that, with his own hands, all beruffled as they were, he used to give change for a shilling, and would turn a half-penny twice over, to make sure that it was a good one. Beyond all question, he had the blood of a petty huckster in his veins, through whatever channel it may have found its way there.

Immediately on his death, the shop-door had been locked, bolted, and barred, and, down to the period of our story, had probably never once been opened. The old counter, shelves, and other fixtures of the little shop remained just as he had left them. It used to be affirmed, that the dead shop-keeper, in a white wig, a faded velvet coat, an apron at his waist, and his ruffles carefully turned back from his wrists, might be seen through the chinks of the shutters, any night of the year, ransacking his till, or poring over the dingy pages of his day-book. From the look of un- utterable woe upon his face, it appeared to be his doom to spend eternity in a vain effort to make his accounts balance.

And now—in a very humble way, as will be seen—we proceed to open our narrative.

## II

### THE LITTLE SHOP-WINDOW

It still lacked half an hour of sunrise, when Miss Hepzibah Pyncheon— we will not say awoke, it being doubtful whether the poor lady had so much as closed her eyes during the brief night of midsummer—but, at all events, arose from her solitary pillow, and began what it would be mock- ery to term the adornment of her person. Far from us be the indecorum of assisting, even in imagination, at a maiden lady's toilet! Our story must therefore await Miss Hepzibah at the threshold of her chamber; only presuming, meanwhile, to note some of the heavy sighs that labored from her bosom, with little restraint as to their lugubrious depth and volume of sound, inasmuch as they could be audible to nobody save a dis- embodied listener like ourself. The Old Maid was alone in the old house. Alone, except for a certain respectable and orderly young man, an artist in the daguerreotype line, who, for about three months back, had been a lodger in a remote gable,—quite a house by itself, indeed,—with locks, bolts, and oaken bars on all the intervening doors. Inaudible, conse- quently, were poor Miss Hepzibah's gusty sighs. Inaudible the creaking joints of her stiffened knees, as she knelt down by the bedside. And in- audible, too, by mortal ear, but heard with all-comprehending love and pity in the farthest heaven, that almost agony of prayer—now whispered, now a groan, now a struggling silence—wherewith she besought the Di- vine assistance through the day! Evidently, this is to be a day of more than ordinary trial to Miss Hepzibah, who, for above a quarter of a century gone by, has dwelt in strict seclusion, taking no part in the business of life, and just as little in its intercourse and pleasures. Not with such fervor prays the torpid recluse, looking forward to the cold, sunless, stagnant calm of a day that is to be like innumerable yesterdays!

The maiden lady's devotions are concluded. Will she now issue forth over the threshold of our story? Not yet, by many moments. First, every drawer in the tall, old-fashioned bureau is to be opened, with difficulty, and with a succession of spasmodic jerks; then, all must close again, with the same fidgety reluctance. There is a rustling of stiff silks; a tread of backward and forward footsteps to and fro across the chamber. We suspect Miss Hepzibah, moreover, of taking a step upward into a chair, in order to give heedful regard to her appearance on all sides, and at full length, in the oval, dingy-framed toilet-glass, that hangs above her table. Truly! well, indeed! who would have thought it! Is all this precious time to be lavished on the matutinal repair and beautifying of an elderly person, who never goes abroad, whom nobody ever visits, and from whom, when she shall have done her utmost, it were the best charity to turn one's eyes another way?

Now she is almost ready. Let us pardon her one other pause; for it is given to the sole sentiment, or, we might better say,—heightened and rendered intense, as it has been, by sorrow and seclusion,—to the strong passion of her life. We heard the turning of a key in a small lock; she has opened a secret drawer of an escritoire, and is probably looking at a certain miniature, done in Malbone's most perfect style, and representing a face worthy of no less delicate a pencil. It was once our good fortune to see this picture. It is a likeness of a young man, in a silken dressing-gown of an old fashion, the soft richness of which is well adapted to the countenance of reverie, with its full, tender lips, and beautiful eyes, that seem to indicate not so much capacity of thought, as gentle and voluptuous emotion. Of the possessor of such features we shall have a right to ask nothing, except that he would take the rude world easily, and make himself happy in it. Can it have been an early lover of Miss Hepzibah? No; she never had a lover—poor thing, how could she?—nor ever knew, by her own experience, what love technically means. And yet, her undying faith and trust, her fresh remembrance, and continual devotedness towards the original of that miniature, have been the only substance for her heart to feed upon.

She seems to have put aside the miniature, and is standing again before the toilet-glass. There are tears to be wiped off. A few more footsteps to and fro; and here, at last,—with another pitiful sigh, like a gust of chill, damp wind out of a long-closed vault, the door of which has accidentally been set ajar,—here comes Miss Hepzibah Pyncheon! Forth she steps into the dusky, time-darkened passage; a tall figure, clad in black silk, with a long and shrunken waist, feeling her way towards the stairs like a near-sighted person, as in truth she is.

The sun, meanwhile, if not already above the horizon, was ascending nearer and nearer to its verge. A few clouds, floating high upward, caught some of the earliest light, and threw down its golden gleam on the windows of all the houses in the street, not forgetting the House of the Seven Gables, which—many such sunrises as it had witnessed—looked cheerfully at the present one. The reflected radiance served to show, pretty distinctly, the aspect and arrangement of the room which Hepzibah entered, after descending the stairs. It was a low-studded room, with a beam across the ceiling, panelled with dark wood, and having a large chimney-piece, set round with pictured tiles, but now closed by an iron fire-board, through which ran the funnel of a modern stove. There was a carpet on the floor, originally of rich texture, but so worn and faded in these latter years that its once brilliant figure had quite vanished into one indistinguishable hue. In the way of furniture, there were two tables: one, constructed with perplexing intricacy and exhibiting as many feet as a centipede; the other, most delicately wrought, with four long and slender legs, so apparently frail that it was almost incredible what a length of time the ancient tea-table had stood upon them. Half a dozen chairs stood about the room, straight and stiff, and so ingeniously contrived for the discomfort of the human person that they were irksome even to sight, and conveyed the ugliest possible idea of the state of society to which they could have been adapted. One exception there was, however, in a very antique elbow-chair, with a high back, carved elaborately in oak, and a roomy depth within its arms, that made up, by its spacious comprehensiveness, for the lack of any of those artistic curves which abound in a modern chair.

As for ornamental articles of furniture, we recollect but two, if such they may be called. One was a map of the Pyncheon territory at the eastward, not engraved, but the handiwork of some skilful old draughtsman, and grotesquely illuminated with pictures of Indians and wild beasts, among which was seen a lion; the natural history of the region being as little known as its geography, which was put down most fantastically awry. The other adornment was the portrait of old Colonel Pyncheon, at two thirds length, representing the stern features of a Puritanic-looking personage, in a skull-cap, with a laced band and a grizzly beard; holding a Bible with one hand, and in the other uplifting an iron sword-hilt. The latter object, being more successfully depicted by the artist, stood out in far greater prominence than the sacred volume. Face to face with this picture, on entering the apartment, Miss Hepzibah Pyncheon came to a pause; regarding it with a singular scowl, a strange contortion of the brow, which, by people who did not know her, would probably have been interpreted as an expression of bitter anger and ill-will. But it was no such thing. She, in fact, felt a reverence for the pictured visage, of which only a far-descended and time-stricken virgin could be susceptible; and this forbidding scowl was the innocent result of her near-sightedness, and an effort so to concentrate her powers of vision as to substitute a firm outline of the object instead of a vague one.

We must linger a moment on this unfortunate expression of poor Hepzibah's brow. Her scowl,—as the world, or such part of it as sometimes caught a transitory glimpse of her at the window, wickedly persisted in calling it,—her scowl had done Miss Hepzibah a very ill office, in establishing her character as an ill-tempered old maid; nor does it appear improbable that, by often gazing at herself in a dim looking-glass, and perpetually encountering her own frown within its ghostly sphere, she had been led to interpret the expression almost as unjustly as the world did. "How miserably cross I look!" she must often have whispered to herself; and ultimately have fancied herself so, by a sense of inevitable doom. But her heart never frowned. It was naturally tender, sensitive, and full of little tremors and palpitations; all of which weaknesses it retained, while her visage was growing so perversely stern, and even fierce. Nor had Hepzibah ever any hardihood, except what came from the very warmest nook in her affections.

All this time, however, we are loitering faint-heartedly on the threshold of our story. In very truth, we have an invincible reluctance to disclose what Miss Hepzibah Pyncheon was about to do.

It has already been observed, that, in the basement story of the gable fronting on the street, an unworthy ancestor, nearly a century ago, had fitted up a shop. Ever since the old gentleman retired from trade, and fell asleep under his coffin-lid, not only the shop-door, but the inner arrangements, had been suffered to remain unchanged; while the dust of ages gathered inch-deep over the shelves and counter, and partly filled an old pair of scales, as if it were of value enough to be weighed. It treasured itself up, too, in the half-open till, where there still lingered a base sixpence, worth neither more nor less than the hereditary pride which had been put to shame. Such had been the state and condition of the little shop in old Hepzibah's childhood, when she and her brother used to play at hide-and-seek in its forsaken precincts. So it had remained, until within a few days past.

But now, though the shop-window was still closely curtained from the public gaze, a remarkable change had taken place in its interior. The rich and heavy festoons of cobweb, which it had cost a long ancestral succession of spiders their life's labor to spin and weave, had been carefully brushed away from the ceiling. The counter, shelves, and floor had all been scoured, and the latter was overstrewn with fresh blue sand. The brown scales, too, had evidently undergone rigid discipline, in an unavailing effort to rub off the rust, which, alas! had eaten through and through their substance. Neither was the little old shop any longer empty of merchantable goods. A curious eye, privileged to take an account of stock, and investigate behind the counter, would have discovered a barrel,—yea, two or three barrels and half ditto,—one containing flour, another apples, and a third, perhaps, Indian meal. There was likewise a square box of pine-wood, full of soap in bars; also, another of the same size, in which were tallow-candles, ten to the pound. A small stock of brown sugar, some white beans and split peas, and a few other commodities of low price, and such as are constantly in demand, made up the bulkier portion of the merchandise. It might have been taken for a ghostly or phantasmagoric reflection of the old shop-keeper Pyncheon's shabbily provided shelves, save that some of the articles were of a description and outward form which could hardly have been known in his day. For instance, there was a glass pickle-jar, filled with fragments of Gibraltar rock; not, indeed, splinters of the veritable stone foundation of the famous fortress, but bits of delectable candy, neatly done up in white paper. Jim Crow, moreover, was seen executing his world-renowned dance, in gingerbread. A party of leaden dragoons were galloping along one of the shelves, in equipments and uniform of modern cut; and there were some sugar figures, with no strong resemblance to the humanity of any epoch, but less unsatisfactorily representing our own fashions than those of a hundred years ago. Another phenomenon, still more strikingly modern, was a package of lucifer matches, which, in old times, would have been thought actually to borrow their instantaneous flame from the nether fires of Tophet.

In short, to bring the matter at once to a point, it was incontrovertibly evident that somebody had taken the shop and fixtures of the long-retired and forgotten Mr. Pyncheon, and was about to renew the enterprise of that departed worthy, with a different set of customers. Who could this bold adventurer be? And, of all places in the world, why had he chosen the House of the Seven Gables as the scene of his commercial speculations?

We return to the elderly maiden. She at length withdrew her eyes from the dark countenance of the Colonel's portrait, heaved a sigh,—indeed, her breast was a very cave of Æolus that morning,—and stept across the room on tiptoe, as is the customary gait of elderly women. Passing through an intervening passage, she opened a door that communicated with the shop, just now so elaborately described. Owing to the projection of the upper story—and still more to the thick shadow of the Pyncheon Elm, which stood almost directly in front of the gable—the twilight, here, was still as much akin to night as morning. Another heavy sigh from Miss Hepzibah! After a moment's pause on the threshold, peering towards the window with her near-sighted scowl, as if frowning down some bitter enemy, she suddenly projected herself into the shop. The haste, and, as it were, the galvanic impulse of the movement, were really quite startling.

Nervously—in a sort of frenzy, we might almost say—she began to busy herself in arranging some children's playthings, and other little wares, on the shelves and at the shop-window. In the aspect of this dark-arrayed, pale-faced, lady-like old figure there was a deeply tragic character that contrasted irreconcilably with the ludicrous pettiness of her employment. It seemed a queer anomaly, that so gaunt and dismal a personage should take a toy in hand; a miracle, that the toy did not vanish in her grasp; a miserably absurd idea, that she should go on perplexing her stiff and sombre intellect with the question how to tempt little boys into her premises! Yet such is undoubtedly her object. Now she places a gingerbread elephant against the window, but with so tremulous a touch that it tumbles upon the floor, with the dismemberment of three legs and its trunk; it has ceased to be an elephant, and has become a few bits of musty gingerbread. There, again, she has upset a tumbler of marbles, all of which roll different ways, and each individual marble, devil-directed, into the most difficult obscurity that it can find. Heaven help our poor old Hepzibah, and forgive us for taking a ludicrous view of her position! As her rigid and rusty frame goes down upon its hands and knees, in quest of the absconding marbles, we positively feel so much the more inclined to shed tears of sympathy, from the very fact that we must needs turn aside and laugh at her. For here,—and if we fail to impress it suitably upon the reader, it is our own fault, not that of the theme,—here is one of the truest points of melancholy interest that occur in ordinary life. It was the final throe of what called itself old gentility. A lady—who had fed herself from childhood with the shadowy food of aristocratic reminiscences, and whose religion it was that a lady's hand soils itself irremediably by doing aught for bread—this born lady, after sixty years of narrowing means, is fain to step down from her pedestal of imaginary rank. Poverty, treading closely at her heels for a lifetime, has come up with her at last. She must earn her own food, or starve! And we have stolen upon Miss Hepzibah Pyncheon, too irreverently, at the instant of time when the patrician lady is to be transformed into the plebeian woman.

In this republican country, amid the fluctuating waves of our social life, somebody is always at the drowning-point. The tragedy is enacted with as continual a repetition as that of a popular drama on a holiday; and, nevertheless, is felt as deeply, perhaps, as when an hereditary noble sinks below his order. More deeply; since, with us, rank is the grosser substance of wealth and a splendid establishment, and has no spiritual existence after the death of these, but dies hopelessly along with them. And, therefore, since we have been unfortunate enough to introduce our heroine at so inauspicious a juncture, we would entreat for a mood of due solemnity in the spectators of her fate. Let us behold, in poor Hepzibah, the immemorial lady,—two hundred years old, on this side of the water, and thrice as many on the other,—with her antique portraits, pedigrees, coats of arms, records and traditions, and her claim, as joint heiress, to that princely territory at the eastward, no longer a wilderness, but a populous fertility,—born, too, in Pyncheon Street, under the Pyncheon Elm, and in the Pyncheon House, where she has spent all her days,—reduced now, in that very house, to be the hucksteress of a cent-shop.

This business of setting up a petty shop is almost the only resource of women, in circumstances at all similar to those of our unfortunate recluse. With her near-sightedness, and those tremulous fingers of hers, at once inflexible and delicate, she could not be a seamstress; although her sampler, of fifty years gone by, exhibited some of the most recondite specimens of ornamental needlework. A school for little children had been often in her thoughts; and, at one time, she had begun a review of her early studies in the New England Primer, with a view to prepare herself for the office of instructress. But the love of children had never been quickened in Hepzibah's heart, and was now torpid, if not extinct; she watched the little people of the neighborhood from her chamber-window, and doubted whether she could tolerate a more intimate acquaintance with them. Besides, in our day, the very A B C has become a science greatly too abstruse to be any longer taught by pointing a pin from letter to letter. A modern child could teach old Hepzibah more than old Hepzibah could teach the child. So—with many a cold, deep heart-quake at the idea of at last coming into sordid contact with the world, from which she had so long kept aloof, while every added day of seclusion had rolled another stone against the cavern-door of her hermitage—the poor thing bethought herself of the ancient shop-window, the rusty scales, and dusty till. She might have held back a little longer; but another circumstance, not yet hinted at, had somewhat hastened her decision. Her humble preparations, therefore, were duly made, and the enterprise was now to be commenced. Nor was she entitled to complain of any remarkable singularity in her fate; for, in the town of her nativity, we might point to several little shops of a similar description, some of them in houses as ancient as that of the Seven Gables; and one or two, it may be, where a decayed gentlewoman stands behind the counter, as grim an image of family pride as Miss Hepzibah Pyncheon herself.

It was overpoweringly ridiculous—we must honestly confess it—the deportment of the maiden lady while setting her shop in order for the public eye. She stole on tiptoe to the window, as cautiously as if she conceived some bloody-minded villain to be watching behind the elm-tree, with intent to take her life. Stretching out her long, lank arm, she put a paper of pearl buttons, a jew's-harp, or whatever the small article might be, in its destined place, and straightway vanished back into the dusk, as if the world need never hope for another glimpse of her. It might have been fancied, indeed, that she expected to minister to the wants of the community unseen, like a disembodied divinity or enchantress, holding forth her bargains to the reverential and awe-stricken purchaser in an invisible hand. But Hepzibah had no such flattering dream. She was well aware that she must ultimately come forward, and stand revealed in her proper individuality; but, like other sensitive persons, she could not bear to be observed in the gradual process, and chose rather to flash forth on the world's astonished gaze at once.

The inevitable moment was not much longer to be delayed. The sunshine might now be seen stealing down the front of the opposite house, from the windows of which came a reflected gleam, struggling through the boughs of the elm-tree, and enlightening the interior of the shop more distinctly than heretofore. The town appeared to be waking up. A baker's cart had already rattled through the street, chasing away the latest vestige of night's sanctity with the jingle-jangle of its dissonant bells. A milkman was distributing the contents of his cans from door to door; and the harsh peal of a fisherman's conch-shell was heard far off, around the corner. None of these tokens escaped Hepzibah's notice. The moment had arrived. To delay longer would be only to lengthen out her misery. Nothing remained, except to take down the bar from the shop-door, leav-

ing the entrance free—more than free—welcome, as if all were household
friends—to every passer-by, whose eyes might be attracted by the commodities at the window. This last act Hepzibah now performed, letting
the bar fall with what smote upon her excited nerves as a most astound-
ing clatter. Then—as if the only barrier betwixt herself and the world
had been thrown down, and a flood of evil consequences would come
tumbling through the gap—she fled into the inner parlor, threw herself
into the ancestral elbow-chair, and wept.

Our miserable old Hepzibah! It is a heavy annoyance to a writer, who
endeavors to represent nature, its various attitudes and circumstances, in
a reasonably correct outline and true coloring, that so much of the mean
and ludicrous should be hopelessly mixed up with the purest pathos which
life anywhere supplies to him. What tragic dignity, for example, can be
wrought into a scene like this! How can we elevate our history of retribution for the sin of long ago, when, as one of our most prominent figures,
we are compelled to introduce—not a young and lovely woman, nor even
the stately remains of beauty, storm-shattered by affliction—but a gaunt,
sallow, rusty-jointed maiden, in a long-waisted silk gown, and with the
strange horror of a turban on her head! Her visage is not even ugly. It is
redeemed from insignificance only by the contraction of her eyebrows
into a near-sighted scowl. And, finally, her great life-trial seems to be,
that, after sixty years of idleness, she finds it convenient to earn comfortable bread by setting up a shop in a small way. Nevertheless, if we
look through all the heroic fortunes of mankind, we shall find this same
entanglement of something mean and trivial with whatever is noblest in
joy or sorrow. Life is made up of marble and mud. And, without all the
deeper trust in a comprehensive sympathy above us, we might hence be
led to suspect the insult of a sneer, as well as an immitigable frown, on
the iron countenance of fate. What is called poetic insight is the gift of
discerning, in this sphere of strangely mingled elements, the beauty and
the majesty which are compelled to assume a garb so sordid.

### III

### THE FIRST CUSTOMER

MISS HEPZIBAH PYNCHEON sat in the oaken elbow-chair, with her hands
over her face, giving way to that heavy down-sinking of the heart which
most persons have experienced, when the image of hope itself seems ponderously moulded of lead, on the eve of an enterprise at once doubtful
and momentous. She was suddenly startled by the tinkling alarum—high,
sharp, and irregular—of a little bell. The maiden lady arose upon her

feet, as pale as a ghost at cock-crow; for she was an enslaved spirit, and this the talisman to which she owed obedience. This little bell,—to speak in plainer terms,—being fastened over the shop-door, was so contrived as to vibrate by means of a steel spring, and thus convey notice to the inner regions of the house when any customer should cross the threshold. Its ugly and spiteful little din (heard now for the first time, perhaps, since Hepzibah's periwigged predecessor had retired from trade) at once set every nerve of her body in responsive and tumultuous vibration. The crisis was upon her! Her first customer was at the door!

Without giving herself time for a second thought, she rushed into the shop, pale, wild, desperate in gesture and expression, scowling portentously, and looking far better qualified to do fierce battle with a housebreaker than to stand smiling behind the counter, bartering small wares for a copper recompense. Any ordinary customer, indeed, would have turned his back and fled. And yet there was nothing fierce in Hepzibah's poor old heart; nor had she, at the moment, a single bitter thought against the world at large, or one individual man or woman. She wished them all well, but wished, too, that she herself were done with them, and in her quiet grave.

The applicant, by this time, stood within the doorway. Coming freshly, as he did, out of the morning light, he appeared to have brought some of its cheery influences into the shop along with him. It was a slender young man, not more than one or two and twenty years old, with rather a grave and thoughtful expression for his years, but likewise a springy alacrity and vigor. These qualities were not only perceptible, physically, in his make and motions, but made themselves felt almost immediately in his character. A brown beard, not too silken in its texture, fringed his chin, but as yet without completely hiding it; he wore a short mustache, too, and his dark, high-featured countenance looked all the better for these natural ornaments. As for his dress, it was of the simplest kind; a summer sack of cheap and ordinary material, thin checkered pantaloons, and a straw hat, by no means of the finest braid. Oak Hall might have supplied his entire equipment. He was chiefly marked as a gentleman—if such, indeed, he made any claim to be—by the rather remarkable whiteness and nicety of his clean linen.

He met the scowl of old Hepzibah without apparent alarm, as having heretofore encountered it and found it harmless.

"So, my dear Miss Pyncheon," said the daguerreotypist,—for it was that sole other occupant of the seven-gabled mansion,—"I am glad to see that you have not shrunk from your good purpose. I merely look in to offer my best wishes, and to ask if I can assist you any further in your preparations."

People in difficulty and distress, or in any manner at odds with the world, can endure a vast amount of harsh treatment, and perhaps be only the stronger for it; whereas they give way at once before the simplest expression of what they perceive to be genuine sympathy. So it proved with poor Hepzibah; for, when she saw the young man's smile,—looking so much the brighter on a thoughtful face,—and heard his kindly tone, she broke first into a hysteric giggle and then began to sob.

"Ah, Mr. Holgrave," cried she, as soon as she could speak, "I never can go through with it! Never, never, never! I wish I were dead, and in the old family-tomb, with all my forefathers! With my father, and my mother, and my sister! Yes, and with my brother, who had far better find me there than here! The world is too chill and hard,—and I am too old, and too feeble, and too hopeless!"

"Oh, believe me, Miss Hepzibah," said the young man, quietly, "these feelings will not trouble you any longer, after you are once fairly in the midst of your enterprise. They are unavoidable at this moment, standing, as you do, on the outer verge of your long seclusion, and peopling the world with ugly shapes, which you will soon find to be as unreal as the giants and ogres of a child's story-book. I find nothing so singular in life, as that everything appears to lose its substance the instant one actually grapples with it. So it will be with what you think so terrible."

"But I am a woman!" said Hepzibah, piteously. "I was going to say, a lady,—but I consider that as past."

"Well; no matter if it be past!" answered the artist, a strange gleam of half-hidden sarcasm flashing through the kindliness of his manner. "Let it go! You are the better without it. I speak frankly, my dear Miss Pyncheon! for are we not friends? I look upon this as one of the fortunate days of your life. It ends an epoch and begins one. Hitherto, the lifeblood has been gradually chilling in your veins as you sat aloof, within your circle of gentility, while the rest of the world was fighting out its battle with one kind of necessity or another. Henceforth, you will at least have the sense of healthy and natural effort for a purpose, and of lending your strength—be it great or small—to the united struggle of mankind. This is success,—all the success that anybody meets with!"

"It is natural enough, Mr. Holgrave, that you should have ideas like these," rejoined Hepzibah, drawing up her gaunt figure, with slightly offended dignity. "You are a man, a young man, and brought up, I suppose, as almost everybody is nowadays, with a view to seeking your fortune. But I was born a lady, and have always lived one; no matter in what narrowness of means, always a lady!"

"But I was not born a gentleman; neither have I lived like one," said Holgrave, slightly smiling; "so, my dear madam, you will hardly expect me to sympathize with sensibilities of this kind; though, unless I deceive myself, I have some imperfect comprehension of them. These names of gentleman and lady had a meaning, in the past history of the world, and conferred privileges, desirable or otherwise, on those entitled to bear them. In the present—and still more in the future condition of society— they imply, not privilege, but restriction!"

"These are new notions," said the old gentlewoman, shaking her head. "I shall never understand them; neither do I wish it."

"We will cease to speak of them, then," replied the artist, with a friendlier smile than his last one, "and I will leave you to feel whether it is not better to be a true woman than a lady. Do you really think, Miss Hepzibah, that any lady of your family has ever done a more heroic thing, since this house was built, than you are performing in it to-day? Never; and if the Pyncheons had always acted so nobly, I doubt whether an old wizard Maule's anathema, of which you told me once, would have had much weight with Providence against them."

"Ah!—no, no!" said Hepzibah, not displeased at this allusion to the sombre dignity of an inherited curse. "If old Maule's ghost, or a descendant of his, could see me behind the counter to-day, he would call it the fulfilment of his worst wishes. But I thank you for your kindness, Mr. Holgrave, and will do my utmost to be a good shop-keeper."

"Pray do," said Holgrave, "and let me have the pleasure of being your first customer. I am about taking a walk to the sea-shore, before going to my rooms, where I misuse Heaven's blessed sunshine by tracing out human features through its agency. A few of those biscuits dipt in sea-water, will be just what I need for breakfast. What is the price of half a dozen?"

"Let me be a lady a moment longer," replied Hepzibah, with a manner of antique stateliness to which a melancholy smile lent a kind of grace. She put the biscuits into his hand, but rejected the compensation. "A Pyncheon must not, at all events under her forefathers' roof, receive money for a morsel of bread from her only friend!"

Holgrave took his departure, leaving her, for the moment, with spirits not quite so much depressed. Soon, however, they had subsided nearly to their former dead level. With a beating heart, she listened to the footsteps of early passengers, which now began to be frequent along the street. Once or twice they seemed to linger; these strangers, or neighbors, as the case might be, were looking at the display of toys and petty commodities in Hepzibah's shop-window. She was doubly tortured; in part, with a sense of overwhelming shame that strange and unloving eyes should have the privilege of gazing, and partly because the idea occurred to her, with ridiculous importunity, that the window was not arranged so skilfully, nor nearly to so much advantage, as it might have been. It seemed as if the whole fortune or failure of her shop might depend on the display of a different set of articles, or substituting a fairer apple for one which appeared to be specked. So she made the change, and straightway fancied that everything was spoiled by it; not recognizing that it was the nervousness of the juncture, and her own native squeamishness as an old maid, that wrought all the seeming mischief.

Anon, there was an encounter, just at the door-step, betwixt two laboring men, as their rough voices denoted them to be. After some slight talk about their own affairs, one of them chanced to notice the shop-window, and directed the other's attention to it.

"See here!" cried he; "what do you think of this? Trade seems to be looking up in Pyncheon Street!"

"Well, well, this is a sight, to be sure!" exclaimed the other. "In the old Pyncheon House, and underneath the Pyncheon Elm! Who would have thought it? Old Maid Pyncheon is setting up a cent-shop!"

"Will she make it go, think you, Dixey?" said his friend. "I don't call it a very good stand. There's another shop just round the corner."

"Make it go!" cried Dixey, with a most contemptuous expression, as if the very idea were impossible to be conceived. "Not a bit of it! Why, her face—I've seen it, for I dug her garden for her one year—her face is enough to frighten the Old Nick himself, if he had ever so great a mind to trade with her. People can't stand it, I tell you! She scowls dreadfully, reason or none, out of pure ugliness of temper!"

"Well, that's not so much matter," remarked the other man. "These sour-tempered folks are mostly handy at business, and know pretty well what they are about. But, as you say, I don't think she'll do much. This business of keeping cent-shops is overdone, like all other kinds of trade, handicraft, and bodily labor. I know it, to my cost! My wife kept a cent-shop three months, and lost five dollars on her outlay!"

"Poor business!" responded Dixey, in a tone as if he were shaking his head,—"poor business!"

For some reason or other, not very easy to analyze there had hardly been so bitter a pang in all her previous misery about the matter as what thrilled Hepzibah's heart, on overhearing the above conversation. The testimony in regard to her scowl was frightfully important; it seemed to hold up her image wholly relieved from the false light of her self-partialities, and so hideous that she dared not look at it. She was absurdly hurt, moreover, by the slight and idle effect that her setting up shop—an event of such breathless interest to herself—appeared to have upon the public, of which these two men were the nearest representatives. A glance; a passing word or two; a coarse laugh; and she was doubtless forgotten before they turned the corner! They cared nothing for her dignity, and just as little for her degradation. Then, also, the augury of ill-success, uttered from the sure wisdom of experience, fell upon her half-dead hope like a clod into a grave. The man's wife had already tried the same experiment, and failed! How could the born lady,—the recluse of half a lifetime, utterly unpractised in the world, at sixty years of age,—how could she ever dream of succeeding, when the hard, vulgar, keen, busy, hackneyed New England woman had lost five dollars on her little outlay! Success presented itself as an impossibility, and the hope of it as a wild hallucination.

Some malevolent spirit, doing his utmost to drive Hepzibah mad, unrolled before her imagination a kind of panorama, representing the great thoroughfare of a city all astir with customers. So many and so magnificent shops as there were! Groceries, toy-shops, drygoods stores, with their immense panes of plate-glass, their gorgeous fixtures, their vast and complete assortments of merchandise, in which fortunes had been invested; and those noble mirrors at the farther end of each establishment, doubling all this wealth by a brightly burnished vista of unrealities! On one side of the street this splendid bazaar, with a multitude of perfumed and glossy salesmen, smirking, smiling, bowing, and measuring out the goods. On the other, the dusky old House of the Seven Gables, with the antiquated shop-window under its projecting story, and Hepzibah herself, in a gown of rusty black silk, behind the counter, scowling at the world as it went by! This mighty contrast thrust itself forward as a fair expression of the odds against which she was to begin her struggle for a subsistence. Success? Preposterous! She would never think of it again! The house might just as well be buried in an eternal fog while all other houses had the sunshine on them; for not a foot would ever cross the threshold, nor a hand so much as try the door!

But, at this instant, the shop-bell, right over her head, tinkled as if it were bewitched. The old gentlewoman's heart seemed to be attached to the same steel spring, for it went through a series of sharp jerks, in unison with the sound. The door was thrust open, although no human form was perceptible on the other side of the half-window. Hepzibah, nevertheless, stood at a gaze, with her hands clasped, looking very much as if she had summoned up an evil spirit, and were afraid, yet resolved, to hazard the encounter.

"Heaven help me!" she groaned, mentally. "Now is my hour of need!"

The door, which moved with difficulty on its creaking and rusty hinges, being forced quite open, a square and sturdy little urchin became apparent, with cheeks as red as an apple. He was clad rather shabbily (but, as it seemed, more owing to his mother's carelessness than his father's poverty), in a blue apron, very wide and short trousers, shoes somewhat out at the toes, and a chip-hat, with the frizzles of his curly hair sticking through its crevices. A book and a small slate, under his arm, indicated that he was on his way to school. He stared at Hepzibah a moment, as an elder customer than himself would have been likely enough to do, not knowing what to make of the tragic attitude and queer scowl wherewith she regarded him.

"Well, child," said she, taking heart at sight of a personage so little formidable,—"well, my child, what did you wish for?"

"That Jim Crow there in the window," answered the urchin, holding out a cent, and pointing to the gingerbread figure that had attracted his notice, as he loitered along to school; "the one that has not a broken foot."

So Hepzibah put forth her lank arm, and, taking the effigy from the shop-window, delivered it to her first customer.

"No matter for the money," said she, giving him a little push towards the door; for her old gentility was contumaciously squeamish at sight of the copper coin, and, besides, it seemed such pitiful meanness to take the child's pocket-money in exchange for a bit of stale gingerbread. "No matter for the cent. You are welcome to Jim Crow."

The child, staring with round eyes at this instance of liberality, wholly unprecedented in his large experience of cent-shops, took the man of gingerbread, and quitted the premises. No sooner had he reached the sidewalk (little cannibal that he was!) than Jim Crow's head was in his mouth. As he had not been careful to shut the door, Hepzibah was at the pains of closing it after him, with a pettish ejaculation or two about the troublesomeness of young people, and particularly of small boys. She had just placed another representative of the renowned Jim Crow at the window, when again the shop-bell tinkled clamorously, and again the door being thrust open, with its characteristic jerk and jar, disclosed the same sturdy little urchin who, precisely two minutes ago, had made his exit. The crumbs and discoloration of the cannibal feast, as yet hardly consummated, were exceedingly visible about his mouth.

"What is it now, child?" asked the maiden lady, rather impatiently; "did you come back to shut the door?"

"No," answered the urchin, pointing to the figure that had just been put up; "I want that other Jim Crow."

"Well, here it is for you," said Hepzibah, reaching it down; but recognizing that this pertinacious customer would not quit her on any other terms, so long as she had a gingerbread figure in her shop, she partly drew back her extended hand, "Where is the cent?"

The little boy had the cent ready, but, like a true-born Yankee, would have preferred the better bargain to the worse. Looking somewhat chagrined, he put the coin into Hepzibah's hand, and departed, sending the second Jim Crow in quest of the former one. The new shopkeeper dropped the first solid result of her commercial enterprise into the till. It was done! The sordid stain of that copper coin could never be washed away from her palm. The little school-boy, aided by the impish figure of the negro dancer, had wrought an irreparable ruin. The structure of ancient aristocracy had been demolished by him, even as if his childish gripe had torn down the seven-gabled mansion. Now let Hepzibah turn the old Pyncheon portraits with their faces to the wall, and take the map of her Eastern territory to kindle the kitchen fire, and blow up the flame with the empty breath of her ancestral traditions! What had she to do with ancestry? Nothing; no more than with posterity! No lady, now, but simply Hepzibah Pyncheon, a forlorn old maid, and keeper of a cent-shop!

Nevertheless, even while she paraded these ideas somewhat ostentatiously through her mind, it is altogether surprising what a calmness had come over her. The anxiety and misgivings which had tormented her, whether asleep or in melancholy day-dreams, ever since her project began to take an aspect of solidity, had now vanished quite away. She felt the novelty of her position, indeed, but no longer with disturbance or affright. Now and then, there came a thrill of almost youthful enjoyment. It was the invigorating breath of a fresh outward atmosphere, after the long torpor and monotonous seclusion of her life. So wholesome is effort! So miraculous the strength that we do not know of! The healthiest glow that Hepzibah had known for years had come now in the dreaded crisis, when, for the first time, she had put forth her hand to help herself. The little circlet of the school-boy's copper coin—dim and lustreless though it was, with the small services which it had been doing here and there about the world—had proved a talisman, fragrant with good, and deserving to be set in gold and worn next her heart. It was as potent, and perhaps endowed with the same kind of efficacy, as a galvanic ring! Hepzibah, at all events, was indebted to its subtile operation both in body and spirit; so much the more, as it inspired her with energy to get some breakfast, at which, still the better to keep up her courage, she allowed herself an extra spoonful in her infusion of black tea.

Her introductory day of shop-keeping did not run on, however, without many and serious interruptions of this mood of cheerful vigor. As a general rule, Providence seldom vouchsafes to mortals any more than just that degree of encouragement which suffices to keep them at a reasonably full exertion of their powers. In the case of our old gentlewoman, after the excitement of new effort had subsided, the despondency of her whole life threatened, ever and anon, to return. It was like the heavy mass of cloud which we may often see obscuring the sky, and making a gray twilight everywhere, until, towards nightfall, it yields temporarily to a glimpse of sunshine. But, always, the envious cloud strives to gather again across the streak of celestial azure.

Customers came in, as the forenoon advanced, but rather slowly; in some cases, too, it must be owned, with little satisfaction either to themselves or Miss Hepzibah; nor, on the whole, with an aggregate of very rich emolument to the till. A little girl, sent by her mother to match a skein of cotton thread, of a peculiar hue, took one that the near-sighted old lady pronounced extremely like, but soon came running back, with a blunt and cross message, that it would not do, and, besides, was very rotten! Then, there was a pale, care-wrinkled woman, not old but haggard, and already with streaks of gray among her hair, like silver ribbons; one of those women, naturally delicate, whom you at once recognize as worn to death by a brute—probably a drunken brute—of a husband, and at least nine children. She wanted a few pounds of flour, and offered the money, which the decayed gentlewoman silently rejected, and gave the poor soul better measure than if she had taken it. Shortly afterwards, a man in a blue cotton frock, much soiled, came in and bought a pipe, filling the whole shop, meanwhile, with the hot odor of strong drink, not only exhaled in the torrid atmosphere of his breath, but oozing out of his entire system, like an inflammable gas. It was impressed on Hepzibah's mind that this was the husband of the care-wrinkled woman. He asked for a paper of tobacco; and as she had neglected to provide herself with the article, her brutal customer dashed down his newly-bought pipe and left the shop, muttering some unintelligible words, which had the tone and bitterness of a curse. Hereupon Hepzibah threw up her eyes, unintentionally scowling in the face of Providence!

No less than five persons, during the forenoon, inquired for ginger-beer, or root-beer, or any drink of a similar brewage, and, obtaining nothing of the kind, went off in an exceedingly bad humor. Three of them left the door open, and the other two pulled it so spitefully in going out that the little bell played the very deuce with Hepzibah's nerves. A round, bustling, fire-ruddy housewife of the neighborhood, burst breathless into the shop, fiercely demanding yeast; and when the poor gentlewoman, with her cold shyness of manner, gave her hot customer to understand that she did not keep the article, this very capable housewife took upon herself to administer a regular rebuke.

"A cent-shop, and no yeast!" quoth she; "that will never do! Who ever heard of such a thing? Your loaf will never rise, no more than mine will to-day. You had better shut up shop at once."

"Well," said Hepzibah, heaving a deep sigh, "perhaps I had!"

Several times, moreover, besides the above instance, her lady-like sensibilities were seriously infringed upon by the familiar, if not rude, tone with which people addressed her. They evidently considered themselves not merely her equals, but her patrons and superiors. Now, Hepzibah had unconsciously flattered herself with the idea that there would be a gleam or halo, of some kind or other, about her person, which would insure an obeisance to her sterling gentility, or, at least, a tacit recognition of it. On the other hand, nothing tortured her more intolerably than when this recognition was too prominently expressed. To one or two rather officious offers of sympathy, her responses were little short of acrimonius; and, we regret to say, Hepzibah was thrown into a positively unchristian state of mind by the suspicion that one of her customers was drawn to the shop, not by any real need of the article which she pretended to seek, but by a wicked wish to stare at her. The vulgar creature was determined to see for herself what sort of a figure a mildewed piece of aristocracy, after wasting all the bloom and much of the decline of her life apart from the world, would cut behind a counter. In this particular case, however mechanical and innocuous it might be at other times, Hepzibah's contortion of brow served her in good stead.

"I never was so frightened in my life!" said the curious customer, in describing the incident to one of her acquaintances. "She's a real old vixen, take my word of it! She says little, to be sure; but if you could only see the mischief in her eye!"

On the whole, therefore, her new experience led our decayed gentlewoman to very disagreeable conclusions as to the temper and manners of what she termed the lower classes, whom heretofore she had looked down upon with a gentle and pitying complaisance, as herself occupying a sphere of unquestionable superiority. But, unfortunately, she had likewise to struggle against a bitter emotion of a directly opposite kind: a sentiment of virulence, we mean, towards the idle aristocracy to which it had so recently been her pride to belong. When a lady, in a delicate and costly summer garb, with a floating veil and gracefully swaying gown, and, altogether an etherial lightness that made you look at her beautifully slippered feet, to see whether she trod on the dust or floated in the air,— when such a vision happened to pass through this retired street, leaving it tenderly and delusively fragrant with her passage, as if a bouquet of tea-roses had been borne along,—then again, it is to be feared, old Hepzibah's scowl could no longer vindicate itself entirely on the plea of near-sightedness.

"For what end," thought she, giving vent to that feeling of hostility which is the only real abasement of the poor in presence of the rich,—"for what good end, in the wisdom of Providence, does that woman live? Must the whole world toil, that the palms of her hands may be kept white and delicate?"

Then, ashamed and penitent, she hid her face.

"May God forgive me!" said she.

Doubtless, God did forgive her. But, taking the inward and outward history of the first half-day into consideration, Hepzibah began to fear that the shop would prove her ruin in a moral and religious point of view, without contributing very essentially towards even her temporal welfare.

## IV

### A DAY BEHIND THE COUNTER

TOWARDS noon, Hepzibah saw an elderly gentleman, large and portly, and of remarkably dignified demeanor, passing slowly along on the opposite side of the white and dusty street. On coming within the shadow of the Pyncheon Elm, he stopt, and (taking off his hat, meanwhile, to wipe the perspiration from his brow) seemed to scrutinize, with especial interest, the dilapidated and rusty-visaged House of the Seven Gables. He himself, in a very different style, was as well worth looking at as the house. No better model need be sought, nor could have been found, of a very high order of respectability, which, by some indescribable magic, not merely expressed itself in his looks and gestures, but even governed the fashion of his garments, and rendered them all proper and essential to the man. Without appearing to differ, in any tangible way, from other people's clothes, there was yet a wide and rich gravity about them that must have been a characteristic of the wearer, since it could not be defined as pertaining either to the cut or material. His gold-headed cane, too,—a serviceable staff, of dark polished wood,—had similar traits, and, had it chosen to take a walk by itself, would have been recognized anywhere as a tolerably adequate representative of its master. This character —which showed itself so strikingly in everything about him, and the effect of which we seek to convey to the reader—went no deeper than his station, habits of life, and external circumstances. One perceived him to be a personage of marked influence and authority; and, especially, you could feel just as certain that he was opulent as if he had exhibited his bank account, or as if you had seen him touching the twigs of the Pyncheon Elm, and, Midas-like, transmuting them to gold.

In his youth, he had probably been considered a handsome man; at his present age, his brow was too heavy, his temples too bare, his remaining hair too gray, his eye too cold, his lips too closely compressed, to bear any relation to mere personal beauty. He would have made a good and massive portrait; better now, perhaps, than at any previous period of his life, although his look might grow positively harsh in the process of being fixed upon the canvas. The artist would have found it desirable to study his face, and prove its capacity for varied expression; to darken it with a frown,—to kindle it up with a smile.

While the elderly gentleman stood looking at the Pyncheon House, both the frown and the smile passed successively over his countenance. His eye rested on the shop-window, and putting up a pair of gold-bowed spectacles, which he held in his hand, he minutely surveyed Hepzibah's little arrangement of toys and commodities. At first it seemed not to please him,—nay, to cause him exceeding displeasure,—and yet, the very next moment, he smiled. While the latter expression was yet on his lips, he caught a glimpse of Hepzibah, who had involuntarily bent forward to the window; and then the smile changed from acrid and disagreeable to the sunniest complacency and benevolence. He bowed, with a happy mixture of dignity and courteous kindliness, and pursued his way.

"There he is!" said Hepzibah to herself, gulping down a very bitter emotion, and, since she could not rid herself of it, trying to drive it back into her heart. "What does he think of it, I wonder? Does it please him? Ah! he is looking back!"

The gentleman had paused in the street, and turned himself half about, still with his eyes fixed on the shop-window. In fact, he wheeled wholly round, and commenced a step or two, as if designing to enter the shop; but, as it chanced, his purpose was anticipated by Hepzibah's first customer, the little cannibal of Jim Crow, who, staring up at the window, was irresistibly attracted by an elephant of gingerbread. What a grand appetite had this small urchin!—Two Jim Crows immediately after breakfast!—and now an elephant, as a preliminary whet before dinner! By the time this latter purchase was completed, the elderly gentleman had resumed his way, and turned the street corner.

"Take it as you like, Cousin Jaffrey!" muttered the maiden lady, as she drew back, after cautiously thrusting out her head, and looking up and down the street,—"take it as you like! You have seen my little shop-window! Well!—what have you to say?—is not the Pyncheon House my own, while I'm alive?"

After this incident, Hepzibah retreated to the back parlor, where she at first caught up a half-finished stocking, and began knitting at it with nervous and irregular jerks; but quickly finding herself at odds with the stitches, she threw it aside, and walked hurriedly about the room. At length, she paused before the portrait of the stern old Puritan, her ancestor, and the founder of the house. In one sense, this picture had almost faded into the canvas, and hidden itself behind the duskiness of age; in another, she could not but fancy that it had been growing more prominent, and strikingly expressive, ever since her earliest familiarity with it as a child. For, while the physical outline and substance were darkening away from the beholder's eye, the bold, hard, and, at the same time, indirect character of the man seemed to be brought out in a kind of spiritual relief. Such an effect may occasionally be observed in pictures of antique date. They acquire a look which an artist (if he have anything like the complacency of artists nowadays) would never dream of presenting to a patron as his own characteristic expression, but which, nevertheless, we at once recognize as reflecting the unlovely truth of a human soul. In such cases, the painter's deep conception of his subject's inward traits has wrought itself into the essence of the picture, and is seen after the superficial coloring has been rubbed off by time.

While gazing at the portrait, Hepzibah trembled under its eye. Her hereditary reverence made her afraid to judge the character of the original so harshly as a perception of the truth compelled her to do. But still she gazed, because the face of the picture enabled her—at least, she fancied so—to read more accurately, and to a greater depth, the face which she had just seen in the street.

"This is the very man!" murmured she to herself. "Let Jaffrey Pyncheon smile as he will, there is that look beneath! Put on him a skull-cap, and a band, and a black cloak, and a Bible in one hand and a sword in the other,—then let Jaffrey smile as he might,—nobody would doubt that it was the old Pyncheon come again! He has proved himself the very man to build up a new house! Perhaps, too, to draw down a new curse!"

Thus did Hepzibah bewilder herself with these fantasies of the old time. She had dwelt too much alone,—too long in the Pyncheon House,—until her very brain was impregnated with the dry-rot of its timbers. She needed a walk along the noonday street to keep her sane.

By the spell of contrast, another portrait rose up before her, painted with more daring flattery than any artist would have ventured upon, but yet so delicately touched that the likeness remained perfect. Malbone's miniature, though from the same original, was far inferior to Hepzibah's air-drawn picture, at which affection and sorrowful remembrance wrought together. Soft, mild, and cheerfully contemplative, with full, red lips, just on the verge of a smile, which the eyes seemed to herald by a gentle kindling-up of their orbs! Feminine traits, moulded inseparably with those of the other sex! The miniature, likewise, had this last peculiarity; so that you inevitably thought of the original as resembling his mother, and she a lovely and lovable woman, with perhaps some beautiful infirmity of character, that made it all the pleasanter to know and easier to love her.

"Yes," thought Hepzibah, with grief of which it was only the more tolerable portion that welled up from her heart to her eyelids, "they persecuted his mother in him! He never was a Pyncheon!"

But here the shop-bell rang; it was like a sound from a remote distance, —so far had Hepzibah descended into the sepulchral depths of her reminiscences. On entering the shop, she found an old man there, a humble resident of Pyncheon Street, and whom, for a great many years past, she had suffered to be a kind of familiar of the house. He was an immemorial personage, who seemed always to have had a white head and wrinkles, and never to have possessed but a single tooth, and that a half-decayed one, in the front of the upper jaw. Well advanced as Hepzibah was, she could not remember when Uncle Venner, as the neighborhood called him, had not gone up and down the street, stooping a little and drawing his feet heavily over the gravel or pavement. But still there was something tough and vigorous about him, that not only kept him in daily breath, but enabled him to fill a place which would else have been vacant in the apparently crowded world. To go of errands with his slow and shuffling gait, which made you doubt how he ever was to arrive anywhere; to saw a small household's foot or two of firewood, or knock to pieces an old barrel, or split up a pine board for kindling-stuff; in summer, to dig the few yards of garden ground appertaining to a low-rented tenement, and share the produce of his labor at the halves; in winter, to shovel away the snow from the sidewalk, or open paths to the woodshed, or along the clothesline; such were some of the essential offices which Uncle Venner performed among at least a score of families. Within that circle, he claimed the same sort of privilege, and probably felt as much warmth of interest, as a clergyman does in the range of his parishioners. Not that he laid claim to the tithe pig; but, as an analogous mode of reverence, he went his rounds, every morning, to gather up the crumbs of the table and overflowings of the dinner-pot, as food for a pig of his own.

In his younger days—for, after all, there was a dim tradition that he had been, not young, but younger—Uncle Venner was commonly regarded as rather deficient, than otherwise, in his wits. In truth he had virtually pleaded guilty to the charge, by scarcely aiming at such success as other men seek, and by taking only that humble and modest part in the intercourse of life which belongs to the alleged deficiency. But now, in his extreme old age,—whether it were that his long and hard experience had actually brightened him, or that his decaying judgment rendered him less capable of fairly measuring himself,—the venerable man made pretensions to no little wisdom, and really enjoyed the credit of it. There was likewise, at times, a vein of something like poetry in him; it was the moss or wall-flower of his mind in its small dilapidation, and gave a charm to what might have been vulgar and commonplace in his earlier and middle life. Hepzibah had a regard for him, because his name was ancient in the town and had formerly been respectable. It was a still better reason for awarding him a species of familiar reverence that Uncle Venner was himself the most ancient existence, whether of man or thing, in Pyncheon Street, except the House of the Seven Gables, and perhaps the elm that overshadowed it.

This patriarch now presented himself before Hepzibah, clad in an old blue coat, which had a fashionable air, and must have accrued to him from the cast-off wardrobe of some dashing clerk. As for his trousers, they were of tow-cloth, very short in the legs, and bagging down strangely in

the rear, but yet having a suitableness to his figure which his other garment entirely lacked. His hat had relation to no other part of his dress,
and but very little to the head that wore it. Thus Uncle Venner was a
miscellaneous old gentleman, partly himself, but, in good measure, somebody else; patched together, too, of different epochs; an epitome of times
and fashions.

"So, you have really begun trade," said he,—"really begun trade!
Well, I'm glad to see it. Young people should never live idle in the world,
nor old ones neither, unless when the rheumatize gets hold of them. It has
given me warning already; and in two or three years longer, I shall think
of putting aside business and retiring to my farm. That's yonder,—the
great brick house, you know,—the workhouse, most folks call it; but I
mean to do my work first, and go there to be idle and enjoy myself. And
I'm glad to see you beginning to do your work, Miss Hepzibah!"

"Thank you, Uncle Venner," said Hepzibah, smiling; for she always
felt kindly towards the simple and talkative old man. Had he been an old
woman, she might probably have repelled the freedom, which she now
took in good part. "It is time for me to begin work, indeed! Or, to speak
the truth, I have just begun when I ought to be giving it up."

"Oh, never say that, Miss Hepzibah!" answered the old man. "You are
a young woman yet. Why, I hardly thought myself younger than I am
now, it seems so little while ago since I used to see you playing about the
door of the old house, quite a small child! Oftener, though, you used to
be sitting at the threshold, and looking gravely into the street; for you
had always a grave kind of way with you,—a grown-up air, when you
were only the height of my knee. It seems as if I saw you now; and your
grandfather with his red cloak, and his white wig, and his cocked hat, and
his cane, coming out of the house, and stepping so grandly up the street!
Those old gentlemen that grew up before the Revolution used to put on
grand airs. In my young days, the great man of the town was commonly
called King; and his wife, not Queen to be sure, but Lady. Nowadays, a
man would not dare to be called King; and if he feels himself a little
above common folks, he only stoops so much the lower to them. I met
your cousin, the Judge, ten minutes ago; and, in my old tow-cloth trousers, as you see, the Judge raised his hat to me, I do believe! At any rate,
the Judge bowed and smiled!"

"Yes," said Hepzibah, with something bitter stealing unawares into her
tone; "my cousin Jaffrey is thought to have a very pleasant smile!"

"And so he has!" replied Uncle Venner. "And that's rather remarkable
in a Pyncheon; for, begging your pardon, Miss Hepzibah, they never had
the name of being an easy and agreeable set of folks. There was no getting
close to them. But now, Miss Hepzibah, if an old man may be bold to ask,
why don't Judge Pyncheon, with his great means, step forward, and tell
his cousin to shut up her little shop at once? It's for your credit to be doing something, but it's not for the Judge's credit to let you!"

"We won't talk of this, if you please, Uncle Venner," said Hepzibah,
coldly. "I ought to say, however, that, if I choose to earn bread for my-

self, it is not Judge Pyncheon's fault. Neither will he deserve the blame," added she, more kindly, remembering Uncle Venner's privileges of age and humble familiarity, "if I should, by and by, find it convenient to retire with you to your farm."

"And it's no bad place, either, that farm of mine!" cried the old man, cheerily, as if there were something positively delightful in the prospect. "No bad place is the great brick farm-house, especially for them that will find a good many old cronies there, as will be my case. I quite long to be among them, sometimes, of the winter evenings; for it is but dull business for a lonesome elderly man, like me, to be nodding, by the hour together, with no company but his air-tight stove. Summer or winter, there's a great deal to be said in favor of my farm! And, take it in the autumn, what can be pleasanter than to spend a whole day on the sunny side of a barn or a wood-pile, chatting with somebody as old as one's self; or, perhaps, idling away the time with a natural-born simpleton, who knows how to be idle, because even our busy Yankees never have found out how to put him to any use? Upon my word, Miss Hepzibah, I doubt whether I've ever been so comfortable as I mean to be at my farm, which most folks call the workhouse. But you,—you're a young woman yet,—you never need go there! Something still better will turn up for you. I'm sure of it!"

Hepzibah fancied that there was something peculiar in her venerable friend's look and tone; insomuch, that she gazed into his face with considerable earnestness, endeavoring to discover what secret meaning, if any, might be lurking there. Individuals whose affairs have reached an utterly desperate crisis almost invariably keep themselves alive with hopes, so much the more airily magnificent as they have the less of solid matter within their grasp whereof to mould any judicious and moderate expectation of good. Thus, all the while Hepzibah was perfecting the scheme of her little shop, she had cherished an unacknowledged idea that some harlequin trick of fortune would intervene in her favor. For example, an uncle—who had sailed for India fifty years before, and never been heard of since—might yet return, and adopt her to be the comfort of his very extreme and decrepit age, and adorn her with pearls, diamonds, and Oriental shawls and turbans, and make her the ultimate heiress of his unreckonable riches. Or the member of Parliament, now at the head of the English branch of the family,—with which the elder stock, on this side of the Atlantic, had held little or no intercourse for the last two centuries,— this eminent gentleman might invite Hepzibah to quit the ruinous House of the Seven Gables, and come over to dwell with her kindred at Pyncheon Hall. But, for reasons the most imperative, she could not yield to his request. It was more probable, therefore, that the descendants of a Pyncheon who had emigrated to Virginia, in some past generation, and became a great planter there,—hearing of Hepzibah's destitution, and impelled by the splendid generosity of character with which their Virginian mixture must have enriched the New England blood,—would send her a remittance of a thousand dollars, with a hint of repeating the favor annually. Or,—and, surely, anything so undeniably just could not be beyond the limits of reasonable anticipation,—the great claim to the heritage of Waldo County might finally be decided in favor of the Pyncheons; so that, instead of keeping a cent-shop, Hepzibah would build a palace, and look down from its highest tower on hill, dale, forest, field, and town, as her own share of the ancestral territory.

These were some of the fantasies which she had long dreamed about; and, aided by these, Uncle Venner's casual attempt at encouragement kindled a strange festal glory in the poor, bare, melancholy chambers of her brain, as if that inner world were suddenly lighted up with gas. But either he knew nothing of her castles in the air—as how should he?—or else her earnest scowl disturbed his recollection, as it might a more courageous man's. Instead of pursuing any weightier topic, Uncle Venner was pleased to favor Hepzibah with some sage counsel in her shop-keeping capacity.

"Give no credit!"—these were some of his golden maxims,—"Never take paper-money! Look well to your change! Ring the silver on the four-pound weight! Shove back all English half-pence and base copper tokens, such as are very plenty about town! At your leisure hours, knit children's woollen socks and mittens! Brew your own yeast, and make your own ginger-beer!"

And while Hepzibah was doing her utmost to digest the hard little pellets of his already uttered wisdom, he gave vent to his final, and what he declared to be his all-important advice, as follows:—

"Put on a bright face for your customers, and smile pleasantly as you hand them what they ask for! A stale article, if you dip it in a good, warm, sunny smile, will go off better than a fresh one that you've scowled upon."

To this last apothegm poor Hepzibah responded with a sigh so deep and heavy that it almost rustled Uncle Venner quite away, like a withered leaf,—as he was,—before an autumnal gale. Recovering himself, however, he bent forward, and, with a good deal of feeling in his ancient visage, beckoned her nearer to him.

"When do you expect him home?" whispered he.

"Whom do you mean?" asked Hepzibah, turning pale.

"Ah? you don't love to talk about it," said Uncle Venner. "Well, well! we'll say no more, though there's word of it all over town. I remember him, Miss Hepzibah, before he could run alone!"

During the remainder of the day poor Hepzibah acquitted herself even less creditably, as a shop-keeper, than in her earlier efforts. She appeared to be walking in a dream; or, more truly, the vivid life and reality assumed by her emotions made all outward occurrences unsubstantial, like the teasing phantasms of a half-conscious slumber. She still responded, mechanically, to the frequent summons of the shop-bell, and, at the demand of her customers, went prying with vague eyes about the shop, proffering them one article after another, and thrusting aside—perversely, as most of them supposed—the identical thing they asked for. There is sad confusion, indeed, when the spirit thus flits away into the past, or into the more awful future, or, in any manner, steps across the spaceless boundary betwixt its own region and the actual world; where the body remains to guide itself as best it may, with little more than the mechanism of animal life. It is like death, without death's quiet privilege,—its freedom from mortal care. Worst of all, when the actual duties are comprised in such petty details as now vexed the brooding soul of the old gentlewoman. As the animosity of fate would have it, there was a great influx of custom in the course of the afternoon. Hepzibah blundered to and fro about her small place of business, committing the most unheard-of errors: now stringing up twelve, and now seven, tallow-candles, instead of ten to the pound; selling ginger for Scotch snuff, pins for needles, and needles for pins; misreckoning her change, sometimes to the public detriment, and much oftener to her own; and thus she went on, doing her utmost to bring chaos back again, until, at the close of the day's labor, to her inexplicable astonishment, she found the money-drawer almost destitute of coin. After all her painful traffic, the whole proceeds were perhaps half a dozen coppers, and a questionable ninepence which ultimately proved to be copper likewise.

At this price, or at whatever price, she rejoined that the day had reached its end. Never before had she had such a sense of the intolerable length of time that creeps between dawn and sunset, and of the miserable irksomeness of having aught to do, and of the better wisdom that it would be to lie down at once, in sullen resignation, and let life, and its toils and vexations, trample over one's prostrate body as they may! Hepzibah's final operation was with the little devourer of Jim Crow and the elephant, who now proposed to eat a camel. In her bewilderment, she offered him first a wooden dragoon, and next a handful of marbles; neither of which being adapted to his else omnivorous appetite, she hastily held out her whole remaining stock of natural history in gingerbread, and huddled the small customer out of the shop. She then muffled the bell in an unfinished stocking, and put up the oaken bar across the door.

During the latter process, an omnibus came to a stand-still under the branches of the elm-tree. Hepzibah's heart was in her mouth. Remote and dusky, and with no sunshine on all the intervening space, was that region of the Past whence her only guest might be expected to arrive! Was she to meet him now?

Somebody, at all events, was passing from the farthest interior of the omnibus towards its entrance. A gentleman alighted; but it was only to offer his hand to a young girl whose slender figure, nowise needing such assistance, now lightly descended the steps, and made an airy little jump from the final one to the sidewalk. She rewarded her cavalier with a smile, the cheery glow of which was seen reflected on his own face as he reëntered the vehicle. The girl then turned towards the House of the Seven Gables, to the door of which, meanwhile,—not the shop-door, but the antique portal,—the omnibus-man had carried a light trunk and a bandbox. First giving a sharp rap of the old iron knocker, he left his passenger and her luggage at the door-step, and departed.

"Who can it be?" thought Hepzibah, who had been screwing her visual organs into the acutest focus of which they were capable. "The girl must have mistaken the house!"

She stole softly into the hall, and, herself invisible, gazed through the dusty side-lights of the portal at the young, blooming, and very cheerful face, which presented itself for admittance into the gloomy old mansion. It was a face to which almost any door would have opened of its own accord.

The young girl, so fresh, so unconventional, and yet so orderly and obedient to common rules, as you at once recognized her to be, was widely in contrast, at that moment, with everything about her. The sordid and ugly luxuriance of gigantic weeds that grew in the angle of the house, and the heavy projection that overshadowed her, and the time-worn framework of the door,—none of these things belonged to her sphere. But, even as a ray of sunshine, fall into what dismal place it may, instantaneously creates for itself a propriety in being there, so did it seem altogether fit that the girl should be standing at the threshold. It was no less evidently proper that the door should swing open to admit her. The maiden lady, herself, sternly inhospitable in her first purposes, soon began to feel that the door ought to be shoved back, and the rusty key be turned in the reluctant lock.

"Can it be Phœbe?" questioned she within herself. "It must be little Phœbe; for it can be nobody else,—and there is a look of her father about her, too! But what does she want here? And how like a country cousin, to come down upon a poor body in this way, without so much as a day's notice, or asking whether she would be welcome! Well; she must have a night's lodging, I suppose; and to-morrow the child shall go back to her mother!"

Phœbe, it must be understood, was that one little offshoot of the Pyncheon race to whom we have already referred, as a native of a rural part of New England, where the old fashions and feelings of relationship are still partially kept up. In her own circle, it was regarded as by no means improper for kinsfolk to visit one another without invitation, or preliminary and ceremonious warning. Yet, in consideration of Miss Hepzibah's recluse way of life, a letter had actually been written and despatched, conveying information of Phœbe's projected visit. This epistle, for three of four days past, had been in the pocket of the penny-postman, who, happening to have no other business in Pyncheon Street, had not yet made it convenient to call at the House of the Seven Gables.

"No!—she can stay only one night," said Hepzibah, unbolting the door. "If Clifford were to find her here, it might disturb him!"

## V

### MAY AND NOVEMBER

PHŒBE PYNCHEON slept, on the night of her arrival, in a chamber that looked down on the garden of the old house. It fronted towards the east, so that at a very seasonable hour a glow of crimson light came flooding through the window, and bathed the dingy ceiling and paper-hangings in its own hue. There were curtains to Phœbe's bed; a dark, antique canopy, and ponderous festoons of a stuff which had been rich, and even magnificent, in its time; but which now brooded over the girl like a cloud, making a night in that one corner, while elsewhere it was beginning to be day. The morning light, however, soon stole into the aperture at the foot of the bed, betwixt those faded curtains. Finding the new guest there,—with a bloom on her cheeks like the morning's own, and a gentle stir of departing slumber in her limbs, as when an early breeze moves the foliage, —the dawn kissed her brow. It was the caress which a dewy maiden— such as the Dawn is, immortally—gives to her sleeping sister, partly from the impulse of irresistible fondness, and partly as a pretty hint that it is time now to unclose her eyes.

At the touch of those lips of light, Phœbe quietly awoke, and, for a moment, did not recognize where she was, nor how those heavy curtains chanced to be festooned around her. Nothing, indeed, was absolutely plain to her, except that it was now early morning, and that, whatever might happen next, it was proper, first of all, to get up and say her prayers. She was the more inclined to devotion from the grim aspect of the chamber and its furniture, especially the tall, stiff chairs; one of which stood close by her bedside, and looked as if some old-fashioned personage had been sitting there all night, and had vanished only just in season to escape discovery.

When Phœbe was quite dressed, she peeped out of the window, and saw a rose-bush in the garden. Being a very tall one, and of luxuriant growth, it had been propped up against the side of the house, and was literally covered with a rare and very beautiful species of white rose. A large portion of them, as the girl afterwards discovered, had blight or mildew at their hearts; but, viewed at a fair distance, the whole rose-bush looked as if it had been brought from Eden that very summer, together with the mould in which it grew. The truth was, nevertheless, that it had been planted by Alice Pyncheon,—she was Phœbe's great-great-grand-aunt,— in soil which, reckoning only its cultivation as a garden-plat, was now unctuous with nearly two hundred years of vegetable decay. Growing as they did, however, out of the old earth, the flowers still sent a fresh and sweet incense up to their Creator; nor could it have been the less pure and acceptable, because Phœbe's young breath mingled with it, as the fragrance floated past the window. Hastening down the creaking and carpetless staircase, she found her way into the garden, gathered some of the most perfect of the roses, and brought them to her chamber.

Little Phœbe was one of those persons who possess, as their exclusive patrimony, the gift of practical arrangement. It is a kind of natural magic that enables these favored ones to bring out the hidden capabilities of things around them; and particularly to give a look of comfort and habitableness to any place which, for however brief a period, may happen to be their home. A wild hut of underbrush, tossed together by wayfarers through the primitive forest, would acquire the home aspect by one night's lodging of such a woman, and would retain it long after her quiet figure had disappeared into the surrounding shade. No less a portion of such homely witchcraft was requisite to reclaim, as it were, Phœbe's waste, cheerless, and dusky chamber, which had been untenanted so long —except by spiders, and mice, and rats, and ghosts—that it was all overgrown with the desolation which watches to obliterate every trace of man's happier hours. What was precisely Phœbe's process we find it impossible to say. She appeared to have no preliminary design, but gave a touch here and another there; brought some articles of furniture to light and dragged others into the shadow; looped up or let down a window-curtain; and, in the course of half an hour, had fully succeeded in throwing a kindly and hospitable smile over the apartment. No longer ago than the night before, it had resembled nothing so much as the old maid's heart; for there was neither sunshine nor household fire in one nor the other, and, save for ghosts and ghostly reminiscences, not a guest, for many years gone by, had entered the heart or the chamber.

There was still another peculiarity of this inscrutable charm. The bed-chamber, no doubt, was a chamber of very great and varied experience, as a scene of human life: the joy of bridal nights had throbbed itself away here; new immortals had first drawn earthly breath here; and here old people had died. But—whether it were the white roses, or whatever the subtile influence might be—a person of delicate instinct would have known at once that it was now a maiden's bedchamber, and had been purified of all former evil and sorrow by her sweet breath and happy thoughts. Her dreams of the past night, being such cheerful ones, had exorcised the gloom, and now haunted the chamber in its stead.

After arranging matters to her satisfaction, Phœbe emerged from her chamber, with a purpose to descend again into the garden. Besides the rose-bush, she had observed several other species of flowers growing there in a wilderness of neglect, and obstructing one another's development (as is often the parallel case in human society) by their uneducated entanglement and confusion. At the head of the stairs, however, she met Hepzibah, who, it being still early, invited her into a room which she would probably have called her boudoir, had her education embraced any such French phrase. It was strewn about with a few old books, and a work-basket, and a dusty writing-desk; and had, on one side, a large, black article of furniture, of very strange appearance, which the old gentlewoman told Phœbe was a harpsichord. It looked more like a coffin than anything else; and, indeed,—not having been played upon, or opened, for years,—there must have been a vast deal of dead music in it, stifled for want of air. Human finger was hardly known to have touched its chords since the days of Alice Pyncheon, who had learned the sweet accomplishment of melody in Europe.

Hepzibah bade her young guest sit down, and, herself taking a chair near by, looked as earnestly at Phœbe's trim little figure as if she expected to see right into its springs and motive secrets.

"Cousin Phœbe," said she, at last, "I really can't see my way clear to keep you with me."

These words, however, had not the inhospitable bluntness with which they may strike the reader; for the two relatives, in a talk before bed-time, had arrived at a certain degree of mutual understanding. Hepzibah knew enough to enable her to appreciate the circumstances (resulting from the second marriage of the girl's mother) which made it desirable for Phœbe to establish herself in another home. Nor did she misinterpret Phœbe's character, and the genial activity pervading it,—one of the most valuable traits of the true New England woman,—which had impelled her forth, as might be said, to seek her fortune, but with a self-respecting purpose to confer as much benefit as she could anywise receive. As one of her nearest kindred, she had naturally betaken herself to Hepzibah, with no idea of forcing herself on her cousin's protection, but only for a visit of a week or two, which might be indefinitely extended, should it prove for the happiness of both.

To Hepzibah's blunt observation, therefore, Phœbe replied, as frankly, and more cheerfully.

"Dear cousin, I cannot tell how it will be," said she. "But I really think we may suit one another much better than you suppose."

"You are a nice girl,—I see it plainly," continued Hepzibah; "and it is not any question as to that point which makes me hesitate. But, Phœbe, this house of mine is but a melancholy place for a young person to be in. It lets in the wind and rain, and the snow, too, in the garret and upper chambers, in winter-time, but it never lets in the sunshine! And as for myself, you see what I am,—a dismal and lonesome old woman (for I begin to call myself old, Phœbe), whose temper, I am afraid, is none of the best, and whose spirits are as bad as can be. I cannot make your life pleasant, Cousin Phœbe, neither can I so much as give you bread to eat."

"You will find me a cheerful little body," answered Phœbe, smiling, and yet with a kind of gentle dignity; "and I mean to earn my bread. You know I have not been brought up a Pyncheon. A girl learns many things in a New England village."

"Ah! Phœbe," said Hepzibah, sighing, "your knowledge would do but little for you here! And then it is a wretched thought that you should fling away your young days in a place like this. Those cheeks would not be so rosy after a month or two. Look at my face!"—and, indeed, the contrast was very striking,—"you see how pale I am! It is my idea that the dust and continual decay of these old houses are unwholesome for the lungs."

"There is the garden,—the flowers to be taken care of," observed Phœbe. "I should keep myself healthy with exercise in the open air."

"And, after all, child," exclaimed Hepzibah, suddenly rising, as if to dismiss the subject, "it is not for me to say who shall be a guest or inhabitant of the old Pyncheon House. Its master is coming."

"Do you mean Judge Pyncheon?" asked Phœbe, in surprise.

"Judge Pyncheon!" answered her cousin, angrily. "He will hardly cross the threshold while I live! No, no! But, Phœbe, you shall see the face of him I speak of."

She went in quest of the miniature already described, and returned with it in her hand. Giving it to Phœbe, she watched her features narrowly, and with a certain jealousy as to the mode in which the girl would show herself affected by the picture.

"How do you like the face?" asked Hepzibah.

"It is handsome!—it is very beautiful!" said Phœbe, admiringly. "It is as sweet a face as a man's can be, or ought to be. It has something of a child's expression,—and yet not childish,—only one feels so very kindly towards him! He ought never to suffer anything. One would bear much for the sake of sparing him toil or sorrow. Who is it, Cousin Hepzibah?"

"Did you never hear," whispered her cousin, bending towards her, "of Clifford Pyncheon?"

"Never! I thought there were no Pyncheons left, except yourself and our cousin Jaffrey," answered Phœbe. "And yet I seem to have heard the name of Clifford Pyncheon. Yes!—from my father or my mother; but has he not been a long while dead?"

"Well, well, child, perhaps he has!" said Hepzibah, with a sad, hollow laugh; "but, in old houses like this, you know, dead people are very apt to come back again! We shall see. And, Cousin Phœbe, since, after all that I have said, your courage does not fail you, we will not part so soon. You are welcome, my child, for the present, to such a home as your kinswoman can offer you."

With this measured, but not exactly cold assurance of a hospitable purpose, Hepzibah kissed her cheek.

They now went below stairs, where Phœbe—not so much assuming the office as attracting it to herself, by the magnetism of innate fitness—took the most active part in preparing breakfast. The mistress of the house, meanwhile, as is usual with persons of her stiff and unmalleable cast, stood mostly aside; willing to lend her aid, yet conscious that her natural inaptitude would be likely to impede the business in hand. Phœbe, and the fire that boiled the teakettle, were equally bright, cheerful, and efficient, in their respective offices. Hepzibah gazed forth from her habitual sluggishness, the necessary result of long solitude, as from another sphere. She could not help being interested, however, and even amused, at the readiness with which her new inmate adapted herself to the circumstances, and brought the house, moreover, and all its rusty old appliances, into a suitableness for her purposes. Whatever she did, too, was done without conscious effort, and with frequent outbreaks of song, which were exceedingly pleasant to the ear. This natural tunefulness made Phœbe seem like a bird in a shadowy tree; or conveyed the idea that the stream of life warbled through her heart as a brook sometimes warbles through a pleasant little dell. It betokened the cheeriness of an active temperament, finding joy in its activity, and, therefore, rendering it beautiful; it was a New England trait,—the stern old stuff of Puritanism with a gold thread in the web.

Hepzibah brought out some old silver spoons with the family crest upon them, and a china tea-set painted over with grotesque figures of man, bird, and beast, in as grotesque a landscape. These pictured people were odd humorists, in a world of their own,—a world of vivid brilliancy, so far as color went, and still unfaded, although the teapot and small cups were as ancient as the custom itself of tea-drinking.

"Your great-great-great-great-grandmother had these cups, when she was married," said Hepzibah to Phœbe. "She was a Davenport, of a good family. They were almost the first teacups ever seen in the colony; and if one of them were to be broken, my heart would break with it. But it is nonsense to speak so about a brittle teacup, when I remember what my heart has gone through without breaking."

The cups—not having been used, perhaps, since Hepzibah's youth—had contracted no small burden of dust, which Phœbe washed away with so much care and delicacy as to satisfy even the proprietor of this invaluable china.

"What a nice little housewife you are!" exclaimed the latter, smiling, and, at the same time, frowning so prodigiously that the smile was sunshine under a thunder-cloud. "Do you do other things as well? Are you as good at your book as you are at washing teacups?"

"Not quite, I am afraid," said Phœbe, laughing at the form of Hepzibah's question. "But I was school-mistress for the little children in our district last summer, and might have been so still."

"Ah! 'tis all very well!" observed the maiden lady, drawing herself up. "But these things must have come to you with your mother's blood. I never knew a Pyncheon that had any turn for them."

It is very queer, but not the less true, that people are generally quite as vain, or even more so, of their deficiencies than of their available gifts; as was Hepzibah of this native inapplicability, so to speak, of the Pyncheons to any useful purpose. She regarded it as an hereditary trait; and so, perhaps, it was, but, unfortunately, a morbid one, such as is often generated in families that remain long above the surface of society.

Before they left the breakfast-table, the shop-bell rang sharply, and Hepzibah set down the remnant of her final cup of tea, with a look of sallow despair that was truly piteous to behold. In cases of distasteful occupation, the second day is generally worse than the first; we return to the rack with all the soreness of the preceding torture in our limbs. At all events, Hepzibah had fully satisfied herself of the impossibility of ever becoming wonted to this peevishly obstreperous little bell. Ring as often as it might, the sound always smote upon her nervous system rudely and suddenly. And especially now, while, with her crested ,teaspoons and antique china, she was flattering herself with ideas of gentility, she felt an unspeakable disinclination to confront a customer.

"Do not trouble yourself, dear cousin!" cried Phœbe, starting lightly up. "I am shop-keeper to-day."

"You, child!" exclaimed Hepzibah. "What can a little country-girl know of such matters?"

"Oh, I have done all the shopping for the family at our village store," said Phœbe. "And I have had a table at a fancy fair, and made better sales than anybody. These things are not to be learnt; they depend upon a knack that comes, I suppose," added she, smiling, "with one's mother's blood. You shall see that I am as nice a little saleswoman as I am a house-wife!"

The old gentlewoman stole behind Phœbe, and peeped from the passage-way into the shop, to note how she would manage her undertaking. It was a case of some intricacy. A very ancient woman, in a white short gown and a green petticoat, with a string of gold beads about her neck, and what looked like a nightcap on her head, had brought a quantity of yarn to barter for the commodities of the shop. She was probably the very last person in town who still kept the time-honored spinning-wheel in constant revolution. It was worth while to hear the croaking and hollow tones of the old lady, and the pleasant voice of Phœbe, mingling in one twisted thread of talk; and still better to contrast their figures,—so light and bloomy,—so decrepit and dusky,—with only the counter betwixt them, in one sense, but more than threescore years, in another. As for the bargain, it was wrinkled slyness and craft pitted against native truth and sagacity.

"Was not that well done?" asked Phœbe, laughing, when the customer was gone.

"Nicely done, indeed, child!" answered Hepzibah. "I could not have gone through with it nearly so well. As you say, it must be a knack that belongs to you on the mother's side."

It is a very genuine admiration, that with which persons too shy or too awkward to take a due part in the bustling world regard the real actors in life's stirring scenes; so genuine, in fact, that the former are usually fain to make it palatable to their self-love, by assuming that these active and forcible qualities are incompatible with others, which they choose to deem higher and more important. Thus, Hepzibah was well content to acknowledge Phœbe's vastly superior gifts as a shop-keeper; she listened, with compliant ear, to her suggestion of various methods whereby the influx of trade might be increased, and rendered profitable, without a hazardous outlay of capital. She consented that the village maiden should manufacture yeast, both liquid and in cakes; and should brew a certain kind of beer, nectareous to the palate, and of rare stomachic virtues; and, moreover, should bake and exhibit for sale some little spice-cakes, which whosoever tasted would longingly desire to taste again. All such proofs of a ready mind and skilful handiwork were highly acceptable to the aristocratic hucksteress, so long as she could murmur to herself with a grim smile, and a half-natural sigh, and a sentiment of mixed wonder, pity, and growing affection,—

"What a nice little body she is! If she could only be a lady, too!—but that's impossible! Phœbe is no Pyncheon. She takes everything from her mother."

As to Phœbe's not being a lady, or whether she were a lady or no, it was a point, perhaps, difficult to decide, but which could hardly have come up for judgment at all in any fair and healthy mind. Out of New England, it would be impossible to meet with a person combining so many lady-like attributes with so many others that form no necessary (if compatible) part of the character. She shocked no canon of taste; she was admirably in keeping with herself, and never jarred against surrounding circumstances. Her figure, to be sure,—so small as to be almost childlike, and so elastic that motion seemed as easy or easier to it than rest,— would hardly have suited one's idea of a countess. Neither did her face— with the brown ringlets on either side, and the slightly piquant nose, and the wholesome bloom, and the clear shade of tan, and the half a dozen freckles, friendly remembrancers of the April sun and breeze—precisely give us a right to call her beautiful. But there was both lustre and depth in her eyes. She was very pretty; as graceful as a bird, and graceful much in the same way; as pleasant about the house as a gleam of sunshine falling on the floor through a shadow of twinkling leaves, or as a ray of firelight that dances on the wall while evening is drawing nigh. Instead of discussing her claim to rank among ladies, it would be preferable to regard Phœbe as the example of feminine grace and availability combined, in a state of society, if there were any such, where ladies did not exist. There it should be woman's office to move in the midst of practical affairs, and to gild them all, the very homeliest,—were it even the scouring of pots and kettles,—with an atmosphere of loveliness and joy.

Such was the sphere of Phœbe. To find the born and educated lady, on the other hand, we need look no farther than Hepzibah, our forlorn old maid, in her rustling and rusty silks, with her deeply cherished and ridiculous consciousness of long descent, her shadowy claims to princely territory, and, in the way of accomplishment, her recollections, it may be, of having formerly thrummed on a harpsichord, and walked a minuet, and worked an antique tapestry-stitch on her sampler. It was a fair parallel between new Plebeianism and old Gentility.

It really seemed as if the battered visage of the House of the Seven Gables, black and heavy-browed as it still certainly looked, must have shown a kind of cheerfulness glimmering through its dusky windows as Phœbe passed to and fro in the interior. Otherwise, it is impossible to explain how the people of the neighborhood so soon became aware of the girl's presence. There was a great run of custom, setting steadily in, from about ten o'clock until towards noon,—relaxing, somewhat, at dinner-time, but recommencing in the afternoon, and, finally, dying away a half an hour or so before the long day's sunset. One of the stanchest patrons was little Ned Higgins, the devourer of Jim Crow and the elephant, who to-day had signalized his omnivorous prowess by swallowing two dromedaries and a locomotive. Phœbe laughed, as she summed up her aggregate of sales upon the slate; while Hepzibah, first drawing on a pair of silk gloves, reckoned over the sordid accumulation of copper coin, not without silver intermixed, that had jingled into the till.

"We must renew our stock, Cousin Hepzibah!" cried the little saleswoman. "The gingerbread figures are all gone, and so are those Dutch wooden milkmaids, and most of our other playthings. There has been constant inquiry for cheap raisins, and a great cry for whistles, and trumpets, and jew's-harps; and at least a dozen little boys have asked for molasses-candy. And we must contrive to get a peck of russet apples, late in the season as it is. But, dear cousin, what an enormous heap of copper! Positively a copper mountain!"

"Well done! well done! well done!" quoth Uncle Venner, who had taken occasion to shuffle in and out of the shop several times in the course of the day. "Here's a girl that will never end her days at my farm! Bless my eyes, what a brisk little soul!"

"Yes, Phœbe is a nice girl!" said Hepzibah, with a scowl of austere approbation. "But, Uncle Venner, you have known the family a great many years. Can you tell me whether there ever was a Pyncheon whom she takes after?"

"I don't believe there ever was," answered the venerable man. "At any rate, it never was my luck to see her like among them, nor, for that matter, anywhere else. I've seen a great deal of the world, not only in people's kitchens and back-yards, but at the street-corners, and on the wharves, and in other places where my business calls me; and I'm free to say, Miss Hepzibah, that I never knew a human creature do her work so much like one of God's angels as this child Phœbe does!"

Uncle Venner's eulogium, if it appear rather too high-strained for the person and occasion, had, nevertheless, a sense in which it was both subtile and true. There was a spiritual quality in Phœbe's activity. The life of the long and busy day—spent in occupations that might so easily have taken a squalid and ugly aspect—had been made pleasant, and even lovely, by the spontaneous grace with which these homely duties seemed to bloom out of her character; so that labor, while she dealt with it, had the easy and flexible charm of play. Angels do not toil, but let their good works grow out of them; and so did Phœbe.

The two relatives—the young maid and the old one—found time before nightfall, in the intervals of trade, to make rapid advances towards affection and confidence. A recluse, like Hepzibah, usually displays remarkable frankness, and at least temporary affability, on being absolutely cornered, and brought to the point of personal intercourse; like the angel

whom Jacob wrestled with, she is ready to bless you when once overcome.

The old gentlewoman took a dreary and proud satisfaction in leading
Phœbe from room to room of the house, and recounting the traditions
with which, as we may say, the walls were lugubriously frescoed. She
showed the indentations made by the lieutenant-governor's sword-hilt in
the door-panels of the apartment where old Colonel Pyncheon, a dead
host, had received his affrighted visitors with an awful frown. The dusky
terror of that frown, Hepzibah observed, was thought to be lingering
ever since in the passage-way. She bade Phœbe step into one of the tall
chairs, and inspect the ancient map of the Pyncheon territory at the eastward. In a tract of land on which she laid her finger, there existed a silver-
mine, the locality of which was precisely pointed out in some memoranda
of Colonel Pyncheon himself, but only to be made known when the
family claim should be recognized by government. Thus it was for the interest of all New England that the Pyncheons should have justice done
them. She told, too, how that there was undoubtedly an immense treasure
of English guineas hidden somewhere about the house, or in the cellar, or
possibly in the garden.

"If you should happen to find it, Phœbe," said Hepzibah, glancing
aside at her with a grim yet kindly smile, "we will tie up the shop-bell for
good and all!"

"Yes, dear cousin," answered Phœbe; "but, in the mean time, I hear
somebody ringing it!"

When the customer was gone, Hepzibah talked rather vaguely, and at
great length, about a certain Alice Pyncheon, who had been exceedingly
beautiful and accomplished in her lifetime, a hundred years ago. The
fragrance of her rich and delightful character still lingered about the
place where she had lived, as a dried rosebud scents the drawer where it
has withered and perished. This lovely Alice had met with some great and
mysterious calamity, and had grown thin and white, and gradually faded
out of the world. But, even now, she was supposed to haunt the House of
the Seven Gables, and, a great many times,—especially when one of the
Pyncheons was to die,—she had been heard playing sadly and beautifully
on the harpsichord. One of these tunes, just as it had sounded from her
spiritual touch, had been written down by an amateur of music; it was
so exquisitely mournful that nobody, to this day, could bear to hear it
played, unless when a great sorrow had made them know the still profounder sweetness of it.

"Was it the same harpsichord that you showed me?" inquired Phœbe.

"The very same," said Hepzibah. "It was Alice Pyncheon's harpsichord. When I was learning music, my father would never let me open
it. So, as I could only play on my teacher's instrument, I have forgotten
all my music long ago."

Leaving these antique themes, the old lady began to talk about the
daguerreotypist, whom, as he seemed to be a well-meaning and orderly

young man, and in narrow circumstances, she had permitted to take up his residence in one of the seven gables. But, on seeing more of Mr. Holgrave, she hardly knew what to make of him. He had the strangest companions imaginable; men with long beards, and dressed in linen blouses, and other such new-fangled and ill-fitting garments; reformers, temperance lecturers, and all manner of cross-looking philanthropists; community-men, and come-outers, as Hepzibah believed, who acknowledged no law, and ate no solid food, but lived on the scent of other people's cookery, and turned up their noses at the fare. As for the daguerreotypist, she had read a paragraph in a penny paper, the other day, accusing him of making a speech full of wild and disorganizing matter, at a meeting of his banditti-like associates. For her own part, she had reason to believe that he practised animal magnetism, and, if such things were in fashion nowadays, should be apt to suspect him of studying the Black Art up there in his lonesome chamber.

"But, dear cousin," said Phœbe, "if the young man is so dangerous, why do you let him stay? If he does nothing worse, he may set the house on fire!"

"Why, sometimes," answered Hepzibah, "I have seriously made it a question, whether I ought not to send him away. But, with all his oddities, he is a quiet kind of a person, and has such a way of taking hold of one's mind, that, without exactly liking him (for I don't know enough of the young man), I should be sorry to lose sight of him entirely. A woman clings to slight acquaintances when she lives so much alone as I do."

"But if Mr. Holgrave is a lawless person!" remonstrated Phœbe, a part of whose essence it was to keep within the limits of law.

"Oh!" said Hepzibah, carelessly,—for, formal as she was, still, in her life's experience, she had gnashed her teeth against human law,—"I suppose he has a law of his own!"

VI

MAULE'S WELL

AFTER an early tea, the little country-girl strayed into the garden. The enclosure had formerly been very extensive, but was now contracted within small compass, and hemmed about, partly by high wooden fences, and partly by the outbuildings of houses that stood on another street. In its centre was a grass-plat, surrounding a ruinous little structure, which showed just enough of its original design to indicate that it had once been a summer-house. A hop-vine, springing from last year's root, was beginning to clamber over it, but would be long in covering the roof with its green mantle. Three of the seven gables either fronted or looked sideways, with a dark solemnity of aspect, down into the garden.

The black, rich soil had fed itself with the decay of a long period of time; such as fallen leaves, the petals of flowers, and the stalks and seed-vessels of vagrant and lawless plants, more useful after their death than ever while flaunting in the sun. The evil of these departed years would naturally have sprung up again, in such rank weeds (symbolic of the transmitted vices of society) as are always prone to root themselves about human dwellings. Phœbe saw, however, that their growth must have been checked by a degree of careful labor, bestowed daily and systematically on the garden. The white double rose-bush had evidently been propped up anew against the house since the commencement of the season; and a pear-tree and three damson-trees, which, except a row of currant-bushes, constituted the only varieties of fruit, bore marks of the recent amputation of several superfluous or defective limbs. There were also a few species of antique and hereditary flowers, in no very flourishing condition, but scrupulously weeded; as if some person, either out of love or curiosity, had been anxious to bring them to such perfection as they were capable of attaining. The remainder of the garden presented a well-selected assortment of esculent vegetables, in a praiseworthy state of advancement. Summer squashes, almost in their golden blossom; cucumbers, now evincing a tendency to spread away from the main stock, and ramble far and wide; two or three rows of string-beans, and as many more that were about to festoon themselves on poles; tomatoes, occupying a site so sheltered and sunny that the plants were already gigantic, and promised an early and abundant harvest.

Phœbe wondered whose care and toil it could have been that had planted these vegetables, and kept the soil so clean and orderly. Not surely her cousin Hepzibah's, who had no taste nor spirits for the lady-like employment of cultivating flowers, and—with her recluse habits, and tendency to shelter herself within the dismal shadow of the house—would hardly have come forth under the speck of open sky to weed and hoe among the fraternity of beans and squashes.

It being her first day of complete estrangement from rural objects, Phœbe found an unexpected charm in this little nook of grass, and foliage, and aristocratic flowers, and plebeian vegetables. The eye of Heaven seemed to look down into it pleasantly, and with a peculiar smile, as if glad to perceive that nature, elsewhere overwhelmed, and driven out of the dusty town, had here been able to retain a breathing-place. The spot acquired a somewhat wilder grace, and yet a very gentle one, from the fact that a pair of robins had built their nest in the pear-tree, and were making themselves exceedingly busy and happy in the dark intricacy of its boughs. Bees, too,—strange, to say,—had thought it worth their while to come hither, possibly from the range of hives beside some farm-house miles away. How many aërial voyages might they have made, in quest of honey, or honey-laden, betwixt dawn and sunset! Yet, late as it now was, there still arose a pleasant hum out of one or two of the squash-blossoms, in the depths of which these bees were plying their golden labor. There was one other object in the garden which Nature might fairly claim as her inalienable property, in spite of whatever man could do to render it his own. This was a fountain, set round with a rim of old mossy stones, and paved, in its bed, with what appeared to be a sort of mosaic-work of variously colored pebbles. The play and slight agitation of the water, in its upward gush, wrought magically with these variegated pebbles, and made a continually shifting apparition of quaint figures, vanishing too suddenly to be definable. Thence, swelling over the rim of moss-grown stones, the water stole away under the fence, through what we regret to call a gutter, rather than a channel.

Nor must we forget to mention a hen-coop of very reverend antiquity that stood in the farther corner of the garden, not a great way from the fountain. It now contained only Chanticleer, his two wives, and a solitary chicken. All of them were pure specimens of a breed which had been transmitted down as an heirloom in the Pyncheon family, and were said, while in their prime, to have attained almost the size of turkeys, and, on the score of delicate flesh, to be fit for a prince's table. In proof of the authenticity of this legendary renown, Hepzibah could have exhibited the shell of a great egg, which an ostrich need hardly have been ashamed of. Be that as it might, the hens were now scarcely larger than pigeons, and had a queer, rusty, withered aspect, and a gouty kind of movement, and a sleepy and melancholy tone throughout all the variations of their clucking and cackling. It was evident that the race had degenerated, like many a noble race besides, in consequence of too strict a watchfulness to keep it pure. These feathered people had existed too long in their distinct variety; a fact of which the present representatives, judging by their lugubrious deportment, seemed to be aware. They kept themselves alive, unquestionably, and laid now and then an egg, and hatched a chicken; not for any pleasure of their own, but that the world might not absolutely lose what had once been so admirable a breed of fowls. The distinguishing mark of the hens was a crest of lamentably scanty growth, in these latter days, but so oddly and wickedly analogous to Hepzibah's turban, that Phœbe—to the poignant distress of her conscience, but inevitably— was led to fancy a general resemblance betwixt these forlorn bipeds and her respectable relative.

The girl ran into the house to get some crumbs of bread, cold potatoes, and other such scraps as were suitable to the accommodating appetite of fowls. Returning, she gave a peculiar call, which they seemed to recognize. The chicken crept through the pales of the coop and ran, with some show of liveliness, to her feet; while Chanticleer and the ladies of his household regarded her with queer, sidelong glances, and then croaked one to another, as if communicating their sage opinions of her character. So wise, as well as antique, was their aspect, as to give color to the idea, not merely that they were the descendants of a time-honored race but that they had existed, in their individual capacity, ever since the House of the Seven Gables was founded, and were somehow mixed up with its destiny. They were a species of tutelary sprite, or Banshee; although winged and feathered differently from most other guardian angels.

"Here, you odd little chicken!" said Phœbe; "here are some nice crumbs for you!"

The chicken, hereupon, though almost as venerable in appearance as its mother,—possessing, indeed, the whole antiquity of its progenitors in miniature,—mustered vivacity enough to flutter upward and alight on Phœbe's shoulder.

"That little fowl pays you a high compliment!" said a voice behind Phœbe.

Turning quickly, she was surprised at sight of a young man, who had found access into the garden by a door opening out of another gable than that whence she had emerged. He held a hoe in his hand, and, while Phœbe was gone in quest of the crumbs, had begun to busy himself with drawing up fresh earth about the roots of the tomatoes.

"The chicken really treats you like an old acquaintance," continued he, in a quiet way, while a smile made his face pleasanter than Phœbe at first fancied it. "Those venerable personages in the coop, too, seem very affably disposed. You are lucky to be in their good graces so soon! They have known me much longer, but never honor me with any familiarity, though hardly a day passes without my bringing them food. Miss Hepzibah, I suppose, will interweave the fact with her other traditions, and set it down that the fowls know you to be a Pyncheon!"

"The secret is," said Phœbe, smiling, "that I have learned how to talk with hens and chickens."

"Ah, but these hens," answered the young man,—"these hens of aristocratic lineage would scorn to understand the vulgar language of a barnyard fowl. I prefer to think—and so would Miss Hepzibah—that they recognize the family tone. For you are a Pyncheon?"

"My name is Phœbe Pyncheon," said the girl, with a manner of some reserve; for she was aware that her new acquaintance could be no other than the daguerreotypist, of whose lawless propensities the old maid had given her a disagreeable idea. "I did not know that my cousin Hepzibah's garden was under another person's care."

"Yes," said Holgrave, "I dig, and hoe, and weed, in this black old earth, for the sake of refreshing myself with what little nature and simplicity may be left in it, after men have so long sown and reaped here. I turn up the earth by way of pastime. My sober occupation, so far as I have any, is with a lighter material. In short, I make pictures out of sunshine; and, not to be too much dazzled with my own trade, I have prevailed with Miss Hepzibah to let me lodge in one of these dusky gables. It is like a bandage over one's eyes, to come into it. But would you like to see a specimen of my productions?"

"A daguerreotype likeness, do you mean?" asked Phœbe, with less reserve; for, in spite of prejudice, her own youthfulness sprang forward to meet his. "I don't much like pictures of that sort,—they are so hard and stern; besides dodging away from the eye, and trying to escape altogether. They are conscious of looking very unamiable, I suppose, and therefore hate to be seen."

"If you would permit me," said the artist, looking at Phœbe, "I should like to try whether the daguerreotype can bring out disagreeable traits on a perfectly amiable face. But there certainly is truth in what you have said. Most of my likenesses do look unamiable; but the very sufficient reason, I fancy, is, because the originals are so. There is a wonderful insight in Heaven's broad and simple sunshine. While we give it credit only for depicting the merest surface, it actually brings out the secret character with a truth that no painter would ever venture upon, even could he detect it. There is, at least, no flattery in my humble line of art. Now, here is a likeness which I have taken over and over again, and still with no better result. Yet the original wears, to common eyes, a very different expression. It would gratify me to have your judgment on this character."

He exhibited a daguerreotype miniature in a morocco case. Phœbe merely glanced at it, and gave it back.

"I know the face," she replied; "for its stern eye has been following me about all day. It is my Puritan ancestor, who hangs yonder in the parlor. To be sure, you have found some way of copying the portrait without its black velvet cap and gray beard, and have given him a modern coat and satin cravat, instead of his cloak and band. I don't think him improved by your alterations."

"You would have seen other differences had you looked a little longer," said Holgrave, laughing, yet apparently much struck. "I can assure you that this is a modern face, and one which you will very probably meet. Now, the remarkable point is, that the original wears, to the world's eye, —and, for aught I know, to his most intimate friends,—an exceedingly pleasant countenance, indicative of benevolence, openness of heart, sunny good-humor, and other praiseworthy qualities of that cast. The sun, as you see, tells quite another story, and will not be coaxed out of it, after half a dozen patient attempts on my part. Here we have the man, sly, subtle, hard, imperious, and, withal, cold as ice. Look at that eye! Would you like to be at its mercy? At that mouth! Could it ever smile? And yet, if you could only see the benign smile of the original! It is so much the more unfortunate, as he is a public character of some eminence, and the likeness was intended to be engraved."

"Well, I don't wish to see it any more," observed Phœbe, turning away her eyes. "It is certainly very like the old portrait. But my cousin Hepzibah has another picture,—a miniature. If the original is still in the world, I think he might defy the sun to make him look stern and hard."

"You have seen that picture, then!" exclaimed the artist, with an expression of much interest. "I never did, but have a great curiosity to do so. And you judge favorably of the face?"

"There never was a sweeter one," said Phœbe. "It is almost too soft and gentle for a man's."

"Is there nothing wild in the eye?" continued Holgrave, so earnestly that it embarrassed Phœbe, as did also the quiet freedom with which he presumed on their so recent acquaintance. "Is there nothing dark or sinister anywhere? Could you not conceive the original to have been guilty of a great crime?"

"It is nonsense," said Phœbe, a little impatiently, "for us to talk about a picture which you have never seen. You mistake it for some other. A crime, indeed! Since you are a friend of my cousin Hepzibah's, you should ask her to show you the picture."

"It will suit my purpose still better to see the original," replied the daguerreotypist coolly. "As to his character, we need not discuss its points; they have already been settled by a competent tribunal, or one which called itself competent. But, stay! Do not go yet, if you please! I have a proposition to make you."

Phœbe was on the point of retreating, but turned back, with some hesitation; for she did not exactly comprehend his manner, although, on better observation, its feature seemed rather to be lack of ceremony than any approach to offensive rudeness. There was an odd kind of authority, too, in what he now proceeded to say, rather as if the garden were his own than a place to which he was admitted merely by Hepzibah's courtesy.

"If agreeable to you," he observed, "it would give me pleasure to turn over these flowers, and those ancient and respectable fowls, to your care. Coming fresh from country air and occupations, you will soon feel the need of some such out-of-door employment. My own sphere does not so much lie among flowers. You can trim and tend them, therefore, as you please; and I will ask only the least trifle of a blossom, now and then, in exchange for all the good, honest kitchen-vegetables with which I propose to enrich Miss Hepzibah's table. So we will be fellow-laborers, somewhat on the community system."

Silently, and rather surprised at her own compliance, Phœbe accordingly betook herself to weeding a flower-bed, but busied herself still more with cogitations respecting this young man, with whom she so unexpectedly found herself on terms approaching to familiarity. She did not altogether like him. His character perplexed the little country-girl, as it might a more practised observer; for, while the tone of his conversation had generally been playful, the impression left on her mind was that of gravity, and, except as his youth modified it, almost sternness. She rebelled, as it were, against a certain magnetic element in the artist's nature, which he exercised towards her, possibly without being conscious of it.

After a little while, the twilight, deepened by the shadows of the fruit-trees and the surrounding buildings, threw an obscurity over the garden.

"There," said Holgrave, "it is time to give over work! That last stroke of the hoe has cut off a beanstalk. Good-night, Miss Phœbe Pyncheon! Any bright day, if you will put one of those rosebuds in your hair, and come to my rooms in Central Street, I will seize the purest ray of sunshine, and make a picture of the flower and its wearer."

He retired towards his own solitary gable, but turned his head, on reaching the door, and called to Phœbe, with a tone which certainly had laughter in it, yet which seemed to be more than half in earnest.

"Be careful not to drink at Maule's well!" said he. "Neither drink nor bathe your face in it!"

"Maule's well!" answered Phœbe. "Is that it with the rim of mossy stones? I have no thought of drinking there,—but why not?"

"Oh," rejoined the daguerreotypist, "because, like an old lady's cup of tea, it is water bewitched!"

He vanished; and Phœbe, lingering a moment, saw a glimmering light, and then the steady beam of a lamp, in a chamber of the gable. On returning into Hepzibah's apartment of the house, she found the low-studded parlor so dim and dusky that her eyes could not penetrate the interior. She was indistinctly aware, however, that the gaunt figure of the old gentlewoman was sitting in one of the straight-backed chairs, a little withdrawn from the window, the faint gleam of which showed the blanched paleness of her cheek, turned sideway towards a corner.

"Shall I light a lamp, Cousin Hepzibah?" she asked.

"Do, if you please, my dear child," answered Hepzibah. "But put it on the table in the corner of the passage. My eyes are weak; and I can seldom bear the lamplight on them."

What an instrument is the human voice! How wonderfully responsive to every emotion of the human soul! In Hepzibah's tone, at that moment, there was a certain rich depth and moisture, as if the words, commonplace as they were, had been steeped in the warmth of her heart. Again, while lighting the lamp in the kitchen, Phœbe fancied that her cousin spoke to her.

"In a moment, cousin!" answered the girl. "These matches just glimmer, and go out."

But, instead of a response from Hepzibah, she seemed to hear the murmur of an unknown voice. It was strangely indistinct, however, and less like articulate words than an unshaped sound, such as would be the utterance of feeling and sympathy, rather than of the intellect. So vague was it, that its impression or echo in Phœbe's mind was that of unreality. She concluded that she must have mistaken some other sound for that of the human voice; or else that it was altogether in her fancy.

She set the lighted lamp in the passage, and again entered the parlor. Hepzibah's form, though its sable outline mingled with the dusk, was now less imperfectly visible. In the remoter parts of the room, however, its walls being so ill adapted to reflect light, there was nearly the same obscurity as before.

"Cousin," said Phœbe, "did you speak to me just now?"

"No, child!" replied Hepzibah.

Fewer words than before, but with the same mysterious music in them! Mellow, melancholy, yet not mournful, the tone seemed to gush up out of the deep well of Hepzibah's heart, all steeped in its profoundest emotion. There was a tremor in it, too, that—as all strong feeling is electric

—partly communicated itself to Phœbe. The girl sat silently for a moment. But soon, her senses being very acute, she became conscious of an irregular respiration in an obscure corner of the room. Her physical organization, moreover, being at once delicate and healthy, gave her a perception, operating with almost the effect of a spiritual medium, that somebody was near at hand.

"My dear cousin," asked she, overcoming an indefinable reluctance, "is there not some one in the room with us?"

"Phœbe, my dear little girl," said Hepzibah, after a moment's pause, "you were up betimes, and have been busy all day. Pray go to bed; for I am sure you must need rest. I will sit in the parlor awhile, and collect my thoughts. It has been my custom for more years, child, than you have lived!"

While thus dismissing her, the maiden lady stept forward, kissed Phœbe, and pressed her to her heart, which beat against the girl's bosom with a strong, high, and tumultuous swell. How came there to be so much love in this desolate old heart, that it could afford to well over thus abundantly?

"Good night, cousin," said Phœbe, strangely affected by Hepzibah's manner. "If you begin to love me, I am glad!"

She retired to her chamber, but did not soon fall asleep, nor then very profoundly. At some uncertain period in the depths of night, and, as it were, through the thin veil of a dream, she was conscious of a footstep mounting the stairs heavily, but not with force and decision. The voice of Hepzibah, with a hush through it, was going up along with the footsteps; and, again, responsive to her cousin's voice, Phœbe heard that strange, vague murmur, which might be likened to an indistinct shadow of human utterance.

## VII

### THE GUEST

WHEN Phœbe awoke,—which she did with the early twittering of the conjugal couple of robins in the pear-tree,—she heard movements below stairs, and, hastening down, found Hepzibah already in the kitchen. She stood by a window, holding a book in close contiguity to her nose, as if with the hope of gaining an olfactory acquaintance with its contents, since her imperfect vision made it not very easy to read them. If any volume could have manifested its essential wisdom in the mode suggested, it would certainly have been the one now in Hepzibah's hand; and the kitchen, in such an event, would forthwith have steamed with the fragrance of venison, turkeys, capons, larded partridges, puddings, cakes, and Christmas pies, in all manner of elaborate mixture and concoction. It was a cookery book, full of innumerable old fashions of English dishes, and illustrated with engravings, which represented the arrangements of the table at such banquets as it might have befitted a nobleman to give in the great hall of his castle. And, amid these rich and potent devices of the culinary art (not one of which, probably, had been tested, within the memory of any man's grandfather), poor Hepzibah was seeking for some nimble little titbit, which, with what skill she had, and such materials as were at hand, she might toss up for breakfast.

Soon, with a deep sigh, she put aside the savory volume, and inquired, of Phœbe whether old Speckle, as she called one of the hens, had laid an egg the preceding day. Phœbe ran to see, but returned without the expected treasure in her hand. At that instant, however, the blast of a fish-dealer's conch was heard, announcing his approach along the street. With energetic raps at the shop-window, Hepzibah summoned the man in, and made purchase of what he warranted as the finest mackerel in his cart, and as fat a one as ever he felt with his finger so early in the season. Requesting Phœbe to roast some coffee,—which she casually observed was the real Mocha, and so long kept that each of the small berries ought to be worth its weight in gold,—the maiden lady heaped fuel into the vast receptacle of the ancient fireplace in such quantity as soon to drive the lingering dusk out of the kitchen. The country-girl, willing to give her utmost assistance, proposed to make an Indian cake, after her mother's peculiar method, of easy manufacture, and which she could vouch for as possessing a richness, and, if rightly prepared, a delicacy, unequalled by any other mode of breakfast-cake. Hepzibah gladly assenting, the kitchen was soon the scene of savory preparation. Perchance, amid their proper element of smoke, which eddied forth from the ill-constructed chimney, the ghosts of departed cook-maids looked wonderingly on, or peeped down the great breadth of the flue, despising the simplicity of the projected meal, yet ineffectually pining to thrust their shadowy hands into each inchoate dish. The half-starved rats, at any rate, stole visibly out of their hiding-places, and sat on their hind-legs, snuffing the fumy atmosphere, and wistfully awaiting an opportunity to nibble.

Hepzibah had no natural turn for cookery, and, to say the truth, had fairly incurred her present meagreness by often choosing to go without her dinner rather than be attendant on the rotation of the spit, or ebullition of the pot. Her zeal over the fire, therefore, was quite an heroic test of sentiment. It was touching, and positively worthy of tears (if Phœbe, the only spectator, except the rats and ghosts aforesaid, had not been better employed than in shedding them), to see her rake out a bed of fresh and glowing coals, and proceed to broil the mackerel. Her usually pale cheeks were all ablaze with heat and hurry. She watched the fish with as much tender care and minuteness of attention as if,—we know not how to express it otherwise,—as if her own heart were on the gridiron, and her immortal happiness were involved in its being done precisely to a turn!

Life, within doors, has few pleasanter prospects than a neatly arranged and well-provisioned breakfast-table. We come to it freshly, in the dewy youth of the day, and when our spiritual and sensual elements are in better accord than at a later period; so that the material delights of the morning meal are capable of being fully enjoyed, without any very grievous reproaches, whether gastric or conscientious, for yielding even a trifle overmuch to the animal department of our nature. The thoughts, too, that run around the ring of familiar guests have a piquancy and mirthfulness, and oftentimes a vivid truth, which more rarely find their way into the elaborate intercourse of dinner. Hepzibah's small and ancient table, supported on its slender and graceful legs, and covered with a cloth of the richest damask, looked worthy to be the scene and centre of one of the cheerfullest of parties. The vapor of the broiled fish arose like incense from the shrine of a barbarian idol, while the fragrance of the Mocha might have gratified the nostrils of a tutelary Lar, or whatever power has scope over a modern breakfast-table. Phœbe's Indian cakes were the sweetest offering of all,—in their hue befitting the rustic altars of the innocent and golden age,—or, so brightly yellow were they, resembling some of the bread which was changed to glistening gold when Midas tried to eat it. The butter must not be forgotten,—butter which Phœbe herself had churned, in her own rural home, and brought it to her cousin as a propitiatory gift,—smelling of clover-blossoms, and diffusing the charm of pastoral scenery through the dark-panelled parlor. All this, with the quaint gorgeousness of the old china cups and saucers, and the crested spoons, and a silver cream-jug (Hepzibah's only other article of plate, and shaped like the rudest porringer), set out a board at which the stateliest of old Colonel Pyncheon's guests need not have scorned to take his place. But the Puritan's face scowled down out of the picture, as if nothing on the table pleased his appetite.

By way of contributing what grace she could, Phœbe gathered some roses and a few other flowers, possessing either scent or beauty, and arranged them in a glass pitcher, which, having long ago lost its handle, was so much the fitter for a flower-vase. The early sunshine—as fresh as that which peeped into Eve's bower while she and Adam sat at breakfast there —came twinkling through the branches of the pear-tree, and fell quite across the table. All was now ready. There were chairs and plates for three. A chair and plate for Hepzibah,—the same for Phœbe,—but what other guest did her cousin look for?

Throughout this preparation there had been a constant tremor in Hepzibah's frame; an agitation so powerful that Phœbe could see the quivering of her gaunt shadow, as thrown by the firelight on the kitchen wall, or by the sunshine on the parlor floor. Its manifestations were so various, and agreed so little with one another, that the girl knew not what to make of it. Sometimes it seemed an ecstasy of delight and happiness. At such moments, Hepzibah would fling out her arms, and infold Phœbe in them, and kiss her cheek as tenderly as ever her mother had; she appeared to do so by an inevitable impulse, and as if her bosom were oppressed with tenderness, of which she must needs pour out a little, in order to gain breathing-room. The next moment, without any visible cause for the change, her unwonted joy shrank back, appalled, as it were, and clothed itself in mourning; or it ran and hid itself, so to speak, in the dungeon of her heart, where it had long lain chained, while a cold, spectral sorrow took the place of the imprisoned joy, that was afraid to be enfranchised,—a sorrow as black as that was bright. She often broke into a little, nervous, hysteric laugh, more touching than any tears could be; and forthwith, as if to try which was the most touching, a gush of tears would follow; or perhaps the laughter and tears came both at once, and surrounded our poor Hepzibah, in a moral sense, with a kind of pale, dim rainbow. Towards Phœbe, as we have said, she was affectionate,—far tenderer than ever before, in their brief acquaintance, except for that one kiss on the preceding night,—yet with a continually recurring pettishness and irritability. She would speak sharply to her; then, throwing aside all the starched reserve of her ordinary manner, ask pardon, and the next instant renew the just-forgiven injury.

At last, when their mutual labor was all finished, she took Phœbe's hand in her own trembling one.

"Bear with me, my dear child," she cried; "for truly my heart is full to the brim! Bear with me; for I love you Phœbe, though I speak so roughly! Think nothing of it, dearest child! By and by, I shall be kind, and only kind!"

"My dearest cousin, cannot you tell me what has happened?" asked Phœbe, with a sunny and tearful sympathy. "What is it that moves you so?"

"Hush! hush! He is coming!" whispered Hepzibah, hastily wiping her eyes. "Let him see you first, Phœbe; for you are young and rosy, and cannot help letting a smile break out whether or no. He always liked bright faces! And mine is old now, and the tears are hardly dry on it. He never could abide tears. There; draw the curtain a little, so that the shadow may fall across his side of the table! But let there be a good deal of sunshine, too; for he never was fond of gloom, as some people are. He has had but little sunshine in his life,—poor Clifford,—and, oh, what a black shadow! Poor, poor Clifford!"

Thus murmuring in an undertone, as if speaking rather to her own heart than to Phœbe, the old gentlewoman stepped on tiptoe about the room, making such arrangements as suggested themselves at the crisis.

Meanwhile there was a step in the passage-way, above stairs. Phœbe recognized it as the same which had passed upward, as through her dream, in the night-time. The approaching guest, whoever it might be, appeared to pause at the head of the staircase; he paused twice or thrice in the descent; he paused again at the foot. Each time, the delay seemed to be without purpose, but rather from a forgetfulness of the purpose which had set him in motion, or as if the person's feet came involuntarily to a stand-still because the motive-power was too feeble to sustain his progress. Finally, he made a long pause at the threshold of the parlor. He took hold of the knob of the door; then loosened his grasp without opening it. Hepzibah, her hands convulsively clasped, stood gazing at the entrance.

"Dear Cousin Hepzibah, pray don't look so!" said Phœbe, trembling; for her cousin's emotion, and this mysteriously reluctant step, made her feel as if a ghost were coming into the room. "You really frighten me! Is something awful going to happen?"

"Hush!" whispered Hepzibah. "Be cheerful! whatever may happen, be nothing but cheerful!"

The final pause at the threshold proved so long, that Hepzibah, unable to endure the suspense, rushed forward, threw open the door, and led in the stranger by the hand. At the first glance, Phœbe saw an elderly personage, in an old-fashioned dressing-gown of faded damask, and wearing his gray or almost white hair of an unusual length. It quite overshadowed his forehead, except when he thrust it back, and stared vaguely about the room. After a very brief inspection of his face, it was easy to conceive that his footstep must necessarily be such an one as that which, slowly, and with as indefinite an aim as a child's first journey across a floor, had just brought him hitherward. Yet there were no tokens that his physical strength might not have sufficed for a free and determined gait. It was the spirit of the man that could not walk. The expression of his countenance —while, notwithstanding, it had the light of reason in it—seemed to waver, and glimmer, and nearly to die away, and feebly to recover itself again. It was like a flame which we see twinkling among half-extinguished embers; we gaze at it more intently than if it were a positive blaze, gushing vividly upward,—more intently, but with a certain impatience, as if it ought either to kindle itself into satisfactory splendor, or be at once extinguished.

For an instant after entering the room, the guest stood still, retaining Hepzibah's hand, instinctively, as a child does that of the grown person who guides it. He saw Phœbe, however, and caught an illumination from her youthful and pleasant aspect, which, indeed, threw a cheerfulness about the parlor, like the circle of reflected brilliancy around the glass vase of flowers that was standing in the sunshine. He made a salutation, or, to speak nearer the truth, an ill-defined, abortive attempt at courtesy. Imperfect as it was, however, it conveyed an idea, or, at least, gave a hint, of indescribable grace, such as no practised art of external manners could have attained. It was too slight to seize upon at the instant; yet, as recollected afterwards, seemed to transfigure the whole man.

"Dear Clifford," said Hepzibah, in the tone with which one soothes a wayward infant, "this is our cousin Phœbe,—little Phœbe Pyncheon,—Arthur's only child, you know. She has come from the country to stay with us awhile; for our old house has grown to be very lonely now."

"Phœbe?—Phœbe Pyncheon?—Phœbe?" repeated the guest, with a strange, sluggish, ill-defined utterance. "Arthur's child! Ah, I forget! No matter! She is very welcome!"

"Come, dear Clifford, take this chair," said Hepzibah, leading him to his place. "Pray, Phœbe, lower the curtain a very little more. Now let us begin breakfast."

The guest seated himself in the place assigned him, and looked strangely around. He was evidently trying to grapple with the present scene, and bring it home to his mind with a more satisfactory distinctness. He desired to be certain, at least, that he was here, in the low-studded, cross-beamed, oaken-panelled parlor, and not in some other spot, which had stereotyped itself into his senses. But the effort was too great to be sustained with more than a fragmentary success. Continually, as we may express it, he faded away out of his place; or, in other words, his mind and consciousness took their departure, leaving his wasted, gray, and melancholy figure—a substantial emptiness, a material ghost—to occupy his seat at table. Again, after a blank moment, there would be a flickering taper-gleam in his eyeballs. It betokened that his spiritual part had returned, and was doing its best to kindle the heart's household fire, and light up intellectual lamps in the dark and ruinous mansion, where it was doomed to be a forlorn inhabitant.

At one of these moments of less torpid, yet still imperfect animation, Phœbe became convinced of what she had at first rejected as too extravagant and startling an idea. She saw that the person before her must have been the original of the beautiful miniature in her cousin Hepzibah's possession. Indeed, with a feminine eye for costume, she had at once identified the damask dressing-gown, which enveloped him, as the same in figure, material, and fashion, with that so elaborately represented in the picture. This old, faded garment, with all its pristine brilliancy extinct, seemed, in some indescribable way, to translate the wearer's untold misfortune, and make it perceptible to the beholder's eye. It was the better to be discerned, by this exterior type, how worn and old were the soul's more immediate garments; that form and countenance, the beauty and grace of which had almost transcended the skill of the most exquisite of artists. It could the more adequately be known that the soul of the man must have suffered some miserable wrong, from its earthly experience. There he seemed to sit, with a dim veil of decay and ruin betwixt him and the world, but through which, at flitting intervals, might be caught the same expression, so refined, so softly imaginative, which Malbone—venturing a happy touch, with suspended breath—had imparted to the miniature! There had been something so innately characteristic in this look, that all the dusky years, and the burden of unfit calamity which had fallen upon him, did not suffice utterly to destroy it.

Hepzibah had now poured out a cup of deliciously fragrant coffee, and presented it to her guest. As his eyes met hers, he seemed bewildered and disquieted.

"Is this you, Hepzibah?" he murmured, sadly; then, more apart, and perhaps unconscious that he was overheard, "How changed! how changed! And is she angry with me? Why does she bend her brow so?"

Poor Hepzibah! It was that wretched scowl which time and her near-sightedness, and the fret of inward discomfort, had rendered so habitual that any vehemence of mood invariably evoked it. But at the indistinct murmur of his words her whole face grew tender, and even lovely, with sorrowful affection; the harshness of her features disappeared, as it were, behind the warm and misty glow.

"Angry!" she repeated; "angry with you, Clifford!"

Her tone, as she uttered the exclamation, had a plaintive and really exquisite melody thrilling through it, yet without subduing a certain something which an obtuse auditor might still have mistaken for asperity. It was as if some transcendent musician should draw a soul-thrilling sweetness out of a cracked instrument, which makes its physical imperfection heard in the midst of ethereal harmony,—so deep was the sensibility that found an organ in Hepzibah's voice!

"There is nothing but love, here, Clifford," she added,—"nothing but love! You are at home!"

The guest responded to her tone by a smile, which did not half light up his face. Feeble as it was, however, and gone in a moment, it had a charm of wonderful beauty. It was followed by a coarser expression; or one that had the effect of coarseness on the fine mould and outline of his countenance, because there was nothing intellectual to temper it. It was a look of appetite. He ate food with what might almost be termed voracity; and seemed to forget himself, Hepzibah, the young girl, and everything else around him, in the sensual enjoyment which the bountifully spread table afforded. In his natural system, though high-wrought and delicately refined, a sensibility to the delights of the palate was probably inherent. It would have been kept in check, however, and even converted into an accomplishment, and one of the thousand modes of intellectual culture, had his more ethereal characteristics retained their vigor. But as it existed now, the effect was painful and made Phœbe droop her eyes.

In a little while the guest became sensible of the fragrance of the yet untasted coffee. He quaffed it eagerly. The subtle essence acted on him like a charmed draught, and caused the opaque substance of his animal being to grow transparent, or, at least, translucent; so that a spiritual gleam was transmitted through it, with a clearer lustre than hitherto.

"More, more!" he cried, with nervous haste in his utterance, as if anxious to retain his grasp of what sought to escape him. "This is what I need! Give me more!"

Under this delicate and powerful influence he sat more erect, and looked out from his eyes with a glance that took note of what it rested on. It was not so much that his expression grew more intellectual; this, though it had its share, was not the most peculiar effect. Neither was what we call the moral nature so forcibly awakened as to present itself in remarkable prominence. But a certain fine temper of being was now not brought out in full relief, but changeably and imperfectly betrayed, of which it was the function to deal with all beautiful and enjoyable things. In a character where it should exist as the chief attribute, it would bestow on its possessor an exquisite taste, and an enviable susceptibility of happiness. Beauty would be his life; his aspirations would all tend toward it; and, allowing his frame and physical organs to be in consonance, his own developments would likewise be beautiful. Such a man should have nothing to do with sorrow; nothing with strife; nothing with the martyrdom which, in an infinite variety of shapes, awaits those who have the heart, and will, and conscience, to fight a battle with the world. To these heroic tempers, such martyrdom is the richest meed in the world's gift. To the individual before us, it could only be a grief, intense in due proportion with the severity of the infliction. He had no right to be a martyr; and, beholding him so fit to be happy and so feeble for all other purposes, a generous, strong, and noble spirit would methinks, have been ready to sacrifice what little enjoyment it might have planned for itself,—it would have flung down the hopes, so paltry in its regard,—if thereby the wintry blasts of our rude sphere might come tempered to such a man.

Not to speak it harshly or scornfully, it seemed Clifford's nature to be a Sybarite. It was perceptible, even there, in the dark old parlor, in the inevitable polarity with which his eyes were attracted towards the quivering play of sunbeams through the shadowy foliage. It was seen in his appreciating notice of the vase of flowers, the scent of which he inhaled with a zest almost peculiar to a physical organization so refined that spiritual ingredients are moulded in with it. It was betrayed in the unconscious smile with which he regarded Phœbe, whose fresh and maidenly figure was both sunshine and flowers,—their essence, in a prettier and more agreeable mode of manifestation. Not less evident was this love and necessity for the Beautiful, in the instinctive caution with which, even so soon, his eyes turned away from his hostess, and wandered to any quarter rather than come back. It was Hepzibah's misfortune,—not Clifford's fault. How could he,—so yellow as she was, so wrinkled, so sad of mien, with that odd uncouthness of a turban on her head, and that most perverse of scowls contorting her brow,—how could he love to gaze at her? But, did he owe her no affection for so much as she had silently given? He owed her nothing. A nature like Clifford's can contract no debts of that kind. It is—we say it without censure, nor in diminution of the claim which it indefeasibly possesses on beings of another mould—it is always selfish in its essence; and we must give it leave to be so, and heap up our heroic and disinterested love upon it so much the more, without a recompense. Poor Hepzibah knew this truth, or, at least, acted on the instinct of it. So long estranged from what was lovely as Clifford had been, she rejoiced—rejoiced, though with a present sigh, and a secret purpose to shed tears in her own chamber—that he had brighter objects now before his eyes than her aged and uncomely features. They never possessed a charm; and if they had, the canker of her grief for him would long since have destroyed it.

The guest leaned back in his chair. Mingled in his countenance with a dreamy delight, there was a troubled look of effort and unrest. He was seeking to make himself more fully sensible of the scene around him; or, perhaps, dreading it to be a dream, or a play of imagination, was vexing the fair moment with a struggle for some added brilliancy and more durable illusion.

"How pleasant!—How delightful!" he murmured, but not as if addressing any one. "Will it last? How balmy the atmosphere through that open window! An open window! How beautiful that play of sunshine! Those flowers, how very fragrant! That young girl's face, how cheerful, how blooming!—a flower with the dew on it, and sunbeams in the dewdrops! Ah! this must be all a dream! A dream! A dream! But it has quite hidden the four stone walls!"

Then his face darkened, as if the shadow of a cavern or a dungeon had come over it; there was no more light in its expression than might have come through the iron grates of a prison window,—still lessening, too, as if he were sinking farther into the depths. Phœbe (being of that quickness and activity of temperament that she seldom long refrained from taking a part, and generally a good one, in what was going forward) now felt herself moved to address the stranger.

"Here is a new kind of rose, which I found this morning in the garden," said she, choosing a small crimson one from among the flowers in the vase. "There will be but five or six on the bush this season. This is the most perfect of them all; not a speck of blight or mildew in it. And how sweet it is!—sweet like no other rose! One can never forget that scent!"

"Ah!—let me see!—let me hold it!" cried the guest, eagerly seizing the flower, which, by the spell peculiar to remembered odors, brought innumerable associations along with the fragrance that it exhaled. "Thank you! This has done me good. I remember how I used to prize this flower, —long ago, I suppose, very long ago!—or was it only yesterday? It makes me feel young again! Am I young? Either this remembrance is singularly distinct, or this consciousness strangely dim! But how kind of the fair young girl! Thank you! Thank you!"

The favorable excitement derived from this little crimson rose afforded Clifford the brightest moment which he enjoyed at the breakfast-table. It might have lasted longer, but that his eyes happened, soon afterwards, to rest on the face of the old Puritan, who, out of his dingy frame and lustreless canvas, was looking down on the scene like a ghost, and a most illtempered and ungenial one. The guest made an impatient gesture of the hand, and addressed Hepzibah with what might easily be recognized as the licensed irritability of a petted member of the family.

"Hepzibah!—Hepzibah!" cried he with no little force and distinctness, "why do you keep that odious picture on the wall? Yes, yes!—that is precisely your taste! I have told you, a thousand times, that it was the evil genius of the house!—my evil genius particularly! Take it down, at once!"

"Dear Clifford," said Hepzibah, sadly, "you know it cannot be!"

"Then, at all events," continued he, still speaking with some energy, "pray cover it with a crimson curtain, broad enough to hang in folds, and with a golden border and tassels. I cannot bear it! It must not stare me in the face!"

"Yes, dear Clifford, the picture shall be covered," said Hepzibah, soothingly. "There is a crimson curtain in a trunk above stairs,—a little faded and moth-eaten, I'm afraid,—but Phœbe and I will do wonders with it."

"This very day, remember!" said he; and then added, in a low, self-communing voice, "Why should we live in this dismal house at all? Why not go to the South of France?—to Italy?—Paris, Naples, Venice, Rome? Hepzibah will say we have not the means. A droll idea that!"

He smiled to himself, and threw a glance of fine sarcastic meaning towards Hepzibah.

But the several moods of feeling, faintly as they were marked, through which he had passed, occurring in so brief an interval of time, had evidently wearied the stranger. He was probably accustomed to a sad monotony of life, not so much flowing in a stream, however sluggish, as stagnating in a pool around his feet. A slumberous veil diffused itself over his countenance, and had an effect, morally speaking, on its naturally delicate and elegant outline, like that which a brooding mist, with no sunshine in it, throws over the features of a landscape. He appeared to become grosser,—almost cloddish. If aught of interest or beauty—even ruined beauty—had heretofore been visible in this man, the beholder might now begin to doubt it, and to accuse his own imagination of deluding him with whatever grace had flickered over that visage, and whatever exquisite lustre had gleamed in those filmy eyes.

Before he had quite sunken away, however, the sharp and peevish tinkle of the shop-bell made itself audible. Striking most disagreeably on Clifford's auditory organs and the characteristic sensibility of his nerves, it caused him to start upright out of his chair.

"Good heavens, Hepzibah! what horrible disturbance have we now in the house?" cried he, wreaking his resentful impatience—as a matter of course, and a custom of old—on the one person in the world that loved him. "I have never heard such a hateful clamor! Why do you permit it? In the name of all dissonance, what can it be?"

It was very remarkable into what prominent relief—even as if a dim picture should leap suddenly from its canvas—Clifford's character was thrown by this apparently trifling annoyance. The secret was, that an individual of his temper can always be pricked more acutely through his sense of the beautiful and harmonious than through his heart. It is even possible—for similar cases have often happened—that if Clifford, in his foregoing life, had enjoyed the means of cultivating his taste to its utmost perfectibility, that subtile attribute might, before this period, have completely eaten out or filed away his affections. Shall we venture to pronounce, therefore, that his long and black calamity may not have had a redeeming drop of mercy at the bottom?

"Dear Clifford, I wish I could keep the sound from your ears," said Hepzibah, patiently, but reddening with a painful suffusion of shame. "It is very disagreeable even to me. But, do you know, Clifford, I have something to tell you? This ugly noise,—pray run, Phœbe, and see who is there!—this naughty little tinkle is nothing but our shop-bell!"

"Shop-bell!" repeated Clifford, with a bewildered stare.

"Yes, our shop-bell," said Hepzibah, a certain natural dignity, mingled with deep emotion, now asserting itself in her manner. "For you must know, dearest Clifford, that we are very poor. And there was no other re-source, but either to accept assistance from a hand that I would push aside (and so would you!) were it to offer bread when we were dying for it,—no help, save from him, or else to earn our subsistence with my own hands! Alone, I might have been content to starve. But you were to be given back to me! Do you think, then, dear Clifford," added she, with a wretched smile, "that I have brought an irretrievable disgrace on the old house, by opening a little shop in the front gable? Our great-great-grand-father did the same, when there was far less need! Are you ashamed of me?"

"Shame! Disgrace! Do you speak these words to me, Hepzibah?" said Clifford,—not angrily, however; for when a man's spirit has been thor-oughly crushed, he may be peevish at small offences, but never resentful of great ones. So he spoke with only a grieved emotion. "It was not kind to say so, Hepzibah! What shame can befall me now?"

And then the unnerved man—he that had been born for enjoyment, but had met a doom so very wretched—burst into a woman's passion of tears. It was but of brief continuance, however; soon leaving him in a quiescent, and, to judge by his countenance, not an uncomfortable state. From this mood, too, he partially rallied for an instant, and looked at Hepzibah with a smile, the keen, half-derisory purport of which was a puzzle to her.

"Are we so very poor, Hepzibah?" said he.

Finally, his chair being deep and softly cushioned, Clifford fell asleep. Hearing the more regular rise and fall of his breath (which, however, even then, instead of being strong and full, had a feeble kind of tremor, corre-sponding with the lack of vigor in his character),—hearing these tokens of settled slumber, Hepzibah seized the opportunity to peruse his face more attentively than she had yet dared to do. Her heart melted away in tears; her profoundest spirit sent forth a moaning voice, low, gentle, but inexpressibly sad. In this depth of grief and pity she felt that there was no irreverence in gazing at his altered, aged, faded, ruined face. But no soon-er was she a little relieved than her conscience smote her for gazing curi-ously at him, now that he was so changed; and, turning hastily away, Hepzibah let down the curtain over the sunny window, and left Clifford to slumber there.

## VIII

### THE PYNCHEON OF TO-DAY

PHŒBE, on entering the shop, beheld there the already familiar face of the little devourer—if we can reckon his mighty deeds aright—of Jim Crow, the elephant, the camel, the dromedaries, and the locomotive. Having expended his private fortune, on the two preceding days, in the purchase of the above unheard-of luxuries, the young gentleman's present errand was on the part of his mother, in quest of three eggs and half a pound of raisins. These articles Phœbe accordingly supplied, and, as a mark of gratitude for his previous patronage, and a slight super-added morsel after breakfast, put likewise into his hand a whale! The great fish, reversing his experience with the prophet of Nineveh, immediately began his progress down the same red pathway of fate whither so varied a caravan had preceded him. This remarkable urchin, in truth, was the very emblem of old Father Time, both in respect of his all-devouring appetite for men and things, and because he, as well as Time, after ingulfing thus much of creation, looked almost as youthful as if he had been just that moment made.

After partly closing the door, the child turned back, and mumbled something to Phœbe, which, as the whale was but half disposed of, she could not perfectly understand.

"What did you say, my little fellow?" asked she.

"Mother wants to know," repeated Ned Higgins, more distinctly, "how Old Maid Pyncheon's brother does? Folks say he has got home."

"My cousin Hepzibah's brother!" exclaimed Phœbe, surprised at this sudden explanation of the relationship between Hepzibah and her guest. "Her brother! And where can he have been?"

The little boy only put his thumb to his broad snub-nose, with that look of shrewdness which a child, spending much of his time in the street, so soon learns to throw over his features, however unintelligent in themselves. Then as Phœbe continued to gaze at him, without answering his mother's message, he took his departure.

As the child went down the steps, a gentleman ascended them, and made his entrance into the shop. It was the portly, and, had it possessed the advantage of a little more height, would have been the stately figure of a man considerably in the decline of life, dressed in a black suit of some thin stuff, resembling broad-cloth as closely as possible. A gold-headed cane, of rare Oriental wood, added materially to the high respectability of his aspect, as did also a neckcloth of the utmost snowy purity, and the conscientious polish of his boots. His dark, square countenance, with its almost shaggy depth of eyebrows, was naturally impressive, and would, perhaps, have been rather stern, had not the gentleman considerately taken upon himself to mitigate the harsh effect by a look of exceeding good-humor and benevolence. Owing, however, to a somewhat massive accumulation of animal substance about the lower region of his face, the look was, perhaps, unctuous, rather than spiritual, and had, so to speak, a kind of fleshly effulgence, not altogether so satisfactory as he doubtless intended it to be. A susceptible observer, at any rate, might have regarded it as affording very little evidence of the general benignity of soul whereof it purported to be the outward reflection. And if the observer chanced to be ill-natured, as well as acute and susceptible, he would probably suspect that the smile on the gentleman's face was a good deal akin to the shine on his boots, and that each must have cost him and his boot-black, respectively, a good deal of hard labor to bring out and preserve them.

As the stranger entered the little shop, where the projection of the second story and the thick foliage of the elm-tree, as well as the commodities at the window, created a sort of gray medium, his smile grew as intense as if he had set his heart on counteracting the whole gloom of the atmosphere (besides any moral gloom pertaining to Hepzibah and her inmates) by the unassisted light of his countenance. On perceiving a young rosebud of a girl, instead of the gaunt presence of the old maid, a look of surprise was manifest. He at first knit his brows; then smiled with more unctuous benignity than ever.

"Ah, I see how it is!" said he, in a deep voice,—a voice which, had it come from the throat of an uncultivated man, would have been gruff, but, by dint of careful training, was now sufficiently agreeable,—"I was not aware that Miss Hepzibah Pyncheon had commenced business under such favorable auspices. You are her assistant, I suppose?"

"I certainly am," answered Phœbe, and added, with a little air of ladylike assumption (for, civil as the gentleman was, he evidently took her to be a young person serving for wages), "I am a cousin of Miss Hepzibah, on a visit to her."

"Her cousin?—and from the country? Pray pardon me, then," said the gentleman, bowing and smiling, as Phœbe never had been bowed to nor smiled on before; "in that case, we must be better acquainted; for, unless I am sadly mistaken, you are my own little kinswoman likewise! Let me see,—Mary?—Dolly?—Phœbe?—yes, Phœbe is the name! Is it possible that you are Phœbe Pyncheon, only child of my dear cousin and classmate, Arthur? Ah, I see your father now, about your mouth! Yes, yes! we must be better acquainted! I am your kinsman, my dear. Surely you must have heard of Judge Pyncheon?"

As Phœbe courtesied in reply, the Judge bent forward, with the pardonable and even praiseworthy purpose—considering the nearness of blood, and the difference of age—of bestowing on his young relative a kiss of acknowledged kindred and natural affection. Unfortunately (without design, or only with such instinctive design as gives no account of itself to the intellect) Phœbe, just at the critical moment, drew back; so that her highly respectable kinsman, with his body bent over the counter, and his lips protruded, was betrayed into the rather absurd predicament of kissing the empty air. It was a modern parallel to the case of Ixion embracing a cloud, and was so much the more ridiculous, as the Judge prided himself on eschewing all airy matter, and never mistaking a shadow for a substance. The truth was,—and it is Phœbe's only excuse,—that, although Judge Pyncheon's glowing benignity might not be absolutely unpleasant to the feminine beholder, with the width of a street, or even an ordinary-sized room, interposed between, yet it became quite too intense, when this dark, full-fed physiognomy (so roughly bearded, too, that no razor could ever make it smooth) sought to bring itself into actual contact with the object of its regards. The man, the sex, somehow or other, was entirely too prominent in the Judge's demonstrations of that sort. Phœbe's eyes sank, and, without knowing why, she felt herself blushing deeply under his look. Yet she had been kissed before, and without any particular squeamishness, by perhaps half a dozen different cousins, younger as well as older than this dark-browed, grisly-bearded, white-neck-clothed, and unctuously-benevolent Judge! Then, why not by him?

On raising her eyes, Phœbe was startled by the change in Judge Pyncheon's face. It was quite as striking, allowing for the difference of scale, as that betwixt a landscape under a broad sunshine and just before a thunder-storm; not that it had the passionate intensity of the latter aspect, but was cold, hard, immitigable, like a day-long brooding cloud.

"Dear me! what is to be done now?" thought the country-girl to herself. "He looks as if there were nothing softer in him than a rock, nor milder than the east wind! I meant no harm! Since he is really my cousin, I would have let him kiss me, if I could!"

Then, all at once, it struck Phœbe that this very Judge Pyncheon was the original of the miniature which the daguerreotypist had shown her in the garden, and that the hard, stern, relentless look, now on his face, was the same that the sun had so inflexibly persisted in bringing out. Was it, therefore, no momentary mood, but, however skilfully concealed, the settled temper of his life? And not merely so, but was it hereditary in him, and transmitted down, as a precious heirloom, from that bearded ancestor, in whose picture both the expression, and, to a singular degree, the features of the modern Judge were shown as by a kind of prophecy? A deeper philosopher than Phœbe might have found something very terrible in this idea. It implied that the weaknesses and defects, the bad passions, the mean tendencies, and the moral diseases which lead to crime are handed down from one generation to another, by a far surer process of transmission than human law has been able to establish in respect to the riches and honors which it seeks to entail upon posterity.

But, as it happened, scarcely had Phœbe's eyes rested again on the Judge's countenance than all its ugly sternness vanished; and she found herself quite overpowered by the sultry, dog-day heat, as it were, of benevolence, which this excellent man diffused out of his great heart into the surrounding atmosphere,—very much like a serpent, which, as a preliminary to fascination, is said to fill the air with his peculiar odor.

"I like that, Cousin Phœbe!" cried he, with an emphatic nod of approbation. "I like it much, my little cousin! You are a good child, and know how to take care of yourself. A young girl—especially if she be a very pretty one—can never be too chary of her lips."

"Indeed, sir," said Phœbe, trying to laugh the matter off, "I did not mean to be unkind."

Nevertheless, whether or no it were entirely owing to the inauspicious commencement of their acquaintance, she still acted under a certain reserve, which was by no means customary to her frank and genial nature. The fantasy would not quit her, that the original Puritan, of whom she had heard so many sombre traditions,—the progenitor of the whole race of New England Pyncheons, the founder of the House of the Seven Gables, and who had died so strangely in it,—had now stept into the shop. In these days of off-hand equipment, the matter was easily enough arranged. On his arrival from the other world, he had merely found it necessary to spend a quarter of an hour at a barber's, who had trimmed down the Puritan's full beard into a pair of grizzled whiskers, then, patronizing a ready-made clothing establishment, he had exchanged his velvet doublet and sable cloak, with the richly worked band under his chin, for a white collar and cravat, coat, vest, and pantaloons; and lastly, putting aside his steel-hilted broadsword to take up a gold-headed cane, the Colonel Pyncheon of two centuries ago steps forward as the Judge of the passing moment!

Of course, Phœbe was far too sensible a girl to entertain this idea in any other way than as matter for a smile. Possibly, also, could the two personages have stood together before her eye, many points of difference would have been perceptible, and perhaps only a general resemblance. The long lapse of intervening years, in a climate so unlike that which had fostered the ancestral Englishman, must inevitably have wrought important changes in the physical system of his descendant. The Judge's volume of muscle could hardly be the same as the Colonel's; there was undoubtedly less beef in him. Though looked upon as a weighty man among his contemporaries in respect of animal substance, and as favored with a remarkable degree of fundamental development, well adapting him for the judicial bench, we conceive that the modern Judge Pyncheon, if weighed in the same balance with his ancestor, would have required at least an old-fashioned fifty-six to keep the scale in equilibrio. Then the Judge's face had lost the ruddy English hue that showed its warmth through all the duskiness of the Colonel's weather-beaten cheek, and had taken a sallow shade, the established complexion of his countrymen. If we mistake not, moreover, a certain quality of nervousness had become more or less manifest, even in so solid a specimen of Puritan descent as the gentleman now under discussion. As one of its effects, it bestowed on his countenance a quicker mobility than the old Englishman's had possessed, and keener vivacity, but at the expense of a sturdier something, on which these acute endowments seemed to act like dissolving acids. This process, for aught we know, may belong to the great system of human progress, which, with every ascending footstep, as it diminishes the necessity for animal force, may be destined gradually to spiritualize us, by refining away our grosser attributes of body. If so, Judge Pyncheon could endure a century or two more of such refinement as well as most other men.

The similarity, intellectual and moral, between the Judge and his ancestor appears to have been at least as strong as the resemblance of mien and feature would afford reason to anticipate. In old Colonel Pyncheon's funeral discourse the clergyman absolutely canonized his deceased parishioner, and opening, as it were, a vista through the roof of the church, and thence through the firmament above, showed him seated, harp in hand, among the crowned choristers of the spiritual world. On his tombstone, too, the record is highly eulogistic; nor does history, so far as he holds a place upon its page, assail the consistency and uprightness of his character. So also, as regards the Judge Pyncheon of to-day, neither clergyman, nor legal critic, nor inscriber of tombstones, nor historian of general or local politics, would venture a word against this eminent person's sincerity as a Christian, or respectability as a man, or integrity as a judge, or courage and faithfulness as the often-tried representative of his political party. But, besides these cold, formal, and empty words of the chisel that inscribes, the voice that speaks, and the pen that writes, for the public eye and for distant time,—and which inevitably lose much of their truth and freedom by the fatal consciousness of so doing,—there were traditions about the ancestor, and private diurnal gossip about the Judge, remarkably accordant in their testimony. It is often instructive to take the woman's, the private and domestic, view of a public man; nor can anything be more curious than the vast discrepancy between portraits intended for engraving and the pencil-sketches that pass from hand to hand behind the original's back.

For example: tradition affirmed that the Puritan had been greedy of wealth; the Judge, too, with all the show of liberal expenditure, was said to be as close-fisted as if his gripe were of iron. The ancestor had clothed himself in a grim assumption of kindliness, a rough heartiness of word and manner, which most people took to be the genuine warmth of nature, making its way through the thick and inflexible hide of a manly character. His descendant, in compliance with the requirements of a nicer age, had etherealized this rude benevolence into that broad benignity of smile, wherewith he shone like a noonday sun along the streets, or glowed like a household fire in the drawing-rooms of his private acquaintance. The Puritan—if not belied by some singular stories, murmured, even at this day, under the narrator's breath—had fallen into certain transgressions to which men of his great animal development, whatever their faith or principles, must continue liable, until they put off impurity, along with the gross earthly substance that involves it. We must not stain our page with any contemporary scandal, to a similar purport, that may have been whispered against the Judge. The Puritan, again, an autocrat in his own household, had worn out three wives, and, merely by the remorseless weight and hardness of his character in the conjugal relation, had sent them, one after another, broken-hearted, to their graves. Here the parallel in some sort, fails. The Judge had wedded but a single wife, and lost her in the third or fourth year of their marriage. There was a fable, however, —for such we choose to consider it, though not impossibly, typical of Judge Pyncheon's marital deportment,—that the lady got her death-blow in the honeymoon, and never smiled again, because her husband compelled her to serve him with coffee every morning at his bedside, in token of fealty to her liege-lord and master.

But it is too fruitful a subject, this of hereditary resemblances,—the frequent recurrence of which, in a direct line, is truly unaccountable, when we consider how large an accumulation of ancestry lies behind every man at the distance of one or two centuries. We shall only add, therefore, that the Puritan—so, at least, says chimney-corner tradition, which often preserves traits of character with marvellous fidelity—was bold, imperious, relentless, crafty; laying his purposes deep, and following them out with an inveteracy of pursuit that knew neither rest nor conscience; trampling on the weak, and, when essential to his ends, doing his utmost to beat down the strong. Whether the Judge in any degree resembled him the further progress of our narrative may show.

Scarcely any of the items in the above-drawn parallel occurred to Phœbe, whose country birth and residence, in truth, had left her pitifully ignorant of most of the family traditions, which lingered, like cobwebs and incrustations of smoke, about the rooms and chimney-corners of the House of the Seven Gables. Yet there was a circumstance, very trifling in itself, which impressed her with an odd degree of horror. She had heard of the anathema flung by Maule, the executed wizard, against Colonel Pyncheon and his posterity,—that God would give them blood to drink, —and likewise of the popular notion, that this miraculous blood might now and then be heard gurgling in their throats. The latter scandal—as became a person of sense, and, more especially, a member of the Pyncheon family—Phœbe had set down for the absurdity which it unquestionably was. But ancient superstitions, after being steeped in human hearts and embodied in human breath, and passing from lip to ear in manifold repetition, through a series of generations, become imbued with an effect of homely truth. The smoke of the domestic hearth has scented them through and through. By long transmission among household facts, they grow to look like them, and have such a familiar way of making themselves at home that their influence is usually greater than we suspect. Thus it happened, that when Phœbe heard a certain noise in Judge Pyncheon's throat,—rather habitual with him, not altogether voluntary, yet indicative of nothing, unless it were a slight bronchial complaint, or, as some people hinted, an apoplectic symptom,—when the girl heard this queer and awkward ingurgitation (which the writer never did hear, and therefore cannot describe), she, very foolishly, started, and clasped her hands.

Of course, it was exceedingly ridiculous in Phœbe to be discomposed by such a trifle, and still more unpardonable to show her discomposure to the individual most concerned in it. But the incident chimed in so oddly with her previous fancies about the Colonel and the Judge, that, for the moment, it seemed quite to mingle their identity.

"What is the matter with you, young woman?" said Judge Pyncheon, giving her one of his harsh looks. "Are you afraid of anything?"

"Oh, nothing, sir,—nothing in the world!" answered Phœbe, with a little laugh of vexation at herself. "But perhaps you wish to speak with my cousin Hepzibah. Shall I call her?"

"Stay a moment, if you please," said the Judge, again beaming sunshine out of his face. "You seem to be a little nervous this morning. The town air, Cousin Phœbe, does not agree with your good, wholesome country habits. Or has anything happened to disturb you?—anything remarkable in Cousin Hepzibah's family?—An arrival, eh? I thought so! No wonder you are out of sorts, my little cousin. To be an inmate with such a guest may well startle an innocent young girl!"

"You quite puzzle me, sir," replied Phœbe, gazing inquiringly at the Judge. "There is no frightful guest in the house, but only a poor, gentle, childlike man, whom I believe to be Cousin Hepzibah's brother. I am afraid (but you, sir, will know better than I) that he is not quite in his sound senses; but so mild and quiet he seems to be, that a mother might trust her baby with him; and I think he would play with the baby as if he were only a few years older than itself. He startle me!—Oh, no indeed!"

"I rejoice to hear so favorable and so ingenuous an account of my cousin Clifford," said the benevolent Judge. "Many years ago, when we were boys and young men together, I had a great affection for him, and still feel a tender interest in all his concerns. You, say, Cousin Phœbe, he appears to be weak-minded. Heaven grant him at least enough of intellect to repent of his past sins!"

"Nobody, I fancy," observed Phœbe, "can have fewer to repent of."

"And is it possible, my dear," rejoined the Judge, with a commiserating look, "that you have never heard of Clifford Pyncheon?—that you know nothing of his history? Well, it is all right; and your mother has shown a very proper regard for the good name of the family with which she connected herself. Believe the best you can of this unfortunate person, and hope the best! It is a rule which Christians should always follow, in their judgments of one another; and especially is it right and wise among near relatives, whose characters have necessarily a degree of mutual dependence. But is Clifford in the parlor? I will just step in and see."

"Perhaps, sir, I had better call my cousin Hepzibah," said Phœbe; hardly knowing, however, whether she ought to obstruct the entrance of so affectionate a kinsman into the private regions of the house. "Her brother seemed to be just falling asleep after breakfast; and I am sure she would not like him to be disturbed. Pray sir, let me give her notice!"

But the Judge showed a singular determination to enter unannounced; and as Phœbe, with the vivacity of a person whose movements unconsciously answer to her thoughts, had stepped towards the door, he used little or no ceremony in putting her aside.

"No, no, Miss Phœbe!" said Judge Pyncheon, in a voice as deep as a thunder-growl, and with a frown as black as the cloud whence it issues. "Stay you here! I know the house, and know my cousin Hepzibah, and know her brother Clifford likewise!—nor need my little country cousin put herself to the trouble of announcing me!"—in these latter words, by the by, there were symptoms of a change from his sudden harshness into his previous benignity of manner. "I am at home here, Phœbe, you must recollect, and you are the stranger. I will just step in, therefore, and see for myself how Clifford is, and assure him and Hepzibah of my kindly feelings and best wishes. It is right, at this juncture, that they should both hear from my own lips how much I desire to serve them. Ha! here is Hepzibah herself!"

Such was the case. The vibrations of the Judge's voice had reached the old gentlewoman in the parlor, where she sat, with face averted, waiting on her brother's slumber. She now issued forth, as would appear, to defend the entrance, looking, we must needs say, amazingly like the dragon which, in fairy tales, is wont to be the guardian over an enchanted beauty. The habitual scowl of her brow was, undeniably, too fierce, at this moment, to pass itself off on the innocent score of near-sightedness; and it was bent on Judge Pyncheon in a way that seemed to confound, if not alarm him, so inadequately had he estimated the moral force of a deeply grounded antipathy. She made a repelling gesture with her hand, and stood a perfect picture of prohibition, at full length, in the dark frame of the doorway. But we must betray Hepzibah's secret, and confess that the native timorousness of her character even now developed itself in a quick tremor, which, to her own perception, set each of her joints at variance with its fellows.

Possibly, the Judge was aware how little true hardihood lay behind Hepzibah's formidable front. At any rate, being a gentleman of steady nerves, he soon recovered himself, and failed not to approach his cousin with outstretched hand; adopting the sensible precaution, however, to cover his advance with a smile, so broad and sultry, that, had it been only half as warm as it looked, a trellis of grapes might at once have turned purple under its summer-like exposure. It may have been his purpose, indeed, to melt poor Hepzibah on the spot, as if she were a figure of yellow wax.

"Hepzibah, my beloved cousin, I am rejoiced!" exclaimed the Judge, most emphatically. "Now, at length, you have something to live for. Yes, and all of us, let me say, your friends and kindred, have more to live for than we had yesterday. I have lost no time in hastening to offer any assistance in my power towards making Clifford comfortable. He belongs to us all. I know how much he requires,—how much he used to require,—with his delicate taste, and his love of the beautiful. Anything in my house,—pictures, books, wine, luxuries of the table,—he may command them all! It would afford me most heart-felt gratification to see him! Shall I step in, this moment?"

"No," replied Hepzibah, her voice quivering too painfully to allow of many words. "He cannot see visitors!"

"A visitor, my dear cousin!—do you call me so?" cried the Judge, whose sensibility, it seems, was hurt by the coldness of the phrase. "Nay, then, let me be Clifford's host, and your own likewise. Come at once to my house. The country air, and all the conveniences—I may say luxuries—that I have gathered about me, will do wonders for him. And you and I, dear Hepzibah, will consult together, and watch together, and labor together, to make our dear Clifford happy. Come! why should we make more words about what is both a duty and a pleasure on my part? Come to me at once!"

On hearing these so hospitable offers, and such generous recognition of the claims of kindred, Phœbe felt very much in the mood of running up to Judge Pyncheon, and giving him, of her own accord, the kiss from which she had so recently shrunk away. It was quite otherwise with Hepzibah; the Judge's smile seemed to operate on her acerbity of heart like sunshine upon vinegar, making it ten times sourer than ever.

"Clifford," said she,—still too agitated to utter more than an abrupt sentence,—"Clifford has a home here!"

"May Heaven forgive you, Hepzibah," said Judge Pyncheon,—reverently lifting his eyes towards that high court of equity to which he appealed,—"if you suffer any ancient prejudice or animosity to weigh with you in this matter! I stand here with an open heart, willing and anxious to receive yourself and Clifford into it. Do not refuse my good offices,—my earnest propositions for your welfare! They are such, in all respects, as it behooves your nearest kinsman to make. It will be a heavy responsibility, cousin, if you confine your brother to this dismal house and stifled air, when the delightful freedom of my country-seat is at his command."

"It would never suit Clifford," said Hepzibah, as briefly as before.

"Woman!" broke forth the Judge, giving way to his resentment, "what is the meaning of all this? Have you other resources? Nay, I suspected as much! Take care, Hepzibah, take care! Clifford is on the brink of as black a ruin as ever befell him yet! But why do I talk with you, woman as you are? Make way!—I must see Clifford!"

Hepzibah spread out her gaunt figure across the door, and seemed really to increase in bulk; looking the more terrible, also, because there was so much terror and agitation in her heart. But Judge Pyncheon's evident purpose of forcing a passage was interrupted by a voice from the inner room; a weak, tremulous, wailing voice, indicating helpless alarm, with no more energy for self-defence than belongs to a frightened infant.

"Hepzibah, Hepzibah!" cried the voice; "go down on your knees to him! Kiss his feet! Entreat him not to come in! Oh, let him have mercy on me! Mercy!—mercy!"

For the instant, it appeared doubtful whether it were not the Judge's resolute purpose to set Hepzibah aside, and step across the threshold into the parlor, whence issued that broken and miserable murmur of entreaty. It was not pity that restrained him, for, at the first sound of the enfeebled voice, a red fire kindled in his eyes, and he made a quick pace forward, with something inexpressibly fierce and grim darkening forth, as it were, out of the whole man. To know Judge Pyncheon, was to see him at that moment. After such a revelation, let him smile with what sultriness he would, he could much sooner turn grapes purple, or pumpkins yellow, than melt the iron-branded impression out of the beholder's memory. And it rendered his aspect not the less, but more frightful, that it seemed not to express wrath or hatred, but a certain hot fellness of purpose, which annihilated everything but itself.

Yet, after all, are we not slandering an excellent and amiable man? Look at the Judge now! He is apparently conscious of having erred, in too energetically pressing his deeds of loving-kindness on persons unable to appreciate them. He will await their better mood, and hold himself as ready to assist them then as at this moment. As he draws back from the door, an all-comprehensive benignity blazes from his visage, indicating that he gathers Hepzibah, little Phœbe, and the invisible Clifford, all three, together with the whole world besides, into his immense heart, and gives them a warm bath in its flood of affection.

"You do me great wrong, dear Cousin Hepzibah!" said he, first kindly offering her his hand, and then drawing on his glove preparatory to departure. "Very great wrong! But I forgive it, and will study to make you think better of me. Of course, our poor Clifford being in so unhappy a state of mind, I cannot think of urging an interview at present. But I shall watch over his welfare as if he were my own beloved brother; nor do I at all despair, my dear cousin, of constraining both him and you to acknowledge your injustice. When that shall happen, I desire no other revenge than your acceptance of the best offices in my power to do you."

With a bow to Hepzibah, and a degree of paternal benevolence in his parting nod to Phœbe, the Judge left the shop, and went smiling along the street. As is customary with the rich, when they aim at the honors of a republic, he apologized, as it were, to the people, for his wealth, prosperity, and elevated station, by a free and hearty manner towards those who knew him; putting off the more of his dignity in due proportion with the humbleness of the man whom he saluted, and thereby proving a haughty consciousness of his advantages as irrefragably as if he had marched forth preceded by a troop of lackeys to clear the way. On this particular forenoon so excessive was the warmth of Judge Pyncheon's kindly aspect, that (such, at least, was the rumor about town) an extra passage of the water-carts was found essential, in order to lay the dust occasioned by so much extra sunshine!

No sooner had he disappeared than Hepzibah grew deadly white, and staggering towards Phœbe, let her head fall on the young girl's shoulder. "O Phœbe!" murmured she, "that man has been the horror of my life! Shall I never, never have the courage,—will my voice never cease from trembling long enough to let me tell him what he is?"

"Is he so very wicked?" asked Phœbe. "Yet his offers were surely kind!"

"Do not speak of them,—he has a heart of iron!" rejoined Hepzibah. "Go, now, and talk to Clifford! Amuse and keep him quiet! It would disturb him wretchedly to see me so agitated as I am. There, go, dear child, and I will try to look after the shop."

Phœbe went, accordingly, but perplexed herself, meanwhile, with queries as to the purport of the scene which she had just witnessed, and also whether judges, clergymen, and other characters of that eminent stamp and respectability, could really, in any single instance, be otherwise than just and upright men. A doubt of this nature has a most disturbing influence, and, if shown to be a fact, comes with fearful and startling effect on minds of the trim, orderly, and limit-loving class, in which we find our little country-girl. Dispositions more boldly speculative may derive a stern enjoyment from the discovery, since there must be evil in the world, that a high man is as likely to grasp his share of it as a low one. A wider scope of view, and a deeper insight, may see rank, dignity, and station, all proved illusory, so far as regards their claim to human reverence, and yet not feel as if the universe were thereby tumbled head-long into chaos. But Phœbe, in order to keep the universe in its old place, was fain to smother, in some degree, her own intuitions as to Judge Pyncheon's character. And as for her cousin's testimony in disparagement of it, she concluded that Hepzibah's judgment was imbittered by one of those family feuds, which render hatred the more deadly by the dead and corrupted love that they intermingle with its native poison.

IX

## CLIFFORD AND PHŒBE

TRULY was there something high, generous, and noble in the native composition of our poor old Hepzibah! Or else,—and it was quite as probably the case,—she had been enriched by poverty, developed by sorrow, elevated by the strong and solitary affection of her life, and thus endowed with heroism, which never could have characterized her in what are called happier circumstances. Through dreary years Hepzibah had looked forward—for the most part despairingly, never with any confidence of hope, but always with the feeling that it was her brightest possibility—to the very position in which she now found herself. In her own behalf, she had asked nothing of Providence but the opportunity of devoting herself to this brother, whom she had so loved,—so admired for what he was, or might have been,—and to whom she had kept her faith, alone of all the world, wholly, unfalteringly, at every instant, and throughout life. And here, in his late decline, the lost one had come back out of his long and strange misfortune, and was thrown on her sympathy, as it seemed, not merely for the bread of his physical existence, but for everything that should keep him morally alive. She had responded to the call. She had come forward,—our poor, gaunt Hepzibah, in her rusty silks, with her rigid joints, and the sad perversity of her scowl,—ready to do her utmost; and with affection enough, if that were all, to do a hundred times as much! There could be few more tearful sights,—and Heaven forgive us if a smile insist on mingling with our conception of it!—few sights with truer pathos in them, than Hepzibah presented on that first afternoon.

How patiently did she endeavor to wrap Clifford up in her great, warm love, and make it all the world to him, so that he should retain no torturing sense of the coldness and dreariness without! Her little efforts to amuse him! How pitiful, yet magnanimous, they were!

Remembering his early love of poetry and fiction, she unlocked a bookcase, and took down several books that had been excellent reading in their day. There was a volume of Pope, with the Rape of the Lock in it, and another of the Tatler, and an odd one of Dryden's Miscellanies, all with tarnished gilding on their covers, and thoughts of tarnished brilliancy inside. They had no success with Clifford. These, and all such writers of society, whose new works glow like the rich texture of a just-woven carpet, must be content to relinquish their charm, for every reader, after an age or two, and could hardly be supposed to retain any portion of it for a mind that had utterly lost its estimate of modes and manners. Hepzibah then took up Rasselas, and began to read of the Happy Valley, with a vague idea that some secret of a contented life had there been elaborated, which might at least serve Clifford and herself for this one day. But the Happy Valley had a cloud over it. Hepzibah troubled her auditor, moreover, by innumerable sins of emphasis, which he seemed to detect, without any reference to the meaning; nor, in fact, did he appear to take much note of the sense of what she read, but evidently felt the tedium of the lecture, without harvesting its profit. His sister's voice, too, naturally harsh, had, in the course of her sorrowful lifetime, contracted a kind of croak, which, when it once gets into the human throat, is as ineradicable as sin. In both sexes, occasionally, this life-long croak, accompanying each word of joy or sorrow, is one of the symptoms of a settled melancholy; and wherever it occurs, the whole history of misfortune is conveyed in its slightest accent. The effect is as if the voice had been dyed black; or,—if we must use a more moderate simile,—this miserable croak, running through all the variations of the voice, is like a black silken thread, on which the crystal beads of speech are strung, and whence they take their hue. Such voices have put on mourning for dead hopes; and they ought to die and be buried along with them!

Discerning that Clifford was not gladdened by her efforts, Hepzibah searched about the house for the means of more exhilarating pastime. At one time, her eyes chanced to rest on Alice Pyncheon's harpsichord. It was a moment of great peril; for,—despite the traditionary awe that had gathered over this instrument of music, and the dirges which spiritual fingers were said to play on it,—the devoted sister had solemn thoughts of thrumming on its chords for Clifford's benefit, and accompanying the performance with her voice. Poor Clifford! Poor Hepzibah! Poor harpsichord! All three would have been miserable together. By some good agency,—possibly, by the unrecognized interposition of the long-buried Alice herself,—the threatening calamity was averted.

But the worst of all—the hardest stroke of fate for Hepzibah to endure, and perhaps for Clifford too—was his invincible distaste for her appearance. Her features, never the most agreeable, and now harsh with age and grief, and resentment against the world for his sake; her dress, and especially her turban; the queer and quaint manners, which had unconsciously grown upon her in solitude,—such being the poor gentlewoman's outward characteristics, it is no great marvel, although the mournfullest of pities, that the instinctive lover of the Beautiful was fain to turn away his eyes. There was no help for it. It would be the latest impulse to die within him. In his last extremity, the expiring breath stealing faintly through Clifford's lips, he would doubtless press Hepzibah's hand, in fervent recognition of all her lavished love, and close his eyes,—but not so much to die, as to be constrained to look no longer on her face! Poor Hepzibah! She took counsel with herself what might be done, and thought of putting ribbons on her turban; but, by the instant rush of several guardian angels, was withheld from an experiment that could hardly have proved less than fatal to the beloved object of her anxiety.

To be brief, besides Hepzibah's disadvantages of person, there was an uncouthness pervading all her deeds; a clumsy something, that could but ill adapt itself for use, and not at all for ornament. She was a grief to Clifford, and she knew it. In this extremity, the antiquated virgin turned to Phœbe. No grovelling jealousy was in her heart. Had it pleased Heaven to crown the heroic fidelity of her life by making her personally the medium of Clifford's happiness, it would have rewarded her for all the past, by a joy with no bright tints, indeed, but deep and true, and worth a thousand gayer ecstasies. This could not be. She therefore turned to Phœbe, and resigned the task into the young girl's hands. The latter took it up cheerfully, as she did everything, but with no sense of a mission to perform, and succeeding all the better for that same simplicity.

By the involuntary effect of a genial temperament, Phœbe soon grew to be absolutely essential to the daily comfort, if not the daily life, of her two forlorn companions. The grime and sordidness of the House of the Seven Gables seemed to have vanished since her appearance there; the gnawing tooth of the dry-rot was stayed among the old timbers of its skeleton frame; the dust had ceased to settle down so densely, from the antique ceilings, upon the floors and furniture of the rooms below,—or, at any rate, there was a little housewife, as light-footed as the breeze that sweeps a garden walk, gliding hither and thither to brush it all away. The shadows of gloomy events that haunted the else lonely and desolate apartments; the heavy, breathless scent which death had left in more than one of the bedchambers, ever since his visits of long ago,—these were less powerful than the purifying influence scattered throughout the atmosphere of the household by the presence of one youthful, fresh, and thoroughly wholesome heart. There was no morbidness in Phœbe; if there had been, the old Pyncheon House was the very locality to ripen it into incurable disease. But now her spirit resembled, in its potency, a minute quantity of ottar of rose in one of Hepzibah's huge, iron-bound trunks, diffusing its fragrance through the various articles of linen and wrought-lace, kerchiefs, caps, stockings, folded dresses, gloves, and whatever else was treasured there. As every article in the great trunk was the sweeter for the rose-scent, so did all the thoughts and emotions of Hepzibah and Clifford, sombre as they might seem, acquire a subtle attribute of happiness from Phœbe's intermixture with them. Her activity of body, intellect, and heart impelled her continually to perform the ordinary little toils that offered themselves around her, and to think the thought proper for the moment, and to sympathize,—now with the twittering gayety of the robins in the pear-tree, and now to such a depth as she could with Hepzibah's dark anxiety, or the vague moan of her brother. This facile adaptation was at once the symptom of perfect health and its best preservative.

A nature like Phœbe's has invariably its due influence, but is seldom regarded with due honor. Its spiritual force, however, may be partially estimated by the fact of her having found a place for herself, amid circumstances so stern as those which surrounded the mistress of the house; and also by the effect which she produced on a character of so much more mass than her own. For the gaunt, bony frame and limbs of Hepzibah, as compared with the tiny lightsomeness of Phœbe's figure, were perhaps in some fit proportion with the moral weight and substance, respectively, of the woman and the girl.

To the guest,—to Hepzibah's brother,—or Cousin Clifford, as Phœbe now began to call him,—she was especially necessary. Not that he could ever be said to converse with her, or often manifest, in any other very definite mode, his sense of a charm in her society. But if she were a long while absent he became pettish and nervously restless, pacing the room to and fro with the uncertainty that characterized all his movements; or else would sit broodingly in his great chair, resting his head on his hands, and evincing life only by an electric sparkle of ill-humor, whenever Hepzibah endeavored to arouse him. Phœbe's presence and the contiguity of her fresh life to his blighted one, was usually all that he required. Indeed, such was the native gush and play of her spirit, that she was seldom perfectly quiet and undemonstrative, any more than a fountain ever ceases to dimple and warble with its flow. She possessed the gift of song, and that, too, so naturally, that you would as little think of inquiring whence she had caught it, or what master had taught her, as of asking the same questions about a bird, in whose small strain of music we recognize the voice of the Creator as distinctly as in the loudest accents of his thunder. So long as Phœbe sang, she might stray at her own will about the house.

Clifford was content, whether the sweet, airy homeliness of her tones came down from the upper chambers, or along the passageway from the shop, or was sprinkled through the foliage of the pear-tree, inward from the garden, with the twinkling sunbeams. He would sit quietly, with a gentle pleasure gleaming over his face, brighter now, and now a little dimmer, as the song happened to float near him, or was more remotely heard. It pleased him best, however, when she sat on a low footstool at his knee.

It is perhaps remarkable, considering her temperament, that Phœbe oftener chose a strain of pathos than of gayety. But the young and happy are not ill pleased to temper their life with a transparent shadow. The deepest pathos of Phœbe's voice and song, moreover, came sifted through the golden texture of a cheery spirit, and was somehow so interfused with the quality thence acquired, that one's heart felt all the lighter for having wept at it. Broad mirth, in the sacred presence of dark misfortune, would have jarred harshly and irreverently with the solemn symphony that rolled its undertone through Hepzibah's and her brother's life. Therefore, it was well that Phœbe so often chose sad themes, and not amiss that they ceased to be so sad while she was singing them.

Becoming habituated to her companionship, Clifford readily showed how capable of imbibing pleasant tints and gleams of cheerful light from all quarters his nature must originally have been. He grew youthful while she sat by him. A beauty,—not precisely real, even in its utmost manifestation, and which a painter would have watched long to seize and fix upon his canvas, and, after all, in vain,—beauty, nevertheless, that was not a mere dream, would sometimes play upon and illuminate his face. It did more than to illuminate; it transfigured him with an expression that could only be interpreted as the glow of an exquisite and happy spirit. That gray hair, and those furrows,—with their record of infinite sorrow so deeply written across his brow, and so compressed, as with a futile effort to crowd in all the tale, that the whole inscription was made illegible,—these, for the moment, vanished. An eye, at once tender and acute, might have beheld in the man some shadow of what he was meant to be. Anon, as age came stealing, like a sad twilight, back over his figure, you would have felt tempted to hold an argument with Destiny, and affirm, that either this being should not have been made mortal, or mortal existence should have been tempered to his qualities. There seemed no necessity for his having drawn breath at all; the world never wanted him; but, as he had breathed, it ought always to have been the balmiest of summer air. The same perplexity will invariably haunt us with regard to natures that tend to feed exclusively upon the Beautiful, let their earthly fate be as lenient as it may.

Phœbe, it is probable, had but a very imperfect comprehension of the character over which she had thrown so beneficent a spell. Nor was it necessary. The fire upon the hearth can gladden a whole semi-circle of faces round about it, but need not know the individuality of one among them all. Indeed, there was something too fine and delicate in Clifford's

traits to be perfectly appreciated by one whose sphere lay so much in the
Actual as Phœbe's did. For Clifford, however, the reality, and simplicity,
and thorough homeliness of the girl's nature, were as powerful a charm
as any that she possessed. Beauty, it is true, and beauty almost perfect in
its own style, was indispensable. Had Phœbe been coarse in feature,
shaped clumsily, of a harsh voice, and uncouthly mannered, she might
have been rich with all good gifts, beneath this unfortunate exterior, and
still, so long as she wore the guise of woman, she would have shocked
Clifford, and depressed him by her lack of beauty. But nothing more
beautiful—nothing prettier, at least—was ever made than Phœbe. And,
therefore, to this man,—whose whole poor and impalpable enjoyment of
existence heretofore, and until both his heart and fancy died within him,
had been a dream,—whose images of women had more and more lost
their warmth and substance, and been frozen, like the pictures of secluded artists, into the chillest ideality,—to him, this little figure of the cheer-
iest household life was just what he required to bring him back into the
breathing world. Persons who have wandered, or been expelled, out of
the common track of things, even were it for a better system, desire
nothing so much as to be led back. They shiver in their loneliness, be it
on a mountain-top or in a dungeon. Now, Phœbe's presence made a home
about her,—that very sphere which the outcast, the prisoner, the potentate,—the wretch beneath mankind, the wretch aside from it, or the
wretch above it,—instinctively pines after,—a home! She was real! Holding her hand, you felt something; a tender something; a substance, and a
warm one: and so long as you should feel its grasp, soft as it was, you
might be certain that your place was good in the whole sympathetic chain
of human nature. The world was no longer a delusion.

By looking a little further in this direction, we might suggest an explanation of an often-suggested mystery. Why are poets so apt to choose
their mates, not for any similarity of poetic endowment, but for qualities
which might make the happiness of the rudest handicraftsman as well as
that of the ideal craftsman of the spirit? Because, probably, at his highest elevation, the poet needs no human intercourse; but he finds it dreary
to descend, and be a stranger.

There was something very beautiful in the relation that grew up between this pair, so closely and constantly linked together, yet with such a
waste of gloomy and mysterious years from his birthday to hers. On Clifford's part it was the feeling of a man naturally endowed with the liveliest sensibility to feminine influence, but who had never quaffed the cup of
passionate love, and knew that it was now too late. He knew it, with the
instinctive delicacy that had survived his intellectual decay. Thus, his
sentiment for Phœbe, without being paternal, was not less chaste than if
she had been his daughter. He was a man, it is true, and recognized her
as a woman. She was his only representative of womankind. He took unfailing note of every charm that appertained to her sex, and saw the ripe-
ness of her lips, and the virginal development of her bosom. All her little
womanly ways, budding out of her like blossoms on a young fruit-tree,

had their effect on him, and sometimes caused his very heart to tingle
with the keenest thrills of pleasure. At such moments,—for the effect was
seldom more than momentary,—the half-torpid man would be full of
harmonious life, just as a long-silent harp is full of sound, when the musician's fingers sweep across it. But, after all, it seemed rather a perception, or a sympathy, than a sentiment belonging to himself as an individual. He read Phœbe, as he would a sweet and simple story; he listened
to her, as if she were a verse of household poetry, which God, in requital of his bleak and dismal lot, had permitted some angel, that most
pitied him, to warble through the house. She was not an actual fact for
him, but the interpretation of all that he had lacked on earth brought
warmly home to his conception; so that this mere symbol, or lifelike picture, had almost the comfort of reality.

But we strive in vain to put the idea into words. No adequate expression of the beauty and profound pathos with which it impresses us is attainable. This being, made only for happiness, and heretofore so miserably failing to be happy,—his tendencies so hideously thwarted, that,
some unknown time ago, the delicate springs of his character, never morally or intellectually strong, had given way, and he was now imbecile,—
this poor, forlorn, voyager from the Islands of the Blest, in a frail bark,
on a tempestuous sea, had been flung, by the last mountain-wave of his
shipwreck, into a quiet harbor. There, as he lay more than half lifeless on
the strand, the fragrance of an earthly rose-bud had come to his nostrils,
and, as odors will, had summoned up reminiscences or visions of all the
living and breathing beauty amid which he should have had his home.
With his native susceptibility of happy influences, he inhales the slight,
ethereal rapture into his soul, and expires!

And how did Phœbe regard Clifford? The girl's was not one of those
natures which are most attracted by what is strange and exceptional in
human character. The path which would best have suited her was the
well-worn track of ordinary life; the companions in whom she would
most have delighted were such as one encounters at every turn. The mystery which enveloped Clifford, so far as it affected her at all, was an annoyance, rather than the piquant charm which many women might have
found in it. Still, her native kindliness was brought strongly into play,
not by what was darkly picturesque in his situation, nor so much, even,
by the finer graces of his character, as by the simple appeal of a heart so
forlorn as his to one so full of genuine sympathy as hers. She gave him an
affectionate regard, because he needed so much love, and seemed to have
received so little. With a ready tact, the result of ever-active and wholesome sensibility, she discerned what was good for him, and did it. Whatever was morbid in his mind and experience she ignored; and thereby
kept their intercourse healthy, by the incautious, but, as it were, heaven-
directed freedom of her whole conduct. The sick in mind, and, perhaps,
in body, are rendered more darkly and hopelessly so by the manifold reflection of their disease, mirrored back from all quarters in the deportment of those about them; they are compelled to inhale the poison of

their own breath, in infinite repetition. But Phœbe afforded her poor patient a supply of purer air. She impregnated it, too, not with a wild-flower scent,—for wildness was no trait of hers,—but with the perfume of garden-roses, pinks, and other blossoms of much sweetness, which nature and man have consented together in making grow from summer to summer, and from century to century. Such a flower was Phœbe, in her relation with Clifford, and such the delight that he inhaled from her.

Yet, it must be said, her petals sometimes drooped a little, in consequence of the heavy atmosphere about her. She grew more thoughtful than heretofore. Looking aside at Clifford's face, and seeing the dim, unsatisfactory elegance and the intellect almost quenched, she would try to inquire what had been his life. Was he always thus? Had this veil been over him from his birth?—this veil, under which far more of his spirit was hidden than revealed, and through which he so imperfectly discerned the actual world,—or was its gray texture woven of some dark calamity? Phœbe loved no riddles, and would have been glad to escape the perplexity of this one. Nevertheless, there was so far a good result of her meditations on Clifford's character, that, when her involuntary conjectures, together with the tendency of every strange circumstance to tell its own story, had gradually taught her the fact, it had no terrible effect upon her. Let the world have done him what vast wrong it might, she knew Cousin Clifford too well—or fancied so—ever to shudder at the touch of his thin delicate fingers.

Within a few days after the appearance of this remarkable inmate, the routine of life had established itself with a good deal of uniformity in the old house of our narrative. In the morning, very shortly after breakfast, it was Clifford's custom to fall asleep in his chair; nor, unless accidentally disturbed, would he emerge from a dense cloud of slumber or the thinner mists that flitted to and fro, until well towards noonday. These hours of drowsihead were the season of the old gentlewoman's attendance on her brother, while Phœbe took charge of the shop; an arrangement which the public speedily understood, and evinced their decided preference of the younger shopwoman by the multiplicity of their calls during her administration of affairs. Dinner over, Hepzibah took her knitting-work,—a long stocking of gray yarn, for her brother's winter-wear,—and with a sigh, and a scowl of affectionate farewell to Clifford, and a gesture enjoining watchfulness on Phœbe, went to take her seat behind the counter. It was now the young girl's turn to be the nurse,—the guardian, the playmate,— or whatever is the fitter phrase,—of the gray-haired man.

X

## THE PYNCHEON GARDEN

CLIFFORD, except for Phœbe's more active instigation, would ordinarily have yielded to the torpor which had crept through all his modes of being, and which sluggishly counselled him to sit in his morning chair till eventide. But the girl seldom failed to propose a removal to the garden, where Uncle Venner and the daguerreotypist had made such repairs on the roof of the ruinous arbor, or summer-house, that it was now a sufficient shelter from sunshine and casual showers. The hop-vine, too, had begun to grow luxuriantly over the sides of the little edifice, and made an interior of verdant seclusion, with innumerable peeps and glimpses into the wider solitude of the garden.

Here, sometimes, in this green play-place of flickering light, Phœbe read to Clifford. Her acquaintance, the artist, who appeared to have a literary turn, had supplied her with works of fiction, in pamphlet-form, and a few volumes of poetry, in altogether a different style and taste from those which Hepzibah selected for his amusement. Small thanks were due to the books, however, if the girl's readings were in any degree more successful than her elderly cousin's. Phœbe's voice had always a pretty music in it, and could either enliven Clifford by its sparkle and gayety of tone, or soothe him by a continued flow of pebbly and brook-like cadences. But the fictions—in which the country-girl, unused to works of that nature, often became deeply absorbed—interested her strange auditor very little, or not at all. Pictures of life, scenes of passion or sentiment, wit, humor, and pathos, were all thrown away, or worse than thrown away, on Clifford; either because he lacked an experience by which to test their truth, or because his own griefs were a touch-stone of reality that few feigned emotions could withstand. When Phœbe broke into a peal of merry laughter at what she read, he would now and then laugh for sympathy, but oftener respond with a troubled, questioning look. If a tear—a maiden's sunshiny tear over imaginary woe—dropped upon some melancholy page, Clifford either took it as a token of actual calamity, or else grew peevish, and angrily motioned her to close the volume. And wisely too! Is not the world sad enough, in genuine earnest, without making a pastime of mock-sorrows?

With poetry it was rather better. He delighted in the swell and subsidence of the rhythm, and the happily recurring rhyme. Nor was Clifford incapable of feeling the sentiment of poetry,—not, perhaps, where it was highest or deepest, but where it was most fitting and ethereal. It was impossible to foretell in what exquisite verse the awakening spell might lurk; but, on raising her eyes from the page to Clifford's face, Phœbe would be made aware, by the light breaking through it, that a more delicate intelligence than her own had caught a lambent flame from

what she read. One glow of this kind, however, was often the precursor of
gloom for many hours afterward; because, when the glow left him, he
seemed conscious of a missing sense and power, and groped about for
them, as if a blind man should go seeking his lost eyesight.

It pleased him more, and was better for his inward welfare, that Phœbe
should talk, and make passing occurrences vivid to his mind by her accompanying description and remarks. The life of the garden offered topics enough for such discourse as suited Clifford best. He never failed to
inquire what flowers had bloomed since yesterday. His feeling for flowers
was very exquisite, and seemed not so much a taste as an emotion; he
was fond of sitting with one in his hand, intently observing it, and looking from its petals into Phœbe's face, as if the garden flower were the sister of the household maiden. Not merely was there a delight in the
flower's perfume, or pleasure in its beautiful form, and the delicacy or
brightness of its hue; but Clifford's enjoyment was accompanied with a
perception of life, character, and individuality, that made him love these
blossoms of the garden, as if they were endowed with sentiment and intelligence. This affection and sympathy for flowers is almost exclusively
a woman's trait. Men, if endowed with it by nature, soon lose, forget, and
learn to despise it, in their contact with coarser things than flowers. Clifford, too, had long forgotten it; but found it again now, as he slowly revived from the chill torpor of his life.

It is wonderful how many pleasant incidents continually came to pass
in that secluded garden-spot when once Phœbe had set herself to look for
them. She had seen or heard a bee there, on the first day of her acquaintance with the place. And often,—almost continually, indeed,—since then,
the bees kept coming thither, Heaven knows why, or by what pertinacious desire, for far-fetched sweets, when, no doubt, there were broad
clover-fields, and all kinds of garden growth, much nearer home than this.
Thither the bees came, however, and plunged into the squash-blossoms,
as if there were no other squash-vines within a long day's flight, or as if
the soil of Hepzibah's garden gave its productions just the very quality
which these laborious little wizards wanted, in order to impart the Hy-
mettus odor to their whole hive of New England honey. When Clifford
heard their sunny, buzzing murmur, in the heart of the great yellow blossoms, he looked about him with a joyful sense of warmth, and blue sky,
and green grass, and of God's free air in the whole height from earth to
heaven. After all, there need be no question why the bees came to that
one green nook in the dusty town. God sent them thither to gladden our
poor Clifford. They brought the rich summer with them, in requital of a
little honey.

When the bean-vines began to flower on the poles, there was one particular variety which bore a vivid scarlet blossom. The daguerreotypist
had found these beans in a garret, over one of the seven gables, treasured
up in an old chest of drawers, by some horticultural Pyncheon of days
gone by, who, doubtless, meant to sow them the next summer, but was
himself first sown in Death's garden-ground. By way of testing whether

there were still a living germ in such ancient seeds, Holgrave had planted some of them; and the result of his experiment was a splendid row of bean-vines, clambering, early, to the full height of the poles, and arraying them, from top to bottom, in a spiral profusion of red blossoms. And, ever since the unfolding of the first bud, a multitude of humming-birds had been attracted thither. At times, it seemed as if for every one of the hundred blossoms there was one of these tiniest fowls of the air,—a thumb's bigness of burnished plumage, hovering and vibrating about the bean-poles. It was with indescribable interest, and even more than childish delight, that Clifford watched the humming-birds. He used to thrust his head softly out of the arbor to see them the better; all the while, too, motioning Phœbe to be quiet, and snatching glimpses of the smile upon her face, so as to heap his enjoyment up the higher with her sympathy. He had not merely grown young;—he was a child again.

Hepzibah, whenever she happened to witness one of these fits of miniature enthusiasm, would shake her head, with a strange mingling of the mother and sister, and of pleasure and sadness, in her aspect. She said that it had always been thus with Clifford when the humming-birds came, —always, from his babyhood,—and that his delight in them had been one of the earliest tokens by which he showed his love for beautiful things. And it was a wonderful coincidence, the good lady thought, that the artist should have planted these scarlet-flowering beans—which the humming-birds sought far and wide, and which had not grown in the Pyncheon garden before for forty years—on the very summer of Clifford's return.

Then would the tears stand in poor Hepzibah's eyes, or overflow them with a too abundant gush, so that she was fain to betake herself into some corner lest Clifford should espy her agitation. Indeed, all the enjoyments of this period were provocative of tears. Coming so late as it did, it was a kind of Indian summer, with a mist in its balmiest sunshine, and decay and death in its gaudiest delight. The more Clifford seemed to taste the happiness of a child, the sadder was the difference to be recognized. With a mysterious and terrible Past, which had annihilated his memory, and a blank Future before him, he had only this visionary and impalpable Now, which, if you once look closely at it, is nothing. He himself, as was perceptible by many symptoms, lay darkly behind his pleasure, and knew it to be a baby-play, which he was to toy and trifle with, instead of thoroughly believing. Clifford saw, it may be, in the mirror of his deeper consciousness, that he was an example and representative of that great class of people whom an inexplicable Providence is continually putting at cross-purposes with the world: breaking what seems its own promise in their nature; withholding their proper food, and setting poison before them for a banquet; and thus—when it might so easily, as one would think, have been adjusted otherwise—making their existence a strangeness, a solitude, and torment. All his life long, he had been learning how to be wretched, as one learns a foreign tongue; and now, with the lesson thoroughly by heart, he could with difficulty comprehend his little airy happiness. Frequently there was a dim shadow of doubt in his eyes. "Take my hand, Phœbe," he would say, "and pinch it hard with your little fingers! Give me a rose, that I may press its thorns, and prove myself awake by the sharp touch of pain!" Evidently, he desired this prick of a trifling anguish, in order to assure himself, by that quality which he best knew to be real, that the garden, and the seven weather-beaten gables, and Hepzibah's scowl, and Phœbe's smile, were real likewise. Without this signet in his flesh, he could have attributed no more substance to them than to the empty confusion of imaginary scenes with which he had fed his spirit, until even that poor sustenance was exhausted.

The author needs great faith in his reader's sympathy; else he must hesitate to give details so minute, and incidents apparently so trifling, as are essential to make up the idea of this garden-life. It was the Eden of a thunder-smitten Adam, who had fled for refuge thither out of the same dreary and perilous wilderness into which the original Adam was expelled.

One of the available means of amusement, of which Phœbe made the most in Clifford's behalf, was that feathered society, the hens, a breed of whom, as we have already said, was an immemorial heirloom in the Pyncheon family. In compliance with a whim of Clifford, as it troubled him to see them in confinement, they had been set at liberty, and now roamed at will about the garden; doing some little mischief but hindered from escape by buildings on three sides, and the difficult peaks of a wooden fence on the other. They spent much of their abundant leisure on the margin of Maule's well, which was haunted by a kind of snail, evidently a titbit to their palates; and the brackish water itself, however nauseous to the rest of the world, was so greatly esteemed by these fowls, that they might be seen tasting, turning up their heads, and smacking their bills, with precisely the air of wine-bibbers round a probationary cask. Their generally quiet, yet often brisk, and constantly diversified talk, one to another, or sometimes in soliloquy,—as they scratched worms out of the rich, black soil, or pecked at such plants as suited their taste,—had such a domestic tone, that it was almost a wonder why you could not establish a regular interchange of ideas about household matters, human and gallinaceous. All hens are well worth studying for the piquancy and rich variety of their manners; but by no possibility can there have been other fowls of such odd appearance and deportment as these ancestral ones. They probably embodied the traditional peculiarities of their whole line of progenitors, derived through an unbroken succession of eggs; or else this individual Chanticleer and his two wives had grown to be humorists, and a little crack-brained withal, on account of their solitary way of life, and out of sympathy for Hepzibah, their lady-patroness.

Queer, indeed, they looked! Chanticleer himself, though stalking on two stilt-like legs, with the dignity of interminable descent in all his gestures, was hardly bigger than an ordinary partridge; his two wives were about the size of quails; and as for the one chicken, it looked small enough to be still in the egg, and, at the same time, sufficiently old, with-

ered, wizened, and experienced, to have been the founder of the antiquated race. Instead of being the youngest of the family, it rather seemed
to have aggregated into itself the ages, not only of these living specimens
of the breed, but of all its forefathers and foremothers, whose united excellences and oddities were squeezed into its little body. Its mother evidently regarded it as the one chicken of the world, and as necessary, in
fact, to the world's continuance, or, at any rate, to the equilibrium of the
present system of affairs, whether in church or state. No lesser sense of
the infant fowl's importance could have justified, even in a mother's eyes,
the perseverance with which she watched over its safety, ruffling her small
person to twice its proper size, and flying in everybody's face that so
much as looked towards her hopeful progeny. No lower estimate could
have vindicated the indefatigable zeal with which she scratched, and her
unscrupulousness in digging up the choicest flower or vegetable, for the
sake of the fat earthworm at its root. Her nervous cluck, when the chicken
happened to be hidden in the long grass or under the squash-leaves; her
gentle croak of satisfaction, while sure of it beneath her wing; her note of
ill-concealed fear and obstreperous defiance, when she saw her arch-
enemy, a neighbor's cat, on the top of the high fence,—one or other of
these sounds was to be heard at almost every moment of the day. By degrees, the observer came to feel nearly as much interest in this chicken of
illustrious race as the mother-hen did.

Phœbe, after getting well acquainted with the old hen, was sometimes
permitted to take the chicken in her hand, which was quite capable of
grasping its cubic inch or two of body. While she curiously examined its
hereditary marks,—the peculiar speckle of its plumage, the funny tuft on
its head, and a knob on each of its legs,—the little biped, as she insisted,
kept giving her a sagacious wink. The daguerreotypist once whispered her
that these marks betokened the oddities of the Pyncheon family, and that
the chicken itself was a symbol of the life of the old house, embodying its
interpretation, likewise, although an unintelligible one, as such clews
generally are. It was a feathered riddle; a mystery hatched out of an egg,
and just as mysterious as if the egg had been addle!

The second of Chanticleer's two wives, ever since Phœbe's arrival, had
been in a state of heavy despondency, caused, as it afterwards appeared,
by her inability to lay an egg. One day, however, by her self-important
gait, the sideway turn of her head, and the cock of her eye, as she pried
into one and another nook of the garden,—croaking to herself, all the
while, with inexpressible complacency,—it was made evident that this
identical hen, much as mankind undervalued her, carried something
about her person the worth of which was not to be estimated either in
gold or precious stones. Shortly after there was a prodigious cackling and
gratulation of Chanticleer and all his family, including the wizened chick-
en, who appeared to understand the matter quite as well as did his sire,
his mother, or his aunt. That afternoon Phœbe found a diminutive egg,—
not in the regular nest, it was far too precious to be trusted there,—but
cunningly hidden under the currant-bushes, on some dry stalks of last

year's grass. Hepzibah, on learning the fact, took possession of the egg and appropriated it to Clifford's breakfast, on account of a certain delicacy of flavor, for which, as she affirmed, these eggs had always been famous. Thus unscrupulously did the old gentlewoman sacrifice the continuance, perhaps, of an ancient feathered race, with no better end than to supply her brother with a dainty that hardly filled the bowl of a teaspoon! It must have been in reference to this outrage that Chanticleer, the next day, accompanied by the bereaved mother of the egg, took his post in front of Phœbe and Clifford, and delivered himself of a harangue that might have proved as long as his own pedigree, but for a fit of merriment on Phœbe's part. Hereupon, the offended fowl stalked away on his long stilts, and utterly withdrew his notice from Phœbe and the rest of human nature, until she made her peace with an offering of spice-cake, which, next to snails, was the delicacy most in favor with his aristocratic taste.

We linger too long, no doubt, beside this paltry rivulet of life that flowed through the garden of the Pyncheon House. But we deem it pardonable to record these mean incidents and poor delights, because they proved so greatly to Clifford's benefit. They had the earth-smell in them, and contributed to give him health and substance. Some of his occupations wrought less desirably upon him. He had a singular propensity, for example, to hang over Maule's well, and look at the constantly shifting phantasmagoria of figures produced by the agitation of the water over the mosaic-work of colored pebbles at the bottom. He said that faces looked upward to him there,—beautiful faces, arrayed in bewitching smiles,— each momentary face so fair and rosy, and every smile so sunny, that he felt wronged at its departure, until the same flitting witchcraft made a new one. But sometimes he would suddenly cry out, "The dark face gazes at me!" and be miserable the whole day afterwards. Phœbe, when she hung over the fountain by Clifford's side, could see nothing of all this, —neither the beauty nor the ugliness,—but only the colored pebbles, looking as if the gush of the waters shook and disarranged them. And the dark face, that so troubled Clifford, was no more than the shadow thrown from a branch of one of the damson-trees, and breaking the inner light of Maule's well. The truth was, however, that his fancy—reviving faster than his will and judgment, and always stronger than they—created shapes of loveliness that were symbolic of his native character, and now and then a stern and dreadful shape that typified his fate.

On Sundays, after Phœbe had been at church,—for the girl had a church-going conscience, and would hardly have been at ease had she missed either prayer, singing, sermon, or benediction,—after church-time, therefore, there was, ordinarily, a sober little festival in the garden. In addition to Clifford, Hepzibah, and Phœbe, two guests made up the company. One was the artist, Holgrave, who, in spite of his consociation with reformers, and his other queer and questionable traits, continued to hold an elevated place in Hepzibah's regard. The other, we are almost ashamed to say, was the venerable Uncle Venner, in a clean shirt, and a broadcloth coat, more respectable than his ordinary wear, inasmuch as it was neatly patched on each elbow, and might be called an entire garment, except for a slight inequality in the length of its skirts. Clifford, on several occasions, had seemed to enjoy the old man's intercourse, for the sake of his mellow, cheerful vein, which was like the sweet flavor of a frost-bitten apple, such as one picks up under the tree in December. A man at the very lowest point of the social scale was easier and more agreeable for the fallen gentleman to encounter than a person at any of the intermediate degrees; and, moreover, as Clifford's young manhood had been lost, he was fond of feeling himself comparatively youthful, now, in apposition with the patriarchal age of Uncle Venner. In fact, it was sometimes observable that Clifford half wilfully hid from himself the consciousness of being stricken in years, and cherished visions of an earthly future still before him; visions, however, too indistinctly drawn to be followed by disappointment —though, doubtless, by depression—when any casual incident or recollection made him sensible of the withered leaf.

So this oddly composed little social party used to assemble under the ruinous arbor. Hepzibah—stately as ever at heart, and yielding not an inch of her old gentility, but resting upon it so much the more, as justifying a princess-like condescension—exhibited a not ungraceful hospitality. She talked kindly to the vagrant artist, and took sage counsel—lady as she was—with the wood-sawyer, the messenger of everybody's petty errands, the patched philosopher. And Uncle Venner, who had studied the world at street-corners, and other posts equally well adapted for just observation, was as ready to give out his wisdom as a town-pump to give water.

"Miss Hepzibah, ma'am," said he once, after they had all been cheerful together, "I really enjoy these quiet little meetings of a Sabbath afternoon. They are very much like what I expect to have after I retire to my farm!"

"Uncle Venner," observed Clifford, in a drowsy, inward tone, "is always talking about his farm. But I have a better scheme for him, by and by. We shall see!"

"Ah, Mr. Clifford Pyncheon!" said the man of patches, "you may scheme for me as much as you please; but I'm not going to give up this one scheme of my own, even if I never bring it really to pass. It does seem to me that men make a wonderful mistake in trying to heap up property upon property. If I had done so, I should feel as if Providence was not bound to take care of me; and, at all events, the city wouldn't be! I'm one of those people who think that infinity is big enough for us all—and eternity long enough."

"Why, so they are, Uncle Venner," remarked Phœbe, after a pause; for she had been trying to fathom the profundity and appositeness of this concluding apothegm. "But for this short life of ours, one would like a house and a moderate garden-spot of one's own."

"It appears to me," said the daguerreotypist, smiling, "that Uncle Venner has the principles of Fourier at the bottom of his wisdom; only they

have not quite so much distinctness, in his mind as in that of the system-
atizing Frenchman."

"Come, Phœbe," said Hepzibah, "it is time to bring the currants."

And then, while the yellow richness of the declining sunshine still fell
into the open space of the garden, Phœbe brought out a loaf of bread and
a china bowl of currants, freshly gathered from the bushes, and crushed
with sugar. These, with water,—but not from the fountain of ill omen,
close at hand,—constituted all the entertainment. Meanwhile, Holgrave
took some pains to establish an intercourse with Clifford, actuated it
might seem, entirely by an impulse of kindliness, in order that the present hour might be cheerfuller than most which the poor recluse had spent,
or was destined yet to spend. Nevertheless, in the artist's deep, thoughtful, all-observant eyes, there was, now and then, an expression, not sinister, but questionable; as if he had some other interest in the scene than a
stranger, a youthful and unconnected adventurer, might be supposed to
have. With great mobility of outward mood, however, he applied himself
to the task of enlivening the party; and with so much success, that even
dark-hued Hepzibah threw off one tint of melancholy, and made what
shift she could with the remaining portion. Phœbe said to herself,—"How
pleasant he can be!" As for Uncle Venner, as a mark of friendship and
approbation, he readily consented to afford the young man his countenance in the way of his profession,—not metaphorically, be it understood,
but literally, by allowing a daguerreotype of his face, so familiar to the
town, to be exhibited at the entrance of Holgrave's studio.

Clifford, as the company partook of their little banquet, grew to be the
gayest of them all. Either it was one of those up-quivering flashes of the
spirit, to which minds in an abnormal state are liable, or else the artist
had subtly touched some chord that made musical vibration. Indeed,
what with the pleasant summer evening, and the sympathy of this little
circle of not unkindly souls, it was perhaps natural that a character so
susceptible as Clifford's should become animated, and show itself readily
responsive to what was said around him. But he gave out his own
thoughts, likewise, with an airy and fanciful glow; so that they glistened,
as it were, through the arbor, and made their escape among the interstices
of the foliage. He had been as cheerful, no doubt, while alone with Phœbe,
but never with such tokens of acute, although partial intelligence.

But, as the sunlight left the peaks of the Seven Gables, so did the excitement fade out of Clifford's eyes. He gazed vaguely and mournfully
about him, as if he missed something precious, and missed it the more
drearily for not knowing precisely what it was.

"I want my happiness!" at last he murmured, hoarsely and indistinctly, hardly shaping out the words. "Many, many years have I waited for
it! It is late! It is late! I want my happiness!"

Alas, poor Clifford! You are old, and worn with troubles that ought
never to have befallen you. You are partly crazy and partly imbecile; a
ruin, a failure, as almost everybody is,—though some in less degree, or
less perceptibly, than their fellows. Fate has no happiness in store for

you; unless your quiet home in the old family residence with the faithful Hepzibah, and your long summer afternoons with Phœbe, and these Sabbath festivals with Uncle Venner and the daguerreotypist, deserve to be called happiness! Why not? If not the thing itself, it is marvellously like it, and the more so for that ethereal and intangible quality which causes it all to vanish at too close an introspection. Take it, therefore, while you may! Murmur not,—question not,—but make the most of it!

XI

## The Arched Window

From the inertness, or what we may term the vegetative character, of his ordinary mood, Clifford would perhaps have been content to spend one day after another, interminably,—or, at least, throughout the summertime,—in just the kind of life described in the preceding pages. Fancying, however, that it might be for his benefit occasionally to diversify the scene, Phœbe sometimes suggested that he should look out upon the life of the street. For this purpose, they used to mount the staircase together, to the second story of the house, where, at the termination of a wide entry, there was an arched window of uncommonly large dimensions, shaded by a pair of curtains. It opened above the porch, where there had formerly been a balcony, the balustrade of which had long since gone to decay, and been removed. At this arched window, throwing it open, but keeping himself in comparative obscurity by means of the curtain, Clifford had an opportunity of witnessing such a portion of the great world's movement as might be supposed to roll through one of the retired streets of a not very populous city. But he and Phœbe made a sight as well worth seeing as any that the city could exhibit. The pale, gray, childish, aged, melancholy, yet often simply cheerful, and sometimes delicately intelligent aspect of Clifford, peering from behind the faded crimson of the curtain,—watching the monotony of every-day occurrences with a kind of inconsequential interest and earnestness, and, at every petty throb of his sensibility, turning for sympathy to the eyes of the bright young girl!

If once he were fairly seated at the window, even Pyncheon Street would hardly be so dull and lonely but that, somewhere or other along its extent, Clifford might discover matter to occupy his eye, and titillate, if not engross, his observation. Things familiar to the youngest child that had begun its outlook at existence seemed strange to him. A cab; an omnibus, with its populous interior, dropping here and there a passenger, and picking up another, and thus typifying that vast rolling vehicle, the world, the end of whose journey is everywhere and nowhere; these objects he followed eagerly with his eyes, but forgot them before the dust raised by the horses and wheels had settled along their track. As regarded novelties (among which cabs and omnibuses were to be reckoned), his mind appeared to have lost its proper gripe and retentiveness. Twice or thrice, for example, during the sunny hours of the day, a water-cart went along by the Pyncheon House, leaving a broad wake of moistened earth, instead of the white dust that had risen at a lady's lightest footfall; it was like a summer shower, which the city authorities had caught and tamed, and compelled it into the commonest routine of their convenience. With the water-cart Clifford could never grow familiar; it always affected him with just the same surprise as at first. His mind took an apparently sharp impression from it, but lost the recollection of this perambulatory shower, before its next reappearance, as completely as did the street itself, along which the heat so quickly strewed white dust again. It was the same with the railroad. Clifford could hear the obstreperous howl of the steam-devil, and, by leaning a little way from the arched window, could catch a glimpse of the trains of cars, flashing a brief transit across the extremity of the street. The idea of terrible energy thus forced upon him was new at every recurrence, and seemed to affect him as disagreeably, and with almost as much surprise, the hundredth time as the first.

Nothing gives a sadder sense of decay than this loss or suspension of the power to deal with unaccustomed things, and to keep up with the swiftness of the passing moment. It can merely be a suspended animation; for, were the power actually to perish, there would be little use of immortality. We are less than ghosts, for the time being, whenever this calamity befalls us.

Clifford was indeed the most inveterate of conservatives. All the antique fashions of the street were dear to him; even such as were characterized by a rudeness that would naturally have annoyed his fastidious senses. He loved the old rumbling and jolting carts, the former track of which he still found in his long-buried remembrance, as the observer of to-day finds the wheel-tracks of ancient vehicles in Herculaneum. The butcher's cart, with its snowy canopy, was an acceptable object; so was the fish-cart, heralded by its horn; so, likewise, was the countryman's cart of vegetables, plodding from door to door, with long pauses of the patient horse, while his owner drove a trade in turnips, carrots, summer-squashes, string-beans, green peas, and new potatoes, with half the house-wives of the neighborhood. The baker's cart, with the harsh music of its bells, had a pleasant effect on Clifford, because, as few things else did, it jingled the very dissonance of yore. One afternoon a scissor-grinder chanced to set his wheel a-going under the Pyncheon Elm, and just in front of the arched window. Children came running with their mothers' scissors, or the carving-knife, or the paternal razor, or anything else that lacked an edge (except, indeed, poor Clifford's wits), that the grinder might apply the article to his magic wheel, and give it back as good as new. Round went the busily revolving machinery, kept in motion by the scissor-grinder's foot, and wore away the hard steel against the hard stone, whence issued an intense and spiteful prolongation of a hiss as fierce as those emitted by Satan and his compeers in Pandemonium, though squeezed into smaller compass. It was an ugly, little, venomous serpent of a noise, as ever did petty violence to human ears. But Clifford listened with rapturous delight. The sound, however disagreeable, had very brisk life in it, and, together with the circle of curious children watching the revolutions of the wheel, appeared to give him a more vivid sense of active, bustling, and sunshiny existence than he had attained in almost any other way. Nevertheless, its charm lay chiefly in the past; for the scissor-grinder's wheel had hissed in his childish ears.

He sometimes made doleful complaint that there were no stage-coaches nowadays. And he asked in an injured tone what had become of all those old square-top chaises, with wings sticking out on either side, that used to be drawn by a plough-horse, and driven by a farmer's wife and daughter, peddling whortleberries and blackberries about the town. Their disappearance made him doubt, he said, whether the berries had not left off growing in the broad pastures and along the shady country lanes.

But anything that appealed to the sense of beauty, in however humble a way, did not require to be recommended by these old associations. This was observable when one of those Italian boys (who are rather a modern feature of our streets) came along with his barrel-organ, and stopped under the wide and cool shadows of the elm. With his quick professional eye he took note of the two faces watching him from the arched window, and, opening his instrument, began to scatter its melodies abroad. He had a monkey on his shoulder, dressed in a Highland plaid; and, to complete the sum of splendid attractions wherewith he presented himself to the public, there was a company of little figures, whose sphere and habitation was in the mahogany case of his organ, and whose principle of life was the music which the Italian made it his business to grind out. In all their variety of occupation,—the cobbler, the blacksmith, the soldier, the lady with her fan, the toper with his bottle, the milkmaid sitting by her cow,— this fortunate little society might truly be said to enjoy a harmonious existence, and to make life literally a dance. The Italian turned a crank; and, behold! every one of these small individuals started into the most curious vivacity. The cobbler wrought upon a shoe; the blacksmith hammered his iron; the soldier waved his glittering blade; the lady raised a tiny breeze with her fan; the jolly toper swigged lustily at his bottle; a scholar opened his book with eager thirst for knowledge, and turned his head to and fro along the page; the milkmaid energetically drained her cow; and a miser counted gold into his strong-box,—all at the same turning of a crank. Yes; and, moved by the self-same impulse, a lover saluted his mistress on her lips! Possibly some cynic, at once merry and bitter, had desired to signify, in this pantomimic scene, that we mortals, whatever our business or amusement,—however serious, however trifling,— all dance to one identical tune, and, in spite of our ridiculous activity, bring nothing finally to pass. For the most remarkable aspect of the affair was, that, at the cessation of the music, everybody was petrified, at once, from the most extravagant life into a dead torpor. Neither was the cobbler's shoe finished, nor the blacksmith's iron shaped out; nor was there a drop less of brandy in the toper's bottle, nor a drop more of milk in the milkmaid's pail, nor one additional coin in the miser's strong-box, nor was the scholar a page deeper in his book. All were precisely in the same condition as before they made themselves so ridiculous by their haste to toil, to enjoy, to accumulate gold, and to become wise. Saddest of all, moreover, the lover was none the happier for the maiden's granted kiss! But, rather than swallow this last too acrid ingredient, we reject the whole moral of the show.

The monkey, meanwhile, with a thick tail curling out into preposterous prolixity from beneath his tartans, took his station at the Italian's feet. He turned a wrinkled and abominable little visage to every passer-by, and to the circle of children that soon gathered round, and to Hepzibah's shop-door, and upward to the arched window, whence Phœbe and Clifford were looking down. Every moment, also, he took off his Highland bonnet, and performed a bow and scrape. Sometimes, moreover, he made personal application to individuals, holding out his small black palm, and otherwise plainly signifying his excessive desire for whatever filthy lucre might happen to be in anybody's pocket. The mean and low, yet strangely man-like expression of his wilted countenance; the prying and crafty glance, that showed him ready to gripe at every miserable advantage; his enormous tail (too enormous to be decently concealed under his gabardine), and the deviltry of nature which it betokened,—take this monkey just as he was, in short, and you could desire no better image of the Mammon of copper coin, symbolizing the grossest form of the love of money. Neither was there any possibility of satisfying the covetous little devil. Phœbe threw down a whole handful of cents, which he picked up with joyless eagerness, handed them over to the Italian for safekeeping, and immediately recommenced a series of pantomimic petitions for more.

Doubtless, more than one New-Englander—or, let him be of what country he might, it is as likely to be the case—passed by, and threw a look at the monkey, and went on, without imagining how nearly his own moral condition was here exemplified. Clifford, however, was a being of another order. He had taken childish delight in the music, and smiled, too, at the figures which it set in motion. But, after looking a while at the long-tailed imp, he was so shockèd by his horrible ugliness, spiritual as well as physical, that he actually began to shed tears; a weakness which men of merely delicate endowments, and destitute of the fiercer, deeper, and more tragic power of laughter, can hardly avoid, when the worst and meanest aspect of life happens to be presented to them.

Pyncheon Street was sometimes enlivened by spectacles of more imposing pretensions than the above, and which brought the multitude along with them. With a shivering repugnance at the idea of personal contact with the world, a powerful impulse still seized on Clifford, whenever the rush and roar of the human tide grew strongly audible to him. This was made evident, one day, when a political procession, with hundreds of flaunting banners, and drums, fifes, clarions, and cymbals, reverberating between the rows of buildings, marched all through town, and trailed its length of trampling footsteps, and most infrequent uproar, past the ordinarily quiet House of the Seven Gables. As a mere object of sight, nothing is more deficient in picturesque features than a procession seen in its passage through narrow streets. The spectator feels it to be fool's play, when he can distinguish the tedious commonplace of each man's visage, with the perspiration and weary self-importance on it, and the very cut of his pantaloons, and the stiffness or laxity of his shirt-collar, and the dust on the back of his black coat. In order to become majestic, it should be viewed from some vantage point, as it rolls its slow and long array through the centre of a wide plain, or the stateliest public square of a city; for then, by its remoteness, it melts all the petty personalities, of which it is made up, into one broad mass of existence,—one great life,—one collected body of mankind, with a vast, homogeneous spirit animating it. But, on the other hand, if an impressible person, standing alone over the brink of one of these processions, should behold it, not in its atoms, but in its aggregate,—as a mighty river of life, massive in its tide, and black with mystery, and, out of its depths, calling to the kindred depth within him,—then the contiguity would add to the effect. It might so fascinate him that he would hardly be restrained from plunging into the surging stream of human sympathies.

So it proved with Clifford. He shuddered; he grew pale; he threw an appealing look at Hepzibah and Phœbe, who were with him at the window. They comprehended nothing of his emotions, and supposed him merely disturbed by the unaccustomed tumult. At last, with tremulous limbs, he started up, set his foot on the window-sill, and in an instant more would have been in the unguarded balcony. As it was, the whole procession might have seen him, a wild, haggard figure, his gray locks floating in the wind that waved their banners; a lonely being, estranged from his race, but now feeling himself man again, by virtue of the irrepressible instinct that possessed him. Had Clifford attained the balcony, he would probably have leaped into the street; but whether impelled by the species of terror that sometimes urges its victim over the very precipice which he shrinks from, or by a natural magnetism, tending towards the great centre of humanity, it were not easy to decide. Both impulses might have wrought on him at once.

But his companions, affrighted by his gesture,—which was that of a man hurried away in spite of himself,—seized Clifford's garment and held him back. Hepzibah shrieked. Phœbe, to whom all extravagance was a horror, burst into sobs and tears.

"Clifford, Clifford! are you crazy?" cried his sister.

"I hardly know, Hepzibah," said Clifford, drawing a long breath. "Fear nothing,—it is over now,—but had I taken that plunge, and survived it, methinks it would have made me another man!"

Possibly, in some sense, Clifford may have been right. He needed a shock; or perhaps he required to take a deep, deep plunge into the ocean of human life, and to sink down and be covered by its profoundness, and then to emerge, sobered, invigorated, restored to the world and to himself. Perhaps, again, he required nothing less than the great final remedy —death!

A similar yearning to renew the broken links of brotherhood with his kind sometimes showed itself in a milder form; and once it was made beautiful by the religion that lay even deeper than itself. In the incident now to be sketched, there was a touching recognition, on Clifford's part, of God's care and love towards him,—towards this poor, forsaken man, who, if any mortal could, might have been pardoned for regarding himself as thrown aside, forgotten, and left to be the sport of some fiend, whose playfulness was an ecstasy of mischief.

It was the Sabbath morning; one of those bright, calm Sabbaths, with its own hallowed atmosphere, when Heaven seems to diffuse itself over the earth's face in a solemn smile, no less sweet than solemn. On such a Sabbath morn, were we pure enough to be its medium, we should be conscious of the earth's natural worship ascending through our frames, on whatever spot of ground we stood. The church-bells, with various tones, but all in harmony, were calling out, and responding to one another,— "It is the Sabbath!—The Sabbath!—Yea; the Sabbath!"—and over the whole city the bells scattered the blessed sounds, now slowly, now with livelier joy, now one bell alone, now all the bells together, crying earnestly, —"It is the Sabbath!" and flinging their accents afar off, to melt into the air, and pervade it with the holy word. The air, with God's sweetest and tenderest sunshine in it, was meet for mankind to breathe into their hearts, and send it forth again as the utterance of prayer.

Clifford sat at the window with Hepzibah, watching the neighbors as they stepped into the street. All of them, however unspiritual on other days, were transfigured by the Sabbath influence; so that their very garments—whether it were an old man's decent coat well brushed for the thousandth time, or a little boy's first sack and trousers finished yesterday by his mother's needle—had somewhat of the quality of ascension-robes. Forth, likewise, from the portal of the old house, stepped Phœbe, putting up her small green sunshade, and throwing upward a glance and smile of parting kindness to the faces at the arched window. In her aspect there was a familiar gladness, and a holiness that you could play with, and yet reverence it as much as ever. She was like a prayer, offered up in the homeliest beauty of one's mother-tongue. Fresh was Phœbe, moreover, and airy and sweet in her apparel; as if nothing that she wore —neither her gown, nor her small straw bonnet, nor her little kerchief, any more than her snowy stockings—had ever been put on before; or, if worn, were all the fresher for it, and with a fragrance as if they had lain among the rose-buds.

The girl waved her hand to Hepzibah and Clifford, and went up the street; a religion in herself, warm, simple, true, with a substance that could walk on earth, and a spirit that was capable of heaven.

"Hepzibah," asked Clifford, after watching Phœbe to the corner, "do you never go to church?"

"No, Clifford!" she replied,—"not these many, many years!"

"Were I to be there," he rejoined, "it seems to me that I could pray once more, when so many human souls were praying all around me!"

She looked into Clifford's face, and beheld there a soft natural effusion; for his heart gushed out, as it were, and ran over at his eyes, in delightful reverence for God, and kindly affection for his human brethren. The emotion communicated itself to Hepzibah. She yearned to take him by the hand, and go and kneel down, they two together,—both so long separate from the world, and, as she now recognized, scarcely friends with Him above,—to kneel down among the people, and be reconciled to God and man at once.

"Dear brother," said she, earnestly, "let us go! We belong nowhere. We have not a foot of space in any church to kneel upon; but let us go to some place of worship, even if we stand in the broad aisle. Poor and forsaken as we are, some pew-door will be opened to us!"

So Hepzibah and her brother made themselves ready,—as ready as they could in the best of their old-fashioned garments, which had hung on pegs, or been laid away in trunks, so long that the dampness and mouldy smell of the past was on them,—made themselves ready, in their faded bettermost, to go to church. They descended the staircase together, —gaunt, sallow Hepzibah, and pale, emaciated, age-stricken Clifford! They pulled open the front door, and stepped across the threshold, and felt, both of them, as if they were standing in the presence of the whole world, and with mankind's great and terrible eye on them alone. The eye of their Father seemed to be withdrawn, and gave them no encouragement. The warm sunny air of the street made them shiver. Their hearts quaked within them at the idea of taking one step farther.

"It cannot be, Hepzibah!—it is too late," said Clifford, with deep sadness. "We are ghosts! We have no right among human beings,—no right anywhere but in this old house, which has a curse on it, and which, therefore, we are doomed to haunt! And, besides," he continued, with a fastidious sensibility, inalienably characteristic of the man, "it would not be fit nor beautiful to go! It is an ugly thought that I should be frightful to my fellow-beings, and that children would cling to their mothers' gowns at sight of me!"

They shrank back into the dusky passage-way, and closed the door. But, going up the staircase again, they found the whole interior of the house tenfold more dismal, and the air closer and heavier, for the glimpse and breath of freedom which they had just snatched. They could not flee; their jailer had but left the door ajar in mockery, and stood behind it to watch them stealing out. At the threshold, they felt his pitiless gripe upon them. For, what other dungeon is so dark as one's own heart! What jailer so inexorable as one's self!

But it would be no fair picture of Clifford's state of mind were we to represent him as continually or prevailingly wretched. On the contrary, there was no other man in the city, we are bold to affirm, of so much as half his years, who enjoyed so many lightsome and griefless moments as himself. He had no burden of care upon him; there were none of those questions and contingencies with the future to be settled which wear away all other lives, and render them not worth having by the very process of providing for their support. In this respect he was a child,—a child for the whole term of his existence, be it long or short. Indeed, his life seemed to be standing still at a period little in advance of childhood, and to cluster all his reminiscences about that epoch; just as, after the torpor of a heavy blow, the sufferer's reviving consciousness goes back to a moment considerably behind the accident that stupefied him. He sometimes told Phœbe and Hepzibah his dreams, in which he invariably played the part of a child, or a very young man. So vivid were they, in his relation of them, that he once held a dispute with his sister as to the particular figure or print of a chintz morning-dress, which he had seen their mother wear, in the dream of the preceding night. Hepzibah, piquing herself on a woman's accuracy in such matters, held it to be slightly different from what Clifford described; but, producing the very gown from an old trunk, it proved to be identical with his remembrance of it. Had Clifford, every time that he emerged out of dreams so lifelike, undergone the torture of transformation from a boy into an old and broken man, the daily recurrence of the shock would have been too much to bear. It would have caused an acute agony to thrill from the morning twilight, all the day through, until bedtime; and even then would have mingled a dull, inscrutable pain, and pallid hue of misfortune, with the visionary bloom and adolescence of his slumber. But the nightly moonshine interwove itself with the morning mist, and enveloped him as in a robe, which he hugged about his person, and seldom let realities pierce through; he was not often quite awake, but slept open-eyed, and perhaps fancied himself most dreaming then.

Thus, lingering always so near his childhood, he had sympathies with children, and kept his heart the fresher thereby, like a reservoir into which rivulets were pouring not far from the fountain-head. Though prevented, by a subtile sense of propriety, from desiring to associate with them, he loved few things better than to look out of the arched window, and see a little girl driving her hoop along the sidewalk, or school-boys at a game of ball. Their voices, also, were very pleasant to him, heard at a distance, all swarming and intermingling together as flies do in a sunny room.

Clifford would, doubtless, have been glad to share their sports. One afternoon he was seized with an irresistible desire to blow soap-bubbles; an amusement, as Hepzibah told Phœbe apart, that had been a favorite one with her brother when they were both children. Behold him, therefore, at the arched window, with an earthern pipe in his mouth! Behold him, with his gray hair, and a wan, unreal smile over his countenance, where still hovered a beautiful grace, which his worst enemy must have acknowledged to be spiritual and immortal, since it had survived so long!

Behold him, scattering airy spheres abroad, from the window into the street! Little impalpable worlds were those soap-bubbles, with the big world depicted, in hues bright as imagination, on the nothing of their surface. It was curious to see how the passers-by regarded these brilliant fantasies, as they came floating down, and made the dull atmosphere imaginative about them. Some stopped to gaze, and, perhaps, carried a pleasant recollection of the bubbles onward as far as the street-corner; some looked angrily upward, as if poor Clifford wronged them by setting an image of beauty afloat so near their dusty pathway. A great many put out their fingers or their walking-sticks to touch, withal; and were perversely gratified, no doubt, when the bubble, with all its pictured earth and sky scene, vanished as if it had never been.

At length, just as an elderly gentleman of very dignified presence happened to be passing, a large bubble sailed majestically down, and burst right against his nose! He looked up,—at first with a stern, keen glance, which penetrated at once into the obscurity behind the arched window,—then with a smile which might be conceived as diffusing a dog-day sultriness for the space of several yards about him.

."Aha, Cousin Clifford!" cried Judge Pyncheon. "What! still blowing soap-bubbles!"

The tone seemed as if meant to be kind and soothing, but yet had a bitterness of sarcasm in it. As for Clifford, an absolute palsy of fear came over him. Apart from any definite cause of dread which his past experience might have given him, he felt that native and original horror of the excellent Judge which is proper to a weak, delicate, and apprehensive character in the presence of massive strength. Strength is incomprehensible by weakness, and, therefore, the more terrible. There is no greater bugbear than a strong-willed relative in the circle, of his own connections.

## XII

### The Daguerreotypist

It must not be supposed that the life of a personage naturally so active as Phœbe could be wholly confined within the precincts of the old Pyncheon House. Clifford's demands upon her time were usually satisfied, in those long days, considerably earlier than sunset. Quiet as his daily existence seemed, it nevertheless drained all the resources by which he lived. It was not physical exercise that overwearied him,—for except that he sometimes wrought a little with a hoe, or paced the garden-walk, or, in rainy weather, traversed a large unoccupied room,—it was his tendency to remain only too quiescent, as regarded any toil of the limbs and muscles.

But, either there was a smouldering fire within him that consumed his vital energy, or the monotony that would have dragged itself with benumbing effect over a mind differently situated was no monotony to Clifford. Possibly, he was in a state of second growth and recovery, and was constantly assimilating nutriment for his spirit and intellect from sights, sounds, and events, which passed as a perfect void to persons more practised with the world. As all is activity and vicissitude to the new mind of a child, so might it be, likewise, to a mind that had undergone a kind of new creation, after its long-suspended life.

Be the cause what it might, Clifford commonly retired to rest, thoroughly exhausted, while the sunbeams were still melting through his window-curtains, or were thrown with late lustre on the chamber wall. And while he thus slept early, as other children do, and dreamed of childhood, Phœbe was free to follow her own tastes for the remainder of the day and evening.

This was a freedom essential to the health even of a character so little susceptible of morbid influences as that of Phœbe. The old house, as we have already said, had both the dry-rot and the damp-rot in its walls; it was not good to breathe no other atmosphere than that. Hepzibah, though she had her valuable and redeeming traits, had grown to be a kind of lunatic, by imprisoning herself so long in one place, with no other company than a single series of ideas, and but one affection, and one bitter sense of wrong. Clifford, the reader may perhaps imagine, was too inert to operate morally on his fellow-creatures, however intimate and exclusive their relations with him. But the sympathy or magnetism among human beings is more subtile and universal than we think; it exists, indeed, among different classes of organized life, and vibrates from one to another. A flower, for instance, as Phœbe herself observed, always began to droop sooner in Clifford's hand, or Hepzibah's, than in her own; and by the same law, converting her whole daily life into a flower-fragrance for these two sickly spirits, the blooming girl must inevitably droop and fade much sooner than if worn on a younger and happier breast. Unless she had now and then indulged her brisk impulses, and breathed rural air in a suburban walk, or ocean breezes along the shore,—had occasionally obeyed the impulse of Nature, in New England girls, by attending a metaphysical or philosophical lecture, or viewing a seven-mile panorama, or listening to a concert,—had gone shopping about the city, ransacking entire depots of splendid merchandise, and bringing home a ribbon,—had employed, likewise, a little time to read the Bible in her chamber, and had stolen a little more to think of her mother and her native place,—unless for such moral medicines as the above, we should soon have beheld our poor Phœbe grow thin and put on a bleached unwholesome aspect, and assume strange, shy ways, prophetic of old-maidenhood and a cheerless future.

Even as it was, a change grew visible; a change partly to be regretted, although whatever charm it infringed upon was repaired by another, perhaps more precious. She was not so constantly gay, but had her moods of thought, which Clifford, on the whole, liked better than her former phase of unmingled cheerfulness; because now she understood him better and more delicately, and sometimes even interpreted him to himself. Her eyes looked larger, and darker, and deeper; so deep, at some silent moments, that they seemed like Artesian wells, down, down, into the infinite. She was less girlish than when we first beheld her alighting from the omnibus; less girlish, but more a woman.

The only youthful mind with which Phœbe had an opportunity of frequent intercourse was that of the daguerreotypist. Inevitably, by the pressure of the seclusion about them, they had been brought into habits of some familiarity. Had they met under different circumstances, neither of these young persons would have been likely to bestow much thought upon the other, unless, indeed, their extreme dissimilarity should have proved a principle of mutual attraction. Both, it is true, were characters proper to New England life, and possessing a common ground, therefore, in their more external developments; but as unlike, in their respective interiors, as if their native climes had been at world-wide distance. During the early part of their acquaintance, Phœbe had held back rather more than was customary with her frank and simple manners from Holgrave's not very marked advances. Nor was she yet satisfied that she knew him well, although they almost daily met and talked together, in a kind, friendly, and what seemed to be a familiar way.

The artist, in a desultory manner, had imparted to Phœbe something of his history. Young as he was, and had his career terminated at the point already attained, there had been enough of incident to fill, very creditably, an autobiographic volume. A romance on the plan of Gil Blas, adapted to American society and manners, would cease to be a romance. The experience of many individuals among us, who think it hardly worth the telling, would equal the vicissitudes of the Spaniard's earlier life; while their ultimate success, or the point whither they tend, may be incomparably higher than any that a novelist would imagine for his hero. Holgrave, as he told Phœbe, somewhat proudly, could not boast of his origin, unless as being exceedingly humble, nor of his education, except that it had been the scantiest possible, and obtained by a few winter-months' attendance at a district school. Left early to his own guidance, he had begun to be self-dependent while yet a boy; and it was a condition aptly suited to his natural force of will. Though now but twenty-two years old (lacking some months, which are years in such a life), he had already been, first, a country schoolmaster; next, a salesman in a country store; and, either at the same time or afterwards, the political editor of a country newspaper. He had subsequently travelled New England and the Middle States, as a pedlar, in the employment of a Connecticut manufactory of cologne-water and other essences. In an episodical way he had studied and practised dentistry, and with very flattering success, especially in many of the factory-towns along our inland streams. As a supernumerary official, of some kind or other, aboard a packet-ship, he had visited Europe, and found means, before his return, to see Italy, and part of France and Germany. At a later period he had spent some months in a community of Fourierists. Still more recently he had been a public lecturer on Mesmerism, for which science (as he assured Phœbe, and, indeed, satisfactorily proved, by putting Chanticleer, who happened to be scratching near by, to sleep) he had very remarkable endowments.

His present phrase, as a daguerreotypist, was of no more importance in his own view, nor likely to be more permanent, than any of the preceding ones. It had been taken up with the careless alacrity of an adventurer, who had his bread to earn. It would be thrown aside as carelessly, whenever he should choose to earn his bread by some other equally digressive means. But what was most remarkable, and, perhaps, showed a more than common poise in the young man, was the fact that, amid all these personal vicissitudes, he had never lost his identity. Homeless as he had been,—continually changing his whereabout, and, therefore, responsible neither to public opinion nor to individuals,—putting off one exterior, and snatching up another, to be soon shifted for a third,—he had never violated the innermost man, but had carried his conscience along with him. It was impossible to know Holgrave without recognizing this to be the fact. Hepzibah had seen it. Phœbe soon saw it, likewise, and gave him the sort of confidence which such a certainty inspires. She was startled, however, and sometimes repelled,—not by any doubt of his integrity to whatever law he acknowledged, but by a sense that his law differed from her own. He made her uneasy, and seemed to unsettle everything around her, by his lack of reverence for what was fixed, unless, at a moment's warning, it could establish its right to hold its ground.

Then, moreover, she scarcely thought him affectionate in his nature. He was too calm and cool an observer. Phœbe felt his eye, often; his heart, seldom or never. He took a certain kind of interest in Hepzibah and her brother, and Phœbe herself. He studied them attentively, and allowed no slightest circumstance of their individualities to escape him. He was ready to do them whatever good he might; but, after all, he never exactly made common cause with them, nor gave any reliable evidence that he loved them better in proportion as he knew them more. In his relations with them, he seemed to be in quest of mental food, not heart-sustenance. Phœbe could not conceive what interested him so much in her friends and herself, intellectually, since he cared nothing for them, or, comparatively, so little, as objects of human affection.

Always, in his interviews with Phœbe, the artist made especial inquiry as to the welfare of Clifford, whom, except at the Sunday festival, he seldom saw.

"Does he still seem happy?" he asked one day.

"As happy as a child," answered Phœbe; "but—like a child, too—very easily disturbed."

"How disturbed?" inquired Holgrave. "By things without, or by thoughts within?"

"I cannot see his thoughts! How should I?" replied Phœbe, with simple piquancy. "Very often his humor changes without any reason that can be

guessed at, just as a cloud comes over the sun. Latterly, since I have be
gun to know him better, I feel it to be not quite right to look closely into
his moods. He has had such a great sorrow, that his heart is made all
solemn and sacred by it. When he is cheerful,—when the sun shines into
his mind,—then I venture to peep in, just as far as the light reaches, but
no further. It is holy ground where the shadow falls!"

"How prettily you express this sentiment!" said the artist. "I can
understand the feeling, without possessing it. Had I your opportunities,
no scruples would prevent me from fathoming Clifford to the full depth
of my plummet-line!"

"How strange that you should wish it!" remarked Phœbe, involuntarily. "What is Cousin Clifford to you?"

"Oh, nothing,—of course, nothing!" answered Holgrave, with a smile.
"Only this is such an odd and incomprehensible world! The more I look
at it the more it puzzles me, and I begin to suspect that a man's bewilderment is the measure of his wisdom. Men and women, and children, too,
are such strange creatures, that one never can be certain that he really
knows them; nor ever guess what they have been, from what he sees them
to be now. Judge Pyncheon! Clifford! What a complex riddle—a complexity of complexities—do they present! It requires intuitive sympathy,
like a young girl's, to solve it. A mere observer, like myself (who never
have any intuitions, and am, at best, only subtile and acute), is pretty
certain to go astray."

The artist now turned the conversation to themes less dark than that
which they had touched upon. Phœbe and he were young together; nor
had Holgrave, in his premature experience of life, wasted entirely that
beautiful spirit of youth, which, gushing forth from one small heart and
fancy, may diffuse itself over the universe, making it all as bright as on
the first day of creation. Man's own youth is the world's youth; at least,
he feels as if it were, and imagines that the earth's granite substance is
something not yet hardened, and which he can mould into whatever shape
he likes. So it was with Holgrave. He could talk sagely about the world's
old age, but never actually believed what he said; he was a young man
still, and therefore looked upon the world—that gray-bearded and
wrinkled profligate, decrepit, without being venerable—as a tender strip-
ling, capable of being improved into all that it ought to be, but scarcely
yet had shown the remotest promise of becoming. He had that sense, or
inward prophecy,—which a young man had better never have been born
than not to have, and a mature man had better die at once than utterly
to relinquish,—that we are not doomed to creep on forever in the old bad
way, but that, this very now, there are the harbingers abroad of a golden
era, to be accomplished in his own life-time. It seemed to Holgrave—as
doubtless it has seemed to the hopeful of every century since the epoch of
Adam's grandchildren—that in this age, more than ever before, the moss-
grown and rotten Past is to be torn down, and lifeless institutions to be
thrust out of the way, and their dead corpses buried, and everything to
begin anew.

As to the main point,—may we never live to doubt it!—as to the better centuries that are coming, the artist was surely right. His error lay in supposing that this age, more than any past or future one, is destined to see the tattered garments of Antiquity exchanged for a new suit, instead of gradually renewing themselves by patchwork; in applying his own little life-span as the measure of an interminable achievement; and, more than all, in fancying that it mattered anything to the great end in view whether he himself should contend for it or against it. Yet it was well for him to think so. This enthusiasm, infusing itself through the calmness of his character, and thus taking an aspect of settled thought and wisdom, would serve to keep his youth pure, and make his aspirations high. And when, with the years settling down more weightily upon him, his early faith should be modified by inevitable experience, it would be with no harsh and sudden revolution of his sentiments. He would still have faith in man's brightening destiny, and perhaps love him all the better, as he should recognize his helplessness in his own behalf; and the haughty faith, with which he began life, would be well bartered for a far humbler one at its close, in discerning that man's best directed effort accomplishes a kind of dream, while God is the sole worker of realities.

Holgrave had read very little, and that little in passing through the thoroughfare of life, where the mystic language of his books was necessarily mixed up with the babble of the multitude, so that both one and the other were apt to lose any sense that might have been properly their own. He considered himself a thinker, and was certainly of a thoughtful turn, but, with his own path to discover, had perhaps hardly yet reached the point where an educated man begins to think. The true value of his character lay in that deep consciousness of inward strength, which made all his past vicissitudes seem merely like a change of garments; in that enthusiasm, so quiet that he scarcely knew of its existence, but which gave a warmth to everything that he laid his hand on; in that personal ambition, hidden—from his own as well as other eyes—among his more generous impulses, but in which lurked a certain efficacy, that might solidify him from a theorist into the champion of some practicable cause. Altogether in his culture and want of culture,—in his crude, wild, and misty philosophy, and the practical experience that counteracted some of its tendencies; in his magnanimous zeal for man's welfare, and his recklessness of whatever the ages had established in man's behalf; in his faith, and in his infidelity; in what he had, and in what he lacked,—the artist might fitly enough stand forth as the representative of many compeers in his native land.

His career it would be difficult to prefigure. There appeared to be qualities in Holgrave, such as, in a country where everything is free to the hand that can grasp it, could hardly fail to put some of the world's prizes within his reach. But these matters are delightfully uncertain. At almost every step in life, we meet with young men of just about Holgrave's age, for whom we anticipate wonderful things, but of whom, even after much and careful inquiry, we never happen to hear another word. The effervescence of youth and passion, and the fresh gloss of the intellect and imagination, endow them with a false brilliancy, which makes fools of themselves and other people. Like certain chintzes, calicoes, and ginghams, they show finely in their first newness, but cannot stand the sun and rain, and assume a very sober aspect after washing-day.

But our business is with Holgrave as we find him on this particular afternoon, and in the arbor of the Pyncheon garden. In that point of view, it was a pleasant sight to behold this young man, with so much faith in himself, and so fair an appearance of admirable powers,—so little harmed, too, by the many tests that had tried his metal,—it was pleasant to see him in his kindly intercourse with Phœbe. Her thought had scarcely done him justice when it pronounced him cold; or, if so, he had grown warmer now. Without such purpose on her part, and unconsciously on his, she made the House of the Seven Gables like a home to him, and the garden a familiar precinct. With the insight on which he prided himself, he fancied that he could look through Phœbe, and all around her, and could read her off like a page of a child's story-book. But these transparent natures are often deceptive in their depth; those pebbles at the bottom of the fountain are farther from us than we think. Thus the artist, whatever he might judge of Phœbe's capacity, was beguiled, by some silent charm of hers, to talk freely of what he dreamed of doing in the world. He poured himself out as to another self. Very possibly, he forgot Phœbe while he talked to her, and was moved only by the inevitable tendency of thought, when rendered sympathetic by enthusiasm and emotion, to flow into the first safe reservoir which it finds. But, had you peeped at them through the chinks of the garden-fence, the young man's earnestness and heightened color might have led you to suppose that he was making love to the young girl!

At length, something was said by Holgrave that made it apposite for Phœbe to inquire what had first brought him acquainted with her cousin Hepzibah, and why he now chose to lodge in the desolate old Pyncheon House. Without directly answering her, he turned from the Future, which had heretofore been the theme of his discourse, and began to speak of the influences of the Past. One subject, indeed, is but the reverberation of the other.

"Shall we never, never get rid of this Past?" cried he, keeping up the earnest tone of his preceding conversation. "It lies upon the Present like a giant's dead body! In fact, the case is just as if a young giant were compelled to waste all his strength in carrying about the corpse of the old giant, his grandfather, who died a long while ago, and only needs to be decently buried. Just think a moment, and it will startle you to see what slaves we are to bygone times,—to Death, if we give the matter the right word!"

"But I do not see it," observed Phœbe.

"For example, then" continued Holgrave: "a dead man, if he happen to have made a will, disposes of wealth no longer his own; or, if he die intestate, it is distributed in accordance with the notions of men much longer dead than he. A dead man sits on all our judgment-seats; and living judges do but search out and repeat his decisions. We read in dead men's books! We laugh at dead men's jokes, and cry at dead men's pathos! We are sick of dead men's diseases, physical and moral, and die of the same remedies with which dead doctors killed their patients! We worship the living Deity according to dead men's forms and creeds. Whatever we seek to do, of our own free motion, a dead man's icy hand obstructs us! Turn our eyes to what point we may, a dead man's white, immitigable face encounters them, and freezes our very heart! And we must be dead ourselves before we can begin to have our proper influence on our own world, which will then be no longer our world, but the world of another generation, with which we shall have no shadow of a right to interfere. I ought to have said, too, that we live in dead men's houses; as, for instance, in this of the Seven Gables!"

"And why not," said Phœbe, "so long as we can be comfortable in them?"

"But we shall live to see the day, I trust," went on the artist, "when no man shall build his house for posterity. Why should he? He might just as reasonably order a durable suit of clothes,—leather, or gutta-percha, or whatever else lasts longest,—so that his great-grandchildren should have the benefit of them, and cut precisely the same figure in the world that he himself does. If each generation were allowed and expected to build its own houses, that single change, comparatively unimportant in itself, would imply almost every reform which society is now suffering for. I doubt whether even our public edifices—our capitols, state-houses, courthouses, city-hall, and churches—ought to be built of such permanent materials as stone or brick. It were better that they should crumble to ruin once in twenty years, or thereabouts, as a hint to the people to examine into and reform the institutions which they symbolize."

"How you hate everything old!" said Phœbe, in dismay. "It makes me dizzy to think of such a shifting world!"

"I certainly love nothing mouldy," answered Holgrave. "Now, this old Pyncheon House! Is it a wholesome place to live in, with its black shingles, and the green moss that shows how damp they are?—its dark, low-studded rooms?—its grime and sordidness, which are the crystallization on its walls of the human breath, that has been drawn and exhaled here in discontent and anguish? The house ought to be purified with fire, —purified till only its ashes remain!"

"Then why do you live in it?" asked Phœbe, a little piqued.

"Oh, I am pursuing my studies here; not in books, however," replied Holgrave. "The house, in my view, is expressive of that odious and abominable Past, with all its bad influences, against which I have just been declaiming. I dwell in it for a while, that I may know the better how to hate it. By the by, did you ever hear the story of Maule, the wizard, and what happened between him and your immeasurably great-grandfather?"

"Yes, indeed!" said Phœbe; "I heard it long ago, from my father, and two or three times from my cousin Hepzibah, in the month that I have been here. She seems to think that all the calamities of the Pyncheons began from that quarrel with the wizard, as you call him. And you, Mr. Holgrave, look as if you thought so too! How singular, that you should believe what is so very absurd, when you reject many things that are a great deal worthier of credit!"

"I do believe it," said the artist, seriously; "not as a superstition, however, but as proved by unquestionable facts, and as exemplifying a theory. Now, see: under those seven gables, at which we now look up,—and which old Colonel Pyncheon meant to be the house of his descendants, in prosperity and happiness, down to an epoch far beyond the present,—under that roof, through a portion of three centuries, there has been perpetual remorse of conscience, a constantly defeated hope, strife amongst kindred, various misery, a strange form of death, dark suspicion, unspeakable disgrace,—all, or most of which calamity I have the means of tracing to the old Puritan's inordinate desire to plant and endow a family. To plant a family! This idea is at the bottom of most of the wrong and mischief which men do. The truth is, that, once in every half-century, at longest, a family should be merged into the great, obscure mass of humanity, and forget all about its ancestors. Human blood, in order to keep its freshness, should run in hidden streams, as the water of an aqueduct is conveyed in subterranean pipes. In the family existence of these Pyncheons, for instance,—forgive me, Phœbe; but I cannot think of you as one of them,—in their brief New England pedigree, there has been time enough to infect them all with one kind of lunacy or another!"

"You speak very unceremoniously of my kindred," said Phœbe, debating with herself whether she ought to take offence.

"I speak true thoughts to a true mind!" answered Holgrave, with a vehemence which Phœbe had not before witnessed in him. "The truth is as I say! Furthermore, the original perpetrator and father of this mischief appears to have perpetuated himself, and still walks the street,—at least, his very image, in mind and body,—with the fairest prospect of transmitting to posterity as rich and as wretched an inheritance as he has received! Do you remember the daguerreotype, and its resemblance to the old portrait?"

"How strangely in earnest you are!" exclaimed Phœbe, looking at him with surprise and perplexity; half alarmed and partly inclined to laugh. "You talk of the lunacy of the Pyncheons; is it contagious?"

"I understand you!" said the artist, coloring and laughing. "I believe I am a little mad. This subject has taken hold of my mind with the strangest tenacity of clutch since I have lodged in yonder old gable. As one method of throwing it off, I have put an incident of the Pyncheon family history, with which I happen to be acquainted, into the form of a legend, and mean to publish it in a magazine."

"Do you write for the magazines?" inquired Phœbe.

"Is it possible you did not know it?" cried Holgrave. "Well, such is literary fame! Yes, Miss Phœbe Pyncheon, among the multitude of my marvellous gifts I have that of writing stories; and my name has figured,

I can assure you, on the covers of Graham and Godey, making as respectable an appearance, for aught I could see, as any of the canonized beadroll with which it was associated. In the humorous line, I am thought to have a very pretty way with me; and as for pathos, I am as provocative of tears as an onion. But shall I read you my story?"

"Yes, if it is not very long," said Phœbe,—and added laughingly,—"nor very dull."

As this latter point was one which the daguerreotypist could not decide for himself, he forthwith produced his roll of manuscript, and, while the late sunbeams gilded the seven gables, began to read.

## XIII

### ALICE PYNCHEON

THERE was a message brought, one day, from the worshipful Gervayse Pyncheon to young Matthew Maule, the carpenter, desiring his immediate presence at the House of the Seven Gables.

"And what does your master want with me?" said the carpenter to Mr. Pyncheon's black servant. "Does the house need any repair? Well it may, by this time; and no blame to my father who built it, neither! I was reading the old Colonel's tombstone, no longer ago than last Sabbath; and, reckoning from that date, the house has stood seven-and-thirty years. No wonder if there should be a job to do on the roof."

"Don't know what massa wants," answered Scipio. "The house is a berry good house, and old Colonel Pyncheon think so too, I reckon;—else why the old man haunt it so, and frighten a poor nigga, as he does?"

"Well, well, friend Scipio; let your master know that I'm coming," said the carpenter, with a laugh. "For a fair, workmanlike job, he'll find me his man. And so the house is haunted, is it? It will take a tighter workman than I am to keep the spirits out of the Seven Gables. Even if the Colonel would be quiet," he added, muttering to himself, "my old grandfather, the wizard, will be pretty sure to stick to the Pyncheons as long as their walls hold together."

"What's that you mutter to yourself, Matthew Maule?" asked Scipio. "And what for do you look so black at me?"

"No matter, darky!" said the carpenter. "Do you think nobody is to look black but yourself? Go tell your master I'm coming; and if you happen to see Mistress Alice, his daughter, give Matthew Maule's humble respects to her. She has brought a fair face from Italy,—fair, and gentle, and proud,—has that same Alice Pyncheon!"

"He talk of Mistress Alice!" cried Scipio, as he returned from his errand. "The low carpenter-man! He no business so much as to look at her a great way off!"

This young Matthew Maule, the carpenter, it must be observed, was a person little understood, and not very generally liked, in the town where he resided; not that anything could be alleged against his integrity, or his skill and diligence in the handicraft which he exercised. The aversion (as it might justly be called) with which many persons regarded him was partly the result of his own character and deportment, and partly an inheritance.

He was the grandson of a former Matthew Maule, one of the early settlers of the town, and who had been a famous and terrible wizard in his day. This old reprobate was one of the sufferers when Cotton Mather, and his brother ministers, and the learned judges, and other wise men, and Sir William Phipps, the sagacious governor, made such laudable efforts to weaken the great enemy of souls, by sending a multitude of his adherents up the rocky pathway of Gallows Hill. Since those days, no doubt, it had grown to be suspected that, in consequence of an unfortunate overdoing of a work praiseworthy in itself, the proceedings against the witches had proved far less acceptable to the Beneficent Father than to that very Arch Enemy whom they were intended to distress and utterly overwhelm. It is not the less certain, however, that awe and terror brooded over the memories of those who died for this horrible crime of witchcraft. Their graves, in the crevices of the rocks, were supposed to be incapable of retaining the occupants who had been so hastily thrust into them. Old Matthew Maule, especially, was known to have as little hesitation or difficulty in rising out of his grave as an ordinary man in getting out of bed, and was as often seen at midnight as living people at noonday. This pestilent wizard (in whom his just punishment seemed to have wrought no manner of amendment) had an inveterate habit of haunting a certain mansion, styled the House of the Seven Gables, against the owner of which he pretended to hold an unsettled claim for ground-rent. The ghost, it appears, —with the pertinacity which was one of his distinguishing characteristics while alive,—insisted that he was the rightful proprietor of the site upon which the house stood. His terms were, that either the aforesaid ground-rent, from the day when the cellar began to be dug, should be paid down, or the mansion itself given up; else he, the ghostly creditor, would have his finger in all the affairs of the Pyncheons, and make everything' go wrong with them, though it should be a thousand years after his death. It was a wild story, perhaps, but seemed not altogether so incredible to those who could remember what an inflexibly obstinate old fellow this wizard Maule had been.

Now, the wizard's grandson, the young Matthew Maule of our story, was popularly supposed to have inherited some of his ancestor's questionable traits. It is wonderful how many absurdities were promulgated in reference to the young man. He was fabled, for example, to have a strange power of getting into people's dreams, and regulating matters there according to his own fancy, pretty much like the stage-manager of a theatre.

There was a great deal of talk among the neighbors, particularly the petticoated ones, about what they called the witchcraft of Maule's eye. Some
said that he could look into people's minds; others, that, by the marvellous power of this eye, he could draw people into his own mind, or send
them, if he pleased, to do errands to his grandfather, in the spiritual
world; others, again, that it was what is termed an Evil Eye, and possessed the valuable faculty of blighting corn, and drying children into
mummies with the heartburn. But, after all, what worked most to the
young carpenter's disadvantage was, first, the reserve and sternness of his
natural disposition, and next, the fact of his not being a church-com-
municant, and the suspicion of his holding heretical tenets in matters of
religion and polity.

After receiving Mr. Pyncheon's message, the carpenter merely tarried
to finish a small job, which he happened to have in hand, and then took
his way towards the House of the Seven Gables. This noted edifice,
though its style might be getting a little out of fashion, was still as respectable a family residence as that of any gentleman in town. The present owner, Gervayse Pyncheon, was said to have contracted a dislike to
the house, in consequence of a shock to his sensibility, in early childhood,
from the sudden death of his grandfather. In the very act of running to
climb Colonel Pyncheon's knee, the boy had discovered the old Puritan
to be a corpse! On arriving at manhood, Mr. Pyncheon had visited England, where he married a lady of fortune, and had subsequently spent
many years, partly in the mother country, and partly in various cities on
the continent of Europe. During this period, the family mansion had been
consigned to the charge of a kinsman, who was allowed to make it his
home for the time being, in consideration of keeping the premises in thorough repair. So faithfully had this contract been fulfilled, that now, as the
carpenter approached the house, his practised eye could detect nothing to
criticise in its condition. The peaks of the seven gables rose up sharply;
the shingled roof looked thoroughly water-tight; and the glittering plas-
ter-work entirely covered the exterior walls, and sparkled in the October
sun, as if it had been new only a week ago.

The house had that pleasant aspect of life which is like the cheery expression of comfortable activity in the human countenance. You could
see, at once, that there was the stir of a large family within it. A huge load
of oak-wood was passing through the gateway, towards the outbuildings
in the rear; the fat cook—or probably it might be the housekeeper—stood
at the side door, bargaining for some turkeys and poultry, which a countryman had brought for sale. Now and then a maid-servant, neatly
dressed, and now the shining sable face of a slave, might be seen bustling
across the windows, in the lower part of the house. At an open window of
a room in the second story, hanging over some pots of beautiful and delicate flowers,—exotics, but which had never known a more genial sunshine
than that of the New England autumn,—was the figure of a young lady,
an exotic, like the flowers, and beautiful and delicate as they. Her presence imparted an indescribable grace and faint witchery to the whole edi-

fice. In other respects, it was a substantial, jolly-looking mansion, and seemed fit to be the residence of a patriarch, who might establish his own headquarters in the front gable and assign one of the remainder to each of his six children, while the great chimney in the centre should symbolize the old fellow's hospitable heart, which kept them all warm, and made a great whole of the seven smaller ones.

There was a vertical sundial on the front gable; and as the carpenter passed beneath it, he looked up and noted the hour.

"Three o'clock!" said he to himself. "My father told me that dial was put up only an hour before the old Colonel's death. How truly it has kept time these seven-and-thirty years past! The shadow creeps and creeps, and is always looking over the shoulder of the sunshine!"

It might have befitted a craftsman, like Matthew Maule, on being sent for to a gentleman's house, to go to the back door, where servants and work-people were usually admitted; or at least to the side entrance, where the better class of tradesmen made application. But the carpenter had a great deal of pride and stiffness in his nature; and, at this moment, moreover, his heart was bitter with the sense of hereditary wrong, because he considered the great Pyncheon House to be standing on soil which should have been his own. On this very site, beside a spring of delicious water, his grandfather had felled the pine-trees and built a cottage, in which children had been born to him; and it was only from a dead man's stiffened fingers that Colonel Pyncheon had wrested away the title-deeds. So young Maule went straight to the principal entrance, beneath a portal of carved oak, and gave such a peal of the iron knocker that you would have imagined the stern old wizard himself to be standing at the threshold.

Black Scipio answered the summons in a prodigious hurry; but showed the whites of his eyes, in amazement on beholding only the carpenter.

"Lord-a-mercy! what a great man he be, this carpenter fellow!" mumbled Scipio, down in his throat. "Anybody think he beat on the door with his biggest hammer!"

"Here I am!" said Maule, sternly. "Show me the way to your master's parlor!"

As he stept into the house, a note of sweet and melancholy music thrilled and vibrated along the passage-way, proceeding from one of the rooms above stairs. It was the harpsichord which Alice Pyncheon had brought with her from beyond the sea. The fair Alice bestowed most of her maiden leisure between flowers and music, although the former were apt to droop, and the melodies were often sad. She was of foreign education, and could not take kindly to the New England modes of life, in which nothing beautiful had ever been developed.

As Mr. Pyncheon had been impatiently awaiting Maule's arrival, black Scipio, of course, lost no time in ushering the carpenter into his master's presence. The room in which this gentleman sat was a parlor of moderate size, looking out upon the garden of the house, and having its windows partly shadowed by the foliage of fruit-trees. It was Mr. Pyncheon's peculiar apartment, and was provided with furniture, in an elegant and costly style, principally from Paris; the floor (which was unusual at that day) being covered with a carpet, so skilfully and richly wrought that it seemed to glow as with living flowers. In one corner stood a marble woman, to whom her own beauty was the sole and sufficient garment. Some pictures—that looked old, and had a mellow tinge diffused through all their artful splendor—hung on the walls. Near the fireplace was a large and very beautiful cabinet of ebony, inlaid with ivory; a piece of antique furniture, which Mr. Pyncheon had bought in Venice, and which he used as the treasure-place for medals, ancient coins, and whatever small and valuable curiosities he had picked up on his travels. Through all this variety of decoration, however, the room showed its original characteristics; its low stud, its cross-beam, its chimney-piece, with the old-fashioned Dutch tiles; so that it was the emblem of a mind industriously stored with foreign ideas, and elaborated into artificial refinement, but neither larger, nor, in its proper self, more elegant than before.

There were two objects that appeared rather out of place in this very handsomely furnished room. One was a large map, or surveyor's plan, of a tract of land, which looked as if it had been drawn a good many years ago, and was now dingy with smoke, and soiled, here and there, with the touch of fingers. The other was a portrait of a stern old man, in a Puritan garb, painted roughly, but with a bold effect, and a remarkably strong expression of character.

At a small table, before a fire of English sea-coal, sat Mr. Pyncheon, sipping coffee, which had grown to be a very favorite beverage with him in France. He was a middle-aged and really handsome man, with a wig flowing down upon his shoulders; his coat was of blue velvet, with lace on the borders and at the button-holes; and the firelight glistened on the spacious breadth of his waistcoat, which was flowered all over with gold. On the entrance of Scipio, ushering in the carpenter, Mr. Pyncheon turned partly round, but resumed his former position, and proceeded deliberately to finish his cup of coffee, without immediate notice of the guest whom he had summoned to his presence. It was not that he intended any rudeness or improper neglect,—which, indeed, he would have blushed to be guilty of,—but it never occurred to him that a person in Maules station had a claim on his courtesy, or would trouble himself about it one way or the other.

The carpenter, however, stepped at once to the hearth, and turned himself about, so as to look Mr. Pyncheon in the face.

"You sent for me," said he. "Be pleased to explain your business, that I may go back to my own affairs."

"Ah! excuse me," said Mr. Pyncheon, quietly. "I did not mean to tax your time without a recompense. Your name, I think, is Maule,—Thomas or Matthew Maule,—a son or grandson of the builder of this house?"

"Matthew Maule," replied the carpenter,—"son of him who built the house,—grandson of the rightful proprietor of the soil."

"I know the dispute to which you allude," observed Mr. Pyncheon with undisturbed equanimity. "I am well aware that my grandfather was compelled to resort to a suit at law, in order to establish his claim to the foundation-site of this edifice. We will not, if you please, renew the discussion. The matter was settled at the time, and by the competent authorities,—equitably, it is to be presumed,—and, at all events, irrevocably. Yet, singularly enough, there is an incidental reference to this very subject in what I am now about to say to you. And this same inveterate grudge,—excuse me, I mean no offence,—this irritability, which you have just shown, is not entirely aside from the matter."

"If you can find anything for your purpose, Mr. Pyncheon," said the carpenter, "in a man's natural resentment for the wrongs done to his blood, you are welcome to it!"

"I take you at your word, Goodman Maule," said the owner of the Seven Gables, with a smile, "and will proceed to suggest a mode in which your hereditary resentments—justifiable, or otherwise—may have had a bearing on my affairs. You have heard, I suppose, that the Pyncheon family, ever since my grandfather's days, have been prosecuting a still unsettled claim to a very large extent of territory at the Eastward?"

"Often," replied Maule,—and it is said that a smile came over his face, —"very often,—from my father!"

"This claim," continued Mr. Pyncheon, after pausing a moment, as if to consider what the carpenter's smile might mean, "appeared to be on the very verge of a settlement and full allowance, at the period of my grandfather's decease. It was well known, to those in his confidence, that he anticipated neither difficulty nor delay. Now, Colonel Pyncheon, I need hardly say, was a practical man, well acquainted with public and private business, and not at all the person to cherish ill-founded hopes, or to attempt the following out of an impracticable scheme. It is obvious to conclude, therefore, that he had grounds, not apparent to his heirs, for his confident anticipation of success in the matter of this Eastern claim. In a word, I believe,—and my legal advisers coincide in the belief, which, moreover, is authorized, to a certain extent, by the family traditions,—that my grandfather was in possession of some deed, or other document, essential to this claim, but which has since disappeared."

"Very likely," said Matthew Maule,—and again, it is said, there was a dark smile on his face,—"but what can a poor carpenter have to do with the grand affairs of the Pyncheon family?"

"Perhaps nothing," returned Mr. Pyncheon,—"possibly, much!"

Here ensued a great many words between Matthew Maule and the proprietor of the Seven Gables, on the subject which the latter had thus broached. It seems (although Mr. Pyncheon had some hesitation in referring to stories so exceedingly absurd in their aspect) that the popular belief pointed to some mysterious connection and dependence, existing between the family of the Maules and these vast unrealized possessions of the Pyncheons. It was an ordinary saying that the old wizard, hanged though he was, had obtained the best end of the bargain in his contest with Colonel Pyncheon; inasmuch as he had got possession of the great Eastern claim, in exchange for an acre or two of garden-ground. A very aged woman, recently dead, had often used the metaphorical expression, in her fireside talk, that miles and miles of the Pyncheon lands had been shovelled into Maule's grave; which, by the by, was but a very shallow nook, between two rocks, near the summit of Gallows Hill. Again, when the lawyers were making inquiry for the missing document, it was a by-word that it would never be found, unless in the wizard's skeleton hand. So much weight had the shrewd lawyers assigned to these fables, that (but Mr. Pyncheon did not see fit to inform the carpenter of the fact) they had secretly caused the wizard's grave to be searched. Nothing was discovered, however, except that, unaccountably, the right hand of the skeleton was gone.

Now, what was unquestionably important, a portion of these popular rumors could be traced, though rather doubtfully and indistinctly, to chance words and obscure hints of the executed wizard's son, and the father of this present Matthew Maule. And here Mr. Pyncheon could bring an item of his own personal evidence into play. Though but a child at the time, he either remembered or fancied that Matthew's father had had some job to perform, on the day before, or possibly the very morning of the Colonel's decease, in the private room where he and the carpenter were at this moment talking. Certain papers belonging to Colonel Pyncheon, as his grandson distinctly recollected, had been spread out on the table.

Matthew Maule understood the insinuated suspicion.

"My father," he said,—but still there was that dark smile, making a riddle of his countenance,—"my father was an honester man than the bloody old Colonel! Not to get his rights back again would he have carried off one of those papers!"

"I shall not bandy words with you," observed the foreign-bred Mr. Pyncheon, with haughty composure. "Nor will it become me to resent any rudeness towards either my grandfather or myself. A gentleman, before seeking intercourse with a person of your station and habits, will first consider whether the urgency of the end may compensate for the disagreeableness of the means. It does so in the present instance."

He then renewed the conversation, and made great pecuniary offers to the carpenter, in case the latter should give information leading to the discovery of the lost document, and the consequent success of the Eastern claim. For a long time Matthew Maule is said to have turned a cold ear to these propositions. At last, however, with a strange kind of laugh, he inquired whether Mr. Pyncheon would make over to him the old wizard's homestead-ground, together with the House of the Seven Gables, now standing on it, in requital of the documentary evidence so urgently required.

The wild, chimney-corner legend (which, without copying all its extravagances, my narrative essentially follows) here gives an account of some very strange behavior on the part of Colonel Pyncheon's portrait. This picture, it must be understood, was supposed to be so intimately connected with the fate of the house, and so magically built into its walls, that, if once it should be removed, that very instant the whole edifice would come thundering down in a heap of dusty ruin. All through the foregoing conversation between Mr. Pyncheon and the carpenter, the portrait had been frowning, clenching its fist, and giving many such proofs of excessive discomposure, but without attracting the notice of either of the two colloquists. And finally, at Matthew Maule's audacious suggestion of a transfer of the seven-gabled structure, the ghostly portrait is averred to have lost all patience, and to have shown itself on the point of descending bodily from its frame. But such incredible incidents are merely to be mentioned aside.

"Give up this house!" exclaimed Mr. Pyncheon, in amazement at the proposal. "Were I to do so, my grandfather would not rest quiet in his grave!"

"He never has, if all stories are true," remarked the carpenter, composedly. "But that matter concerns his grandson more than it does Matthew Maule. I have no other terms to propose."

Impossible as he at first thought it to comply with Maule's conditions, still, on a second glance, Mr. Pyncheon was of opinion that they might at least be made matter of discussion. He himself had no personal attachment for the house, nor any pleasant associations connected with his childish residence in it. On the contrary, after seven-and-thirty years, the presence of his dead grandfather seemed still to pervade it, as on that morning when the affrighted boy had beheld him, with so ghastly an aspect, stiffening in his chair. His long abode in foreign parts, moreover, and familiarity with many of the castles and ancestral halls of England, and the marble palaces of Italy, had caused him to look contemptuously at the House of the Seven Gables, whether in point of splendor or convenience. It was a mansion exceedingly inadequate to the style of living which it would be incumbent on Mr. Pyncheon to support, after realizing his territorial rights. His steward might deign to occupy it, but never, certainly, the great landed proprietor himself. In the event of success, indeed, it was his purpose to return to England; nor, to say the truth, would he recently have quitted that more congenial home, had not his own fortune, as well as his deceased wife's, begun to give symptoms of exhaustion. The Eastern claim once fairly settled, and put upon the firm basis of actual possession, Mr. Pyncheon's property—to be measured by miles, not acres—would be worth an earldom, and would reasonably entitle him to solicit, or enable him to purchase, that elevated dignity from the British monarch. Lord Pyncheon!—or the Earl of Waldo!—how could such a magnate be expected to contract his grandeur within the pitiful compass of seven shingled gables?

In short, on an enlarged view of the business, the carpenter's terms appeared so ridiculously easy that Mr. Pyncheon could scarcely forbear laughing in his face. He was quite ashamed, after the foregoing reflections, to propose any diminution of so moderate a recompense for the immense service to be rendered.

"I consent to your proposition, Maule," cried he. "Put me in possession of the document essential to establish my rights, and the House of the Seven Gables is your own!"

According to some versions of the story, a regular contract to the above effect was drawn up by a lawyer, and signed and sealed in the presence of witnesses. Others say that Matthew Maule was contented with a private written agreement, in which Mr. Pyncheon pledged his honor and integrity to the fulfilment of the terms concluded upon. The gentleman then ordered wine, which he and the carpenter drank together, in confirmation of their bargain. During the whole preceding discussion and subsequent formalities, the old Puritan's portrait seems to have persisted in its shadowy gestures of disapproval; but without effect, except that, as Mr. Pyncheon set down the emptied glass, he thought he beheld his grandfather frown.

"This sherry is too potent a wine for me; it has affected my brain already," he observed, after a somewhat startled look at the picture. "On returning to Europe, I shall confine myself to the more delicate vintages of Italy and France, the best of which will not bear transportation."

"My Lord Pyncheon may drink what wine he will, and wherever he pleases," replied the carpenter, as if he had been privy to Mr. Pyncheon's ambitious projects. "But first, sir, if you desire tidings of this lost document, I must crave the favor of a little talk with your fair daughter Alice!"

"You are mad, Maule!" exclaimed Mr. Pyncheon, haughtily; and now, at last, there was anger mixed up with his pride. "What can my daughter have to do with a business like this?"

Indeed, at this new demand on the carpenter's part, the proprietor of the Seven Gables was even more thunder-struck than at the cool proposition to surrender his house. There was, at least, an assignable motive for the first stipulation; there appeared to be none whatever for the last. Nevertheless, Matthew Maule sturdily insisted on the young lady being summoned, and even gave her father to understand, in a mysterious kind of explanation,—which made the matter considerably darker than it looked before,—that the only chance of acquiring the requisite knowledge was through the clear, crystal medium of a pure and virgin intelligence, like that of the fair Alice. Not to encumber our story with Mr. Pyncheon's scruples, whether of conscience, pride, or fatherly affection, he at length ordered his daughter to be called. He well knew that she was in her chamber, and engaged in no occupation that could not readily be laid aside; for, as it happened, ever since Alice's name had been spoken, both her father and the carpenter had heard the sad and sweet music of her harpsichord, and the airier melancholy of her accompanying voice.

So Alice Pyncheon was summoned and appeared. A portrait of this young lady, painted by a Venetian artist, and left by her father in England, is said to have fallen into the hands of the present Duke of Devonshire, and to be now preserved at Chatsworth; not on account of any associations with the original, but for its value as a picture, and the high character of beauty in the countenance. If ever there was a lady born, and set apart from the world's vulgar mass by a certain gentle and cold state-liness, it was this very Alice Pyncheon. Yet there was the womanly mix--ture in her; the tenderness, or, at least, the tender capabilities. For the sake of that redeeming quality, a man of generous nature would have for-given all her pride, and have been content, almost, to lie down in her path, and let Alice set her slender foot upon his heart. All that he would have required was simply the acknowledgment that he was indeed a man, and a fellow-being, moulded of the same elements as she.

As Alice came into the room, her eyes fell upon the carpenter, who was standing near its centre, clad in a green woollen jacket, a pair of loose breeches, open at the knees, and with a long pocket for his rule, the end of which protruded; it was as proper a mark of the artisan's calling, as Mr. Pyncheon's full-dress sword of that gentleman's aristocratic preten-sions. A glow of artistic approval brightened over Alice Pyncheon's face; she was struck with admiration—which she made no attempt to conceal —of the remarkable comeliness, strength, and energy of Maule's figure. But that admiring glance (which most other men, perhaps, would have cherished as a sweet recollection, all through life) the carpenter never forgave. It must have been the devil himself that made Maule so subtile in his perception.

"Does the girl look at me as if I were a brute beast?" thought he, set-ting his teeth. "She shall know whether I have a human spirit; and the worse for her, if it prove stronger than her own!"

"My father, you sent for me," said Alice, in her sweet and harp-like voice. "But, if you have business with this young man, pray let me go again. You know I do not love this room, in spite of that Claude, with which you try to bring back sunny recollections."

"Stay a moment, young lady, if you please!" said Matthew Maule. "My business with your father is over. With yourself, it is now to begin!"

Alice looked towards her father, in surprise and inquiry.

"Yes, Alice," said Mr. Pyncheon, with some disturbance and confusion. "This young man—his name is Matthew Maule—professes, so far as I can understand him, to be able to discover, through your means, a certain paper or parchment, which was missing long before your birth. The im-portance of the document in question renders it advisable to neglect no possible, even if improbable, method of regaining it. You will therefore oblige me, my dear Alice, by answering this person's inquiries, and com-plying with his lawful and reasonable requests, so far as they may appear to have the aforesaid object in view. As I shall remain in the room, you need apprehend no rude nor unbecoming deportment, on the young man's part; and, at your slightest wish, of course, the investigation, or whatever we may call it, shall immediately be broken off.

"Mistress Alice Pyncheon," remarked Matthew Maule, with the ut-most deference, but yet a half-hidden sarcasm in his look and tone, "will no doubt feel herself quite safe in her father's presence, and under his all-sufficient protection."

"I certainly shall entertain no manner of apprehension, with my father at hand," said Alice, with maidenly dignity. "Neither do I conceive that a lady, while true to herself, can have aught to fear from whomsoever, or in any circumstances!"

Poor Alice! By what unhappy impulse did she thus put herself at once on terms of defiance against a strength which she could not estimate?

"Then, Mistress Alice," said Matthew Maule, handing a chair,—gracefully enough, for a craftsman,—"will it please you only to sit down, and do me the favor (though altogether beyond a poor carpenter's deserts) to fix your eyes on mine!"

Alice complied. She was very proud. Setting aside all advantages of rank, this fair girl deemed herself conscious of a power—combined of beauty, high, unsullied purity, and the preservative force of womanhood —that could make her sphere impenetrable, unless betrayed by treachery within. She instinctively knew, it may be, that some sinister or evil potency was now striving to pass her barriers; nor would she decline the contest. So Alice put woman's might against man's might; a match not often equal on the part of woman.

Her father meanwhile had turned away, and seemed absorbed in the contemplation of a lanscapee by Claude, where a shadowy and sun-streaked vista penetrated so remotely into an ancient wood, that it would have been no wonder if his fancy had lost itself in the picture's bewildering depths. But, in truth, the picture was no more to him at that moment than the blank wall against which it hung. His mind was haunted with the many and strange tales which he had heard, attributing mysterious if not supernatural endowments to these Maules, as well the grandson here present as his two immediate ancestors. Mr. Pyncheon's long residence abroad, and intercourse with men of wit and fashion,—courtiers, world-lings, and free-thinkers,—had done much towards obliterating the grim Puritan superstitions, which no man of New England birth at that early period could entirely escape. But, on the other hand, had not a whole community believed Maule's grandfather to be a wizard? Had not the crime been proved? Had not the wizard died for it? Had he not be-queathed a legacy of hatred against the Pyncheons to this only grandson, who, as it appeared, was now about to exercise a subtle influence over the daughter of his enemy's house? Might not this influence be the same that was called witchcraft?

Turning half around, he caught a glimpse of Maule's figure in the look-ing-glass. At some paces from Alice, with his arms uplifted in the air, the carpenter made a gesture as if directing downward a slow, ponderous, and invisible weight upon the maiden.

"Stay, Maule!" exclaimed Mr. Pyncheon, stepping forward. "I forbid your proceeding further!"

"Pray, my dear father, do not interrupt the young man," said Alice, without changing her position. "His efforts, I assure you, will prove very harmless."

Again Mr. Pyncheon turned his eyes towards the Claude. It was then his daughter's will, in opposition to his own, that the experiment should be fully tried. Henceforth, therefore, he did but consent, not urge it. And was it not for her sake far more than for his own that he desired its success? That lost parchment once restored, the beautiful Alice Pyncheon, with the rich dowry which he could then bestow, might wed an English duke or a German reigning-prince, instead of some New England clergyman or lawyer! At the thought, the ambitious father almost consented, in his heart, that, if the devil's power were needed to the accomplishment of this great object, Maule might evoke him. Alice's own purity would be her safeguard.

With his mind full of imaginary magnificence, Mr. Pyncheon heard a half-uttered exclamation from his daughter. It was very faint and low; so indistinct that there seemed but half a will to shape out the words, and too undefined a purport to be intelligible. Yet it was a call for help!— his conscience never doubted it;—and, little more than a whisper to his ear, it was a dismal shriek, and long reëchoed so, in the region round his heart! But this time the father did not turn.

After a further interval, Maule spoke.

"Behold your daughter!" said he.

Mr. Pyncheon came hastily forward. The carpenter was standing erect in front of Alice's chair, and pointing his finger towards the maiden with an expression of triumphant power the limits of which could not be defined, as, indeed, its scope stretched vaguely towards the unseen and the infinite. Alice sat in an attitude of profound repose, with the long brown lashes drooping over her eyes.

"There she is!" said the carpenter. "Speak to her!"

"Alice! My daughter!" exclaimed Mr. Pyncheon. "My own Alice!"

She did not stir.

"Louder!" said Maule, smiling.

"Alice! Awake!" cried her father. "It troubles me to see you thus! Awake!"

He spoke loudly, with terror in his voice, and close to that delicate ear which had always been so sensitive to every discord. But the sound evidently reached her not. It is indescribable what a sense of remote, dim, unattainable distance, betwixt himself and Alice, was impressed on the father by this impossibility of reaching her with his voice.

"Best touch her!" said Matthew Maule. "Shake the girl, and roughly too! My hands are hardened with too much use of axe, saw, and plane,— else I might help you!"

Mr. Pyncheon took her hand, and pressed it with the earnestness of startled emotion. He kissed her, with so great a heart-throb in the kiss, that he thought she must needs feel it. Then, in a gust of anger at her insensibility, he shook her maiden form with a violence which, the next moment, it affrighted him to remember. He withdrew his encircling arms, and Alice—whose figure, though flexible, had been wholly impassive— relapsed into the same attitude as before these attempts to arouse her. Maule having shifted his position, her face was turned towards him slightly, but with what seemed to be a reference of her very slumber to his guidance.

Then it was a strange sight to behold how the man of conventionalities shook the powder out of his periwig; how the reserved and stately gentle-man forgot his dignity; how the gold-embroidered waistcoat flickered and glistened in the firelight with the convulsion of rage, terror, and sorrow in the human heart that was beating under it.

"Villain!" cried Mr. Pyncheon, shaking his clenched fist at Maule. "You and the fiend together have robbed me of my daughter! Give her back, spawn of the old wizard, or you shall climb Gallows Hill in your grandfather's footsteps!"

"Softly, Mr. Pyncheon!" said the carpenter, with scornful composure. "Softly, an it please your worship, else you will spoil those rich lace ruffles at your wrists! Is it my crime if you have sold your daughter for the mere hope of getting a sheet of yellow parchment into your clutch? There sits Mistress Alice quietly asleep! Now let Matthew Maule try whether she be as proud as the carpenter found her awhile since."

He spoke, and Alice responded, with a soft, subdued, inward acqui-escence, and a bending of her form towards him, like the flame of a torch when it indicates a gentle draught of air. He beckoned with his hand, and, rising from her chair,—blindly, but undoubtingly, as tending to her sure and inevitable centre,—the proud Alice approached him. He waved her back, and, retreating, Alice sank again into her seat.

"She is mine!" said Matthew Maule. "Mine, by the right of the strong-est spirit!"

In the further progress of the legend, there is a long, grotesque, and oc-casionally awe-striking account of the carpenter's incantations (if so they are to be called), with a view of discovering the lost document. It appears to have been his object to convert the mind of Alice into a kind of teles-copic medium, through which Mr. Pyncheon and himself might obtain a glimpse into the spiritual world. He succeeded, accordingly, in holding an imperfect sort of intercourse, at one remove, with the departed person-ages, in whose custody the so much valued secret had been carried be-yond the precincts of earth. During her trance, Alice described three fig-ures as being present to her spiritualized perception. One was an aged, dignified, stern-looking gentleman, clad as for a solemn festival in grave and costly attire, but with a great bloodstain on his richly wrought band; the second, an aged man, meanly dressed, with a dark and malign coun-tenance, and a broken halter about his neck; the third, a person not so advanced in life as the former two, but beyond the middle age, wearing a coarse woollen tunic and leather breeches, and with a carpenter's rule sticking out of his side pocket. These three visionary characters possessed a mutual knowledge of the missing document. One of them, in truth,—it was he with the blood-stain on his band,—seemed, unless his gestures were misunderstood, to hold the parchment to his immediate keeping, but was prevented, by his two partners in the mystery, from disburdening himself of the trust. Finally, when he showed a purpose of shouting forth the secret, loudly enough to be heard from his own sphere into that of mortals, his companions struggled with him, and pressed their hands over his mouth; and forthwith—whether that he were choked by it, or that the secret itself was of a crimson hue—there was a fresh flow of blood upon his band. Upon this, the two meanly dressed figures mocked and jeered at the much-abashed old dignitary, and pointed their fingers at the stain.

At this juncture, Maule turned to Mr. Pyncheon.

"It will never be allowed," said he. "The custody of this secret, that would so enrich his heirs, makes part of your grandfather's retribution. He must choke with it until it is no longer of any value. And keep you the House of the Seven Gables! It is too dear bought an inheritance, and too heavy with the curse upon it, to be shifted yet awhile from the Colonel's posterity!"

Mr. Pyncheon tried to speak, but—what with fear and passion—could make only a gurgling murmur in his throat. The carpenter smiled.

"Aha, worshipful sir!—so you have old Maule's blood to drink!" said he, jeeringly.

"Fiend in man's shape! why dost thou keep dominion over my child?" cried Mr. Pyncheon, when his choked utterance could make way. "Give me back by daughter! Then go thy ways; and may we never meet again!"

"Your daughter!" said Matthew Maule. "Why, she is fairly mine! Nevertheless, not to be too hard with fair Mistress Alice, I will leave her in your keeping; but I do not warrant you that she shall never have occasion to remember Maule, the carpenter."

He waved his hands with an upward motion; and, after a few repetitions of similar gestures, the beautiful Alice Pyncheon awoke from her strange trance. She awoke, without the slightest recollection of her visionary experience; but as one losing herself in a momentary reverie, and returning to the consciousness of actual life, in almost as brief an interval as the down-sinking flame of the hearth should quiver again up the chimney. On recognizing Matthew Maule, she assumed an air of somewhat cold but gentle dignity, the rather, as there was a certain peculiar smile on the carpenter's visage that stirred the native pride of the fair Alice. So ended, for that time, the quest for the lost title-deed of the Pyncheon territory at the Eastward; nor, though often subsequently renewed, has it ever yet befallen a Pyncheon to set his eye upon that parchment.

But, alas for the beautiful, the gentle, yet too haughty Alice! A power that she little dreamed of had laid its grasp upon her maiden soul. A will, most unlike her own, constrained her to do its grotesque and fantastic bidding. Her father, as it proved, had martyred his poor child to an inordinate desire for measuring his land by miles instead of acres. And, therefore, while Alice Pyncheon lived, she was Maule's slave, in a bondage more humiliating, a thousand-fold, than that which binds its chain around the body. Seated by his humble fireside, Maule had but to wave his hand; and, wherever the proud lady chanced to be,—whether in her chamber, or entertaining her father's stately guests, or worshipping at church,—whatever her place or occupation, her spirit passed from beneath her own control, and bowed itself to Maule. "Alice, laugh!"—the carpenter, beside his hearth, would say; or perhaps intensely will it, without a spoken word. And, even were it prayer-time, or at a funeral, Alice must break into wild laughter. "Alice, be sad!"—and, at the instant, down would come her tears, quenching all the mirth of those around her like sudden rain upon a bonfire. "Alice, dance!"—and dance she would, not in such court-like measures as she had learned abroad, but some high-paced jig, or hop-skip rigadoon, befitting the brisk lasses at a rustic merry-making. It seemed to be Maule's impulse, not to ruin Alice, nor to visit her with any black or gigantic mischief, which would have crowned her sorrows with the grace of tragedy, but to wreak a low, ungenerous scorn upon her. Thus all the dignity of life was lost. She felt herself too much abased, and longed to change natures with some worm!

One evening, at a bridal-party (but not her own; for, so lost from self-control, she would have deemed it sin to marry), poor Alice was beckoned forth by her unseen despot, and constrained, in her gossamer white dress and satin slippers, to hasten along the street to the mean dwelling of a laboring-man. There was laughter and good cheer within; for Matthew Maule, that night, was to wed the laborer's daughter, and had summoned proud Alice Pyncheon to wait upon his bride. And so she did; and when the twain were one, Alice awoke out of her enchanted sleep. Yet, no longer proud,—humbly, and with a smile all steeped in sadness,—she kissed Maule's wife, and went her way. It was an inclement night; the southeast wind drove the mingled snow and rain into her thinly sheltered bosom; her satin slippers were wet through and through, as she trod the muddy sidewalks. The next day a cold; soon, a settled cough; anon, a hectic cheek, a wasted form, that sat beside the harpsichord, and filled the house with music! Music, in which a strain of the heavenly choristers was echoed! Oh, joy! For Alice had borne her last humiliation! Oh, greater joy! For Alice was penitent of her one earthly sin, and proud no more!

The Pyncheons made a great funeral for Alice. The kith and kin were there, and the whole respectability of the town besides. But, last in the procession, came Matthew Maule, gnashing his teeth, as if he would have bitten his own heart in twain,—the darkest and wofullest man that ever walked behind a corpse! He meant to humble Alice, not to kill her; but he had taken a woman's delicate soul into his rude gripe, to play with—and she was dead!

XIV

PHŒBE'S GOOD-BYE

HOLGRAVE, plunging into his tale with the energy and absorption natural to a young author, had given a good deal of action to the parts capable of being developed and exemplified in that manner. He now observed that a certain remarkable drowsiness (wholly unlike that with which the reader possibly feels himself affected) had been flung over the senses of his auditress. It was the effect, unquestionably, of the mystic gesticulations by which he had sought to bring bodily before Phœbe's perception the figure of the mesmerizing carpenter. With the lids drooping over her eyes,— now lifted for an instant, and drawn down again as with leaden weights, —she leaned slightly towards him, and seemed almost to regulate her breath by his. Holgrave gazed at her, as he rolled up his manuscript, and recognized an incipient stage of that curious psychological condition, which, as he had himself told Phœbe, he possessed more than an ordinary faculty of producing. A veil was beginning to be muffled about her, in which she could behold only him, and live only in his thoughts and emotions. His glance, as he fastened it on the young girl, grew involuntarily more concentrated; in his attitude there was the consciousness of power, investing his hardly mature figure with a dignity that did not belong to its physical manifestation. It was evident, that, with but one wave of his hand and a corresponding effort of his will, he could complete his mastery over Phœbe's yet free and virgin spirit: he could establish an influence over this good, pure, and simple child, as dangerous, and perhaps as disastrous, as that which the carpenter of his legend had acquired and exercised over the ill-fated Alice.

To a disposition like Holgrave's, at once speculative and active, there is no temptation so great as the opportunity of acquiring empire over the human spirit; nor any idea more seductive to a young man than to become the arbiter of a young girl's destiny. Let us, therefore,—whatever his defects of nature and education, and in spite of his scorn for creeds and institutions,—concede to the daguerreotypist the rare and high quality of reverence for another's individuality. Let us allow him integrity, also, forever after to be confided in; since he forbade himself to twine that one link more which might have rendered his spell over Phœbe indissoluble.

He made a slight gesture upward with his hand.

"You really mortify me, my dear Miss Phœbe!" he exclaimed, smiling half-sarcastically at her. "My poor story it is but too evident, will never do for Godey or Graham! Only think of your falling asleep at what I hoped the newspaper critics would pronounce a most brilliant, powerful, imaginative, pathetic, and original winding up! Well, the manuscript must serve to light lamps with;—if, indeed, being so imbued with my gentle dulness, it is any longer capable of flame!"

"Me asleep! How can you say so?" answered Phœbe, as unconscious of the crisis through which she had passed as an infant of the precipice to the verge of which it has rolled. "No, no! I consider myself as having been very attentive; and, though I don't remember the incidents quite distinctly, yet I have an impression of a vast deal of trouble and calamity, —so, no doubt, the story will prove exceedingly attractive."

By this time the sun had gone down, and was tinting the clouds towards the zenith with those bright hues which are not seen there until some time after sunset, and when the horizon has quite lost its richer brilliancy. The moon, too, which had long been climbing overhead, and unobtrusively melting its disk into the azure,—like an ambitious demagogue, who hides his aspiring purpose by assuming the prevalent hue of popular sentiment, —now began to shine out, broad and oval, in its middle pathway. These silvery beams were already powerful enough to change the character of the lingering daylight. They softened and embellished the aspect of the old house; although the shadows fell deeper into the angles of its many gables, and lay brooding under the projecting story, and within the half-open door. With the lapse of every moment, the garden grew more picturesque; the fruit-trees, shrubbery, and flower-bushes had a dark obscurity among them. The commonplace characteristics—which, at noon-tide, it seemed to have taken a century of sordid life to accumulate—were now transfigured by a charm of romance. A hundred mysterious years were whispering among the leaves, whenever the slight sea-breeze found its way thither and stirred them. Through the foliage that roofed the little summer-house the moonlight flickered to and fro, and fell silvery white on the dark floor, the table, and the circular bench, with a continual shift and play, according as the chinks and wayward crevices among the twigs admitted or shut out the glimmer.

So sweetly cool was the atmosphere, after all the feverish day, that the summer eve might be fancied as sprinkling dews and liquid moonlight, with a dash of icy temper in them, out of a silver vase. Here and there, a few drops of this freshness were scattered on a human heart, and gave it youth again, and sympathy with the eternal youth of nature. The artist chanced to be one on whom the reviving influence fell. It made him feel— what he sometimes almost forgot, thrust so early as he had been into the rude struggle of man with man—how youthful he still was.

"It seems to me," he observed, "that I never watched the coming of so beautiful an eve, and never felt anything so very much like happiness as at this moment. After all, what a good world we live in! How good, and beautiful! How young it is, too, with nothing really rotten or age-worn in it! This old house, for example, which sometimes has positively oppressed my breath with its smell of decaying timber! And this garden, where the black mould always clings to my spade, as if I were a sexton delving in a graveyard! Could I keep the feeling that now possesses me, the garden would every day be virgin soil, with the earth's first freshness in the flavor of its beans and squashes; and the house!—it would be like a bower in Eden, blossoming with the earliest roses that God ever made. Moonlight, and the sentiment in man's heart responsive to it, are the greatest of renovators and reformers. And all other reform and renovation, I suppose, will prove to be no better than moonshine!"

"I have been happier than I am now; at least, much gayer," said Phœbe, thoughtfully. "Yet I am sensible of a great charm in this brightening moonlight; and I love to watch how the day, tired as it is, lags away reluctantly, and hates to be called yesterday so soon. I never cared much about moonlight before. What is there, I wonder, so beautiful in it, to-night?"

"And you have never felt it before?" inquired the artist, looking earnestly at the girl through the twilight.

"Never," answered Phœbe; "and life does not look the same, now that I have felt it so. It seems as if I had looked at everything, hitherto, in broad daylight, or else in the ruddy light of a cheerful fire, glimmering and dancing through a room. Ah, poor me!" she added, with a half-melancholy laugh. "I shall never be so merry as before I knew Cousin Hepzibah and poor Cousin Clifford. I have grown a great deal older, in this little time. Older, and, I hope, wiser, and,—not exactly sadder,—but, certainly, with not half so much lightness in my spirits! I have given them my sunshine, and have been glad to give it; but, of course, I cannot both give and keep it. They are welcome, notwithstanding!"

"You have lost nothing, Phœbe, worth keeping, nor which it was possible to keep," said Holgrave, after a pause. "Our first youth is of no value; for we are never conscious of it until after it is gone. But sometimes —always, I suspect, unless one is exceedingly unfortunate—there comes a sense of second youth, gushing out of the heart's joy at being in love; or, possibly, it may come to crown some other grand festival in life, if any other such there be. This bemoaning of one's self (as you do now) over the first, careless, shallow gayety of youth departed, and this profound happiness at youth regained,—so much deeper and richer than that we lost,—are essential to the soul's development. In some cases, the two states come almost simultaneously, and mingle the sadness and the rapture in one mysterious emotion."

"I hardly think I understand you," said Phœbe.

"No wonder," replied Holgrave, smiling; "for I have told you a secret which I hardly began to know before I found myself giving it utterance. Remember it, however; and when the truth becomes clear to you, then think of this moonlight scene!"

"It is entirely moonlight now, except only a little flush of faint crimson, upward from the west, between those buildings," remarked Phœbe. "I must go in. Cousin Hepzibah is not quick at figures, and will give herself a headache over the day's accounts, unless I help her."

But Holgrave detained her a little longer.

"Miss Hepzibah tells me," observed he, "that you return to the country in a few days."

"Yes, but only for a little while," answered Phœbe; "for I look upon this as my present home. I go to make a few arrangements, and to take a more deliberate leave of my mother and friends. It is pleasant to live where one is much desired and very useful; and I think I may have the satisfaction of feeling myself so here."

"You surely may, and more than you imagine," said the artist. "Whatever health, comfort, and natural life exists in the house, is embodied in your person. These blessings came along with you, and will vanish when you leave the threshold. Miss Hepzibah, by secluding herself from society, has lost all true relation with it, and is, in fact, dead; although she galvanizes herself into a semblance of life, and stands behind her counter, afflicting the world with a greatly-to-be-deprecated scowl. Your poor cousin Clifford is another dead and long-buried person, on whom the governor and council have wrought a necromantic miracle. I should not wonder if he were to crumble away, some morning, after you are gone, and nothing be seen of him more, except a heap of dust. Miss Hepzibah, at any rate, will lose what little flexibility she has. They both exist by you."

"I should be very sorry to think so," answered Phœbe, gravely. "But it is true that my small abilities were precisely what they needed; and I have a real interest in their welfare,—an odd kind of motherly sentiment, —which I wish you would not laugh at! And let me tell you frankly, Mr. Holgrave, I sometimes puzzled to know whether you wish them well or ill."

"Undoubtedly," said the daguerreotypist, "I do feel an interest in this antiquated, poverty-stricken old maiden lady, and this degraded and shattered gentleman,—this abortive lover of the beautiful. A kindly interest, too, helpless old children that they are! But you have no conception what a different kind of heart mine is from your own. It is not my impulse, as regards these two individuals, either to help or hinder; but to look on, to analyze, to explain matters to myself, and to comprehend the drama which, for almost two hundred years, has been dragging its slow length over the ground where you and I now tread. If permitted to witness the close, I doubt not to derive a moral satisfaction from it, go matters how they may. There is a conviction within me that the end draws nigh. But, though Providence sent you hither to help, and sends me only as a privileged and meet spectator, I pledge myself to lend these unfortunate beings whatever aid I can!"

"I wish you would speak more plainly," cried Phœbe, perplexed and displeased; "and, above all, that you would feel more like a Christian and a human being! How is it possible to see people in distress, without desiring, more than anything else, to help and comfort them? You talk as if this old house were a theatre; and you seem to look at Hepzibah's and Clifford's misfortunes, and those of generations before them, as a tragedy, such as I have seen acted in the hall of a country hotel, only the present one appears to be played exclusively for your amusement. I do not like this. The play costs the performers too much, and the audience is too cold-hearted."

"You are severe," said Holgrave, compelled to recognize a degree of truth in this piquant sketch of his own mood.

"And then," continued Phœbe, "what can you mean by your conviction, which you tell me of, that the end is drawing near? Do you know of any new trouble hanging over my poor relatives? If so, tell me at once, and I will not leave them!"

"Forgive me, Phœbe!" said the daguerreotypist, holding out his hand, to which the girl was constrained to yield her own. "I am somewhat of a mystic, it must be confessed. The tendency is in my blood, together with the faculty of mesmerism, which might have brought me to Gallows Hill, in the good old times of witchcraft. Believe me, if I were really aware of any secret, the disclosure of which would benefit your friends,—who are my own friends, likewise,—you should learn it before we part. But I have no such knowledge."

"You hold something back!" said Phœbe.

"Nothing,—no secrets but my own," answered Holgrave. "I can perceive, indeed, that Judge Pyncheon still keeps his eye on Clifford, in whose ruin he had so large a share. His motives and intentions, however, are a mystery to me. He is a determined and relentless man, with the genuine character of an inquisitor; and had he any object to gain by putting Clifford to the rack, I verily believe that he would wrench his joints from their sockets, in order to accomplish it. But, so wealthy and eminent as he is,—so powerful in his own strength, and in the support of society on all sides,—what can Judge Pyncheon have to hope or fear from the imbecile, branded, half-torpid Clifford?"

"Yet," urged Phœbe, "you did speak as if misfortune were impending!"

"Oh, that was because I am morbid!" replied the artist. "My mind has a twist aside, like almost everybody's mind, except your own. Moreover, it is so strange to find myself an inmate of this old Pyncheon House, and sitting in this old garden—(hark, how Maule's well is murmuring!)—that, were it only for this one circumstance, I cannot help fancying that Destiny is arranging its fifth act for a catastrophe."

"There!" cried Phœbe with renewed vexation; for she was by nature as hostile to mystery as the sunshine to a dark corner. "You puzzle me more than ever!"

"Then let us part friends!" said Holgrave, pressing her hand. "Or, if not friends, let us part before you entirely hate me. You, who love everybody else in the world!"

"Good-by, then," said Phœbe, frankly. "I do not mean to be angry a great while, and should be sorry to have you think so. There has Cousin Hepzibah been standing in the shadow of the doorway, this quarter of an hour past! She thinks I stay too long in the damp garden. So, good-night, and good-by!"

On the second morning thereafter, Phœbe might have been seen, in her straw bonnet, with a shawl on one arm and a little carpet-bag on the other, bidding adieu to Hepzibah and Cousin Clifford. She was to take a seat in the next train of cars, which would transport her to within half a dozen miles of her country village.

The tears were in Phœbe's eyes; a smile, dewy with affectionate regret, was glimmering around her pleasant mouth. She wondered how it came to pass, that her life of a few weeks, here in this heavy-hearted old mansion, had taken such hold of her, and so melted into her associations, as now to seem a more important centre-point of remembrance than all which had gone before. How had Hepzibah—grim, silent, and irresponsive to her overflow of cordial sentiment—contrived to win so much love? And Clifford,—in his abortive decay, with the mystery of fearful crime

upon him, and the close prison-atmosphere yet lurking in his breath,—
how had he transformed himself into the simplest child, whom Phœbe
felt bound to watch over, and be, as it were, the providence of his uncon-
sidered hours! Everything, at that instant of farewell, stood out prominently to her view. Look where she would, lay her hand on what she might,
the object responded to her consciousness, as if a moist human heart were
in it.

She peeped from the window into the garden, and felt herself more regretful at leaving this spot of black earth, vitiated with such an age-long
growth of weeds, than joyful at the idea of again scenting her pine forests and fresh clover-fields. She called Chanticleer, his two wives, and
the venerable chicken, and threw them some crumbs of bread from the
breakfast-table. These being hastily gobbled up, the chicken spread its
wings, and alighted close by Phœbe on the window-sill, where it looked
gravely into her face and vented its emotions in a croak. Phœbe bade it
be a good old chicken during her absence, and promised to bring it a little
bag of buckwheat.

"Ah, Phœbe!" remarked Hepzibah, "you do not smile so naturally as
when you came to us! Then, the smile chose to shine out; now, you
choose it should. It is well that you are going back, for a little while, into
your native air. There has been too much weight on your spirits. The
house is too gloomy and lonesome; the shop is full of vexations; and as
for me, I have no faculty of making things look brighter than they are.
Dear Clifford has been your only comfort!"

"Come hither, Phœbe," suddenly cried her cousin Clifford, who had
said very little all the morning. "Close!—closer!—and look me in the
face!"

Phœbe put one of her small hands on each elbow of his chair; and
leaned her face towards him, so that he might peruse it as carefully as he
would. It is probable that the latent emotions of this parting hour had
revived, in some degree, his bedimmed and enfeebled faculties. At any
rate, Phœbe soon felt that, if not the profound insight of a seer, yet a
more than feminine delicacy of appreciation, was making her heart the
subject of its regard. A moment before, she had known nothing which she
would have sought to hide. Now, as if some secret were hinted to her own
consciousness through the medium of another's perception, she was fain
to let her eyelids droop beneath Clifford's gaze. A blush, too,—the redder, because she strove hard to keep it down,—ascended higher and
higher, in a tide of fitful progress, until even her brow was all suffused
with it.

"It is enough, Phœbe," said Clifford, with a melancholy smile. "When I
first saw you, you were the prettiest little maiden in the world; and now
you have deepened into beauty! Girlhood has passed into womanhood;
the bud is a bloom! Go, now!—I feel lonelier than I did."

Phœbe took leave of the desolate couple, and passed through the shop,
twinkling her eyelids to shake off a dew-drop; for—considering how brief
her absence was to be, and therefore the folly of being cast down about it

—she would not so far acknowledge her tears as to dry them with her handkerchief. On the doorstep, she met the little urchin whose marvellous feats of gastronomy have been recorded in the earlier pages of our narrative. She took from the window some specimen or other of natural history,—her eyes being too dim with moisture to inform her accurately whether it was a rabbit or a hippopotamus,—put it into the child's hand, as a parting gift, and went her way. Old Uncle Venner was just coming out of his door, with a wood-horse and saw on his shoulder; and, trudging along the street, he scrupled not to keep company with Phœbe, so far as their paths lay together; nor, in spite of his patched coat and rusty beaver, and the curious fashion of his tow-cloth trousers, could she find it in her heart to outwalk him.

"We shall miss you, next Sabbath afternoon," observed the street philosopher. "It is unaccountable how little while it takes some folks to grow just as natural to a man as his own breath; and, begging your pardon, Miss Phœbe (though there can be no offence in an old man's saying it), that's just what you've grown to me! My years have been a great many, and your life is but just beginning; and yet, you are somehow as familiar to me as if I had found you at my mother's door, and you had blossomed, like a running vine, all along my pathway since. Come back soon, or I shall be gone to my farm; for I begin to find these wood-sawing jobs a little too tough for my back-ache."

"Very soon, Uncle Venner," replied Phœbe.

"And let it be all the sooner, Phœbe, for the sake of those poor souls yonder," continued her companion. "They can never do without you, now,—never, Phœbe, never!—no more than if one of God's angels had been living with them, and making their dismal house pleasant and comfortable! Don't it seem to you they'd be in a sad case, if, some pleasant summer morning like this, the angel should spread his wings, and fly to the place he came from? Well, just so they feel, now that you're going home by the railroad! They can't bear it, Miss Phœbe; so be sure to come back!"

"I am no angel, Uncle Venner," said Phœbe, smiling, as she offered him her hand at the street-corner. "But, I suppose, people never feel so much like angels as when they are doing what little good they may. So I shall certainly come back!"

Thus parted the old man and the rosy girl; and Phœbe took the wings of the morning, and was soon flitting almost as rapidly away as if endowed with the aerial locomotion of the angels to whom Uncle Venner had so graciously compared her.

## THE SCOWL AND SMILE

SEVERAL days passed over the Seven Gables, heavily and drearily enough. In fact (not to attribute the whole gloom of sky and earth to the one inauspicious circumstance of Phœbe's departure), an easterly storm had set in, and indefatigably applied itself to the task of making the black roof and walls of the old house look more cheerless than ever before. Yet was the outside not half so cheerless as the interior. Poor Clifford was cut off, at once, from all his scanty resources of enjoyment. Phœbe was not there; nor did the sunshine fall upon the floor. The garden, with its muddy walks, and the chill, dripping foliage of its summer-house, was an image to be shuddered at. Nothing flourished in the cold, moist, pitiless atmosphere, drifting with the brackish scud of sea-breezes, except the moss along the joints of the shingle-roof, and the great bunch of weeds, that had lately been suffering from drought, in the angle between the two front gables.

As for Hepzibah, she seemed not merely possessed with the east wind, but to be, in her very person, only another phase of this gray and sullen spell of weather; the east wind itself, grim and disconsolate, in a rusty black silk gown, and with a turban of cloud-wreaths on its head. The custom of the shop fell off, because a story got abroad that she soured her small beer and other damageable commodities, by scowling on them. It is, perhaps, true that the public had something reasonably to complain of in her deportment; but towards Clifford she was neither ill-tempered nor unkind, nor felt less warmth of heart than always, had it been possible to make it reach him. The inutility of her best efforts, however, palsied the poor old gentlewoman. She could do little else than sit silently in a corner of the room, when the wet pear-tree branches, sweeping across the small windows, created a noon-day dusk, which Hepzibah unconsciously darkened with her woe-begone aspect. It was no fault of Hepzibah's. Everything—even the old chairs and tables, that had known what weather was for three or four such lifetimes as her own—looked as damp and chill as if the present were their worst experience. The picture of the Puritan Colonel shivered on the wall. The house itself shivered, from every attic of its seven gables, down to the great kitchen fireplace, which served all the better as an emblem of the mansion's heart, because, though built for warmth, it was now so comfortless and empty.

Hepzibah attempted to enliven matters by a fire in the parlor. But the storm-demon kept watch above, and, whenever a flame was kindled, drove the smoke back again, choking the chimney's sooty throat with its own breath. Nevertheless, during four days of this miserable storm, Clifford wrapt himself in an old cloak, and occupied his customary chair. On the morning of the fifth, when summoned to breakfast, he responded only by a broken-hearted murmur, expressive of a determination not to leave his bed. His sister made no attempt to change his purpose. In fact, entirely as she loved him, Hepzibah could hardly have borne any longer the wretched duty—so impracticable by her few and rigid faculties—of seeking pastime for a still sensitive, but ruined mind, critical and fastidious, without force or volition. It was, at least, something short of positive despair, that, to-day, she might sit shivering alone, and not suffer continually a new brief, and unreasonable pang of remorse, at every fitful sigh of her fellow-sufferer.

But Clifford, it seemed, though he did not make his appearance below stairs, had, after all, bestirred himself in quest of amusement. In the course of the forenoon, Hepzibah heard a note of music, which (there being no other tuneful contrivance in the House of the Seven Gables) she knew must proceed from Alice Pyncheon's harpsichord. She was aware that Clifford, in his youth, had possessed a cultivated taste for music, and a considerable degree of skill in its practice. It was difficult, however, to conceive of his retaining an accomplishment to which daily exercise is so essential, in the measure indicated by the sweet, airy, and delicate, though most melancholy strain, that now stole upon her ear. Nor was it less marvellous that the long-silent instrument should be capable of so much melody. Hepzibah involuntarily thought of the ghostly harmonies, prelusive of death in the family, which were attributed to the legendary Alice. But it was, perhaps, proof of the agency of other than spiritual fingers, that, after a few touches, the chords seemed to snap asunder with their own vibrations, and the music ceased.

But a harsher sound succeeded to the mysterious notes; nor was the easterly day fated to pass without an event sufficient in itself to poison, for Hepzibah and Clifford, the balmiest air that ever brought the humming-birds along with it. The final echoes of Alice Pyncheon's performance (or Clifford's, if his we must consider it) were driven away by no less vulgar a dissonance than the ringing of the shop-bell. A foot was heard scraping itself on the threshold, and thence somewhat ponderously stepping on the floor. Hepzibah delayed a moment, while muffling herself in a faded shawl, which had been her defensive armor in a forty years' warfare against the east wind. A characteristic sound, however,—neither a cough nor a hem, but a kind of rumbling and reverberating spasm in somebody's capacious depth of chest,—impelled her to hurry forward, with that aspect of fierce faint-heartedness so common to women in cases of perilous emergency. Few of her sex, on such occasions, have ever looked so terible as our poor scowling Hepzibah. But the visitor quietly closed the shop-door behind him, stood up his umbrella against the counter, and turned a visage of composed benignity, to meet the alarm and anger which his appearance had excited.

Hepzibah's presentiment had not deceived her. It was no other than Judge Pyncheon, who, after in vain trying the front door, had now effected his entrance into the shop.

"How do you do, Cousin Hepzibah?—and how does this most inclement weather affect our poor Clifford?" began the Judge; and wonderful it seemed, indeed, that the easterly storm was not put to shame,
or, at any rate, a little mollified, by the genial benevolence of his smile.
"I could not rest without calling to ask, once more, whether I can in any
manner promote his comfort, or your own."

"You can do nothing," said Hepzibah, controlling her agitation as
well as she could. "I devote myself to Clifford. He has every comfort
which his situation admits of."

"But allow me to suggest, dear cousin," rejoined the Judge, "you err,
—in all affection and kindness, no doubt, and with the very best intentions,—but you do err, nevertheless, in keeping your brother so secluded.
Why insulate him thus from all sympathy and kindness? Clifford, alas!
has had too much of solitude. Now let him try society,—the society, that
is to say, of kindred and old friends. Let me, for instance, but see Clifford, and I will answer for the good effect of the interview."

"You cannot see him," answered Hepzibah. "Clifford has kept his bed
since yesterday."

"What! How! Is he ill?" exclaimed Judge Pyncheon, starting with
what seemed to be angry alarm; for the very frown of the old Puritan
darkened through the room as he spoke. "Nay, then, I must and will see
him! What if he should die?"

"He is in no danger of death," said Hepzibah,—and added, with bitterness that she could repress no longer, "none; unless he shall be persecuted to death, now, by the same man who long ago attempted it!"

"Cousin Hepzibah," said the Judge, with an impressive earnestness of
manner, which grew even to tearful pathos as he proceeded, "is it possible that you do not perceive how unjust, how unkind, how unchristian, is this constant, this long-continued bitterness against me, for a
part which I was constrained by duty and conscience, by the force of
law, and at my own peril, to act? What did I do, in detriment to Clifford, which it was possible to leave undone? How could you, his sister,—
if, for your never-ending sorrow, as it has been for mine, you had known
what I did,—have shown greater tenderness? And do you think, cousin,
that it had cost me no pang?—that it has left no anguish in my bosom,
from that day to this, amidst all the prosperity with which Heaven has
blessed me?—or that I do not now rejoice, when it is deemed consistent
with the dues of public justice and the welfare of society that this dear
kinsman, this early friend, this nature so delicately and beautifully constituted,—so unfortunate, let us pronounce him, and forbear to say, so
guilty,—that our own Clifford, in fine, should be given back to life, and
its possibilities of enjoyment? Ah, you little know me, Cousin Hepzibah!
You little know this heart! It now throbs at the thought of meeting him!
There lives not the human being (except yourself,—and you not more
than I) who has shed so many tears for Clifford's calamity! You behold
some of them now. There is none who would so delight to promote his

happiness! Try me, Hepzibah!—try me, cousin!—try the man whom you have treated as your enemy and Clifford's!—try Jaffrey Pyncheon, and you shall find him true, to the heart's core!'"

"In the name of Heaven," cried Hepzibah, provoked only to intenser indignation by this outgush of the inestimable tenderness of a stern nature,—"in God's name, whom you insult, and whose power I could almost question, since he hears you utter so many false words without palsying your tongue,—give over, I beseech you, this loathsome pretence of affection for your victim! You hate him! Say so, like a man! You cherish, at this moment, some black purpose against him in your heart! Speak it out, at once!—or, if you hope so to promote it better, hide it till you can triumph in its success! But never speak again of your love for my poor brother! I cannot bear it! It will drive me beyond a woman's decency! It will drive me mad! Forbear! Not another word! It will make me spurn you!"

For once, Hepzibah's wrath had given her courage. She had spoken. But, after all, was this unconquerable distrust of Judge Pyncheon's integrity, and this utter denial, apparently, of his claim to stand in the ring of human sympathies,—were they founded in any just perception of his character, or merely the off-spring of a woman's unreasonable prejudice, deduced from nothing?

The Judge, beyond all question, was a man of eminent respectability. The church acknowledged it; the state acknowledged it. It was denied by nobody. In all the very extensive sphere of those who knew him, whether in his public or private capacities, there was not an individual—except Hepzibah, and some lawless mystic, like the daguerreotypist, and, possibly, a few political opponents—who would have dreamed of seriously disputing his claim to a high and honorable place in the world's regard. Nor (we must do him the further justice to say) did Judge Pyncheon himself, probably, entertain many or very frequent doubts, that his enviable reputation accorded with his deserts. His conscience, therefore, usually considered the surest witness to a man's integrity,—his conscience, unless it might be for the little space of five minutes in the twenty-four hours, or, now and then, some black day in the whole year's circle,—his conscience bore an accordant testimony with the world's laudatory voice. And yet, strong as this evidence may seem to be, we should hesitate to peril our own conscience on the assertion, that the Judge and the consenting world were right, and that poor Hepzibah, with her solitary prejudice was wrong. Hidden from mankind,—forgotten by himself, or buried so deeply under a sculptured and ornamented pile of ostentatious deeds that his daily life could take no note of it,—there may have lurked some evil and unsightly thing. Nay, we could almost venture to say, further, that a daily guilt might have been acted by him, continually renewed, and reddening forth afresh, like the miraculous bloodstain of a murder, without his necessarily and at every moment being aware of it.

Men of strong minds, great force of character, and a hard texture of the sensibilities, are very capable of falling into mistakes of this kind. They are ordinarily men to whom forms are of paramount importance. Their field of action lies among the external phenomena of life. They possess vast ability in grasping, and arranging, and appropriating to themselves, the big, heavy, solid unrealities, such as gold, landed estate, offices of trust and emolument, and public honors. With these materials, and with deeds of goodly aspect, done in the public eye, an individual of this class builds up, as it were, a tall and stately edifice, which, in the view of other people, and ultimately in his own view, is no other than the man's character, or the man himself. Behold, therefore, a palace! Its splendid halls, and suites of spacious apartments, are floored with a mosaic-work of costly marbles; its windows, the whole height of each room, admit the sunshine through the most transparent of plate-glass; its high cornices are gilded, and its ceilings gorgeously painted; and a lofty dome—through which, from the central pavement, you may gaze up to the sky, as with no obstructing medium between—surmounts the whole. With what fairer and nobler emblem could any man desire to shadow forth his character? Ah! but in some low and obscure nook,—some narrow closet on the ground-floor, shut, locked and bolted, and the key flung away,—or beneath the marble pavement, in a stagnant water-puddle, with the richest pattern of mosaic-work above,—may lie a corpse, half decayed, and still decaying, and diffusing its death-scent all through the palace! The inhabitant will not be conscious of it, for it has long been his daily breath! Neither will the visitors, for they smell only the rich odors which the master sedulously scatters through the palace, and the incense which they bring, and delight to burn before him! Now and then, perchance, comes in a seer, before whose sadly gifted eye the whole structure melts into thin air, leaving only the hidden nook, the bolted closet, with the cobwebs festooned over its forgotten door, or the deadly hole under the pavement, and the decaying corpse within. Here, then, we are to seek the true emblem of the man's character, and of the deed that gives whatever reality it possesses to his life. And, beneath the show of a marble palace, that pool of stagnant water, foul with many impurities, and, perhaps, tinged with blood,—that secret abomination, above which, possibly, he may say his prayers, without remembering it,—is this man's miserable soul!

To apply this train of remark somewhat more closely to Judge Pyncheon. We might say (without in the least imputing crime to a personage of his eminent respectability) that there was enough of splendid rubbish in his life to cover up and paralyze a more active and subtile conscience than the Judge was ever troubled with. The purity of his judicial character, while on the bench; the faithfulness of his public service in subsequent capacities; his devotedness to his party, and the rigid consistency with which he had adhered to its principles, or, at all events, kept pace with its organized movements; his remarkable zeal as president of a Bible society; his unimpeachable integrity as treasurer of a widow's and orphan's fund; his benefits to horticulture, by producing two much-esteemed varieties of the pear, and to agriculture, through the agency of the famous Pyncheon bull; the cleanliness of his moral deportment, for a great many years past; the severity with which he had frowned upon, and finally cast off, an expensive and dissipated son, delaying forgiveness until within the final quarter of an hour of the young man's life; his prayers at morning and eventide, and graces at meal-time; his efforts in furtherance of the temperance cause; his confining himself, since the last attack of the gout, to five diurnal glasses of old sherry wine; the snowy whiteness of his linen, the polish of his boots, the handsomeness of his gold-headed cane, the square and roomy fashion of his coat, and the fineness of its material, and, in general, the studied propriety of his dress and equipment; the scrupulousness with which he paid public notice, in the street, by a bow, a lifting of the hat, a nod, or a motion of the hand, to all and sundry of his acquaintances, rich or poor; the smile of broad benevolence wherewith he made it a point to gladden the whole world,—what room could possibly be found for darker traits in a portrait made up of lineaments like these? This proper face was what he beheld in the looking-glass. This admirably arranged life was what he was conscious of in the progress of every day. Then, might not he claim to be its result and sum, and say to himself and the community, "Behold Judge Pyncheon there"?

And allowing that, many, many years ago, in his early and reckless youth, he had committed some one wrong act,—or that, even now, the inevitable force of circumstances should occasionally make him do one questionable deed among a thousand praiseworthy, or, at least, blameless ones,—would you characterize the Judge by that one necessary deed, and that half-forgotten act, and let it overshadow the fair aspect of a lifetime? What is there so ponderous in evil, that a thumb's bigness of it should outweigh the mass of things not evil which were heaped into the other scale! This scale and balance system is a favorite one with people of Judge Pyncheon's brotherhood. A hard, cold man, thus unfortunately situated, seldom or never looking inward, and resolutely taking his idea of himself from what purports to be his image as reflected in the mirror of public opinion, can scarcely arrive at true self-knowledge, except through loss of property and reputation. Sickness will not always help him do it; not always the death-hour!

But our affair now is with Judge Pyncheon as he stood confronting the fierce outbreak of Hepzibah's wrath. Without premeditation, to her own surprise, and indeed terror, she had given vent, for once, to the inveteracy of her resentment, cherished against this kinsman for thirty years.

Thus far the Judge's countenance had expressed mild forbearance,—grave and almost gentle deprecation of his cousin's unbecoming violence,—free and Christian-like forgiveness of the wrong inflicted by her words. But when those words were irrevocably spoken his look assumed sternness, the sense of power, and immitigable resolve; and this with so natural and imperceptible a change, that it seemed as if the iron man had stood there from the first, and the meek man not at all. The effect was as when the light, vapory clouds, with their soft coloring, suddenly vanish from the stony brow of a precipitous mountain, and leave there the frown which you at once feel to be eternal. Hepzibah almost adopted the insane belief that it was her old Puritan ancestor, and not the modern Judge, on whom she had just been wreaking the bitterness of her heart. Never did a man show stronger proof of the lineage attributed to him than Judge Pyncheon, at this crisis, by his unmistakable resemblance to the picture in the inner room.

"Cousin Hepzibah," said he, very calmly, "it is time to have done with this."

"With all my heart!" answered she. "Then, why do you persecute us any longer? Leave poor Clifford and me in peace. Neither of us desires anything better!"

"It is my purpose to see Clifford before I leave this house," continued the Judge. "Do not act like a madwoman, Hepzibah! I am his only friend, and an all-powerful one. Has it never occurred to you,—are you so blind as not to have seen,—that, without not merely my consent, but my efforts, my representations, the exertion of my whole influence, political, official, personal, Clifford would never have been what you call free? Did you think his release a triumph over me? Not so, my good cousin; not so, by any means! The furthest possible from that! No; but it was the accomplishment of a purpose long entertained on my part. I set him free!"

"You!" answered Hepzibah. "I never will believe it! He owed his dungeon to you; his freedom to God's providence!"

"I set him free!" reaffirmed Judge Pyncheon, with the calmest composure. "And I came hither now to decide whether he shall retain his freedom. It will depend upon himself. For this purpose, I must see him."

"Never!—it would drive him mad!" exclaimed Hepzibah, but with an irresoluteness sufficiently perceptible to the keen eye of the Judge; for, without the slightest faith in his good intentions, she knew not whether there was most to dread in yielding or resistance. "And why should you wish to see this wretched, broken man, who retains hardly a fraction of his intellect, and will hide even that from an eye which has no love in it?"

"He shall see love enough in mine, if that be all!" said the Judge, with well-grounded confidence in the benignity of his aspect. "But, Cousin Hepzibah, you confess a great deal, and very much to the purpose. Now, listen, and I will frankly explain my reasons for insisting on this interview. At the death, thirty years since, of our uncle Jaffrey, it was found, —I know not whether the circumstance ever attracted much of your attention, among the sadder interests that clustered round that event,—but it was found that his visible estate, of every kind, fell far short of any estimate ever made of it. He was supposed to be immensely rich. Nobody doubted that he stood among the weightiest men of his day. It was one of his eccentricities, however,—and not altogether a folly, neither,—to conceal the amount of his property by making distant and foreign investments, perhaps under other names than his own, and by various means, familiar enough to capitalists, but unnecessary here to be specified. By

Uncle Jaffrey's last will and testament, as you are aware, his entire property was bequeathed to me, with the single exception of a life interest to yourself in this old family mansion, and the strip of patrimonial estate remaining attached to it."

"And do you seek to deprive us of that?" asked Hepzibah, unable to restrain her bitter contempt. "Is this your price for ceasing to persecute poor Clifford?"

"Certainly not, my dear cousin!" answered the Judge, smiling benevolently. "On the contrary, as you must do me the justice to own, I have constantly expressed my readiness to double or treble your resources, whenever you should make up your mind to accept any kindness of that nature at the hands of your kinsman. No, no! But here lies the gist of the matter. Of my uncle's unquestionably great estate, as I have said, not the half—no, not one third, as I am fully convinced—was apparent after his death. Now, I have the best possible reasons for believing that your brother Clifford can give me a clew to the recovery of the remainder."

"Clifford!—Clifford know of any hidden wealth?—Clifford have it in his power to make you rich?" cried the old gentlewoman, affected with a sense of something like ridicule, at the idea. "Impossible! You deceive yourself! It is really a thing to laugh at!"

"It is as certain as that I stand here!" said Judge Pyncheon, striking his gold-headed cane on the floor, and at the same time stamping his foot, as if to express his conviction the more forcibly by the whole emphasis of his substantial person. "Clifford told me so himself!"

"No, no!" exclaimed Hepzibah, incredulously. "'You are dreaming, Cousin Jaffrey!'"

"I do not belong to the dreaming class of men," said the Judge, quietly. "Some months before my uncle's death, Clifford boasted to me of the possession of the secret of incalculable wealth. His purpose was to taunt me, and excite my curiosity. I know it well. But, from a pretty distinct recollection of the particulars of our conversation, I am thoroughly convinced that there was truth in what he said. Clifford, at this moment, if he chooses,—and choose he must!—can inform me where to find the schedule, the documents, the evidences, in whatever shape they exist, of the vast amount of Uncle Jaffrey's missing property. He has the secret. His boast was no idle word. It had a directness, an emphasis, a particularity, that showed a backbone of solid meaning within the mystery of his expression."

"But what could have been Clifford's object," asked Hepzibah, "in concealing it so long?"

"It was one of the bad impulses of our fallen nature," replied the Judge, turning up his eyes. "He looked upon me as his enemy. He considered me as the cause of his overwhelming disgrace, his imminent peril of death, his irretrievable ruin. There was no great probability, therefore, of his volunteering information, out of his dungeon, that should elevate me still higher on the ladder of prosperity. But the moment has now come when he must give up his secret."

"And what if he should refuse?" inquired Hepzibah. "Or,—as I steadfastly believe,—what if he has no knowledge of this wealth?"

"My dear cousin," said Judge Pyncheon, with a quietude which he had the power of making more formidable than any violence, "since your brother's return, I have taken the precaution (a highly proper one in the near kinsman and natural guardian of an individual so situated) to have his deportment and habits constantly and carefully overlooked. Your neighbors have been eye-witnesses to whatever has passed in the garden. The butcher, the baker, the fish-monger, some of the customers of your shop, and many a prying old woman, have told me several of the secrets of your interior. A still larger circle—I myself, among the rest—can testify to his extravagances at the arched window. Thousands beheld him, a week or two ago, on the point of flinging himself thence into the street. From all this testimony, I am led to apprehend—reluctantly, and with deep grief—that Clifford's misfortunes have so affected his intellect, never very strong, that he cannot safely remain at large. The alternative, you must be aware,—and its adoption will depend entirely on the decision which I am now about to make,—the alternative is his confinement, probably for the remainder of his life, in a public asylum for persons in his unfortunate state of mind."

"You cannot mean it!" shrieked Hepzibah.

"Should my cousin Clifford," continued Judge Pyncheon, wholly undisturbed, "from mere malice, and hatred of one whose interests ought naturally to be dear to him,—a mode of passion that, as often as any other, indicates mental disease,—should he refuse me the information so important to myself, and which he assuredly possesses, I shall consider it the one needed jot of evidence to satisfy my mind of his insanity. And, once sure of the course pointed out by conscience, you know me too well, Cousin Hepzibah, to entertain a doubt that I shall pursue it."

"O, Jaffrey,—Cousin Jaffrey!" cried Hepzibah, mournfully, not passionately, "it is you that are diseased in mind, not Clifford! You have forgotten that a woman was your mother!—that you have had sisters, brothers, children of your own!—or that there ever was affection between man and man, or pity from one man to another, in this miserable world! Else, how could you have dreamed of this? You are not young, Cousin Jaffrey!—no, nor middle-aged,—but already an old man! The hair is white upon your head! How many years have you to live? Are you not rich enough for that little time? Shall you be hungry—shall you lack clothes, or a roof to shelter you,—between this point and the grave? No! but, with the half of what you now possess, you could revel in costly food and wines, and build a house twice as splendid as you now inhabit, and make a far greater show to the world,—and yet leave riches to your only son, to make him bless the hour of your death! Then, why should you do this cruel, cruel thing?—so mad a thing, that I know not whether to call it wicked! Alas, Cousin Jaffrey, this hard and grasping spirit has run in our blood these two hundred years. You are but doing over again, in another shape, what your ancestor before you did, and sending down to your posterity the curse inherited from him!"

"Talk sense, Hepzibah, for Heaven's sake!" exclaimed the Judge, with the impatience natural to a reasonable man, on hearing anything so utterly absurd as the above, in a discussion about matters of business. "I have told you my determination. I am not apt to change. Clifford must give up his secret or take the consequences. And let him decide quickly; for I have several affairs to attend to this morning, and an important dinner engagement with some political friends."

"Clifford has no secret!" answered Hepzibah. "And God will not let you do the thing you meditate!"

"We shall see," said the unmoved Judge. "Meanwhile, choose whether you will summon Clifford, and allow this business to be amicably settled by an interview between two kinsmen, or drive me to harsher measures, which I should be most happy to feel myself justified in avoiding. The responsibility is altogether on your part."

"You are stronger than I," said Hepzibah, after a brief consideration; "and you have no pity in your strength! Clifford is not now insane; but the interview which you insist upon may go far to make him so. Nevertheless, knowing you as I do, I believe it to be my best course to allow you to judge for yourself as to the improbability of his possessing any valuable secret. I will call Clifford. Be merciful in your dealings with him!—be far more merciful than your heart bids you be!—for God is looking at you, Jaffrey Pyncheon!"

The Judge followed his cousin from the shop, where the foregoing conversation had passed, into the parlor, and flung himself heavily into the great ancestral chair. Many a former Pyncheon had found repose in its capacious arms: rosy children, after their sports; young men, dreamy with love; grown men, weary with cares; old men, burdened with winters, —they had mused, and slumbered, and departed to a yet profounder sleep. It had been a long tradition, though a doubtful one, that this was the very chair, seated in which, the earliest of the Judge's New England forefathers—he whose picture still hung upon the wall—had given a dead man's silent and stern reception to the throng of distinguished guests. From that hour of evil omen until the present, it may be,—though we know not the secret of his heart,—but it may be that no wearier and sadder man had ever sunk into the chair than this same Judge Pyncheon, whom we have just beheld so immitigably hard and resolute. Surely, it must have been at no slight cost that he had thus fortified his soul with iron. Such calmness is a mightier effort than the violence of weaker men. And there was yet a heavy task for him to do. Was it a little matter,—a trifle to be prepared for in a single moment, and to be rested from in another moment,—that he must now, after thirty years, encounter a kinsman risen from a living tomb, and wrench a secret from him, or else consign him to a living tomb again?

"Did you speak?" asked Hepzibah, looking in from the threshold of the parlor; for she imagined that the Judge had uttered some sound which she was anxious to interpret as a relenting impulse. "I thought you called me back."

"No, no!" gruffly answered Judge Pyncheon, with a harsh frown, while his brow grew almost a black purple, in the shadow of the room. "Why should I call you back? Time flies! Bid Clifford come to me!"

The Judge had taken his watch from his vest-pocket and now held it in his hand, measuring the interval which was to ensue before the appearance of Clifford.

## XVI

### CLIFFORD'S CHAMBER

NEVER had the old house appeared so dismal to poor Hepzibah as when she departed on that wretched errand. There was a strange aspect in it. As she trod along the foot-worn passages, and opened one crazy door after another, and ascended the creaking staircase, she gazed wistfully and fearfully around. It would have been no marvel, to her excited mind, if, behind or beside her, there had been the rustle of dead people's garments, or pale visages awaiting her on the landing-place above. Her nerves were set all ajar by the scene of passion and terror through which she had just struggled. Her colloquy with Judge Pyncheon, who so perfectly represented the person and attributes of the founder of the family, had called back the dreary past. It weighed upon her heart. Whatever she had heard, from lengendary aunts and grandmothers, concerning the good or evil fortunes of the Pyncheons,—stories which had heretofore been kept warm in her remembrance by the chimney-corner glow that was associated with them,—now recurred to her, sombre, ghastly, cold, like most passages of family history, when brooded over in melancholy mood. The whole seemed little else but a series of calamity, reproducing itself in successive generations, with one general hue, and varying in little, save the outline. But Hepzibah now felt as if the Judge, and Clifford, and herself,—they three together,—were on the point of adding another incident to the annals of the house, with a bolder relief of wrong and sorrow, which would cause it to stand out from all the rest. Thus it is that the grief of the passing moment takes upon itself an individuality, and a character of climax, which it is destined to lose after a while, and to fade into the dark gray tissue common to the grave or glad events of many years ago. It is but for a moment, comparatively, that anything looks strange or startling,—a truth that has the bitter and the sweet in it.

But Hepzibah could not rid herself of the sense of something unprecedented at that instant passing and soon to be accomplished. Her nerves were in a shake. Instinctively she paused before the arched window, and looked out upon the street, in order to seize its permanent objects with her mental grasp, and thus to steady herself from the reel and vibration which affected her more immediate sphere. It brought her up, as we may say, with a kind of shock, when she beheld everything under the same appearance as the day before, and numberless preceding days, except for the difference between sunshine and sullen storm. Her eyes travelled along the street, from doorstep to doorstep, noting the wet sidewalks, with here and there a puddle in hollows that had been imperceptible until filled with water. She screwed her dim optics to their acutest point, in the hope of making out, with greater distinctness, a certain window, where she half saw, half guessed, that a tailor's seamstress was sitting at her work. Hepzibah flung herself upon that unknown woman's companionship, even thus far off. Then she was attracted by a chaise rapidly passing, and watched its moist and glistening top, and its splashing wheels, until it had turned the corner, and refused to carry any further her idly trifling, because appalled and overburdened, mind. When the vehicle had disappeared, she allowed herself still another loitering moment; for the patched figure of good Uncle Venner was now visible, coming slowly from the head of the street downward, with a rheumatic limp, because the east wind had got into his joints. Hepzibah wished that he would pass yet more slowly, and befriend her shivering solitude a little longer. Anything that would take her out of the grievous present, and interpose human beings betwixt herself and what was nearest to her,—whatever would defer for an instant, the inevitable errand on which she was bound,—all such impediments were welcome. Next to the lightest heart, the heaviest is apt to be most playful.

Hepzibah had little hardihood for her own proper pain and far less for what she must inflict on Clifford. Of so slight a nature, and so shattered by his previous calamities, it could not well be short of utter ruin to bring him face to face with the hard, relentless man, who had been his evil destiny through life. Even had there been no bitter recollections, nor any hostile interest now at stake between them, the mere natural repugnance of the more sensitive system to the massive, weighty, and unimpressible one, must, in itself, have been disastrous to the former. It would be like flinging a porcelain vase, with already a crack in it, against a granite column. Never before had Hepzibah so adequately estimated the powerful character of her cousin Jaffrey,—powerful by intellect, energy of will, the long habit of acting among men, and, as she believed, by his unscrupulous pursuit of selfish ends through evil means. It did but increase the difficulty that Judge Pyncheon was under a delusion as to the secret which he supposed Clifford to possess. Men of his strength of purpose, and customary sagacity, if they chance to adopt a mistaken opinion in practical matters, so wedge it and fasten it among things known to be true, that to wrench it out of their minds is hardly less difficult than pulling up an oak. Thus, as the Judge required an impossibility of Clifford, the latter, as he could not perform it, must needs perish. For what, in the grasp of a man like this, was to become of Clifford's soft poetic nature, that never should have had a task more stubborn than to set a life of beautiful enjoyment to the flow and rhythm of musical cadences! Indeed, what had become of it already? Broken! Blighted! All but annihilated! Soon to be wholly so!

For a moment, the thought crossed Hepzibah's mind, whether Clifford might not really have such knowledge of their deceased uncle's vanished estate as the Judge imputed to him. She remembered some vague intimations, on her brother's part, which—if the supposition were not essentially preposterous—might have been so interpreted. There had been schemes of travel and residence abroad, day-dreams of brilliant life at home, and splendid castles in the air, which it would have required boundless wealth to build and realize. Had this wealth been in her power, how gladly would Hepzibah have bestowed it all upon her iron-hearted kinsman, to buy for Clifford the freedom and seclusion of the desolate old house! But she believed that her brother's schemes were as destitute of actual substance and purpose as a child's pictures of its future life, while sitting in a little chair by its mother's knee. Clifford had none but shadowy gold at his command; and it was not the stuff to satisfy Judge Pyncheon!

Was there no help, in their extremity? It seemed strange that there should be none, with a city round about her. It would be so easy to throw up the window, and send forth a shriek, at the strange agony of which everybody would come hastening to the rescue, well understanding it to be the cry of a human soul, at some dreadful crisis! But how wild, how almost laughable, the fatality,—and yet how continually it comes to pass, thought Hepzibah, in this dull delirium of a world,—that whosoever, and with however kindly a purpose, should come to help, they would be sure to help the strongest side! Might and wrong combined, like iron magnetized, are endowed with irresistible attraction. There would be Judge Pyncheon,—a person eminent in the public view, of high station and great wealth, a philanthropist, a member of Congress and of the church, and intimately associated with whatever else bestows good name,—so imposing, in these advantageous lights, that Hepzibah herself could hardly help shrinking from her own conclusions as to his hollow integrity. The Judge, on one side! And who, on the other? The guilty Clifford! Once a byword! Now, an indistinctly remembered ignominy!

Nevertheless, in spite of this perception that the Judge would draw all human aid to his own behalf, Hepzibah was so unaccustomed to act for herself, that the least word of counsel would have swayed her to any mode of action. Little Phœbe Pyncheon would at once have lighted up the whole scene, if not by any available suggestion, yet simply by the warm vivacity of her character. The idea of the artist occurred to Hepzibah. Young and unknown, mere vagrant adventurer as he was, she had been conscious of a force in Holgrave which might well adapt him to be the champion of a crisis. With this thought in her mind, she unbolted a door, cobwebbed and long disused, but which had served as a former medium of communication between her own part of the house and the gable where the wandering daguerreotypist had now established his temporary home. He was not there. A book, face downward, on the table, a roll of manuscript, a half-written sheet, a newspaper, some tools of his present occupation, and several rejected daguerreotypes, conveyed an impression as if he were close at hand. But, at this period of the day, as Hepzibah might have anticipated, the artist was at his public rooms. With an impulse of idle curiosity, that flickered among her heavy thoughts, she looked at one of the daguerreotypes, and beheld Judge Pyncheon frowning at her. Fate stared her in the face. She turned back from her fruitless quest, with a heart-sinking sense of disappointment. In all her years of seclusion, she had never felt, as now, what it was to be alone. It seemed as if the house stood in a desert, or, by some spell, was made invisible to those who dwelt around, or passed beside it; so that any mode of misfortune, miserable accident, or crime might happen in it without the possibility of aid. In her grief and wounded pride, Hepzibah had spent her life in divesting herself of friends; she had wilfully cast off the support which God has ordained his creatures to need from one another; and it was now her punishment, that Clifford and herself would fall the easier victims to their kindred enemy.

Returning to the arched window, she lifted her eyes,—scowling, poor, dim-sighted Hepzibah, in the face of Heaven!—and strove hard to send up a prayer through the dense gray pavement of clouds. Those mists had gathered, as if to symbolize a great, brooding mass of human trouble, doubt, confusion, and chill indifference, between earth and the better regions. Her faith was too weak; the prayer too heavy to be thus uplifted. It fell back, a lump of lead, upon her heart. It smote her with the wretched conviction that Providence intermeddled not in these petty wrongs of one individual to his fellow, nor had any balm for these little agonies of a solitary soul; but shed its justice, and its mercy, in a broad, sunlike sweep, over half the universe at once. Its vastness made it nothing. But Hepzibah did not see that, just as there comes a warm sunbeam into every cottage window, so comes a lovebeam of God's care and pity for every separate need.

At last, finding no other pretext for deferring the torture that she was to inflict on Clifford,—her reluctance to which was the true cause of her loitering at the window, her search for the artist, and even her abortive prayer,—dreading, also, to hear the stern voice of Judge Pyncheon from below stairs, chiding her delay,—she crept slowly, a pale, grief-stricken figure, a dismal shape of woman, with almost torpid limbs, slowly to her brother's door, and knocked!

There was no reply!

And how should there have been? Her hand, tremulous with the shrinking purpose which directed it, had smitten so feebly against the door that the sound could hardly have gone inward. She knocked again. Still, no response! Nor was it to be wondered at. She had struck with the entire force of her heart's vibration, communicating, by some subtle magnetism, her own terror to the summons. Clifford would turn his face to the pillow, and cover his head beneath the bedclothes, like a startled child at midnight. She knocked a third time, three regular strokes, gently, but perfectly distinct, and with meaning in them; for, modulate it with what cautious art we will, the hand cannot help playing some tune of what we feel, upon the senseless wood.

Clifford returned no answer.

"Clifford! dear brother!" said Hepzibah. "Shall I come in?"

A silence.

Two or three times, and more, Hepzibah repeated his name, without result; till, thinking her brother's sleep unwontedly profound, she undid the door, and entering, found the chamber vacant. How could he have come forth, and when, without her knowledge? Was it possible that, in spite of the stormy day, and worn out with the irksomeness within doors, he had betaken himself to his customary haunt in the garden, and was now shivering under the cheerless shelter of the summer-house? She hastily threw up a window, thrust forth her turbaned head and the half of her gaunt figure, and searched the whole garden through, as completely as her dim vision would allow. She could see the interior of the summer-house, and its circular seat, kept moist by the droppings of the roof. It had no occupant. Clifford was not thereabouts; unless, indeed, he had crept for concealment (as, for a moment, Hepzibah fancied might be the case) into a great, wet mass of tangled and broad-leaved shadow, where the squash-vines were clambering tumultuously upon an old wooden framework, set casually aslant against the fence. This could not be, however; he was not there; for, while Hepzibah was looking, a strange grimalkin stole forth from the very spot, and picked his way across the garden. Twice he paused to snuff the air, and then anew directed his course towards the parlor window. Whether it was only on account of the stealthy, prying manner common to the race, or that this cat seemed to have more than ordinary mischief in his thoughts, the old gentlewoman, in spite of her much perplexity, felt an impulse to drive the animal away, and accordingly flung down a window-stick. The cat stared up at her, like a detected thief or murderer, and, the next instant, took to flight. No other living creature was visible in the garden. Chanticleer and his family had either not left their roost, disheartened by the interminable rain, or had done the next wisest thing, by seasonably returning to it. Hepzibah closed the window.

But where was Clifford? Could it be that, aware of the presence of his Evil Destiny, he had crept silently down the staircase, while the Judge and Hepzibah stood talking in the shop, and had softly undone the fastenings of the outer door, and made his escape into the street? With that thought, she seemed to behold his gray, wrinkled, yet childlike aspect, in the old-fashioned garments which he wore about the house; a figure such as one sometimes imagines himself to be, with the world's eye upon him, in a troubled dream. This figure of her wretched brother would go wandering through the city, attracting all eyes, and everybody's wonder and repugnance, like a ghost, the more to be shuddered at because visible at noontide. To incur the ridicule of the younger crowd, that knew him not, —the harsher scorn and indignation of a few old men, who might recall his once familiar features! To be the sport of boys, who, when old enough to run about the streets, have no more reverence for what is beautiful and holy, nor pity for what is sad,—no more sense of sacred misery, sanctifying the human shape in which it embodies itself,—than if Satan were the father of them all! Goaded by their taunts, their loud, shrill cries, and cruel laughter,—insulted by the filth of the public ways, which they would fling upon him,—or, as it might well be, distracted by the mere strangeness of his situation, though nobody should afflict him with so much as a thoughtless word,—what wonder if Clifford were to break into some wild extravagance which was certain to be interpreted as lunacy? Thus Judge Pyncheon's fiendish scheme would be ready accomplished to his hands!

Then Hepzibah reflected that the town was almost completely water-girdled. The wharves stretched out towards the centre of the harbor, and, in this inclement weather, were deserted by the ordinary throng of merchants, laborers, and sea-faring men; each wharf a solitude, with the vessels moored stem and stern, along its misty length. Should her brother's aimless footsteps stray thitherward, and he but bend, one moment, over the deep, black tide, would he not bethink himself that here was the sure refuge within his reach, and that, with a single step, or the slightest over-balance of his body, he might be forever beyond his kinsman's gripe? Oh, the temptation! To make of his ponderous sorrow a security! To sink, with its leaden weight upon him, and never rise again!

The horror of this last conception was too much for Hepzibah. Even Jaffrey Pyncheon must help her now! She hastened down the staircase, shrieking as she went.

"Clifford is gone!" she cried. "I cannot find my brother! Help, Jaffrey Pyncheon! Some harm will happen to him!"

She threw open the parlor-door. But, what with the shade of branches across the windows, and the smoke-blackened ceiling, and the dark oak-panelling of the walls, there was hardly so much daylight in the room that Hepzibah's imperfect sight could accurately distinguish the Judge's figure. She was certain, however, that she saw him sitting in the ancestral armchair, near the centre of the floor, with his face somewhat averted, and looking towards a window. So firm and quiet is the nervous system of such men as Judge Pyncheon, that he had perhaps stirred not more than once since her departure, but, in the hard composure of his temperament, retained the position into which accident had thrown him.

"I tell you, Jaffrey," cried Hepzibah, impatiently, as she turned from the parlor-door to search other rooms, "my brother is not in his chamber! You must help me seek him!"

But Judge Pyncheon was not the man to let himself be startled from an easy-chair with haste ill-befitting either the dignity of his character or his broad personal basis, by the alarm of an hysteric woman. Yet, considering his own interest in the matter, he might have bestirred himself with a little more alacrity.

"Do you hear me, Jaffrey Pyncheon?" screamed Hepzibah, as she again approached the parlor-door, after an ineffectual search elsewhere. "Clifford is gone!"

At this instant, on the threshold of the parlor, emerging from within, appeared Clifford himself! His face was preternaturally pale; so deadly white, indeed, that, through all the glimmering indistinctness of the passage-way, Hepzibah could discern his features, as if a light fell on them alone. Their vivid and wild expression seemed likewise sufficient to illuminate them; it was an expression of scorn and mockery, coinciding with the emotions indicated by his gesture. As Clifford stood on the threshold, partly turning back, he pointed his finger within the parlor, and shook it slowly as though he would have summoned, not Hepzibah alone, but the whole world, to gaze at some object inconceivably ridiculous. This action, so ill-timed and extravagant,—accompanied, too, with a look that showed more like joy than any other kind of excitement,—compelled Hepzibah to dread that her stern kinsman's ominous visit had driven her poor brother to absolute insanity. Nor could she otherwise account for the Judge's quiescent mood than by supposing him craftily on the watch, while Clifford developed these symptoms of a distracted mind.

"Be quiet, Clifford!" whispered his sister, raising her hand to impress caution. "Oh, for Heaven's sake, be quiet!"

"Let him be quiet! What can he do better?" answered Clifford, with a still wilder gesture, pointing into the room which we had just quitted. "As for us, Hepzibah, we can dance now!—we can sing, laugh, play, do what we will! The weight is gone, Hepzibah! it is gone off this weary old world, and we may be as light-hearted as little Phœbe herself!"

And, in accordance with his words, he began to laugh, still pointing his finger at the object, invisible to Hepzibah, within the parlor. She was seized with a sudden intuition of some horrible thing. She thrust herself past Clifford, and disappeared into the room; but almost immediately returned, with a cry choking in her throat. Gazing at her brother with an affrighted glance of inquiry, she beheld him all in a tremor and a quake, from head to foot, while, amid these commoted elements of passion or alarm, still flickered his gusty mirth.

"My God! what is to become of us?" gasped Hepzibah.

"Come!" said Clifford, in a tone of brief decision, most unlike what was usual with him. "We stay here too long! Let us leave the old house to our cousin Jaffrey! He will take good care of it!"

Hepzibah now noticed that Clifford had on a cloak,—a garment of long ago,—in which he had constantly muffled himself during these days of easterly storm. He beckoned with his hand, and intimated, so far as she could comprehend him, his purpose that they should go together from the house. There are chaotic, blind, or drunken moments, in the lives of persons who lack real force of character,—moments of test, in which courage would most assert itself,—but where these individuals, if left to themselves, stagger aimlessly along, or follow implicitly whatever guidance may befall them, even if it be a child's. No matter how preposterous or insane, a purpose is a God-send to them. Hepzibah had reached this point. Unaccustomed to action or responsibility,—full of horror at what she had seen, and afraid to inquire, or almost to imagine, how it had come to pass,—affrighted at the fatality which seemed to pursue her brother,—stupefied by the dim, thick, stifling atmosphere of dread, which filled the house as with a death-smell, and obliterated all definiteness of thought,—she yielded without a question, and on the instant, to the will which Clifford expressed. For herself, she was like a person in a dream, when the will always sleeps. Clifford, ordinarily so destitute of this faculty, had found it in the tension of the crisis.

"Why do you delay so?" cried he, sharply. "Put on your cloak and hood, or whatever it pleases you to wear! No matter what; you cannot look beautiful nor brilliant, my poor Hepzibah! Take your purse, with money in it, and come along!"

Hepzibah obeyed these instructions, as if nothing else were to be done or thought of. She began to wonder, it is true, why she did not wake up, and at what still more intolerable pitch of dizzy trouble her spirit would struggle out of the maze, and make her conscious that nothing of all this had actually happened. Of course it was not real; no such black, easterly day as this had yet begun to be; Judge Pyncheon had not talked with her; Clifford had not laughed, pointed, beckoned her away with him; but she had merely been afflicted—as lonely sleepers often are—with a great deal of unreasonable misery, in a morning dream!

"Now—now—I shall certainly awake!" thought Hepzibah, as she went to and fro, making her little preparations. "I can bear it no longer! I must wake up now!"

But it came not, that awakening moment! It came not, even when, just before they left the house, Clifford stole to the parlor-door, and made a parting obeisance to the sole occupant of the room.

"What an absurd figure the old fellow cuts now!" whispered he to Hepzibah. "Just when he fancied he had me completely under his thumb! Come, come; make haste! or he will start up, like Giant Despair in pursuit of Christian and Hopeful, and catch us yet!"

As they passed into the street, Clifford directed Hepzibah's attention to something on one of the posts of the front door. It was merely the initials of his own name, which, with somewhat of his characteristic grace about the forms of the letters, he had cut there when a boy. The brother and sister departed, and left Judge Pyncheon sitting in the old home of his forefathers, all by himself; so heavy and lumpish that we can liken him to nothing better than a defunct nightmare, which had perished in the midst of its wickedness, and left its flabby corpse on the breast of the tormented one, to ge gotten rid of as it might!

## XVII

### THE FLIGHT OF TWO OWLS

SUMMER as it was, the east wind set poor Hepzibah's few remaining teeth chattering in her head, as she and Clifford faced it, on their way up Pyncheon Street, and towards the centre of the town. Not merely was it the shiver which this pitiless blast brought to her frame (although her feet and hands, especially, had never seemed so death-a-cold as now), but there was a moral sensation, mingling itself with the physical chill, and causing her to shake more in spirit than in body. The world's broad, bleak atmosphere was all so comfortless! Such, indeed, is the impression which it makes on every new adventurer, even if he plunge into it while the warmest tide of life is bubbling through his veins. What, then, must it have been to Hepzibah and Clifford,—so time-stricken as they were, yet so like children in their inexperience,—as they left the doorstep, and passed from beneath the wide shelter of the Pyncheon Elm! They were wandering all abroad, on precisely such a pilgrimage as a child often meditates, to the world's end, with perhaps a sixpence and a biscuit in his pocket. In Hepzibah's mind, there was the wretched consciousness of being adrift. She had lost the faculty of self-guidance; but, in view of the difficulties around her, felt it hardly worth an effort to regain it, and was, moreover, incapable of making one.

As they proceeded on their strange expedition she now and then cast a look sidelong at Clifford, and could not but observe that he was possessed and swayed by a powerful excitement. It was this, indeed, that gave him the control which he had at once, and so irresistibly, established over his movements. It not a little resembled the exhilaration of wine. Or, it might more fancifully be compared to a joyous piece of music, played with wild vivacity, but upon a disordered instrument. As the cracked jarring note might always be heard, and as it jarred loudest amid the loftiest exultation of the melody, so was there a continual quake through Clifford, causing him most to quiver while he wore a triumphant smile, and seemed almost under a necessity to skip in his gait.

They met few people abroad, even on passing from the retired neighborhood of the House of the Seven Gables into what was ordinarily the more thronged and busier portion of the town. Glistening sidewalks, with little pools of rain, here and there, along their unequal surface; umbrellas displayed ostentatiously in the shop-windows, as if the life of trade had concentred itself in that one article; wet leaves of the horse-chestnut or elm-trees, torn off untimely by the blast and scattered along the public way; an unsightly accumulation of mud in the middle of the street, which perversely grew the more unclean for its long and laborious washing,— these were the more definable points of a very sombre picture. In the way of movement, and human life, there was the hasty rattle of a cab or coach, its driver protected by a water-proof cap over his head and shoulders; the forlorn figure of an old man, who seemed to have crept out of some subterranean sewer, and was stooping along the kennel, and poking the wet rubbish with a stick, in quest of rusty nails; a merchant or two, at the door of the post-office, together with an editor, and a miscellaneous politician, awaiting a dilatory mail; a few visages of retired sea-captains at the window of an insurance office, looking out vacantly at the vacant street, blaspheming at the weather, and fretting at the dearth as well of public news as local gossip. What a treasure-trove to these venerable quidnuncs, could they have guessed the secret which Hepzibah and Clifford were carrying along with them! But their two figures attracted hardly so much notice as that of a young girl, who passed at the same instant, and happened to raise her skirt a trifle too high above her ankles. Had it been a sunny and cheerful day, they could hardly have gone through the streets without making themselves obnoxious to remark. Now, probably, they were felt to be in keeping with the dismal and bitter weather, and therefore did not stand out in strong relief; as if the sun were shining on them, but melted into the gray gloom and were forgotten as soon as gone.

Poor Hepzibah! Could she have understood this fact, it would have brought her some little comfort; for, to all her other troubles,—strange to say!—there was added the womanish and old-maiden-like misery arising from a sense of unseemliness in her attire. Thus, she was fain to shrink deeper into herself, as it were, as if in the hope of making people suppose that here was only a cloak and hood, threadbare and wofully faded, taking an airing in the midst of the storm, without any wearer!

As they went on, the feeling of indistinctness and unreality kept dimly hovering round about her, and so diffusing itself into her system that one of her hands was hardly palpable to the touch of the other. Any certainty would have been preferable to this. She whispered to herself, again and again, "Am I awake?—Am I awake?" and sometimes exposed her face to the chill spatter of the wind, for the sake of its rude assurance that she was. Whether it was Clifford's purpose, or only chance, had led them thither, they now found themselves passing beneath the arched entrance of a large structure of gray stone. Within, there was spacious breadth, and an airy height from floor to roof, now partially filled with smoke and steam, which eddied voluminously upward and formed a mimic cloud-region over their heads. A train of cars was just ready for a start; the locomotive was fretting and fuming, like a steed impatient for a headlong rush; and the bell rang out its hasty peal, so well expressing the brief summons which life vouchsafes to us in its hurried career. Without question or delay,—with the irresistible decision, if not rather to be called recklessness, which had so strangely taken possession of him, and through him of Hepzibah,—Clifford impelled her towards the cars, and assisted her to enter. The signal was given; the engine puffed forth its short, quick breaths; the train began its movement; and, along with a hundred other passengers, these two unwonted travellers sped onward like the wind.

At last, therefore, and after so long estrangement from everything that the world acted or enjoyed, they had been drawn into the great current of human life, and were swept away with it, as by the suction of fate itself.

Still haunted with the idea that not one of the past incidents, inclusive of Judge Pyncheon's visit, could be real, the recluse of the Seven Gables murmured in her brother's ear,—

"Clifford! Clifford! Is not this a dream?"

"A dream, Hepzibah!" repeated he, almost laughing in her face. "On the contrary, I have never been awake before!"

Meanwhile, looking from the window, they could see the world racing past them. At one moment, they were rattling through a solitude; the next, a village had grown up around them; a few breaths more, and it had vanished, as if swallowed by an earthquake. The spires of meeting-houses seemed set adrift from their foundations; the broad-based hills glided away. Everything was unfixed from its age-long rest, and moving at whirlwind speed in a direction opposite to their own.

Within the car there was the usual interior life of the railroad, offering little to the observation of other passengers, but full of novelty for this pair of strangely enfranchised prisoners. It was novelty enough, indeed, that there were fifty human beings in close relation with them, under one long and narrow roof, and drawn onward by the same mighty influence that had taken their two selves into its grasp. It seemed marvellous how all these people could remain so quietly in their seats, while so much noisy strength was at work in their behalf. Some, with tickets in their hats (long travellers these, before whom lay a hundred miles of railroad), had plunged into the English scenery and adventures of pamphlet novels, and were keeping company with dukes and earls. Others, whose briefer span forbade their devoting themselves to studies so abstruse, beguiled the little tedium of the way with penny-papers. A party of girls, and one young man, on opposite sides of the car, found huge amusement in a game of ball. They tossed it to and fro, with peals of laughter that might be measured by mile-lengths; for, faster than the nimble ball could fly, the merry players fled unconsciously along, leaving the trail of their mirth afar behind, and ending their game under another sky than had witnessed its commencement. Boys, with apples, cakes, candy, and rolls of variously tinctured lozenges,—merchandise that reminded Hepzibah of her deserted shop,—appeared at each momentary stopping-place, doing up their business in a hurry, or breaking it short off, lest the market should ravish them away with it. New people continually entered. Old acquaintances—for such they soon grew to be, in this rapid current of affairs—continually departed. Here and there, amid the rumble and the tumult sat one asleep. Sleep; sport; business; graver or lighter study; and the common and inevitable movement onward! It was life itself!

Clifford's naturally poignant sympathies were all aroused. He caught the color of what was passing about him, and threw it back more vividly than he received it, but mixed, nevertheless, with a lurid and portentous hue. Hepzibah, on the other hand, felt herself more apart from human kind than even in the seclusion which she had just quitted.

"You are not happy, Hepzibah!" said Clifford, apart, in a tone of reproach. "You are thinking of that dismal old house, and of Cousin Jaffrey,"—here came the quake through him,—"and of Cousin Jaffrey sitting there, all by himself! Take my advice,—follow my example,—and let such things slip aside. Here we are, in the world, Hepzibah!—in the midst of life!—in the throng of our fellow-beings! Let you and I be happy! As happy as that youth, and those pretty girls, at their game of ball!"

"Happy!" thought Hepzibah, bitterly conscious, at the word, of her dull and heavy heart, with the frozen pain in it,—"happy! He is mad already; and, if I could once feel myself broad awake, I should go mad too!"

If a fixed idea be madness, she was perhaps not remote from it. Fast and far as they had rattled and clattered along the iron track, they might just as well, as regarded Hepzibah's mental images, have been passing up and down Pyncheon Street. With miles and miles of varied scenery between, there was no scene for her, save the seven old gable-peaks, with their moss, and the tuft of weeds in one of the angles, and the shop-window, and a customer shaking the door, and compelling the little bell to jingle fiercely, but without disturbing Judge Pyncheon! This one old house was everywhere! It transported its great, lumbering bulk with more than railroad speed, and set itself phlegmatically down on whatever spot she glanced at. The quality of Hepzibah's mind was too unmalleable to take new impressions so readily as Clifford's. He had a winged nature; she was rather of the vegetable kind, and could hardly be kept long alive, if drawn up by the roots. Thus it happened that the relation heretofore existing between her brother and herself was changed. At home, she was his guardian; here, Clifford had become hers, and seemed to comprehend whatever belonged to their new position with a singular rapidity of intelligence. He had been startled into manhood and intellectual vigor; or, at least into a condition that resembled them, though it might be both diseased and transitory.

The conductor now applied for their tickets; and Clifford, who had made himself the purse-bearer, put a bank-note into his hand, as he had observed others do.

"For the lady and yourself?" asked the conductor. "And how far?"

"As far as that will carry us," said Clifford. "It is no great matter. We are riding for pleasure merely!"

"You choose a strange day for it, sir!" remarked a gimlet-eyed old gentleman, on the other side of the car, looking at Clifford and his companion, as if curious to make them out. "The best chance of pleasure, in an easterly rain, I take it, is in a man's own house, with a nice little fire in the chimney."

"I cannot precisely agree with you," said Clifford, courteously bowing to the old gentleman, and at once taking up the clew of conversation which the latter had proffered. "It had just occurred to me, on the contrary, that this admirable invention of the railroad—with the vast and inevitable improvements to be looked for, both as to speed and convenience—is destined to do away with those stale ideas of home and fireside, and substitute something better."

"In the name of common-sense," asked the old gentleman, rather testily, "what can be better for a man than his own .parlor and chimney-corner?"

"These things have not the merit which many good people attribute to them," replied Clifford. "They may be said, in few and pithy words, to have ill served a poor purpose. My impression is, that our wonderfully increased and still increasing facilities of locomotion are destined to bring us round again to the nomadic state. You are aware, my dear sir,—you must have observed it in your own experience,—that all human progress is in a circle; or, to use a more accurate and beautiful figure, in an ascending spiral curve. While we fancy ourselves going straight forward, and attaining, at every step, an entirely new position of affairs, we do actually return to something long ago tried and abandoned, but which we now find etherealized, refined, and perfected to its ideal. The past is but a coarse and sensual prophecy of the present and the future. To apply this truth to the topic now under discussion. In the early epochs of our race, men dwelt in temporary huts, of bowers of branches, as easily constructed as a bird's-nest, and which they built,—if it should be called building, when such sweet homes of a summer solstice rather grew than were made with hands,—which Nature, we will say, assisted them to rear where fruit abounded, where fish and game were plentiful, or, most especially, where the sense of beauty was to be gratified by a lovelier shade than elsewhere, and a more exquisite arrangement of lake, wood, and hill. This life possessed a charm, which, ever since man quitted it, has vanished from existence. And it typified something better than itself. It had its drawbacks; such as hunger and thirst, inclement weather, hot sunshine, and weary and foot-blistering marches over barren and ugly tracts, that lay between the sites desirable for their fertility and beauty. But in our ascending spiral, we escape all this. These railroads—could but the whistle be made musical, and the rumble and the jar got rid of—are positively the greatest blessing that the ages have wrought out for us. They give us wings; they annihilate the toil and dust of pilgrimage; they spiritualize travel! Transition being so facile, what can be any man's inducement to tarry in one spot? Why, therefore, should he build a more cumbrous habitation than can readily be carried off with him? Why should he make himself a prisoner for life in brick, and stone, and old worm-eaten timber, when he may just as easily dwell, in one sense, nowhere,—in a better sense, wherever the fit and beautiful shall offer him a home?"

Clifford's countenance glowed, as he divulged this theory; a youthful character shone out from within, converting the wrinkles and pallid duskiness of age into an almost transparent mask. The merry girls let their ball drop upon the floor, and gazed at him. They said to themselves, perhaps, that, before his hair was gray and the crow's-feet tracked his temples, this now decaying man must have stamped the impress of his features on many a woman's heart. But, alas! no woman's eye had seen his face while it was beautiful.

"I should scarcely call it an improved state of things," observed Clifford's new acquaintance, "to live everywhere and nowhere!"

"Would you not?" exclaimed Clifford, with singular energy. "It is as clear to me as sunshine,—were there any in the sky,—that the greatest possible stumbling-blocks in the path of human happiness and improvement are these heaps of bricks and stones, consolidated with mortar, or hewn timber, fastened together with spike-nails, which men painfully contrive for their own torment, and call them house and home! The soul needs air; a wide sweep and frequent change of it. Morbid influences, in a thousand-fold variety, gather about hearths, and pollute the life of households. There is no such unwholesome atmosphere as that of an old home, rendered poisonous by one's defunct forefathers and relatives. I speak of what I know. There is a certain house within my familiar recollection,—one of those peaked-gable (there are seven of them), projecting-storied edifices, such as you occasionally see in our older towns,—a rusty, crazy, creaky, dry-rotted, damp-rotted, dingy, dark, and miserable old dungeon, with an arched window over the porch, and a little shop-door on one side, and a great melancholy elm before it! Now, sir, whenever my thoughts recur to this seven-gabled mansion (the fact is so very curious that I must needs mention it), immediately I have a vision or image of an elderly man, of remarkably stern countenance, sitting in an oaken elbow-chair, dead, stone-dead, with an ugly flow of blood upon his shirt-bosom! Dead, but with open eyes! He taints the whole house, as I remember it. I could never flourish there, nor be happy, nor do nor enjoy what God meant me to do and enjoy!"

His face darkened, and seemed to contract, and shrivel itself up, and wither into age.

"Never, sir!" he repeated. "I could never draw cheerful breath there!"

"I should think not," said the old gentleman, eying Clifford earnestly, and rather apprehensively. "I should conceive not, sir, with that notion in your head!"

"Surely not," continued Clifford; "and it were a relief to me if that house could be torn down, or burnt up, and so the earth be rid of it, and grass be sown abundantly over its foundation. Not that I should ever visit its site again! for, sir, the farther I get away from it, the more does the joy, the lightsome freshness, the heart-leap, the intellectual dance, the youth, in short,—yes, my youth, my youth!—the more does it come back to me. No longer ago than this morning, I was old. I remember looking in the glass, and wondering at my own gray hair, and the wrinkles, many and deep, right across my brow, and the furrows down my cheeks, and the prodigious trampling of crow's-feet about my temples! It was too soon! I could not bear it! Age had no right to come! I had not lived! But now do I look old? If so, my aspect belies me strangely; for—a great weight being off my mind—I feel in the very heyday of my youth, with the world and my best days before me!"

"I trust you may find it so," said the old gentleman, who seemed rather embarrassed, and desirous of avoiding the observation which Clifford's wild talk drew on them both. "You have my best wishes for it."

"For Heaven's sake, dear Clifford, be quiet!" whispered his sister. "They think you mad."

"Be quiet yourself, Hepzibah!" returned her brother. "No matter what they think! I am not mad. For the first time in thirty years my thoughts gush up and find words ready for them. I must talk, and I will!"

He turned again towards the old gentleman, and renewed the conversation.

"Yes, my dear sir," said he, "it is my firm belief and hope that these terms of roof and hearth-stone, which have so long been held to embody something sacred, are soon to pass out of men's daily use, and be forgotten. Just imagine, for a moment, how much of human evil will crumble away, with this one change! What we call real estate—the solid ground to build a house on—is the broad foundation on which nearly all the guilt of this world rests. A man will commit almost any wrong,—he will heap up an immense pile of wickedness, as hard as granite, and which will weigh as heavily upon his soul, to eternal ages,—only to build a great, gloomy, dark-chambered mansion, for himself to die in, and for his posterity to be miserable in. He lays his own dead corpse beneath the underpinning, as one may say, and hangs his frowning picture on the wall, and, after thus converting himself into an evil destiny, expects his remotest great-grand-children to be happy there! I do not speak wildly. I have just such a house in my mind's eye!"

"Then, sir," said the old gentleman, getting anxious to drop the subject, "you are not to blame for leaving it."

"Within the lifetime of the child already born," Clifford went on, "all this will be done away. The world is growing too ethereal and spiritual to bear these enormities a great while longer. To me,—though, for a considerable period of time, I have lived chiefly in retirement, and know less of such things than most men,—even to me, the harbingers of a better era are unmistakable. Mesmerism, now! Will that effect nothing, think you, towards purging away the grossness out of human life?"

"All a humbug!" growled the old gentleman.

"These rapping spirits, that little Phœbe told us of, the other day," said Clifford,—"what are these but the messengers of the spiritual world, knocking at the door of substance? And it shall be flung wide open!"

"A humbug, again!" cried the old gentleman, growing more and more testy, at these glimpses of Clifford's metaphysics. "I should like to rap with a good stick on the empty pates of the dolts who circulate such nonsense!"

"Then there is electricity,—the demon, the angel, the mighty physical power, the all-pervading intelligence!" exclaimed Clifford. "Is that a humbug, too? Is it a fact—or have I dreamt it—that, by means of electricity, the world of matter has become a great nerve, vibrating thousands of miles in a breathless point of time? Rather, the round globe is a vast head, a brain, instinct with intelligence! Or, shall we say, it is itself a thought, nothing but thought, and no longer the substance which we deemed it!"

"If you mean the telegraph," said the old gentleman, glancing his eye toward its wire, alongside the rail-track, "it is an excellent thing,—that is, of course, if the speculators in cotton and politics don't get possession of it. A great thing, indeed, sir, particularly as regards the detection of bank-robbers and murderers."

"I don't quite like it, in that point of view," replied Clifford. "A bank-robber, and what you call a murderer, likewise, has his rights, which men of enlightened humanity and conscience should regard in so much the more liberal spirit, because the bulk of society is prone to controvert their existence. An almost spiritual medium, like the electric telegraph, should be consecrated to high, deep, joyful, and holy missions. Lovers, day by day,—hour by hour, if so often moved to do it,—might send their heart-throbs from Maine to Florida, with some such words as these, 'I love you forever!'—'My heart runs over with love!'—'I love you more than I can!' and, again, at the next message, 'I have lived an hour longer, and love you twice as much!' Or, when a good man has departed, his distant friend should be conscious of an electric thrill, as from the world of happy spirits, telling him, 'Your dear friend is in bliss!' Or, to an absent husband, should come tidings thus, 'An immortal being, of whom you are the father, has this moment come from God!' and immediately its little voice would seem to have reached so far, and to be echoing in his heart. But for these poor rogues, the bank-robbers,—who after all, are about as honest as nine people in ten, except that they disregard certain formalities, and prefer to transact business at midnight rather than 'Change-hours,—and for these murderers, as you phrase it, who are often excusable in the motives of their deed, and deserve to be ranked among public benefactors, if we consider only its result,—for unfortunate individuals like these, I really cannot applaud the enlistment of an immateral and miraculous power in the universal world-hunt at their heels!"

"You can't, hey?" cried the old gentleman, with a hard look.

"Positively, no!" answered Clifford. "It puts them too miserably at disadvantage. For example, sir, in a dark, low, cross-beamed, panelled room of an old house, let us suppose a dead man, sitting in an arm-chair, with a blood-stain on his shirt-bosom,—and let us add to our hypothesis another man, issuing from the house, which he feels to be over-filled with the dead man's presence,—and let us lastly imagine him fleeing, Heaven knows whither, at the speed of a hurricane, by railroad! Now, sir, if the fugitive alight in some distant town, and find all the people babbling about that self-same dead man, whom he has fled so far to avoid the sight and thought of, will you not allow that his natural rights have been infringed? He has been deprived of his city of refuge, and, in my humble opinion, has suffered infinite wrong!"

"You are a strange man, sir!" said the old gentleman, bringing his gimlet-eye to a point on Clifford, as if determined to bore right into him. "I can't see through you!"

"No, I'll be bound you can't!" cried Clifford, laughing. "And yet, my dear sir, I am as transparent as the water of Maule's well! But come, Hepzibah! We have flown far enough for once. Let us alight, as the birds do, and perch ourselves on the nearest twig, and consult whither we shall fly next!"

Just then, as it happened, the train reached a solitary way-station. Taking advantage of the brief pause, Clifford left the car, and drew Hepzibah along with him. A moment afterwards, the train—with all the life of its interior, amid which Clifford had made himself so conspicuous an object—was gliding away in the distance, and rapidly lessening to a point, which, in another moment, vanished. The world had fled away from these two wanderers. They gazed drearily about them. At a little distance stood a wooden church, black with age, and in a dismal state of ruin and decay, with broken windows, a great rift through the main body of the edifice, and a rafter dangling from the top of the square tower. Farther off was a farm-house, in the old style, as venerably black as the church, with a roof sloping downward from the three-story peak, to within a man's height of the ground. It seemed uninhabited. There were the relics of a wood-pile, indeed, near the door, but with grass sprouting up among the chips and scattered logs. The small rain-drops came down aslant; the wind was not turbulent, but sullen, and full of chilly moisture.

Clifford shivered from head to foot. The wild effervescence of his mood—which had so readily supplied thoughts, fantasies, and a strange aptitude of words, and impelled him to talk from the mere necessity of giving vent to this bubbling-up gush of ideas—had entirely subsided. A powerful excitement had given him energy and vivacity. Its operation over, he forthwith began to sink.

"You must take the lead now, Hepzibah!" murmured he, with a torpid and reluctant utterance. "Do with me as you will!"

She knelt down upon the platform where they were standing and lifted her clasped hands to the sky. The dull, gray weight of clouds made it invisible; but it was no hour for disbelief,—no juncture this to question that there was a sky above, and an Almighty Father looking from it!

"O God!"—ejaculated poor, gaunt Hepzibah,—then paused a moment, to consider what her prayer should be,—"O God,—our Father,—are we not thy children? Have mercy on us!"

## XVIII

### GOVERNOR PYNCHEON

JUDGE PYNCHEON, while his two relatives have fled away with such ill-considered haste, still sits in the old parlor, keeping house, as the familiar phrase is, in the absence of its ordinary occupants. To him, and to the venerable House of the Seven Gables, does our story now betake itself, like an owl, bewildered in the daylight, and hastening back to his hollow tree.

The Judge has not shifted his position for a long while now. He has not stirred hand or foot, nor withdrawn his eyes so much as a hair's-breadth from their fixed gaze towards the corner of the room, since the footsteps of Hepzibah and Clifford creaked along the passage, and the outer door was closed cautiously behind their exit. He holds his watch in his left hand, but clutched in such a manner that you cannot see the dial-plate. How profound a fit of meditation! Or, supposing him asleep, how infantile a quietude of conscience, and what wholesome order in the gastric region, are betokened by slumber so entirely undisturbed with starts, cramp, twitches, muttered dream-talk, trumpet-blasts through the nasal organ, or any the slightest irregularity of breath! You must hold your own breath, to satisfy yourself whether he breathes at all. It is quite inaudible. You hear the ticking of his watch; his breath you do not hear. A most refreshing slumber, doubtless! And yet, the Judge cannot be asleep. His eyes are open! A veteran politician, such as he, would never fall asleep with wide-open eyes, lest some enemy or mischief-maker, taking him thus at unawares, should peep through these windows into his consciousness, and make strange discoveries among the reminiscences, projects, hopes, apprehensions, weaknesses, and strong points, which he has heretofore shared with nobody. A cautious man is proverbially said to sleep with one eye open. That may be wisdom. But not with both; for this were heedlessness! No, no! Judge Pyncheon cannot be asleep.

It is odd, however, that a gentleman so burdened with engagements,—and noted, too, for punctuality,—should linger thus in an old lonely mansion, which he has never seemed very fond of visiting. The oaken chair, to be sure, may tempt him with its roominess. It is, indeed, a spacious, and, allowing for the rude age that fashioned it, a moderately easy seat, with capacity enough, at all events, and offering no restraint to the Judge's breadth of beam. A bigger man might find ample accommodation in it. His ancestor, now pictured upon the wall, with all his English beef about him, used hardly to present a front extending from elbow to elbow of this chair, or a base that would cover its whole cushion. But there are better chairs than this,—mahogany, black-walnut, rosewood, spring-seated and damask-cushioned, with varied slopes, and innumerable artifices to make them easy, and obviate the irksomeness of too tame an ease,—a score of such might be at Judge Pyncheon's service. Yes! in a score of drawing-rooms he would be more than welcome. Mamma would advance to meet him, with outstretched hand; the virgin daughter, elderly as he has now got to be,—an old widower, as he smilingly describes himself,—would shake up the cushion for the Judge, and do her pretty little utmost to make him comfortable. For the Judge is a prosperous man. He cherishes his schemes, moreover, like other people, and reasonably brighter than most others; or did so, at least, as he lay abed this morning, in an agreeable half-drowse, planning the business of the day, and speculating on the probabilities of the next fifteen years. With his firm health, and the little inroad that age has made upon him, fifteen years or twenty—yes, or perhaps five-and-twenty!—are no more than he may fairly call his own. Five-and-twenty years for the enjoyment of his real estate in town and country, his railroad, bank, and insurance shares, his United States stock,—his wealth, in short, however invested, now in possession, or soon to be acquired; together with the public honors that have fallen upon him, and the weightier ones that are yet to fall! It is good! It is excellent! It is enough!

Still lingering in the old chair! If the Judge has a little time to throw away, why does not he visit the insurance office, as is his frequent custom, and sit awhile in one of their leathern-cushioned arm-chairs, listening to the gossip of the day, and dropping some deeply designed chance-word, which will be certain to become the gossip of to-morrow! And have not the bank directors a meeting at which it was the Judge's purpose to be present, and his office to preside? Indeed they have; and the hour is noted on a card, which is, or ought to be, in Judge Pyncheon's right vest-pocket. Let him go thither, and loll at ease upon his money-bags! He has lounged long enough in the old chair!

This was to have been such a busy day! In the first place, the interview with Clifford. Half an hour, by the Judge's reckoning, was to suffice for that; it would probably be less, but—taking into consideration that Hepzibah was first to be dealt with, and that these women are apt to make many words where a few would do much better—it might be safest to allow half an hour. Half an hour? Why, Judge, it is already two hours, by your own undeviatingly accurate chronometer! Glance your eye down at it and see! Ah! he will not give himself the trouble either to bend his head, or elevate his hand, so as to bring the faithful time-keeper within his range of vision! Time, all at once, appears to have become a matter of no moment with the Judge!

And has he forgotten all the other items of his memoranda? Clifford's affair arranged, he was to meet a State Street broker, who has undertaken to procure a heavy percentage, and the best of paper, for a few loose thousands which the Judge happens to have by him, uninvested. The wrinkled note-shaver will have taken his railroad trip in vain. Half an hour later, in the street next to this, there was to be an auction of real estate, including a portion of the old Pyncheon property, originally belonging to Maule's garden-ground. It has been alienated from the Pyncheons these four-score years; but the Judge had kept it in his eye, and had set his heart on reannexing it to the small demesne still left around the Seven Gables; and now, during this odd fit of oblivion, the fatal hammer must have fallen, and transferred our ancient patrimony to some alien possessor! Possibly, indeed, the sale may have been postponed till fairer weather. If so, will the Judge make it convenient to be present, and favor the auctioneer with his bid, on the proximate occasion?

The next affair was to buy a horse for his own driving. The one heretofore his favorite stumbled, this very morning, on the road to town, and must be at once discarded. Judge Pyncheon's neck is too precious to be risked on such a contingency as a stumbling steed. Should all the above business be seasonably got through with, he might attend the meeting of a charitable society; the very name of which, however, in the multiplicity of his benevolence, is quite forgotten; so that this engagement may pass unfulfilled, and no great harm done. And if he have time, amid the press of more urgent matters, he must take measures for the renewal of Mrs. Pyncheon's tombstone, which, the sexton tells him, has fallen on its marble face, and is cracked quite in twain. She was a praise-worthy woman enough, thinks the Judge, in spite of her nervousness, and the tears that she was so oozy with, and her foolish behavior about the coffee; and as she took her departure so seasonably, he will not grudge the second tombstone. It is better, at least, than if she had never needed any! The next item on his list was to give orders for some fruit-trees, of a rare variety, to be deliverable at his country-seat, in the ensuing autumn. Yes, buy them, by all means; and may the peaches be luscious in your mouth, Judge Pyncheon! After this comes something more important. A committee of his political party has besought him for a hundred or two of dollars, in addition to his previous disbursements, towards carrying on the fall campaign. The Judge is a patriot; the fate of the country is staked on the November election; and besides, as will be shadowed forth in another paragraph, he has no trifling stake of his own in the same great game. He will do what the committee asks; nay, he will be liberal beyond their expectations; they shall have a check for five hundred dollars, and more anon, if it be needed. What next? A decayed widow, whose husband was Judge Pyncheon's early friend, has laid her case of destitution before him, in a very moving letter. She and her fair daughter have scarcely bread to eat. He partly intends to call on her, to-day,—perhaps so—perhaps not,—accordingly as he may happen to have leisure, and a small bank-note.

Another business, which, however, he puts no great weight on (it is well, you know, to be heedful, but not over-anxious, as respects one's personal health),—another business, then, was to consult his family physician. About what, for Heaven's sake? Why, it is rather difficult to describe the symptoms. A mere dimness of sight and dizziness of brain, was it?—or a disagreeable choking, or stifling, or gurgling, or bubbling, in the region of the thorax, as the anatomists say?—or was it a pretty severe throbbing and kicking of the heart, rather creditable to him than otherwise, as showing that the organ had not been left out of the Judge's physical contrivance? No matter what it was. The doctor, probably, would smile at the statement of such trifles to his professional ear; the Judge would smile in his turn; and meeting one another's eyes, they would enjoy a hearty laugh together! But a fig for medical advice! The Judge will never need it.

Pray, pray, Judge Pyncheon, look at your watch, now! What—not a glance! It is within ten minutes of the dinner-hour! It surely cannot have slipped your memory that the dinner of to-day is to be the most import-ant, in its consequences, of all the dinners you ever ate. Yes, precisely the most important; although, in the course of your somewhat eminent ca-reer, you have been placed high towards the head of the table, at splendid banquets, and have poured out your festive eloquence to ears yet echoing with Webster's mighty organ-tones. No public dinner this, however. It is merely a gathering of some dozen or so of friends from several districts of the State; men of distinguished character and influence, assembling, al-most casually, at the house of a common friend, likewise distinguished, who will make them welcome to a little better than his ordinary fare. Nothing in the way of French cookery, but an excellent dinner neverthe-less. Real turtle, we understand, and salmon, tautog, canvas-backs, pig, English mutton, good roast-beef, or dainties of that serious kind, fit for substantial country gentlemen, as these honorable persons mostly are. The delicacies of the season, in short, and flavored by a brand of old Madeira which has been the pride of many seasons. It is the Juno brand; a glorious wine, fragrant, and full of gentle might; a bottled-up happi-ness, put up for use; a golden liquid, worth more than liquid gold; so rare and admirable, that veteran wine-bibbers count it among their epochs to have tasted it! It drives away the heart-ache, and substitutes no head-ache! Could the Judge but quaff a glass, it might enable him to shake off the unaccountable lethargy which (for the ten intervening min-utes, and five to boot, are already past) has made him such a laggard at this momentous dinner. It would all but revive a dead man! Would you like to sip it now, Judge Pyncheon?

Alas, this dinner! Have you really forgotten its true object? Then let us whisper it, that you may start at once out of the oaken chair, which really seems to be enchanted, like the one in Comus, or that in which Moll Pitcher imprisoned your own grandfather. But ambition is a talisman more powerful than witchcraft. Start up, then, and, hurrying through the streets, burst in upon the company, that they may begin before the fish is spoiled! They wait for you; and it is little for your interest that they should wait. These gentlemen—need you be told it?—have assembled, not without purpose, from every quarter of the State. They are practised politicians, every man of them, and skilled to adjust those preliminary measures which steal from the people, without its knowledge, the power of choosing its own rulers. The popular voice, at the next gubernatorial election, though loud as thunder, will be really but an echo of what these gentlemen shall speak, under their breath, at your friend's festive board.

They meet to decide upon their candidate. This little knot of subtle schemers will control the convention, and, through it, dictate to the party. And what worthier candidate,—more wise and learned, more noted for philanthropic liberality, truer to safe principles, tried oftener by public trusts, more spotless in private character, with a larger stake in the common welfare, and deeper grounded, by hereditary descent, in the faith and practice of the Puritans,—what man can be presented for the suffrage of the people, so eminently combining all these claims to the chief-rulership as Judge Pyncheon here before us?

Make haste, then! Do your part! The meed for which you have toiled, and fought, and climbed, and crept, is ready for your grasp! Be present at this dinner!—drink a glass or two of that noble wine!—make your pledges in as low a whisper as you will!—and you rise up from table virtually governor of the glorious old State! Governor Pyncheon of Massachusetts!

And is there no potent and exhilarating cordial in a certainty like this? It has been the grand purpose of half your lifetime to obtain it. Now, when there needs little more than to signify your acceptance, why do you sit so lumpishly in your great-great-grandfather's oaken chair, as if preferring it to the gubernatorial one? We have all heard of King Log; but, in these jostling times, one of that royal kindred will hardly win the race for an elective chief-magistracy.

Well! it is absolutely too late for dinner! Turtle, salmon, tautog, woodcock, boiled turkey, South-Down mutton, pig, roast-beef, have vanished, or exist only in fragments, with lukewarm potatoes, and gravies crusted over with cold fat. The Judge, had he done nothing else, would have achieved wonders with his knife and fork. It was he, you know, of whom it used to be said, in reference to his ogre-like appetite, that his Creator made him a great animal, but that the dinner-hour made him a great beast. Persons of his large sensual endowments must claim indulgence, at their feeding-time. But, for once, the Judge is entirely too late for dinner! Too late, we fear, even to join the party at their wine! The guests are warm and merry; they have given up the Judge; and, concluding that the Free-Soilers have him, they will fix upon another candidate. Were our friend now to stalk in among them, with that wide-open stare, at once wild and stolid, his ungenial presence would be apt to change their cheer. Neither would it be seemly in Judge Pyncheon, generally so scrupulous in his attire, to show himself at a dinner-table with that crimson stain upon his shirt-bosom. By the by, how came it there? It is an ugly sight, at any rate; and the wisest way for the Judge is to button his coat closely over his breast, and, taking his horse and chaise from the livery-stable, to make all speed to his own house. There, after a glass of brandy and water, and a mutton-chop, a beefsteak, a broiled fowl, or some such hasty little dinner and supper all in one, he had better spend the evening by the fireside. He must toast his slippers a long while, in order to get rid of the chilliness which the air of this vile old house has sent curdling through his veins.

Up, therefore, Judge Pyncheon, up! You have lost a day. But to-morrow will be here anon. Will you rise, betimes, and make the most of it? To-morrow! To-morrow! To-morrow! We, that are alive, may rise betimes to-morrow. As for him that has died to-day, his morrow will be the resurrection morn.

Meanwhile the twilight is glooming upward out of the corners of the room. The shadows of the tall furniture grow deeper, and at first become more definite; then, spreading wider, they lose their distinctness of outline in the dark gray tide of oblivion, as it were, that creeps slowly over the various objects, and the one human figure sitting in the midst of them. The gloom has not entered from without; it has brooded here all day, and now, taking its own inevitable time, will possess itself of everything. The Judge's face, indeed, rigid, and singularly white, refuses to melt into this universal solvent. Fainter and fainter grows the light. It is as if another double-handful of darkness had been scattered through the air. Now it is no longer gray, but sable. There is still a faint appearance at the window; neither a glow, nor a gleam, nor a glimmer,—any phrase of light would express something far brighter than this doubtful perception, or sense, rather, that there is a window there. Has it yet vanished? No!—yes!—not quite! And there is still the swarthy whiteness, —we shall venture to marry these ill-agreeing words,—the swarthy whiteness of Judge Pyncheon's face. The features are all gone: there is only the paleness of them left. And how looks it now? There is no window! There is no face! An infinite, inscrutable blackness has annihilated sight! Where is our universe? All crumbled away from us; and we, adrift in chaos, may hearken to the gusts of homeless wind, that go sighing and murmuring about, in quest of what was once a world!

Is there no other sound? One other, and a fearful one. It is the ticking of the Judge's watch, which, ever since Hepzibah left the room in search of Clifford, he has been holding in his hand. Be the cause what it may, this little, quiet, never-ceasing throb of Time's pulse, repeating its small strokes with such busy regularity, in Judge Pyncheon's motionless hand, has an effect of terror, which we do not find in any other accompaniment of the scene.

But, listen! That puff of the breeze was louder; it had a tone unlike the dreary and sullen one which has bemoaned itself, and afflicted all mankind with miserable sympathy, for five days past. The wind has veered about! It now comes boisterously from the northwest, and, taking hold of the aged framework of the Seven Gables, gives it a shake, like a wrestler that would try strength with his antagonist. Another and another sturdy tussle with the blast! The old house creaks again, and makes a vociferous but somewhat unintelligible bellowing in its sooty throat (the big flue, we mean, of its wide chimney), partly in complaint at the rude wind, but rather, as befits their century and a half of hostile intimacy, in tough defiance. A rumbling kind of a bluster roars behind the fire-board. A door has slammed above stairs. A window, perhaps, has been left open, or else is driven in by an unruly gust. It is not to be conceived, beforehand, what wonderful wind-instruments are these old timber mansions, and how haunted with the strangest noises, which immediately begin to sing, and sigh, and sob, and shriek,—and to smite with sledge-hammers, airy but ponderous, in some distant chamber,—and to tread along the entries as with stately footsteps, and rustle up and down the staircase, as with silks miraculously stiff,—whenever the gale catches the house with a window open, and gets fairly into it. Would that we were not an attendant spirit here! It is too awful! This clamor of the wind through the lonely house; the Judge's quietude, as he sits invisible; and that pertinacious ticking of his watch!

As regards Judge Pyncheon's invisibility, however, that matter will soon be remedied. The northwest wind has swept the sky clear. The window is distinctly seen. Through its panes, moreover, we dimly catch the sweep of the dark, clustering foliage, outside, fluttering with a constant irregularity of movement, and letting in a peep of starlight, now here, now there. Oftener than any other object, these glimpses illuminate the Judge's face. But here comes more effectual light. Observe that silvery dance upon the upper branches of the pear-tree, and now a little lower, and now on the whole mass of boughs, while, through their shifting intricacies, the moonbeams fall aslant into the room. They play over the Judge's figure and show that he has not stirred throughout the hours of darkness. They follow the shadows, in changeful sport, across his unchanging features. They gleam upon his watch. His grasp conceals the dial-plate; but we know that the faithful hands have met; for one of the city clocks tells midnight.

A man of sturdy understanding, like Judge Pyncheon, cares no more for twelve o'clock at night than for the corresponding hour of noon. However just the parallel drawn, in some of the preceding pages, between his Puritan ancestor and himself, it fails in this point. The Pyncheon of two centuries ago, in common with most of his contemporaries, professed his full belief in spiritual ministrations, although reckoning them chiefly of a malignant character. The Pyncheon of to-night, who sits in yonder arm-chair, believes in no such nonsense. Such, at least, was his creed, some few hours since. His hair will not bristle, therefore, at the stories which—in times when chimney-corners had benches in them, where old people sat poking into the ashes of the past, and raking out traditions like live coals—used to be told about this very room of his ancestral house. In fact, these tales are too absurd to bristle even childhood's hair. What sense, meaning, or moral, for example, such as even ghost-stories should be susceptible of, can be traced in the ridiculous legend, that, at midnight, all the dead Pyncheons are bound to assemble in this parlor? And, pray, for what? Why, to see whether the portrait of their ancestor still keeps its place upon the wall, in compliance with his testamentary directions! Is it worth while to come out of their graves for that?

We are tempted to make a little sport with the idea. Ghost-stories are hardly to be treated seriously, any longer. The family-party of the defunct Pyncheons, we presume, goes off in this wise.

First comes the ancestor himself, in his black cloak, steeple-hat, and trunk-breeches, girt about the waist with a leathern belt, in which hangs his steel-hilted sword; he has a long staff in his hand, such as gentlemen in advanced life used to carry, as much for the dignity of the thing as for the support to be derived from it. He looks up at the portrait; a thing of no substance, gazing at its own painted image! All is safe. The picture is still there. The purpose of his brain has been kept sacred thus long after the man himself has sprouted up in graveyard grass. See! he lifts his ineffectual hand, and tries the frame. All safe! But is that a smile?—is it not, rather, a frown of deadly import, that darkens over the shadow of his features? The stout Colonel is dissatisfied! So decided is his look of discontent as to impart additional distinctness to his features; through which, nevertheless, the moonlight passes, and flickers on the wall beyond. Something has strangely vexed the ancestor! With a grim shake of the head, he turns away. Here come other Pyncheons, the whole tribe, in their half a dozen generations, jostling and elbowing one another, to reach the picture. We behold aged men and grandames, a clergyman with the Puritanic stiffness still in his garb and mien, and a red-coated officer of the old French war; and there comes the shop-keeping Pyncheon of a century ago, with the ruffles turned back from his wrists; and there the periwigged and brocaded gentleman of the artist's legend, with the beautiful and pensive Alice, who brings no pride out of her virgin grave. All try the picture-frame. What do these ghostly people seek? A mother lifts her child, that his little hands may touch it! There is evidently a mystery about the picture, that perplexes these poor Pyncheons when they ought to be at rest. In a corner, meanwhile, stands the figure of an elderly man, in a leather jerkin and breeches, with a carpenter's rule sticking out of his side pocket; he points his finger at the bearded Colonel and his descendants, nodding, jeering, mocking, and finally bursting into obstreperous, though inaudible laughter.

Indulging our fancy in this freak, we have partly lost the power of restraint and guidance. We distinguish an unlooked-for figure in our visionary scene. Among those ancestral people there is a young man, dressed in the very fashion of to-day: he wears a dark frock-coat, almost destitute of skirts, gray pantaloons, gaiter boots of patent leather, and has a finely wrought gold chain across his breast, and a little silver-headed whalebone stick in his hand. Were we to meet this figure at noonday, we should greet him as young Jaffrey Pyncheon, the Judge's only surviving child, who has been spending the last two years in foreign travel. If still in life, how comes his shadow hither? If dead, what a misfortune! The old Pyncheon property, together with the great estate acquired by the young man's father, would devolve on whom? On poor, foolish Clifford, gaunt Hepzibah, and rustic little Phœbe! But another and a greater marvel greets us! Can we believe our eyes? A stout, elderly gentleman has made his appearance; he has an aspect of eminent respectability, wears a black coat and pantaloons, of roomy width, and might be pronounced scrupulously neat in his attire, but for a broad crimson stain across his snowy neckcloth and down his shirt-bosom. Is it the Judge, or no? How can it be Judge Pyncheon? We discern his figure, as plainly as the flickering moonbeams can show us anything, still seated in the oaken chair! Be the apparition whose it may, it advances to the picture, seems to seize the frame, tries to peep behind it, and turns away, with a frown as black as the ancestral one.

The fantastic scene just hinted at must by no means be considered as forming an actual portion of our story. We were betrayed into this brief extravagance by the quiver of the moonbeams; they dance hand-in-hand with shadows, and are reflected in the looking-glass, which, you are aware, is always a kind of window or doorway into the spiritual world. We needed relief, moreover, from our too long and exclusive contemplation of that figure in the chair. This wild wind, too, has tossed our thoughts into strange confusion, but without tearing them away from their one determined centre. Yonder leaden Judge sits immovably upon our soul. Will he never stir again? We shall go mad unless he stirs! You may the better estimate his quietude by the fearlessness of a little mouse, which sits on its hind legs, in a streak of moonlight, close by Judge Pyncheon's foot, and seems to meditate a journey of exploration over this great black bulk. Ha! what has startled the nimble little mouse? Is it the visage of grimalkin, outside of the window, where he appears to have posted himself for a deliberate watch. This grimalkin has a very ugly look. Is it a cat watching for a mouse, or the devil for a human soul? Would we could scare him from the window!

Thank Heaven, the night is wellnigh past! The moonbeams have no longer so silvery a gleam, nor contrast so strongly with the blackness of the shadows among which they fall. They are paler, now; the shadows look gray, not black. The boisterous wind is hushed. What is the hour? Ah! the watch has at last ceased to tick; for the Judge's forgetful fingers neglected to wind it up, as usual, at ten o'clock, being half an hour or so before his ordinary bedtime,—and it has run down, for the first time in five years. But the great world-clock of Time still keeps its beat. The dreary night—for, oh, how dreary seems its haunted waste, behind us!— gives place to a fresh, transparent cloudless morn. Blessed, blessed radiance! The day-beam—even what little of it finds its way into this always dusky parlor—seems part of the universal benediction, annulling evil, and rendering all goodness possible, and happiness attainable. Will Judge Pyncheon now rise up from his chair? Will he go forth, and receive the early sunbeams on his brow? Will he begin this new day,—which God has smiled upon, and blessed, and given to mankind,—will he begin it with better purposes than the many that have been spent amiss? Or are all the deep-laid schemes of yesterday as stubborn in his heart, and as busy in his brain, as ever?

In this latter case, there is much to do. Will the Judge still insist with Hepzibah on the interview with Clifford? Will he buy a safe, elderly gentleman's horse? Will he persuade the purchaser of the old Pyncheon property to relinquish the bargain, in his favor? Will he see his family phy-

sician, and obtain a medicine that shall preserve him, to be an honor and
blessing to his race, until the utmost term of patriarchal longevity? Will
Judge Pyncheon, above all, make due apologies to that company of honorable friends, and satisfy them that his absence from the festive board
was unavoidable, and so fully retrieve himself in their good opinion that
he shall yet be Governor of Massachusetts? And all these great purposes
accomplished, will he walk the streets again, with that dog-day smile of
elaborate benevolence, sultry enough to tempt flies to come and buzz in
it? Or will he, after the tomb-like seclusion of the past day and night, go
forth a humbled and repentant man, sorrowful, gentle, seeking no profit,
shrinking from worldly honor, hardly daring to love God, but bold to love
his fellowman, and to do him what good he may? Will he bear about with
him,—no odious grin of feigned benignity, insolent in its pretence, and
loathsome in its falsehood,—but the tender sadness of a contrite heart,
broken, at last, beneath its own weight of sin? For it is our belief, whatever show of honor he may have piled upon it, that there was heavy sin
at the base of this man's being.

Rise up, Judge Pyncheon! The morning sunshine glimmers through the
foliage, and, beautiful and holy as it is, shuns not to kindle up your face.
Rise up, thou subtle, worldly, selfish, iron-hearted hypocrite, and make
thy choice whether still to be subtle, worldly, selfish, iron-hearted, and
hypocritical, or to tear these sins out of thy nature, though they bring the
life-blood with them! The Avenger is upon thee! Rise up, before it be
too late!

What! Thou art not stirred by this last appeal? No, not a jot! And
there we see a fly,—one of your common house-flies, such as are always
buzzing on the window-pane,—which has smelt out Governor Pyncheon,
and alights, now on his forehead, now on his chin, and now, Heaven help
us! is creeping over the bridge of his nose, towards the would-be chief-
magistrate's wide-open eyes! Canst thou not brush the fly away? Art
thou too sluggish? Thou man, that hadst so many busy projects yesterday! Art thou too weak, that wast so powerful? Not brush away a fly?
Nay, then, we give thee up!

And hark! the shop-bell rings. After hours like these latter ones,
through which we have borne our heavy tale, it is good to be made sensible that there is a living world, and that even this old, lonely mansion retains some manner of connection with it. We breathe more freely, emerging from Judge Pyncheon's presence into the street before the Seven
Gables.

## XIX

## ALICE'S POSIES

UNCLE VENNER, trundling a wheelbarrow, was the earliest person stirring in the neighborhood the day after the storm.

Pyncheon Street, in front of the House of the Seven Gables, was a far pleasanter scene than a by-lane, confined by shabby fences, and bordered with wooden dwellings of the meaner class, could reasonably be expected to present. Nature made sweet amends, that morning, for the five unkindly days which had preceded it. It would have been enough to live for, merely to look up at the wide benediction of the sky, or as much of it as was visible between the houses, genial once more with sunshine. Every object was agreeable, whether to be gazed at in the breadth, or examined more minutely. Such, for example, were the well-washed pebbles and gravel of the sidewalk; even the sky-reflecting pools in the centre of the street; and the grass, now freshly verdant, that crept along the base of the fences, on the other side of which, if one peeped over, was seen the multifarious growth of gardens. Vegetable productions, of whatever kind, seemed more than negatively happy, in the juicy warmth and abundance of their life. The Pyncheon Elm, throughout its great circumference, was all alive, and full of the morning sun and a sweet-tempered little breeze, which lingered within this verdant sphere, and set a thousand leafy tongues a-whispering all at once. This aged tree appeared to have suffered nothing from the gale. It had kept its boughs unshattered, and its full complement of leaves; and the whole in perfect verdure, except a single branch, that, by the earlier change with which the elm-tree sometimes prophesies the autumn, had been transmuted to bright gold. It was like the golden branch that gained Æneas and the Sibyl admittance into Hades.

This one mystic branch hung down before the main entrance of the Seven Gables, so nigh the ground that any passer-by might have stood on tiptoe and plucked it off. Presented at the door, it would have been a symbol of his right to enter, and be made acquainted with all the secrets of the house. So little faith is due to external appearance, that there was really an inviting aspect over the venerable edifice, conveying an idea that its history must be a decorous and happy one, and such as would be delightful for a fireside tale. Its windows gleamed cheerfully in the slanting sunlight. The lines and tufts of green moss, here and there, seemed pledges of familiarity and sisterhood with Nature; as if this human dwelling-place, being of such old date, had established its prescriptive title among primeval oaks and whatever other objects, by virtue of their long continuance, have acquired a gracious right to be. A person of imaginative temperament, while passing by the house, would turn, once and again, and peruse it well: its many peaks, consenting together in the clustered chimney; the deep projection over its basement-story; the arched window, imparting a look, if not of grandeur, yet of antique gentility, to the broken portal over which it opened; the luxuriance of gigantic burdocks, near the threshold; he would note all these characteristics, and be conscious of something deeper than he saw. He would conceive the mansion to have been the residence of the stubborn old Puritan, Integrity, who, dying in some forgotten generation, had left a blessing in all its rooms and chambers, the efficacy of which was to be seen in the religion, honesty, moderate competence, or upright poverty and solid happiness, of his descendants, to this day.

One object, above all others, would take root in the imaginative observer's memory. It was the great tuft of flowers,—weeds, you would have called them, only a week ago,—the tuft of crimson-spotted flowers, in the angle between the two front gables. The old people used to give them the name of Alice's Posies, in remembrance of fair Alice Pyncheon, who was believed to have brought their seeds from Italy. They were flaunting in rich beauty and full bloom to-day, and seemed, as it were, a mystic expression that something within the house was consummated.

It was but little after sunrise, when Uncle Venner made his appearance, as aforesaid, impelling a wheelbarrow along the street. He was going his matutinal rounds to collect cabbage-leaves, turnip-tops, potato-skins, and the miscellaneous refuse of the dinner-pot, which the thrifty housewives of the neighborhood were accustomed to put aside, as fit only to feed a pig. Uncle Venner's pig was fed entirely, and kept in prime order, on these eleemosynary contributions; insomuch that the patched philosopher used to promise that, before retiring to his farm, he would make a feast of the portly grunter, and invite all his neighbors to partake of the joints and spare-ribs which they had helped to fatten. Miss Hepzibah Pyncheon's housekeeping had so greatly improved, since Clifford became a member of the family, that her share of the banquet would have been no lean one; and Uncle Venner, accordingly, was a good deal disappointed not to find the large earthen pan, full of fragmentary eatables, that ordinarily awaited his coming at the back doorstep of the Seven Gables.

"I never knew Miss Hepzibah so forgetful before," said the patriarch to himself. "She must have had a dinner yesterday,—no question of that! She always has one, nowadays. So where's the pot-liquor and potato-skins, I ask? Shall I knock, and see if she's stirring yet? No, no—'t won't do! If little Phœbe was about the house, I should not mind knocking: but Miss Hepzibah, likely as not, would scowl down at me out of the window, and look cross, even if she felt pleasantly. So, I'll come back at noon."

With these reflections, the old man was shutting the gate of the little back-yard. Creaking on its hinges, however, like every other gate and door about the premises, the sound reached the ears of the occupant of the northern gable, one of the windows of which had a side-view towards the gate.

Good morning, Uncle Venner!" said the daguerreotypist, leaning out of the window. "Do you hear nobody stirring?"

"Not a soul," said the man of patches. "But that 's no wonder. 'T is barely half an hour past sunrise, yet. But I'm really glad to see you, Mr. Holgrave! There 's a strange, lonesome look about this side of the house; so that my heart misgave me, somehow or other, and I felt as if there was nobody alive in it. The front of the house looks a good deal cheerier; and Alice's Posies are blooming there beautifully; and if I were a young man, Mr. Holgrave, my sweetheart should have one of those flowers in her bosom, though I risked my neck climbing for it! Well, and did the wind keep you awake last night?"

"It did, indeed!" answered the artist, smiling. "If I were a believer in ghosts,—and I don't quite know whether I am or not,—I should have concluded that all the old Pyncheons were running riot in the lower rooms, especially in Miss Hepzibah's part of the house. But it is very quiet now."

"Yes, Miss Hepzibah will be apt to over-sleep herself, after being disturbed, all night, with the racket," said Uncle Venner. "But it would be odd, now, would n't it, if the Judge had taken both his cousins into the country along with him? I saw him go into the shop yesterday."

"At what hour?" inquired Holgrave.

"Oh, along in the forenoon," said the old man. "Well, well! I must go my rounds, and so must my wheelbarrow. But I'll be back here at dinner-time; for my pig likes a dinner as well as a breakfast. No meal-time, and no sort of victuals, ever seems to come amiss to my pig. Good morning to you! And, Mr. Holgrave, if I were a young man, like you, I 'd get one of Alice's Posies, and keep it in water till Phœbe comes back."

"I have heard," said the daguerreotypist, as he drew in his head, "that the water of Maule's well suits those flowers best."

Here the conversation ceased, and Uncle Venner went on his way. For half an hour longer, nothing disturbed the repose of the Seven Gables; nor was there any visitor, except a carrier-boy, who, as he passed the front doorstep, threw down one of his newspapers; for Hepzibah, of late, had regularly taken it in. After a while, there came a fat woman, making prodigious speed, and stumbling as she ran up the steps of the shop-door. Her face glowed with fire-heat, and, it being a pretty warm morning, she bubbled and hissed, as it were, as if all a-fry with chimney-warmth, and summer-warmth, and the warmth of her own corpulent velocity. She tried the shop-door; it was fast. She tried it again, with so angry a jar that the bell tingled angrily back at her.

"The deuce take Old Maid Pyncheon!" muttered the irascible house-wife. "Think of her pretending to set up a cent-shop, and then lying abed till noon! These are what she calls gentlefolk's airs, I suppose! But I 'll either start her ladyship, or break the door down!"

She shook it accordingly, and the bell, having a spiteful little temper of its own, rang obstreperously, making its remonstrances heard,—not, indeed, by the ears for which they were intended,—but by a good lady on the opposite side of the street. She opened her window, and addressed the impatient applicant.

"You 'll find nobody there, Mrs. Gubbins."

"But I must and will find somebody here!" cried Mrs. Gubbins, inflicting another outrage on the bell. "I want a half-pound of pork, to fry some first-rate flounders, for Mr. Gubbins's breakfast; and, lady or not, Old Maid Pyncheon shall get up and serve me with it!"

"But do hear reason, Mrs. Gubbins!" responded the lady opposite. "She, and her brother too, have both gone to their cousin, Judge Pyncheon's at his country-seat. There 's not a soul in the house, but that young daguerreotype-man that sleeps in the north gable. I saw old Hepzibah and Clifford go away yesterday; and a queer couple of ducks they were, paddling through the mud-puddles! They 're gone, I'll assure you."

"And how do you know they 're gone to the Judge's?" asked Mrs. Gubbins. "He 's a rich man; and there 's been a quarrel between him and Hepzibah, this many a day because he won't give her a living. That 's the main reason of her setting up a cent-shop."

"I know that well enough," said the neighbor. "But they 're gone,— that 's one thing certain. And who but a blood relation, that could n't help himself, I ask you, would take in that awful-tempered old maid, and that dreadful Clifford? That 's it, you may be sure."

Mrs. Gubbins took her departure, still brimming over with hot wrath against the absent Hepzibah. For another half-hour, or, perhaps, considerably more, there was almost as much quiet on the outside of the house as within. The elm, however, made a pleasant, cheerful, sunny sigh, responsive to the breeze that was elsewhere imperceptible; a swarm of insects buzzed merrily under its drooping shadow, and became specks of light whenever they darted into the sunshine; a locust sang, once or twice, in some inscrutable seclusion of the tree; and a solitary little bird, with plumage of pale gold, came and hovered about Alice's Posies.

At last our small acquaintance, Ned Higgins, trudged up the street, on his way to school; and happening, for the first time in a fortnight, to be the possessor of a cent, he could by no means get past the shop-door of the Seven Gables. But it would not open. Again and again, however, and half a dozen other agains, with the inexorable pertinacity of a child intent upon some object important to itself, did he renew his efforts for admittance. He had, doubtless, set his heart upon an elephant; or, possibly, with Hamlet, he meant to eat a crocodile. In response to his more violent attacks, the bell gave, now and then, a moderate tinkle, but could not be stirred into clamor by any exertion of the little fellow's childish and tip-toe strength. Holding by the door-handle, he peeped through a crevice of the curtain, and saw that the inner door, communicating with the passage towards the parlor, was closed.

"Miss Pyncheon!" screamed the child, rapping on the window-pane, "I want an elephant!"

There being no answer to several repetitions of the summons, Ned began to grow impatient; and his little pot of passion quickly boiling over, he picked up a stone, with a naughty purpose to fling it through the window; at the same time blubbering and sputtering with wrath. A man—one of two who happened to be passing by—caught the urchin's arm.

"What 's the trouble, old gentleman?" he asked.

"I want old Hepzibah, or Phœbe, or any of them!" answered Ned, sobbing. "They won't open the door; and I can't get my elephant!"

"Go to school, you little scamp!" said the man. "There 's another cent-shop round the corner. 'T is very strange, Dixey," added he to his companion, "what 's become of all these Pyncheons! Smith, the livery-stable keeper, tells me Judge Pyncheon put his horse up yesterday, to stand till after dinner, and has not taken him away yet. And one of the Judge's hired men has been in, this morning, to make inquiry about him. He 's a kind of person, they say, that seldom breaks his habits, or stays out o' nights."

"Oh, he 'll turn up safe enough!" said Dixey. "And as for Old Maid Pyncheon, take my word for it, she has run in debt, and gone off from her creditors. I foretold, you remember, the first morning she set up shop, that her devilish scowl would frighten away customers. They could n't stand it!"

"I never thought she 'd make it go," remarked his friend. "This business of cent-shops is overdone among the womenfolks. My wife tried it, and lost five dollars on her outlay!"

"Poor business!" said Dixey, shaking his head. "Poor business!"

In the course of the morning, there were various other attempts to open a communication with the supposed inhabitants of this silent and impenetrable mansion. The man of root-beer came, in his neatly painted wagon, with a couple of dozen full bottles, to be exchanged for empty ones; the baker, with a lot of crackers which Hepzibah had ordered for her retail custom; the butcher, with a nice titbit which he fancied she would be eager to secure for Clifford. Had any observer of these proceedings been aware of the fearful secret hidden within the house, it would have affected him with a singular shape and modification of horror, to see the current of human life making this small eddy hereabouts,—whirling sticks, straws, and all such trifles, round and round, right over the black depth where a dead corpse lay unseen!

The butcher was so much in earnest with his sweet-bread of lamb, or whatever the dainty might be, that he tried every accessible door of the Seven Gables, and at length came round again to the shop, where he ordinarily found admittance.

"It's a nice article, and I know the old lady would jump at it," said he to himself. "She can't be gone away! In fifteen years that I have driven my cart through Pyncheon Street, I 've never known her to be away from home; though often enough, to be sure, a man might knock all day without bringing her to the door. But that was when she 'd only herself to provide for."

Peeping through the same crevice of the curtain where, only a little while before, the urchin of elephantine appetite had peeped, the butcher beheld the inner door, not closed, as the child had seen it, but ajar, and almost wide open. However it might have happened, it was the fact. Through the passage-way there was a dark vista into the lighter but still obscure interior of the parlor. It appeared to the butcher that he could pretty clearly discern what seemed to be the stalwart legs, clad in black pantaloons, of a man sitting in a large oaken chair, the back of which concealed all the remainder of his figure. This contemptuous tranquillity on the part of an occupant of the house, in response to the butcher's indefatigable efforts to attract notice, so piqued the man of flesh that he determined to withdraw.

"So," thought he, "there sits Old Maid Pyncheon's bloody brother, while I 've been giving myself all this trouble! Why, if a hog had n't more manners, I 'd stick him! I call it demeaning a man's business to trade with such people; and from this time forth, if they want a sausage or an ounce of liver, they shall run after the cart for it!"

He tossed the titbit angrily into his cart, and drove off in a pet.

Not a great while afterwards there was a sound of music turning the corner, and approaching down the street, with several intervals of silence, and then a renewed and nearer outbreak of brisk melody. A mob of children was seen moving onward, or stopping, in unison with the sound, which appeared to proceed from the centre of the throng; so that they were loosely bound together by slender strains of harmony, and drawn along captive; with ever and anon an accession of some little fellow in an apron and straw-hat, capering forth from door or gateway. Arriving under the shadow of the Pyncheon Elm, it proved to be the Italian boy, who, with his monkey and show of puppets, had once before played his hurdy-gurdy beneath the arched window. The pleasant face of Phœbe —and doubtless, too, the liberal recompense which she had flung him— still dwelt in his remembrance. His expressive features kindled up, as he recognized the spot where this trifling incident of his erratic life had chanced. He entered the neglected yard (now wilder than ever, with its growth of hog-weed and burdock), stationed himself on the doorstep of the main entrance, and, opening his show-box, began to play. Each individual of the automatic community forthwith set to work, according to his or her proper vocation: the monkey, taking off his Highland bonnet, bowed and scraped to the by-standers most obsequiously, with ever an observant eye to pick up a stray cent; and the young foreigner himself, as he turned the crank of his machine, glanced upward to the arched window, expectant of a presence that would make his music the livelier and sweeter. The throng of children stood near; some on the sidewalk; some within the yard; two or three establishing themselves on the very door-step; and one squatting on the threshold. Meanwhile, the locust kept singing in the great old Pyncheon Elm.

"I don't hear anybody in the house," said one of the children to another. "The monkey won't pick up anything here."

"There is somebody at home," affirmed the urchin on the threshold. "I heard a step!"

Still the young Italian's eye turned sidelong upward; and it really seemed as if the touch of genuine, though slight and almost playful, emotion communicated a juicier sweetness to the dry, mechanical process of his minstrelsy. These wanderers are readily responsive to any natural kindness—be it no more than a smile, or a word itself not understood, but only a warmth in it—which befalls them on the roadside of life. They remember these things, because they are the little enchantments which, for the instant,—for the space that reflects a landscape in a soap-bubble,—build up a home about them. Therefore, the Italian boy would not be discouraged by the heavy silence with which the old house seemed resolute to clog the vivacity of his instrument. He persisted in his melodious appeals; he still looked upward, trusting that his dark, alien countenance would soon be brightened by Phœbe's sunny aspect. Neither could he be willing to depart without again beholding Clifford, whose sensibility, like Phœbe's smile, had talked a kind of heart's language to the foreigner. He repeated all his music over and over again, until his auditors were getting weary. So were the little wooden people in his show-box, and the monkey most of all. There was no response, save the singing of the locust.

"No children live in this house," said a school-boy, at last. "Nobody lives here but an old maid and an old man. You 'll get nothing here! Why don't you go along?"

"You fool, you, why do you tell him?" whispered a shrewd little Yankee, caring nothing for the music, but a good deal for the cheap rate at which it was had. "Let him play as long as he likes! If there 's nobody to pay him, that 's his own lookout!"

Once more, however, the Italian ran over his round of melodies. To the common observer—who could understand nothing of the case, except the music and the sunshine on the hither side of the door—it might have been amusing to watch the pertinacity of the street-performer. Will he succeed at last? Will that stubborn door be suddenly flung open? Will a group of joyous children, the young ones of the house, come dancing, shouting, laughing, into the open air, and cluster round the show-box, looking with eager merriment at the puppets, and tossing each a copper for long-tailed Mammon, the monkey, to pick up?

But to us, who know the inner heart of the Seven Gables as well as its exterior face, there is a ghastly effect in this repetition of light popular tunes at its door-step. It would be an ugly business, indeed, if Judge Pyncheon (who would not have cared a fig for Paganini's fiddle in his most harmonious mood) should make his appearance at the door, with a bloody shirt-bosom, and a grim frown on his swarthily white visage, and motion the foreign vagabond away! Was ever before such a grinding out of jigs and waltzes, where nobody was in the cue to dance? Yes, very often. This contrast, or intermingling of tragedy with mirth, happens daily, hourly, momently. The gloomy and desolate old house, deserted of life, and with awful Death sitting sternly in its solitude, was the emblem of many a human heart, which, nevertheless, is compelled to hear the thrill and echo of the world's gayety around it.

Before the conclusion of the Italian's performance, a couple of men happened to be passing, on their way to dinner.

"I say, you young French fellow!" called out one of them,—"come away from that doorstep, and go somewhere else with your nonsense! The Pyncheon family live there; and they are in great trouble, just about this time. They don't feel musical to-day. It is reported all over town that Judge Pyncheon, who owns the house, has been murdered; and the city marshal is going to look into the matter. So be off with you, at once!"

As the Italian shouldered his hurdy-gurdy, he saw on the doorstep a card, which had been covered, all the morning, by the newspaper that the carrier had flung upon it, but was now shuffled into sight. He picked it up, and perceiving something written in pencil, gave it to the man to read. In fact, it was an engraved card of Judge Pyncheon's with certain pencilled memoranda on the back, referring to various businesses which it had been his purpose to transact during the preceding day. It formed a prospective epitome of the day's history; only that affairs had not turned out altogether in accordance with the programme. The card must have been lost from the Judge's vest-pocket, in his preliminary attempt to gain access by the main entrance of the house. Though well soaked with rain, it was still partially legible.

"Look here, Dixey!" cried the man. "This has something to do with Judge Pyncheon. See!—here 's his name printed on it; and here, I suppose, is some of his handwriting."

"Let 's go to the city marshal with it!" said Dixey. "It may give him just the clew he wants. After all," whispered he in his companion's ear, "it would be no wonder if the Judge has gone into that door and never come out again! A certain cousin of his may have been at his old tricks. And Old Maid Pyncheon having got herself in debt by the cent-shop,—and the Judge's pocket-book being well filled,—and bad blood amongst them already! Put all these things together and see what they make!"

"Hush, hush!" whispered the other. "It seems like a sin to be the first to speak of such a thing. But I think, with you, that we had better go to the city marshal."

"Yes, yes!" said Dixey. "Well!—I always said there was something devilish in that woman's scowl!"

The men wheeled about, accordingly, and retraced their steps up the street. The Italian, also, made the best of his way off, with a parting glance up at the arched window. As for the children, they took to their heels, with one accord, and scampered as if some giant or ogre were in pursuit, until, at a good distance from the house, they stopped as suddenly and simultaneously as they had set out. Their susceptible nerves took an indefinite alarm from what they had overheard. Looking back at the grotesque peaks and shadowy angles of the old mansion, they fancied a gloom diffused about it which no brightness of the sunshine could dispel. An imaginary Hepzibah scowled and shook her finger at them, from several windows at the same moment. An imaginary Clifford—for (and it would have deeply wounded him to know it) he had always been a horror to these small people—stood behind the unreal Hepzibah, making awful gestures, in a faded dressing-gown. Children are even more apt, if possible, than grown people, to catch the contagion of a panic terror. For the rest of the day, the more timid went whole streets about, for the sake of avoiding the Seven Gables; while the bolder signalized their hardihood by challenging their comrades to race past the mansion at full speed.

It could not have been more than half an hour after the disappearance of the Italian boy, with his unseasonable melodies, when a cab drove down the street. It stopped beneath the Pyncheon Elm; the cabman took a trunk, a canvas bag, and a bandbox, from the top of his vehicle, and deposited them on the doorstep of the old house; a straw bonnet, and then the pretty figure of a young girl, came into view from the interior of the cab. It was Phœbe! Though not altogether so blooming as when she first tripped into our story,—for, in the few intervening weeks, her experiences had made her graver, more womanly, and deeper-eyed, in token of a heart that had begun to suspect its depths,—still there was the quiet glow of natural sunshine over her. Neither had she forfeited her proper gift of making things look real, rather than fantastic, within her sphere. Yet we feel it to be a questionable venture, even for Phœbe, at this juncture, to cross the threshold of the Seven Gables. Is her healthful presence potent enough to chase away the crowd of pale, hideous, and sinful phantoms, that have gained admittance there since her departure? Or will she, likewise, fade, sicken, sadden, and grow into deformity, and be only another pallid phantom, to glide noiselessly up and down the stairs, and affright children as she pauses at the window?

At least, we would gladly forewarn the unsuspecting girl that there is nothing in human shape or substance to receive her, unless it be the figure of Judge Pyncheon, who—wretched spectacle that he is, and frightful in our remembrance, since our night-long vigil with him!—still keeps his place in the oaken chair.

Phœbe first tried the shop-door. It did not yield to her hand; and the white curtain, drawn across the window which formed the upper section of the door, struck her quick perceptive faculty as something unusual. Without making another effort to enter here, she betook herself to the great portal, under the arched window. Finding it fastened, she knocked. A reverberation came from the emptiness within. She knocked again, and a third time; and, listening intently, fancied that the floor creaked, as if Hepzibah were coming, with her ordinary tiptoe movement, to admit her. But so dead a silence ensued upon this imaginary sound, that she began to question whether she might not have mistaken the house, familiar as she thought herself with its exterior.

Her notice was now attracted by a child's voice, at some distance. It appeared to call her name. Looking in the direction whence it proceeded, Phœbe saw little Ned Higgins, a good way down the street, stamping, shaking his head violently, making deprecatory gestures with both hands, and shouting to her at mouth-wide screech.

"No, no, Phœbe?" he screamed. "Don't you go in! There's something wicked there! Don't—don't—don't go in!"

But, as the little personage could not be induced to approach near enough to explain himself, Phœbe concluded that he had been frightened, on some of his visits to the shop, by her cousin Hepzibah; for the good lady's manifestations, in truth, ran about an equal chance of scaring children out of their wits, or compelling them to unseemly laughter. Still, she felt the more, for this incident, how unaccountably silent and impenetrable the house had become. As her next resort, Phœbe made her way into the garden, where on so warm and bright a day as the present, she had little doubt of finding Clifford, and perhaps Hepzibah also, idling away the noontide in the shadow of the arbor. Immediately on her entering the garden-gate, the family of hens half ran, half flew, to meet her; while a strange grimalkin, which was prowling under the parlor window, took to his heels, clambered hastily over the fence, and vanished. The arbor was vacant, and its floor, table, and circular bench were still damp, and bestrewn with twigs, and the disarray of the past storm. The growth of the garden seemed to have got quite out of bounds; the weeds had taken advantage of Phœbe's absence, and the long-continued rain, to run rampant over the flowers and kitchen-vegetables. Maule's well had overflowed its stone border, and made a pool of formidable breadth in that corner of the garden.

The impression of the whole scene was that of a spot where no human foot had left its print for many preceding days,—probably not since Phœbe's departure,—for she saw a side-comb of her own under the table of the arbor, where it must have fallen on the last afternoon when she and Clifford sat there.

The girl knew that her two relatives were capable of far greater oddities than that of shutting themselves up in their old house, as they appeared now to have done. Nevertheless, with indistinct misgivings of something amiss, and apprehensions to which she could not give shape, she approached the door that formed the customary communication between the house and garden. It was secured within, like the two which she had already tried. She knocked, however; and immediately, as if the application had been expected, the door was drawn open, by a considerable exertion of some unseen person's strength, not wide, but far enough to afford her a side-long entrance. As Hepzibah, in order not to expose herself to inspection from without, invariably opened a door in this manner, Phœbe necessarily concluded that it was her cousin who now admitted her.

Without hesitation, therefore, she stepped across the threshold, and had no sooner entered than the door closed behind her.

## XX

### The Flower of Eden

PHŒBE, coming so suddenly from the sunny daylight, was altogether be-dimmed in such density of shadow as lurked in most of the passages of the old house. She was not at first aware by whom she had been admitted. Before her eyes had adapted themselves to the obscurity, a hand grasped her own, with a firm but gentle and warm pressure, thus imparting a wel-come which caused her heart to leap and thrill with an indefinable shiver of enjoyment. She felt herself drawn along, not towards the parlor, but into a large and unoccupied apartment, which had formerly been the grand reception-room of the Seven Gables. The sunshine came freely into all the uncurtained windows of this room, and fell upon the dusty floor; so that Phœbe now clearly saw—what, indeed, had been no secret, after the encounter of a warm hand with hers—that it was not Hepzibah nor Clifford, but Holgrave, to whom she owed her reception. The subtile, in-tuitive communication, or, rather, the vague and formless impression of something to be told, had made her yield unresistingly to his impulse. Without taking away her hand, she looked eagerly in his face, not quick to forebode evil, but unavoidably conscious that the state of the family had changed since her departure, and therefore anxious for an explana-tion.

The artist looked paler than ordinary; there was a thoughtful and se-vere contraction of his forehead, tracing a deep, vertical line between the eyebrows. His smile, however, was full of genuine warmth, and had in it a joy, by far the most vivid expression that Phœbe had ever witnessed, shin-ing out of the New England reserve with which Holgrave habitually masked whatever lay near his heart. It was the look wherewith a man, brooding alone over some fearful object, in a dreary forest, or illimitable desert, would recognize the familiar aspect of his dearest friend, bringing up all the peaceful ideas that belong to home, and the gentle current of every-day affairs. And yet, as he felt the necessity of responding to her look of inquiry, the smile disappeared.

"I ought not to rejoice that you have come, Phœbe," said he. "We meet at a strange moment!"

"What has happened?" she exclaimed. "Why is the house so deserted? Where are Hepzibah and Clifford?"

"Gone! I cannot imagine where they are!" answered Holgrave. "We are alone in the house!"

"Hepzibah and Clifford gone?" cried Phœbe. "It is not possible! And why have you brought me into this room, instead of the parlor? Ah, some-thing terrible has happened! I must run and see!"

"No, no, Phœbe!" said Holgrave, holding her back. "It is as I have told you. They are gone, and I know not whither. A terrible event has, indeed, happened, but not to them, nor, as I undoubtingly believe, through any agency of theirs. If I read your character rightly, Phœbe," he continued, fixing his eyes on hers, with stern anxiety, intermixed with tenderness, "gentle as you are, and seeming to have your sphere among common things, you yet possess remarkable strength. You have wonderful poise, and a faculty which, when tested, will prove itself capable of dealing with matters that fall far out of the ordinary rule."

"Oh no, I am very weak!" replied Phœbe, trembling. "But tell me what has,happened!"

"You are strong!" persisted Holgrave. "You must be both strong and wise; for I am all astray, and need your counsel. It may be you can suggest the one right thing to do!"

"Tell me!—tell me!" said Phœbe, all in a tremble. "It oppresses,—it terrifies me,—this mystery! Anything else I can bear!"

The artist hesitated. Notwithstanding what he had just said, and most sincerely, in regard to the self-balancing power with which Phœbe impressed him, it still seemed almost wicked to bring the awful secret of yesterday to her knowledge. It was like dragging a hideous shape of death into the cleanly and cheerful space before a household fire, where it would present all the uglier aspect, amid the decorousness of everything about it. Yet it could not be concealed from her; she must needs know it.

"Phœbe," said he, "do you remember this?"

He put into her hand a daguerreotype; the same that he had shown her at their first interview in the garden, and which so strikingly brought out the hard and relentless traits of the original.

"What has this to do with Hepzibah and Clifford?" asked Phœbe, with impatient surprise that Holgrave should so trifle with her at such a moment. "It is Judge Pyncheon! You have shown it to me before!"

"But here is the same face, taken within this half-hour," said the artist, presenting her with another miniature. "I had just finished it, when I heard you at the door."

"This is death!" shuddered Phœbe, turning very pale. "Judge Pyncheon dead!"

"Such as there represented," said Holgrave, "he sits in the next room. The Judge is dead, and Clifford and Hepzibah have vanished! I know no more. All beyond is conjecture. On returning to my solitary chamber, last evening, I noticed no light, either in the parlor, or Hepzibah's room, or Clifford's; no stir nor footstep about the house. This morning, there was the same death-like quiet. From my window, I overheard the testimony of a neighbor, that your relatives were seen leaving the house, in the midst of yesterday's storm. A rumor reached me, too, of Judge Pyncheon being missed. A feeling which I cannot describe—an indefinite sense of some catastrophe, or consummation—impelled me to make my way into this part of the house, where I discovered what you see. As a point of evidence that may be useful to Clifford, and also as a memorial valuable to myself, —for, Phœbe, there are hereditary reasons that connect me strangely with that man's fate,—I used the means at my disposal to preserve this pictorial record of Judge Pyncheon's death."

Even in her agitation, Phœbe could not help remarking the calmness of Holgrave's demeanor. He appeared, it is true, to feel the whole awfulness of the Judge's death, yet had received the fact into his mind without any mixture of surprise, but as an event preordained, happening inevitably, and so fitting itself into past occurrences that it could almost have been prophesied.

"Why have you not thrown open the doors, and called in witnesses?" inquired she, with a painful shudder. "It is terrible to be here alone!"

"But Clifford!" suggested the artist. "Clifford and Hepzibah! We must consider what is best to be done in their behalf. It is a wretched fatality that they should have disappeared! Their flight will throw the worst coloring over this event of which it is susceptible. Yet how easy is the explanation, to those who know them! Bewildered and terror-stricken by the similarity of this death to a former one, which was attended with such disastrous consequences to Clifford, they have had no idea but of removing themselves from the scene. How miserably unfortunate! Had Hepzibah but shrieked aloud,—had Clifford flung wide the door, and proclaimed Judge Pyncheon's death,—it would have been, however awful in itself, an event fruitful of good consequences to them. As I view it, it would have gone far towards obliterating the black stain on Clifford's character."

"And how," asked Phœbe, "could any good come from what is so very dreadful?"

"Because," said the artist, "if the matter can be fairly considered and candidly interpreted, it must be evident that Judge Pyncheon could not have come unfairly to his end. This mode of death has been an idiosyncrasy with his family, for generations past; not often occurring, indeed, but, when it does occur, usually attacking individuals about the Judge's time of life, and generally in the tension of some mental crisis, or, perhaps, in an access of wrath. Old Maule's prophecy was probably founded on a knowledge of this physical predisposition in the Pyncheon race. Now, there is a minute and almost exact similarity in the appearances connected with the death that occurred yesterday and those recorded of the death of Clifford's uncle thirty years ago. It is true, there was a certain arrangement of circumstances, unnecessary to be recounted, which made it possible—nay, as men look at these things, probable, or even certain—that old Jaffrey Pyncheon came to a violent death, and by Clifford's hands."

"Whence came those circumstances?" exclaimed Phœbe; "he being innocent, as we know him to be!"

"They were arranged," said Holgrave,—"at least such has long been my conviction,—they were arranged after the uncle's death, and before it was made public, by the man who sits in yonder parlor. His own death, so like that former one, yet attended by none of those suspicious circumstances, seems the stroke of God upon him, at once a punishment for his wickedness, and making plain the innocence of Clifford. But this flight,—

it distorts everything! He may be in concealment, near at hand. Could we but bring him back before the discovery of the Judge's death the evil might be rectified."

"We must not hide this thing a moment longer!" said Phœbe. "It is dreadful to keep it so closely in our hearts. Clifford is innocent. God will make it manifest! Let us throw open the doors, and call all the neighborhood to see the truth!"

"You are right, Phœbe," rejoined Holgrave. "Doubtless you are right."

Yet the artist did not feel the horror, which was proper to Phœbe's sweet and order-loving character, at thus finding herself at issue with society, and brought in contact with an event that transcended ordinary rules. Neither was he in haste, like her, to betake himself within the precincts of common life. On the contrary, he gathered a wild enjoyment,— as it were, a flower of strange beauty, growing in a desolate spot, and blossoming in the wind,—such a flower of momentary happiness he gathered from his present position. It separated Phœbe and himself from the world, and bound them to each other, by their exclusive knowledge of Judge Pyncheon's mysterious death, and the counsel which they were forced to hold respecting it. The secret, so long as it should continue such, kept them within the circle of a spell, a solitude in the midst of men, a remoteness as entire as that of an island in mid-ocean; once divulged, the ocean would flow betwixt them, standing on its widely sundered shores. Meanwhile, all the circumstances of their situation seemed to draw them together; they were like two children who go hand in hand, pressing closely to one another's side, through a shadow-haunted passage. The image of awful Death, which filled the house, held them united by his stiffened grasp.

These influences hastened the development of emotions that might not otherwise have flowered so. Possibly, indeed, it had been Holgrave's purpose to let them die in their undeveloped germs.

"Why do we delay so?" asked Phœbe. "This secret takes away my breath! Let us throw open the doors!"

"In all our lives there can never come another moment like this!" said Holgrave. "Phœbe, is it all terror?—nothing but terror? Are you conscious of no joy, as I am, that has made this the only point of life worth living for?"

"It seems a sin," replied Phœbe, trembling, "to think of joy at such a time!"

"Could you but know, Phœbe, how it was with me the hour before you came!" exclaimed the artist. "A dark, cold, miserable hour! The presence of yonder dead man threw a great black shadow over everything; he made the universe, so far as my perception could reach, a scene of guilt and of retribution more dreadful than the guilt. The sense of it took away my youth. I never hoped to feel young again! The world looked strange, wild, evil, hostile; my past life, so lonesome and dreary; my future, a shapeless gloom, which I must mould into gloomy shapes! But, Phœbe, you crossed the threshold; and hope, warmth, and joy came in with you! The black moment became at once a blissful one. It must not pass without the spoken word. I love you!"

"How can you love a simple girl like me?" asked Phœbe, compelled by his earnestness to speak. "You have many, many thoughts, with which I should try in vain to sympathize. And I,—I, too,—I have tendencies with which you would sympathize as little. That is less matter. But I have not scope enough to make you happy."

"You are my only possibility of happiness!" answered Holgrave. "I have no faith in it, except as you bestow it on me!"

"And then—I am afraid!" continued Phœbe, shrinking towards Holgrave, even while she told him so frankly the doubts with which he affected her. "You will lead me out of my own quiet path. You will make me strive to follow you where it is pathless. I cannot do so. It is not my nature. I shall sink down and perish!"

"Ah, Phœbe!" exclaimed Holgrave, with almost a sigh, and a smile that was burdened with thought. "It will be far otherwise than as you forebode. The world owes all its onward impulses to men ill at ease. The happy man inevitably confines himself within ancient limits. I have a presentiment that, hereafter, it will be my lot to set out trees, to make fences,—perhaps, even, in due time, to build a house for another generation,—in a word, to conform myself to laws, and the peaceful practice of society. Your poise will be more powerful than any oscillating tendency of mine."

"I would not have it so!" said Phœbe, earnestly.

"Do you love me?" asked Holgrave. "If we love one another, the moment has room for nothing more. Let us pause upon it, and be satisfied. Do you love me, Phœbe?"

"You look into my heart," said she, letting her eyes drop. "You know I love you!"

And it was in this hour, so full of doubt and awe, that the one miracle was wrought, without which every human existence is a blank. The bliss which makes all things true, beautiful, and holy shone around this youth and maiden. They were conscious of nothing sad nor old. They transfigured the earth, and made it Eden again, and themselves the two first dwellers in it. The dead man, so close beside them, was forgotten. At such a crisis, there is no death; for immortality is revealed anew, and embraces everything in its hallowed atmosphere.

But how soon the heavy earth-dream settled down again!

"Hark!" whispered Phœbe. "Somebody is at the street-door!"

"Now let us meet the world!" said Holgrave. "No doubt, the rumor of Judge Pyncheon's visit to this house, and the flight of Hepzibah and Clifford, is about to lead to the investigation of the premises. We have no way but to meet it. Let us open the door at once."

But, to their surprise, before they could reach the street-door,—even before they quitted the room in which the foregoing interview had passed, —they heard footsteps in the farther passage. The door, therefore, which they supposed to be securely locked,—which Holgrave, indeed, had seen to be so, and at which Phœbe had vainly tried to enter,—must have been opened from without. The sound of footsteps was not harsh, bold, decided, and intrusive, as the gait of strangers would naturally be, making authoritative entrance into a dwelling where they knew themselves unwelcome. It was feeble, as of persons either weak or weary; there was the mingled murmur of two voices, familiar to both the listeners.

"Can it be?" whispered Holgrave.

"It is they!" answered Phœbe. "Thank God!—thank God!"

And then, as if in sympathy with Phœbe's whispered ejaculation, they heard Hepzibah's voice, more distinctly.

"Thank God, my brother, we are at home!"

"Well!—Yes!—thank God!" responded Clifford. "A dreary home, Hepzibah! But you have done well to bring me hither! Stay! That parlor door is open. I cannot pass by it! Let me go and rest me in the arbor, where I used,—oh, very long ago, it seems to me, after what has befallen us,—where I used to be so happy with little Phœbe!"

But the house was not altogether so dreary as Clifford imagined it. They had not made many steps,—in truth, they were lingering in the entry, with the listlessness of an accomplished purpose, uncertain what to do next,—when Phœbe ran to meet them. On beholding her, Hepzibah burst into tears. With all her might, she had staggered onward beneath the burden of grief and responsibility, until now that it was safe to fling it down. Indeed, she had not energy to fling it down, but had ceased to uphold it, and suffered it to press her to the earth. Clifford appeared the stronger of the two.

"It is our own little Phœbe!—Ah! and Holgrave with her," exclaimed he, with a glance of keen and delicate insight, and a smile, beautiful, kind, but melancholy. "I thought of you both, as we came down the street, and beheld Alice's Posies in full bloom. And so the flower of Eden has bloomed, likewise, in this old, darksome house to-day."

## XXI

### THE DEPARTURE

THE sudden death of so prominent a member of the social world as the Honorable Judge Jaffrey Pyncheon created a sensation (at least, in the circles more immediately connected with the deceased) which had hardly quite subsided in a fortnight.

It may be remarked, however, that, of all the events which constitute a person's biography, there is scarcely one—none, certainly, of anything like a similar importance—to which the world so easily reconciles itself as to his death. In most other cases and contingencies, the individual is present among us, mixed up with the daily revolution of affairs, and affording a definite point for observation. At his decease, there is only a vacancy, and a momentary eddy,—very small, as compared with the apparent magnitude of the ingurgitated object,—and a bubble or two, ascending out of the black depth and bursting at the surface. As regarded Judge Pyncheon, it seemed probable, at first blush, that the mode of his final departure might give him a larger and longer posthumous vogue than ordinarily attends the memory of a distinguished man. But when it came to be understood, on the highest professional authority, that the event was a natural, and—except for some unimportant particulars, denoting a slight idiosyncrasy—by no means an unusual form of death, the public, with its customary alacrity, proceeded to forget that he had ever lived. In short, the honorable Judge was beginning to be a stale subject before half the county newspapers had found time to put their columns in mourning, and publish his exceedingly eulogistic obituary.

Nevertheless, creeping darkly through the places which this excellent person had haunted in his life-time, there was a hidden stream of private talk, such as it would have shocked all decency to speak loudly at the street-corners. It is very singular, how the fact of a man's death often seems to give people a truer idea of his character, whether for good or evil, than they have ever possessed while he was living and acting among them. Death is so genuine a fact that it excludes falsehood, or betrays its emptiness; it is a touchstone that proves the gold, and dishonors the baser metal. Could the departed, whoever he may be, return in a week after his decease, he would almost invariably find himself at a higher or lower point than he had formerly occupied, on the scale of public appreciation. But the talk, or scandal, to which we now allude, had reference to matters of no less old a date than the supposed murder, thirty or forty years ago, of the late Judge Pyncheon's uncle. The medical opinion, with regard to his own recent and regretted decease, had almost entirely obviated the idea that a murder was committed in the former case. Yet, as the record showed, there were circumstances irrefragably indicating that some person had gained access to old Jaffrey Pyncheon's private apartments, at or near the moment of his death. His desk and private drawers, in a room contiguous to his bedchamber, had been ransacked; money and valuable articles were missing; there was a bloody hand-print on the old man's linen; and, by a powerfully welded chain of deductive evidence, the guilt of the robbery and apparent murder had been fixed on Clifford, then residing with his uncle in the House of the Seven Gables.

Whencesoever originating, there now arose a theory that undertook so to account for these circumstances as to exclude the idea of Clifford's agency. Many persons affirmed that the history and elucidation of the facts, long so mysterious, had been obtained by the daguerreotypist from one of those mesmerical seers, who, nowadays, so strangely perplex the aspect of human affairs, and put everybody's natural vision to the blush, by the marvels which they see with their eyes shut.

According to this version of the story, Judge Pyncheon, exemplary as we have portrayed him in our narrative, was, in his youth, an apparently irreclaimable scapegrace. The brutish, the animal instincts, as is often the case, had been developed earlier than the intellectual qualities, and the force of character, for which he was afterwards remarkable. He had shown himself wild, dissipated, addicted to low pleasures, little short of ruffianly in his propensities, and recklessly expensive, with no other resources than the bounty of his uncle. This course of conduct had alienated the old bachelor's affection, once strongly fixed upon him. Now it is averred,—but whether on authority available in a court of justice, we do not pretend to have investigated,—that the young man was tempted by the devil, one night, to search his uncle's private drawers, to which he had unsuspected means of access. While thus criminally occupied, he was startled by the opening of the chamber-door. There stood old Jaffrey Pyncheon, in his nightclothes! The surprise of such a discovery, his agitation, alarm, and horror, brought on the crisis of a disorder to which the old bachelor had an hereditary liability; he seemed to choke with blood, and fell upon the floor, striking his temple a heavy blow against the corner of a table. What was to be done? The old man was surely dead! Assistance would come too late! What a misfortune, indeed, should it come too soon, since his reviving consciousness would bring the recollection of the ignominious offence which he had beheld his nephew in the very act of committing!

But he never did revive. With the cool hardihood that always pertained to him, the young man continued his search of the drawers, and found a will, of recent date, in favor of Clifford,—which he destroyed,—and an older one, in his own favor, which he suffered to remain. But before retiring, Jaffrey bethought himself of the evidence, in these ransacked drawers, that some one had visited the chamber with sinister purposes. Suspicion, unless averted, might fix upon the real offender. In the very presence of the dead man, therefor, he laid a scheme that should free himself at the expense of Clifford, his rival, for whose character he had at once a contempt and a repugnance. It is not probable, be it said, that he acted with any set purpose of involving Clifford in a charge of murder. Knowing that his uncle did not die by violence, it may not have occurred to him, in the hurry of the crisis, that such an inference might be drawn. But, when the affair took this darker aspect, Jaffrey's previous steps had already pledged him to those which remained. So craftily had he arranged the circumstances, that, at Clifford's trial, his cousin hardly found it necessary to swear to anything false, but only to withhold the one decisive explanation, by refraining to state what he had himself done and witnessed.

Thus Jaffrey Pyncheon's inward criminality, as regarded Clifford, was, indeed, black and damnable; while its mere outward show and positive commission was the smallest that could possibly consist with so great a sin. This is just the sort of guilt that a man of eminent respectability finds it easiest to dispose of. It was suffered to fade out of sight or be reckoned a venial matter, in the Honorable Judge Pyncheon's long subsequent survey of his own life. He shuffled it aside, among the forgotten and forgiven frailties of his youth, and seldom thought of it again.

We leave the Judge to his repose. He could not be styled fortunate at the hour of death. Unknowingly, he was a childless man, while striving to add more wealth to his only child's inheritance. Hardly a week after his decease, one of the Cunard steamers brought intelligence of the death, by cholera, of Judge Pyncheon's son, just at the point of embarkation for his native land. By this misfortune Clifford became rich; so did Hepzibah; so did our little village maiden, and, through her, that sworn foe of wealth and all manner of conservatism,—the wild reformer,—Holgrave!

It was now far too late in Clifford's life for the good opinion of society to be worth the trouble and anguish of a formal vindication. What he needed was the love of a very few; not the admiration, or even the respect, of the unknown many. The latter might probably have been won for him, had those on whom the guardianship of his welfare had fallen deemed it advisable to expose Clifford to a miserable resuscitation of past ideas, when the condition of whatever comfort he might expect lay in the calm of forgetfulness. After such wrong as he had suffered, there is no reparation. The pitiable mockery of it, which the world might have been ready enough to offer, coming so long after the agony had done its utmost work, would have been fit only to provoke bitterer laughter than poor Clifford was ever capable of. It is a truth (and it would be a very sad one but for the higher hopes which it suggests) that no great mistake, whether acted or endured, in our mortal sphere, is ever really set right. Time, the continual vicissitude of circumstances, and the invariable inopportunity of death, render it impossible. If, after long lapse of years, the right seems to be in our power, we find no niche to set it in. The better remedy is for the sufferer to pass on, and leave what he once thought his irreparable ruin far behind him.

The shock of Judge Pyncheon's death had a permanently invigorating and ultimately beneficial effect on Clifford. That strong and ponderous man had been Clifford's nightmare. There was no free breath to be drawn, within the sphere of so malevolent an influence. The first effect of freedom, as we have witnessed in Clifford's aimless flight, was a tremulous exhilaration. Subsiding from it, he did not sink into his former intellectual apathy. He never, it is true, attained to nearly the full measure of what might have been his faculties. But he recovered enough of them partially to light up his character, to display some outline of the marvellous grace that was abortive in it, and to make him the object of no less deep, although less melancholy interest than heretofore. He was evidently happy. Could we pause to give another picture of his daily life, with all the appliances now at command to gratify his instinct for the Beautiful, the garden scenes, that seemed so sweet to him, would look mean and trivial in comparison.

Very soon after their change of fortune, Clifford, Hepzibah, and little Phœbe, with the approval of the artist, concluded to remove from the dismal old House of the Seven Gables, and take up their abode, for the present, at the elegant country-seat of the late Judge Pyncheon. Chanticleer and his family had already been transported thither, where the two hens had forthwith begun an indefatigable process of egg-laying, with an evident design, as a matter of duty and conscience, to continue their illustrious breed under better auspices than for a century past. On the day set for their departure, the principal personages of our story, including good Uncle Venner, were assembled in the parlor.

"The country-house is certainly a very fine one, so far as the plan goes," observed Holgrave, as the party were discussing their future arrangements. "But I wonder that the late Judge—being so opulent, and with a reasonable prospect of transmitting his wealth to descendants of his own —should not have felt the propriety of embodying so excellent a piece of domestic architecture in stone, rather than in wood. Then, every generation of the family might have altered the interior, to suit its own taste and convenience; while the exterior, through the lapse of years, might have been adding venerableness to its original beauty, and thus giving that impression of permanence which I consider essential to the happiness of any one moment."

"Why," cried Phœbe, gazing into the artist's face with infinite amazement, "how wonderfully your ideas are changed! A house of stone, indeed! It is but two or three weeks ago that you seemed to wish people to live in something as fragile and temporary as a bird's-nest!"

"Ah, Phœbe, I told you how it would be!" said the artist, with a half-melancholy laugh. "You find me a conservative already! Little did I think ever to become one. It is especially unpardonable in this dwelling of so much hereditary misfortune, and under the eye of yonder portrait of a model conservative, who, in that very character, rendered himself so long the evil destiny of his race."

"That picture!" said Clifford, seeming to shrink from its stern glance. "Whenever I look at it, there is an old dreamy recollection haunting me, but keeping just beyond the grasp of my mind. Wealth it seems to say!— boundless wealth!—unimaginable wealth! I could fancy that, when I was a child, or a youth, that portrait had spoken, and told me a rich secret, or had held forth its hand, with the written record of hidden opulence. But those old matters are so dim with me, nowadays! What could this dream have been?"

"Perhaps I can recall it," answered Holgrave. "See! There are a hundred chances to one that no person, unacquainted with the secret, would ever touch this spring."

"A secret spring!" cried Clifford. "Ah, I remember now! I did discover it, one summer afternoon, when I was idling and dreaming about the house, long long ago. But the mystery escapes me."

The artist put his finger on the contrivance to which he had referred. In former days, the effect would probably have been to cause the picture to start forward. But, in so long a period of concealment, the machinery had been eaten through with rust; so that at Holgrave's pressure, the portrait, frame and all, tumbled suddenly from its position, and lay face downward on the floor. A recess in the wall was thus brought to light, in which lay an object so covered with a century's dust that it could not immediately be recognized as a folded sheet of parchment. Holgrave opened it, and displayed an ancient deed, signed with the hieroglyphics of several Indian sagamores, and conveying to Colonel Pyncheon and his heirs, forever, a vast extent of territory at the Eastward.

"This is the very parchment the attempt to recover which cost the beautiful Alice Pyncheon her happiness and life," said the artist, alluding to his legend. "It is what the Pyncheons sought in vain, while it was valuable; and now that they find the treasure, it has long been worthless."

"Poor Cousin Jaffrey! This is what deceived him," exclaimed Hepzibah. "When they were young together, Clifford probably made a kind of fairy-tale of this discovery. He was always dreaming hither and thither about the house, and lighting up its dark corners with beautiful stories. And poor Jaffrey, who took hold of everything as if it were real, thought my brother had found out his uncle's wealth. He died with this delusion in his mind!"

"But," said Phœbe, apart to Holgrave, "how came you to know the secret?"

"My dearest Phœbe," said Holgrave, "how will it please you to assume the name of Maule? As for the secret, it is the only inheritance that has come down to me from my ancestors. You should have known sooner (only that I was afraid of frightening you away) that, in this long drama of wrong and retribution, I represent the old wizard, and am probably as much a wizard as ever he was. The son of the executed Matthew Maule, while building this house, took the opportunity to construct that recess, and hide away the Indian deed, on which depended the immense land-claim of the Pyncheons. Thus they bartered their Eastern territory for Maule's garden-ground."

"And now," said Uncle Venner, "I suppose their whole claim is not worth one man's share in my farm yonder!"

"Uncle Venner," cried Phœbe, taking the patched philosopher's hand, "you must never talk any more about your farm! You shall never go there, as long as you live! There is a cottage in our new garden,—the prettiest little yellowish-brown cottage you ever saw; and the sweetest-looking place, for it looks just as if it were made of gingerbread,—and we are going to fit it up and furnish it, on purpose for you. And you shall do nothing but what you choose, and shall be as happy as the day is long, and shall keep Cousin Clifford in spirits with the wisdom and pleasantness which is always dropping from your lips!"

"Ah! my dear child," quoth good Uncle Venner, quite overcome, "if you were to speak to a young man as you do to an old one, his chance of keeping his heart another minute would not be worth one of the buttons on my waistcoat! And—soul alive!—that great sigh, which you made me heave, has burst off the very last of them! But, never mind! It was the happiest sigh I ever did heave; and it seems as if I must have drawn in a gulp of heavenly breath, to make it with. Well, well Miss Phœbe! They'll miss me in the gardens hereabouts, and round by the back doors; and Pyncheon Street, I'm afraid, will hardly look the same without old Uncle Venner, who remembers it with a mowing field on one side, and the garden of the Seven Gables on the other. But either I must go to your country-seat, or you must come to my farm,—that's one of two things certain; and I leave you to choose which!"

"Oh, come with us, by all means, Uncle Venner!" said Clifford, who had a remarkable enjoyment of the old man's mellow, quiet, and simple spirit. "I want you always to be within five minutes' saunter of my chair. You are the only philosopher I ever knew of whose wisdom has not a drop of bitter essence at the bottom!"

"Dear me!" cried Uncle Venner, beginning partly to realize what manner of man he was. "And yet folks used to set me down among the simple ones, in my younger days! But I suppose I am like a Roxbury russet,—a great deal the better, the longer I can be kept. Yes; and my words of wisdom, that you and Phœbe tell me of, are like the golden dandelions, which never grow in the hot months, but may be seen glistening among the withered grass, and under the dry leaves, sometimes as late as December. And you are welcome, friends, to my mess of dandelions, if there were twice as many!"

A plain, but handsome, dark-green barouche had now drawn up in front of the ruinous portal of the old mansion-house. The party came forth, and (with the exception of good Uncle Venner, who was to follow in a few days) proceeded to take their places. They were chatting and laughing very pleasantly together; and—as proves to be often the case, at moments when we ought to palpitate with sensibility—Clifford and Hepzibah bade a final farewell to the abode of their forefathers, with hardly more emotion than if they had made it their arrangement to return thither at tea-time. Several children were drawn to the spot by so unusual a spectacle as the barouche and pair of gray horses. Recognizing little Ned Higgins among them, Hepzibah put her hand into her pocket, and presented the urchin, her earliest and staunchest customer, with silver enough to people the Domdaniel cavern of his interior with as various a procession of quadrupeds as passed into the ark.

Two men were passing, just as the barouche drove off.

"Well, Dixey," said one of them, "what do you think of this? My wife kept a cent-shop three months, and lost five dollars on her outlay. Old Maid Pyncheon has been in trade just about as long, and rides off in her carriage with a couple of hundred thousand,—reckoning her share, and Clifford's, and Phœbe's,—and some say twice as much! If you choose to call it luck, it is all very well; but if we are to take it as the will of Providence, why, I can't exactly fathom it!"

"Pretty good business!" quoth the sagacious Dixey,—"pretty good business!"

Maule's well, all this time, though left in solitude, was throwing up a succession of kaleidoscopic pictures, in which a gifted eye might have seen foreshadowed the coming fortunes of Hepzibah and Clifford, and the descendant of the legendary wizard, and the village maiden, over whom he had thrown Love's web of sorcery. The Pyncheon Elm, moreover, with what foliage the September gale had spared to it, whispered unintelligible prophecies. And wise Uncle Venner, passing slowly from the ruinous porch, seemed to hear a strain of music, and fancied that sweet Alice Pyncheon—after witnessing these deeds, this bygone woe and this present happiness, of her kindred mortals—had given one farewell touch of a spirit's joy upon her harpsichord, as she floated heavenward from the HOUSE OF THE SEVEN GABLES!

# THE

# BLITHEDALE ROMANCE

# Preface

IN the "BLITHEDALE" of this volume many readers will, probably, suspect a faint and not very faithful shadowing of BROOK FARM, in Roxbury, which (now a little more than ten years ago) was occupied and cultivated by a company of socialists. The author does not wish to deny that he had this community in his mind, and that (having had the good fortune, for a time, to be personally connected with it) he has occasionally availed himself of his actual reminiscences, in the hope of giving a more life-like tint to the fancy-sketch in the following pages. He begs it to be understood, however, that he has considered the institution itself as not less fairly the subject of fictitious handling than the imaginary personages whom he has introduced there. His whole treatment of the affair is altogether incidental to the main purpose of the romance; nor does he put forward the slightest pretensions to illustrate a theory, or elicit a conclusion, favorable or otherwise, in respect to socialism.

In short, his present concern with the socialist community is merely to establish a theatre, a little removed from the highway of ordinary travel, where the creatures of his brain may play their phantasmagorical antics, without exposing them to too close a comparison with the actual events of real lives. In the old countries, with which fiction has long been conversant, a certain conventional privilege seems to be awarded to the romancer; his work is not put exactly side by side with nature; and he is allowed a license with regard to every-day probability, in view of the improved effects which he is bound to produce thereby. Among ourselves, on the contrary, there is as yet no such Faery Land, so like the real world, that, in a suitable remoteness, one cannot well tell the difference, but with an atmosphere of strange enchantment, beheld through which the inhabitants have a propriety of their own. This atmosphere is what the American romancer needs. In its absence, the beings of imagination are compelled to show themselves in the same category as actually living mortals; a necessity that generally renders the paint and pasteboard of their composition but too painfully discernible. With the idea of partially obviating this difficulty (the sense of which has always pressed very heavily upon him), the author has ventured to make free with his old and affectionately remembered home at BROOK FARM, as being certainly the most romantic episode of his own life,—essentially a day-dream, and yet a fact,—and thus offering an available foothold between fiction and reality. Furthermore, the scene was in good keeping with the personages whom he desired to introduce.

These characters, he feels it right to say, are entirely fictitious. It would, indeed (considering how few amiable qualities he distributes among his imaginary progeny), be a most grievous wrong to his former excellent associates, were the author to allow it to be supposed that he has been sketching any of their likenesses. Had he attempted it, they would at least have recognized the touches of a friendly pencil. But he has done nothing of the kind. The self-concentrated Philanthropist; the high-spirited Woman, bruising herself against the narrow limitations of her sex; the weakly Maiden, whose tremulous nerves endow her with Sibylline attributes; the Minor Poet, beginning life with strenuous aspirations which die out with his youthful fervor,—all these might have been looked for at BROOK FARM, but, by some accident, never made their appearance there.

The author cannot close his reference to this subject without expressing a most earnest wish that some one of the many cultivated and philosophic minds, which took an interest in that enterprise, might now give the world its history. Ripley, with whom rests the honorable paternity of the institution, Dana, Dwight, Channing, Burton, Parker, for instance,—with others, whom he dares not name, because they veil themselves from the public eye,—among these is the ability to convey both the outward narrative and the inner truth and spirit of the whole affair, together with the lessons which those years of thought and toil must have elaborated, for the behoof of future experimentalists. Even the brilliant Howadji might find as rich a theme in his youthful reminiscences of BROOK FARM, and a more novel one,—close at hand as it lies,—than those which he has since made so distant a pilgrimage to seek, in Syria and along the current of the Nile.

CONCORD, MASS., *May,* 1852.

# THE BLITHEDALE ROMANCE

## I

### OLD MOODIE

THE evening before my departure for Blithedale, I was returning to my bachelor apartments, after attending the wonderful exhibition of the Veiled Lady, when an elderly man, of rather shabby appearance, met me in an obscure part of the street.

"Mr. Coverdale," said he, softly, "can I speak with you a moment?"

As I have casually alluded to the Veiled Lady, it may not be amiss to mention, for the benefit of such of my readers, as are unacquainted with her now forgotten celebrity, that she was a phenomenon in the mesmeric line; one of the earliest that had indicated the birth of a new science, or the revival of an old humbug. Since those times her sisterhood have grown too numerous to attract much individual notice; nor, in fact, has any one of them come before the public under such skilfully contrived circumstances of stage-effect as those which at once mystified and illuminated the remarkable performances of the lady in question. Nowadays, in the management of his "subject," "clairvoyant," or "medium," the exhibitor affects the simplicity and openness of scientific experiment; and even if he profess to tread a step or two across the boundaries of the spiritual world, yet carries with him the laws of our actual life, and extends them over his preternatural conquests. Twelve or fifteen years ago, on the contrary, all the arts of mysterious arrangement, of picturesque disposition, and artistically contrasted light and shade, were made available, in order to set the apparent miracle in the strongest attitude of opposition to ordinary facts. In the case of the Veiled Lady, moreover, the interest of the spectator was further wrought up by the enigma of her identity, and an absurd rumor (probably set afloat by the exhibitor, and at one time very prevalent) that a beautiful young lady, of family and fortune, was enshrouded within the misty drapery of the veil. It was white, with somewhat of a subdued silver sheen, like the sunny side of a cloud; and, falling over the wearer from head to foot, was supposed to insulate her from the material world, from time and space, and to endow her with many of the privileges of a disembodied spirit.

Her pretensions, however, whether miraculous or otherwise, have little to do with the present narrative; except, indeed, that I had propounded, for the Veiled Lady's prophetic solution, a query as to the success of our Blithedale enterprise. The response, by the by, was of the true Sibylline stamp,—nonsensical in its first aspect, yet, on closer study, unfolding a

441

variety of interpretations, one of which has certainly accorded with the event. I was turning over this riddle in my mind, and trying to catch its slippery purport by the tail, when the old man above mentioned interrupted me.

"Mr. Coverdale!—Mr. Coverdale!" said he, repeating my name twice, in order to make up for the hesitating and ineffectual way in which he uttered it. "I ask your pardon, sir, but I hear you are going to Blithedale to-morrow."

I knew the pale, elderly face, with the red-tipt nose, and the patch over one eye; and likewise saw something characteristic in the old fellow's way of standing under the arch of a gate, only revealing enough of himself to make me recognize him as an acquaintance. He was a very shy personage, this Mr. Moodie; and the trait was the more singular, as his mode of getting his bread necessarily brought him into the stir and hubbub of the world more than the generality of men.

"Yes, Mr. Moodie," I answered, wondering what interest he could take in the fact, "it is my intention to go to Blithedale to-morrow. Can I be of any service to you before my departure?"

"If you pleased, Mr. Coverdale," said he, "you might do me a very great favor."

"A very great one?" repeated I, in a tone that must have expressed but little alacrity of beneficence, although I was ready to do the old man any amount of kindness involving no special trouble to myself. "A very great favor, do you say? My time is brief, Mr. Moodie, and I have a good many preparations to make. But be good enough to tell me what you wish."

"Ah, sir," replied Old Moodie, "I don't quite like to do that; and, on further thoughts, Mr. Coverdale, perhaps I had better apply to some older gentleman, or to some lady, if you would have the kindness to make me known to one, who may happen to be going to Blithedale. You are a young man, sir!"

"Does that fact lessen my availability for your purpose?" asked I. "However, if an older man will suit you better, there is Mr. Hollingsworth, who has three or four years the advantage of me in age, and is a much more solid character, and a philanthropist to boot. I am only a poet, and, so the critics tell me, no great affair at that! But what can this business be, Mr. Moodie? It begins to interest me; especially since your hint that a lady's influence might be found desirable  Come, I am really anxious to be of service to you."

But the old fellow, in his civil and demure manner, was both freakish and obstinate; and he had now taken some notion or other into his head that made him hesitate in his former design.

"I wonder, sir," said he, "whether you know a lady whom they call Zenobia?"

"Not personally," I answered, "although I expect that pleasure to-morrow, as she has got the start of the rest us, and is already a resident at Blithedale. But have you a literary turn, Mr. Moodie? or have you taken up the advocacy of women's rights? or what else can have interested you in this lady? Zenobia, by the by, as I suppose you know, is merely her public name; a sort of mask in which she comes before the world, retaining all the privileges of privacy,—a contrivance, in short, like the white drapery of the Veiled Lady, only a little more transparent. But it is late. Will you tell me what I can do for you?"

"Please to excuse me to-night, Mr. Coverdale," said Moodie. "You are very kind; but I am afraid I have troubled you, when, after all, there may be no need. Perhaps, with your good leave, I will come to your lodgings to-morrow morning, before you set out for Blithedale. I wish you a good-night, sir, and beg pardon for stopping you."

And so he slipt away; and, as he did not show himself the next morning, it was only through subsequent events that I ever arrived at a plausible conjecture as to what his business could have been. Arriving at my room, I threw a lump of cannel coal upon the grate, lighted a cigar, and spent an hour in musings of every hue, from the brightest to the most sombre; being, in truth, not so very confident as at some former periods that this final step, which would mix me up irrevocably with the Blithedale affair, was the wisest that could possibly be taken. It was nothing short of midnight when I went to bed, after drinking a glass of particularly fine sherry, on which I used to pride myself in those days. It was the very last bottle; and I finished it, with a friend, the next forenoon, before setting out for Blithedale.

## II

### BLITHEDALE

THERE can hardly remain for me (who am really getting to be a frosty bachelor, with another white hair, ever week or so, in my mustache), there can hardly flicker up again so cheery a blaze upon the hearth, as that which I remember, the next day, at Blithedale. It was a wood-fire, in the parlor of an old farm-house, on an April afternoon, but with the fitful gusts of a wintry snow-storm roaring in the chimney. Vividly does that fireside re-create itself, as I rake away the ashes from the embers in my memory, and blow them up with a sigh, for lack of more inspiring breath. Vividly, for an instant, but, anon, with the dimmest gleam, and with just as little fervency for my heart as for my finger-ends! The staunch oaken logs were long ago burnt out. Their genial glow must be represented, if at all, by the merest phosphoric glimmer, like that which exudes, rather than shines, from damp fragments of decayed trees, deluding the benighted wanderer through a forest. Around such chill mockery of a fire some few of us might sit on the withered leaves, spreading out each a palm towards the imaginary warmth, and talk over our exploded scheme for beginning the life of Paradise anew.

Paradise, indeed! Nobody else in the world, I am bold to affirm—nobody, at least, in our bleak little world of New England,—had dreamed of Paradise that day, except as the pole suggests the tropic. Nor, with such materials as were at hand, could the most skilful architect have constructed any better imitation of Eve's bower than might be seen in the snow-hut of an Equimaux. But we made a summer of it, in spite of the wild drifts.

It was an April day, as already hinted, and well towards the middle of the month. When morning dawned upon me, in town, its temperature was mild enough to be pronounced even balmy, by a lodger, like myself, in one of the midmost houses of a brick block,—each house partaking of the warmth of all the rest, besides the sultriness of its individual furnace-heat. But, towards noon, there had come snow, driven along the street by a northeasterly blast, and whitening the roofs and sidewalks with a business-like perseverance that would have done credit to our severest January tempest. It set about its task apparently as much in earnest as if it had been guaranteed from a thaw for months to come. The greater, surely, was my heroism, when, puffing out a final whiff of cigar-smoke, I quitted my cosey pair of bachelor-rooms,—with a good fire burning in the grate, and a closet right at hand, where there was still a bottle or two in the champagne-basket, and a residuum of claret in a box,—quitted, I say, these comfortable quarters, and plunged into the heart of the pitiless snow-storm, in quest of a better life.

The better life! Possibly, it would hardly look so, now; it is enough if it looked so then. The greatest obstacle to being heroic is the doubt whether one may not be going to prove one's self a fool; the truest heroism is to resist the doubt; and the profoundest wisdom to know when it ought to be resisted, and when to be obeyed.

Yet, after all, let us acknowledge it wiser, if not more sagacious, to follow out one's day-dream to its natural consummation, although, if the vision have been worth the having, it is certain never to be consummated otherwise than by a failure. And what of that? Its airiest fragments, impalpable as they may be, will possess a value that lurks not in the most ponderous realities of any practicable scheme. They are not the rubbish of the mind. Whatever else I may repent of, therefore, let it be reckoned neither among my sins nor follies that I once had faith and force enough to form generous hopes of the world's destiny,—yes!—and to do what in me lay for their accomplishment; even to the extent of quitting a warm fireside, flinging away a freshly lighted cigar, and travelling far beyond the strike of city clocks, through a drifting snow-storm.

There were four of us who rode together through the storm; and Hollingsworth, who had agreed to be of the number, was accidentally delayed, and set forth at a later hour alone. As we threaded the streets, I remember how the buildings on either side seemed to press too closely upon us, insomuch that our mighty hearts found barely room enough to throb between them. The snowfall, too, looked inexpressibly dreary (I had almost called it dingy), coming down through an atmosphere of city smoke, and alighting on the sidewalk only to be moulded into the impress of somebody's patched boot or overshoe. Thus the track of an old conventionalism was visible on what was freshest from the sky. But when we left the pavements, and our muffled hoof-tramps beat upon a desolate extent of country road, and were effaced by the unfettered blast as soon as stamped, then there was better air to breathe. Air that had not been breathed once and again! air that had not been spoken into words of falsehood, formality, and error, like all the air of the dusky city!

"How pleasant it is!" remarked I, while the snow-flakes flew into my mouth the moment it was opened. "How very mild and balmy is this country air!"

"Ah, Coverdale, don't laugh at what little enthusiasm you have left!" said one of my companions. "I maintain that this nitrous atmosphere is really exhilarating; and, at any rate, we can never call ourselves regenerated men till a February northeaster shall be as grateful to us as the softest breeze of June!"

So we all of us took courage, riding fleetly and merrily along, by stone fences that were half buried in the wave-like drifts; and through patches of woodland, where the tree-trunks opposed a snow-incrusted side towards the northeast; and within ken of deserted villas, with no footprints in their avenues; and passed scattered dwellings, whence puffed the smoke of country fires, strongly impregnated with the pungent aroma of burning peat. Sometimes, encountering a traveller, we shouted a friendly greeting; and he, unmuffling his ears to the bluster and the snow-spray, and listening eagerly, appeared to think our courtesy worth less than the trouble which it cost him. The churl! He understood the shrill whistle of the blast, but had no intelligence for our blithe tones of brotherhood. This lack of faith in our cordial sympathy, on the traveller's part, was one among the innumerable tokens how difficult a task we had in hand, for the reformation of the world. We rode on, however, with still unflagging spirits, and made such good companionship with the tempest that, at our journey's end, we professed ourselves almost loath to bid the rude blusterer good-by. But, to own the truth, I was little better than an icicle, and began to be suspicious that I had caught a fearful cold.

And now we were seated by the brisk fireside of the old farm-house,—the same fire that glimmers so faintly among my reminiscences at the beginning of this chapter. There we sat, with the snow melting out of our hair and beards, and our faces all ablaze, what with the past inclemency and present warmth. It was, indeed, a right good fire that we found awaiting us, built up of great, rough logs, and knotty limbs, and splintered fragments of an oak-tree, such as farmers are wont to keep for their own hearths,—since these crooked and unmanageable boughs could never be measured into merchantable cords for the market. A family of the old Pilgrims might have swung their kettle over precisely such a fire as this, only, no doubt, a bigger one; and, contrasting it with my coal-grate, I felt so much the more that we had transported ourselves a world-wide distance from the system of society that shackled us at breakfast-time.

Good, comfortable Mrs. Foster (the wife of stout Silas Foster, who was to manage the farm, at a fair stipend, and be our tutor in the art of husbandry) bade us a hearty welcome. At her back—a back of generous breadth—appeared two young women, smiling most hospitably, but looking rather awkward withal, as not well knowing what was to be their position in our new arrangement of the world. We shook hands affectionately all round, and congratuated ourselves that the blessed state of brotherhood and sisterhood, at which we aimed, might fairly be dated from this moment. Our greetings were hardly concluded when the door opened, and Zenobia,—whom I had never before seen, important as was her place in our enterprise,—Zenobia entered the parlor.

This (as the reader, if at all acquainted with our literary biography, need scarcely be told) was not her real name. She had assumed it, in the first instance, as her magazine signature; and, as it accorded well with something imperial which her friends attributed to this lady's figure and deportment, they half-laughingly, adopted it in their familiar intercourse with her. She took the appellation in good part, and even encouraged its constant use; which, in fact, was thus far appropriate, that our Zenobia, however humble looked her new philosophy, had as much native pride as any queen would have known what to do with.

## III

### A Knot of Dreamers

ZENOBIA bade us welcome, in a fine, frank, mellow voice, and gave each of us her hand, which was very soft and warm. She had something appropriate, I recollect, to say to every individual; and what she said to myself was this:—

"I have long wished to know you, Mr. Coverdale, and to thank you for your beautiful poetry, some of which I have learned by heart; or, rather, it has stolen into my memory, without my exercising any choice or volition about the matter. Of course—permit me to say—you do not think of relinquishing an occupation in which you have done yourself so much credit. I would almost rather give you up as an associate, than that the world should lose one of its true poets!"

"Ah, no; there will not be the slightest danger of that, especially after this inestimable praise from Zenobia," said I, smiling, and blushing, no doubt, with excess of pleasure. "I hope, on the contrary, now to produce something that shall really deserve to be called poetry,—true, strong, natural, and sweet, as is the life which we are going to lead,—something that shall have the notes of wild birds twittering through it, or a strain like the wind-anthems in the woods, as the case may be."

"Is it irksome to you to hear your own verses sung?" asked Zenobia, with a gracious smile. "If so, I am very sorry, for you will certainly hear me singing them, sometimes, in the summer evenings."

"Of all things," answered I, "that is what will delight me most."

While this passed, and while she spoke to my companions, I was taking note of Zenobia's aspect; and it impressed itself on me so distinctly, that I can now summon her up, like a ghost, a little wanner than the life, but otherwise identical with it. She was dressed as simply as possible, in an American print (I think the dry-goods people call it so), but with a silken kerchief, between which and her gown there was one glimpse of a white shoulder. It struck me as a great piece of good fortune that there should be just that glimpse. Her hair, which was dark, glossy, and of singular abundance, was put up rather soberly and primly, without curls, or other ornament, except a single flower. It was an exotic, of rare beauty, and as fresh as if the hot-house gardener had just clipt it from the stem. That flower has struck deep root into my memory. I can both see it and smell it, at this moment. So brilliant, so rare, so costly, as it must have been, and yet enduring only for a day, it was more indicative of the pride and pomp which had a luxuriant growth in Zenobia's character than if a great diamond had sparkled among her hair.

Her hand, though very soft, was larger than most women would like to have, or than they could afford to have, though not a whit too large in proportion with the spacious plan of Zenobia's entire development. It did one good to see a fine intellect (as hers really was, although its natural tendency lay in another direction than towards literature) so fitly cased. She was, indeed, an admirable figure of a woman, just on the hither verge of her richest maturity, with a combination of features which it is safe to call remarkably beautiful, even if some fastidious persons might pronounce them a little deficient in softness and delicacy. But we find enough of those attributes everywhere. Preferable—by way of variety, at least— was Zenobia's bloom, health, and vigor, which she possessed in such over-flow that a man might well have fallen in love with her for their sake only. In her quiet moods, she seemed rather indolent; but when really in earnest, particularly if there were a spice of bitter feeling, she grew all alive, to her finger-tips.

"I am the first comer," Zenobia went on to say, while her smile beamed warmth upon us all; "so I take the part of hostess, for to-day, and welcome you as if to my own fireside. You shall be my guests, too, at supper. To-morrow, if you please, we will be brethren and sisters, and begin our new life from daybreak."

"Have we our various parts assigned?" asked some one.

"Oh, we of the softer sex," responded Zenobia, with her mellow, almost broad laugh,—most delectable to hear, but not in the least like an ordinary woman's laugh,—"we women (there are four of us here already) will take the domestic and in-door part of the business, as a matter of course. To bake, to boil, to roast, to fry, to stew,—to wash, and iron, and scrub, and sweep,—and, at our idler intervals, to repose ourselves on knitting and sewing,—these, I suppose, must be feminine occupations, for the present. By and by, perhaps, when our individual adaptations begin to develop themselves, it may be that some of us who wear the petticoat will go afield, and leave the weaker brethren to take our places in the kitchen."

"What a pity," I remarked, "that the kitchen, and the house-work generally, cannot be left out of our system altogether! It is odd enough that the kind of labor which falls to the lot of women is just that which chiefly distinguishes artificial life—the life of degenerated mortals—from the life of Paradise. Eve had no dinner-pot, and no clothes to mend, and no washing-day."

"I am afraid," said Zenobia, with mirth gleaming out of her eyes, "we shall find some difficulty in adopting the paradisiacal system for at least a month to come. Look at that snow-drift sweeping past the window! Are there any figs ripe, do you think? Have the pine-apples been gathered to-day? Would you like a bread-fruit, or a cocoa-nut? Shall I run out and pluck you some roses? No no, Mr. Coverdale; the only flower hereabouts is the one in my hair, which I got out of a green-house this morning. As for the garb of Eden," added she, shivering playfully, "I shall not assume it till after May-day!"

Assuredly, Zenobia could not have intended it,—the fault must have been entirely in my imagination. But these last words, together with something in her manner, irresistibly brough up a picture of that fine, perfectly developed figure, in Eve's earliest garment. Her free, careless, generous modes of expression often had this effect of creating images which though pure, are hardly felt to be quite decorus when born of a thought that passes between man and woman. I imputed it, at that time, to Zenobia's noble courage, conscious of no harm, and scorning the petty restraints which take the life and color out of other women's conversation. There was another peculiarity about her. We seldom meet with women nowadays, and in this country, who impress us as being women at all,— their sex fades away, and goes for nothing, in ordinary intercourse. Not so with Zenobia. One felt an influence breathing out of her such as we might suppose to come from Eve, when she was just made, and her Creator brought her to Adam, saying, "Behold! here is a woman!" Not that I would convey the idea of especial gentleness, grace, modesty, and shyness, but of a certain warm and rich characteristic, which seems, for the most part, to have been refined away out of the feminine system.

"And now," continued Zenobia, "I must go and help get supper. Do you think you can be content, instead of figs, pine-apples, and all the other delicacies of Adam's supper-table, with tea and toast, and a certain modest supply of ham and tongue, which, with the instinct of a house-wife, I brought hither in a basket? And there shall be bread and milk, too, if the innocence of your taste demands it."

The whole sisterhood now went about their domestic avocations, utterly declining our offers to assist, further than by bringing wood, for the kitchen fire, from a huge pile in the back-yard. After heaping up more than a sufficient quantity, we returned to the sitting-room, drew our chairs close to the hearth, and began to talk over our prospects. Soon, with a tremendous stamping in the entry, appeared Silas Foster, lank, stalwart, uncouth, and grisly-bearded. He came from foddering the cattle in the barn, and from the field, where he had been ploughing, until the depth of the snow rendered it impossible to draw a furrow. He greeted us in pretty much the same tone as if he were speaking to his oxen, took a quid from his iron tobacco-box, pulled off his wet cowhide boots, and sat down before the fire in his stocking-feet. The steam arose from his soaked garments, so that the stout yeoman looked vaporous and spectre-like.

"Well, folks," remarked Silas, "you'll be wishing yourselves back to town again, if this weather holds."

And, true enough, there was a look of gloom, as the twilight fell silently and sadly out of the sky, its gray or sable flakes intermingling themselves with the fast-descending snow. The storm, in its evening aspect, was decidedly dreary. It seemed to have arisen for our especial behoof,— a symbol of the cold, desolate, distrustful phantoms that invariably haunt the mind, on the eve of adventurous enterprises, to warn us back within the boundaries of ordinary life.

But our courage did not quail. We would not allow ourselves to be depressed by the snow-drift trailing past the window, any more than if it had been the sigh of a summer wind among rustling boughs. There have been few brighter seasons for us than that. If ever men might lawfully dream awake, and give utterance to their wildest visions without dread of laughter or scorn on the part of the audience,—yes, and speak of earthly happiness, for themselves and mankind, as an object to be hopefully striven for, and probably attained,—we who made that little semicircle round the blazing fire were those very men. We had left the rusty iron framework of society behind us; we had broken through many hindrances that are powerful enough to keep most people on the weary tread-mill of the established system, even while they feel its irksomeness almost as intolerable as we did. We had stepped down from the pulpit; we had flung aside the pen; we had shut up the ledger; we had thrown off that sweet, bewitching, enervating indolence, which is better, after all, than most of the enjoyments within mortal grasp. It was our purpose—a generous one, certainly, and absurd, no doubt, in full proportion with its generosity—to give up whatever we had heretofore attained, for the sake of showing mankind the example of a life governed by other than the false and cruel principles on which human society has all along been based.

And, first of all, we had divorced ourselves from pride, and were striving to supply its place with familiar love. We meant to lessen the laboring man's great burden of toil, by performing our due share of it at the cost of our own thews and sinews. We sought our profit by mutual aid, instead of wresting it by the strong hand from an enemy, or filching it craftily from those less shrewd than ourselves (if, indeed, there were any such in New England), or winning it by selfish competition with a neighbor; in one or another of which fashions every son of woman both perpetrates and suffers his share of the common evil, whether he chooses it or no. And, as the basis of our institution, we purposed to offer up the earnest toil of our bodies, as a prayer no less than an effort for the advancement of our race.

Therefore, if we built splendid castles (phalansteries perhaps they might be more fitly called), and pictured beautiful scenes, among the fervid coals of the hearth around which we were clustering, and if all went to rack with the crumbling embers and have never since arisen out of the ashes, let us take to ourselves no shame. In my own behalf, I rejoice that I could once think better of the world's improvability than it deserved. It is a mistake into which men seldom fall twice in a lifetime; or, if so, the rarer and higher is the nature that can thus magnanimously persist in error.

Stout Silas Foster mingled little in our conversation; but when he did speak, it was very much to some practical purpose. For instance:—

"Which man among you," quoth he, "is the best judge of swine? Some of us must go to the next Brighton fair, and buy half a dozen pigs."

Pigs! Good heavens! had we come out from among the swinish multitude for this? And, again, in reference to some discussion about raising early vegetables for the market:—

"We shall never make any hand at market-gardening," said Silas Foster, "unless the women-folks will undertake to do all the weeding. We haven't team enough for that and the regular farm-work, reckoning three of your city folks as worth one common field-hand. No, no; I tell you, we should have to get up a little too early in the morning, to compete with the market-gardeners round Boston."

It struck me as rather odd, that one of the first questions raised, after our separation from the greedy, struggling, self-seeking world, should relate to the possibility of getting the advantage over the outside barbarians in their own field of labor. But, to own the truth, I very soon became sensible that, as regarded society at large, we stood in a position of new hostility, rather than new brotherhood. Nor could this fail to be the case, in some degree, until the bigger and better half of society should range itself on our side. Constituting so pitiful a minority as now, we were inevitably estranged from the rest of mankind in pretty fair proportion with the strictness of our mutual bond among ourselves.

This dawning idea, however, was driven back into my inner consciousness by the entrance of Zenobia. She came with the welcome intelligence that supper was on the table. Looking at herself in the glass, and perceiving that her one magnificent flower had grown rather languid (probably by being exposed to the fervency of the kitchen fire), she flung it on the floor, as unconcernedly as a village girl would throw away a faded violet. The action seemed proper to her character, although, methought, it would still more have befitted the bounteous nature of this beautiful woman to scatter fresh flowers from her hand, and to revive faded ones by her touch. Nevertheless, it was a singular but irresistible effect; the presence of Zenobia caused our heroic enterprise to show like an illusion, a masquerade, a pastoral, a counterfeit Arcadia, in which we grown-up men and women were making a play-day of the years that were given us to live in. I tried to analyze this impression, but not with much success.

"It really vexes me," observed Zenobia, as we left the room, "that Mr. Hollingsworth should be such a laggard. I should not have thought him at all the sort of person to be turned back by a puff of contrary wind, or a few snow-flakes drifting into his face."

"Do you know Hollingsworth personally?" I inquired.

"No; only as an auditor—auditress, I mean—of some of his lectures," said she. "What a voice he has! and what a man he is! Yet not so much an intellectual man, I should say, as a great heart; at least, he moved me more deeply than I think myself capable of being moved, except by the stroke of a true, strong heart against my own. It is a sad pity that he should have devoted his glorious powers to such a grimy, unbeautiful, and positively hopeless object as this reformation of criminals, about which he makes himself and his wretchedly small audiences so very miserable. To tell you a secret, I never could tolerate a philanthropist before. Could you?"

"By no means," I answered; "neither can I now."

"They are, indeed, an odiously disagreeable set of mortals," continued Zenobia. "I should like Mr. Hollingsworth a great deal better, if the philanthropy had been left out. At all events, as a mere matter of taste, I wish he would let the bad people alone, and try to benefit those who are not already past his help. Do you suppose he will be content to spend his life, or even a few months of it, among tolerably virtuous and comfortable individuals, like ourselves?"

"Upon my word, I doubt it," said I. "If we wish to keep him with us, we must systematically commit, at least, one crime apiece! Mere peccadilloes will not satisfy him."

Zenobia turned, sidelong, a strange kind of a glance upon me; but, before I could make out what it meant, we had entered the kitchen, where, in accordance with the rustic simplicity of our new life, the supper-table was spread.

## IV

### THE SUPPER-TABLE

THE pleasant firelight! I must still keep harping on it.

The kitchen hearth had an old-fashioned breadth, depth, and spaciousness, far within which lay what seemed the butt of a good-sized oak-tree, with the moisture bubbling merrily out at both ends. It was now half an hour beyond dusk. The blaze from an armful of substantial sticks, rendered more combustible by brushwood and pine, flickered powerfully on the smoke-blackened walls, and so cheered our spirits that we cared not what inclemency might rage and roar on the other side of our illuminated windows. A yet sultrier warmth was bestowed by a goodly quantity of peat, which was crumbling to white ashes among the burning brands, and incensed the kitchen with its not ungrateful fragrance. The exuberance of this household fire would alone have sufficed to bespeak us no true farmers; for the New England yeoman, if he have the misfortune to dwell within practicable distance of a wood-market, is as niggardly of each stick as if it were a bar of California gold.

But it was fortunate for us, on that wintry eve of our untried life, to enjoy the warm and radiant luxury of a somewhat too abundant fire. If it served no other purpose, it made the men look so full of youth, warm blood, and hope, and the women—such of them, at least, as were anywise convertible by its magic—so very beautiful, that I would cheerfully have spent my last dollar to prolong the blaze. As for Zenobia, there was a glow in her cheeks that made me think of Pandora, fresh from Vulcan's workshop, and full of the celestial warmth by dint of which he had tempered and moulded her.

"Take your places, my dear friends all," cried she; "seat yourselves without ceremony, and you shall be made happy with such tea as not many of the world's working-people, except yourselves, will find in their cups to-night. After this one supper, you may drink buttermilk, if you please. To-night we will quaff this nectar, which, I assure you, could not be bought with gold."

We all sat down,—grisly Silas Foster, his rotund helpmate, and the two bouncing handmaidens, included,—and looked at one another in a friendly but rather awkward way. It was the first practical trial of our theories of equal brotherhood and sisterhood; and we people of superior cultivation and refinement (for as such, I presume, we unhesitatingly reckoned ourselves) felt as if something were already accomplished towards the millennium of love. The truth is, however, that the laboring-oar was with our unpolished companions; it being far easier to condescend than to accept of condescension. Neither did I refrain from questioning, in secret, whether some of us—and Zenobia among the rest—would so quietly have taken our places among these good people, save for the cherished consciousness that it was not by necessity, but choice. Though we saw fit to drink our tea out of earthen cups to-night, and in earthen company, it was at our own option to use pictured porcelain and handle silver forks again to-morrow. This same salve, as to the power of regaining our former position, contributed much, I fear, to the equanimity with which we subsequently bore many of the hardships and humiliations of a life of toil. If ever I have deserved (which has not often been the case, and, I think, never), but if ever I did deserve to be soundly cuffed by a fellow-mortal, for secretly putting weight upon some imaginary social advantage, it must have been while I was striving to prove myself ostentatiously his equal, and no more. It was while I sat beside him on·his cobbler's bench, or clinked my hoe against his own in the cornfield, or broke the same crust of bread, my earth-grimed hand to his, at our noontide lunch. The poor, proud man should look at both sides of sympathy like this.

The silence which followed upon our sitting down to table grew rather oppressive; indeed, it was hardly broken by a word, during the first round of Zenobia's fragrant tea.

"I hope," said I, at last, "that our blazing windows will be visible a great way off. There is nothing so pleasant and encouraging to a solitary traveller, on a stormy night, as a flood of firelight seen amid the gloom. These ruddy window-panes cannot fail to cheer the hearts of all that look at them. Are they not warm with the beacon-fire which we have kindled for humanity?"

"The blaze of that brushwood will only last a minute or two longer," observed Silas Foster; but whether he meant to insinuate that our moral illumination would have as brief a term, I cannot say.

"Meantime," said Zenobia, "it may serve to guide some wayfarer to a shelter."

And, just as she said this, there came a knock at the house-door.

"There is one of the world's wayfarers," said I.

"Ay, ay, just so!" quoth Silas Foster. "Our fire light will draw stragglers, just as a candle draws dorbugs, on a summer night."

Whether to enjoy a dramatic suspense, or that we were selfishly contrasting our own comfort with the chill and dreary situation of the unknown person at the threshold, or that some of us city-folk felt a little startled at the knock which came so unseasonably, through night and storm, to the door of the lonely farm-house,—so it happened that nobody, for an instant or two, arose to answer the summons. Pretty soon there came another knock. The first had been moderately loud; the second was smitten so forcibly that the knuckles of the applicant must have left their mark in the door-panel.

"He knocks as if he had a right to come in," said Zenobia, laughing. "And what are we thinking of? It must be Mr. Hollingsworth!"

Hereupon I went to the door, unbolted, and flung it wide open. There, sure enough, stood Hollingsworth, his shaggy great-coat all covered with snow, so that he looked quite as much like a polar bear as a modern philanthropist.

"Sluggish hospitality this!" said he, in those deep tones of his, which seemed to come out of a chest as capacious as a barrel. "It would have served you right if I had lain down and spent the night on the doorstep, just for the sake of putting you to shame. But here is a guest who will need a warmer and softer bed."

And, stepping back to the wagon in which he had journeyed hither, Hollingsworth received into his arms and deposited on the doorstep a figure enveloped in a cloak. It was evidently a woman; or, rather,—judging from the ease with which he lifted her, and the little space which she seemed to fill in his arms,—a slim and unsubstantial girl. As she showed some hesitation about entering the door, Hollingsworth, with his usual directness and lack of ceremony, urged her forward not merely within the entry, but into the warm and strongly lighted kitchen.

"Who is this?" whispered I, remaining behind with him, while he was taking off his great-coat.

"Who? Really, I don't know," answered Hollingsworth, looking at me with some surprise. "It is a young person who belongs here, however; and, no doubt, she has been expected. Zenobia, or some of the women-folks, can tell you all about it."

"I think not," said I, glancing towards the newcomer and the other occupants of the kitchen. "Nobody seems to welcome her. I should hardly judge that she was an expected guest."

"Well, well," said Hollingsworth, quietly. "We'll make it right."

The stranger, or whatever she were, remained standing precisely on that spot of the kitchen floor to which Hollingsworth's kindly hand had impelled her. The cloak falling partly off, she was seen to be a very young woman dressed in a poor but decent gown, made high in the neck, and without any regard to fashion or smartness. Her brown hair fell down from beneath a hood, not in curls but with only a slight wave; her face was of a wan, almost sickly hue, betokening habitual seclusion from the sun and free atmosphere, like a flower-shrub that had done its best to blossom in too scanty light. To complete the pitiableness of her aspect, she shivered either with cold, or fear, or nervous excitement, so that you might have beheld her shadow vibrating on the fire-lighted wall. In short, there has seldom been seen so depressed and sad a figure as this young girl's; and it was hardly possible to help being angry with her, from mere despair of doing anything for her comfort. The fantasy occurred to me that she was some desolate kind of a creature, doomed to wander about in snow-storms; and that, though the ruddiness of our window-panes had tempted her into a human dwelling, she would not remain long enough to melt the icicles out of her hair.

Another conjecture likewise came into my mind. Recollecting Hollingsworth's sphere of philanthropic action, I deemed it possible that he might have brought one of his guilty patients, to be wrought upon, and restored to spiritual health, by the pure influences which our mode of life would create.

As yet the girl had not stirred. She stood near the door, fixing a pair of large, brown, melancholy eyes upon Zenobia,—only upon Zenobia!—she evidently saw nothing else in the room, save that bright, fair, rosy, beautiful woman. It was the strangest look I ever witnessed; long a mystery to me, and forever a memory. Once she seemed about to move forward and greet her,—I know not with what warmth, or with what words,—but, finally, instead of doing so, she dropped down upon her knees, clasped her hands, and gazed piteously into Zenobia's face. Meeting no kindly reception, her head fell on her bosom.

I never thoroughly forgave Zenobia for her conduct on this occasion.

But women are always more cautious in their casual hospitalities than men.

"What does the girl mean?" cried she in rather a sharp tone. "Is she crazy? Has she no tongue?"

And here Hollingsworth stepped forward.

"No wonder if the poor child's tongue is frozen in her mouth," said he; and I think he positively frowned at Zenobia. "The very heart will be frozen in her bosom, unless you women can warm it, among you, with the warmth that ought to be in your own!"

Hollingsworth's appearance was very striking at this moment. He was then about thirty years old, but looked several years older, with his great shaggy head, his heavy brow, his dark complexion, his abundant beard, and the rude strength with which his features seemed to have been hammered out of iron, rather than chiselled or moulded from any finer or softer material. His figure was not tall, but massive and brawny, and well befitting his original occupation, which—as the reader probably knows,—was that of a blacksmith. As for external polish, or mere courtesy of manner, he never possessed more than a tolerably educated bear; although, in his gentler moods, there was a tenderness in his voice, eyes, mouth, in his gesture, and in every indescribable manifestation, which few men could resist, and no woman. But he now looked stern and reproachful; and it was with that inauspicious meaning in his glance that Hollingsworth first met Zenobia's eyes, and began his influence upon her life.

To my surprise, Zenobia—of whose haughty spirit I had been told so many examples—absolutely changed color, and seemed mortified and confused.

"You do not quite do me justice, Mr. Hollingsworth," said she, almost humbly. "I am willing to be kind to the poor girl. Is she a *protégée* of yours? What can I do for her?"

"Have you anything to ask of this lady?" said Hollingsworth, kindly, to the girl. "I remember you mentioned her name before we left town."

"Only that she will shelter me," replied the girl, tremulously. "Only that she will let me be always near her."

"Well, indeed," exclaimed Zenobia, recovering herself, and laughing, "this is an adventure, and well worthy to be the first incident in our life of love and free-heartedness! But I accept it, for the present, without further question,—only," added she, "it would be a convenience if we knew your name."

"Priscilla," said the girl; and it appeared to me that she hesitated whether to add anything more, and decided in the negative. "Pray do not ask me my other name,—at least not yet,—if you will be so kind to a forlorn creature."

Priscilla!—Priscilla! I repeated the name to myself, three or four times; and in that little space, this quaint and prim cognomen had so amalgamated itself with my idea of the girl, that it seemed as if no other name could have adhered to her for a moment. Heretofore, the poor thing had not shed any tears; but now that she found herself received, and at least temporarily established, the big drops began to ooze out from beneath her eyelids, as if she were full of them. Perhaps it showed the iron substance of my heart, that I could not help smiling at this odd scene of unknown and unaccountable calamity, into which our cheerful party had been entrapped, without the liberty of choosing whether to sympathize or no. Hollingsworth's behavior was certainly a great deal more creditable than mine.

"Let us not pry further into her secrets," he said to Zenobia and the rest of us, apart; and his dark, shaggy face looked really beautiful with its expression of thoughtful benevolence. "Let us conclude that Providence has sent her to us, as the first-fruits of the world, which we have undertaken to make happier than we find it. Let us warm her poor, shivering body with this good fire, and her poor, shivering heart with our best kindness. Let us feed her, and make her one of us. As we do by this friendless girl, so shall we prosper. And, in good time, whatever is desirable for us to know will be melted out of her, as inevitably as those tears which we see now."

"At least," remarked I, "you may tell us how and where you met with her."

"An old man brought her to my lodgings," answered Hollingsworth, "and begged me to convey her to Blithedale, where—so I understood him—she had friends; and this is positively all I know about the matter."

Grim Silas Foster, all this while, had been busy at the supper-table, pouring out his own tea and gulping it down with no more sense of its exquisiteness than if it were a decoction of catnip; helping himself to pieces of dipt toast on the flat of his knife-blade, and dropping half of it on the table-cloth; using the same serviceable implement to cut slice after slice of ham; perpetrating terrible enormities with the butter-plate; and, in all other respects, behaving less like a civilized Christian than the worst kind of an ogre. Being by this time fully gorged, he crowned his amiable exploits with a draught from the water-pitcher, and then favored us with his opinion about the business in hand. And, certainly, though they proceeded out of an unwiped mouth, his expressions did him honor.

"Give the girl a hot cup of tea, and a thick slice of this first-rate bacon," said Silas, like a sensible man as he was. "That's what she wants. Let her stay with us as long as she likes, and help in the kitchen, and take the cow-breath at milking-time; and, in a week or two, she'll begin to look like a creature of this world."

So we sat down again to supper, and Priscilla along with us.

V

UNTIL BEDTIME

SILAS FOSTER, by the time we concluded our meal, had stript off his coat, and planted himself on a low chair by the kitchen fire, with a lap-stone, a hammer, a piece of sole-leather, and some waxed-ends, in order to cobble an old pair of cowhide boots; he being, in his own phrase, "something of a dab" (whatever degree of skill that may imply) at the shoe-making business. We heard the tap of his hammer, at intervals, for the rest of the evening. The remainder of the party adjourned to the sitting-room. Good Mrs. Foster took her knitting-work, and soon fell fast asleep, still keeping her needles in brisk movement, and, to the best of my observation, absolutely footing a stocking out of the texture of a dream. And a very substantial stocking it seemed to be. One of the two handmaidens hemmed a towel, and the other appeared to be making a ruffle, for her Sunday's wear, out of a little bit of embroidered muslin which Zenobia had probably given her.

It was curious to observe how trustingly, and yet how timidly, our poor Priscilla betook herself into the shadow of Zenobia's protection. She sat beside her on a stool, looking up, every now and then, with an expression of humble delight, at her new friend's beauty. A brilliant woman is often an object of the devoted admiration—it might almost be termed worship, or idolatry—of some young girl, who perhaps beholds the cynosure only at an awful distance, and has as little hope of personal intercourse as of climbing among the stars of heaven. We men are too gross to comprehend it. Even a woman, of mature age, despises or laughs at such a passion. There occurred to me no mode of accounting for Priscilla's behavior, except by supposing that she had read some of Zenobia's stories (as such literature goes everywhere), or her tracts in defence of the sex, and had come hither with the one purpose of being her slave. There is nothing parallel to this, I believe,—nothing so foolishly disinterested, and hardly anything so beautiful,—in the masculine nature, at whatever epoch of life; or, if there be, a fine and rare development of character might reasonably be looked for from the youth who should prove himself capable of such self-forgetful affection.

Zenobia happening to change her seat, I took the opportunity, in an undertone, to suggest some such notion as the above.

"Since you see the young woman in so poetical a light," replied she, in the same tone, "you had better turn the affair into a ballad. It is a grand subject, and worthy of supernatural machinery. The storm, the startling knock at the door, the entrance of the sable knight Hollingsworth and this shadowy snow-maiden, who, precisely at the stroke of midnight, shall melt away at my feet in a pool of ice-cold water and give me my death with a pair of wet slippers! And when the verses are written, and polished quite to your mind, I will favor you with my idea as to what the girl really is."

"Pray let me have it now," said I; "it shall be woven into the ballad."

"She is neither more nor less," answered Zenobia, "than a seamstress from the city; and she has probably no more transcendental purpose than to do my miscellaneous sewing, for I suppose she will hardly expect to make my dresses."

"How can you decide upon her so easily?" I inquired.

"Oh, we women judge one another by tokens that escape the obtuseness of masculine perceptions!" said Zenobia. "There is no proof which you would be likely to appreciate, except the needle-marks on the tip of her forefinger. Then, my supposition perfectly accounts for her paleness, her nervousness, and her wretched fragility. Poor thing! She has been stifled with the heat of a salamander-stove, in a small, close room, and has drunk coffee, and fed upon doughnuts, raisins, candy, and all such trash, till she is scarcely half alive; and so, as she has hardly any physique, a poet, like Mr. Miles Coverdale, may be allowed to think her spiritual."

"Look at her now!" whispered I.

Priscilla was gazing towards us, with an inexpressible sorrow in her wan face, and great tears running down her cheeks. It was difficult to resist the impression that, cautiously as we had lowered our voices, she must have overheard and been wounded by Zenobia's scornful estimate of her character and purposes.

"What ears the girl must have!" whispered Zenobia, with a look of vexation, partly comic and partly real. "I will confess to you that I cannot quite make her out. However, I am positively not an ill-natured person, unless when very grievously provoked; and as you, and especially Mr. Hollingsworth, take so much interest in this odd creature,—and as she knocks with a very slight tap against my own heart, likewise,—why, I mean to let her in. From this moment, I will be reasonably kind to her. There is no pleasure in tormenting a person of one's own sex, even if she do favor one with a little more love than one can conveniently dispose of; and that, let me say, Mr. Coverdale, is the most troublesome offence you can offer to a woman."

"Thank you," said I, smiling; "I don't mean to be guilty of it."

She went towards Priscilla, took her hand, and passed her own rosy finger-tips, with a pretty, caressing movement, over the girl's hair. The touch had a magical effect. So vivid a look of joy flushed up beneath those fingers, that it seemed as if the sad and wan Priscilla had been snatched away, and another kind of creature substituted in her place. This one caress, bestowed voluntarily by Zenobia, was evidently received as a pledge of all that the stranger sought from her, whatever the unuttered boon might be. From that instant, too, she melted in quietly amongst us, and was no longer a foreign element. Though always an object of peculiar interest, a riddle, and a theme of frequent discussion, her tenure at Blithedale was thenceforth fixed. We no more thought of questioning it, than if Priscilla had been recognized as a domestic sprite, who had haunted the rustic fireside, of old, before we had ever been warmed by its blaze.

She now produced, out of a work-bag that she had with her, some little wooden instruments (what they are called I never knew), and proceeded to knit, or net, an article which ultimately took the shape of a silk purse. As the work went on, I remembered to have seen just such purses before; indeed, I was the possessor of one. Their peculiar excellence, besides the great delicacy and beauty of the manufacture, lay in the almost impossibility that any uninitiated person should discover the aperture; although, to a practised touch, they would open as wide as charity or prodigality might wish. I wondered if it were not a symbol of Priscilla's own mystery.

Notwithstanding the new confidence with which Zenobia had inspired her, our guest showed herself disquieted by the storm. When the strong puffs of wind spattered the snow against the windows, and made the oaken frame of the farm-house creak, she looked at us apprehensively, as if to inquire whether these tempestuous outbreaks did not betoken some unusual mischief in the shrieking blast. She had been bred up, no doubt, in some close nook, some inauspiciously sheltered court of the city, where the uttermost rage of a tempest, though it might scatter down the slates of the roof into the bricked area, could not shake the casement of her little room. The sense of vast, undefined space, pressing from the outside against the black panes of our uncurtained windows, was fearful to the poor girl, heretofore accustomed to the narrowness of human limits, with the lamps of neighboring tenements glimmering across the street. The house probably seemed to her adrift on the great ocean of the night. A little parallelogram of sky was all that she had hitherto known of nature, so that she felt the awfulness that really exists in its limitless extent. Once, while the blast was bellowing, she caught hold of Zenobia's robe, with precisely the air of one who hears her own name spoken at a distance, but is unutterably reluctant to obey the call.

We spent rather an incommunicative evening. Hollingsworth hardly said a word, unless when repeatedly and pertinaciously addressed. Then, indeed, he would glare upon us from the thick shrubbery of his meditations like a tiger out of a jungle, make the briefest reply possible, and betake himself back into the solitude of his heart and mind. The poor fellow had contracted this ungracious habit from the intensity with which he contemplated his own ideas, and the infrequent sympathy which they met with from his auditors,—a circumstance that seemed only to strengthen the implicit confidence that he awarded to them. His heart, I imagine, was never really interested in our socialist scheme, but was forever busy with his strange, and, as most people thought it, impracticable plan, for the reformation of criminals through an appeal to their higher instincts. Much as I liked Hollingsworth, it cost me many a groan to tolerate him on this point. He ought to have commenced his investigation of the subject by perpetrating some huge sin in his proper person, and examining the condition of his higher instincts afterwards.

The rest of us formed ourselves into a committee for providing our infant community with an appropriate name,—a matter of greatly more difficulty than the uninitiated reader would suppose. Blithedale was neither good nor bad. We should have resumed the old Indian name of the premises, had it possessed the oil-and-honey flow which the aborigines were so often happy in communicating to their local appellations; but it chanced to be a harsh, ill-connected, and interminable word, which seemed to fill the mouth with a mixture of very stiff clay and very crumbly pebbles. Zenobia suggested "Sunny Glimpse," as expressive of a vista into a better system of society. This we turned over and over, for a while, acknowledging its prettiness, but concluded it to be rather too fine and sentimental a name (a fault inevitable by literary ladies, in such attempts) for sunburnt men to work under. I ventured to whisper "Utopia," which, however, was unanimously scouted down, and the proposer very harshly maltreated, as if he had intended a latent satire. Some were for calling our institution "The Oasis," in view of its being the one green spot in the moral sand-waste of the world; but others insisted on a proviso for reconsidering the matter at a twelvemonth's end, when a final decision might be had, whether to name it "The Oasis," or "Sahara." So, at last, finding it impracticable to hammer out anything better, we resolved that the spot should still be Blithedale, as being of good augury enough.

The evening wore on, and the outer solitude looked in upon us through the windows, gloomy, wild, and vague, like another state of existence, close beside the little sphere of warmth and light in which we were the prattlers and bustlers of a moment. By and by, the door was opened by Silas Foster, with a cotton handkerchief about his head, and a tallow-candle in his hand.

"Take my advice, brother farmers," said he, with a great, broad, bottomless yawn, "and get to bed as soon as you can. I shall sound the horn at daybreak; and we've got the cattle to fodder, and nine cows to milk, and a dozen other things to do, before breakfast."

Thus ended the first evening at Blithedale. I went shivering to my fireless chamber, with the miserable consciousness (which had been growing upon me for several hours past) that I had caught a tremendous cold, and should probably awaken, at the blast of the horn, a fit subject for a hospital. The night proved a feverish one. During the greater part of it, I was in that vilest of states when a fixed idea remains in the mind, like the nail in Sisera's brain, while innumerable other ideas go and come, and flutter to and fro, combining constant transition with intolerable sameness. Had I made a record of that night's half-waking dreams, it is my belief that it would have anticipated several of the chief incidents of this narrative, including a dim shadow of its catastrophe. Starting up in bed, at length, I saw that the storm was past, and the moon was shining on the snowy landscape, which looked like a lifeless copy of the world in marble.

From the bank of the distant river, which was shimmering in the moonlight, came the black shadow of the only cloud in heaven, driven swiftly by the wind, and passing over meadow and hillock, vanishing amid tufts of leafless trees, but reappearing on the hither side, until it swept across our doorstep.

How cold an Arcadia was this!

## VI

### COVERDALE'S SICK-CHAMBER

THE horn sounded at daybreak, as Silas Foster had forewarned us, harsh, uproarious, inexorably drawn out, and as sleep-dispelling as if this hard-hearted old yeoman had got hold of the trump of doom.

On all sides I could hear the creaking of the bedsteads, as the brethren of Blithedale started from slumber, and thrust themselves into their habiliments, all awry, no doubt, in their haste to begin the reformation of the world. Zenobia put her head into the entry, and besought Silas Foster to cease his clamor, and to be kind enough to leave an armful of firewood and a pail of water at her chamber-door. Of the whole household,—unless, indeed, it were Priscilla, for whose habits, in this particular, I cannot vouch,—of all our apostolic society, whose mission was to bless mankind, Hollingsworth, I apprehend, was the only one who began the enterprise with prayer. My sleeping-room being but thinly partitioned from his, the solemn murmur of his voice made its way to my ears, compelling me to be an auditor of his awful privacy with the Creator. It affected me with a deep reverence for Hollingsworth, which no familiarity then existing, or that afterwards grew more intimate between us,—no, nor my subsequent perception of his own great errors,—ever quite effaced. It is so rare, in these times, to meet with a man of prayerful habits (except, of course, in the pulpit), that such an one is decidedly marked out by a light of transfiguration, shed upon him in the divine interview from which he passes into his daily life.

As for me, I lay abed; and if I said my prayers, it was backward, cursing my day as bitterly as patient Job himself. The truth was, the hot-house warmth of a town residence, and the luxurious life in which I indulged myself, had taken much of the pith out of my physical system; and the wintry blast of the preceding day, together with the general chill of our airy old farm-house, had got fairly into my heart and the marrow of my bones. In this predicament, I seriously wished—selfish as it may appear—that the reformation of society had been postponed about half a century, or, at all events, to such a date as should have put my intermeddling with it entirely out of the question.

What, in the name of common-sense, had I to do with any better society than I had always lived in? It had satisfied me well enough. My pleasant bachelor-parlor, sunny and shadowy, curtained and carpeted, with the bedchamber adjoining; my centre-table, strewn with books and periodicals; my writing-desk with a half-finished poem, in a stanza of my own contrivance; my morning lounge at the reading-room or picture-gallery; my noontide walk along the cheery pavement, with the suggestive succession of human faces, and the brisk throb of human life, in which I shared; my dinner at the Albion, where I had a hundred dishes at command, and could banquet as delicately as the wizard Michael Scott when the Devil fed him from the king of France's kitchen; my evening at the billiard-club, the concert, the theatre, or at somebody's party, if I pleased,—what could be better than all this? Was it better to hoe, to mow, to toil and moil amidst the accumulations of a barnyard; to be the chambermaid of two yoke of oxen and a dozen cows; to eat salt beef, and earn it with the sweat of my brow, and thereby take the tough morsel out of some wretch's mouth, into whose vocation I had thrust myself? Above all, was it better to have a fever and die blaspheming, as I was like to do?

In this wretched plight, with a furnace in my heart, and another in my head, by the heat of which I was kept constantly at the boiling point, yet shivering at the bare idea of extruding so much as a finger into the icy atmosphere of the room, I kept my bed until breakfast-time, when Hollingsworth knocked at the door, and entered.

"Well, Coverdale," cried he, "you bid fair to make an admirable farmer! Don't you mean to get up to-day?"

"Neither to-day nor to-morrow," said I, hopelessly. "I doubt if I ever rise again!"

"What is the matter, now?" he asked.

I told him my piteous case, and besought him to send me back to town in a close carriage.

"No, no!" said Hollingsworth, with kindly seriousness. "If you are really sick, we must take care of you."

Accordingly, he built a fire in my chamber, and, having little else to do while the snow lay on the ground, established himself as my nurse. A doctor was sent for, who, being homœopathic, gave me as much medicine, in the course of a fortnight's attendance, as would have laid on the point of a needle. They fed me on water-gruel, and I speedily became a skeleton above ground. But, after all, I have many precious recollections connected with that fit of sickness.

Hollingsworth's more than brotherly attendance gave me inexpressible comfort. Most men—and certainly I could not always claim to be one of the exceptions—have a natural indifference, if not an absolutely hostile feeling, towards those whom disease, or weakness, or calamity of any kind causes to falter and faint amid the rude jostle of our selfish existence. The education of Christianity, it is true, the sympathy of a like experience and the example of women, may soften, and, possibly, subvert this ugly characteristic of our sex; but it is originally there, and has likewise its analogy in the practice of our brute brethren, who hunt the sick or disabled member of the herd from among them, as an enemy. It is for this reason that the stricken deer goes apart, and the sick lion grimly withdraws himself into his den. Except in love, or the attachments of kindred, or other very long and habitual affection, we really have no tenderness. But there was something of the woman moulded into the great, stalwart frame of Hollingsworth; nor was he ashamed of it, as men often are of what is best in them, nor seemed ever to know that there was such a soft place in his heart. I knew it well, however, at that time, although afterwards it came nigh to be forgotten. Methought there could not be two such men alive as Hollingsworth. There never was any blaze of a fireside that warmed and cheered me, in the down-sinkings and shiverings of my spirit, so effectually as did the light out of those eyes, which lay so deep and dark under his shaggy brows.

Happy the man that has such a friend beside him when he comes to die! and unless a friend like Hollingsworth be at hand,—as most probably there will not,—he had better make up his mind to die alone. How many men, I wonder, does one meet with in a lifetime, whom he would choose for his death-bed companions! At the crisis of my fever, I besought Hollingsworth to let nobody else enter the room, but continually to make me sensible of his own presence, by a grasp of the hand, a word, a prayer, if he thought good to utter it; and that then he should be the witness how courageously I would encounter the worst. It still impresses me as almost a matter of regret that I did not die then, when I had tolerably made up my mind to it; for Hollingsworth would have gone with me to the hither verge of life, and have sent his friendly and hopeful accents far over on the other side, while I should be treading the unknown path. Now, were I to send for him, he would be hardly come to my bedside, nor should I depart the easier for his presence.

"You are not going to die, this time," said he, gravely smiling. "You know nothing about sickness, and think your case a great deal more desperate than it is."

"Death should take me while I am in the mood," replied I, with a little of my customary levity.

"Have you nothing to do in life," asked Hollingsworth, "that you fancy yourself so ready to leave it?"

"Nothing," answered I; "nothing that I know of, unless to make pretty verses, and play a part, with Zenobia and the rest of the amateurs, in our pastoral. It seems but an unsubstantial sort of business, as viewed through a mist of fever. But, dear Hollingsworth, your own vocation is evidently to be a priest, and to spend your days and nights in helping your fellow-creatures to draw peaceful dying breaths."

"And by which of my qualities," inquired he, "can you suppose me fitted for this awful ministry?"

"By your tenderness," I said. "It seems to me the reflection of God's own love."

"And you call me tender!" repeated Hollingsworth, thoughtfully. "I should rather say that the most marked trait in my character is an inflexible severity of purpose. Mortal man has no right to be so inflexible as it is my nature and necessity to be."

"I do not believe it," I replied.

But, in due time, I remembered what he said.

Probably, as Hollingsworth suggested, my disorder was never so serious as, in my ignorance of such matters, I was inclined to consider it. After so much tragical preparation, it was positively rather mortifying to find myself on the mending hand.

All the other members of the Community showed me kindness, according to the full measure of their capacity. Zenobia brought me my gruel, every day, made by her own hands (not very skilfully, if the truth must be told), and whenever I seemed inclined to converse, would sit by my bedside, and talk with so much vivacity as to add several gratuitous throbs to my pulse. Her poor little stories and tracts never half did justice to her intellect. It was only the lack of a fitter avenue that drove her to seek development in literature. She was made (among a thousand other things that she might have been) for a stump-oratress. I recognized no severe culture in Zenobia; her mind was full of weeds. It startled me sometimes, in my state of moral as well as bodily faint-heartedness, to observe the hardihood of her philosophy. She made no scruple of oversetting all human institutions, and scattering them as with a breeze from her fan. A female reformer, in her attacks upon society, has an instinctive sense of where the life lies, and is inclined to aim directly at that spot. Especially the relation between the sexes is naturally among the earliest to attract her notice.

Zenobia was truly a magnificent woman. The homely simplicity of her dress could not conceal, nor scarcely diminish, the queenliness of her presence. The image of her form and face should have been multiplied all over the earth. It was wronging the rest of mankind to retain her as the spectacle of only a few. The stage would have been her proper sphere. She should have made it a point of duty, moreover, to sit endlessly to painters and sculptors, and preferably to the latter; because the cold decorum of the marble would consist with the utmost scantiness of drapery, so that the eye might chastely be gladdened with her material perfection in its entirety. I know not well how to express, that the native glow of coloring in her cheeks, and even the flesh-warmth over her round arms, and what was visible of her full bust,—in a word, her womanliness incarnated,—compelled me sometimes to close my eyes, as if it were not quite the privilege of modesty to gaze at her. Illness and exhaustion, no doubt, had made me morbidly sensitive.

I noticed—and wondered how Zenobia contrived it—that she had always a new flower in her hair. And still it was a hot-house flower,—an outlandish flower,—a flower of the tropics, such as appeared to have sprung passionately out of a soil the very weeds of which would be fervid and spicy. Unlike as was the flower of each successive day to the preceding one, it yet so assimilated its richness to the rich beauty of the woman, that I thought it the only flower fit to be worn; so fit, indeed, that Nature had evidently created this floral gem, in a happy exuberance, for the one purpose of worthily adorning Zenobia's head. It might be that my feverish fantasies clustered themselves about this peculiarity, and caused it to look more gorgeous and wonderful than if beheld with temperate eyes. In the height of my illness, as I well recollect, I went so far as to pronounce it preternatural.

"Zenobia is an enchantress!" whispered I once to Hollingsworth. "She is a sister of the Veiled Lady. That flower in her hair is a talisman. If you were to snatch it away, she would vanish, or be transformed into something else."

"What does he say?" asked Zenobia.

"Nothing that has an atom of sense in it," answered Hollingsworth. "He is a little beside himself, I believe, and talks about your being a witch, and of some magical property in the flower that you wear in your hair."

"It is an idea worthy of a feverish poet," said she, laughing rather compassionately, and taking out the flower. "I scorn to owe anything to magic. Here, Mr. Hollingsworth, you may keep the spell while it has any virtue in it; but I cannot promise you not to appear with a new one tomorrow. It is the one relic of my more brilliant, my happier days!"

The most curious part of the matter was, that long after my slight delirium had passed away,—as long, indeed, as I continued to know this remarkable woman,—her daily flower affected my imagination, though more slightly, yet in very much the same way. The reason must have been that, whether intentionally on her part or not, this favorite ornament was actually a subtile expression of Zenobia's character.

One subject, about which—very impertinently, moreover—I perplexed myself with a great many conjectures, was, whether Zenobia had ever been married. The idea, it must be understood, was unauthorized by any circumstance or suggestion that had made its way to my ears. So young as I beheld her, and the freshest and rosiest woman of a thousand, there was certainly no need of imputing to her a destiny already accomplished; the probability was far greater that her coming years had all life's richest gifts to bring. If the great event of a woman's existence had been consummated, the world knew nothing of it, although the world seemed to know Zenobia well. It was a ridiculous piece of romance, undoubtedly, to imagine that this beautiful personage, wealthy as she was, and holding a position that might fairly enough be called distinguished, could have given herself away so privately, but that some whisper and suspicion, and, by degrees, a full understanding of the fact, would eventually be blown abroad. But then, as I failed not to consider, her original home was at a distance of many hundred miles. Rumors might fill the social atmosphere, or might once have filled it, there, which would travel but slowly, against the wind, towards our Northeastern metropolis, and perhaps melt into thin air before reaching it.

There was not—and I distinctly repeat it—the slightest foundation in my knowledge for any surmise of the kind. But there is a species of intuition,—either a spiritual lie, or the subtile recognition of a fact,—which comes to us in a reduced state of the corporeal system. The soul gets the better of the body, after wasting illness, or when a vegetable diet may have mingled too much ether in the blood. Vapors then rise up to the brain, and take shapes that often image falsehood, but sometimes truth. The spheres of our companions have, at such periods, a vastly greater influence upon our own than when robust health gives us a repellent and self-defensive energy. Zenobia's sphere, I imagine, impressed itself powerfully on mine, and transformed me, during this period of my weakness, into something like a mesmerical clairvoyant.

Then, also, as anybody could observe, the freedom of her deportment (though, to some tastes, it might commend itself as the utmost perfection of manner in a youthful widow or a blooming matron) was not exactly maiden-like. What girl had ever laughed as Zenobia did? What girl had ever spoken in her mellow tones? Her unconstrained and inevitable manifestation, I said often to myself, was that of a woman to whom wedlock had thrown wide the gates of mystery. Yet sometimes I strove to be ashamed of these conjectures. I acknowledged it as a masculine grossness —a sin of wicked interpretation, of which man is often guilty towards the other sex—thus to mistake the sweet, liberal, but womanly frankness of a noble and generous disposition. Still, it was of no avail to reason with myself nor to upbraid myself. Pertinaciously the thought, "Zenobia is a wife; Zenobia has lived and loved! There is no folded petal, no latent dew-drop, in this perfectly developed rose!"—irresistibly that thought drove out all other conclusions, as often as my mind reverted to the subject.

Zenobia was conscious of my observation, though not, I presume, of the point to which it led me.

"Mr. Coverdale," said she one day, as she saw me watching her, while she arranged my gruel on the table, "I have been exposed to a great deal of eye-shot in the few years of my mixing in the world, but never, I think, to precisely such glances as you are in the habit of favoring me with. I seem to interest you very much; and yet—or else a woman's instinct is for once deceived—I cannot reckon you as an admirer. What are you seeking to discover in me?"

"The mystery of your life," answered I, surprised into the truth by the unexpectedness of her attack. "And you will never tell me."

She bent her head towards me, and let me look into her eyes, as if challenging me to drop a plummet-line down into the depths of her consciousness.

"I see nothing now," said I, closing my own eyes, "unless it be the face of a sprite laughing at me from the bottom of a deep well."

A bachelor always feels himself defrauded, when he knows or suspects that any woman of his acquaintance has given herself away. Otherwise, the matter could have been no concern of mine. It was purely speculative, for I should not, under any circumstances, have fallen in love with Zenobia. The riddle made me so nervous, however, in my sensitive condition of mind and body, that I most ungratefully began to wish that she would let me alone. Then, too, her gruel was very wretched stuff, with almost invariably the smell of pine smoke upon it, like the evil taste that is said to mix itself up with a witch's best concocted dainties. Why could not she have allowed one of the other women to take the gruel in charge? Whatever else might be her gifts, Nature certainly never intended Zenobia for a cook. Or, if so, she should have meddled only with the richest and spiciest dishes, and such as are to be tasted at banquets, between draughts of intoxicating wine.

## VII

### THE CONVALESCENT

As soon as my incommodities allowed me to think of past occurrences, I failed not to inquire what had become of the odd little guest whom Hollingsworth had been the medium of introducing among us. It now appeared that poor Priscilla had not so literally fallen out of the clouds, as we were at first inclined to suppose. A letter, which should have introduced her, had since been received from one of the city missionairies, containing a certificate of character, and an allusion to circumstances which, in the writer's judgment, made it especially desirable that she should find shelter in our Community. There was a hint, not very intelligible, implying either that Priscilla had recently escaped from some particular peril or irksomeness of position, or else that she was still liable to this danger or difficulty, whatever it might be. We should ill have deserved the reputation of a benevolent fraternity, had we hesitated to entertain a petitioner in such need, and so strongly recommended to our kindness; not to mention, moreover, that the strange maiden had set herself diligently to work, and was doing good service with her needle. But a slight mist of uncertainty still floated about Priscilla, and kept her, as yet, from taking a very decided place among creatures of flesh and blood.

The mysterious attraction, which, from her first entrance on our scene, she evinced for Zenobia, had lost nothing of its force. I often heard her footsteps, soft and low, accompanying the light but decided tread of the latter up the staircase, stealing along the passage-way by her new friend's side, and pausing while Zenobia entered my chamber. Occasionally, Zenobia would be a little annoyed by Priscilla's too close attendance. In an authoritative and not very kindly tone, she would advise her to breathe the pleasant air in a walk, or to go with her work into the barn, holding out half a promise to come and sit on the hay with her, when at leisure.

Evidently, Priscilla found but scanty requital for her love. Hollingsworth was likewise a great favorite with her. For several minutes together, sometimes, while my auditory nerves retained the susceptibility of delicate health, I used to hear a low, pleasant murmur, ascending from the room below; and at last ascertained it to be Priscilla's voice, babbling like a little brook to Hollingsworth. She talked more largely and freely with him than with Zenobia, towards whom, indeed, her feelings seemed not so much to be confidence as involuntary affection. I should have thought all the better of my own qualities had Priscilla marked me out for the third place in her regards. But, though she appeared to like me tolerably well, I could never flatter myself with being distinguished by her as Hollingsworth and Zenobia were.

One forenoon, during my convalescence, there came a gentle tap at my chamber-door. I immediately said, "Come in, Priscilla!" with an acute sense of the applicant's identity. Nor was I deceived. It was really Priscilla,—a pale, large-eyed little woman (for she had gone far enough into her teens to be, at least, on the outer limit of girlhood), but much less wan than at my previous view of her, and far better conditioned both as to health and spirits. As I first saw her, she had reminded me of plants that one sometimes observes doing their best to vegetate among the bricks of an enclosed court, where there is scanty soil, and never any sunshine. At present, though with no approach to bloom, there were indications that the girl had human blood in her veins.

Priscilla came softly to my bedside, and held out an article of snow-white linen, very carefully and smoothly ironed. She did not seem bashful, nor anywise embarrassed. My weakly condition, I suppose, supplied a medium in which she could approach me.

"Do not you need this?" asked she. "I have made it for you."

It was a nightcap!

"My dear Priscilla," said I, smiling, "I never had on a nightcap in my life! But perhaps it will be better for me to wear one, now that I am a miserable invalid. How admirably you have done it! No, no; I never can think of wearing such an exquisitely wrought nightcap as this, unless it be in the daytime, when I sit up to receive company."

"It is for use, not beauty," answered Priscilla. "I could have embroidered it, and made it much prettier if I pleased."

While holding up the nightcap, and admiring the fine needlework, I perceived that Priscilla had a sealed letter, which she was waiting for me to take. It had arrived from the village post-office that morning. As I did not immediately offer to receive the letter, she drew it back, and held it against her bosom, with both hands clasped over it, in a way that had probably grown habitual to her. Now, on turning my eyes from the nightcap to Priscilla, it forcibly struck me that her air, though not her figure, and the expression of her face, but not its features, had a resemblance to what I had often seen in a friend of mine, one of the most gifted women of the age. I cannot describe it. The points easiest to convey to the reader were, a certain curve of the shoulders, and a partial closing of the eyes, which seemed to look more penetratingly into my own eyes, through the narrowed apertures, than if they had been open at full width. It was a singular anomaly of likeness coexisting with perfect dissimilitude.

"Will you give me the letter, Priscilla?" said I.

She started, put the letter into my hand, and quite lost the look that had drawn my notice.

"Priscilla," I inquired, "did you ever see Miss Margaret Fuller?"

"No," she answered.

"Because," said I, "you reminded me of her, just now; and it happens, strangely enough, that this very letter is from her."

Priscilla, for whatever reason, looked very much discomposed.

"I wish people would not fancy such odd things in me!" she said, rater petulantly. "How could I possibly make myself resemble this lady, merely by holding her letter in my hand?"

"Certainly, Priscilla, it would puzzle me to explain it," I replied; "nor do I suppose that the letter had anything to do with it. It was just a coincidence, nothing more."

She hastened out of the room, and this was the last that I saw of Priscilla until I ceased to be an invalid.

Being much alone, during my recovery, I read interminably in Mr. Emerson's Essays, "The Dial," Carlyle's works, George Sand's romances (lent me by Zenobia), and other books which one or another of the brethren or sisterhood had brought with them. Agreeing in little else, most of these utterances were like the cry of some solitary sentinel, whose station was on the outposts of the advance-guard of human progression; or, sometimes, the voice came sadly from among the shattered ruins of the past, but yet had a hopeful echo in the future. They were well adapted (better, at least, than any other intellectual products, the volatile essence of which had heretofore tinctured a printed page) to pilgrims like ourselves, whose present bivouac was considerably further into the waste of chaos than any mortal army of crusaders had ever marched before. Fourier's works, also, in a series of horribly tedious volumes, attracted a good deal of my attention, from the analogy which I could not but recognize between his system and our own. There was far less resemblance, it is true, than the world chose to imagine, inasmuch as the two theories differed, as widely as the zenith from the nadir, in their main principles.

I talked about Fourier to Hollingsworth, and translated, for his benefit, some of the passages that chiefly impressed me.

"When, as a consequence of human improvement," said I, "the globe shall arrive at its final perfection, the great ocean is to be converted into a particular kind of lemonade, such as was fashionable at Paris in Fourier's time. He calls it *limonade à cèdre*. It is positively a fact! Just imagine the city-docks filled, every day, with a flood-tide of this delectable beverage!"

"Why did not the Frenchman make punch of it, at once?" asked Hollingsworth. "The jack-tars would be delighted to go down in ships and do business in such an element."

I further proceeded to explain, as well as I modestly could, several points of Fourier's system, illustrating them with here and there a page or two, and asking Hollingsworth's opinion as to the expediency of introducing these beautiful peculiarities into our own practice.

"Let me hear no more of it!" cried he, in utter disgust. "I never will forgive this fellow! He has committed the unpardonable sin; for what more monstrous iniquity could the Devil himself contrive than to choose the selfish principle,—the principle of all human wrong, the very blackness of man's heart, the portion of ourselves which we shudder at, and which it is the whole aim of spiritual discipline to eradicate,—to choose it as the master-workman of his system? To seize upon and foster whatever vile, petty, sordid, filthy, bestial, and abominable corruptions have cankered into our nature, to be the efficient instruments of his infernal regeneration! And his consummated Paradise, as he pictures it, would be worthy of the agency which he counts upon for establishing it. The nauseous villain!"

"Nevertheless," remarked I, "in consideration of the promised delights of his system,—so very proper, as they certainly are, to be appreciated by Fourier's countrymen,—I cannot but wonder that universal France did not adopt his theory, at a moment's warning. But is there not something very characteristic of his nation in Fourier's manner of putting forth his view? He makes no claim to inspiration. He has not persuaded himself— as Swedenborg did, and as any other than a Frenchman would, with a mission of like importance to communicate—that he speaks with authority from above. He promulgates his system, so far as I can perceive, entirely on his own responsibility. He has searched out and discovered the whole counsel of the Almighty, in respect to mankind, past, present, and for exactly seventy thousand years to come, by the mere force and cunning of his individual intellect!"

"Take the book out of my sight," said Hollingsworth, with great virulence of expression, "or, I tell you fairly, I shall fling it in the fire! And as for Fourier, let him make a Paradise, if he can, of Gehenna, where, as I conscientiously believe, he is floundering at this moment!"

"And bellowing, I suppose," said I,—not that I felt any ill-will towards Fourier, but merely wanted to give the finishing touch to Hollingsworth's image,—"bellowing for the least drop of his beloved *limonade à cèdre!*"

There is but little profit to be expected in attempting to argue with a man who allows himself to declaim in this manner; so I dropt the subject, and never took it up again.

But had the system at which he was so enraged combined almost any amount of human wisdom, spiritual insight, and imaginative beauty, I question whether Hollingsworth's mind was in a fit condition to receive it. I began to discern that he had come among us actuated by no real sympathy with our feelings and our hopes, but chiefly because we were estranging ourselves from the world, with which his lonely and exclusive object in life had already put him at odds. Hollingsworth must have been originally endowed with a great spirit of benevolence, deep enough and warm enough to be the source of as much disinterested good as Provi- dence often allows a human being the privilege of conferring upon his fel- lows. This native instinct yet lived within him. I myself had profited by it, in my necessity. It was seen, too, in his treatment of Priscilla. Such casual circumstances as were here involved would quicken his divine power of sympathy, and make him seem, while their influence lasted, the tenderest man and the truest friend on earth. But, by and by, you missed the tenderness of yesterday, and grew drearily conscious that Hollings- worth had a closer friend than ever you could be; and this friend was the cold, spectral monster which he had himself conjured up, and on which he was wasting all the warmth of his heart, and of which, at last,—as these men of a mighty purpose so invariably do,—he had grown to be the bond-slave. It was his philanthropic theory.

This was a result exceedingly sad to contemplate, considering that it had been mainly brought about by the very ardor and exuberance of his philanthropy. Sad, indeed, but by no means unusual: he had taught his benevolence to pour its warm tide exclusively through one channel; so that there was nothing to spare for other great manifestations of love to man, nor scarcely for the nutriment of individual attachments, unless they could minister, in some way, to the terrible egotism which he mis- took for an angel of God. Had Hollingsworth's education been more en- larged, he might not so inevitably have stumbled into this pitfall. But this identical pursuit had educated him. He knew absolutely nothing, except in a single direction, where he had thought so energetically, and felt to such a debt, that, no doubt, the entire reason and justice of the universe appeared to be concentrated thitherward.

It is my private opinion that, at this period of his life, Hollingsworth was fast going mad; and, as with other crazy people (among whom I in- clude humorists of every degree), it required all the constancy of friend- ship to restrain his associates from pronouncing him an intolerable bore. Such prolonged fiddling upon one string,—such multiform presentation of one idea! His specific object (of which he made the public more than suf- ficiently aware, through the medium of lectures and pamphlets) was to obtain funds for the construction of an edifice, with a sort of collegiate endowment. On this foundation, he purposed to devote himself and a few disciples to the reform and mental culture of our criminal brethren. His visionary edifice was Hollingsworth's one castle in the air; it was the ma- terial type in which his philanthropic dream strove to embody itself; and he made the scheme more definite, and caught hold of it the more strong- ly, and kept his clutch the more pertinaciously, by rendering it visible to the bodily eye. I have seen him, a hundred times, with a pencil and sheet of paper, sketching the facade, the side-view, or the rear of the structure, or planning the internal arrangements, as lovingly as another man might plan those of the projected home where he meant to be happy with his wife and children. I have known him to begin a model of the building with little stones, gathered at the brook-side, whither we had gone to cool ourselves in the sultry noon of haying-time. Unlike all other ghosts, his spirit haunted an edifice, which, instead of being time-worn, and full of storied love, and joy, and sorrow, had never yet come into existence.

"Dear friend," said I, once, to Hollingsworth, before leaving my sick-chamber, "I heartily wish that I could make your schemes my schemes, because it would be so great a happiness to find myself treading the same path with you. But I am afraid there is not stuff in me stern enough for a philanthropist,—or not in this peculiar direction,—or, at all events, not solely in this. Can you bear with me, if such should prove to be the case?"

"I will at least wait awhile," answered Hollingsworth, gazing at me sternly and gloomily. "But how can you be my life-long friend, except you strive with me towards the great object of my life?"

Heaven forgive me! A horrible suspicion crept into my heart, and stung the very core of it as with the fangs of an adder. I wondered whether it were possible that Hollingsworth could have watched by my bedside, with all that devoted care, only for the ulterior purpose of making me a proselyte to his views!

## VIII

## A MODERN ARCADIA

MAY-DAY—I forget whether by Zenobia's sole decree, or by the unanimous vote of our community—had been declared a movable festival. It was deferred until the sun should have had a reasonable time to clear away the snow-drifts along the lee of the stone walls, and bring out a few of the readiest wild-flowers. On the forenoon of the substituted day, after admitting some of the balmy air into my chamber, I decided that it was nonsense and effeminacy to keep myself a prisoner any longer. So I descended to the sitting-room, and finding nobody there, proceeded to the barn, whence I had already heard Zenobia's voice, and along with it a girlish laugh, which was not so certainly recognizable. Arriving at the spot it a little surprised me to discover that these merry outbreaks came from Priscilla.

The two had been a-maying together. They had found anemones in abundance, houstonias by the handful, some columbines, a few long-stalked violets, and a quantity of white everlasting-flowers, and had filled up their basket with the delicate spray of shrubs and trees. None were prettier than the maple-twigs, the leaf of which looks like a scarlet bud in May, and like a plate of vegetable gold in October. Zenobia, who showed no conscience in such matters, had also rifled a cherry-tree of one of its blossomed boughs, and, with all this variety of sylvan ornament, had been decking out Priscilla. Being done with a good deal of taste, it made her look more charming than I should have thought possible, with my recollection of the wan, frost-nipt girl, as heretofore described. Nevertheless, among those fragrant blossoms, and conspicuously, too, had been stuck a weed of evil odor and ugly aspect, which, as soon as I detected it, destroyed the effect of all the rest. There was a gleam of latent mischief —not to call it deviltry—in Zenobia's eye, which seemed to indicate a slightly malicious purpose in the arrangement.

As for herself, she scorned the rural buds and leaflets, and wore nothing but her invariable flower of the tropics.

"What do you think of Priscilla now, Mr. Coverdale?" asked she, surveying her as a child does its doll. "Is not she worth a verse or two?"

"There is only one thing amiss," answered I.

Zenobia laughed, and flung the malignant weed away.

"Yes; she deserves some verses now," said I, "and from a better poet than myself. She is the very picture of the New England spring; subdued in tint, and rather cool, but with a capacity of sunshine, and bringing us a few Alpine blossoms, as earnest of something richer, though hardly more beautiful, hereafter. The best type of her is one of those anemones."

"What I find most singular in Priscilla, as her health improves," observed Zenobia, "is her wildness. Such a quiet little body as she seemed, one would not have expected that. Why, as we strolled the woods together, I could hardly keep her from scrambling up the trees, like a squirrel. She has never before known what it is to live in the free air, and so it intoxicates her as if she were sipping wine. And she thinks it such a paradise here, and all of us, particularly Mr. Hollingsworth and myself, such angels! It is quite ridiculous, and provokes one's malice, almost, to see a creature so happy—especially a feminine creature."

"They are always happier than male creatures," said I.

"You must correct that opinion, Mr. Coverdale," replied Zenobia contemptuously, "or I shall think you lack the poetic insight. Did you ever see a happy woman in your life? Of course, I do not mean a girl, like Priscilla, and a thousand others,—for they are all alike, while on the sunny side of experience,—but a grown woman. How can she be happy, after discovering that fate has assigned her but one single event, which she must contrive to make the substance of her whole life? A man has his choice of innumerable events."

"A woman, I suppose," answered I, "by constant repetition of her one event, may compensate for the lack of variety."

"Indeed!" said Zenobia.

While we were talking, Priscilla caught sight of Hollingsworth, at a distance, in a blue frock, and with a hoe over his shoulder, returning from the field. She immediately set out to meet him, running and skipping, with spirits as light as the breeze of the May morning, but with limbs too little exercised to be quite responsive; she clapped her hands, too, with great exuberance of gesture, as is the custom of young girls when their electricity overcharges them. But, all at once, midway to Hollingsworth, she paused, looked round about her, towards the river, the road, the woods, and back towards us, appearing to listen, as if she heard some one calling her name, and knew not precisely in what direction.

"Have you bewitched her?" I exclaimed.

"It is no sorcery of mine," said Zenobia; "but I have seen the girl do that identical thing once or twice before. Can you imagine what is the matter with her?"

"No; unless," said I, "she has the gift of hearing those 'airy tongues that syllable men's names,' which Milton tells about."

From whatever cause, Priscilla's animation seemed entirely to have deserted her. She seated herself on a rock, and remained there until Hollingsworth came up; and when he took her hand and led her back to us, she rather resembled my original image of the wan and spiritless Priscilla than the flowery May-queen of a few moments ago. These sudden transformations, only to be accounted for by an extreme nervous susceptibility, always continued to characterize the girl, though with diminished frequency as her health progressively grew more robust.

I was now on my legs again. My fit of illness had been an avenue between two existences; the low-arched and darksome doorway, through which I crept out of a life of old conventionalisms, on my hands and knees, as it were, and gained admittance into the freer region that lay beyond. In this respect, it was like death. And, as with death, too, it was good to have gone through it. No otherwise could I have rid myself of a thousand follies, fripperies, prejudices, habits, and other such worldly dust as inevitably settles upon the crowd along the broad highway, giving them all one sordid aspect before noon-time, however freshly they may have begun their pilgrimage in the dewy morning. The very substance upon my bones had not been fit to live with in any better, truer, or more energetic mode than that to which I was accustomed. So it was taken off me and flung aside, like any other worn-out or unseasonable garment; and, after shivering a little while in my skeleton, I began to be clothed anew, and much more satisfactorily than in my previous suit. In literal and physical truth, I was quite another man. I had a lively sense of the exultation with which the spirit will enter on the next stage of its eternal progress after leaving the heavy burden of its mortality in an early grave, with as little concern for what may become of it as now affected me for the flesh which I had lost.

Emerging into the genial sunshine, I half fancied that the labors of the brotherhood had already realized some of Fourier's predictions. Their enlightened culture of the soil, and the virtues with which they sanctified their life, had begun to produce an effect upon the material world and its climate. In my new enthusiasm, man looked strong and stately,—and woman, oh how beautiful!—and the earth a green garden, blossoming with many-colored delights. Thus Nature, whose laws I had broken in various artificial ways, comported herself towards me as a strict but loving mother, who uses the rod upon her little boy for his naughtiness, and then gives him a smile, a kiss, and some pretty playthings to console the urchin for her severity.

In the interval of my seclusion, there had been a number of recruits to our little army of saints and martyrs. They were mostly individuals who had gone through such an experience as to disgust them with ordinary pursuits, but who were not yet so old, nor had suffered so deeply, as to lose their faith in the better time to come. On comparing their minds one with another they often discovered that this idea of a Community had been growing up, in silent and unknown sympathy, for years. Thoughtful, strongly lined faces were among them; sombre brows, but eyes that did not require spectacles, unless prematurely dimmed by the student's lamplight, and hair that seldom showed a thread of silver. Age, wedded to the past, incrusted over with a stony layer of habits, and retaining nothing fluid in its possibilities, would have been absurdly out of place in an enterprise like this. Youth, too, in its early dawn, was hardly more adapted to our purpose; for it would behold the morning radiance of its own spirit beaming over the very same spots of withered grass and barren sand whence most of us had seen it vanish. We had very young people with us, it is true,—downy lads, rosy girls in their first teens, and children of all heights above one's knee; but these had chiefly been sent hither for education, which it was one of the objects and methods of our institution to supply. Then we had boarders, from town and elsewhere, who lived with us in a familiar way, sympathized more or less in our theories, and sometimes shared in our labors.

On the whole, it was a society such as has seldom met together; nor, perhaps, could it reasonably be expected to hold together long. Persons of marked individuality—crooked sticks, as some of us might be called— are not exactly the easiest to bind up into a fagot. But, so long as our union should subsist, a man of intellect and feeling, with a free nature in him, might have sought far and near without finding so many points of attraction as would allure him hitherward. We were of all creeds and opinions, and generally tolerant of all, on every imaginable subject. Our bond, it seems to me, was not affirmative, but negative. We had individually found one thing or another to quarrel with in our past life, and were pretty well agreed as to the inexpediency of lumbering along with the old system any further. As to what should be substituted, there was much less unanimity. We did not greatly care—at least, I never did —for the written constitution under which our millennium had commenced. My hope was, that, between theory and practice, a true and available mode of life might be struck out; and that, even should we ultimately fail, the months or years spent in the trial would not have been wasted, either as regarded passing enjoyment, or the experience which makes men wise.

Arcadians though we were, our costume bore no resemblance to the beribboned doublets, silk breeches and stockings, and slippers fastened with artificial roses, that distinguish the pastoral people of poetry and the stage. In outward show, I humbly conceive, we looked rather like a gang of beggars, or banditti, than either a company of honest laboring-men, or a conclave of philosophers. Whatever might be our points of difference, we all of us seemed to have come to Blithedale with the one thrifty and laudable idea of wearing out our old clothes. Such garments as had an airing, whenever we strode afield! Coats with high collars and with no collars, broad-skirted or swallow-tailed, and with the waist at every point between the hip and arm-pit; pantaloons of a dozen successive epochs, and greatly defaced at the knees by the humiliations of the wearer before his lady-love,—in short, we were a living epitome of defunct fashions, and the very raggedest presentment of men who had seen better days. It was gentility in tatters. Often retaining a scholarlike or clerical air, you might have taken us for the denizens of Grub Street, intent on getting a comfortable livelihood by agricultural labor; or, Coleridge's projected Pantisocracy in full experiment; or, Candide and his motley associates at work in their cabbage-garden; or anything else that was miserably out at elbows, and most clumsily patched in the rear. We might have been sworn comrades to Falstaff's ragged regiment. Little skill as we boasted in other points of husbandry, every mother's son of us would have served admirably to stick up for a scarecrow. And the worst of the matter was, that the first energetic movement essential to one downright stroke of real labor was sure to put a finish to these poor habiliments. So we gradually flung them all aside, and took to honest homespun and linsey-woolsey, as preferable, on the whole, to the plan recommended, I think, by Virgil,—"*Ara nudus; sere nudus,*"—which as Silas Foster remarked, when I translated the maxim, would be apt to astonish the women-folks.

After a reasonable training, the yeoman life throve well with us. Our faces took the sunburn kindly; our chests gained in compass, and our shoulders in breadth and squareness; our great brown fists looked as if they had never been capable of kid gloves. The plough, the hoe, the scythe, and the hay-fork grew familiar to our grasp. The oxen responded to our voices. We could do almost as fair a day's work as Silas Foster himself, sleep dreamlessly after it, and awake at daybreak with only a little stiffness of the joints, which was usually quite gone by breakfast-time.

To be sure, our next neighbors pretended to be incredulous as to our real proficiency in the business which we had taken in hand. They told slanderous fables about our inability to yoke our own oxen, or to drive them afield when yoked, or to release the poor brutes from their conjugal bond at nightfall. They had the face to say, too, that the cows laughed at our awkwardness at milking-time, and invariably kicked over the pails; partly in consequence of our putting the stool on the wrong side, and partly because, taking offence at the whisking of their tails, we were in the habit of holding these natural fly-flappers with one hand and milking with the other. They further averred that we hoed up whole acres of Indian corn and other crops, and drew the earth carefully about the weeds; and that we raised five hundred tufts of burdock, mistaking them for cabbages; and that, by dint of unskilful planting few of our seeds ever came up at all, or, if they did come up it was stern-foremost; and that we spent the better part of the month of June in reversing a field of beans, which had thrust themselves out of the ground in this unseemly way. They quoted it as nothing more than an ordinary occurrence for one or other of us to crop off two or three fingers, of a morning, by our clumsy use of the hay-cutter. Finally, and as an ultimate catastrophe, these mendacious rogues circulated a report that we communitarians were exterminated, to the last man, by severing ourselves asunder, with the sweep of our own scythes!—and that the world had lost nothing by this little accident.

But this was pure envy and malice on the part of the neighboring farmers. The peril of our new way of life was not lest we should fail in becoming practical agriculturists, but that we should probably cease to be anything else. While our enterprise lay all in theory, we had pleased ourselves with delectable visions of the spiritualization of labor. It was to be our form of prayer and ceremonial of worship. Each stroke of the hoe was to uncover some aromatic root of wisdom, heretofore hidden from the sun. Pausing in the field, to let the wind exhale the moisture from our foreheads, we were to look upward, and catch glimpses into the far-off soul of truth. In this point of view, matters did not turn out quite so well as we anticipated. It is very true that, sometimes, gazing casually around me, out of the midst of my toil, I used to discern a richer picturesqueness in the visible scene of earth and sky. There was, at such moments, a novelty, an unwonted aspect, on the face of Nature, as if she had been taken by surprise and seen at unawares, with no opportunity to put off her real look, and assume the mask with which she mysteriously hides herself from mortals. But this was all. The clods of earth, which we so constantly belabored and turned over and over, were never etherealized into thought. Our thoughts, on the contrary, were fast becoming cloddish. Our labor symbolized nothing, and left us mentally sluggish in the dusk of the evening. Intellectual activity is incompatible with any large amount of bodily exercise. The yeoman and the scholar—the yeoman and the man of finest moral culture, though not the man of sturdiest sense and integrity—are two distinct individuals, and can never be melted or welded into one substance.

Zenobia soon saw this truth, and gibed me about it, one evening, as Hollingsworth and I lay on the grass, after a hard day's work.

"I am afraid you did not make a song, to-day, while loading the hay-cart," said she, "as Burns did, when he was reaping barley."

"Burns never made a song in haying-time," I answered, very positively. "He was no poet while a farmer, and no farmer while a poet."

"And on the whole, which of the two characters do you like best?" asked Zenobia. "For I have an idea that you cannot combine them any better than Burns did. Ah, I see, in my mind's eye, what sort of an individual you are to be, two or three years hence. Grim Silas Foster is your prototype, with his palm of sole-leather, and his joints of rusty iron (which all through summer keep the stiffness of what he calls his winter's rheumatize), and his brain of—I don't know what his brain is made of, unless it be a Savoy cabbage; but yours may be cauliflower, as a rather more delicate variety. Your physical man will be transmuted into salt beef and friend pork, at the rate, I should imagine, of a pound and a half a day; that being about the average which we find necessary in the kitchen. You will make your toilet for the day (still like this delightful Silas Foster) by rinsing your fingers and the front part of your face in a little tin pan of water at the doorstep, and teasing your hair with a wooden pocket-comb before a seven-by-nine-inch looking-glass. Your only pastime will be to smoke some very vile tobacco in the black stump of a pipe."

"Pray, spare me!" cried I. "But the pipe is not Silas's only mode of solacing himself with the weed."

"Your literature," continued Zenobia, apparently delighted with her description, "will be the 'Farmer's Almanac;' for I observe our friend Foster never gets so far as the newspaper. When you happen to sit down, at odd moments, you will fall asleep, and make nasal proclamation of the fact, as he does; and invariably you must be jogged out of a nap, after supper, by the future Mrs. Coverdale, and persuaded to go regularly to bed. And on Sundays, when you put on a blue coat with brass buttons, you will think of nothing else to do, but to go and lounge over the stone walls and rail fences, and stare at the corn growing. And you will look with a knowing eye at oxen, and will have a tendency to clamber over into pigsties, and feel of the hogs, and give a guess how much they will weigh after you shall have stuck and dressed them. Already I have noticed you begin to speak through your nose, and with a drawl. Pray, if you really did make any poetry to-day, let us hear it in that kind of utterance!"

"Coverdale has given up making verses now," said Hollingsworth, who never had the slightest appreciation of my poetry. "Just think of him penning a sonnet with a fist like that! There is at least this good in a life of toil, that it takes the nonsense and fancy-work out of a man, and leaves nothing but what truly belongs to him. If a farmer can make poetry at the plough-tail, it must be because his nature insists on it; and if that be the case, let him make it, in Heaven's name!"

"And how is it with you?" asked Zenobia, in a different voice; for she never laughed at Hollingsworth, as she often did at me. "You, I think, cannot have ceased to live a life of thought and feeling."

"I have always been in earnest," answered Hollingsworth. "I have hammered thought out of iron, after heating the iron in my heart! It matters little what my outward toil may be. Were I a slave at the bottom of a mine, I should keep the same purpose, the same faith in its ultimate accomplishment, that I do now. Miles Coverdale is not in earnest, either as a poet or a laborer."

"You give me hard measure, Hollingsworth," said I, a little hurt. "I have kept pace with you in the field; and my bones feel as if I had been in earnest, whatever may be the case with my brain!"

"I cannot conceive," observed Zenobia, with great emphasis,—and, no doubt, she spoke fairly the feeling of the moment,—"I cannot conceive of being so continually as Mr. Coverdale is within the sphere of a strong and noble nature, without being strengthened and ennobled by its influence!"

This amiable remark of the fair Zenobia confirmed me in what I had already begun to suspect, that Hollingsworth, like many other illustrious prophets, reformers, and philanthropists, was likely to make at least two proselytes among the women to one among the men. Zenobia and Priscilla! These, I believe (unless my unworthy self might be reckoned for a third), were the only disciples of his mission; and I spent a great deal of time, uselessly, in trying to conjecture what Hollingsworth meant to do with them—and they with him!

## IX

### HOLLINGSWORTH, ZENOBIA, PRISCILLA

IT is not, I apprehend, a healthy kind of mental occupation, to devote ourselves too exclusively to the study of individual men and women. If the person under examination be one's self, the result is pretty certain to be diseased action of the heart, almost before we can snatch a second glance. Or, if we take the freedom to put a friend under our microscope, we thereby insulate him from many of his true relations, magnify his peculiarities, inevitably tear him into parts, and, of course, patch him very clumsily together again. What wonder, then, should we be frightened by the aspect of a monster, which, after all,—though we can point to every feature of his deformity in the real personage,—may be said to have been created mainly by ourselves.

Thus, as my conscience has often whispered me, I did Hollingsworth a great wrong by prying into his character; and am perhaps doing him as great a one, at this moment, by putting faith in the discoveries which I seemed to make. But I could not help it. Had I loved him less, I might have used him better. He and Zenobia and Priscilla—both for their own sakes and as connected with him—were separated from the rest of the Community, to my imagination, and stood forth as the indices of a problem which it was my business to solve. Other associates had a portion of my time; other matters amused me; passing occurrences carried me along with them, while they lasted. But here was the vortex of my meditations, around which they revolved, and whitherward they too continually tended. In the midst of cheerful society, I had often a feeling of loneliness. For it was impossible not to be sensible that, while these three characters figured so largely on my private theatre, I—though probably reckoned as a friend by all—was at best but a secondary or tertiary personage with either of them.

I loved Hollingsworth, as has already been enough expressed. But it impressed me, more and more, that there was a stern and dreadful peculiarity in this man, such as could not prove otherwise than pernicious to the happiness of those who should be drawn into too intimate a connection with him. He was not altogether human. There was something else in Hollingsworth besides flesh and blood, and sympathies and affections and celestial spirit.

This is always true of those men who have surrendered themselves to an overruling purpose. It does not so much impel them from without, nor even operate as a motive power within, but grows incorporate with all that they think and feel, and finally converts them into little else save that one principle. When such begins to be the predicament, it is not cowardice, but wisdom to avoid these victims. They have no heart, no sympathy, no reason, no conscience. They will keep no friend, unless he make himself the mirror of their purpose; they will smite and slay you, and trample your dead corpse under foot, all the more readily, if you take the first step with them, and cannot take the second, and the third, and every other step of their terribly strait path. They have an idol to which they consecrate themselves high-priest, and deem it holy work to offer sacrifices of whatever is most precious; and never once seem to suspect—so cunning has the Devil been with them—that this false deity, in whose iron features, immitigable to all the rest of mankind, they see only benignity and love, is but a spectrum of the very priest himself, projected upon the surrounding darkness. And the higher and purer the original object, and the more unselfishly it may have been taken up, the slighter is the probability that they can be led to recognize the process by which godlike benevolence has been debased into all-devouring egotism.

Of course I am perfectly aware that the above statement is exaggerated, in the attempt to make it adequate. Professed philanthropists have gone far; but no originally good man, I presume, ever went quite so far as this. Let the reader abate whatever he deems fit. The paragraph may remain, however, both for its truth and its exaggeration, as strongly expressive of the tendencies which were really operative in Hollingsworth, and as exemplifying the kind of error into which my mode of observation was calculated to lead me. The issue was, that in solitude I often shuddered at my friend. In my recollection of his dark and impressive countenance, the features grew more sternly prominent than the reality, duskier in their depth and shadow, and more lurid in their light; the frown, that had merely flitted across his brow, seemed to have contorted it with an adamantine wrinkle. On meeting him again, I was often filled with remorse, when his deep eyes beamed kindly upon me, as with the glow of a household fire that was burning in a cave. "He is a man after all," thought

I; "his Maker's own truest image, a philanthropic man!—not that steel engine of the Devil's contrivance, a philanthropist!" But in my wood-walks, and in my silent chamber, the dark face frowned at me again.

When a young girl comes within the sphere of such a man, she is as perilously situated as the maiden whom, in the old classical myths, the people used to expose to a dragon. If I had any duty whatever, in reference to Hollingsworth, it was to endeavor to save Priscilla from that kind of personal worship which her sex is generally prone to lavish upon saints and heroes. It often requires but one smile out of the hero's eyes into the girl's or woman's heart, to transform this devotion, from a sentiment of the highest approval and confidence, into passionate love. Now, Hollingsworth smiled much upon Priscilla,—more than upon any other person. If she thought him beautiful, it was no wonder. I often thought him so, with the expression of tender human care and gentlest sympathy which she alone seemed to have power to call out upon his features. Zenobia, I suspect, would have given her eyes, bright as they were, for such a look; it was the least that our poor Priscilla could do, to give her heart for a great many of them. There was the more danger of this, inasmuch as the footing on which we all associated at Blithedale was widely different from that of conventional society. While inclining us to the soft affections of the golden age, it seemed to authorize any individual, of either sex, to fall in love with any other, regardless of what would elsewhere be judged suitable and prudent. Accordingly the tender passion was very rife among us, in various degrees of mildness or virulence, but mostly passing away with the state of things that had given it origin. This was all well enough; but, for a girl like Priscilla and a woman like Zenobia to jostle one another in their love of a man like Hollingsworth, was likely to be no child's play.

Had I been as cold-hearted as I sometimes thought myself, nothing would have interested me more than to witness the play of passions that must thus have been evolved. But, in honest truth, I would really have gone far to save Priscilla, at least, from the catastrophe in which such a drama would be apt to terminate.

Priscilla had now grown to be a very pretty girl, and still kept budding and blossoming, and daily putting on some new charm, which you no sooner became sensible of than you thought it worth all that she had previously possessed. So unformed, vague, and without substance, as she had come to us, it seemed as if we could see Nature shaping out a woman before our very eyes, and yet had only a more reverential sense of the mystery of a woman's soul and frame. Yesterday, her cheek was pale,—to-day, it had a bloom. Priscilla's smile, like a baby's first one, was a wondrous novelty. Her imperfections and short-comings affected me with a kind of playful pathos, which was as absolutely bewitching a sensation as ever I experienced. After she had been a month or two at Blithedale, her animal spirits waxed high, and kept her pretty constantly in a state of bubble and ferment, impelling her to far more bodily activity than she had yet strength to endure. She was very fond of playing with the other girls out of doors. There is hardly another sight in the world so pretty as that of a company of young girls, almost women grown, at play, and so giving themselves up to their airy impulse that their tiptoes barely touch the ground.

Girls are incomparably wilder and more effervescent than boys, more untamable, and regardless of rule and limit, with an ever-shifting variety, breaking continually into new modes of fun, yet with a harmonious propriety through all. Their steps, their voices, appear free as the wind, but keep consonance with a strain of music inaudible to us. Young men and boys, on the other hand, play, according to recognized law, old, traditionary games, permitting no caprioles of fancy, but with scope enough for the outbreak of savage instincts. For, young or old, in play or in earnest, man is prone to be a brute.

Especially is it delightful to see a vigorous young girl run a race, with her head thrown back, her limbs moving more friskily than they need, and an air between that of a bird and a young colt. But Priscilla's peculiar charm, in a foot-race, was the weakness and irregularity with which she ran. Growing up without exercise, except to her poor little fingers, she had never yet acquired the perfect use of her legs. Setting buoyantly forth, therefore, as if no rival less swift than Atalanta could compete with her, she ran falteringly, and often tumbled on the grass. Such an incident —though it seems too slight to think of—was a thing to laugh at, but which brought the water into one's eyes, and lingered in the memory after far greater joys and sorrows were wept out of it, as antiquated trash. Priscilla's life, as I beheld it, was full of trifles that affected me in just this way.

When she had come to be quite at home among us, I used to fancy that Priscilla played more pranks, and perpetrated more mischief, than any other girl in the Community. For example, I once heard Silas Foster, in a very gruff voice, threatening to rivet three horse-shoes round Priscilla's neck and chain her to a post, because she, with some other young people, had clambered upon a load of hay, and caused it to slide off the cart. How she made her peace I never knew; but very soon afterwards I saw old Silas, with his brawny hands round Priscilla's waist, swinging her to and fro, and finally depositing her on one of the oxen, to take her first lessons in riding. She met with terrible mishaps in her efforts to milk a cow; she let the poultry into the garden; she generally spoilt whatever part of the dinner she took in charge; she broke crockery; she dropt our biggest pitcher into the well; and—except with her needle, and those little wooden instruments for purse-making—was as unserviceable a member of society as any young lady in the land. There was no other sort of efficiency about her. Yet everybody was kind to Priscilla; everybody loved her and laughed at her to her face, and did not laugh behind her back; everybody would have given her half of his last crust, or the bigger share of his plum-cake. These were pretty certain indications that we were all conscious of a pleasant weakness in the girl, and considered her not quite able to look after her own interests, or fight her battle with the world. And Hollingsworth—perhaps because he had been the means of introducing Priscilla to her new abode—appeared to recognize her as his own especial charge.

Her simple, careless, childish flow of spirits often made me sad. She seemed to me like a butterfly at play in a flickering bit of sunshine, and mistaking it for a broad and eternal summer. We sometimes hold mirth to a stricter accountability than sorrow; it must show good cause, or the echo of its laughter comes back drearily. Priscilla's gayety, moreover, was of a nature that showed me how delicate an instrument she was, and what fragile harp-strings were her nerves. As they made sweet music at the airiest touch, it would require but a stronger one to burst them all asunder. Absurd as it might be, I tried to reason with her, and persuade her not to be so joyous, thinking that, if she would draw less lavishly upon her fund of happiness, it would last the longer. I remember doing so, one summer evening, when we tired laborers sat looking on, like Goldsmith's old folks under the village thorn-tree, while the young people were at their sports.

"What is the use or sense of being so very gay?" I said to Priscilla, while she was taking breath, after a great frolic. "I love to see a sufficient cause for everything, and I can see none for this. Pray tell me, now, what kind of a world you imagine this to be, which you are so merry in."

"I never think about it at all," answered Priscilla, laughing. "But this I am sure of, that it is a world where everybody is kind to me, and where I love everybody. My heart keeps dancing within me, and all the foolish things which you see me do are only the motions of my heart. How can I be dismal, if my heart will not let me?"

"Have you nothing dismal to remember?" I suggested. "If not, then, indeed, you are very fortunate!"

"Ah!" said Priscilla, slowly.

And then came that unintelligible gesture, when she seemed to be listening to a distant voice.

"For my part," I continued, beneficently seeking to overshadow her with my own sombre humor, "my past life has been a tiresome one enough; yet I would rather look backward ten times than forward once. For, little as we know of our life to come, we may be very sure, for one thing, that the good we aim at will not be attained. People never do get just the good they seek. If it come at all, it is something else, which they never dreamed of, and did not particularly want. Then, again, we may rest certain that our friends of to-day will not be our friends of a few years hence; but, if we keep one of them, it will be at the expense of the others; and, most probably, we shall keep none. To be sure, there are more to be had; but who cares about making a new set of friends, even should they be better than those around us?"

"Not I!" said Priscilla. "I will live and die with these!"

"Well; but let the future go," resumed I. "As for the present moment, if we could look into the hearts where we wish to be most valued, what should you expect to see? One's own likeness, in the innermost, holiest niche? Ah! I don't know! It may not be there at all. It may be a dusty image, thrust aside into a corner, and by and by to be flung out of doors, where any foot may trample upon it. If not to-day, then to-morrow! And so, Priscilla, I do not see much wisdom in being so very merry in this kind of a world."

It had taken me nearly seven years of worldly life to hive up the bitter honey which I here offered to Priscilla. And she rejected it!

"I don't believe one word of what you say!" she replied, laughing anew. "You made me sad, for a minute, by talking about the past; but the past never comes back again. Do we dream the same dream twice? There is nothing else that I am afraid of."

So away she ran, and fell down on the green grass, as it was often her luck to do, but got up again, without any harm.

"Priscilla, Priscilla!" cried Hollingsworth, who was sitting on the doorstep; "you had better not run any more to-night. You will weary yourself too much. And do not sit down out of doors, for there is a heavy dew beginning to fall."

At his first word, she went and sat down under the porch, at Hollingsworth's feet, entirely contented and happy. What charm was there in his rude massiveness that so attracted and soothed this shadow-like girl? It appeared to me, who have always been curious in such matters, that Priscilla's vague and seemingly causeless flow of felicitous feeling was that with which love blesses inexperienced hearts, before they begin to suspect what is going on within them. It transports them to the seventh heaven; and, if you ask what brought them thither, they neither can tell nor care to learn, but cherish an ecstatic faith that there they shall abide forever.

Zenobia was in the doorway, not far from Hollingsworth. She gazed at Priscilla in a very singular way. Indeed, it was a sight worth gazing at, and a beautiful sight, too, as the fair girl sat at the feet of that dark, powerful figure. Her air, while perfectly modest, delicate, and virgin-like, denoted her as swayed by Hollingsworth, attracted to him, and unconsciously seeking to rest upon his strength. I could not turn away my own eyes, but hoped that nobody, save Zenobia and myself, were witnessing this picture. It is before me now, with the evening twilight a little deepened by the dusk of memory.

"Come hither, Priscilla," said Zenobia. "I have something to say to you."

She spoke in little more than a whisper. But it is strange how expressive of moods a whisper may often be. Priscilla felt at once that something had gone wrong.

"Are you angry with me?" she asked, rising slowly, and standing before Zenobia in a drooping attitude. "What have I done? I hope you are not angry!"

"No, no, Priscilla!" said Hollingsworth, smiling, "I will answer for it, she is not. You are the one little person in the world with whom nobody can be angry!"

"Angry with you, child? What a silly idea!" exclaimed Zenobia, laughing. "No, indeed! But, my dear Priscilla, you are getting to be so very pretty that you absolutely need a duenna; and, as I am older than you, and have had my own little experience of life, and think myself exceedingly sage, I intend to fill the place of a maiden aunt. Every day, I shall give you a lecture, a quarter of an hour in length, on the morals, manners, and proprieties of social life. When our pastoral shall be quite played out, Priscilla, my worldly wisdom may stand you in good stead."

"I am afraid you are angry with me!" repeated Priscilla, sadly; for, while she seemed as impressible as wax, the girl often showed a persistency in her own ideas as stubborn as it was gentle.

"Dear me, what can I say to the child!" cried Zenobia, in a tone of humorous vexation. "Well, well; since you insist on my being angry, come to my room, this moment, and let me beat you!"

Zenobia bade Hollingsworth good-night very sweetly, and nodded to me with a smile. But, just as she turned aside with Priscilla, into the dimness of the porch, I caught another glance at her countenance. It would have made the fortune of a tragic actress, could she have borrowed it for the moment when she fumbles in her bosom for the concealed dagger, or the exceedingly sharp bodkin, or mingles the ratsbane in her lover's bowl of wine or her rival's cup of tea. Not that I in the least anticipated any such catastrophe,—it being a remarkable truth that custom has in no one point a greater sway than over our modes of wreaking our wild passions. And besides, had we been in Italy, instead of New England, it was hardly yet a crisis for the dagger or the bowl.

It often amazed me, however, that Hollingsworth should show himself so recklessly tender towards Priscilla, and never once seem to think of the effect which it might have upon her heart. But the man, as I have endeavored to explain, was thrown completely off his moral balance, and quite bewildered as to his personal relations, by his great excrescence of a philanthropic scheme. I used to see, or fancy, indications that he was not altogether obtuse to Zenobia's influence as a woman. No doubt, however, he had a still more exquisite enjoyment of Priscilla's silent sympathy with his purposes, so unalloyed with criticism, and therefore more grateful than any intellectual approbation, which always involves a possible reserve of latent censure. A man—poet, prophet, or whatever he may be—readily persuades himself of his right to all the worship that is voluntarily tendered. In requital of so rich benefits as he was to confer upon mankind, it would have been hard to deny Hollingsworth the simple solace of a young girl's heart, which he held in his hand, and smelled to, like a rosebud. But what if, while pressing out its fragrance, he should crush the tender rosebud in his grasp!

As for Zenobia, I saw no occasion to give myself any trouble. With her native strength, and her experience of the world, she could not be supposed to need any help of mine. Nevertheless, I was really generous enough to feel some little interest likewise for Zenobia. With all her faults (which might have been a great many besides the abundance that I knew of), she possessed noble traits, and a heart which must, at least, have been valuable while new. And she seemed ready to fling it away as uncalculatingly as Priscilla herself. I could not but suspect that, if merely at play with Hollingsworth, she was sporting with a power which she did not fully estimate. Or, if in earnest, it might chance, between Zenobia's passionate force and his dark, self-delusive egotism, to turn out such earnest as would develop itself in some sufficiently tragic catastrophe, though the dagger and the bowl should go for nothing in it.

Meantime, the gossip of the Community set them down as a pair of lovers. They took walks together, and were not seldom encountered in the wood-paths: Hollingsworth deeply discoursing, in tones solemn and sternly pathetic; Zenobia, with a rich glow on her cheeks, and her eyes softened from their ordinary brightness, looked so beautiful, that had her companion been ten times a philanthropist, it seemed impossible but that one glance should melt him back into a man. Oftener than anywhere else, they went to a certain point on the slope of a pasture, commanding near-ly the whole of our own domain, besides a view of the river, and an airy prospect of many distant hills. The bond of our Community was such, that the members had the privilege of building cottages for their own residence within our precincts, thus laying a hearth-stone and fencing in a home private and peculiar to all desirable extent, while yet the inhabi-tants should continue to share the advantages of an associated life. It was inferred that Hollingsworth and Zenobia intended to rear their dwelling on this favorite spot.

I mentioned those rumors to Hollingsworth, in a playful way.

"Had you consulted me," I went on to observe, "I should have recom-mended a site farther to the left, just a little withdrawn into the wood, with two or three peeps at the prospect, among the trees. You will be in the shady vale of years, long before you can raise any better kind of shade around your cottage, if you build it on this bare slope."

"But I offer my edifice as a spectacle to the world," said Hollings-worth, "that it may take example and build many another like it. There-fore, I mean to set it on the open hill-side."

Twist these words how I might, they offered no very satisfactory im-port. It seemed hardly probable that Hollingsworth should care about educating the public taste in the department of cottage architecture, de-sirable as such improvement certainly was.

## X

### A VISITOR FROM TOWN

HOLLINGSWORTH and I—we had been hoeing potatoes, that forenoon, while the rest of the fraternity were engaged in a distant quarter of the farm—sat under a clump of maples, eating our eleven-o'clock lunch, when we saw a stranger approaching along the edge of the field. He had admitted himself from the roadside through a turnstile, and seemed to have a purpose of speaking with us.

And, by the by, we were favored with many visits at Blithedale, especially from people who sympathized with our theories, and perhaps held themselves ready to unite in our actual experiment as soon as there should appear a reliable promise of its success. It was rather ludicrous, indeed (to me, at least, whose enthusiasm had insensibly been exhaled, together with the perspiration of many a hard day's toil), it was absolutely funny, therefore, to observe what a glory was shed about our life and labors, in the imagination of these longing proselytes. In their view, we were as poetical as Arcadians, besides being as practical as the hardest-fisted husbandmen in Massachusetts. We did not, it is true, spend much time in piping to our sheep, or warbling our innocent loves to the sisterhood. But they gave us credit for imbuing the ordinary rustic occupations with a kind of religious poetry, insomuch that our very cow-yards and pigsties were as delightfully fragrant as a flower-garden. Nothing used to please me more than to see one of these lay enthusiasts snatch up a hoe, as they were very prone to do, and set to work with a vigor that perhaps carried him through about a dozen ill-directed strokes. Men are wonderfully soon satisfied, in this day of shameful bodily enervation, when, from one end of life to the other, such multitudes never taste the sweet weariness that follows accustomed toil. I seldom saw the new enthusiasm that did not grow as flimsy and flaccid as the proselyte's moistened shirt-collar, with a quarter of an hour's active labor under a July sun.

But the person now at hand had not at all the air of one of these amiable visionaries. He was an elderly man, dressed rather shabbily, yet decently enough, in a gray frock-coat, faded towards a brown hue, and wore a broad-brimmed white hat, of the fashion of several years gone by. His hair was perfect silver, without a dark thread in the whole of it; his nose, though it had a scarlet tip, by no means indicated the jollity of which a red nose is the generally admitted symbol. He was a subdued, undemonstrative old man, who would doubtless drink a glass of liquor, now and then, and probably more than was good for him,—not, however, with a purpose of undue exhilaration, but in the hope of bringing his spirits up to the ordinary level of the world's cheerfulness. Drawing nearer, there was a shy look about him, as if he were ashamed of his poverty, or, at any rate, for some reason or other, would rather have us glance at him sidelong than take a full front view. He had a queer appearance of hiding himself behind the patch on his left eye.

"I know this old gentleman," said I to Hollingsworth, as we sat observing him; "that is, I have met him a hundred times in town, and have often amused my fancy with wondering what he was before he came to be what he is. He haunts restaurants and such places, and has an odd way of lurking in corners or getting behind a door whenever practicable, and holding out his hand with some little article in it which he wishes you to buy. The eye of the world seems to trouble him, although he necessarily lives so much in it. I never expected to see him in an open field."

"Have you learned anything of his history?" asked Hollingsworth.

"Not a circumstance," I answered; "but there must be something curious in it. I take him to be a harmless sort of a person, and a tolerably honest one; but his manners, being so furtive, remind me of those of a rat,—a rat without the mischief, the fierce eye, the teeth to bite with, or the desire to bite. See, now! He means to skulk along that fringe of bushes, and approach us on the other side of our clump of maples."

We soon heard the old man's velvet tread on the grass, indicating that he had arrived within a few feet of where we sat.

"Good morning, Mr. Moodie," said Hollingsworth, addressing the stranger as an acquaintance; "you must have had a hot and tiresome walk from the city. Sit down, and take a morsel of our bread and cheese."

The visitor made a grateful little murmur of acquiescence, and sat down in a spot somewhat removed; so that, glancing round, I could see his gray pantaloons and dusty shoes, while his upper part was mostly hidden behind the shrubbery. Nor did he come forth from this retirement during the whole of the interview that followed. We handed him such food as we had, together with a brown jug of molasses and water, (would that it had been brandy, or something better, for the sake of his chill old heart!) like priests offering dainty sacrifice to an enshrined and invisible idol. I have no idea that he really lacked sustenance; but it was quite touching, nevertheless, to hear him nibbling away at our crusts.

"Mr. Moodie," said I, "do you remember selling me one of those very pretty little silk purses, of which you seem to have a monopoly in the market? I keep it to this day, I can assure you."

"Ah, thank you," said our guest. "Yes, Mr. Coverdale, I used to sell a good many of those little purses."

He spoke languidly, and only those few words, like a watch with an inelastic spring, that just ticks a moment or two, and stops again. He seemed a very forlorn old man. In the wantonness of youth, strength, and comfortable condition,—making my prey of people's individualities, as my custom was,—I tried to identify my mind with the old fellow's, and take his view of the world, as if looking through a smoke-blackened glass at the sun. It robbed the landscape of all its life. Those pleasantly swelling slopes of our farm, descending towards the wide meadows, through which sluggishly circled the brimful tide of the Charles, bathing the long sedges on its hither and farther shores; the broad, sunny gleam over the winding water; that peculiar picturesqueness of the scene where capes and headlands put themselves boldly forth upon the perfect level of the meadow, as into a green lake, with inlets between the promontories; the shadowy woodland, with twinkling showers of light falling into its depths; the sultry heat-vapor, which rose everywhere like incense, and in which my soul delighted, as indicating so rich a fervor in the passionate day, and in the earth that was burning with its love,—I beheld all these things as through old Moodie's eyes. When my eyes are dimmer than they have yet come to be, I will go thither again, and see if I did not catch the tone of his mind aright, and if the cold and lifeless tint of his perceptions be not then repeated in my own.

Yet it was unaccountable to myself, the interest that I felt in him.

"Have you any objection," said I, "to telling me who made those little purses?"

"Gentlemen have often asked me that," said Moodie, slowly; "but I shake my head, and say little or nothing, and creep out of the way as well as I can. I am a man of few words; and if gentlemen were to be told one thing, they would be very apt, I suppose, to ask me another. But it happens, just now, Mr. Coverdale, that you can tell me more about the maker of those little purses than I can tell you."

"Why do you trouble him with needless questions, Coverdale?" interrupted Hollingsworth. "You must have known, long ago, that it was Priscilla. And so, my good friend, you have come to see her? Well, I am glad of it. You will find her altered very much for the better, since that winter evening when you put her into my charge. Why, Priscilla has a bloom in her cheeks, now!"

"Has my pale little girl a bloom?" repeated Moodie, with a kind of slow wonder. "Priscilla with a bloom in her cheeks! Ah, I am afraid I shall not know my little girl. And is she happy?"

"Just as happy as a bird," answered Hollingsworth.

"Then, gentlemen," said our guest, apprehensively, "I don't think it well for me to go any farther. I crept hitherward only to ask about Priscilla; and now that you have told me such good news, perhaps I can do no better than to creep back again. If she were to see this old face of mine, the child would remember some very sad times which we have spent together. Some very sad times, indeed! She has forgotten them, I know,—them and me,—else she could not be so happy, nor have a bloom in her cheeks. Yes—yes—yes," continued he, still with the same torpid utterance; "with many thanks to you, Mr. Hollingsworth, I will creep back to town again."

"You shall do no such thing, Mr. Moodie," said Hollingsworth, bluffly. "Priscilla often speaks of you; and if there lacks anything to make her cheeks bloom like two damask roses, I 'll venture to say it is just the sight of your face. Come,—we will go and find her."

"Mr. Hollingsworth!" said the old man, in his hesitating way.

"Well," answered Hollingsworth.

"Has there been any call for Priscilla?" asked Moodie; and though his face was hidden from us, his tone gave a sure indication of the mysterious nod and wink with which he put the question. "You know, I think, sir, what I mean."

"I have not the remotest suspicion what you mean, Mr. Moodie," replied Hollingsworth; "nobody, to my knowledge, has called for Priscilla, except yourself. But come; we are losing time, and I have several things to say to you by the way."

"And, Mr. Hollingsworth!" repeated Moodie.

"Well, again!" cried my friend, rather impatiently. "What now?"

"There is a lady here," said the old man; and his voice lost some of its wearisome hesitation. "You will account it a very strange matter for me to talk about; but I chanced to know this lady when she was but a little child. If I am rightly informed, she has grown to be a very fine woman, and makes a brilliant figure in the world, with her beauty, and her talents, and her noble way of spending her riches. I should recognize this lady, so people tell me, by a magnificent flower in her hair."

"What a rich tinge it gives to his colorless ideas, when he speaks of Zenobia!" I whispered to Hollingsworth. "But how can there possibly be any interest or connecting link between him and her?"

"The old man, for years past," whispered Hollingsworth, "has been a little out of his right mind, as you probably see."

"What I would inquire," resumed Moodie, "is, whether this beautiful lady is kind to my poor Priscilla."

"Very kind," said Hollingsworth.

"Does she love her?" asked Moodie.

"It should seem so," answered my friend. "They are always together."

"Like a gentlewoman and her maid-servant, I fancy?" suggested the old man.

There was something so singular in his way of saying this, that I could not resist the impulse to turn quite round, so as to catch a glimpse of his face, almost imagining that I should see another person than old Moodie. But there he sat, with the patched side of his face towards me.

"Like an elder and younger sister, rather," replied Hollingsworth.

"Ah!" said Moodie, more complacently,—for his latter tones had harshness and acidity in them,—"it would gladden my old heart to witness that. If one thing would make me happier than another, Mr. Hollingsworth, it would be to see that beautiful lady holding my little girl by the hand."

"Come along," said Hollingsworth, "and perhaps you may."

After a little more delay on the part of our freakish visitor, they set forth together, old Moodie keeping a step or two behind Hollingsworth, so that the latter could not very conveniently look him in the face. I remained under the tuft of maples, doing my utmost to draw an inference from the scene that had just passed. In spite of Hollingsworth's off-hand explanation, it did not strike me that our strange guest was really beside himself, but only that his mind needed screwing up, like an instrument long out of tune, the strings of which have ceased to vibrate smartly and sharply. Methought it would be profitable for us, projectors of a happy life, to welcome this old gray shadow, and cherish him as one of us, and let him creep about our domain, in order that he might be a little merrier for our sakes, and we, sometimes, a little sadder for his. Human destinies look ominous without some perceptible intermixture of the sable or the gray. And then, too, should any of our fraternity grow ferverish with an over-exulting sense of prosperity, it would be a sort of cooling regimen to slink off into the woods, and spend an hour, or a day, or as many days as might be requisite to the cure, in uninterrupted communion with this deplorable old Moodie!

Going homeward to dinner, I had a glimpse of him, behind the trunk of a tree, gazing earnestly towards a particular window of the farmhouse; and, by and by, Priscilla appeared at this window, playfully drawing along Zenobia, who looked as bright as the very day that was blazing down upon us, only not, by many degrees, so well advanced towards her noon. I was convinced that this pretty sight must have been purposely arranged by Priscilla for the old man to see. But either the girl held her too long, or her fondness was resented as too great a freedom; for Zenobia suddenly put Priscilla decidedly away, and gave her a haughty look, as from a mistress to a dependant. Old Moodie shook his head; and again and again I saw him shake it, as he withdrew along the road; and, at the last point whence the farm-house was visible, he turned and shook his uplifted staff.

XI

THE WOOD-PATH

NOT long after the preceding incident, in order to get the ache of too constant labor out of my bones, and to relieve my spirit of the irksomeness of a settled routine, I took a holiday. It was my purpose to spend it, all alone, from breakfast-time till twilight, in the deepest wood-seclusion that lay anywhere around us. Though fond of society, I was so constituted as to need these occasional retirements, even in a life like that of Blithedale, which was itself characterized by a remoteness from the world. Unless renewed by a yet further withdrawal towards the inner circle of self-communion, I lost the better part of my individuality. My thoughts became of little worth, and my sensibilities grew as arid as a tuft of moss (a thing whose life is in the shade, the rain, or the noontide dew), crumbling in the sunshine after long expectance of a shower. So, with my heart full of a drowsy pleasure, and cautious not to dissipate my mood by previous intercourse with any one, I hurried away, and was soon pacing a wood-path, arched overhead with boughs, and dusky-brown beneath my feet.

At first, I walked very swiftly, as if the heavy flood-tide of social life were roaring at my heels, and would outstrip and overwhelm me, without all the better diligence in my escape. But, threading the more distant windings of the track, I abated my pace, and looked about me for some side-aisle, that should admit me into the innermost sanctuary of this green cathedral, just as, in human acquaintanceship, a casual opening some-times lets us, all of a sudden, into the long-sought intimacy of a myster-ious heart. So much was I absorbed in my reflections,—or, rather, in my mood, the substance of which was as yet too shapeless to be called thought,—that footsteps rustled on the leaves, and a figure passed me by, almost without impressing either the sound or sight upon my conscious-ness.

A moment afterwards, I heard a voice at a little distance behind me, speaking so sharply and impertinently that it made a complete discord with my spiritual state, and caused the latter to vanish as abruptly as when you thrust a finger into a soap-bubble.

"Halloo, friend!" cried this most unseasonable voice. "Stop a moment, I say! I must have a word with you!"

I turned about, in a humor ludicrously irate. In the first place, the in-terruption, at any rate, was a grievous injury; then, the tone displeased me. And, finally, unless there be real affection in his heart, a man cannot, —such is the bad state to which the world has brought itself,—cannot more effectually show his contempt for a brother-moral, nor more gall-ingly assume a position of superiority, than by addressing him as "friend." Especially does the misapplication of this phrase bring out that latent hostility which is sure to animate peculiar sects, and those who, with however generous a purpose, have sequestered themselves from the crowd; a feeling, it is true, which may be hidden in some dog-kennel of the heart, grumbling there in the darkness, but is never quite extinct, un-til the dissenting party have gained power and scope enough to treat the world generously. For my part, I should have taken it as far less an insult to be styled "fellow," "clown," or "bumpkin." To either of these appella-tions my rustic garb (it was a linen blouse, with checked shirt and striped pantaloons, a chip hat on my head, and a rough hickory-stick in my hand) very fairly entitled me. As the case stood, my temper darted at once to the opposite pole; not friend, but enemy!

"What do you want with me?" said I, facing about.

"Come a little nearer, friend," said the stranger, beckoning.

"No," answered I. "If I can do anything for you without too much trouble to myself, say so. But recollect, if you please, that you are not speaking to an acquaintance, much less a friend!"

"Upon my word, I believe not!" retorted he, looking at me with some curiosity; and, lifting his hat, he made me a salute which had enough of sarcasm to be offensive, and just enough of doubtful courtesy to render any resentment of it absurd. "But I ask your pardon! I recognize a little mistake. If I may take the liberty to suppose it, you, sir, are probably one of the æsthetic—or shall I rather say ecstatic?—laborers, who have plant-ed themselves hereabouts. This is your forest of Arden; and you are either the banished Duke in person, or one of the chief nobles in his train. The melancholy Jacques, perhaps? Be it so. In that case, you can prob-ably do me a favor."

I never, in my life, felt less inclined to confer a favor on any man.

"I am busy," said I.

So unexpectedly had the stranger made me sensible of his presence, that he had almost the effect of an apparition; and certainly a less appropriate one (taking into view the dim woodland solitude about us) than if the salvage man of antiquity, hirsute and cinctured with a leafy girdle, had started out of a thicket. He was still young, seemingly a little under thirty, of a tall and well-developed figure, and as handsome a man as ever I beheld. The style of his beauty, however, though a masculine style, did not at all commend itself to my taste. His countenance—I hardly know how to describe the peculiarity—had an indecorum in it, a kind of rudeness, a hard, coarse, forth-putting freedom of expression, which no degree of external polish could have abated one single jot. Not that it was vulgar. But he had no fineness of nature; there was in his eyes (although they might have artifice enough of another sort) the naked exposure of something that ought not to be left prominent. With these vague allusions to what I have seen in other faces as well as his, I leave the quality to be comprehended best—because with an intuitive repugnance—by those who possess least of it.

His hair, as well as his beard and mustache, was coal-black; his eyes, too, were black and sparkling, and his teeth remarkably brilliant. He was rather carelessly but well and fashionably dressed, in a summer-morning costume. There was a gold chain, exquisitely wrought, across his vest. I never saw a smoother or whiter gloss than that upon his shirt-bosom, which had a pin in it, set with a gem that glimmered, in the leafy shadow where he stood, like a living tip of fire. He carried a stick with a wooden head, carved in vivid imitation of that of a serpent. I hated him, partly, I do believe, from a comparison of my own homely garb with his well-ordered foppishness.

"Well, sir," said I, a little ashamed of my first irritation, but still with no waste of civility, "be pleased to speak at once, as I have my own business in hand."

"I regret that my mode of addressing you was a little unfortunate," said the stranger, smiling; for he seemed a very acute sort of person, and saw, in some degree, how I stood affected towards him. "I intended no offence, and shall certainly comport myself with due ceremony hereafter. I merely wish to make a few inquiries respecting a lady, formerly of my acquaintance, who is now resident in your Community, and, I believe, largely concerned in your social enterprise. You call her, I think, Zenobia."

"That is her name in literature," observed I; "a name, too, which possibly she may permit her private friends to know and address her by,—but not one which they feel at liberty to recognize when used of her personally by a stranger or casual acquaintance."

"Indeed!" answered this disagreeable person; and he turned aside his face for an instant with a brief laugh, which struck me as a noteworthy expression of his character. "Perhaps I might put forward a claim, on your own grounds, to call the lady by a name so appropriate to her splendid qualities. But I am willing to know her by any cognomen that you may suggest."

Heartily wishing that he would be either a little more offensive, or a good deal less so, or break off our intercourse altogether, I mentioned Zenobia's real name.

"True," said he; "and, in general society, I have never heard her called otherwise. And, after all, our discussion of the point has been gratuitous. My object is only to inquire when, where, and how this lady may most conveniently be seen."

"At her present residence, of course," I replied. "You have but to go thither and ask for her. This very path will lead you within sight of the house; so I wish you good morning."

"One moment, if you please," said the stranger. "The course you indicate would certainly be the proper one, in an ordinary morning call. But my business is private, personal, and somewhat peculiar. Now, in a community like this, I should judge that any little occurrence is likely to be discussed rather more minutely than would quite suit my views. I refer solely to myself, you understand, and without intimating that it would be other than a matter of entire indifference to the lady. In short, I especially desire to see her in private. If her habits are such as I have known them, she is probably often to be met with in the woods, or by the riverside; and I think you could do me the favor to point out some favorite walk, where, about this hour, I might be fortunate enough to gain an interview."

I reflected that it would be quite a supererogatory piece of Quixotism in me to undertake the guardianship of Zenobia, who, for my pains, would only make me the butt of endless ridicule, should the fact ever come to her knowledge. I therefore described a spot which, as often as any other, was Zenobia's resort at this period of the day; nor was it so remote from the farm-house as to leave her in much peril, whatever might be the stranger's character.

"A single word more," said he; and his black eyes sparkled at me, whether with fun or malice I knew not, but certainly as if the Devil were peeping out of them. "Among your fraternity, I understand, there is a certain holy and benevolent blacksmith; a man of iron, in more senses than one; a rough, cross-grained, well-meaning individual, rather boorish in his manners, as might be expected, and by no means of the highest intellectual cultivation. He is a philanthropical lecturer, with two or three disciples, and a scheme of his own, the preliminary step in which involves a large purchase of land, and the erection of a spacious edifice, at an expense considerably beyond his means; inasmuch as these are to be reckoned in copper or old iron much more conveniently than in gold or silver. He hammers away upon his one topic as lustily as ever he did upon a horseshoe! Do you know such a person?"

I shook my head, and was turning away.

"Our friend," he continued, "is described to me as a brawny, shaggy, grim, and ill-favored personage, not particularly well calculated, one would say, to insinuate himself with the softer sex. Yet, so far has this honest fellow succeeded with one lady whom we wot of, that he anticipates, from her abundant resources, the necessary funds for realizing his plan in brick and mortar!"

Here the stranger seemed to be so much amused with his sketch of Hollingsworth's character and purposes, that he burst into a fit of merriment, of the same nature as the brief, metallic laugh, already alluded to, but immensely prolonged and enlarged. In the excess of his delight, he opened his mouth wide, and disclosed a gold band around the upper part of his teeth, thereby making it apparent that every one of his brilliant grinders and incisors was a sham. This discovery affected me very oddly. I felt as if the whole man were a moral and physical humbug; his wonderful beauty of face, for aught I knew, might be removable like a mask; and, tall and comely as his figure looked, he was perhaps but a wizened little elf, gray and decrepit, with nothing genuine about him, save the wicked expression of his grin. The fantasy of his spectral character so wrought upon me, together with the contagion of his strange mirth on my sympathies, that I soon began to laugh as loudly as himself.

By and by, he paused all at once; so suddenly, indeed, that my own cachinnation lasted a moment longer.

"Ah, excuse me!" said he. "Our interview seems to proceed more merrily than it began."

"It ends here," answered I. "And I take shame to myself that my folly has lost me the right of resenting your ridicule of a friend."

"Pray allow me," said the stranger, approaching a step nearer, and laying his gloved hand on my sleeve. "One other favor I must ask of you. You have a young person, here at Blithedale, of whom I have heard,—whom, perhaps, I have known,—and in whom, at all events, I take a peculiar interest. She is one of those delicate, nervous young creatures, not uncommon in New England, and whom I suppose to have become what we find them by the gradual refining away of the physical system among your women. Some philosophers choose to glorify this habit of body by terming it spiritual; but, in my opinion, it is rather the effect of unwholesome food, bad air, lack of out-door exercise, and neglect of bathing, on the part of these damsels and their female progenitors, all resulting in a kind of hereditary dyspepsia. Zenobia, even with her uncomfortable surplus of vitality, is far the better model of womanhood. But—to revert again to this young person—she goes among you by the name of Priscilla. Could you possibly afford me the means of speaking with her?"

"You have made so many inquiries of me," I observed, "that I may at least trouble you with one. What is your name?"

He offered me a card, with "Professor Westervelt" engraved on it. At the same time, as if to vindicate his claim to the professorial dignity, so often assumed on very questionable grounds, he put on a pair of spectacles, which so altered the character of his face that I hardly knew him again. But I liked the present aspect no better than the former one.

"I must decline any further connection with your affairs," said I, drawing back. "I have told you where to find Zenobia. As for Priscilla, she has closer friends than myself, through whom, if they see fit, you can gain access to her."

"In that case," returned the Professor, ceremoniously raising his hat, "good morning to you."

He took his departure, and was soon out of sight among the windings of the wood-path. But after a little reflection, I could not help regretting that I had so peremptorily broken off the interview while the stranger seemed inclined to continue it. His evident knowledge of matters affecting my three friends might have led to disclosures or inferences that would perhaps have been serviceable. I was particularly struck with the fact that, ever since the appearance of Priscilla, it had been the tendency of events to suggest and establish a connection between Zenobia and her. She had come, in the first instance, as if with the sole purpose of claiming Zenobia's protection. Old Moodie's visit, it appeared, was chiefly to ascertain whether this object had been accomplished. And here, to-day, was the questionable Professor, linking one with the other in his inquiries, and seeking communication with both.

Meanwhile, my inclination for a ramble having been balked, I lingered in the vicinity of the farm, with perhaps a vague idea that some new event would grow out of Westervelt's proposed interview with Zenobia. My own part in these transactions was singularly surbordinate. It resembled that of the Chorus in a classic play, which seems to be set aloof from the possibility of personal concernment, and bestows the whole measure of its hope or fear, its exultation or sorrow, on the fortunes of others, between whom and itself this sympathy is the only bond. Destiny, it may be,—the most skilful of stage-managers,—seldom chooses to arrange its scenes, and carry forward its drama, without securing the presence of at least one calm observer. It is his office to give applause when due, and sometimes an inevitable tear, to detect the final fitness of incident to character, and distil in his long-brooding thought the whole morality of the performance.

Not to be out of the way, in case there were need of me in my vocation, and, at the same time, to avoid thrusting myself where neither destiny nor mortals might desire my presence, I remained pretty near the verge of the woodlands. My position was off the track of Zenobia's customary walk, yet not so remote but that a recognized occasion might speedily have brought me thither.

## XII

### COVERDALE'S HERMITAGE

LONG since, in this part of our circumjacent wood, I had found out for myself a little hermitage. It was a kind of leafy cave, high upward into the air, among the midmost branches of a white-pine tree. A wild grape-vine, of unusual size and luxuriance, had twined and twisted itself up into the tree, and, after wreathing the entanglement of its tendrils almost around every bough, had caught hold of three or four neighboring trees, and married the whole clump with a perfectly inextricable knot of polygamy. Once, while sheltering myself from a summer shower, the fancy had taken me to clamber up into this seemingly impervious mass of foliage. The branches yielded me a passage, and closed again beneath, as if only a squirrel or a bird had passed. Far aloft, around the stem of the central pine, behold a perfect nest for Robinson Crusoe or King Charles! A hollow chamber of rare seclusion had been formed by the decay of some of the pine branches, which the vine had lovingly strangled with its embrace, burying them from the light of day in an aerial sepulchre of its own leaves. It cost me but little ingenuity to enlarge the interior, and open loopholes through the verdant walls. Had it ever been my fortune to spend a honeymoon, I should have thought seriously of inviting my bride up thither, where our next neighbors would have been two orioles in another part of the clump.

It was an admirable place to make verses, tuning the rhythm to the breezy symphony that so often stirred among the vine-leaves; or to meditate an essay for "The Dial," in which the many tongues of Nature whispered mysteries, and seemed to ask only a little stronger puff of wind to speak out the solution of its riddle. Being so pervious to air-currents, it was just the nook, too, for the enjoyment of a cigar. This hermitage was my one exclusive possession while I counted myself a brother of the socialists. It symbolized my individuality, and aided me in keeping it inviolate. None ever found me out in it, except, once, a squirrel. I brought thither no guest, because, after Hollingsworth failed me, there was no longer the man alive with whom I could think of sharing all. So there I used to sit, owl-like, yet not without liberal and hospitable thoughts. I counted the innumerable clusters of my vine, and fore-reckoned the abundance of my vintage. It gladdened me to anticipate the surprise of the Community, when, like an allegorical figure of rich October, I should make my appearance, with shoulders bent beneath the burden of ripe grapes, and some of the crushed ones crimsoning my brow as with a blood-stain.

Ascending into this natural turret, I peeped in turn out of several of its small windows. The pine-tree, being ancient, rose high above the rest of the wood, which was of comparatively recent growth. Even where I sat, about midway between the root and the topmost bough, my position was lofty enough to serve as an observatory, not for starry investigations, but for those sublunary matters in which lay a lore as infinite as that of the planets. Through one loophole I saw the river lapsing calmly onward, while in the meadow, near its brink, a few of the brethren were digging peat for our winter's fuel. On the interior cart-road of our farm, I discerned Hollingsworth, with a yoke of oxen hitched to a drag of stones, that were to be piled into a fence, on which we employed ourselves at the odd intervals of other labor. The harsh tones of his voice, shouting to the sluggish steers, made me sensible, even at such a distance, that he was ill at ease, and that the balked philanthropist had the battle-spirit in his heart.

"Haw, Buck!" quoth he. "Come along there, ye lazy ones! What are ye about, now? Gee!"

"Mankind, in Hollingsworth's opinion," thought I, "is but another yoke of oxen, as stubborn, stupid, and sluggish as our old Brown and Bright. He vituperates us aloud, and curses us in his heart, and will begin to prick us with the goad-stick, by and by. But are we his oxen? And what right has he to be the driver? And why, when there is enough else to do, should we waste our strength in dragging home the ponderous load of his philanthropic absurdities? At my height above the earth, the whole matter looks ridiculous!"

Turning towards the farm-house, I saw Priscilla (for, though a great way off, the eye of faith assured me that it was she) sitting at Zenobia's window, and making little purses, I suppose; or, perhaps, mending the Community's old linen. A bird flew past my tree; and, as it clove its way onward into the sunny atmosphere, I flung it a message for Priscilla.

"Tell her," said I, "that her fragile thread of life has inextricably knotted itself with other and tougher threads, and most likely it will be broken. Tell her that Zenobia will not be long her friend. Say that Hollingsworth's heart is on fire with his own purpose, but icy for all human affection; and that, if she has given him her love, it is like casting a flower into a sepulchre. And say that if any mortal really cares for her, it is myself; and not even I, for her realities,—poor little seamstress, as Zenobia rightly called her!—but for the fancy-work with which I have idly decked her out!"

The pleasant scent of the wood, evolved by the hot sun, stole up to my nostrils, as if I had been an idol in its niche. Many trees mingled their fragrance into a thousand-fold odor. Possibly there was a sensual influence in the broad light of noon that lay beneath me. It may have been the cause, in part, that I suddenly found myself possessed by a mood of disbelief in moral beauty or heroism, and a conviction of the folly of attempting to benefit the world. Our especial scheme of reform, which, from my observatory, I could take in with the bodily eye, looked so ridiculous that it was impossible not to laugh aloud.

"But the joke is a little too heavy," thought I. "If I were wise, I should get out of the scrape with all diligence, and then laugh at my companions for remaining in it."

While thus musing, I heard, with perfect distinctness, somewhere in the wood beneath, the peculiar laugh which I have described as one of the disagreeable characteristics of Professor Westervelt. It brought my thoughts back to our recent interview. I recognized as chiefly due to this man's influence the sceptical and sneering view which, just now had filled my mental vision, in regard to all life's better purposes. And it was through his eyes, more than my own, that I was looking at Hollingsworth, with his glorious, if impracticable dream, and at the noble earthliness of Zenobia's character, and even at Priscilla, whose impalpable grace lay so singularly between disease and beauty. The essential charm of each had vanished. There are some spheres the contact with which inevitably degrades the high, debases the pure, deforms the beautiful. It must be a mind of uncommon strength, and little impressibility, that can permit itself the habit of such intercourse, and not be permanently deteriorated; and yet the Professor's tone represented that of worldly society at large, where a cold scepticism smothers what it can of our spiritual aspirations, and makes the rest ridiculous. I detested this kind of man; and all the more because a part of my own nature showed itself responsive to him.

Voices were now approaching through the region of the wood which lay in the vicinity of my tree. Soon I caught glimpses of two figures—a woman and a man—Zenobia and the stranger—earnestly talking together as they advanced.

Zenobia had a rich, though varying color. It was, most of the while, a flame, and anon a sudden paleness. Her eyes glowed, so that their light sometimes flashed upward to me, as when the sun throws a dazzle from some bright object on the ground. Her gestures were free, and strikingly impressive. The whole woman was alive with a passionate intensity, which I now perceived to be the phase in which her beauty culminated. Any passion would have become her well; and passionate love, perhaps, the best of all. This was not love, but anger, largely intermixed with scorn. Yet the idea strangely forced itself upon me, that there was a sort of familiarity between these two companions, necessarily the result of an intimate love,—on Zenobia's part, at least,—in days gone by, but which had prolonged itself into as intimate a hatred, for all futurity. As they passed among the trees, reckless as her movement was, she took good heed that even the hem of her garment should not brush against the stranger's person. I wondered whether there had always been a chasm, guarded so religiously, betwixt these two.

As for Westervelt, he was not a whit more warmed by Zenobia's passion than a salamander by the heat of its native furnace. He would have been absolutely statuesque, save for a look of slight perplexity, tinctured strongly with derision. It was a crisis in which his intellectual perceptions could not altogether help him out. He failed to comprehend, and cared but little for comprehending, why Zenobia should put herself into such a fume; but satisfied his mind that it was all folly, and only another shape of a woman's manifold absurdity, which men can never understand. How many a woman's evil fate has yoked her with a man like this! Nature thrusts some of us into the world miserably incomplete on the emotional side, with hardly any sensibilities except what pertain to us as animals. No passion, save of the senses; no holy tenderness, nor the delicacy that results from this. Externally they bear a close resemblance to other men, and have perhaps all save the finest grace; but when a woman wrecks herself on such a being, she ultimately finds that the real womanhood within her has no corresponding part in him. Her deepest voice lacks a response; the deeper her cry, the more dead his silence. The fault may be none of his; he cannot give her what never lived within his soul. But the wretchedness on her side, and the moral deterioration attendant on a false and shallow life, without strength enough to keep itself sweet, are among the most pitiable wrongs that mortals suffer.

Now, as I looked down from my upper region at this man and woman, —outwardly so fair a sight, and wandering like two lovers in the wood,— I imagined that Zenobia, at an earlier period of youth, might have fallen into the misfortune above indicated. And when her passionate womanhood, as was inevitable, had discovered its mistake, here had ensued the character of eccentricity and defiance which distinguished the more public portion of her life.

Seeing how aptly matters had chanced thus far, I began to think it the design of fate to let me into all Zenobia's secrets, and that therefore the couple would sit down beneath my tree, and carry on a conversation which would leave me nothing to inquire. No doubt, however, had it so happened, I should have deemed myself honorably bound to warn them of a listener's presence, by flinging down a handful of unripe grapes, or by sending an unearthly groan out of my hiding-place, as if this were one of the trees of Dante's ghostly forest. But real life never arranges itself exactly like a romance. In the first place, they did not sit down at all. Secondly, even while they passed beneath the tree, Zenobia's utterance was so hasty and broken, and Westervelt's so cool and low, that I hardly could make out an intelligible sentence on either side. What I seem to remember, I yet suspect, may have been patched together, by my fancy, in brooding over the matter afterwards.

"Why not fling the girl off," said Westervelt, "and let her go?"

"She clung to me from the first," replied Zenobia. "I neither know nor care what it is in me that so attaches her. But she loves me, and I will not fail her."

"She will plague you, then," said he, "in more ways than one."

"The poor child!" exclaimed Zenobia. "She can do me neither good nor harm. How should she?"

I know not what reply Westervelt whispered; nor did Zenobia's subsequent exclamation give me any clew, except that it evidently inspired her with horror and disgust.

"With what kind of a being am I linked?" cried she. "If my Creator cares aught for my soul, let him release me from this miserable bond!"

"I did not think it weighed so heavily," said her companion.

"Nevertheless," answered Zenobia, "it will strangle me, at last!"

And then I heard her utter a helpless sort of moan; a sound which, struggling out of the heart of a person of her pride and strength, affected me more than if she had made the wood dolorously vocal with a thousand shrieks and wails.

Other mysterious words, besides what are above written, they spoke together; but I understood no more, and even question whether I fairly understood so much as this. By long brooding over our recollections, we subtilize them into something akin to imaginary stuff, and hardly capable of being distinguished from it. In a few moments, they were completely beyond ear-shot. A breeze stirred after them, and awoke the leafy tongues of the surrounding trees, which forthwith began to babble, as if innumerable gossips had all at once got wind of Zenobia's secret. But, as the breeze grew stronger, its voice among the branches was as if it said, "Hush! Hush!" and I resolved that to no mortal would I disclose what I had heard. And, though there might be room for casuistry, such, I conceive, is the most equitable rule in all similar conjunctures.

## XIII

### ZENOBIA'S LEGEND

THE illustrious Society of Blithedale, though it toiled in downright earnest for the good of mankind, yet not unfrequently illuminated its laborious life with an afternoon or evening of pastime. Picnics under the trees were considerably in vogue; and, within doors, fragmentary bits of theatrical performance, such as single acts of tragedy or comedy, or dramatic proverbs and charades. Zenobia, besides, was fond of giving us readings from Shakespeare, and often with the depth of tragic power, or breadth of comic effect, that made one feel it an intolerable wrong to the world that she did not at once go upon the stage. Tableaux vivants were another of our occasional modes of amusement, in which scarlet shawls, old silken robes, ruffs, velvets, furs, and all kinds of miscellaneous trumpery converted our familiar companions into the people of a pictorial world. We had been thus engaged on the evening after the incident narrated in the last chapter. Several splendid works of art—either arranged after engravings from the old masters, or original illustrations of scenes in history or romance—had been presented, and we were earnestly entreating Zenobia for more.

She stood, with a meditative air, holding a large piece of gauze, or some such ethereal stuff, as if considering what picture should next occupy the frame: while at her feet lay a heap of many-colored garments, which her quick fancy and magic skill could so easily convert into gorgeous draperies for heroes and princesses.

"I am getting weary of this," said she, after a moment's thought. "Our own features, and our own figures and airs, show a little too intrusively through all the characters we assume. We have so much familiarity with one another's realities, that we cannot remove ourselves, at pleasure, into an imaginary sphere. Let us have no more pictures to-night; but, to make you what poor amends I can, how would you like to have me trump up a wild, spectral legend, on the spur of the moment?"

Zenobia had the gift of telling a fanciful little story, off-hand, in a way that made it greatly more effective than it was usually found to be when she afterwards elaborated the same production with her pen. Her proposal, therefore, was greeted with acclamation.

"Oh, a story, a story, by all means!" cried the young girls. "No matter how marvellous; we will believe it, every word. And let it be a ghost-story, if you please."

"No, not exactly a ghost-story," answered Zenobia; "but something so nearly like it that you shall hardly tell the difference. And, Priscilla, stand you before me, where I may look at you, and get my inspiration out of your eyes. They are very deep and dreamy tonight."

I know not whether the following version of her story will retain any portion of its pristine character; but, as Zenobia told it wildly and rapidly, hesitating at no extravagance, and dashing at absurdities which I am too timorous to repeat,—giving it the varied emphasis of her inimitable voice, and the pictorial illustration of her mobile face, while through it all we caught the freshest aroma of the thoughts, as they came bubbling out of her mind,—thus narrated, and thus heard, the legend seemed quite a remarkable affair. I scarcely knew, at the time, whether she intended us to laugh or be more seriously impressed. From beginning to end, it was undeniable nonsense, but not necessarily the worse for that.

### THE SILVERY VEIL

You have heard, my dear friends, of the Veiled Lady, who grew suddenly so very famous, a few months ago. And have you never thought how remarkable it was that this marvellous creature should vanish, all at once, while her renown was on the increase, before the public had grown weary of her, and when the enigma of her character, instead of being solved, presented itself more mystically at every exhibition? Her last appearance, as you know, was before a crowded audience. The next evening, —although the bills had announced her, at the corner of every street, in red letters of a gigantic size,—there was no Veiled Lady to be seen! Now, listen to my simple little tale, and you shall hear the very latest incident in the known life—(if life it may be called, which seemed to have no more reality than the candle-light image of one's self which peeps at us outside of a dark window-pane)—the life of this shadowy phenomenon.

A party of young gentlemen, you are to understand, were enjoying themselves, one afternoon,—as young gentlemen are sometimes fond of doing,—over a bottle or two of champagne; and, among other ladies less mysterious, the subject of the Veiled Lady, as was very natural, happened to come up before them for discussion. She rose, as it were, with the sparkling effervescence of their wine, and appeared in a more airy and fantastic light on account of the medium through which they saw her. They repeated to one another, between jest and earnest, all the wild stories that were in vogue; nor, I presume, did they hesitate to add any small circumstance that the inventive whim of the moment might suggest, to heighten the marvellousness of their theme.

"But what an audacious report was that," observed one, "which pretended to assert the identity of this strange creature with a young lady," —and here he mentioned her name,—"the daughter of one of our most distinguished families!"

"Ah, there is more in that story than can well be accounted for," remarked another. "I have it on good authority, that the young lady in question is invariably out of sight, and not to be traced, even by her own family, at the hours when the Veiled Lady is before the public; nor can any satisfactory explanation be given of her disappearance. And just look at the thing: Her brother is a young fellow of spirit. He cannot but be aware of these rumors in reference to his sister. Why, then, does he not come forward to defend her character, unless he is conscious that an investigation would only make the matter worse?"

It is essential to the purposes of my legend to distinguish one of these young gentlemen from his companions; so, for the sake of a soft and pretty name (such as we of the literary sisterhood invariably bestow upon our heroes), I deem it fit to call him Theodore.

"Pshaw!" exclaimed Theodore; "her brother is no such fool! Nobody, unless his brain be as full of bubbles as this wine, can seriously think of crediting that ridiculous rumor. Why, if my senses did not play me false (which never was the case yet), I affirm that I saw that very lady, last evening, at the exhibition, while this veiled phenomenon was playing off her juggling tricks! What can you say to that?"

"Oh, it was a spectral illusion that you saw!" replied his friends, with a general laugh. "The Veiled Lady is quite up to such a thing."

However, as the above-mentioned fable could not hold its ground against Theodore's downright refutation, they went on to speak of other stories which the wild babble of the town had set afloat. Some upheld that the veil covered the most beautiful countenance in the world; others,—and certainly with more reason, considering the sex of the Veiled Lady,—that the face was the most hideous and horrible, and that this was her sole motive for hiding it. It was the face of a corpse; it was the head of a skeleton; it was a monstrous visage, with snaky locks, like Medusa's, and one great red eye in the centre of the forehead. Again, it was affirmed that there was no single and unchangeable set of features beneath the veil; but that whosoever should be bold enough to lift it would behold the features of that person, in all the world, who was destined to be his fate; perhaps he would be greeted by the tender smile of the woman whom he loved, or, quite as probably, the deadly scowl of his bitterest enemy would throw a blight over his life. They quoted, moreover, this startling explanation of the whole affair: that the magician who exhibited the Veiled Lady—and who, by the by, was the handsomest man in the whole world —had bartered his own soul for seven years' possession of a familiar fiend, and that the last year of the contract was wearing towards its close.

If it were worth our while, I could keep you till an hour beyond midnight listening to a thousand such absurdities as these. But finally our friend Theodore, who prided himself upon his common-sense, found the matter getting quite beyond his patience.

"I offer any wager you like," cried he, setting down his glass so forcibly as to break the stem of it, "that this very evening I find out the mystery of the Veiled Lady!"

Young men, I am told, boggle at nothing over their wine; so, after a little more talk, a wager of considerable amount was actually laid, the money staked, and Theodore left to choose his own method of settling the dispute.

How he managed it I know not, nor is it of any great importance to this veracious legend. The most natural way, to be sure, was by bribing the door-keeper,—or possibly he preferred clambering in at the window. But, at any rate, that very evening, while the exhibition was going forward in the hall, Theodore contrived to gain admittance into the private withdrawing-room whither the Veiled Lady was accustomed to retire at the close of her performances. There he waited, listening, I suppose, to the stifled hum of the great audience; and no doubt he could distinguish the deep tones of the magician, causing the wonders that he wrought to appear more dark and intricate, by his mystic pretence of an explanation. Perhaps, too, in the intervals of the wild breezy music which accompanied the exhibition, he might hear the low voice of the Veiled Lady, conveying her sibylline responses. Firm as Theodore's nerves might be, and much as he prided himself on his sturdy perception of realities, I should not be surprised if his heart throbbed at a little more than its ordinary rate.

Theodore concealed himself behind a screen. In due time, the performance was brought to a close, and, whether the door was softly opened, or whether her bodiless presence came through the wall, is more than I can say, but, all at once, without the young man's knowing how it happened, a veiled figure stood in the centre of the room. It was one thing to be in presence of this mystery in the hall of exhibition, where the warm, dense life of hundreds of other mortals kept up the beholder's courage, and distributed her influence among so many; it was another thing to be quite alone with her, and that, too, with a hostile, or, at least, an unauthorized and unjustifiable purpose. I rather imagine that Theodore now began to be sensible of something more serious in his enterprise than he had been quite aware of while he sat with his boon-companions over their sparkling wine.

Very strange, it must be confessed, was the movement with which the figure floated to and fro over the carpet, with the silvery veil covering her from head to foot; so impalpable, so ethereal, so without substance, as the texture seemed, yet hiding her every outline in an impenetrability like that of midnight. Surely, she did not walk! She floated, and flitted, and hovered about the room; no sound of a footstep, no perceptible motion of a limb; it was as if a wondering breeze wafted her before it, at its own wild and gentle pleasure. But, by and by, a purpose began to be discernible, throughout the seeming vagueness of her unrest. She was in quest of something. Could it be that a subtile presentiment had informed her of the young man's presence? And if so, did the Veiled Lady seek or did she shun him? The doubt in Theodore's mind was speedily resolved; for, after a moment or two of these erratic flutterings, she advanced more decidedly, and stood motionless before the screen.

"Thou art here!" said a soft, low voice. "Come forth, Theodore!"

Thus summoned by his name, Theodore, as a man of courage, had no choice. He emerged from his concealment, and presented himself before the Veiled Lady, with the wine-flush, it may be, quite gone out of his cheeks.

"What wouldst thou with me?" she inquired, with the same gentle composure that was in her former utterance.

"Mysterious creature," replied Theodore, "I would know who and what you are!"

"My lips are forbidden to betray the secret," said the Veiled Lady.

"At whatever risk, I must discover it," rejoined Theodore.

"Then," said the Mystery, "there is no way save to lift my veil."

And Theodore, partly recovering his audacity, stept forward on the instant, to do as the Veiled Lady had suggested. But she floated backward to the opposite side of the room, as if the young man's breath had possessed power enough to waft her away.

"Pause, one little instant," said the soft, low voice, "and learn the conditions of what thou art so bold to undertake! Thou canst go hence, and think of me no more; or, at thy option, thou canst lift this mysterious veil, beneath which I am a sad and lonely prisoner, in a bondage which is worse to me than death. But, before raising it, I entreat thee, in all maiden modesty, to bend forward and impress a kiss where my breath stirs the veil; and my virgin lips shall come forward to meet thy lips; and from that instant, Theodore, thou shalt be mine, and I thine, with never more a veil between us. And all the felicity of earth and of the future world shall be thine and mine together. So much may a maiden say behind the veil. If thou shrinkest from this, there is yet another way."

"And what is that?" asked Theodore.

"Dost thou hesitate," said the Veiled Lady, "to pledge thyself to me, by meeting these lips of mine, while the veil yet hides my face? Has not thy heart recognized me? Dost thou come hither, not in holy faith, nor with a pure and generous purpose, but in scornful scepticism and idle curiosity? Still, thou mayest lift the veil! But, from that instant, Theodore, I am doomed to be thy evil fate; nor wilt thou ever taste another breath of happiness!"

There was a shade of inexpressible sadness in the utterance of these last words. But Theodore, whose natural tendency was towards scepticism, felt himself almost injured and insulted by the Veiled Lady's proposal that he should pledge himself, for life and eternity, to so questionable a creature as herself; or even that she should suggest an inconsequential kiss, taking into view the probability that her face was none of the most bewitching. A delightful idea, truly, that he should salute the lips of a dead girl, or the jaws of a skeleton, or the grinning cavity of a monster's mouth! Even should she prove a comely maiden enough in other respects, the odds were ten to one that her teeth were defective; a terrible drawback on the delectableness of a kiss.

"Excuse me, fair lady," said Theodore,—and I think he nearly burst into a laugh,—"if I prefer to lift the veil first; and for this affair of the kiss, we may decide upon it afterwards."

"Thou hast made thy choice," said the sweet, sad voice behind the veil; and there seemed a tender but unresentful sense of wrong done to womanhood by the young man's contemptuous interpretation of her offer. "I must not counsel thee to pause, although thy fate is still in thine own hand!"

Grasping at the veil, he flung it upward, and caught a glimpse of a pale, lovely face beneath; just one momentary glimpse, and then the apparition vanished, and the silvery veil fluttered slowly down and lay upon the floor. Theodore was alone. Our legend leaves him there. His retribution was, to pine forever and ever for another sight of that dim, mournful face, —which might have been his life-long household fireside joy,—to desire, and waste life in a feverish quest, and never meet it more.

But what, in good sooth, had become of the Veiled Lady? Had all her existence been comprehended within that mysterious veil, and was she now annihilated? Or was she a spirit, with a heavenly essence, but which might have been tamed down to human bliss, had Theodore been brave and true enough to claim her? Hearken, my sweet friends,—and hearken, dear Priscilla,—and you shall learn the little more that Zenobia can tell you.

Just at the moment, so far as can be ascertained, when the Veiled Lady vanished, a maiden, pale and shadowy, rose up amid a knot of visionary people, who were seeking for the better life. She was so gentle and so sad, —a nameless melancholy gave her such hold upon their sympathies,— that they never thought of questioning whence she came. She might have heretofore existed, or her thin substance might have been moulded out of air at the very instant when they first beheld her. It was all one to them; they took her to their hearts. Among them was a lady, to whom, more than to all the rest, this pale, mysterious girl attached herself.

But one morning the lady was wandering in the woods, and there met her a figure in an Oriental robe, with a dark beard, and holding in his hand a silvery veil. He motioned her to stay. Being a woman of some nerve, she did not shriek, nor run away, nor faint, as many ladies would have been apt to do, but stood quietly, and bade him speak. The truth was, she had seen his face before, but had never feared it, although she knew him to be a terrible magician.

"Lady," said he, with a warning gesture, "you are in peril!"

"Peril!" she exclaimed. "And of what nature?"

"There is a certain maiden," replied the magician, "who has come out of the realm of mystery, and made herself your most intimate companion. Now, the fates have so ordained it, that, whether by her own will or no, this stranger is your deadliest enemy. In love, in worldly fortune, in all your pursuit of happiness, she is doomed to fling a blight over your prospects. There is but one possibility of thwarting her disastrous influence."

"Then tell me that one method," said the lady.

"Take this veil," he answered, holding forth the silvery texture. "It is a spell; it is a powerful enchantment, which I wrought for her sake, and beneath which she was once my prisoner. Throw it, at unawares, over the head of this secret foe, stamp your foot, and cry, 'Arise, Magician! Here is the Veiled Lady!' and immediately I will rise up through the earth, and seize her; and from that moment you are safe!"

So the lady took the silvery veil, which was like woven air, or like some substance airier than nothing, and that would float upward and be lost among the clouds, were she once to let it go. Returning homeward, she found the shadowy girl, amid the knot of visionary transcendentalists, who were still seeking for the better life. She was joyous now, and had a rose-bloom in her cheeks, and was one of the prettiest creatures, and seemed one of the happiest, that the world could show. But the lady stole noiselessly behind her and threw the veil over her head. As the slight, ethereal texture sank inevitably down over her figure, the poor girl strove to raise it, and met her dear friend's eyes with one glance of mortal terror, and deep, deep reproach. It could not change her purpose.

"Arise, Magician!" she exclaimed, stamping her foot upon the earth. "Here is the Veiled Lady!"

At the word, uprose the bearded man in the Oriental robes,—the beautiful, the dark magician, who had bartered away his soul! He threw his arms around the Veiled Lady, and she was his bond-slave for evermore!

Zenobia, all this while, had been holding the piece of gauze, and so managed it as greatly to increase the dramatic effect of the legend at those points where the magic veil was to be described. Arriving at the catastrophe, and uttering the fatal words, she flung the gauze over Priscilla's head; and for an instant her auditors held their breath, half expecting, I verily believe, that the magician would start up through the floor, and carry off our poor little friend, before our eyes.

As for Priscilla, she stood droopingly in the midst of us, making no attempt to remove the veil.

"How do you find yourself, my love?" said Zenobia, lifting a corner of the gauze, and peeping beneath it, with a mischievous smile. "Ah, the dear little soul! Why, she is really going to faint! Mr. Coverdale, Mr. Coverdale, pray bring a glass of water!"

Her nerves being none of the strongest, Priscilla hardly recovered her equanimity during the rest of the evening. This, to be sure, was a great pity; but, nevertheless we thought it a very bright idea of Zenobia's to bring her legend to so effective a conclusion.

## XIV

### ELIOT'S PULPIT

OUR Sundays at Blithedale were not ordinarily kept with such rigid observance as might have befitted the descendants of the Pilgrims, whose high enterprise, as we sometimes flattered ourselves, we had taken up, and were carrying it onward and aloft, to a point which they never dreamed of attaining.

On that hallowed day, it is true, we rested from our labors. Our oxen, relieved from their week-day yoke, roamed at large through the pasture; each yoke-fellow, however, keeping close beside his mate, and continuing to acknowledge, from the force of habit and sluggish sympathy, the union which the taskmaster had imposed for his own hard ends. As for us human yoke-fellows, chosen companions of toil, whose hoes had clinked together throughout the week, we wandered off, in various directions, to enjoy our interval of repose. Some, I believe, went devoutly to the village church. Others, it may be, ascended a city or a country pulpit, wearing the clerical robe with so much dignity that you would scarcely have suspected the yeoman's frock to have been flung off only since milking-time. Others took long rambles among the rustic lanes and by-paths, pausing to look at black old farm-houses, with their sloping roofs; and at the modern cottage, so like a plaything that it seemed as if real joy or sorrow could have no scope within; and at the more pretending villa, with its range of wooden columns supporting the needless insolence of a great portico. Some betook themselves into the wide, dusky barn, and lay there for hours together on the odorous hay; while the sunstreaks and the shadows strove together,—these to make the barn solemn, those to make it cheerful,—and both were conquerors; and the swallows twittered a cheery anthem, flashing into sight, or vanishing as they darted to and fro among the golden rules of sunshine. And others went a little way into the woods, and threw themselves on mother earth, pillowing their heads on a heap of moss, the green decay of an old log; and, dropping asleep, the humble-bees and mosquitoes sung and buzzed about their ears, causing the slumberers to twitch and start, without awaking.

With Hollingsworth, Zenobia, Priscilla, and myself, it grew to be a custom to spend the Sabbath afternoon at a certain rock. It was known to us under the name of Eliot's pulpit, from a tradition that the venerable

Apostle Eliot had preached there, two centuries gone by, to an Indian auditory. The old pine forest, through which the Apostle's voice was wont to sound, had fallen, an immemorial time ago. But the soil, being of the rudest and most broken surface, had apparently never been brought under tillage; other growths, maple and beech and birch, had succeeded to the primeval trees; so that it was still as wild a tract of woodland as the great-great-great-great-grandson of one of Eliot's Indians (had any such posterity been in existence) could have desired, for the site and shelter of his wigwam. These after-growths, indeed, lose the stately solemnity of the original forest. If left in due neglect, however, they run into an entanglement of softer wildness, among the rustling leaves of which the sun can scatter cheerfulness as it never could among the dark-browed pines.

The rock itself rose some twenty or thirty feet, a shattered granite bowlder, or heap of bowlders, with an irregular outline and many fissures, out of which sprang shrubs, bushes, and even trees; as if the scanty soil within those crevices were sweeter to their roots than any other earth. At the base of the pulpit, the broken bowlders inclined towards each other, so as to form a shallow cave, within which our little party had sometimes found protection from a summer shower. On the threshold, or just across it, grew a tuft of pale columbines, in their season, and violets, sad and shadowy recluses, such as Priscilla was when we first knew her; children of the sun, who had never seen their father, but dwelt among damp mosses, though not akin to them. At the summit, the rock was overshadowed by the canopy of a birch-tree which served as a sounding-board for the pulpit. Beneath this shade (with my eyes of sense half shut, and those of the imagination widely opened) I used to see the holy Apostle of the Indians, with the sunlight flickering down upon him through the leaves, and glorifying his figure as with the half-perceptible glow of a transfiguration.

I the more minutely describe the rock, and this little Sabbath solitude, because Hollingsworth, at our solicitation, often ascended Eliot's pulpit, and not exactly preached, but talked to us, his few disciples, in a strain that rose and fell as naturally as the wind's breath among the leaves of the birch-tree. No other speech of man has ever moved me like some of those discourses. It seemed most pitiful—a positive calamity to the world —that a treasury of golden thoughts should thus be scattered, by the liberal handful, down among us three, when a thousand hearers might have been the richer for them; and Hollingsworth the richer, likewise, by the sympathy of multitudes. After speaking much or little, as might happen, he would descend from his gray pulpit, and generally fling himself at full length on the ground, face downward. Meanwhile, we talked around him on such topics as were suggested by the discourse.

Since her interview with Westervelt, Zenobia's continual inequalities of temper had been rather difficult for her friends to bear. On the first Sunday after that incident, when Hollingsworth had clambered down from Eliot's pulpit, she declaimed with great earnestness and passion, nothing short of anger, on the injustice which the world did to women, and equally to itself, by not allowing them, in freedom and honor, and with the fullest welcome, their natural utterance in public.

"It shall not always be so!" cried she. "If I live another year, I will lift up my own voice in behalf of woman's wider liberty!"

She, perhaps, saw me smile.

"What matter of ridicule do you find in this, Miles Coverdale?" exclaimed Zenobia, with a flash of anger in her eyes. "That smile, permit me to say, makes me suspicious of a low tone of feeling and shallow thought. It is my belief—yes, and my prophecy, should I die before it happens—that, when my sex shall achieve its rights there will be ten eloquent women where there is now one eloquent man. Thus far, no woman in the world has ever once spoken out her whole heart and her whole mind. The mistrust and disapproval of the vast bulk of society throttles us, as with two gigantic hands at our throats! We mumble a few weak words, and leave a thousand better ones unsaid. You let us write a little, it is true, on a limited range of subjects. But the pen is not for woman. Her power is too natural and immediate. It is with the living voice alone that she can compel the world to recognize the light of her intellect and the depth of her heart!"

Now,—though I could not well say so to Zenobia,—I had not smiled from any unworthy estimate of woman, or in denial of the claims which she is beginning to put forth. What amused and puzzled me was the fact, that women, however intellectually superior, so seldom disquiet themselves about the rights or wrongs of their sex, unless their own individual affections chance to lie in idleness, or to be ill at ease. They are not natural reformers, but become such by the pressure of exceptional misfortune. I could measure Zenobia's inward trouble by the animosity with which she now took up the general quarrel of woman against man.

"I will give you leave, Zenobia," replied I, "to fling your utmost scorn upon me, if you ever hear me utter a sentiment unfavorable to the widest liberty which woman has yet dreamed of. I would give her all she asks, and add a great deal more, which she will not be the party to demand, but which men, if they were generous and wise, would grant of their own free motion. For instance, I should love dearly—for the next thousand years, at least—to have all government devolve into the hands of women. I hate to be ruled by my own sex; it excites my jealousy, and wounds my pride. It is the iron sway of bodily force which abases us, in our compelled submission. But how sweet the free-generous courtesy, with which I would kneel before a woman-ruler!"

"Yes, if she were young and beautiful," said Zenobia, laughing. "But how if she were sixty, and a fright?"

"Ah! it is you that rate womanhood low," said I. "But let me go on. I have never found it possible to suffer a bearded priest so near my heart and conscience as to do me any spiritual good. I blush at the very thought! Oh, in the better order of things, Heaven grant that the ministry of souls may be left in charge of women! The gates of the Blessed City will be thronged with the multitude that enter in, when that day comes!

The task belongs to woman. God meant it for her. He has endowed her with the religious sentiment in its utmost depth and purity, refined from that gross, intellectual alloy with which every masculine theologist—save only One, who merely veiled himself in mortal and masculine shape, but was, in truth, divine—has been prone to mingle it. I have always envied the Catholics their faith in that sweet, sacred Virgin Mother, who stands between them and the Deity, intercepting somewhat of his awful splendor, but permitting his love to stream upon the worshipper more intelligibly to human comprehension through the medium of a woman's tenderness. Have I not said enough, Zenobia?"

"I cannot think that this is true," observed Priscilla, who had been gazing at me with great, disapproving eyes. "And I am sure I do not wish it to be true!"

"Poor child!" exclaimed Zenobia, rather contemptuously. "She is the type of womanhood, such as man has spent centuries in making it. He is never content unless he can degrade himself by stooping towards what he loves. In denying us our rights, he betrays even more blindness to his own interests than profligate disregard of ours!"

"Is this true?" asked Priscilla, with simplicity, turning to Hollingsworth. "Is it all true, that Mr. Coverdale and Zenobia have been saying?"

"No, Priscilla!" answered Hollingsworth, with his customary bluntness. "They have neither of them spoken one true word yet."

"Do you despise woman?" said Zenobia. "Ah, Hollingsworth, that would be most ungrateful!"

"Despise her? No!" cried Hollingsworth, lifting his great shaggy head and shaking it at us, while his eyes glowed almost fiercely. "She is the most admirable handiwork of God, in her true place and character. Her place is at man's side. Her office, that of the sympathizer; the unreserved, unquestioning believer; the recognition, withheld in every other manner, but given, in pity, through woman's heart, lest man should utterly lose faith in himself; the echo of God's own voice, pronouncing, 'It is well done!' All the separate action of woman is, and ever has been, and always shall be, false, foolish, vain, destructive of her own best and holiest qualities, void of every good effect, and productive of intolerable mischiefs! Man is a wretch without woman; but woman is a monster—and, thank Heaven, an almost impossible and hitherto imaginary monster—without man as her acknowledged principal! As true as I had once a mother whom I loved, were there any possible prospect of woman's taking the social stand which some of them,—poor, miserable, abortive creatures, who only dream of such things because they have missed woman's peculiar happiness, or because nature made them really neither man nor woman?—if there were a chance of their attaining the end which these petticoated monstrosities have in view, I would call upon my own sex to use its physical force, that unmistakable evidence of sovereignty, to scourge them back within their proper bounds! But it will not be needful. The heart of true womanhood knows where its own sphere is, and never seeks to stray beyond it!"

Never was mortal blessed—if blessing it were—with a glance of such entire acquiescence and unquestioning faith, happy in its completeness, as our little Priscilla unconsciously bestowed on Hollingsworth. She seemed to take the sentiment from his lips into her heart, and brood over it in perfect content. The very woman whom he pictured—the gentle parasite, the soft reflection of a more powerful existence—sat there at his feet.

I looked at Zenobia, however, fully expecting her to resent—as I felt, by the indignant ebullition of my own blood, that she ought—this outrageous affirmation of what struck me as the intensity of masculine egotism. It centred everything in itself, and deprived woman of her very soul, her inexpressible and unfathomable all, to make it a mere incident in the great sum of man. Hollingsworth had boldly uttered what he, and millions of despots like him, really felt. Without intending it, he had disclosed the well-spring of all these troubled waters. Now, if ever, it surely behooved Zenobia to be the champion of her sex.

But, to my surprise, and indignation too, she only looked humbled. Some tears sparkled in her eyes, but they were wholly of grief, not anger.

"Well, be it so," was all she said. "I, at least, have deep cause to think you right. Let man be but manly and godlike, and woman is only too ready to become to him what you say!"

I smiled—somewhat bitterly, it is true—in contemplation of my own ill-luck. How little did these two women care for me, who had freely conceded all their claims, and a great deal more, out of the fulness of my heart; while Hollingsworth, by some necromancy of his horrible injustice, seemed to have brought them both to his feet!

"Women almost invariably behave thus," thought I. "What does the fact mean? Is it their nature? Or, is it, at last, the result of ages of compelled degradation? And, in either case, will it be possible ever to redeem them?"

An intuition now appeared to possess all the party, that, for this time, at least, there was no more to be said. With one accord, we arose from the ground, and made our way through the tangled undergrowth towards one of those pleasant wood-paths that wound among the over-arching trees. Some of the branches hung so low as partly to conceal the figures that went before from those who followed. Priscilla had leaped up more lightly than the rest of us, and ran along in advance, with as much airy activity of spirit as was typified in the motion of a bird, which chanced to be flitting from tree to tree, in the same direction as herself. Never did she seem so happy as that afternoon. She skipt, and could not help it, from very playfulness of heart.

Zenobia and Hollingsworth went next, in close contiguity, but not with arm in arm. Now, just when they had passed the impending bough of a birch-tree, I plainly saw Zenobia take the hand of Hollingsworth in both her own, press it to her bosom, and let it fall again!

The gesture was sudden, and full of passion; the impulse had evidently taken her by surprise; it expressed all! Had Zenobia knelt before him, or flung herself upon his breast, and gasped out, "I love you, Hollingsworth!" I could not have been more certain of what it meant. They then walked onward, as before. But, methought, as the declining sun threw Zenobia's magnified shadow along the path, I beheld it tremulous; and the delicate stem of the flower which she wore in her hair was likewise responsive to her agitation.

Priscilla—through the medium of her eyes at least—could not possibly have been aware of the gesture above described. Yet, at that instant, I saw her droop. The buoyancy, which just before had been so bird-like, was utterly departed; the life seemed to pass out of her, and even the substance of her figure to grow thin and gray. I almost imagined her a shadow, fading gradually into the dimness of the wood. Her pace became so slow that Hollingsworth and Zenobia passed by, and I, without hastening my footsteps, overtook her.

"Come, Priscilla," said I, looking her intently in the face, which was very pale and sorrowful, "we must make haste after our friends. Do you feel suddenly ill? A moment ago, you flitted along so lightly that I was comparing you to a bird. Now, on the contrary, it is as if you had a heavy heart, and very little strength to bear it with. Pray take my arm!"

"No," said Priscilla, "I do not think it would help me. It is my heart, as you say, that makes me heavy; and I know not why. Just now, I felt very happy."

No doubt it was a kind of sacrilege in me to attempt to come within her maidenly mystery; but, as she appeared to be tossed aside by her other friends, or carelessly let fall, like a flower which they had done with, I could not resist the impulse to take just one peep beneath her folded petals.

"Zenobia and yourself are dear friends of late," I remarked. "At first, —that first evening when you came to us,—she did not receive you quite so warmly as might have been wished."

"I remember it," said Priscilla. "No wonder she hesitated to love me, who was then a stranger to her, and a girl of no grace or beauty,—she being herself so beautiful!"

"But she loves you now, of course?" suggested I. "And at this very instant you feel her to be your dearest friend?"

"Why do you ask me that question?" exclaimed Priscilla, as if frightened at the scrutiny into her feelings which I compelled her to make. "It somehow puts strange thoughts into my mind. But I do love Zenobia dearly! If she only loves me half as well, I shall be happy!"

"How is it possible to doubt that, Priscilla?" I rejoined. "But observe how pleasantly and happily Zenobia and Hollingsworth are walking together. I call it a delightful spectacle. It truly rejoices me that Hollingsworth has found so fit and affectionate a friend! So many people in the world mistrust him,—so many disbelieve and ridicule, while hardly any do him justice, or acknowledge him for the wonderful man he is,—that it is really a blessed thing for him to have won the sympathy of such a woman as Zenobia. Any man might be proud of that. Any man, even if he be as great as Hollingsworth, might love so magnificent a woman. How very beautiful Zenobia is! And Hollingsworth knows it, too."

There may have been some petty malice in what I said. Generosity is a very fine thing, at a proper time and within due limits. But it is an insufferable bore to see one man engrossing every thought of all the women, and leaving his friend to shiver in outer seclusion, without even the alternative of solacing himself with what the more fortunate individual has rejected. Yes, it was out of a foolish bitterness of heart that I had spoken.

"Go on before," said Priscilla, abruptly, and with true feminine imperiousness, which heretofore I had never seen her exercise. "It pleases me best to loiter along by myself. I do not walk so fast as you."

With her hand, she made a little gesture of dismissal. It provoked me; yet, on the whole, was the most bewitching thing that Priscilla had ever done. I obeyed her, and strolled moodily homeward, wondering—as I had wondered a thousand times already—how Hollingsworth meant to dispose of these two hearts, which (plainly to my perception, and, as I could not but now suppose, to his) he had engrossed into his own huge egotism.

There was likewise another subject hardly less fruitful of speculation. In what attitude did Zenobia present herself to Hollingsworth? Was it in that of a free woman, with no mortgage on her affections nor claimant to her hand, but fully at liberty to surrender both, in exchange for the heart and hand which she apparently expected to receive? But was it a vision that I had witnessed in the wood? Was Westervelt a goblin? Were those words of passion and agony, which Zenobia had uttered in my hearing, a mere stage declamation? Were they formed of a material lighter than common air? Or, supposing them to bear sterling weight, was it a perilous and dreadful wrong which she was meditating towards herself and Hollingsworth?

Arriving nearly at the farm-house, I looked back over the long slope of pasture-land, and beheld them standing together, in the light of sunset, just on the spot where, according to the gossip of the Community, they meant to build their cottage. Priscilla, alone and forgotten, was lingering in the shadow of the wood.

XV

A CRISIS

THUS the summer was passing away,—a summer of toil, of interest, of something that was not pleasure, but which went deep into my heart, and there became a rich experience. I found myself looking forward to years, if not to a lifetime, to be spent on the same system. The Community were now beginning to form their permanent plans. One of our purposes was to erect a Phalanstery (as I think we called it, after Fourier; but the phraseology of those days is not very fresh in my remembrance), where the great and general family should have its abiding-place. Individual members, too, who made it a point of religion to preserve the sanctity of an exclusive home, were selecting sites for their cottages, by the woodside, or on the breezy swells, or in the sheltered nook of some little valley, according as their taste might lean towards snugness or the picturesque. Altogether, by projecting our minds outward, we had imparted a show of novelty to existence, and contemplated it as hopefully as if the soil beneath our feet had not been fathom-deep with the dust of deluded generations, on every one of which, as on ourselves, the world had imposed itself as a hitherto unwedded bride.

Hollingsworth and myself had often discussed these prospects. It was easy to perceive, however, that he spoke with little or no fervor, but either as questioning the fulfilment of our anticipations, or, at any rate, with a quiet consciousness that it was no personal concern of his. Shortly after the scene at Eliot's pulpit, while he and I were repairing an old stone fence, I amused myself with sallying forward into the future time.

"When we come to be old men," I said, "they will call us uncles, or fathers,—Father Hollingsworth and Uncle Coverdale,—and we will look back cheerfully to these early days, and make a romantic story for the young people (and if a little more romantic than truth may warrant, it will be no harm) out of our severe trials and hardships. In a century or two, we shall, every one of us, be mythical personages, or exceedingly picturesque and poetical ones, at all events. They will have a great public hall, in which your portrait, and mine, and twenty other faces that are living now, shall be hung up; and as for me, I will be painted in my shirt-sleeves, and with the sleeves rolled up, to show my muscular development. What stories will be rife among them about our mighty strength!" continued I, lifting a big stone and putting it into its place, "though our posterity will really be far stronger than ourselves, after several generations of a simple, natural, and active life. What legends of Zenobia's beauty, and Priscilla's slender and shadowy grace, and those mysterious qualities which make her seem diaphanous with spiritual light. In due course of ages, we must all figure heroically in an epic poem; and we will ourselves —at least, I will—bend unseen over the future poet, and lend him inspiration while he writes it."

"You seem," said Hollingsworth, "to be trying how much nonsense you can pour out in a breath."

"I wish you would see fit to comprehend," retorted I, "that the profoundest wisdom must be mingled with nine tenths of nonsense, else it is not worth the breath that utters it. But I do long for the cottages to be built, that the creeping plants may begin to run over them, and the moss to gather on the walls, and the trees—which we will set out—to cover them with a breadth of shadow. This spick-and-span novelty does not quite suit my taste. It is time, too, for children to be born among us. The first-born child is still to come. And I shall never feel as if this were a real, practical, as well as poetical system of human life, until somebody has sanctified it by death."

"A pretty occasion for martyrdom, truly!" said Hollingsworth.

"As good as any other," I replied. "I wonder, Hollingsworth, who, of all these strong men, and fair women and maidens, is doomed the first to die. Would it not be well, even before we have absolute need of it, to fix upon a spot for a cemetery? Let us choose the rudest, roughest, most uncultivable spot, for Death's garden-ground; and Death shall teach us to beautify it, grave by grave. By our sweet, calm way of dying, and the airy elegance out of which we will shape our funeral rites, and the cheerful allegories which we will model into tombstones, the final scene shall lose its terrors; so that hereafter it may be happiness to live, and bliss to die. None of us must die young. Yet, should Providence ordain it so, the event shall not be sorrowful, but affect us with a tender, delicious, only half-melancholy, and almost smiling pathos!"

"That is to say," muttered Hollingsworth, "you will die like a heathen, as you certainly live like one. But, listen to me, Coverdale. Your fantastic anticipations make me discern all the more forcibly what a wretched, unsubstantial scheme is this, on which we have wasted a precious summer of our lives. Do you seriously imagine that any such realities as you, and many others here, have dreamed of, will ever be brought to pass?"

"Certainly, I do," said I. "Of course, when the reality comes, it will wear the every-day, commonplace, dusty, and rather homely garb, that reality always does put on. But, setting aside the ideal charm, I hold that our highest anticipations have a solid footing on common-sense."

"You only half believe what you say," rejoined Hollingsworth; "and as for me, I neither have faith in your dream, nor would care the value of this pebble for its realization, were that possible. And what more do you want of it? It has given you a theme for poetry. Let that content you. But now I ask you to be, at last, a man of sobriety and earnestness, and aid me in an enterprise which is worth all our strength, and the strength of a thousand mightier than we."

There can be no need of giving in detail the conversation that ensued. It is enough to say that Hollingsworth once more brought forward his rigid and unconquerable idea,—a scheme for the reformation of the wicked by methods moral, intellectual, and industrial, by the sympathy of pure, humble, and yet exalted minds, and by opening to his pupils the possibility of a worthier life than that which had become their fate. It appeared, unless he over-estimated his own means, that Hollingsworth held it at his choice (and he did so choose) to obtain possession of the very ground on which we had planted our Community, and which had not yet been made irrevocably ours, by purchase. It was just the foundation that he desired. Our beginnings might readily be adapted to his great end. The arrangements already completed would work quietly into his system. So plausible looked his theory, and, more than that, so practical,— such an air of reasonableness had he, by patient thought, thrown over it, —each segment of it was contrived to dovetail into all the rest with such a complicated applicability, and so ready was he with a response for every objection, that, really, so far as logic and argument went, he had the matter all his own way.

"But," said I, "whence can you, having no means of your own, derive the enormous capital which is essential to this experiment? State Street, I imagine, would not draw its purse-strings very liberally in aid of such a speculation."

"I have the funds—as much, at least, as is needed for a commencement—at command," he answered. "They can be produced within a month, if necessary."

My thoughts reverted to Zenobia. It could only be her wealth which Hollingsworth was appropriating so lavishly. And on what conditions was it to be had? Did she fling it into the scheme with the uncalculating generosity that characterizes a woman when it is her impulse to be generous at all? And did she fling herself along with it? But Hollingsworth did not volunteer an explanation.

"And have you no regrets," I inquired, "in overthrowing this fair system of our new life, which has been planned so deeply, and is now beginning to flourish so hopefully around us? How beautiful it is, and, so far as we can yet see, how practicable! The ages have waited for us, and here we are, the very first that have essayed to carry on our mortal existence in love and mutual help! Hollingsworth, I would be loath to take the ruin of this enterprise upon my conscience."

"Then let it rest wholly upon mine!" he answered, knitting his black brows. "I see through the system. It is full of defects,—irremediable and damning ones!—from first to last, there is nothing else! I grasp it in my hand, and find no substance whatever. There is not human nature in it."

"Why are you so secret in your operations?" I asked. "God forbid that I should accuse you of intentional wrong; but the besetting sin of a philanthropist, it appears to me, is apt to be a moral obliquity. His sense of honor ceases to be the sense of other honorable men. At some point of his course—I know not exactly when or where—he is tempted to palter with the right, and can scarcely forbear persuading himself that the importance of his public ends renders it allowable to throw aside his private conscience. Oh my dear friend, beware this error! If you meditate the overthrow of this establishment, call together our companions, state your design, support it with all your eloquence, but allow them an opportunity of defending themselves."

"It does not suit me," said Hollingsworth. "Nor is it my duty to do so."

"I think it is," replied I.

Hollingsworth frowned; not in passion, but, like fate, inexorably.

"I will not argue the point," said he. "What I desire to know of you is, —and you can tell me in one word,—whether I am to look for your co-operation in this great scheme of good? Take it up with me! Be my brother in it! It offers you (what you have told me, over and over again, that you most need) a purpose in life, worthy of the extremest self-devotion,—worthy of martyrdom, should God so order it! In this view, I

present it to you. You can greatly benefit mankind. Your peculiar faculties, as I shall direct them, are capable of being so wrought into this
enterprise that not one of them need lie idle. Strike hands with me, and
from this moment you shall never again feel the languor and vague
wretchedness of an indolent or half-occupied man. There may be no more
aimless beauty in your life; but, in its stead, there shall be strength,
courage, immitigable will,—everything that a manly and generous nature
should desire! We shall succeed! We shall have done our best for this
miserable world; and happiness (which never comes but incidentally)
will come to us unawares."

It seemed his intention to say no more. But, after he had quite broken
off, his deep eyes filled with tears, and he held out both his hands to me.

"Coverdale," he murmured, "there is not the man in this wide world
whom I can love as I could you. Do not forsake me!"

As I look back upon this scene, through the coldness and dimness of so
many years, there is still a sensation as if Hollingsworth had caught hold
of my heart, and were pulling it towards him with an almost irresistible
force. It is a mystery to me how I withstood it. But, in truth, I saw in his
scheme of philanthropy nothing but what was odious. A loathsomeness
that was to be forever in my daily work! A great black ugliness of sin,
which he proposed to collect out of a thousand human hearts, and that
we should spend our lives in an experiment of transmuting it into virtue!
Had I but touched his extended hand, Hollingsworth's magnetism would
perhaps have penetrated me with his own conception of all these matters.
But I stood aloof. I fortified myself with doubts whether his strength of
purpose had not been too gigantic for his integrity, impelling him to
trample on considerations that should have been paramount to every
other.

"Is Zenobia to take a part in your enterprise?" I asked.

"She is," said Hollingsworth.

"She!—the beautiful!—the gorgeous!" I exclaimed. "And how have
you prevailed with such a woman to work in this squalid element?"

"Through no base methods, as you seem to suspect," he answered;
"but by addressing whatever is best and noblest in her."

Hollingsworth was looking on the ground. But, as he often did so,—
generally, indeed, in his habitual moods of thought,—I could not judge
whether it was from any special unwillingness now to meet my eyes. What
it was that dictated my next question, I cannot precisely say. Nevertheless, it rose so inevitably into my mouth, and, as it were, asked itself so
involuntarily, that there must needs have been an aptness in it.

"What is to become of Priscilla?"

Hollingsworth looked at me fiercely, and with glowing eyes. He could
not have shown any other kind of expression than that, had he meant to
strike me with a sword.

"Why do you bring in the names of these women?" said he, after a moment of pregnant silence. "What have they to do with the proposal which

I make you? I must have your answer! Will you devote yourself, and sacrifice all to this great end, and be my friend of friends forever?"

"In Heaven's name, Hollingsworth," cried I, getting angry, and glad to be angry, because so only was it possible to oppose his tremendous concentrativeness and indomitable will, "cannot you conceive that a man may wish well to the world, and struggle for its good, on some other plan than precisely that which you have laid down? And will you cast off a friend for no unworthiness, but merely because he stands upon his right as an individual being, and looks at matters through his own optics, instead of yours?"

"Be with me," said Hollingsworth, "or be against me! There is no third choice for you."

"Take this, then, as my decision," I answered. "I doubt the wisdom of your scheme. Furthermore, I greatly fear that the methods by which you allow yourself to pursue it are such as cannot stand the scrutiny of an unbiased conscience."

"And you will not join me?"

"No!"

I never said the word—and certainly can never have it to say hereafter—that cost me a thousandth part so hard an effort as did that one syllable. The heart-pang was not merely figurative, but an absolute torture of the breast. I was gazing steadfastly at Hollingsworth. It seemed to me that it struck him, too, like a bullet. A ghastly paleness—always so terrific on a swarthy face—overspread his features. There was a convulsive movement of his throat, as if he were forcing down some words that struggled and fought for utterance. Whether words of anger, or words of grief, I cannot tell; although many and many a time I have vainly tormented myself with conjecturing which of the two they were. One other appeal to my friendship,—such as once, already, Hollingsworth had made,—taking me in the revulsion that followed a strenuous exercise of opposing will, would completely have subdued me. But he left the matter there.

"Well!" said he.

And that was all! I should have been thankful for one word more, even had it shot me through the heart, as mine did him. But he did not speak it; and, after a few moments, with one accord, we set to work again, repairing the stone fence. Hollingsworth, I observed, wrought like a Titan; and, for my own part, I lifted stones which at this day—or, in a calmer mood, at that one—I should no more have thought it possible to stir than to carry off the gates of Gaza on my back.

## LEAVE-TAKINGS

A FEW days after the tragic passage-at-arms between Hollingsworth and me, I appeared at the dinner-table actually dressed in a coat, instead of my customary blouse; with a satin cravat, too, a white vest, and several other things that made me seem strange and outlandish to myself. As for my companions, this unwonted spectacle caused a great stir upon the wooden benches that bordered either side of our homely board.

"What's in the wind now, Miles?" asked one of them. "Are you deserting us?"

"Yes, for a week or two," said I. "It strikes me that my health demands a little relaxation of labor, and a short visit to the sea-side, during the dog-days."

"You look like it!" grumbled Silas Foster, not greatly pleased with the idea of losing an efficient laborer before the stress of the season was well over. "Now, here's a pretty fellow! His shoulders have broadened a matter of six inches, since he came among us; he can do his day's work, if he likes, with any man or ox on the farm; and yet he talks about going to the sea-shore for his health! Well, well, old woman," added he to his wife, "let me have a plateful of that pork and cabbage! I begin to feel in a very weakly way. When the others have had their turn, you and I will take a jaunt to Newport or Saratoga!"

"Well, but, Mr. Foster," said I, "you must allow me to take a little breath."

"Breath!" retorted the old yeoman. "Your lungs have the play of a pair of blacksmith's bellows already. What on earth do you want more? But go along! I understand the business. We shall never see your face here again. Here ends the reformation of the world, so far as Miles Coverdale has a hand in it!"

"By no means," I replied. "I am resolute to die in the last ditch, for the good of the cause."

"Die in a ditch!" muttered gruff Silas, with genuine Yankee intolerance of any intermission of toil, except on Sunday, the Fourth of July, the autumnal cattle-show, Thanksgiving, or the annual Fast,—"die in a ditch! I believe, in my conscience, you would, if there were no steadier means than your own labor to keep you out of it!"

The truth was, that an intolerable discontent and irksomeness had come over me. Blithedale was no longer what it had been. Everything was suddenly faded. The sunburnt and arid aspect of our woods and pastures, beneath the August sky, did but imperfectly symbolize the lack of dew and moisture, that, since yesterday, as it were, had blighted my fields of thought, and penetrated to the innermost and shadiest of my contemplative recesses. The change will be recognized by many, who, after a period of happiness, have endeavored to go on with the same kind of life, in the same scene, in spite of the alteration or withdrawal of some principal circumstance. They discover (what heretofore, perhaps, they had not known) that it was this which gave the bright color and vivid reality to the whole affair.

I stood on other terms than before, not only with Hollingsworth, but with Zenobia and Priscilla. As regarded the two latter, it was that dreamlike and miserable sort of change that denies you the privilege to complain, because you can assert no positive injury, nor lay your finger on anything tangible. It is a matter which you do not see, but feel, and which, when you try to analyze it, seems to lose its very existence, and resolve itself into a sickly humor of your own. Your understanding, possibly, may put faith in this denial. But your heart will not so easily rest satisfied. It incessantly remonstrates, though, most of the time, in a bassnote, which you do not separately distinguish; but, now and then, with a sharp cry, importunate to be heard, and resolute to claim belief. "Things are not as they were!" it keeps saying. "You shall not impose on me! I will never be quiet! I will throb painfully! I will be heavy, and desolate, and shiver with cold! For I, your deep heart, know when to be miserable, as once I knew when to be happy! All is changed for us! You are beloved no more!" And were my life to be spent over again, I would invariably lend my ear to this Cassandra of the inward depths, however clamorous the music and the merriment of a more superficial region.

My outbreak with Hollingsworth, though never definitely known to our associates, had really an effect upon the moral atmosphere of the Community. It was incidental to the closeness of relationship into which we had brought ourselves, that an unfriendly state of feeling could not occur between any two members without the whole society being more or less commoted and made uncomfortable thereby. This species of nervous sympathy (though a pretty characteristic enough, sentimentally considered, and apparently betokening an actual bond of love among us) was yet found rather inconvenient in its practical operation; mortal tempers being so infirm and variable as they are. If one of us happened to give his neighbor a box on the ear, the tingle was immediately felt on the same side of everybody's head. Thus, even on the supposition that we were far less quarrelsome than the rest of the world, a great deal of time was necessarily wasted in rubbing our ears.

Musing on all these matters, I felt an inexpressible longing for at least a temporary novelty. I thought of going across the Rocky Mountains, or to Europe, or up the Nile; of offering myself a volunteer on the Exploring Expedition; of taking a ramble of years, no matter in what direction, and coming back on the other side of the world. Then, should the colonists of Blithedale have established their enterprise on a permanent basis, I might fling aside my pilgrim staff and dusty shoon, and rest as peacefully here as elsewhere. Or, in case Hollingsworth should occupy the ground with his School of Reform, as he now purposed, I might plead earthly guilt enough, by that time, to give me what I was inclined to think the only trustworthy hold on his affections. Meanwhile, before deciding on any ultimate plan, I determined to remove myself to a little distance, and take an exterior view of what we had all been about.

In truth, it was dizzy work, amid such fermentation of opinions as was going on in the general brain of the Community. It was a kind of Bedlam, for the time being, although out of the very thoughts that were wildest and most destructive might grow a wisdom, holy, calm, and pure, and that should incarnate itself with the substance of a noble and happy life. But, as matters now were, I felt myself (and, having a decided tendency towards the actual, I never liked to feel it) getting quite out of my reckoning, with regard to the existing state of the world. I was beginning to lose the sense of what kind of a world it was, among innumerable schemes of what it might or ought to be. It was impossible, situated as we were, not to imbibe the idea that everything in nature and human existence was fluid, or fast becoming so; that the crust of the earth in many places was broken, and its whole surface portentously upheaving; that it was a day of crisis, and that we ourselves were in the critical vortex. Our great globe floated in the atmosphere of infinite space like an unsubstantial bubble. No sagacious man will long retain his sagacity, if he live exclusively among reformers and progressive people, without periodically returning into the settled system of things, to correct himself by a new observation from that old stand-point.

It was now time for me, therefore, to go and hold a little talk with the conservatives, the writers of "The North American Review," the merchants, the politicians, the Cambridge men, and all those respectable old blockheads, who still, in this intangibility and mistiness of affairs, kept a death-grip on one or two ideas which had not come into vogue since yesterday morning.

The brethren took leave of me with cordial kindness; and as for the sisterhood, I had serious thoughts of kissing them all round, but forbore to do so, because, in all such general salutations, the penance is fully equal to the pleasure. So I kissed none of them; and nobody, to say the truth, seemed to expect it.

"Do you wish me," I said to Zenobia, "to announce in town, and at the watering-places, your purpose to deliver a course of lectures on the rights of women?"

"Women possess no rights," said Zenobia, with a half-melancholy smile; "or, at all events, only little girls and grandmothers would have the force to exercise them."

She gave me her hand freely and kindly, and looked at me, I thought, with a pitying expression in her eyes; nor was there any settled light of joy in them on her own behalf, but a troubled and passionate flame, flickering and fitful.

"I regret, on the whole, that you are leaving us," she said; "and all the more, since I feel that this phase of our life is finished, and can never be lived over again. Do you know, Mr. Coverdale, that I have been several times on the point of making you my confidant, for lack of a better and wiser one? But you are too young to be my father confessor; and you would not thank me for treating you like one of those good little handmaidens who share the bosom secrets of a tragedy-queen."

"I would, at least, be loyal and faithful," answered I; "and would counsel you with an honest purpose, if not wisely."

"Yes," said Zenobia, "you would be only too wise, too honest. Honesty and wisdom are such a delightful pastime, at another person's expense!"

"Ah, Zenobia," I exclaimed, "if you would but let me speak!"

"By no means," she replied, "especially when you have just resumed the whole series of social conventionalisms, together with that strait-bodied coat. I would as lief open my heart to a lawyer or a clergyman! No, no, Mr. Coverdale; if I choose a counsellor, in the present aspect of my affairs, it must be either an angel or a madman; and I rather apprehend that the latter would be likeliest of the two to speak the fitting word. It needs a wild steersman when we voyage through chaos! The anchor is up,—farewell!"

Priscilla, as soon as dinner was over, had betaken herself into a corner, and set to work on a little purse. As I approached her, she let her eyes rest on me with a calm, serious look; for, with all her delicacy of nerves, there was a singular self-possession in Priscilla, and her sensibilities seemed to lie sheltered from ordinary commotion, like the water in a deep well.

"Will you give me that purse, Priscilla," said I, "as a parting keepsake?"

"Yes," she answered, "if you will wait till it is finished."

"I must not wait, even for that," I replied. "Shall I find you here, on my return?"

"I never wish to go away," said she.

"I have sometimes thought," observed I, smiling, "that you, Priscilla, are a little prophetess, or, at least, that you have spiritual intimations respecting matters which are dark to us grosser people. If that be the case, I should like to ask you what is about to happen; for I am tormented with a strong foreboding that, were I to return even so soon as tomorrow morning, I should find everything changed. Have you any impressions of this nature?"

"Ah, no," said Priscilla, looking at me, apprehensively. "If any such misfortune is coming, the shadow has not reached me yet. Heaven forbid! I should be glad if there might never be any change, but one summer follow another, and all just like this."

"No summer ever came back, and no two summers ever were alike," said I, with a degree of Orphic wisdom that astonished myself. "Times change, and people change; and if our hearts do not change as readily, so much the worse for us. Good-by, Priscilla!"

I gave her hand a pressure, which, I think, she neither resisted nor retuned. Priscilla's heart was deep, but of small compass; it had room but for a very few dearest ones, among whom she never reckoned me.

On the doorstep I met Hollingsworth. I had a momentary impulse to hold out my hand, or at least, to give a parting nod, but resisted both. When a real and strong affection has come to an end, it is not well to mock the sacred past with any show of those commonplace civilities that belong to ordinary intercourse. Being dead henceforth to him, and he to me, there could be no propriety in our chilling one another with the touch of two corpse-like hands, or playing at looks of courtesy with eyes that were impenetrable beneath the glaze and the film. We passed, therefore, as if mutually invisible.

I can nowise explain what sort of whim, prank, or perversity it was, that, after all these leave-takings, induced me to go to the pigsty, and take leave of the swine! There they lay, buried as deeply among the straw as they could burrow, four huge black grunters, the very symbols of slothful ease and sensual comfort. They were asleep, drawing short and heavy breaths, which heaved their big sides up and down. Unclosing their eyes, however, at my approach, they looked dimly forth at the outer world, and simultaneously uttered a gentle grunt; not putting themselves to the trouble of an additional breath for that particular purpose, but grunting with their ordinary inhalation. They were involved, and almost stifled and buried alive, in their own corporeal substance. The very unreadiness and oppression wherewith these greasy citizens gained breath enough to keep their life-machinery in sluggish movement, appeared to make them only the more sensible of the ponderous and fat satisfaction of their existence. Peeping at me, an instant, out of their small, red, hardly perceptible eyes, they dropt asleep again; yet not so far asleep but that their unctuous bliss was still present to them, betwixt dream and reality.

"You must come back in season to eat part of a spare-rib," said Silas Foster, giving my hand a mighty squeeze. "I shall have these fat fellows hanging up by the heels, heads downward, pretty soon, I tell you!"

"O cruel Silas, what a horrible idea!" cried I. "All the rest of us, men, women, and live-stock, save only these four porkers, are bedevilled with one grief or another; they alone are happy,—and you mean to cut their throats and eat them! It would be more for the general comfort to let them eat us; and bitter and sour morsels we should be!"

## XVII

### THE HOTEL

ARRIVING in town (where my bachelor-rooms, long before this time, had received some other occupant), I established myself, for a day or two, in a certain respectable hotel. It was situated somewhat aloof from my former track in life; my present mood inclining me to avoid most of my old companions, from whom I was now sundered by other interests, and who would have been likely enough to amuse themselves at the expense of the amateur workingman. The hotel-keeper put me into a back room of the third story of his spacious establishment. The day was lowering, with occasional gusts of rain, and an ugly-tempered east-wind, which seemed to come right off the chill and melancholy sea, hardly mitigated by sweeping over the roofs, and amalgamating itself with the dusky element of city smoke. All the effeminacy of past days had returned upon me at once. Summer as it still was, I ordered a coal-fire in the rusty grate, and was glad to find myself growing a little too warm with an artificial temperature.

My sensations were those of a traveller, long sojourning in remote regions, and at length sitting down again amid customs once familiar. There was a newness and an oldness oddly combining themselves into one impression. It made me acutely sensible how strange a piece of mosaic-work had lately been wrought into my life. True, if you look at it in one way, it had been only a summer in the country. But, considered in a profounder relation, it was part of another age, a different state of society, a segment of an existence peculiar in its aims and methods, a leaf of some mysterious volume interpolated into the current history which time was writing off. At one moment, the very circumstances now surrounding me—my coal-fire, and the dingy room in the bustling hotel— appeared far off and intangible; the next instant Blithedale looked vague, as if it were at a distance both in time and space, and so shadowy that a question might be raised whether the whole affair had been anything more than the thoughts of a speculative man. I had never before experienced a mood that so robbed the actual world of its solidity. It nevertheless involved a charm, on which—a devoted epicure of my own emotions—I resolved to pause, and enjoy the moral sillabub until quite dissolved away.

Whatever had been my taste for solitude and natural scenery, yet the thick, foggy, stifled element of cities, the entangled life of many men together, sordid as it was, and empty of the beautiful, took quite as strenuous a hold upon my mind. I felt as if there could never be enough of it. Each characteristic sound was too suggestive to be passed over unnoticed. Beneath and around me, I heard the stir of the hotel; the loud voices of guests, landlord, or bar-keeper; steps echoing on the staircase; the ringing of a bell, announcing arrivals or departures; the porter lumbering past my door with baggage, which he thumped down upon the floors of neighboring chambers; the lighter feet of chambermaids scudding along the passages;—it is ridiculous to think what an interest they had for me! From the street came the tumult of the pavements, pervading the whole house with a continual uproar, so broad and deep that only an unaccustomed ear would dwell upon it. A company of the city soldiery, with a full military band, marched in front of the hotel, invisible to me, but stirringly audible both by its foot-tramp and the clangor of its instruments. Once or twice all the city bells jangled together, announcing a fire, which brought out the engine-men and their machines, like an army with its artillery rushing to battle. Hour by hour the clocks in many steeples responded one to another. In some public hall, not a great way off, there seemed to be an exhibition of a mechanical diorama; for three times during the day occurred a repetition of obstreperous music, winding up with the rattle of imitative cannon and musketry, and a huge final explosion. Then ensued the applause of the spectators, with clap of hands and thump of sticks, and the energetic pounding of their heels. All this was just as valuable, in its way, as the sighing of the breeze among the birch-trees that overshadowed Eliot's pulpit.

Yet I felt a hesitation about plunging into this muddy tide of human activity and pastime. It suited me better, for the present, to linger on the brink, or hover in the air above it. So I spent the first day, and the greater part of the second, in the laziest manner possible, in a rocking-chair, inhaling the fragrance of a series of cigars, with my legs and slippered feet horizontally disposed, and in my hand a novel purchased of a railroad bibliopolist. The gradual waste of my cigar accomplished itself with an easy and gentle expenditure of breath. My book was of the dullest, yet had a sort of sluggish flow, like that of a stream in which your boat is as often aground as afloat. Had there been a more impetuous rush, a more absorbing passion of the narrative, I should the sooner have struggled out of its uneasy current, and have given myself up to the swell and subsidence of my thoughts. But, as it was, the torpid life of the book served as an unobtrusive accompaniment to the life within me and about me. At intervals, however, when its effect grew a little too soporific,—not for my patience, but for the possibility of keeping my eyes open,—I bestirred myself, started from the rocking-chair, and looked out of the window.

A gray sky; the weathercock of a steeple, that rose beyond the opposite range of buildings, pointing from the eastward; a sprinkle of small, spiteful-looking rain-drops on the window-pane. In that ebb-tide of my energies, had I thought of venturing abroad, these tokens would have checked the abortive purpose.

After several such visits to the window, I found myself getting pretty well acquainted with that little portion of the backside of the universe which it presented to my view. Over against the hotel and its adjacent houses, at the distance of forty or fifty yards, was the rear of a range of buildings, which appeared to be spacious, modern, and calculated for fashionable residences. The interval between was apportioned into grass-plots, and here and there an apology for a garden, pertaining severally to these dwellings. There were apple-trees, and pear and peach-trees, too, the fruit on which looked singularly large, luxuriant, and abundant, as well it might, in a situation so warm and sheltered, and where the soil had doubtless been enriched to a more than natural fertility.  In two or three places grape-vines clambered upon trellises, and bore clusters already purple, and promising the richness of Malta or Madeira in their ripened juice. The blighting winds of our rigid climate could not molest these trees and vines; the sunshine, though descending late into this area, and too early intercepted by the height of the surrounding houses, yet lay tropically there, even when less than temperate in every other region. Dreary as was the day, the scene was illuminated by not a few sparrows and other birds, which spread their wings, and flitted and fluttered, and alighted now here, now there, and busily scratched their food out of the wormy earth. Most of these winged people seemed to have their domicile in a robust and healthy buttonwood-tree. It aspired upward, high above the roof of the houses, and spread a dense head of foliage half across the area.

There was a cat—as there invariably is in such places—who evidently thought herself entitled to the privileges of forest-life in this close heart of city conventionalisms. I watched her creeping along the low, flat roofs of the offices, descending a flight of wooden steps, gliding among the grass, and besieging the buttonwood-tree, with murderous purpose against its feathered citizens. But, after all, they were birds of city breeding, and doubtless knew how to guard themselves against the peculiar perils of their position.

Bewitching to my fancy are all those nooks and crannies, where Nature, like a stray partridge, hides her head among the long-established haunts of men! It is likewise to be remarked, as a general rule, that there is far more of the picturesque, more truth to native and characteristic tendencies, and vastly greater suggestiveness in the back view of a residence, whether in town or country, than in its front. The latter is always artificial; it is meant for the world's eye, and is therefore a veil and a concealment. Realities keep in the rear, and put forward an advance-guard of show and humbug. The posterior aspect of any old farmhouse, behind which a railroad has unexpectedly been opened, is so different from that looking upon the immemorial highway, that the spectator gets new ideas of rural life and individuality in the puff or two of steam-breath which shoots him past the premises. In a city, the distinction between what is offered to the public and what is kept for the family is certainly not less striking.

But, to return to my window, at the back of the hotel. Together with a due contemplation of the fruit-trees, the grape-vines, the buttonwood-tree, the cat, the birds, and many other particulars, I failed not to study the row of fashionable dwellings to which all these appertained. Here, it must be confessed, there was a general sameness. From the upper story to the first floor, they were so much alike, that I could only conceive of the inhabitants as cut out on one identical pattern, like little wooden toy-people of German manufacture. One long, united roof, with its thousands of slates glittering in the rain, extended over the whole. After the distinctness of separate characters, to which I had recently been accustomed, it perplexed and annoyed me not to be able to resolve this combination of human interests into well-defined elements. It seemed hardly worth while for more than one of those families to be in existence, since they all had the same glimpse of the sky, all looked into the same area, all received just their equal share of sunshine through the front windows, and all listened to precisely the same noises of the street on which they boarded. Men are so much alike in their nature, that they grow intolerable unless varied by their circumstances.

Just about this time, a waiter entered my room. The truth was, I had rung the bell and ordered a sherry-cobbler.

"Can you tell me," I inquired, "what families reside in any of those houses opposite?"

"The one right opposite is a rather stylish boarding-house," said the waiter. "Two of the gentlemen-boarders keep horses at the stable of our establishment. They do things in very good style, sir, the people that live there."

I might have found out nearly as much for myself, on examining the house a little more closely. In one of the upper chambers I saw a young man in a dressing gown, standing before the glass and brushing his hair, for a quarter of an hour together. He then spent an equal space of time in the elaborate arrangement of his cravat, and finally made his appearance in a dress-coat, which I suspected to be newly come from the tailor's, and now first put on for a dinner-party. At a window of the next story below, two children, prettily dressed, were looking out. By and by, a middle-aged gentleman came softly behind them, kissed the little girl, and playfully pulled the little boy's ear. It was a papa, no doubt, just come in from his counting-room or office; and anon appeared mamma, stealing as softly behind papa as he had stolen behind the children, and laying her hand on his shoulder, to surprise him. Then followed a kiss between papa and mamma; but a noiseless one, for the children did not turn their heads.

"I bless God for these good folks!" thought I to myself. "I have not seen a prettier bit of nature, in all my summer in the country, than they have shown me here, in a rather stylish boarding-house. I will pay them a little more attention by and by.

On the first floor, an iron balustrade ran along in front of the tall and spacious windows, evidently belonging to a back drawing-room; and, far into the interior, through the arch of the sliding-doors, I could discern a gleam from the windows of the front apartment. There were no signs of present occupancy in this suite of rooms; the curtains being enveloped in a protective covering, which allowed but a small portion of their crimson material to be seen. But two house-maids were industriously at work; so that there was good prospect that the boarding-house might not long suffer from the absence of its most expensive and profitable guests. Meanwhile, until they should appear, I cast my eyes downward to the lower regions. There, in the dusk that so early settles into such places, I saw the red glow of the kitchen-range. The hot cook, or one of her subordinates, with a ladle in her hand, came to draw a cool breath at the back door. As soon as she disappeared, an Irish man-servant, in a white jacket, crept slyly forth, and threw away the fragments of a china dish, which, unquestionably, he had just broken. Soon afterwards, a lady, showily dressed, with a curling front of what must have been false hair, and reddish-brown, I suppose, in hue,—though my remoteness allowed me only to guess at such particulars,—this respectable mistress of the boarding-house made a momentary transit across the kitchen-window, and appeared no more. It was her final, comprehensive glance, in order to make sure that soup, fish, and flesh were in a proper state of readiness, before the serving up of dinner.

There was nothing else worth noticing about the house, unless it be that on the peak of one of the dormer-windows which opened out of the roof sat a dove, looking very dreary and forlorn; insomuch that I wondered why she chose to sit there, in the chilly rain, while her kindred were doubtless nestling in a warm and comfortable dove-cote. All at once, this dove spread her wings, and, launching herself in the air, came flying so straight across the intervening space that I fully expected her to alight directly on my window-sill. In the latter part of her course, however, she swerved aside, flew upward, and vanished, as did, likewise, the slight, fantastic pathos with which I had invested her.

## XVIII

### THE BOARDING-HOUSE

THE next day, as soon as I thought of looking again towards the opposite house, there sat the dove again, on the peak of the same dormer-window!

It was by no means an early hour, for, the preceding evening, I had ultimately mustered enterprise enough to visit the theatre, had gone late to bed, and slept beyond all limit, in my remoteness from Silas Foster's awakening horn. Dreams had tormented me throughout the night. The train of thoughts which, for months past, had worn a track through my mind, and to escape which was one of my chief objects in leaving Blithedale, kept treading remorselessly to and fro in their old footsteps, while slumber left me impotent to regulate them. It was not till I had quitted my three friends that they first began to encroach upon my dreams. In those of the last night, Hollingsworth and Zenobia, standing on either side of my bed, had bent across it to exchange a kiss of passion. Priscilla, beholding this,—for she seemed to be peeping in at the chamber-window, —had melted gradually away, and left only the sadness of her expression in my heart. There it still lingered, after I awoke; one of those unreasonable sadnesses that you know not how to deal with, because it involves nothing for common-sense to clutch.

It was a gray and dripping forenoon; gloomy enough in town, and still gloomier in the haunts to which my recollections persisted in transporting me. For, in spite of my efforts to think of something else, I thought how the gusty rain was drifting over the slopes and valleys of our farm; how wet must be the foliage that overshadowed the pulpit-rock; how cheer-less, in such a day, my hermitage,—the tree-solitude of my owl-like hu-mors,—in the vine-encircled heart of the tall pine! It was a phase of homesickness. I had wrenched myself too suddenly out of an accustomed sphere. There was no choice, now, but to bear the pang of whatever heart-strings were snapt asunder, and that illusive torment (like the ache of a limb long ago cut off) by which a past mode of life prolongs itself into the succeeding one. I was full of idle and shapeless regrets. The thought im-pressed itself upon me that I had left duties unperformed. With the pow-er, perhaps, to act in the place of destiny and avert misfortune from my friends, I had resigned them to their fate. That cold tendency, between in-stinct and intellect, which made me pry with a speculative interest into people's passions and impulses, appeared to have gone far towards un-humanizing my heart.

But a man cannot always decide for himself whether his own heart is cold or warm. It now impresses me that, if I erred at all in regard to Hol-lingsworth, Zenobia, and Priscilla, it was through too much sympathy, rather than too little.

To escape the irksomeness of these meditations, I resumed my post at the window. At first sight, there was nothing new to be noticed. The gen-eral aspect of affairs was the same as yesterday, except that the more de-cided inclemency of to-day had driven the sparrows to shelter, and kept the cat within doors; whence, however, she soon emerged, pursued by the cook, and with what looked like the better half of a roast chicken in her mouth. The young man in the dress-coat was invisible; the two children, in the story below, seemed to be romping about the room, under the su-perintendence of a nursery-maid. The damask curtains of the drawing-room, on the first floor, were now fully displayed, festooned gracefully from top to bottom of the windows, which extended from the ceiling to the carpet. A narrower window, at the left of the drawing-room, gave light to what was probably a small boudoir, within which I caught the faintest imaginable glimpse of a girl's figure, in airy drapery. Her arm was in regu-lar movement, as if she were busy with her German worsted, or some other such pretty and unprofitable handiwork.

While intent upon making out this girlish shape, I became sensible that a figure had appeared at one of the windows of the drawing-room. There was a presentiment in my mind; or perhaps my first glance, imperfect and sidelong as it was, had sufficed to convey subtle information of the truth. At any rate, it was with no positive surprise, but as if I had all along expected the incident, that, directing my eyes thitherward, I beheld—like a full-length picture, in the space between the heavy festoons of the win-dow-curtains—no other than Zenobia! At the same instant, my thoughts made sure of the identity of the figure in the boudoir. It could only be Priscilla.

Zenobia was attired, not in the almost rustic costume which she had heretofore worn, but in a fashionable morning-dress. There was, never-theless, one familiar point. She had, as usual, a flower in her hair, brilliant

and of a rare variety, else it had not been Zenobia. After a brief pause at
the window, she turned away, exemplifying, in the few steps that removed
her out of sight, that noble and beautiful motion which characterized her
as much as any other personal charm. Not one woman in a thousand could
move so admirably as Zenobia. Many women can sit gracefully; some can
stand gracefully; and a few, perhaps, can assume a series of graceful positions. But natural movement is the result and expression of the whole being, and cannot be well and nobly performed unless responsive to something in the character. I often used to think that music—light and airy,
wild and passionate, or the full harmony of stately marches, in accordance with her varying mood—should have attended Zenobia's footsteps.

I waited for her reappearance. It was one peculiarity, distinguishing
Zenobia from most of her sex, that she needed for her moral well-being,
and never would forego, a large amount of physical exercise. At Blithedale, no inclemency of sky or muddiness of earth had ever impeded her
daily walks. Here, in town, she probably preferred to tread the extent of
the two drawing-rooms, and measure out the miles by spaces of forty feet,
rather than bedraggle her skirts over the sloppy pavements. Accordingly,
in about the time requisite to pass through the arch of the sliding-doors to
the front window, and to return upon her steps, there she stood again, between the festoons of the crimson curtains. But another personage was
now added to the scene. Behind Zenobia appeared that face which I had
first encountered in the wood-path; the man who had passed, side by side
with her, in such mysterious familiarity and estrangement, beneath my
vine-curtained hermitage in the tall pine-tree. It was Westervelt. And
though he was looking closely over her shoulder, it still seemed to me, as
on the former occasion, that Zenobia repelled him,—that perchance, they
mutually repelled each other, by some incompatibility of their spheres.

This impression, however, might have been altogether the result of
fancy and prejudice in me. The distance was so great as to obliterate any
play of feature by which I might otherwise have been made a partaker of
their counsels.

There now needed only Hollingsworth and old Moodie to complete the
knot of characters, whom a real intricacy of events, greatly assisted by
my method of insulating them from other relations, had kept so long upon
my mental stage, as actors in a drama. In itself, perhaps, it was no very
remarkable event that they should thus come across me, at the moment
when I imagined myself free. Zenobia, as I well knew, had retained an establishment in town, and had not unfrequently withdrawn herself from
Blithedale during brief intervals, on one of which occasions she had taken
Priscilla along with her. Nevertheless, there seemed something fatal in the
coincidence that had borne me to this one spot, of all others in a great city,
and transfixed me there, and compelled me again to waste my already
wearied sympathies on affairs which were none of mine, and persons who
cared little for me. It irritated my nerves; it affected me with a kind of
heart-sickness. After the effort which it cost me to fling them off,—after
consummating my escape, as I thought, from these goblins of flesh and

blood, and pausing to revive myself with a breath or two of an atmosphere in which they should have no share,—it was a positive despair, to find the same figures arraying themselves before me, and presenting their old problem in a shape that made it more insoluble than ever.

I began to long for a catastrophe. If the noble temper of Hollingsworth's soul were doomed to be utterly corrupted by the too powerful purpose which had grown out of what was noblest in him; if the rich and generous qualities of Zenobia's womanhood might not save her; if Priscilla must perish by her tenderness and faith, so simple and so devout,—then be it so! Let it all come! As for me, I would look on, as it seemed my part to do, understandingly, if my intellect could fathom the meaning and the moral, and, at all events, reverently and sadly. The curtain fallen, I would pass onward with my poor individual life, which was now attenuated of much of its proper substance, and diffused among many alien interests.

Meanwhile, Zenobia and her companion had retreated from the window. Then followed an interval, during which I directed my eyes towards the figure in the boudoir. Most certainly it was Priscilla, although dressed with a novel and fanciful elegance. The vague perception of it, as viewed so far off, impressed me as if she had suddenly passed out of a chrysalis state and put forth wings. Her hands were not now in motion. She had dropt her work, and sat with her head thrown back, in the same attitude that I had seen several times before, when she seemed to be listening to an imperfectly distinguished sound.

Again the two figures in the drawing-room became visible. They were now a little withdrawn from the window, face to face, and, as I could see by Zenobia's emphatic gestures, were discussing some subject in which she, at least, felt a passionate concern. By and by she broke away, and vanished beyond my ken. Westervelt approached the window, and leaned his forehead against a pane of glass, displaying the sort of smile on his handsome features which, when I before met him, had let me into the secret of his gold-bordered teeth. Every human being, when given over to the Devil, is sure to have the wizard mark upon him, in one form or another. I fancied that this smile, with its peculiar revelation, was the Devil's signet on the Professor.

This man, as I had soon reason to know, was endowed with a cat-like circumspection; and though precisely the most unspiritual quality in the world, it was almost as effective as spiritual insight in making him acquainted with whatever it suited him to discover. He now proved it, considerably to my discomfiture, by detecting and recognizing me, at my post of observation. Perhaps I ought to have blushed at being caught in such an evident scrutiny of Professor Westervelt and his affairs. Perhaps I did blush. Be that as it might, I retained presence of mind enough not to make my position yet more irksome, by the poltroonery of drawing back.

Westervelt looked into the depths of the drawing-room, and beckoned. Immediately afterwards Zenobia appeared at the window, with color much heightened, and eyes which, as my conscience whispered me, were shooting bright arrows, barbed with scorn, across the intervening space, directed full at my sensibilities as a gentleman. If the truth must be told, far as her flight-shot was, those arrows hit the mark. She signified her recognition of me by a gesture with her head and hand, comprising at once a salutation and dismissal. The next moment, she administered one of those pitiless rebukes which a woman always has at hand, ready for any offence (and which she so seldom spares on due occasion), by letting down a white linen curtain between the festoons of the damask ones. It fell like the drop-curtain of a theatre, in the interval between the acts.

Priscilla had disappeared from the boudoir. But the dove still kept her desolate perch on the peak of the attic-window.

## XIX

### ZENOBIA'S DRAWING-ROOM

THE remainder of the day, so far as I was concerned, was spent in meditating on these recent incidents. I contrived, and alternately rejected, innumerable methods of accounting for the presence of Zenobia and Priscilla, and the connection of Westervelt with both. It must be owned, too, that I had a keen, revengeful sense of the insult inflicted by Zenobia's scornful recognition, and more particularly by her letting down the curtain; as if such were the proper barrier to be interposed between a character like hers and a perceptive faculty like mine. For, was mine a mere vulgar curiosity? Zenobia should have known me better than to suppose it. She should have been able to appreciate that quality of the intellect and the heart which impelled me (often against my own will, and to the detriment of my own comfort) to live in other lives, and to endeavor—by generous sympathies, by delicate intuitions, by taking note of things too slight for record, and by bringing my human spirit into manifold accordance with the companions whom God assigned me—to learn the secret which was hidden even from themselves.

Of all possible observers, methought a woman like Zenobia and a man like Hollingsworth should have selected me. And now when the event has long been past, I retain the same opinion of my fitness for the office. True, I might have condemned them. Had I been judge as well as witness, my sentence might have been stern as that of destiny itself. But, still, no trait of original nobility of character, no struggle against temptation,—no iron necessity of will, on the one hand, nor extenuating circumstance to be derived from passion and despair, on the other,—no remorse that might co-exist with error, even if powerless to prevent it,—no proud repentance that should claim retribution as a meed,—would go unappreciated. True, again, I might give my full assent to the punishment which was sure to follow. But it would be given mournfully, and with undiminished love. And, after all was finished, I would come, as if to gather up the white ashes of those who had perished at the stake, and to tell the world—the wrong being now atoned for—how much had perished there which it had never yet known how to praise.

I sat in my rocking-chair, too far withdrawn from the window to expose myself to another rebuke like that already inflicted. My eyes still wandered towards the opposite house, but without effecting any new discoveries. Late in the afternoon, the weather-cock on the church-spire indicated a change of wind; the sun shone dimly out as if the golden wine of its beams were mingled half-and-half with water. Nevertheless, they kindled up the whole range of edifices, threw a glow over the windows, glistened on the wet roofs, and, slowly withdrawing upward, perched upon the chimney-tops; thence they took a higher flight, and lingered an instant on the tip of the spire, making it the final point of more cheerful light in the whole sombre scene. The next moment, it was all gone. The twilight fell into the area like a shower of dusky snow, and before it was quite dark, the gong of the hotel summoned me to tea.

When I returned to my chamber, the glow of an astral-lamp was penetrating mistily through the white curtain of Zenobia's drawing-room. The shadow of a passing figure was now and then cast upon this medium, but with too vague an outline for even my adventurous conjectures to read the hieroglyphic that it presented.

All at once, it occurred to me how very absurd was my behavior in thus tormenting myself with crazy hypotheses as to what was going on within that drawing-room, when it was at my option to be personally present there. My relations with Zenobia, as yet unchanged,—as a familiar friend, and associated in the same life-long enterprise,—gave me the right, and made it no more than kindly courtesy demanded, to call on her. Nothing, except our habitual independence of conventional rules at Blithedale, could have kept me from sooner recognizing this duty. At all events, it should now be performed.

In compliance with this sudden impulse, I soon found myself actually within the house, the rear of which, for two days past, I had been so sedulously watching. A servant took my card, and immediately returning, ushered me up stairs. On the way, I heard a rich, and, as it were, triumphant burst of music from a piano, in which I felt Zenobia's character, although heretofore I had known nothing of her skill upon the instrument. Two or three canary-birds, excited by this gush of sound, sang piercingly, and did their utmost to produce a kindred melody. A bright illumination streamed through the door of the front drawing-room; and I had barely stept across the threshold before Zenobia came forward to meet me, laughing, and with an extended hand.

"Ah, Mr. Coverdale," said she, still smiling, but, as I thought, with a good deal of scornful anger underneath, "it has gratified me to see the interest which you continue to take in my affairs! I have long recognized you as a sort of transcendental Yankee, with all the native propensity of your countrymen to investigate matters that come within their range, but rendered almost poetical, in your case, by the refined methods which you adopt for its gratification. After all, it was an unjustifiable stroke, on my part,—was it not?—to let down the window-curtain!"

"I cannot call it a very wise one," returned I, with a secret bitterness, which, no doubt, Zenobia appreciated. "It is really impossible to hide anything, in this world, to say nothing of the next. All that we ought to ask, therefore, is, that the witnesses of our conduct, and the speculators on our motives, should be capable of taking the highest view which the circumstances of the case may admit. So much being secured, I, for one, would be most happy in feeling myself followed everywhere by an indefatigable human sympathy."

"We must trust for intelligent sympathy to our guardian angels, if any there be," said Zenobia. "As long as the only spectator of my poor tragedy is a young man at the window of his hotel, I must still claim the liberty to drop the curtain."

While this passed, as Zenobia's hand was extended, I had applied the very slightest touch of my fingers to her own. In spite of an external freedom, her manner made me sensible that we stood upon no real terms of confidence. The thought came sadly across me, how great was the contrast betwixt this interview and our first meeting. Then, in the warm light of the country fireside, Zenobia had greeted me cheerily and hopefully, with a full sisterly grasp of the hand, conveying as much kindness in it as other women could have evinced by the pressure of both arms around my neck, or by yielding a cheek to the brotherly salute. The difference was as complete as between her appearance at that time—so simply attired, and with only the one superb flower in her hair—and now, when her beauty was set off by all that dress and ornament could do for it. And they did much. Not, indeed, that they created or added anything to what Nature had lavishly done for Zenobia. But, those costly robes which she had on, those flaming jewels on her neck, served as lamps to display the personal advantages which required nothing less than such an illumination to be fully seen. Even her characteristic flower, though it seemed to be still there, had undergone a cold and bright transfiguration; it was a flower exquisitely imitated in jeweller's work, and imparting the last touch that transformed Zenobia into a work of art.

"I scarcely feel," I could not forbear saying, "as if we had ever met before. How many years ago it seems since we last sat beneath Eliot's pulpit, with Hollingsworth extended on the fallen leaves, and Priscilla at his feet! Can it be, Zenobia, that you ever really numbered yourself with our little band of earnest, thoughtful, philanthropic laborers?"

"Those ideas have their time and place," she answered, coldly. "But I fancy it must be a very circumscribed mind that can find room for no other."

Her manner bewildered me. Literally, moreover, I was dazzled by the brilliancy of the room. A chandelier hung down in the centre, glowing with I know not how many lights; there were separate lamps, also, on two or three tables, and on marble brackets, adding their white radiance to that of the chandelier. The furniture was exceedingly rich. Fresh from our old farm-house, with its homely board and benches in the dining-room, and a few wicker chairs in the best parlor, it struck me that here was the fulfilment of every fantasy of an imagination revelling in various methods of costly self-indulgence and splendid ease. Pictures, marbles, vases,—in brief, more shapes of luxury than there could be any object in enumerating, except for an auctioneer's advertisement,—and the whole repeated and doubled by the reflection of a great mirror, which showed me Zenobia's proud figure, likewise, and my own. It cost me, I acknowledge, a bitter sense of shame, to perceive in myself a positive effort to bear up against the effect which Zenobia sought to impose on me. I reasoned against her, in my secret mind, and strove so to keep my footing. In the gorgeousness with which she had surrounded herself,—in the redundance of personal ornament, which the largeness of her physical nature and the rich type of her beauty caused to seem so suitable,—I malevolently beheld the true character of the woman, passionate, luxurious, lacking simplicity, not deeply refined, incapable of pure and perfect taste.

But, the next instant, she was too powerful for all my opposing struggles. I saw how fit it was that she should make herself as gorgeous as she pleased, and should do a thousand things that would have been ridiculous in the poor, thin, weakly characters of other women. To this day, however, I hardly know whether I then beheld Zenobia in her truest attitude, or whether that were the truer one in which she had presented herself at Blithedale. In both, there was something like the illusion which a great actress flings around her.

"Have you given up Blithedale forever?" I inquired.

"Why should you think so?" asked she.

"I cannot tell," answered I; "except that it appears all like a dream that we were ever there together."

"It is not so to me," said Zenobia. "I should think it a poor and meagre nature that is capable of but one set of forms, and must convert all the past into a dream merely because the present happens to be unlike it. Why should we be content with our homely life of a few months past, to the exclusion of all other modes? It was good; but there are other lives as good, or better. Not, you will understand, that I condemn those who give themselves up to it more entirely than I, for myself, should deem it wise to do."

It irritated me, this self-complacent, condescending, qualified approval and criticism of a system to which many individuals—perhaps as highly endowed as our gorgeous Zenobia—had contributed their all of earthly endeavor, and their loftiest aspirations. I determined to make proof if there were any spell that would exorcise her out of the part which she seemed to be acting. She should be compelled to give me a glimpse of something true; some nature, some passion, no matter whether right or wrong, provided it were real.

"Your allusion to that class of circumscribed characters, who can live only in one mode of life," remarked I, coolly, "reminds me of our poor friend Hollingsworth. Possibly he was in your thoughts when you spoke thus. Poor fellow! It is a pity that, by the fault of a narrow education, he should have so completely immolated himself to that one idea of his, especially as the slightest modicum of common-sense would teach him its utter impracticability. Now that I have returned into the world, and can look at his project from a distance, it requires quite all my real regard for this respectable and well-intentioned man, to prevent me laughing at him, —as I find society at large does."

Zenobia's eyes darted lightning, her cheeks flushed, the vividness of her expression was like the effect of a powerful light flaming up suddenly within her. My experiment had fully succeeded. She had shown me the true flesh and blood of her heart, by thus involuntarily resenting my slight, pitying, half-kind, half-scornful mention of the man who was all in all with her. She herself probably felt this; for it was hardly a moment before she tranquillized her uneven breath, and seemed as proud and self-possessed as ever.

"I rather imagine," said she, quietly, "that your appreciation falls short of Mr. Hollingsworth's just claims. Blind enthusiasm, absorption in one idea, I grant, is generally ridiculous, and must be fatal to the respectability of an ordinary man; it requires a very high and powerful character to make it otherwise. But a great man—as, perhaps, you do not know —attains his normal condition only through the inspiration of one great idea. As a friend of Mr. Hollingsworth, and, at the same time, a calm observer, I must tell you that he seems to me such a man. But you are very pardonable for fancying him ridiculous. Doubtless, he is so—to you! There can be no truer test of the noble and heroic, in any individual, than the degree in which he possesses the faculty of distinguishing heroism from absurdity."

I dared make no retort to Zenobia's concluding apothegm. In truth, I admired her fidelity. It gave me a new sense of Hollingsworth's native power, to discover that his influence was no less potent with this beautiful woman, here, in the midst of artificial life, than it had been at the foot of the gray rock, and among the wild birch-trees of the wood-path, when she so passionately pressed his hand against her heart. The great, rude, shaggy, swarthy man! And Zenobia loved him!

"Did you bring Priscilla with you?" I resumed. "Do you know I have sometimes fancied it not quite safe, considering the susceptibility of her temperament, that she should be so constantly within the sphere of a man like Hollingsworth. Such tender and delicate natures, among your sex, have often, I believe, a very adequate appreciation of the heroic element in men. But then, again, I should suppose them as likely as any other women to make a reciprocal impression. Hollingsworth could hardly give his affections to a person capable of taking an independent stand, but only to one whom he might absorb into himself. He has certainly shown great tenderness for Priscilla."

Zenobia had turned aside. But I caught the reflection of her face in the mirror, and saw that it was very pale,—as pale, in her rich attire, as if a shroud were round her.

"Priscilla is here," said she, her voice a little lower than usual. "Have not you learnt as much from your chamber-window? Would you like to see her?"

She made a step or two into the back drawing-room, and called, "Priscilla! Dear Priscilla!"

## XX

### They Vanish

Priscilla immediately answered the summons, and made her appearance through the door of the boudoir.

I had conceived the idea, which I now recognized as a very foolish one, that Zenobia would have taken measures to debar me from an interview with this girl, between whom and herself there was so utter an opposition of their dearest interests, that, on one part or the other, a great grief, if not likewise a great wrong, seemed a matter of necessity. But, as Priscilla was only a leaf floating on the dark current of events, without influencing them by her own choice or plan,—as she probably guessed not whither the stream was bearing her, nor perhaps even felt its inevitable movement,—there could be no peril of her communicating to me any intelligence with regard to Zenobia's purposes.

On perceiving me, she came forward with great quietude of manner; and when I held out my hand, her own moved slightly towards it, as if attracted by a feeble degree of magnetism.

"I am glad to see you, my dear Priscilla," said I, still holding her hand; "but everything that I meet with nowadays makes me wonder whether I am awake. You, especially, have always seemed like a figure in a dream, and now more than ever."

"Oh, there is substance in these fingers of mine," she answered, giving my hand the faintest possible pressure, and then taking away her own. "Why do you call me a dream? Zenobia is much more like one than I; she is so very, very beautiful! And, I suppose," added Priscilla, as if thinking aloud, "everybody sees it, as I do."

But, for my part, it was Priscilla's beauty, not Zenobia's, of which I was thinking at that moment. She was a person who could be quite obliterated, so far as beauty went, by anything unsuitable in her attire; her charm was not positive and material enough to bear up against a mistaken choice of color, for instance, or fashion. It was safest, in her case, to attempt no art of dress; for it demanded the most perfect taste, or else the happiest accident in the world, to give her precisely the adornment which she needed. She was now dressed in pure white, set off with some kind of a gauzy fabric, which—as I bring up her figure in my memory, with a faint gleam on her shadowy hair, and her dark eyes bent shyly on mine, through all the vanished years—seems to be floating about her like a mist. I wondered what Zenobia meant by evolving so much loveliness out of this poor girl. It was what few women could afford to do; for, as I looked from one to the other, the sheen and splendor of Zenobia's presence took nothing from Priscilla's softer spell, if it might not rather be thought to add to it.

"What do you think of her?" asked Zenobia.

I could not understand the look of melancholy kindness with which Zenobia regarded her. She advanced a step, and beckoning Priscilla near her, kissed her cheek; then, with a slight gesture of repulse, she moved to the other side of the room. I followed.

"She is a wonderful creature," I said. "Ever since she came among us, I have been dimly sensible of just this charm which you have brought out. But it was never absolutely visible till now. She is as lovely as a flower!"

"Well, say so if you like," answered Zenobia. "You are a poet,—at least, as poets go nowadays,—and must be allowed to make an opera-glass of your imagination, when you look at women. I wonder, in such Arcadian freedom of falling in love as we have lately enjoyed, it never occurred to you to fall in love with Priscilla. In society, indeed, a genuine American never dreams of stepping across the inappreciable air-line which separates one class from another. But what was rank to the colonists of Blithedale?"

"There were other reasons," I replied, "why I should have demonstrated myself an ass, had I fallen in love with Priscilla. By the by, has Hollingsworth ever seen her in this dress?"

"Why do you bring up his name at every turn?" asked Zenobia, in an undertone, and with a malign look which wandered from my face to Priscilla's. "You know not what you do! It is dangerous, sir, believe me, to tamper thus with earnest human passions, out of your own mere idleness, and for your sport. I will endure it no longer! Take care that it does not happen again! I warn you!"

"You partly wrong me, if not wholly," I responded. "It is an uncertain sense of some duty to perform, that brings my thoughts, and therefore my words, continually to that one point."

"Oh, this stale excuse of duty!" said Zenobia, in a whisper so full of scorn that it penetrated me like the hiss of a serpent. "I have often heard it before, from those who sought to interfere with me, and I know precisely what it signifies. Bigotry; self-conceit; an insolent curiosity; a meddlesome temper; a cold-blooded criticism, founded on a shallow interpretation of half-perceptions; a monstrous scepticism in regard to any conscience or any wisdom, except one's own; a most irreverent propensity to thrust Providence aside, and substitute one's self in its awful place,—out of these, and other motives as miserable as these, comes your idea of duty! But, beware, sir! With all your fancied acuteness, you step blindfold into these affairs. For any mischief that may follow your interference, I hold you responsible!"

It was evident that, with but a little further provocation, the lioness would turn to bay; if, indeed, such were not her attitude already. I bowed, and not very well knowing what else to do, was about to withdraw. But, glancing again towards Priscilla, who had retreated into a corner, there fell upon my heart an intolerable burden of despondency, the purport of which I could not tell, but only felt it to bear reference to her. I approached and held out my hand; a gesture, however, to which she made no response. It was always one of her peculiarities that she seemed to shrink from even the most friendly touch, unless it were Zenobia's or Hollingsworth's. Zenobia, all this while, stood watching us, but with a careless expression, as if it mattered very little what might pass.

"Priscilla," I inquired, lowering my voice, "when do you go back to Blithedale?"

"Whenever they please to take me," said she.

"Did you come away of your own free will?" I asked.

"I am blown about like a leaf," she replied. "I never have any free will."

"Does Hollingsworth know that you are here? said I.

"He bade me come," answered Priscilla.

She looked at me, I thought, with an air of surprise as if the idea were incomprehensible that she should have taken this step without his agency.

"What a gripe this man has laid upon her whole being!" muttered I, between my teeth. "Well, as Zenobia so kindly intimates, I have no more business here. I wash my hands of it all. On Hollingsworth's head be the consequences! Priscilla," I added aloud, "I know not that ever we may meet again. Farewell!"

As I spoke the word, a carriage had rumbled along the street, and stopt before the house. The door-bell rang, and steps were immediately afterwards heard on the staircase. Zenobia had thrown a shawl over her dress.

"Mr. Coverdale," said she, with cool courtesy, "you will perhaps excuse us. We have an engagement, and are going out."

"Whither?" I demanded.

"Is not that a little more than you are entitled to inquire?" said she, with a smile. "At all events, it does not suit me to tell you."

The door of the drawing-room opened, and Westervelt appeared. I observed that he was elaborately dressed, as if for some grand entertainment. My dislike for this man was infinite. At that moment it amounted to nothing less than a creeping of the flesh, as when, feeling about in a dark place, one touches something cold and slimy, and questions what the secret hatefulness may be. And still I could not but acknowledge that, for personal beauty, for polish of manner, for all that externally befits a gentleman, there was hardly another like him. After bowing to Zenobia, and graciously saluting Priscilla in her corner, he recognized me by a slight but courteous inclination.

"Come, Priscilla," said Zenobia; "it is time. Mr. Coverdale, good evening."

As Priscilla moved slowly forward, I met her in the middle of the drawing-room.

"Priscilla," said I, in the hearing of them all, "do you know whither you are going?"

"I do not know," she answered.

"Is it wise to go, and is it your choice to go?" I asked. "If not, I am your friend, and Hollingsworth's friend. Tell me so, at once."

"Possibly," observed Westervelt, smiling, "Priscilla sees in me an older friend than either Mr. Coverdale or Mr. Hollingsworth. I shall willingly leave the matter at her option."

While thus speaking, he made a gesture of kindly invitation, and Priscilla passed me, with the gliding movement of a sprite, and took his offered arm. He offered the other to Zenobia; but she turned her proud and beautiful face upon him, with a look which—judging from what I caught of it in profile—would undoubtedly have smitten the man dead, had he possessed any heart, or had this glance attained to it. It seemed to rebound, however, from his courteous visage, like an arrow from polished steel. They all three descended the stairs; and when I likewise reached the street-door, the carriage was already rolling away.

## XXI

### AN OLD ACQUAINTANCE

THUS excluded from everybody's confidence, and attaining no further, by my most earnest study, than to an uncertain sense of something hidden from me, it would appear reasonable that I should have flung off all these alien perplexities. Obviously, my best course was to betake myself to new scenes. Here I was only an intruder. Elsewhere there might be circumstances in which I could establish a personal interest, and people who would respond, with a portion of their sympathies, for so much as I should bestow of mine.

Nevertheless, there occurred to me one other thing to be done. Remembering old Moodie, and his relationship with Priscilla, I determined to seek an interview, for the purpose of ascertaining whether the knot of affairs was as inextricable on that side as I found it on all others. Being tolerably well acquainted with the old man's haunts, I went, the next day, to the saloon of a certain establishment about which he often lurked. It was a reputable place enough, affording good entertainment in the way of meat, drink, and fumigation; and there, in my young and idle days and nights, when I was neither nice nor wise, I had often amused myself with watching the staid humors and sober jollities of the thirsty souls around me.

At my first entrance, old Moodie was not there. The more patiently to await him, I lighted a cigar, and establishing myself in a corner, took a quiet, and, by sympathy, a boozy kind of pleasure in the customary life that was going forward. The saloon was fitted up with a good deal of taste. There were pictures on the walls, and among them an oil-painting of a beefsteak, with such an admirable show of juicy tenderness, that the beholder sighed to think it merely visionary, and incapable of ever being put upon a gridiron. Another work of high art was the life-like representation of a noble sirloin; another, the hindquarters of a deer, retaining the hoofs and tawny fur; another, the head and shoulders of a salmon; and, still more exquisitely finished, a brace of canvas-back ducks, in which the mottled feathers were depicted with the accuracy of a daguerreotype. Some very hungry painter, I suppose, had wrought these subjects of still-life, heightening his imagination with his appetite, and earning, it is to be hoped, the privilege of a daily dinner off whichever of his pictorial viands he liked best. Then, there was a fine old cheese, in which you could almost discern the mites; and some sardines, on a small plate, very richly done, and looking as if oozy with the oil in which they had been smothered. All these things were so perfectly imitated, that you seemed to have the genuine article before you, and yet with an indescribable ideal charm; it took away the grossness from what was fleshiest and fattest, and thus helped the life of man, even in its earthliest relations, to appear rich and noble, as well as warm, cheerful, and substantial. There were pictures, too, of gallant revellers,—those of the old time,—Flemish, apparently,—with doublets and slashed sleeves,—drinking their wine out of fantastic long-stemmed glasses; quaffing joyously, quaffing forever, with inaudible laughter and song, while the Champagne bubbled immortally against their mustaches or the purple tide of Burgundy ran inexhaustibly down their throats.

But, in an obscure corner of the saloon, there was a little picture—excellently done, moreover—of a ragged, bloated New England toper, stretched out on a bench, in the heavy, apoplectic sleep of drunkenness. The death-in-life was too well portrayed. You smelt the fumy liquor that had brought on this syncope. Your only comfort lay in the forced reflection, that, real as he looked, the poor caitiff was but imaginary,—a bit of painted canvas, whom no delirium tremens, nor so much as a retributive headache, awaited, on the morrow.

By this time, it being past eleven o'clock, the two barkeepers of the saloon were in pretty constant activity. One of these young men had a rare faculty in the concoction of gin-cocktails. It was a spectacle to behold, how, with a tumbler in each hand, he tossed the contents from one to the other. Never conveying it awry, nor spilling the least drop, he compelled the frothy liquor, as it seemed to me, to spout forth from one glass and descend into the other, in a great parabolic curve, as well defined and calculable as a planet's orbit. He had a good forehead, with a particularly large development just above the eyebrows; fine intellectual gifts, no doubt, which he had educated to this profitable end; being famous for nothing but gin-cocktails, and commanding a fair salary by his one accomplishment. These cocktails, and other artificial combinations of liquor (of which there were at least a score, though mostly, I suspect, fantastic in their differences), were much in favor with the younger class of customers, who, at furthest, had only reached the second stage of potatory life. The staunch old soakers, on the other hand, —men who, if put on tap, would have yielded a red alcoholic liquor by way of blood,—usually confined themselves to plain brandy-and-water, gin, or West India rum; and, oftentimes, they prefaced their dram with some medicinal remark as to the wholesomeness and stomachic qualities of that particular drink. Two or three appeared to have bottles of their own behind the counter; and, winking one red eye to the barkeeper, he forthwith produced these choicest and peculiar cordials, which it was a matter of great interest and favor, among their acquaintances, to obtain a sip of.

Agreeably to the Yankee habit, under whatever circumstances, the deportment of all these good fellows, old or young, was decorous and thoroughly correct. They grew only the more sober in their cups; there was no confused babble nor boisterous laughter. They sucked in the joyous fire of the decanters and kept it smouldering in their inmost recesses, with a bliss known only to the heart which it warmed and comforted. Their eyes twinkled a little, to be sure; they hemmed vigorously after each glass, and laid a hand upon the pit of the stomach, as if the pleasant titillation there was what constituted the tangible part of their enjoyment. In that spot, unquestionably, and not in the brain, was the acme of the whole affair. But the true purpose of their drinking—and one that will induce men to drink, or do something equivalent, as long as this weary world shall endure—was the renewed youth and vigor, the brisk, cheerful sense of things present and to come, with which, for about a quarter of an hour, the dram permeated their systems. And when such quarters of an hour can be obtained in some mode less baneful to the great sum of a man's life,—but, nevertheless, with a little spice of impropriety, to give it a wild flavor,—we temperance people may ring out our bells for victory!

The prettiest object in the saloon was a tiny fountain, which threw up its feathery jet through the counter, and sparkled down again into an oval basin, or lakelet, containing several gold-fishes. There was a bed of bright sand at the bottom, strewn with coral and rock-work; and the fishes went gleaming about, now turning up the sheen of a golden side, and now vanishing into the shadows of the water, like the fanciful thoughts that coquet with a poet in his dream. Never before, I imagine.

did a company of water-drinkers remain so entirely uncontaminated by the bad example around them; nor could I help wondering that it had not occurred to any freakish inebriate to empty a glass of liquor into their lakelet. What a delightful idea! Who would not be a fish, if he could inhale jollity with the essential element of his existence!

I had begun to despair of meeting old Moodie, when, all at once, I recognized his hand and arm protruding from behind a screen that was set up for the accommodation of bashful topers. As a matter of course, he had one of Priscilla's little purses, and was quietly insinuating it under the notice of a person who stood near. This was always old Moodie's way. You hardly ever saw him advancing towards you, but became aware of his proximity without being able to guess how he had come thither. He glided about like a spirit, assuming visibility close to your elbow, offering his petty trifles of merchandise, remaining long enough for you to purchase, if so disposed, and then taking himself off, between two breaths, while you happened to be thinking of something else.

By a sort of sympathetic impulse that often controlled me in those more impressible days of my life, I was induced to approach this old man in a mode as undemonstrative as his own. Thus, when, according to his custom, he was probably just about to vanish, he found me at his elbow.

"Ah!" said he, with more emphasis than was usual with him. "It is Mr. Coverdale!"

"Yes, Mr. Moodie, your old acquaintance," answered I. "It is some time now since we ate luncheon together at Blithedale, and a good deal longer since our little talk together at the street-corner."

"That was a good while ago," said the old man.

And he seemed inclined to say not a word more. His existence looked so colorless and torpid,—so very faintly shadowed on the canvas of reality,—that I was half afraid lest he should altogether disappear, even while my eyes were fixed full upon his figure. He was certainly the wretchedest old ghost in the world, with his crazy hat, the dingy handkerchief about his throat, his suit of threadbare gray, and especially that patch over his right eye, behind which he always seemed to be hiding himself. There was one method, however, of bringing him out into somewhat stronger relief. A glass of brandy would effect it. Perhaps the gentler influence of a bottle of claret might do the same. Nor could I think it a matter for the recording angel to write down against me, if— with my painful consciousness of the frost in this old man's blood, and the positive ice that had congealed about his heart—I should thaw him out, were it only for an hour, with the summer warmth of a little wine. What else could possibly be done for him? How else could he be imbued with energy enough to hope for a happier state hereafter? How else be inspired to say his prayers? For there are states of our spiritual system when the throb of the soul's life is too faint and weak to render us capable of religious aspiration.

"Mr. Moodie," said I, "shall we lunch together? And would you like to drink a glass of wine?"

His one eye gleamed. He bowed; and it impressed me that he grew to be more of a man at once, either in anticipation of the wine, or as a grateful response to my good fellowship in offering it.

"With pleasure," he replied.

The barkeeper, at my request, showed us into a private room, and soon afterwards set some fried oysters and a bottle of claret on the table; and I saw the old man glance curiously at the label of the bottle, as if to learn the brand.

"It should be good wine," I remarked, "if it have any right to its label."

"You cannot suppose, sir," said Moodie, with a sigh, "that a poor old fellow like me knows any difference in wines."

And yet, in his way of handling the glass, in his preliminary snuff at the aroma, in his first cautious sip of the wine, and the gustatory skill with which he gave his palate the full advantage of it, it was impossible not to recognize the connoisseur.

"I fancy, Mr. Moodie," said I, "you are a much better judge of wines than I have yet learned to be. Tell me fairly,—did you never drink it where the grape grows?"

"How should that have been, Mr. Coverdale?" answered old Moodie, shyly; but then he took courage, as it were, and uttered a feeble little laugh. "The flavor of this wine," added he, "and its perfume still more than its taste, makes me remember that I was once a young man."

"I wish, Mr. Moodie," suggested I,—not that I greatly cared about it, however, but was only anxious to draw him into some talk about Priscilla and Zenobia,—"I wish, while we sit over our wine, you would favor me with a few of those youthful reminiscences."

"Ah," said he, shaking his head, "they might interest you more than you suppose. But I had better be silent, Mr. Coverdale. If this good wine,—though claret, I suppose, is not apt to play such a trick,—but if it should make my tongue run too freely, I could never look you in the face again."

"You never did look me in the face, Mr. Moodie," I replied, "until this very moment."

"Ah!" sighed old Moodie.

It was wonderful, however, what an effect the mild grape-juice wrought upon him. It was not in the wine, but in the associations which it seemed to bring up. Instead of the mean, slouching, furtive, painfully depressed air of an old city vagabond, more like a gray kennel-rat than any other living thing, he began to take the aspect of a decayed gentleman. Even his garments—especially after I had myself quaffed a glass or two—looked less shabby than when we first sat down. There was, by and by, a certain exuberance and elaborateness of gesture and manner, oddly in contrast with all that I had hitherto seen of him. Anon, with hardly any impulse from me, old Moodie began to talk. His communications referred exclusively to a long-past and more fortunate period of his life, with only a few unavoidable allusions to the circumstances that had reduced him to his present state. But, having once got the clew, my subsequent researches acquainted me with the main facts of the following narrative; although, in writing it out, my pen has perhaps allowed itself a trifle of romantic and legendary license, worthier of a small poet than of a grave biographer.

## XXII

### FAUNTLEROY

FIVE-AND-TWENTY years ago, at the epoch of this story, there dwelt in one of the Middle States a man whom we shall call Fauntleroy; a man of wealth, and magnificent tastes, and prodigal expenditure. His home might almost be styled a palace; his habits, in the ordinary sense, princely. His whole being seemed to have crystallized itself into an external splendor, wherewith he glittered in the eyes of the world, and had no other life than upon this gaudy surface. He had married a lovely woman, whose nature was deeper than his own. But his affection for her, though it showed largely, was superficial, like all his other manifestations and developments; he did not so truly keep this noble creature in his heart, as wear her beauty for the most brilliant ornament of his outward state. And there was born to him a child, a beautiful daughter, whom he took from the beneficent hand of God with no just sense of her immortal value, but as a man already rich in gems would receive another jewel. If he loved her, it was because she shone.

After Fauntleroy had thus spent a few empty years, coruscating continually an unnatural light, the source of it—which was merely his gold —began to grow more shallow, and finally became exhausted. He saw himself in imminent peril of losing all that had heretofore distinguished him; and, conscious of no innate worth to fall back upon, he recoiled from this calamity with the instinct of a soul shrinking from annihilation. To avoid it—wretched man!—or, rather to defer it, if but for a month, a day, or only to procure himself the life of a few breaths more amid the false glitter which was now less his own than ever,—he made himself guilty of a crime. It was just the sort of crime, growing out of its artificial state which society (unless it should change its entire constitution for this man's unworthy sake) neither could nor ought to pardon. More safely might it pardon murder. Fauntleroy's guilt was discovered. He fled; his wife perished, by the necessity of her innate nobleness, in its alliance with a being so ignoble; and betwixt her mother's death and her father's ignominy, his daughter was left worse than orphaned.

There was no pursuit after Fauntleroy. His family connections, who had great wealth, made such arrangements with those whom he had attempted to wrong as secured him from the retribution that would have overtaken an unfriended criminal. The wreck of his estate was divided among his creditors. His name, in a very brief space, was forgotten by the multitude who had passed it so diligently from mouth to mouth. Seldom, indeed, was it recalled, even by his closest former intimates. Nor could it have been otherwise. The man had laid no real touch on any mortal's heart. Being a mere image, an optical delusion, created by the sunshine of prosperity, it was his law to vanish into the shadow of the first intervening cloud. He seemed to leave no vacancy; a phenomenon which, like many others that attended his brief career, went far to prove the illusiveness of his existence.

Not, however, that the physical substance of Fauntleroy had literally melted into vapor. He had fled northward to the New England metropolis, and had taken up his abode, under another name, in a squalid street or court of the older portion of the city. There he dwelt among poverty-stricken wretches, sinners, and forlorn good people, Irish, and whomsoever else were neediest. Many families were clustered in each house together, above stairs and below, in the little peaked garrets, and even in the dusky cellars. The house where Fauntleroy paid weekly rent for a chamber and a closet had been a stately habitation in its day. An old colonial governor had built it, and lived there, long ago, and held his levees in a great room where now slept twenty Irish bedfellows; and died in Fauntleroy's chamber, which his embroidered and white-wigged ghost still haunted. Tattered hangings, a marble hearth, traversed with many cracks and fissures, a richly carved oaken mantel-piece, partly hacked away for kindling-stuff, a stuccoed ceiling, defaced with great, unsightly patches of the naked laths,—such was the chamber's aspect, as if, with its splinters and rags of dirty splendor, it were a kind of practical gibe at this poor, ruined man of show.

At first, and at irregular intervals, his relatives allowed Fauntleroy a little pittance to sustain life; not from any love, perhaps, but lest poverty should compel him, by new offences, to add more shame to that with which he had already stained them. But he showed no tendency to further guilt. His character appeared to have been radically changed (as, indeed, from its shallowness, it well might) by his miserable fate; or, it may be, the traits now seen in him were portions of the same character, presenting itself in another phase. Instead of any longer seeking to live in the sight of the world, his impulse was to shrink into the nearest obscurity, and to be unseen of men, were it possible, even while standing before their eyes. He had no pride; it was all trodden in the dust. No ostentation; for how could it survive, when there was nothing left of Fauntleroy, save penury and shame! His very gait demonstrated that he would gladly have faded out of view, and have crept about invisibly, for the sake of sheltering himself from the irksomeness of a human glance. Hardly, it was averred, within the memory of those who knew him now, had he the hardihood to show his full front to the world. He skulked in corners, and crept about in a sort of noonday twilight, making himself gray and misty, at all hours, with his morbid intolerance of sunshine.

In his torpid despair, however, he had done an act which that condition of the spirit seems to prompt almost as often as prosperity and hope. Fauntleroy was again married. He had taken to wife a forlorn, meek-spirited, feeble young woman, a seamstress, whom he found dwelling with her mother in a contiguous chamber of the old gubernatorial residence. This poor phantom—as the beautiful and noble companion of his former life had done—brought him a daughter. And sometimes, as from one dream into another, Fauntleroy looked forth out of his present grimy environment into that past magnificence, and wondered whether the grandee of yesterday or the pauper of to-day were real. But, in my mind, the one and the other were alike impalpable. In truth, it was Fauntleroy's fatality to behold whatever he touched dissolve. After a few years, his second wife (dim shadow that she had always been) faded finally out of the world, and left Fauntleroy to deal as he might with their pale and nervous child. And, by this time, among his distant relatives,—with whom he had grown a weary thought, linked with contagious infamy, and which they were only too willing to get rid of,—he was himself supposed to be no more.

The younger child, like his elder one, might be considered as the true offspring of both parents, and as the reflection of their state. She was a tremulous little creature, shrinking involuntarily from all mankind, but in timidity, and no sour repugnance. There was a lack of human substance in her; it seemed as if, were she to stand up in a sunbeam, it would pass right through her figure, and trace out the cracked and dusty window-panes upon the naked floor. But, nevertheless, the poor child had a heart; and from her mother's gentle character she had inherited a profound and still capacity of affection. And so her life was one of love. She bestowed it partly on her father, but in greater part on an idea.

For Fauntleroy, as they sat by their cheerless fireside,—which was no fireside, in truth, but only a rusty stove,—had often talked to the little girl about his former wealth, the noble loveliness of his first wife, and the beautiful child whom she had given him. Instead of the fairy tales which other parents tell, he told Priscilla this. And, out of the loneliness of her sad little existence, Priscilla's love grew, and tended upward, and twined itself perseveringly around this unseen sister; as a grape-vine might strive to clamber out of a gloomy hollow among the rocks, and embrace a young tree standing in the sunny warmth above. It was almost like worship, both in its earnestness and its humility; nor was it the less humble,—though the more earnest,—because Priscilla could claim human kindred with the being whom she so devoutly loved. As with worship, too, it gave her soul the refreshment of a purer atmosphere. Save for this singular, this melancholy, and yet beautiful affec-

ion, the child could hardly have lived; or, had she lived, with a heart
shrunken for lack of any sentiment to fill it, she must have yielded to
the barren miseries of her position, and have grown to womanhood char-
acterless and worthless. But now, amid all the sombre coarseness of her
father's outward life, and of her own, Priscilla had a higher and imag-
native life within. Some faint gleam thereof was often visible upon her
face. It was as if, in her spiritual visits to her brilliant sister, a portion
of the latter's brightness had permeated our dim Priscilla, and still lingered, shedding a faint illumination through the cheerless chamber, after
she came back.

As the child grew up, so pallid and so slender, and with much unaccountable nervousness, and all the weaknesses of neglected infancy still
haunting her, the gross and simple neighbors whispered strange things
about Priscilla. The big, red, Irish matrons, whose innumerable progeny swarmed out of the adjacent doors, used to mock at the pale
Western child. They fancied—or, at least, affirmed it, between jest and
earnest—that she was not so solid flesh and blood as other children, but
mixed largely with a thinner element. They called her ghost-child, and
said that she could indeed vanish when she pleased, but could never, in
her densest moments, make herself quite visible. The sun, at midday,
would shine through her; in the first gray of the twilight, she lost all
the distinctness of her outline; and, if you followed the dim thing into
a dark corner, behold! she was not there. And it was true that Priscilla
had strange ways; strange ways, and stranger words, when she uttered
any words at all. Never stirring out of the old governor's dusky house,
she sometimes talked of distant places and splendid rooms, as if she had
just left them. Hidden things were visible to her (at least so the people
inferred from obscure hints escaping unawares out of her mouth), and
silence was audible. And in all the world there was nothing so difficult
to be endured, by those who had any dark secret to conceal, as the
glance of Priscilla's timid and melancholy eyes.

Her peculiarities were the theme of continual gossip among the other
inhabitants of the gubernatorial mansion. The rumor spread thence into
a wider circle. Those who knew old Moodie, as he was now called, used
often to jeer him, at the very street-corners, about his daughter's gift of
second-sight and prophecy. It was a period when science (though mostly through its empirical professors) was bringing forward, anew, a hoard
of facts and imperfect theories, that had partially won credence in elder
times, but which modern scepticism had swept away as rubbish. These
things were now tossed up again, out of the surging ocean of human
thought and experience. The story of Priscilla's preternatural manifestations, therefore, attracted a kind of notice of which it would have been
deemed wholly unworthy a few years earlier. One day a gentleman ascended the creaking staircase, and inquired which was old Moodie's
chamber-door. And, several times, he came again. He was a marvellously handsome man,—still youthful, too, and fashionably dressed.
Except that Priscilla, in those days, had no beauty, and, in the languor

of her existence, had not yet blossomed into womanhood, there would have been rich food for scandal in these visits; for the girl was unquestionably their sole object, although her father was supposed always to be present. But, it must likewise be added, there was something about Priscilla that calumny could not meddle with; and thus far was she privileged, either by the preponderance of what was spiritual, or the thin and watery blood that left her cheek so pallid.

Yet, if the busy tongues of the neighborhood spared Priscilla in one way, they made themselves amends by renewed and wilder babble on another score. They averred that the strange gentleman was a wizard, and that he had taken advantage of Priscilla's lack of earthly substance to subject her to himself, as his familiar spirit, through whose medium he gained cognizance of whatever happened, in regions near or remote. The boundaries of his power were defined by the verge of the pit of Tartarus on the one hand, and the third sphere of the celestial world on the other. Again, they declared their suspicion that the wizard, with all his show of manly beauty, was really an aged and wizened figure, or else that his semblance of a human body was only a necromantic, or perhaps a mechanical contrivance, in which a demon walked about. In proof of it, however, they could merely instance a gold band around his upper teeth, which had once been visible to several old women, when he smiled at them from the top of the governor's staircase. Of course, this was all absurdity, or mostly so. But, after every possible deduction, there remained certain very mysterious points about the stranger's character, as well as the connection that he established with Priscilla. Its nature at that period was even less understood than now, when miracles of this kind have grown so absolutely stale, that I would gladly, if the truth allowed, dismiss the whole matter from my narrative.

We must now glance backward, in quest of the beautiful daughter of Fauntleroy's prosperity. What had become of her? Fauntleroy's only brother, a bachelor, and with no other relative so near, had adopted the forsaken child. She grew up in affluence, with native graces clustering luxuriantly about her. In her triumphant progress towards womanhood, she was adorned with every variety of feminine accomplishment. But she lacked a mother's care. With no adequate control, on any hand (for a man, however stern, however wise, can never sway and guide a female child), her character was left to shape itself. There was good in it, and evil. Passionate, self-willed, and imperious, she had a warm and generous nature; showing the richness of the soil, however, chiefly by the weeds that flourished in it, and choked up the herbs of grace. In her girlhood her uncle died. As Fauntleroy was supposed to be likewise dead, and no other heir was known to exist, his wealth devolved on her, although, dying suddenly, the uncle left no will. After his death, there were obscure passages in Zenobia's history. There were whispers of an attachment, and even a secret marriage, with a fascinating and accomplished but unprincipled young man. The incidents and appearances,

however, which led to this surmise, soon passed away, and were forgotten.

Nor was her reputation seriously affected by the report. In fact, so
great was her native power and influence, and such seemed the careless
purity of her nature, that whatever Zenobia did was generally acknowledged as right for her to do. The world never criticised her so harshly
as it does most women who transcend its rules. It almost yielded its
assent, when it beheld her stepping out of the common path, and asserting the more extensive privileges of her sex, both theoretically and by
her practice. The sphere of ordinary womanhood was felt to be narrower than her development required.

A portion of Zenobia's more recent life is told in the foregoing pages.
Partly in earnest,—and, I imagine, as was her disposition, half in a
proud jest, or in a kind of recklessness that had grown upon her, out of
some hidden grief,—she had given her countenance, and promised liberal pecuniary aid, to our experiment of a better social state. And
Priscilla followed her to Blithedale. The sole bliss of her life had been a
dream of this beautiful sister, who had never so much as known of her
existence. By this time, too, the poor girl was inthralled in an intolerable bondage, from which she must either free herself or perish. She
deemed herself safest near Zenobia, into whose large heart she hoped to
nestle.

One evening, months after Priscilla's departure, when Moodie (or
shall we call him Fauntleroy?) was sitting alone in the state-chamber
of the old governor, there came footsteps up the staircase. There was a
pause on the landing-place. A lady's musical yet haughty accents were
heard making an inquiry from some denizen of the house, who had
thrust a head out of a contiguous chamber. There was then a knock at
Moodie's door.

"Come in!" said he.

And Zenobia entered. The details of the interview that followed being unknown to me—while, notwithstanding, it would be a pity quite to
lose the picturesqueness of the situation,—I shall attempt to sketch it,
mainly from fancy, although with some general grounds of surmise in
regard to the old man's feelings.

She gazed wonderingly at the dismal chamber. Dismal to her, who
beheld it only for an instant; and how much more so to him, into whose
brain each bare spot on the ceiling, every tatter of the paper-hangings,
and all the splintered carvings of the mantel-piece, seen wearily through
long years, had worn their several prints! Inexpressibly miserable is
this familiarity with objects that have been from the first disgustful.

"I have received a strange message," said Zenobia, after a moment's
silence, "requesting, or rather enjoining it upon me, to come hither.
Rather from curiosity than any other motive,—and because, though a
woman, I have not all the timidity of one,—I have complied. Can it be
you, sir, who thus summoned me?"

"It was," answered Moodie.

"And what was your purpose?" she continued. "You require charity, perhaps? In that case, the message might have been more fitly worded. But you are old and poor, and age and poverty should be allowed their privileges. Tell me, therefore, to what extent you need my aid."

"Put up your purse," said the supposed mendicant, with an inexplicable smile. "Keep it,—keep all your wealth,—until I demand it all, or none! My message had no such end in view. You are beautiful, they tell me; and I desired to look at you."

He took the one lamp that showed the discomfort and sordidness of his abode, and approaching Zenobia held it up, so as to gain the more perfect view of her, from top to toe. So obscure was the chamber, that you could see the reflection of her diamonds thrown upon the dingy wall, and flickering with the rise and fall of Zenobia's breath. It was the splendor of those jewels on her neck, like lamps that burn before some fair temple, and the jewelled flower in her hair, more than the murky, yellow light, that helped him to see her beauty. But he beheld it, and grew proud at heart; his own figure, in spite of his mean habiliments, assumed an air of state and grandeur.

"It is well," cried old Moodie. "Keep your wealth. You are right worthy of it. Keep it, therefore, but with one condition only."

Zenobia thought the old man beside himself, and was moved with pity.

"Have you none to care for you?" asked she. "No daughter?—no kind-hearted neighbor?—no means of procuring the attendance which you need? Tell me once again, can I do nothing for you?"

"Nothing," he replied. "I have beheld what I wished. Now leave me. Linger not a moment longer, or I may be tempted to say what would bring a cloud over that queenly brow. Keep all your wealth, but with only this one condition: Be kind—be no less kind than sisters are—to my poor Priscilla!"

And, it may be, after Zenobia withdrew, Fauntleroy paced his gloomy chamber, and communed with himself as follows,—or, at all events, it is the only solution which I can offer of the enigma presented in his character:—

"I am unchanged,—the same man as of yore!" said he. "True, my brother's wealth—he dying intestate—is legally my own. I know it; yet of my own choice, I live a beggar, and go meanly clad, and hide myself behind a forgotten ignominy. Looks this like ostentation? Ah! but in Zenobia I live again! Beholding her, so beautiful,—so fit to be adorned with all imaginable splendor of outward state,—the cursed vanity, which, half a lifetime since, dropt off like tatters of once gaudy apparel from my debased and ruined person, is all renewed for her sake. Were I to reappear, my shame would go with me from darkness into daylight. Zenobia has the splendor, and not the shame. Let the world admire her, and be dazzled by her, the brilliant child of my prosperity! It is Fauntleroy that still shines through her!"

But then, perhaps, another thought occurred to him.

"My poor Priscilla! And am I just to her, in surrendering all to this beautiful Zenobia? Priscilla! I love her best,—I love her only!—but with shame, not pride. So dim, so pallid, so shrinking,—the daughter of my long calamity! Wealth were but a mockery in Priscilla's hands. What is its use, except to fling a golden radiance around those who grasp it? Yet let Zenobia take heed! Priscilla shall have no wrong!"

But, while the man of show thus meditated,—that very evening, so far as I can adjust the dates of these strange incidents,—Priscilla— poor, pallid flower!—was either snatched from Zenobia's hand, or flung wilfully away!

### XXIII

### A VILLAGE HALL

WELL, I betook myself away, and wandered up and down, like an exorcised spirit that had been driven from its old haunts after a mighty struggle. It takes down the solitary pride of man, beyond most other things, to find the impracticability of flinging aside affections that have grown irksome. The bands that were silken once are apt to become iron fetters when we desire to shake them off. Our souls, after all, are not our own. We convey a property in them to those with whom we associate; but to what extent can never be known, until we feel the tug, the agony, of our abortive effort to resume an exclusive sway over ourselves. Thus, in all the weeks of my absence, my thoughts continually reverted back, brooding over the bygone months, and bringing up incidents that seemed hardly to have left a trace of themselves in their passage. I spent painful hours in recalling these trifles, and rendering them more misty and unsubstantial than at first by the quantity of speculative musing thus kneaded in with them. Hollingsworth, Zenobia, Priscilla! These three had absorbed my life into themselves. Together with an inexpressible longing to know their fortunes, there was likewise a morbid resentment of my own pain, and a stubborn reluctance to come again within their sphere.

All that I learned of them, therefore, was comprised in a few brief and pungent squibs, such as the newspapers were then in the habit of bestowing on our socialist enterprise. There was one paragraph, which if I rightly guessed its purport, bore reference to Zenobia, but was too darkly hinted to convey even thus much of certainty. Hollingsworth, too, with his philanthropic project, afforded the penny-a-liners a theme for some savage and bloody-minded jokes; and, considerably to my surprise, they affected me with as much indignation as if we had still been friends.

Thus passed several weeks; time long enough for my brown and toil-hardened hands to reaccustom themselves to gloves. Old habits, such as were merely external, returned upon me with wonderful promptitude. My superficial talk, too, assumed altogether a worldly tone. Meeting former acquaintances, who showed themselves inclined to ridicule my heroic devotion to the cause of human welfare, I spoke of the recent phase of my life as indeed fair matter for a jest. But, I also gave them to understand that it was, at most, only an experiment, on which I had staked no valuable amount of hope or fear. It had enabled me to pass the summer in a novel and agreeable way, had afforded me some grotesque specimens of artificial simplicity, and could not, therefore, so far as I was concerned, be reckoned a failure. In no one instance, however, did I voluntarily speak of my three friends. They dwelt in a profounder region. The more I consider myself as I then was, the more do I recognize how deeply my connection with those three had affected all my being.

As it was already the epoch of annihilated space, I might in the time I was away from Blithedale have snatched a glimpse at England, and been back again. But my wanderings were confined within a very limited sphere. I hopped and fluttered, like a bird with a string about its leg, gyrating round a small circumference, and keeping up a restless activity to no purpose. Thus it was still in our familiar Massachusetts—in one of its white country-villages—that I must next particularize an incident.

The scene was one of those lyceum-halls, of which almost every village has now its own, dedicated to that sober and pallid, or rather drab-colored, mode of winter-evening entertainment, the lecture. Of late years, this has come strangely into vogue, when the natural tendency of things would seem to be to substitute lettered for oral methods of addressing the public. But, in halls like this, besides the winter course of lectures, there is a rich and varied series of other exhibitions. Hither comes the ventriloquist, with all his mysterious tongues; the thaumaturgist, too, with his miraculous transformations of plates, doves, and rings, his pancakes smoking in your hat, and his cellar of choice liquors represented in one small bottle. Here, also, the itinerant professor instructs separate classes of ladies and gentlemen in physiology, and demonstrates his lessons by the aid of real skeletons, and manikins in wax, from Paris. Here is to be heard the choir of Ethiopian melodists, and to be seen the diorama of Moscow or Bunker Hill, or the moving panorama of the Chinese wall. Here is displayed the museum of wax figures, illustrating the wide catholicism of earthly renown, by mixing up heroes and statesmen, the pope and the Mormon prophet, kings, queens, murderers, and beautiful ladies; every sort of person, in short, except authors, of whom I never beheld even the most famous done in wax. And here, in this many-purposed hall (unless the selectmen of the village chance to have more than their share of the Puritanism, which, however diversified with later patchwork, still gives its prevailing tint to New England character), here the company of strolling players sets up its little stage, and claims patronage for the legitimate drama.

But, on the autumnal evening which I speak of, a number of printed handbills—stuck up in the barroom, and on the sign-post of the hotel, and on the meeting-house porch, and distributed largely through the village—had promised the inhabitants an interview with that celebrated and hitherto inexplicable phenomenon, the Veiled Lady!

The hall was fitted up with an amphitheatrical descent of seats towards a platform, on which stood a desk, two lights, a stool, and a capacious antique chair. The audience was of a generally decent and respectable character: old farmers, in their Sunday black coats, with shrewd, hard, sun-dried faces, and a cynical humor, oftener than any other expression, in their eyes; pretty girls, in many-colored attire; pretty young men,—the schoolmaster, the lawyer, or student at law, the shop-keeper,—all looking rather suburban than rural. In these days, there is absolutely no rusticity, except when the actual labor of the soil leaves its earth-mould on the person. There was likewise a considerable proportion of young and middle-aged women, many of them stern in feature, with marked foreheads, and a very definite line of eyebrow; a type of womanhood in which a bold intellectual development seems to be keeping pace with the progressive delicacy of the physical constitution. Of all these people I took note, at first, according to my custom. But I ceased to do so the moment that my eyes fell on an individual who sat two or three seats below me, immovable, apparently deep in thought, with his back, of course, towards me, and his face turned steadfastly upon the platform.

After sitting awhile in contemplation of this person's familiar contour, I was irresistibly moved to step over the intervening benches, lay my hand on his shoulder, put my mouth close to his ear, and address him in a sepulchral, melodramatic whisper:—

"Hollingsworth! where have you left Zenobia?"

His nerves, however, were proof against my attack. He turned half around, and looked me in the face with great, sad eyes, in which there was neither kindness nor resentment, nor any perceptible surprise.

"Zenobia, when I last saw her," he answered, "was at Blithedale."

He said no more. But there was a great deal of talk going on near me, among a knot of people who might be considered as representing the mysticism, or rather the mystic sensuality, of this singular age. The nature of the exhibition that was about to take place had probably given the turn to their conversation.

I heard, from a pale man in blue spectacles, some stranger stories than ever were written in a romance; told, too, with a simple, unimaginative steadfastness, which was terribly efficacious in compelling the auditor to receive them into the category of established facts. He cited instances of the miraculous power of one human being over the will and passions of another; insomuch that settled grief was but a shadow beneath the influence of a man possessing this potency, and the strong love of years melted away like a vapor. At the bidding of one of these wizards, the maiden, with her lover's kiss still burning on her lips, would turn from him with icy indifference; the newly made widow would dig up her buried heart out of her young husband's grave before the sods had taken root upon it; a mother with her babe's milk in her bosom, would thrust away her child. Human character was but soft wax in his hands; and guilt, or virtue, only the forms into which he should see fit to mould it. The religious sentiment was a flame which he could blow up with his breath, or a spark that he could utterly extinguish. It is unutterable, the horror and disgust with which I listened, and saw that, if these things were to be believed, the individual soul was virtually annihilated, and all that is sweet and pure in our present life debased, and that the idea of man's eternal responsibility was made ridiculous, and immortality rendered at once impossible, and not worth acceptance. But I would have perished on the spot sooner than believe it.

The epoch of rapping spirits, and all the wonders that have followed in their train,—such as tables upset by invisible agencies, bells self-tolled at funerals, and ghostly music performed on jewsharps,—had not yet arrived. Alas, my countrymen, methinks we have fallen on an evil age! If these phenomena have not humbug at the bottom, so much the worse for us. What can they indicate, in a spiritual way, except that the soul of man is descending to a lower point than it has ever before reached while incarnate? We are pursuing a downward course in the eternal march, and thus bring ourselves into the same range with beings whom death, in requital of their gross and evil lives, has degraded below humanity! To hold intercourse with spirits of this order, we must stoop and grovel in some element more vile than earthly dust. These goblins, if they exist at all, are but the shadows of past mortality, outcasts, mere refuse-stuff, adjudged unworthy of the eternal world, and, on the most favorable supposition, dwindling gradually into nothingness. The less we have to say to them the better, lest we share their fate!

The audience now began to be impatient; they signified their desire for the entertainment to commence by thump of sticks and stamp of boot-heels. Nor was it a great while longer before, in response to their call, there appeared a bearded personage in Oriental robes, looking like one of the enchanters of the Arabian Nights. He came upon the platform from a side door, saluted the spectators, not with a salaam, but a bow, took his station at the desk, and first blowing his nose with a white handkerchief, prepared to speak. The environment of the homely village hall, and the absence of many ingenious contrivances of stage-effect with which the exhibition had heretofore been set off, seemed to bring the artifice of this character more openly upon the surface. No sooner did I behold the bearded enchanter, than, laying my hand again on Hollingsworth's shoulder, I whispered in his ear,—

"Do you know him?"

"I never saw the man before," he muttered, without turning his head.

But I had seen him three times already. Once, on occasion of my first visit to the Veiled Lady; a second time, in the wood-path at Blithedale; and lastly, in Zenobia's drawing-room. It was Westervelt. A quick association of ideas made me shudder from head to foot; and again, like an evil spirit, bringing up reminiscences of a man's sins, I whispered a question in Hollingsworth's ear,—

"What have you done with Priscilla?"

He gave a convulsive start, as if I had thrust a knife into him, writhed himself round on his seat, glared fiercely into my eyes, but answered not a word.

The Professor began his discourse, explanatory of the psychological phenomena, as he termed them, which it was his purpose to exhibit to the spectators. There remains no very distinct impression of it on my memory. It was eloquent, ingenious, plausible, with a delusive show of spirituality, yet really imbued throughout with a cold and dead materialism. I shivered, as at a current of chill air issuing out of a sepulchral vault, and bringing the smell of corruption along with it. He spoke of a new era that was dawning upon the world; an era that would link soul to soul, and the present life to what we call futurity, with a closeness that should finally convert both worlds into one great, mutually conscious brotherhood. He described (in a strange, philosophical guise, with terms of art, as if it were a matter of chemical discovery) the agency by which this mighty result was to be effected; nor would it have surprised me, had he pretended to hold up a portion of his universally pervasive fluid, as he affirmed it to be, in a glass phial.

At the close of his exordium, the Professor beckoned with his hand, —once, twice, thrice,—and a figure came gliding upon the platform, enveloped in a long veil of silvery whiteness. It fell about her like the texture of a summer cloud, with a kind of vagueness, so that the outline of the form beneath it could not be accurately discerned. But the movement of the Veiled Lady was graceful, free, and unembarrassed, like that of a person accustomed to be the spectacle of thousands; or, possibly, a blindfold prisoner within the sphere with which this dark earthly magician had surrounded her, she was wholly unconscious of being the central object to all those straining eyes.

Pliant to his gesture (which had even an obsequious courtesy, but at the same time a remarkable decisiveness), the figure placed itself in the great chair. Sitting there, in such visible obscurity, it was, perhaps, as much like the actual presence of a disembodied spirit as anything that stage trickery could devise. The hushed breathing of the spectators proved how high-wrought were their anticipations of the wonders to be performed through the medium of this incomprehensible creature. I, too, was in breathless suspense, but with a far different presentiment of some strange event at hand.

"You see before you the Veiled Lady," said the bearded Professor, advancing to the verge of the platform. "By the agency of which I have just spoken, she is at this moment in communion with the spiritual world. That silvery veil is, in one sense, an enchantment, having been dipped, as it were, and essentially imbued, through the potency of my art, with the fluid medium of spirits. Slight and ethereal as it seems, the limitations of time and space have no existence within its folds. This hall—these hundreds of faces, encompassing her within so narrow an amphitheatre—are of thinner substance, in her view, than the airiest vapor that the clouds are made of. She beholds the Absolute!"

As preliminary to other and far more wonderful psychological experiments, the exhibitor suggested that some of his auditors should endeavor to make the Veiled Lady sensible of their presence by such methods—provided only no touch were laid upon her person—as they might deem best adapted to that end. Accordingly, several deep-lunged country-fellows, who looked as if they might have blown the apparition away with a breath, ascended the platform. Mutually encouraging one another, they shouted so close to her ear that the veil stirred like a wreath of vanishing mist; they smote upon the floor with bludgeons; they perpetrated so hideous a clamor, that methought it might have reached, at least, a little way into the eternal sphere. Finally, with the assent of the Professor, they laid hold of the great chair, and were startled, apparently, to find it soar upward, as if lighter than the air through which it rose. But the Veiled Lady remained seated and motionless, with a composure that was hardly less than awful, because implying so immeasurable a distance betwixt her and these rude persecutors.

"These efforts are wholly without avail," observed the Professor, who had been looking on with an aspect of serene indifference. "The roar of a battery of cannon would be inaudible to the Veiled Lady. And yet, were I to will it, sitting in this very hall, she could hear the desert wind sweeping over the sands as far off as Arabia; the icebergs grinding one against the other in the polar seas; the rustle of a leaf in an East-Indian forest; the lowest whispered breath of the bashfullest maiden in the world, uttering the first confession of her love. Nor does there exist the moral inducement, apart from my own behest, that could persuade her to lift the silvery veil, or arise out of that chair."

Greatly to the Professor's discomposure, however, just as he spoke these words, the Veiled Lady arose. There was a mysterious tremor that shook the magic veil. The spectators, it may be, imagined that she was about to take flight into that invisible sphere, and to the society of those purely spiritual beings with whom they reckoned her so near akin. Hollingsworth, a moment ago, had mounted the platform, and now stood gazing at the figure, with a sad intentness that brought the whole power of his great, stern, yet tender soul into his glance.

"Come," said he, waving his hand towards her. "You are safe!"

She threw off the veil, and stood before that multitude of people pale, tremulous, shrinking, as if only then had she discovered that a thousand eyes were gazing at her. Poor maiden! How strangely had she been betrayed! Blazoned abroad as a wonder of the world, and performing what were adjudged as miracles,—in the faith of many, a seeress and a prophetess; in the harsher judgment of others, a mountebank,—she had kept, as I religiously believe, her virgin reserve and sanctity of soul throughout it all. Within that encircling veil, though an evil hand had flung it over her, there was as deep a seclusion as if this forsaken girl had, all the while, been sitting under the shadow of Eliot's pulpit, in the Blithedale woods, at the feet of him who now summoned her to the shelter of his arms. And the true heart-throb of a woman's affection was too powerful for the jugglery that had hitherto environed her. She uttered a shriek, and fled to Hollingsworth, like one escaping from her deadliest enemy, and was safe forever.

## XXIV

### THE MASQUERADERS

Two nights had passed since the foregoing occurrences, when, in a breezy September forenoon, I set forth from town, on foot, towards Blithedale.

It was the most delightful of all days for a walk, with a dash of invigorating ice-temper in the air, but a coolness that soon gave place to the brisk glow of exercise, while the vigor remained as elastic as before. The atmosphere had a spirit and sparkle in it. Each breath was like a sip of ethereal wine, tempered, as I said, with a crystal lump of ice. I had started on this expedition in an exceedingly sombre mood, as well befitted one who found himself tending towards home, but was conscious that nobody would be quite overjoyed to greet him there. My feet were hardly off the pavement, however, when this morbid sensation began to yield to the lively influences of air and motion. Nor had I gone far, with fields yet green on either side, before my step became as swift and light as if Hollingsworth were waiting to exchange a friendly handgrip, and Zenobia's and Priscilla's open arms would welcome the wanderer's reappearance. It has happened to me on other occasions, as well as this, to prove how a state of physical well-being can create a kind of joy, in spite of the profoundest anxiety of mind.

The pathway of that walk still runs along, with sunny freshness, through my memory. I know not why it should be so. But my mental eye can even now discern the September grass, bordering the pleasant roadside with a brighter verdure than while the summer heats were scorching it; the trees, too, mostly green, although here and there a branch or shrub has donned its vesture of crimson and gold a week or two before its fellows. I see the tufted barberry-bushes, with their small clusters of scarlet fruit; the toadstools, likewise,—some spotlessly white, others yellow or red,—mysterious growths, springing suddenly from no root or seed, and growing nobody can tell how or wherefore. In this respect they resembled many of the emotions in my breast. And I still see the little rivulẹts, chill, clear, and bright, that murmured beneath the road, through subterranean rocks, and deepened into mossy pools, where tiny fish were darting to and fro, and within which lurked the hermit-frog. But no,—I never can account for it, that, with a yearning interest to learn the upshot of all my story, and returning to Blithedale for that sole purpose, I should examine these things so like a peaceful-bosomed naturalist. Nor why, amid all my sympathies and fears, there shot, at times, a wild exhilaration through my frame.

Thus I pursued my way along the line of the ancient stone wall that Paul Dudley built, and through white villages, and past orchards of ruddy apples, and fields of ripening maize, and patches of woodland, and all such sweet rural scenery as looks the fairest, a little beyond the suburbs of a town. Hollingsworth, Zenobia, Priscilla! They glided mistily before me, as I walked. Sometimes, in my solitude, I laughed with the bitterness of self-scorn, remembering how unreservedly I had given up my heart and soul to interests that were not mine. What had I ever had to do with them? And why, being now free, should I take this thraldom on me once again? It was both sad and dangerous, I whispered to myself, to be in too close affinity with the passions, the errors, and the misfortunes of individuals who stood within a circle of their own, into which, if I stept at all, it must be as an intruder, and at a peril that I could not estimate.

Drawing nearer to Blithedale, a sickness of the spirits kept alternating with my flights of causeless buoyancy. I indulged in a hundred odd and extravagant conjectures. Either there was no such place as Blithedale, nor ever had been, nor any brotherhood of thoughtful laborers, like what I seemed to recollect there, or else it was all changed during my absence. It had been nothing but dream-work and enchantment. I should seek in vain for the old farm-house, and for the greensward, the potato-fields, the root-crops, and acres of Indian corn, and for all that configuration of the land which I had imagined. It would be another spot, and an utter strangeness.

These vagaries were of the spectral throng so apt to steal out of an unquiet heart. They partly ceased to haunt me, on my arriving at a point whence, through the trees, I began to catch glimpses of the Blithedale farm. That surely was something real. There was hardly a square foot of all those acres on which I had not trodden heavily, in one or another kind of toil. The curse of Adam's posterity—and, curse or blessing be it, it gives substance to the life around us—had first come upon me there. In the sweat of my brow I had there earned bread and eaten it, and so established my claim to be on earth, and my fellowship with all the sons of labor. I could have knelt down, and have laid my breast against that soil. The red clay of which my frame was moulded seemed nearer akin to those crumbling furrows than to any other portion of the world's dust. There was my home, and there might be my grave.

I felt an invincible reluctance, nevertheless, at the idea of presenting myself before my old associates, without first ascertaining the state in which they were. A nameless foreboding weighed upon me. Perhaps, should I know all the circumstances that had occurred, I might find it my wisest course to turn back, unrecognized, unseen, and never look at Blithedale more. Had it been evening, I would have stolen softly to some lighted window of the old farm-house, and peeped darkling in, to see all their well-known faces round the supper-board. Then, were there a vacant seat, I might noiselessly unclose the door, glide in, and take my place among them, without a word. My entrance might be so quiet, my aspect so familiar, that they would forget how long I had been away, and suffer me to melt into the scene, as a wreath of vapor melts into a larger cloud. I dreaded a boisterous greeting. Beholding me at table, Zenobia, as a matter of course, would send me a cup of tea, and Hollingsworth fill my plate from the great dish of pandowdy, and Priscilla, in her quiet way, would hand the cream, and others help me to the bread and butter. Being one of them again, the knowledge of what had happened would come to me without a shock. For still, at every turn of my shifting fantasies, the thought stared me in the face that some evil thing had befallen us, or was ready to befall.

Yielding to this ominous impression, I now turned aside into the woods, resolving to spy out the posture of the Community, as craftily as the wild Indian before he makes his onset. I would go wandering about the outskirts of the farm, and, perhaps, catching sight of a solitary acquaintance, would approach him amid the brown shadows of the trees (a kind of medium fit for spirits departed and revisitant, like myself), and entreat him to tell me how all things were.

The first living creature that I met was a partridge which sprung up beneath my feet, and whirred away; the next was a squirrel, who chattered angrily at me from an overhanging bough. I trod along by the dark, sluggish river, and remember pausing on the bank, above one of its blackest and most placid pools (the very spot, with the barkless stump of a tree aslantwise over the water, is depicting itself to my fancy at this instant), and wondering how deep it was, and if any over-laden soul had ever flung its weight of mortality in thither, and if it thus escaped the burden, or only made it heavier. And perhaps the skeleton of the drowned wretch still lay beneath the inscrutable depth, clinging to some sunken log at the bottom with the gripe of its old despair. So slight, however, was the track of these gloomy ideas, that I soon forgot them in the contemplation of a brood of wild ducks, which were floating on the river, and anon took flight, leaving each a bright streak over the black surface. By and by, I came to my hermitage, in the heart of the white-pine tree, and clambering up into it, sat down to rest. The grapes, which I had watched throughout the summer, now dangled around me in abundant clusters of the deepest purple, deliciously sweet to the taste, and, though wild, yet free from that ungentle flavor which distinguishes nearly all our native and uncultivated grapes. Methought a wine might be pressed out of them possessing a passionate zest, and endowed with a new kind of intoxicating quality, attended with such bacchanalian ecstasies as the tamer grapes of Madeira, France, and the Rhine are inadequate to produce. And I longed to quaff a great goblet of it that moment!

While devouring the grapes, I looked on all sides out of the peepholes of my hermitage, and saw the farm-house, the fields, and almost every part of our domain, but not a single human figure in the landscape. Some of the windows of the house were open, but with no more signs of life than in a dead man's unshut eyes. The barn-door was ajar, and swinging in the breeze. The big old dog,—he was a relic of the former dynasty of the farm,—that hardly ever stirred out of the yard, was nowhere to be seen. What, then, had become of all the fraternity and sisterhood? Curious to ascertain this point, I let myself down out of the tree, and going to the edge of the wood, was glad to perceive our herd of cows chewing the cud or grazing not far off. I fancied, by their manner, that two or three of them recognized me (as, indeed, they ought, for I had milked them and been their chamberlain times without number); but, after staring me in the face a little while, they phlegmatically began grazing and chewing their cuds again. Then I grew foolishly angry at so cold a reception, and flung some rotten fragments of an old stump at these unsentimental cows.

Skirting farther round the pasture, I heard voices and much laughter proceeding from the interior of the wood. Voices, male and feminine; laughter, not only of fresh young throats, but the bass of grown people, as if solemn organ-pipes should pour out airs of merriment. Not a voice spoke, but I knew it better than my own; not a laugh, but its cadences were familiar. The wood, in this portion of it, seemed as full of jollity as if Comus and his crew were holding their revels in one of its usually lonesome glades. Stealing onward as far as I durst, without hazard of discovery, I saw a concourse of strange figures beneath the overshadowing branches. They appeared, and vanished, and came again, confusedly with the streaks of sunlight glimmering down upon them.

Among them was an Indian chief, with blanket, feathers and war-paint, and uplifted tomahawk; and near him, looking fit to be his woodland-bride, the goddess Diana, with the crescent on her head, and attended by our big lazy dog, in lack of any fleeter hound. Drawing an arrow from her quiver, she let it fly at a venture, and hit the very tree behind which I happened to be lurking. Another group consisted of a Bavarian broom-girl, a negro of the Jim Crow order, one or two foresters of the Middle Ages, a Kentucky woodsman in his trimmed hunting-shirt and deerskin leggings, and a Shaker elder, quaint, demure, broad-brimmed, and square-skirted. Shepherds of Arcadia, and allegoric figures from the Faerie Queen, were oddly mixed up with these. Arm in arm, or otherwise huddled together in strange discrepancy, stood grim Puritans, gay Cavaliers, and Revolutionary officers with three-cornered cocked hats, and queues longer than their swords. A bright-complexioned, dark-haired, vivacious little gypsy, with a red shawl over her head, went from one group to another, telling fortunes by palmistry; and Moll Pitcher, the renowned old witch of Lynn, broomstick in hand, showed herself prominently in the midst, as if announcing all these apparitions to be the offspring of her necromantic art. But Silas Foster, who leaned against a tree near by, in his customary blue frock, and smoking a short pipe, did more to disenchant the scene, with his look of shrewd, acrid, Yankee observation, than twenty witches and necromancers could have done in the way of rendering it weird and fantastic.

A little farther off, some old-fashioned skinkers and drawers, all with portentously red noses, were spreading a banquet on the leaf-strewn earth; while a horned and long-tailed gentleman (in whom I recognized the fiendish musician erst seen by Tam O'Shanter) tuned his fiddle, and summoned the whole motley rout to a dance, before partaking of the festal cheer. So they joined hands in a circle, whirling round so swiftly, so madly, and so merrily, in time and tune with the Satanic music, that their separate incongruities were blended all together, and they became a kind of entanglement that went nigh to turn one's brain with merely looking at it. Anon they stopt all of a sudden, and staring at one another's figures, set up a roar of laughter; whereat a shower of the September leaves (which, all day long, had been hesitating whether to fall or no) were shaken off by the movement of the air, and came eddying down upon the revellers.

Then, for lack of breath, ensued a silence, at the deepest point of which, tickled by the oddity of surprising my grave associates in this masquerading trim, I could not possibly refrain from a burst of laughter on my own separate account.

"Hush!" I heard the pretty gypsy fortune-teller say. "Who is that laughing?"

"Some profane intruder!" said the goddess Diana. "I shall send an arrow through his heart, or change him into a stag, as I did Actæon, if he peeps from behind the trees!"

"Me take his scalp!" cried the Indian chief, brandishing his tomahawk, and cutting a great caper in the air.

"I'll root him in the earth with a spell that I have at my tongue's end!" squeaked Moll Pitcher. "And the green moss shall grow all over him, before he gets free again!"

"The voice was Miles Coverdale's," said the fiendish fiddler, with a whisk of his tail and a toss of his horns. "My music has brought him hither. He is always ready to dance to the Devil's tune!"

Thus put on the right track, they all recognized the voice at once, and set up a simultaneous shout.

"Miles! Miles! Miles Coverdale, where are you?" they cried. "Zenobia! Queen Zenobia! here is one of your vassals lurking in the wood. Command him to approach and pay his duty!"

The whole fantastic rabble forthwith streamed off in pursuit of me, so that I was like a mad poet hunted by chimeras. Having fairly the

THE WORKS OF HAWTHORNE

start of them, however, I succeeded in making my escape, and soon left their merriment and riot at a good distance in the rear. Its fainter tones assumed a kind of mournfulness, and were finally lost in the hush and solemnity of the wood. In my haste, I stumbled over a heap of logs and sticks that had been cut for fire-wood, a great while ago, by some former possessor of the soil, and piled up square, in order to be carted or sledded away to the farm-house. But, being forgotten, they had lain there perhaps fifty years, and possibly much longer; until, by the accumulation of moss, and the leaves falling over them, and decaying there, from autumn to autumn, a green mound was formed, in which the softened outline of the wood-pile was still perceptible. In the fitful mood that then swayed my mind, I found something strangely affecting in this simple circumstance. I imagined the long-dead woodman, and his long-dead wife and children, coming out of their chill graves, and essaying to make a fire with this heap of mossy fuel!

From this spot I strayed onward, quite lost in reverie, and neither knew nor cared whither I was going, until a low, soft, well-remembered voice spoke, at a little distance.

"There is Mr. Coverdale!"

"Miles Coverdale!" said another voice,—and its tones were very stern. "Let him come forward, then!"

"Yes, Mr. Coverdale," cried a woman's voice,—clear and melodious, but, just then, with something unnatural in its chord,—"you are welcome! But you come half an hour too late, and have missed a scene which you would have enjoyed!"

I looked up and found myself nigh Eliot's pulpit, at the base of which sat Hollingsworth, with Priscilla at his feet, and Zenobia standing before them.

## XXV

### THE THREE TOGETHER

HOLLINGSWORTH was in his ordinary working-dress. Priscilla wore a pretty and simple gown, with a kerchief about her neck, and a calash, which she had flung back from her head, leaving it suspended by the strings. But Zenobia (whose part among the maskers, as may be supposed, was no inferior one) appeared in a costume of fanciful magnificence, with her jewelled flower as the central ornament of what resembled a leafy crown, or coronet. She represented the Oriental princess by whose name we were accustomed to know her. Her attitude was free and noble; yet, if a queen's, it was not that of a queen triumphant, but dethroned, on trial for her life, or, perchance, condemned already. The spirit of the conflict seemed, nevertheless, to be alive in her. Her eyes were on fire; her cheeks had each a crimson spot, so exceedingly vivid, and marked with so definite an outline, that I at first doubted whether it were not artificial. In a very brief space, however, this idea was shamed by the paleness that ensued, as the blood sunk suddenly away. Zenobia now looked like marble.

One always feels the fact, in an instant, when he has intruded on those who love, or those who hate, at some acme of their passion that puts them into a sphere of their own, where no other spirit can pretend to stand on equal ground with them. I was confused,—affected even with a species of terror,—and wished myself away. The intenseness of their feelings gave them the exclusive property of the soil and atmosphere, and left me no right to be or breathe there.

"Hollingsworth,—Zenobia,—I have just returned to Blithedale," said I, "and had no thought of finding you here. We shall meet again at the house. I will retire."

"This place is free to you," answered Hollingsworth.

"As free as to ourselves," added Zenobia. "This long while past, you have been following up your game, groping for human emotions in the dark corners of the heart. Had you been here a little sooner, you might have seen them dragged into the daylight. I could even wish to have my trial over again, with you standing by to see fair play! Do you know, Mr. Coverdale, I have been on trial for my life?"

She laughed, while speaking thus. But, in truth, as my eyes wandered from one of the group to another, I saw in Hollingsworth all that an artist could desire for the grim portrait of a Puritan magistrate holding inquest of life and death in a case of witchcraft: in Zenobia, the sorceress herself, not aged, wrinkled, and decrepit, but fair enough to tempt Satan with a force reciprocal to his own; and, in Priscilla, the pale victim, whose soul and body had been wasted by her spells. Had a pile of fagots been heaped against the rock, this hint of impending doom would have completed the suggestive picture.

"It was too hard upon me," continued Zenobia, addressing Hollingsworth, "that judge, jury, and accuser should all be comprehended in one man! I demur, as I think the lawyers say, to the jurisdiction. But let the learned Judge Coverdale seat himself on the top of the rock, and you and me stand at its base, side by side, pleading our cause before him! There might, at least, be two criminals instead of one."

"You forced this on me," replied Hollingsworth, looking her sternly in the face. "Did I call you hither from among the masqueraders yonder? Do I assume to be your judge? No; except so far as I have an unquestionable right of judgment, in order to settle my own line of behavior towards those with whom the events of life bring me in contact. True, I have already judged you, but not on the world's part,—neither do I pretend to pass a sentence!"

"Ah, this is very good!" cried Zenobia, with a smile. "What strange beings you men are, Mr. Coverdale!—is it not so? It is the simplest thing in the world with you to bring a woman before your secret tribunals, and judge and condemn her unheard, and then tell her to go free without a sentence. The misfortune is, that this same secret tribunal chances to be the only judgment-seat that a true woman stands in awe of, and that any verdict short of acquittal is equivalent to a death-sentence!"

The more I looked at them, and the more I heard, the stronger grew my impression that a crisis had just come and gone. On Hollingsworth's brow it had left a stamp like that of irrevocable doom, of which his own will was the instrument. In Zenobia's whole person, beholding her more closely, I saw a riotous agitation; the almost delirious disquietude of a great struggle, at the close of which the vanquished one felt her strength and courage still mighty within her, and longed to renew the contest. My sensations were as if I had come upon a battle-field before the smoke was as yet cleared away.

And what subjects had been discussed here? All, no doubt, that for so many months past had kept my heart and my imagination idly feverish. Zenobia's whole character and history; the true nature of her mysterious connection with Westervelt; her later purposes towards Hollingsworth, and, reciprocally, his in reference to her; and, finally, the degree in which Zenobia had been cognizant of the plot against Priscilla, and what, at last, had been the real object of that scheme. On these points, as before, I was left to my own conjectures. One thing, only, was certain. Zenobia and Hollingsworth were friends no longer. If their heart-strings were ever intertwined, the knot had been adjudged an entanglement, and was now violently broken.

But Zenobia seemed unable to rest content with the matter in the posture which it had assumed.

"Ah! do we part so?" exclaimed she, seeing Hollingsworth about to retire.

"And why not?" said he, with almost rude abruptness. "What is there further to be said between us?"

"Well, perhaps nothing," answered Zenobia, looking him in the face, and smiling. "But we have come many times before to this gray rock, and we have talked very softly among the whisperings of the birch-trees. They were pleasant hours! I love to make the latest of them, though not altogether so delightful, loiter away as slowly as may be. And, besides, you have put many queries to me at this, which you design to be our last interview; and being driven, as I must acknowledge, into a corner, I have responded with reasonable frankness. But now, with your free consent, I desire the privilege of asking a few questions, in my turn."

"I have no concealments," said Hollingsworth.

"We shall see," answered Zenobia. "I would first inquire whether you have supposed me to be wealthy?"

"On that point," observed Hollingsworth, "I have had the opinion which the world holds."

"And I held it likewise," said Zenobia. "Had I not, Heaven is my witness the knowledge should have been as free to you as me. It is only three days since I knew the strange fact that threatens to make me poor; and your own acquaintance with it, I suspect, is of at least as old a date. I fancied myself affluent. You are aware, too, of the disposition which I purposed making of the larger portion of my imaginary opulence,—nay, were it all, I had not hesitated. Let me ask you, further, did I ever propose or intimate any terms of compact, on which depended this—as the world would consider it—so important sacrifice?"

"You certainly spoke of none," said Hollingsworth.

"Nor meant any," she responded. "I was willing to realize your dream, freely,—generously, as some might think,—but, at all events, fully, and heedless though it should prove the ruin of my fortune. If, in your own thoughts, you have imposed any conditions of this expenditure, it is you that must be held responsible for whatever is sordid and unworthy in them. And now one other question. Do you love this girl?"

"O Zenobia!" exclaimed Priscilla, ·shrinking back, as if longing for the rock to topple over and hide her.

"Do you love her?" repeated Zenobia.

"Had you asked me that question a short time since," replied Hollingsworth, after a pause, during which, it seemed to me, even the birch-trees held their whispering breath, "I should have told you—'No!' My feelings for Priscilla differed little from those of an elder brother, watching tenderly over the gentle sister whom God has given him to protect."

"And what is your answer now?" persisted Zenobia.

"I do love her!" said Hollingsworth, uttering the words with a deep inward breath, instead of speaking them outright. "As well declare it thus as in any other way. I do love her!"

"Now, God be judge between us," cried Zenobia, breaking into sudden passion, "which of us two has most mortally offended Him! At least, I am a woman, with every fault, it may be, that a woman ever had,—weak, vain, unprincipled (like most of my ·sex; for our virtues, when we have any, are merely impulsive and intuitive), passionate, too, and pursuing my foolish and unattainable ends by indirect and cunning, though absurdly chosen means, as an hereditary bondslave must; false, moreover, to the whole circle of good, in my reckless truth to the little good I saw before me,—but still a woman! A creature whom only a little change of earthly fortune, a little kinder smile of Him who sent me hither, and one true heart to encourage and direct me, might have made all that a woman can be! But how is it with you? Are you a man? No; but a monster! A cold, heartless, self-beginning and self-ending piece of mechanism!"

"With what, then, do you charge me!" asked Hollingsworth, aghast, and greatly disturbed by this attack. "Show me one selfish end, in all I ever aimed at, and you may cut it out of my bosom with a knife!"

"It is all self!" answered Zenobia, with still intenser bitterness. "Nothing else; nothing but self, self, self! The fiend, I doubt not, has made his choicest mirth ·of you these seven years past, and especially in the mad summer which we have spent together. I see it now! I am awake, disenchanted, disinthralled! Self, self, self! You have embodied yourself in a project. You are a better masquerader than the witches and gypsies yonder; for your disguise is a self-deception. See whither it has brought you! First, you aimed a death-blow, and a treacherous one, at this scheme of a purer and higher life, which so many noble spirits had wrought out. Then, because Coverdale could not be quite your slave, you threw him ruthlessly away. And you took me, too, into your plan, as long as there was hope of my being available, and now fling me aside again, a broken tool! But, foremost and blackest of your sins, you stifled down your inmost consciousness!—you did a deadly wrong to your own heart!—you were ready to sacrifice this girl, whom, if God ever visibly showed a purpose, He put into your charge, and through whom He was striving to redeem you!"

"This is a woman's view," said Hollingsworth, growing deadly pale, —"a woman's, whose whole sphere of action is in the heart, and who can conceive of no higher nor wider one!"

"Be silent!" cried Zenobia, imperiously. "You know neither man nor woman! The utmost that can be said in your behalf—and because I would not be wholly despicable in my own eyes, but would fain excuse my wasted feelings, nor own it wholly a delusion, therefore I say it—is, that a great and rich heart has been ruined in your breast. Leave me, now. You have done with me, and I with you. Farewell!"

"Priscilla," said Hollingsworth, "come."

Zenobia smiled; possibly I did so too. Not often, in human life, has a gnawing sense of injury found a sweeter morsel of revenge than was conveyed in the tone with which Hollingsworth spoke those two words. It was the abased and tremulous tone of a man whose faith in himself was shaken, and who sought, at last, to lean on an affection. Yes; the strong man bowed himself and rested on this poor Priscilla! Oh, could she have failed him, what a triumph for the lookers-on!

And, at first, I half imagined that she was about to fail him. She rose up, stood shivering like the birch-leaves that trembled over her head, and then slowly tottered, rather than walked, towards Zenobia. Arriving at her feet, she sank down there, in the very same attitude which she had assumed on their first meeting, in the kitchen of the old farm-house. Zenobia remembered it.

"Ah, Priscilla!" said she, shaking her head, "how much is changed since then! You kneel to a dethroned princess. You, the victorious one! But he is waiting for you. Say what you wish, and leave me."

"We are sisters!" gasped Priscilla.

I fancied that I understood the word and action. It meant the offering of herself, and all she had, to be at Zenobia's disposal. But the latter would not take it thus.

"True, we are sisters!" she replied; and, moved by the sweet word, she stooped down and kissed Priscilla; but not lovingly, for a sense of fatal harm received through her seemed to be lurking in Zenobia's heart.

"We had one father! You knew it from the first; I, but a little while,—else some things that have chanced might have been spared you. But I never wished you harm. You stood between me and an end which I desired. I wanted a clear path. No matter what I meant. It is over now. Do you forgive me?"

"O Zenobia," sobbed Priscilla, "it is I that feel like the guilty one!"

"No, no, poor little thing!" said Zenobia, with a sort of contempt. "You have been my evil fate; but there never was a babe with less strength or will to do an injury. Poor child! Methinks you have but a melancholy lot before you, sitting all alone in that wide, cheerless heart, where, for aught you know,—and as I, alas! believe,—the fire which you have kindled may soon go out. Ah, the thought makes me shiver for you! What will you do, Priscilla, when you find no spark among the ashes?"

"Die!" she answered.

"That was well said!" responded Zenobia, with an approving smile. "There is all a woman in your little compass, my poor sister. Meanwhile, go with him, and live!"

She waved her away, with a queenly gesture, and turned her own face to the rock. I watched Priscilla, wondering what judgment she would pass between Zenobia and Hollingsworth; how interpret his behavior, so as to reconcile it with true faith both towards her sister and herself; how compel her love for him to keep any terms whatever with her sisterly affection! But, in truth, there was no such difficulty as I imagined. Her engrossing love made it all clear. Hollingsworth could have no fault. That was the one principle at the centre of the universe. And the doubtful guilt or possible integrity of other people, appearances, self-evident facts, the testimony of her own senses,—even Hollingsworth's self-accusation, had he volunteered it,—would have weighed not the value of a mote of thistle-down on the other side. So secure was she of his right, that she never thought of comparing it with another's wrong, but left the latter to itself.

Hollingsworth drew her arm within his, and soon disappeared with her among the trees. I cannot imagine how Zenobia knew when they were out of sight; she never glanced again towards them. But, retaining a proud attitude so long as they might have thrown back a retiring look, they were no sooner departed,—utterly departed,—than she began slowly to sink down. It was as if a great, invisible, irresistible weight were pressing her to the earth. Settling upon her knees, she leaned her forehead against the rock, and sobbed convulsively; dry sobs they seemed to be, such as have nothing to do with tears.

## XXVI

### ZENOBIA AND COVERDALE

ZENOBIA had entirely forgotten me. She fancied herself alone with her great grief. And had it been only a common pity that I felt for her,—the pity that her proud nature would have repelled, as the one worst wrong which the world yet held in reserve,—the sacredness and awfulness of the crisis might have impelled me to steal away silently, so that not a dry leaf should rustle under my feet. I would have left her to struggle, in that solitude, with only the eye of God upon her. But, so it happened, I never once dreamed of questioning my right to be there now, as I had questioned it just before, when I came so suddenly upon Hollingsworth and herself, in the passion of their recent debate. It suits me not to explain what was the analogy that I saw or imagined, between Zenobia's situation and mine; nor, I believe, will the reader detect this one secret, hidden beneath many a revelation which perhaps concerned me less. In simple truth, however, as Zenobia leaned her forehead against the rock, shaken with that tearless agony, it seemed to me that the self-same pang, with hardly mitigated torment, leaped thrilling from her heart-strings to my own. Was it wrong, therefore, if I felt myself consecrated to the priesthood by sympathy like this, and called upon to minister to this woman's affliction, so far as mortal could?

But, indeed, what could mortal do for her? Nothing! The attempt would be a mockery and an anguish. Time, it is true, would steal away her grief, and bury it and the best of her heart in the same grave. But Destiny itself, methought, in its kindliest mood, could do no better for Zenobia, in the way of quick relief, than to cause the impending rock to impend a little farther, and fall upon her head. So I leaned against a tree, and listened to her sobs, in unbroken silence. She was half prostrate, half kneeling, with her forehead still pressed against the rock. Her sobs were the only sound; she did not groan, nor give any other utterance to her distress. It was all involuntary.

At length she sat up, put back her hair, and stared about her with a bewildered aspect, as if not distinctly recollecting the scene through which she had passed, nor cognizant of the situation in which it left her. Her face and brow were almost purple with the rush of blood. They whitened, however, by and by, and for some time retained this death-like hue. She put her hand to her forehead, with a gesture that made me forcibly conscious of an intense and living pain there.

Her glance, wandering wildly to and fro, passed over me several times, without appearing to inform her of my presence. But, finally, a look of recognition gleamed from her eyes into mine.

"Is it you, Miles Coverdale?" said she, smiling. "Ah, I perceive what you are about! You are turning this whole affair into a ballad. Pray let me hear as many stanzas as you happen to have ready."

"Oh, hush, Zenobia!" I answered. "Heaven knows what an ache is in my soul!"

"It is genuine tragedy, is it not?" rejoined Zenobia, with a sharp, light laugh. "And you are willing to allow, perhaps, that I have had hard measure. But it is a woman's doom, and I have deserved it like a woman; so let there be no pity, as, on my part, there shall be no complaint. It is all right, now, or will shortly be so. But, Mr. Coverdale, by all means write this ballad, and put your soul's ache into it, and turn your sympathy to good account, as other poets do, and as poets must, unless they choose to give us glittering icicles instead of lines of fire. As for the moral, it shall be distilled into the final stanza, in a drop of bitter honey."

"What shall it be, Zenobia?" I inquired, endeavoring to fall in with her mood.

"Oh, a very old one will serve the purpose," she replied. "There are no new truths, much as we have prided ourselves on finding some. A moral? Why, this: That, in the battle-field of life, the downright stroke, that would fall only on a man's steel head-piece, is sure to light on a woman's heart, over which she wears no breast-plate, and whose wisdom it is, therefore to keep out of the conflict. Or, this: That the whole universe, her own sex and yours, and Providence, or Destiny, to boot, make common cause against the woman who swerves one hair's-breadth, out of the beaten track. Yes; and add (for I may as well own it, now) that, with that one hair's-breadth, she goes all astray and never sees the world in its true aspect afterwards."

"This last is too stern a moral," I observed. "Cannot we soften it a little?"

"Do it if you like, at your own peril, not on my responsibility," she answered. Then, with a sudden change of subject, she went on: "After all, he has flung away what would have served him better than the poor, pale flower he kept. What can Priscilla do for him? Put passionate warmth into his heart, when it shall be chilled with frozen hopes? Strengthen his hands, when they are weary with much doing and no performance? No! but only tend towards him with a blind, instinctive love, and hang her little, puny weakness for a clog upon his arm! She cannot even give him such sympathy as is worth the name. For will he never, in many an hour of darkness, need that proud intellectual sympathy which he might have had from me?—the sympathy that would flash light along his course, and guide as well as cheer him? Poor Hollingsworth! Where will he find it now?"

"Hollingsworth has a heart of ice!" said I, bitterly. "He is a wretch!"

"Do him no wrong," interrupted Zenobia, turning haughtily upon me. "Presume not to estimate a man like Hollingsworth. It was my fault, all along, and none of his. I see it now! He never sought me. Why should he seek me? What had I to offer him? A miserable, bruised, and battered heart, spoilt long before he met me. A life, too, hopelessly entangled with a villain's! He did well to cast me off. God be praised, he did it! And yet, had he trusted me, and borne with me a little longer, I would have saved him all this trouble."

She was silent for a time, and stood with her eyes fixed on the ground. Again raising them, her look was more mild and calm.

"Miles Coverdale!" said she.

"Well, Zenobia," I responded. "Can I do you any service?"

"Very little," she replied. "But it is my purpose, as you may well imagine, to remove from Blithedale; and, most likely, I may not see Hollingsworth again. A woman in my position, you understand, feels scarcely at her ease among former friends. New faces,—unaccustomed looks,—those only can she tolerate. She would pine among familiar scenes; she would be apt to blush, too, under the eyes that knew her secret; her heart might throb uncomfortably; she would mortify herself, I suppose, with foolish notions of having sacrificed the honor of her sex at the foot of proud, contumacious man. Poor womanhood, with its rights and wrongs! Here will be new matter for my course of lectures, at the idea of which you smiled, Mr. Coverdale, a month or two ago. But, as you have really a heart and sympathies, as far as they go, and as I shall depart without seeing Hollingsworth, I must entreat you to be a messenger between him and me."

"Willingly," said I, wondering at the strange way in which her mind seemed to vibrate from the deepest earnest to mere levity. "What is the message?"

"True,—what is it?" exclaimed Zenobia. "After all, I hardly know. On better consideration, I have no message. Tell him,—tell him something pretty and pathetic, that will come nicely and sweetly into your ballad,—anything you please, so it be tender and submissive enough. Tell him he has murdered me! Tell him that I'll haunt him!"—She spoke these words with the wildest energy.—"And give him—no, give Priscilla—this!"

Thus saying, she took the jewelled flower out of her hair; and it struck me as the act of a queen, when worsted in a combat, discrowning herself, as if she found a sort of relief in abasing all her pride.

"Bid her wear this for Zenobia's sake," she continued. "She is a pretty little creature, and will make as soft and gentle a wife as the veriest Bluebeard could desire. Pity that she must fade so soon! These delicate and puny maidens always do. Ten years hence, let Hollingsworth look at my face and Priscilla's, and then choose betwixt them. Or, if he pleases, let him do it now."

How magnificently Zenobia looked as she said this! The effect of her beauty was even heightened by the over-consciousness and self-recognition of it, into which, I suppose, Hollingsworth's scorn had driven her. She understood the look of admiration in my face; and—Zenobia to the last—it gave her pleasure.

"It is an endless pity," said she, "that I had not bethought myself of

winning your heart, Mr. Coverdale, instead of Hollingsworth's. I think
I should have succeeded, and many women would have deemed you the
worthier conquest of the two. You are certainly much the handsomest
man. But there is a fate in these things. And beauty, in a man, has been
of little account with me, since my earliest girlhood, when, for once, it
turned my head. Now, farewell!"

"Zenobia, whither are you going?" I asked.

"No matter where," said she. "But I am weary of this place, and
sick to death of playing at philanthropy and progress. Of all varieties of
mock-life, we have surely blundered into the very emptiest mockery in
our effort to establish the one true system. I have done with it; and
Blithedale must find another woman to superintend the laundry, and
you, Mr. Coverdale, another nurse to make your gruel, the next time
you fall ill. It was, indeed, a foolish dream! Yet it gave us some pleasant summer days, and bright hopes, while they lasted. It can do no
more; nor will it avail us to shed tears over a broken bubble. Here is
my hand! Adieu!"

She gave me her hand, with the same free, whole-souled gesture as on
the first afternoon of our acquaintance, and, being greatly moved, I bethought me of no better method of expressing my deep sympathy than
to carry it to my lips. In so doing, I perceived that this white hand—so
hospitably warm when I first touched it, five months since—was now
cold as a veritable piece of snow.

"How very cold!" I exclaimed, holding it between both my own, with
the vain idea of warming it. "What can be the reason? It is really death-
like!"

"The extremities die first, they say," answered Zenobia, laughing.
"And so you kiss this poor, despised, rejected hand! Well, my dear
friend, I thank you. You have reserved your homage for the fallen. Lip
of man will never touch my hand again. I intend to become a Catholic,
for the sake of going into a nunnery. When you next hear of Zenobia,
her face will be behind the black veil; so look your last at it now,—for
all is over. Once more, farewell!"

She withdrew her hand, yet left a lingering pressure, which I felt long
afterwards. So intimately connected as I had been with perhaps the
only man in whom she was ever truly interested, Zenobia looked on me
as the representative of all the past, and was conscious that, in bidding
me adieu, she likewise took final leave of Hollingsworth, and of this
whole epoch of her life. Never did her beauty shine out more lustrously
than in the last glimpse that I had of her. She departed, and was soon
hidden among the trees.

But, whether it was the strong impression of the foregoing scene, or
whatever else the cause, I was affected with a fantasy that Zenobia had
not actually gone, but was still hovering about the spot and haunting it.
I seemed to feel her eyes upon me. It was as if the vivid coloring of her
character had left a brilliant stain upon the air. By degrees, however,
the impression grew less distinct. I flung myself upon the fallen leaves

at the base of Eliot's pulpit. The sunshine withdrew up the tree-trunks, and flickered on the topmost boughs; gray twilight made the wood obscure; the stars brightened out; the pendent boughs became wet with chill autumnal dews. But I was listless, worn out with emotion on my own behalf and sympathy for others, and had no heart to leave my comfortless lair beneath the rock.

I must have fallen asleep, and had a dream, all the circumstances of which utterly vanished at the moment when they converged to some tragical catastrophe, and thus grew too powerful for the thin sphere of slumber that enveloped them. Starting from the ground, I found the risen moon shining upon the rugged face of the rock, and myself all in a tremble.

## XXVII

### MIDNIGHT

IT could not have been far from midnight when I came beneath Hollingsworth's window, and, finding it open, flung in a tuft of grass with earth at the roots, and heard it fall upon the floor. He was either awake or sleeping very lightly; for scarcely a moment had gone by, before he looked out and discerned me standing in the moonlight.

"Is it you, Coverdale?" he asked. "What is the matter?"

"Come down to me, Hollingsworth!" I answered. "I am anxious to speak with you."

The strange tone of my own voice startled me, and him, probably, no less. He lost no time, and soon issued from the house-door, with his dress half arranged.

"Again, what is the matter?" he asked, impatiently.

"Have you seen Zenobia," said I, "since you parted from her at Eliot's pulpit?"

"No," answered Hollingsworth; "nor did I expect it."

His voice was deep, but had a tremor in it. Hardly had he spoken, when Silas Foster thrust his head, done up in a cotton handkerchief, out of another window, and took what he called—as it literally was—a squint at us.

"Well, folks, what are ye about here?" he demanded. "Aha! are you there, Miles Coverdale? You have been turning night into day since you left us, I reckon; and so you find it quite natural to come prowling about the house at this time o' night, frightening my old woman out of her wits, and making her disturb a tired man out of his best nap. In with you, you vagabond, and to bed!"

"Dress yourself quickly, Foster," said I. "We want your assistance."

I could not, for the life of me, keep that strange tone out of my voice. Silas Foster, obtuse as were his sensibilities, seemed to feel the ghastly earnestness that was conveyed in it as well as Hollingsworth did. He immediately withdrew his head, and I heard him yawning, muttering to his wife, and again yawning heavily, while he hurried on his clothes. Meanwhile, I showed Hollingsworth a delicate handkerchief, marked with a well-known cipher, and told where I had found it, and other circumstances, which had filled me with a suspicion so terrible that I left him, if he dared, to shape it out for himself. By the time, my brief explanation was finished, we were joined by Silas Foster, in his blue woollen frock.

"Well, boys," cried he, peevishly, "what is to pay now?"

"Tell him, Hollingsworth," said I.

Hollingsworth shivered, perceptibly, and drew in a hard breath betwixt his teeth. He steadied himself, however, and, looking the matter more firmly in the face than I had done, explained to Foster my suspicions, and the grounds of them, with a distinctness from which, in spite of my utmost efforts, my words had swerved aside. The tough-nerved yeoman, in his comment, put a finish on the business, and brought out the hideous idea in its full terror, as if he were removing the napkin from the face of a corpse.

"And so you think she 's drowned herself?" he cried. I turned away my face.

"What on earth should the young woman do that for?" exclaimed Silas, his eyes half out of his head with mere surprise. "Why, she has more means than she can use or waste, and lacks nothing to make her comfortable, but a husband, and that 's an article she could have, any day. There 's some mistake about this, I tell you!"

"Come," said I, shuddering; "let us go and ascertain the truth."

"Well, well," answered Silas Foster; "just as you say. We'll take the long pole, with the hook at the end, that serves to get the bucket out of the draw-well, when the rope is broken. With that, and a couple of long-handled hay-rakes, I 'll answer for finding her, if she 's anywhere to be found. Strange enough! Zenobia drown herself! No, no; I don't believe it. She had too much sense, and too much means, and enjoyed life a great deal too well."

When our few preparations were completed, we hastened, by a shorter than the customary route, through fields and pastures, and across a portion of the meadow, to the particular spot on the river-bank which I had paused to contemplate in the course of my afternoon's ramble. A nameless presentiment had again drawn me thither, after leaving Eliot's pulpit. I showed my companions where I had found the handkerchief, and pointed to two or three footsteps, impressed into the clayey margin, and tending towards the water. Beneath its shallow verge, among the water-weeds, there were further traces, as yet unobliterated by the sluggish current, which was there almost at a stand-still. Silas Foster thrust his face down close to these footsteps, and picked up a shoe that had escaped my observation, being half imbedded in the mud.

"There 's a kid shoe that never was made on a Yankee last," observed he. "I know enough of shoemaker's craft to tell that. French manufacture; and, see what a high instep! and how evenly she trod in it! There never was a woman that stept handsomer in her shoes than Zenobia did. Here," he added, addressing Hollingsworth, "would you like to keep the shoe?"

Hollingsworth started back.

"Give it to me, Foster," said I.

I dabbled it in the water, to rinse off the mud, and have kept it ever since. Not far from this spot lay an old, leaky punt, drawn up on the oozy river-side, and generally half full of water. It served the angler to go in quest of pickerel, or the sportsman to pick up his wild ducks. Setting this crazy bark afloat, I seated myself in the stern with the paddle, while Hollingsworth sat in the bows with the hooked pole, and Silas Foster amidships with a hay-rake.

"It puts me in mind of my young days," remarked Silas, "when I used to steal out of bed to go bobbing for hornpouts and eels. Heigh-ho!—well, life and death together make sad work for us all! Then I was a boy, bobbing for fish; and now I am getting to be an old fellow, and here I be, groping for a dead body! I tell you what, lads; if I thought anything had really happened to Zenobia, I should feel kind o' sorrowful."

"I wish, at least, you would hold your tongue," muttered I.

The moon, that night, though past the full, was still large and oval, and having risen between eight and nine o'clock, now shone aslantwise over the river, throwing the high, opposite bank, with its woods, into deep shadow, but lighting up the hither shore pretty effectually. Not a ray appeared to fall on the river itself. It lapsed imperceptibly away, a broad, black, inscrutable depth, keeping its own secrets from the eye of man, as impenetrably as mid-ocean could.

"Well, Miles Coverdale," said Foster, "you are the helmsman. How do you mean to manage this business?"

"I shall let the boat drift, broadside foremost, past that stump," I replied. "I know the bottom, having sounded it in fishing. The shore, on this side, after the first step or two, goes off very abruptly; and there is a pool, just by the stump, twelve or fifteen feet deep. The current could not have force enough to sweep any sunken object, even if partially buoyant, out of that hollow."

"Come, then," said Silas; "but I doubt whether I can touch bottom with this hay-rake, if it 's as deep as you say. Mr. Hollingsworth, I think you 'll be the lucky man to-night, such luck as it is."

We floated past the stump. Silas Foster plied his rake manfully, poking it as far as he could into the water, and immersing the whole length of his arm besides. Hollingsworth at first sat motionless, with the hooked pole elevated in the air. But, by and by, with a nervous and jerky movement, he began to plunge it into the blackness that upbore us, setting his teeth, and making precisely such thrusts, methought, as if he were stabbing at a deadly enemy. I bent over the side of the boat. So obscure, however, so awfully mysterious, was that dark stream, that—and the thought made me shiver like a leaf—I might as well have tried to look into the enigma of the eternal world, to discover what had become of Zenobia's soul, as into the river's depths, to find her body. And there, perhaps, she lay, with her face upward, while the shadow of the boat, and my own pale face peering downward, passed slowly betwixt her and the sky!

Once, twice, thrice, I paddled the boat up stream, and again suffered it to glide, with the river's slow, funereal motion, downward. Silas Foster had raked up a large mass of stuff, which, as it came towards the surface, looked somewhat like a flowing garment, but proved to be a monstrous tuft of water-weeds. Hollingsworth, with a gigantic effort, upheaved a sunken log. When once free of the bottom, it rose partly out of water,— all weedy and slimy, a devilish-looking object, which the moon had not shone upon for half a hundred years,—then plunged again, and sullenly returned to its old resting-place, for the remnant of the century.

"That looked ugly!" quoth Silas. "I half thought it was the Evil One, on the same errand as ourselves,—searching for Zenobia."

"He shall never get her," said I, giving the boat a strong impulse.

"That's not for you to say, my boy," retorted the yeoman. "Pray God he never has, and never may. Slow work this, however! I should really be glad to find something! Pshaw! What a notion that is, when the only good luck would be to paddle, and drift, and poke, and grope, here-abouts, till morning, and have our labor for our pains! For my part, I should n't wonder if the creature had only lost her shoe in the mud, and saved her soul alive, after all. My stars! how she will laugh at us, to-mor-row morning!"

It is indescribable what an image of Zenobia—at the breakfast-table, full of warm and mirthful life—this surmise of Silas Foster's brought before my mind. The terrible phantasm of her death was thrown by it into the remotest and dimmest background, where it seemed to grow as improbable as a myth.

"Yes, Silas, it may be as you say," cried I.

The drift of the stream had again borne us a little below the stump, when I felt—yes, felt, for it was as if the iron hook had smote my breast —felt Hollingsworth's pole strike some object at the bottom of the river! He started up, and almost overset the boat.

"Hold on!" cried Foster; "you have her!"

Putting a fury of strength into the effort, Hollingsworth heaved amain, and up came a white swash to the surface of the river. It was the flow of a woman's garments. A little higher, and we saw her dark hair streaming down the current. Black River of Death, thou hadst yielded up thy vic-tim! Zenobia was found!

Silas Foster laid hold of the body; Hollingsworth, likewise, grappled with it; and I steered towards the bank, gazing all the while at Zenobia, whose limbs were swaying in the current close at the boat's side. Arriving near the shore, we all three stept into the water, bore her out, and laid her on the ground beneath a tree.

"Poor child!" said Foster,—and his dry old heart, I verily believe, vouchsafed a tear,—"I 'm sorry for her!"

Were I to describe the perfect horror of the spectacle, the reader might justly reckon it to me for a sin and shame. For more than twelve long years I have borne it in my memory, and could now reproduce it as freshly as if it were still before my eyes. Of all modes of death, methinks it is the ugliest. Her wet garments swathed limbs of terrible inflexibility. She was the marble image of a death-agony. Her arms had grown rigid in the act of struggling, and were bent before her with clenched hands; her knees, too, were bent, and—thank God for it!—in the attitude of prayer. Ah, that rigidity! It is impossible to bear the terror of it. It seemed,—I must needs impart so much of my own miserable idea,—it seemed as if her body must keep the same position in the coffin, and that her skeleton would keep it in the grave; and that when Zenobia rose at the day of judgment, it would be in just the same attitude as now!

One hope I had, and that too was mingled half with fear. She knelt as if in prayer. With the last, choking consciousness, her soul, bubbling out through her lips, it may be, had given itself up to the Father, reconciled and penitent. But her arms! They were bent before her, as if she struggled against Providence in never-ending hostility. Her hands! They were clenched in immitigable defiance. Away with the hideous thought. The flitting moment after Zenobia sank into the dark pool—when her breath was gone, and her soul at her lips—was as long, in its capacity of God's infinite forgiveness, as the lifetime of the world!

Foster bent over the body, and carefully examined it.

"You have wounded the poor thing's breast," said he to Hollingsworth; "close by her heart, too!"

"Ha!" cried Hollingsworth, with a start.

And so he had, indeed, both before and after death!

"See!" said Foster. "That's the place where the iron struck her. It looks cruelly, but she never felt it!"

He endeavored to arrange the arms of the corpse decently by its side. His utmost strength, however, scarcely sufficed to bring them down; and rising again, the next instant, they bade him defiance, exactly as before. He made another effort, with the same result.

"In God's name, Silas Foster," cried I, with bitter indignation, "let that dead woman alone!"

"Why, man, it 's not decent!" answered he, staring at me in amazement. "I can't bear to see her looking so! Well, well," added he, after a third effort, " 't is of no use, sure enough; and we must leave the women to do their best with her, after we get to the house. The sooner that 's done, the better."

We took two rails from a neighboring fence, and formed a bier by laying across some boards from the bottom of the boat. And thus we bore Zenobia homeward. Six hours before, how beautiful! At midnight, what a horror! A reflection occurs to me that will show ludicrously, I doubt not, on my page, but must come in, for its sterling truth. Being the woman that she was, could Zenobia have foreseen all these ugly circumstances of death,—how ill it would become her, the altogether unseemly aspect which she must put on, and especially old Silas Foster's efforts to improve the matter,—she would no more have committed the dreadful act than have exhibited herself to a public assembly in a badly fitting garment! Zenobia, I have often thought, was not quite simple in her death. She had seen pictures, I suppose, of drowned persons in lithe and graceful attitudes. And she deemed it well and decorous to die as so many village maidens have, wronged in their first love, and seeking peace in the bosom of the old familiar stream,—so familiar that they could not dread it,—where, in childhood, they used to bathe their little feet, wading midleg deep, unmindful of wet skirts. But in Zenobia's case there was some tint of the Arcadian affectation that had been visible enough in all our lives for a few months past.

This, however, to my conception, takes nothing from the tragedy. For, has not the world come to an awfully sophisticated pass, when, after a certain degree of acquaintance with it, we cannot even put ourselves to death in whole-hearted simplicity?

Slowly, slowly, with many a dreary pause,—resting the bier often on some rock or balancing it across a mossy log, to take fresh hold,—we bore our burden onward through the moonlight, and at last laid Zenobia on the floor of the old farm-house. By and by came three or four withered women, and stood whispering around the corpse, peering at it through their spectacles, holding up their skinny hands, shaking their night-capped heads, and taking counsel of one another's experience what was to be done.

With those tire-women we left Zenobia.

## XXVIII

### BLITHEDALE PASTURE

BLITHEDALE, thus far in its progress, had never found the necessity of a burial-ground. There was some consultation among us in what spot Zenobia might most fitly be laid. It was my own wish that she should sleep at the base of Eliot's pulpit, and that on the rugged front of the rock the name by which we familiarly knew her,—ZENOBIA,—and not another word, should be deeply cut, and left for the moss and lichens to fill up at their long leisure. But Hollingsworth (to whose ideas on this point great deference was due) made it his request that her grave might be dug on the gently sloping hill-side, in the wide pasture, where, as we once supposed, Zenobia and he had planned to build their cottage. And thus it was done, accordingly.

She was buried very much as other people have been for hundreds of years gone by. In anticipation of a death, we Blithedale colonists had sometimes set our fancies at work to arrange a funereal ceremony, which should be the proper symbolic expression of our spiritual faith and eternal hopes; and this we meant to substitute for those customary rites which were moulded originally out of the Gothic gloom, and by long use, like an old velvet pall, have so much more than their first death-smell in them. But when the occasion came we found it the simplest and truest thing, after all, to content ourselves with the old-fashion, taking away what we could, but interpolating no novelties, and particularly avoiding all frippery of flowers and cheerful emblems. The procession moved from the farm-house. Nearest the dead walked an old man in deep mourning, his face mostly concealed in a white handkerchief, and with Priscilla leaning on his arm. Hollingsworth and myself came next. We all stood around the narrow niche in the cold earth; all saw the coffin lowered in; all heard the rattle of the crumbly soil upon its lid,—that final sound, which mortality awakens on the utmost verge of sense, as if in the vain hope of bringing an echo from the spiritual world.

I noticed a stranger,—a stranger to most of those present, though known to me,—who, after the coffin had descended, took up a handful of earth, and flung it first into the grave. I had given up Hollingsworth's arm, and now found myself near this man.

"It was an idle thing—a foolish thing—for Zenobia to do," said he. "She was the last woman in the world to whom death could have been necessary. It was too absurd! I have no patience with her."

"Why so?" I inquired, smothering my horror at his cold comment, in my eager curiosity to discover some tangible truth as to his relation with Zenobia. "If any crisis could justify the sad wrong she offered to herself, it was surely that in which she stood. Everything had failed her; prosperity in the world's sense, for her opulence was gone,—the heart's prosperity, in love. And there was a secret burden on her, the nature of which is best known to you. Young as she was, she had tried life fully, had no more to hope, and something, perhaps, to fear. Had Providence taken her away in its own holy hand, I should have thought it the kindest dispensation that could be awarded to one so wrecked."

"You mistake the matter completely," rejoined Westervelt.

"What, then, is your own view of it?" I asked.

"Her mind was active, and various in its powers," said he. "Her heart had a manifold adaptation; her constitution an infinite buoyancy, which (had she possessed only a little patience to await the reflux of her troubles) would have borne her upward triumphantly for twenty years to come. Her beauty would not have waned—or scarcely so, and surely not beyond the reach of art to restore it—in all that time. She had life's summer all before her, and a hundred varieties of brilliant success. What an actress Zenobia might have been! It was one of her least valuable capabilities. How forcibly she might have wrought upon the world, either directly in her own person, or by her influence upon some man, or a series of men, of controlling genius! Every prize that could be worth a woman's having—and many prizes which other women are too timid to desire—lay within Zenobia's reach."

"In all this," I observed, "there would have been nothing to satisfy her heart."

"Her heart!" answered Westervelt, contemptuously. "That troublesome organ (as she had hitherto found it) would have been kept in its due place and degree, and have had all the gratification it could fairly claim. She would soon have established a control over it. Love had failed her, you say. Had it never failed her before? Yet she survived it, and loved again,—possibly not once alone, nor twice either. And now to drown herself for yonder dreamy philanthropist!"

"Who are you," I exclaimed, indignantly, "that dare to speak thus of the dead? You seem to intend a eulogy, yet leave out whatever was noblest in her, and blacken while you mean to praise. I have long considered you as Zenobia's evil fate. Your sentiments confirm me in the idea, but leave me still ignorant as to the mode in which you have influenced her life. The connection may have been indissoluble, except by death. Then, indeed,—always in the hope of God's infinite mercy,—I cannot deem it a misfortune that she sleeps in yonder grave!"

"No matter what I was to her," he answered, gloomily, yet without actual emotion. "She is now beyond my reach. Had she lived, and harkened to my counsels, we might have served each other well. But there Zenobia lies in yonder pit, with the dull earth over her. Twenty years of a brilliant lifetime thrown away for a mere woman's whim!"

Heaven deal with Westervelt according to his nature and deserts!—that is to say, annihilate him. He was altogether earthy, worldly, made for time and its gross objects, and incapable—except by a sort of dim reflection caught from other minds—of so much as one spiritual idea. Whatever stain Zenobia had was caught from him; nor does it seldom happen that a character of admirable qualities loses its better life because the atmosphere that should sustain it is rendered poisonous by such breath as this man mingled with Zenobia's. Yet his reflections possessed their share of truth. It was a woful thought, that a woman of Zenobia's diversified capacity should have fancied herself irretrievably defeated on the broad battle-field of life, and with no refuge, save to fall on her own sword, merely because Love had gone against her. It is nonsense, and a miserable wrong,—the result, like so many others, of masculine egotism, —that the success or failure of woman's existence should be made to depend wholly on the affections, and on one species of affection, while man has such a multitude of other chances, that this seems but an incident. For its own sake, if it will do no more, the world should throw open all its avenues to the passport of a woman's bleeding heart.

As we stood around the grave, I looked often towards Priscilla, dreading to see her wholly overcome with grief. And deeply grieved, in truth, she was. But a character so simply constituted as hers has room only for a single predominant affection. No other feeling can touch the heart's inmost core, nor do it any deadly mischief. Thus, while we see that such a being responds to every breeze with tremulous vibration, and imagine that she must be shattered by the first rude blast, we find her retaining her equilibrium amid shocks that might have overthrown many a sturdier frame. So with Priscilla; her one possible misfortune was Hollingsworth's unkindness; and that was destined never to befall her,—never yet, at least, for Priscilla has not died.

But Hollingsworth! After all the evil that he did, are we to leave him thus, blest with the entire devotion of this one true heart, and with wealth at his disposal to execute the long-contemplated project that had led him so far astray? What retribution is there here? My mind being vexed with precisely this query, I made a journey, some years since, for the sole purpose of catching a last glimpse of Hollingsworth, and judging for myself whether he were a happy man or no. I learned that he inhabited a small cottage, that his way of life was exceedingly retired, and that my only chance of encountering him or Priscilla was to meet them in a secluded lane, where, in the latter part of the afternoon, they were accustomed to walk. I did meet them, accordingly. As they approached me, I observed in Hollingsworth's face a depressed and melancholy look, that seemed habitual; the powerfully built man showed a self-distrustful weakness, and a childlike or childish tendency to press close, and closer still, to the side of the slender woman whose arm was within his. In Priscilla's manner there was a protective and watchful quality, as if she felt herself the guardian of her companion; but, likewise, a deep, submissive, unquestioning reverence, and also a veiled happiness in her fair and quiet countenance.

Drawing nearer, Priscilla recognized me, and gave me a kind and friendly smile, but with a slight gesture, which I could not help interpreting as an entreaty not to make myself known to Hollingsworth. Nevertheless, an impulse took possession of me, and compelled me to address him.

"I have come, Hollingsworth," said I, "to view your grand edifice for the reformation of criminals. Is it finished yet?"

"No, nor begun," answered he, without raising his eyes. "A very small one answers all my purposes."

Priscilla threw me an upbraiding glance. But I spoke again, with a bitter and revengeful emotion, as if flinging a poisoned arrow at Hollingsworth's heart.

"Up to this moment," I inquired, "how many criminals have you reformed?"

"Not one," said Hollingsworth, with his eyes still fixed on the ground. "Ever since we parted, I have been busy with a single murderer."

Then the tears gushed into my eyes, and I forgave him; for I remembered the wild energy, the passionate shriek, with which Zenobia had spoken those words,—"Tell him he has murdered me! Tell him that I'll haunt him!"—and I knew what murderer he meant, and whose vindictive shadow dogged the side where Priscilla was not.

The moral which presents itself to my reflections, as drawn from Hollingsworth's character and errors, is simply this,—that, admitting what is called philanthropy, when adopted as a profession, to be often useful by its energetic impulse to society at large, it is perilous to the individual whose ruling passion, in one exclusive channel, it thus becomes. It ruins, or is fearfully apt to ruin, the heart, the rich juices of which God never meant should be pressed violently out, and distilled into alcoholic liquor, by an unnatural process, but should render life sweet, bland, and gently beneficent, and insensibly influence other hearts and other lives to the same blessed end. I see in Hollingsworth an exemplification of the most awful truth in Bunyan's book of such,—from the very gate of heaven there is a by-way to the pit!

But, all this while, we have been standing by Zenobia's grave. I have never since beheld it, but make no question that the grass grew all the better, on that little parallelogram of pasture-land, for the decay of the beautiful woman who slept beneath. How Nature seems to love us! And how readily, nevertheless, without a sigh or a complaint, she converts us to a meaner purpose, when her highest one—that of a conscious intellectual life and sensibility—has been untimely balked! While Zenobia lived, Nature was proud of her, and directed all eyes upon that radiant presence, as her fairest handiwork. Zenobia perished. Will not Nature shed a tear? Ah, no!—she adopts the calamity at once into her system, and is just as well pleased, for aught we can see, with the tuft of ranker vegetation that grew out of Zenobia's heart, as with all the beauty which has bequeathed us no earthly representative except in this crop of weeds. It is because the spirit is inestimable that the lifeless body is so little valued.

## XXIX

### MILES COVERDALE'S CONFESSION

It remains only to say a few words about myself. Not improbably, the reader might be willing to spare me the trouble; for I have made but a poor and dim figure in my own narrative, establishing no separate interest, and suffering my colorless life to take its hue from other lives. But one still retains some little consideration for one's self; so I keep these last two or three pages for my individual and sole behoof.

But what, after all, have I to tell? Nothing, nothing, nothing! I left Blithedale within the week after Zenobia's death, and went back thither no more. The whole soil of our farm, for a long time afterwards, seemed but the sodded earth over her grave. I could not toil there, nor live upon its products. Often, however, in these years that are darkening around me, I remember our beautiful scheme of a noble and unselfish life; and how fair, in that first summer, appeared the prospect that it might endure for generations, and be perfected, as the ages rolled away, into the system of a people and a world! Were my former associates now there,— were there only three or four of those true-hearted men still laboring in the sun,—I sometimes fancy that I should direct my world-weary footsteps thitherward, and entreat them to receive me, for old friendship's sake. More and more I feel that we had struck upon what ought to be a truth. Posterity may dig it up, and profit by it. The experiment, so far as its original projectors were concerned, proved, long ago, a failure; first lapsing into Fourierism, and dying, as it well deserved, for this infidelity to its own higher spirit. Where once we toiled with our whole hopeful hearts, the town-paupers, aged, nerveless, and disconsolate, creep sluggishly afield. Alas, what faith is requisite to bear up against such results of generous effort!

My subsequent life has passed,—I was going to say happily,—but, at all events, tolerably enough. I am now at middle age,—well, well, a step or two beyond the midmost point, and I care not a fig who knows it!—a bachelor, with no very decided purpose of ever being otherwise. I have been twice to Europe, and spent a year or two rather agreeably at each visit. Being well to do in the world, and having nobody but myself to care for, I live very much at my ease, and fare sumptuously every day. As for poetry, I have given it up, notwithstanding that Dr. Griswold—as the reader, of course, knows—has placed me at a fair elevation among our minor minstrelsy, on the strength of my pretty little volume, published ten years ago. As regards human progress (in spite of my irrepressible yearnings over the Blithedale reminiscences), let them believe in it who can, and aid in it who choose. If I could earnestly do either, it might be all the better for my comfort. As Hollingsworth once told me, I lack a purpose. How strange! He was ruined, morally, by an overplus of the very same ingredient, the want of which, I occasionally suspect, has rendered my own life all an emptiness. I by no means wish to die. Yet, were there any cause, in this whole chaos of human struggle, worth a sane man's dying for, and which my death would benefit, then—provided, however, the effort did not involve an unreasonable amount of trouble— methinks I might be bold to offer up my life. If Kossuth, for example, would pitch the battlefield of Hungarian rights within an easy ride of my abode, and choose a mild, sunny morning, after breakfast, for the conflict, Miles Coverdale would gladly be his man, for one brave rush upon the levelled bayonets. Further than that, I should be loath to pledge myself.

I exaggerate my own defects. The reader must not take my own word for it, nor believe me altogether changed from the young man who once hoped strenuously, and struggled not so much amiss. Frostier heads than mine have gained honor in the world; frostier hearts have imbibed new warmth, and been newly happy. Life, however, it must be owned, has come to rather an idle pass with me. Would my friends like to know what brought it thither? There is one secret,—I have concealed it all along, and never meant to let the least whisper of it escape,—one foolish little secret, which possibly may have had something to do with these inactive years of meridian manhood, with my bachelorship, with the unsatisfied retrospect that I fling back on life, and my listless glance towards the future. Shall I reveal it? It is an absurd thing for a man in his afternoon,— a man of the world, moreover, with these three white hairs in his brown mustache and that deepening track of a crow's-foot on each temple,—an absurd thing ever to have happened, and quite the absurdest for an old bachelor, like me, to talk about. But it rises to my throat; so let it come.

I perceive, moreover, that the confession, brief as it shall be, will throw a gleam of light over my behavior throughout the foregoing incidents, and is, indeed, essential to the full understanding of my story. The reader, therefore, since I have disclosed so much, is entitled to this one word more. As I write it, he will charitably suppose me to blush, and turn away my face:—

I—I myself—was in love—with—PRISCILLA!

# THE MARBLE FAUN

## OR

# THE ROMANCE OF MONTE BENI

# PREFACE

IT is now seven or eight years (so many, at all events, that I cannot precisely remember the epoch) since the author of this romance last appeared before the Public. It had grown to be a custom with him to introduce each of his humble publications with a familiar kind of preface, addressed nominally to the Public at large, but really to a character with whom he felt entitled to use far greater freedom. He meant it for that one congenial friend,—more comprehensive of his purposes, more appreciative of his success, more indulgent of his shortcomings, and, in all respects, closer and kinder than a brother,—that all-sympathizing critic, in short, whom an author never actually meets, but to whom he implicitly makes his appeal whenever he is conscious of having done his best.

The antique fashion of Prefaces recognized this genial personage as the "Kind Reader," the "Gentle Reader," the "Beloved," the "Indulgent," or, at coldest, the "Honored Reader," to whom the prim old author was wont to make his preliminary explanations and apologies, with the certainty that they would be favorably received. I never personally encountered, nor corresponded through the post with this representative essence of all delightful and desirable qualities which a reader can possess. But, fortunately for myself, I never therefore concluded him to be merely a mythic character. I had always a sturdy faith in his actual existence, and wrote for him year after year, during which the great eye of the Public (as well it might) almost utterly overlooked my small productions.

Unquestionably, this gentle, kind, benevolent, indulgent, and most beloved and honored Reader did once exist for me, and (in spite of the infinite chances against a letter's reaching its destination without a definite address) duly received the scrolls which I flung upon whatever wind was blowing, in the faith that they would find him out. But, is he extant now? In these many years, since he last heard from me, may he not have deemed his earthly task accomplished, and have withdrawn to the paradise of gentle readers, wherever it may be, to the enjoyments of which his kindly charity on my behalf must surely have entitled him? I have a sad foreboding that this may be the truth. The "Gentle Reader," in the case of any individual author, is apt to be extremely short-lived; he seldom outlasts a literary fashion, and, except in very rare instances, closes his weary eyes before the writer has half done with him. If I find him at all, it will probably be under some mossy-gravestone, inscribed with a half-obliterated name which I shall never recognize.

Therefore, I have little heart or confidence (especially, writing as I do, in a foreign land, and after a long, long absence from my own) to presume upon the existence of that friend of friends, that unseen brother of the soul, whose apprehensive sympathy has so often encouraged me to be egotistical in my prefaces, careless though unkindly eyes should skim over what was never meant for them. I stand upon ceremony now; and, after stating a few particulars about the work which is here offered to the Public, must make my most reverential bow, and retire behind the curtain.

This Romance was sketched out during a residence of considerable length in Italy, and has been rewritten and prepared for the press in England. The author proposed to himself merely to write a fanciful story, evolving a thoughtful moral, and did not propose attempting a portraiture of Italian manners and character. He has lived too long abroad not to be aware that a foreigner seldom acquires that knowledge of a country at once flexible and profound, which may justify him in endeavoring to idealize its traits.

Italy, as the site of his Romance, was chiefly valuable to him as affording a sort of poetic or fairy precinct, where actualities would not be so terribly insisted upon as they are, and must needs be, in America. No author, without a trial, can conceive of the difficulty of writing a romance about a country where there is no shadow, no antiquity, no mystery, no picturesque and gloomy wrong, nor anything but a commonplace prosperity, in broad and simple daylight, as is happily the case with my dear native land. It will be very long, I trust, before romance-writers may find congenial and easily handled themes, either in the annals of our stalwart republic, or in any characteristic and probable events of our individual lives. Romance and poetry, ivy, lichens, and wall-flowers, need ruin to make them grow.

In rewriting these volumes, the author was somewhat surprised to see the extent to which he had introduced descriptions of various Italian objects, antique, pictorial, and statuesque. Yet these things fill the mind everywhere in Italy, and especially in Rome, and cannot easily be kept from flowing out upon the page when one writes freely, and with self-enjoyment. And, again, while reproducing the book, on the broad and dreary sands of Redcar, with the gray German Ocean tumbling in upon me, and the northern blast always howling in my ears, the complete change of scene made these Italian reminiscences shine out so vividly that I could not find it in my heart to cancel them.

An act of justice remains to be performed towards two men of genius with whose productions the author has allowed himself to use a quite unwarrantable freedom. Having imagined a sculptor in this Romance, it was necessary to provide him with such works in marble as should be in keeping with the artistic ability which he was supposed to possess. With this view, the author laid felonious hands upon a certain bust of Milton, and a statue of a pearl-diver, which he found in the studio of Mr. PAUL AKERS, and secretly conveyed them to the premises of his imaginary friend, in the Via Frezza. Not content even with these spoils, he committed a further robbery upon a magnificent statue of Cleopatra, the production of Mr. WILLIAM W. STORY, an artist whom his country and the world will not long fail to appreciate. He had thoughts of appropriating, likewise, a certain door of bronze by Mr. RANDOLPH ROGERS, representing the history of Columbus in a series of admirable bas-reliefs, but was deterred by an unwillingness to meddle with public property. Were he capable of stealing from a lady, he would certainly have made free with Miss HOSMER's admirable statue of Zenobia.

He now wishes to restore the above-mentioned beautiful pieces of sculpture to their proper owners, with many thanks, and the avowal of his sincere admiration. What he has said of them in the Romance does not partake of the fiction in which they are imbedded, but expresses his genuine opinion, which, he has little doubt, will be found in accordance with that of the Public. It is, perhaps, unnecessary to say, that, while stealing their designs, the Author has not taken a similar liberty with the personal characters of either of these gifted sculptors; his own man of marble being entirely imaginary.

LEAMINGTON, *December* 15, 1859.

# THE ROMANCE OF MONTE BENI

## CHAPTER I

### MIRIAM, HILDA, KENYON, DONATELLO

FOUR individuals, in whose fortunes we should be glad to interest the reader, happened to be standing in one of the saloons of the sculpture gallery in the Capitol at Rome. It was that room (the first, after ascending the staircase) in the centre of which reclines the noble and most pathetic figure of the Dying Gladiator, just sinking into his death-swoon. Around the walls stand the Antinous, the Amazon, the Lycian Apollo, the Juno; all famous productions of antique sculpture, and still shining in the undiminished majesty and beauty of their ideal life, although the marble that embodies them is yellow with time, and perhaps corroded by the damp earth in which they lay buried for centuries. Here, likewise, is seen a symbol (as apt at this moment as it was two thousand years ago) of the Human Soul, with its choice of Innocence or Evil close at hand, in the pretty figure of a child, clasping a dove to her bosom, but assaulted by a snake.

From one of the windows of this saloon, we may see a flight of broad stone steps, descending alongside the antique and massive foundation of the Capitol, towards the battered triumphal arch of Septimius Severus, right below. Farther on, the eye skirts along the edge of the desolate Forum (where Roman washer-women hang out their linen to the sun), passing over a shapeless confusion of modern edifices, piled rudely up with ancient brick and stone, and over the domes of Christian churches, built on the old pavements of heathen temples, and supported by the very pillars that once upheld them. At a distance beyond—yet but a little way, considering how much history is heaped into the intervening space—rises the great sweep of the Coliseum, with the blue sky brightening through its upper tier of arches. Far off, the view is shut in by the Alban Mountains, looking just the same, amid all this decay and change, as when Romulus gazed thitherward over his half-finished wall.

We glance hastily at these things,—at this bright sky, and those blue distant mountains, and at the ruins, Etruscan, Roman, Christian, venerable with a threefold antiquity, and at the company of world-famous statues in the saloon,—in the hope of putting the reader into that state of feeling which is experienced oftenest at Rome. It is a vague sense of ponderous remembrances; a perception of such weight and density in a by-gone life, of which this spot was the centre, that the present moment is pressed down or crowded out, and our individual affairs and interests are but half as real here as elsewhere. Viewed through this medium, our narrative—into which are woven some airy and unsubstantial threads, intermixed with others, twisted out of the commonest stuff of human existence—may seem not widely different from the texture of all our lives.

Side by side with the massiveness of the Roman Past, all matters that we handle or dream of nowadays look evanescent and visionary alike.

It might be that the four persons whom we are seeking to introduce were conscious of this dreamy character of the present, as compared with the square blocks of granite wherewith the Romans built their lives. Perhaps it even contributed to the fanciful merriment which was just now their mood. When we find ourselves fading into shadows and unrealities, it seems hardly worth while to be sad, but rather to laugh as gayly as we may, and ask little reason wherefore.

Of these four friends of ours, three were artists, or connected with art; and, at this moment, they had been simultaneously struck by a resemblance between one of the antique statues, a well-known masterpiece of Grecian sculpture, and a young Italian, the fourth member of their party.

"You must needs confess, Kenyon," said a dark-eyed young woman, whom her friends called Miriam, "that you never chiselled out of marble, nor wrought in clay, a more vivid likeness than this, cunning a bust-maker as you think yourself. The portraiture is perfect in character, sentiment, and feature. If it were a picture, the resemblance might be half illusive and imaginary; but here, in this Pentelic marble, it is a substantial fact, and may be tested by absolute touch and measurement. Our friend Donatello is the very Faun of Praxiteles. Is it not true, Hilda?"

"Not quite—almost—yes, I really think so," replied Hilda, a slender, brown-haired, New England girl, whose perceptions of form and expression were wonderfully clear and delicate. "If there is any difference between the two faces, the reason may be, I suppose, that the Faun dwelt in woods and fields, and consorted with his like; whereas, Donatello has known cities a little, and such people as ourselves. But the resemblance is very close, and very strange."

"Not so strange," whispered Miriam, mischievously; "for no Faun in Arcadia was ever a greater simpleton than Donatello. He has hardly a man's share of wit, small as that may be. It is a pity there are no longer any of this congenial race of rustic creatures for our friend to consort with!"

"Hush, naughty one!" returned Hilda. "You are very ungrateful, for you well know he has wit enough to worship you, at all events."

"Then the greater fool he!" said Miriam, so bitterly that Hilda's quiet eyes were somewhat startled.

"Donatello, my dear friend," said Kenyon, in Italian, "pray gratify us all by taking the exact attitude of this statue."

The young man laughed, and threw himself into the position in which the statue has been standing for two or three thousand years. In truth, allowing for the difference of costume, and if a lion's skin could have been substituted for his modern talma, and a rustic pipe for his stick, Donatello might have figured perfectly as the marble Faun, miraculously softened into flesh and blood.

"Yes; the resemblance is wonderful," observed Kenyon, after examining the marble and the man with the accuracy of a sculptor's eye. "There is one point, however, or, rather, two points, in respect to which our friend Donatello's abundant curls will not permit us to say whether the likeness is carried into minute detail."

And the sculptor directed the attention of the party to the ears of the beautiful statue which they were contemplating.

But we must do more than merely refer to this exquisite work of art; it must be described, however inadequate may be the effort to express its magic peculiarity in words.

The Faun is the marble image of a young man, leaning his right arm on the trunk or stump of a tree; one hand hangs carelessly by his side; in the other he holds the fragment of a pipe, or some such sylvan instrument of music. His only garment—a lion's skin, with the claws upon his shoulder—falls half-way down his back, leaving the limbs and entire front of the figure nude. The form, thus displayed, is marvellously graceful, but has a fuller and more rounded outline, more flesh, and less of heroic muscle, than the old sculptors were wont to assign to their types of masculine beauty. The character of the face corresponds with the figure; it is most agreeable in outline and feature, but rounded and somewhat voluptuously developed, especially about the throat and chin; the nose is almost straight, but very slightly curves inward, thereby acquiring an indescribable charm of geniality and humor. The mouth, with its full yet delicate lips, seems so nearly to smile outright, that it calls forth a responsive smile. The whole statue—unlike anything else that ever was wrought in that severe material of marble—conveys the idea of an amiable and sensual creature, easy, mirthful, apt for jollity, yet not incapable of being touched by pathos. It is impossible to gaze long at this stone image without conceiving a kindly sentiment towards it, as if its substance were warm to the touch, and imbued with actual life. It comes very close to some of our pleasantest sympathies.

Perhaps it is the very lack of moral severity, of any high and heroic ingredient in the character of the Faun, that makes it so delightful an object to the human eye and to the frailty of the human heart. The being here represented is endowed with no principle of virtue, and would be incapable of comprehending such; but he would be true and honest by dint of his simplicity. We should expect from him no sacrifice or effort for an abstract cause; there is not an atom of martyr's stuff in all that softened marble; but he has a capacity for strong and warm attachment, and might act devotedly through its impulse, and even die for it at need. It is possible, too, that the Faun might be educated through the medium of his emotions, so that the coarser animal portion of his nature might eventually be thrown into the background, though never utterly expelled.

The animal nature, indeed, is a most essential part of the Faun's composition; for the characteristics of the brute creation meet and combine with those of humanity in this strange yet true and natural conception of antique poetry and art. Praxiteles has subtly diffused throughout his work that mute mystery which so hopelessly perplexes us whenever we attempt to gain an intellectual or sympathetic knowledge of the lower orders of creation. The riddle is indicated, however, only by two definite signs; these are the two ears of the Faun, which are leaf-shaped, terminating in little peaks, like those of some species of animals. Though not so seen in the marble, they are probably to be considered as clothed in fine, downy fur. In the coarser representations of this class of mythological creatures, there is another token of brute kindred,—a certain caudal appendage; which, if the Faun of Praxiteles must be supposed to possess it at all, is hidden by the lion's skin that forms his garment. The pointed and furry ears, therefore, are the sole indications of his wild, forest nature.

Only a sculptor of the finest imagination, the most delicate taste, the sweetest feeling, and the rarest artistic skill—in a word, a sculptor and a poet too—could have first dreamed of a Faun in this guise, and then have succeeded in imprisoning the sportive and frisky thing in marble. Neither man nor animal, and yet no monster, but a being in whom both races meet on friendly ground. The idea grows coarse as we handle it, and hardens in our grasp. But, if the spectator broods long over the statue, he will be conscious of its spell; all the pleasantness of sylvan life, all the genial and happy characteristics of creatures that dwell in woods and fields, will seem to be mingled and kneaded into one substance, along with the kindred qualities in the human soul. Trees, grass, flowers, woodland streamlets, cattle, deer, and unsophisticated man. The essence of all these was compressed long ago, and still exists, within that discolored marble surface of the Faun of Praxiteles.

And, after all, the idea may have been no dream, but rather a poet's reminiscence of a period when man's affinity with nature was more strict, and his fellowship with every living thing more intimate and dear.

## CHAPTER II

### THE FAUN

"DONATELLO," playfully cried Miriam, "do not leave us in this perplexity! Shake aside those brown curls, my friend, and let us see whether this marvellous resemblance extends to the very tips of the ears. If so, we shall like you all the better!"

"No, no, dearest signorina," answered Donatello, laughing, but with a certain earnestness. "I entreat you to take the tips of my ears for granted." As he spoke, the young Italian made a skip and jump, light enough for a veritable faun; so as to place himself quite beyond the reach of the fair hand that was outstretched, as if to settle the matter by actual examination. "I shall be like a wolf of the Apennines," he continued, taking his stand on the other side of the Dying Gladiator, "if you touch my ears ever so softly. None of my race could endure it. It has always been a tender point with my forefathers and me."

He spoke in Italian, with the Tuscan rusticity of accent, and an unshaped sort of utterance, betokening that he must heretofore have been chiefly conversant with rural people.

"Well, well," said Miriam, "your tender point—your two tender points, if you have them—shall be safe, so far as I am concerned. But how strange this likeness is, after all! and how delightful, if it really includes the pointed ears! Oh, it is impossible, of course," she continued, in English, "with a real and commonplace young man like Donatello; but you see how this peculiarity defines the position of the Faun; and, while putting him where he cannot exactly assert his brotherhood, still disposes us kindly towards the kindred creature. He is not supernatural, but just on the verge of nature, and yet within it. What is the nameless charm of this idea, Hilda? You can feel it more delicately than I."

"It perplexes me," said Hilda, thoughtfully, and shrinking a little; "neither do I quite like to think about it."

"But, surely," said Kenyon, "you agree with Miriam and me that there is something very touching and impressive in this statue of the Faun. In some long-past age, he must really have existed. Nature needed, and still needs, this beautiful creature; standing betwixt man and animal, sympathizing with each, comprehending the speech of either race, and interpreting the whole existence of one to the other. What a pity that he has forever vanished from the hard and dusty paths of life,—unless," added the sculptor, in a sportive whisper, "Donatello be actually he!"

"You cannot conceive how this fantasy takes hold of me," responded Miriam, between jest and earnest. "Imagine, now, a real being, similar to this mythic Faun; how happy, how genial, how satisfactory would be his life, enjoying the warm, sensuous, earthy side of nature; revelling in the merriment of woods and streams; living as our four-footed kindred do,—as mankind did in its innocent childhood; before sin, sorrow or morality itself had ever been thought of! Ah! Kenyon, if Hilda and you and I—if I, at least—had pointed ears! For I suppose the Faun had no conscience, no remorse, no burden on the heart, no troublesome recollections of any sort; no dark future either."

"What a tragic tone was that last, Miriam!" said the sculptor; and, looking into her face, he was startled to behold it pale and tear-stained. "How suddenly this mood has come over you!"

"Let it go as it came," said Miriam, "like a thunder-shower in this Roman sky. All is sunshine again, you see!"

Donatello's refractoriness as regarded his ears had evidently cost him something, and he now came close to Miriam's side, gazing at her with an appealing air, as if to solicit forgiveness. His mute, helpless gesture of entreaty had something pathetic in it, and yet might well enough excite a laugh, so like it was to what you may see in the aspect of a hound when he thinks himself in fault or disgrace. It was difficult to make out the character of this young man. So full of animal life as he was, so joyous in his deportment, so handsome, so physically well-developed, he made no impression of incompleteness, of maimed or stinted nature. And yet, in social intercourse, these familiar friends of his habitually and instinctively allowed for him, as for a child or some other lawless thing, exacting no strict obedience to conventional rules, and hardly noticing his eccentricities enough to pardon them. There was an indefinable characteristic about Donatello that set him outside of rules.

He caught Miriam's hand, kissed it, and gazed into her eyes without saying a word. She smiled, and bestowed on him a little careless caress, singularly like what one would give to a pet dog when he puts himself in the way to receive it. Not that it was so decided a caress either, but only the merest touch, somewhere between a pat and a tap of the finger; it might be a mark of fondness, or perhaps a playful pretence of punishment. At all events, it appeared to afford Donatello exquisite pleasure; insomuch that he danced quite round the wooden railing that fences in the Dying Gladiator.

"It is the very step of the Dancing Faun," said Miriam, apart, to Hilda. "What a child, or what a simpleton, he is! I continually find myself treating Donatello as if he were the merest unfledged chicken; and yet he can claim no such privileges in the right of his tender age, for he is at least—how old should you think him, Hilda?"

"Twenty years, perhaps," replied Hilda, glancing at Donatello; "but, indeed, I cannot tell; hardly so old, on second thoughts, or possibly older. He has nothing to do with time, but has a look of eternal youth in his face."

"All underwitted people have that look," said Miriam, scornfully.

"Donatello has certainly the gift of eternal youth, as Hilda suggests," observed Kenyon, laughing; "for, judging by the date of this statue, which, I am more and more convinced, Praxiteles carved on purpose for him, he must be at least twenty-five centuries old, and he still looks as young as ever."

"What age have you, Donatello?" asked Miriam.

"Signorina, I do not know," he answered; "no great age, however; for I have only lived since I met you."

"Now, what old man of society could have turned a silly compliment more smartly than that!" exclaimed Miriam. "Nature and art are just at one sometimes. But what a happy ignorance is this of our friend Donatello! Not to know his own age! It is equivalent to being immortal on earth. If I could only forget mine!"

"It is too soon to wish that," observed the sculptor; "you are scarcely older than Donatello looks."

"I shall be content, then," rejoined Miriam, "if I could only forget one day of all my life." Then she seemed to repent of this allusion, and hastily added, "A woman's days are so tedious that it is a boon to leave even one of them out of the account."

The foregoing conversation had been carried on in a mood in which all imaginative people, whether artists or poets, love to indulge. In this frame of mind, they sometimes find their profoundest truths side by side with the idlest jest, and utter one or the other, apparently without distinguishing which is the most valuable, or assigning any considerable value to either. The resemblance between the marble Faun and their living companion had made a deep, half-serious, half-mirthful impression on these three friends, and had taken them into a certain airy region, lifting up, as it is so pleasant to feel them lifted, their heavy earthly feet from the actual soil of life. The world had been set afloat, as it were, for a moment, and relieved them, for just so long, of all customary responsibility for what they thought and said.

It might be under this influence—or, perhaps, because sculptors always abuse one another's works—that Kenyon threw in a criticism upon the Dying Gladiator.

"I used to admire this statue exceedingly," he remarked, "but, latterly, I find myself getting weary and annoyed that the man should be such a length of time leaning on his arm in the very act of death. If he is so terribly hurt, why does he not sink down and die without further ado? Flitting moments, imminent emergencies, imperceptible intervals between two breaths, ought not to be incrusted with the eternal repose of marble; in any sculptural subject, there should be a moral stand-still, since there must of necessity be a physical one. Otherwise, it is like flinging a block of marble up into the air, and, by some trick of enchantment, causing it to stick there. You feel that it ought to come down, and are dissatisfied that it does not obey the natural law."

"I see," said Miriam, mischievously, "you think that sculpture should be a sort of fossilizing process. But, in truth, your frozen art has nothing like the scope and freedom of Hilda's and mine. In painting there is no similar objection to the representation of brief snatches of time; perhaps, because a story can be so much more fully told in picture, and buttressed about with circumstances that give it an epoch. For instance, a painter never would have sent down yonder Faun out of his far antiquity, lonely and desolate, with no companion to keep his simple heart warm."

"Ah, the Faun!" cried Hilda, with a little gesture of impatience; "I have been looking at him too long; and now, instead of a beautiful statue, immortally young, I see only a corroded and discolored stone. This change is very apt to occur in statues."

"And a similar one in pictures, surely," retorted the sculptor. "It is the spectator's mood that transfigures the Transfiguration itself. I defy any painter to move and elevate me without my own consent and assistance."

"Then you are deficient of a sense," said Miriam.

The party now strayed onward from hall to hall of that rich gallery, pausing here and there, to look at the multitude of noble and lovely shapes, which have been dug up out of the deep grave in which old Rome lies buried. And still, the realization of the antique Faun, in the person of Donatello, gave a more vivid character to all these marble ghosts. Why should not each statue grow warm with life! Antinous might lift his brow, and tell us why he is forever sad. The Lycian Apollo might strike his lyre; and, at the first vibration, that other Faun in red marble, who keeps up a motionless dance, should frisk gayly forth, leading yonder Satyrs, with shaggy goat-shanks, to clatter their little hoofs upon the floor, and all join hands with Donatello! Bacchus, too, a rosy flush diffusing itself over his time-stained surface, could come down from his pedestal, and offer a cluster of purple grapes to Donatello's lips; because the god recognizes him as the woodland elf who so often shared his revels. And here, in this sarcophagus, the exquisitely carved figures might assume life, and chase one another round its verge with that wild merriment which is so strangely represented on those old burial coffers: though still with some subtile allusion to death, carefully veiled, but forever peeping forth amid emblems of mirth and riot.

As the four friends descended the stairs, however, their play of fancy subsided into a much more sombre mood; a result apt to follow upon such exhilaration as that which had so recently taken possession of them.

"Do you know," said Miriam, confidentially to Hilda, "I doubt the reality of this likeness of Donatello to the Faun, which we have been talking so much about? To say the truth, it never struck me so forcibly as it did Kenyon and yourself, though I gave in to whatever you were pleased to fancy, for the sake of a moment's mirth and wonder."

"I was certainly in earnest, and you seemed equally so," replied Hilda, glancing back at Donatello, as if to reassure herself of the resemblance. "But faces change so much, from hour to hour, that the same set of features has often no keeping with itself; to an eye, at least, which looks at expression more than outline. How sad and sombre he has grown all of a sudden!"

"Angry too, methinks! nay, it is anger much more than sadness," said Miriam. "I have seen Donatello in this mood once or twice before. If you consider him well, you will observe an odd mixture of the bulldog, or some other equally fierce brute, in our friend's composition; a trait of savageness hardly to be expected in such a gentle creature as he usually is. Donatello is a very strange young man. I wish he would not haunt my footsteps so continually."

"You have bewitched the poor lad," said the sculptor, laughing. "You have a faculty of bewitching people, and it is providing you with a singular train of followers. I see another of them behind yonder pillar; and it is his presence that has aroused Donatello's wrath."

They had now emerged from the gateway of the palace; and partly concealed by one of the pillars of the portico stood a figure such as may often be encountered in the streets and piazzas of Rome, and nowhere else. He looked as if he might just have stepped out of a picture, and, in truth, was likely enough to find his way into a dozen pictures; being no other than one of those living models, dark, bushy-bearded, wild of aspect and attire, whom artists convert into saints or assassins, according as their pictorial purposes demand.

"Miriam," whispered Hilda, a little startled, "it is your model!"

CHAPTER III

SUBTERRANEAN REMINISCENCES

MIRIAM'S model has so important a connection with our story, that it is essential to describe the singular mode of his first appearance, and how he subsequently became a self-appointed follower of the young female artist. In the first place, however, we must devote a page or two to certain peculiarities in the position of Miriam herself.

There was an ambiguity about this young lady, which, though it did not necessarily imply anything wrong, would have operated unfavorably as regarded her reception in society, anywhere but in Rome. The truth was, that nobody knew anything about Miriam, either for good or evil. She had made her appearance without introduction, had taken a studio, put her card upon the door, and showed very considerable talent as a painter in oils. Her fellow-professors of the brush, it is true, showered abundant criticisms upon her pictures, allowing them to be well enough for the idle half-efforts of an amateur, but lacking both the trained skill and the practice that distinguish the works of a true artist.

Nevertheless, be their faults what they might, Miriam's pictures met with good acceptance among the patrons of modern art. Whatever technical merit they lacked, its absence was more than supplied by a warmth and passionateness, which she had the faculty of putting into her productions, and which all the world could feel. Her nature had a great deal of color, and, in accordance with it, so likewise had her pictures.

Miriam had great apparent freedom of intercourse; her manners were so far from evincing shyness, that it seemed easy to become acquainted with her, and not difficult to develop a casual acquaintance into intimacy. Such, at least, was the impression which she made, upon brief contact, but not such the ultimate conclusion of those who really sought to know her. So airy, free, and affable was Miriam's deportment towards all who came within her sphere, that possibly they might never be conscious of the fact; but so it was, that they did not get on, and were seldom any further advanced into her good graces to-day than yesterday. By some subtile quality, she kept people at a distance, without so much as letting them know that they were excluded from her inner circle. She resembled one of those images of light, which conjurers evoke and cause to shine before us, in apparent tangibility, only an arm's-length beyond our grasp: we make a step in advance, expecting to seize the illusion, but find it still precisely so far out of our reach. Finally, society began to recognize the impossibility of getting nearer to Miriam, and gruffly acquiesced.

There were two persons, however, whom she appeared to acknowledge as friends in the closer and truer sense of the word; and both of these more favored individuals did credit to Miriam's selection. One was a young American sculptor, of high promise and rapidly increasing celebrity; the other, a girl of the same country, a painter like Miriam herself, but in a widely different sphere of art. Her heart flowed out towards these two; she requited herself by their society and friendship (and especially by Hilda's) for all the loneliness with which, as regarded the rest of the world, she chose to be surrounded. Her two friends were conscious of the strong, yearning grasp which Miriam laid upon them, and gave her their affection in full measure; Hilda, indeed, responding with the fervency of a girl's first friendship, and Kenyon with a manly regard, in which there was nothing akin to what is distinctively called love.

A sort of intimacy subsequently grew up between these three friends and a fourth individual; it was a young Italian, who, casually visiting Rome, had been attracted by the beauty which Miriam possessed in a remarkable degree. He had sought her, followed her, and insisted, with simple perseverance, upon being admitted at least to her acquaintance; a boon which had been granted, when a more artful character, seeking it by a more subtle mode of pursuit, would probably have failed to obtain it. This young man, though anything but intellectually brilliant, had many agreeable characteristics which won him the kindly and half-contemptuous regard of Miriam and her two friends. It was he whom they called Donatello, and whose wonderful resemblance to the Faun of Praxiteles forms the keynote of our narrative.

Such was the position in which we find Miriam some few months after her establishment at Rome. It must be added, however, that the world did not permit her to hide her antecedents without making her the subject of a good deal of conjecture; as was natural enough, considering the abundance of her personal charms, and the degree of notice that she attracted as an artist. There were many stories about Miriam's origin and previous life, some of which had a very probable air, while others were evidently wild and romantic fables. We cite a few, leaving the reader to designate them either under the probable or the romantic head.

It was said, for example, that Miriam was the daughter and heiress of a great Jewish banker (an idea perhaps suggested by a certain rich Oriental character in her face), and had fled from her paternal home to escape a union with a cousin, the heir of another of that golden brotherhood; the object being, to retain their vast accumulation of wealth within the family. Another story hinted that she was a German princess, whom, for reasons of state, it was proposed to give in marriage either to a decrepit sovereign, or a prince still in his cradle. According to a third statement, she was the offspring of a Southern American planter, who had given her an elaborate education and endowed her with his wealth; but the one burning drop of African blood in her veins so affected her with a sense of ignominy, that she relinquished all and fled her country. By still another account she was the lady of an English nobleman; and, out of mere love and honor of art, had thrown aside the splendor of her rank, and come to seek a subsistence by her pencil in a Roman studio.

In all the above cases, the fable seemed to be instigated by the large and bounteous impression which Miriam invariably made, as if necessity and she could have nothing to do with one another. Whatever deprivations she underwent must needs be voluntary. But there were other surmises, taking such a common-place view as that Miriam was the daughter of a merchant or financier, who had been ruined in a great commercial crisis; and, possessing a taste for art, she had attempted to support herself by the pencil, in preference to the alternative of going out as governess.

Be these things how they might, Miriam, fair as she looked, was plucked up out of a mystery, and had its roots still clinging to her. She was a beautiful and attractive woman, but based, as it were, upon a cloud, and all surrounded with misty substance; so that the result was to render her sprite-like in her most ordinary manifestations. This was the case even in respect to Kenyon and Hilda, her especial friends. But such was the effect of Miriam's natural language, her generosity, kindliness, and native truth of character, that these two received her as a dear friend into their hearts, taking her good qualities as evident and genuine, and never imagining that what was hidden must be therefore evil.

We now proceed with our narrative.

The same party of friends, whom we have seen at the sculpture gallery of the Capitol, chanced to have gone together, some months before, to the catacomb of St. Calixtus. They went joyously down into that vast tomb, and wandered by torchlight through a sort of dream, in which reminiscences of church-aisles and grimy cellars—and chiefly the latter,—seemed to be broken into fragments, and hopelessly intermingled. The intricate passages along which they followed their guide had been hewn, in some forgotten age, out of a dark-red, crumbly stone. On either side were horizontal niches, where, if they held their torches closely, the shape of a human body was discernible in white ashes, into which the entire mortality of a man or woman had resolved itself. Among all this extinct dust, there might perchance be a thigh-bone, which crumbled at a touch; or possibly a skill, grinning at its own wretched plight, as is the ugly and empty habit of the thing.

Sometimes their gloomy pathway tended upward, so that, through a crevice, a little daylight glimmered down upon them, or even a streak of sunshine peeped into a burial niche; then again, they went downward by gradual descent, or by abrupt, rudely hewn steps, into deeper and deeper recesses of the earth. Here and there the narrow and tortuous passages widened somewhat, developing themselves into small chapels; which once, no doubt, had been adorned with marble-work and lighted with ever-burning lamps and tapers. All such illumination and ornament, however, had long since been extinguished and stript away; except, indeed, that the low roofs of a few of these ancient sites of worship were covered with dingy stucco, and frescoed with scriptural scenes and subjects, in the dreariest stage of ruin.

In one such chapel, the guide showed them a low arch, beneath which the body of St. Cecilia had been buried after her martyrdom, and where it lay till a sculptor saw it, and rendered it forever beautiful in marble.

In a similar spot they found two sarcophagi, one containing a skeleton, and the other a shrivelled body, which still wore the garments of its former lifetime.

"How dismal all this is!" said Hilda, shuddering. "I do not know why we came here, nor why we should stay a moment longer."

"I hate it all!" cried Donatello, with peculiar energy. "Dear friends, let us hasten back into the blessed daylight!"

From the first, Donatello had shown little fancy for the expedition; for, like most Italians, and in especial accordance with the law of his own simple and physically happy nature, this young man had an infinite repugnance to graves and skulls, and to all that ghastliness which the Gothic mind loves to associate with the idea of death. He shuddered, and looked fearfully round, drawing nearer to Miriam, whose attractive influence alone had enticed him into that gloomy region.

"What a child you are, poor Donatello!" she observed, with the freedom which she always used towards him. "You are afraid of ghosts!"

"Yes, signorina; terribly afraid!" said the truthful Donatello.

"I also believe in ghosts," answered Miriam, "and could tremble at them, in a suitable place. But these sepulchres are so old, and these skulls and white ashes so very dry, that methinks they have ceased to be haunted. The most awful idea connected with the catacombs is their interminable extent, and the possibility of going astray into this labyrinth of darkness, which broods around the little glimmer of our tapers."

"Has any one ever been lost here?" asked Kenyon of the guide.

"Surely, signor; one, no longer ago than my father's time," said the guide; and he added, with the air of a man who believed what he was telling, "but the first that went astray here was a pagan of old Rome, who hid himself in order to spy out and betray the blessed saints, who then dwelt and worshipped in these dismal places. You have heard the story, signor? A miracle was wrought upon the accursed one; and, ever since (for fifteen centuries at least), he has been groping in the darkness, seeking his way out of the catacomb."

"Has he ever been seen?" asked Hilda, who had great and tremulous faith in marvels of this kind.

"These eyes of mine never beheld him, signorina; the saints forbid!" answered the guide. "But it is well known that he watches near parties that come into the catacomb, especially if they be heretics, hoping to lead some straggler astray. What this lost wretch pines for, almost as much as for the blessed sunshine, is a companion to be miserable with him."

"Such an intense desire for sympathy indicates something amiable in the poor fellow, at all events," observed Kenyon.

They had now reached a larger chapel than those heretofore seen; it was of a circular shape, and, though hewn out of the solid mass of red sandstone, had pillars, and a carved roof, and other tokens of a regular architectural design. Nevertheless, considered as a church, it was exceedingly minute, being scarcely twice a man's stature in height, and only two or three paces from wall to wall; and while their collected torches illuminated this one small, consecrated spot, the great darkness spread all round it, like that immenser mystery which envelops our little life, and into which friends vanish from us, one by one.

"Why, where is Miriam?" cried Hilda.

The party gazed hurriedly from face to face, and became aware that one of their party had vanished into the great darkness, even while they were shuddering at the remote possibility of such a misfortune.

## CHAPTER IV

### THE SPECTRE OF THE CATACOMB

"SURELY, she cannot be lost!" exclaimed Kenyon. "It is but a moment since she was speaking."

"No, no!" said Hilda, in great alarm. "She was behind us all; and it is a long while since we have heard her voice!"

"Torches! torches!" cried Donatello, desperately. "I will seek her, be the darkness ever so dismal!"

But the guide held him back, and assured them all that there was no possibility of assisting their lost companion, unless by shouting at the very top of their voices. As the sound would go very far along these close and narrow passages, there was a fair probability that Miriam might hear the call, and be able to retrace her steps.

Accordingly, they all—Kenyon with his bass voice; Donatello with his tenor; the guide with that high and hard Italian cry, which makes the streets of Rome so resonant; and Hilda with her slender scream, piercing farther than the united uproar of the rest—began to shriek, halloo, and bellow, with the utmost force of their lungs. And, not to prolong the reader's suspense (for we do not particularly seek to interest him in this scene, telling it only on account of the trouble and strange entanglement which followed), they soon heard a responsive call, in a female voice.

"It was the signorina!" cried Donatello, joyfully.

"Yes; it was certainly dear Miriam's voice," said Hilda. "And here she comes! Thank Heaven! Thank Heaven!"

The figure of their friend was now discernible by her own torchlight, approaching out of one of the cavernous passages. Miriam came forward, but not with the eagerness and tremulous joy of a fearful girl, just rescued from a labyrinth of gloomy mystery. She made no immediate response to their inquiries and tumultuous congratulations; and, as they afterwards remembered, there was something absorbed, thoughtful, and self-concentrated in her deportment. She looked pale, as well she might, and held her torch with a nervous grasp, the tremor of which was seen in the irregular twinkling of the flame. This last was the chief perceptible sign of any recent agitation or alarm.

"Dearest, dearest Miriam," exclaimed Hilda, throwing her arms about her friend, "where have you been straying from us? Blessed be Providence, which has rescued you out of that miserable darkness!"

"Hush, dear Hilda!" whispered Miriam, with a strange little laugh. "Are you quite sure that it was Heaven's guidance which brought me back. If so, it was by an odd messenger, as you will confess. See; there he stands."

Startled at Miriam's words and manner, Hilda gazed into the duskiness whither she pointed, and there beheld a figure standing just on the doubtful limit of obscurity, at the threshold of the small, illuminated chapel. Kenyon discerned him at the same instant, and drew nearer with his torch; although the guide attempted to dissuade him, averring that, once beyond the consecrated precincts of the chapel, the apparition would have power to tear him limb from limb. It struck the sculptor, however, when he afterwards recurred to these circumstances, that the guide manifested no such apprehension on his own account as he professed on behalf of others; for he kept pace with Kenyon as the latter approached the figure, though still endeavoring to restrain him.

In fine, they both drew near enough to get as good a view of the spectre as the smoky light of their torches, struggling with the massive gloom, could supply.

The stranger was of exceedingly picturesque, and even melodramatic aspect. He was clad in a voluminous cloak, that seemed to be made of a buffalo's hide, and a pair of those goat-skin breeches, with the hair outward, which are still commonly worn by the peasants of the Roman Campagna. In this garb, they look like antique Satyrs; and, in truth, the Spectre of the Catacomb might have represented the last survivor of that vanished race, hiding himself in sepulchral gloom, and mourning over his lost life of woods and streams.

Furthermore, he had on a broad-brimmed, conical hat, beneath the shadow of which a wild visage was indistinctly seen, floating away, as it were, into a dusky wilderness of mustache and beard. His eyes winked, and turned uneasily from the torches, like a creature to whom midnight would be more congenial than noonday.

On the whole, the spectre might have made a considerable impression on the sculptor's nerves, only that he was in the habit of observing similar figures, almost every day, reclining on the Spanish steps, and waiting for some artist to invite them within the magic realm of picture. Nor, even thus familiarized with the stranger's peculiarities of appearance, could Kenyon help wondering to see such a personage, shaping himself so suddenly out of the void darkness of the catacomb.

"What are you?" said the sculptor, advancing his torch nearer. "And how long have you been wandering here?"

"A thousand and five hundred years!" muttered the guide, loud enough to be heard by all the party. "It is the old pagan phantom that I told you of, who sought to betray the blessed saints!"

"Yes; it is a phantom!" cried Donatello, with a shudder. "Ah, dearest signorina, what a fearful thing has beset you in those dark corridors!"

"Nonsense, Donatello," said the sculptor. "The man is no more a phantom than yourself. The only marvel is, how he comes to be hiding himself in the catacomb. Possibly, our guide might solve the riddle."

The spectre himself here settled the point of his tangibility, at all events, and physical substance, by approaching a step nearer, and laying his hand on Kenyon's arm.

"Inquire not what I am, nor wherefore I abide in the darkness," said he, in a hoarse, harsh voice, as if a great deal of damp were clustering in his throat. "Henceforth, I am nothing but a shadow behind her footsteps. She came to me when I sought her not. She has called me forth, and must abide the consequences of my reappearance in the world."

"Holy Virgin! I wish the signorina joy of her prize," said the guide, half to himself. "And in any case, the catacomb is well rid of him."

We need follow the scene no further. So much is essential to the subsequent narrative, that, during the short period while astray in those tortuous passages, Miriam had encountered an unknown man, and led him forth with her, or was guided back by him, first into the torchlight, thence into the sunshine.

It was the further singularity of this affair, that the connection, thus briefly and casually formed, did not terminate with the incident that gave it birth. As if her service to him, or his service to her, whichever it might be, had given him an indefeasible claim on Miriam's regard and protecton, the Spectre of the Catacomb never long allowed her to lose sight of him, from that day forward. He haunted her footsteps with more than the customary persistency of Italian mendicants, when once they have recognized a benefactor. For days together, it is true, he occasionally vanished, but always reappeared, gliding after her through the narrow streets, or climbing the hundred steps of her staircase and sitting at her threshold.

Being often admitted to her studio, he left his features, or some shadow or reminiscence of them, in many of her sketches and pictures. The moral atmosphere of these productions was thereby so influenced, that rival painters pronounced it a case of hopeless mannerism, which would destroy all Miriam's prospects of true excellence in art.

The story of this adventure spread abroad, and made its way beyond the usual gossip of the Forestieri, even into Italian circles, where, enhanced by a still potent spirit of superstition, it grew far more wonderful than as above recounted. Thence, it came back among the Anglo-Saxons, and was communicated to the German artists, who so richly supplied it with romantic ornaments and excrescences, after their fashion, that it became a fantasy worthy of Tieck or Hoffmann. For nobody has any conscience about adding to the improbabilities of a marvellous tale.

The most reasonable version of the incident, that could anywise be rendered acceptable to the auditors, was substantially the one suggested by the guide of the catacomb, in his allusion to the legend of Memmius. This man, or demon, or man-demon, was a spy during the persecutions of the early Christians, probably under the Emperor Diocletian, and penetrated into the catacomb of St. Calixtus, with the malignant purpose of tracing out the hiding-places of the refugees. But, while he stole craftily through those dark corridors, he chanced to come upon a little chapel, where tapers were burning before an altar and a crucifix, and a priest was in the performance of his sacred office. By divine indulgence, there was a single moment's grace allowed to Memmius, during which, had he been capable of Christian faith and love, he might have knelt before the cross, and received the holy light into his soul, and so have been blest forever. But he resisted the sacred impulse. As soon, therefore, as that one moment had glided by, the light of the consecrated tapers, which represent all truth, bewildered the wretched man with everlasting error, and the blessed cross itself was stamped as a seal upon his heart, so that it should never open to receive conviction.

Thenceforth, this heathen Memmius has haunted the wide and dreary precincts of the catacomb, seeking, as some say, to beguile new victims into his own misery; but, according to other statements, endeavoring to prevail on any unwary visitor to take him by the hand, and guide him out into the daylight. Should his wiles and entreaties take effect, however, the man-demon would remain only a little while above ground. He would gratify his fiendish malignity by perpetrating signal mischief on his benefactor, and perhaps bringing some old pestilence or other forgotten and long-buried evil on society; or, possibly, teaching the modern world some decayed and dusty kind of crime, which the antique Romans knew; and then would hasten back to the catacomb, which, after so long haunting it, has grown his most congenial home.

Miriam herself, with her chosen friends, the sculptor and the gentle Hilda, often laughed at the monstrous fictions that had gone abroad in reference to her adventure. Her two confidants (for such they were, on all ordinary subjects) had not failed to ask an explanation of the mystery, since undeniably a mystery there was, and one sufficiently perplexing in itself, without any help from the imaginative faculty. And, sometimes responding to their inquiries with a melancholy sort of playfulness, Miriam let her fancy run off into wilder fables than any which German ingenuity or Italian superstition had contrived.

For example, with a strange air of seriousness over all her face, only belied by a laughing gleam in her dark eyes, she would aver that the spectre (who had been an artist in his mortal lifetime) had promised to teach her a long lost, but invaluable secret of old Roman fresco-painting. The knowledge of this process would place Miriam at the head of modern art; the sole condition being agreed upon, that she should return with him into his sightless gloom, after enriching a certain extent of stuccoed wall with the most brilliant and lovely designs. And what true votary of art would not purchase unrivalled excellence, even at so vast a sacrifice!

Or, if her friends still solicited a soberer account, Miriam replied, that, meeting the old infidel in one of the dismal passages of the catacomb, she had entered into controversy with him, hoping to achieve the glory and satisfaction of converting him to the Christian faith. For the sake of so excellent a result, she had even staked her own salvation against his, binding herself to accompany him back into his penal gloom, if, within a twelve-month's space, she should not have convinced him of the errors through which he had so long groped and stumbled. But, alas! up to the present time, the controversy had gone direfully in favor of the man-demon; and Miriam (as she whispered in Hilda's ear) had awful forebodings, that, in a few more months, she must take an eternal farewell of the sun!

It was somewhat remarkable that all her romantic fantasies arrived at this self-same dreary termination; it appeared impossible for her even to imagine any other than a disastrous result from her connection with her ill-omened attendant.

This singularity might have meant nothing, however, had it not suggested a despondent state of mind, which was likewise indicated by many other tokens. Miriam's friends had no difficulty in perceiving that, in one way or another, her happiness was very seriously compromised. Her spirits were often depressed into deep melancholy. If ever she was gay, it was seldom with a healthy cheerfulness. She grew moody, moreover, and subject to fits of passionate ill-temper; which usually wreaked itself on the heads of those who loved her best. Not that Miriam's indifferent acquaintances were safe from similar outbreaks of her displeasure, especially if they ventured upon any allusion to the model. In such cases, they were left with little disposition to renew the subject, but inclined, on the other hand, to interpret the whole matter as much to her discredit as the least favorable coloring of the facts would allow.

It may occur to the reader, that there was really no demand for so much rumor and speculation in regard to an incident, which might well enough have been explained without going many steps beyond the limits of probability. The spectre might have been merely a Roman beggar, whose fraternity often harbor in stranger shelters than the catacombs; or one of those pilgrims, who still journey from remote countries to kneel and worship at the holy sites, among which these haunts of the early Christians are esteemed especially sacred. Or, as was perhaps a more plausible theory, he might be a thief of the city, a robber of the Campagna, a political offender, or an assassin, with blood upon his hand; whom the negligence or connivance of the police allowed to take refuge in those subterranean fastnesses, where such outlaws have been accustomed to hide themselves from a far antiquity downward. Or he might have been a lunatic, fleeing instinctively from man, and making it his dark pleasure to dwell among the tombs, like him whose awful cry echoes afar to us from Scripture times.

And, as for the stranger's attaching himself so devotedly to Miriam, her personal magnetism might be allowed a certain weight in the explanation. For what remains, his pertinacity need not seem so very singular to those who consider how slight a link serves to connect these vagabonds of idle Italy with any person that may have the ill-hap to bestow charity, or be otherwise serviceable to them, or betray the slightest interest in their fortunes.

Thus little would remain to be accounted for, except the deportment of Miriam herself; her reserve, her brooding melancholy, her petulance, and moody passion. If generously interpreted, even these morbid symptoms might have sufficient cause in the stimulating and exhaustive influences of imaginative art, exercised by a delicate young woman, in the nervous and unwholesome atmosphere of Rome. Such, at least, was the view of the case which Hilda and Kenyon endeavored to impress on their own minds, and impart to those whom their opinions might influence.

One of Miriam's friends took the matter sadly to heart. This was the young Italian. Donatello, as we have seen, had been an eye-witness of the stranger's first appearance, and had ever since nourished a singular prejudice against the mysterious, dusky, death-scented apparition. It resembled not so much a human dislike or hatred, as one of those instinctive, unreasoning antipathies which the lower animals sometimes display, and which generally prove more trustworthy than the acutest insight into character. The shadow of the model, always flung into the light which Miriam diffused around her, caused no slight trouble to Donatello. Yet he was of a nature so remarkably genial and joyous, so simply happy, that he might well afford to have something subtracted from his comfort, and make tolerable shift to live upon what remained.

CHAPTER V

MIRIAM'S STUDIO

THE court-yard and staircase of a palace built three hundred years ago are a peculiar feature of modern Rome, and interest the stranger more than many things of which he has heard loftier descriptions. You pass through the grand breadth and height of a squalid entrance-way, and perhaps see a range of dusky pillars, forming a sort of cloister round the court, and in the intervals, from pillar to pillar, are strewn fragments of antique statues, headless and legless torsos, and busts that have invariably lost—what it might be well if living men could lay aside in that unfragrant atmosphere—the nose. Bas-reliefs, the spoil of some far older palace, are set in the surrounding walls, every stone of which has been ravished from the Coliseum, or any other imperial ruin which earlier barbarism had not already levelled with the earth. Between two of the pillars, moreover, stands an old sarcophagus without its lid, and with all its more prominently projecting sculptures broken off; perhaps it once held famous dust, and the bony framework of some historic man, although now only a receptacle for the rubbish of the court-yard, and a half-worn broom.

In the centre of the court, under the blue Italian sky, and with the hundred windows of the vast palace gazing down upon it, from four sides, appears a fountain. It brims over from one stone basin to another, or gushes from a Naiad's urn, or spurts its many little jets from the mouths of nameless monsters, which were merely grotesque and artificial when Bernini, or whoever was their unnatural father, first produced them; but now the patches of moss, the tufts of grass, the trailing maiden-hair, and all sorts of verdant weeds that thrive in the cracks and crevices of moist marble, tell us that Nature takes the fountain back into her great heart, and cherishes it as kindly as if it were a woodland spring. And, hark, the pleasant murmur, the gurgle, the plash! You might hear just those tinkling sounds from any tiny waterfall in the forest, though here they gain a delicious pathos from the stately echoes that reverberate their natural language. So the fountain is not altogether glad, after all its three centuries at play!

In one of the angles of the court-yard, a pillared door-way gives access to the staircase, with its spacious breadth of low, marble steps, up which, in former times, have gone the princes and cardinals of the great Roman family who built this palace. Or they have come down, with still grander and loftier mien, on their way to the Vatican or the Quirinal, there to put off their scarlet hats in exchange for the triple crown. But, in fine, all these illustrious personages have gone down their hereditary staircase for the last time, leaving it to be the thoroughfare of ambassadors, English noblemen, American millionnaires, artists, tradesmen, washerwomen, and people of every degree; all of whom find such gilded and marble-panelled saloons as their pomp and luxury demand, or such homely garrets as their necessity can pay for, within this one multifarious abode. Only, in not a single nook of the palace (built for splendor, and the accommodation of a vast retinue, but with no vision of a happy fireside or any mode of domestic enjoyment) does the humblest or the haughtiest occupant find comfort.

Up such a staircase, on the morning after the scene at the sculpture gallery, sprang the light foot of Donatello. He ascended from story to story, passing lofty door-ways, set within rich frames of sculptured marble, and climbing unweariedly upward, until the glories of the first piano and the elegance of the middle height were exchanged for a sort of Alpine region, cold and naked in its aspect. Steps of rough stone, rude wooden balustrades, a brick pavement in the passages, a dingy whitewash on the walls; these were here the palatial features. Finally, he paused before an oaken door, on which was pinned a card, bearing the name of Miriam Schaefer, artist in oils. Here Donatello knocked, and the door immediately fell somewhat ajar; its latch having been pulled up by means of a string on the inside. Passing through a little anteroom, he found himself in Miriam's presence.

"Come in, wild Faun," she said, "and tell me the latest news from Arcady!"

The artist was not just then at her easel, but was busied with the feminine task of mending a pair of gloves.

There is something extremely pleasant, and even touching,—at least, of very sweet, soft, and winning effect,—in this peculiarity of needlework, distinguishing women from men. Our own sex is incapable of any such by-play aside from the main business of life; but women—be they of what earthly rank they may, however gifted with intellect or genius, or endowed with awful beauty—have always some little handiwork ready to fill the tiny gap of every vacant moment. A needle is familiar to the fingers of them all. A queen, no doubt, plies it on occasion; the woman poet can use it as adroitly as her pen; the woman's eye, that has discovered a new star, turns from its glory to send the polished little instrument gleaming along the hem of her kerchief, or to darn a casual fray in her dress. And they have greatly the advantage of us in this respect. The slender thread of silk or cotton keeps them united with the small, familiar, gentle interests of life, the continually operating influences of which do so much for the health of the character, and carry off what would otherwise be a dangerous accumulation of morbid sensibility. A vast deal of human sympathy runs along this electric line, stretching from the throne to the wicker chair of the humblest seamstress, and keeping high and low in a species of communion with their kindred beings. Methinks it is a token of healthy and gentle characteristics, when women of high thoughts and accomplishments love to sew; especially as they are never more at home with their own hearts than while so occupied.

And when the work falls in a woman's lap, of its own accord, and the needle involuntarily ceases to fly, it is a sign of trouble, quite as trustworthy as the throb of the heart itself. This was what happened to Miriam. Even while Donatello stood gazing at her, she seemed to have forgotten his presence, allowing him to drop out of her thoughts, and the torn glove to fall from her idle fingers. Simple as he was, the young man knew by his sympathies that something was amiss.

"Dear lady, you are sad," said he, drawing close to her.

"It is nothing, Donatello," she replied, resuming her work; "yes; a little sad, perhaps; but that is not strange for us people of the ordinary

world, especially for women. You are of a cheerfuller race, my friend, and
know nothing of this disease of sadness. But why do you come into this
shadowy room of mine?"

"Why do you make it so shadowy?" asked he.

"We artists purposely exclude sunshine, and all but a partial light,"
said Miriam, "because we think it necessary to put ourselves at odds with
Nature before trying to imitate her. That strikes you very strangely, does
it not? But we make very pretty pictures sometimes with our artfully arranged lights and shadows. Amuse yourself with some of mine, Donatello, and by and by I shall be in the mood to begin the portrait we were
talking about."

The room had the customary aspect of a painter's studio; one of those
delightful spots that hardly seem to belong to the actual world, but
rather to be the outward type of a poet's haunted imagination, where
there are glimpses, sketches, and half-developed hints of beings and objects grander and more beautiful than we can anywhere find in reality.
The windows were closed with shutters, or deeply curtained, except one,
which was partly open to a sunless portion of the sky, admitting only
from high upward that partial light which, with its strongly marked contrast of shadow, is the first requisite towards seeing objects pictorially.
Pencil-drawings were pinned against the wall or scattered on the tables.
Unframed canvases turned their backs on the spectator, presenting only a
blank to the eye, and churlishly concealing whatever riches of scenery or
human beauty Miriam's skill had depicted on the other side.

In the obscurest part of the room Donatello was half startled at perceiving duskily a woman with long dark hair, who threw up her arms with
a wild gesture of tragic despair, and appeared to beckon him into the
darkness along with her.

"Do not be afraid, Donatello," said Miriam, smiling to see him peering doubtfully into the mysterious dusk. "She means you no mischief,
nor could perpetrate any if she wished it ever so much. It is a lady of
exceedingly pliable disposition; now a heroine of romance, and now a
rustic maid; yet all for show; being created, indeed, on purpose to wear
rich shawls and other garments in a becoming fashion. This is the true
end of her being, although she pretends to assume the most varied duties
and perform many parts in life, while really the poor puppet has nothing
on earth to do. Upon my word, I am satirical unawares, and seem to be
describing nine women out of ten in the person of my lay-figure. For
most purposes she has the advantage of the sisterhood. Would I were like
her!"

"How it changes her aspect," exclaimed Donatello, "to know that she
is but a jointed figure! When my eyes first fell upon her, I thought her
arms moved, as if beckoning me to help her in some direful peril."

"Are you often troubled with such sinister freaks of fancy?" asked
Miriam. "I should not have supposed it."

"To tell you the truth, dearest signorina," answered the young Italian,
"I am apt to be fearful in old, gloomy houses, and in the dark. I love no

dark or dusky corners, except it be in a grotto, or among the thick green leaves of an arbor, or in some nook of the woods, such as I know many in the neighborhood of my home. Even there, if a stray sunbeam steal in, the shadow is all the better for its cheerful glimmer."

"Yes; you are a Faun, you know," said the fair artist, laughing at the remembrance of the scene of the day before. "But the world is sadly changed nowadays; grievously changed, poor Donatello, since those happy times when your race used to dwell in the Arcadian woods, playing hide-and-seek with the nymphs in grottos and nooks of shrubbery. You have reappeared on earth some centuries too late."

"I do not understand you now," answered Donatello, looking perplexed; "only signorina, I am glad to have my lifetime while you live; and where you are, be it in cities or fields, I would fain be there too."

"I wonder whether I ought to allow you to speak in this way," said Miriam, looking thoughtfully at him. "Many young women would think it behoved them to be offended. Hilda would never let you speak so, I dare say. But he is a mere boy," she added, aside, "a simple boy, putting his boyish heart to the proof on the first woman whom he chances to meet. If yonder lay-figure had had the luck to meet him first, she would have smitten him as deeply as I."

"Are you angry with me?" asked Donatello, dolorously.

"Not in the least," answered Miriam, frankly giving him her hand. "Pray look over some of these sketches till I have leisure to chat with you a little. I hardly think I am in spirits enough to begin your portrait to-day."

Donatello was as gentle and docile as a pet spaniel; as playful, too, in his general disposition, or saddening with his mistress's variable mood like that or any other kindly animal which has the faculty of bestowing its sympathies more completely than men or women can ever do. Accordingly, as Miriam bade him, he tried to turn his attention to a great pile and confusion of pen-and-ink sketches and pencil-drawings which lay tossed together on a table. As it chanced, however, they gave the poor youth little delight.

The first that he took up was a very impressive sketch, in which the artist had jotted down her rough ideas for a picture of Jael driving the nail through the temples of Sisera. It was dashed off with remarkable power, and showed a touch or two that were actually life-like and death-like, as if Miriam had been standing by when Jael gave the first stroke of her murderous hammer, or as if she herself were Jael, and felt irresistibly impelled to make her bloody confession in this guise.

Her first conception of the stern Jewess had evidently been that of perfect womanhood, a lovely form, and a high, heroic face of lofty beauty; but, dissatisfied either with her own work or the terrible story itself, Miriam had added a certain wayward quirk of her pencil, which at once converted the heroine into a vulgar murderess. It was evident that a Jael like this would be sure to search Sisera's pockets as soon as the breath was out of his body.

In another sketch she had attempted the story of Judith, which we see represented by the old masters so often, and in such various styles. Here, too, beginning with a passionate and fiery conception of the subject in all earnestness, she had given the last touches in utter scorn, as it were, of the feelings which at first took such powerful possession of her hand. The head of Holofernes (which by the by had a pair of twisted mustaches, like those of a certain potentate of the day) being fairly cut off, was screwing its eyes upward and twirling its features into a diabolical grin of triumphant malice, which it flung right in Judith's face. On her part, she had the startled aspect that might be conceived of a cook if a calf's head should sneer at her when about to be popped into the dinner-pot.

Over and over again, there was the idea of woman, acting the part of a revengeful mischief towards man. It was, indeed, very singular to see how the artist's imagination seemed to run on these stories of blood-shed, in which woman's hand was crimsoned by the stain; and how, too, —in one form or another, grotesque or sternly sad,—she failed not to bring out the moral, that woman must strike through her own heart to reach a human life, whatever were the motive that impelled her.

One of the sketches represented the daughter of Herodias receiving the head of John the Baptist in a charger. The general conception appeared to be taken from Bernardo Luini's picture, in the Uffizzi Gallery at Florence; but Miriam had imparted to the saint's face a look of gentle and heavenly reproach, with sad and blessed eyes fixed upward at the maiden; by the force of which miraculous glance, her whole womanhood was at once awakened to love and endless remorse.

These sketches had a most disagreeable effect on Donatello's peculiar temperament. He gave a shudder; his face assumed a look of trouble, fear, and disgust; he snatched up one sketch after another, as if about to tear it in pieces. Finally, shoving away the pile of drawings, he shrank back from the table and clasped his hands over his eyes.

"What is the matter, Donatello?" asked Miriam, looking up from a letter which she was now writing. "Ah! I did not mean you to see those drawings. They are ugly phantoms that stole out of my mind; not things that I created, but things that haunt me. See! here are some trifles that perhaps will please you better."

She gave him a portfolio, the sketches in which indicated a happier mood of mind, and one, it is to be hoped, more truly characteristic of the artist. Supposing neither of these classes of subject to show anything of her own individuality, Miriam had evidently a great scope of fancy, and a singular faculty of putting what looked like heart into her productions. The latter sketches were domestic and common scenes, so finely and subtilely idealized that they seemed such as we may see at any moment, and everywhere; while still there was the indefinable something added, or taken away, which makes all the difference between sordid life and an earthly paradise. The feeling and sympathy in all of them were deep and true. There was the scene, that comes once in every life, of the lover winning the soft and pure avowal of bashful affection from the maiden whose slender form half leans towards his arm, half shrinks from it, we know not which. There was wedded affection in its successive stages, represented in a series of delicately conceived designs, touched with a holy fire, that burned from youth to age in those two hearts, and gave one identical beauty to the faces throughout all the changes of feature.

There was a drawing of an infant's shoe, half worn out, with the airy print of the blessed foot within; a thing that would make a mother smile or weep out of the very depths of her heart; and yet an actual mother would not have been likely to appreciate the poetry of the little shoe, until Miriam revealed it to her. It was wonderful, the depth and force with which the above, and other kindred subjects, were depicted, and the profound significance which they often acquired. The artist, still in her fresh youth, could not probably have drawn any of these dear and rich experiences from her own life; unless, perchance, that first sketch of all, the avowal of maiden affection, were a remembered incident, and not a prophecy. But it is more delightful to believe that, from first to last, they were the productions of a beautiful imagination, dealing with the warm and pure suggestions of a woman's heart, and thus idealizing a truer and lovelier picture of the life that belongs to woman, than an actual acquaintance with some of its hard and dusty facts could have inspired. So considered, the sketches intimated such a force and variety of imaginative sympathies as would enable Miriam to fill her life richly with the bliss and suffering of womanhood, however barren it might individually be.

There was one observable point, indeed, betokening that the artist relinquished, for her personal self, the happiness which she could so profoundly appreciate for others. In all those sketches of common life, and the affections that spiritualize it, a figure was portrayed apart; now it peeped between the branches of a shrubbery, amid which two lovers sat; now it was looking through a frosted window, from the outside, while a young wedded pair sat at their new fireside within; and once it leaned from a chariot, which six horses were whirling onward in pomp and pride, and gazed at a scene of humble enjoyment by a cottage-door. Always it was the same figure, and always depicted with an expression of deep sadness; and in every instance, slightly as they were brought out, the face and form had the traits of Miriam's own.

"Do you like these sketches better, Donatello?" asked Miriam.

"Yes," said Donatello, rather doubtfully.

"Not much, I fear," responded she, laughing. "And what should a boy like you—a Faun, too—know about the joys and sorrows, the intertwining light and shadow, of human life? I forgot that you were a Faun. You cannot suffer deeply; therefore you can but half enjoy. Here, now, is a subject which you can better appreciate."

The sketch represented merely a rustic dance, but with such extravagance of fun as was delightful to behold; and here there was no drawback, except that strange sigh and sadness which always come when we are merriest.

"I am going to paint the picture in oils," said the artist; "and I want you, Donatello, for the wildest dancer of them all. Will you sit for me, some day?—or, rather, dance for me?"

"Oh, most gladly, signorina!" exclaimed Donatello. "See; it shall be like this."

And forthwith he began to dance, and flit about the studio, like an incarnate sprite of jollity, pausing at last on the extremity of one toe, as if that were the only portion of himself whereby his frisky nature could come in contact with the earth. The effect in that shadowy chamber, whence the artist had so carefully excluded the sunshine, was as enlivening as if one bright ray had contrived to shimmer in the frolic around the walls, and finally rest just in the centre of the floor.

"That was admirable!" said Miriam, with an approving smile. "If I can catch you on my canvas, it will be a glorious picture; only I am afraid you will dance out of it, by the very truth of the representation, just when I shall have given it the last touch. We will try it one of these days. And now, to reward you for that jolly exhibition, you shall see what has been shown to no one else."

She went to her easel, on which was placed a picture with its back turned towards the spectator. Reversing the position, there appeared the portrait of a beautiful woman, such as one sees only two or three, if even so many times, in all a lifetime; so beautiful, that she seemed to get into your consciousness and memory, and could never afterwards be shut out, but haunted your dreams, for pleasure or for pain; holding your inner realm as a conquered territory, though without deigning to make herself at home there.

She was very youthful, and had what was usually thought to be a Jewish aspect; a complexion in which there was no roseate bloom, yet neither was it pale; dark eyes, into which you might look as deeply as your glance would go, and still be conscious of a depth that you had not sounded, though it lay open to the day. She had black, abundant hair, with none of the vulgar glossiness of other women's sable locks; if she were really of Jewish blood, then this was Jewish hair, and a dark glory such as crowns no Christian maiden's head. Gazing at this portrait, you saw what Rachel might have been, when Jacob deemed her worth the wooing seven years, and seven more; or perchance she might ripen to be what Judith was, when she vanquished Holofernes with her beauty, and slew him for too much adoring it.

Miriam watched Donatello's contemplation of the picture, and seeing his simple rapture, a smile of pleasure brightened on her face, mixed with a little scorn; at least, her lips curled, and her eyes gleamed, as if she disdained either his admiration or her own enjoyment of it.

"Then you like the picture, Donatello?" she asked.

"Oh, beyond what I can tell!" he answered. "So beautiful!—so beautiful!"

"And do you recognize the likeness?"

"Signorina," exclaimed Donatello, turning from the picture to the artist, in astonishment that she should ask the question, "the resemblance is as little to be mistaken as if you had bent over the smooth surface of a fountain, and possessed the witchcraft to call forth the image that you made there! It is yourself!"

Donatello said the truth; and we forbore to speak descriptively of Miriam's beauty earlier in our narrative, because we foresaw this occasion to bring it perhaps more forcibly before the reader.

We know not whether the portrait were a flattered likeness; probably not, regarding it merely as the delineation of a lovely face; although Miriam, like all self-painters, may have endowed herself with certain graces which other eyes might not discern. Artists are fond of painting their own portraits; and, in Florence, there is a gallery of hundreds of them, including the most illustrious, in all of which there are autobiographical characteristics, so to peak; traits, expressions, loftinesses, and amenities, which would have been invisible, had they not been painted from within. Yet their reality and truth are none the less. Miriam, in like manner, had doubtless conveyed some of the intimate results of her heart-knowledge into her own portrait, and perhaps wished to try whether they would be perceptible to so simple and natural an observer as Donatello.

"Does the expression please you?" she asked.

"Yes," said Donatello, hesitatingly; "if it would only smile so like the sunshine as you sometimes do. No, it is sadder than I thought at first. Cannot you make yourself smile a little, signorina?"

"A forced smile is uglier than a frown," said Miriam, a bright, natural smile breaking out over her face even as she spoke.

"Oh, catch it now!" cried Donatello, clapping his hands. "Let it shine upon the picture! There! it has vanished already! And you are sad again, very sad; and the picture gazes sadly forth at me, as if some evil had befallen it in the little time since I looked last."

"How perplexed you seem, my friend!" answered Miriam. "I really half believe you are a Faun, there is such a mystery and terror for you in these dark moods, which are just as natural as daylight to us people of ordinary mould. I advise you, at all events, to look at other faces with those innocent and happy eyes, and never more to gaze at mine!"

"You speak in vain," replied the young man, with a deeper emphasis than she had ever before heard in his voice; "shroud yourself in what gloom you will, I must needs follow you."

"Well, well, well," said Miriam, impatiently; "but leave me now; for to speak plainly, my good friend, you grow a little wearisome. I walk this afternoon in the Borghese grounds. Meet me there, if it suits your pleasure."

## CHAPTER VI

## THE VIRGIN'S SHRINE

AFTER Donatello had left the studio, Miriam herself came forth, and taking her way through some of the intricacies of the city, entered what might be called either a widening of a street, or a small piazza. The neighborhood comprised a baker's oven, emitting the usual fragrance of sour bread; a shoe-shop; a linen-draper's shop; a pipe and cigar shop; a lottery office; a station for French soldiers, with a sentinel pacing in front; and a fruit-stand, at which a Roman matron was selling the dried kernels of chestnuts, wretched little figs, and some bouquets of yesterday. A church, of course, was near at hand, the façade of which ascended into lofty pinnacles, whereon were perched two or three winged figures of stone, either angelic or allegorical, blowing stone trumpets in close vicinity to the upper windows of an old and shabby palace. This palace was distinguished by a feature not very common in the architecture of Roman edifices; that is to say, a mediæval tower, square, massive, lofty, and battlemented and machicolated at the summit.

At one of the angles of the battlements stood a shrine of the Virgin, such as we see everywhere at the street-corners of Rome, but seldom or never, except in this solitary instance, at a height above the ordinary level of men's views and aspirations. Connected with this old tower and its lofty shrine, there is a legend which we cannot here pause to tell; but for centuries a lamp has been burning before the Virgin's image, at noon, at midnight, and at all hours of the twenty-four, and must be kept burning forever, as long as the tower shall stand; or else the tower itself, the palace, and whatever estate belongs to it, shall pass from its hereditary possessor, in accordance with an ancient vow, and become the property of the Church.

As Miriam approached, she looked upward, and saw,—not, indeed, the flame of the never-dying lamp, which was swallowed up in the broad sunlight that brightened the shrine, but a flock of white doves, skimming, fluttering, and wheeling about the topmost height of the tower, their silver wings flashing in the pure transparency of the air. Several of them sat on the ledge of the upper window, pushing one another off by their eager struggle for this favorite station, and all tapping their beaks and flapping their wings tumultuously against the panes; some had alighted in the street, far below, but flew hastily upward, at the sound of the window being thrust ajar, and, opening in the middle, on rusty hinges, as Roman windows do.

A fair young girl, dressed in white, showed herself at the aperture for a single instant, and threw forth as much as her two small hands could hold of some kind of food, for the flock of eleemosynary doves. It seemed greatly to the taste of the feathered people; for they tried to snatch beak-fuls of it from her grasp, caught it in the air, and rushed downward after it upon the pavement.

"What a pretty scene this is," thought Miriam, with a kindly smile, "and how like a dove she is herself, the fair, pure creature! The other doves know her for a sister, I am sure."

Miriam passed beneath the deep portal of the palace, and turning to the left, began to mount flight after flight of a staircase, which, for the loftiness of its aspiration, was worthy to be Jacob's ladder, or, at all events, the staircase of the Tower of Babel. The city bustle, which is heard even in Rome, the rumble of wheels over the uncomfortable pav-ing-stones, the hard harsh cries reëchoing in the high and narrow streets, grew faint and died away; as the turmoil of the world will always die, if we set our faces to climb heavenward. Higher, and higher still; and now, glancing through the successive windows that threw in their narrow light upon the stairs, her view stretched across the roofs of the city, unim-peded even by the stateliest palaces. Only the domes of churches ascend into this airy region, and hold up their golden crosses on a level with her eye; except, that, out of the very heart of Rome, the column of Antoninus thrusts itself upward, with St. Paul upon its summit, the sole human form that seems to have kept her company.

Finally, the staircase came to an end; save that, on one side of the lit-tle entry where it terminated, a flight of a dozen steps gave access to the roof of the tower and the legendary shrine. On the other side was a door, at which Miriam knocked, but rather as a friendly announcement of her presence than with any doubt of hospitable welcome; for, awaiting no re-sponse, she lifted the latch and entered.

"What a hermitage you have found for yourself, dear Hilda!" she ex-claimed. "You breathe sweet air, above all the evil scents of Rome; and even so, in your maiden elevation, you dwell above our vanities and pas-sions, our moral dust and mud, with the doves and the angels for your nearest neighbors. I should not wonder if the Catholics were to make a saint of you, like your namesake of old; especially as you have almost avowed yourself of their religion, by undertaking to keep the lamp alight before the Virgin's shrine."

"No, no, Miriam!" said Hilda, who had come joyfully forward to greet her friend. "You must not call me a Catholic. A Christian girl—even a daughter of the Puritans—may surely pay honor to the idea of divine Womanhood, without giving up the faith of her forefathers. But how kind you are to climb into my dove-cote!"

"It is no trifling proof of friendship, indeed," answered Miriam; "I should think there were three hundred stairs at least."

"But it will do you good," continued Hilda. "A height of some fifty feet above the roofs of Rome gives me all the advantages that I could get from fifty miles of distance. The air so exhilarates my spirits, that some-times I feel half inclined to attempt a flight from the top of my tower, in the faith that I should float upward."

"Oh, pray don't try it!" said Miriam, laughing. "If it should turn out that you are less than an angel, you would find the stones of the Roman pavement very hard; and if an angel, indeed, I am afraid you would never come down among us again."

This young American girl was an example of the freedom of life which it is possible for a female artist to enjoy at Rome. She dwelt in her tower, as free to descend into the corrupted atmosphere of the city beneath, as one of her companion doves to fly downward into the street;—all alone, perfectly independent, under her own sole guardianship, unless watched over by the Virgin, whose shrine she tended; doing what she liked without a suspicion or a shadow upon the snowy whiteness of her fame. The customs of artist life bestow such liberty upon the sex, which is elsewhere restricted within so much narrower limits; and it is perhaps an indication that, whenever we admit women to a wider scope of pursuits and professions, we must also remove the shackles of our present conventional rules, which would then become an insufferable restraint on either maid or wife. The system seems to work unexceptionably in Rome; and in many other cases, as in Hilda's, purity of heart and life are allowed to assert themselves, and to be their own proof and security, to a degree unknown in the society of other cities.

Hilda, in her native land, had early shown what was pronounced by connoisseurs a decided genius for the pictorial art. Even in her schooldays—still not so very distant—she had produced sketches that were seized upon by men of taste, and hoarded as among the choicest treasures of their portfolios; scenes delicately imagined, lacking, perhaps, the reality which comes only from a close acquaintance with life, but so softly touched with feeling and fancy, that you seemed to be looking at humanity with angels' eyes. With years and experience she might be expected to attain a darker and more forcible touch, which would impart to her designs the relief they needed. Had Hilda remained in her own country, it is not improbable that she might have produced original works worthy to hang in that gallery of native art which, we hope, is destined to extend its rich length through many future centuries. An orphan, however, without near relatives, and possessed of a little property, she had found it within her possibilities to come to Italy; that central clime, whither the eyes and the heart of every artist turn, as if pictures could not be made to glow in any other atmosphere, as if statues could not assume grace and expression, save in that land of whitest marble.

Hilda's gentle courage had brought her safely over land and sea; her mild, unflagging perseverance had made a place for her in the famous city, even like a flower that finds a chink for itself, and a little earth to grow in, on whatever ancient wall its slender roots may fasten. Here she dwelt, in her tower, possessing a friend or two in Rome, but no home companion except the flock of doves, whose cote was in a ruinous chamber contiguous to her own. They soon became as familiar with the fair-haired Saxon girl as if she were a born sister of their brood; and her customary white robe bore such an analogy to their snowy plumage that the confraternity of artists called Hilda the Dove, and recognized her aerial apartment as the Dove-cote. And while the other doves flew far and wide in quest of what was good for them, Hilda likewise spread her wings, and sought such ethereal and imaginative sustenance as God ordains for creatures of her kind.

We know not whether the result of her Italian studies, so far as it could yet be seen, will be accepted as a good or desirable one. Certain it is, that since her arrival in the pictorial land, Hilda seemed to have entirely lost the impulse of original design, which brought her thither. No doubt the girl's early dreams had been of sending forms and hues of beauty into the visible world out of her own mind; of compelling scenes of poetry and history to live before men's eyes, through conceptions and by methods individual to herself. But more and more, as she grew familiar with the miracles of art that enrich so many galleries in Rome, Hilda had ceased to consider herself as an original artist. No wonder that this change should have befallen her. She was endowed with a deep and sensitive faculty of appreciation; she had the gift of discerning and worshipping excellence in a most unusual measure. No other person, it is probable, recognized so adequately, and enjoyed with such deep delight, the pictorial wonders that were here displayed. She saw—no, not saw, but felt—through and through a picture; she bestowed upon it all the warmth and richness of a woman's sympathy; not by any intellectual effort, but by this strength of heart, and this guiding light of sympathy, she went straight to the central point, in which the master had conceived his work. Thus, she viewed it, as it were, with his own eyes, and hence her comprehension of any picture that interested her was perfect.

This power and depth of appreciation depended partly upon Hilda's physical organization, which was at once healthful and exquisitely delicate; and, connected with this advantage, she had a command of hand, a nicety and force of touch, which is an endowment separate from pictorial genius, though indispensable to its exercise.

It has probably happened in many other instances, as it did in Hilda's case, that she ceased to aim at original achievement in consequence of the very gifts which so exquisitely fitted her to profit by familiarity with the works of the mighty old masters. Reverencing these wonderful men so deeply, she was too grateful for all they bestowed upon her, too loyal, too humble, in their awful presence, to think of enrolling herself in their society. Beholding the miracles of beauty which they had achieved, the world seemed already rich enough in original designs, and nothing more was so desirable as to diffuse those self-same beauties more widely among mankind. All the youthful hopes and ambitions, the fanciful ideas which she had brought from home, of great pictures to be conceived in her feminine mind, were flung aside, and, so far as those most intimate with her could discern, relinquished without a sigh. All that she would henceforth attempt—and that most reverently, not to say religiously—was to catch and reflect some of the glory which had been shed upon canvas from the immortal pencils of old.

So Hilda became a copyist: in the Pinacotheca of the Vatican, in the galleries of the Pamfili-Doria palace, the Borghese, the Corsini, the Sciarra, her easel was set up before many a famous picture by Guido, Domenichino, Raphael, and the devout painters of earlier schools than these. Other artists and visitors from foreign lands beheld the slender, girlish figure in front of some world-known work, absorbed, unconscious of everything around her, seeming to live only in what she sought to do. They smiled, no doubt, at the audacity which led her to dream of copying those mighty achievements. But, if they paused to look over her shoulder, and had sensibility enough to understand what was before their eyes, they soon felt inclined to believe that the spirits of the old masters were hovering over Hilda, and guiding her delicate white hand. In truth, from whatever realm of bliss and many-colored beauty those spirits might descend, it would have been no unworthy errand to help so gentle and pure a worshipper of their genius in giving the last divine touch to her repetitions of their works.

Her copies were indeed marvellous. Accuracy was not the phrase for them; a Chinese copy is accurate. Hilda's had that evanescent and ethereal life—that flitting fragrance, as it were, of the originals—which it is as difficult to catch and retain as it would be for a sculptor to get the very movement and varying color of a living man into his marble bust. Only by watching the efforts of the most skilful copyists—men who spend a lifetime, as some of them do, in multiplying copies of a single picture—and observing how invariably they leave out just the indefinable charm that involves the last, inestimable value, can we understand the difficulties of the task which they undertake.

It was not Hilda's general practice to attempt reproducing the whole of a great picture, but to select some high, noble, and delicate portion of it, in which the spirit and essence of the picture culminated: the Virgin's celestial sorrow, for example, or a hovering angel, imbued with immortal light, or a saint with the glow of heaven in his dying face,—and these would be rendered with her whole soul. If a picture had darkened into an indistinct shadow through time and neglect, or had been injured by cleaning, or retouched by some profane hand, she seemed to possess the faculty of seeing it in its pristine glory. The copy would come from her hands with what the beholder felt must be the light which the old master had left upon the original in bestowing his final and most ethereal touch. In some instances even (at least, so those believed who best appreciated Hilda's power and sensibility) she had been enabled to execute what the great master had conceived in his imagination, but had not so perfectly succeeded in putting upon canvas; a result surely not impossible when such depth of sympathy as she possessed was assisted by the delicate skill and accuracy of her slender hand. In such cases the girl was but a finer instrument, a more exquisitely effective piece of mechanism, by the help of which the spirit of some great departed painter now first achieved his ideal, centuries after his own earthly hand, that other tool, had turned to dust.

Not to describe her as too much a wonder, however, Hilda, or the Dove, as her well-wishers half laughingly delighted to call her, had been pronounced by good judges incomparably the best copyist in Rome. After minute examination of her works, the most skilful artists declared that she had been led to her results by following precisely the same process step by step through which the original painter had trodden to the development of his idea. Other copyists—if such they are worthy to be called—attempt only a superficial imitation. Copies of the old masters in this sense are produced by thousands; there are artists, as we have said, who spend their lives in painting the works, or perhaps one single work, of one illustrious painter over and over again: thus they convert themselves into Guido machines, or Raphaelic machines. Their performances, it is true, are often wonderfully deceptive to a careless eye; but working entirely from the outside, and seeking only to reproduce the surface, these men are sure to leave out that indefinable nothing, that inestimable something, that constitutes the life and soul through which the picture gets its immortality. Hilda was no such machine as this; she wrought religiously, and therefore wrought a miracle.

It strikes us that there is something far higher and nobler in all this, in her thus sacrificing herself to the devout recognition of the highest excellence in art, than there would have been in cultivating her not inconsiderable share of talent for the production of works from her own ideas. She might have set up for herself, and won no ignoble name; she might have helped to fill the already crowded and cumbered world with pictures, not destitute of merit, but falling short, if by ever so little, of the best that has been done; she might thus have gratified some tastes that were incapable of appreciating Raphael. But this could be done only by lowering the standard of art to the comprehension of the spectator. She chose the better and loftier and more unselfish part, laying her individual hopes, her fame, her prospects of enduring remembrance, at the feet of those great departed ones, whom she so loved and venerated; and therefore the world was the richer for this feeble girl.

Since the beauty and glory of a great picture are confined within itself, she won out that glory by patient faith and self-devotion, and multiplied it for mankind. From the dark, chill corner of a gallery,—from some curtained chapel in a church, where the light came seldom and aslant,—from the prince's carefully guarded cabinet, where not one eye in thousands was permitted to behold it,—she brought the wondrous picture into daylight, and gave all its magic splendor for the enjoyment of the world. Hilda's faculty of genuine admiration is one of the rarest to be found in human nature; and let us try to recompense her in kind by admiring her generous self-surrender, and her brave, humble magnanimity in choosing to be the handmaid of those old magicians, instead of a minor enchantress within a circle of her own.

The handmaid of Raphael, whom she loved with a virgin's love! Would it have been worth Hilda's while to relinquish this office for the sake of giving the world a picture or two which it would call original; pretty fancies of snow and moonlight; the counterpart in picture of so many femine achievements in literature!

CHAPTER VII

## BEATRICE

MIRIAM was glad to find the Dove in her turret-home; for being endowed with an infinite activity, and taking exquisite delight in the sweet labor of which her life was full, it was Hilda's practice to flee abroad betimes, and haunt the galleries till dusk. Happy were those (but they were very few) whom she ever chose to be the companions of her day; they saw the art-treasures of Rome, under her guidance, as they had never seen them before. Not that Hilda could dissertate, or talk learnedly about pictures; she would probably have been puzzled by the technical terms of her own art. Not that she had much to say about what she most profoundly admired; but even her silent sympathy was so powerful that it drew your own along with it, endowing you with a second-sight that enabled you to see excellences with almost the depth and delicacy of her own perceptions.

All the Anglo-Saxon denizens of Rome, by this time, knew Hilda by sight. Unconsciously, the poor child had become one of the spectacles of the Eternal City, and was often pointed out to strangers, sitting at her easel among the wild-bearded young men, the white-haired old ones, and the shabbily dressed, painfully plain women, who make up the throng of copyists. The old custodes knew her well, and watched over her as their own child. Sometimes a young artist, instead of going on with a copy of the picture before which he had placed his easel, would enrich his canvas with an original portrait of Hilda at her work. A lovelier subject could not have been selected, nor one which required nicer skill and insight in doing it anything like justice. She was pretty at all times, in our native New England style, with her light-brown ringlets, her delicately tinged, but healthful cheek, her sensitive, intelligent, yet most feminine and kindly face. But, every few moments, this pretty and girlish face grew beautiful and striking, as some inward thought and feeling brightened, rose to the surface, and then, as it were, passed out of sight again; so that, taking into view this constantly recurring change, it really seemed as if Hilda were only visible by the sunshine of her soul.

In other respects, she was a good subject for a portrait, being distinguished by a gentle picturesqueness, which was perhaps unconsciously bestowed by some minute peculiarity of dress, such as artists seldom fail to assume. The effect was to make her appear like an inhabitant of picture-land, a partly ideal creature, not to be handled, nor even approached too closely. In her feminine self, Hilda was natural, and of pleasant deportment, endowed with a mild cheerfulness of temper, not overflowing with animal spirits, but never long despondent. There was a certain simplicity that made every one her friend, but it was combined with a subtile attribute of reserve, that insensibly kept those at a distance who were not suited to her sphere.

Miriam was the dearest friend whom she had ever known. Being a year or two the elder, of longer acquaintance with Italy, and better fitted to deal with its crafty and selfish inhabitants, she had helped Hilda to arrange her way of life, and had encouraged her through those first weeks, when Rome is so dreary to every new-comer.

"But how lucky that you are at home to-day," said Miriam, continuing the conversation which was begun, many pages back. "I hardly hoped to find you, though I had a favor to ask,—a commission to put into your charge. But what picture is this?"

"See!" said Hilda, taking her friend's hand, and leading her in front of the easel. "I wanted your opinion of it."

"If you have really succeeded," observed Miriam, recognizing the picture at the first glance, "it will be the greatest miracle you have yet achieved."

The picture represented simply a female head; a very youthful, girlish, perfectly beautiful face, enveloped in white drapery, from beneath which strayed a lock or two of what seemed a rich, though hidden luxuriance of auburn hair. The eyes were large and brown, and met those of the spectator, but evidently with a strange, ineffectual effort to escape. There was a little redness about the eyes, very slightly indicated, so that you would question whether or no the girl had been weeping. The whole face was quiet; there was no distortion or disturbance of any single feature; nor was it easy to see why the expression was not cheerful, or why a single touch of the artist's pencil should not brighten it into joyousness. But, in fact, it was the very saddest picture ever painted or conceived; it involved an unfathomable depth of sorrow, the sense of which came to the observer by a sort of intuition. It was a sorrow that removed this beautiful girl out of the sphere of humanity, and set her in a far-off region, the remoteness of which—while yet her face is so close before us—makes us shiver as at a spectre.

"Yes, Hilda," said her friend, after closely examining the picture, "you have done nothing else so wonderful as this. But by what unheard-of solicitations or secret interest have you obtained leave to copy Guido's Beatrice Cenci? It is an unexampled favor; and the impossibility of getting a genuine copy has filled the Roman picture-shops with Beatrices, gay, grievous, or coquettish, but never a true one among them."

"There has been one exquisite copy, I have heard," said Hilda, "by an artist capable of appreciating the spirit of the picture. It was Thompson, who brought it away piecemeal, being forbidden (like the rest of us) to set up his easel before it. As for me, I knew the Prince Barberini would be deaf to all entreaties; so I had no resource but to sit down before the picture, day after day, and let it sink into my heart. I do believe it is now photographed there. It is a sad face to keep so close to one's heart; only, what is so very beautiful can never be quite a pain. Well; after studying it in this way, I know not how many times, I came home, and have done my best to transfer the image to canvas."

"Here it is then," said Miriam, contemplating Hilda's work with great interest and delight, mixed with the painful sympathy that the picture excited. "Everywhere we see oil-paintings, crayon-sketches, cameos, engravings, lithographs, pretending to be Beatrice, and representing the poor girl with blubbered eyes, a leer of coquetry, a merry look as if she were dancing, a piteous look as if she were beaten, and twenty other modes of fantastic mistake. But here is Guido's very. Beatrice; she that slept in the dungeon, and awoke, betimes, to ascend the scaffold. And now that you have done it, Hilda, can you interpret what the feeling is, that gives this picture such a mysterious force? For my part, though deeply sensible of its influence, I cannot seize it."

"Nor can I, in words," replied her friend. "But while I was painting her, I felt all the time as if she were trying to escape from my gaze. She knows that her sorrow is so strange and so immense, that she ought to be solitary forever, both for the world's sake and her own; and this is the reason we feel such a distance between Beatrice and ourselves, even when our eyes meet hers. It is infinitely heart-breaking to meet her glance, and to feel that nothing can be done to help or comfort her; neither does she ask help or comfort, knowing the hopelessness of her case better than we do. She is a fallen angel,—fallen, and yet sinless; and it is only this depth of sorrow, with its weight and darkness, that keeps her down upon earth, and brings her within our view even while it sets her beyond our reach."

"You deem her sinless?" asked Miriam; "that is not so plain to me. If I can pretend to see at all into that dim region, whence she gazes so strangely and sadly at us, Beatrice's own conscience does not acquit her of something evil, and never to be forgiven!"

"Sorrow so black as hers oppresses her very nearly as sin would," said Hilda.

"Then," inquired Miriam, "do you think that there was no sin in the deed for which she suffered?"

"Ah!" replied Hilda, shuddering, "I really had quite forgotten Beatrice's history, and was thinking of her only as the picture seems to reveal her character. Yes, yes; it was terrible guilt, an inexpiable crime, and she feels it to be so. Therefore it is that the forlorn creature so longs to elude our eyes, and forever vanish away into nothingness! Her doom is just!"

"O Hilda, your innocence is like a sharp steel sword!" exclaimed her friend. "Your judgments are often terribly severe, though you seem all made up of gentleness and mercy. Beatrice's sin may not have been so great: perhaps it was no sin at all, but the best virtue possible in the cir-

cumstances. If she viewed it as a sin, it may have been because her nature was too feeble for the fate imposed upon her. Ah!" continued Miriam, passionately, "if I could only get within her consciousness!—if I
could but clasp Beatrice Cenci's ghost, and draw it into myself! I would
give my life to know whether she thought herself innocent, or the one
great criminal since time began."

As Miriam gave utterance to these words, Hilda looked from the picture into her face, and was startled to observe that her friend's expression had become almost exactly that of the portrait; as if her passionate
wish and struggle to penetrate poor Beatrice's mystery had been successful.

"Oh, for Heaven's sake, Miriam, do not look so!" she cried. "What an
actress you are! And I never guessed it before. Ah! now you are yourself
again!" she added, kissing her. "Leave Beatrice to me in future."

"Cover up your magical picture, then," replied her friend, "else I never
can look away from it. It is strange, dear Hilda, how an innocent, delicate, white soul like yours has been able to seize the subtle mystery of
this portrait; as you surely must, in order to reproduce it so perfectly.
Well; we will not talk of it any more. Do you know, I have come to you
this morning on a small matter of business. Will you undertake it for
me?"

"Oh, certainly," said Hilda, laughing; "if you choose to trust me with
business."

"Nay, it is not a matter of any difficulty," answered Miriam; "merely
to take charge of this packet, and keep it for me awhile."

"But why not keep it yourself?" asked Hilda.

"Partly because it will be safer in your charge," said her friend. "I am
a careless sort of person in ordinary things; while you, for all you dwell
so high above the world, have certain little housewifely ways of accuracy
and order. The packet is of some slight importance; and yet, it may be, I
shall not ask you for it again. In a week or two, you know, I am leaving
Rome. You, setting at defiance the malarial fever, mean to stay here and
haunt your beloved galleries through the summer. Now, four months
hence, unless you hear more from me, I would have you deliver the
packet according to its address."

Hilda read the direction; it was to Signore Luca Barboni, at the Palazzo Cenci, third piano.

"I will deliver it with my own hand," said she, "precisely four months
from to-day, unless you bid me to the contrary. Perhaps I shall meet the
ghost of Beatrice in that grim old palace of her forefathers."

"In that case," rejoined Miriam, "do not fail to speak to her, and try
to win her confidence. Poor thing! she would be all the better for pouring
her heart out freely, and would be glad to do it, if she were sure of sympathy. It irks my brain and heart to think of her, all shut up within herself." She withdrew the cloth that Hilda had drawn over the picture, and
took another long look at it,—"Poor sister Beatrice! for she was still a
woman, Hilda, still a sister, be her sin or sorrow what they might. How

well you have done it, Hilda! I know not whether Guido will thank you, or be jealous of your rivalship."

"Jealous, indeed!" exclaimed Hilda. "If Guido had not wrought through me, my pains would have been thrown away."

"After all," resumed Miriam, "if a woman had painted the original picture, there might have been something in it which we miss now. I have a great mind to undertake a copy myself, and try to give it what it lacks. Well; good-by. But, stay! I am going for a little airing to the grounds of the Villa Borghese this afternoon. You will think it very foolish, but I always feel the safer in your company, Hilda, slender little maiden as you are. Will you come?"

"Ah, not to-day, dearest Miriam," she replied, "I have set my heart on giving another touch or two to this picture, and shall not stir abroad till nearly sunset."

"Farewell, then," said her visitor. "I leave you in your dove-cote. What a sweet, strange life you lead here; conversing with the souls of the old masters, feeding and fondling your sister-doves, and trimming the Virgin's lamp! Hilda, do you ever pray to the Virgin while you tend her shrine?"

"Sometimes I have been moved to do so," replied the Dove, blushing, and lowering her eyes; "she was a woman once. Do you think it would be wrong?"

"Nay, that is for you to judge," said Miriam; "but when you pray next, dear friend, remember me!"

She went down the long descent of the lower staircase, and just as she reached the street the flock of doves again took their hurried flight from the pavement to the topmost window. She threw her eyes upward and beheld them hovering about Hilda's head; for, after her friend's departure, the girl had been more impressed than before by something very sad and troubled in her manner. She was, therefore, leaning forth from her airy abode, and flinging down a kind, maidenly kiss, and a gesture of farewell, in the hope that these might alight upon Miriam's heart, and comfort its unknown sorrow a little. Kenyon the sculptor, who chanced to be passing the head of the street, took note of that ethereal kiss, and wished that he could have caught it in the air and got Hilda's leave to keep it.

## CHAPTER VIII

### THE SUBURBAN VILLA

DONATELLO, while it was still a doubtful question betwixt afternoon and morning, set forth to keep the appointment which Miriam had carelessly tendered him in the grounds of the Villa Borghese.

The entrance to these grounds (as all my readers know, for everybody nowadays has been in Rome) is just outside of the Porta del Popolo. Passing beneath that not very impressive specimen of Michael Angelo's architecture, a minute's walk will transport the visitor from the small, uneasy, lava stones of the Roman pavement into broad, gravelled carriage-drives, whence a little farther stroll brings him to the soft turf of a beautiful seclusion. A seclusion, but seldom a solitude; for priest, noble, and populace, stranger and native, all who breathe Roman air, find free admission, and come hither to taste the languid enjoyment of the day-dream that they call life.

But Donatello's enjoyment was of a livelier kind. He soon began to draw long and delightful breaths among those shadowy walks. Judging by the pleasure which the sylvan character of the scene excited in him, it might be no merely fanciful theory to set him down as a kinsman, not far remote, of that wild, sweet, playful, rustic creature, to whose marble image he bore so striking a resemblance. How mirthful a discovery would it be (and yet with a touch of pathos in it), if the breeze which sported fondly with his clustering locks were to waft them suddenly aside, and show a pair of leaf-shaped, furry ears! What an honest strain of wildness would it indicate! and into what regions of rich mystery would it extend Donatello's sympathies, to be thus linked (and by no monstrous chain) with what we call the inferior tribes of being, whose simplicity, mingled with his human intelligence, might partly restore what man has lost of the divine!

The scenery amid which the youth now strayed was such as arrays itself in the imagination when we read the beautiful old myths, and fancy a brighter sky, a softer turf, a more picturesque arrangement of venerable trees, than we find in the rude and untrained landscapes of the Western world. The ilex-trees, so ancient and time-honored were they, seemed to have lived for ages undisturbed, and to feel no dread of profanation by the axe any more than overthrow by the thunder-stroke. It had already passed out of their dreamy old memories that only a few years ago they were grievously imperilled by the Gaul's last assault upon the walls of Rome. As if confident in the long peace of their lifetime, they assumed attitudes of indolent repose. They leaned over-the green turf in ponderous grace, throwing abroad their great branches without danger of interfering with other trees, though other majestic trees grew near enough for dignified society, but too distant for constraint. Never was there a more venerable quietude than that which slept among their sheltering boughs; never a sweeter sunshine than that now gladdening the gentle gloom which these leafy patriarchs strove to diffuse over the swelling and subsiding lawns.

In other portions of the grounds the stone-pines lifted their dense clump of branches upon a slender length of stem, so high that they looked like green islands in the air, flinging down a shadow upon the turf so far off that you hardly knew which tree had made it. Again, there were avenues of cypress, resembling dark flames of huge funeral candles, which spread dusk and twilight round about them instead of cheerful radiance. The more open spots were all a-bloom, even so early in the season, with anemones of wondrous size, both white and rose-colored, and violets that betrayed themselves by their rich fragrance, even if their blue eyes failed to meet your own. Daisies, too, were abundant, but larger than the modest little English flower, and therefore of small account.

These wooded and flowery lawns are more beautiful than the finest of English park-scenery, more touching, more impressive, through the neglect that leaves Nature so much to her own ways and methods. Since man seldom interferes with her, she sets to work in her quiet way and makes herself at home. There is enough of human care, it is true, bestowed, long ago and still bestowed, to prevent wildness from growing into deformity; and the result is an ideal landscape, a woodland scene that seems to have been projected out of the poet's mind. If the ancient Faun were other than a mere creation of old poetry, and could have reappeared anywhere, it must have been in such a scene as this.

In the openings of the wood there are fountains plashing into marble basins, the depths of which are shaggy with water-weeds; or they tumble like natural cascades from rock to rock, sending their murmur afar, to make the quiet and silence more appreciable. Scattered here and there with careless artifice, stand old altars bearing Roman inscriptions. Statues, gray with the long corrosion of even that soft atmosphere, half hide and half reveal themselves, high on pedestals, or perhaps fallen and broken on the turf. Terminal figures, columns of marble or granite porticos, arches, are seen in the vistas of the wood-paths, either veritable relics of antiquity, or with so exquisite a touch of artful ruin on them that they are better than if really antique. At all events, grass grows on the tops of the shattered pillars, and weeds and flowers root themselves in the chinks of the massive arches and fronts of temples, and clamber at large over their pediments, as if this were the thousandth summer since their winged seeds alighted there.

What a strange idea—what a needless labor—to construct artificial ruins in Rome, the native soil of ruin! But even these sportive imitations, wrought by man in emulation of what time has done to temples and palaces, are perhaps centuries old, and, beginning as illusions, have grown to be venerable in sober earnest. The result of all is a scene, pensive, lovely, dream-like, enjoyable and sad, such as is to be found nowhere save in these princely villa-residences in the neighborhood of Rome; a scene that must have required generations and ages, during which growth, decay, and man's intelligence wrought kindly together, to render it so gently wild as we behold it now.

The final charm is bestowed by the malaria. There is a piercing, thrilling, delicious kind of regret in the idea of so much beauty thrown away, or only enjoyable at its half-development, in winter and early spring, and never to be dwelt amongst, as the home-scenery of any human being. For if you come hither in summer, and stray through these glades in the golden sunset, fever walks arm in arm with you, and death awaits you at the end of the dim vista. Thus the scene is like Eden in its loveliness; like Eden, too, in the fatal spell that removes it beyond the scope of man's actual possessions. But Donatello felt nothing of this dream-like melancholy that haunts the spot. As he passed among the sunny shadows, his spirit seemed to acquire new elasticity. The flicker of the sunshine, the sparkle of the fountain's gush, the dance of the leaf upon the bough, the woodland fragrance, the green freshness, the old sylvan peace and freedom, were all intermingled in those long breaths which he drew.

The ancient dust, the mouldiness of Rome, the dead atmosphere in which he had wasted so many months, the hard pavements, the smell of ruin and decaying generations, the chill palaces, the convent-bells, the heavy incense of altars, the life that he had led in those dark, narrow streets, among priests, soldiers, nobles, artists, and women,—all the sense of these things rose from the young man's consciousness like a cloud which had darkened over him without his knowing how densely.

He drank in the natural influences of the scene, and was intoxicated as by an exhilarating wine. He ran races with himself along the gleam and shadow of the wood-paths. He leapt up to catch the overhanging bough of an ilex, and swinging himself by it alighted far onward, as if he had flown thither through the air. In a sudden rapture, he embraced the trunk of a sturdy tree, and seemed to imagine it a creature worthy of affection and capable of a tender response; he clasped it closely in his arms, as a Faun might have clasped the warm feminine grace of the nymph, whom antiquity supposed to dwell within that rough, encircling rind. Then, in order to bring himself closer to the genial earth, with which his kindred instincts linked him so strongly, he threw himself at full length on the turf, and pressed down his lips, kissing the violets and daisies, which kissed him back again, though shyly, in their maiden fashion.

While he lay there, it was pleasant to see how the green and blue lizards, who had been basking on some rock or on a fallen pillar that absorbed the warmth of the sun, scrupled not to scramble over him with their small feet; and how the birds alighted on the nearest twigs and sang their little roundelays unbroken by any chirrup of alarm; they recognized him, it may be, as something akin to themselves, or else they fancied that he was rooted and grew there; for these wild pets of nature dreaded him no more in his buoyant life than if a mound of soil and grass and flowers had long since covered his dead body, converting it back to the sympathies from which human existence had estranged it.

All of us, after a long abode in cities, have felt the blood gush more joyously through our veins with the first breath of rural air; few could feel it so much as Donatello, a creature of simple elements, bred in the sweet sylvan life of Tuscany, and for months back dwelling amid the mouldy gloom and dim splendor of old Rome. Nature has been shut out for numberless centuries from those stony-hearted streets, to which he had latterly grown accustomed; there is no trace of her, except for what blades of grass spring out of the pavements of the less trodden piazzas, or what weeds cluster and tuft themselves on the cornices of ruins. Therefore his joy was like that of a child that had gone astray from home, and finds him suddenly in his mother's arms again.

At last, deeming it full time for Miriam to keep her tryst, he climbed to the tiptop of the tallest tree, and thence looked about him, swaying to and fro in the gentle breeze, which was like the respiration of that great leafy, living thing. Donatello saw beneath him the whole circuit of the enchanted ground; the statues and columns pointing upward from among the shrubbery, the fountains flashing in the sunlight, the paths winding hither and thither, and continually finding out some nook of new and ancient pleasantness. He saw the villa, too, with its marble front incrusted all over with bas-reliefs, and statues in its many niches. It was as beautiful as a fairy palace, and seemed an abode in which the lord and lady of this fair domain might fitly dwell, and come forth each morning to enjoy as sweet a life as their happiest dreams of the past night could have depicted. All this he saw, but his first glance had taken in too wide a sweep, and it was not till his eyes fell almost directly beneath him, that Donatello beheld Miriam just turning into the path that led across the roots of his very tree.

He descended among the foliage, waiting for her to come close to the trunk, and then suddenly dropped from an impending bough, and alighted at her side. It was as if the swaying of the branches had let a ray of sunlight through. The same ray likewise glimmered among the gloomy meditations that encompassed Miriam, and lit up the pale, dark beauty of her face, while it responded pleasantly to Donatello's glance.

"I hardly know," said she, smiling, "whether you have sprouted out of the earth, or fallen from the clouds. In either case you are welcome."

And they walked onward together.

## CHAPTER IX

### THE FAUN AND NYMPH

MIRIAM's sadder mood, it might be, had at first an effect on Donatello's spirits. It checked the joyous ebullition into which they would otherwise have effervesced when he found himself in her society, not, as heretofore, in the old gloom of Rome, but under that bright soft sky and in those Arcadian woods. He was silent for a while; it being, indeed, seldom Donatello's impulse to express himself copiously in words. His usual modes of demonstration were by the natural language of gesture, the instinctive movement of his agile frame, and the unconscious play of his features, which, within a limited range of thought and emotion, would speak volumes in a moment.

By and by, his own mood seemed to brighten Miriam's, and was reflected back upon himself. He began inevitably, as it were, to dance along the wood-path, flinging himself into attitudes of strange comic grace. Often, too, he ran a little way in advance of his companion, and then stood to watch her as she approached along the shadowy and sun-fleckered path. With every step she took, he expressed his joy at her nearer and nearer presence by what might be thought an extravagance of gesticulation, but which doubtless was the language of the natural man, though laid aside and forgotten by other men, now that words have been feebly substituted in the place of signs and symbols. He gave Miriam the idea of a being not precisely man, nor yet a child, but, in a high and beautiful sense, an animal,—a creature in a state of development less than what mankind has attained, yet the more perfect within itself for that very deficiency. This idea filled her mobile imagination with agreeable fantasies, which, after smiling at them herself, she tried to convey to the young man.

"What are you, my friend?" she exclaimed, always keeping in mind his singular resemblance to the Faun of the Capitol. "If you are, in good truth, that wild and pleasant creature whose face you wear, pray make me known to your kindred. They will be found hereabouts, if anywhere. Knock at the rough rind of this ilex-tree, and summon forth the Dryad! Ask the water-nymph to rise dripping from yonder fountain, and exchange a moist pressure of the hand with me! Do not fear that I shall shrink, even if one of your rough cousins, a hairy Satyr, should come capering on his goat-legs out of the haunts of far antiquity, and propose to dance with me among these lawns! And will not Bacchus,—with whom you consorted so familiarly of old, and who loved you so well,—will he not meet us here, and squeeze rich grapes into his cup for you and me?"

Donatello smiled; he laughed heartily, indeed, in sympathy with the mirth that gleamed out of Miriam's deep, dark eyes. But he did not seem quite to understand her mirthful talk, nor to be disposed to explain what kind of creature he was, or to inquire with what divine or poetic kindred his companion feigned to link him. He appeared only to know that Miriam was beautiful, and that she smiled graciously upon him; that the present moment was very sweet, and himself most happy, with the sunshine, the sylvan scenery, and woman's kindly charm, which it enclosed within its small circumference. It was delightful to see the trust which he reposed in Miriam, and his pure joy in her propinquity; he asked nothing, sought nothing, save to be near the beloved object, and brimmed over with ecstacy at that simple boon. A creature of the happy tribes below us sometimes shows the capacity of this enjoyment; a man, seldom or never.

"Donatello," said Miriam, looking at him thoughtfully, but amused, yet not without a shade of sorrow, "you seem very happy; what makes you so?"

"Because I love you!" answered Donatello.

He made this momentous confession as if it were the most natural thing

in the world; and on her part,—such was the contagion of his simplicity,
—Miriam heard it without anger or disturbance, though with no responding emotion. It was as if they had strayed across the limits of Arcadia,
and come under a civil polity where young men might avow their passion
with as little restraint as a bird pipes its note to a similar purpose.

"Why should you love me, foolish boy?" said she. "We have no points
of sympathy at all. There are not two creatures more unlike, in this wide
world, than you and I!"

"You are yourself, and I am Donatello," replied he. "Therefore I love
you! There needs no other reason."

Certainly, there was no better or more explicable reason. It might have
been imagined that Donatello's unsophisticated heart would be more
readily attracted to a feminine nature of clear simplicity like his own,
than to one already turbid with grief or wrong, as Miriam's seemed to be.
Perhaps, on the other hand, his character needed the dark element, which
it found in her. The force and energy of will, that sometimes flashed
through her eyes, may have taken him captive; or, not improbably, the
varying lights and shadows of her temper, now so mirthful, and anon so
sad with mysterious gloom, had bewitched the youth. Analyze the matter as we may, the reason assigned by Donatello himself was as satisfactory as we are likely to attain.

Miriam could not think seriously of the avowal that had passed. He
held out his love so freely, in his open palm, that she felt it could be
nothing but a toy, which she might play with for an instant, and give
back again. And yet Donatello's heart was so fresh a fountain, that, had
Miriam been more world-worn than she was, she might have found it
exquisite to slake her thirst with the feelings that welled up and brimmed
over from it. She was far, very far, from the dusty mediæval epoch, when
some women have a taste for such refreshment. Even for her, however,
there was an inexpressible charm in the simplicity that prompted Donatello's words and deeds; though, unless she caught them in precisely the
true light, they seemed but folly, the offspring of a maimed or imperfectly developed intellect. Alternately, she almost admired, or wholly
scorned him, and knew not which estimate resulted from the deeper appreciation. But it could not, she decided for herself, be other than an innocent pastime, if they two—sure to be separated by their different paths in
life, to-morrow—were to gather up some of the little pleasures that
chanced to grow about their feet, like the violets and wood-anemones,
to-day.

Yet an impulse of rectitude impelled Miriam to give him what she still
held to be a needless warning against an imaginary peril.

"If you were wiser, Donatello, you would think me a dangerous person," said she. "If you follow my footsteps, they will lead you to no good.
You ought to be afraid of me."

"I would as soon think of fearing the air we breathe," he replied.

"And well you may, for it is full of malaria," said Miriam; she went
on, hinting at an intangible confession, such as persons with overbur-

dened hearts often make to children or dumb animals, or to holes in the earth, where they think their secrets may be at once revealed and buried. "Those who come too near me are in danger of great mischiefs, I do assure you. Take warning, therefore! It is a sad fatality that has brought you from your home among the Apennines,—some rusty old castle, I suppose, with a village at its foot, and an Arcadian environment of vineyards, fig-trees, and olive-orchards,—a sad mischance, I say, that has transported you to my side. You have had a happy life hitherto,—have you not, Donatello?"

"Oh, yes," answered the young man; and, though not of a retrospective turn, he made the best effort he could to send his mind back into the past. "I remember thinking it happiness to dance with the contadinas at a village feast; to taste the new, sweet wine at vintage-time, and the old, ripened wine, which our podere is famous for, in the cold winter evenings; and to devour great, luscious figs, and apricots, peaches, cherries, and melons. I was often happy in the woods, too, with hounds and horses, and very happy in watching all sorts of creatures and birds that haunt the leafy solitudes. But never half so happy as now!"

"In these delightful groves?" she asked.

"Here, and with you," answered Donatello. "Just as we are now."

"What a fulness of content in him! How silly, and how delightful!" said Miriam to herself. Then addressing him again: "But, Donatello, how long will this happiness last?"

"How long!" he exclaimed; for it perplexed him even more to think of the future than to remember the past. "Why should it have any end? How long! Forever! forever! forever!"

"The child! the simpleton!" said Miriam, with sudden laughter, and checking it as suddenly. "But is he a simpleton indeed? Here, in those few natural words, he has expressed that deep sense, that profound conviction of its own immortality, which genuine love never fails to bring. He perplexes me,—yes, and bewitches me,—wild, gentle, beautiful creature that he is! It is like playing with a young greyhound!"

Her eyes filled with tears, at the same time that a smile shone out of them. Then first she became sensible of a delight and grief at once, in feeling this zephyr of a new affection, with its untainted freshness, blow over her weary, stifled heart, which had no right to be revived by it. The very exquisiteness of the enjoyment made her know that it ought to be a forbidden one.

"Donatello," she hastily exclaimed, "for your own sake, leave me! It is not such a happy thing as you imagine it, to wander in these woods with me, a girl from another land, burdened with a doom that she tells to none. I might make you dread me,—perhaps hate me,—if I chose; and I must choose, if I find you loving me too well!"

"I fear nothing!" said Donatello, looking into her unfathomable eyes with perfect trust. "I love always!"

"I speak in vain," thought Miriam within herself.

"Well, then, for this one hour, let me be such as he imagines me. To-morrow will be time enough to come back to my reality. My reality! what is it? Is the past so indestructible? the future so immitigable? Is the dark dream, in which I walk, of such solid, stony substance, that there can be no escape out of its dungeon? Be it so! There is, at least, that ethereal quality in my spirit, that it can make me as gay as Donatello himself,—for this one hour?"

And immediately she brightened up, as if an inward flame, heretofore stifled, were now permitted to fill her with its happy lustre, glowing through her cheeks and dancing in her eye-beams.

Donatello, brisk and cheerful as he seemed before, showed a sensibility to Miriam's gladdened mood by breaking into still wilder and ever-varying activity. He frisked around her, bubbling over with joy, which clothed itself in words that had little individual meaning, and in snatches of song that seemed as natural as bird-notes. Then they both laughed together, and heard their own laughter returning in the echoes, and laughed again at the response, so that the ancient and solemn grove became full of merriment for these two blithe spirits. A bird happening to sing cheerily, Donatello gave a peculiar call, and the little feathered creature came fluttering about his head, as if it had known him through many summers.

"How close he stands to nature!" said Miriam, observing this pleasant familiarity between her companion and the bird. "He shall make me as natural as himself for this one hour."

As they strayed through that sweet wilderness, she felt more and more the influence of his elastic temperament. Miriam was an impressible and impulsive creature, as unlike herself, in different moods, as if a melancholy maiden and a glad one were both bound within the girdle about her waist, and kept in magic thraldom by the brooch that clasped it. Naturally, it is true, she was the more inclined to melancholy, yet fully capable of that high frolic of the spirits which richly compensates for many gloomy hours; if her soul was apt to lurk in the darkness of a cavern, she could sport madly in the sunshine before the cavern's mouth. Except the freshest mirth of animal spirits, like Donatello's, there is no merriment, no wild exhilaration, comparable to that of melancholy people escaping from the dark region in which it is their custom to keep themselves imprisoned.

So the shadowy Miriam almost outdid Donatello on his own ground. They ran races with each other, side by side, with shouts and laughter; they pelted one another with early flowers, and gathering them up twined them with green leaves into garlands for both their heads. They played together like children, or creatures of immortal youth. So much had they flung aside the sombre habitudes of daily life, that they seemed born to be sportive forever, and endowed with eternal mirthfulness instead of any deeper joy. It was a glimpse far backward into Arcadian life, or, further still, into the Golden Age, before mankind was burdened with sin and sorrow, and before pleasure had been darkened with those shadows that bring it into high relief, and make it happiness.

"Hark!" cried Donatello, stopping short, as he was about to bind Miriam's fair hands with flowers, and lead her along in triumph, "there is music somewhere in the grove!"

"It is your kinsman, Pan, most likely," said Miriam, "playing on his pipe. Let us go seek him, and make him puff out his rough cheeks and pipe his merriest air! Come; the strain of music will guide us onward like a gayly colored thread of silk."

"Or like a chain of flowers," responded Donatello, drawing her along by that which he had twined. "This way!—Come!"

CHAPTER X

## The Sylvan Dance

As the music came fresher on their ears, they danced to its cadence, extemporizing new steps and attitudes. Each varying movement had a grace which might have been worth putting into marble, for the long delight of days to come, but vanished with the movement that gave it birth, and was effaced from memory by another. In Miriam's motion, freely as she flung herself into the frolic of the hour, there was still an artful beauty; in Donatello's, there was a charm of indescribable grotesqueness hand in hand with grace; sweet, bewitching, most provocative of laughter, and yet akin to pathos, so deeply did it touch the heart. This was the ultimate peculiarity, the final touch, distinguishing between the sylvan creature and the beautiful companion at his side. Setting apart only this, Miriam resembled a Nymph, as much as Donatello did a Faun.

There were flitting moments, indeed, when she played the sylvan character as perfectly as he. Catching glimpses of her, then, you would have fancied that an oak had sundered its rough bark to let her dance freely forth, endowed with the same spirit in her human form as that which rustles in the leaves; or that she had emerged through the pebbly bottom of a fountain, a water-nymph, to play and sparkle in the sunshine, flinging a quivering light around her, and suddenly disappearing in a shower of rainbow drops.

As the fountain sometimes subsides into its basin, so in Miriam there were symptoms that the frolic of her spirits would at last tire itself out.

"Ah! Donatello," cried she, laughing, as she stopped to take breath; "you have an unfair advantage over me! I am no true creature of the woods; while you are a real Faun, I do believe. When your curls shook just now, methought I had a peep at the pointed ears."

Donatello snapped his fingers above his head, as fauns and satyrs taught us first to do, and seemed to radiate jollity out of his whole nimble person. Nevertheless, there was a kind of dim apprehension in his

face, as if he dreaded that a moment's pause might break the spell, and
snatch away the sportive companion whom he had waited for through so
many dreary months.

"Dance! dance!" cried he, joyously. "If we take breath, we shall be as
we were yesterday. There, now, is the music, just beyond this clump of
trees. Dance, Miriam, dance!"

They had now reached an open, grassy glade (of which there are many
in that artfully constructed wilderness), set round with stone seats, on
which the aged moss had kindly essayed to spread itself instead of
cushions. On one of the stone benches sat the musicians, whose strains
had enticed our wild couple thitherward. They proved to be a vagrant
band, such as Rome, and all Italy, abounds with; comprising a harp, a
flute, and a violin, which, though greatly the worse for wear, the performers had skill enough to provoke and modulate into tolerable harmony. It chanced to be a feast-day; and, instead of playing in the sun-
scorched piazzas of the city, or beneath the windows of some unrespons-
ive palace, they had bethought themselves to try the echoes of these
woods; for, on the festas of the Church, Rome scatters its merry-makers
all abroad, ripe for the dance or any other pastime.

As Miriam and Donatello emerged from among the trees, the musicians
scraped, tinkled, or blew, each according to his various kind of instrument, more inspiringly than ever. A dark-cheeked little girl, with bright
black eyes, stood by, shaking a tambourine set round with tinkling bells,
and thumping it on its parchment head. Without interrupting his brisk,
though measured movement, Donatello snatched away this unmelodious
contrivance, and flourishing it above his head, produced music of indescribable potency, still dancing with frisky step, and striking the tambourine, and ringing its little bells, all in one jovial act.

It might be that there was magic in the sound, or contagion, at least, in
the spirit which had got possession of Miriam and himself, for very soon
a number of festal people were drawn to the spot, and struck into the
dance, singly, or in pairs, as if they were all gone mad with jollity. Among
them were some of the plebeian damsels whom we meet bareheaded in
the Roman streets, with silver stilettos thrust through their glossy hair;
the contadinas, too, from the Campagna and the villages, with their rich
and picturesque costumes of scarlet and all bright hues, such as fairer
maidens might not venture to put on. Then came the modern Roman
from Trastevere, perchance, with his old cloak drawn about him like a
toga, which anon, as his active motion heated him, he flung aside. Three
French soldiers capered freely into the throng, in wide scarlet trousers,
their short swords dangling at their sides; and three German artists in
gray flaccid hats and flaunting beards; and one of the Pope's Swiss
guardsmen in the strange motley garb which Michael Angelo contrived
for them. Two young English tourists (one of them a lord) took conta-
dine partners and dashed in, as did also a shaggy man in goat-skin
breeches, who looked like rustic Pan in person, and footed it as merrily as
he. Besides the above there was a herdsman or two from the Campagna,

and a few peasants in sky-blue jackets, and small-clothes tied with ribbons at the knees; haggard and sallow were these last, poor serfs, having little to eat and nothing but the malaria to breathe; but still they plucked up a momentary spirit and joined hands in Donatello's dance.

Here, as it seemed, had the Golden Age come back again within the precincts of this sunny glade, thawing mankind out of their cold formalities, releasing them from irksome restraint, mingling them together in such childlike gayety that new flowers (of which the old bosom of the earth is full) sprang up beneath their footsteps. The sole exception to the geniality of the moment, as we have understood, was seen in a countryman of our own, who sneered at the spectacle, and declined to compromise his dignity by making part of it.

The harper thrummed with rapid fingers; the violin-player flashed his bow back and forth across the strings; the flautist poured his breath in quick puffs of jollity, while Donatello shook the tambourine above his head, and led the merry throng with unweariable steps. As they followed one another in a wild ring of mirth, it seemed the realization of one of those bas-reliefs where a dance of nymphs, satyrs, or bacchanals is twined around the circle of an antique vase; or it was like the sculptured scene on the front and sides of a sarcophagus, where, as often as any other device, a festive procession mocks the ashes and white bones that are treasured up within. You might take it for a marriage-pageant; but after a while, if you look at these merry-makers, following them from end to end of the marble coffin, you doubt whether their gay movement is leading them to a happy close. A youth has suddenly fallen in the dance; a chariot is overturned and broken, flinging the charioteer headlong to the ground; a maiden seems to have grown faint or weary and is drooping on the bosom of a friend. Always some tragic incident is shadowed forth or thrust sidelong into the spectacle; and when once it has caught your eye you can look no more at the festal portions of the scene, except with reference to this one slightly suggested doom and sorrow.

As in its mirth, so in the darker characteristic here alluded to, there was an analogy between the sculptured scene on the sarcophagus and the wild dance which we have been describing. In the midst of its madness and riot Miriam found herself suddenly confronted by a strange figure that shook its fantastic garments in the air, and pranced before her on its tip-toes, almost vying with the agility of Donatello himself. It was the model.

A moment afterwards Donatello was aware that she had retired from the dance. He hastened towards her, and flung himself on the grass beside the stone bench on which Miriam was sitting. But a strange distance and unapproachableness had all at once enveloped her; and though he saw her within reach of his arm, yet the light of her eyes seemed as far off as that of a star, nor was there any warmth in the melancholy smile with which she regarded him.

"Come back!" cried he. "Why should this happy hour end so soon?"

"It must end here, Donatello," said she, in answer to his words and

outstretched hand; "and such hours, I believe, do not often repeat themselves in a lifetime. Let me go, my friend; let me vanish from you quietly
among the shadows of these trees. See, the companions of our pastime are
vanishing already!"

Whether it was that the harp-strings were broken, the violin out of
tune, or the flautist out of breath, so it chanced that the music had ceased,
and the dancers come abruptly to a pause. All that motley throng of rioters was dissolved as suddenly as it had been drawn together. In Miriam's
remembrance the scene had a character of fantasy. It was as if a company of satyrs, fauns, and nymphs, with Pan in the midst of them, had
been disporting themselves in these venerable woods only a moment ago;
and now in another moment, because some profane eye had looked at
them too closely, or some intruder had cast a shadow on their mirth, the
sylvan pageant had utterly disappeared. If a few of the merry-makers
lingered among the trees, they had hidden their racy peculiarities under
the garb and aspect of ordinary people, and sheltered themselves in the
weary commonplace of daily life. Just an instant before it was Arcadia
and the Golden Age. The spell being broken, it was now only that old
tract of pleasure-ground, close by the people's gate of Rome,—a tract
where the crimes and calamities of ages, the many battles, blood recklessly poured out, and deaths of myriads, have corrupted all the soil, creating an influence that makes the air deadly to human lungs.

"You must leave me," said Miriam to Donatello, more imperatively
than before; "have I not said it? Go; and look not behind you."

"Miriam," whispered Donatello, grasping her hand forcibly, "who is it
that stands in the shadow yonder, beckoning you to follow him?"

"Hush; leave me!" repeated Miriam. "Your hour is past; his hour has
come."

Donatello still gazed in the direction which he had indicated, and the
expression of his face was fearfully changed, being so disordered, perhaps
with terror,—at all events with anger and invincible repugnance,—that
Miriam hardly knew him. His lips were drawn apart so as to disclose his
set teeth, thus giving him a look of animal rage, which we seldom see except in persons of the simplest and rudest natures. A shudder seemed to
pass through his very bones.

"I hate him!" muttered he.

"Be satisfied; I hate him too!" said Miriam.

She had no thought of making this avowal, but was irresistibly drawn
to it by the sympathy of the dark emotion in her own breast with that so
strongly expressed by Donatello. Two drops of water or of blood do not
more naturally flow into each other than did her hatred into his.

"Shall I clutch him by the throat?" whispered Donatello, with a savage scowl. "Bid me do so, and we are rid of him forever."

"In Heaven's name, no violence!" exclaimed Miriam, affrighted out of
the scornful control which she had hitherto held over her companion, by
the fierceness that he so suddenly developed. "Oh, have pity on me, Donatello, if for nothing else, yet because in the midst of my wretchedness I let

myself be your playmate for this one wild hour! Follow me no farther. Henceforth, leave me to my doom. Dear friend,—kind, simple, loving friend,—make me not more wretched by the remembrance of having thrown fierce hates or loves into the wellspring of your happy life!"

"Not follow you!" repeated Donatello, soothed from anger into sorrow, less by the purport of what she said, than by the melancholy sweetness of her voice,—"not follow you! What other path have I?"

"We will talk of it once again," said Miriam, still soothingly; "soon— to-morrow—when you will; only leave me now."

## CHAPTER XI

### FRAGMENTARY SENTENCES

IN the Borghese Grove, so recently uproarious with merriment and music, there remained only Miriam and her strange follower.

A solitude had suddenly spread itself around them. It perhaps symbolized a peculiar character in the relation of these two, insulating them, and building up an insuperable barrier between their life-streams and other currents, which might seem to flow in close vicinity. For it is one of the chief earthly incommodities of some species of misfortune, or of a great crime, that it makes the actor in the one, or the sufferer of the other, an alien in the world, by interposing a wholly unsympathetic medium betwixt himself and those whom he yearns to meet.

Owing, it may be, to this moral estrangement,—this chill remoteness of their position,—there have come to us but a few vague whisperings of what passed in Miriam's interview that afternoon with the sinister personage who had dogged her footsteps ever since the visit to the catacomb. In weaving these mystic utterances into a continuous scene, we undertake a task resembling in its perplexity that of gathering up and piecing together the fragments of a letter which has been torn and scattered to the winds. Many words of deep significance, many entire sentences, and those possibly the most important ones, have flown too far on the winged breeze to be recovered. If we insert our own conjectural amendments, we perhaps give a purport utterly at variance with the true one. Yet unless we attempt something in this way, there must remain an unsightly gap, and a lack of continuousness and dependence in our narrative; so that it would arrive at certain inevitable catastrophes without due warning of their imminence.

Of so much we are sure, that there seemed to be a sadly mysterious fascination in the influence of this ill-omened person over Miriam; it was such as beasts and reptiles of subtle and evil nature sometimes exercise upon their victims. Marvellous it was to see the hopelessness with which —being naturally of so courageous a spirit—she resigned herself to the thraldom in which he held her. That iron chain, of which some of the massive links were round her feminine waist, and the others in his ruthless hand,—or which, perhaps, bound the pair together by a bond equally torturing to each,—must have been forged in some such unhallowed furnace as is only kindled by evil passions and fed by evil deeds.

Yet, let us trust, there may have been no crime in Miriam, but only one of those fatalities which are among the most insoluble riddles propounded to mortal comprehension; the fatal decree by which every crime is made to be the agony of many innocent persons, as well as of the single guilty one.

It was, at any rate, but a feeble and despairing kind of remonstrance which she had now the energy to oppose against his persecution.

"You follow me too closely," she said, in low, faltering accents; "you allow me too scanty room to draw my breath. Do you know what will be the end of this?"

"I know well what must be the end," he replied.

"Tell me, then," said Miriam, "that I may compare your foreboding with my own. Mine is a very dark one."

"There can be but one result, and that soon," answered the model. You must throw off your present mask and assume another. You must vanish out of the scene: quit Rome with me, and leave no trace whereby to follow you. It is in my power, as you well know, to compel your acquiescence in my bidding. You are aware of the penalty of a refusal."

"Not that penalty with which you would terrify me," said Miriam; "another there may be, but not so grievous."

"What is that other?" he inquired.

"Death! simply death!" she answered.

"Death," said her persecutor, "is not so simple and opportune a thing as you imagine. You are strong and warm with life. Sensitive and irritable as your spirit is, these many months of trouble, this latter thraldom in which I hold you, have scarcely made your cheek paler than I saw it in your girlhood. Miriam,—for I forbear to speak another name, at which these leaves would shiver above our heads,—Miriam, you cannot die!"

"Might not a dagger find my heart?" said she, for the first time meeting his eyes. "Would not poison make an end of me? Will not the Tiber drown me?"

"It might," he answered; "for I allow that you are mortal. But, Miriam, believe me, it is not your fate to die while there remains so much to be sinned and suffered in the world. We have a destiny which we must needs fulfil together. I, too, have struggled to escape it. I was as anxious as yourself to break the tie between us,—to bury the past in a fathomless grave,—to make it impossible that we should ever meet, until you confront me at the bar of Judgment! You little can imagine what steps I took to render all this secure; and what was the result? Our strange interview in the bowels of the earth convinced me of the futility of my design."

"Ah, fatal chance!" cried Miriam, covering her face with her hands.

"Yes, your heart trembled with horror when you recognized me," rejoined he; "but you did not guess that there was an equal horror in my own!"

"Why would not the weight of earth above our heads have crumbled down upon us both, forcing us apart, but burying us equally?" cried Miriam, in a burst of vehement passion. "Oh, that we could have wandered in those dismal passages till we both perished, taking opposite paths in the darkness, so that when we lay down to die our last breaths might not mingle!"

"It were vain to wish it," said the model. "In all that labyrinth of midnight paths, we should have found one another out to live or die together. Our fates cross and are entangled. The threads are twisted into a strong cord, which is dragging us to an evil doom. Could the knots be severed, we might escape. But neither can your slender fingers untie these knots, nor my masculine force break them. We must submit!"

"Pray for rescue, as I have," exclaimed Miriam. "Pray for deliverance from me, since I am your evil genius, as you mine. Dark as your life has been, I have known you to pray in times past!"

At these words of Miriam, a tremor and horror appeared to seize upon her persecutor, insomuch that he shook and grew ashy pale before her eyes. In this man's memory, there was something that made it awful for him to think of prayer; nor would any torture be more intolerable than to be reminded of such divine comfort and succor as await pious souls merely for the asking. This torment was perhaps the token of a native temperament deeply susceptible of religious impressions, but which had been wronged, violated, and debased, until, at length, it was capable only of terror from the sources that were intended for our purest and loftiest consolation. He looked so fearfully at her, and with such intense pain struggling in his eyes, that Miriam felt pity.

And, now, all at once, it struck her that he might be mad. It was an idea that had never before seriously occurred to her mind, although, as soon as suggested, it fitted marvellously into many circumstances that lay within her knowledge. But, alas! such was her evil fortune, that, whether mad or no, his power over her remained the same, and was likely to be used only the more tyrannously, if exercised by a lunatic.

"I would not give you pain," she said, soothingly; "your faith allows you the consolations of penance and absolution. Try what help there may be in these, and leave me to myself."

"Do not think it, Miriam," said he; "we are bound together, and can never part again."

"Why should it seem so impossible?" she rejoined. "Think how I had escaped from all the past! I had made for myself a new sphere, and found new friends, new occupations, new hopes and enjoyments. My heart, methinks, was almost as unburdened as if there had been no miserable life behind me. The human spirit does not perish of a single wound, nor exhaust itself in a single trial of life. Let us but keep asunder, and all may go well for both."

"We fancied ourselves forever sundered," he replied. "Yet we met once, in the bowels of the earth; and, were we to part now, our fates would fling us together again in a desert, on a mountain-top, or in whatever spot seemed safest. You speak in vain, therefore."

"You mistake your own will for an iron necessity," said Miriam; "otherwise, you might have suffered me to glide past you like a ghost, when we met among those ghosts of ancient days. Even now you might bid me pass as freely."

"Never!" said he, with unmitigable will; "your reappearance has destroyed the work of years. You know the power that I have over you. Obey my bidding; or, within a short time, it shall be exercised: nor will I cease to haunt you till the moment comes."

"Then," said Miriam, more calmly, "I foresee the end, and have already warned you of it. It will be death!"

"Your own death, Miriam,—or mine?" he asked, looking fixedly at her.

"Do you imagine me a murderess?" said she, shuddering; "you, at least, have no right to think me so!"

"Yet," rejoined he, with a glance of dark meaning, "men have said that this white hand had once a crimson stain." He took her hand as he spoke, and held it in his own, in spite of the repugnance, amounting to nothing short of agony, with which she struggled to regain it. Holding it up to the fading light (for there was already dimness among the trees), he appeared to examine it closely, as if to discover the imaginary blood-stain with which he taunted her. He smiled as he let it go. "It looks very white," said he; "but I have known hands as white, which all the water in the ocean would not have washed clean."

"It had no stain," retorted Miriam, bitterly, "until you grasped it in your own."

The wind has blown away whatever else they may have spoken.

They went together towards the town, and, on their way, continued to make reference, no doubt, to some strange and dreadful history of their former life, belonging equally to this dark man and to the fair and youthful woman whom he persecuted. In their words, or in the breath that uttered them, there seemed to be an odor of guilt, and a scent of blood. Yet, how can we imagine that a stain of ensanguined crime should attach to Miriam! Or how, on the other hand, should spotless innocence be subjected to a thraldom like that which she endured from the spectre, whom she herself had evoked out of the darkness! Be this as it might, Miriam, we have reason to believe, still continued to beseech him, humbly, passionately, wildly, only to go his way, and leave her free to follow her own sad path.

Thus they strayed onward through the green wilderness of the Borghese grounds, and soon came near the city wall, where, had Miriam raised her eyes, she might have seen Hilda and the sculptor leaning on the parapet. But she walked in a mist of trouble, and could distinguish little beyond its limits. As they came within public observation, her persecutor fell behind, throwing off the imperious manner which he had assumed during their solitary interview. The Porta del Popolo swarmed with life. The merry-makers, who had spent the feast-day outside the walls, were now thronging in; a party of horsemen were entering beneath the arch; a travelling-carriage had been drawn up just within the verge, and was passing through the villanous ordeal of the papal custom-house. In the broad piazza, too, there was a motley crowd.

But the stream of Miriam's trouble kept its way through this flood of human life, and neither mingled with it nor was turned aside. With a sad kind of feminine ingenuity, she found a way to kneel before her tyrant undetected, though in full sight of all the people, still beseeching him for freedom, and in vain.

CHAPTER XII

A STROLL ON THE PINCIAN

HILDA, after giving the last touches to the picture of Beatrice Cenci, had flown down from her dove-cote, late in the afternoon, and gone to the Pincian Hill, in the hope of hearing a strain or two of exhilarating music. There, as it happened, she met the sculptor; for, to say the truth, Kenyon had well noted the fair artist's ordinary way of life, and was accustomed to shape his own movements, so as to bring him often within her sphere.

The Pincian Hill is the favorite promenade of the Roman aristocracy. At the present day, however, like most other Roman possessions, it belongs less to the native inhabitants than to the barbarians from Gaul, Great Britain, and beyond the sea, who have established a peaceful usurpation over whatever is enjoyable or memorable in the Eternal City. These foreign guests are indeed ungrateful, if they do not breathe a prayer for Pope Clement, or whatever Holy Father it may have been, who levelled the summit of the mount so skilfully, and bounded it with the parapet of the city wall; who laid out those broad walks and drives, and overhung them with the deepening shade of many kinds of tree; who scattered the flowers of all seasons, and of every clime, abundantly over those green, central lawns; who scooped out hollows, in fit places, and, setting great basins of marble in them, caused ever-gushing fountains to fill them to the brim; who reared up the immemorial obelisk out of the soil that had long hidden it; who placed pedestals along the borders of the avenues, and crowned them with busts of that multitude of worthies

—statesmen, heroes, artists, men of letters and of song—whom the whole world claims as its chief ornaments, though Italy produced them all. In a word, the Pincian garden is one of the things that reconcile the stranger (since he fully appreciates the enjoyment, and feels nothing of the cost) to the rule of an irresponsible dynasty of Holy Fathers, who seem to have aimed at making life as agreeable an affair as it can well be.

In this pleasant spot, the red-trousered French soldiers are always to be seen; bearded and grizzled veterans, perhaps with medals of Algiers or the Crimea on their breasts. To them is assigned the peaceful duty of seeing that children do not trample on the flower-beds, nor any youthful lover rifle them of their fragrant blossoms to stick in the beloved one's hair. Here sits (drooping upon some marble bench, in the treacherous sunshine) the consumptive girl, whose friends have brought her, for cure, to a climate that instils poison into its very purest breath. Here, all day, come nursery-maids, burdened with rosy English babies, or guiding the footsteps of little travellers from the far Western world. Here, in the sunny afternoons, roll and rumble all kinds of equipages, from the cardinal's old-fashioned and gorgeous purple carriage to the gay barouche of modern date. Here horsemen gallop on thoroughbred steeds. Here, in short, all the transitory population of Rome, the world's great watering-place, rides, drives, or promenades! Here are beautiful sunsets; and here, whichever way you turn your eyes, are scenes as well worth gazing at, both in themselves and for their historic interest, as any that the sun ever rose and set upon. Here, too, on certain afternoons of the week, a French military band flings out rich music over the poor old city, floating her with strains as loud as those of her own echoless triumphs.

Hilda and the sculptor (by the contrivance of the latter, who loved best to be alone with his young country-woman) had wandered beyond the throng of promenaders, whom they left in a dense cluster around the music. They strayed, indeed, to the farthest point of the Pincian Hill, and leaned over the parapet, looking down upon the Muro Torto, a massive fragment of the oldest Roman wall, which juts over, as if ready to tumble down by its own weight, yet seems still the most indestructible piece of work that men's hands ever piled together. In the blue distance rose Soracte, and other heights, which have gleamed afar, to our imaginations, but look scarcely real to our bodily eyes, because, being dreamed about so much, they have taken the aerial tints which belong only to a dream. These, nevertheless, are the solid frame-work of hills that shut in Rome, and its wide surrounding Campagna; no land of dreams, but the broadest page of history, crowded so full with memorable events that one obliterates another; as if Time had crossed and recrossed his own records till they grew illegible.

But, not to meddle with history,—with which our narrative is no otherwise concerned, than that the very dust of Rome is historic, and inevitably settles on our page and mingles with our ink,—we will return to our two friends, who were still leaning over the wall. Beneath them lay the broad sweep of the Borghese grounds, covered with trees, amid which appeared the white gleam of pillars and statues, and the flash of an up-springing fountain, all to be overshadowed at a later period of the year by the thicker growth of foliage.

The advance of vegetation, in this softer climate, is less abrupt than the inhabitant of the cold North is accustomed to observe. Beginning earlier, —even in February,—Spring is not compelled to burst into Summer with such headlong haste; there is time to dwell upon each opening beauty, and to enjoy the budding leaf, the tender green, the sweet youth and freshness of the year; it gives us its maiden charm, before settling into the married Summer, which, again, does not so soon sober itself into matronly Autumn. In our own country, the virgin Spring hastens to its bridal too abruptly. But, here, after a month or two of kindly growth, the leaves of the young trees, which cover that portion of the Borghese grounds nearest the city wall, were still in their tender half-development.

In the remoter depths, among the old groves of ilex-trees, Hilda and Kenyon heard the faint sound of music, laughter, and mingling voices. It was probably the uproar—spreading even so far as the walls of Rome, and growing faded and melancholy in its passage—of that wild sylvan merriment, which we have already attempted to describe. By and by, it ceased; although the two listeners still tried to distinguish it between the bursts of nearer music from the military band. But there was no renewal of that distant mirth. Soon afterwards, they saw a solitary figure advancing along one of the paths that lead from the obscurer part of the ground towards the gateway.

"Look! is it not Donatello?" said Hilda.

"He it is, beyond a doubt," replied the sculptor. "But how gravely he walks, and with what long looks behind him! He seems either very weary, or very sad. I should not hesitate to call it sadness, if Donatello were a creature capable of the sin and folly of low spirits. In all these hundred paces, while we have been watching him, he has not made one of those little caprioles in the air which are characteristic of his natural gait. I begin to doubt whether he is a veritable Faun."

"Then," said Hilda, with perfect simplicity, "you have thought him—and do think him—one of that strange, wild, happy race of creatures, that used to laugh and sport in the woods, in the old, old times? So do I, indeed! But I never quite believed, till now, that fauns existed anywhere but in poetry."

The sculptor at first merely smiled. Then, as the idea took further possession of his mind, he laughed outright, and wished from the bottom of his heart (being in love with Hilda, though he had never told her so) that he could have rewarded or punished her for its pretty absurdity with a kiss.

"O Hilda, what a treasure of sweet faith and pure imagination you hide under that little straw hat!" cried he, at length. "A Faun! a Faun! Great Pan is not dead, then, after all! The whole tribe of mythical creatures yet live in the moonlit seclusion of a young girl's fancy, and find it a lovelier abode and play-place, I doubt not, than their Arcadian haunts of yore. What bliss, if a man of marble, like myself, could stray thither, too!"

"Why do you laugh so?" asked Hilda, reddening; for she was a little disturbed at Kenyon's ridicule, however kindly expressed. "What can I have said, that you think so very foolish?"

"Well, not foolish, then," rejoined the sculptor, "but wiser, it may be, than I can fathom. Really, however, the idea does strike one as delightfully fresh, when we consider Donatello's position and external environment. Why, my dear Hilda, he is a Tuscan born, of an old noble race in that part of Italy; and he has a moss-grown tower among the Apennines, where he and his forefathers have dwelt, under their own vines and fig-trees, from an unknown antiquity. His boyish passion for Miriam has introduced him familiarly to our little circle; and our republican and artistic simplicity of intercourse has included this young Italian, on the same terms as one of ourselves. But, if we paid due respect to rank and title, we should bend reverentially to Donatello, and salute him as his Excellency the Count di Monte Beni."

"That is a droll idea,—much droller than his being a Faun!" said Hilda, laughing in her turn. "This does not quite satisfy me, however, especially as you yourself recognized and acknowledged his wonderful resemblance to the statue."

"Except as regards the pointed ears," said Kenyon; adding, aside, "and one other little peculiarity, generally observable in the statues of fauns."

"As for his Excellency the Count di Monte Beni's ears," replied Hilda, smiling again at the dignity with which this title invested their playful friend, "you know we could never see their shape, on account of his clustering curls. Nay, I remember, he once started back, as shyly as a wild deer, when Miriam made a pretense of examining them. How do you explain that?"

"Oh, I certainly shall not contend against such a weight of evidence; the fact of his faunship being otherwise so probable," answered the sculptor, still hardly retaining his gravity. "Faun or not, Donatello—or the Count di Monte Beni—is a singularly wild creature, and, as I have remarked on other occasions, though very gentle, does not love to be touched. Speaking in no harsh sense, there is a great deal of animal nature in him, as if he had been born in the woods, and had run wild all his childhood, and were as yet but imperfectly domesticated. Life, even in our day, is very simple and unsophisticated in some of the shaggy nooks of the Apennines."

"It annoys me very much," said Hilda, "this inclination, which most people have, to explain away the wonder and the mystery out of everything. Why could not you allow me—and yourself, too—the satisfaction of thinking him a Faun?"

"Pray keep your belief, dear Hilda, if it makes you any happier," said the sculptor; "and I shall do my best to become a convert. Donatello has asked me to spend the summer with him, in his ancestral tower, where I purpose investigating the pedigree of these sylvan counts, his forefatners; and if their shadows beckon me into dreamland, I shall willingly follow. By the by, speaking of Donatello, there is a point on which I should like to be enlightened."

"Can I help you, then?" said Hilda, in answer to his look.

"Is there the slightest chance of his winning Miriam's affections?" suggested Kenyon.

"Miriam! she, so accomplished and gifted!" exclaimed Hilda; "and he, a rude, uncultivated boy! No, no, no!"

"It would seem impossible," said the sculptor. "But, on the other hand, a gifted woman flings away her affections so unaccountably, sometimes! Miriam, of late, has been very morbid and miserable, as we both know. Young as she is, the morning light seems already to have faded out of her life; and now comes Donatello, with natural sunshine enough for himself and her, and offers her the opportunity of making her heart and life all new and cheery again. People of high intellectual endowments do not require similar ones in those they love. They are just the persons to appreciate the wholesome gush of natural feeling, the honest affection, the simple joy, the fulness of contentment with what he loves, which Miriam sees in Donatello. True; she may call him a simpleton. It is a necessity of the case; for a man loses the capacity for this kind of affection, in proportion as he cultivates and refines himself."

"Dear me!" said Hilda, drawing imperceptibly away from her companion. "Is this the penalty of refinement? Pardon me; I do not believe it. It is because you are a sculptor, that you think nothing can be finely wrought except it be cold and hard, like the marble in which your ideas take shape. I am a painter, and know that the most delicate beauty may be softened and warmed throughout."

"I said a foolish thing, indeed," answered the sculptor. "It surprises me, for I might have drawn a wiser knowledge out of my own experience. It is the surest test of genuine love, that it brings back our early simplicity to the worldliest of us."

Thus talking, they loitered slowly along beside the parapet which borders the level summit of the Pincian with its irregular sweep. At intervals they looked through the lattice-work of their thoughts at the varied prospects that lay before and beneath them.

From the terrace where they now stood there is an abrupt descent towards the Piazza del Popolo; and looking down into its broad space they beheld the tall palatial edifices, the church-domes, and the ornamented gateway, which grew and were consolidated out of the thought of Michael Angelo. They saw, too, the red granite obelisk, oldest of things, even in Rome, which rises in the centre of the piazza, with a fourfold fountain at its base. All Roman works and ruins (whether of the empire, the far-off republic, or the still more distant kings) assume a transient, visionary, and impalpable character when we think that this indestructible monument supplied one of the recollections which Moses and the Israelites bore from Egypt into the desert. Perchance, on beholding the cloudy pillar and the fiery column, they whispered awe-stricken to one another, "In its shape it is like that old obelisk which we and our fathers have so often seen on the borders of the Nile." And now that very obelisk, with hardly a trace of decay upon it, is the first thing that the modern traveller sees after entering the Flaminian Gate!

Lifting their eyes, Hilda and her companion gazed westward, and saw beyond the invisible Tiber the Castle of St. Angelo; that immense tomb of a pagan emperor, with the archangel at its summit.

Still farther off appeared a mighty pile of buildings, surmounted by the vast dome, which all of us have shaped and swelled outward, like a huge bubble, to the utmost scope of our imaginations, long before we see it floating over the worship of the city. It may be most worthily seen from precisely the point where our two friends were now standing. At any nearer view the grandeur of St. Peter's hides itself behind the immensity of its separate parts, so that we see only the front, only the sides, only the pillared length and loftiness of the portico, and not the mighty whole. But at this distance the entire outline of the world's cathedral, as well as that of the palace of the world's chief priest, is taken in at once. In such remoteness, moreover, the imagination is not debarred from lending its assistance, even while we have the reality before our eyes, and helping the weakness of human sense to do justice to so grand an object. It requires both faith and fancy to enable us to feel, what is nevertheless so true, that yonder, in front of the purple outline of hills, is the grandest edifice ever built by man, painted against God's loveliest sky.

After contemplating a little while a scene which their long residence in Rome had made familiar to them, Kenyon and Hilda again let their glances fall into the piazza at their feet. They there beheld Miriam, who had just entered the Porta del Popolo, and was standing by the obelisk and fountain. With a gesture that impressed Kenyon as at once suppliant and imperious, she seemed to intimate to a figure which had attended her thus far, that it was now her desire to be left alone. The pertinacious model, however, remained immovable.

And the sculptor here noted a circumstance, which, according to the interpretation he might put upon it, was either too trivial to be mentioned, or else so mysteriously significant that he found it difficult to believe his eyes. Miriam knelt down on the steps of the fountain; so far there could be no question of the fact. To other observers, if any there were, she probably appeared to take this attitude merely for the convenience of dipping her fingers into the gush of water from the mouth of one of the stone lions. But as she clasped her hands together after thus bathing them, and glanced upward at the model, an idea took strong possession of Kenyon's mind that Miriam was kneeling to this dark follower there in the world's face!

"Do you see it?" he said to Hilda.

"See what?" asked she, surprised at the emotion of his tone. "I see

Miriam, who has just bathed her hands in that delightfully cool water. I often dip my fingers into a Roman fountain, and think of the brook that used to be one of my playmates in my New England village."

"I fancied I saw something else," said Kenyon; "but it was doubtless a mistake."

But, allowing that he had caught a true glimpse into the hidden significance of Miriam's gesture, what a terrible thraldom did it suggest! Free as she seemed to be,—beggar as he looked,—the nameless vagrant must then be dragging the beautiful Miriam through the streets of Rome, fettered and shackled more cruelly than any captive queen of yore following in an emperor's triumph. And was it conceivable that she would have been thus enthralled unless some great error—how great Kenyon dared not think—or some fatal weakness had given this dark adversary a vantage-ground?

"Hilda," said he, abruptly, "who and what is Miriam? Pardon me; but are you sure of her?"

"Sure of her!" repeated Hilda, with an angry blush, for her friend's sake. "I am sure that she is kind, good, and generous; a true and faithful friend, whom I love dearly, and who loves me as well! What more than this need I be sure of?"

"And your delicate instincts say all this in her favor?—nothing against her?" continued the sculptor, without heeding the irritation of Hilda's tone. "These are my own impressions, too. But she is such a mystery! We do not even know whether she is a countrywoman of ours, or an English-woman, or a German. There is Anglo-Saxon blood in her veins, one would say, and a right English accent on her tongue, but much that is not English breeding, nor American. Nowhere else but in Rome, and as an artist, could she hold a place in society without giving some clew to her past life."

"I love her dearly," said Hilda, still with displeasure in her tone, "and trust her most entirely."

"My heart trusts her at least, whatever my head may do," replied Kenyon; "and Rome is not like one of our New England villages, where we need the permission of each individual neighbor for every act that we do, every word that we utter, and every friend that we make or keep. In these particulars the papal despotism allows us freer breath than our native air; and if we like to take generous views of our associates, we can do so, to a reasonable extent, without ruining ourselves."

"The music has ceased," said Hilda; "I am going now."

There are three streets that, beginning close beside each other, diverge from the Piazza del Popolo towards the heart of Rome: on the left, the Via del Babuino; on the right, the Via della Ripetta; and between these two that world-famous avenue, the Corso. It appeared that Miriam and her strange companion were passing up the first-mentioned of these three, and were soon hidden from Hilda and the sculptor.

The two latter left the Pincian by the broad and stately walk that skirts along its brow. Beneath them, from the base of the abrupt descent, the city spread wide away in a close contiguity of red-earthen roofs, above which rose eminent the domes of a hundred churches, beside here and there a tower, and the upper windows of some taller or higher situated palace, looking down on a multitude of palatial abodes. At a distance, ascending out of the central mass of edifices, they could see the top of the Antonine column, and near it the circular roof of the Pantheon looking heavenward with its ever-open eye.

Except these two objects, almost everything that they beheld was mediæval, though built, indeed, of the massive old stones and indestructible bricks of imperial Rome; for the ruins of the Coliseum, the Golden House, and innumerable temples of Roman gods, and mansions of Cæsars and senators, had supplied the material for all those gigantic hovels, and their walls were cemented with mortar of inestimable cost, being made of precious antique statues, burnt long ago for this petty purpose.

Rome, as it now exists, has grown up under the Popes, and seems like nothing but a heap of broken rubbish, thrown into the great chasm between our own days and the Empire, merely to fill it up; and, for the better part of two thousand years, its annals of obscure policies, and wars, and continually recurring misfortunes, seem also but broken rubbish, as compared with its classic history.

If we consider the present city as at all connected with the famous one of old, it is only because we find it built over its grave. A depth of thirty feet of soil has covered up the Rome of ancient days, so that it lies like the dead corpse of a giant, decaying for centuries, with no survivor mighty enough even to bury it, until the dust of all those years has gathered slowly over its recumbent form and made a casual sepulchre.

We know not how to characterize, in any accordant and compatible terms, the Rome that lies before us; its sunless alleys, and streets of palaces; its churches, lined with the gorgeous marbles that were originally polished for the adornment of pagan temples; its thousands of evil smells, mixed up with fragrance of rich incense, diffused from as many censers; its little life, deriving feeble nutriment from what has long been dead. Everywhere, some fragment of ruin suggesting the magnificence of a former epoch; everywhere, moreover, a Cross,—and nastiness at the foot of it. As the sum of all, there are recollections that kindle the soul, and a gloom and languor that depress it beyond any depth of melancholic sentiment that can be elsewhere known.

Yet how is it possible to say an unkind or irreverential word of Rome? The city of all time, and of all the world! The spot for which man's great life and deeds have done so much, and for which decay has done whatever glory and dominion could not do! At this moment, the evening sunshine is flinging its golden mantle over it, making all that we thought mean magnificent; the bells of all the churches suddenly ring out, as if it were a peal of triumph because Rome is still imperial.

"I sometimes fancy," said Hilda, on whose susceptibility the scene always made a strong impression, "that Rome—mere Rome—will crowd everything else out of my heart."

"Heaven forbid!" ejaculated the sculptor.

They had now reached the grand stairs that ascend from the Piazza di Spagna to the hither brow of the Pincian Hill. Old Beppo, the millionnaire of his ragged fraternity,—it is a wonder that no artist paints him as the cripple whom St. Peter heals at the Beautiful Gate of the Temple,—was just mounting his donkey to depart, laden with the rich spoil of the day's beggary.

Up the stairs, drawing his tattered cloak about his face, came the model, at whom Beppo looked askance, jealous of an encroacher on his rightful domain. The figure passed away, however, up the Via Sistina. In the piazza below, near the foot of the magnificent steps, stood Miriam, with her eyes bent on the ground, as if she were counting those little, square, uncomfortable paving-stones, that make it a penitential pilgrimage to walk in Rome. She kept this attitude for several minutes, and when, at last, the importunities of a beggar disturbed her from it, she seemed bewildered and pressed her hand upon her brow.

"She has been in some sad dream or other, poor thing!" said Kenyon, sympathizingly; "and even now, she is imprisoned there in a kind of cage, the iron bars of which are made of her own thoughts."

"I fear she is not well," said Hilda. "I am going down the stairs, and will join Miriam."

"Farewell, then," said the sculptor. "Dear Hilda, this is a perplexed and troubled world! It soothes me inexpressibly to think of you in your tower, with white doves and white thoughts for your companions, so high above us all, and with the Virgin for your household friend. You know not how far it throws its light, that lamp which you keep burning at her shrine! I passed beneath the tower last night, and the ray cheered me,— because you lighted it."

"It has for me a religious significance," replied Hilda, quietly, "and yet I am no Catholic."

They parted, and Kenyon made haste along the Via Sistina, in the hope of overtaking the model, whose haunts and character he was anxious to investigate, for Miriam's sake. He fancied that he saw him a long way in advance, but before he reached the Fountain of the Triton, the dusky figure had vanished.

## CHAPTER XIII

### A SCULPTOR'S STUDIO

ABOUT this period, Miriam seems to have been goaded by a weary restlessness that drove her abroad on any errand or none. She went one morning to visit Kenyon in his studio, whither he had invited her to see a new statue, on which he had staked many hopes, and which was now almost completed in the clay. Next to Hilda, the person for whom Miriam felt most affection and confidence was Kenyon; and in all the difficulties that beset her life, it was her impulse to draw near Hilda for feminine sympathy, and the sculptor for brotherly counsel.

Yet it was to little purpose that she approached the edge of the voiceless gulf between herself and them. Standing on the utmost verge of that dark chasm, she might stretch out her hand, and never clasp a hand of theirs; she might strive to call out, "Help, friends! help!" but, as with dreamers when they shout, her voice would perish inaudibly in the remoteness that seemed such a little way. This perception of an infinite, shivering solitude, amid which we cannot come close enough to human beings to be warmed by them, and where they turn to cold, chilly shapes of mist, is one of the most forlorn results of any accident, misfortune, crime, or peculiarity of character, that puts an individual ajar with the world. Very often, as in Miriam's case, there is an insatiable instinct that demands friendship, love, and intimate communion, but is forced to pine in empty forms; a hunger of the heart, which finds only shadows to feed upon.

Kenyon's studio was in a cross-street, or, rather, an ugly and dirty little lane, between the Corso and the Via della Ripetta; and though chill, narrow, gloomy, and bordered with tall and shabby structures, the lane was not a whit more disagreeable than nine tenths of the Roman streets. Over the door of one of the houses was a marble tablet, bearing an inscription, to the purport that the sculpture-rooms within had formerly been occupied by the illustrious artist Canova. In these precincts (which Canova's genius was not quite of a character to render sacred, though it certainly made them interesting) the young American sculptor had now established himself.

The studio of a sculptor is generally but a rough and dreary-looking place, with a good deal the aspect, indeed, of a stone-mason's workshop. Bare floors of brick or plank, and plastered walls; an old chair or two, or perhaps only a block of marble (containing, however, the possibility of ideal grace within it) to sit down upon; some hastily scrawled sketches of nude figures on the whitewash of the wall. These last are probably the sculptor's earliest glimpses of ideas that may hereafter be solidified into imperishable stone, or perhaps may remain as impalpable as a dream. Next there are a few very roughly modelled little figures in clay or plaster, exhibiting the second stage of the idea as it advances towards a marble immortality; and then is seen the exquisitely designed shape of clay, more interesting than even the final marble, as being the intimate production of the sculptor himself, moulded throughout with his loving hands, and nearest to his imagination and heart. In the plaster-cast, from this clay model, the beauty of the statue strangely disappears, to shine forth again with pure white radiance, in the precious marble of Carrara. Works in all these stages of advancement, and some with the final touch upon them, might be found in Kenyon's studio.

Here might be witnessed the process of actually chiselling the marble, with which (as it is not quite satisfactory to think) a sculptor in these days has very little to do. In Italy, there is a class of men whose merely mechanical skill is perhaps more exquisite than was possessed by the ancient artificers, who wrought out the designs of Praxiteles; or, very possibly, by Praxiteles himself. Whatever of illusive representation can be effected in marble, they are capable of achieving, if the object be before their eyes. The sculptor has but to present these men with a plaster-cast of his design, and a sufficient block of marble, and tell them that the figure is imbedded in the stone, and must be freed from its encumbering superfluities; and, in due time, without the necessity of his touching the work with his own finger, he will see before him the statue that is to make him renowned. His creative power has wrought it with a word.

In no other art, surely, does genius find such effective instruments, and so happily relieve itself of the drudgery of actual performance; doing wonderfully nice things by the hands of other people, when it may be suspected they could not always be done by the sculptor's own. And how much of the admiration which our artists get for their buttons and button-holes, their shoe-ties, their neck-cloths,—and these, at our present epoch of taste, make a large share of the renown,—would be abated, if we were generally aware that the sculptor can claim no credit for such pretty performances, as immortalized in marble! They are not his work, but that of some nameless machine in human shape.

Miriam stopped an instant in an antechamber, to look at a half-finished bust, the features of which seemed to be struggling out of the stone; and, as it were, scattering and dissolving its hard substance by the glow of feeling and intelligence. As the skilful workman gave stroke after stroke of the chisel with apparent carelessness, but sure effect, it was impossible not to think that the outer marble was merely an extraneous environment; the human countenance within its embrace must have existed there since the limestone ledges of Carrara were first made. Another bust was nearly completed, though still one of Kenyon's most trustworthy assistants was at work, giving delicate touches, shaving off an impalpable something, and leaving little heaps of marble-dust to attest it.

"As these busts in the block of marble," thought Miriam, "so does our individual fate exist in the limestone of time. We fancy that we carve it out; but its ultimate shape is prior to all our action."

Kenyon was in the inner room, but, hearing a step in the antechamber, he threw a veil over what he was at work upon, and came out to receive his visitor. He was dressed in a gray blouse, with a little cap on the top of his head; a costume which became him better than the formal garments which he wore, whenever he passed out of his own domains. The sculptor had a face which, when time had done a little more for it, would offer a worthy subject for as good an artist as himself: features finely cut, as if already marble; an ideal forehead, deeply set eyes, and a mouth much hidden in a light-brown beard, but apparently sensitive and delicate.

"I will not offer you my hand," said he; "it is grimy with Cleopatra's clay."

"No; I will not touch clay; it is earthy and human," answered Miriam. "I have come to try whether there is any calm and coolness among your marbles. My own art is too nervous, too passionate, too full of agitation, for me to work at it whole days together, without intervals of repose. So, what have you to show me?"

"Pray look at everything here," said Kenyon. "I love to have painters see my work. Their judgment is unprejudiced, and more valuable than that of the world generally, from the light which their own art throws on mine. More valuable, too, than that of my brother sculptors, who never judge me fairly,—nor I them, perhaps."

To gratify him, Miriam looked round at the specimens in marble or plaster, of which there were several in the room, comprising originals or casts of most of the designs that Kenyon had thus far produced. He was still too young to have accumulated a large gallery of such things. What he had to show were chiefly the attempts and experiments, in various directions, of a beginner in art, acting as a stern tutor to himself, and profiting more by his failures than by any successes of which he was yet capable. Some of them, however, had great merit; and in the pure, fine glow of the new marble, it may be, they dazzled the judgment into awarding them higher praise than they deserved. Miriam admired the statue of a beautiful youth, a pearl-fisher, who had got entangled in the weeds at the bottom of the sea, and lay dead among the pearl-oysters, the rich shells, and the sea-weeds, all of like value to him now.

"The poor young man has perished among the prizes that he sought," remarked she. "But what a strange efficacy there is in death! If we cannot all win pearls, it causes an empty shell to satisfy us just as well. I like this statue, though it is too cold and stern in its moral lesson; and, physically, the form has not settled itself into sufficient repose."

In another style, there was a grand, calm head of Milton, not copied from any one bust or picture, yet more authentic than any of them, because all known representations of the poet had been profoundly studied, and solved in the artist's mind. The bust over the tomb in Grey Friars Church, the original miniatures and pictures, wherever to be found, had mingled each its special truth in this one work; wherein, likewise, by long perusal and deep love of the "Paradise Lost," the "Comus," the "Lycidas," and "L'Allegro," the sculptor had succeeded, even better than he knew, in spiritualizing his marble with the poet's mighty genius. And this was a great thing to have achieved, such a length of time after the dry bones and dust of Milton were like those of any other dead man.

There were also several portrait-busts, comprising those of two or three of the illustrious men of our own country, whom Kenyon, before he left America, had asked permission to model. He had done so, because he sincerely believed that, whether he wrought the busts in marble or bronze, the one would corrode and the other crumble in the long lapse of time, beneath these great men's immortality. Possibly, however, the young artist may have under-estimated the durability of his material. Other faces there were, too, of men who (if the brevity of their remembrance, after death, can be augured from their little value in life) should have been represented in snow rather than marble. Posterity will be puzzled what to do with busts like these, the concretions and petrifactions of a vain self-estimate; but will find, no doubt, that they serve to build into stone-walls, or burn into quick-lime, as well as if the marble had never been blocked into the guise of human heads.

But it is an awful thing, indeed, this endless endurance, this almost indestructibility, of a marble bust! Whether in our own case, or that of other men, it bids us sadly measure the little, little time during which our lineaments are likely to be of interest to any human being. It is especially singular that Americans should care about perpetuating themselves in this mode. The brief duration of our families, as a hereditary household, renders it next to a certainty that the great-grandchildren will not know their father's grandfather, and that half a century hence at furthest, the hammer of the auctioneer will thump its knock-down blow against his blockhead, sold at so much for the pound of stone! And it ought to make us shiver, the idea of leaving our features to be a dusty-white ghost among strangers of another generation, who will take our nose between their thumb and fingers (as we have seen men do by Cæsar's), and infallibly break it off if they can do so without detection!

"Yes," said Miriam, who had been revolving some such thoughts as the above, "it is a good state of mind for mortal man, when he is content to leave no more definite memorial than the grass, which will sprout kindly and speedily over his grave, if we do not make the spot barren with marble. Methinks, too, it will be a fresher and better world, when it flings off this great burden of stony memories, which the ages have deemed it a piety to heap upon its back."

"What you say," remarked Kenyon, "goes against my whole art. Sculpture, and the delight which men naturally take in it, appear to me a proof that it is good to work with all time before our view."

"Well, well," answered Miriam, "I must not quarrel with you for flinging your heavy stones at poor Posterity; and, to say the truth, I think you are as li'ely to hit the mark as anybody. These busts, now, much as I seem to scorn them, make me feel as if you were a magician. You turn feverish men into cool, quiet marble. What a blessed change for them! Would you could do as much for me!"

"Oh, gladly!" cried Kenyon, who had long wished to model that beautiful and most expressive face. "When will you begin to sit?"

"Poh! that was not what I meant," said Miriam. "Come, show me something else."

"Do you recognize this?" asked the sculptor.

He took out of his desk a little old-fashioned ivory coffer, yellow with age; it was richly carved with antique figures and foliage; and had Kenyon thought fit to say that Benvenuto Cellini wrought this precious box,

the skill and elaborate fancy of the work would by no means have discredited his word, nor the old artist's fame. At least, it was evidently a
production of Benvenuto's school and century, and might once have been
the jewel-case of some grand lady at the court of the De' Medici.

Lifting the lid, however, no blaze of diamonds was disclosed, but only,
lapped in fleecy cotton, a small, beautifully shaped hand, most delicately
sculptured in marble. Such loving care and nicest art had been lavished
here, that the palm really seemed to have a tenderness in its very substance. Touching those lovely fingers,—had the jealous sculptor allowed
you to touch,—you could hardly believe that a virgin warmth would not
steal from them into your heart.

"Ah, this is very beautiful!" exclaimed Miriam, with a genial smile.
"It is as good in its way as Loulie's hand with its baby-dimples, which
Powers showed me at Florence, evidently valuing it as much as if he had
wrought it out of a piece of his great heart. As good as Harriet Hosmer's
clasped hands of Browning and his wife, symbolizing the individuality
and heroic union of two high, poetic lives! Nay, I do not question that it
is better than either of those, because you must have wrought it passionately, in spite of its maiden palm and dainty finger-tips."

"Then you do recognize it?" asked Kenyon.

"There is but one right hand on earth that could have supplied the
model," answered Miriam; "so small and slender, so perfectly symmetri-
cal, and yet with a character of delicate energy. I have watched it a hundred times at its work; but I did not dream that you had won Hilda so
far! How have you persuaded that shy maiden to let you take her hand
in marble?"

"Never! She never knew it!" hastily replied Kenyon, anxious to vindicate his mistress's maidenly reserve. "I stole it from her. The hand is a
reminiscence. After gazing at it so often, and even holding it once for an
instant, when Hilda was not thinking of me, I should be a bungler indeed,
if I could not now reproduce it to something like the life."

"May you win the original one day!" said Miriam, kindly.

"I have little ground to hope it," answered the sculptor, despondingly;
"Hilda does not dwell in our mortal atmosphere; and gentle and soft as
she appears, it will be as difficult to win her heart as to entice down a
white bird from its sunny freedom in the sky. It is strange, with all her
delicacy and fragility, the impression she makes of being utterly sufficient
to herself. No; I shall never win her. She is abundantly capable of sympathy, and delights to receive it, but she has no need of love."

"I partly agree with you," said Miriam. "It is a mistaken idea, which
men generally entertain, that nature has made women especially prone to
throw their whole being into what is technically called love. We have, to
say the least, no more necessity for it than yourselves; only we have
nothing else to do with our hearts. When women have other objects in life,
they are not apt to fall in love. I can think of many women distinguished
in art, literature, and science,—and multitudes whose hearts and minds
find good employment in less ostentatious ways,—who lead high, lonely

lives, and are conscious of no sacrifice so far as your sex is concerned."

"And Hilda will be one of these!" said Kenyon, sadly; "the thought makes me shiver for myself, and—and for her, too."

"Well," said Miriam, smiling, "perhaps she may sprain the delicate wrist which you have sculptured to such perfection. In that case you may hope. These old masters to whom she has vowed herself, and whom her slender hand and woman's heart serve so faithfully, are your only rivals."

The sculptor sighed as he put away the treasure of Hilda's marble hand into the ivory coffer, and thought how slight was the possibility that he should ever feel responsive to his own the tender clasp of the original. He dared not even kiss the image that he himself had made: it had assumed its share of Hilda's remote and shy divinity.

"And now," said Miriam, "show me the new statue which you asked me hither to see."

## CHAPTER XIV

### CLEOPATRA

"MY new statue!" said Kenyon, who had positively forgotten it in the thought of Hilda; "here it is, under this veil."

"Not a nude figure, I hope," observed Miriam. "Every young sculptor seems to think that he must give the world some specimen of indecorous womanhood, and call it Eve, Venus, a Nymph, or any name that may apologize for a lack of decent clothing. I am weary, even more than I am ashamed, of seeing such things. Nowadays people are as good as born in their clothes, and there is practically not a nude human being in existence. An artist, therefore, as you must candidly confess, cannot sculpture nudity with a pure heart, if only because he is compelled to steal guilty glimpses at hired models. The marble inevitably loses its chastity under such circumstances. An old Greek sculptor, no doubt, found his models in the open sunshine, and among pure and princely maidens, and thus the nude statues of antiquity are as modest as violets, and sufficiently draped in their own beauty. But as for Mr. Gibson's colored Venuses (stained, I believe, with tobacco-juice), and all other nudities of to-day, I really do not understand what they have to say to this generation, and would be glad to see as many heaps of quicklime in their stead."

"You are severe upon the professors of my art," said Kenyon, half smiling, half seriously; "not that you are wholly wrong, either. We are bound to accept drapery of some kind, and make the best of it. But what are we to do? Must we adopt the costume of to-day, and carve, for example, a Venus in a hoop-petticoat?"

"That would be a bowlder, indeed!" rejoined Miriam, laughing. "But the difficulty goes to confirm me in my belief that, except for portrait-busts, sculpture has no longer a right to claim any place among living arts. It has wrought itself out, and come fairly to an end. There is never a new group nowadays; never even so much as a new attitude. Greenough (I take my examples among men of merit) imagined nothing new; nor Crawford either, except in the tailoring line. There are not, as you will own, more than half a dozen positively original statues or groups in the world, and these few are of immemorial antiquity. A person familiar with the Vatican, the Uffizzi Gallery, the Naples Gallery, and the Louvre, will at once refer any modern production to its antique prototype; which, moreover, had begun to get out of fashion, even in old Roman days."

"Pray stop, Miriam," cried Kenyon, "or I shall fling away the chisel forever!"

"Fairly own to me, then, my friend," rejoined Miriam, whose disturbed mind found a certain relief in this declamation, "that you sculptors are, of necessity, the greatest plagiarists in the world."

"I do not own it," said Kenyon, "yet cannot utterly contradict you, as regards the actual state of the art. But as long as the Carrara quarries still yield pure blocks, and while my own country has marble mountains, probably as fine in quality, I shall steadfastly believe that future sculptors will revive this noblest of the beautiful arts, and people the world with new shapes of delicate grace and massive grandeur. Perhaps," he added, smiling, "mankind will consent to wear a more manageable costume; or, at worst, we sculptors shall get the skill to make broadcloth transparent, and render a majestic human character visible through the coats and trousers of the present day."

"Be it so!" said Miriam; "you are past my counsel. Show me the veiled figure, which I am afraid, I have criticised beforehand. To make amends, I am in the mood to praise it now."

But, as Kenyon was about to take the cloth off the clay model, she laid her hand on his arm.

"Tell me first what is the subject," said she, "for I have sometimes incurred great displeasure from members of your brotherhood by being too obtuse to puzzle out the purport of their productions. It is so difficult, you know, to compress and define a character or story, and make it patent at a glance, within the narrow scope attainable by sculpture! Indeed I fancy it is still the ordinary habit with sculptors, first to finish their group of statuary,—in such development as the particular block of marble will allow,—and then to choose the subject; as John of Bologna did with his 'Rape of the Sabines.' Have you followed that good example?"

"No; my statue is intended for Cleopatra," replied Kenyon, a little disturbed by Miriam's raillery. "The special epoch of her history you must make out for yourself."

He drew away the cloth that had served to keep the moisture of the clay model from being exhaled. The sitting figure of a woman was seen. She was draped from head to foot in a costume minutely and scrupulously studied from that of ancient Egypt, as revealed by the strange sculpture of that country, its coins, drawings, painted mummy-cases, and whatever other tokens have been dug out of its pyramids, graves, and catacombs. Even the stiff Egyptian head-dress was adhered to, but had been softened into a rich feminine adornment, without losing a particle of its truth. Difficulties that might well have seemed insurmountable had been courageously encountered and made flexible to purposes of grace and dignity; so that Cleopatra sat attired in a garb proper to her historic and queenly state, as a daughter of the Ptolemies, and yet such as the beautiful woman would have put on as best adapted to heighten the magnificence of her charms, and kindle a tropic fire in the cold eyes of Octavius.

A marvellous repose—that rare merit in statuary, except it be the lumpish repose native to the block of stone—was diffused throughout the figure. The spectator felt that Cleopatra had sunk down out of the fever and turmoil of her life, and for one instant—as it were, between two pulse-throbs—had relinquished all activity, and was resting throughout every vein and muscle. It was the repose of despair, indeed; for Octavius had seen her, and remained insensible to her enchantments. But still there was a great smouldering furnace deep down in the woman's heart. The repose, no doubt, was as complete as if she were never to stir hand or foot again; and yet, such was the creature's latent energy and fierceness, she might spring upon you like a tigress, and stop the very breath that you were now drawing midway in your throat.

The face was a miraculous success. The sculptor had not shunned to give the full Nubian lips, and other characteristics of the Egyptian physiognomy. His courage and integrity had been abundantly rewarded; for Cleopatra's beauty shone out richer, warmer, more triumphantly beyond comparison, than if, shrinking timidly from the truth, he had chosen the tame Grecian type. The expression was of profound, gloomy, heavily revolving thought; a glance into her past life and present emergencies, while her spirit gathered itself up for some new struggle, or was getting sternly reconciled to impending doom. In one view, there was a certain softness and tenderness,—how breathed into the statue, among so many strong and passionate elements, it is impossible to say. Catching another glimpse, you beheld her as implacable as a stone and cruel as fire.

In a word, all Cleopatra—fierce, voluptuous, passionate, tender, wicked, terrible, and full of poisonous and rapturous enchantment—was kneaded into what, only a week or two before, had been a lump of wet clay from the Tiber. Soon, apotheosized in an indestructible material, she would be one of the images that men keep forever, finding a heat in them which does not cool down, throughout the centuries.

"What a woman is this!" exclaimed Miriam, after a long pause. "Tell me, did she ever try, even while you were creating her, to overcome you with her fury or her love? Were you not afraid to touch her, as she grew more and more towards hot life beneath your hand? My dear friend, it is a great work! How have you learned to do it?"

"It is the concretion of a good deal of thought, emotion, and toil of brain and hand," said Kenyon, not without a perception that his work was good; "but I know not how it came about at last. I kindled a great fire within my mind, and threw in the material,—as Aaron threw the gold of the Israelites into the furnace,—and in the midmost heat uprose Cleopatra, as you see her."

"What I most marvel at," said Miriam, "is the womanhood that you have so thoroughly mixed up with all those seemingly discordant elements. Where did you get that secret? You never found it in your gentle Hilda, yet I recognize its truth."

"No, surely, it was not in Hilda," said Kenyon. "Her womanhood is of the ethereal type, and incompatible with any shadow of darkness or evil."

"You are right," rejoined Miriam; "there are women of that ethereal type as you term it, and Hilda is one of them. She would die of her first wrong-doing,—supposing for a moment that she could be capable of doing wrong. Of sorrow, slender as she seems, Hilda might bear a great burden; of sin, not a feather's weight. Methinks now, were it my doom, I could bear either, or both at once; but my conscience is still as white as Hilda's. Do you question it?"

"Heaven forbid, Miriam!" exclaimed the sculptor.

He was startled at the strange turn which she had so suddenly given to the conversation. Her voice, too,—so much emotion was stifled rather than expressed in it,—sounded unnatural.

"Oh, my friend," cried she, with sudden passion, "will you be my friend indeed? I am lonely, lonely, lonely! There is a secret in my heart that burns me,—that tortures me! Sometimes I fear to go mad of it; sometimes I hope to die of it; but neither of the two happens. Ah, if I could but whisper it to only one human soul! And you—you see far into womanhood; you receive it widely into your large view. Perhaps—perhaps, but Heaven only knows, you might understand me! Oh, let me speak!"

"Miriam, dear friend," replied the sculptor, "if I can help you, speak freely, as to a brother."

"Help me? No!" said Miriam.

Kenyon's respose had been perfectly frank and kind; and yet the subtlety of Miriam's emotion detected a certain reserve and alarm in his warmly expressed readiness to hear her story. In his secret soul, to say the truth, the sculptor doubted whether it were well for this poor, suffering girl to speak what she so yearned to say, or for him to listen. If there were any active duty of friendship to be performed, then, indeed, he would joyfully have come forward to do his best. But if it were only a pent-up heart that sought an outlet? in that case it was by no means so certain that a confession would do good. The more her secret struggled and fought to be told, the more certain would it be to change all former relations that had subsisted between herself and the friend to whom she might reveal it. Unless he could give her all the sympathy, and just the kind of sympathy that the occasion required, Miriam would hate him by and by, and herself still more, if he let her speak.

This was what Kenyon said to himself; but his reluctance, after all, and whether he were conscious of it or no, resulted from a suspicion that had crept into his heart and lay there in a dark corner. Obscure as it was, when Miriam looked into his eyes, she detected it at once.

"Ah, I shall hate you!" cried she, echoing the thought which he had not spoken; she was half choked with the gush of passion that was thus turned back upon her. "You are as cold and pitiless as your own marble."

"No; but full of sympathy, God knows!" replied he.

In truth his suspicions, however warranted by the mystery in which Miriam was enveloped, had vanished in the earnestness of his kindly and sorrowful emotion. He was now ready to receive her trust.

"Keep your sympathy, then, for sorrows that admit of such solace," said she, making a strong effort to compose herself. "As for my griefs, I know how to manage them. It was all a mistake: you can do nothing for me, unless you petrify me into a marble companion for your Cleopatra there; and I am not of her sisterhood, I do assure you. Forget this foolish scene, my friend, and never let me see a reference to it in your eyes when they meet mine hereafter."

"Since you desire it, all shall be forgotten," answered the sculptor, pressing her hand as she departed; "or, if ever I can serve you, let my readiness to do so be remembered. Meanwhile, dear Miriam, let us meet in the same clear, friendly light as heretofore."

"You are less sincere than I thought you," said Miriam, "if you try to make me think that there will be no change."

As he attended her through the antechamber, she pointed to the statue of the pearl-diver.

"My secret is not a pearl," said she; "yet a man might drown himself in plunging after it."

After Kenyon had closed the door, she went wearily down the staircase, but paused midway, as if debating with herself whether to return.

"The mischief was done," thought she; "and I might as well have had the solace that ought to come with it. I have lost,—by staggering a little way beyond the mark, in the blindness of my distress,—I have lost, as we shall hereafter find, the genuine friendship of this clear-minded, honorable, true-hearted young man, and all for nothing. What if I should go back this moment and compel him to listen?"

She ascended two or three of the stairs, but again paused, murmured to herself, and shook her head.

"No, no, no," she thought; "and I wonder how I ever came to dream of it. Unless I had his heart for my own,—and that is Hilda's, nor would I steal it from her,—it should never be the treasure-place of my secret. It is no precious pearl, as I just now told him; but my dark-red carbuncle—red as blood—is too rich a gem to put into a stranger's casket."

She went down the stairs, and found her Shadow waiting for her in the street.

CHAPTER XV

An Æsthetic Company

On the evening after Miriam's visit to Kenyon's studio, there was an assemblage composed almost entirely of Anglo-Saxons, and chiefly of American artists, with a sprinkling of their English brethren; and some few of the tourists who still lingered in Rome, now that Holy Week was past. Miriam, Hilda, and the sculptor were all three present, and, with them, Donatello, whose life was so far turned from its natural bent, that, like a pet spaniel, he followed his beloved mistress wherever he could gain admittance.

The place of meeting was in the palatial, but somewhat faded and gloomy apartment of an eminent member of the æsthetic body. It was no more formal an occasion than one of those weekly receptions, common among the foreign residents of Rome, at which pleasant people—or disagreeable ones, as the case may be—encounter one another with little ceremony.

If anywise interested in art, a man must be difficult to please who cannot find fit companionship among a crowd of persons, whose ideas and pursuits all tend towards the general purpose of enlarging the world's stock of beautiful productions.

One of the chief causes that make Rome the favorite residence of artists—their ideal home which they sigh for in advance, and are so loath to migrate from, after once breathing its enchanted air—is, doubtless, that they there find themselves in force, and are numerous enough to create a congenial atmosphere. In every other clime they are isolated strangers; in this land of art, they are free citizens.

Not that, individually, or in the mass, there appears to be any large stock of mutual affection among the brethren of the chisel and the pencil. On the contrary, it will impress the shrewd observer that the jealousies and petty animosities, which the poets of our day have flung aside, still irritate and gnaw into the hearts of this kindred class of imaginative men. It is not difficult to suggest reasons why this should be the fact. The public, in whose good graces lie the sculptor's or the painter's prospects of success, is infinitely smaller than the public to which literary men make their appeal. It is composed of a very limited body of wealthy patrons; and these, as the artist well knows, are but blind judges in matters that require the utmost delicacy of perception. Thus, success in art is apt to become partly an affair of intrigue; and it is almost inevitable that even a gifted artist should look askance at his gifted brother's fame, and be chary of the good word that might help him to sell still another statue or picture. You seldom hear a painter heap generous praise on anything in his special line of art; a sculptor never has a favorable eye for any marble but his own.

Nevertheless, in spite of all these professional grudges, artists are conscious of a social warmth from each other's presence and contiguity. They shiver at the remembrance of their lonely studios in the unsympathizing cities of their native land. For the sake of such brotherhood as they can find, more than for any good that they get from galleries, they linger year after year in Italy, while their originality dies out of them, or is polished away as a barbarism.

The company this evening included several men and women whom the world has heard of, and many others, beyond all question, whom it ought to know. It would be a pleasure to introduce them upon our humble pages, name by name, and—had we confidence enough in our own taste —to crown each well-deserving brow according to its deserts. The opportunity is tempting, but not easily manageable, and far too perilous, both in respect to those individuals whom we might bring forward, and the far greater number that must needs be left in the shade. Ink, moreover, is apt to have a corrosive quality, and might chance to raise a blister, instead of any more agreeable titillation, on skins so sensitive as those of artists. We must therefore forego the delight of illuminating this chapter with personal allusions to men whose renown glows richly on canvas, or gleams in the white moonlight of marble.

Otherwise we might point to an artist who has studied Nature with such tender love that she takes him to her intimacy, enabling him to reproduce her in landscapes that seem the reality of a better earth, and yet are but the truth of the very scenes around us, observed by the painter's insight and interpreted for us by his skill. By his magic, the moon throws her light far out of the picture, and the crimson of the summer night absolutely glimmers on the beholder's face. Or we might indicate a poet-painter, whose song has the vividness of picture, and whose canvas is peopled with angels, fairies, and water-sprites, done to the ethereal life, because he saw them face to face in his poetic mood. Or we might bow before an artist, who has wrought too sincerely, too religiously, with too earnest a feeling, and too delicate a touch, for the world at once to recognize how much toil and thought are compressed into the stately brow of Prospero, and Miranda's maiden loveliness; or from what a depth within this painter's heart the Angel is leading forth St. Peter.

Thus it would be easy to go on, perpetrating a score of little epigrammatical allusions, like the above, all kindly meant, but none of them quite hitting the mark, and often striking where they were not aimed. It may be allowable to say, however, that American art is much better represented at Rome in the pictorial than in the sculpturesque department. Yet the men of marble appear to have more weight with the public than the men of canvas; perhaps on account of the greater destiny and solid substance of the material in which they work, and the sort of physical advantage which their labors thus acquire over the illusive unreality of color. To be a sculptor seems a distinction in itself; whereas a painter is nothing, unless individually eminent.

One sculptor there was, an Englishman, endowed with a beautiful fancy, and possessing at his fingers' ends the capability of doing beautiful things. He was a quiet, simple, elderly personage, with eyes brown and bright, under a slightly impending brow, and a Grecian profile, such as he might have cut with his own chisel. He had spent his life, for forty years, in making Venuses, Cupids, Bacchuses, and a vast deal of other marble progeny of dream-work, or rather frost-work: it was all a vapory exhalation out of the Grecian mythology, crystallizing on the dull window-panes of to-day. Gifted with a more delicate power than any other man alive, he had foregone to be a Christian reality, and perverted himself into a Pagan idealist, whose business or efficacy, in our present world, it would be exceedingly difficult to define. And, loving and reverencing the pure material in which he wrought, as surely this admirable sculptor did, he had nevertheless robbed the marble of its chastity, by giving it an artificial warmth of hue. Thus it became a sin and shame to look at his nude goddesses. They had revealed themselves to his imagination, no doubt, with all their deity about them; but, bedaubed with buff-color, they stood forth to the eyes of the profane in the guise of naked women. But, whatever criticism may be ventured on his style, it was good to meet a man so modest and yet imbued with such thorough and simple conviction of his own right principles and practice, and so quietly satisfied that his kind of antique achievement was all that sculpture could effect for modern life.

This eminent person's weight and authority among his artistic brethren were very evident; for beginning unobtrusively to utter himself on a topic of art, he was soon the centre of a little crowd of younger sculptors. They drank in his wisdom, as if it would serve all the purposes of original inspiration; he, meanwhile, discoursing with gentle calmness, as if there could possibly be no other side, and often ratifying, as it were, his own conclusions by a mildly emphatic "Yes."

The veteran sculptor's unsought audience was composed mostly of our own countrymen. It is fair to say, that they were a body of very dexterous and capable artists, each of whom had probably given the delighted public a nude statue, or had won credit for even higher skill by the nice carving of button-holes, shoe-ties, coat-seams, shirt-bosoms, and other such graceful peculiarities of modern costume. Smart, practical men they doubtless were, and some of them far more than this, but, still, not precisely what an uninitiated person looks for in a sculptor. A sculptor, indeed, to meet the demands which our preconceptions make upon him, should be even more indispensably a poet than those who deal in measured verse and rhyme. His material, or instrument, which serves him in the stead of shifting and transitory language, is a pure, white, undecaying substance. It insures immortality to whatever is wrought in it, and therefore makes it a religious obligation to commit no idea to its mighty guardianship, save such as may repay the marble for its faithful care, its incorruptible fidelity, by warming it with an ethereal life. Under this aspect, marble assumes a sacred character; and no man should dare to touch it unless he feels within himself a certain consecration and a priesthood, the only evidence of which, for the public eye, will be the high treatment of heroic subjects, or the delicate evolution of spiritual, through material beauty.

No ideas such as the foregoing—no misgivings suggested by them—probably troubled the self-complacency of most of these clever sculptors. Marble, in their view, had no such sanctity as we impute to it. It was merely a sort of white limestone from Carrara, cut into convenient blocks, and worth, in that state, about two or three dollars per pound; and it was susceptible of being wrought into certain shapes (by their own mechanical ingenuity, or that of artisans in their employment) which would enable them to sell it again at a much higher figure. Such men, on the strength of some small knack in handling clay, which might have been fitly employed in making wax-work, are bold to call themselves sculptors. How terrible should be the thought, that the nude woman whom the modern artist patches together, bit by bit, from a dozen heterogeneous models, meaning nothing by her, shall last as long as the Venus of the Capitol!—that his group of—no matter what, since it has no moral or intellectual existence—will not physically crumble any sooner than the immortal agony of the Laocoön!

Yet we love the artists, in every kind; even these, whose merits we are not quite able to appreciate. Sculptors, painters, crayon-sketchers, or whatever branch of æsthetics they adopted, were certainly pleasanter people, as we saw them that evening, than the average whom we meet in ordinary society. They were not wholly confined within the sordid compass of practical life; they had a pursuit which, if followed faithfully out, would lead them to the beautiful, and always had a tendency thitherward, even if they lingered to gather up golden dross by the wayside. Their actual business (though they talked about it very much as other men talk of cotton, politics, flour-barrels, and sugar) necessarily illuminated their conversation with something akin to the ideal. So, when the guests collected themselves in little groups, here and there in the wide saloon, a cheerful and airy gossip began to be heard. The atmosphere ceased to be precisely that of common life; a faint, mellow tinge, such as we see in pictures, mingled itself with the lamplight.

This good effect was assisted by many curious little treasures of art, which the host had taken care to strew upon his tables. They were principally such bits of antiquity as the soil of Rome and its neighborhood are still rich in; seals, gems, small figures of bronze, mediæval carvings in ivory; things which had been obtained at little cost, yet might have borne no inconsiderable value in the museum of a virtuoso.

As interesting as any of these relics was a large portfolio of old drawings, some of which, in the opinion of their possessor, bore evidence on their faces of the touch of master-hands. Very ragged and ill-conditioned they mostly were, yellow with time, and tattered with rough usage; and, in their best estate, the designs had been scratched rudely with pen and ink, on coarse paper, or, if drawn with charcoal or a pencil, were now half rubbed out. You would not anywhere see rougher and homelier things than these. But this hasty rudeness made the sketches only the more valuable; because the artist seemed to have bestirred himself at the pinch of the moment, snatching up whatever material was nearest, so as to seize the first glimpse of an idea that might vanish in the twinkling of an eye. Thus, by the spell of a creased, soiled, and discolored scrap of paper, you were enabled to steal close to an old master, and watch him in the very effervescence of his genius.

According to the judgment of several connoisseurs, Raphael's own hand had communicated its magnetism to one of these sketches; and, if genuine, it was evidently his first conception of a favorite Madonna, now hanging in the private apartment of the Grand Duke, at Florence. Another drawing was attributed to Leonardo da Vinci, and appeared to be a somewhat varied design for his picture of Modesty and Vanity, in the Sciarra Palace. There were at least half a dozen others, to which the owner assigned as high an origin. It was delightful to believe in their authenticity, at all events; for these things make the spectator more vividly sensible of a great painter's power, than the final glow and perfected art of the most consummate picture that may have been elaborated from them. There is an effluence of divinity in the first sketch; and there, if anywhere, you find the pure light of inspiration, which the subsequent toil of the artist serves to bring out in stronger lustre, indeed, but likewise adulterates it with what belongs to an inferior mood. The aroma and fragrance of new thought were perceptible in these designs, after three centuries of wear and tear. The charm lay partly in their very imperfection; for this is suggestive, and sets the imagination at work; whereas, the finished picture, if a good one, leaves the spectator nothing to do, and, if bad, confuses, stupefies, disenchants, and disheartens him.

Hilda was greatly interested in this rich portfolio. She lingered so long over one particular sketch, that Miriam asked her what discovery she had made.

"Look at it carefully," replied Hilda, putting the sketch into her hands. "If you take pains to disentangle the design from those pencil-marks that seem to have been scrawled over it, I think you will see something very curious."

"It is a hopeless affair, I am afraid," said Miriam. "I have neither your faith, dear Hilda, nor your perceptive faculty. Fie! what a blurred scrawl it is indeed!"

The drawing had originally been very slight, and had suffered more from time and hard usage than almost any other in the collection; it appeared, too, that there had been an attempt (perhaps by the very hand that drew it) to obliterate the design. By Hilda's help, however, Miriam pretty distinctly made out a winged figure with a drawn sword, and a dragon, or a demon, prostrate at his feet.

"I am convinced," said Hilda, in a low, reverential tone, "that Guido's own touches are on that ancient scrap of paper! If so, it must be his original sketch for the picture of the Archangel Michael setting his foot upon the demon, in the Church of the Cappuccini. The composition and general arrangement of the sketch are the same with those of the picture; the only difference being, that the demon has a more upturned face, and scowls vindictively at the Archangel, who turns away his eyes in painful disgust."

"No wonder!" responded Miriam. "The expression suits the daintiness of Michael's character, as Guido represents him. He never could have looked the demon in the face!"

"Miriam!" exclaimed her friend, reproachfully, "you grieve me, and you know it, by pretending to speak contemptuously of the most beautiful and the divinest figure that mortal painter ever drew."

"Forgive me, Hilda!" said Miriam. "You take these matters more religiously than I can, for my life. Guido's Archangel is a fine picture, of course, but it never impressed me as it does you."

"Well; we will not talk of that," answered Hilda. "What I wanted you to notice, in this sketch, is the face of the demon. It is entirely unlike the demon of the finished picture. Guido, you know, always affirmed that the resemblance to Cardinal Pamfili was either casual or imaginary. Now, here is the face as he first conceived it."

"And a more energetic demon, altogether, than that of the finished picture," said Kenyon, taking the sketch into his hand. "What a spirit is conveyed into the ugliness of this strong, writhing, squirming dragon, under the Archangel's foot! Neither is the face an impossible one. Upon my word, I have seen it somewhere, and on the shoulders of a living man!"

"And so have I," said Hilda. "It was what struck me from the first."

"Donatello, look at this face!" cried Kenyon.

The young Italian, as may be supposed, took little interest in matters of art, and seldom or never ventured an opinion respecting them. After holding the sketch a single instant in his hand, he flung it from him with a shudder of disgust and repugnance, and a frown that had all the bitterness of hatred.

"I know the face well!" whispered he. "It is Miriam's model!"

It was acknowledged both by Kenyon and Hilda that they had detected, or fancied, the resemblance which Donatello so strongly affirmed; and it added not a little to the grotesque and weird character which, half playfully, half seriously, they assigned to Miriam's attendant, to think of him as personating the demon's part in a picture of more than two centuries ago. Had Guido, in his effort to imagine the utmost of sin and misery, which his pencil could represent, hit ideally upon just this face? Or was it an actual portrait of somebody, that haunted the old master, as Miriam was haunted now? Did the ominous shadow follow him through all the sunshine of his earlier career, and into the gloom that gathered about its close? And when Guido died, did the spectre betake himself to those ancient sepulchres, there awaiting a new victim, till it was Miriam's ill-hap to encounter him?

"I do not acknowledge the resemblance at all," said Miriam, looking narrowly at the sketch; "and, as I have drawn the face twenty times, I think you will own that I am the best judge."

A discussion here arose, in reference to Guido's Archangel, and it was agreed that these four friends should visit the Church of the Cappuccini the next morning, and critically examine the picture in question; the similarity between it and the sketch being, at all events, a very curious circumstance.

It was now a little past ten o'clock, when some of the company, who had been standing in a balcony, declared the moonlight to be resplendent. They proposed a ramble through the streets, taking in their way some of those scenes of ruin which produced their best effects under the splendor of the Italian moon.

CHAPTER XVI

A MOONLIGHT RAMBLE

THE proposal for a moonlight ramble was received with acclamation by all the younger portion of the company. They immediately set forth and descended from story to story, dimly lighting their way by waxen tapers, which are a necessary equipment to those whose thoroughfare, in the night-time, lies up and down a Roman staircase. Emerging from the courtyard of the edifice, they looked upward and saw the sky full of light, which seemed to have a delicate purple or crimson lustre, or, at least, some richer tinge than the cold, white moonshine of other skies. It gleamed over the front of the opposite palace, showing the architectural ornaments of its cornice and pillared portal, as well as the iron-barred basement-windows, that gave such a prison-like aspect to the structure, and the shabbiness and squalor that lay along its base. A cobbler was just shutting up his little shop, in the basement of the palace; a cigar-vender's lantern flared in the blast that came through the archway; a French sentinel paced to and fro before the portal; a homeless dog, that haunted thereabouts, barked as obstreperously at the party as if he were the domestic guardian of the precincts.

The air was quietly full of the noise of falling water, the cause of which was nowhere visible, though apparently near at hand. This pleasant, natural sound, not unlike that of a distant cascade in the forest, may be heard in many of the Roman streets and piazzas, when the tumult of the city is hushed; for consuls, emperors, and popes, the great men of every age, have found no better way of immortalizing their memories, than by the shifting, indestructible, ever new, yet unchanging, upgush and downfall of water. They have written their names in that unstable element, and proved it a more durable record than brass or marble.

"Donatello, you had better take one of those gay, boyish artists for your companion," said Miriam, when she found the Italian youth at her side. "I am not now in a merry mood, as when we set all the world a-dancing the other afternoon, in the Borghese grounds."

"I never wish to dance any more," answered Donatello.

"What a melancholy was in that tone!" exclaimed Miriam. "You are getting spoilt in this dreary Rome, and will be as wise and as wretched as all the rest of mankind, unless you go back soon to your Tuscan vineyards. Well; give me your arm then! But take care that no friskiness comes over you. We must walk evenly and heavily to-night!"

The party arranged itself according to its natural affinities or casual likings; a sculptor generally choosing a painter, and a painter a sculptor, for his companion, in preference to brethren of their own art. Kenyon would gladly have taken Hilda to himself, and have drawn her a little aside from the throng of merry wayfarers. But she kept near Miriam, and seemed, in her gentle and quiet way, to decline a separate alliance either with him or any other of her acquaintances.

So they set forth, and had gone but a little way, when the narrow street emerged into a piazza, on one side of which glistening, and dimpling in the moonlight, was the most famous fountain in Rome. Its murmur—not to say its uproar—had been in the ears of the company, ever since they came into the open air. It was the Fountain of Trevi, which draws its precious water from a source far beyond the walls, whence it flows hitherward through old subterranean aqueducts, and sparkles forth as pure as the virgin who first led Agrippa to its well-spring, by her father's door.

"I shall sip as much of this water as the hollow of my hand will hold," said Miriam. "I am leaving Rome in a few days; and the tradition goes, that a parting draught at the Fountain of Trevi insures the traveller's return, whatever obstacles and improbabilities may seem to beset him. Will you drink, Donatello?"

"Signorina, what you drink, I drink," said the youth.

They and the rest of the party descended some steps to the water's brim, and, after a sip or two, stood gazing at the absurd design of the fountain, where some sculptor of Bernini's school had gone absolutely mad in marble. It was a great palace-front, with niches and many bas-reliefs, out of which looked Agrippa's legendary virgin, and several of the allegoric sisterhood; while, at the base, appeared Neptune, with his floundering steeds, and Tritons blowing their horns about him, and twenty other artificial fantasies, which the calm moonlight soothed into better taste than was native to them.

And, after all, it was as magnificent a piece of work as ever human skill contrived. At the foot of the palatial façade was strown, with careful art and ordered irregularity, a broad and broken heap of massive rock, looking as if it might have lain there since the deluge. Over a central precipice fell the water, in a semicircular cascade; and from a hundred crevices, on all sides, snowy jets gushed up, and streams spouted out of the mouths and nostrils of stone monsters, and fell in glistening drops; while other rivulets, that had run wild, came leaping from one rude step to another,

over stones that were mossy, slimy, and green with sedge, because, in a
century of their wild play, Nature had adopted the Fountain of Trevi,
with all its elaborate devices, for her own. Finally, the water, tumbling,
sparkling, and dashing, with joyous haste and never-ceasing murmur,
poured itself into a great marble-brimmed reservoir, and filled it with a
quivering tide; on which was seen, continually, a snowy semicircle of momentary foam from the principal cascade, as well as a multitude of snow-
points from smaller jets. The basin occupied the whole breadth of the
piazza, whence flights of steps descended to its border. A boat might float,
and make voyages from one shore to another in this mimic lake.

In the daytime, there is hardly a livelier scene in Rome than the neighborhood of the Fountain of Trevi; for the piazza is then filled with the
stalls of vegetable and fruit-dealers, chestnut-roasters, cigar-venders, and
other people, whose petty and wandering traffic is transacted in the open
air. It is likewise thronged with idlers, lounging over the iron railing, and
with Forestieri, who came hither to see the famous fountain. Here, also,
are seen men with buckets, urchins with cans, and maidens (a picture as
old as the patriarchal times) bearing their pitchers upon their heads. For
the water of Trevi is in request, far and wide, as the most refreshing
draught for feverish lips, the pleasantest to mingle with wine, and the
wholesomest to drink, in its native purity, that can anywhere be found.
But now, at early midnight, the piazza was a solitude; and it was a delight to behold this untamable water, sporting by itself in the moonshine,
and compelling all the elaborate trivialities of art to assume a natural aspect, in accordance with its own powerful simplicity.

"What would be done with this water-power," suggested an artist, "if
we had it in one of our American cities? Would they employ it to turn the
machinery of a cotton-mill, I wonder?"

"The good people would pull down those rampant marble deities," said
Kenyon, "and, possibly, they would give me a commission to carve the
one-and-thirty (is that the number?) sister States, each pouring a silver
stream from a separate can into one vast basin, which should represent
the grand reservoir of national prosperity."

"Or, if they wanted a bit of satire," remarked an English artist, "you
could set those same one-and-thirty States to cleansing the national flag
of any stains that it may have incurred. The Roman washer-women at the
lavatory yonder, plying their labor in the open air, would serve admirably
as models."

"I have often intended to visit this fountain by moonlight," said Miriam, "because it was here that the interview took place between Corinne
and Lord Neville, after their separation and temporary estrangement.
Pray come behind me, one of you, and let me try whether the face can be
recognized in the water."

Leaning over the stone brim of the basin she heard footsteps stealing
behind her, and knew that somebody was looking over her shoulder. The
moonshine fell directly behind Miriam, illuminating the palace-front and
the whole scene of statues and rocks, and filling the basin, as it were, with

tremulous and palpable light. Corinne, it will be remembered, knew Lord Neville by the reflection of his face in the water. In Miriam's case, however (owing to the agitation of the water, its transparency, and the angle at which she was compelled to lean over), no reflected image appeared; nor, from the same causes, would it have been possible for the recognition between Corinne and her lover to take place. The moon, indeed, flung Miriam's shadow at the bottom of the basin, as well as two more shadows of persons who had followed her, on either side.

"Three shadows!" exclaimed Miriam. "Three separate shadows, all so black and heavy that they sink in the water! There they lie on the bottom, as if all three were drowned together. This shadow on my right is Donatello; I know him by his curls, and the turn of his head. My left-hand companion puzzles me; a shapeless mass, as indistinct as the premonition of calamity! Which of you can it be? Ah!"

She had turned round, while speaking, and saw beside her the strange creature, whose attendance on her was already familiar, as a marvel and a jest, to the whole company of artists. A general burst of laughter followed the recognition; while the model leaned towards Miriam, as she shrank from him, and muttered something that was inaudible to those who witnessed the scene. By his gestures, however, they concluded that he was inviting her to bathe her hands.

"He cannot be an Italian; at least not a Roman," observed an artist. "I never knew one of them to care about ablution. See him now! It is as if he were trying to wash off the time-stains and earthly soil of a thousand years!"

Dipping his hands into the capacious washbowl before him, the model rubbed them together with the utmost vehemence. Ever and anon, too, he peeped into the water, as if expecting to see the whole Fountain of Trevi turbid with the results of his ablution. Miriam looked at him, some little time, with an aspect of real terror, and even imitated him by leaning over to peep into the basin. Recovering herself, she took up some of the water in the hollow of her hand, and practised an old form of exorcism by flinging it in her persecutor's face.

"In the name of all the Saints," cried she, "vanish, Demon, and let me be free of you now and forever!"

"It will not suffice," said some of the mirthful party, "unless the Fountain of Trevi gushes with holy water."

In fact, the exorcism was quite ineffectual upon the pertinacious demon, or whatever the apparition might be. Still he washed his brown, bony talons; still he peered into the vast basin, as if all the water of that great drinking-cup of Rome must needs be stained black or sanguine; and still he gesticulated to Miriam to follow his example. The spectators laughed loudly, but yet with a kind of constraint; for the creature's aspect was strangely repulsive and hideous.

Miriam felt her arm seized violently by Donatello. She looked at him, and beheld a tiger-like fury gleaming from his wild eyes.

"Bid me drown him!" whispered he, shuddering between rage and horrible disgust. "You shall hear his death-gurgle in another instant!"

"Peace, peace, Donatello!" said Miriam, soothingly, for this naturally gentle and sportive being seemed all aflame with animal rage. "Do him no mischief! He is mad; and we are as mad as he, if we suffer ourselves to be disquieted by his antics. Let us leave him to bathe his hands till the fountain run dry, if he find solace and pastime in it. What is it to you or me, Donatello? There, there! Be quiet, foolish boy!"

Her tone and gesture were such as she might have used in taming down the wrath of a faithful hound, that had taken upon himself to avenge some supposed affront to his mistress. She smoothed the young man's curls (for his fierce and sudden fury seemed to bristle among his hair), and touched his cheek with her soft palm, till his angry mood was a little assuaged.

"Signorina, do I look as when you first knew me?" asked he, with a heavy, tremulous sigh, as they went onward, somewhat apart from their companions. "Methinks there has been a change upon me, these many months; and more and more, these last few days. The joy is gone out of my life; all gone! all gone! Feel my hand! Is it not very hot? Ah; and my heart burns hotter still!"

"My poor Donatello, you are ill!" said Miriam, with deep sympathy and pity. "This melancholy and sickly Rome is stealing away the rich, joyous life that belongs to you. Go back, my dear friend, to your home among the hills, where (as I gather from what you have told me) your days were filled with simple and blameless delights. Have you found aught in the world that is worth what you there enjoyed? Tell me truly, Donatello!"

"Yes!" replied the young man.

"And what, in Heaven's name?" asked she.

"This burning pain in my heart," said Donatello; "for you are in the midst of it."

By this time, they had left the Fountain of Trevi considerably behind them. Little further allusion was made to the scene at its margin; for the party regarded Miriam's persecutor as diseased in his wits, and were hardly to be surprised by an eccentricity in his deportment.

Threading several narrow steets, they passed though the Piazza of the Holy Apostles, and soon came to Trajan's Forum. All over the surface of what once was Rome, it seems to be the effort of Time to bury up the ancient city, as if it were a corpse, and he the sexton; so that, in eighteen centuries, the soil over its grave has grown very deep, by the slow scattering of dust, and the accumulation of more modern decay upon older ruin.

This was the fate, also, of Trajan's Forum, until some papal antiquary, a few hundred years ago, began to hollow it out again, and disclosed the full height of the gigantic column wreathed round with bas-reliefs of the old emperor's warlike deeds. In the area before it stands a grove of stone, consisting of the broken and unequal shafts of a vanished temple, still keeping a majestic order, and apparently incapable of further demolition. The modern edifices of the piazza (wholly built, no doubt, out of the spoil of its old magnificence) look down into the hollow space whence these pillars rise.

One of the immense gray granite shafts lay.in the piazza, on the verge of the area. It was a great, solid fact of the Past, making old Rome actually sensible to the touch and eye; and no study of history, nor force of thought, nor magic of song, could so vitally assure us that Rome once existed, as this sturdy specimen of what its rulers and people wrought.

"And see!" said Kenyon, laying his hand upon it, "there is still a polish remaining on the hard substance of the pillar; and even now, late as it is, I can feel very sensibly the warmth of the noonday sun, which did its best to heat it through. This shaft will endure forever. The polish of eighteen centuries ago, as yet but half rubbed off, and the heat of to-day's sunshine, lingering into the night, seem almost equally ephemeral in relation to it."

"There is comfort to be found in the pillar," remarked Miriam, "hard and heavy as it is. Lying here forever, as it will, it makes all human trouble appear but a momentary annoyance."

"And human happiness as evanescent too," observed Hilda, sighing; "and beautiful art hardly less so! I do not love to think that this dull stone, merely by its massiveness, will last infinitely longer than any picture, in spite of the spiritual life that ought to give it immortality!"

"My poor little Hilda," said Miriam, kissing her compassionately, "would you sacrifice this greatest mortal consolation, which we derive from the transitoriness of all things,—from the right of saying, in every conjecture, 'This, too, will pass away,'—would you give up this unspeakable boon, for the sake of making a picture eternal?"

Their moralizing strain was interrupted by a demonstration from the rest of the party, who, after talking and laughing together, suddenly joined their voices, and shouted at full pitch,—

"Trajan! Trajan!"

"Why do you deafen us with such an uproar?" inquired Miriam.

In truth, the whole piazza had been filled with their idle vociferation; the echoes from the surrounding houses reverberating the cry of "Trajan," on all sides; as if there was a great search for that imperial personage, and not so much as a handful of his ashes to be found.

"Why, it was a good opportunity to air our voices in this resounding piazza," replied one of the artists. "Besides, we had really some hopes of summoning Trajan to look at his column, which, you know, he never saw in his lifetime. Here is your model (who, they say, lived and sinned before Trajan's death) still wandering about Rome; and why not the Emperor Trajan?"

"Dead emperors have very little delight in their columns, I am afraid," observed Kenyon. "All that rich sculpture of Trajan's bloody warfare, twining from the base of the pillar to its capital, may be but an ugly spectacle for his ghostly eyes, if he considers that this huge, storied shaft must be laid before the judgment-seat, as a piece of the evidence of what he did in the flesh. If ever I am employed to sculpture a hero's monument, I shall think of this, as I put in the bas-reliefs of the pedestal!"

"There are sermons in stones," said Hilda, thoughtfully, smiling at Kenyon's morality; "and especially in the stones of Rome."

The party moved on, but deviated a little from the straight way, in order to glance at the ponderous remains of the temple of Mars Ultor, within which a convent of nuns is now established,—a dove-cote, in the war-god's mansion. At only a little distance, they passed the portico of a Temple of Minerva, most rich and beautiful in architecture, but wofully gnawed by time and shattered by violence, besides being buried midway in the accumulation of soil, that rises over dead Rome like a flood-tide. Within this edifice of antique sanctity, a baker's shop was now established, with an entrance on one side; for, everywhere, the remnants of old grandeur and divinity have been made available for the meanest necessities of to-day.

"The baker is just drawing his loaves out of the oven," remarked Kenyon. "Do you smell how sour they are? I should fancy that Minerva (in revenge for the desecration of her temple) had slyly poured vinegar into the batch, if I did not know that the modern Romans prefer their bread in the acetous fermentation."

They turned into the Via Alessandria, and thus gained the rear of the Temple of Peace, and, passing beneath its great arches, pursued their way along a hedge-bordered lane. In all probability, a stately Roman street lay buried beneath that rustic-looking pathway; for they had now emerged from the close and narrow avenues of the modern city, and were treading on a soil where the seeds of antique grandeur had not yet produced the squalid crop that elsewhere sprouts from them. Grassy as the lane was, it skirted along heaps of shapeless ruin, and the bare site of the vast temple that Hadrian planned and built. It terminated on the edge of a somewhat abrupt descent, at the foot of which, with a muddy ditch between, rose, in the bright moonlight, the great curving wall and multitudinous arches of the Coliseum.

CHAPTER XVII

MIRIAM'S TROUBLE

As usual of a moonlight evening, several carriages stood at the entrance of this famous ruin, and the precincts and interior were anything but a solitude. The French sentinel on duty beneath the principal archway eyed our party curiously, but offered no obstacle to their admission. Within, the moonlight filled and flooded the great empty space; it glowed upon tier above tier of ruined, grass-grown arches, and made them even too distinctly visible. The splendor of the revelation took away that inestimable effect of dimness and mystery by which the imagination might be assisted to build a grander structure than the Coliseum, and to shatter it with a more picturesque decay. Byron's celebrated description is better than the reality. He beheld the scene in his mind's eye, through the witchery of many intervening years, and faintly illuminated it as if with starlight instead of this broad glow of moonshine.

The party of our friends sat down, three or four of them on a prostrate column, another on a shapeless lump of marble, once a Roman altar; others on the steps of one of the Christian shrines. Goths and barbarians though they were, they chatted as gayly together as if they belonged to the gentle and pleasant race of people who now inhabit Italy. There was much pastime and gayety just then in the area of the Coliseum, where so many gladiators and wild beasts had fought and died, and where so much blood of Christian martyrs had been lapped up by that fiercest of wild beasts, the Roman populace of yore. Some youths and maidens were running merry races across the open space, and playing at hide-and-seek a little way within the duskiness of the ground-tier of arches, whence now and then you could hear the half-shriek, half-laugh of a frolicsome girl, whom the shadow had betrayed into a young man's arms. Elder groups were seated on the fragments of pillars and blocks of marble that lay round the verge of the arena, talking in the quick, short ripple of the Italian tongue. On the steps of the great black cross in the centre of the Coliseum sat a party singing scraps of songs, with much laughter and merriment between the stanzas.

It was a strange place for song and mirth. That black cross marks one of the special blood-spots of the earth where, thousands of times over, the dying gladiator fell, and more of human agony has been endured for the mere pastime of the multitude than on the breadth of many battle-fields. From all this crime and suffering, however, the spot has derived a more than common sanctity. An inscription promises seven years' indulgence, seven years of remission from the pains of purgatory, and earlier enjoyment of heavenly bliss, for each separate kiss imprinted on the black cross. What better use could be made of life, after middle-age, when the accumulated sins are many and the remaining temptations few, than to spend it all in kissing the black cross of the Coliseum!

Besides its central consecration, the whole area has been made sacred by a range of shrines, which are erected round the circle, each commemorating some scene or circumstance of the Saviour's passion and suffering. In accordance with an ordinary custom a pilgrim was making his progress from shrine to shrine upon his knees, and saying a penitential prayer at each. Light-footed girls ran across the path along which he crept, or sported with their friends close by the shrines where he was kneeling. The pilgrim took no heed, and the girls meant no irreverence; for in Italy religion jostles along side by side with business and sport, after a fashion of its own, and people are accustomed to kneel down and pray, or see others praying, between two fits of merriment, or between two sins.

To make an end of our description, a red twinkle of light was visible amid the breadth of shadow that fell across the upper part of the Coliseum. Now it glimmered through a line of arches, or threw a broader gleam as it rose out of some profound abyss of ruin; now it was muffled by a heap of shrubbery which had adventurously clambered to that dizzy height; and so the red light kept ascending to loftier and loftier ranges of the structure, until it stood like a star where the blue sky rested against the Coliseum's topmost wall. It indicated a party of English or Americans paying the inevitable visit by moonlight, and exalting themselves with raptures that were Byron's, not their own.

Our company of artists sat on the fallen column, the pagan altar, and the steps of the Christian shrine, enjoying the moonlight and shadow, the present gayety and the gloomy reminiscences of the scene, in almost equal share. Artists, indeed, are lifted by the ideality of their pursuits a little way off the earth, and are therefore able to catch the evanescent fragrance that floats in the atmosphere of life above the heads of the ordinary crowd. Even if they seem endowed with little imagination individually, yet there is a property, a gift, a talisman, common to their class, entitling them to partake somewhat more bountifully than other people in the thin delights of moonshine and romance.

"How delightful this is!" said Hilda; and she sighed for very pleasure.

"Yes," said Kenyon, who sat on the column, at her side. "The Coliseum is far more delightful, as we enjoy it now, than when eighty thousand persons sat squeezed together, row above row, to see their fellow-creatures torn by lions and tigers limb from limb. What a strange thought that the Coliseum was really built for us, and has not come to its best uses till almost two thousand years after it was finished!"

"The Emperor Vespasian scarcely had us in his mind," said Hilda, smiling; "but I thank him none the less for building it."

"He gets small thanks, I fear, from the people whose bloody instincts he pampered," rejoined Kenyon. "Fancy a nightly assemblage of eighty thousand melancholy and remorseful ghosts, looking down from those tiers of broken arches, striving to repent of the savage pleasures which they once enjoyed, but still longing to enjoy them over again."

"You bring a Gothic horror into this peaceful moonlight scene," said Hilda.

"Nay, I have good authority for peopling the Coliseum with phantoms," replied the sculptor. "Do you remember that veritable scene in Benvenuto Cellini's autobiography, in which a necromancer of his acquaintance draws a magic circle—just where the black cross stands now, I suppose—and raises myriads of demons? Benvenuto saw them with his own eyes,—giants, pygmies, and other creatures of frightful aspect,—capering and dancing on yonder walls. Those spectres must have been Romans, in their lifetime, and frequenters of this bloody amphitheatre."

"I see a spectre, now!" said Hilda, with a little thrill of uneasiness.

"Have you watched that pilgrim, who is going round the whole circle of shrines, on his knees, and praying with such fervency at every one? Now that he has revolved so far in his orbit, and has the moonshine on his face as he turns towards us, methinks I recognize him!"

"And so do I," said Kenyon. "Poor Miriam! Do you think she sees him?"

They looked round, and perceived that Miriam had risen from the steps of the shrine and disappeared. She had shrunk back, in fact, into the deep obscurity of an arch that opened just behind them.

Donatello, whose faithful watch was no more to be eluded than that of a hound, had stolen after her, and became the innocent witness of a spectacle that had its own kind of horror. Unaware of his presence, and fancying herself wholly unseen, the beautiful Miriam began to gesticulate extravagantly, gnashing her teeth, flinging her arms wildly abroad, stamping with her foot. It was as if she had stepped aside for an instant, solely to snatch the relief of a brief fit of madness. Persons in acute trouble, or laboring under strong excitement, with a necessity for concealing it, are prone to relieve their nerves in this wild way; although, when practicable, they find a more effectual solace in shrieking aloud.

Thus, as soon as she threw off her self-control, under the dusky arches of the Coliseum, we may consider Miriam as a mad woman, concentrating the elements of a long insanity into that instant.

"Signorina! signorina! have pity on me!" cried Donatello, approaching her; "this is too terrible!"

"How dare you look at me!" exclaimed Miriam, with a start; then, whispering below her breath, "men have been struck dead for a less offence!"

"If you desire it, or need it," said Donatello, humbly, "I shall not be loath to die."

"Donatello," said Miriam, coming close to the young man, and speaking low, but still the almost insanity of the moment vibrating in her voice, "if you love yourself; if you desire those earthly blessings, such as you, of all men, were made for; if you would come to a good old age among your olive-orchards and your Tuscan vines, as your forefathers did; if you would leave children to enjoy the same peaceful, happy, innocent life, then flee from me. Look not behind you! Get you gone without another word." He gazed sadly at her, but did not stir. "I tell you," Miriam went on, "there is a great evil hanging over me! I know it; I see it in the sky; I feel it in the air! It will overwhelm me as utterly as if this arch should crumble down upon our heads! It will crush you, too, if you stand at my side! Depart, then; and make the sign of the cross, as your faith bids you, when an evil spirit is nigh. Cast me off, or you are lost forever."

A higher sentiment brightened upon Donatello's face than had hitherto seemed to belong to its simple expression and sensuous beauty.

"I will never quit you," he said; "you cannot drive me from you."

"Poor Donatello!" said Miriam, in a changed tone, and rather to herself than him. "Is there no other that seeks me out,—follows me,—is obstinate to share my affliction and my doom,—but only you! They call me beautiful; and I used to fancy that, at my need, I could bring the whole world to my feet. And lo! here is my utmost need; and my beauty and my gifts have brought me only this poor, simple boy. Half-witted, they call him; and surely fit for nothing but to be happy. And I accept his aid! To-morrow, to-morrow, I will tell him all! Ah! what a sin to stain his joyous nature with the blackness of a woe like mine!"

She held out her hand to him, and smiled sadly as Donatello pressed it to his lips. They were now about to emerge from the depth of the arch; but, just then, the kneeling pilgrim, in his revolution round the orbit of the shrines, had reached the one on the steps of which Miriam had been sitting. There, as at the other shrines, he prayed, or seemed to pray. It struck Kenyon, however,—who sat close by, and saw his face distinctly, —that the suppliant was merely performing an enjoined penance, and without the penitence that ought to have given it effectual life. Even as he knelt, his eyes wandered, and Miriam soon felt that he had detected her, half hidden as she was within the obscurity of the arch.

"He is evidently a good Catholic, however," whispered one of the party. "After all, I fear we cannot identify him with the ancient pagan who haunts the catacombs."

"The doctors of the Propaganda may have converted him," said another; "they have had fifteen hundred years to perform the task."

The company now deemed it time to continue their ramble. Emerging from a side entrance of the Coliseum, they had on their left the Arch of Constantine, and, above it, the shapeless ruins of the Palace of the Cæsars; portions of which have taken shape anew, in mediæval convents and modern villas. They turned their faces cityward, and, treading over the broad flagstones of the old Roman pavement, passed through the Arch of Titus. The moon shone brightly enough within it, to show the seven-branched Jewish candlestick, cut in the marble of the interior. The original of that awful trophy lies buried, at this moment, in the yellow mud of the Tiber; and, could its gold of Ophir again be brought to light, it would be the most precious relic of past ages, in the estimation of both Jew and Gentile.

Standing amid so much ancient dust, it is difficult to spare the reader the commonplaces of enthusiasm, on which hundreds of tourists have already insisted. Over this half-worn pavement, and beneath this Arch of Titus, the Roman armies had trodden in their outward march, to fight battles, a world's width away. Returning victorious, with royal captives and inestimable spoil, a Roman triumph, that most gorgeous pageant of earthly pride, had streamed and flaunted in hundred-fold succession over these same flagstones, and through this yet stalwart archway. It is politic, however, to make few allusions to such a past; nor, if we would create an interest in the characters of our story, is it wise to suggest how Cicero's foot may have stepped on yonder stone, or how Horace was wont to stroll near by, making his footsteps chime with the measure of the ode that was ringing in his mind. The very ghosts of that massive and stately epoch have so much density that the actual people of to-day seem the thinner of the two, and stand more ghostlike by the arches and columns, letting the rich sculpture be discerned through their ill-compacted substance.

The party kept onward, often meeting pairs and groups of midnight strollers like themselves. On such a moonlight night as this, Rome keeps itself awake and stirring, and is full of song and pastime, the noise of which mingles with your dreams, if you have gone betimes to bed. But it is better to be abroad, and take our own share of the enjoyable time; for the languor what weighs so heavily in the Roman atmosphere by day is lightened beneath the moon and stars.

They had now reached the precincts of the Forum.

CHAPTER XVIII

ON THE EDGE OF A PRECIPICE

"LET us settle it," said Kenyon, stamping his foot firmly down, "that this is precisely the spot where the chasm opened, into which Curtius precipitated his good steed and himself. Imagine the great, dusky gap, impenetrably deep, and with half-shaped monsters and hideous faces looming upward out of it, to the vast affright of the good citizens who peeped over the brim! There, now, is a subject, hitherto unthought of, for a grim and ghastly story, and, methinks, with a moral as deep as the gulf itself. Within it, beyond a question, there were prophetic visions,—intimations of all the future calamities of Rome,—shades of Goths, and Gauls, and even of the French soldiers of to-day. It was a pity to close it up so soon! I would give much for a peep into such a chasm."

"I fancy," remarked Miriam, "that every person takes a peep into it in moments of gloom and despondency; that is to say, in his moments of deepest insight."

"Where is it, then?" asked Hilda. "I never peeped into it."

"Wait, and it will open for you," replied her friend. "The chasm was merely one of the orifices of that pit of blackness that lies beneath us, everywhere. The firmest substance of human happiness is but a thin crust spread over it, with just reality enough to bear up the illusive stage-scenery amid which we tread. It needs no earthquake to open the chasm. A footstep, a little heavier than ordinary, will serve; and we must step very daintily, not to break through the crust at any moment. By and by, we inevitably sink! It was a foolish piece of heroism in Curtius to precipitate himself there, in advance; for all Rome, you see, has been swallowed up in that gulf, in spite of him. The Palace of the Cæsars has gone down thither, with a hollow, rumbling sound of its fragments! All the temples have tumbled into it; and thousands of statues have been thrown after! All the armies and the triumphs have marched into the great chasm, with their martial music playing, as they stepped over the brink. All the heroes, the statesmen, and the poets! All piled upon poor Curtius, who thought to have saved them all! I am loath to smile at the self-conceit of that gallant horseman, but cannot well avoid it."

"It grieves me to hear you speak thus, Miriam," said Hilda, whose natural and cheerful piety was shocked by her friend's gloomy view of human destinies. "It seems to me that there is no chasm, nor any hideous emptiness under our feet, except what the evil within us digs. If there be such a chasm, let us bridge it over with good thoughts and deeds, and we shall tread safely to the other side. It was the guilt of Rome, no doubt, that caused this gulf to open; and Curtius filled it up with his heroic self-sacrifice and patriotism, which was the best virtue that the old Romans knew. Every wrong thing makes the gulf deeper; every right one helps to fill it up. As the evil of Rome was far more than its good, the whole commonwealth finally sank into it, indeed, but of no original necessity."

"Well, Hilda, it came to the same thing at last," answered Miriam, despondingly.

"Doubtless, too," resumed the sculptor (for his imagination was greatly excited by the idea of this wondrous chasm), "all the blood that the Romans shed, whether on battle-fields, or in the Coliseum, or on the cross,— in whatever public or private murder,—ran into this fatal gulf, and formed a mighty subterranean lake of gore, right beneath our feet. The blood from the thirty wounds in Cæsar's breast flowed hitherward, and that pure little rivulet from Virginia's bosom, too! Virginia, beyond all question, was stabbed by her father, precisely where we are standing."

"Then the spot is hallowed forever!" said Hilda.

"Is there such blessed potency in bloodshed?" asked Miriam. "Nay, Hilda, do not protest! I take your meaning rightly."

They again moved forward. And still, from the Forum and the Via Sacra, from beneath the arches of the Temple of Peace on one side, and the acclivity of the Palace of the Cæsars on the other, there arose singing voices of parties that were strolling through the moonlight. Thus, the air was full of kindred melodies that encountered one another, and twined themselves into a broad, vague music, out of which no single strain could be disentangled. These good examples, as well as the harmonious influences of the hour, incited our artist-friends to make proof of their own vocal powers. With what skill and breath they had, they set up a choral strain,—"Hail, Columbia!" we believe,—which those old Roman echoes must have found it exceeding difficult to repeat aright. Even Hilda poured the slender sweetness of her note into her country's song. Miriam was at first silent, being perhaps unfamiliar with the air and burden. But, suddenly, she threw out such a swell and gush of sound, that it seemed to pervade the whole choir of other voices, and then to rise above them all, and become audible in what would else have been the silence of an upper region. That volume of melodious voice was one of the tokens of a great trouble. There had long been an impulse upon her—amounting, at last, to a necessity—to shriek aloud; but she had struggled against it, till the thunderous anthem gave her an opportunity to relieve her heart by a great cry.

They passed the solitary Column of Phocas, and looked down into the excavated space, where a confusion of pillars, arches, pavements, and shattered blocks and shafts—the crumbs of various ruin dropped from the devouring maw of Time—stand, or lie, at the base of the Capitoline Hill. That renowned hillock (for it is little more) now arose abruptly above them. The ponderous masonry, with which the hill-side is built up, is as old as Rome itself, and looks likely to endure while the world retains any substance or permanence. It once sustained the Capitol, and now bears up the great pile which the mediæval builders raised on the antique foundation, and that still loftier tower, which looks abroad upon a larger page of deeper historic interest than any other scene can show. On the same pedestal of Roman masonry, other structures will doubtless rise, and vanish like ephemeral things.

To a spectator on the spot, it is remarkable that the events of Roman history, and Roman life itself, appear not so distant as the Gothic ages which succeeded them. We stand in the Forum, or on the height of the Capitol, and seem to see the Roman epoch close at hand. We forget that a chasm extends between it and ourselves, in which lie all those dark, rude, unlettered centuries, around the birth-time of Christianity, as well as the age of chivalry and romance, the feudal system, and the infancy of a better civilization than that of Rome. Or, if we remember these mediæval times, they look further off than the Augustan age. The reason may be, that the old Roman literature survives, and creates for us an intimacy with the classic ages, which we have no means of forming with the subsequent ones.

The Italian climate, moreover, robs age of its reverence and makes it look newer than it is. Not the Coliseum, nor the tombs of the Appian Way, nor the oldest pillar in the Forum, nor any other Roman ruin, be it as dilapidated as it may, ever give the impression of venerable antiquity which we gather, along with the ivy, from the gray walls of an English abbey or castle. And yet every brick or stone, which we pick up among the former, had fallen ages before the foundation of the latter was begun. This is owing to the kindliness with which Nature takes an English ruin to her heart, covering it with ivy, as tenderly as Robin Redbreast covered the dead babes with forest leaves. She strives to make it a part of herself, gradually obliterating the handiwork of man, and supplanting it with her own mosses and trailing verdure, till she has won the whole structure back. But, in Italy, whenever man has once hewn a stone, Nature forthwith relinquishes her right to it, and never lays her finger on it again. Age after age finds it bare and naked, in the barren sunshine, and leaves it so. Besides this natural disadvantage, too, each succeeding century, in Rome, has done its best to ruin the very ruins, so far as their picturesque effect is concerned, by stealing away the marble and hewn stone, and leaving only yellow bricks, which never can look venerable.

The party ascended the winding way that leads from the Forum to the Piazza of the Campidoglio on the summit of the Capitoline Hill. They stood awhile to contemplate the bronze equestrian statue of Marcus Aurelius. The moonlight glistened upon traces of the gilding which had once covered both rider and steed; these were almost gone, but the aspect of dignity was still perfect, clothing the figure as it were with an imperial robe of light. It is the most majestic representation of the kingly character that ever the world has seen. A sight of the old heathen emperor is enough to create an evanescent sentiment of loyalty even in a democratic bosom, so august does he look, so fit to rule, so worthy of man's profoundest homage and obedience, so inevitably attractive of his love. He stretches forth his hand with an air of grand beneficence and unlimited authority, as if uttering a decree from which no appeal was permissible, but in which the obedient subject would find his highest interests consulted; a command that was in itself a benediction.

"The sculptor of this statue knew what a king should be," observed Kenyon, "and knew, likewise, the heart of mankind, and how it craves a true ruler, under whatever title, as a child its father."

"Oh, if there were but one such man as this!" exclaimed Miriam. "One such man in an age, and one in all the world; then how speedily would the strife, wickedness, and sorrow of us poor creatures be relieved. We would come to him with our griefs, whatever they might be,—even a poor, frail woman burdened with her heavy heart,—and lay them at his feet, and never need to take them up again. The rightful king would see to all."

"What an idea of the regal office and duty!" said Kenyon, with a smile. "It is a woman's idea of the whole matter to perfection. It is Hilda's, too, no doubt?"

"No," answered the quiet Hilda; "I should never look for such assistance from an earthly king."

"Hilda, my religious Hilda," whispered Miriam, suddenly drawing the girl close to her, "do you know how it is with me? I would give all I have or hope—my life, oh how freely—for one instant of your trust in God! You little guess my need of it. You really think, then, that He sees and cares for us?"

"Miriam, you frighten me."

"Hush, hush! do not let them hear you!" whispered Miriam. "I frighten you, you say; for Heaven's sake, how? Am I strange? is there anything wild in my behavior?"

"Only for that moment," replied Hilda, "because you seemed to doubt God's providence."

"We will talk of that another time," said her friend. "Just now it is very dark to me."

On the left of the Piazza of the Campidoglio, as you face cityward, and at the head of the long and stately flight of steps descending from the

Capitoline Hill to the level of lower Rome, there is a narrow lane or passage. Into this the party of our friends now turned. The path ascended a little, and ran along under the walls of a palace, but soon passed through a gateway, and terminated in a small paved court-yard. It was bordered by a low parapet.

The spot, for some reason or other, impressed them as exceedingly lonely. On one side was the great height of the palace, with the moonshine falling over it, and showing all the windows barred and shuttered. Not a human eye could look down into the little courtyard, even if the seemingly deserted palace had a tenant. On all other sides of its narrow compass there was nothing but the parapet, which as it now appeared was built right on the edge of a steep precipice. Gazing from its imminent brow, the party beheld a crowded confusion of roofs spreading over the whole space between them and the line of hills that lay beyond the Tiber. A long, misty wreath, just dense enough to catch a little of the moonshine, floated above the houses, midway towards the hilly line, and showed the course of the unseen river. Far away on the right, the moon gleamed on the dome of St. Peter's as well as on many lesser and nearer domes.

"What a beautiful view of the city!" exclaimed Hilda; "and I never saw Rome from this point before."

"It ought to afford a good prospect," said the sculptor; "for it was from this point—at least we are at liberty to think so, if we choose—that many a famous Roman caught his last glimpse of his native city, and of all other earthly things. This is one of the sides of the Tarpeian Rock. Look over the parapet, and see what a sheer tumble there might still be for a traitor, in spite of the thirty feet of soil that have accumulated at the foot of the precipice."

They all bent over, and saw that the cliff fell perpendicularly downward to about the depth, or rather more, at which the tall palace rose in height above their heads. Not that it was still the natural, shaggy front of the original precipice; for it appeared to be cased in ancient stone-work, through which the primeval rock showed its face here and there grimly and doubtfully. Mosses grew on the slight projections, and little shrubs sprouted out of the crevices, but could not much soften the stern aspect of the cliff. Brightly as the Italian moonlight fell a-down the height, it scarcely showed what portion of it was man's work, and what was nature's, but left it all in very much the same kind of ambiguity and half-knowledge in which antiquarians generally leave the identity of Roman remains.

The roofs of some poor-looking houses, which had been built against the base and sides of the cliff, rose nearly midway to the top; but from an angle of the parapet there was a precipitous plunge straight downward into a stone-paved court.

"I prefer this to any other site as having been veritably the Traitor's Leap," said Kenyon, "because it was so convenient to the Capitol. It was an admirable idea of those stern old fellows to fling their political criminals down from the very summit on which stood the Senate House and

Jove's Temple, emblems of the institutions which they sought to violate. It symbolizes how sudden was the fall in those days from the utmost height of ambition to its profoundest ruin."

"Come, come; it is midnight," cried another artist, "too late to be moralizing here. We are literally dreaming on the edge of a precipice. Let us go home."

"It is time, indeed," said Hilda.

The sculptor was not without hopes that he might be favored with the sweet charge of escorting Hilda to the foot of her tower. Accordingly, when the party prepared to turn back, he offered her his arm. Hilda at first accepted it; but when they had partly threaded the passage between the little court-yard and the Piazza del Campidoglio, she discovered that Miriam had remained behind.

"I must go back," said she, withdrawing her arm from Kenyon's; "but pray do not come with me. Several times this evening I have had a fancy that Miriam had something on her mind, some sorrow or perplexity, which, perhaps, it would relieve her to tell me about. No, no; do not turn back! Donatello will be a sufficient guardian for Miriam and me."

The sculptor was a good deal mortified, and perhaps a little angry; but he knew Hilda's mood of gentle decision and independence too well not to obey her. He therefore suffered the fearless maiden to return alone.

Meanwhile Miriam had not noticed the departure of the rest of the company; she remained on the edge of the precipice and Donatello along with her.

"It would be a fatal fall, still," she said to herself, looking over the parapet, and shuddering as her eye measured the depth. "Yes; surely yes! Even without the weight of an overburdened heart, a human body would fall heavily enough upon those stones to shake all its joints asunder. How soon it would be over!"

Donatello, of whose presence she was possibly not aware, now pressed closer to her side; and he, too, like Miriam, bent over the low parapet and trembled violently. Yet he seemed to feel that perilous fascination which haunts the brow of precipices, tempting the unwary one to fling himself over for the very horror of the thing, for, after drawing hastily back, he again looked down, thrusting himself out farther than before. He then stood silent a brief space, struggling, perhaps, to make himself conscious of the historic associations of the scene.

"What are you thinking of, Donatello?" asked Miriam.

"Who are they," said he, looking earnestly in her face, "who have been flung over here in days gone by?"

"Men that cumbered the world," she replied. "Men whose lives were the bane of their fellow-creatures. Men who poisoned the air, which is the common breath of all, for their own selfish purposes. There was short work with such men in old Roman times. Just in the moment of their triumph, a hand, as of an avenging giant, clutched them, and dashed the wretches down this precipice."

"Was it well done?" asked the young man.

"It was well done," answered Miriam; "innocent persons were saved by the destruction of a guilty one, who deserved his doom."

While this brief conversation passed, Donatello had once or twice glanced aside with a watchful air, just as a hound may often be seen to take sidelong note of some suspicious object, while he gives his more direct attention to something nearer at hand. Miriam seemed now first to become aware of the silence that had followed upon the cheerful talk and laughter of a few moments before.

Looking round, she perceived that all her company of merry friends had retired, and Hilda, too, in whose soft and quiet presence she had always an indescribable feeling of security. All gone; and only herself and Donatello left hanging over the brow of the ominous precipice.

Not so, however; not entirely alone! In the basement wall of the palace, shaded from the moon, there was a deep, empty niche, that had probably once contained a statue; not empty, either; for a figure now came forth from it and approached Miriam. She must have had cause to dread some unspeakable evil from this strange persecutor, and to know that this was the very crisis of her calamity; for, as he drew near, such a cold, sick despair crept over her, that it impeded her breath, and benumbed her natural promptitude of thought. Miriam seemed dreamily to remember falling on her knees; but, in her whole recollection of that wild moment, she beheld herself as in a dim show, and could not well distinguish what was done and suffered; no, not even whether she were really an actor and sufferer in the scene.

Hilda, meanwhile, had separated herself from the sculptor, and turned back to rejoin her friend. At a distance, she still heard the mirth of her late companions, who were going down the cityward descent of the Capitoline Hill; they had set up a new stave of melody, in which her own soft voice, as well as the powerful sweetness of Miriam's, was sadly missed.

The door of the little court-yard had swung upon its hinges, and partly closed itself. Hilda (whose native gentleness pervaded all her movements) was quietly opening it, when she was startled, midway, by the noise of a struggle within, beginning and ending all in one breathless instant. Along with it, or closely succeeding it, was a loud, fearful cry, which quivered upward through the air, and sank quivering downward to the earth. Then, a silence! Poor Hilda had looked into the court-yard, and saw the whole quick passage of a deed, which took but that little time to grave itself in the eternal adamant.

## CHAPTER XIX

### THE FAUN'S TRANSFORMATION

THE door of the court-yard swung slowly, and closed itself of its own accord. Miriam and Donatello were now alone there. She clasped her hands, and looked wildly at the young man, whose form seemed to have dilated, and whose eyes blazed with the fierce energy that had suddenly inspired him. It had kindled him into a man; it had developed within him an intelligence which was no native characteristic of the Donatello whom we have heretofore known. But that simple and joyous creature was gone forever.

"What have you done?" said Miriam, in a horror-stricken whisper.

The glow of rage was still lurid on Donatello's face, and now flashed out again from his eyes.

"I did what ought to be done to a traitor!" he replied. "I did what your eyes bade me do, when I asked them with mine, as I held the wretch over the precipice!"

These last words struck Miriam like a bullet. Could it be so? Had her eyes provoked or assented to this deed? She had not known it. But, alas! looking back into the frenzy and turmoil of the scene just acted, she could not deny—she was not sure whether it might be so, or no—that a wild joy had flamed up in her heart, when she beheld her persecutor in his mortal peril. Was it horror?—or ecstasy?—or both in one? Be the emotion what it might, it had blazed up more madly, when Donatello flung his victim off the cliff, and more and more, while his shriek went quivering downward. With the dead thump upon the stones below, had come an unutterable horror.

"And my eyes bade you do it!" repeated she.

They both leaned over the parapet, and gazed downward as earnestly as if some inestimable treasure had fallen over, and were yet recoverable. On the pavement, below, was a dark mass, lying in a heap, with little or nothing human in its appearance, except that the hands were stretched out, as if they might have clutched, for a moment, at the small square stones. But there was no motion in them now. Miriam watched the heap of mortality while she could count a hundred, which she took pains to do. No stir; not a finger moved!

"You have killed him, Donatello! He is quite dead!" said she. "Stone dead! Would I were so, too!"

"Did you not mean that he should die?" sternly asked Donatello, still in the glow of that intelligence which passion had developed in him. "There was short time to weigh the matter; but he had his trial in that breath or two while I held him over the cliff, and his sentence in that one glance, when your eyes responded to mine! Say that I have slain him against your will,—say that he died without your whole consent,—and, in another breath, you shall see me lying beside him."

"Oh, never!" cried Miriam. "My one, own friend! Never, never, never!"

She turned to him,—the guilty, blood-stained, lonely woman,—she turned to her fellow-criminal, the youth, so lately innocent, whom she had drawn into her doom. She pressed him close, close to her bosom, with a clinging embrace that brought their two hearts together, till the horror and agony of each was combined into one emotion, and that a kind of rapture.

"Yes, Donatello, you speak the truth!" said she; "my heart consented to what you did. We two slew yonder wretch. The deed knots us together, for time and eternity, like the coil of a serpent!"

They threw one other glance at the heap of death below, to assure themselves that it was there; so like a dream was the whole thing. Then they turned from that fatal precipice, and came out of the court-yard, arm in arm, heart in heart. Instinctively, they were heedful not to sever themselves so much as a pace or two from one another, for fear of the terror and deadly chill that would thenceforth wait for them in solitude. Their deed—the crime which Donatello wrought, and Miriam accepted on the instant—had wreathed itself, as she said, like a serpent, in inextricable links about both their souls, and drew them into one, by its terrible contractile power. It was closer than a marriage-bond. So intimate, in those first moments, was the union, that it seemed as if their new sympathy annihilated all other ties, and that they were released from the chain of humanity; a new sphere, a special law, had been created for them alone. The world could not come near them; they were safe!

When they reached the flight of steps leading downward from the Capitol, there was a far-off noise of singing and laughter. Swift, indeed, had been the rush of the crisis that was come and gone! This was still the merriment of the party that had so recently been their companions. They recognized the voices which, a little while ago, had accorded and sung in cadence with their own. But they were familiar voices no more; they sounded strangely, and, as it were, out of the depths of space; so remote was all that pertained to the past life of these guilty ones, in the moral seclusion that had suddenly extended itself around them. But how close, and ever closer, did the breath of the immeasurable waste, that lay between them and all brotherhood or sisterhood, now press them one within the other!

"O friend!" cried Miriam, so putting her soul into the word that it took a heavy richness of meaning, and seemed never to have been spoken before,—"O friend, are you conscious, as I am, of this companionship that knits our heart-strings together?"

"I feel it, Miriam," said Donatello. "We draw one breath; we live one life!"

"Only yesterday," continued Miriam; "nay, only a short half-hour ago, I shivered in an icy solitude. No friendship, no sisterhood, could come near enough to keep the warmth within my heart. In an instant, all is changed! There can be no more loneliness!"

"None, Miriam!" said Donatello.

"None, my beautiful one!" responded Miriam, gazing in his face, which had taken a higher, almost an heroic aspect, from the strength of passion. "None, my innocent one! Surely, it is no crime that we have committed. One wretched and worthless life has been sacrificed to cement two other lives for evermore."

"For evermore, Miriam!" said Donatello; "cemented with his blood!"

The young man started at the word which he had himself spoken; it may be that it brought home, to the simplicity of his imagination, what he had not before dreamed of,—the ever-increasing loathsomeness of a union that consists in guilt. Cemented with blood, which would corrupt and grow more noisome forever and forever, but bind them none the less strictly for that.

"Forget it! Cast it all behind you!" said Miriam, detecting, by her sympathy, the pang that was in his heart. "The deed has done its office, and has no existence any more."

They flung the past behind them, as she counselled, or else distilled from it a fiery intoxication, which sufficed to carry them triumphantly through those first moments of their doom. For, guilt has its moment of rapture too. The foremost result of a broken law is ever an ecstatic sense of freedom. And thus there exhaled upward (out of their dark sympathy, at the base of which lay a human corpse) a bliss, or an insanity, which the unhappy pair imagined to be well worth the sleepy innocence that was forever lost to them.

As their spirits rose to the solemn madness of the occasion, they went onward,—not stealthily, not fearfully,—but with a stately gait and aspect. Passion lent them (as it does to meaner shapes) its brief nobility of carriage. They trod through the streets of Rome, as if they, too, were among the majestic and guilty shadows, that, from ages long gone by, have haunted the blood-stained city. And, at Miriam's suggestion, they turned aside, for the sake of treading loftily past the old site of Pompey's Forum.

"For there was a great deed done here!" she said,—"a deed of blood like ours! Who knows, but we may meet the high and ever-sad fraternity of Cæsar's murderers, and exchange a salutation?"

"Are they our brethren, now?" asked Donatello.

"Yes; all of them," said Miriam; "and many another, whom the world little dreams of, has been made our brother or our sister, by what we have done within this hour!"

And, at the thought, she shivered. Where, then, was the seclusion, the remoteness, the strange, lonesome Paradise, into which she and her one companion had been transported by their crime? Was there, indeed, no such refuge, but only a crowded thoroughfare and jostling throng of criminals? And was it true, that whatever hand had a blood-stain on it,— or had poured out poison,—or strangled a babe at its birth,—or clutched

a grandsire's throat, he sleeping, and robbed him of his few last breaths,
—had now the right to offer itself in fellowship with their two hands? Too
certainly, that right existed. It is a terrible thought, that an individual
wrong-doing melts into the great mass of human crime, and makes us,—
who dreamed only of our own little separate sin,—makes us guilty of the
whole. And thus Miriam and her lover were not an insulated pair, but
members of an innumerable confraternity of guilty ones, all shuddering
at each other.

"But not now; not yet," she murmured to herself. "To-night, at least,
there shall be no remorse!"

Wandering without a purpose, it so chanced that they turned into a
street, at one extremity of which stood Hilda's tower. There was a light in
her high chamber; a light, too, at the Virgin's shrine; and the glimmer of
these two was the loftiest light beneath the stars. Miriam drew Donatello's arm, to make him stop, and while they stood at some distance
looking at Hilda's window, they beheld her approach and throw it open.
She leaned far forth, and extended her clasped hands towards the sky.

"The good, pure, child! She is praying, Donatello," said Miriam, with
a kind of simple joy at witnessing the devoutness of her friend. Then her
own sin rushed upon her, and she shouted, with the rich strength of her
voice, "Pray for us, Hilda; we need it!"

Whether Hilda heard and recognized the voice we cannot tell. The
window was immediately closed, and her form disappeared from behind
the snowy curtain. Miriam felt this to be a token that the cry of her condemned spirit was shut out of heaven.

CHAPTER XX

THE BURIAL CHANT

THE Church of the Capuchins (where, as the reader may remember, some
of our acquaintances had made an engagement to meet) stands a little
aside from the Piazza Barberini. Thither, at the hour agreed upon, on
the morning after the scenes last described, Miriam and Donatello directed their steps. At no time are people so sedulously careful to keep their
trifling appointments, attend to their ordinary occupations, and thus put
a commonplace aspect on life, as when conscious of some secret that if
suspected would make them look monstrous in the general eye.

Yet how tame and wearisome is the impression of all ordinary things in
the contrast with such a fact! How sick and tremulous, the next morning, is the spirit that has dared so much only the night before! How icy
cold is the heart, when the fervor, the wild ecstasy of passion, has faded

away, and sunk down among the dead ashes of the fire that blazed so fiercely, and was fed by the very substance of its life! How faintly does the criminal stagger onward, lacking the impulse of that strong madness that hurried him into guilt, and treacherously deserts him in the midst of it!

When Miriam and Donatello drew near the church, they found only Kenyon awaiting them on the steps. Hilda had likewise promised to be of the party, but had not yet appeared. Meeting the sculptor, Miriam put a force upon herself and succeeded in creating an artificial flow of spirits, which, to any but the nicest observation, was quite as effective as a natural one. She spoke sympathizingly to the sculptor on the subject of Hilda's absence, and somewhat annoyed him by alluding in Donatello's hearing to an attachment which had never been openly avowed, though perhaps plainly enough betrayed. He fancied that Miriam did not quite recognize the limits of the strictest delicacy; he even went so far as to generalize, and conclude within himself, that this deficiency is a more general failing in woman than in man, the highest refinement being a masculine attribute.

But the idea was unjust to the sex at large, and especially so to this poor Miriam, who was hardly responsible for her frantic efforts to be gay. Possibly, moreover, the nice action of the mind is set ajar by any violent shock, as of great misfortune or great crime, so that the finer perceptions may be blurred thenceforth, and the effect be traceable in all the minutest conduct of life.

"Did you see anything of the dear child after you left us?" asked Miriam, still keeping Hilda as her topic of conversation. "I missed her sadly on my way homeward; for nothing insures me such delightful and innocent dreams (I have experienced it twenty times) as a talk late in the evening with Hilda."

"So I should imagine," said the sculptor, gravely; "but it is an advantage that I have little or no opportunity of enjoying. I know not what became of Hilda after my parting from you. She was not especially my companion in any part of our walk. The last I saw of her she was hastening back to rejoin you in the court-yard of the Palazzo Caffarelli."

"Impossible!" cried Miriam, starting.

"Then did you not see her again?" inquired Kenyon, in some alarm.

"Not there," answered Miriam, quietly; "indeed, I followed pretty closely on the heels of the rest of the party. But do not be alarmed on Hilda's account; the Virgin is bound to watch over the good child, for the sake of the piety with which she keeps the lamp alight at her shrine. And, besides, I have always felt that Hilda is just as safe in these evil streets of Rome as her white doves when they fly downwards from the tower-top, and run to and fro among the horses' feet. There is certainly a providence on purpose for Hilda, if for no other human creature."

"I religiously believe it," rejoined the sculptor; "and yet my mind would be the easier, if I knew that she had returned safely to her tower."

"Then make yourself quite easy," answered Miriam. "I saw her (and it is the last sweet sight that I remember) leaning from her window midway between earth and sky!"

Kenyon now looked at Donatello.

"You seem out of spirits, my dear friend," he observed. "This languid Roman atmosphere is not the airy wine that you were accustomed to breathe at home. I have not forgotten your hospitable invitation to meet you this summer at your castle among the Apennines. It is my fixed purpose to come, I assure you. We shall both be the better for some deep draughts of the mountain-breezes."

"It may be," said Donatello, with unwonted sombreness; "the old house seemed joyous when I was a child. But as I remember it now it was a grim place, too."

The sculptor looked more attentively at the young man, and was surprised and alarmed to observe how entirely the fine, fresh glow of animal spirits had departed out of his face. Hitherto, moreover, even while he was standing perfectly still, there had been a kind of possible gambol indicated in his aspect. It was quite gone now. All his youthful gayety, and with it his simplicity of manner, was eclipsed, if not utterly extinct.

"You are surely ill, my dear fellow," exclaimed Kenyon.

"Am I? Perhaps so," said Donatello indifferently; "I never have been ill, and know not what it may be."

"Do not make the poor lad fancy-sick," whispered Miriam, pulling the sculptor's sleeve. "He is of a nature to lie down and die at once, if he finds himself drawing such melancholy breaths as we ordinary people are enforced to burden our lungs withal. But we must get him away from this old, dreamy, and dreary Rome, where nobody but himself ever thought of being gay. Its influences are too heavy to sustain the life of such a creature."

The above conversation had passed chiefly on the steps of the Cappuccini; and, having said so much, Miriam lifted the leathern curtain that hangs before all church-doors in Italy.

"Hilda has forgotten her appointment," she observed, "or else her maiden slumbers are very sound this morning. We will wait for her no longer."

They entered the nave. The interior of the church was of moderate compass, but of good architecture, with a vaulted roof over the nave, and a row of dusky chapels on either side of it instead of the customary side-aisles. Each chapel had its saintly shrine, hung round with offerings; its picture above the altar, although closely veiled, if by any painter of renown; and its hallowed tapers, burning continually, to set alight the devotion of the worshippers. The pavement of the nave was chiefly of marble, and looked old and broken, and was shabbily patched here and there with tiles of brick; it was inlaid, moreover, with tombstones of the mediæval taste, on which were quaintly sculptured borders, figures, and portraits in bas-relief, and Latin epitaphs, now grown illegible by the tread of footsteps over them. The church appertains to a convent of Capuchin monks; and, as usually happens when a reverend brotherhood have such an edifice in charge, the floor seemed never to have been scrubbed or swept, and had as little the aspect of sanctity as a kennel; whereas, in all churches of nunneries, the maiden sisterhood invariably show the purity of their own hearts by the virgin cleanliness and visible consecration of the walls and pavement.

As our friends entered the church, their eyes rested at once on a remarkable object in the centre of the nave. It was either the actual body, or, as might rather have been supposed at first glance, the cunningly wrought waxen face and suitably draped figure of a dead monk. This image of wax or clay-cold reality, whichever it might be, lay on a slightly elevated bier, with three tall candles burning on each side, another tall candle at the head, and another at the foot. There was music, too, in harmony with so funereal a spectacle. From beneath the pavement of the church came the deep, lugubrious strain of a *De Profundis*, which sounded like an utterance of the tomb itself; so dismally did it rumble through the burial vaults, and ooze up among the flat gravestones and sad epitaphs, filling the church as with a gloomy mist.

"I must look more closely at that dead monk before we leave the church," remarked the sculptor. "In the study of my art, I have gained many a hint from the dead, which the living could never have given me."

"I can well imagine it," answered Miriam. "One clay image is readily copied from another. But let us first see Guido's picture. The light is favorable now."

Accordingly, they turned into the first chapel on the right hand, as you enter the nave; and there they beheld,—not the picture, indeed,—but a closely drawn curtain. The churchmen of Italy make no scruple of sacrificing the very purpose for which a work of sacred art has been created; that of opening the way for religious sentiment through the quick medium of sight, by bringing angels, saints, and martyrs down visibly upon earth; of sacrificing this high purpose, and, for aught they know, the welfare of many souls along with it, to the hope of a paltry fee. Every work by an artist of celebrity is hidden behind a veil, and seldom revealed, except to Protestants, who scorn it as an object of devotion, and value it only for its artistic merit.

The sacristan was quickly found, however, and lost no time in disclosing the youthful Archangel, setting his divine foot on the head of his fallen adversary. It was an image of that greatest of future events, which we hope for so ardently,—at least, while we are young,—but find so very long in coming,—the triumph of goodness over the evil principle.

"Where can Hilda be?" exclaimed Kenyon. "It is not her custom ever to fail in an engagement; and the present one was made entirely on her account. Except herself, you know, we were all agreed in our recollection of the picture."

"But we were wrong, and Hilda right, as you perceive," said Miriam, directing his attention to the point on which their dispute of the night before had arisen. "It is not easy to detect her astray as regards any picture on which those clear, soft eyes of hers have ever rested."

"And she has studied and admired few pictures so much as this," observed the sculptor. "No wonder; for there is hardly another so beautiful in the world. What an expression of heavenly severity in the Archangel's face! There is a degree of pain, trouble, and disgust at being brought in contact with sin, even for the purpose of quelling and punishing it; and yet a celestial tranquillity pervades his whole being."

"I have never been able," said Miriam, "to admire this picture nearly so much as Hilda does, in its moral and intellectual aspect. If it cost her more trouble to be good, if her soul were less white and pure, she would be a more competent critic of this picture, and would estimate it not half so high. I see its defects to-day more clearly than ever before."

"What are some of them?" asked Kenyon.

"That Archangel, now," Miriam continued; "how fair he looks, with his unruffled wings, with his unhacked sword, and clad in his bright armor, and that exquisitely fitting sky-blue tunic, cut in the latest Paradisiacal mode! What a dainty air of the first celestial society! With what half-scornful delicacy he sets his prettily sandalled foot on the head of his prostrate foe! But, is it thus that virtue looks the moment after its death-struggle with evil? No, no; I could have told Guido better. A full third of the Archangel's feathers should have been torn from his wings; the rest all ruffled, till they looked like Satan's own! His sword should be streaming with blood, and perhaps broken half-way to the hilt; his armor crushed, his robes rent, his breast gory; a bleeding gash on his brow, cutting right across the stern scowl of battle! He should press his foot hard down upon the old serpent, as if his very soul depended upon it, feeling him squirm mightily, and doubting whether the fight were half over yet, and how the victory might turn! And, with all this fierceness, this grimness, this unutterable horror, there should still be something high, tender, and holy in Michael's eyes, and around his mouth. But the battle never was such child's play as Guido's dapper Archangel seems to have found it."

"For Heaven's sake, Miriam," cried Kenyon, astonished at the wild energy of her talk; "paint the picture of man's struggle against sin according to your own idea! I think it will be a masterpiece."

"The picture would have its share of truth, I assure you," she answered; "but I am sadly afraid the victory would fall on the wrong side. Just fancy a smoke-blackened, fiery-eyed demon, bestriding that nice young angel, clutching his white throat with one of his hinder claws; and giving a triumphant whisk of his scaly tail, with a poisonous dart at the end of it! That is what they risk, poor souls, who do battle with Michael's enemy."

It now, perhaps, struck Miriam that her mental disquietude was impelling her to an undue vivacity; for she paused, and turned away from the picture, without saying a word more about it. All this while, moreover, Donatello had been very ill at ease, casting awe-stricken and inquiring glances at the dead monk; as if he could look nowhere but at that ghastly object, merely because it shocked him. Death has probably a peculiar horror and ugliness, when forced upon the contemplation of a person so naturally joyous as Donatello, who lived with completeness in the present moment, and was able to form but vague images of the future.

"What is the matter, Donatello?" whispered Miriam, soothingly. "You are quite in a tremble, my poor friend! What is it?"

"This awful chant from beneath the church," answered Donatello; "it oppresses me; the air is so heavy with it that I can scarcely draw my breath. And yonder dead monk! I feel as if he were lying right across my heart."

"Take courage!" whispered she again; "come, we will approach close to the dead monk. The only way, in such cases, is to stare the ugly horror right in the face; never a sidelong glance, nor half-look, for those are what show a frightful thing in its frightfullest aspect. Lean on me, dearest friend! My heart is very strong for both of us. Be brave; and all is well."

Donatello hung back for a moment, but then pressed close to Miriam's side, and suffered her to lead him up to the bier. The sculptor followed. A number of persons, chiefly women, with several children among them, were standing about the corpse; and as our three friends drew nigh, a mother knelt down, and caused her little boy to kneel, both kissing the beads and crucifix that hung from the monk's girdle. Possibly he had died in the odor of sanctity; or, at all events, death and his brown frock and cowl made a sacred image of this reverend father.

## CHAPTER XXI

### THE DEAD CAPUCHIN

THE dead monk was clad, as when alive, in the brown woollen frock of the Capuchins, with the hood drawn over his head, but so as to leave the features and a portion of the beard uncovered. His rosary and cross hung at his side; his hands were folded over his breast; his feet (he was of a barefooted order in his lifetime, and continued so in death) protruded from beneath his habit, stiff and stark, with a more waxen look than even his face. They were tied together at the ankles with a black ribbon.

The countenance, as we have already said, was fully displayed. It had a purplish hue upon it, unlike the paleness of an ordinary corpse, but as little resembling the flush of natural life. The eyelids were but partially drawn down, and showed the eyeballs beneath; as if the deceased friar were stealing a glimpse at the by-standers, to watch whether they were duly impressed with the solemnity of his obsequies. The shaggy eyebrows gave sternness to the look.

Miriam passed between two of the lighted candles, and stood close beside the bier.

"My God!" murmured she. "What is this?"

She grasped Donatello's hand, and, at the same instant, felt him give a convulsive shudder, which she knew to have been caused by a sudden and terrible throb of the heart. His hand, by an instantaneous change, became like ice within hers, which likewise grew so icy, that their insensible fingers might have rattled, one against the other. No wonder that their blood curdled; no wonder that their hearts leaped and paused! The dead face of the monk, gazing at them beneath its half-closed eyelids, was the same visage that had glared upon their naked souls, the past midnight, as Donatello flung him over the precipice.

The sculptor was standing at the foot of the bier, and had not yet seen the monk's features.

"Those naked feet!" said he. "I know not why, but they affect me strangely. They have walked to and fro over the hard pavements of Rome, and through a hundred other rough ways of this life, where the monk went begging for his brotherhood; along the cloisters and dreary corridors of his convent, too, from his youth upward! It is a suggestive idea, to track those worn feet backward through all the paths they have trodden, ever since they were the tender and rosy little feet of a baby, and (cold as they now are) were kept warm in his mother's hand."

As his companions, whom the sculptor supposed to be close by him, made no response to his fanciful musing, he looked up, and saw them at the head of the bier. He advanced thither himself.

"Ha!" exclaimed he.

He cast a horror-stricken and bewildered glance at Miriam, but withdrew it immediately. Not that he had any definite suspicion, or, it may be, even a remote idea, that she could be held responsible, in the least degree, for this man's sudden death. In truth, it seemed too wild a thought to connect, in reality, Miriam's persecutor of many past months and the vagabond of the preceding night, with the dead Capuchin of to-day. It resembled one of those unaccountable changes and interminglings of identity, which so often occur among the personages of a dream. But Kenyon, as befitted the professor of an imaginative art, was endowed with an exceedingly quick sensibility, which was apt to give him intimations of the true state of matters that lay beyond his actual vision. There was a whisper in his ear; it said, "Hush!" Without asking himself wherefore, he resolved to be silent as regarded the mysterious discovery which he had made, and to leave any remark or exclamation to be voluntarily offered by Miriam. If she never spoke, then let the riddle be unsolved.

And now occurred a circumstance that would seem too fantastic to be told, if it had not actually happened, precisely as we set it down. As the three friends stood by the bier, they saw that a little stream of blood had begun to ooze from the dead monk's nostrils; it crept slowly towards the thicket of his beard, where, in the course of a moment or two, it hid itself.

"How strange!" ejaculated Kenyon. "The monk died of apoplexy, I suppose, or by some sudden accident, and the blood has not yet congealed."

"Do you consider that a sufficient explanation?" asked Miriam, with a smile from which the sculptor involuntarily turned away his eyes. "Does it satisfy you?"

"And why not?" he inquired.

"Of course, you know the old superstition about this phenomenon of blood flowing from a dead body," she rejoined. "How can we tell but that the murderer of this monk (or, possibly, it may be only that privileged murderer, his physician) may have just entered the church?"

"I cannot jest about it," said Kenyon. "It is an ugly sight!"

"True, true; horrible to see, or dream of!" she replied, with one of those long, tremulous sighs, which so often betray a sick heart by escaping unexpectedly. "We will not look at it any more. Come away, Donatello. Let us escape from this dismal church. The sunshine will do you good."

When had ever a woman such a trial to sustain as this! By no possible supposition could Miriam explain the identity of the dead Capuchin, quietly and decorously laid out in the nave of his convent church, with that of her murdered persecutor, flung heedlessly at the foot of the precipice. The effect upon her imagination was as if a strange and unknown corpse had miraculously, while she was gazing at it, assumed the likeness of that face, so terrible henceforth in her remembrance. It was a symbol, perhaps, of the deadly iteration with which she was doomed to behold the image of her crime reflected back upon her in a thousand ways, and converting the great, calm face of Nature, in the whole, and in its innumerable details, into a manifold reminiscence of that one dead visage.

No sooner had Miriam turned away from the bier, and gone a few steps, than she fancied the likeness altogether an illusion, which would vanish at a closer and colder view. She must look at it again, therefore, and at once; or else the grave would close over the face, and leave the awful fantasy that had connected itself therewith fixed ineffaceably in her brain.

"Wait for me, one moment!" she said to her companions. "Only a moment!"

So she went back, and gazed once more at the corpse. Yes; these were the features that Miriam had known so well; this was the visage that she remembered from a far longer date than the most intimate of her friends suspected; this form of clay had held the evil spirit which blasted her sweet youth, and compelled her, as it were, to stain her womanhood with crime. But, whether it were the majesty of death, or something originally noble and lofty in the character of the dead, which the soul had stamped upon the features, as it left them; so it was that Miriam now quailed and shook, not for the vulgar horror of the spectacle, but for the severe, reproachful glance that seemed to come from between those half-closed lids. True, there had been nothing, in his lifetime, viler than this man. She knew it; there was no other fact within her consciousness that she felt to be so certain; and yet, because her persecutor found himself safe and irrefutable in death, he frowned upon his victim, and threw back the blame on her!

"Is it thou, indeed?" she murmured, under her breath. "Then thou hast no right to scowl upon me so! But art thou real, or a vision?"

She bent down over the dead monk, till one of her rich curls brushed against his forehead. She touched one of his folded hands with her finger.

"It is he," said Miriam. "There is the scar, that I know so well, on his brow. And it is no vision; he is palpable to my touch! I will question the fact no longer, but deal with it as I best can."

It was wonderful to see how the crisis developed in Miriam its own proper strength, and the faculty of sustaining the demands which it made upon her fortitude. She ceased to tremble; the beautiful woman gazed sternly at her dead enemy, endeavoring to meet and quell the look of accusation that he threw from between his half-closed eyelids.

"No; thou shalt not scowl me down!" said she. "Neither now, nor when we stand together at the judgment-seat. I fear not to meet thee there. Farewell, till that next encounter!"

Haughtily waving her hand, Miriam rejoined her friends, who were awaiting her at the door of the church. As they went out, the sacristan stopped them, and proposed to show the cemetery of the convent, where the deceased members of the fraternity are laid to rest in sacred earth, brought long ago from Jerusalem.

"And will yonder monk be buried there?" she asked.

"Brother Antonio?" exclaimed the sacristan. "Surely, our good brother will be put to bed there! His grave is already dug, and the last occupant has made room for him. Will you look at it, signorina?"

"I will!" said Miriam.

"Then excuse me," observed Kenyon; "for I shall leave you. One dead monk has more than sufficed me; and I am not bold enough to face the whole mortality of the convent."

It was easy to see, by Donatello's looks, that he, as well as the sculptor, would gladly have escaped a visit to the famous cemetery of the Cappuccini. But Miriam's nerves were strained to such a pitch, that she anticipated a certain solace and absolute relief in passing from one ghastly spectacle to another of long-accumulated ugliness; and there was, besides, a singular sense of duty which impelled her to look at the final resting-place of the being whose fate had been so disastrously involved with her own. She therefore followed the sacristan's guidance, and drew her companion along with her, whispering encouragement as they went.

The cemetery is beneath the church, but entirely above ground, and lighted by a row of iron-grated windows without glass. A corridor runs along beside these windows, and gives access to three or four vaulted recesses, or chapels, of considerable breadth and height, the floor of which consists of the consecrated earth of Jerusalem. It is smoothed decorously over the deceased brethren of the convent, and is kept quite free from grass or weeds, such as would grow even in these gloomy recesses, if pains were not bestowed to root them up. But, as the cemetery is small, and it is a precious privilege to sleep in holy ground, the brotherhood are immemorially accustomed, when one of their number dies, to take the longest-buried skeleton out of the oldest grave, and lay the new slumberer there instead. Thus, each of the good friars, in his turn, enjoys the luxury of a consecrated bed, attended with the slight drawback of being forced to get up long before daybreak, as it were, and make room for another lodger.

The arrangement of the unearthed skeletons is what makes the special interest of the cemetery. The arched and vaulted walls of the burial recesses are supported by massive pillars and pilasters made of thigh-bones and skulls; the whole material of the structure appears to be of a similar kind; and the knobs and embossed ornaments of this strange architecture are represented by the joints of the spine, and the more delicate tracery by the smaller bones of the human frame. The summits of the arches are adorned with entire skeletons, looking as if they were wrought most skilfully in bas-relief. There is no possibility of describing how ugly and grotesque is the effect, combined with a certain artistic merit, nor how much perverted ingenuity has been shown in this queer way, nor what a multitude of dead monks, through how many hundred years, must have contributed their bony framework to build up these great arches of mortality. On some of the skulls there are inscriptions, purporting that such a monk, who formerly made use of that particular headpiece, died on such a day and year; but vastly the greater number are piled up indistinguishably into the architectural design, like the many deaths that make up the one glory of a victory.

In the side walls of the vaults are niches where skeleton monks sit or stand, clad in the brown habits that they wore in life, and labelled with their names and the dates of their decease. Their skulls (some quite bare, and others still covered with yellow skin, and hair that has known the earth-damps) look out from beneath their hoods, grinning hideously repulsive. One reverend father has his mouth wide open, as if he had died in the midst of a howl of terror and remorse, which perhaps is even now screeching through eternity. As a general thing, however, these frocked and hooded skeletons seem to take a more cheerful view of their position, and try with ghastly smiles to turn it into a jest. But the cemetery of the Capuchins is no place to nourish celestial hopes: the soul sinks forlorn and wretched under all this burden of dusty death; the holy earth from Jerusalem, so imbued is it with mortality, has grown as barren of the flowers of Paradise as it is of earthly weeds and grass. Thank Heaven for its blue sky; it needs a long, upward gaze to give us back our faith. Not here can we feel ourselves immortal, where the very altars in these chapels of horrible consecration are heaps of human bones.

Yet let us give the cemetery the praise that it deserves. There is no disagreeable scent, such as might have been expected from the decay of so many holy persons, in whatever odor of sanctity they may have taken their departure. The same number of living monks would not smell half so unexceptionably.

Miriam went gloomily along the corridor, from one vaulted Golgotha to another, until in the farthest recess she beheld an open grave.

"Is that for him who lies yonder in the nave?" she asked.

"Yes, signorina, this is to be the resting-place of Brother Antonio, who came to his death last night," answered the sacristan; "and in yonder niche, you see, sits a brother who was buried thirty years ago, and has risen to give him place."

"It is not a satisfactory idea," observed Miriam, "that you poor friars cannot call even your graves permanently your own. You must lie down in them, methinks, with a nervous anticipation of being disturbed, like weary men who know that they shall be summoned out of bed at midnight. Is it not possible (if money were to be paid for the privilege) to leave Brother Antonio—if that be his name—in the occupancy of that narrow grave till the last trumpet sounds?"

"By no means, signorina; neither is it needful or desirable," answered the sacristan. "A quarter of a century's sleep in the sweet earth of Jerusalem is better than a thousand years in any other soil. Our brethren find good rest there. No ghost was ever known to steal out of this blessed cemetery.

"That is well," responded Miriam; "may he whom you now lay to sleep prove no exception to the rule!"

As they left the cemetery she put money into the sacristan's hand to an amount that made his eyes open wide and glisten, and requested that it might be expended in masses for the repose of Father Antonio's soul.

## CHAPTER XXII

### THE MEDICI GARDENS

"DONATELLO," said Miriam, anxiously, as they came through the Piazza Barberini, "what can I do for you, my beloved friend? You are shaking as with the cold fit of the Roman fever."

"Yes," said Donatello; "my heart shivers."

As soon as she could collect her thoughts, Miriam led the young man to the gardens of the Villa Medici, hoping that the quiet shade and sunshine of that delightful retreat would a little revive his spirits. The grounds are there laid out in the old fashion of straight paths, with borders of box, which form hedges of great height and density, and are shorn and trimmed to the evenness of a wall of stone, at the top and sides. There are green alleys, with long vistas overshadowed by ilex-trees; and at each intersection of the paths, the visitor finds seats of lichen-covered stone to repose upon, and marble statues that look forlornly at him, regretful of their lost noses. In the more open portions of the garden, before the sculptured front of the villa, you see fountains and flower-beds, and, in their season, a profusion of roses, from which the genial sun of Italy distils a fragrance, to be scattered abroad by the no less genial breeze.

But Donatello drew no delight from these things. He walked onward in silent apathy, and looked at Miriam with strangely half-awakened and bewildered eyes, when she sought to bring his mind into sympathy with hers, and so relieve his heart of the burden that lay lumpishly upon it.

She made him sit down on a stone bench, where two embowered alleys crossed each other; so that they could discern the approach of any casual intruder a long way down the path.

"My sweet friend," she said, taking one of his passive hands in both of hers, "what can I say to comfort you?"

"Nothing!" replied Donatello, with sombre reserve. "Nothing will ever comfort me."

"I accept my own misery," continued Miriam, "my own guilt, if guilt it be; and, whether guilt or misery, I shall know how to deal with it. But you, dearest friend, that were the rarest creature in all this world, and seemed a being to whom sorrow could not cling,—you, whom I half fancied to belong to a race that had vanished forever, you only surviving, to show mankind how genial and how joyous life used to be, in some long-gone age,—what had you to do with grief or crime?"

"They came to me as to other men," said Donatello, broodingly. "Doubtless I was born to them."

"No, no; they came with me," replied Miriam. "Mine is the responsibility! Alas! wherefore was I born? Why did we ever meet? Why did I not drive you from me, knowing,—for my heart foreboded it—that the cloud in which I walked would likewise envelop you!"

Donatello stirred uneasily, with the irritable impatience that is often combined with a mood of leaden despondency. A brown lizard with two tails—a monster often engendered by the Roman sunshine—ran across his foot, and made him start. Then he sat silent awhile, and so did Miriam, trying to dissolve her whole heart into sympathy, and lavish it all upon him, were it only for a moment's cordial.

The young man lifted his hand to his breast, and, unintentionally, as Miriam's hand was within his, he lifted that along with it.

"I have a great weight here!" said he.

The fancy struck Miriam (but she drove it resolutely down) that Donatello almost imperceptibly shuddered, while, in pressing his own hand against his heart, he pressed hers there too.

"Rest your heart on me, dearest one!" she resumed. "Let me bear all its weight; I am well able to bear it; for I am a woman, and I love you! I love you, Donatello! Is there no comfort for you in this avowal? Look at me! Heretofore, you have found me pleasant to your sight. Gaze into my eyes! Gaze into my soul! Search as deeply as you may, you can never see half the tenderness and devotion that I henceforth cherish for you. All that I ask is your acceptance of the utter self-sacrifice (but it shall be no sacrifice, to my great love) with which I seek to remedy the evil you have incurred for my sake!"

All this fervor on Miriam's part; on Donatello's, a heavy silence.

"Oh, speak to me!" she exclaimed. "Only promise me to be, by and by, a little happy!"

"Happy?" murmured Donatello. "Ah, never again; never again!"

"Never? Ah, that is a terrible word to say to me!" answered Miriam. "A terrible word to let fall upon a woman's heart, when she loves you, and is conscious of having caused your misery! If you love me, Donatello, speak it not again. And surely you did love me?"

"I did," replied Donatello, gloomily and absently.

Miriam released the young man's hand, but suffered one of her own to lie close to his, and waited a moment to see whether he would make any effort to retain it. There was much depending upon that simple experiment.

With a deep sigh—as when, sometimes, a slumberer turns over in a troubled dream—Donatello changed his position, and clasped both his hands over his forehead. The genial warmth of a Roman April kindling into May was in the atmosphere around them; but when Miriam saw that involuntary movement and heard that sigh of relief (for so she interpreted it), a shiver ran through her frame, as if the iciest wind of the Apennines were blowing over her.

"He has done himself a greater wrong than I dreamed of," thought she, with unutterable compassion. "Alas! it was a sad mistake! He might have had a kind of bliss in the consequences of this deed, had he been impelled to it by a love vital enough to survive the frenzy of that terrible moment, —mighty enough to make its own law, and justify itself against the natural remorse. But to have perpetrated a dreadful murder (and such was his crime, unless love, annihilating moral distinctions, made it otherwise) on no better warrant than a boy's idle fantasy! I pity him from the very depths of my soul! As for myself, I am past my own or other's pity."

She arose from the young man's side, and stood before him with a sad, commiserating aspect; it was the look of a ruined soul, bewailing, in him, a grief less than what her profounder sympathies imposed upon herself.

"Donatello, we must part," she said, with melancholy firmness. "Yes; leave me! Go back to your old tower, which overlooks the green valley you have told me of among the Apennines. Then, all that has passed will be recognized as but an ugly dream. For, in dreams, the conscience sleeps, and we often stain ourselves with guilt of which we should be incapable in our waking moments. The deed you seemed to do, last night, was no more than such a dream; there was as little substance in what you fancied yourself doing. Go; and forget it all!"

"Ah, that terrible face!" said Donatello, pressing his hands over his eyes. "Do you call that unreal?"

"Yes; for you beheld it with dreaming eyes," replied Miriam. "It was unreal; and, that you may feel it so, it is requisite that you see this face of mine no more. Once, you may have thought it beautiful; now, it has lost its charm. Yet it would still retain a miserable potency to bring back the past illusion, and, in its train, the remorse and anguish that would darken all your life. Leave me, therefore, and forget me."

"Forget you, Miriam!" said Donatello, roused somewhat from his apathy of despair. "If I could remember you, and behold you, apart from that frightful visage which stares at me over your shoulder, that were a consolation, at least, if not a joy."

"But since that visage haunts you along with mine," rejoined Miriam, glancing behind her, "we needs must part. Farewell, then! But if ever—in distress, peril, shame, poverty, or whatever anguish is most poignant, whatever burden heaviest—you should require a life to be given wholly, only to make your own a little easier, then summon me! As the case now stands between us, you have bought me dear, and find me of little worth. Fling me away, therefore! May you never need me more! But, if otherwise, a wish—almost an unuttered wish—will bring me to you!"

She stood a moment, expecting a reply. But Donatello's eyes had again fallen on the ground, and he had not, in his bewildered mind and overburdened heart, a word to respond.

"That hour I speak of may never come," said Miriam. "So farewell,—farewell forever."

"Farewell," said Donatello.

His voice hardly made its way through the environment of unaccustomed thoughts and emotions which had settled over him like a dense and dark cloud. Not improbably, he beheld Miriam through so dim a medium that she looked visionary; heard her speak only in a thin, faint echo.

She turned from the young man, and, much as her heart yearned towards him, she would not profane that heavy parting by an embrace, or even a pressure of the hand. So soon after the semblance of such mighty love, and after it had been the impulse to so terrible a deed, they parted, in all outward show, as coldly as people part whose whole mutual intercourse has been encircled within a single hour.

And Donatello, when Miriam had departed, stretched himself at full length on the stone bench, and drew his hat over his eyes, as the idle and light-hearted youths of dreamy Italy are accustomed to do, when they lie down in the first convenient shade, and snatch a noonday slumber. A stupor was upon him, which he mistook for such drowsiness as he had known in his innocent past life. But, by and by, he raised himself slowly and left the garden. Sometimes poor Donatello started, as if he heard a shriek; sometimes he shrank back, as if a face, fearful to behold, were thrust close to his own. In this dismal mood, bewildered with the novelty of sin and grief, he had little left of that singular resemblance, on account of which, and for their sport, his three friends had fantastically recognized him as the veritable Faun of Praxiteles.

## CHAPTER XXIII

### MIRIAM AND HILDA

ON leaving the Medici Gardens Miriam felt herself astray in the world; and having no special reason to seek one place more than another, she suffered chance to direct her steps as it would. Thus it happened, that, involving herself in the crookedness of Rome, she saw Hilda's tower rising before her, and was put in mind to climb to the young girl's eyry, and ask why she had broken her engagement at the church of the Capuchins. People often do the idlest acts of their lifetime in their heaviest and most anxious moments; so that it would have been no wonder had Miriam been impelled only by so slight a motive of curiosity as we have indicated. But she remembered, too, and with a quaking heart, what the sculptor had mentioned of Hilda's retracing her steps towards the court-yard of the Palazzo Caffarelli in quest of Miriam herself. Had she been compelled to choose between infamy in the eyes of the whole world, or in Hilda's eyes alone, she would unhesitatingly have accepted the former, on condition of remaining spotless in the estimation of her white-souled friend. This possibility, therefore, that Hilda had witnessed the scene of the past night, was unquestionably the cause that drew Miriam to the tower, and made her linger and falter as she approached it.

As she drew near, there were tokens to which her disturbed mind gave a sinister interpretation. Some of her friend's airy family, the doves, with their heads imbedded disconsolately in their bosoms, were huddled in a corner of the piazza; others had alighted on the heads, wings, shoulders, and trumpets of the marble angels which adorned the façade of the neighboring church; two or three had betaken themselves to the Virgin's shrine; and as many as could find room were sitting on Hilda's window-sill. But all of them, so Miriam fancied, had a look of weary expectation and disappointment,—no flights, no flutterings, no cooing murmur; something that ought to have made their day glad and bright was evidently left out of this day's history. And, furthermore, Hilda's white window-curtain was closely drawn, with only that one little aperture at the side, which Miriam remembered noticing the night before.

"Be quiet," said Miriam to her own heart, pressing her hand hard upon it. "Why shouldst thou throb now? Hast thou not endured more terrible things than this?"

Whatever were her apprehensions, she would not turn back. It might be—and the solace would be worth a world—that Hilda, knowing nothing of the past night's calamity, would greet her friend with a sunny smile, and so restore a portion of the vital warmth, for lack of which her soul was frozen. But could Miriam, guilty as she was, permit Hilda to kiss her cheek, to clasp her hand, and thus be no longer so unspotted from the world as heretofore?

"I will never permit her sweet touch again," said Miriam, toiling up the staircase, "if I can find strength of heart to forbid it. But, oh! it would be so soothing in this wintry fever-fit of my heart. There can be no harm to my white Hilda in one parting kiss. That shall be all!"

But, on reaching the upper landing-place, Miriam paused, and stirred not again till she had brought herself to an immovable resolve.

"My lips, my hand, shall never meet Hilda's more," said she.

Meanwhile, Hilda sat listlessly in her painting-room. Had you looked into the little adjoining chamber, you might have seen the slight imprint of her finger on the bed, but would also have detected at once that the white counterpane had not been turned down. The pillow was more disturbed; she had turned her face upon it, the poor child, and bedewed it with some of those tears (among the most chill and forlorn that gush from human sorrow) which the innocent heart pours forth at its first actual discovery that sin is in the world. The young and pure are not apt to find out that miserable truth until it is brought home to them by the guiltiness of some trusted friend. They may have heard much of the evil of the world, and seem to know it, but only as an impalpable theory. In due time, some mortal, whom they reverence too highly, is commissioned by Providence to teach them this direful lesson; he perpetrates a sin; and Adam falls anew, and Paradise, heretofore in unfaded bloom, is lost again, and closed forever, with the fiery swords gleaming at its gates.

The chair in which Hilda sat was near the portrait of Beatrice Cenci, which had not yet been taken from the easel. It is a peculiarity of this picture, that its profoundest expression eludes a straightforward glance, and can only be caught by side glimpses, or when the eye falls casually upon it; even as if the painted face had a life and consciousness of its own, and, resolving not to betray its secret of grief or guilt, permitted the true tokens to come forth only when it imagined itself unseen. No other such magical effect has ever been wrought by pencil.

Now, opposite the easel hung a looking-glass, in which Beatrice's face and Hilda's were both reflected. In one of her weary, nerveless changes of position, Hilda happened to throw her eyes on the glass, and took in both these images at one unpremeditated glance. She fancied—nor was it without horror—that Beatrice's expression, seen aside and vanishing in a moment, had been depicted in her own face likewise, and flitted from it as timorously.

"Am I, too, stained with guilt?" thought the poor girl, hiding her face in her hands.

Not so, thank Heaven! But, as regards Beatrice's picture, the incident suggests a theory which may account for its unutterable grief and mysterious shadow of guilt, without detracting from the purity which we love to attribute to that ill-fated girl. Who, indeed, can look at that mouth,— with its lips half apart, as innocent as a baby's that has been crying,— and not pronounce Beatrice sinless? It was the intimate consciousness of her father's sin that threw its shadow over her, and frightened her into a remote and inaccessible region, where no sympathy could come. It was the knowledge of Miriam's guilt that lent the same expression to Hilda's face.

But Hilda nervously moved her chair, so that the images in the glass should be no longer visible. She now watched a speck of sunshine that came through a shuttered window, and crept from object to object, indicating each with a touch of its bright finger, and then letting them all vanish successively. In like manner, her mind, so like sunlight in its natural cheerfulness, went from thought to thought, but found nothing that it could dwell upon for comfort. Never before had this young, energetic, active spirit known what it is to be despondent. It was the unreality of the world that made her so. Her dearest friend, whose heart seemed the most solid and richest of Hilda's possessions, had no existence for her any more; and in that dreary void, out of which Miriam had disappeared, the substance, the truth, the integrity of life, the motives of effort, the joy of success, had departed along with her.

It was long past noon, when a step came up the staircase. It had passed beyond the limits where there was communication with the lower regions of the palace, and was mounting the successive flights which led only to Hilda's precincts. Faint as the tred was, she heard and recognized it. It startled her into sudden life. Her first impulse was to spring to the door of the studio, and fasten it with lock and bolt. But a second thought made her feel that this would be an unworthy cowardice, on her own part, and also that Miriam—only yesterday her closest friend—had a right to be told, face to face, that thenceforth they must be forever strangers.

She heard Miriam pause, outside of the door. We have already seen what was the latter's resolve with respect to any kiss or pressure of the hand between Hilda and herself. We know not what became of the resolution. As Miriam was of a highly impulsive character, it may have vanished at the first sight of Hilda; but, at all events, she appeared to have dressed herself up in a garb of sunshine, and was disclosed, as the door swung open, in all the glow of her remarkable beauty. The truth was, her heart leaped conclusively towards the only refuge that it had, or hoped. She forgot, just one instant, all cause for holding herself aloof. Ordinarily there was a certain reserve in Miriam's demonstrations of affection, in consonance with the delicacy of her friend. To-day, she opened her arms to take Hilda in.

"Dearest, darling Hilda!" she exclaimed. "It gives me new life to see you!"

Hilda was standing in the middle of the room. When her friend made a step or two from the door, she put forth her hands with an involuntary repellent gesture, so expressive, that Miriam at once felt a great chasm opening itself between them two. They might gaze at one another from the opposite side, but without the possibility of ever meeting more; or, at least, since the chasm could never be bridged over, they must tread the whole round of Eternity to meet on the other side. There was even a terror in the thought of their meeting again. It was as if Hilda or Miriam were dead, and could no longer hold intercourse without violating a spiritual law.

Yet, in the wantonness of her despair, Miriam made one more step towards the friend whom she had lost.

"Do not come nearer, Miriam!" said Hilda.

Her look and tone were those of sorrowful entreaty, and yet they expressed a kind of confidence, as if the girl were conscious of a safeguard that could not be violated.

"What has happened between us, Hilda?" asked Miriam. "Are we not friends?"

"No, no!" said Hilda, shuddering.

"At least we have been friends," continued Miriam. "I loved you dearly! I love you still! You were to me as a younger sister; yes, dearer than sisters of the same blood; for you and I were so lonely, Hilda, that the whole world pressed us together by its solitude and strangeness. Then, will you not touch my hand? Am I not the same as yesterday?"

"Alas! no, Miriam!" said Hilda.

"Yes, the same,—the same for you, Hilda," rejoined her lost friend. "Were you to touch my hand, you would find it as warm to your grasp as ever. If you were sick or suffering, I would watch night and day for you. It is in such simple offices that true affection shows itself; and so I speak of them. Yet now, Hilda, your very look seems to put me beyond the limits of human kind!"

"It is not I, Miriam," said Hilda; "not I that have done this."

"You, and you only, Hilda," replied Miriam, stirred up to make her own cause good by the repellent force which her friend opposed to her. "I am a woman, as I was yesterday; endowed with the same truth of nature, the same warmth of heart, the same genuine and earnest love, which you have always known in me. In any regard that concerns yourself, I am not changed. And believe me, Hilda, when a human being has chosen a friend out of all the world, it is only some faithlessness between themselves, rendering true intercourse impossible, that can justify either friend in severing the bond. Have I deceived you? Then cast me off! Have I wronged you personally? Then forgive me, if you can. But, have I sinned against God and man, and deeply sinned? Then be more my friend than ever, for I need you more."

"Do not bewilder me thus, Miriam!" exclaimed Hilda, who had not forborne to express, by look and gesture, the anguish which this interview inflicted on her. "If I were one of God's angels, with a nature incapable of stain, and garments that never could be spotted, I would keep ever at your side, and try to lead you upward. But I am a poor, lonely girl, whom God has set here in an evil world, and given her only a white robe, and bid her wear it back to Him, as white as when she put it on. Your powerful magnetism would be too much for me. The pure, white atmosphere, in which I try to discern what things are good and true, would be discolored. And, therefore, Miriam, before it is too late, I mean to put faith in this awful heart-quake, which warns me henceforth to avoid you."

"Ah, this is hard! Ah, this is terrible!" murmured Miriam, dropping her forehead in her hands. In a moment or two she looked up again, as pale as death, but with a composed countenance: "I always said, Hilda, that you were merciless; for I had a perception of it, even while you loved me best. You have no sin, nor any conception of what it is; and therefore you are so terribly severe! As an angel, you are not amiss; but, as a human creature, and a woman among earthly men and women, you need a sin to soften you."

"God forgive me," said Hilda, "if I have said a needlessly cruel word!"

"Let it pass," answered Miriam; "I, whose heart it has smitten upon, forgive you. And tell me, before we part forever, what have you seen or known of me, since we last met?"

"A terrible thing, Miriam," said Hilda, growing paler than before.

"Do you see it written in my face, or painted in my eyes?" inquired Miriam, her trouble seeking relief in a half-frenzied raillery. "I would fain know how it is that Providence, or fate, brings eye-witnesses to watch us, when we fancy ourselves acting in the remotest privacy. Did all Rome see it, then? Or, at least, our merry company of artists? Or is it some blood-stain on me, or death-scent in my garments? They say that monstrous deformities sprout out of fiends, who once were lovely angels. Do you perceive such in me already? Tell me, by our past friendship, Hilda, all you know."

Thus adjured, and frightened by the wild emotion which Miriam could not suppress, Hilda strove to tell what she had witnessed.

"After the rest of the party had passed on, I went back to speak to you," she said; "for there seemed to be a trouble on your mind, and I wished to share it with you, if you could permit me. The door of the little court-yard was partly shut; but I pushed it open, and saw you within, and Donatello, and a third person, whom I had before noticed in the shadow of a niche. He approached you, Miriam. You knelt to him!—I saw Donatello spring upon him! I would have shrieked, but my throat was dry. I would have rushed forward, but my limbs seemed rooted to the earth. It was like a flash of lightning. A look passed from your eyes to Donatello's—a look"—

"Yes, Hilda, yes!" exclaimed Miriam, with intense eagerness. "Do not pause now! That look?"

"It revealed all your heart, Miriam," continued Hilda, covering her eyes as if to shut out the recollection; "a look of hatred, triumph, vengeance, and, as it were, joy at some unhoped-for relief."

"Ah! Donatello was right, then," murmured Miriam, who shook throughout all her frame. "My eyes bade him do it! Go on, Hilda."

"It all passed so quickly,—all like a glare of lightning," said Hilda, "and yet it seemed to me that Donatello had paused, while one might draw a breath. But that look!—Ah, Miriam, spare me. Need I tell more?"

"No more; there needs no more, Hilda," replied Miriam, bowing her head, as if listening to a sentence of condemnation from a supreme tribunal. "It is enough! You have satisfied my mind on a point where it was greatly disturbed. Henceforward, I shall be quiet. Thank you, Hilda."

She was on the point of departing, but turned back again from the threshold.

"This is a terrible secret to be kept in a young girl's bosom," she observed; "what will you do with it, my poor child?"

"Heaven help and guide me," answered Hilda, bursting into tears; "for the burden of it crushes me to the earth! It seems a crime to know of such a thing, and to keep it to myself. It knocks within my heart continually, threatening, imploring, insisting to be let out! Oh, my mother! —my mother! Were she yet living, I would travel over land and sea to tell her this dark secret, as I told all the little troubles of my infancy. But I am alone—alone! Miriam, you were my dearest, only friend. Advise me what to do."

This was a singular appeal, no doubt, from the stainless maiden to the guilty woman, whom she had just banished from her heart forever. But it bore striking testimony to the impression which Miriam's natural uprightness and impulsive generosity had made on the friend who knew her best; and it deeply comforted the poor criminal, by proving to her that the bond between Hilda and herself was vital yet.

As far as she was able, Miriam at once responded to the girl's cry for help.

"If I deemed it good for your peace of mind," she said, "to bear testimony against me for this deed, in the face of all the world, no consideration of myself should weigh with me an instant. But I believe that you would find no relief in such a course. What men call justice lies chiefly in outward formalities, and has never the close application and fitness that would be satisfactory to a soul like yours. I cannot be fairly tried and judged before an earthly tribunal; and of this, Hilda, you would perhaps become fatally conscious when it was too late. Roman justice, above all things, is a byword. What have you to do with it? Leave all such thoughts aside! Yet, Hilda, I would not have you keep my secret imprisoned in your heart if it tries to leap out, and stings you, like a wild, venomous thing, when you thrust it back again. Have you no other friend, now that you have been forced to give me up?"

"No other," answered Hilda, sadly.

"Yes; Kenyon!" rejoined Miriam.

"He cannot be my friend," said Hilda, "because—because—I have fancied that he sought to be something more."

"Fear nothing!" replied Miriam, shaking her head, with a strange smile. "This story will frighten his new-born love out of its little life, if that be what you wish. Tell him the secret, then, and take his wise and honorable counsel as to what should next be done. I know not what else to say."

"I never dreamed," said Hilda,—"how could you think it?—of betraying you to justice. But I see how it is, Miriam. I must keep your secret, and die of it, unless God sends me some relief by methods which are now beyond my power to imagine. It is very dreadful. Ah! now I understand how the sins of generations past have created an atmosphere of sin for those that follow. While there is a single guilty person in the universe, each innocent one must feel his innocence tortured by that guilt. Your deed, Miriam, has darkened the whole sky!"

Poor Hilda turned from her unhappy friend, and, sinking on her knees in a corner of the chamber, could not be prevailed upon to utter another word. And Miriam, with a long regard from the threshold, bade farewell to this doves' nest, this one little nook of pure thoughts and innocent enthusiasms, into which she had brought such trouble. Every crime destroys more Edens than our own!

## CHAPTER XXIV

### The Tower Among the Apennines

It was in June that the sculptor, Kenyon, arrived on horseback at the gate of an ancient country-house (which, from some of its features, might almost be called a castle) situated in a part of Tuscany somewhat remote from the ordinary track of tourists. Thither we must now accompany him, and endeavor to make our story flow onward, like a streamlet, past a gray tower that rises on the hill-side, overlooking a spacious valley, which is set in the grand framework of the Apennines.

The sculptor had left Rome with the retreating tide of foreign residents. For, as summer approaches, the Niobe of Nations is made to bewail anew, and doubtless with sincerity, the loss of that large part of her population, which she derives from other lands, and on whom depends much of whatever remnant of prosperity she still enjoys. Rome, at this season, is pervaded and overhung with atmospheric terrors, and insulated within a charmed and deadly circle. The crowd of wandering tourists betake themselves to Switzerland, to the Rhine, or, from this central home of the world, to their native homes in England or America, which they are apt thenceforward to look upon as provincial, after once having yielded to the spell of the Eternal City. The artist, who contemplates an indefinite succession of winters in this home of art (though his first thought was merely to improve himself by a brief visit), goes forth, in the summer time, to sketch scenery and costume among the Tuscan hills, and pour, if he can, the purple air of Italy over his canvas. He studies the old schools of art in the mountain-towns where they were born, and where they are still to be seen in the faded frescos of Giotto and Cimabue, on the walls of many a church, or in the dark chapels, in which the sacristan draws aside the veil from a treasured picture of Perugino. Thence, the happy painter goes to walk the long, bright galleries of Florence, or to steal glowing colors from the miraculous works, which he finds in a score of Venetian palaces. Such summers as these, spent amid whatever is exquisite in art, or wild and picturesque in nature, may not inadequately repay him for the chill neglect and disappointment through which he has probably languished, in his Roman winter. This sunny, shadowy, breezy, wandering life, in which he seeks for beauty as his treasure, and gathers for his winter's honey what is but a passing fragrance to all other men, is worth living for, come afterwards what may. Even if he die unrecognized, the artist has had his share of enjoyment and success.

Kenyon had seen, at a distance of many miles, the old villa or castle, towards which his journey lay, looking from its height over a broad expanse of valley. As he drew nearer, however, it had been hidden among the inequalities of the hill-side, until the winding road brought him almost to the iron gateway. The sculptor found this substantial barrier fastened with lock and bolt. There was no bell, nor other instrument of sound; and, after summoning the invisible garrison with his voice, instead of a trumpet, he had leisure to take a glance at the exterior of the fortress.

About thirty yards within the gateway rose a square tower, lofty enough to be a very prominent object in the landscape, and more than sufficiently massive in proportion to its height. Its antiquity was evidently such, that, in a climate of more abundant moisture, the ivy would have mantled it from head to foot in a garment that might, by this time, have been centuries old, though ever new. In the dry Italian air, however, Nature had only so far adopted this old pile of stone-work as to cover almost every hand's-breadth of it with close-clinging lichens and yellow moss; and the immemorial growth of these kindly productions rendered the general hue of the tower soft and venerable, and took away the aspect of nakedness which would have made its age drearier than now.

Up and down the height of the tower were scattered three or four windows, the lower ones grated with iron bars, the upper ones vacant both of window-frames and glass. Besides these larger openings, there were several square loopholes and little square apertures, which might be supposed to light the staircase, that doubtless climbed the interior towards the battlemented and machicolated summit. With this last-mentioned war-like garniture upon its stern old head and brow, the tower seemed evidently a stronghold of times long past. Many a cross-bowman had shot his shafts from those windows and loopholes, and from the vantage-height of those gray battlements; many a flight of arrows, too, had hit all round about the embrasures above, or the apertures below, where the helmet of a defender had momentarily glimmered. On festal nights, moreover, a hundred lamps had often gleamed afar over the valley, suspended from the iron hooks that were ranged for the purpose beneath the battlements and every window.

Connected with the tower, and extending behind it, there seemed to be a very spacious residence, chiefly of more modern date. It perhaps owed much of its fresher appearance, however, to a coat of stucco and yellow wash, which is a sort of renovation very much in vogue with the Italians.

Kenyon noticed over a doorway, in the portion of the edifice immediately adjacent to the tower, a cross, which, with a bell suspended above the roof, indicated that this was a consecrated precinct, and the chapel of the mansion.

Meanwhile, the hot sun so incommoded the unsheltered traveller, that he shouted forth another impatient summons. Happening, at the same moment, to look upward, he saw a figure leaning from an embrasure of the battlements, and gazing down at him.

"Ho, Signore Count!" cried the sculptor, waving his straw hat, for he recognized the face, after a moment's doubt. "This is a warm reception, truly! Pray bid your porter let me in, before the sun shrivels me quite into a cinder."

"I will come myself," responded Donatello, flinging down his voice out of the clouds, as it were; "old Tomaso and old Stella are both asleep, no doubt, and the rest of the people are in the vineyard. But I have expected you, and you are welcome!"

The young Count—as perhaps we had better designate him in his ancestral tower—vanished from the battlements; and Kenyon saw his figure appear successively at each of the windows, as he descended. On every reappearance, he turned his face towards the sculptor and gave a nod and smile; for a kindly impulse prompted him thus to assure his visitor of a welcome, after keeping him so long at an inhospitable threshold.

Kenyon, however (naturally and professionally expert at reading the expression of the human countenance), had a vague sense that this was not the young friend whom he had known so familiarly in Rome; not the sylvan and untutored youth, whom Miriam, Hilda, and himself had liked, laughed at, and sported with; not the Donatello whose identity they had so playfully mixed up with that of the Faun of Praxiteles.

Finally, when his host had emerged from a side portal of the mansion, and approached the gateway, the traveller still felt that there was something lost, or something gained (he hardly knew which), that set the Donatello of to-day irreconcilably at odds with him of yesterday. His very gait showed it, in a certain gravity, a weight and measure of step, that had nothing in common with the irregular buoyancy which used to distinguish him. His face was paler and thinner, and the lips less full and less apart.

"I have looked for you a long while," said Donatello; and, though his voice sounded differently, and cut out its words more sharply than had been its wont, still there was a smile shining on his face, that, for the moment, quite brought back the Faun. "I shall be more cheerful, perhaps, now that you have come. It is very solitary here."

"I have come slowly along, often lingering, often turning aside," replied Kenyon; "for I found a great deal to interest me in the mediæval sculpture hidden away in the churches hereabouts. An artist, whether painter or sculptor, may be pardoned for loitering through such a region. But what a fine old tower! Its tall front is like a page of black-letter, taken from the history of the Italian republics."

"I know little or nothing of its history," said the Count, glancing upward at the battlements, where he had just been standing. "But I thank my forefathers for building it so high. I like the windy summit better than the world below, and spend much of my time there, nowadays."

"It is a pity you are not a star-gazer," observed Kenyon, also looking up. "It is higher than Galileo's tower, which I saw, a week or two ago, outside of the walls of Florence."

"A star-gazer? I am one," replied Donatello. "I sleep in the tower, and often watch very late on the battlements. There is a dismal old staircase to climb, however, before reaching the top, and a succession of dismal chambers, from story to story. Some of them were prison chambers in times past, as old Tomaso will tell you."

The repugnance intimated in his tone at the idea of this gloomy staircase and these ghostly, dimly lighted rooms, reminded Kenyon of the original Donatello, much more than his present custom of midnight vigils on the battlements.

"I shall be glad to share your watch," said the guest; "especially by moonlight. The prospect of this broad valley must be very fine. But I was not aware, my friend, that these were your country habits. I have fancied you in a sort of Arcadian life, tasting rich figs, and squeezing the juice out of the sunniest grapes, and sleeping soundly all night, after a day of simple pleasures."

"I may have known such a life, when I was younger," answered the Count, gravely. "I am not a boy now. Time flies over us, but leaves its shadow behind."

The sculptor could not but smile at the triteness of the remark, which, nevertheless, had a kind of originality as coming from Donatello. He had thought it out from his own experience, and perhaps considered himself as communicating a new truth to mankind.

They were now advancing up the court-yard; and the long extent of the villa, with its iron-barred lower windows and balconied upper ones, became visible, stretching back towards a grove of trees.

"At some period of your family history," observed Kenyon, "the Counts of Monte Beni must have led a patriarchal life in this vast house. A great-grandsire and all his descendants might find ample verge here, and with space, too, for each separate brood of little ones to play within its own precincts. Is your present household a large one?"

"Only myself," answered Donatello, "and Tomaso, who has been butler since my grandfather's time, and old Stella, who goes sweeping and dusting about the chambers, and Girolamo, the cook, who has but an idle life of it. He shall send you up a chicken forthwith. But, first of all, I must summon one of the contadini from the farm-house yonder, to take your horse to the stable."

Accordingly, the young Count shouted amain, and with such effect, that, after several repetitions of the outcry, an old gray woman protruded her head and a broom-handle from a chamber window; the venerable butler emerged from a recess in the side of the house, where was a well, or reservoir, in which he had been cleansing a small wine-cask; and a sunburnt contadino, in his shirt-sleeves, showed himself on the outskirts of the vineyard, with some kind of a farming tool in his hand. Donatello found employment for all these retainers in providing accommodation for his guest and steed, and then ushered the sculptor into the vestibule of the house.

It was a square and lofty entrance-room, which, by the solidity of its construction, might have been an Etruscan tomb, being paved and walled with heavy blocks of stone, and vaulted almost as massively overhead. On two sides, there were doors, opening into long suites of anterooms and saloons; on the third side, a stone staircase, of spacious breadth, ascending, by dignified degrees and with wide resting-places, to another floor of similar extent. Through one of the doors, which was ajar, Kenyon beheld an almost interminable vista of apartments, opening one beyond the other, and reminding him of the hundred rooms in Blue Beard's castle, or the countless halls in some palace of the Arabian Nights.

It must have been a numerous family, indeed, that could ever have sufficed to people with human life so large an abode as this, and impart social warmth to such a wide world within doors. The sculptor confessed to himself, that Donatello could allege reason enough for growing melancholy, having only his own personality to vivify it all.

"How a woman's face would brighten it up!" he ejaculated, not intending to be overheard.

But, glancing at Donatello, he saw a stern and sorrowful look in his eyes, which altered his youthful face as if it had seen thirty years of trouble; and, at the same moment, old Stella showed herself through one of the doorways, as the only representative of her sex at Monte Beni.

## CHAPTER XXV

### SUNSHINE

"COME," said the Count, "I see you already find the old house dismal. So do I, indeed! And yet it was a cheerful place in my boyhood. But, you see, in my father's days (and the same was true of all my endless line of grandfathers, as I have heard), there used to be uncles, aunts, and all manner of kindred, dwelling together as one family. They were a merry and kindly race of people, for the most part, and kept one another's hearts warm."

"Two hearts might be enough for warmth," observed the sculptor, "even in so large a house as this. One solitary heart, it is true, may be apt to shiver a little. But, I trust, my friend, that the genial blood of your race still flows in many veins besides your own?"

"I am the last," said Donatello, gloomily. "They have all vanished from me, since my childhood. Old Tomaso will tell you that the air of Monte Beni is not so favorable to length of days as it used to be. But that is not the secret of the quick extinction of my kindred."

"Then you are aware of a more satisfactory reason?" suggested Kenyon.

"I thought of one, the other night, while I was gazing at the stars," answered Donatello; "but, pardon me, I do not mean to tell it. One cause, however, of the longer and healthier life of my forefathers was, that they had many pleasant customs, and means of making themselves glad, and their guests and friends along with them. Nowadays we have but one!"

"And what is that?" asked the sculptor.

"You shall see!" said his young host.

By this time, he had ushered the sculptor into one of the numberless saloons; and, calling for refreshment, old Stella placed a cold fowl upon the table, and quickly followed it with a savory omelet, which Girolamo had lost no time in preparing. She also brought some cherries, plums, and apricots, and a plate full of particularly delicate figs, of last year's growth. The butler showing his white head at the door, his master beckoned to him.

"Tomaso, bring some Sunshine!" said he.

The readiest method of obeying this order, one might suppose, would have been, to fling wide the green window-blinds, and let the glow of the summer noon into the carefully shaded room. But, at Monte Beni, with provident caution against the wintry days, when there is little sunshine, and the rainy ones, when there is none, it was the hereditary custom to keep their Sunshine stored away in the cellar. Old Tomaso quickly produced some of it in a small, straw-covered flask, out of which he extracted the cork, and inserted a little cotton wool, to absorb the olive-oil that kept the precious liquid from the air.

"This is a wine," observed the Count, "the secret of making which has been kept in our family for centuries upon centuries; nor would it avail any man to steal the secret, unless he could also steal the vineyard, in which alone the Monte Beni grape can be produced. There is little else left me, save that patch of vines. Taste some of their juices, and tell me whether it is worthy to be called Sunshine! for that is its name."

"A glorious name, too!" cried the sculptor.

"Taste it," said Donatello, filling his friend's glass, and pouring likewise a little into his own. "But first smell its fragrance; for the wine is very lavish of it, and will scatter it all abroad."

"Ah, how exquisite!" said Kenyon. "No other wine has a bouquet like this. The flavor must be rare, indeed, if it fulfil the promise of this fragrance, which is like the airy sweetness of youthful hopes, that no realities will ever satisfy!"

This invaluable liquor was of a pale golden hue, like other of the rarest Italian wines, and, if carelessly and irreligiously quaffed, might have been mistaken for a very fine sort of champagne. It was not, however, an effervescing wine, although its delicate piquancy produced a somewhat similar effect upon the palate. Sipping, the guest longed to sip again; but the wine demanded so deliberate a pause, in order to detect the hidden peculiarities and subtile exquisiteness of its flavor, that to drink it was really more a moral than a physical enjoyment. There was a deliciousness in it that eluded analysis, and—like whatever else is superlatively good —was perhaps better appreciated in the memory than by present consciousness.

One of its most ethereal charms lay in the transitory life of the wine's richest qualities; for, while it required a certain leisure and delay, yet, if you lingered too long upon the draught, it became disenchanted both of its fragrance and its flavor.

The lustre should not be forgotten, among the other admirable endowments of the Monte Beni wine; for, as it stood in Kenyon's glass, a little circle of light glowed on the table round about it, as if it were really so much golden sunshine.

"I feel myself a better man for that ethereal potation," observed the sculptor. "The finest Orvieto, or that famous wine, the Est Est Est of Montefiascone, is vulgar in comparison. This is surely the wine of the Golden Age, such as Bacchus himself first taught mankind to press from the choicest of his grapes. My dear Count, why is it not illustrious? The pale, liquid gold, in every such flask as that, might be solidified into golden scudi, and would quickly make you a millionnaire!"

Tomaso, the old butler, who was standing by the table, and enjoying the praises of the wine quite as much as if bestowed upon himself, made answer,—

"We have a tradition, signore," said he, "that this rare wine of our vineyard would lose all its wonderful qualities, if any of it were sent to market. The Counts of Monte Beni have never parted with a single flask of it for gold. At their banquets, in the olden time, they have entertained princes, cardinals, and once an emperor, and once a pope, with this delicious wine, and always, even to this day, it has been their custom to let it flow freely, when those whom they love and honor sit at the board. But the grand duke himself could not drink that wine, except it were under this very roof!"

"What you tell me, my good friend," replied Kenyon, "makes me venerate the Sunshine of Monte Beni even more abundantly than before. As I understand you, it is a sort of consecrated juice, and symbolizes the holy virtues of hospitality and social kindness?"

"Why, partly so, Signore," said the old butler, with a shrewd twinkle in his eye; "but, to speak out all the truth, there is another excellent reason why neither a cask nor a flask of our precious vintage should ever be sent to market. The wine, Signore, is so fond of its native home, that a transportation of even a few miles turns it quite sour. And yet it is a wine that keeps well in the cellar, underneath this floor, and gathers fragrance, flavor, and brightness, in its dark dungeon. That very flask of Sunshine, now, has kept itself for you, sir guest (as a maid reserves her sweetness till her lover come for it), ever since a merry vintage-time, when the Signore Count here was a boy!"

"You must not wait for Tomaso to end his discourse about the wine, before drinking off your glass," observed Donatello. "When once the flask is uncorked, its finest qualities lose little time in making their escape. I doubt whether your last sip will be quite so delicious as you found the first."

And, in truth, the sculptor fancied that the Sunshine became almost imperceptibly clouded, as he approached the bottom of the flask. The effect of the wine, however, was a gentle exhilaration, which did not so speedily pass away.

Being thus refreshed. Kenyon looked around him at the antique saloon in which they sat. It was constructed in a most ponderous style, with a stone floor, on which heavy pilasters were planted against the wall, supporting arches that crossed one another in the vaulted ceiling. The upright walls, as well as the compartments of the roof, were completely covered with frescos, which doubtless had been brilliant when first executed, and perhaps for generations afterwards. The designs were of a festive and joyous character, representing Arcadian scenes, where nymphs, fauns, and satyrs disported themselves among mortal youths and maidens; and Pan, and the god of wine, and he of sunshine and music, disdained not to brighten some sylvan merry-making with the scarcely veiled glory of their presence. A wreath of dancing figures, in admirable variety of shape and motion, was festooned quite round the cornice of the room.

In its first splendor, the saloon must have presented an aspect both gorgeous and enlivening; for it invested some of the cheerfullest ideas and emotions of which the human mind is susceptible with the external reality of beautiful form, and rich, harmonious glow and variety of color. But the frescos were now very ancient. They had been rubbed and scrubbed by old Stella and many a predecessor, and had been defaced in one spot, and retouched in another, and had peeled from the walls in patches, and had hidden some of their brightest portions under dreary dust, till the joyousness had quite vanished out of them all. It was often difficult to puzzle out the design; and even where it was more readily intelligible, the figures showed like the ghosts of dead and buried joys,—the closer their resemblance to the happy past, the gloomier now. For it is thus, that with only an inconsiderable change, the gladdest objects and existences become the saddest; hope fading into disappointment; joy darkening into grief, and festal splendor into funereal duskiness; and all evolving, as their moral, a grim identity between gay things and sorrowful ones. Only give them a little time, and they turn out to be just alike!

"There has been much festivity in this saloon, if I may judge by the character of its frescos," remarked Kenyon, whose spirits were still upheld by the mild potency of the Monte Beni wine. "Your forefathers, my dear Count, must have been joyous fellows, keeping up the vintage merriment throughout the year. It does me good to think of them gladdening the hearts of men and women, with their wine of Sunshine, even in the

Iron Age, as Pan and Bacchus, whom we see yonder, did in the Golden one!"

"Yes; there have been merry times in the banquet-hall of Monte Beni, even within my own remembrance," replied Donatello, looking gravely at the painted walls. "It was meant for mirth, as you see; and when I brought my own cheerfulness into the saloon, these frescos looked cheerful too. But, methinks, they have all faded since I saw them last."

"It would be a good idea," said the sculptor, falling into his companion's vein, and helping him out with an illustration which Donatello himself could not have put into shape, "to convert this saloon into a chapel; and when the priest tells his hearers of the instability of earthly joys, and would show how drearily they vanish, he may point to these pictures, that were so joyous and are so dismal. He could not illustrate his theme so aptly in any other way."

"True, indeed," answered the Count, his former simplicity strangely mixing itself up with an experience that had changed him; "and yonder, where the minstrels used to stand, the altar shall be placed. A sinful man might do all the more effective penance in this old banquet-hall."

"But I should regret to have suggested so ungenial a transformation in your hospitable saloon," continued Kenyon, duly noting the change in Donatello's characteristics. "You startle me, my friend, by so ascetic a design! It would hardly have entered your head, when we first met. Pray do not,—if I may take the freedom of a somewhat elder man to advise you," added he, smiling,—"pray do not, under a notion of improvement, take upon yourself to be sombre, thoughtful, and penitential, like all the rest of us."

Donatello made no answer, but sat awhile, appearing to follow with his eyes one of the figures, which was repeated many times over in the groups upon the walls and ceiling. It formed the principal link of an allegory, by which (as is often the case in such pictorial designs) the whole series of frescos were bound together, but which it would be impossible, or, at least, very wearisome, to unravel. The sculptor's eyes took a similar direction, and soon began to trace through the vicissitudes,—once gay, now sombre,—in which the old artist had involved it, the same individual figure. He fancied a resemblance in it to Donatello himself; and it put him in mind of one of the purposes with which he had come to Monte Beni.

"My dear Count," said he, "I have a proposal to make. You must let me employ a little of my leisure in modelling your bust. You remember what a striking resemblance we all of us—Hilda, Miriam, and I—found between your features and those of the Faun of Praxiteles. Then, it seemed an identity; but now that I know your face better, the likeness is far less apparent. Your head in marble would be a treasure to me. Shall I have it?"

"I have a weakness which I fear I cannot overcome," replied the Count, turning away his face. "It troubles me to be looked at steadfastly."

"I have observed it since we have been sitting here, though never before," rejoined the sculptor. "It is a kind of nervousness, I apprehend, which you caught in the Roman air, and which grows upon you, in your solitary life. It need be no hindrance to my taking your bust; for I will catch the likeness and expression by side glimpses, which (if portrait-painters and bust-makers did but know it) always bring home richer results than a broad stare."

"You may take me if you have the power," said Donatello; but, even as he spoke, he turned away his face; "and if you can see what makes me shrink from you, you are welcome to put it in the bust. It is not my will, but my necessity, to avoid men's eyes. Only," he added, with a smile which made Kenyon doubt whether he might not as well copy the Faun as model a new bust,—"only, you know, you must not insist on my un-covering these ears of mine!"

"Nay; I never should dream of such a thing," answered the sculptor, laughing, as the young Count shook his clustering curls. "I could not hope to persuade you, remembering how Miriam once failed!"

Nothing is more unaccountable than the spell that often lurks in a spoken word. A thought may be present to the mind, so distinctly that no utterance could make it more so; and two minds may be conscious of the same thought, in which one or both take the profoundest interest; but as long as it remains unspoken, their familiar talk flows quietly over the hidden idea, as a rivulet may sparkle and dimple over something sunken in its bed. But, speak the word; and it is like bringing up a drowned body out of the deepest pool of the rivulet, which has been aware of the hor-rible secret all along, in spite of its smiling surface.

And even so, when Kenyon chanced to make a distinct reference to Donatello's relations with Miriam (though the subject was already in both their minds), a ghastly emotion rose up out of the depths of the young Count's heart. He trembled either with anger or terror, and glared at the sculptor with wild eyes, like a wolf that meets you in the forest, and hesitates whether to flee or turn to bay. But, as Kenyon still looked calmly at him, his aspect gradually became less disturbed, though far from resuming its former quietude.

"You have spoken her name," said he, at last, in an altered and tremu-lous tone; "tell me, now, all that you know of her."

"I scarcely think that I have any later intelligence than yourself," an-swered Kenyon; "Miriam left Rome at about the time of your own de-parture. Within a day or two after our last meeting at the Church of the Capuchins, I called at her studio and found it vacant. Whither she has gone, I cannot tell."

Donatello asked no further questions.

They rose from table, and strolled together about the premises, whil-ing away the afternoon with brief intervals of unsatisfactory conversa-tion, and many shadowy silences. The sculptor had a perception of change in his companion,—possibly of growth and development, but certainly of change,—which saddened him, because it took away much of the simple grace that was the best of Donatello's peculiarities.

Kenyon betook himself to repose that night in a grim, old, vaulted apartment, which, in the lapse of five or six centuries, had probably been the birth, bridal, and death chamber of a great many generations of the Monte Beni family. He was aroused, soon after daylight, by the clamor of a tribe of beggars who had taken their stand in a little rustic lane that crept beside that portion of the villa, and were addressing their petitions to the open windows. By and by, they appeared to have received alms, and took their departure.

"Some charitable Christian has sent those vagabonds away," thought the sculptor, as he resumed his interrupted nap; "who could it be? Donatello has his own rooms in the tower; Stella, Tomaso, and the cook are a world's width off; and I fancied myself the only inhabitant in this part of the house."

In the breadth and space which so delightfully characterize an Italian villa, a dozen guests might have had each his suite of apartments without infringing upon one another's ample precincts. But, so far as Kenyon knew, he was the only visitor beneath Donatello's widely extended roof.

CHAPTER XXVI

THE PEDIGREE OF MONTE BENI

FROM the old butler, whom he found to be a very gracious and affable personage, Kenyon soon learned many curious particulars about the family history and hereditary peculiarities of the Counts of Monte Beni. There was a pedigree, the later portion of which—that is to say, for a little more than a thousand years—a genealogist would have found delight in tracing out, link by link, and authenticating by records and documentary evidences. It would have been as difficult, however, to follow up the stream of Donatello's ancestry to its dim source, as travellers have found it to reach the mysterious fountains of the Nile. And, far beyond the region of definite and demonstrable fact, a romancer might have strayed into a region of old poetry, where the rich soil, so long uncultivated and untrodden, had lapsed into nearly its primeval state of wilderness. Among those antique paths, now overgrown with tangled and riotous vegetation, the wanderer must needs follow his own guidance, and arrive nowhither at last.

The race of Monte Beni, beyond a doubt, was one of the oldest in Italy, where families appear to survive at least, if not to flourish, on their half-decayed roots, oftener than in England or France. It came down in a broad track from the Middle Ages; but, at epochs anterior to those, it was distinctly visible in the gloom of the period before chivalry put forth its flower; and further still, we are almost afraid to say, it was seen, though with a fainter and wavering course, in the early morn of Christendom, when the Roman Empire had hardly begun to show symptoms of decline. At that venerable distance, the heralds gave up the lineage in despair.

But where written record left the genealogy of Monte Beni, tradition took it up, and carried it without dread or shame beyond the Imperial ages into the times of the Roman republic; beyond those, again, into the epoch of kingly rule. Nor even so remotely among the mossy centuries did it pause, but strayed onward into that gray antiquity of which there is no token left, save its cavernous tombs, and a few bronzes, and some quaintly wrought ornaments of gold, and gems with mystic figures and inscriptions. There, or thereabouts, the line was supposed to have had its origin in the sylvan life of Etruria, while Italy was yet guiltless of Rome.

Of course, as we regret to say, the earlier and very much the larger portion of this respectable descent—and the same is true of many briefer pedigrees—must be looked upon as altogether mythical. Still, it threw a romantic interest around the unquestionable antiquity of the Monte Beni family, and over that tract of their own vines and fig-trees, beneath the shade of which they had unquestionably dwelt for immemorial ages. And there they had laid the foundations of their tower, so long ago that one half of its height was said to be sunken under the surface and to hide subterranean chambers which once were cheerful with the olden sunshine.

One story, or myth, that had mixed itself up with their mouldy genealogy, interested the sculptor by its wild, and perhaps grotesque, yet not unfascinating peculiarity. He caught at it the more eagerly, as it afforded a shadowy and whimsical semblance of explanation for the likeness which he, with Miriam and Hilda, had seen or fancied, between Donatello and the Faun of Praxiteles.

The Monte Beni family, as this legend averred, drew their origin from the Pelasgic race, who peopled Italy in times that may be called prehistoric. It was the same noble breed of men, of Asiatic birth, that settled in Greece; the same happy and poetic kindred who dwelt in Arcadia, and—whether they ever lived such life or not—enriched the world with dreams, at least, and fables, lovely, if unsubstantial, of a Golden Age. In those delicious times, when deities and demigods appeared familiarly on earth, mingling with its inhabitants as friend with friend,—when nymphs, satyrs, and the whole train of classic faith or fable hardly took pains to hide themselves in the primeval woods,—at that auspicious period the lineage of Monte Beni had its rise. Its progenitor was a being not altogether human, yet partaking so largely of the gentlest human qualities, as to be neither awful nor shocking to the imagination. A sylvan creature, native among the woods, had loved a mortal maiden, and—perhaps by kindness, and the subtile courtesies which love might teach to his simplicity, or possibly by a ruder wooing—had won her to his haunts. In due time, he gained her womanly affection; and, making their bridal bower, for aught we know, in the hollow of a great tree, the pair spent a happy wedded life in that ancient neighborhood where now stood Donatello's tower.

From this union sprang a vigorous progeny that took its place unquestioned among human families. In that age, however, and long afterwards, it showed the ineffaceable lineaments of its wild paternity: it was a pleasant and kindly race of men, but capable of savage fierceness, and never quite restrainable within the trammels of social law. They were strong, active, genial, cheerful as the sunshine, passionate as the tornado. Their lives were rendered blissful by an unsought harmony with nature.

But, as centuries passed away, the Faun's wild blood had necessarily been attempered with constant intermixtures from the more ordinary streams of human life. It lost many of its original qualities, and served, for the most part, only to bestow an unconquerable vigor, which kept the family from extinction, and enabled them to make their own part good throughout the perils and rude emergencies of their interminable descent. In the constant wars with which Italy was plagued, by the dissensions of her petty states and republics, there was a demand for native hardihood.

The successive members of the Monte Beni family showed valor and policy enough, at all events, to keep their hereditary possessions out of the clutch of grasping neighbors, and probably differed very little from the other feudal barons with whom they fought and feasted. Such a degree of conformity with the manners of the generations, through which it survived, must have been essential to the prolonged continuance of the race.

It is well known, however, that any hereditary peculiarity—as a supernumerary finger, or an anomalous shape of feature, like the Austrian lip—is wont to show itself in a family after a very wayward fashion. It skips at its own pleasure along the line, and, latent for half a century or so, crops out again in a great-grandson. And thus, it was said, from a period beyond memory or record, there had ever and anon been a descendant of the Monte Benis bearing nearly all the characteristics that were attributed to the original founder of the race. Some traditions even went so far as to enumerate the ears, covered with a delicate fur, and shaped like a pointed leaf, among the proofs of authentic descent which were seen in these favored individuals. We appreciate the beauty of such tokens of a nearer kindred to the great family of nature than other mortals bear; but it would be idle to ask credit for a statement which might be deemed to partake so largely of the grotesque.

But it was indisputable that, once in a century, or oftener, a son of Monte Beni gathered into himself the scattered qualities of his race, and reproduced the character that had been assigned to it from immemorial times. Beautiful, strong, brave, kindly, sincere, of honest impulses, and endowed with simple tastes and the love of homely pleasures, he was believed to possess gifts by which he could associate himself with the wild things of the forests, and with the fowls of the air, and could feel a sympathy even with the trees, among which it was his joy to dwell. On the other hand, there were deficiencies both of intellect and heart, and especially, as it seemed, in the development of the higher portion of man's nature. These defects were less perceptible in early youth, but showed themselves more strongly with advancing age, when, as the animal spirits settled down upon a lower level, the representative of the Monte Benis was apt to become sensual, addicted to gross pleasures, heavy, unsympathizing, and insulated within the narrow limits of a surly selfishness.

A similar change, indeed, is no more than what we constantly observe to take place in persons who are not careful to substitute other graces for those which they inevitably lose along with the quick sensibility and joyous vivacity of youth. At worst, the reigning Count of Monte Beni, as his hair grew white, was still a jolly old fellow over his flask of wine,—the wine that Bacchus himself was fabled to have taught his sylvan ancestor how to express, and from what choicest grapes, which would ripen only in a certain divinely favored portion of the Monte Beni vineyard.

The family, be it observed, were both proud and ashamed of these legends; but whatever part of them they might consent to incoporate into their ancestral history, they steadily repudiated all that referred to their one distinctive feature, the pointed and furry ears. In a great many years past, no sober credence had been yielded to the mythical portion of the pedigree. It might, however, be considered as typifying some such assemblage of qualities—in this case, chiefly remarkable for their simplicity and naturalness—as, when they reappear in successive generations, constitute what we call family character. The sculptor found, moreover, on the evidence of some old portraits, that the physical features of the race had long been similar to what he now saw them in Donatello. With accumulating years, it is true, the Monte Beni face had a tendency to look grim and savage; and, in two or three instances, the family pictures glared at the spectator in the eyes like some surly animal, that had lost its good-humor when it outlived its playfulness.

The young Count accorded his guest full liberty to investigate the personal annals of these pictured worthies, as well as all the rest of his progenitors; and ample materials were at hand in many chests of worm-eaten papers and yellow parchments, that had been gathering into larger and dustier piles ever since the dark ages. But, to confess the truth, the information afforded by these musty documents was so much more prosaic than what Kenyon acquired from Tomaso's legends, that even the superior authenticity of the former could not reconcile him to its dulness.

What especially delighted the sculptor was the analogy between Donatello's character, as he himself knew it, and those peculiar traits which the old butler's narrative assumed to have been long hereditary in the race. He was amused at finding, too, that not only Tomaso but the peasantry of the estate and neighboring village recognized his friend as a genuine Monte Beni, of the original type. They seemed to cherish a great affection for the young Count, and were full of stories about his sportive childhood; how he had played among the little rustics, and been at once the wildest and the sweetest of them all; and how, in his very infancy, he had plunged into the deep pools of the streamlets and never been drowned, and had clambered to the topmost branches of tall trees without ever breaking his neck. No such mischance could happen to the sylvan child, because, handling all the elements of nature so fearlessly and freely, nothing had either the power or the will to do him harm.

He grew up, said these humble friends, the playmate not only of all mortal kind, but of creatures of the woods; although, when Kenyon pressed them for some particulars of this latter mode of companionship, they could remember little more than a few anecdotes of a pet fox, which used to growl and snap at everybody save Donatello himself.

But they enlarged—and never were weary of the theme—upon the blithesome effects of Donatello's presence in his rosy childhood and budding youth. Their hovels had always glowed like sunshine when he entered them; so that, as the peasants expressed it, their young master had never darkened a doorway in his life. He was the soul of vintage festivals. While he was a mere infant, scarcely able to run alone, it had been the custom to make him tread the wine-press with his tender little feet, if it were only to crush one cluster of the grapes. And the grape-juice that gushed beneath his childish tread, be it ever so small in quantity, sufficed to impart a pleasant flavor to a whole cask of wine. The race of Monte Beni—so these rustic chroniclers assured the sculptor—had possessed the gift from the oldest of old times of expressing good wine from ordinary grapes, and a ravishing liquor from the choice growth of their vineyard.

In a word, as he listened to such tales as these, Kenyon could have imagined that the valleys and hill-sides about him were a veritable Arcadia; and that Donatello was not merely a sylvan faun, but the genial wine-god in his very person. Making many allowances for the poetic fancies of Italian peasants, he set it down for fact, that his friend, in a simple way, and among rustic folks, had been an exceedingly delightful fellow in his younger days.

But the contadini sometimes added, shaking their heads and sighing, that the young Count was sadly changed since he went to Rome. The village girls now missed the merry smile with which he used to greet them.

The sculptor inquired of his good friend Tomaso, whether he, too, had noticed the shadow which was said to have recently fallen over Donatello's life.

"Ah, yes, Signore!" answered the old butler, "it is even so, since he came back from that wicked and miserable city. The world has grown either too evil, or else too wise and sad, for such men as the old Counts of Monte Beni used to be. His very first taste of it, as you see, has changed and spoilt my poor young lord. There had not been a single count in the family these hundred years or more, who was so true a Monte Beni, of the antique stamp, as this poor signorino; and now it brings the tears into my eyes to hear him sighing over a cup of Sunshine! Ah, it is a sad world now!"

"Then you think there was a merrier world once?" asked Kenyon.

"Surely, Signore," said Tomaso; "a merrier world, and merrier Counts of Monte Beni to live in it! Such tales of them as I have heard, when I was a child on my grandfather's knee! The good old man remembered a lord of Monte Beni—at least, he had heard of such a one, though I will not make oath upon the holy crucifix that my grandsire lived in his time —who used to go into the woods and call pretty damsels out of the fountains, and out of the trunks of the old trees. That merry lord was known to dance with them a whole long summer afternoon! When shall we see such frolics in our days?"

"Not soon, I am afraid," acquiesced the sculptor. "You are right, excellent Tomaso; the world is sadder now!"

And, in truth, while our friend smiled at these wild fables, he sighed in the same breath to think how the once genial earth produces, in every successive generation, fewer flowers than used to gladden the preceding ones. Not that the modes and seeming possibilities of human enjoyment are rarer in our refined and softened era,—on the contrary, they never before were nearly so abundant,—but that mankind are getting so far beyond the childhood of their race that they scorn to be happy any longer. A simple and joyous character can find no place for itself among the sage and sombre figures that would put his unsophisticated cheerfulness to shame. The entire system of man's affairs, as at present established, is built up purposely to exclude the careless and happy soul. The very children would upbraid the wretched individual who should endeavor to take life and the world as—what we might naturally suppose them meant for —a place and opportunity for enjoyment.

It is the iron rule in our day to require an object and a purpose in life. It makes us all parts of a complicated scheme of progress, which can only result in our arrival at a colder and drearier region than we were born in. It insists upon everybody's adding somewhat—a mite, perhaps, but earned by incessant effort—to an accumulated pile of usefulness, of which the only use will be, to burden our posterity with even heavier thoughts and more inordinate labor than our own. No life now wanders like an unfettered stream; there is a mill-wheel for the tiniest rivulet to turn. We go all wrong, by too strenuous a resolution to go all right.

Therefore it was—so, at least, the sculptor thought, although partly suspicious of Donatello's darker misfortune—that the young Count found it impossible nowadays to be what his forefathers had been. He could not live their healthy life of animal spirits, in their sympathy with nature, and brotherhood with all that breathed around them. Nature, in beast, fowl, and tree, and earth, flood, and sky, is what it was of old; but sin, care, and self-consciousness have set the human portion of the world askew; and thus the simplest character is ever the soonest to go astray.

"At any rate, Tomaso," said Kenyon, doing his best to comfort the old man, "let us hope that your young lord will still enjoy himself at vintage-time. By the aspect of the vineyard, I judge that this will be a famous year for the golden wine of Monte Beni. As long as your grapes produce that admirable liquor, sad as you think the world, neither the Count nor his guests will quite forget to smile."

"Ah, Signore," rejoined the butler with a sigh, "but he scarcely wets his lips with the sunny juice."

"There is yet another hope," observed Kenyon; "the young Count may fall in love, and bring home a fair and laughing wife to chase the gloom out of yonder old, frescoed saloon. Do you think he could do a better thing, my good Tomaso?"

"Maybe not, Signore," said the sage butler, looking earnestly at him; "and, maybe, not a worse!"

The sculptor fancied that the good old man had it partly in his mind to make some remark, or communicate some fact, which, on second thoughts, he resolved to keep concealed in his own breast. He now took his departure cellarward, shaking his white head and muttering to himself, and did not reappear till dinner-time, when he favored Kenyon, whom he had taken far into his good graces, with a choicer flask of Sunshine than had yet blessed his palate.

To say the truth, this golden wine was no unnecessary ingredient towards making the life of Monte Beni palatable. It seemed a pity that Donatello did not drink a little more of it, and go jollily to bed at least, even if he should awake with an accession of darker melancholy the next morning.

Nevertheless, there was no lack of outward means for leading an agreeable life in the old villa. Wandering musicians haunted the precincts of Monte Beni, where they seemed to claim a prescriptive right; they made the lawn and shrubbery tuneful with the sound of fiddle, harp, and flute, and now and then with the tangled squeaking of a bagpipe. Improvvisatori likewise came and told tales or recited verses to the contadini—among whom Kenyon was often an auditor—after their day's work in the vineyard. Jugglers, too, obtained permission to do feats of magic in the hall, where they set even the sage Tomaso, and Stella, Girolamo, and the peasant-girls from the farm-house, all of a broad grin, between merriment and wonder. These good people got food and lodging for their pleasant pains, and some of the small wine of Tuscany, and a reasonable handful of the Grand Duke's copper coin, to keep up the hospitable renown of Monte Beni. But very seldom had they the young Count as a listener or a spectator.

There were sometimes dances by moonlight on the lawn, but never since he came from Rome did Donatello's presence deepen the blushes of the pretty contadinas, or his footstep weary out the most agile partner or competitor, as once it was sure to do.

Paupers—for this kind of vermin infested the house of Monte Beni worse than any other spot in beggar-haunted Italy—stood beneath all the windows, making loud supplication, or even establishing themselves on the marble steps of the grand entrance. They ate and drank, and filled their bags, and pocketed the little money that was given them, and went forth on their devious ways, showering blessings innumerable on the mansion and its lord, and on the souls of his deceased forefathers, who had always been just such simpletons as to be compassionate to beggary. But, in spite of their favorable prayers,—by which Italian philanthropists set great store,—a cloud seemed to hang over these once Arcadian precincts, and to be darkest around the summit of the tower where Donatello was wont to sit and brood.

### CHAPTER XXVII

### MYTHS

AFTER the sculptor's arrival, however, the young Count sometimes came down from his forlorn elevation, and rambled with him among the neighboring woods and hills. He led his friend to many enchanting nooks, with which he himself had been familiar in his childhood. But of late, as he remarked to Kenyon, a sort of strangeness had overgrown them, like clusters of dark shrubbery, so that he hardly recognized the places which he had known and loved so well.

To the sculptor's eye, nevertheless, they were still rich with beauty. They were picturesque in that sweetly impressive way where wildness, in a long lapse of years, has crept over scenes that have been once adorned with the careful art and toil of man; and when man could do no more for them, time and nature came, and wrought hand in hand to bring them to a soft and venerable perfection. There grew the fig-tree that had run wild and taken to wife the vine, which likewise had gone rampant out of all human control; so that the two wild things had tangled and knotted themselves into a wild marriage-bond, and hung their various progeny—the luscious figs, the grapes, oozy with the Southern juice, and both endowed with a wild flavor that added the final charm—on the same bough together.

In Kenyon's opinion, never was any other nook so lovely as a certain little dell which he and Donatello visited. It was hollowed in among the hills, and open to a glimpse of the broad, fertile valley. A fountain had its birth here, and fell into a marble basin, which was all covered with moss and shaggy with water-weeds. Over the gush of the small stream, with an urn in her arms, stood a marble nymph, whose nakedness the moss had kindly clothed as with a garment; and the long trails and tresses of the maidenhair had done what they could in the poor thing's behalf, by hanging themselves about her waist. In former days—it might be a remote antiquity—this lady of the fountain had first received the infant tide into her urn and poured it thence into the marble basin. But now the sculptured urn had a great crack from top to bottom; and the discontented nymph was compelled to see the basin fill itself through a channel which she could not control, although with water long ago consecrated to her.

For this reason, or some other, she looked terribly forlorn; and you might have fancied that the whole fountain was but the overflow of her lonely tears.

"This was a place that I used greatly to delight in," remarked Donatello, sighing. "As a child, and as a boy, I have been very happy here."

"And, as a man, I should ask no fitter place to be happy in," answered Kenyon. "But you, my friend, are of such a social nature, that I should hardly have thought these lonely haunts would take your fancy. It is a place for a poet to dream in, and people it with the beings of his imagination."

"I am no poet, that I know of," said Donatello, "but yet, as I tell you, I have been very happy here, in the company of this fountain and this nymph. It is said that a Faun, my oldest forefather, brought home hither to this very spot a human maiden, whom he loved and wedded. This spring of delicious water was their household well."

"It is a most enchanting fable!" exclaimed Kenyon; "that is, if it be not a fact."

"And why not a fact?" said the simple Donatello. "There is, likewise, another sweet old story connected with this spot. But, now that I remember it, it seems to me more sad than sweet, though formerly the sorrow, in which it closes, did not so much impress me. If I had the gift of tale-telling, this one would be sure to interest you mightily."

"Pray tell it," said Kenyon; "no matter whether well or ill. These wild legends have often the most powerful charm when least artfully told."

So the young Count narrated a myth of one of his progenitors,—he might have lived a century ago, or a thousand years, or before the Christian epoch, for anything that Donatello knew to the contrary,—who had made acquaintance with a fair creature belonging to this fountain. Whether woman or sprite was a mystery, as was all else about her, except that her life and soul were somehow interfused throughout the gushing water. She was a fresh, cool, dewy thing, sunny and shadowy, full of pleasant little mischiefs, fitful and changeable with the whim of the moment, but yet as constant as her native stream, which kept the same gush and flow forever, while marble crumbled over and around it. The fountain woman loved the youth,—a knight, as Donatello called him,—for, according to the legend, his race was akin to hers. At least, whether kin or no, there had been friendship and sympathy of old betwixt an ancestor of his, with furry ears, and the long-lived lady of the fountain. And, after all those ages, she was still as young as a May morning, and as frolicsome as a bird upon a tree, or a breeze that makes merry with the leaves.

She taught him how to call her from her pebbly source, and they spent many a happy hour together, more especially in the fervor of the summer days. For often as he sat waiting for her by the margin of the spring, she would suddenly fall down around him in a shower of sunny rain-drops, with a rainbow glancing through them, and forthwith gather herself up into the likeness of a beautiful girl, laughing—or was it the warble of the rill over the pebbles?—to see the youth's amazement.

Thus, kind maiden that she was, the hot atmosphere became delicious-ly cool and fragrant for this favored knight; and, furthermore, when he knelt down to drink out of the spring, nothing was more common than for a pair of rosy lips to come up out of its little depths, and touch his mouth with the thrill of a sweet, cool, dewy kiss!

"It is a delightful story for the hot noon of your Tuscan summer," ob-served the sculptor, at this point. "But the deportment of the watery lady must have had a most chilling influence in midwinter. Her lover would find it, very literally, a cold reception!"

"I suppose," said Donatello, rather sulkily, "you are making fun of the story. But I see nothing laughable in the thing itself, nor in what you say about it."

He went on to relate, that for a long while the knight found infinite pleasure and comfort in the friendship of the fountain nymph. In his mer-riest hours, she gladdened him with her sportive humor. If ever he was an-noyed with earthly trouble, she laid her moist hand upon his brow, and charmed the fret and fever quite away.

But one day—one fatal noontide—the young knight came rushing with hasty and irregular steps to the accustomed fountain. He called the nymph; but—no doubt because there was something unusual and fright-ful in his tone—she did not appear, nor answer him. He flung himself down, and washed his hands and bathed his feverish brow in the cool, pure water. And then, there was a sound of woe; it might have been a woman's voice; it might have been only the sighing of the brook over the pebbles. The water shrank away from the youth's hands, and left his brow as dry and feverish as before.—

Donatello here came to a dead pause.

"Why did the water shrink from this unhappy knight?" inquired the sculptor.

"Because he had tried to wash off a blood-stain!" said the young Count, in a horror-stricken whisper. "The guilty man had polluted the pure water. The nymph might have comforted him in sorrow, but could not cleanse his conscience of a crime."

"And did he never behold her more?" asked Kenyon.

"Never but once," replied his friend. "He never beheld her blessed face but once again, and then there was a blood-stain on the poor nymph's brow; it was the stain his guilt had left in the fountain where he tried to wash it off. He mourned for her his whole life long, and employed the best sculptor of the time to carve this statue of the nymph from his descrip-tion of her aspect. But, though my ancestor would fain have had the im-age wear her happiest look, the artist, unlike yourself, was so impressed with the mournfulness of the story, that, in spite of his best efforts, he made her forlorn, and forever weeping, as you see!"

Kenyon found a certain charm in this simple legend. Whether so in-tended or not, he understood it as an apologue, typifying the soothing and genial effects of an habitual intercourse with nature, in all ordinary cares and griefs; while, on the other hand, her mild influences fall short in their effect upon the ruder passions, and are altogether powerless in the dread fever-fit or deadly chill of guilt.

"Do you say," he asked, "that the nymph's face has never since been shown to any mortal? Methinks you, by your native qualities are as well entitled to her favor as ever your progenitor could have been. Why have you not summoned her?'"

"I called her often when I was a silly child," answered Donatello; and he added, in an inward voice, "Thank Heaven, she did not come!"

"Then you never saw her?" said the sculptor.

"Never in my life!" rejoined the Count. "No, my dear friend, I have not seen the nymph; although here, by her fountain, I used to make many strange acquaintances; for, from my earliest childhood, I was familiar with whatever creatures haunt the woods. You would have laughed to see the friends I had among them; yes, among the wild, nimble things, that reckon man their deadliest enemy! How it was first taught me, I cannot tell; but there was a charm—a voice, a murmur, a kind of chant—by which I called the woodland inhabitants, the furry people, and the feathered people, in a language that they seemed to understand."

"I have heard of such a gift," responded the sculptor, gravely, "but never before met with a person endowed with it. Pray, try the charm; and lest I should frighten your friends away, I will withdraw into this thicket, and merely peep at them."

"I doubt," said Donatello, "whether they will remember my voice now. It changes, you know, as the boy grows towards manhood."

Nevertheless, as the young Count's good-nature and easy persuadability were among his best characteristics, he set about complying with Kenyon's request. The latter, in his concealment among the shrubberies, heard him send forth a sort of modulated breath, wild, rude, yet harmonious. It struck the auditor as at once the strangest and the most natural utterance that had ever reached his ears. Any idle boy, it should seem, singing to himself and setting his wordless song to no other or more definite tune than the play of his own pulses, might produce a sound almost identical with this; and yet, it was as individual as a murmur of the breeze. Donatello tried it, over and over again, with many breaks, at first, and pauses of uncertainty; then with more confidence, and a fuller swell, like a wayfarer groping out of obscurity into the light, and moving with freer footsteps as it brightens around him.

Anon, his voice appeared to fill the air, yet not with an obtrusive clangor. The sound was of a murmurous character, soft, attractive, persuasive, friendly. The sculptor fancied that such might have been the original voice and utterance of the natural man, before the sophistication of the human intellect formed what we now call language. In this broad dialect —broad as the sympathies of nature—the human brother might have spoken to his inarticulate brotherhood that prowl the woods, or soar upon the wing, and have been intelligible to such extent as to win their confidence.

The sound had its pathos too. At some of its simple cadences, the tears came quietly into Kenyon's eyes. They welled up slowly from his heart, which was thrilling with an emotion more delightful than he had often felt before, but which he forbore to analyze, lest, if he seized it, it should at once perish in his grasp.

Donatello paused two or three times, and seemed to listen; then, recommencing, he poured his spirit and life more earnestly into the strain. And, finally,—or else the sculptor's hope and imagination deceived him, —soft treads were audible upon the fallen leaves. There was a rustling among the shrubbery; a whir of wings, moreover, that hovered in the air. It may have been all an illusion; but Kenyon fancied that he could distinguish the stealthy, cat-like movement of some small forest citizen, and that he could even see its doubtful shadow, if not really its substance. But, all at once, whatever might be the reason, there ensued a hurried rush and scamper of little feet; and then the sculptor heard a wild, sorrowful cry, and through the crevices of the thicket beheld Donatello fling himself on the ground.

Emerging from his hiding-place, he saw no living thing, save a brown lizard (it was of the tarantula species) rustling away through the sunshine. To all present appearance, this venomous reptile was the only creature that had responded to the young Count's efforts to renew his intercourse with the lower orders of nature.

"What has happened to you?" exclaimed Kenyon, stooping down over his friend, and wondering at the anguish which he betrayed.

"Death, death!" sobbed Donatello. "They know it!"

He grovelled beside the fountain, in a fit of such passionate sobbing and weeping, that it seemed as if his heart had broken, and spilt its wild sorrows upon the ground. His unrestrained grief and childish tears made Kenyon sensible in how small a degree the customs and restaints of society had really acted upon this young man, in spite of the quietude of his ordinary deportment. In response to his friend's efforts to console him, he murmured words hardly more articulate than the strange chant which he had so recently been breathing into the air.

"They know it!" was all that Kenyon could yet distinguish,—"they know it!"

"Who know it?" asked the sculptor. "And what is it they know?"

"They know it!" repeated Donatello, trembling. "They shun me! All nature shrinks from me, and shudders at me! I live in the midst of a curse, that hems me round with a circle of fire! No innocent thing can come near me."

"Be comforted, my dear friend," said Kenyon, kneeling beside him. "You labor under some illusion, but no curse. As for this strange, natural spell, which you have been exercising, and of which I have heard before, though I never believed in, nor expected to witness it, I am satisfied that you still possess it. It was my own half-concealed presence, no doubt, and some involuntary little movement of mine, that scared away your forest friends."

"They are friends of mine no longer," answered Donatello.

"We all of us, as we grow older," rejoined Kenyon, "lose somewhat of our proximity to nature. It is the price we pay for experience."

"A heavy price, then!" said Donatello, rising from the ground. "But we will speak no more of it. Forget this scene, my dear friend. In your eyes, it must look very absurd. It is a grief, I presume, to all men, to find the pleasant privileges and properties of early life departing from them. That grief has now befallen me. Well; I shall waste no more tears for such a cause!"

Nothing else made Kenyon so sensible of a change in Donatello, as his newly acquired power of dealing with his own emotions, and, after a struggle more or less fierce, thrusting them down into the prison-cells where he usually kept them confined. The restraint, which he now put upon himself, and the mask of dull composure which he succeeded in clasping over his still beautiful, and once faun-like face, affected the sensitive sculptor more sadly than even the unrestrained passion of the preceding scene. It is a very miserable epoch, when the evil necessities of life, in our tortuous world, first get the better of us so far as to compel us to attempt throwing a cloud over our transparency. Simplicity increases in value the longer we can keep it, and the further we carry it onward into life; the loss of a child's simplicity, in the inevitable lapse of years, causes but a natural sigh or two, because even his mother feared that he could not keep it always. But after a young man has brought it through his childhood, and has still worn it in his bosom, not as an early dew-drop, but as a diamond of pure, white, lustre,—it is a pity to lose it, then. And thus, when Kenyon saw how much his friend had now to hide, and how well he hid it, he would have wept, although his tears would have been even idler than those which Donatello had just shed.

They parted on the lawn before the house, the Count to climb his tower, and the sculptor to read an antique edition of Dante, which he had found among some old volumes of Catholic devotion, in a seldom-visited room. Tomaso met him in the entrance-hall, and showed a desire to speak.

"Our poor signorino looks very sad to-day!" he said.

"Even so, good Tomaso," replied the sculptor. "Would that we could raise his spirits a little!"

"There might be means, Signore," answered the old butler, "if one might but be sure that they were the right ones. We men are but rough nurses for a sick body or a sick spirit."

"Women, you would say, my good friend, are better," said the sculptor, struck by an intelligence in the butler's face. "That is possible! But it depends."

"Ah; we will wait a little longer," said Tomaso, with the customary shake of his head.

## CHAPTER XXVIII

## THE OWL TOWER

"WILL you not show me your tower?" said the sculptor one day to his friend.

"It is plainly enough to be seen, methinks," answered the Count, with a kind of sulkiness that often appeared in him, as one of the little symptoms of inward trouble.

"Yes; its exterior is visible far and wide," said Kenyon. "But such a gray, moss-grown tower as this, however valuable as an object of scenery, will certainly be quite as interesting inside as out. It cannot be less than six hundred years old; the foundations and lower story are much older than that, I should judge; and traditions probably cling to the walls within quite as plentifully as the gray and yellow lichens cluster on its face without."

"No doubt," replied Donatello; "but I know little of such things, and never could comprehend the interest which some of you Forestieri take in them. A year or two ago an English signore, with a venerable white beard —they say he was a magician, too—came hither from as far off as Florence, just to see my tower."

"Ah, I have seen him at Florence," observed Kenyon. "He is a necromancer, as you say, and dwells in an old mansion of the Knights Templars, close by the Ponte Vecchio, with a great many ghostly books, pictures, and antiquities, to make the house gloomy, and one bright-eyed little girl, to keep it cheerful!"

"I know him only by his white beard," said Donatello; "but he could have told you a great deal about the tower, and the sieges which it has stood, and the prisoners who have been confined in it. And he gathered up all the traditions of the Monte Beni family, and, among the rest, the sad one which I told you at the fountain the other day. He had known mighty poets, he said, in his earlier life; and the most illustrious of them would have rejoiced to preserve such a legend in immortal rhyme,—especially if he could have had some of our wine of Sunshine to help out his inspiration!"

"Any man might be a poet, as well as Byron, with such wine and such a theme," rejoined the sculptor. "But, shall we climb your tower? The thunder-storm gathering yonder among the hills will be a spectacle worth witnessing."

"Come, then," said the Count, adding, with a sigh, "it has a weary staircase, and dismal chambers, and it is very lonesome at the summit!"

"Like a man's life, when he has climbed to eminence," remarked the sculptor; "or, let us rather say, with its difficult steps, and the dark prison-cells you speak of, your tower resembles the spiritual experience of many a sinful soul, which, nevertheless, may struggle upward into the pure air and light of Heaven at last!"

Donatello sighed again, and led the way up into the tower.

Mounting the broad staircase that ascended from the entrance-hall, they traversed the great wilderness of a house, through some obscure passages, and came to a low, ancient doorway. It admitted them to a narrow turret-stair which zigzagged upward, lighted in its progress by loopholes and iron-barred windows. Reaching the top of the first flight, the Count threw open a door of worm-eaten oak, and disclosed a chamber that occupied the whole area of the tower. It was most pitiably forlorn of aspect, with a brick-paved floor, bare holes through the massive walls, grated with iron, instead of windows, and for furniture an old stool, which increased the dreariness of the place tenfold, by suggesting an idea of its having once been tenanted.

"This was a prisoner's cell in the old days," said Donatello; "the white-bearded necromancer, of whom I told you, found out that a certain famous monk was confined here, about five hundred years ago. He was a very holy man, and was afterwards burned at the stake in the Grand-ducal Square at Firenze. There have always been stories, Tomaso says, of a hooded monk creeping up and down these stairs, or standing in the doorway of this chamber. It must needs be the ghost of the ancient prisoner. Do you believe in ghosts?"

"I can hardly tell," replied Kenyon; "on the whole, I think not."

"Neither do I," responded the Count; "for, if spirits ever come back, I should surely have met one within these two months past. Ghosts never rise! So much I know, and am glad to know it!"

Following the narrow staircase still higher, they came to another room of similar size and equally forlorn, but inhabited by two personages of a race which from time immemorial have held proprietorship and occupancy in ruined towers. These were a pair of owls, who, being doubtless acquainted with Donatello, showed little sign of alarm at the entrance of visitors. They gave a dismal croak or two, and hopped aside into the darkest corner, since it was not yet their hour to flap duskily abroad.

"They do not desert me, like my other feathered acquaintances," observed the young Count, with a sad smile, alluding to the scene which Kenyon had witnessed at the fountain-side. "When I was a wild, playful boy, the owls did not love me half so well."

He made no further pause here, but led his friend up another flight of steps; while, at every stage, the windows and narrow loopholes afforded Kenyon more extensive eyeshots over hill and valley, and allowed him to taste the cool purity of mid-atmosphere. At length they reached the topmost chamber, directly beneath the roof of the tower.

"This is my own abode," said Donatello; "my own owl's nest."

In fact, the room was fitted up as a bedchamber, though in a style of the utmost simplicity. It likewise served as an oratory; there being a crucifix in one corner, and a multitude of holy emblems, such as Catholics judge it necessary to help their devotion withal. Several ugly little prints, representing the sufferings of the Saviour, and the martyrdoms of saints, hung on the wall; and, behind the crucifix, there was a good copy of Titian's Magdalen of the Pitti Palace, clad only in the flow of her golden ringlets. She had a confident look (but it was Titian's fault, not the penitent woman's), as if expecting to win heaven by the free display of her earthly charms. Inside of a glass case appeared an image of the sacred Bambino, in the guise of a little waxen boy, very prettily made, reclining among flowers, like a Cupid, and holding up a heart that resembled a bit of red sealing-wax. A small vase of precious marble was full of holy water.

Beneath the crucifix, on a table, lay a human skull, which looked as if it might have been dug up out of some old grave. But, examining it more closely, Kenyon saw that it was carved in gray alabaster, most skilfully done to the death, with accurate imitation of the teeth, the sutures, the empty eye-caverns, and the fragile little bones of the nose. This hideous emblem rested on a cushion of white marble, so nicely wrought that you seemed to see the impression of the heavy skull in a silken and downy substance.

Donatello dipped his fingers into the holy-water vase, and crossed himself. After doing so he trembled.

"I have no right to make the sacred symbol on a sinful breast!" he said.

"On what mortal breast can it be made, then?" asked the sculptor. "Is there one that hides no sin?"

"But these blessed emblems make you smile, I fear," resumed the Count, looking askance at his friend. "You heretics, I know, attempt to pray without even a crucifix to kneel at."

"I, at least, whom you call a heretic, reverence that holy symbol," answered Kenyon. "What I am most inclined to murmur at is this death's-head. I could laugh, moreover, in its ugly face! It is absurdly monstrous, my dear friend, thus to fling the deadweight of our mortality upon our immortal hopes. While we live on earth, 't is true, we must needs carry our skeletons about with us; but, for Heaven's sake, do not let us burden our spirits with them, in our feeble efforts to soar upward! Believe me, it will change the whole aspect of death, if you can once disconnect it, in your idea, with that corruption from which it disengages our higher part."

"I do not well understand you," said Donatello; and he took up the alabaster skull, shuddering, and evidently feeling it a kind of penance to touch it. "I only know that this skull has been in my family for centuries. Old Tomaso has a story that it was copied by a famous sculptor from the skull of that same unhappy knight who loved the fountain-lady, and lost her by a blood-stain. He lived and died with a deep sense of sin upon him, and, on his death-bed, he ordained that this token of him should go down to his posterity. And my forefathers, being a cheerful race of men in their natural disposition, found it needful to have the skull often before their eyes, because they dearly loved life and its enjoyments, and hated the very thought of death."

"I am afraid," said Kenyon, "they liked it none the better, for seeing its face under this abominable mask."

Without further discussion, the Count led the way up one more flight of stairs, at the end of which they emerged upon the summit of the tower. The sculptor felt as if his being were suddenly magnified a hundred-fold; so wide was the Umbrian valley that suddenly opened before him, set in its grand framework of nearer and more distant hills. It seemed as if all Italy lay under his eyes in that one picture. For there was the broad, sunny smile of God, which we fancy to be spread over that favored land more abundantly than on other regions, and, beneath it, glowed a most rich and varied fertility. The trim vineyards were there, and the fig-trees, and the mulberries, and the smoky-hued tracts of the olive-orchards; there, too, were fields of every kind of grain, among which waved the Indian corn, putting Kenyon in mind of the fondly remembered acres of his father's homestead. White villas, gray convents, church-spires, villages, towns, each with its battlemented walls and towered gateway, were scattered upon this spacious map; a river gleamed across it; and lakes opened their blue eyes in its face, reflecting heaven, lest mortals should forget that better land when they beheld the earth so beautiful.

What made the valley look still wider was the two or three varieties of weather that were visible on its surface, all at the same instant of time. Here lay the quiet sunshine; there fell the great black patches of ominous shadow from the clouds; and behind them, like a giant of league-long strides, came hurrying the thunder-storm, which had already swept midway across the plain. In the rear of the approaching tempest, brightened forth again the sunny splendor, which its progress had darkened with so terrible a frown.

All round this majestic landscape, the bald-peaked or forest-crowned mountains descended boldly upon the plain. On many of their spurs and midway declivities, and even on their summits, stood cities, some of them famous of old; for these had been the seats and nurseries of early art, where the flower of beauty sprang out of a rocky soil, and in a high, keen atmosphere, when the richest and most sheltered gardens failed to nourish it.

"Thank God for letting me again behold this scene!" said the sculptor, a devout man in his way, reverently taking off his hat. "I have viewed it from many points, and never without as full a sensation of gratitude as my heart seems capable of feeling. How it strengthens the poor human spirit in its reliance on His providence, to ascend but this little way above the common level, and so attain a somewhat wider glimpse of His dealings with mankind! He doeth all things right! His will be done!"

"You discern something that is hidden from me," observed Donatello, gloomily, yet striving with unwonted grasp to catch the analogies which so cheered his friend. "I see sunshine on one spot, and cloud in another, and no reason for it in either case. The sun on you; the cloud on me! What comfort can I draw from this?"

"Nay; I cannot preach," said Kenyon, "with a page of heaven and a page of earth spread wide open before us! Only begin to read it, and you will find it interpreting itself without the aid of words. It is a great mistake to try to put our best thoughts into human language. When we ascend into the higher regions of emotion and spiritual enjoyment, they are only expressible by such grand hieroglyphics as these around us."

They stood awhile, contemplating the scene; but, as inevitably happens after a spiritual flight, it was not long before the sculptor felt his wings flagging in the rarity of the upper atmosphere. He was glad to let himself quietly downward out of the mid-sky, as it were, and alight on the solid platform of the battlemented tower. He looked about him, and beheld growing out of the stone pavement, which formed the roof, a little shrub, with green and glossy leaves. It was the only green thing there; and Heaven knows how its seeds had ever been planted, at that airy height, or how it had found nourishment for its small life in the chinks of the stones; for it had no earth, and nothing more like soil than the crumbling mortar, which had been crammed into the crevices in a long-past age.

Yet the plant seemed fond of its native site; and Donatello said it had always grown there, from his earliest remembrance, and never, he believed, any smaller or any larger than they saw it now.

"I wonder if the shrub teaches you any good lesson," said he, observing the interest with which Kenyon examined it. "If the wide valley has a great meaning, the plant ought to have at least a little one; and it has been growing on our tower long enough to have learned how to speak it."

"Oh, certainly!" answered the sculptor; "the shrub has its moral, or it would have perished long ago. And, no doubt, it is for your use and edification, since you have had it before your eyes all your lifetime, and now are moved to ask what may be its lesson."

"It teaches me nothing," said the simple Donatello, stooping over the plant, and perplexing himself with a minute scrutiny. "But here was a worm that would have killed it; an ugly creature, which I will fling over the battlements."

## CHAPTER XXIX

### ON THE BATTLEMENTS

THE sculptor now looked through an embrasure, and threw down a bit of lime, watching its fall, till it struck upon a stone bench at the rocky foundation of the tower, and flew into many fragments.

"Pray pardon me for helping Time to crumble away your ancestral walls," said he. "But I am one of those persons who have a natural tendency to climb heights, and to stand on the verge of them, measuring the depth below. If I were to do just as I like, at this moment, I should fling myself down after that bit of lime. It is a very singular temptation, and all but irresistible; partly, I believe, because it might be so easily done, and partly because such momentous consequences would ensue, without my being compelled to wait a moment for them. Have you never felt this strange impulse of an evil spirit at your back, shoving you towards a precipice?"

"Ah, no!" cried Donatello, shrinking from the battlemented wall with a face of horror. "I cling to life in a way which you cannot conceive; it has been so rich, so warm, so sunny!—and beyond its verge, nothing but the chilly dark! And then a fall from a precipice is such an awful death!"

"Nay; if it be a great height," said Kenyon, " a man would leave his life in the air, and never feel the hard shock at the bottom."

"That is not the way with this kind of death!" exclaimed Donatello, in a low, horror-stricken voice, which grew higher and more full of emotion as he proceeded. "Imagine a fellow-creature,—breathing, now, and looking you in the face,—and now tumbling down, down, down, with a long shriek wavering after him, all the way! He does not leave his life in the air! No; but it keeps in him till he thumps against the stones, a horribly long while; then he lies there frightfully quiet, a dead heap of bruised flesh and broken bones! A quiver runs through the crushed mass; and no more movement after that! No; not if you would give your soul to make him stir a finger! Ah, terrible! Yes, yes; I would fain fling myself down for the very dread of it, that I might endure it once for all, and dream of it no more!"

"How forcibly, how frightfully you conceive this!" said the sculptor, aghast at the passionate horror which was betrayed in the Count's words, and still more in his wild gestures and ghastly look. "Nay, if the height of your tower affects your imagination thus, you do wrong to trust yourself here in solitude, and in the night-time, and at all unguarded hours. You are not safe in your chamber. It is but a step or two; and what if a vivid dream should lead you up hither, at midnight, and act itself out as a reality!"

Donatello had hidden his face in his hands, and was leaning against the parapet.

"No fear of that!" said he. "Whatever the dream may be, I am too genuine a coward to act out my own death in it."

The paroxysm passed away, and the two friends continued their desultory talk, very much as if no such interruption had occurred. Nevertheless, it affected the sculptor with infinite pity to see this young man, who had been born to gladness as an assured heritage, now involved in a misty bewilderment of grievous thoughts, amid which he seemed to go staggering blindfold. Kenyon, not without an unshaped suspicion of the definite fact, knew that his condition must have resulted from the weight and gloom of life, now first, through the agency of a secret trouble, making themselves felt on a character that had heretofore breathed only an atmosphere of joy. The effect of this hard lesson, upon Donatello's intellect and disposition, was very striking. It was perceptible that he had already had glimpses of strange and subtle matters in those dark caverns, into which all men must descend, if they would know anything beneath the surface and illusive pleasures of existence. And when they emerge, though dazzled and blinded by the first glare of daylight, they take truer and sadder views of life forever afterwards.

From some mysterious source, as the sculptor felt assured, a soul had been inspired into the young Count's simplicity, since their intercourse in Rome. He now showed a far deeper sense, and an intelligence that began to deal with high subjects, though in a feeble and childish way. He evinced, too, a more definite and nobler individuality, but developed out of grief and pain, and fearfully conscious of the pangs that had given it birth. Every human life, if it ascends to truth or delves down to reality, must undergo a similar change; but sometimes, perhaps, the instruction comes without the sorrow; and oftener the sorrow teaches no lesson that abides with us. In Donatello's case, it was pitiful, and almost ludicrous, to observe the confused struggle that he made; how completely he was taken by surprise; how ill-prepared he stood, on this old battle-field of the world, to fight with such an inevitable foe as mortal calamity, and sin for its stronger ally.

"And yet," thought Kenyon, "the poor fellow bears himself like a hero, too! If he would only tell me his trouble, or give me an opening to speak frankly about it, I might help him; but he finds it too horrible to be uttered, and fancies himself the only mortal that ever felt the anguish of remorse. Yes; he believes that nobody ever endured his agony before; so that—sharp enough in itself—it has all the additional zest of a torture just invented to plague him individually."

The sculptor endeavored to dismiss the painful subject from his mind; and, leaning against the battlements, he turned his face southward and westward, and gazed across the breadth of the valley. His thoughts flew far beyond even those wide boundaries, taking an air-line from Donatello's tower to another turret that ascended into the sky of the summer afternoon, invisibly to him, above the roofs of distant Rome. Then rose tumultuously into his consciousness that strong love for Hilda, which it was his habit to confine in one of the heart's inner chambers, because he had found no encouragement to bring it forward. But now, he felt a strange pull at his heartstrings. It could not have been more perceptible, if all the way between these battlements and Hilda's dove-cote had stretched an exquisitely sensitive cord, which, at the hither end, was knotted with his aforesaid heartstrings, and, at the remoter one, was grasped by a gentle hand. His breath grew tremulous. He put his hand to his breast; so distinctly did he seem to feel that cord drawn once, and again, and again, as if—though still it was bashfuly intimated—there were an importunate demand for his presence. Oh, for the white wings of Hilda's doves, that he might have flown thither, and alighted at the Virgin's shrine!

But lovers, and Kenyon knew it well, project so lifelike a copy of their mistresses out of their own imaginations, that it can pull at the heartstrings almost as perceptibly as the genuine original. No airy intimations are to be trusted; no evidences of responsive affection less positive than whispered and broken words, or tender pressures of the hand, allowed and half returned; or glances, that distil many passionate avowals into one gleam of richly colored light. Even these should be weighed rigorously, at the instant; for, in another instant, the imagination seizes on them as its property, and stamps them with its own arbitrary value. But Hilda's maidenly reserve had given her lover no such tokens, to be interpreted either by his hopes or fears.

"Yonder, over mountain and valley, lies Rome," said the sculptor; "shall you return thither in the autumn?"

"Never! I hate Rome," answered Donatello; "and have good cause."

"And yet it was a pleasant winter that we spent there," observed Kenyon, "and with pleasant friends about us. You would meet them again there,—all of them."

"All?" asked Donatello.

"All, to the best of my belief," said the sculptor; "but you need not go to Rome to seek them. If there were one of those friends whose lifetime was twisted with your own, I am enough of a fatalist to feel assured that you will meet that one again, wander whither you may. Neither can we escape the companions whom Providence assigns for us, by climbing an old tower like this."

"Yet the stairs are steep and dark," rejoined the Count; "none but yourself would seek me here, or find me, if they sought."

As Donatello did not take advantage of this opening which his friend had kindly afforded him to pour out his hidden troubles, the latter again threw aside the subject, and returned to the enjoyment of the scene before him. The thunder-storm, which he had beheld striding across the valley, had passed to the left of Monte Beni, and was continuing its march towards the hills that formed the boundary on the eastward. Above the whole valley, indeed, the sky was heavy with tumbling vapors, interspersed with which were tracts of blue, vividly brightened by the sun; but, in the east, where the tempest was yet trailing its ragged skirts, lay a dusky region of cloud and sullen mist, in which some of the hills appeared of a dark-purple hue. Others became so indistinct, that the spectator could not tell rocky height from impalpable cloud. Far into this misty cloud-region, however,—within the domain of chaos, as it were,—hill-tops were seen brightening in the sunshine; they looked like fragments of the world, broken adrift and based on nothingness, or like portions of a sphere destined to exist, but not yet finally compacted.

The sculptor, habitually drawing many of the images and illustrations of his thoughts from the plastic art, fancied that the scene represented the process of the Creator, when he held the new, imperfect earth in his hand, and modelled it.

"What a magic is in mist and vapor among the mountains!" he exclaimed. "With their help, one single scene becomes a thousand. The cloud-scenery gives such variety to a hilly landscape that it would be worth while to journalize its aspect from hour to hour. A cloud, however, —as I have myself experienced,—is apt to grow solid and as heavy as a stone the instant that you take in hand to describe it. But in my own heart, I have found great use in clouds. Such silvery ones as those to the northward, for example, have often suggested sculpturesque groups, figures, and attitudes; they are especially rich in attitudes of living repose, which a sculptor only hits upon by the rarest good fortune. When I go back to my dear native land, the clouds along the horizon will be my only gallery of art!"

"I can see cloud-shapes, too," said Donatello; "yonder is one that shifts strangely; it has been like people whom I knew. And now, if I watch it a little longer, it will take the figure of a monk reclining, with his cowl about his head and drawn partly over his face, and—well! did I not tell you so?"

"I think," remarked Kenyon, "we can hardly be gazing at the same cloud. What I behold is a reclining figure, to be sure, but feminine, and with a despondent air, wonderfully well expressed in the wavering outline from head to foot. It moves my very heart by something indefinable that it suggests."

"I see the figure, and almost the face," said the Count; adding, in a lower voice, "It is Miriam's!"

"No, not Miriam's," answered the sculptor.

While the two gazers thus found their own reminiscences and presentiments floating among the clouds, the day drew to its close, and now showed them the fair spectacle of an Italian sunset. The sky was soft and bright, but not so gorgeous as Kenyon had seen it, a thousand times, in America; for there the western sky is wont to be set aflame with breadths and depths of color with which poets seek in vain to dye their verses, and which painters never dare to copy. As beheld from the tower of Monte Beni, the scene was tenderly magnificent, with mild gradations of hue, and a lavish outpouring of gold, but rather such gold as we see on the leaf of a bright flower than the burnished glow of metal from the mine. Or, if metallic, it looked airy and unsubstantial, like the glorified dreams of an alchemist. And speedily—more speedily than in our own clime—came the twilight, and, brightening through its gray transparency, the stars.

A swarm of minute insects that had been hovering all day round the battlements were now swept away by the freshness of a rising breeze. The two owls in the chamber beneath Donatello's uttered their soft melancholy cry,—which, with national avoidance of harsh sounds, Italian owls substitute for the hoot of their kindred in other countries,—and flew darkling forth among the shrubbery. A convent-bell rang out near at hand, and was not only echoed among the hills, but answered by another bell, and still another, which doubtless had farther and farther responses, at various distances along the valley; for, like the English drumbeat around the globe, there is a chain of convent-bells from end to end, and crosswise, and in all possible directions over priest-ridden Italy.

"Come," said the sculptor, "the evening air grows cool. It is time to descend."

"Time for you, my friend," replied the Count; and he hesitated a little before adding, "I must keep a vigil here for some hours longer. It is my frequent custom to keep vigils; and sometimes the thought occurs to me whether it were not better to keep them in yonder convent, the bell of which just now seemed to summon me. Should I do wisely, do you think, to exchange this old tower for a cell?"

"What! Turn monk?" exclaimed his friend. "A horrible idea!"

"True," said Donatello, sighing. "Therefore, if at all, I purpose doing it."

"Then think of it no more, for Heaven's sake!" cried the sculptor. "There are a thousand better and more poignant methods of being miserable than that, if to be miserable is what you wish. Nay; I question whether a monk keeps himself up to the intellectual and spiritual height which misery implies. A monk—I judge from their sensual physiognomies, which meet me at every turn—is inevitably a beast! Their souls, if they have any to begin with, perish out of them, before their sluggish, swinish existence is half done. Better, a million times, to stand star-gazing on these airy battlements, than to smother your new germ of a higher life in a monkish cell!"

"You make me tremble," said Donatello, "by your bold aspersion of men who have devoted themselves to God's service!"

"They serve neither God nor man, and themselves least of all, though their motives be utterly selfish," replied Kenyon. "Avoid the convent, my dear friend, as you would shun the death of the soul! But, for my own part, if I had an insupportable burden,—if, for any cause, I were bent upon sacrificing every earthly hope as a peace-offering towards Heaven, —I would make the wide world my cell, and good deeds to mankind my prayer. Many penitent men have done this, and found peace in it."

"Ah, but you are a heretic!" said the Count.

Yet his face brightened beneath the stars; and, looking at it through the twilight, the sculptor's remembrance went back to that scene in the Capitol, where, both in features and expression, Donatello had seemed identical with the Faun. And still there was a resemblance; for now, when first the idea was suggested of living for the welfare of his fellow-creatures, the original beauty, which sorrow had partly effaced, came back elevated and spiritualized. In the black depths, the Faun had found a soul, and was struggling with it towards the light of heaven.

The illumination, it is true, soon faded out of Donatello's face. The idea of life-long and unselfish effort was too high to be received by him with more than a momentary comprehension. An Italian, indeed, seldom dreams of being philanthropic, except in bestowing alms among the paupers, who appeal to his beneficence at every step; nor does it occur to him that there are fitter modes of propitiating Heaven than by penances, pilgrimages, and offerings at shrines. Perhaps, too, their system has its share of moral advantages; they, at all events, cannot well pride themselves, as our own more energetic benevolence is apt to do, upon sharing in the counsels of Providence and kindly helping out its otherwise impracticable designs.

And now the broad valley twinkled with lights, that glimmered through its duskiness, like the fire-flies in the garden of a Florentine palace. A gleam of lightning from the rear of the tempest showed the circumference of hills, and the great space between, as the last cannon-flash of a retreating army reddens across the field where it has fought. The sculptor was on the point of descending the turret-stair, when, somewhere in the darkness that lay beneath them, a woman's voice was heard, singing a low, sad strain.

"Hark!" said he, laying his hand on Donatello's arm.

And Donatello had said, "Hark!" at the same instant.

The song, if song it could be called, that had only a wild rhythm, and flowed forth in the fitful measure of a wind-harp, did not clothe itself in the sharp brilliancy of the Italian tongue. The words, so far as they could be distinguished, were German, and therefore unintelligible to the Count, and hardly less so to the sculptor; being softened and molten, as it were, into the melancholy richness of the voice that sung them. It was as the murmur of a soul bewildered amid the sinful gloom of earth, and retaining only enough memory of a better state to make sad music of the wail, which would else have been a despairing shriek. Never was there profounder pathos than breathed through that mysterious voice; it brought the tears into the sculptor's eyes, with remembrances and forebodings of whatever sorrow he had felt or apprehended; it made Donatello sob, as chiming in with the anguish that he found unutterable, and giving it the expression which he vaguely sought.

But, when the emotion was at its profoundest depth, the voice rose out of it, yet so gradually that a gloom seemed to pervade it, far upward from the abyss, and not entirely to fall away as it ascended into a higher and purer region. At last, the auditors would have fancied that the melody, with its rich sweetness all there, and much of its sorrow gone, was floating around the very summit of the tower.

"Donatello," said the sculptor, when there was silence again, "had that voice no message for your ear?"

"I dare not receive it," said Donatello; "the anguish of which it spoke abides with me: the hope dies away with the breath that brought it hither. It is not good for me to hear that voice."

The sculptor sighed, and left the poor penitent keeping his vigil on the tower.

## CHAPTER XXX

### DONATELLO'S BUST

KENYON, it will be remembered, had asked Donatello's permission to model his bust. The work had now made considerable progress, and necessarily kept the sculptor's thoughts brooding much and often upon his host's personal characteristics. These it was his difficult office to bring out from their depths, and interpret them to all men, showing them what they could not discern for themselves, yet must be compelled to recognize at a glance, on the surface of a block of marble.

He had never undertaken a portrait-bust which gave him so much trouble as Donatello's; not that there was any special difficulty in hitting the likeness, though even in this respect the grace and harmony of the features seemed inconsistent with a prominent expression of individuality; but he was chiefly perplexed how to make this genial and kind type of countenance the index of the mind within. His acuteness and his sympathies, indeed, were both somewhat at fault in their efforts to enlighten him as to the moral phase through which the Count was now passing. If at one sitting he caught a glimpse of what appeared to be a genuine and permanent trait, it would probably be less perceptible on a second occasion, and perhaps have vanished entirely at a third. So evanescent a show of character threw the sculptor into despair; not marble or clay, but cloud and vapor, was the material in which it ought to be represented. Even the ponderous depression which constantly weighed upon Donatello's heart could not compel him into the kind of repose which the plastic art requires.

Hopeless of a good result, Kenyon gave up all preconceptions about the character of his subject, and let his hands work uncontrolled with the clay, somewhat as a spiritual medium, while holding a pen, yields it to an unseen guidance other than that of her own will. Now and then he fancied that this plan was destined to be the successful one. A skill and insight beyond his consciousness seemed occasionally to take up the task. The mystery, the miracle, of imbuing an inanimate substance with thought, feeling, and all the intangible attributes of the soul, appeared on the verge of being wrought. And now, as he flattered himself, the true image of his friend was about to emerge from the facile material, bringing with it more of Donatello's character than the keenest observer could detect at any one moment in the face of the original. Vain expectation! some touch, whereby the artist thought to improve or hasten the result, interfered with the design of his unseen spiritual assistant, and spoilt the whole. There was still the moist, brown clay, indeed, and the features of Donatello, but without any semblance of intelligent and sympathetic life.

"The difficulty will drive me mad, I verily believe!" cried the sculptor, nervously. "Look at the wretched piece of work yourself, my dear friend, and tell me whether you recognize any manner of likeness to your inner man?"

"None," replied Donatello, speaking the simple truth. "It is like looking a stranger in the face."

This frankly unfavorable testimony so wrought with the sensitive artist, that he fell into a passion with the stubborn image, and cared not what might happen to it thenceforward. Wielding that wonderful power which sculptors possess over moist clay, however refractory it may show itself in certain respects, he compressed, elongated, widened, and otherwise altered the features of the bust in mere recklessness, and at every change inquired of the Count whether the expression became anywise more satisfactory.

"Stop!" cried Donatello, at last, catching the sculptor's hand. "Let it remain so!"

By some accidental handling of the clay, entirely independent of his own will, Kenyon had given the countenance a distorted and violent look, combining animal fierceness with intelligent hatred. Had Hilda, or had Miriam, seen the bust, with the expression which it had now assumed, they might have recognized Donatello's face as they beheld it at that terrible moment when he held his victim over the edge of the precipice.

"What have I done?" said the sculptor, shocked at his own casual production. "It were a sin to let the clay which bears your features harden into a look like that. Cain never wore an uglier one."

"For that very reason, let it remain!" answered the Count, who had grown pale as ashes at the aspect of his crime, thus strangely presented to him in another of the many guises under which guilt stares the criminal in the face. "Do not alter it! Chisel it, rather, in eternal marble! I will set it up in my oratory and keep it continually before my eyes. Sadder and more horrible is a face like this, alive with my own crime, than the dead skull which my forefathers handed down to me!"

But, without in the least heeding Donatello's remonstrances, the sculptor again applied his artful fingers to the clay, and compelled the bust to dismiss the expression that had so startled them both.

"Believe me," said he, turning his eyes upon his friend, full of grave and tender sympathy, "you know not what is requisite for your spiritual growth, seeking, as you do, to keep your soul perpetually in the unwholesome region of remorse. It was needful for you to pass through that dark valley, but it is infinitely dangerous to linger there too long; there is poison in the atmosphere, when we sit down and brood in it, instead of girding up our loins to press onward. Not despondency, not slothful anguish, is what you now require,—but effort! Has there been an unalterable evil in your young life? Then crowd it out with good, or it will lie corrupting there forever, and cause your capacity for better things to partake its noisome corruption!"

"You stir up many thoughts," said Donatello, pressing his hand upon his brow, "but the multitude and the whirl of them make me dizzy."

They now left the sculptor's temporary studio, without observing that his last accidental touches, with which he hurriedly effaced the look of deadly rage, had given the bust a higher and sweeter expression than it had hitherto worn. It is to be regretted that Kenyon had not seen it; for only an artist, perhaps, can conceive the irksomeness, the irritation of brain, the depression of spirits, that resulted from his failure to satisfy himself, after so much toil and thought as he had bestowed on Donatello's bust. In case of success, indeed, all this thoughtful toil would have been reckoned, not only as well bestowed, but as among the happiest hours of his life; whereas, deeming himself to have failed, it was just so much of life that had better never have been lived; for thus does the good or ill result of his labor throw back sunshine or gloom upon the artist's mind. The sculptor, therefore, would have done well to glance again at his work; for here were still the features of the antique Faun, but now illuminated with a higher meaning, such as the old marble never bore.

Donatello having quitted him, Kenyon spent the rest of the day strolling about the pleasant precincts of Monte Beni, where the summer was now so far advanced that it began, indeed, to partake of the ripe wealth of autumn. Apricots had long been abundant, and had passed away, and plums and cherries along with them. But now came great, juicy pears, melting and delicious, and peaches of goodly size and tempting aspect, though cold and watery to the palate, compared with the sculptor's rich reminiscences of that fruit in America. The purple figs had already enjoyed their day, and the white ones were luscious now. The contadini (who, by this time, knew Kenyon well) found many clusters of ripe grapes for him, in every little globe of which was included a fragrant draught of the sunny Monte Beni wine.

Unexpectedly, in a nook, close by the farm-house, he happened upon a spot where the vintage had actually commenced. A great heap of early ripened grapes had been gathered, and thrown into a mighty tub. In the middle of it stood a lusty and jolly contadino, nor stood, merely, but stamped with all his might, and danced amain; while the red juice bathed his feet, and threw its foam midway up his brown and shaggy legs. Here, then, was the very process that shows so picturesquely in Scripture and in poetry, of treading out the wine-press and dyeing the feet and garments with the crimson effusion as with the blood of a battle-field. The memory of the process does not make the Tuscan wine taste more deliciously. The contadini hospitably offered Kenyon a sample of the new liquor, that had already stood fermenting for a day or two. He had tried a similar draught, however, in years past, and was little inclined to make proof of it again; for he knew that it would be a sour and bitter juice, a wine of woe and tribulation, and that the more a man drinks of such liquor, the sorrier he is likely to be.

The scene reminded the sculptor of our New England vintages, where the big piles of golden and rosy apples lie under the orchard trees, in the mild, autumnal sunshine; and the creaking cider-mill, set in motion by a circumgyratory horse, is all a-gush with the luscious juice. To speak frankly, the cider-making is the more picturesque sight of the two, and the new, sweet cider an infinitely better drink than the ordinary, unripe Tuscan wine. Such as it is, however, the latter fills thousands upon thousands of small, flat barrels, and, still growing thinner and sharper, loses the little life it had, as wine, and becomes apotheosized as a more praiseworthy vinegar.

Yet all these vineyard scenes, and the processes connected with the culture of the grape, had a flavor of poetry about them. The toil that produces those kindly gifts of nature which are not the substance of life, but its luxury, is unlike other toil. We are inclined to fancy that it does not bend the sturdy frame and stiffen the overwrought muscles, like the labor that is devoted in sad, hard earnest to raise grain for sour bread. Certainly, the sunburnt young men and dark-cheeked, laughing girls, who weeded the rich acres of Monte Beni, might well enough have passed for inhabitants of an unsophisticated Arcadia. Later in the season, when the true vintage-time should come, and the wine of Sunshine gush into the vats, it was hardly too wild a dream that Bacchus himself might revisit the haunts which he loved of old. But, alas! where now would he find the Faun with whom we see him consorting in so many an antique group?

Donatello's remorseful anguish saddened this primitive and delightful life. Kenyon had a pain of his own, moreover, although not all a pain, in the never-quiet, never-satisfied yearning of his heart towards Hilda. He was authorized to use little freedom towards that shy maiden, even in his visions; so that he almost reproached himself when sometimes his imagination pictured in detail the sweet years that they might spend together, in a retreat like this. It had just that rarest quality of remoteness from the actual and ordinary world—a remoteness through which all delights might visit them freely, sifted from all troubles—which lovers so reasonably insist upon, in their ideal arrangements for a happy union. It is possible, indeed, that even Donatello's grief and Kenyon's pale, sunless affection lent a charm to Monte Beni, which it would not have retained amid a more abundant joyousness. The sculptor strayed amid its vineyards and orchards, its dells and tangled shrubberies, with somewhat the sensations of an adventurer who should find his way to the site of ancient Eden, and behold its loveliness through the transparency of that gloom which has been brooding over those haunts of innocence ever since the fall. Adam saw it in a brighter sunshine, but never knew the shade of pensive beauty which Eden won from his expulsion.

It was in the decline of the afternoon that Kenyon returned from his long, musing ramble. Old Tomaso—between whom and himself for some time past there had been a mysterious understanding,—met him in the entrance-hall, and drew him a little aside.

"The signorina would speak with you," he whispered.

"In the chapel?" asked the sculptor.

"No; in the saloon beyond it," answered the butler: "the entrance—you once saw the signorina appear through it—is near the altar, hidden behind the tapestry."

Kenyon lost no time in obeying the summons.

## CHAPTER XXXI

### THE MARBLE SALOON

IN an old Tuscan villa, a chapel ordinarily makes one among the numerous apartments; though it often happens that the door is permanently closed, the key lost, and the place left to itself, in dusty sanctity, like that chamber in man's heart where he hides his religious awe. This was very much the case with the chapel of Monte Beni. One rainy day, however, in his wanderings through the great, intricate house, Kenyon had unexpectedly found his way into it, and been impressed by its solemn aspect. The arched windows, high upward in the wall, and darkened with dust and cobweb, threw down a dim light that showed the altar, with a picture of a martyrdom above, and some tall tapers ranged before it. They had apparently been lighted, and burned an hour or two, and been extinguished perhaps half a century before. The marble vase at the entrance held some hardened mud at the bottom, accruing from the dust that had settled in it during the gradual evaporation of the holy water; and a spider (being an insect that delights in pointing the moral of desolation and neglect) had taken pains to weave a prodigiously thick tissue across the circular brim. An old family banner, tattered by the moths, drooped from the vaulted roof. In niches there were some mediæval busts of Donatello's forgotten ancestry; and among them, it might be, the forlorn visage of that hapless knight between whom and the fountain-nymph had occurred such tender love-passages.

Throughout all the jovial prosperity of Monte Beni, this one spot within the domestic walls had kept itself silent, stern, and sad. When the individual or the family retired from song and mirth, they here sought those realities which men do not invite their festive associates to share. And here, on the occasion above referred to, the sculptor had discovered—accidentally, so far as he was concerned, though with a purpose on her part —that there was a guest under Donatello's roof, whose presence the Count did not suspect. An interview had since taken place, and he was now summoned to another.

He crossed the chapel, in compliance with Tomaso's instructions, and, passing through the side entrance, found himself in a saloon, of no great size, but more magnificent than he had supposed the villa to contain. As it was vacant, Kenyon had leisure to pace it once or twice, and examine it with a careless sort of scrutiny, before any person appeared.

This beautiful hall was floored with rich marbles, in artistically arranged figures and compartments. The walls, likewise, were almost entirely cased in marble of various kinds, the prevalent variety being giallo antico, intermixed with verd-antique, and others equally precious. The splendor of the giallo antico, however, was what gave character to the saloon; and the large and deep niches, apparently intended for full-length statues, along the walls, were lined with the same costly material. Without visiting Italy, one can have no idea of the beauty and magnificence that are produced by these fittings-up of polished marble. Without such experience, indeed, we do not even know what marble means, in any sense, save as the white limestone of which we carve our mantel-pieces. This rich hall of Monte Beni, moreover, was adorned, at its upper end, with two pillars that seemed to consist of Oriental alabaster; and wherever there was a space vacant of precious and variegated marble, it was frescoed with ornaments in arabesque. Above, there was a coved and vaulted ceiling, glowing with pictured scenes, which affected Kenyon with a vague sense of splendor, without his twisting his neck to gaze at them.

It is one of the special excellences of such a saloon of polished and richly colored marble, that decay can never tarnish it. Until the house crumbles down upon it, it shines indestructibly, and, with a little dusting, looks just as brilliant in its three hundredth year as the day after the final slab of giallo antico was fitted into the wall. To the sculptor, at this first view of it, it seemed a hall where the sun was magically imprisoned, and must always shine. He anticipated Miriam's entrance, arrayed in queenly robes, and beaming with even more than the singular beauty that had heretofore distinguished her.

While this thought was passing through his mind, the pillared door, at the upper end of the saloon, was partly opened, and Miriam appeared. She was very pale, and dressed in deep mourning. As she advanced towards the sculptor, the feebleness of her step was so apparent that he made haste to meet her, apprehending that she might sink down on the marble floor, without the instant support of his arm.

But, with a gleam of her natural self-reliance, she declined his aid, and, after touching her cold hand to his, went and sat down on one of the cushioned divans that were ranged against the wall.

"You are very ill, Miriam!" said Kenyon, much shocked at her appearance. "I had not thought of this."

"No; not so ill as I seem to you," she answered; adding despondently, "yet I am ill enough I believe, to die, unless some change speedily occurs."

"What, then, is your disorder?" asked the sculptor; "and what the remedy?"

"The disorder!" repeated Miriam. "There is none that I know of save too much life and strength, without a purpose for one or the other. It is my too redundant energy that is slowly—or perhaps rapidly—wearing me away, because I can apply it to no use. The object, which I am bound to consider my only one on earth, fails me utterly. The sacrifice which I yearn to make of myself, my hopes, my everything, is coldly put aside. Nothing is left for me but to brood, brood, brood, all day, all night, in unprofitable longings and repinings."

"This is very sad, Miriam," said Kenyon.

"Ay, indeed; I fancy so," she replied, with a short unnatural laugh.

"With all your activity of mind," resumed he, "so fertile in plans as I have known you, can you imagine no method of bringing your resources into play?"

"My mind is not active any longer," answered Miriam, in a cold, indifferent tone. "It deals with one thought and no more. One recollection paralyzes it. It is not remorse; do not think it! I put myself out of the question, and feel neither regret nor penitence on my own behalf. But what benumbs me, what robs me of all power,—it is no secret for a woman to tell a man, yet I care not though you know it,—is the certainty that I am, and must ever be, an object of horror in Donatello's sight."

The sculptor—a young man, and cherishing a love which insulated him from the wild experiences which some men gather—was startled to perceive how Miriam's rich, ill-regulated nature impelled her to fling herself, conscience and all, on one passion, the object of which intellectually seemed far beneath her.

"How have you obtained the certainty of which you speak?" asked he, after a pause.

"Oh, by a sure token," said Miriam; "a gesture, merely; a shudder, a cold shiver, that ran through him one sunny morning when his hand happened to touch mine! But it was enough."

"I firmly believe, Miriam," said the sculptor, "that he loves you still."

She started, and a flush of color came tremulously over the paleness of her cheek.

"Yes," repeated Kenyon, "if my interest in Donatello—and in yourself, Miriam—endows me with any true insight, he not only loves you still, but with a force and depth proportioned to the stronger grasp of his faculties, in their new development."

"Do not deceive me," said Miriam, growing pale again.

"Not for the world!" replied Kenyon. "Here is what I take to be the truth. There was an interval, no doubt, when the horror of some calamity, which I need not shape out in my conjectures, threw Donatello into a stupor of misery. Connected with the first shock there was an intolerable pain and shuddering repugnance attaching themselves to all the circumstances and surroundings of the event that so terribly affected him. Was his dearest friend involved within the horror of that moment? He would shrink from her as he shrank most of all from himself. But as his mind roused itself,—as it rose to a higher life than he had hitherto experienced,—whatever had been true and permanent within him revived by the self-same impulse. So has it been with his love."

"But, surely," said Miriam, "he knows that I am here! Why, then, except that I am odious to him, does he not bid me welcome?"

"He is, I believe, aware of your presence here," answered the sculptor. "Your song, a night or two ago, must have revealed it to him, and, in truth, I had fancied that there was already a consciousness of it in his mind. But, the more passionately he longs for your society, the more religiously he deems himself bound to avoid it. The idea of a life-long penance has taken strong possession of Donatello. He gropes blindly about him for some method of sharp self-torture, and finds, of course, no other so efficacious as this."

"But, he loves me," repeated Miriam, in a low voice, to herself. "Yes; he loves me!"

It was strange to observe the womanly softness that came over her, as she admitted that comfort into her bosom. The cold, unnatural indifference of her manner, a kind of frozen passionateness which had shocked and chilled the sculptor, disappeared. She blushed, and turned away her eyes, knowing that there was more surprise and joy in their dewy glances than any man save one ought to detect there.

"In other respects," she inquired at length, "is he much changed?"

"A wonderful process is going forward in Donatello's mind," answered the sculptor. "The germs of faculties that have heretofore slept are fast springing into activity. The world of thought is disclosing itself to his inward sight. He startles me, at times, with his perception of deep truths; and, quite as often, it must be owned, he compels me to smile by the intermixture of his former simplicity with a new intelligence. But, he is bewildered with the revelations that each day brings. Out of his bitter agony, a soul and intellect, I could almost say, have been inspired into him."

"Ah, I could help him here!" cried Miriam, clasping her hands. "And how sweet a toil and bend and adapt my whole nature to do him good! To instruct, to elevate, to enrich his mind with the wealth that would flow in upon me, had I such a motive for acquiring it! Who else can perform the task? Who else has the tender sympathy which he requires? Who else, save only me,—a woman, a sharer in the same dread secret, a partaker in one identical guilt,—could meet him on such terms of intimate equality as the case demands? With this object before me, I might feel a right to live! Without it, it is a shame for me to have lived so long."

"I fully agree with you," said Kenyon, "that your true place is by his side."

"Surely it is," replied Miriam. "If Donatello is entitled to aught on earth, it is to my complete self-sacrifice for his sake. It does not weaken his claim, methinks, that my only prospect of happiness—a fearful word, however—lies in the good that may accrue to him from our intercourse. But he rejects me! He will not listen to the whisper of his heart, telling him that she, most wretched, who beguiled him into evil, might guide him to a higher innocence than that from which he fell. How is this first, great difficulty to be obviated?"

"It lies at your own option, Miriam, to do away the obstacle, at any moment," remarked the sculptor. "It is but to ascend Donatello's tower, and you will meet him there, under the eye of God."

"I dare not," answered Miriam. "No; I dare not!"

"Do you fear," asked the sculptor, "the dread eye-witness whom I have named?"

"No; for, as far as I can see into that cloudy and inscrutable thing, my heart, it has none but pure motives," replied Miriam. "But, my friend,

you little know what a weak or what a strong creature a woman is! I fear
not Heaven, in this case, at least, but—shall I confess it?—I am greatly
in dread of Donatello. Once he shuddered at my touch. If he shudder
once again, or frown, I die!"

Kenyon could not but marvel at the subjection into which this proud
and self-dependent woman had wilfully flung herself, hanging her life
upon the chance of an angry or favorable regard from a person who, a little while before, had seemed the plaything of a moment. But, in Miriam's
eyes, Donatello was always, thenceforth, invested with the tragic dignity
of their hour of crime; and, furthermore, the keen and deep insight, with
which her love endowed her, enabled her to know him far better than he
could be known by ordinary observation. Beyond all question, since she
loved him so, there was a force in Donatello worthy of her respect and
love.

"You see my weakness," said Miriam, flinging out her hands, as a person does when a defect is acknowledged, and beyond remedy. "What I
need, now, is an opportunity to show my strength."

"It has occurred to me," Kenyon remarked, "that the time is come
when it may be desirable to remove Donatello from the complete seclusion in which he buries himself. He has struggled long enough with one
idea. He now needs a variety of thought, which cannot be otherwise so
readily supplied to him, as through the medium of a variety of scenes. His
mind is awakened, now; his heart, though full of pain, is no longer benumbed. They should have food and solace. If he linger here much longer,
I fear that he may sink back, into a lethargy. The extreme excitability,
which circumstances have imparted to his moral system, has its dangers
and its advantages; it being one of the dangers, that an obdurate scar
may supervene upon its very tenderness. Solitude has done what it could
for him; now, for a while, let him be enticed into the outer world."

"What is your plan, then?" asked Miriam.

"Simply," replied Kenyon, "to persuade Donatello to be my companion in a ramble among these hills and valleys. The little adventures and
vicissitudes of travel will do him infinite good. After his recent profound
experience, he will re-create the world by the new eyes with which he will
regard it. He will escape, I hope, out of a morbid life, and find his way
into a healthy one."

"And what is to be my part in this process?" inquired Miriam, sadly,
and not without jealousy. "You are taking him from me, and putting
yourself, and all manner of living interests, into the place which I ought
to fill!"

"It would rejoice me, Miriam, to yield the entire responsibility of this
office to yourself," answered the sculptor. "I do not pretend to be the
guide and counsellor whom Donatello needs; for, to mention no other obstacle, I am a man, and between man and man there is always an insuperable gulf. They can never quite grasp each other's hands; and therefore
man never derives any intimate help, any heart sustenance, from his

brother man, but from woman,—his mother, his sister, or his wife. Be Donatello's friend at need, therefore, and most gladly will I resign him!"

"It is not kind to taunt me thus," said Miriam. "I have told you that I cannot do what you suggest, because I dare not."

"Well, then," rejoined the sculptor, "see if there is any possibility of adapting yourself to my scheme. The incidents of a journey often fling people together in the oddest and therefore the most natural way. Supposing you were to find yourself on the same route, a reunion with Donatello might ensue, and Providence have a larger hand in it than either of us."

"It is not a hopeful plan," said Miriam, shaking her head, after a moment's thought; "yet I will not reject it without a trial. Only in case it fail, here is a resolution to which I bind myself, come what come may! You know the bronze statue of Pope Julius in the great square of Perugia? I remember standing in the shadow of that statue one sunny noontime, and being impressed by its paternal aspect, and fancying that a blessing fell upon me from its outstretched hand. Ever since, I have had a superstition,—you will call it foolish, but sad and ill-fated persons always dream such things,—that, if I waited long enough in that same spot, some good event would come to pass. Well, my friend, precisely a fortnight after you begin your tour,—unless we sooner meet,—bring Donatello, at noon, to the base of the statue. You will find me there!"

Kenyon assented to the proposed arrangement, and, after some conversation respecting his contemplated line of travel, prepared to take his leave. As he met Miriam's eyes, in bidding farewell, he was surprised at the new, tender gladness that beamed out of them, and at the appearance of health and bloom, which, in this little while, had overspread her face.

"May I tell you, Miriam," said he, smiling, "that you are still as beautiful as ever?"

"You have a right to notice it," she replied, "for, if it be so, my faded bloom has been revived by the hopes you give me. Do you, then, think me beautiful? I rejoice, most truly. Beauty—if I possess it—shall be one of the instruments by which I will try to educate and elevate him, to whose good I solely dedicate myself."

The sculptor had nearly reached the door, when, hearing her call him, he turned back, and beheld Miriam still standing where he had left her, in the magnificent hall which seemed only a fit setting for her beauty. She beckoned him to return.

"You are a man of refined taste," said she; "more than that,—a man of delicate sensibility. Now tell me frankly, and on your honor! Have I not shocked you many times during this interview by my betrayal of woman's cause, my lack of feminine modesty, my reckless, passionate, most indecorous avowal, that I live only in the life of one who, perhaps, scorns and shudders at me?"

Thus adjured, however difficult the point to which she brought him, the sculptor was not a man to swerve aside from the simple truth.

"Miriam," replied he, "you exaggerate the impression made upon my mind; but it has been painful, and somewhat of the character which you suppose."

"I knew it," said Miriam, mournfully, and with no resentment. "What remains of my finer nature would have told me so, even if it had not been perceptible in all your manner. Well, my dear friend, when you go back to Rome, tell Hilda what her severity has done! She was all womanhood to me; and when you cast me off, I had no longer any terms to keep with the reserves and decorums of my sex. Hilda has set me free! Pray tell her so, from Miriam, and thank her!"

"I shall tell Hilda nothing that will give her pain," answered Kenyon. "But, Miriam,—though I know not what passed between her and yourself,—I feel,—and let the noble frankness of your disposition forgive me if I say so,—I feel that she was right. You have a thousand admirable qualities. Whatever mass of evil may have fallen into your life,—pardon me, but your own words suggest it,—you are still as capable as ever of many high and heroic virtues. But the white shining purity of Hilda's nature is a thing apart; and she is bound, by the undefiled material of which God moulded her, to keep that severity which I, as well as you, have recognized."

"Oh, you are right!" said Miriam; "I never questioned it; though, as I told you, when she cast me off, it severed some few remaining bonds between me and decorous womanhood. But were there anything to forgive, I do forgive her. May you win her virgin heart; for methinks there can be few men in this evil world who are not more unworthy of her than yourself."

## CHAPTER XXXII

### Scenes by the Way

WHEN it came to the point of quitting the reposeful life of Monte Beni, the sculptor was not without regrets, and would willingly have dreamed a little longer of the sweet paradise on earth that Hilda's presence there might make. Nevertheless, amid all its repose, he had begun to be sensible of a restless melancholy, to which the cultivators of the ideal arts are more liable than sturdier men. On his own part, therefore, and leaving Donatello out of the case, he would have judged it well to go. He made parting visits to the legendary dell, and to other delightful spots with which he had grown familiar; he climbed the tower again, and saw a sunset and a moonrise over the great valley; he drank, on the eve of his departure, one flask, and then another, of the Monte Beni Sunshine, and stored up its flavor in his memory, as the standard of what is exquisite in wine. These things accomplished, Kenyon was ready for the journey.

Donatello had not very easily been stirred out of the peculiar sluggishness, which inthralls and bewitches melancholy people. He had offered merely a passive resistance, however, not an active one, to his friend's schemes; and when the appointed hour came, he yielded to the impulse which Kenyon failed not to apply; and was started upon the journey before he had made up his mind to undertake it. They wandered forth at large, like two knights-errant among the valleys, and the mountains, and the old mountain-towns of that picturesque and lovely region. Save to keep the appointment with Miriam, a fortnight thereafter, in the great square of Perugia, there was nothing more definite in the sculptor's plan, than that they should let themselves be blown hither and thither like winged seeds, that mount upon each wandering breeze. Yet there was an idea of fatality implied in the simile of the winged seeds which did not altogether suit Kenyon's fancy; for, if you look closely into the matter, it will be seen that whatever appears most vagrant, and utterly purposeless, turns out, in the end, to have been impelled the most surely on a preordained and unswerving track. Chance and change love to deal with men's settled plans, not with their idle vagaries. If we desire unexpected and unimaginable events, we should contrive an iron framework, such as we fancy may compel the future to take one inevitable shape; then comes in the unexpected, and shatters our design in fragments.

The travellers set forth on horseback, and purposed to perform much of their aimless journeyings under the moon, and in the cool of the morning or evening twilight; the midday sun, while summer had hardly begun to trail its departing skirts over Tuscany, being still too fervid to allow of noontide exposure.

For a while, they wandered in that same broad valley which Kenyon had viewed with such delight from the Monte Beni tower. The sculptor soon began to enjoy the idle activity of their new life, which the lapse of a day or two sufficed to establish as a kind of system; it is so natural for mankind to be nomadic, that a very little taste of that primitive mode of existence subverts the settled habits of many preceding years. Kenyon's cares, and whatever gloomy ideas before possessed him, seemed to be left at Monte Beni, and were scarcely remembered by the time that its gray tower grew undistinguishable on the brown hill-side. His perceptive faculties, which had found little exercise of late, amid so thoughtful a way of life, became keen, and kept his eyes busy with a hundred agreeable scenes.

He delighted in the picturesque bits of rustic character and manners, so little of which ever comes upon the surface of our life at home. There, for example, were the old women, tending pigs or sheep by the wayside. As they followed the vagrant steps of their charge, these venerable ladies kept spinning yarn with that elsewhere forgotten contrivance, the distaff; and so wrinkled and stern-looking were they, that you might have taken them for the Parcæ, spinning the threads of human destiny. In contrast with their great-grandmothers were the children, leading goats of shaggy beard, tied by the horns, and letting them browse on branch and shrub. It is the fashion of Italy to add the petty industry of age and childhood to the hum of human toil. To the eyes of an observer from the Western world, it was a strange spectacle to see sturdy, sunburnt creatures, in petticoats, but otherwise manlike, toiling side by side with male laborers, in the rudest work of the fields. These sturdy women (if as such we must recognize them) wore the high-crowned, broad-brimmed hat of Tuscan straw, the customary female head-apparel; and, as every breeze blew back its breadth of brim, the sunshine constantly added depth to the brown glow of their cheeks. The elder sisterhood, however, set off their witch-like ugliness to the worst advantage with black felt hats, bequeathed them, one would fancy, by their long-buried husbands.

Another ordinary sight, as sylvan as the above, and more agreeable, was a girl, bearing on her back a huge bundle of green twigs and shrubs, or grass, intermixed with scarlet poppies and blue flowers; the verdant burden being sometimes of such size as to hide the bearer's figure, and seem a self-moving mass of fragrant bloom and verdure. Oftener, however, the bundle reached only half-way down the back of the rustic nymph, leaving in sight her well-developed lower limbs, and the crooked knife, hanging behind her, with which she had been reaping this strange harvest sheaf. A pre-Raphaelite artist (he, for instance, who painted so marvellously a wind-swept heap of autumnal leaves) might find an admirable subject in one of these Tuscan girls, stepping with a free, erect, and graceful carriage. The miscellaneous herbage and tangled twigs and blossoms of her bundle, crowning her head (while her ruddy, comely face looks out between the hanging side festoons like a larger flower), would give the painter boundless scope for the minute delineation which he loves.

Though mixed up with what was rude and earthlike, there was still a remote, dream-like, Arcadian charm, which is scarcely to be found in the daily toil of other lands. Among the pleasant features of the wayside were always the vines, clambering on fig-trees, or other sturdy trunks; they wreathed themselves in huge and rich festoons, from one tree to another, suspending clusters of ripening grapes in the interval between. Under such careless mode of culture, the luxuriant vine is a lovelier spectacle than where it produces a more precious liquor, and is therefore more artificially restrained and trimmed. Nothing can be more picturesque than an old grape-vine, with almost a trunk of its own, clinging fast around its supporting tree. Nor does the picture lack its moral. You might twist it to more than one grave purpose, as you saw how the knotted, serpentine growth imprisoned within its strong embrace the friend that had supported its tender infancy; and how (as seemingly flexible natures are prone to do) it converted the sturdier tree entirely to its own selfish ends, extending its innumerable arms on every bough, and permitting hardly a leaf to sprout except its own. It occurred to Kenyon, that the enemies of the vine, in his native land, might here have seen an emblem of the remorseless gripe, which the habit of vinous enjoyment lays upon its victim, possessing him wholly, and letting him live no life but such as it bestows.

The scene was not less characteristic when their path led the two wanderers through some small, ancient town. There, besides the peculiarities of present life, they saw tokens of the life that had long ago been lived and flung aside. The little town, such as we see in our mind's eye, would have its gate and its surrounding walls, so ancient and massive that ages had not sufficed to crumble them away; but in the lofty upper portion of the gateway, still standing over the empty arch, where there was no longer a gate to shut, there would be a dove-cote, and peaceful doves for the only warders. Pumpkins lay ripening in the open chambers of the structure. Then, as for the town-wall, on the outside an orchard extends peacefully along its base, full, not of apple-trees, but of those old humorists with gnarled trunks and twisted boughs, the olives. Houses have been built upon the ramparts, or burrowed out of their ponderous foundation. Even the gray, martial towers, crowned with ruined turrets, have been converted into rustic habitations, from the windows of which hang ears of Indian corn. At a door, that has been broken through the massive stonework, where it was meant to be strongest, some contadini are winnowing grain. Small windows, too, are pierced through the whole line of ancient wall, so that it seems a row of dwellings with one continuous front, built in a strange style of needless strength; but remnants of the old battlements and machicolations are interspersed with the homely chambers and earthen-tiled house-tops; and all along its extent both grape-vines and running flower-shrubs are encouraged to clamber and sport over the roughness of its decay.

Finally the long grass, intermixed with weeds and wild-flowers, waves on the uppermost height of the shattered rampart; and it is exceedingly pleasant in the golden sunshine of the afternoon to behold the warlike precinct so friendly in its old days, and so overgrown with rural peace. In its guard-rooms, its prison-chambers, and scooped out of its ponderous breadth, there are dwellings nowadays where happy human lives are spent. Human parents and broods of children nestle in them, even as the swallows nestle in the little crevices along the broken summit of the wall.

Passing through the gateway of this same little town, challenged only by those watchful sentinels, the pigeons, we find ourselves in a long, narrow street, paved from side to side with flagstones, in the old Roman fashion. Nothing can exceed the grim ugliness of the houses, most of which are three or four stories high, stone built, gray, dilapidated, or half-covered with plaster in patches, and contiguous all along from end to end of the town. Nature, in the shape of tree, shrub, or grassy sidewalk, is as much shut out from the one street of the rustic village as from the heart of any swarming city. The dark and half-ruinous habitations, with their small windows, many of which are drearily closed with wooden shutters, are but magnified hovels, piled story upon story, and squalid with the grime that successive ages have left behind them. It would be a hideous scene to contemplate in a rainy day, or when no human life pervaded it.

In the summer-noon, however, it possesses vivacity enough to keep itself cheerful; for all the within-doors of the village then bubbles over upon the flagstones, or looks out from the small windows, and from here and there a balcony. Some of the populace are at the butcher's shop; others are at the fountain, which gushes into a marble basin that resembles an antique sarcophagus. A tailor is sewing before his door with a young priest seated sociably beside him; a burly friar goes by with an empty wine-barrel on his head; children are at play; women, at their own door-steps, mend clothes, embroider, weave hats of Tuscan straw, or twirl the distaff. Many idlers, meanwhile, strolling from one group to another, let the warm day slide by in the sweet, interminable task of doing nothing.

From all these people there comes a babblement that seems quite dis-proportioned to the number of tongues that make it. So many words are not uttered in a New England village throughout the year—except it be at a political canvass or town-meeting—as are spoken here, with no espe-cial purpose, in a single day. Neither so many words, nor so much laugh-ter; for people talk about nothing as if they were terribly in earnest, and make merry at nothing as if it were the best of all possible jokes. In so long a time as they have existed, and within such narrow precincts, these little walled towns are brought into a closeness of society that makes them but a larger household. All the inhabitants are akin to each, and each to all; they assemble in the street as their common saloon, and thus live and die in a familiarity of intercourse, such as never can be known where a village is open at either end, and all roundabout, and has ample room within itself.

Stuck up beside the door of one house, in this village street, is a with-ered bough; and on a stone seat, just under the shadow of the bough, sits a party of jolly drinkers, making proof of the new wine, or quaffing the old, as their often-tried and comfortable friend. Kenyon draws bridle here (for the bough, or bush, is a symbol of the wine-shop at this day in Italy, as it was three hundred years ago in England), and calls for a goblet of the deep, mild, purple juice, well diluted with water from the fountain. The Sunshine of Monte Beni would be welcome now. Meanwhile, Dona-tello has ridden onward, but alights where a shrine, with a burning lamp before it, is built into the wall of an inn-stable. He kneels, and crosses himself, and mutters a brief prayer, without attracting notice from the passers-by, many of whom are parenthetically devout, in a similar fash-ion. By this time the sculptor has drunk off his wine-and-water, and our two travellers resume their way, emerging from the opposite gate of the village.

Before them, again, lies the broad valley, with a mist so thinly scat-tered over it as to be perceptible only in the distance, and most so in the nooks of the hills. Now that we have called it mist, it seems a mistake not rather to have called it sunshine; the glory of so much light being min-gled with so little gloom, in the airy material of that vapor. Be it mist or sunshine, it adds a touch of ideal beauty to the scene, almost persuading the spectator that this valley and those hills are visionary, because their visible atmosphere is so like the substance of a dream.

Immediately about them, however, there were abundant tokens that the country was not really the paradise it looked to be, at a casual glance. Neither the wretched cottages nor the dreary farm-houses seemed to partake of the prosperity, with which so kindly a climate, and so fertile a portion of Mother Earth's bosom, should have filled them, one and all. But, possibly, the peasant inhabitants do not exist in so grimy a poverty, and in homes so comfortless, as a stranger, with his native ideas of those matters, would be likely to imagine. The Italians appear to possess none of that emulative pride which we see in our New England villages, where every householder, according to his taste and means, endeavors to make his homestead an ornament to the grassy and elm-shadowed wayside. In Italy there are no neat doorsteps and thresholds; no pleasant, vine-sheltered porches; none of those grass-plots or smoothly shorn lawns, which hospitably invite the imagination into the sweet domestic interiors of English life. Everything, however sunny and luxuriant may be the scene around, is especially disheartening in the immediate neighborhood of an Italian home.

An artist, it is true, might often thank his stars for those old houses, so picturesquely time-stained, and with the plaster falling in blotches from the ancient brick-work. The prison-like, iron-barred windows, and the wide-arched, dismal entrance, admitting on one hand to the stable, on the other to the kitchen, might impress him as far better worth his pencil than the newly painted pine boxes, in which—if he be an American—his countrymen live and thrive. But there is reason to suspect that a people are waning to decay and ruin the moment that their life becomes fascinating either in the poet's imagination or the painter's eye.

As usual, on Italian waysides, the wanderers passed great, black crosses, hung with all the instruments of the sacred agony and passion: there were the crown of thorns, the hammer and nails, the pincers, the spear, the sponge; and perched over the whole, the cock that crowed to St. Peter's remorseful conscience. Thus, while the fertile scene showed the never-failing beneficence of the Creator towards man in his transitory state, these symbols reminded each wayfarer of the Saviour's infinitely greater love for him as an immortal spirit. Beholding these consecrated stations, the idea seemed to strike Donatello of converting the other wise aimless journey into a penitential pilgrimage. At each of them he alighted to kneel and kiss the cross, and humbly press his forehead against its foot; and this so invariably, that the sculptor soon learned to draw bridle of his own accord. It may be, too, heretic as he was, that Kenyon likewise put up a prayer, rendered more fervent by the symbols before his eyes, for the peace of his friend's conscience, and the pardon of the sin that so oppressed him.

Not only at the crosses did Donatello kneel, but at each of the many shrines, where the Blessed Virgin in fresco—faded with sunshine and half washed out with showers—looked benignly at her worshipper; or where she was represented in a wooden image, or a bas-relief of plaster or marble, as accorded with the means of the devout person who built, or restored from a mediæval antiquity, these places of wayside worship. They were everywhere: under arched niches, or in little penthouses with a brick tiled roof, just large enough to shelter them; or perhaps in some bit of old Roman masonry, the founders of which had died before the Advent; or in the wall of a country inn or farm-house; or at the midway point of a bridge; or in the shallow cavity of a natural rock; or high upward in the deep cuts of the road. It appeared to the sculptor that Donatello prayed the more earnestly and the more hopefully at these shrines, because the mild face of the Madonna promised him to intercede as a tender mother betwixt the poor culprit and the awfulness of judgment.

It was beautiful to observe, indeed, how tender was the soul of man and woman towards the Virgin mother, in recognition of the tenderness which, as their faith taught them, she immortally cherishes towards all human souls. In the wire-work screen, before each shrine, hung offerings of roses, or whatever flower was sweetest and most seasonable; some already wilted and withered, some fresh with that very morning's dew-drops. Flowers there were, too, that, being artificial, never bloomed on earth, nor would ever fade. The thought occurred to Kenyon, that flower-pots with living plants might be set within the niches, or even that rose-trees, and all kinds of flowering shrubs, might be reared under the shrines, and taught to twine and wreathe themselves around; so that the Virgin should dwell within a bower of verdure, bloom, and fragrant freshness, symbolizing a homage perpetually new. There are many things in the religious customs of these people that seem good; many things, at least, that might be both good and beautiful, if the soul of goodness and the sense of beauty were as much alive in the Italians now as they must have been when those customs were first imagined and adopted. But, instead of blossoms on the shrub, or freshly gathered, with the dew-drops on their leaves, their worship, nowadays, is best symbolized by the artificial flower.

The sculptor fancied, moreover (but perhaps it was his heresy that suggested the idea), that it would be of happy influence to place a comfortable and shady seat beneath every wayside shrine. Then the weary and sun-scorched traveller, while resting himself under her protecting shadow, might thank the Virgin for her hospitality. Nor, perchance, were he to regale himself, even in such a consecrated spot, with the fragrance of a pipe, would it rise to heaven more offensively than the smoke of priestly incense. We do ourselves wrong, and too meanly estimate the Holiness above us, when we deem that any act or enjoyment, good in itself, is not good to do religiously.

Whatever may be the iniquities of the papal system, it was a wise and lovely sentiment that set up the frequent shrine and cross along the roadside. No wayfarer, bent on whatever worldly errand, can fail to be reminded, at every mile or two, that this is not the business which most concerns him. The pleasure-seeker is silently admonished to look heavenward for a joy infinitely greater than he now possesses. The wretch in temptation beholds the cross, and is warned that, if he yield, the Saviour's agony for his sake will have been endured in vain. The stubborn criminal, whose heart has long been like a stone, feels it throb anew with dread and hope; and our poor Donatello, as he went kneeling from shrine to cross, and from cross to shrine, doubtless found an efficacy in these symbols that helped him towards a higher penitence.

Whether the young Count of Monte Beni noticed the fact, or no, there was more than one incident of their journey that led Kenyon to believe that they were attended, or closely followed, or preceded, near at hand, by some one who took an interest in their motions. As it were, the step, the sweeping garment, the faintly heard breath, of an invisible companion, was beside them, as they went on their way. It was like a dream that had strayed out of their slumber, and was haunting them in the daytime, when its shadowy substance could have neither density nor outline, in the too obtrusive light. After sunset, it grew a little more distinct.

"On the left of that last shrine," asked the sculptor, as they rode, under the moon, "did you observe the figure of a woman kneeling, with her face hidden in her hands?"

"I never looked that way," replied Donatello. "I was saying my own prayer. It was some penitent, perchance. May the Blessed Virgin be the more gracious to the poor soul, because she is a woman."

## CHAPTER XXXIII

### PICTURED WINDOWS

AFTER wide wanderings through the valley, the two travellers directed their course towards its boundary of hills. Here, the natural scenery and men's modifications of it immediately took a different aspect from that of the fertile and smiling plain. Not unfrequently there was a convent on the hill-side; or, on some insulated promontory, a ruined castle, once the den of a robber chieftain, who was accustomed to dash down from his commanding height upon the road that wound below. For ages back, the old fortress had been flinging down its crumbling ramparts, stone by stone, towards the grimy village at its foot.

Their road wound onward among the hills, which rose steep and lofty from the scanty level space that lay between them. They continually thrust their great bulks before the wayfarers, as if grimly resolute to forbid their passage, or closed abruptly behind them, when they still dared to proceed. A gigantic hill would set its foot right down before them, and only at the last moment would grudgingly withdraw it, just far enough to let them creep towards another obstacle. Adown these rough heights were visible the dry tracks of many a mountain-torrent that had lived a life too fierce and passionate to be a long one. Or, perhaps, a stream was yet hurrying shyly along the edge of a far wider bed of pebbles and shelving rock than it seemed to need, though not too wide for the swollen rage of which this shy rivulet was capable. A stone bridge bestrode it, the ponderous arches of which were upheld and rendered indestructible by the weight of the very stones that threatened to crush them down. Old Roman toil was perceptible in the foundations of that massive bridge; the first weight that it ever bore was that of an army of the Republic.

Threading these defiles, they would arrive at some immemorial city, crowning the high summit of a hill with its cathedral, its many churches, and public edifices, all of Gothic architecture. With no more level ground than a single piazza, in the midst, the ancient town tumbled its crooked and narrow streets down the mountain-side, through arched passages, and by steps of stone. The aspect of everything was awfully old; older, indeed, in its effect on the imagination, than Rome itself, because history does not lay its finger on these forgotten edifices and tell us all about their origin. Etruscan princes may have dwelt in them. A thousand years, at all events, would seem but a middle age for these structures. They are built of such huge, square stones, that their appearance of ponderous durability distresses the beholder with the idea that they can never fall,—never crumble away,—never be less fit than now for human habitation. Many of them may once have been palaces, and still retain a squalid grandeur. But, gazing at them, we recognize how undesirable it is to build the tabernacle of our brief lifetime out of permanent materials, and with a view to their being occupied by future generations.

All towns should be made capable of purification by fire, or of decay, within each half-century. Otherwise, they become the hereditary haunts of vermin and noisomeness, besides standing apart from the possibility of such improvements as are constantly introduced into the rest of man's contrivances and accommodations. It is beautiful, no doubt, and exceedingly satisfactory to some of our natural instincts, to imagine our far posterity dwelling under the same roof-tree as ourselves. Still, when people insist on building indestructible houses, they incur, or their children do, a misfortune analogous to that of the Sibyl, when she obtained the grievous boon of immortality. So, we may build almost immortal habitations, it is true; but we cannot keep them from growing old, musty, unwholesome, dreary, full of death-scents, ghosts, and murder-stains; in short, such habitations as one sees everywhere in Italy, be they hovels or palaces.

"You should go with me to my native country," observed the sculptor to Donatello. "In that fortunate land, each generation has only its own sins and sorrows to bear. Here, it seems as if all the weary and dreary Past were piled upon the back of the Present. If I were to lose my spirits in this country,—if I were to suffer any heavy misfortune here,—methinks it would be impossible to stand up against it, under such adverse influences."

"The sky itself is an old roof, now," answered the Count; "and, no doubt, the sins of mankind have made it gloomier than it used to be."

"Oh, my poor Faun," thought Kenyon to himself, "how art thou changed!"

A city, like this of which we speak, seems a sort of stony growth out of the hill-side, or a fossilized town; so ancient and strange it looks, without enough of life and juciness in it to be any longer susceptible of decay. An earthquake would afford it the only chance of being ruined, beyond its present ruin.

Yet, though dead to all the purposes for which we live to-day, the place has its glorious recollections, and not merely rude and warlike ones, but those of brighter and milder triumphs, the fruits of which we still enjoy. Italy can count several of these lifeless towns which, four or five hundred years ago, were each the birthplace of its own school of art; nor have they yet forgotten to be proud of the dark, old pictures, and the faded frescos, the pristine beauty of which was a light and gladness to the world. But now, unless one happens to be a painter, these famous works make us miserably desperate. They are poor, dim ghosts of what, when Giotto or Cimabue first created them, threw a splendor along the stately aisles; so far gone towards nothingness, in our day, that scarcely a hint of design or expression can glimmer through the dusk. Those early artists did well to paint their frescos. Glowing on the church-walls, they might be looked upon as symbols of the living spirit that made Catholicism a true religion, and that glorified it as long as it retained a genuine life; they filled the transepts with a radiant throng of saints and angels, and threw around the high altar a faint reflection—as much as mortals could see, or bear—of a Diviner Presence. But now that the colors are so wretchedly bedimmed,—now that blotches of plastered wall dot the frescos all over, like a mean reality thrusting itself through life's brightest illusions,—the next best artist to Cimabue or Giotto or Ghirlandaio or Pinturicchio will be he that shall reverently cover their ruined masterpieces with whitewash!

Kenyon, however, being an earnest student and critic of Art, lingered long before these pathetic relics; and Donatello, in his present phase of penitence, thought no time spent amiss while he could be kneeling before an altar. Whenever they found a cathedral, therefore, or a Gothic church, the two travellers were of one mind to enter it. In some of these holy edifices they saw pictures that time had not dimmed nor injured in the least, though they perhaps belonged to as old a school of Art as any that were perishing around them. These were the painted windows; and as often as he gazed at them the sculptor blessed the mediæval time, and its gorgeous contrivances of splendor; for surely the skill of man has never accomplished, nor his mind imagined, any other beauty or glory worthy to be compared with these.

It is the special excellence of pictured glass, that the light, which falls merely on the outside of other pictures, is here interfused throughout the work; it illuminates the design, and invests it with a living radiance; and in requital the unfading colors transmute the common daylight into a miracle of richness and glory in its passage through the heavenly substance of the blessed and angelic shapes which throng the high-arched window.

"It is a woful thing," cried Kenyon, while one of these frail yet enduring and fadeless pictures threw its hues on his face, and on the pavement of the church around him,—"a sad necessity that any Christian soul should pass from earth without once seeing an antique painted window, with the bright Italian sunshine glowing through it! There is no other such true symbol of the glories of the better world, where a celestial radiance will be inherent in all things and persons, and render each continually transparent to the sight of all."

"But what a horror it would be," said Donatello, sadly, "if there were a soul among them through which the light could not be transfused!"

"Yes; and perhaps this is to be the punishment of sin," replied the sculptor; "not that it shall be made evident to the universe, which can profit nothing by such knowledge, but that it shall insulate the sinner from all sweet society by rendering him impermeable to light, and, therefore, unrecognizable in the abode of heavenly simplicity and truth. Then, what remains for him, but the dreariness of infinite and eternal solitude?"

"That would be a horrible destiny, indeed!" said Donatello.

His voice as he spoke the words had a hollow and dreary cadence, as if he anticipated some such frozen solitude for himself. A figure in a dark robe was lurking in the obscurity of a side-chapel close by, and made an impulsive movement forward, but hesitated as Donatello spoke again.

"But there might be a more miserable torture than to be solitary forever," said he. "Think of having a single companion in eternity, and instead of finding any consolation, or at all events variety of torture, to see your own weary, weary sin repeated in that inseparable soul."

"I think, my dear Count, you have never read Dante," observed Kenyon. "That idea is somewhat in his style, but I cannot help regretting that it came into your mind just then."

The dark-robed figure had shrunk back, and was quite lost to sight among the shadows of the chapel.

"There was an English poet," resumed Kenyon, turning again towards the window, "who speaks of the 'dim, religious light,' transmitted through painted glass. I always admired this richly descriptive phrase; but, though he was once in Italy, I question whether Milton ever saw any but the dingy pictures in the dusty windows of English cathedrals, imperfectly shown by the gray English daylight. He would else have illuminated that word 'dim' with some epithet that should not chase away the dimness, yet should make it glow like a million of rubies, sapphires, emeralds, and topazes. Is it not so with yonder window? The pictures are most brilliant in themselves, yet dim with tenderness and reverence, because God himself is shining through them."

"The pictures fill me with emotion, but not such as you seem to experience," said Donatello. "I tremble at those awful saints; and, most of all, at the figure above them. He glows with Divine wrath!"

"My dear friend," said Kenyon, "how strangely your eyes have transmuted the expression of the figure! It is divine love, not wrath!"

"To my eyes," said Donatello, stubbornly, "it is wrath, not love! Each must interpret for himself."

The friends left the church, and looking up, from the exterior, at the window which they had just been contemplating within, nothing was visible but the merest outline of dusky shapes. Neither the individual likeness of saint, angel, nor Saviour, and far less the combined scheme and purport of the picture, could anywise be made out. That miracle of radiant art, thus viewed, was nothing better than an incomprehensible obscurity, without a gleam of beauty to induce the beholder to attempt unravelling it.

"All this," thought the sculptor, "is a most forcible emblem of the different aspect of religious truth and sacred story, as viewed from the warm interior of belief, or from its cold and dreary outside. Christian faith is a grand cathedral, with divinely pictured windows. Standing without, you see no glory, nor can possibly imagine any; standing within, every ray of light reveals a harmony of unspeakable splendors."

After Kenyon and Donatello emerged from the church, however, they had better opportunity for acts of charity and mercy than for religious contemplation; being immediately surrounded by a swarm of beggars, who are the present possessors of Italy, and share the spoil of the stranger with the fleas and mosquitoes, their formidable allies. These pests—the human ones—had hunted the two travellers at every stage of their journey. From village to village, ragged boys and girls kept almost under the horses' feet; hoary grandsires and grandames caught glimpses of their approach, and hobbled to intercept them at some point of vantage; blind men stared them out of countenance with their sightless orbs; women held up their unwashed babies; cripples displayed their wooden legs, their grievous scars, their dangling, boneless arms, their broken backs, their burden of a hump, or whatever infirmity or deformity Providence had assigned them for an inheritance. On the highest mountain summit—in the most shadowy ravine—there was a beggar waiting for them. In one small village, Kenyon had the curiosity to count merely how many children were crying, whining, and bellowing all at once for alms. They proved to be more than forty of as ragged and dirty little imps as any in the world; besides whom, all the wrinkled matrons, and most of the village maids, and not a few stalwart men, held out their hands grimly, piteously, or smilingly in the forlorn hope of whatever trifle of coin might remain in pockets alread so fearfully taxed. Had they been permitted, they would gladly have knelt down and worshipped the travellers, and have cursed them, without rising from their knees, if the expected boon failed to be awarded.

Yet they were not so miserably poor but that the grown people kept houses over their heads. In the way of food, they had, at least, vegetables in their little gardens, pigs and chickens to kill, eggs to fry into omelets with oil, wine to drink, and many other things to make life comfortable. As for the children, when no more small coin appeared to be forthcoming, they began to laugh and play, and turn heels over head, showing themselves jolly and vivacious brats, and evidently as well fed as needs be. The truth is, the Italian peasantry look upon strangers as the almoners of Providence, and therefore feel no more shame in asking and receiving alms, than in availing themselves of providential bounties in whatever other form.

In accordance with his nature, Donatello was always exceedingly charitable to these ragged battalions, and appeared to derive a certain consolation from the prayers which many of them put up in his behalf. In Italy a copper coin of minute value, will often make all the difference between a vindictive curse—death by apoplexy being the favorite one—mumbled in an old witch's toothless jaws and a prayer from the same lips, so earnest that it would seem to reward the charitable soul with at least a puff of grateful breath to help him heavenward. Good wishes being so cheap, though possibly not very efficacious, and anathemas so exceedingly bitter,—even if the greater portion of their poison remain in the mouth that utters them,—it may be wise to expend some reasonable amount in the purchase of the former. Donatello invariably did so; and as he distributed his alms under the pictured window, of which we have been speaking, no less than seven ancient women lifted their hands and besought blessings on his head.

"Come," said the sculptor, rejoicing at the happier expression which he saw in his friend's face. "I think your steed will not stumble with you today. Each of these old dames looks as much like Horace's Atra Cura as can well be conceived; but, though there are seven of them, they will make your burden on horseback lighter instead of heavier."

"Are we to ride far?" asked the Count.

"A tolerable journey betwixt now and to-morrow noon," Kenyon replied; "for, at that hour, I purpose to be standing by the Pope's statue in the great square of Perugia."

### CHAPTER XXXIV

### MARKET-DAY IN PERUGIA

PERUGIA, on its lofty hill-top, was reached by the two travellers before the sun had quite kissed away the early freshness of the morning. Since midnight, there had been a heavy rain, bringing infinite refreshment to the scene of verdure and fertility amid which this ancient civilization stands; insomuch that Kenyon loitered, when they came to the gray city-wall, and was loath to give up the prospect of the sunny wilderness that lay below. It was as green as England, and bright as Italy alone. There was all the wide valley, sweeping down and spreading away on all sides from the weed-grown ramparts, and bounded afar by mountains, which lay asleep in the sun, with thin mists and silvery clouds floating about their heads by way of morning dreams.

"It lacks still two hours of noon," said the sculptor to his friend, as they stood under the arch of the gateway, waiting for their passports to be examined; "will you come with me to see some admirable frescos by Perugino? There is a hall in the Exchange, of no great magnitude, but covered with what must have been—at the time it was painted—such magnificence and beauty as the world had not elsewhere to show."

"It depresses me to look at old frescos," responded the Count; "it is a pain, yet not enough of a pain to answer as a penance."

"Will you look at some pictures by Fra Angelico in the Church of San Domenico?" asked Kenyon; "they are full of religious sincerity. When one studies them faithfully, it is like holding a conversation about heavenly things with a tender and devout-minded man."

"You have shown me some of Fra Angelico's pictures, I remember," answered Donatello; "his angels look as if they had never taken a flight out of heaven; and his saints seem to have been born saints, and always to have lived so. Young maidens, and all innocent persons, I doubt not, may find great delight and profit in looking at such holy pictures. But they are not for me."

"Your criticism, I fancy, has great moral depth," replied Kenyon; "and I see in it the reason why Hilda so highly appreciates Fra Angelico's pictures. Well; we will let all such matters pass for to-day, and stroll about this fine old city till noon."

They wandered to and fro, accordingly, and lost themselves among the strange, precipitate passages, which, in Perugia, are called streets. Some of them are like caverns, being arched all over, and plunging down abruptly towards an unknown darkness; which, when you have fathomed its depths, admits you to a daylight that you scarcely hoped to behold again. Here they met shabby men, and the careworn wives and mothers of the people, some of whom guided children in leading-strings through those dim and antique thoroughfares, where a hundred generations had passed before the little feet of to-day began to tread them. Thence they climbed upward again, and came to the level plateau, on the summit of the hill, where are situated the grand piazza and the principal public edifices.

It happened to be market-day in Perugia. The great square, therefore, presented a far more vivacious spectacle than would have been witnessed in it at any other time of the week, though not so lively as to overcome the gray solemnity of the architectural portion of the scene. In the shadow of the cathedral and other old Gothic structures—seeking shelter from the sunshine that fell across the rest of the piazza—was a crowd of people, engaged as buyers or sellers in the petty traffic of a country-fair. Dealers had erected booths and stalls on the pavement, and overspread them with scanty awnings, beneath which they stood, vociferously crying their merchandise; such as shoes, hats and caps, yarn stockings, cheap jewelry and cutlery, books, chiefly little volumes of a religious character, and a few French novels; toys, tin-ware, old iron, cloth, rosaries of beads, crucifixes, cakes, biscuits, sugar-plums, and innumerable little odds and ends, which we see no object in advertising. Baskets of grapes, figs, and pears stood on the ground. Donkeys, bearing panniers stuffed out with kitchen vegetables, and requiring an ample roadway, roughly shouldered aside the throng.

Crowded as the square was, a juggler found room to spread out a white cloth upon the pavement, and cover it with cups, plates, balls, cards,— the whole material of his magic, in short,—wherewith he proceeded to work miracles under the noonday sun. An organ-grinder at one point, and a clarion and a flute at another, accomplished what they could towards filling the wide space with tuneful noise. Their small uproar, however, was nearly drowned by the multitudinous voices of the people, bargaining, quarrelling, laughing, and babbling copiously at random; for the briskness of the mountain atmosphere, or some other cause, made everybody so loquacious, that more words were wasted in Perugia on this one market-day, than the noisiest piazza of Rome would utter in a month.

Through all this petty tumult, which kept beguiling one's eyes and upper strata of thought, it was delightful to catch glimpses of the grand old architecture that stood around the square. The life of the flitting moment, existing in the antique shell of an age gone by, has a fascination which we do not find in either the past or present, taken by themselves. It might seem irreverent to make the gray cathedral and the tall, time-worn palaces echo back the exuberant vociferation of the market; but they did so, and caused the sound to assume a kind of poetic rhythm, and themselves looked only the more majestic for their condescension.

On one side, there was an immense edifice devoted to public purposes, with an antique gallery, and a range of arched and stone-mullioned windows, running along its front; and by way of entrance it had a central Gothic arch, elaborately wreathed around with sculptured semicircles, within which the spectator was aware of a stately and impressive gloom. Though merely the municipal council-house and exchange of a decayed country town, this structure was worthy to have held in one portion of it the parliament-hall of a nation, and in the other, the state apartments of its ruler. On another side of the square rose the mediæval front of the cathedral, where the imagination of a Gothic architect had long ago flowered out indestructibly, in the first place, a grand design, and then covering it with such abundant detail of ornament, that the magnitude of the work seemed less a miracle than its minuteness. You would suppose that he must have softened the stone into wax, until his most delicate fancies were modelled in the pliant material, and then had hardened it into stone again. The whole was a vast, black-letter page of the richest and quaintest poetry. In fit keeping with all this old magnificence was a great marble fountain, where again the Gothic imagination showed its overflow and gratuity of device in the manifold sculptures which it lavished as freely as the water did its shifting shapes.

Besides the two venerable structures which we have described, there were lofty palaces, perhaps of as old a date, rising story above story, and adorned with balconies, whence, hundreds of years ago, the princely occupants had been accustomed to gaze down at the sports, business, and popular assemblages of the piazza. And, beyond all question, they thus witnessed the erection of a bronze statue, which, three centuries since, was placed on the pedestal that it still occupies.

"I never come to Perugia," said Kenyon, "without spending as much time as I can spare in studying yonder statue of Pope Julius the Third. Those sculptors of the Middle Age have fitter lessons for the professors of my art than we can find in the Grecian masterpieces. They belong to our Christian civilization; and, being earnest works, they always express something which we do not get from the antique. Will you look at it?"

"Willingly," replied the Count, "for I see, even so far off, that the statue is bestowing a benediction, and there is a feeling in my heart that I may be permitted to share it."

Remembering the similar idea which Miriam a short time before had expressed, the sculptor smiled hopefully at the coincidence. They made their way through the throng of the market-place, and approached close to the iron railing that protected the pedestal of the statue.

It was the figure of a pope, arrayed in his pontifical robes, and crowned with the tiara. He sat in a bronze chair, elevated high above the pavement, and seemed to take kindly yet authoritative cognizance of the busy scene which was at that moment passing before his eye. His right hand was raised and spread abroad, as if in the act of shedding forth a benediction, which every man—so broad, so wise, and so serenely affectionate was the bronze pope's regard—might hope to feel quietly descending upon the need, or the distress, that he had closest at his heart. The statue had life and observation in it, as well as patriarchal majesty. An imaginative spectator could not but be impressed with the idea that this benignly awful representative of divine and human authority might rise from his brazen chair, should any great public exigency demand his interposition, and encourage or restrain the people by his gesture, or even by prophetic utterances worthy of so grand a presence.

And, in the long, calm intervals, amid the quiet lapse of ages, the pontiff watched the daily turmoil around his seat, listening with majestic patience to the market cries, and all the petty uproar that awoke the echoes of the stately old piazza. He was the enduring friend of these men, and of their forefathers and children,—the familiar face of generations.

"The pope's blessing, methinks, has fallen upon you," observed the sculptor, looking at his friend.

In truth, Donatello's countenance indicated a healthier spirit than while he was brooding in his melancholy tower. The change of scene, the breaking up of custom, the fresh flow of incidents, the sense of being homeless, and therefore free, had done something for our poor Faun; these circumstances had at least promoted a reaction, which might else have been slower in its progress. Then, no doubt, the bright day, the gay spectacle of the market-place, and the sympathetic exhilaration of so many people's cheerfulness, had each their suitable effect on a temper naturally prone to be glad. Perhaps, too, he was magnetically conscious of a presence that formerly sufficed to make him happy. Be the cause what it might, Donatello's eyes shone with a serene and hopeful expression while looking upward at the bronze pope, to whose widely diffused blessing, it may be, he attributed all this good influence.

"Yes, my dear friend," said he, in reply to the sculptor's remark, "I feel the blessing upon my spirit."

"It is wonderful," said Kenyon, with a smile, "wonderful and delightful to think how long a good man's beneficence may be potent, even after his death. How great, then, must have been the efficacy of this excellent pontiff's blessing while he was alive!"

"I have heard," remarked the Count, "that there was a brazen image set up in the wilderness, the sight of which healed the Israelites of their poisonous and rankling wounds. If it be the Blessed Virgin's pleasure, why should not this holy image before us do me equal good? A wound has long been rankling in my soul, and filling it with poison."

"I did wrong to smile," answered Kenyon. "It is not for me to limit Providence in its operations on man's spirit."

While they stood talking, the clock in the neighboring cathedral told the hour, with twelve reverberating strokes, which it flung down upon the crowded market-place, as if warning one and all to take advantage of the bronze pontiff's benediction, or of Heaven's blessing, however proffered, before the opportunity were lost.

"High noon," said the sculptor. "It is Miriam's hour!"

## CHAPTER XXXV

### THE BRONZE PONTIFF'S BENEDICTION

WHEN the last of the twelve strokes had fallen from the cathedral clock, Kenyon threw his eyes over the busy scene of the market-place, expecting to discern Miriam somewhere in the crowd. He looked next towards the cathedral itself, where it was reasonable to imagine that she might have taken shelter, while awaiting her appointed time. Seeing no trace of her in either direction, his eyes came back from their quest somewhat disappointed, and rested on a figure which was leaning, like Donatello and himself, on the iron balustrade that surrounded the statue. Only a moment before, they two had been alone.

It was the figure of a woman, with her head bowed on her hands, as if she deeply felt—what we have been endeavoring to convey into our feeble description—the benign and awe-inspiring influence which the pontiff's statue exercises upon a sensitive spectator. No matter though it were modelled for a Catholic chief priest, the desolate heart, whatever be its religion, recognizes in that image the likeness of a father.

"Miriam," said the sculptor, with a tremor in his voice, "is it yourself?"

"It is I," she replied; "I am faithful to my engagement, though with many fears."

She lifted her head, and revealed to Kenyon—revealed to Donatello likewise—the well-remembered features of Miriam. They were pale and worn, but distinguished even now, though less gorgeously, by a beauty that might be imagined bright enough to glimmer with its own light in a dim cathedral aisle, and had no need to shrink from the severer test of the mid-day sun. But she seemed tremulous, and hardly able to go through with a scene which at a distance she had found courage to undertake.

"You are most welcome, Miriam!" said the sculptor, seeking to afford her the encouragement which he saw she so greatly required. "I have a hopeful trust that the result of this interview will be propitious. Come; let me lead you to Donatello."

"No, Kenyon, no!" whispered Miriam, shrinking back; "unless of his own accord he speaks my name,—unless he bids me stay,—no word shall ever pass between him and me. It is not that I take upon me to be proud at this late hour. Among other feminine qualities, I threw away my pride when Hilda cast me off."

"If not pride, what else restrains you?" Kenyon asked, a little angry at her unseasonable scruples, and also at this half-complaining reference to Hilda's just severity. "After daring so much, it is no time for fear! If we let him part from you without a word, your opportunity of doing him inestimable good is lost forever."

"True; it will be lost forever!" repeated Miriam, sadly, "But, dear friend, will it be my fault? I willingly fling my woman's pride at his feet. But—do you not see?—his heart must be left freely to its own decision whether to recognize me, because on his voluntary choice depends the whole question whether my devotion will do him good or harm. Except he feel an infinite need of me, I am a burden and fatal obstruction to him!"

"Take your own course, then, Miriam," said Kenyon; "and, doubtless, the crisis being what it is, your spirit is better instructed for its emergencies than mine."

While the foregoing words passed between them they had withdrawn a little from the immediate vicinity of the statue, so as to be out of Donatello's hearing. Still, however, they were beneath the pontiff's outstretched hand; and Miriam, with her beauty and her sorrow, looked up into his benignant face, as if she had come thither for his pardon and paternal affection, and despaired of so vast a boon.

Meanwhile, she had not stood thus long in the public square of Perugia, without attracting the observation of many eyes. With their quick sense of beauty, these Italians had recognized her loveliness, and spared not to take their fill of gazing at it; though their native gentleness and courtesy made their homage far less obtrusive than that of Germans, French, or Anglo-Saxons might have been. It is not improbable that Miriam had planned this momentous interview, on so public a spot and at high noon, with an eye to the sort of protection that would be thrown over it by a multitude of eye-witnesses. In circumstances of profound feeling and passion, there is often a sense that too great a seclusion cannot be endured; there is an indefinite dread of being quite alone with the object of our deepest interest. The species of solitude that a crowd harbors within itself is felt to be preferable, in certain conditions of the heart, to the remoteness of a desert or the depths of an untrodden wood. Hatred, love, or whatever kind of too intense emotion, or even indifference, where emotion has once been, instinctively seeks to interpose some barrier between itself and the corresponding passion in another breast. This, we suspect, was what Miriam had thought of, in coming to the thronged piazza; partly this, and partly, as she said, her superstition that the benign statue held good influences in store.

But Donatello remained leaning against the balustrade. She dared not glance towards him, to see whether he were pale and agitated, or calm as ice. Only, she knew that the moments were fleetly lapsing away, and that his heart must call her soon, or the voice would never reach her. She turned quite away from him and spoke again to the sculptor.

"I have wished to meet you," said she, "for more than one reason. News has come to me respecting a dear friend of ours. Nay, not of mine! I dare not call her a friend of mine, though once the dearest."

"Do you speak of Hilda?" exclaimed Kenyon, with quick alarm. "Has anything befallen her? When I last heard of her, she was still in Rome, and well."

"Hilda remains in Rome," replied Miriam, "nor is she ill as regards physical health, though much depressed in spirits. She lives quite alone in her dove-cote; not a friend near her, not one in Rome, which, you know, is deserted by all but its native inhabitants. I fear for her health, if she continue long in such solitude, with despondency preying on her mind. I tell you this, knowing the interest which the rare beauty of her character has awakened in you."

"I will go to Rome!" said the sculptor, in great emotion. "Hilda has never allowed me to manifest more than a friendly regard; but, at least, she cannot prevent my watching over her at a humble distance. I will set out this very hour."

"Do not leave us now!" whispered Miriam, imploringly, and laying her hand on his arm. "One moment more! Ah; he has no word for me!"

"Miriam!" said Donatello.

Though but a single word, and the first that he had spoken, its tone was a warrant of the sad and tender depth from which it came. It told Miriam things of infinite importance, and, first of all, that he still loved her. The sense of their mutual crime had stunned, but not destroyed, the vitality of his affection; it was therefore indestructible. That tone, too, bespoke an altered and deepened character; it told of a vivified intellect, and of spiritual instruction that had come through sorrow and remorse; so that instead of the wild boy, the thing of sportive, animal nature, the sylvan Faun, here was now the man of feeling and intelligence.

She turned towards him, while his voice still reverberated in the depths of her soul.

"You have called me!" said she.

"Because my deepest heart has need of you!" he replied. "Forgive, Miriam, the coldness, the hardness with which I parted from you! I was bewildered with strange horror and gloom."

"Alas! and it was I that brought it on you," said she. "What repentance, what self-sacrifice, can atone for that infinite wrong? There was something so sacred in the innocent and joyous life which you were leading! A happy person is such an unaccustomed and holy creature in this sad world! And, encountering so rare a being, and gifted with the power of sympathy with his sunny life, it was my doom, mine, to bring him within the limits of sinful, sorrowful mortality! Bid me depart, Donatello! Fling me off! No good, through my agency, can follow upon such a mighty evil!"

"Miriam," said he, "our lot lies together. Is it not so? Tell me, in Heaven's name, if it be otherwise."

Donatello's conscience was evidently perplexed with doubt, whether the communion of a crime, such as they two were jointly stained with, ought not to stifle all the instinctive motions of their hearts, impelling them one towards the other. Miriam, on the other hand, remorsefully questioned with herself whether the misery, already accruing from her influence, should not warn her to withdraw from his path. In this momentous interview, therefore, two souls were groping for each other in the darkness of guilt and sorrow, and hardly were bold enough to grasp the cold hands that they found.

The sculptor stood watching the scene with earnest sympathy.

"It seems irreverent," said he, at length; "intrusive, if not irreverent, for a third person to thrust himself between the two solely concerned in a crisis like the present. Yet, possibly as a by-stander, though a deeply interested one, I may discern somewhat of truth that is hidden from you both; nay, at least interpret or suggest some ideas which you might not so readily convey to each other."

"Speak!" said Miriam. "We confide in you."

"Speak!" said Donatello. "You are true and upright."

"I well know," rejoined Kenyon, "that I shall not succeed in uttering the few, deep words which, in this matter, as in all others, include the absolute truth. But here, Miriam, is one whom a terrible misfortune has begun to educate; it has taken him, and through your agency, out of a wild and happy state, which, within circumscribed limits, gave him joys that he cannot elsewhere find on earth. On his behalf, you have incurred a responsibility which you cannot fling aside. And here, Donatello, is one whom Providence marks out as intimately connected with your destiny. The mysterious process, by which our earthly life instructs us for another state of being, was begun for you by her. She has rich gifts of heart and mind, a suggestive power, a magnetic influence, a sympathetic knowledge, which, wisely and religiously exercised, are what your condition needs. She possesses what you require, and, with utter self-devotion, will use it for your good. The bond betwixt you, therefore, is a true one, and never —except by Heaven's own act—should be rent asunder."

"Ah; he has spoken the truth!" cried Donatello, grasping Miriam's hand.

"The very truth, dear friend," cried Miriam.

"But take heed," resumed the sculptor, anxious not to violate the integrity of his own conscience,—"take heed; for you love one another, and yet your bond is twined with such black threads that you must never look upon it as identical with the ties that unite other loving souls. It is for mutual support; it is for one another's final good; it is for effort, for sacrifice, but not for earthly happiness. If such be your motive, believe me, friends, it were better to relinquish each other's hands at this sad moment. There would be no holy sanction on your wedded life."

"None," said Donatello, shuddering. "We know it well."

"None," repeated Miriam, also shuddering. "United—miserably entangled with me, rather—by a bond of guilt, our union might be for eternity, indeed, and most intimate; but, through all that endless duration, I should be conscious of his horror."

"Not for earthly bliss, therefore," said Kenyon, "but for mutual elevation, and encouragement towards a severe and painful life, you take each other's hands. And if, out of toil, sacrifice, prayer, penitence, and earnest effort towards right things, there comes, at length, a sombre and thoughtful happiness, taste it, and thank Heaven! So that you live not for it,— so that it be a wayside flower, springing along a path that leads to higher ends,—it will be Heaven's gracious gift, and a token that it recognizes your union here below."

"Have you no more to say?" asked Miriam, earnestly. "There is matter of sorrow and lofty consolation strangely mingled in your words."

"Only this, dear Miriam," said the sculptor; "if ever in your lives the highest duty should require from either of you the sacrifice of the other, meet the occasion without shrinking. This is all."

While Kenyon spoke, Donatello had evidently taken in the ideas which he propounded, and had ennobled them by the sincerity of his reception. His aspect unconsciously assumed a dignity, which, elevating his former beauty, accorded with the change that had long been taking place in his interior self. He was a man, revolving grave and deep thoughts in his breast. He still held Miriam's hand; and there they stood, the beautiful man, the beautiful woman, united forever, as they felt, in the presence of these thousand eye-witnesses, who gazed so curiously at the unintelligible scene. Doubtless, the crowd recognized them as lovers, and fancied this a betrothal that was destined to result in life-long happiness. And, possibly, it might be so. Who can tell where happiness may come; or where, though an expected guest, it may never show its face? Perhaps—shy, subtle thing —it had crept into this sad marriage-bond, when the partners would have trembled at its presence as a crime.

"Farewell!" said Kenyon; "I go to Rome."

"Farewell, true friend!" said Miriam.

"Farewell!" said Donatello too. "May you be happy. You have no guilt to make you shrink from happiness."

At this moment it so chanced that all the three friends by one impulse glanced upward at the statue of Pope Julius; and there was the majestic figure stretching out the hand of benediction over them, and bending down upon this guilty and repentant pair its visage of grand benignity. There is a singular effect oftentimes when, out of the midst of engrossing thought and deep absorption, we suddenly look up, and catch a glimpse of external objects. We seem at such moments to look farther and deeper into them, than by any premeditated observation; it is as if they met our eyes alive, and with all their hidden meaning on the surface, but grew again inanimate and inscrutable the instant that they became aware of our glances. So now, at that unexpected glimpse, Miriam, Donatello, and the sculptor, all three imagined that they beheld the bronze pontiff endowed with spiritual life. A blessing was felt descending upon them from his outstretched hand; he approved by look and gesture the pledge of a deep union that had passed under his auspices.

## CHAPTER XXXVI

### HILDA'S TOWER

WHEN we have once known Rome, and left her where she lies, like a long-decaying corpse, retaining a trace of the noble shape it was, but with accumulated dust and a fungous growth overspreading all its more admirable features,—left her in utter weariness, no doubt, of her narrow, crooked, intricate streets, so uncomfortably paved with little squares of lava that to tread over them is a penitential pilgrimage, so indescribably ugly, moreover, so cold, so alley-like, into which the sun never falls, and where a chill wind forces its deadly breath into our lungs,—left her, tired of the sight of those immense seven-storied, yellow-washed hovels, or call them palaces, where all that is dreary in domestic life seems magnified and multiplied, and weary of climbing those staircases, which ascend from a ground-floor of cook-shops, cobblers' stalls, stables, and regiments of cavalry, to a middle region of princes, cardinals, and ambassadors, and an upper tier of artists, just beneath the unattainable sky,—left her, worn out with shivering at the cheerless and smoky fireside by day, and feasting with our own substance the ravenous little populace of a Roman bed at night,—left her, sick at heart of Italian trickery, which has uprooted whatever faith in man's integrity had endured till now, and sick at stomach of sour bread, sour wine, rancid butter, and bad cookery, needlessly bestowed on evil meats,—left her, disgusted with the pretence of holiness and the reality of nastiness, each equally omnipresent,—left her, half lifeless from the languid atmosphere, the vital principle of which has been used up long ago, or corrupted by myriads of slaughters,—left her, crushed down in spirit with the desolation of her ruin, and the hopelessness of her future,—left her, in short, hating her with all our might, and adding our individual curse to the infinite anathema which her old crimes have unmistakably brought down,—when we have left Rome in such mood as this, we are astonished by the discovery, by and by, that our heart-strings have mysteriously attached themselves to the Eternal City, and are drawing us thitherward again, as if it were more familiar, more intimately our home, than even the spot where we were born.

It is with a kindred sentiment, that we now follow the course of our story back through the Flaminian Gate, and, treading our way to the Via Portoghese, climb the staircase to the upper chamber of the tower where we last saw Hilda.

Hilda all along intended to pass the summer in Rome; for she had laid out many high and delightful tasks, which she could the better complete while her favorite haunts were deserted by the multitude that thronged them throughout the winter and early spring. Nor did she dread the summer atmosphere, although generally held to be so pestilential. She had already made trial of it, two years before, and found no worse effect than a kind of dreamy languor, which was dissipated by the first cool breezes that came with autumn. The thickly populated centre of the city, indeed, is never affected by the feverish influence that lies in wait in the Campagna, like a besieging foe, and nightly haunts those beautiful lawns and woodlands, around the suburban villas, just at the season when they most resemble Paradise. What the flaming sword was to the first Eden, such is the malaria to these sweet gardens and groves. We may wander through them, of an afternoon, it is true, but they cannot be made a home and a reality, and to sleep among them is death. They are but illusions, therefore, like the show of gleaming waters and shadowy foliage in a desert.

But Rome, within the walls, at this dreaded season, enjoys its festal days, and makes itself merry with characteristic and hereditary pastimes, for which its broad piazzas afford abundant room. It leads its own life with a freer spirit, now that the artists and foreign visitors are scattered abroad. No bloom, perhaps, would be visible in a cheek that should be unvisited, throughout the summer, by more invigorating winds than any within fifty miles of the city; no bloom, but yet, if the mind kept its healthy energy, a subdued and colorless well-being. There was conse-

quently little risk in Hilda's purpose to pass the summer days in the galleries of Roman palaces, and her nights in that aerial chamber, whither
the heavy breath of the city and its suburbs could not aspire. It would
probably harm her no more than it did the white doves, who sought the
same high atmosphere at sunset, and, when morning came, flew down into
the narrow streets, about their daily business, as Hilda likewise did.

With the Virgin's aid and blessing, which might be hoped for even by a
heretic, who so religiously lit the lamp before her shrine, the New England girl would sleep securely in her old Roman tower, and go forth on
her pictorial pilgrimages without dread or peril. In view of such a summer, Hilda had anticipated many months of lonely, but unalloyed enjoyment. Not that she had a churlish disinclination to society, or needed to
be told that we taste one intellectual pleasure twice, and with double the
result, when we taste it with a friend. But, keeping a maiden heart within
her bosom, she rejoiced in the freedom that enabled her still to choose her
own sphere, and dwell in it, if she pleased, without another inmate.

Her expectation, however, of a delightful summer was wofully disappointed. Even had she formed no previous plan of remaining there, it
is improbable that Hilda would have gathered energy to stir from Rome.
A torpor, heretofore unknown to her vivacious though quiet temperament,
had possessed itself of the poor girl, like a half-dead serpent knotting its
cold, inextricable wreaths about her limbs. It was that peculiar despair,
that chill and heavy misery, which only the innocent can experience, although it possesses many of the gloomy characteristics that mark a sense
of guilt. It was that heart-sickness, which, it is to be hoped, we may all of
us have been pure enough to feel, once in our lives, but the capacity for
which is usually exhausted early, and perhaps with a single agony. It was
that dismal certainty of the existence of evil in the world, which, though
we may fancy ourselves fully assured of the sad mystery long before,
never becomes a portion of our practical belief until it takes substance
and reality from the sin of some guide, whom we have deeply trusted and
revered, or some friend whom we have dearly loved.

When that knowledge comes, it is as if a cloud had suddenly gathered
over the morning light; so dark a cloud, that there seems to be no longer
any sunshine behind it or above it. The character of our individual beloved one having invested itself with all the attributes of right,—that one
friend being to us the symbol and representative of whatever is good and
true,—when he falls, the effect is amost as if the sky fell with him, bringing down in chaotic ruin the columns that upheld our faith. We struggle
forth again, no doubt, bruised and bewildered. We stare wildly about us,
and discover—or, it may be, we never make the discovery—that it was
not actually the sky that has tumbled down, but merely a frail structure
of our own rearing, which never rose higher than the house-tops, and has
fallen because we founded it on nothing. But the crash, and the affright
and trouble, are as overwhelming, for the time, as if the catastrophe involved the whole moral world. Remembering these things, let them suggest one generous motive for walking heedfully amid the defilement of

earthly ways! Let us reflect, that the highest path is pointed out by the pure Ideal of those who look up to us, and who, if we tread less loftily, may never look so high again.

Hilda's situation was made infinitely more wretched by the necessity of confining all her trouble within her own consciousness. To this inno-cent girl, holding the knowledge of Miriam's crime within her tender and delicate soul, the effect was almost the same as if she herself had par-ticipated in the guilt. Indeed, partaking the human nature of those who could perpetrate such deeds, she felt her own spotlessness impugned.

Had there been but a single friend,—or, not a friend, since friends were no longer to be confided in, after Miriam had betrayed her trust,—but, had there been any calm, wise mind, any sympathizing intelligence; or, if not these, any dull, half-listening ear into which she might have flung the dreadful secret, as into an echoless cavern,—what a relief would have ensued! But this awful loneliness! It enveloped her whithersoever she went. It was a shadow in the sunshine of festal days; a mist between her eyes and the pictures at which she strove to look; a chill dungeon, which kept her in its gray twilight and fed her with its unwholesome air, fit only for a criminal to breathe and pine in! She could not escape from it. In the effort to do so, straying farther into the intricate passages of our nature, she stumbled, ever and again, over this deadly idea of mortal guilt.

Poor sufferer for another's sin! Poor well-spring of a virgin's heart, into which a murdered corpse had casually fallen, and whence it could not be drawn forth again, but lay there, day after day, night after night, tainting its sweet atmosphere with the scent of crime and ugly death!

The strange sorrow that had befallen Hilda did not fail to impress its mysterious seal upon her face, and to make itself perceptible to sensitive observers in her manner and carriage. A young Italian artist, who fre-quented the same galleries which Hilda haunted, grew deeply interested in her expression. One day, while she stood before Leonardo da Vinci's picture of Joanna of Aragon, but evidently without seeing it,—for, though it had attracted her eyes, a fancied resemblance to Miriam had immediate-ly drawn away her thoughts,—this artist drew a hasty sketch which he afterwards elaborated into a finished portrait. It represented Hilda as gazing with sad and earnest horror at a blood-spot which she seemed just then to have discovered on her white robe. The picture attracted consider-able notice. Copies of an engraving from it may still be found in the print-shops along the Corso. By many connoisseurs, the idea of the face was supposed to have been suggested by the portrait of Beatrice Cenci; and, in fact, there was a look somewhat similar to poor Beatrice's forlorn gaze out of the dreary isolation and remoteness, in which a terrible doom had involved a tender soul. But the modern artist strenuously upheld the originality of his own picture, as well as the stainless purity of its subject, and chose to call it—and was laughed at for his pains—"Innocence, dying of a blood-stain!"

"Your picture, Signore Panini, does you credit," remarked the picture-dealer, who had bought it of the young man for fifteen scudi, and afterwards sold it for ten times the sum; "but it would be worth a better price if you had given it a more intelligible title. Looking at the face and expression of this fair signorina, we seem to comprehend readily enough, that she is undergoing one or another of those troubles of the heart to which young ladies are but too liable. But what is this blood-stain? And what has innocence to do with it? Has she stabbed her perfidious lover with a bodkin?"

"She! she commit a crime!" cried the young artist. "Can you look at the innocent anguish in her face, and ask that question? No; but, as I read the mystery, a man has been slain in her presence, and the blood, spurting accidentally on her white robe, has made a stain which eats into her life."

"Then, in the name of her patron saint," exclaimed the picture-dealer, "why don't she get the robe made white again at the expense of a few baiocchi to her washer-woman? No, no, my dear Panini. The picture being now my property, I shall call it 'The Signorina's Vengeance.' She has stabbed her lover overnight, and is repenting it betimes the next morning. So interpreted, the picture becomes an intelligible and very natural representation of a not uncommon fact."

Thus coarsely does the world translate all finer griefs that meet its eye. It is more a coarse world than an unkind one.

But Hilda sought nothing either from the world's delicacy or its pity, and never dreamed of its misinterpretations. Her doves often flew in through the windows of the tower, winged messengers, bringing her what sympathy they could, and uttering soft, tender, and complaining sounds, deep in their bosoms, which soothed the girl more than a distincter utterance might. And sometimes Hilda moaned quietly among the doves, teaching her voice to accord with theirs, and thus finding a temporary relief from the burden of her incommunicable sorrow, as if a little portion of it, at least, had been told to these innocent friends, and been understood and pitied.

When she trimmed the lamp before the Virgin's shrine, Hilda gazed at the sacred image, and, rude as was the workmanship, beheld, or fancied, expressed with the quaint, powerful simplicity which sculptors sometimes had five hundred years ago, a woman's tenderness responding to her gaze. If she knelt, if she prayed, if her oppressed heart besought the sympathy of divine womanhood afar in bliss, but not remote, because forever humanized by the memory of mortal griefs, was Hilda to be blamed? It was not a Catholic kneeling at an idolatrous shrine, but a child lifting its tear-stained face to seek comfort from a mother.

## CHAPTER XXXVII

### THE EMPTINESS OF PICTURE GALLERIES

HILDA descended, day by day, from her dove-cote, and went to one or another of the great, old palaces,—the Pamfili Doria, the Corsini, the Sciarra, the Borghese, the Colonna,—where the door-keepers knew her well, and offered her a kindly greeting. But they shook their heads and sighed, on observing the languid step with which the poor girl toiled up the grand marble staircases. There was no more of that cheery alacrity with which she used to flit upward, as if her doves had lent her their wings, nor of that glow of happy spirits which had been wont to set the tarnished gilding of the picture-frames and the shabby splendor of the furniture all a-glimmer, as she hastened to her congenial and delightful toil.

An old German artist, whom she often met in the galleries, once laid a paternal hand on Hilda's head, and bade her go back to her own country.

"Go back soon," he said, with kindly freedom and directness, "or you will go never more. And, if you go not, why, at least, do you spend the whole summer-time in Rome? The air has been breathed too often, in so many thousand years, and is not wholesome for a little foreign flower like you, my child, a delicate wood-anemone from the western forest-land."

"I have no task nor duty anywhere but here," replied Hilda. "The old masters will not set me free!"

"Ah, those old masters!" cried the veteran artist, shaking his head. "They are a tyrannous race! You will find them of too mighty a spirit to be dealt with, for long together, by the slender hand, the fragile mind, and the delicate heart, of a young girl. Remember that Raphael's genius wore out that divinest painter before half his life was lived. Since you feel his influence powerfully enough to reproduce his miracles so well, it will assuredly consume you like a flame."

"That might have been my peril once," answered Hilda. "It is not so now."

"Yes, fair maiden, you stand in that peril now!" insisted the kind old man; and he added, smiling, yet in a melancholy vein, and with a German grotesqueness of idea, "Some fine morning, I shall come to the Pinacotheca of the Vatican, with my palette and my brushes, and shall look for my little American artist that sees into the very heart of the grand pictures! And what shall I behold? A heap of white ashes on the marble floor, just in front of the divine Raphael's picture of the Madonna da Foligno! Nothing more, upon my word! The fire, which the poor child feels so fervently, will have gone into her innermost, and burnt her quite up!"

"It would be a happy martyrdom!" said Hilda, faintly smiling. "But I am far from being worthy of it. What troubles me much, among other troubles, is quite the reverse of what you think. The old masters hold me here, it is true, but they no longer warm me with their influence. It is not flame consuming, but torpor chilling me, that helps to make me wretched."

"Perchance, then," said the German, looking keenly at her, "Raphael has a rival in your heart? He was your first-love; but young maidens are not always constant, and one flame is sometimes extinguished by another!"

Hilda shook her head, and turned away.

She had spoken the truth, however, in alleging that torpor, rather than fire, was what she had now to dread. In those gloomy days that had befallen her, it was a great additional calamity that she felt conscious of the present dimness of an insight, which she once possessed in more than ordinary measure. She had lost—and she trembled lest it should have departed forever—the faculty of appreciating those great works of art, which heretofore had made so large a portion of her happiness. It was no wonder.

A picture, however admirable the painter's art, and wonderful his power, requires of the spectator a surrender of himself, in due proportion with the miracle which has been wrought. Let the canvas glow as it may, you must look with the eye of faith, or its highest excellence escapes you. There is always the necessity of helping out the painter's art with your own resources of sensibility and imagination. Not that these qualities shall really add anything to what the master has effected; but they must be put so entirely under his control, and work along with him to such an extent, that, in a different mood, when you are cold and critical, instead of sympathetic, you will be apt to fancy that the loftier merits of the picture were of your own dreaming, not of his creating.

Like all revelations of the better life, the adequate perception of a great work of art demands a gifted simplicity of vision. In this, and in her self-surrender, and the depth and tenderness of her sympathy, had lain Hilda's remarkable power as a copyist of the old masters. And now that her capacity of emotion was choked up with a horrible experience, it inevitably followed that she should seek in vain, among those friends so venerated and beloved, for the marvels which they had heretofore shown her. In spite of a reverence that lingered longer than her recognition, their poor worshipper became almost an infidel, and sometimes doubted whether the pictorial art be not altogether a delusion.

For the first time in her life, Hilda now grew acquainted with that icy demon of weariness, who haunts great picture galleries. He is a plausible Mephistopheles, and possesses the magic that is the destruction of all other magic. He annihilates color, warmth, and, more especially, sentiment and passion, at a touch. If he spare anything, it will be some such matter as an earthen pipkin, or a bunch of herrings by Teniers; a brass kettle, in which you can see your face, by Gerard Douw; a furred robe, or the silken texture of a mantle, or a straw hat, by Van Mieris; or a long-stalked wine-glass, transparent and full of shifting reflection, or a bit of bread and cheese, or an over-ripe peach, with a fly upon it, truer than reality itself, by the school of Dutch conjurers. These men, and a few Flemings, whispers the wicked demon, were the only painters. The mighty Italian masters, as you deem them, were not human, nor addressed their work to human sympathies, but to a false intellectual taste, which they themselves were the first to create. Well might they call their doings "art," for they substituted art instead of nature. Their fashion is past, and ought, indeed, to have died and been buried along with them.

Then there is such a terrible lack of variety in their subjects. The churchmen, their great patrons, suggested most of their themes, and a dead mythology the rest. A quarter-part, probably, of any large collection of pictures, consist of Virgins and infant Christs, repeated over and over again in pretty much an identical spirit, and generally with no more mixture of the Divine than just enough to spoil them as representations of maternity and childhood, with which everybody's heart might have something to do. Half of the other pictures are Magdalens, Flights into Egypt, Crucifixions, Depositions from the Cross, Pietas, Noli-me-tangeres, or the Sacrifice of Abraham, or martyrdoms of saints, originally painted as altar-pieces, or for the shrines of chapels, and wofully lacking the accompaniments which the artist had in view.

The remainder of the gallery comprises mythological subjects, such as nude Venuses, Ledas, Graces, and, in short, a general apotheosis of nudity, once fresh and rosy perhaps, but yellow and dingy in our day, and retaining only a traditionary charm. These impure pictures are from the same illustrious and impious hands that adventured to call before us the august forms of Apostles and Saints, the Blessed Mother of the Redeemer, and her Son, at his death, and in his glory, and even the awfulness of Him, to whom the martyrs, dead a thousand years ago, have not yet dared to raise their eyes. They seem to take up one task or the other —the disrobed woman whom they call Venus, or the type of highest and tenderest womanhood in the mother of their Saviour—with equal readiness, but to achieve the former with far more satisfactory success. If an artist sometimes produced a picture of the Virgin, possessing warmth enough to excite devotional feelings, it was probably the object of his earthly love to whom he thus paid the stupendous and fearful homage of setting up her portrait to be worshipped, not figuratively as a mortal, but by religious souls in their earnest aspirations towards Divinity. And who can trust the religious sentiment of Raphael, or receive any of his Virgins as heaven-descended likenesses, after seeing, for example, the Fornarina of the Barberini Palace, and feeling how sensual the artist must have been to paint such a brazen trollop of his own accord, and lovingly? Would the Blessed Mary reveal herself to his spiritual vision, and favor him with sittings alternately with that type of glowing earthliness, the Fornarina?

But no sooner have we given expression to this irreverent criticism, than a throng of spiritual faces look reproachfully upon us. We see cherubs by Raphael, whose baby-innocence could only have been nursed in paradise; angels by Raphael as innocent as they, but whose serene intelligence embraces both earthly and celestial things; madonnas by Raphael, on whose lips he has impressed a holy and delicate reserve, implying sanctity on earth, and into whose soft eyes he has thrown a light which he never could have imagined except by raising his own eyes with a pure aspiration heavenward. We remember, too, that divinest countenance in the Transfiguration, and withdraw all that we have said.

Poor Hilda, however, in her gloomiest moments, was never guilty of the high treason suggested in the above remarks against her beloved and honored Raphael. She had a faculty (which, fortunately for themselves, pure women often have) of ignoring all moral blotches in a character that won her admiration. She purified the objects of her regard by the mere act of turning such spotless eyes upon them.

Hilda's despondency, nevertheless, while it dulled her perceptions in one respect, had deepened them in another; she saw beauty less vividly, but felt truth, or the lack of it, more profoundly. She began to suspect that some, at least, of her venerated painters, had left an inevitable hollowness in their works, because, in the most renowned of them, they essayed to express to the world what they had not in their own souls. They deified their light and wandering affections, and were continually playing off the tremendous jest, alluded to above, of offering the features of some venal beauty to be enshrined in the holiest places. A deficiency of earnestness and absolute truth is generally discoverable in Italian pictures, after the art had become consummate. When you demand what is deepest, these painters have not wherewithal to respond. They substituted a keen intellectual perception, and a marvellous knack of external arrangement, instead of live sympathy and sentiment which should have been their inspiration. And hence it happens, that shallow and worldly men are among the best critics of their works; a taste for pictorial art is often no more than a polish upon the hard enamel of an artificial character. Hilda had lavished her whole heart upon it, and found (just as if she had lavished it upon a human idol) that the greater part was thrown away.

For some of the earlier painters, however, she still retained much of her former reverence. Fra Angelico, she felt, must have breathed a humble aspiration between every two touches of his brush, in order to have made the finished picture such a visible prayer as we behold it, in the guise of a prim angel, or a saint without the human nature. Through all these dusky centuries, his works may still help a struggling heart to pray. Perugino was evidently a devout man; and the Virgin, therefore, revealed herself to him in loftier and sweeter faces of celestial womanhood, and yet with a kind of homeliness in their human mould, than even the genius of Raphael could imagine. Sodoma, beyond a question, both prayed and wept, while painting his fresco, at Siena, of Christ bound to a pillar.

In her present need and hunger for a spiritual revelation, Hilda felt a vast and weary longing to see this last-mentioned picture once again. It is inexpressibly touching. So weary is the Saviour, and utterly worn out with agony, that his lips have fallen apart from mere exhaustion; his eyes seem to be set; he tries to lean his head against the pillar, but is kept from sinking down upon the ground only by the cords that bind him. One of the most striking effects produced is the sense of loneliness. You behold Christ deserted both in heaven and earth; that despair is in him which wrung forth the saddest utterance man ever made, "Why hast Thou forsaken me?" Even in this extremity, however, he is still divine. The great and reverent painter has not suffered the Son of God to be merely an object of pity, though depicting him in a state so profoundly pitiful. He is rescued from it, we know not how,—by nothing less than miracle,—by a celestial majesty and beauty, and some quality of which these are the outward garniture. He is as much, and as visibly, our Redeemer, there bound, there fainting, and bleeding from the scourge, with the cross in view, as if he sat on his throne of glory in the heavens! Sodoma, in this matchless picture, has done more towards reconciling the incongruity of Divine Omnipotence and outraged, suffering Humanity, combined in one person, than the theologians ever did.

This hallowed work of genius shows what pictorial art, devoutly exercised, might effect in behalf of religious truth; involving, as it does, deeper mysteries of revelation, and bringing them closer to man's heart, and making him tenderer to be impressed by them, than the most eloquent words of preacher or prophet.

It is not of pictures like the above that galleries, in Rome or elsewhere, are made up, but of productions immeasurably below them, and requiring to be appreciated by a very different frame of mind. Few amateurs are endowed with a tender susceptibility to the sentiment of a picture; they are not won from an evil life, nor anywise morally improved by it. The love of art, therefore, differs widely in its influence from the love of nature; whereas, if art had not strayed away from its legitimate paths and aims, it ought to soften and sweeten the lives of its worshippers, in even a more exquisite degree than the contemplation of natural objects. But, of its own potency, it has no such effect; and it fails, likewise, in that other test of its moral value which poor Hilda was now involuntarily trying' upon it. It cannot comfort the heart in affliction; it grows dim when the shadow is upon us.

So the melancholy girl wandered through those long galleries, and over the mosaic pavements of vast, solitary saloons, wondering what had become of the splendor that used to beam upon her from the walls. She grew sadly critical, and condemned almost everything that she was wont to admire. Heretofore, her sympathy went deeply into a picture, yet seemed to leave a depth which it was inadequate to sound; now, on the contrary, her perceptive faculty penetrated the canvas like a steel probe, and found but a crust of paint over an emptiness. Not that she gave up all art as worthless; only it had lost its consecration. One picture in ten thousand, perhaps, ought to live in the applause of mankind, from generation to generation, until the colors fade and blacken out of sight, or the canvas rot entirely away. For the rest, let them be piled in garrets, just as the tolerable poets are shelved, when their little day is over. Is a painter more sacred than a poet?

And as for these galleries of Roman palaces, they were to Hilda,—though she still trod them with the forlorn hope of getting back her sympathies,—they were drearier than the whitewashed walls of a prison corridor. If a magnificent palace were founded, as was generally the case, on hardened guilt and a stony conscience,—if the prince or cardinal who stole the marble of his vast mansion from the Coliseum, or some Roman temple, had perpetrated still deadlier crimes, as probably he did,—there could be no fitter punishment for his ghost than to wander perpetually through these long suites of rooms, over the cold marble or mosaic of the floors, growing chiller at every eternal footstep. Fancy the progenitor of the Dorias thus haunting those heavy halls where his posterity reside! Nor would it assuage his monotonous misery, but increase it manifold, to be compelled to scrutinize those masterpieces of art, which he collected with so much cost and care, and gazing at them unintelligently, still leave a further portion of his vital warmth at every one.

Such, or of a similar kind, is the torment of those who seek to enjoy pictures in an uncongenial mood. Every haunter of picture galleries, we should imagine, must have experienced it, in greater or less degree; Hilda never till now, but now most bitterly.

And now, for the first time in her lengthened absence, comprising so many years of her young life, she began to be acquainted with the exile's pain. Her pictorial imagination brought up vivid scenes of her native village, with its great, old elm-trees; and the neat, comfortable houses, scattered along the wide, grassy margin of its street, and the white meeting-house, and her mother's very door, and the stream of gold-brown water, which her taste for color had kept flowing, all this while, through her remembrance. Oh, dreary streets, palaces, churches, and imperial sepulchres of hot and dusty Rome, with the muddy Tiber eddying through the midst, instead of the gold-brown rivulet! How she pined under this crumbly magnificence, as if it were piled all upon her human heart! How she yearned for that native homeliness, those familiar sights, those faces which she had known always, those days that never brought any strange event; that life of sober week-days, and a solemn sabbath at the close! The peculiar fragrance of a flower-bed, which Hilda used to cultivate, came freshly to her memory, across the windy sea, and through the long years since the flowers had withered. Her heart grew faint at the hundred reminiscences that were awakened by that remembered smell of dead blossoms; it was like opening a drawer, where many things were laid away, and every one of them scented with lavender and dried rose-leaves.

We ought not to betray Hilda's secret; but it is the truth, that being so sad, and so utterly alone, and in such great need of sympathy, her thoughts sometimes recurred to the sculptor. Had she met him now, her heart, indeed, might not have been won, but her confidence would have flown to him like a bird to its nest. One summer afternoon, especially,

Hilda leaned upon the battlements of her tower, and looked over Rome towards the distant mountains, whither Kenyon had told her that he was going.

"Oh, that he were here!" she sighed; "I perish under this terrible secret; and he might help me to endure it. Oh, that he were here!"

That very afternoon, as the reader may remember, Kenyon felt Hilda's hand pulling at the silken cord that was connected with his heartstrings, as he stood looking towards Rome from the battlements of Monte Beni.

## CHAPTER XXXVIII

### ALTARS AND INCENSE

ROME has a certain species of consolation readier at hand, for all the necessitous, than any other spot under the sky; and Hilda's despondent state made her peculiarly liable to the peril, if peril it can justly be termed, of seeking, or consenting, to be thus consoled.

Had the Jesuits known the situation of this troubled heart, her inheritance of New England Puritanism would hardly have protected the poor girl from the pious strategy of those good fathers. Knowing, as they do, how to work each proper engine, it would have been ultimately impossible for Hilda to resist the attractions of a faith, which so marvellously adapts itself to every human need. Not, indeed, that it can satisfy the soul's cravings, but, at least, it can sometimes help the soul towards a higher satisfaction than the faith contains within itself. It supplies a multitude of external forms, in which the spiritual may be clothed and manifested; it has many painted windows, as it were, through which the celestial sunshine, else disregarded, may make itself gloriously perceptible in visions of beauty and splendor. There is no one want or weakness of human nature for which Catholicism will own itself without a remedy; cordials, certainly, it possesses in abundance, and sedatives in inexhaustible variety, and what may once have been genuine medicaments, though a little the worse for long keeping.

To do it justice, Catholicism is such a miracle of fitness for its own ends, many of which might seem to be admirable ones, that it is difficult to imagine it a contrivance of mere man. Its mighty machinery was forged and put together, not on middle earth, but either above or below. If there were but angels to work it, instead of the very different class of engineers who now manage its cranks and safety-valves, the system would soon vindicate the dignity and holiness of its origin.

Hilda had heretofore made many pilgrimages among the churches of Rome, for the sake of wondering at their gorgeousness. Without a glimpse at these palaces of worship, it is impossible to imagine the magnificence of the religion that reared them. Many of them shine with burnished gold. They glow with pictures. Their walls, columns, and arches seem a quarry of precious stones, so beautiful and costly are the marbles with which they are inlaid. Their pavements are often a mosaic, of rare workmanship. Around their lofty cornices hover flights of sculptured angels; and within the vault of the ceiling and the swelling interior of the dome, there are frescos of such brilliancy, and wrought with so artful a perspective, that the sky, peopled with sainted forms, appears to be opened, only a little way above the spectator. Then there are chapels, opening from the side-aisles and transepts, decorated by princes for their own burial-places, and as shrines for their especial saints. In these, the splendor of the entire edifice is intensified and gathered to a focus. Unless words were gems, that would flame with many-colored light upon the page, and throw thence a tremulous glimmer into the reader's eyes, it were vain to attempt a description of a princely chapel.

Restless with her trouble, Hilda now entered upon another pilgrimage among these altars and shrines. She climbed the hundred steps of the Ara Cœli; she trod the broad, silent nave of St. John Lateran; she stood in the Pantheon, under the round opening in the dome, through which the blue sunny sky still gazes down, as it used to gaze when there were Roman deities in the antique niches. She went into every church that rose before her, but not now to wonder at its magnificence, when she hardly noticed more than if it had been the pine-built interior of a New England meeting-house.

She went—and it was a dangerous errand—to observe how closely and comfortingly the popish faith applied itself to all human occasions. It was impossible to doubt that multitudes of people found their spiritual advantage in it, who would find none at all in our own formless mode of worship; which, besides, so far as the sympathy of prayerful souls is concerned, can be enjoyed only at stated and too unfrequented periods. But here, whenever the hunger for divine nutriment came upon the soul, it could on the instant he appeased. At one or another altar, the incense was forever ascending; the mass always being performed, and carrying upward with it the devotion of such as had not words for their own prayer. And yet, if the worshipper had his individual petition to offer, his own heart-secret to whisper below his breath, there were divine auditors ever ready to receive it from his lips; and what encouraged him still more, these auditors had not always been divine, but kept, within their heavenly memories, the tender humility of a human experience. Now a saint in heaven, but once a man on earth.

Hilda saw peasants, citizens, soldiers, nobles, women with bare heads, ladies in their silks, entering the churches individually, kneeling for moments, or for hours, and directing their inaudible devotions to the shrine of some saint of their own choice. In his hallowed person, they felt themselves possessed of an own friend in heaven. They were too humble to approach the Deity directly. Conscious of their unworthiness, they asked the mediation of their sympathizing patron, who, on the score of his ancient martyrdom, and after many ages of celestial life, might venture to talk with the Divine Presence, almost as friend with friend. Though dumb before its Judge, even despair could speak, and pour out the misery of its soul like water, to an advocate so wise to comprehend the case, and eloquent to plead it, and powerful to win pardon, whatever were the guilt. Hilda witnessed what she deemed to be an example of this species of confidence between a young man and his saint. He stood before a shrine, writhing, wringing his hands, contorting his whole frame in an agony of remorseful recollection, but finally knelt down to weep and pray. If this youth had been a Protestant, he would have kept all that torture pent up in his heart, and let it burn there till it seared him into indifference.

Often and long, Hilda lingered before the shrines and chapels of the Virgin, and departed from them with reluctant steps. Here, perhaps, strange as it may seem, her delicate appreciation of art stood her in good stead, and lost Catholicism a convert. If the painter had represented Mary with a heavenly face, poor Hilda was now in the very mood to worship her, and adopt the faith in which she held so elevated a position. But she saw that it was merely the flattered portrait of an earthly beauty; the wife, at best, of the artist; or, it might be, a peasant-girl of the Campagna, or some Roman princess, to whom he desired to pay his court. For love, or some even less justifiable motive, the old painter had apotheosized these women; he thus gained for them, as far as his skill would go, not only the meed of immortality, but the privilege of presiding over Christian altars, and of being worshipped with far holier fervors than while they dwelt on earth. Hilda's fine sense of the fit and decorous could not be betrayed into kneeling at such a shrine.

She never found just the virgin mother whom she needed. Here, it was an earthly mother, worshipping the earthly baby in her lap, as any and every mother does, from Eve's time downward. In another picture, there was a dim sense, shown in the mother's face, of some divine quality in the child. In a third, the artist seemed to have had a higher perception, and had striven hard to shadow out the Virgin's joy at bringing the Saviour into the world, and her awe and love, inextricably mingled, of the little form which she pressed against her bosom. So far was good. But still, Hilda looked for something more; a face of celestial beauty, but human as well as heavenly, and with the shadow of past grief upon it; bright with immortal youth, yet matronly and motherly; and endowed with a queenly dignity, but infinitely tender, as the highest and deepest attribute of her divinity.

"Ah," thought Hilda to herself, "why should not there be a woman to listen to the prayers of women? a mother in heaven for all motherless girls like me? In all God's thought and care for us, can he have withheld this boon, which our weakness so much needs?"

Oftener than to the other churches, she wandered into St. Peter's. Within its vast limits, she thought, and beneath the sweep of its great

dome, there should be space for all forms of Christian truth; room both
for the faithful and the heretic to kneel; due help for every creature's
spiritual want.

Hilda had not always been adequately impressed by the grandeur of
this mighty cathedral. When she first lifted the heavy leathern curtain, at
one of the doors, a shadowy edifice in her imagination had been dazzled
out of sight by the reality. Her preconception of St. Peter's was a structure of no definite outline, misty in its architecture, dim and gray and
huge, stretching into an interminable perspective, and over-arched by a
dome like the cloudy firmament. Beneath that vast breadth and height,
as she had fancied them, the personal man might feel his littleness, and
the soul triumph in its immensity. So, in her earlier visits, when the com-
passed splendor of the actual interior glowed before her eyes, she had pro-
fanely called it a great prettiness; a gay piece of cabinet-work, on a Titanic scale; a jewel-casket, marvellously magnified.

This latter image best pleased her fancy; a casket, all inlaid, in the inside, with precious stones of various hue, so that there should not be a
hair's-breadth of the small interior unadorned with its resplendent gem.
Then, conceive this minute wonder of a mosaic box, increased to the magnitude of a cathedral, without losing the intense lustre of its littleness, but
all its petty glory striving to be sublime. The magic transformation from
the minute to the vast has not been so cunningly effected but that the rich
adornment still counteracts the impression of space and loftiness. The
spectator is more sensible of its limits than of its extent.

Until after many visits, Hilda continued to mourn for that dim, illimitable interior, which with her eyes shut she had seen from childhood, but
which vanished at her first glimpse through the actual door. Her childish
vision seemed preferable to the cathedral which Michael Angelo, and all
the great architects, had built; because, of the dream edifice, she had
said, "How vast it is!" while of the real St. Peter's she could only say,
"After all, it is not so immense!" Besides, such as the church is, it can
nowhere be made visible at one glance. It stands in its own way. You
see an aisle, or a transept; you see the nave, or the tribune; but, on account of its ponderous piers and other obstructions, it is only by this
fragmentary process that you get an idea of the cathedral.

There is no answering such objections. The great church smiles calmly
upon its critics, and, for all response, says, "Look at me!" and if you still
murmur for the loss of your shadowy perspective, there comes no reply,
save, "Look at me!" in endless repetition, as the one thing to be said.
And, after looking many times, with long intervals between, you discover that the cathedral has gradually extended itself over the whole compass of your idea; it covers all the site of your visionary temple, and has
room for its cloudy pinnacles beneath the dome.

One afternoon, as Hilda entered St. Peter's in sombre mood, its interior beamed upon her with all the effect of a new creation. It seemed an
embodiment of whatever the imagination could conceive, or the heart desire, as a magnificent, comprehensive, majestic symbol of religious faith.

All splendor was included within its verge, and there was space for all. She gazed with delight even at the multiplicity of ornament. She was glad at the cherubim that fluttered upon the pilasters, and of the marble doves, hovering unexpectedly, with green olive-branches of precious stones. She could spare nothing, now, of the manifold magnificence that had been lavished, in a hundred places, richly enough to have made world-famous shrines in any other church, but which here melted away into the vast sunny breadth, and were of no separate account. Yet each contributed its little all towards the grandeur of the whole.

She would not have banished one of those grim popes, who sit each over his own tomb, scattering cold benedictions out of their marble hands; nor a single frozen sister of the Allegoric family, to whom—as, like hired mourners at an English funeral, it costs them no wear and tear of heart —is assigned the office of weeping for the dead. If you choose to see these things, they present themselves; if you deem them unsuitable and out of place, they vanish, individually, but leave their life upon the walls.

The pavement! it stretched out illimitably, a plain of many-colored marble, where thousands of worshippers might kneel together, and shadowless angels tread among them without brushing their heavenly garments against those earthly ones. The roof! the dome! Rich, gorgeous, filled with sunshine, cheerfully sublime, and fadeless after centuries, those lofty depths seemed to translate the heavens to mortal comprehension, and help the spirit upward to a yet higher and wider sphere. Must not the faith, that built this matchless edifice, and warmed, illuminated, and overflowed from it, include whatever can satisfy human aspirations at the loftiest, or minister to human necessity at the sorest? If Religion had a material home, was it not here?

As the scene which we but faintly suggest shone calmly before the New England maiden at her entrance, she moved, as if by very instinct, to one of the vases of holy water, upborne against a column by two mighty cherubs. Hilda dipped her fingers, and had almost signed the cross upon her breast, but forbore, and trembled, while shaking the water from her finger-tips. She felt as if her mother's spirit, somewhere within the dome, were looking down upon her child, the daughter of Puritan forefathers, and weeping to behold her ensnared by these gaudy superstitions. So she strayed sadly onward, up the nave, and towards the hundred golden lights that swarm before the high altar. Seeing a woman, a priest, and a soldier kneel to kiss the toe of the brazen St. Peter, who protrudes it beyond his pedestal, for the purpose, polished bright with former salutations, while a child stood on tiptoe to do the same, the glory of the church was darkened before Hilda's eyes. But again she went onward into remoter regions. She turned into the right transept, and thence found her way to a shrine, in the extreme corner of the edifice, which is adorned with a mosaic copy of Guido's beautiful Archangel, treading on the prostrate fiend.

This was one of the few pictures, which, in these dreary days, had not faded nor deteriorated in Hilda's estimation; not that it was better than many in which she no longer took an interest; but the subtile delicacy of the painter's genius was peculiarly adapted to her character. She felt, while gazing at it, that the artist had done a great thing, not merely for the Church of Rome, but for the cause of Good. The moral of the picture, the immortal youth and loveliness of Virtue, and its irresistible might against ugly Evil, appealed as much to Puritans as Catholics.

Suddenly, and as if it were done in a dream, Hilda found herself kneeling before the shrine, under the ever-burning lamp that throws its rays upon the Archangel's face. She laid her forehead on the marble steps before the altar, and sobbed out a prayer; she hardly knew to whom, whether Michael, the Virgin, or the Father; she hardly knew for what, save only a vague longing, that thus the burden of her spirit might be lightened a little.

In an instant she snatched herself up, as it were, from her knees, all a-throb with the emotions which were struggling to force their way out of her heart by the avenue that had so nearly been opened for them. Yet there was a strange sense of relief won by that momentary, passionate prayer; a strange joy, moreover, whether from what she had done, or for what she had escaped doing, Hilda could not tell. But she felt as one half stifled, who has stolen a breath of air.

Next to the shrine where she had knelt, there is another, adorned with a picture by Guercino, representing a maiden's body in the jaws of the sepulchre, and her lover weeping over it; while her beatified spirit looks down upon the scene, in the society of the Saviour and a throng of saints. Hilda wondered if it were not possible, by some miracle of faith, so to rise above her present despondency that she might look down upon what she was, just as Petronilla in the picture looked at her own corpse. A hope, born of hysteric trouble, fluttered in her heart. A presentiment, or what she fancied such, whispered her, that, before she had finished the circuit of the cathedral, relief would come.

The unhappy are continually tantalized by similar delusions of succor near at hand; at least, the despair is very dark that has no such will-o'-the-wisp to glimmer in it.

## CHAPTER XXXIX

### THE WORLD'S CATHEDRAL

STILL gliding onward, Hilda now looked up into the dome, where the sunshine came through the western windows, and threw across long shafts of light. They rested upon the mosaic figures of two evangelists above the cornice. These great beams of radiance, traversing what seemed the empty space, were made visible in misty glory, by the holy cloud of incense, else unseen, which had risen into the middle dome. It was to Hilda as if she beheld the worship of the priest and people ascending heavenward, purified from its alloy of earth, and acquiring celestial substance in the golden atmosphere to which it aspired. She wondered if angels did not sometimes hover within the dome, and show themselves, in brief glimpses, floating amid the sunshine and the glorified vapor, to those who devoutly worshipped on the pavement.

She had now come into the southern transept. Around this portion of the church are ranged a number of confessionals. They are small tabernacles of carved wood, with a closet for the priest in the centre; and, on either side, a space for a penitent to kneel, and breathe his confession through a perforated auricle into the good father's ear. Observing this arrangement, though already familiar to her, our poor Hilda was anew impressed with the infinite convenience—if we may use so poor a phrase —of the Catholic religion to its devout believers.

Who, in truth, that considers the matter, can resist a similar impression! In the hottest fever-fit of life, they can always find, ready for their need, a cool, quiet, beautiful place of worship. They may enter its sacred precincts at any hour, leaving the fret and trouble of the world behind them, and purifying themselves with a touch of holy water at the threshold. In the calm interior, fragrant of rich and soothing incense, they may hold converse with some saint, their awful, kindly friend. And, most precious privilege of all, whatever perplexity, sorrow, guilt, may weigh upon their souls, they can fling down the dark burden at the foot of the cross, and go forth—to sin no more, nor be any longer disquieted; but to live again in the freshness and elasticity of innocence.

"Do not these inestimable advantages," thought Hilda, "or some of them at least, belong to Christianity itself? Are they not a part of the blessings which the system was meant to bestow upon mankind? Can the faith in which I was born and bred be perfect, if it leave a weak girl like me to wander, desolate, with this great trouble crushing me down?"

A poignant anguish thrilled within her breast; it was like a thing that had life, and was struggling to get out.

"Oh, help! Oh, help!" cried Hilda; "I cannot, cannot bear it!"

Only by the reverberations that followed—arch echoing the sound to arch, and a pope of bronze repeating it to a pope of marble, as each sat enthroned over his tomb—did Hilda become aware that she had really spoken above her breath. But, in that great space, there is no need to hush up the heart within one's own bosom, so carefully as elsewhere; and if the cry reached any distant auditor, it came broken into many fragments, and from various quarters of the church.

Approaching one of the confessionals, she saw a woman kneeling within. Just as Hilda drew near, the penitent rose, came forth, and kissed the hand of the priest, who regarded her with a look of paternal benignity, and appeared to be giving her some spiritual counsel, in a low voice. She then knelt to receive his blessing, which was fervently bestowed. Hilda was so struck with the peace and joy in the woman's face, that, as the latter retired, she could not help speaking to her.

"You look very happy!" said she. "Is it so sweet, then, to go to the confessional?"

"Oh, very sweet, my dear signorina!" answered the woman, with moistened eyes and an affectionate smile; for she was so thoroughly softened with what she had been doing, that she felt as if Hilda were her younger sister. "My heart is at rest now. Thanks be to the Saviour, and the Blessed Virgin and the saints, and this good father, there is no more trouble for poor Teresa!"

"I am glad for your sake," said Hilda, sighing for her own. "I am a poor heretic, but a human sister; and I rejoice for you!"

She went from one to another of the confessionals, and, looking at each, perceived that they were inscribed with gilt letters: on one, PRO ITALICA LINGUA; on another, PRO FLANDRICA LINGUA; on a third, PRO POLONICA LINGUA; on a fourth, PRO ILLYRICA LINGUA; on a fifth, PRO HISPANICA LINGUA. In this vast and hospitable cathedral, worthy to be the religious heart of the whole world, there was room for all nations; there was access to the Divine Grace for every Christian soul; there was an ear for what the overburdened heart might have to murmur, speak in what native tongue it would.

When Hilda had almost completed the circuit of the transept, she came to a confessional—the central part was closed, but a mystic rod protruded from it, indicating the presence of a priest within—on which was inscribed, PRO ANGLICA LINGUA.

It was the word in season! If she had heard her mother's voice from within the tabernacle, calling her, in her own mother-tongue, to come and lay her poor head in her lap, and sob out all her troubles, Hilda could not have responded with a more inevitable obedience. She did not think; she only felt. Within her heart was a great need. Close at hand, within the veil of the confessional, was the relief. She flung herself down in the penitent's place; and, tremulously, passionately, with sobs, tears, and the turbulent overflow of emotion too long repressed, she poured out the dark story which had infused its poison into her innocent life.

Hilda had not seen, nor could she now see the visage of the priest. But, at intervals, in the pauses of that strange confession, half choked by the struggle of her feelings toward an outlet, she heard a mild, calm voice, somewhat mellowed by age. It spoke soothingly; it encouraged her; it led her on by apposite questions that seemed to be suggested by a great and tender interest, and acted like magnetism in attracting the girl's confidence to this unseen friend. The priest's share in the interview, indeed, resembled that of one who removes the stones, clustered branches, or whatever entanglements impede the current of a swollen stream. Hilda could have imagined—so much to the purpose were his inquiries—that he was already acquainted with some outline of what she strove to tell him.

Thus assisted, she revealed the whole of her terrible secret! The whole, except that no name escaped her lips.

And, ah, what a relief! When the hysteric gasp, the strife between words and sobs, had subsided, what a torture had passed away from her soul! It was all gone; her bosom was as pure now as in her childhood. She was a girl again; she was Hilda of the dove-cote; not that doubtful creature whom her own doves had hardly recognized as their mistress and playmate, by reason of the death-scent that clung to her garments!

After she had ceased to speak, Hilda heard the priest bestir himself with an old man's reluctant movement. He stepped out of the confessional; and as the girl was still kneeling in the penitential corner, he summoned her forth.

"Stand up, my daughter," said the mild voice of the confessor; "what we have further to say must be spoken face to face."

Hilda did his bidding, and stood before him with a downcast visage, which flushed and grew pale again. But it had the wonderful beauty which we may often observe in those who have recently gone through a great struggle, and won the peace that lies just on the other side. We see it in a new mother's face; we see it in the faces of the dead; and in Hilda's countenance—which had always a rare natural charm for her friends—this glory of peace made her as lovely as an angel.

On her part, Hilda beheld a venerable figure with hair as white as snow, and a face strikingly characterized by benevolence. It bore marks of thought, however, and penetrative insight; although the keen glances of the eyes were now somewhat bedimmed with tears, which the aged shed, or almost shed, on lighter stress of emotion than would elicit them from younger men.

"It has not escaped my observation, daughter," said the priest, "that this is your first acquaintance with the confessional. How is this?"

"Father," replied Hilda, raising her eyes, and again letting them fall, "I am of New England birth, and was bred as what you call a heretic."

"From New England!" exclaimed the priest. "It was my own birthplace, likewise; nor have fifty years of absence made me cease to love it. But, a heretic! And are you reconciled to the Church?"

"Never, father," said Hilda.

"And, that being the case," demanded the old man, "on what ground, my daughter, have you sought to avail yourself of these blessed privileges, confined exclusively to members of the one true Church, of confession and absolution?"

"Absolution, father?" exclaimed Hilda, shrinking back. "Oh no, no! I never dreamed of that! Only our Heavenly Father can forgive my sins; and it is only by sincere repentance of whatever wrong I may have done, and by my own best efforts towards a higher life, that I can hope for his forgiveness! God forbid that I should ask absolution from mortal man!"

"Then, wherefore," rejoined the priest, with somewhat less mildness in his tone,—"wherefore, I ask again, have you taken possession, as I may term it, of this holy ordinance; being a heretic, and neither seeking to share, nor having faith in, the unspeakable advantages which the Church offers to its penitents?"

"Father," answered Hilda, trying to tell the old man the simple truth, "I am a motherless girl, and a stranger here in Italy. I had only God to take care of me, and be my closest friend; and the terrible, terrible crime, which I have revealed to you, thrust itself between him and me; so that I groped for him in the darkness, as it were, and found him not,—found nothing but a dreadful solitude, and this crime in the midst of it! I could not bear it. It seemed as if I made the awful guilt my own, by keeping it hidden in my heart. I grew a fearful thing to myself. I was going mad!"

"It was a grievous trial, my poor child!" observed the confessor. "Your relief, I trust, will prove to be greater than you yet know!"

"I feel already how immense it is!" said Hilda, looking gratefully in his face. "Surely, father, it was the hand of Providence that led me hither, and made me feel that this vast temple of Christianity, this great home of religion, must needs contain some cure, some ease, at least, for my unutterable anguish. And it has proved so. I have told the hideous secret; told it under the sacred seal of the confessional; and now it will burn my poor heart no more!"

"But, daughter," answered the venerable priest, not unmoved by what Hilda said, "you forget! you mistake!—you claim a privilege to which you have not entitled yourself! The seal of the confessional, do you say? God forbid that it should ever be broken where it has been fairly impressed; but it applies only to matters that have been confided to its keeping in a certain prescribed method, and by persons, moreover, who have faith in the sanctity of the ordinance. I hold myself, and any learned casuist of the Church would hold me, as free to disclose all the particulars of what you term your confession, as if they had come to my knowledge in a secular way."

"This is not right, father!" said Hilda, fixing her eyes on the old man's.

"Do not you see, child," he rejoined, with some little heat, "with all your nicety of conscience, cannot you recognize it as my duty to make the story known to the proper authorities; a great crime against public justice being involved, and further evil consequences likely to ensue?"

"No, father, no!" answered Hilda, courageously, her cheeks flushing and her eyes brightening as she spoke. "Trust a girl's simple heart sooner than any casuist of your Church, however learned he may be. Trust your own heart, too! I came to your confessional, father, as I devoutly believe, by the direct impulse of Heaven, which also brought you hither to-day, in its mercy and love, to relieve me of a torture that I could no longer bear. I trusted in the pledge which your Church has always held sacred between the priest and the human soul, which, through his medium, is struggling towards its Father above. What I have confided to you lies sacredly between God and yourself. Let it rest there, father; for this is right, and if you do otherwise, you will perpetrate a great wrong, both as a priest and a man! And, believe me, no question, no torture, shall ever force my lips to utter what would be necessary, in order to make my confession available towards the punishment of the guilty ones. Leave Providence to deal with them!"

"My quiet little countrywoman," said the priest, with half a smile on his kindly old face, "you can pluck up a spirit, I perceive, when you fancy an occasion for one."

"I have spirit only to do what I think right," replied Hilda, simply. "In other respects I am timorous."

"But you confuse yourself between right feelings and very foolish inferences," continued the priest, "as is the wont of women,—so much I have learnt by long experience in the confessional,—be they young or old. However, to set your heart at rest, there is no probable need for me to reveal the matter. What you have told, if I mistake not, and perhaps more, is already known in the quarter which it most concerns."

"Known!" exclaimed Hilda. "Known to the authorities of Rome! And what will be the consequence?"

"Hush," answered the confessor, laying his finger on his lips. "I tell you my supposition—mind, it is no assertion of the fact—in order that you may go the more cheerfully on your way, not deeming yourself burdened with any responsibility as concerns this dark deed. And now, daughter, what have you to give in return for an old man's kindness and sympathy?"

"My grateful remembrance," said Hilda, fervently, "as long as I live!"

"And nothing more?" the priest inquired, with a persuasive smile. "Will you not reward him with a great joy; one of the last joys that he may know on earth, and a fit one to take with him into the better world? In a word, will you not allow me to bring you, as a stray lamb into the true fold? You have experienced some little taste of the relief and comfort which the Church keeps abundantly in store for all its faithful children. Come home, dear child,—poor wanderer, who hast caught a glimpse of the heavenly light,—come home, and be at rest."

"Father," said Hilda, much moved by his kindly earnestness; in which, however, genuine as it was, there might still be a leaven of professional craft, "I dare not come a step farther than Providence shall guide me. Do not let it grieve you, therefore, if I never return to the confessional; never dip my fingers in holy water; never sign my bosom with the cross. I am a daughter of the Puritans. But, in spite of my heresy," she added with a sweet, tearful smile, "you may one day see the poor girl, to whom you have done this great Christian kindness, coming to remind you of it, and thank you for it, in the Better Land."

The old priest shook his head. But as he stretched out his hands at the same moment, in the act of benediction, Hilda knelt down and received the blessing with as devout a simplicity as any Catholic of them all.

## CHAPTER XL

## HILDA AND A FRIEND

WHEN Hilda knelt to receive the priest's benediction, the act was witnessed by a person who stood leaning against the marble balustrade that surrounds the hundred golden lights, before the high altar. He had stood there, indeed, from the moment of the girl's entrance into the confessional. His start of surprise, at first beholding her, and the anxious gloom that afterwards settled on his face, sufficiently betokened that he felt a deep and sad interest in what was going forward.

After Hilda had bidden the priest farewell, she came slowly towards the high altar. The individual, to whom we have alluded, seemed irresolute whether to advance or retire. His hesitation lasted so long, that the maiden, straying through a happy reverie, had crossed the wide extent of the pavement between the confessional and the altar, before he had decided whether to meet her. At last, when within a pace or two, she raised her eyes and recognized Kenyon.

"It is you!" she exclaimed, with joyful surprise. "I am so happy."

In truth, the sculptor had never before seen, nor hardly imagined, such a figure of peaceful beatitude as Hilda now presented. While coming towards him in the solemn radiance which, at that period of the day, is diffused through the transept, and showered down beneath the dome, she seemed of the same substance as the atmosphere that enveloped her. He could scarcely tell whether she was imbued with sunshine, or whether it was a glow of happiness that shone out of her.

At all events, it was a marvellous change from the sad girl, who had entered the confessional bewildered with anguish, to this bright, yet softened image of religious consolation that emerged from it. It was as if one of the throng of angelic people, who might be hovering in the sunny depths of the dome, had alighted on the pavement. Indeed, this capability of transfiguration, which we often see wrought by inward delight on persons far less capable of it than Hilda, suggests how angels come by their beauty. It grows out of their happiness, and lasts forever only because that is immortal.

She held out her hand, and Kenyon was glad to take it in his own, if only to assure himself that she was made of earthly material.

"Yes, Hilda, I see that you are very happy," he replied, gloomily, and withdrawing his hand after a single pressure. "For me, I never was less so than at this moment."

"Has any misfortune befallen you?" asked Hilda, with earnestness. "Pray tell me, and you shall have my sympathy, though I must still be very happy. Now, I know how it is, that the saints above are touched by the sorrows of distressed people on earth, and yet are never made wretched by them. Not that I profess to be a saint, you know," she added, smiling radiantly. "But the heart grows so large, and so rich, and so variously endowed, when it has a great sense of bliss, that it can give smiles to some, and tears to others, with equal sincerity, and enjoy its own peace throughout all."

"Do not say you are no saint!" answered Kenyon, with a smile, though he felt that the tears stood in his eyes. "You will still be Saint Hilda, whatever church may canonize you."

"Ah! you would not have said so, had you seen me but an hour ago!" murmured she. "I was so wretched, that there seemed a grievous sin in it."

"And what has made you so suddenly happy?" inquired the sculptor. "But first, Hilda, will you not tell me why you were so wretched?"

"Had I met you yesterday, I might have told you that," she replied. "To-day, there is no need."

"Your happiness, then?" said the sculptor, as sadly as before. "Whence comes it?"

"A great burden has been lifted from my heart,—from my conscience, I had almost said,"—answered Hilda, without shunning the glance that he fixed upon her. "I am a new creature, since this morning, Heaven be praised for it! It was a blessed hour—a blessed impulse—that brought me to this beautiful and glorious cathedral. I shall hold it in loving remembrance while I live, as the spot where I found infinite peace after infinite trouble."

Her heart seemed so full, that it spilt its new gush of happiness, as it were, like rich and sunny wine out of an over-brimming goblet. Kenyon saw that she was in one of those moods of elevated feeling, when the soul is upheld by a strange tranquillity, which is really more passionate, and less controllable, than emotions far exceeding it in violence. He felt that there would be indelicacy, if he ought not rather to call it impiety, in his stealing upon Hilda, while she was thus beyond her own guardianship, and surprising her out of secrets which she might afterwards bitterly regret betraying to him. Therefore, though yearning to know what had happened, he resolved to forbear further question.

Simple and earnest people, however, being accustomed to speak from their genuine impulses, cannot easily, as craftier men do, avoid the subject which they have at heart. As often as the sculptor unclosed his lips, such words as these were ready to burst out:—

"Hilda, have you flung your angelic purity into that mass of unspeakable corruption, the Roman Church?"

"What were you saying?" she asked, as Kenyon forced back an almost uttered exclamation of this kind.

"I was thinking of what you have just remarked about the cathedral," said he, looking up into the mighty hollow of the dome. "It is indeed a magnificent structure, and an adequate expression of the Faith which built it. When I behold it in a proper mood,—that is to say, when I bring my mind into a fair relation with the minds and purposes of its spiritual and material architects,—I see but one or two criticisms to make. One is, that it needs painted windows."

"Oh, no!" said Hilda. "They would be quite inconsistent with so much richness of color in the interior of the church. Besides, it is a Gothic ornament, and only suited to that style of architecture, which requires a gorgeous dimness."

"Nevertheless," continued the sculptor, "yonder square apertures, filled with ordinary panes of glass, are quite out of keeping with the superabundant splendor of everything about them. They remind me of that portion of Aladdin's palace which he left unfinished, in order that his royal father-in-law might put the finishing touch. Daylight, in its natural state, ought not to be admitted here. It should stream through a brilliant illusion of saints and hierarchies, and old scriptural images, and symbolized dogmas, purple, blue, golden, and a broad flame of scarlet. Then, it would be just such an illumination as the Catholic faith allows to its believers. But, give me—to live and die in—the pure, white light of heaven!"

"Why do you look so sorrowfully at me?" asked Hilda, quietly meeting his disturbed gaze. "What would you say to me? I love the white light too!"

"I fancied so," answered Kenyon. "Forgive me, Hilda; but I must needs speak. You seemed to me a rare mixture of impressibility, sympathy, sensitiveness to many influences, with a certain quality of common sense;—no, not that, but a higher and finer attribute, for which I find no better word. However tremulously you might vibrate, this quality, I supposed, would always bring you back to the equipoise. You were a creature of imagination, and yet as truly a New England girl as any with whom you grew up in your native village. If there were one person in the world whose native rectitude of thought, and something deeper, more reliable, than thought, I would have trusted against all the arts of a priesthood,—whose taste alone, so exquisite and sincere that it rose to be a moral virtue, I would have rested upon as a sufficient safeguard,—it was yourself!"

"I am conscious of no such high and delicate qualities as you allow me," answered Hilda. "But what have I done that a girl of New England birth and culture, with the right sense that her mother taught her, and the conscience that she developed in her, should not do?"

"Hilda, I saw you at the confessional!" said Kenyon.

"Ah, well, my dear friend," replied Hilda casting down her eyes, and looking somewhat confused, yet not ashamed, "you must try to forgive me for that,—if you deem it wrong,—because it has saved my reason, and made me very happy. Had you been here yesterday, I would have confessed to you."

"Would to Heaven I had!" ejaculated Kenyon.

"I think," Hilda resumed, "I shall never go to the confessional again; for there can scarcely come such a sore trial twice in my life. If I had been a wiser girl, a stronger, and a more sensible, very likely I might not have gone to the confessional at all. It was the sin of others that drove me thither; not my own, though it almost seemed so. Being what I am, I must either have done what you saw me doing, or have gone mad. Would that have been better?"

"Then you are not a Catholic?" asked the sculptor, earnestly.

"Really, I do not quite know what I am," replied Hilda, encountering his eyes with a frank and simple gaze. "I have a great deal of faith, and Catholicism seems to have a great deal of good. Why should not I be a Catholic, if I find there what I need, and what I cannot find elsewhere? The more I see of this worship, the more I wonder at the exuberance with which it adapts itself to all the demands of human infirmity. If its ministers were but a little more than human, above all error, pure from all iniquity, what a religion would it be!"

"I need not fear your conversion to the Catholic faith," remarked Kenyon, "if you are at all aware of the bitter sarcasm implied in your last observation. It is very just. Only the exceeding ingenuity of the system stamps it as the contrivance of man, or some worse author; not an emanation of the broad and simple wisdom from on high."

"It may be so," said Hilda; "but I meant no sarcasm."

Thus conversing, the two friends went together down the grand extent of the nave. Before leaving the church, they turned to admire again its mighty breadth, the remoteness of the glory behind the altar, and the effect of visionary splendor and magnificence imparted by the long bars of smoky sunshine, which travelled so far before arriving at a place of rest.

"Thank Heaven for having brought me hither!" said Hilda, fervently.

Kenyon's mind was deeply disturbed by his idea of her Catholic propensities; and now what he deemed her disproportionate and misapplied veneration for the sublime edifice stung him into irreverence.

"The best thing I know of St. Peter's," observed he, "is its equable temperature. We are now enjoying the coolness of last winter, which, a few months hence, will be the warmth of the present summer. It has no cure, I suspect, in all its length and breadth, for a sick soul, but it would make an admirable atmospheric hospital for sick bodies. What a delightful shelter would it be for the invalids who throng to Rome, where the sirocco steals away their strength, and the tramontana stabs them through and through, like cold steel with a poisoned point! But within these walls, the thermometer never varies. Winter and summer are married at the high altar, and dwell together in perfect harmony."

"Yes," said Hilda; "and I have always felt this soft, unchanging climate of St. Peter's to be another manifestation of its sanctity."

"That is not precisely my idea," replied Kenyon. "But what a delicious life it would be, if a colony of people with delicate lungs—or merely with delicate fancies—could take up their abode in this ever-mild and tranquil air. These architectural tombs of the popes might serve for dwellings, and each brazen sepulchral doorway would become a domestic threshold. Then the lover, if he dared, might say to his mistress, 'Will you share my tomb with me?' and, winning her soft consent, he would lead her to the altar, and thence to yonder sepulchre of Pope Gregory, which should be their nuptial home. What a life would be theirs, Hilda, in their marble Eden!"

"It is not kind, nor like yourself," said Hilda, gently, "to throw ridicule on emotions which are genuine. I revere this glorious church for itself and its purposes; and love it, moreover, because here I have found sweet peace, after a great anguish."

"Forgive me," answered the sculptor, "and I will do so no more. My heart is not so irreverent as my words."

They went through the piazza of St. Peter's and the adjacent streets, silently at first; but, before reaching the bridge of St. Angelo, Hilda's flow of spirits began to bubble forth, like the gush of a streamlet that has been shut up, by frost, or by a heavy stone over its source. Kenyon had never found her so delightful as now; so softened out of the chillness of her virgin pride; so full of fresh thoughts, at which he was often moved to smile, although, on turning them over a little more, he sometimes discovered that they looked fanciful only because so absolutely true.

But, indeed, she was not quite in a normal state. Emerging from gloom into sudden cheerfulness, the effect upon Hilda was as if she were just now created. After long torpor, receiving back her intellectual activity, she derived an exquisite pleasure from the use of her faculties, which were set in motion by causes that seemed inadequate. She continually brought to Kenyon's mind the image of a child, making its plaything of every object, but sporting in good faith, and with a kind of seriousness. Looking up, for example, at the statue of St. Michael, on the top of Hadrian's castellated tomb, Hilda fancied an interview between the Archangel and the old emperor's ghost, who was naturally displeased at finding his mausoleum, which he had ordained for the stately and solemn repose of his ashes, converted to its present purposes.

"But St. Michael, no doubt," she thoughtfully remarked, "would finally convince the Emperor Hadrian that where a warlike despot is sown as the seed, a fortress and a prison are the only possible crop."

They stopped on the bridge to look into the swift eddying flow of the yellow Tiber, a mud-puddle in strenuous motion; and Hilda wondered whether the seven-branched golden candlestick,—the holy candlestick of the Jews,—which was lost at the Ponte Molle, in Constantine's time, had yet been swept as far down the river as this.

"It probably stuck where it fell," said the sculptor; "and, by this time, is imbedded thirty feet deep in the mud of the Tiber. Nothing will ever bring it to light again."

"I fancy you are mistaken," replied Hilda, smiling. "There was a meaning and purpose in each of its seven branches, and such a candlestick cannot be lost forever. When it is found again, and seven lights are kindled and burning in it, the whole world will gain the illumination which it needs. Would not this be an admirable idea for a mystic story or parable, or seven-branched allegory, full of poetry, art, philosophy, and religion? It shall be called 'The Recovery of the Sacred Candlestick.' As each branch is lighted, it shall have a differently colored lustre from the other six; and when all the seven are kindled, their radiance shall combine into the intense white light of truth."

"Positively, Hilda, this is a magnificent conception," cried Kenyon. "The more I look at it, the brighter it burns."

"I think so too," said Hilda, enjoying a childlike pleasure in her own idea. "The theme is better suited for verse than prose; and when I go home to America, I will suggest it to one of our poets. Or, seven poets might write the poem together, each lighting a separate branch of the Sacred Candlestick."

"Then you think of going home?" Kenyon asked.

"Only yesterday," she replied, "I longed to flee away. Now, all is changed, and, being happy again, I should feel deep regret at leaving the Pictorial Land. But, I cannot tell. In Rome, there is something dreary and awful, which we can never quite escape. At least, I thought so yesterday."

When they reached the Via Portoghese, and approached Hilda's tower, the doves, who were waiting aloft, flung themselves upon the air, and came floating down about her head. The girl caressed them, and responded to their cooings with similar sounds from her own lips, and with words of endearment; and their joyful flutterings and airy little flights, evidently impelled by pure exuberance of spirits, seemed to show that the doves had a real sympathy with their mistress's state of mind. For peace had descended upon her like a dove.

Bidding the sculptor farewell, Hilda climbed her tower, and came forth upon its summit to trim the Virgin's lamp. The doves, well knowing her custom, had flown up thither to meet her, and again hovered about her head; and very lovely was her aspect, in the evening sunlight, which had little further to do with the world, just then, save to fling a golden glory on Hilda's hair, and vanish.

Turning her eyes down into the dusky street which she had just quitted, Hilda saw the sculptor still there, and waved her hand to him.

"How sad and dim he looks, down there in that dreary street!" she said to herself. "Something weighs upon his spirits. Would I could comfort him!"

"How like a spirit she looks, aloft there, with the evening glory round her head, and those winged creatures claiming her as akin to them!" thought Kenyon, on his part. "How far above me! how unattainable! Ah, if I could lift myself to her region! Or,—if it be not a sin to wish it,—would that I might draw her down to an earthly fireside!"

What a sweet reverence is that, when a young man deems his mistress a little more than mortal, and almost chides himself for longing to bring her close to his heart! A trifling circumstance, but such as lovers make much of, gave him hope. One of the doves, which had been resting on Hilda's shoulder, suddenly flew downward, as if recognizing him as its mistress's dear friend; and, perhaps commissioned with an errand of regard, brushed his upturned face with its wings, and again soared aloft.

The sculptor watched the bird's return, and saw Hilda greet it with a smile.

## CHAPTER XLI

### SNOW-DROPS AND MAIDENLY DELIGHTS

IT being still considerably earlier than the period at which artists and tourists are accustomed to assemble in Rome, the sculptor and Hilda found themselves comparatively alone there. The dense mass of native Roman life, in the midst of which they were, served to press them near one another. It was as if they had been thrown together on a desert island. Or, they seemed to have wandered, by some strange chance, out of the common world, and encountered each other in a depopulated city, where there were streets of lonely palaces, and unreckonable treasures of beautiful and admirable things, of which they two became the sole inheritors.

In such circumstances, Hilda's gentle reserve must have been stronger than her kindly disposition permitted, if the friendship between Kenyon and herself had not grown as warm as a maiden's friendship can ever be, without absolutely and avowedly blooming into love. On the sculptor's side, the amaranthine flower was already in full blow. But it is very beautiful, though the lover's heart may grow chill at the perception, to see how the snow will sometimes linger in a virgin's breast, even after the spring is well advanced. In such alpine soils, the summer will not be anticipated; we seek vainly for passionate flowers, and blossoms of fervid hue and spicy fragrance, finding only snow-drops and sunless violets, when it is almost the full season for the crimson rose.

With so much tenderness as Hilda had in her nature, it was strange that she so reluctantly admitted the idea of love; especially, as, in the sculptor, she found both congeniality and variety of taste, and likenesses and differences of character; these being as essential as those to any poignancy of mutual emotion.

So Hilda, as far as Kenyon could discern, still did not love him, though she admitted him within the quiet circle of her affections as a dear friend and trusty counsellor. If we knew what is best for us, or could be content with what is reasonably good, the sculptor might well have been satisfied, for a season, with this calm intimacy, which so sweetly kept him a stranger in her heart, and a ceremonious guest; and yet allowed him the free enjoyment of all but its deeper recesses. The flowers that grow outside of those minor sanctities have a wild, hasty charm, which it is well to prove; there may be sweeter ones within the sacred precinct, but none that will die while you are handling them, and bequeath you a delicious legacy, as these do, in the perception of their evanescence and unreality.

And this may be the reason, after all, why Hilda, like so many other maidens, lingered on the hither side of passion; her finer instinct and keener sensibility made her enjoy those pale delights in a degree of which men are incapable. She hesitated to grasp a richer happiness, as possessing already such measure of it as her heart could hold, and of a quality most agreeable to her virgin tastes.

Certainly, they both were very happy. Kenyon's genius, unconsciously wrought upon by Hilda's influence, took a more delicate character than heretofore. He modelled, among other things, a beautiful little statue of maidenhood gathering a snow-drop. It was never put into marble, however, because the sculptor soon recognized it as one of those fragile creations which are true only to the moment that produces them, and are wronged if we try to imprison their airy excellence in a permanent material.

On her part, Hilda returned to her customary occupations with a fresh love for them, and yet with a deeper look into the heart of things; such as those necessarily acquire who have passed from picture galleries into dungeon gloom, and thence come back to the picture gallery again. It is questionable whether she was ever so perfect a copyist thenceforth. She could not yield herself up to the painter so unreservedly as in times past; her character had developed a sturdier quality, which made her less pliable to the influence of other minds. She saw into the picture as profoundly as ever, and perhaps more so, but not with the devout sympathy that had formerly given her entire possession of the old master's idea. She had known such a reality, that it taught her to distinguish inevitably the large portion that is unreal, in every work of art. Instructed by sorrow, she felt that there is something beyond almost all which pictorial genius has produced; and she never forgot those sad wanderings from gallery to gallery, and from church to church, where she had vainly sought a type of the Virgin Mother, or the Saviour, or saint, or martyr, which a soul in extreme need might recognize as the adequate one.

How, indeed, should she have found such? How could holiness be revealed to the artist of an age when the greatest of them put genius and imagination in the place of spiritual insight, and when, from the pope downward, all Christendom was corrupt?

Meanwhile, months wore away, and Rome received back that large portion of its life-blood which runs in the veins of its foreign and temporary population. English visitors established themselves in the hotels, and in all the sunny suites of apartments, in the streets convenient to the Piazza di Spagna; the English tongue was heard familiarly along the Corso, and English children sported in the Pincian Gardens.

The native Romans, on the other hand, like the butterflies and grasshoppers, resigned themselves to the short, sharp misery which winter brings to a people whose arrangements are made almost exclusively with a view to summer. Keeping no fire within doors, except possibly a spark or two in the kitchen, they crept out of their cheerless houses into the narrow, sunless, sepulchral streets, bringing their firesides along with them, in the shape of little earthen pots, vases, or pipkins, full of lighted charcoal and warm ashes, over which they held their tingling finger-ends. Even in this half-torpid wretchedness, they still seemed to dread a pestilence in the sunshine, and kept on the shady side of the piazzas, as scrupulously as in summer. Through the open doorways—no need to shut them when the weather within was bleaker than without—a glimpse into the interior of their dwellings showed the uncarpeted brick floors, as dismal as the pavement of a tomb.

They drew their old cloaks about them, nevertheless, and threw the corners over their shoulders, with the dignity of attitude and action that have come down to these modern citizens, as their sole inheritance from the togated nation. Somehow or other, they managed to keep up their poor, frost-bitten hearts against the pitiless atmosphere with a quiet and uncomplaining endurance that really seems the most respectable point in the present Roman character. For, in New England, or in Russia, or scarcely in a hut of the Esquimaux, there is no such discomfort to be borne as by Romans in wintry weather, when the orange-trees bear icy fruit in the gardens; and when the rims of all the fountains are shaggy with icicles, and the Fountain of Trevi skimmed almost across with a glassy surface; and when there is a slide in the piazza of St. Peter's, and a fringe of brown, frozen foam along the eastern shore of the Tiber, and sometimes a fall of great snow-flakes into the dreary lanes and alleys of the miserable city. Cold blasts, that bring death with them, now blow upon the shivering invalids, who came hither in the hope of breathing balmy airs.

Wherever we pass our summers, may all our inclement months, from November to April, henceforth be spent in some country that recognizes winter as an integral portion of its year!

Now, too, there was especial discomfort in the stately picture galleries, where nobody, indeed,—not the princely or priestly founders, nor any who have inherited their cheerless magnificence,—ever dreamed of such an impossibility as fireside warmth, since those great palaces were built. Hilda, therefore, finding her fingers so much benumbed that the spiritual influence could not be transmitted to them, was persuaded to leave her easel before a picture, on one of these wintry days, and pay a visit to Kenyon's studio. But neither was the studio anything better than a dismal den, with its marble shapes shivering around the walls, cold as the snow-images which the sculptor used to model in his boyhood, and sadly behold them weep themselves away at the first thaw.

Kenyon's Roman artisans, all this while, had been at work on the Cleopatra. The fierce Egyptian queen had now struggled almost out of the imprisoning stone; or, rather, the workmen had found her within the mass of marble, imprisoned there by magic, but still fervid to the touch with fiery life, the fossil woman of an age that produced statelier, stronger, and more passionate creatures than our own. You already felt her compressed heat, and were aware of a tiger-like character even in her repose. If Octavius should make his appearance, though the marble still held her within its embrace, it was evident that she would tear herself forth in a twinkling, either to spring enraged at his throat, or, sinking into his arms, to make one more proof of her rich blandishments, or, falling lowly at his feet, to try the efficacy of a woman's tears.

"I am ashamed to tell you how much I admire this statue," said Hilda. "No other sculptor could have done it."

"This is very sweet for me to hear," replied Kenyon; "and since your reserve keeps you from saying more, I shall imagine you expressing everything that an artist would wish to hear said about his work."

"You will not easily go beyond my genuine opinion," answered Hilda, with a smile.

"Ah, your kind word makes me very happy," said the sculptor, "and I need it, just now, on behalf of my Cleopatra. That inevitable period has come,—for I have found it inevitable, in regard to all my works,—when I look at what I fancied to be a statue, lacking only breath to make it live, and find it a mere lump of senseless stone, into which I have not really succeeded in moulding the spiritual part of my idea. I should like, now,— only it would be such shameful treatment for a discrowned queen, and my own offspring too,—I should like to hit poor Cleopatra a bitter blow on her Egyptian nose with this mallet."

"That is a blow which all statues seemed doomed to receive, sooner or later, though seldom from the hand that sculptured them," said Hilda, laughing. "But you must not let yourself be too much disheartened by the decay of your faith in what you produce. I have heard a poet express similar distaste for his own most exquisite poem, and I am afraid that this final despair, and sense of short-coming, must always be the reward and punishment of those who try to grapple with a great or beautiful idea. It only proves that you have been able to imagine things too high for mortal faculties to execute. The idea leaves you an imperfect image of itself, which you at first mistake for the ethereal reality, but soon find that the latter has escaped out of your closest embrace."

"And the only consolation is," remarked Kenyon, "that the blurred and imperfect image may still make a very respectable appearance in the eyes of those who have not seen the original."

"More than that," rejoined Hilda; "for there is a class of spectators whose sympathy will help them to see the perfect through a mist of imperfection. Nobody, I think, ought to read poetry, or look at pictures or statues, who cannot find a great deal more in them than the poet or artist has actually expressed. Their highest merit is suggestiveness."

"You, Hilda, are yourself the only critic in whom I have much faith," said Kenyon. "Had you condemned Cleopatra, nothing should have saved her."

"You invest me with such an awful responsibility," she replied, "that I shall not dare to say a single word about your other works."

"At least," said the sculptor, "tell me whether you recognize this bust?"

He pointed to the bust of Donatello. It was not the one which Kenyon had begun to model at Monte Beni, but a reminiscence of the Count's face, wrought under the influence of all the sculptor's knowledge of his history, and of his personal and hereditary character. It stood on a wooden pedestal, not nearly finished, but with fine white dust and small chips of marble scattered about it, and itself incrusted all round with the white, shapeless substance of the block. In the midst appeared the features, lacking sharpness, and very much resembling a fossil countenance, —but we have already used this simile, in reference to Cleopatra,—with the accumulations of long-past ages clinging to it.

And yet, strange to say, the face had an expression, and a more recognizable one than Kenyon had succeeded in putting into the clay model at Monte Beni. The reader is probably acquainted with Thorwaldsen's three-fold analogy,—the clay model, the Life; the plaster cast, the Death; and the sculptured marble, the Resurrection,—and it seemed to be made good by the spirit that was kindling up these imperfect features, like a lambent flame.

"I was not quite sure, at first glance, that I knew the face," observed Hilda; "the likeness surely is not a striking one. There is a good deal of external resemblance, still, to the features of the Faun of Praxiteles, between whom and Donatello, you know, we once insisted that there was a perfect twin-brotherhood. But the expression is now so very different!"

"What do you take it to be?" asked the sculptor.

"I hardly know how to define it," she answered. "But it has an effect as if I could see this countenance gradually brightening while I look at it. It gives the impression of a growing intellectual power and moral sense. Donatello's face used to evince little more than a genial, pleasurable sort of vivacity, and capability of enjoyment. But, here, a soul is being breathed into him; it is the Faun, but advancing towards a state of higher development."

"Hilda, do you see all this?" exclaimed Kenyon, in considerable surprise. "I may have had such an idea in my mind, but was quite unaware that I had succeeded in conveying it into the marble."

"Forgive me," said Hilda, "but I question whether this striking effect has been brought about by any skill or purpose on the sculptor's part. Is it not, perhaps, the chance result of the bust being just so far shaped out, in the marble, as the process of moral growth had advanced in the original? A few more strokes of the chisel might change the whole expression, and so spoil it for what it is now worth."

"I believe you are right," answered Kenyon, thoughtfully examining his work; "and, strangely enough, it was the very expression that I tried unsuccessfully to produce in the clay model. Well; not another chip shall be struck from the marble."

And, accordingly, Donatello's bust (like that rude, rough mass of the head of Brutus, by Michael Angelo, at Florence) has ever since remained in an unfinished state. Most spectators mistake it for an unsuccessful attempt towards copying the features of the Faun of Praxiteles. One observer in a thousand is conscious of something more, and lingers long over this mysterious face, departing from it reluctantly, and with many a glance thrown backward. What perplexes him is the riddle that he sees propounded there; the riddle of the soul's growth, taking its first impulse amid remorse and pain, and struggling through the incrustations of the senses. It was the contemplation of this imperfect portrait of Donatello that originally interested us in his history, and impelled us to elicit from Kenyon what he knew of his friend's adventures.

CHAPTER XLII

REMINISCENCES OF MIRIAM

WHEN Hilda and himself turned away from the unfinished bust, the sculptor's mind still dwelt upon the reminiscences which it suggested.

"You have not seen Donatello recently," he remarked, "and therefore cannot be aware how sadly he is changed."

"No wonder!" exclaimed Hilda, growing pale.

The terrible scene which she had witnessed, when Donatello's face gleamed out in so fierce a light, came back upon her memory, almost for the first time since she knelt at the confessional. Hilda, as is sometimes the case with persons whose delicate organization requires a peculiar safeguard, had an elastic faculty of throwing off such recollections as would be too painful for endurance. The first shock of Donatello's and Miriam's crime had, indeed, broken through the frail defence of this voluntary forgetfulness; but, once enabled to relieve herself of the ponderous anguish over which she had so long brooded, she had practised a subtile watchfulness in preventing its return.

"No wonder, do you say?" repeated the sculptor, looking at her with interest, but not exactly with surprise; for he had long suspected that Hilda had a painful knowledge of events which he himself little more than surmised. "Then you know!—you have heard! But what can you possibly have heard, and through what channel?"

"Nothing!" replied Hilda, faintly. "Not one word has reached my ears from the lips of any human being. Let us never speak of it again! No, no! never again!"

"And Miriam!" said Kenyon, with irrepressible interest. "Is it also forbidden to speak of her?"

"Hush! do not even utter her name! Try not to think of it!" Hilda whispered. "It may bring terrible consequences!"

"My dear Hilda!" exclaimed Kenyon, regarding her with wonder and deep sympathy. "My sweet friend, have you had this secret hidden in your delicate, maidenly heart, through all these many months! No wonder that your life was withering out of you."

"It was so, indeed!" said Hilda, shuddering. "Even now, I sicken at the recollection."

"And how could it have come to your knowledge?" continued the sculptor. "But, no matter! Do not torture yourself with referring to the subject. Only, if at any time it should be a relief to you, remember that we can speak freely together, for Miriam has herself suggested a confidence between us."

"Miriam has suggested this!" exclaimed Hilda. "Yes, I remember, now, her advising that the secret should be shared with you. But I have survived the death-struggle that it cost me, and need make no further revelations. And Miriam has spoken to you! What manner of woman can she be, who, after sharing in such a deed, can make it a topic of conversation with her friends?"

"Ah, Hilda," replied Kenyon, "you do not know, for you could never learn it from your own heart, which is all purity and rectitude, what a mixture of good there may be in things evil; and how the greatest criminal, if you look at his conduct from his own point of view, or from any side-point, may seem not so unquestionably guilty, after all. So with Miriam; so with Donatello. They are, perhaps, partners in what we must call awful guilt; and yet, I will own to you,—when I think of the original cause, the motives, the feelings, the sudden concurrence of circumstances thrusting them onward, the urgency of the moment, and the sublime unselfishness on either part,—I know not well how to distinguish it from much that the world calls heroism. Might we not render some such verdict as this?—'Worthy of Death, but not unworthy of Love!'"

"Never!" answered Hilda, looking at the matter through the clear crystal medium of her own integrity. "This thing, as regards its causes, is all a mystery to me, and must remain so. But there is, I believe, only one right and one wrong; and I do not understand, and may God keep me from ever understanding, how two things so totally unlike can be mistaken for one another; nor how two mortal foes, as Right and Wrong surely are, can work together in the same deed. This is my faith; and I should be led astray, if you could persuade me to give it up."

"Alas for poor human nature, then!" said Kenyon, sadly, and yet half smiling at Hilda's unworldly and impracticable theory. "I always felt you, my dear friend, a terribly severe judge, and have been perplexed to conceive how such tender sympathy could coexist with the remorselessness of a steel blade. You need no mercy, and therefore know not how to show any."

"That sounds like a bitter gibe," said Hilda, with the tears springing into her eyes. "But I cannot help it. It does not alter my perception of the truth. If there be any such dreadful mixture of good and evil as you affirm,—and which appears to me almost more shocking than pure evil,—then the good is turned to poison, not the evil to wholesomeness."

The sculptor seemed disposed to say something more, but yielded to the gentle steadfastness with which Hilda declined to listen. She grew very sad; for a reference to this one dismal topic had set, as it were, a prison-door ajar, and allowed a throng of torturing recollections to escape from their dungeons into the pure air and white radiance of her soul. She bade

Kenyon a briefer farewell than ordinary, and went homeward to her tower.

In spite of her efforts to withdraw them to other subjects, her thoughts dwelt upon Miriam; and, as had not heretofore happened, they brought with them a painful doubt whether a wrong had not been committed on Hilda's part, towards the friend once so beloved. Something that Miriam had said, in their final conversation, recurred to her memory, and seemed now to deserve more weight than Hilda had assigned to it, in her horror at the crime just perpetrated. It was not that the deed looked less wicked and terrible in the retrospect; but she asked herself whether there were not other questions to be considered, aside from that single one of Miriam's guilt or innocence; as, for example, whether a close bond of friendship, in which we once voluntarily engage, ought to be severed on account of any unworthiness, which we subsequently detect in our friend. For, in these unions of hearts,—call them marriage, or whatever else,—we take each other for better for worse. Availing ourselves of our friend's intimate affection, we pledge our own, as to be relied upon in every emergency. And what sadder, more desperate emergency could there be, than had befallen Miriam? Who more need the tender succor of the innocent, than wretches stained with guilt! And must a selfish care for the spotlessness of our own garments keep us from pressing the guilty ones close to our hearts, wherein, for the very reason that we are innocent, lies their securest refuge from further ill?

It was a sad thing for Hilda to find this moral enigma propounded to her conscience; and to feel that, whichever way she might settle it, there would be a cry of wrong on the other side. Still, the idea stubbornly came back, that the tie between Miriam and herself had been real, the affection true, and that therefore the implied compact was not to be shaken off.

"Miriam loved me well," thought Hilda, remorsefully, "and I failed her at her sorest need."

Miriam loved her well; and not less ardent had been the affection which Miriam's warm, tender, and generous characteristics had excited in Hilda's more reserved and quiet nature. It had never been extinguished; for, in part, the wretchedness which Hilda had since endured was but the struggle and writhing of her sensibility, still yearning towards her friend. And now, at the earliest encouragement, it awoke again, and cried out piteously, complaining of the violence that had been done it.

Recurring to the delinquencies of which she fancied (we say "fancied," because we do not unhesitatingly adopt Hilda's present view, but rather suppose her misled by her feelings)—of which she fancied herself guilty towards her friend, she suddenly remembered a sealed packet that Miriam had confided to her. It had been put into her hands with earnest injunctions of secrecy and care, and if unclaimed after a certain period, was to be delivered according to its address. Hilda had forgotten it; or, rather, she had kept the thought of this commission in the background of her consciousness, with all other thoughts referring to Miriam.

But now the recollection of this packet, and the evident stress which

Miriam laid upon its delivery at the specified time, impelled Hilda to hurry up the staircase of her tower, dreading lest the period should already have elapsed.

No; the hour had not gone by, but was on the very point of passing. Hilda read the brief note of instruction, on a corner of the envelope, and discovered, that, in case of Miriam's absence from Rome, the packet was to be taken to its destination that very day.

"How nearly I had violated my promise!" said Hilda. "And, since we are separated forever, it has the sacredness of an injunction from a dead friend. There is no time to be lost."

So Hilda set forth in the decline of the afternoon, and pursued her way towards the quarter of the city in which stands the Palazzo Cenci. Her habit of self-reliance was so simply strong, so natural, and now so well established by long use, that the idea of peril seldom or never occurred to Hilda, in her lonely life.

She differed, in this particular, from the generality of her sex; although the customs and character of her native land often produce women who meet the world with gentle fearlessness, and discover that its terrors have been absurdly exaggerated by the tradition of mankind. In ninety-nine cases out of a hundred, the apprehensiveness of women is quite gratuitous. Even as matters now stand, they are really safer in perilous situations and emergencies than men; and might be still more so, if they trusted themselves more confidingly to the chivalry of manhood. In all her wanderings about Rome, Hilda had gone and returned as securely as she had been accustomed to tread the familiar street of her New England village, where every face wore a look of recognition. With respect to whatever was evil, foul, and ugly, in this populous and corrupt city, she trod as if invisible, and not only so, but blind. She was altogether unconscious of anything wicked that went along the same pathway, but without jostling or impeding her, any more than gross substance hinders the wanderings of a spirit. Thus it is, that, bad as the world is said to have grown, innocence continues to make a paradise around itself, and keep it still unfallen.

Hilda's present expedition led her into what was—physically, at least —the foulest and ugliest part of Rome. In that vicinity lies the Ghetto, where thousands of Jews are crowded within a narrow compass, and lead a close, unclean, and multitudinous life, resembling that of maggots when they over-populate a decaying cheese.

Hilda passed on the borders of this region, but had no occasion to step within it. Its neighborhood, however, naturally partook of characteristics like its own. There was a confusion of black and hideous houses, piled massively out of the ruins of former ages; rude and destitute of plan, as a pauper would build his hovel, and yet displaying here and there an arched gateway, a cornice, a pillar, or a broken arcade, that might have adorned a palace. Many of the houses, indeed, as they stood, might once have been palaces, and possessed still a squalid kind of grandeur. Dirt was everywhere, strewing the narrow streets, and incrusting the tall shabbiness of the edifices, from the foundations to the roofs; it lay upon the thresholds, and looked out of the windows, and assumed the guise of human life in the children that seemed to be engendered out of it. Their father was the sun, and their mother—a heap of Roman mud.

It is a question of speculative interest, whether the ancient Romans were as unclean a people as we everywhere find those who have succeeded them. There appears to be a kind of malignant spell in the spots that have been inhabited by these masters of the world, or made famous in their history; an inherited and inalienable curse, impelling their successors to fling dirt and defilement upon whatever temple, column, ruined palace, or triumphal arch may be nearest at hand, and on every monument that the old Romans built. It is most probably a classic trait, regularly transmitted downward, and perhaps a little modified by the better civilization of Christianity; so that Cæsar may have trod narrower and filthier ways in his path to the Capitol, than even those of modern Rome.

As the paternal abode of Beatrice, the gloomy old palace of the Cencis had an interest for Hilda, although not sufficiently strong, hitherto, to overcome the disheartening effect of the exterior, and draw her over its threshold. The adjacent piazza, of poor aspect, contained only an old woman selling roasted chestnuts and baked squash-seeds; she looked sharply at Hilda, and inquired whether she had lost her way.

"No," said Hilda; "I seek the Palazzo Cenci."

"Yonder it is, fair signorina," replied the Roman matron. "If you wish that packet delivered, which I see in your hand, my grandson Pietro shall run with it for a baiocco. The Cenci palace is a spot of ill-omen for young maidens."

Hilda thanked the old dame, but alleged the necessity of doing her errand in person. She approached the front of the palace, which, with all its immensity, had but a mean appearance, and seemed an abode which the lovely shade of Beatrice would not be apt to haunt, unless her doom made it inevitable. Some soldiers stood about the portal, and gazed at the brown-haired, fair-cheeked Anglo-Saxon girl, with approving glances, but not indecorously. Hilda began to ascend the staircase, three lofty flights of which were to be surmounted, before reaching the door whither she was bound.

CHAPTER XLIII

THE EXTINCTION OF A LAMP

BETWEEN Hilda and the sculptor there had been a kind of half-expressed understanding, that both were to visit the galleries of the Vatican the day subsequent to their meeting at the studio. Kenyon, accordingly, failed not to be there, and wandered through the vast ranges of apartments, but saw nothing of his expected friend. The marble faces, which stand innumerable along the walls, and have kept themselves so calm through the vicissitudes of twenty centuries, had no sympathy for his disappointment; and he, on the other hand, strode past these treasures and marvels of antique art, with the indifference which any preoccupation of the feelings is apt to produce, in reference to objects of sculpture. Being of so cold and pure a substance, and mostly deriving their vitality more from thought than passion, they require to be seen through a perfectly transparent medium.

And, moreover, Kenyon had counted so much upon Hilda's delicate perceptions in enabling him to look at two or three of the statues, about which they had talked together, that the entire purpose of his visit was defeated by her absence. It is a delicious sort of mutual aid, when the united power of two sympathetic, yet dissimilar, intelligences is brought to bear upon a poem by reading it aloud, or upon a picture or statue by viewing it in each other's company. Even if not a word of criticism be uttered, the insight of either party is wonderfully deepened, and the comprehension broadened; so that the inner mystery of a work of genius, hidden from one, will often reveal itself to two. Missing such help, Kenyon saw nothing at the Vatican which he had not seen a thousand times before, and more perfectly than now.

In the chill of his disappointment, he suspected that it was a very cold art to which he had devoted himself. He questioned, at that moment, whether sculpture really ever softens and warms the material which it handles; whether carved marble is anything but limestone, after all; and whether the Apollo Belvedere itself possesses any merit above its physical beauty, or is beyond criticism even in that generally acknowledged excellence. In flitting glances, heretofore, he had seemed to behold this statue, as something ethereal and godlike, but not now.

Nothing pleased him, unless it were the group of the Laocoön, which, in its immortal agony, impressed Kenyon as a type of the long, fierce struggle of man, involved in the knotted entanglements of Error and Evil, those two snakes, which, if no divine help intervene, will be sure to strangle him and his children in the end. What he most admired was the strange calmness diffused through this bitter strife; so that it resembled the rage of the sea made calm by its immensity, or the tumult of Niagara which ceases to be tumult because it lasts forever. Thus, in the Laocoön, the horror of a moment grew to be the fate of interminable ages. Kenyon looked upon the group as the one triumph of sculpture, creating the repose, which is essential to it, in the very acme of turbulent effort; but, in truth, it was his mood of unwonted despondency that made him so sensitive to the terrible magnificence, as well as to the sad moral, of this work. Hilda herself could not have helped him to see it with nearly such intelligence.

A good deal more depressed than the nature of the disappointment warranted, Kenyon went to his studio, and took in hand a great lump of clay. He soon found, however, that his plastic cunning had departed from him for the time. So he wandered forth again into the uneasy streets of Rome, and walked up and down the Corso, where, at that period of the day, a throng of passers-by and loiterers choked up the narrow sidewalk. A penitent was thus brought in contact with the sculptor.

It was a figure in a white robe, with a kind of featureless mask over the face, through the apertures of which the eyes threw an unintelligible light. Such odd, questionable shapes are often seen gliding through the streets of Italian cities, and are understood to be usually persons of rank, who quit their palaces, their gayeties, their pomp, and pride, and assume the penitential garb for a season, with a view of thus expiating some crime, or atoning for the aggregate of petty sins that make up a worldly life. It is their custom to ask alms, and perhaps to measure the duration of their penance by the time requisite to accumulate a sum of money out of the little droppings of individual charity. The avails are devoted to some beneficent or religious purpose; so that the benefit accruing to their own souls is, in a manner, linked with a good done, or intended, to their fellowmen. These figures have a ghastly and startling effect, not so much from any very impressive peculiarity in the garb, as from the mystery which they bear about with them, and the sense that there is an acknowledged sinfulness as the nucleus of it.

In the present instance, however, the penitent asked no alms of Kenyon; although, for the space of a minute or two, they stood face to face, the hollow eyes of the mask encountering the sculptor's gaze. But, just as the crowd was about to separate them, the former spoke, in a voice not unfamiliar to Kenyon, though rendered remote and strange by the guilty veil through which it penetrated.

"Is all well with you, Signore?" inquired the penitent, out of the cloud in which he walked.

"All is well," answered Kenyon. "And with you?"

But the masked penitent returned no answer, being borne away by the pressure of the throng.

The sculptor stood watching the figure, and was almost of a mind to hurry after him and follow up the conversation that had been begun; but it occurred to him that there is a sanctity (or, as we might rather term it, an inviolable etiquette) which prohibits the recognition of persons who choose to walk under the veil of penitence.

"How strange!" thought Kenyon to himself. "It was surely Donatello! What can bring him to Rome, where his recollections must be so painful, and his presence not without peril? And Miriam! Can she have accompanied him?"

He walked on, thinking of the vast change in Donatello, since those days of gayety and innocence, when the young Italian was new in Rome, and was just beginning to be sensible of a more poignant felicity than he had yet experienced, in the sunny warmth of Miriam's smile. The growth of a soul, which the sculptor half imagined that he had witnessed in his friend, seemed hardly worth the heavy price that it had cost, in the sacrifice of those simple enjoyments that were gone forever. A creature of antique healthfulness had vanished from the earth; and, in his stead, there was only one other morbid and remorseful man, among millions that were cast in the same indistinguishable mould.

The accident of thus meeting Donatello—the glad Faun of his imagination and memory, now transformed into a gloomy penitent—contributed to deepen the cloud that had fallen over Kenyon's spirits. It caused him to fancy, as we generally do, in the petty troubles which extend not a hand's-breadth beyond our own sphere, that the whole world was saddening around him. It took the sinister aspect of an omen, although he could not distinctly see what trouble it might forebode.

If it had not been for a peculiar sort of pique, with which lovers are much conversant, a preposterous kind of resentment which endeavors to wreak itself on the beloved object, and on one's own heart, in requital of mishaps for which neither is in fault, Kenyon might at once have betaken himself to Hilda's studio, and asked why the appointment was not kept. But the interview of to-day was to have been so rich in present joy, and its results so important to his future life, that the bleak failure was too much for his equanimity. He was angry with poor Hilda, and censured her without a hearing; angry with himself, too, and therefore inflicted on this latter criminal the severest penalty in his power; angry with the day that was passing over him, and would not permit its latter hours to redeem the disappointment of the morning.

To confess the truth, it had been the sculptor's purpose to stake all his hopes on that interview in the galleries of the Vatican. Straying with Hilda through those long vistas of ideal beauty, he meant, at last, to utter himself upon that theme which lovers are fain to discuss in village lanes, in wood-paths, on sea-side sands, in crowded streets; it little matters where, indeed, since roses are sure to blush along the way, and daisies and violets to spring beneath the feet, if the spoken word be graciously received. He was resolved to make proof whether the kindness that Hilda evinced for him was the precious token of an individual preference, or merely the sweet fragrance of her disposition, which other friends might share as largely as himself. He would try if it were possible to take this shy, yet frank, and innocently fearless creature captive, and imprison her in his heart, and make her sensible of a wider freedom there, than in all the world besides.

It was hard, we must allow, to see the shadow of a wintry sunset falling upon a day that was to have been so bright, and to find himself just where yesterday had left him, only with a sense of being drearily balked, and defeated without an opportunity for struggle. So much had been anticipated from these now vanished hours, that it seemed as if no other day could bring back the same golden hopes.

In a case like this, it is doubtful whether Kenyon could have done a much better thing than he actually did, by going to dine at the Café Nuovo, and drinking a flask of Montefiascone; longing, the while, for a beaker or two of Donatello's Sunshine. It would have been just the wine to cure a lover's melancholy, by illuminating his heart with tender light and warmth, and suggestions of undefined hopes, too ethereal for his morbid humor to examine and reject them.

No decided improvement resulting from the draught of Montefiascone, he went to the Teatro Argentino, and sat gloomily to see an Italian comedy, which ought to have cheered him somewhat, being full of glancing merriment, and effective over everybody's risibilities except his own. The sculptor came out, however, before the close of the performance, as disconsolate as he went in.

As he made his way through the complication of narrow streets, which perplex that portion of the city, a carriage passed him. It was driven rapidly, but not too fast for the light of a gas-lamp to flare upon a face within; especially as it was bent forward, appearing to recognize him, while a beckoning hand was protruded from the window. On his part, Kenyon at once knew the face, and hastened to the carriage, which had now stopped.

"Miriam! you in Rome?" he exclaimed. "And your friends know nothing of it?"

"Is all well with you?" she asked.

This inquiry, in the identical words which Donatello had so recently addressed to him, from beneath the penitent's mask, startled the sculptor. Either the previous disquietude of his mind, or some tone in Miriam's voice, or the unaccountableness of beholding her there at all, made it seem ominous.

"All is well, I believe," answered he, doubtfully. "I am aware of no misfortune. Have you any to announce?"

He looked still more earnestly at Miriam, and felt a dreamy uncertainty whether it was really herself to whom he spoke. True; there were those beautiful features, the contour of which he had studied too often, and with a sculptor's accuracy of perception, to be in any doubt that it was Miriam's identical face. But he was conscious of a change, the nature of which he could not satisfactorily define; it might be merely her dress, which, imperfect as the light was, he saw to be richer than the simple garb that she had usually worn. The effect, he fancied, was partly owing to a gem which she had on her bosom; not a diamond, but something that glimmered with a clear, red lustre, like the stars in a southern sky. Somehow or other, this colored light seemed an emanation of herself, as if all that was passionate and glowing, in her native disposition, had crystallized upon her breast, and were just now scintillating more brilliantly than ever, in sympathy with some emotion of her heart.

Of course there could be no real doubt that it was Miriam, his artist friend, with whom and Hilda he had spent so many pleasant and familiar hours, and whom he had last seen at Perugia, bending with Donatello beneath the bronze pope's benediction. It must be that self-same Miriam; but the sensitive sculptor felt a difference of manner, which impressed him more than he conceived it possible to be affected by so external a thing. He remembered the gossip so prevalent in Rome on Miriam's first appearance; how that she was no real artist, but the daughter of an illustrious or golden lineage, who was merely playing at necessity; mingling with human struggle for her pastime; stepping out of her native sphere only for an interlude, just as a princess might alight from her gilded equipage to go on foot through a rustic lane. And now, after a mask in which love and death had performed their several parts, she had resumed her proper character.

"Have you anything to tell me?" cried he, impatiently; for nothing causes a more disagreeable vibration of the nerves than this perception of ambiguousness in familiar persons or affairs. "Speak; for my spirits and patience have been much tried to-day."

Miriam put her finger on her lips, and seemed desirous that Kenyon should know of the presence of a third person. He now saw, indeed, that there was some one beside her in the carriage, hitherto concealed by her attitude; a man, it appeared, with a sallow Italian face, which the sculptor distinguished but imperfectly, and did not recognize.

"I can tell you nothing," she replied; and leaning towards him, she whispered,—appearing then more like the Miriam whom he knew than in what had before passed,—"Only, when the lamp goes out do not despair."

The carriage drove on, leaving Kenyon to muse over this unsatisfactory interview, which seemed to have served no better purpose than to fill his mind with more ominous forebodings than before. Why were Donatello and Miriam in Rome, where both, in all likelihood, might have much to dread? And why had one and the other addressed him with a question that seemed prompted by a knowledge of some calamity, either already fallen on his unconscious head, or impending closely over him?

"I am sluggish," muttered Kenyon, to himself; "a weak, nerveless fool, devoid of energy and promptitude; or neither Donatello nor Miriam could have escaped me thus! They are aware of some misfortune that concerns me deeply. How soon am I to know it too?"

There seemed but a single calamity possible to happen within so narrow a sphere as that with which the sculptor was connected; and even to that one mode of evil he could assign no definite shape, but only felt that it must have some reference to Hilda.

Flinging aside the morbid hesitation, and the dallyings with his own wishes, which he had permitted to influence his mind throughout the day, he now hastened to the Via Portoghese. Soon the old palace stood before him, with its massive tower rising into the clouded night; obscured from view at its midmost elevation, but revealed again, higher upward, by the Virgin's lamp that twinkled on the summit. Feeble as it was, in the broad, surrounding gloom, that little ray made no inconsiderable illumination among Kenyon's sombre thoughts; for, remembering Miriam's last words, a fantasy had seized him that he should find the sacred lamp extinguished.

And, even while he stood gazing, as a mariner at the star in which he put his trust, the light quivered, sank, gleamed up again, and finally went out, leaving the battlements of Hilda's tower in utter darkness. For the first time in centuries, the consecrated and legendary flame, before the loftiest shrine in Rome, had ceased to burn.

CHAPTER XLIV

THE DESERTED SHRINE

KENYON knew the sanctity which Hilda (faithful Protestant, and daughter of the Puritans, as the girl was) imputed to this shrine. He was aware of the profound feeling of responsibility, as well earthly as religious, with which her conscience had been impressed, when she became the occupant of her aerial chamber, and undertook the task of keeping the consecrated lamp alight. There was an accuracy and a certainty about Hilda's movements, as regarded all matters that lay deep enough to have their roots in right or wrong, which made it as possible and safe to rely upon the timely and careful trimming of this lamp (if she were in life, and able to creep up the steps), as upon the rising of to-morrow's sun, with lustre undiminished from to-day.

The sculptor could scarcely believe his eyes, therefore, when he saw the flame flicker and expire. His sight had surely deceived him. And now, since the light did not reappear, there must be some smoke-wreath or impenetrable mist brooding about the tower's gray old head, and obscuring it from the lower world. But no! For right over the dim battlements, as the wind chased away a mass of clouds, he beheld a star, and, moreover, by an earnest concentration of his sight, was soon able to discern even the darkened shrine itself. There was no obscurity around the tower; no infirmity of his own vision. The flame had exhausted its supply of oil, and become extinct. But where was Hilda?

A man in a cloak happened to be passing; and Kenyon—anxious to distrust the testimony of his senses, if he could get more acceptable evidence on the other side—appealed to him.

"Do me the favor, Signore," said he, "to look at the top of yonder tower, and tell me whether you see the lamp burning at the Virgin's shrine."

"The lamp, Signore?" answered the man, without at first troubling himself to look up. "The lamp that has burned these four hundred years! how is it possible, Signore, that it should not be burning now?"

"But look!" said the sculptor, impatiently.

With good-natured indulgence for what he seemed to consider as the whim of an eccentric Forestiero, the Italian carelessly threw his eyes upwards; but, as soon as he perceived that there was really no light, he lifted his hands with a vivid expression of wonder and alarm.

"The lamp is extinguished!" cried he. "The lamp that has been burning these four hundred years! This surely must portend some great misfortune; and, by my advice, Signore, you will hasten hence, lest the tower tumble on our heads. A priest once told me, that, if the Virgin withdrew her blessing, and the light went out, the old Palazzo del Torre would sink into the earth, with all that dwell in it. There will be a terrible crash before morning!"

The stranger made the best of his way from the doomed premises; while Kenyon—who would willingly have seen the tower crumble down before his eyes, on condition of Hilda's safety—determined, late as it was, to attempt ascertaining if she were in her dove-cote.

Passing through the arched entrance,—which, as is often the case with Roman entrances, was as accessible at midnight as at noon,—he groped his way to the broad staircase, and, lighting his wax taper, went glimmering up the multitude of steps that led to Hilda's door. The hour being so unseasonable, he intended merely to knock, and, as soon as her voice from within should reassure him, to retire, keeping his explanations and apologies for a fitter time. Accordingly, reaching the lofty height where the maiden, as he trusted, lay asleep, with angels watching over her, though the Virgin seemed to have suspended her care, he tapped lightly at the door-panels,—then knocked more forcibly,—then thundered an impatient summons. No answer came; Hilda, evidently, was not there.

After assuring himself that this must be the fact, Kenyon descended the stairs, but made a pause at every successive stage, and knocked at the door of its apartment, regardless whose slumbers he might disturb, in his anxiety to learn where the girl had last been seen. But, at each closed entrance, there came those hollow echoes, which a chamber, or any dwelling, great or small, never sends out, in response to human knuckles or iron hammer, as long as there is life within to keep its heart from getting dreary.

Once, indeed, on the lower landing-place, the sculptor fancied that there was a momentary stir, inside the door, as if somebody were listening at the threshold. He hoped, at least, that the small, iron-barred aperture would be unclosed, through which Roman housekeepers are wont to take careful cognizance of applicants for admission, from a traditionary dread, perhaps, of letting in a robber or assassin. But it remained shut; neither was the sound repeated; and Kenyon concluded that his excited nerves had played a trick upon his senses, as they are apt to do when we most wish for the clear evidence of the latter.

There was nothing to be done, save to go heavily away, and await whatever good or ill to-morrow's daylight might disclose.

Betimes in the morning, therefore, Kenyon went back to the Via Portoghese, before the slant rays of the sun had descended half-way down the gray front of Hilda's tower. As he drew near its base, he saw the doves perched in full session, on the sunny height of the battlements, and a pair of them—who were probably their mistress's especial pets, and the confidants of her bosom-secrets, if Hilda had any—came shooting down, and made a feint of alighting on his shoulder. But, though they evidently recognized him, their shyness would not yet allow so decided a demonstration. Kenyon's eyes followed them as they flew upward, hoping that they might have come as joyful messengers of the girl's safety, and that he should discern her slender form, half hidden by the parapet, trimming the extinguished lamp at the Virgin's shrine, just as other maidens set about the little duties of a household. Or, perhaps, he might see her gentle and sweet face smiling down upon him, midway towards heaven, as if she had flown thither for a day or two, just to visit her kindred, but had been drawn earthward again by the spell of unacknowledged love.

But his eyes were blessed by no such fair vision or reality; nor, in truth, were the eager, unquiet flutterings of the doves indicative of any joyful intelligence, which they longed to share with Hilda's friend, but of anxious inquiries that they knew not how to utter. They could not tell, any more than he, whither their lost companion had withdrawn herself, but were in the same void despondency with him, feeling their sunny and airy lives darkened and grown imperfect, now that her sweet society was taken out of it.

In the brisk morning air, Kenyon found it much easier to pursue his researches than at the preceding midnight, when, if any slumberers heard the clamor that he made, they had responded only with sullen and drowsy maledictions, and turned to sleep again. It must be a very dear and intimate reality for which people will be content to give up a dream. When the sun was fairly up, however, it was quite another thing. The heterogeneous population, inhabiting the lower floor of the old tower, and the other extensive regions of the palace, were now willing to tell all they knew, and imagine a great deal more. The amiability of these Italians, assisted by their sharp and nimble wits, caused them to overflow with plausible suggestions, and to be very bounteous in their avowals of interest for the lost Hilda. In a less demonstrative people, such expressions would have implied an eagerness to search land and sea, and never rest till she were found. In the mouths that uttered them, they meant good wishes, and were, so far, better than indifference. There was little doubt that many of them felt a genuine kindness for the shy, brown-haired, delicate, young foreign maiden, who had flown from some distant land to alight upon their tower, where she consorted only with the doves. But their energy expended itself in exclamation, and they were content to leave all more active measures to Kenyon, and to the Virgin, whose affair it was, to see that the faithful votary of her lamp received no harm.

In a great Parisian domicile, multifarious as its inhabitants might be, the concierge under the archway would be cognizant of all their incomings and issuings forth. But, except in rare cases, the general entrance and main staircase of a Roman house are left as free as the street, of which they form a sort of by-lane. The sculptor, therefore, could hope to find information about Hilda's movements only from casual observers.

On probing the knowledge of these people to the bottom, there was various testimony as to the period when the girl had last been seen. Some said that it was four days since there had been a trace of her; but an English lady, in the second piano of the palace, was rather of opinion that she had met her, the morning before, with a drawing-book in her hand. Having no acquaintance with the young person, she had taken little notice and might have been mistaken. A count, on the piano next above, was very certain that he had lifted his hat to Hilda, under the archway, two afternoons ago. An old woman, who had formerly tended the shrine, threw some light upon the matter, by testifying that the lamp required to be replenished once, at least, in three days, though its reservoir of oil was exceedingly capacious.

On the whole, though there was other evidence enough to create some perplexity, Kenyon could not satisfy himself that she had been visible since the afternoon of the third preceding day, when a fruit-seller remembered her coming out of the arched passage, with a sealed packet in her hand. As nearly as he could ascertain, this was within an hour after Hilda had taken leave of the sculptor, at his own studio, with the understanding that they were to meet at the Vatican the next day. Two nights, therefore, had intervened, during which the lost maiden was unaccounted for.

The door of Hilda's apartments was still locked, as on the preceding night; but Kenyon sought out the wife of the person who sublet them, and prevailed on her to give him admittance by means of the duplicate key, which the good woman had in her possession. On entering, the maidenly neatness and simple grace, recognizable in all the arrangements, made him visibly sensible that this was the daily haunt of a pure soul, in whom religion and love of beauty were at one.

Thence, the sturdy Roman matron led the sculptor across a narrow passage, and threw open the door of a small chamber, on the threshold of which he reverently paused. Within, there was a bed, covered with white drapery, enclosed with snowy curtains, like a tent, and of barely width enough for a slender figure to repose upon it. The sight of this cool, airy, and secluded bower caused the lover's heart to stir as if enough of Hilda's gentle dreams were lingering there to make him happy for a single instant. But then came the closer consciousness of her loss, bringing along with it a sharp sting of anguish.

"Behold, Signore," said the matron; "here is the little staircase by which the signorina used to ascend and trim the Blessed Virgin's lamp. She was worthy to be a Catholic, such pains the good child bestowed to keep it burning; and doubtless the Blessed Mary will intercede for her, in consideration of her pious offices, heretic though she was. What will become of the old palazzo, now that the lamp is extinguished, the saints above us only know! Will you mount, Signore, to the battlements, and see if she has left any trace of herself there?"

The sculptor stepped across the chamber and ascended the little staircase, which gave him access to the breezy summit of the tower. It affected him inexpressibly to see a bouquet of beautiful flowers beneath the shrine, and to recognize in them an offering of his own to Hilda, who had put them in a vase of water, and dedicated them to the Virgin, in a spirit partly fanciful, perhaps, but still partaking of the religious sentiment which so profoundly influenced her character. One rose-bud, indeed, she had selected for herself from the rich mass of flowers; for Kenyon well remembered recognizing it in her bosom when he last saw her at his studio.

"That little part of my great love she took," said he to himself. "The remainder she would have devoted to Heaven; but has left it withering in the sun and wind. Ah! Hilda, Hilda, had you given me a right to watch over you, this evil had not come!"

"Be not downcast, signorino mio," said the Roman matron, in response to the deep sigh which struggled out of Kenyon's breast. "The dear little maiden, as we see, has decked yonder blessed shrine as devoutly as I myself, or any other good Catholic woman, could have done. It is a religious act, and has more than the efficacy of a prayer. The signorina will as surely come back as the sun will fall through the window tomorrow no less than to-day. Her own doves have often been missing for a day or two, but they were sure to come fluttering about her head again, when she least expected them. So will it be with this dove-like child."

"It might be so," thought Kenyon, with yearning anxiety, "if a pure maiden were as safe as a dove, in this evil world of ours."

As they returned through the studio, with the furniture and arrangements of which the sculptor was familiar, he missed a small ebony writing-desk that he remembered as having always been placed on a table there. He knew that it was Hilda's custom to deposit her letters in this desk, as well as other little objects of which she wished to be specially careful.

"What has become of it?" he suddenly inquired, laying his hand on the table.

"Become of what, pray?" exclaimed the woman, a little disturbed. "Does the Signore suspect a robbery, then?"

"The signorina's writing-desk is gone," replied Kenyon; "it always stood on this table, and I myself saw it there only a few days ago."

"Ah, well!" said the woman, recovering her composure, which she seemed partly to have lost. "The signorina has doubtless taken it away with her. The fact is of good omen; for it proves that she did not go unexpectedly, and is likely to return when it may best suit her convenience."

"This is very singular," observed Kenyon. "Have the rooms been entered by yourself, or any other person, since the signorina's disappearance?"

"Not by me, Signore, so help me Heaven and the saints!" said the matron. "And I question whether there are more than two keys in Rome that will suit this strange old lock. Here is one; and as for the other, the signorina carries it in her pocket."

The sculptor had no reason to doubt the word of this respectable dame. She appeared to be well-meaning and kind-hearted, as Roman matrons generally are; except when a fit of passion incites them to shower horrible curses on an obnoxious individual, or perhaps to stab him with the steel stiletto that serves them for a hair-pin. But Italian asseverations of any questionable fact, however true they may chance to be, have no witness of their truth in the faces of those who utter them. Their words are spoken with strange earnestness, and yet do not vouch for themselves as coming from any depth, like roots drawn out of the substance of the soul, with some of the soil clinging to them. There is always a something inscrutable, instead of frankness, in their eyes. In short, they lie so much like truth, and speak truth so much as if they were telling a lie, that their auditor suspects himself in the wrong, whether he believes or disbelieves them; it being the one thing certain, that falsehood is seldom an intolerable burden to the tenderest of Italian consciences.

"It is very strange what can have become of the desk!" repeated Kenyon, looking the woman in the face.

"Very strange, indeed, Signore," she replied meekly, without turning away her eyes in the least, but checking his insight of them at about half an inch below the surface. "I think the signorina must have taken it with her."

It seemed idle to linger here any longer. Kenyon therefore departed, after making an arrangement with the woman, by the terms of which she was to allow the apartments to remain in their present state, on his assuming the responsibility for the rent.

He spent the day in making such further search and investigation as he found practicable; and, though at first trammelled by an unwillingness to draw public attention to Hilda's affairs, the urgency of the circumstances soon compelled him to be thoroughly in earnest. In the course of a week, he tried all conceivable modes of fathoming the mystery, not merely by his personal efforts and those of his brother-artists and friends, but through the police, who readily undertook the task, and expressed strong confidence of success. But the Roman police has very little efficiency, except in the interest of the despotism of which it is a tool. With their cocked hats, shoulder-belts, and swords, they wear a sufficiently imposing aspect, and doubtless keep their eyes open wide enough to track a political offender, but are too often blind to private outrage, be it murder or any lesser crime. Kenyon counted little upon their assistance, and profited by it not at all.

Remembering the mystic words which Miriam had addressed to him, he was anxious to meet her, but knew not whither she had gone, nor how to obtain an interview either with herself or Donatello. The days wore away, and still there were no tidings of the lost one; no lamp rekindled before the Virgin's shrine; no light shining into the lover's heart; no star of Hope—he was ready to say, as he turned his eyes almost reproachfully upward—in heaven itself!

### CHAPTER XLV

### The Flight of Hilda's Doves

Along with the lamp on Hilda's tower, the sculptor now felt that a light had gone out, or, at least, was ominously obscured, to which he owed whatever cheerfulness had heretofore illuminated his cold, artistic life.

The idea of this girl had been like a taper of virgin wax, burning with a pure and steady flame, and chasing away the evil spirits out of the magic circle of its beams. It had darted its rays afar, and modified the whole sphere in which Kenyon had his being. Beholding it no more, he at once found himself in darkness and astray.

This was the time, perhaps, when Kenyon first became sensible what a dreary city is Rome, and what a terrible weight is there imposed on human life, when any bloom within the heart corresponds to the spell of ruin, that has been thrown over the site of ancient empire. He wandered, as it were, and stumbled over the fallen columns, and among the tombs, and groped his way into the sepulchral darkness of the catacombs, and found no path emerging from them. The happy may well enough continue to be such, beneath the brilliant sky of Rome. But, if you go thither in melancholy mood,—if you go with a ruin in your heart, or with a vacant site there, where once stood the airy fabric of happiness, now vanished,— all the ponderous gloom of the Roman Past will pile itself upon that spot, and crush you down as with the heaped-up marble and granite, the earth-mounds, and multitudinous bricks of its material decay.

It might be supposed that a melancholy man would here make acquaintance with a grim philosophy. He should learn to bear patiently his individual griefs, that endure only for one little lifetime, when here are the tokens of such infinite misfortune on an imperial scale, and when so many far landmarks of time, all around him, are bringing the remoteness of a thousand years ago into the sphere of yesterday. But it is in vain that you seek this shrub of bitter sweetness among the plants that root themselves on the roughness of massive walls, or trail downward from the capitals of pillars, or spring out of the green turf in the palace of the Cæsars. It does not grow in Rome; not even among the five hundred various weeds which deck the grassy arches of the Coliseum. You look through a vista of century beyond century,—through much shadow, and a little sunshine,—through barbarism and civilization, alternating with one another like actors that have prearranged their parts,—through a broad pathway of progressive generations bordered by palaces and temples, and bestridden by old, triumphal arches, until, in the distance, you behold the obelisks, with their unintelligible inscriptions, hinting at a past infinitely more remote than history can define. Your own life is as nothing, when compared with that immeasurable distance; but still you demand, none the less earnestly, a gleam of sunshine, instead of a speck of shadow, on the step or two that will bring you to your quiet rest.

How exceedingly absurd! All men, from the date of the earliest obelisk,—and of the whole world, moreover, since that far epoch, and before, —have made a similar demand, and seldom had their wish. If they had it, what are they the better now? But, even while you taunt yourself with this sad lesson, your heart cries out obstreperously for its small share of earthly happiness, and will not be appeased by the myriads of dead hopes that lie crushed into the soil of Rome. How wonderful that this our narrow foothold of the Present should hold its own so constantly, and, while

every moment changing, should still be like a rock betwixt the encountering tides of the long Past and the infinite To-come!

Man of marble though he was, the sculptor grieved for the Irrevocable.
Looking back upon Hilda's way of life, he marvelled at his own blind stupidity, which had kept him from remonstrating—as a friend, if with no
stronger right—against the risks that she continually encountered. Being
so innocent, she had no means of estimating those risks, nor even a possibility of suspecting their existence. But he—who had spent years in
Rome, with a man's far wider scope of observation and experience—knew
things that made him shudder. It seemed to Kenyon, looking through the
darkly colored medium of his fears, that all modes of crime were crowded
into the close intricacy of Roman streets, and that there was no redeeming element, such as exists in other dissolute and wicked cities.

For here was a priesthood, pampered, sensual, with red and bloated
cheeks, and carnal eyes. With apparently a grosser development of animal life than most men, they were placed in an unnatural relation with
woman, and thereby lost the healthy, human conscience that pertains to
other human beings, who own the sweet household ties connecting them
with wife and daughter. And here was an indolent nobility, with no high
aims or opportunities, but cultivating a vicious way of life, as if it were an
art, and the only one which they cared to learn. Here was a population,
high and low, that had no genuine belief in virtue; and if they recognized
any act as criminal, they might throw off all care, remorse, and memory
of it, by kneeling a little while at the confessional, and rising unburdened,
active, elastic, and incited by fresh appetite for the next ensuing sin. Here
was a soldiery who felt Rome to be their conquered city, and doubtless
considered themselves the legal inheritors of the foul license which Gaul,
Goth, and Vandal have here exercised in days gone by.

And what localities for new crime existed in those guilty sites, where
the crime of departed ages used to be at home, and had its long, hereditary haunt! What street in Rome, what ancient ruin, what one place
where man had standing-room, what fallen stone was there, unstained
with one or another kind of guilt! In some of the vicissitudes of the city's
pride, or its calamity, the dark tide of human evil had swelled over it, far
higher than the Tiber ever rose against the acclivities of the seven hills.
To Kenyon's morbid view, there appeared to be a contagious element,
rising foglike from the ancient depravity of Rome, and brooding over the
dead and half-rotten city, as nowhere else on earth. It prolonged the tendency to crime, and developed an instantaneous growth of it, whenever an
opportunity was found. And where could it be found so readily as here!
In those vast palaces, there were a hundred remote nooks where Innocence might shriek in vain. Beneath meaner houses there were unsuspected dungeons that had once been princely chambers, and open to the daylight; but, on account of some wickedness there perpetrated, each passing
age had thrown its handful of dust upon the spot, and buried it from
sight. Only ruffians knew of its existence, and kept it for murder, and
worse crime.

Such was the city through which Hilda, for three years past, had been wandering without a protector or a guide. She had trodden lightly over the crumble of old crimes; she had taken her way amid the grime and corruption which Paganism had left there, and a perverted Christianity had made more noisome; walking saint-like through it all, with white, innocent feet; until, in some dark pitfall that lay right across her path, she had vanished out of sight. It was terrible to imagine what hideous outrage might have thrust her into that abyss!

Then the lover tried to comfort himself with the idea that Hilda's sanctity was a sufficient safeguard. Ah, yes; she was so pure! The angels, that were of the same sisterhood, would never let Hilda come to harm. A miracle would be wrought on her behalf, as naturally as a father would stretch out his hand to save a best-beloved child. Providence would keep a little area and atmosphere about her as safe and wholesome as heaven itself, although the flood of perilous iniquity might hem her round, and its black waves hang curling above her head! But these reflections were of slight avail. No doubt they were the religious truth. Yet the ways of Providence are utterly inscrutable; and many a murder has been done, and many an innocent virgin has lifted her white arms, beseeching its aid in her extremity, and all in vain; so that, though Providence is infinitely good and wise,—and perhaps for that very reason,—it may be half an eternity before the great circle of its scheme shall bring us the superabundant recompense for all these sorrows! But what the lover asked was such prompt consolation as might consist with the brief span of mortal life; the assurance of Hilda's present safety, and her restoration within that very hour.

An imaginative man, he suffered the penalty of his endowment in the hundred-fold variety of gloomily tinted scenes that it presented to him, in which Hilda was always a central figure. The sculptor forgot his marble. Rome ceased to be anything, for him, but a labyrinth of dismal streets, in one or another of which the lost girl had disappeared. He was haunted with the idea, that some circumstance, most important to be known, and, perhaps, easily discoverable, had hitherto been overlooked, and that, if he could lay hold of this one clew, it would guide him directly in the track of Hilda's footsteps. With this purpose in view, he went, every morning, to the Via Portoghese, and made it the starting-point of fresh investigations. After nightfall, too, he invariably returned thither, with a faint hope fluttering at his heart that the lamp might again be shining on the summit of the tower, and would dispel this ugly mystery out of the circle consecrated by its rays. There being no point of which he could take firm hold, his mind was filled with unsubstantial hopes and fears. Once, Kenyon had seemed to cut his life in marble; now he vaguely clutched at it, and found it vapor.

In his unstrung and despondent mood, one trifling circumstance affected him with an idle pang. The doves had at first been faithful to their lost mistress. They failed not to sit in a row upon her window-sill, or to alight on the shrine, or the church-angels, and on the roofs and portals of the neighboring houses, in evident expectation of her reappearance. After the second week, however, they began to take flight, and dropping off by pairs, betook themselves to other dove-cotes. Only a single dove remained, and brooded drearily beneath the shrine. The flock, that had departed, were like the many hopes that had vanished from Kenyon's heart; the one that still lingered, and looked so wretched,—was it a Hope, or already a Despair?

In the street, one day, the sculptor met a priest of mild and venerable aspect; and as his mind dwelt continually upon Hilda, and was especially active in bringing up all incidents that had ever been connected with her, it immediately struck him that this was the very father with whom he had seen her at the confessional. Such trust did Hilda inspire in him, that Kenyon had never asked what was the subject of the communication between herself and this old priest. He had no reason for imagining that it could have any relation with her disappearance, so long subsequently; but, being thus brought face to face with a personage, mysteriously associated, as he now remembered, with her whom he had lost, an impulse ran before his thoughts and led the sculptor to address him.

It might be that the reverend kindliness of the old man's expression took Kenyon's heart by surprise; at all events, he spoke as if there were a recognized acquaintanceship, and an object of mutual interest between them.

"She has gone from me, father," said he.

"Of whom do you speak, my son?" inquired the priest.

"Of that sweet girl," answered Kenyon, "who knelt to you at the confessional. Surely, you remember her, among all the mortals to whose confessions you have listened! For she alone could have had no sins to reveal."

"Yes; I remember," said the priest, with a gleam of recollection in his eyes. "She was made to bear a miraculous testimony to the efficacy of the divine ordinances of the Church, by seizing forcibly upon one of them, and finding immediate relief from it, heretic though she was. It is my purpose to publish a brief narrative of this miracle, for the edification of mankind, in Latin, Italian, and English, from the printing-press of the Propaganda. Poor child! Setting apart her heresy, she was spotless, as you say. And is she dead?"

"Heaven forbid, father!" exclaimed Kenyon, shrinking back. "But she has gone from me, I know not whither. It may be—yes, the idea seizes upon my mind—that what she revealed to you will suggest some clew to the mystery of her disappearance."

"None, my son, none," answered the priest, shaking his head; "nevertheless, I bid you be of good cheer. That young maiden is not doomed to die a heretic. Who knows what the Blessed Virgin may at this moment be doing for her soul! Perhaps, when you next behold her, she will be clad in the shining white robe of the true faith."

This latter suggestion did not convey all the comfort which the old priest possibly intended by it; but he imparted it to the sculptor, along with his blessing, as the two best things that he could bestow, and said nothing further, except to bid him farewell.

When they had parted, however, the idea of Hilda's conversion to Catholicism recurred to her lover's mind, bringing with it certain reflections, that gave a new turn to his surmises about the mystery into which she had vanished. Not that he seriously apprehended—although the superabundance of her religious sentiment might mislead her for a moment —that the New England girl would permanently succumb to the scarlet superstitions which surrounded her in Italy. But the incident of the confessional—if known, as probably it was, to the eager propagandists who prowl about for souls, as cats to catch a mouse—would surely inspire the most confident expectations of bringing her over to the faith. With so pious an end in view, would Jesuitical morality be shocked at the thought of kidnapping the mortal body, for the sake of the immortal spirit that might otherwise be lost forever? Would not the kind old priest, himself, deem this to be infinitely the kindest service that he could perform for the stray lamb, who had so strangely sought his aid?

If these suppositions were well founded, Hilda was most likely a prisoner in one of the religious establishments that are so numerous in Rome. The idea, according to the aspect in which it was viewed, brought now a degree of comfort, and now an additional perplexity. On the one hand, Hilda was safe from any but spiritual assaults; on the other, where was the possibility of breaking through all those barred portals, and searching a thousand convent-cells, to set her free?

Kenyon, however, as it happened, was prevented from endeavoring to follow out this surmise, which only the state of hopeless uncertainty, that almost bewildered his reason, could have led him for a moment to entertain. A communication reached him by an unknown hand, in consequence of which, and within an hour after receiving it, he took his way through one of the gates of Rome.

CHAPTER XLVI

A WALK ON THE CAMPAGNA

It was a bright forenoon of February; a month in which the brief severity of a Roman winter is already past, and when violets and daisies begin to show themselves in spots favored by the sun. The sculptor came out of the city by the gate of San Sebastiano, and walked briskly along the Appian Way.

For the space of a mile or two beyond the gate, this ancient and famous road is as desolate and disagreeable as most of the other Roman avenues.

It extends over small, uncomfortable paving-stones, between brick and plastered walls, which are very solidly constructed, and so high as almost to exclude a view of the surrounding country. The houses are of most uninviting aspect, neither picturesque, nor homelike and social; they have seldom or never a door opening on the wayside, but are accessible only from the rear, and frown inhospitably upon the traveller through iron-grated windows. Here and there appears a dreary inn, or a wine-shop, designated by the withered bush beside the entrance, within which you discern a stone-built and sepulchral interior, where guests refresh themselves with sour bread and goats'-milk cheese, washed down with wine of dolorous acerbity.

At frequent intervals along the roadside uprises the ruin of an ancient tomb. As they stand now, these structures are immensely high and broken mounds of conglomerated brick, stone, pebbles, and earth, all molten by time into a mass as solid and indestructible as if each tomb were composed of a single bowlder of granite. When first erected, they were cased externally, no doubt, with slabs of polished marble, artfuly wrought bas-reliefs, and all such suitable adornments, and were rendered majestically beautiful by grand architectural designs. This antique splendor has long since been stolen from the dead, to decorate the palaces and churches of the living. Nothing remains to the dishonored sepulchres, except their massiveness.

Even the pyramids form hardly a stranger spectacle, or are more alien from human sympathies, than the tombs of the Appian Way, with their gigantic height, breadth, and solidity, defying time and the elements, and far too mighty to be demolished by an ordinary earthquake. Here you may see a modern dwelling, and a garden with its vines and olive-trees, perched on the lofty dilapidation of a tomb, which forms a precipice of fifty feet in depth on each of the four sides. There is a home on that funereal mound, where generations of children have been born, and successive lives been spent, undisturbed by the ghost of the stern Roman whose ashes were so preposterously burdened. Other sepulchres wear a crown of grass, shrubbery, and forest-trees, which throw out a broad sweep of branches, having had time, twice over, to be a thousand years of age. On one of them stands a tower, which, though immemorially more modern than the tomb, was itself built by immemorial hands, and is now rifted quite from top to bottom by a vast fissure of decay; the tomb-hillock, its foundation, being still as firm as ever, and likely to endure until the last trump shall rend it wide asunder, and summon forth its unknown dead.

Yes; its unknown dead! For, except in one or two doubtful instances, these mountainous sepulchral edifices have not availed to keep so much as the bare name of an individual or a family from oblivion. Ambitious of everlasting remembrance, as they were, the slumberers might just as well have gone quietly to rest, each in his pigeon-hole of a columbarium, or under his little green hillock, in a graveyard, without a headstone to mark the spot. It is rather satisfactory than otherwise, to think that all these idle pains have turned out so utterly abortive.

About two miles, or more, from the city-gate, and right upon the road-side, Kenyon passed an immense round pile, sepulchral in its original purposes, like those already mentioned. It was built of great blocks of hewn stone, on a vast, square foundation of rough, agglomerated material, such as composes the mass of all the other ruinous tombs. But whatever might be the cause, it was in a far better state of preservation than they. On its broad summit rose the battlements of a mediæval fortress, out of the midst of which (so long since had time begun to crumble the supplemental structure, and cover it with soil, by means of wayside dust) grew trees, bushes, and thick festoons of ivy. This tomb of a woman had become the citadel and donjon-keep of a castle; and all the care that Cecilia Metella's husband could bestow, to secure endless peace for her beloved relics, had only sufficed to make that handful of precious ashes the nucleus of battles, long ages after her death.

A little beyond this point, the sculptor turned aside from the Appian Way, and directed his course across the Campagna, guided by tokens that were obvious only to himself. On one side of him, but at a distance, the Claudian aqueduct was striding over fields and water-courses. Before him, many miles away, with a blue atmosphere between, rose the Alban hills, brilliantly silvered with snow and sunshine.

He was not without a companion. A buffalo-calf, that seemed shy and sociable by the self-same impulse, had begun to make acquaintance with him, from the moment when he left the road. This frolicsome creature gambolled along, now before, now behind; standing a moment to gaze at him, with wild, curious eyes, he leaped aside and shook his shaggy head, as Kenyon advanced too nigh; then, after loitering in the rear, he came galloping up, like a charge of cavalry, but halted, all of a sudden, when the sculptor turned to look, and bolted across the Campagna, at the slightest signal of nearer approach. The young sportive thing, Kenyon half fancied, was serving him as a guide, like the heifer that led Cadmus to the site of his destined city; for, in spite of a hundred vagaries, his general course was in the right direction, and along by several objects which the sculptor had noted as landmarks of his way.

In this natural intercourse with a rude and healthy form of animal life, there was something that wonderfully revived Kenyon's spirits. The warm rays of the sun, too, were wholesome for him in body and soul; and so was a breeze that bestirred itself occasionally, as if for the sole purpose of breathing upon his cheek, and dying softly away, when he would fain have felt a little more decided kiss. This shy, but loving breeze reminded him strangely of what Hilda's deportment had sometimes been towards himself.

The weather had very much to do, no doubt, with these genial and delightful sensations, that made the sculptor so happy with mere life, in spite of a head and heart full of doleful thoughts, anxieties, and fears, which ought in all reason to have depressed him. It was like no weather that exists anywhere, save in Paradise and in Italy; certainly not in America, where it is always too strenuous on the side either of heat or cold. Young as the season was, and wintry as it would have been under a more rigid sky, it resembled summer rather than what we New-Englanders recognize in our idea of spring. But there was an indescribable something, sweet, fresh, and remotely affectionate, which the matronly summer loses, and which thrilled, and, as it were, tickled Kenyon's heart with a feeling partly of the senses, yet far more a spiritual delight. In a word, it was as if Hilda's delicate breath were on his cheek.

After walking at a brisk pace for about half an hour, he reached a spot where an excavation appeared to have been begun, at some not very distant period. There was a hollow space in the earth, looking exceedingly like a deserted cellar, being enclosed within old subterranean walls, constructed of thin Roman bricks, and made accessible by a narrow flight of stone steps. A suburban villa had probably stood over this site, in the imperial days of Rome, and these might have been the ruins of a bath-room, or some other apartment that was required to be wholly or partly under ground. A spade can scarcely be put into that soil, so rich in lost and forgotten things, without hitting upon some discovery which would attract all eyes, in any other land. If you dig but a little way, you gather bits of precious marble, coins, rings, and engraved gems; if you go deeper, you break into columbaria, or into sculptured and richly frescoed apartments that look like festive halls, but were only sepulchres.

The sculptor descended into the cellar-like cavity, and sat down on a block of stone. His eagerness had brought him thither sooner than the appointed hour. The sunshine fell slantwise into the hollow, and happened to be resting on what Kenyon at first took to be a shapeless fragment of stone, possibly marble, which was partly concealed by the crumbling down of earth.

But his practised eye was soon aware of something artistic in this rude object. To relieve the anxious tedium of his situation, he cleared away some of the soil, which seemed to have fallen very recently, and discovered a headless figure of marble. It was earth-stained, as well it might be, and had a slightly corroded surface, but at once impressed the sculptor as a Greek production, and wonderfully delicate and beautiful. The head was gone; both arms were broken off at the elbow. Protruding from the loose earth, however, Kenyon beheld the fingers of a marble hand; it was still appended to its arm, and a little further search enabled him to find the other. Placing these limbs in what the nice adjustment of the fractures proved to be their true position, the poor, fragmentary woman forthwith showed that she retained her modest instincts to the last. She had perished with them, and snatched them back at the moment of revival. For these long-buried hands immediately disposed themselves in the manner that nature prompts, as the antique artist knew, and as all the world has seen, in the Venus de' Medici.

"What a discovery is here!" thought Kenyon to himself. "I seek for Hilda, and find a marble woman! Is the omen good or ill?"

In a corner of the excavation lay a small round block of stone, much incrusted with earth that had dried and hardened upon it. So, at least, you would have described this object, until the sculptor lifted it, turned it hither and thither in his hands, brushed off the clinging soil, and finally placed it on the slender neck of the newly discovered statue. The effect was magical. It immediately lighted up and vivified the whole figure, endowing it with personality, soul, and intelligence. The beautiful Idea at once asserted its immortality, and converted that heap of forlorn fragments into a whole, as perfect to the mind, if not to the eye, as when the new marble gleamed with snowy lustre; nor was the impression marred by the earth that still hung upon the exquisitely graceful limbs, and even filled the lovely crevice of the lips. Kenyon cleared it away from between them, and almost deemed himself rewarded with a living smile.

It was either the prototype or a better repetition of the Venus of the Tribune. But those who have been dissatisfied with the small head, the narrow, soulless face, the button-hole eyelids, of that famous statue, and its mouth such as nature never moulded, should see the genial breadth of this far nobler and sweeter countenance. It is one of the few works of antique sculpture in which we recognize womanhood, and that, moreover, without prejudice to its divinity.

Here, then, was a treasure for the sculptor to have found! How happened it to be lying there, beside its grave of twenty centuries? Why were not the tidings of its discovery already noised abroad? The world was richer than yesterday, by something far more precious than gold. Forgotten beauty had come back, as beautiful as ever; a goddess had risen from her long slumber, and was a goddess still. Another cabinet in the Vatican was destined to shine as lustrously as that of the Apollo Belvedere; or, if the aged pope should resign his claim, an emperor would woo this tender marble, and win her as proudly as an imperial bride!

Such were the thoughts with which Kenyon exaggerated to himself the importance of the newly discovered statue, and strove to feel at least a portion of the interest which this event would have inspired in him a little while before. But, in reality, he found it difficult to fix his mind upon the subject. He could hardly, we fear, be reckoned a consummate artist, because there was something dearer to him than his art; and, by the greater strength of a human affection, the divine statue seemed to fall asunder again, and become only a heap of worthless fragments.

While the sculptor sat listlessly gazing at it, there was a sound of small hoofs, clumsily galloping on the Campagna; and, soon, his frisky acquaintance, the buffalo-calf, came and peeped over the edge of the excavation. Almost at the same moment, he heard voices, which approached nearer and nearer; a man's voice, and a feminine one, talking the musical tongue of Italy. Besides the hairy visage of his four-footed friend, Kenyon now saw the figures of a peasant and a contadina, making gestures of salutation to him, on the opposite verge of the hollow space.

## CHAPTER XLVII

### THE PEASANT AND CONTADINA

THEY descended into the excavation: a young peasant, in the short blue
jacket, the small-clothes buttoned at the knee, and buckled shoes, that
compose one of the ugliest dresses ever worn by man, except the wearer's
form have a grace which any garb, or the nudity of an antique statue,
would equally set off; and, hand in hand with him, a village girl, in one of
those brilliant costumes largely kindled up with scarlet, and decorated
with gold embroidery, in which the contadinas array themselves on feast-
days. But Kenyon was not deceived; he had recognized the voices of his
friends, indeed, even before their disguised figures came between him and
the sunlight. Donatello was the peasant; the contadina, with the airy
smile, half mirthful, though it shone out of melancholy eyes,—was
Miriam.

They both greeted the sculptor with a familiar kindness which reminded him of the days when Hilda and they and he had lived so happily together, before the mysterious adventure of the catacomb. What a succession of sinister events had followed one spectral figure out of that gloomy
labyrinth.

"It is carnival time, you know," said Miriam, as if in explanation of
Donatello's and her own costume. "Do you remember how merrily we
spent the Carnival, last year?"

"It seems many years ago," replied Kenyon. "We are all so changed!"

When individuals approach one another with deep purposes on both
sides, they seldom come at once to the matter which they have most at
heart. They dread the electric shock of a too sudden contact with it. A
natural impulse leads them to steal gradually onward, hiding themselves,
as it were, behind a closer, and still a closer topic, until they stand face to
face with the true point of interest. Miriam was conscious of this impulse,
and partially obeyed it.

"So, your instincts as a sculptor have brought you into the presence of
our newly discovered statue," she observed. "It is not beautiful? A far
truer image of immortal womanhood than the poor little damsel at Florence, world-famous though she be."

"Most beautiful," said Kenyon, casting an indifferent glance at the
Venus. "The time has been when the sight of this statue would have been
enough to make the day memorable."

"And will it not do so, now?" Miriam asked. "I fancied so, indeed,
when we discovered it two days ago. It is Donatello's prize. We were sitting here together, planning an interview with you, when his keen eyes
detected the fallen goddess, almost entirely buried under that heap of
earth, which the clumsy excavators showered down upon her, I suppose.
We congratulated ourselves, chiefly for your sake. The eyes of us three

are the only ones to which she has yet revealed herself. Does it not frighten you a little, like the apparition of a lovely woman that lived of old, and has long lain in the grave?"

"Ah, Miriam! I cannot respond to you," said the sculptor, with irrepressible impatience. "Imagination and the love of art have both died out of me."

"Miriam," interposed Donatello, with gentle gravity, "why should we keep our friend in suspense? We know what anxiety he feels. Let us give him what intelligence we can."

"You are so direct and immediate, my beloved friend!" answered Miriam with an unquiet smile. "There are several reasons why I should like to play round this matter a little while, and cover it with fanciful thoughts, as we strew a grave with flowers."

"A grave!" exclaimed the sculptor.

"No grave in which your heart need be buried," she replied; "you have no such calamity to dread. But I linger and hesitate, because every word I speak brings me nearer to a crisis from which I shrink. Ah, Donatello! let us live a little longer the life of these last few days! It is so bright, so airy, so childlike, so without either past or future! Here, on the wild Campagna, you seem to have found, both for yourself and me, the life that belonged to you in early youth; the sweet irresponsible life which you inherited from your mythic ancestry, the Fauns of Monte Beni. Our stern and black reality will come upon us speedily enough. But, first, a brief time more of this strange happiness."

"I dare not linger upon it," answered Donatello, with an expression that reminded the sculptor of the gloomiest days of his remorse at Monte Beni. "I dare to be so happy as you have seen me, only because I have felt the time to be so brief."

"One day, then!" pleaded Miriam. "One more day in the wild freedom of this sweet-scented air."

"Well, one more day," said Donatello, smiling; and his smile touched Kenyon with a pathos beyond words, there being gayety and sadness both melted into it; "but here is Hilda's friend, and our own. Comfort him, at least, and set his heart at rest, since you have it partly in your power."

"Ah, surely he might endure his pangs a little longer!" cried Miriam, turning to Kenyon with a tricksy, fitful kind of mirth, that served to hide some solemn necessity, too sad and serious to be looked at in its naked aspect. "You love us both, I think, and will be content to suffer for our sakes, one other day. Do I ask too much?"

"Tell me of Hilda," replied the sculptor; "tell me only that she is safe, and keep back what else you will."

"Hilda is safe," said Miriam. "There is a Providence purposely for Hilda, as I remember to have told you long ago. But a great trouble—an evil deed, let us acknowledge it—has spread out its dark branches so widely, that the shadow falls on innocence as well as guilt. There was one slight link that connected your sweet Hilda with a crime which it was her unhappy fortune to witness, but of which I need not say she was as guiltless as the angels that looked out of heaven, and saw it too. No matter, now, what the consequence has been. You shall have your lost Hilda back, and—who knows?—perhaps tenderer than she was."

"But when will she return?" persisted the sculptor; "tell me the when, and where, and how!"

"A little patience. Do not press me so," said Miriam; and again Kenyon was struck by the spritelike, fitful characteristic of her manner, and a sort of hysteric gayety, which seemed to be a will-o'-the-wisp from a sorrow stagnant at her heart. "You have more time to spare than I. First, listen to something that I have to tell. We will talk of Hilda by and by."

Then Miriam spoke of her own life, and told facts that threw a gleam of light over many things which had perplexed the sculptor in all his previous knowledge of her. She described herself as springing from English parentage, on the mother's side, but with a vein, likewise, of Jewish blood; yet connected, through her father, with one of those few princely families of Southern Italy, which still retain great wealth and influence. And she revealed a name, at which her auditor started, and grew pale; for it was one that, only a few years before, had been familiar to the world in connection with a mysterious and terrible event. The reader—if he think it worth while to recall some of the strange incidents which have been talked of, and forgotten, within no long time past—will remember Miriam's name.

"You shudder at me, I perceive," said Miriam, suddenly interrupting her narrative.

"No; you were innocent," replied the sculptor. "I shudder at the fatality that seems to haunt your footsteps, and throws a shadow of crime about your path, you being guiltless."

"There was such a fatality," said Miriam; "yes; the shadow fell upon me, innocent, but I went astray in it, and wandered—as Hilda could tell you—into crime."

She went on to say, that, while yet a child, she had lost her English mother. From a very early period of her life, there had been a contract of betrothal between herself and a certain marchese, the representative of another branch of her paternal house,—a family arrangement between two persons of disproportioned ages, and in which feeling went for nothing. Most Italian girls of noble rank would have yielded themselves to such a marriage, as an affair of course. But there was something in Miriam's blood, in her mixed race, in her recollections of her mother,—some characteristic, finally, in her own nature,—which had given her freedom of thought, and force of will, and made this prearranged connection odious to her. Moreover, the character of her destined husband would have been a sufficient and insuperable objection; for it betrayed traits so evil, so treacherous, so vile, and yet so strangely subtle, as could only be accounted for by the insanity which often develops itself in old, close-kept races of men, when long unmixed with newer blood. Reaching the age when the marriage contract should have been fulfilled, Miriam had utterly repudiated it.

Some time afterwards had occurred that terrible event to which Miriam had alluded, when she revealed her name; an event, the frightful and mysterious circumstances of which will recur to many minds, but of which few or none can have found for themselves a satisfactory explanation. It only concerns the present narrative, inasmuch as the suspicion of being at least an accomplice in the crime fell darkly and directly upon Miriam herself.

"But you know that I am innocent!" she cried, interrupting herself again, and looking Kenyon in the face.

"I know it by my deepest consciousness," he answered; "and I know it by Hilda's trust and entire affection, which you never could have won had you been capable of guilt."

"That is sure ground, indeed, for pronouncing me innocent," said Miriam with the tears gushing into her eyes. "Yet I have since become a horror to your saint-like Hilda, by a crime which she herself saw me help to perpetrate!"

She proceeded with her story. The great influence of her family connections had shielded her from some of the consequences of her imputed guilt. But, in her despair, she had fled from home, and had surrounded her flight with such circumstances as rendered it the most probable conclusion that she had committed suicide. Miriam, however, was not of the feeble nature which takes advantage of that obvious and poor resource in earthly difficulties. She flung herself upon the world, and speedily created a new sphere, in which Hilda's gentle purity, the sculptor's sensibility, clear thought, and genius, and Donatello's genial simplicity, had given her almost her first experience of happiness. Then came that ill-omened adventure of the catacomb. The spectral figure which she encountered there was the evil fate that had haunted her through life.

Looking back upon what had happened, Miriam observed, she now considered him a madman. Insanity must have been mixed up with his original composition, and developed by those very acts of depravity which it suggested, and still more intensified, by the remorse that ultimately followed them. Nothing was stranger in his dark career than the penitence which often seemed to go hand in hand with crime. Since his death, she had ascertained that it finally led him to a convent, where his severe and self-inflicted penance had even acquired him the reputation of unusual sanctity, and had been the cause of his enjoying greater freedom than is commonly allowed to monks.

"Need I tell you more?" asked Miriam, after proceeding thus far. "It is still a dim and dreary mystery, a gloomy twilight into which I guide you; but possibly you may catch a glimpse of much that I myself can explain only by conjecture. At all events, you can comprehend what my situation must have been, after that fatal interview in the catacomb. My persecutor had gone thither for penance, but followed me forth with fresh impulses to crime. He had me in his power. Mad as he was, and wicked as he was, with one word he could have blasted me in the belief of all the world. In your belief too, and Hilda's! Even Donatello would have shrunk from me with horror!"

"Never," said Donatello, "my instinct would have known you innocent."

"Hilda and Donatello and myself,—we three would have acquitted you," said Kenyon, "let the world say what it might. Ah, Miriam, you should have told us this sad story sooner!"

"I thought often of revealing it to you," answered Miriam; "on one occasion, especially,—it was after you had shown me your Cleopatra; it seemed to leap out of my heart, and got as far as my very lips. But finding you cold to accept my confidence, I thrust it back again. Had I obeyed my first impulse, all would have turned out differently."

"And Hilda!" resumed the sculptor. "What can have been her connection with these dark incidents?"

"She will, doubtless, tell you with her own lips," replied Miriam. "Through sources of information which I possess in Rome, I can assure you of her safety. In two days more—by the help of the special Providence that, as I love to tell you, watches over Hilda—she shall rejoin you."

"Still two days more!" murmured the sculptor.

"Ah, you are cruel now! More cruel than you know!" exclaimed Miriam, with another gleam of that fantastic, fitful gayety, which had more than once marked her manner, during this interview. "Spare your poor friends!"

"I know not what you mean, Miriam," said Kenyon.

"No matter," she replied; "you will understand hereafter. But could you think it? Here is Donatello haunted with strange remorse, and an unmitigable resolve to obtain what he deems justice upon himself. He fancies, with a kind of direct simplicity, which I have vainly tried to combat, that, when a wrong has been done, the doer is bound to submit himself to whatsoever tribunal takes cognizance of such things, and abide its judgment. I have assured him that there is no such thing as earthly justice, and especially none here, under the head of Christendom."

"We will not argue the point again," said Donatello, smiling. "I have no head for argument, but only a sense, an impulse, an instinct, I believe, which sometimes leads me right. But why do we talk now of what may make us sorrowful? There are still two days more. Let us be happy!"

It appeared to Kenyon that since he last saw Donatello, some of the sweet and delightful characteristics of the antique Faun had returned to him. There were slight, careless graces, pleasant and simple peculiarities, that had been obliterated by the heavy grief through which he was passing at Monte Beni, and out of which he had hardly emerged, when the sculptor parted with Miriam and him beneath the bronze pontiff's outstretched hand. These happy blossoms had now reappeared. A playfulness came out of his heart, and glimmered like firelight in his actions, alternating, or even closely intermingled, with profound sympathy and serious thought.

"Is he not beautiful?" said Miriam, watching the sculptor's eye as it dwelt admiringly on Donatello. "So changed, yet still, in a deeper sense, so much the same! He has travelled in a circle, as all things heavenly and earthly do, and now comes back to his original self, with an inestimable treasure of improvement won from an experience of pain. How wonderful is this! I tremble at my own thoughts, yet must needs probe them to their depths. Was the crime—in which he and I were wedded—was it a blessing, in that strange disguise? Was it a means of education, bringing a simple and imperfect nature to a point of feeling and intelligence which it could have reached under no other discipline?"

"You stir up deep and perilous matter, Miriam," replied Kenyon. "I dare not follow you into the unfathomable abysses whither you are tending."

"Yet there is a pleasure in them! I delight to brood on the verge of this great mystery," returned she. "The story of the fall of man! Is it not repeated in our romance of Monte Beni? And may we follow the analogy yet further? Was that very sin,—into which Adam precipitated himself and all his race,—was it the destined means by which, over a long pathway of toil and sorrow, we are to attain a higher, brighter, and profounder happiness, than our lost birthright gave? Will not this idea account for the permitted existence of sin, as no other theory can?"

"It is too dangerous, Miriam! I cannot follow you!" repeated the sculptor. "Mortal man has no right to tread on the ground where you now set your feet."

"Ask Hilda what she thinks of it," said Miriam, with a thoughtful smile. "At least, she might conclude that sin—which man chose instead of good—has been so beneficently handled by omniscience and omnipotence, that, whereas our dark enemy sought to destroy us by it, it has really become an instrument most effective in the education of intellect and soul."

Miriam paused a little longer among these meditations, which the sculptor, rightly felt to be so perilous; she then pressed his hand, in token of farewell.

"The day after to-morrow," said she, "an hour before sunset, go to the Corso, and stand in front of the fifth house on your left, beyond the Antonine column. You will learn tidings of a friend."

Kenyon would have besought her for more definite intelligence, but she shook her head, put her finger on her lips, and turned away with an illusive smile. The fancy impressed him, that she, too, like Donatello, had reached a wayside paradise, in their mysterious life-journey, where they both threw down the burden of the before and after, and, except for this interview with himself, were happy in the flitting moment. Today, Donatello was the sylvan Faun; to-day, Miriam was his fit companion, a Nymph of grove or fountain; to-morrow,—a remorseful man and woman, linked by a marriage-bond of crime,—they would set forth towards an inevitable goal.

## CHAPTER XLVIII

### A Scene in the Corso

On the appointed afternoon, Kenyon failed not to make his appearance in the Corso, and at an hour much earlier than Miriam had named.

It was carnival time. The merriment of this famous festival was in full progress; and the stately avenue of the Corso was peopled with hundreds of fantastic shapes, some of which probably represented the mirth of ancient times, surviving through all manner of calamity, ever since the days of the Roman Empire. For a few afternoons of early spring, this mouldy gayety strays into the sunshine; all the remainder of the year, it seems to be shut up in the catacombs or some other sepulchral storehouse of the past.

Besides these hereditary forms, at which a hundred generations have laughed, there were others of modern date, the humorous effluence of the day that was now passing. It is a day, however, and an age, that appears to be remarkably barren, when compared with the prolific originality of former times, in productions of a scenic and ceremonial character, whether grave or gay. To own the truth, the Carnival is alive, this present year, only because it has existed through centuries gone by. It is traditionary, not actual. If decrepit and melancholy Rome smiles, and laughs broadly, indeed, at carnival time, it is not in the old simplicity of real mirth, but with a half-conscious effort, like our self-deceptive pretence of jollity at a threadbare joke. Whatever it may once have been, it is now but a narrow stream of merriment, noisy of set purpose, running along the middle of the Corso, through the solemn heart of the decayed city, without extending its shallow influence on either side. Nor, even within its own limits, does it affect the mass of spectators, but only a comparatively few, in street and balcony, who carry on the warfare of nosegays and counterfeit sugar-plums. The populace look on with staid composure; the nobility and priesthood take little or no part in the matter; and, but for the hordes of Anglo-Saxons who annually take up the flagging mirth, the Carnival might long ago have been swept away, with the snow-drifts of confetti that whiten all the pavement.

No doubt, however, the worn-out festival is still new to the youthful and light-hearted, who make the worn-out world itself as fresh as Adam found it on his first forenoon in Paradise. It may be only age and care that chill the life out of its grotesque and airy riot, with the impertinence of their cold criticism.

Kenyon, though young, had care enough within his breast to render the Carnival the emptiest of mockeries. Contrasting the stern anxiety of his present mood with the frolic spirit of the preceding year, he fancied that so much trouble had, at all events, brought wisdom in its train. But there is a wisdom that looks grave, and sneers at merriment; and again a deeper wisdom, that stoops to be gay as often as occasion serves, and oftenest avails itself of shallow and trifling grounds of mirth; because, if we wait for more substantial ones, we seldom can be gay at all. Therefore, had it been possible, Kenyon would have done well to mask himself in some wild, hairy visage, and plunge into the throng of other maskers, as at the Carnival before. Then, Donatello had danced along the Corso in all the equipment of a Faun, doing the part with wonderful felicity of execution, and revealing furry ears, which looked absolutely real; and Miriam had been, alternately, a lady of the antique régime, in powder and brocade, and the prettiest peasant-girl of the Campagna, in the gayest of costumes; while Hilda, sitting demurely in a balcony, had hit the sculptor with a single rose-bud,—so sweet and fresh a bud that he knew at once whose hand had flung it.

These were all gone; all those dear friends whose sympathetic mirth had made him gay. Kenyon felt as if an interval of many years had passed since the last Carnival. He had grown old, the nimble jollity was tame, and the maskers dull and heavy; the Corso was but a narrow and shabby street of decaying palaces; and even the long, blue streamer of Italian sky, above it, not half so brightly blue as formerly.

Yet, if he could have beheld the scene with his clear, natural eyesight, he might still have found both merriment and splendor in it. Everywhere, and all day long, there had been tokens of the festival, in the baskets brimming over with bouquets, for sale at the street-corners, or borne about on people's heads; while bushels upon bushels of variously colored confetti were displayed, looking just like veritable sugar-plums; so that a stranger would have imagined that the whole commerce and business of stern old Rome lay in flowers and sweets. And, now, in the sunny afternoon, there could hardly be a spectacle more picturesque than the vista of that noble street, stretching into the interminable distance between two rows of lofty edifices, from every window of which, and many a balcony, flaunted gay and gorgeous carpets, bright silks, scarlet cloths with rich golden fringes, and Gobelin tapestry, still lustrous with varied hues, though the product of antique looms. Each separate palace had put on a gala-dress, and looked festive for the occasion, whatever sad or guilty secret it might hide within. Every window, moreover, was alive with the faces of women, rosy girls, and children, all kindled into brisk and mirthful expression, by the incidents in the street below. In the balconies that projected along the palace fronts stood groups of ladies, some beautiful, all richly dressed, scattering forth their laughter, shrill, yet sweet, and the musical babble of their voices, to thicken into an airy tumult over the heads of common mortals.

All these innumerable eyes looked down into the street, the whole capacity of which was thronged with festal figures, in such fantastic variety that it had taken centuries to contrive them; and through the midst of the mad, merry stream of human life, rolled slowly onward a never-ending procession of all the vehicles in Rome, from the ducal carriage, with the powdered coachman high in front, and the three golden lackeys, clinging in the rear, down to the rustic cart drawn by its single donkey. Among this various crowd, at windows and in balconies, in cart, cab, barouche, or gorgeous equipage, or bustling to and fro afoot, there was a sympathy of nonsense; a true and genial brotherhood and sisterhood, based on the honest purpose—and a wise one, too—of being foolish, all together. The sport of mankind, like its deepest earnest, is a battle; so these festive people fought one another with an ammunition of sugar-plums and flowers.

Not that they were veritable sugar-plums, however, but something that resembled them only as the apples of Sodom look like better fruit. They were concocted mostly of lime, with a grain of oat, or some other worthless kernel, in the midst. Besides the hail-storm of confetti, the combatants threw handfuls of flour or lime into the air, where it hung like smoke over a battle-field, or, descending, whitened a black coat or priestly robe, and made the curly locks of youth irreverently hoary.

At the same time with this acrid contest of quicklime, which caused much effusion of tears from suffering eyes, a gentler warfare of flowers was carried on, principally between knights and ladies. Originally, no doubt, when this pretty custom was first instituted, it may have had a sincere and modest import. Each youth and damsel, gathering bouquets of field-flowers, or the sweetest and fairest that grew in their own gardens, all fresh and virgin blossoms, flung them, with true aim, at the one, or few, whom they regarded with a sentiment of shy partiality at least, if not with love. Often, the lover in the Corso may thus have received from his bright mistress, in her father's princely balcony, the first sweet intimation that his passionate glances had not struck against a heart of marble. What more appropriate mode of suggesting her tender secret could a maiden find than by the soft hit of a rose-bud against a young man's cheek.

This was the pastime and the earnest of a more innocent and homelier age. Nowadays, the nosegays are gathered and tied up by sordid hands, chiefly of the most ordinary flowers, and are sold along the Corso, at mean price, yet more than such venal things are worth. Buying a basketful, you find them miserably wilted, as if they had flown hither and thither through two or three carnival days already; muddy, too, having been fished up from the pavement, where a hundred feet have trampled on them. You may see throngs of men and boys who thrust themselves beneath the horses' hoofs to gather up bouquets that were aimed amiss from balcony and carriage; these they sell again, and yet once more, and ten times over, defiled as they all are with the wicked filth of Rome.

Such are the flowery favors—the fragrant bunches of sentiment—that fly between cavalier and dame, and back again, from one end of the Corso to the other. Perhaps they may symbolize, more aptly than was intended, the poor, battered, wilted hearts of those who fling them; hearts which—crumpled and crushed by former possessors, and stained with various mishap—have been passed from hand to hand along the muddy streetway of life, instead of being treasured in one faithful bosom.

These venal and polluted flowers, therefore, and those deceptive bon-bons, are types of the small reality that still subsists in the observance of the Carnival. Yet the government seemed to imagine that there might be excitement enough,—wild mirth, perchance, following its antics beyond law, and frisking from frolic into earnest,—to render it expedient to guard the Corso with an imposing show of military power. Besides the ordinary force of gendarmes, a strong patrol of papal dragoons, in steel helmets and white cloaks, were stationed at all the street-corners. Detachments of French infantry stood by their stacked muskets in the Piazza del Popolo, at one extremity of the course, and before the palace of the Austrian embassy, at the other, and by the column of Antoninus, midway between. Had that chained tiger-cat, the Roman populace, shown only so much as the tip of his claws, the sabres would have been flashing and the bullets whistling, in right earnest, among the combatants who now pelted one another with mock sugar-plums and wilted flowers.

But, to do the Roman people justice, they were restrained by a better safeguard than the sabre or the bayonet; it was their own gentle courtesy, which imparted a sort of sacredness to the hereditary festival. At first sight of a spectacle so fantastic and extravagant, a cool observer might have imagined the whole town gone mad; but, in the end, he would see that all this apparently unbounded license is kept strictly within a limit of its own; he would admire a people who can so freely let loose their mirthful propensities, while muzzling those fiercer ones that tend to mischief. Everybody seemed lawless; nobody was rude. If any reveller overstepped the mark, it was sure to be no Roman, but an Englishman or an American; and even the rougher play of this Gothic race was still softened by the insensible influence of a moral atmosphere more delicate, in some respects, than we breathe at home. Not that, after all, we like the fine Italian spirit better than our own; popular rudeness is sometimes the symptom of rude moral health. But, where a Carnival is in question, it would probably pass off more decorously, as well as more airily and delightfully, in Rome, than in any Anglo-Saxon city.

When Kenyon emerged from a side-lane into the Corso, the mirth was at its height. Out of the seclusion of his own feelings, he looked forth at the tapestried and damask-curtained palaces, the slow-moving, double line of carriages, and the motley maskers that swarmed on foot, as if he were gazing through the iron lattice of a prison-window. So remote from the scene were his sympathies, that it affected him like a thin dream, through the dim, extravagant material of which he could discern more substantial objects, while too much under its control to start forth broad awake. Just at that moment, too, there came another spectacle, making its way right through the masquerading throng.

It was, first and foremost, a full band of martial music, reverberating, in that narrow and confined, though stately avenue, between the walls of the lofty palaces, and roaring upward to the sky, with melody so powerful that it almost grew to discord. Next came a body of cavalry and mounted gendarmes, with great display of military pomp. They were escorting a long train of equipages, each and all of which shone as gorgeously as Cinderella's coach, with paint and gilding. Like that, too, they were provided with coachmen, of mighty breadth, and enormously tall footmen, in immense, powdered wigs, and all the splendor of gold-laced, three-cornered hats, and embroidered silk coats and breeches. By the old-fashioned magnificence of this procession, it might worthily have included his Holiness in person, with a suite of attendant Cardinals, if those sacred dignitaries would kindly have lent their aid to heighten the frolic of the Carnival. But, for all its show of a martial escort, and its antique splendor of costume, it was but a train of the municipal authorities of Rome, —illusive shadows, every one, and among them a phantom, styled the Roman Senator,—proceeding to the Capitol.

The riotous interchange of nosegays and confetti was partially suspended, while the procession passed. One well-directed shot, however,—it was a double handful of powdered lime, flung by an impious New-Englander,—hit the coachman of the Roman Senator full in the face, and hurt his dignity amazingly. It appeared to be his opinion, that the Republic was again crumbling into ruin, and that the dust of it now filled his nostrils; though, in fact, it would hardly be distinguished from the official powder with which he was already plentifully bestrewn.

While the sculptor, with his dreamy eyes, was taking idle note of this trifling circumstance, two figures passed before him, hand in hand. The countenance of each was covered with an impenetrable black mask; but one seemed a peasant of the Campagna; the other, a contadina in her holiday costume.

## CHAPTER XLIX

### A FROLIC OF THE CARNIVAL

THE crowd and confusion, just at that moment, hindered the sculptor from pursuing these figures,—the peasant and contadina,—who, indeed, were but two of a numerous tribe that thronged the Corso, in similar costume. As soon as he could squeeze a passage, Kenyon tried to follow in their footsteps, but quickly lost sight of them, and was thrown off the track by stopping to examine various groups of masqueraders, in which he fancied the objects of his search to be included. He found many a sallow peasant or herdsman of the Campagna, in such a dress as Donatello wore; many a contadina, too, brown, broad, and sturdy, in her finery of scarlet, and decked out with gold or coral beads, a pair of heavy earrings, a curiously wrought cameo or mosaic brooch, and a silver comb or long stiletto among her glossy hair. But those shapes of grace and beauty, which he sought, had vanished.

As soon as the procession of the Senator had passed, the merry-makers resumed their antics with fresh spirit, and the artillery of bouquets and sugar-plums, suspended for a moment, began anew. The sculptor himself, being probably the most anxious and unquiet spectator there, was especially a mark for missiles from all quarters, and for the practical jokes which the license of the Carnival permits. In fact, his sad and contracted brow so ill accorded with the scene, that the revellers might be pardoned for thus using him as the butt of their idle mirth, since he evidently could not otherwise contribute to it.

Fantastic figures, with bulbous heads, the circumference of a bushel, grinned enormously in his face. Harlequins struck him with their wooden swords, and appeared to expect his immediate transformation into some jollier shape. A little, long-tailed, horned fiend sidled up to him, and suddenly blew at him through a tube, enveloping our poor friend in a whole harvest of winged seeds. A biped, with an ass's snout, brayed close to his ear, ending his discordant uproar with a peal of human laughter. Five strapping damsels—so, at least, their petticoats bespoke them, in spite of an awful freedom in the flourish of their legs,—joined hands, and danced around him, inviting him by their gestures to perform a hornpipe in the midst. Released from these gay persecutors, a clown in motley rapped him on the back with a blown bladder, in which a handful of dried peas rattled horribly.

Unquestionably, a care-stricken mortal has no business abroad, when the rest of mankind are at high carnival; they must either pelt him and absolutely martyr him with jests, and finally bury him beneath the aggregate heap; or else the potency of his darker mood, because the tissue of human life takes a sad dye more readily than a gay one, will quell their holiday humors, like the aspect of a death's-head at a banquet. Only that we know Kenyon's errand, we could hardly forgive him for venturing into the Corso with that troubled face.

Even yet, his merry martyrdom was not half over. There came along a gigantic female figure, seven feet high, at least, and taking up a third of the street's breadth with the preposterously swelling sphere of her crinoline skirts. Singling out the sculptor, she began to make a ponderous assault upon his heart, throwing amorous glances at him out of her great goggle-eyes, offering him a vast bouquet of sunflowers and nettles, and soliciting his pity by all sorts of pathetic and passionate dumb-show. Her suit meeting no favor, the rejected Titaness made a gesture of despair and rage; then suddenly drawing a huge pistol, she took aim right at the obdurate sculptor's breast, and pulled the trigger. The shot took effect, for the abominable plaything went off by a spring, like a boy's popgun, covering Kenyon with a cloud of lime-dust, under shelter of which the revengeful damsel strode away.

Hereupon, a whole host of absurd figures surrounded him pretending to sympathize in his mishap. Clowns and party-colored harlequins; orang-outangs; bear-headed, bull-headed, and dog-headed individuals; faces that would have been human, but for their enormous noses; one terrific creature, with a visage right in the centre of his breast; and all other imaginable kinds of monstrosity and exaggeration. These apparitions appeared to be investigating the case, after the fashion of a coroner's jury, poking their pasteboard countenances close to the sculptor's with an unchangeable grin, that gave still more ludicrous effect to the comic alarm and sorrow of their gestures. Just then, a figure came by, in a gray wig and rusty gown, with an inkhorn at his button-hole, and a pen behind his ear; he announced himself as a notary, and offered to make the last will and testament of the assassinated man. This solemn duty, however, was interrupted by a surgeon, who brandished a lancet, three feet long, and proposed to him to let him take blood.

The affair was so like a feverish dream, that Kenyon resigned himself to let it take its course. Fortunately the humors of the Carnival pass from one absurdity to another, without lingering long enough on any, to wear out even the slightest of them. The passiveness of his demeanor afforded too little scope for such broad merriment as the masqueraders sought. In a few moments they vanished from him, as dreams and spectres do, leaving him at liberty to pursue his quest, with no impediment except the crowd that blocked up the footway.

He had not gone far when the peasant and the contadina met him. They were still hand in hand, and appeared to be straying through the grotesque and animated scene, taking as little part in it as himself. It might be because he recognized them, and knew their solemn secret, that the sculptor fancied a melancholy emotion to be expressed by the very movement and attitudes of these two figures; and even the grasp of their hands, uniting them so closely, seemed to set them in a sad remoteness from the world at which they gazed.

"I rejoice to meet you," said Kenyon.

But they looked at him through the eye-holes of their black masks, without answering a word.

"Pray give me a little light on the matter which I have so much at heart," said he; "if you know anything of Hilda, for Heaven's sake, speak!"

Still, they were silent; and the sculptor began to imagine that he must have mistaken the identity of these figures, there being such a multitude in similar costume. Yet there was no other Donatello, no other Miriam. He felt, too, that spiritual certainty which impresses us with the presence of our friends, apart from any testimony of the senses.

"You are unkind," resumed he,—"knowing the anxiety which oppresses me,—not to relieve it, if in your power."

The reproach evidently had its effect; for the contadina now spoke, and it was Miriam's voice.

"We gave you all the light we could," said she. "You are yourself unkind, though you little think how much so, to come between us at this hour. There may be a sacred hour, even in carnival time."

In another state of mind, Kenyon could have been amused by the impulsiveness of this response, and a sort of vivacity that he had often noted in Miriam's conversation. But he was conscious of a profound sadness in her tone, overpowering its momentary irritation, and assuring him that a pale, tear-stained face was hidden behind her mask.

"Forgive me!" said he.

Donatello here extended his hand,—not that which was clasping Miriam's,—and she, too, put her free one into the sculptor's left; so that they were a linked circle of three, with many reminiscences and forebodings flashing through their hearts. Kenyon knew intuitively that these once familiar friends were parting with him, now.

"Farewell!" they all three said, in the same breath.

No sooner was the word spoken, than they loosed their hands; and the uproar of the Carnival swept like a tempestuous sea over the spot, which they had included within their small circle of isolated feeling.

By this interview, the sculptor had learned nothing in reference to Hilda; but he understood that he was to adhere to the instructions already received, and await a solution of the mystery in some mode that he could not yet anticipate. Passing his hands over his eyes, and looking about him,—for the event just described had made the scene even more dreamlike than before,—he now found himself approaching that broad piazza bordering on the Corso, which has for its central object the sculptured column of Antoninus. It was not far from this vicinity that Miriam had bid him wait. Struggling onward, as fast as the tide of merry-makers, setting strong against him, would permit, he was now beyond the Palazzo Colonna, and began to count the houses. The fifth was a palace, with a long front upon the Corso, and of stately height, but somewhat grim with age.

Over its arched and pillared entrance there was a balcony, richly hung with tapestry and damask, and tenanted, for the time, by a gentleman of venerable aspect, and a group of ladies. The white hair and whiskers of the former, and the winter-roses in his cheeks, had an English look; the ladies, too, showed a fair-haired Saxon bloom, and seemed to taste the mirth of the Carnival with the freshness of spectators to whom the scene was new. All the party, the old gentleman with grave earnestness, as if he were defending a rampart, and his young companions with exuberance of frolic, showered confetti inexhaustibly upon the passers-by.

In the rear of the balcony, a broad-brimmed, ecclesiastical beaver was visible. An abbate, probably an acquaintance and cicerone of the English family, was sitting there, and enjoying the scene, though partially withdrawn from view, as the decorum for his order dictated.

There seemed no better nor other course for Kenyon, than to keep watch at this appointed spot, waiting for whatever should happen next. Clasping his arm around a lamp-post, to prevent being carried away by the turbulent stream of wayfarers, he scrutinized every face, with the idea that some one of them might meet his eyes with a glance of intelligence. He looked at each mask,—harlequin, ape, bulbous-headed monster, or anything that was absurdest,—not knowing but that the messenger might come, even in such fantastic guise. Or, perhaps, one of those quaint figures, in the stately ruff, the cloak, tunic, and trunk-hose, of three centuries ago, might bring him tidings of Hilda, out of that long-past age. At times, his disquietude took a hopeful aspect; and he fancied that Hilda might come by, her own sweet self, in some shy disguise which the instinct of his love would be sure to penetrate. Or, she might be borne past on a triumphal car, like the one just now approaching, its slow-moving wheels encircled and spoked with foliage, and drawn by horses, that were harnessed and wreathed with flowers. Being, at best, so far beyond the bounds of reasonable conjecture, he might anticipate the wildest event, or find either his hopes or fears disappointed in what appeared most probable.

The old Englishman and his daughters, in the opposite balcony, must have seen something unutterably absurd in the sculptor's deportment, poring into this whirlpool of nonsense so earnestly, in quest of what was to make his life dark or bright. Earnest people, who try to get a reality out of human existence, are necessarily absurd in the view of the revellers and masqueraders. At all events, after a good deal of mirth at the expense of his melancholy visage, the fair occupants of the balcony favored Kenyon with a salvo of confetti, which came rattling about him like a hail-storm. Looking up, instinctively, he was surprised to see the abbate in the background lean forward and give a courteous sign of recognition.

It was the same old priest with whom he had seen Hilda, at the confessional; the same with whom he had talked of her disappearance on meeting him in the street.

Yet, whatever might be the reason, Kenyon did not now associate this ecclesiastical personage with the idea of Hilda. His eyes lighted on the old man, just for an instant, and then returned to the eddying throng of the Corso, on his minute scrutiny of which depended, for aught he knew, the sole chance of ever finding any trace of her. There was, about this moment, a bustle on the other side of the street, the cause of which Kenyon did not see, nor exert himself to discover. A small party of soldiers or gendarmes appeared to be concerned in it; they were perhaps arresting some disorderly character, who, under the influence of an extra flask of wine, might have reeled across the mystic limitation of carnival proprieties.

The sculptor heard some people near him talking of the incident.

"That contadina, in a black mask, was a fine figure of a woman."

"She was not amiss," replied a female voice; "but her companion was far the handsomer figure of the two. Could they be really a peasant and a contadina, do you imagine?"

"No, no," said the other. "It is some frolic of the Carnival, carried a little too far."

This conversation might have excited Kenyon's interest; only that, just as the last words were spoken, he was hit by two missiles, both of a kind that were flying abundantly on that gay battle-field. One, we are ashamed to say, was a cauliflower, which, flung by a young man from a passing carriage, came with a prodigious thump against his shoulder; the other was a single rose-bud, so fresh that it seemed that moment gathered.

It flew from the opposite balcony, smote gently on his lips, and fell into his hand. He looked upward, and beheld the face of his lost Hilda!

She was dressed in a white domino, and looked pale and bewildered, and yet full of tender joy. Moreover, there was a gleam of delicate mirthfulness in her eyes, which the sculptor had seen there only two or three times, in the course of their acquaintance, but thought it the most bewitching and fairy-like of all Hilda's expressions. That soft, mirthful smile caused her to melt, as it were, into the wild frolic of the Carnival, and become not so strange and alien to the scene, as her unexpected apparition must otherwise have made her.

Meanwhile, the venerable Englishman and his daughters were staring at poor Hilda in a way that proved them altogether astonished, as well as inexpressibly shocked, by her sudden intrusion into their private balcony. They looked,—as, indeed, English people of respectability would, if an angel were to alight in their circle, without due introduction from somebody whom they knew, in the court above,—they looked as if an unpardonable liberty had been taken, and a suitable apology must be made; after which, the intruder would be expected to withdraw.

The abbate, however, drew the old gentleman aside, and whispered a few words that served to mollify him; he bestowed on Hilda a sufficiently benignant, though still a perplexed and questioning regard, and invited her, in dumb-show, to put herself at her ease.

But, whoever was in fault, our shy and gentle Hilda had dreamed of no intrusion. Whence she had come, or where she had been hidden, during this mysterious interval, we can but imperfectly surmise, and do not mean, at present, to make it a matter of formal explanation with the reader. It is better, perhaps, to fancy that she had been snatched away to a land of picture; that she had been straying with Claude in the golden light which he used to shed over his landscapes, but which he could never have beheld with his waking eyes till he awoke in the better clime. We will imagine that, for the sake of the true simplicity with which she loved them, Hilda had been permitted, for a season, to converse with the great, departed masters of the pencil, and behold the diviner works which they have painted in heavenly colors. Guido had shown her another portrait of Beatrice Cenci, done from the celestial life, in which that forlorn mystery of the earthly countenance was exchanged for a radiant joy. Perugino had allowed her a glimpse at his easel, on which she discerned what seemed a woman's face, but so divine, by the very depth and softness of its womanhood, that a gush of happy tears blinded the maiden's eyes before she had time to look. Raphael had taken Hilda by the hand,—that fine, forcible hand which Kenyon sculptured,—and drawn aside the curtain of gold-fringed cloud that hung before his latest masterpiece. On earth, Raphael painted the Transfiguration. What higher scene may he have since depicted, not from imagination, but as revealed to his actual sight!

Neither will we retrace the steps by which she returned to the actual world. For the present, be it enough to say that Hilda had been summoned forth from a secret place, and led we know not through what mysterious passages, to a point where the tumult of life burst suddenly upon her ears. She heard the tramp of footsteps, the rattle of wheels, and the mingled hum of a multitude of voices, with strains of music and loud laughter breaking through. Emerging into a great, gloomy hall, a curtain was drawn aside; she found herself gently propelled into an open balcony, whence she looked out upon the festal street, with gay tapestries flaunting over all the palace fronts, the windows thronged with merry faces, and a crowd of maskers rioting upon the pavement below.

Immediately, she seemed to become a portion of the scene. Her pale, large-eyed, fragile beauty, her wondering aspect and bewildered grace, attracted the gaze of many; and there fell around her a shower of bouquets, and bonbons—freshest blossoms and sweetest sugar-plums, sweets to the sweet—such as the revellers of the Carnival reserve as tributes to especial loveliness. Hilda pressed her hand across her brow; she let her eyelids fall, and, lifting them again, looked through the grotesque and gorgeous show, the chaos of mad jollity, in quest of some object by which she might assure herself that the whole spectacle was not an illusion.

Beneath the balcony, she recognized a familiar and fondly remembered face. The spirit of the hour and the scene exercised its influence over her quick and sensitive nature; she caught up one of the rose-buds that had been showered upon her, and aimed it at the sculptor. It hit the mark; he turned his sad eyes upward, and there was Hilda, in whose gentle presence his own secret sorrow and the obtrusive uproar of the Carnival alike died away from his perception.

That night, the lamp beneath the Virgin's shrine burned as brightly as if it had never been extinguished; and though the one faithful dove had gone to her melancholy perch, she greeted Hilda rapturously the next morning, and summoned her less constant companions, whithersoever they had flown, to renew their homage.

## CHAPTER L

### MIRIAM, HILDA, KENYON, DONATELLO

THE gentle reader, we trust, would not thank us for one of those minute elucidations, which are so tedious, and, after all, so unsatisfactory, in clearing up the romantic mysteries of a story. He is too wise to insist upon looking closely at the wrong side of the tapestry, after the right one has been sufficiently displayed to him, woven with the best of the artist's skill, and cunningly arranged with a view to the harmonious exhibition of its colors. If any brilliant, or beautiful, or even tolerable effect have been produced, this pattern of kindly readers will accept it at its worth, without tearing its web apart, with the idle purpose of discovering how the threads have been knit together; for the sagacity by which he is distinguished will long ago have taught him that any narrative of human action and adventure—whether we call it history or romance—is certain to be a fragile handiwork, more easily rent than mended. The actual experience of even the most ordinary life is full of events that never explain themselves, either as regards their origin or their tendency.

It would be easy, from conversations which we have held with the sculptor, to suggest a clew to the mystery of Hilda's disappearance; although, as long as she remained in Italy, there was a remarkable reserve in her communications upon this subject, even to her most intimate friends. Either a pledge of secrecy had been exacted, or a prudential motive warned her not to reveal the stratagems of a religious body, or the secret acts of a despotic government—whichever might be responsible in the present instance—while still within the scope of their jurisdiction. Possibly, she might not herself be fully aware what power had laid its grasp upon her person. What has chiefly perplexed us, however, among Hilda's adventures, is the mode of her release, in which some inscrutable tyranny or other seemed to take part in the frolic of the Carnival. We can only account for it, by supposing that the fitful and fantastic imagination of a woman—sportive, because she must otherwise be desperate—had arranged this incident, and made it the condition of a step which her conscience, or the conscience of another, required her to take.

A few days after Hilda's reappearance, she and the sculptor were straying together through the streets of Rome. Being deep in talk, it so happened that they found themselves near the majestic, pillared portico, and huge, black rotundity of the Pantheon. It stands almost at the central point of the labyrinthine intricacies of the modern city, and often presents itself before the bewildered stranger, when he is in search of other objects. Hilda, looking up, proposed that they should enter.

"I never pass it without going in," she said, "to pay my homage at the tomb of Raphael."

"Nor I," said Kenyon, "without stopping to admire the noblest edifice which the barbarism of the early ages, and the more barbarous pontiffs and princes of later ones, have spared to us."

They went in, accordingly, and stood in the free space of that great circle, around which are ranged the arched recesses and stately altars, formerly dedicated to heathen gods, but Christianized through twelve centuries gone by. The world has nothing else like the Pantheon. So grand it is, that the pasteboard statues over the lofty cornice do not disturb the effect, any more than the tin crowns and hearts, the dusty artificial flowers, and all manner of trumpery gewgaws, hanging at the saintly shrines. The rust and dinginess that have dimmed the precious marble on the walls; the pavement, with its great squares and rounds of porphyry and granite, cracked crosswise and in a hundred directions, showing how roughly the troublesome ages have trampled here; the gray dome above, with its opening to the sky, as if heaven were looking down into the interior of this place of worship, left unimpeded for prayers to ascend the more freely: all these things make an impression of solemnity, which St. Peter's itself fails to produce.

"I think," said the sculptor, "it is to the aperture in the dome—that great Eye, gazing heavenward—that the Pantheon owes the peculiarity of its effect. It is so heathenish, as it were,—so unlike all the snugness of our modern civilization! Look, too, at the pavement, directly beneath the open space! So much rain has fallen there, in the last two thousand years, that it is green with small, fine moss, such as grows over tombstones in a damp English churchyard."

"I like better," replied Hilda, "to look at the bright, blue sky, roofing the edifice where the builders left it open. It is very delightful, in a breezy day, to see the masses of white cloud float over the opening, and then the sunshine fall through it again, fitfully, as it does now. Would it be any wonder if we were to see angels hovering there, partly in and partly out, with genial, heavenly faces, not intercepting the light, but only transmuting it into beautiful colors? Look at that broad, golden beam—a sloping cataract of sunlight—which comes down from the aperture and rests upon the shrine, at the right hand of the entrance!"

"There is a dusky picture over that altar," observed the sculptor. "Let us go and see if this strong illumination brings out any merit in it."

Approaching the shrine, they found the picture little worth looking at, but could not forbear smiling, to see that a very plump and comfortable tabby-cat—whom we ourselves have often observed haunting the Pantheon—had established herself on the altar, in the genial sunbeam, and was fast asleep among the holy tapers. Their footsteps disturbing her, she awoke, raised herself, and sat blinking in the sun, yet with a certain dignity and self-possession, as if conscious of representing a saint.

"I presume," remarked Kenyon, "that this is the first of the feline race that has ever set herself up as an object of worship, in the Pantheon or elsewhere, since the days of ancient Egypt. See; there is a peasant from the neighboring market, actually kneeling to her! She seems a gracious and benignant saint enough."

"Do not make me laugh," said Hilda, reproachfully, "but help me to drive the creature away. It distresses me to see that poor man, or any human being, directing his prayers so much amiss."

"Then, Hilda," answered the sculptor, more seriously, "the only place in the Pantheon for you and me to kneel is on the pavement beneath the central aperture. If we pray at a saint's shrine, we shall give utterance to earthly wishes; but if we pray face to face with the Deity, we shall feel it impious to petition for aught that is narrow and selfish. Methinks, it is this that makes the Catholics so delight in the worship of saints; they can bring up all their little worldly wants and whims, their individualities and human weaknesses, not as things to be repented of, but to be humored by the canonized humanity to which they pray. Indeed, it is very tempting!"

What Hilda might have answered must be left to conjecture; for as she turned from the shrine, her eyes were attracted to the figure of a female penitent, kneeling on the pavement just beneath the great central eye, in the very spot which Kenyon had designated as the only one whence prayers should ascend. The upturned face was invisible, behind a veil or mask, which formed a part of the garb.

"It cannot be!" whispered Hilda, with emotion. "No; it cannot be!"

"What disturbs you?" asked Kenyon. "Why do you tremble so?"

"If it were possible," she replied, "I should fancy that kneeling figure to be Miriam!"

"As you say, it is impossible," rejoined the sculptor. "We know too well what has befallen both her and Donatello."

"Yes; it is impossible!" repeated Hilda.

Her voice was still tremulous, however, and she seemed unable to withdraw her attention from the kneeling figure. Suddenly, and as if the idea of Miriam had opened the whole volume of Hilda's reminiscences, she put this question to the sculptor:—

"Was Donatello really a Faun?"

"If you had ever studied the pedigree of the far-descended heir of Monte Beni, as I did," answered Kenyon, with an irrepressible smile, "you would have retained few doubts on that point. Faun or not, he had a genial nature, which, had the rest of mankind been in accordance with it, would have made earth a paradise to our poor friend. It seems the moral of his story, that human beings of Donatello's character, compounded especially for happiness, have no longer any business on earth, or elsewhere. Life has grown so sadly serious, that such men must change their nature, or else perish, like the antediluvian creatures, that required, as the condition of their existence, a more summer-like atmosphere than ours."

"I will not accept your moral!" replied the hopeful and happy-natured Hilda.

"Then here is another; take your choice!" said the sculptor, remembering what Miriam had recently suggested, in reference to the same point. "He perpetrated a great crime; and his remorse, gnawing into his soul, has awakened it; developing a thousand high capabilities, moral and intellectual, which we never should have dreamed of asking for, within the scanty compass of the Donatello whom we knew."

"I know not whether this is so," said Hilda. "But what then?"

"Here comes my perplexity," continued Kenyon. "Sin has educated Donatello, and elevated him. Is sin, then,—which we deem such a dreadful blackness in the universe,—is it, like sorrow, merely an element of human education, through which we struggle to a higher and purer state than we could otherwise have attained? Did Adam fall, that we might ultimately rise to a far loftier paradise than his?"

"Oh, hush!" cried Hilda, shrinking from him with an expression of horror which wounded the poor, speculative sculpture to the soul. "This is terrible; and I could weep for you, if you indeed believe it. Do not you

perceive what a mockery your creed makes, not only of all religious sentiments, but of moral law? and how it annuls and obliterates whatever pre-
cepts of Heaven are written deepest within us? You have shocked me beyond words!"

"Forgive me, Hilda!" exclaimed the sculptor, startled by her agitation;
"I never did believe it! But the mind wanders wild and wide; and, so
lonely as I live and work, I have neither pole-star above nor light of cot-
tage-windows here below, to bring me home. Were you my guide, my
counsellor, my inmost friend, with that white wisdom which clothes you
as a celestial garment, all would go well. O Hilda, guide me home!"

"We are both lonely; both far from home!" said Hilda, her eyes filling
with tears. "I am a poor, weak girl, and have no such wisdom as you
fancy in me."

What further may have passed between these lovers, while standing
before the pillared shrine, and the marble Madonna that marks Raphael's
tomb, whither they had now wandered, we are unable to record. But when
the kneeling figure beneath the open eye of the Pantheon arose, she looked
towards the pair, and extended her hands with a gesture of benediction.
Then they knew that it was Miriam. They suffered her to glide out of the
portal, however, without a greeting; for those extended hands, even while
they blessed, seemed to repel, as if Miriam stood on the other side of a
fathomless abyss, and warned them from its verge.

So Kenyon won the gentle Hilda's shy affection, and her consent to be
his bride. Another hand must henceforth trim the lamp before the Virgin's shrine; for Hilda was coming down from her old tower, to be herself enshrined and worshipped as a household saint, in the light of her
husband's fireside. And, now that life had so much human promise in it,
they resolved to go back to their own land; because the years, after all,
have a kind of emptiness, when we spend too many of them on a foreign
shore. We defer the reality of life, in such cases, until a future moment,
when we shall again breathe our native air; but, by and by, there are no
future moments; or, if we do return, we find that the native air has lost
its invigorating quality, and that life has shifted its reality to the spot
where we have deemed ourselves only temporary residents. Thus, between
two countries, we have none at all, or only that little space of either, in
which we finally lay down our discontented bones. It is wise, therefore, to
come back betimes, or never.

Before they quitted Rome, a bridal gift was laid on Hilda's table. It
was a bracelet, evidently of great cost, being composed of seven ancient
Etruscan gems, dug out of seven sepulchres, and each one of them the
signet of some princely personage, who had lived an immemorial time
ago. Hilda remembered this precious ornament. It had been Miriam's;
and once, with the exuberance of fancy that distinguished her, she had
amused herself with telling a mythical and magic legend for each gem,
comprising the imaginary adventures and catastrophe of its former wearer. Thus, the Etruscan bracelet became the connecting bond of a series
of seven wondrous tales, all of which, as they were dug out of seven sepul-

chres, were characterized by a seven-fold sepulchral gloom; such as Miriam's imagination, shadowed by her own misfortunes, was wont to fling over its most sportive flights.

And now, happy as Hilda was, the bracelet brought the tears into her eyes, as being, in its entire circle, the symbol of as sad a mystery as any that Miriam had attached to the separate gems. For, what was Miriam's life to be? And where was Donatello? But Hilda had a hopeful soul, and saw sunlight on the mountain-tops.

## CONCLUSION

THERE comes to the author, from many readers of the foregoing pages, a demand for further elucidations respecting the mysteries of the story.

He reluctantly avails himself of the opportunity afforded by a new edition, to explain such incidents and passages as may have been left too much in the dark; reluctantly, he repeats, because the necessity makes him sensible that he can have succeeded but imperfectly, at best, in throwing about this Romance the kind of atmosphere essential to the effect at which he aimed.

He designed the story and the characters to bear, of course, a certain relation to human nature and human life, but still to be so artfully and airily removed from our mundane sphere, that some laws and proprieties of their own should be implicitly and insensibly acknowledged.

The idea of the modern Faun, for example, loses all the poetry and beauty which the Author fancied in it, and becomes nothing better than a grotesque absurdity, if we bring it into the actual light of day. He had hoped to mystify this anomalous creature between the Real and the Fantastic, in such a manner that the reader's sympathies might be excited to a certain pleasurable degree, without impelling him to ask how Cuvier would have classified poor Donatello, or to insist upon being told, in so many words, whether he had furry ears or no. As respects all who ask such questions, the book is, to that extent, a failure.

Nevertheless, the Author fortunately has it in his power to throw light upon several matters in which some of his readers appear to feel an interest. To confess the truth, he was himself troubled with a curiosity similar to that which he has just deprecated on the part of his readers, and once took occasion to cross-examine his friends, Hilda and the sculptor, and to pry into several dark recesses of the story, with which they had heretofore imperfectly acquainted him.

We three had climbed to the top of St. Peter's, and were looking down upon the Rome we were soon to leave, but which (having already sinned sufficiently in that way) it is not my purpose further to describe. It occurred to me, that, being so remote in the upper air, my friends might safely utter, here, the secrets which it would be perilous even to whisper on lower earth.

"Hilda," I began, "can you tell me the contents of that mysterious packet which Miriam intrusted to your charge, and which was addressed to Signore Luca Barboni, at the Palazzo Cenci?"

"I never had any further knowledge of it," replied Hilda, "nor felt it right to let myself be curious upon the subject."

"As to its precise contents," interposed Kenyon, "it is impossible to speak. But Miriam, isolated as she seemed, had family connections in Rome, one of whom, there is reason to believe, occupied a position in the papal government.

"This Signore Luca Barboni was either the assumed name of the personage in question, or the medium of communication between that individual and Miriam. Now, under such a government as that of Rome, it is obvious that Miriam's privacy and isolated life could only be maintained through the connivance and support of some influential person connected with the administration of affairs. Free and self-controlled as she appeared, her every movement was watched and investigated far more thoroughly by the priestly rulers than by her dearest friends.

"Miriam, if I mistake not, had a purpose to withdraw herself from this irksome scrutiny, and to seek real obscurity in another land; and the packet, to be delivered long after her departure, contained a reference to this design, besides certain family documents, which were to be imparted to her relative as from one dead and gone."

"Yes, it is clear as a London fog," I remarked. "On this head no further elucidation can be desired. But when Hilda went quietly to deliver the packet, why did she so mysteriously vanish?"

"You must recollect," replied Kenyon, with a glance of friendly commiseration at my obtuseness, "that Miriam had utterly disappeared, leaving no trace by which her whereabouts could be known. In the meantime, the municipal authorities had become aware of the murder of the Capuchin; and from many preceding circumstances, such as his persecution of Miriam, they must have seen an obvious connection between herself and that tragical event. Furthermore, there is reason to believe that Miriam was suspected of connection with some plot, or political intrigue, of which there may have been tokens in the packet. And when Hilda appeared, as the bearer of this missive, it was really quite a matter of course, under a despotic government, that she should be detained."

"Ah, quite a matter of course, as you say," answered I. "How excessively stupid in me not to have seen it sooner! But there are other riddles. On the night of the extinction of the lamp, you met Donatello, in a penitent's garb, and afterwards saw and spoke to Miriam, in a coach, with a gem glowing on her bosom. What was the business of these two guilty ones in Rome, and who was Miriam's companion?"

"Who!" repeated Kenyon, "why her official relative, to be sure; and as to their business, Donatello's still gnawing remorse had brought him hitherward, in spite of Miriam's entreaties, and kept him lingering in the neighborhood of Rome, with the ultimate purpose of delivering himself up to justice. Hilda's disappearance, which took place the day before, was known to them through a secret channel, and had brought them into the city, where Miriam, as I surmise, began to make arrangements, even then, for that sad frolic of the Carnival."

"And where was Hilda all that dreary time between?" inquired I.

"Where were you, Hilda?" asked Kenyon, smiling.

Hilda threw her eyes on all sides, and seeing that there was not even a bird of the air to fly away with the secret, nor any human being nearer than the loiterers by the obelisk, in the piazza below, she told us about her mysterious abode.

"I was a prisoner in the Convent of the Sacré Cœur, in the Trinità de' Monte," said she, "but in such kindly custody of pious maidens, and watched over by such a dear old priest, that—had it not been for one or two disturbing recollections, and also because I am a daughter of the Puritans—I could willingly have dwelt there forever.

"My entanglement with Miriam's misfortunes, and the good abbate's mistaken hope of a proselyte, seem to me a sufficient clew to the whole mystery."

"The atmosphere is getting delightfully lucid," observed I, "but there are one or two things that still puzzle me. Could you tell me—and it shall be kept a profound secret, I assure you—what were Miriam's real name and rank, and precisely the nature of the troubles that led to all those direful consequences?"

"Is it possible that you need an answer to those questions?" exclaimed Kenyon, with an aspect of vast surprise. "Have you not even surmised Miriam's name? Think awhile, and you will assuredly remember it. If not, I congratulate you most sincerely; for it indicates that your feelings have never been harrowed by one of the most dreadful and mysterious events that have occurred within the present century!"

"Well," resumed I, after an interval of deep consideration, "I have but few things more to ask. Where, at this moment, is Donatello?"

"The Castle of Saint Angelo," said Kenyon, sadly, turning his face towards that sepulchral fortress, "'is no longer a prison; but there are others which have dungeons as deep, and in one of them, I fear, lies our poor Faun."

"And why, then, is Miriam at large?" I asked.

"Call it cruelty if you like, not mercy," answered Kenyon. "But, after all, her crime lay merely in a glance. She did no murder!"

"Only one question more," said I, with intense earnestness. "Did Donatello's ears resemble those of the Faun of Praxiteles?"

"I know, but may not tell," replied Kenyon, smiling mysteriously. "On that point, at all events, there shall be not one word of explanation."

Leamington, *March* 14, 1860.

# FROM TWICE-TOLD TALES

# THE GRAY CHAMPION

THERE was once a time when New England groaned under the actual pressure of heavier wrongs than those threatened ones which brought on the Revolution. James II., the bigoted successor of Charles the Voluptuous, had annulled the charters of all the colonies, and sent a harsh and unprincipled soldier to take away our liberties and endanger our religion. The administration of Sir Edmund Andros lacked scarcely a single characteristic of tyranny: a Governor and Council, holding office from the King, and wholly independent of the country; laws made and taxes levied without concurrence of the people immediate or by their representatives; the rights of private citizens violated, and the titles of all landed property declared void; the voice of complaint stifled by restrictions on the press; and, finally, disaffection overawed by the first band of mercenary troops that ever marched on our free soil. For two years our ancestors were kept in sullen submission by that filial love which had invariably secured their allegiance to the mother country, whether its head chanced to be a Parliament, Protector, or Popish Monarch. Till these evil times, however, such allegiance had been merely nominal, and the colonists had ruled themselves, enjoying far more freedom than is even yet the privilege of the native subjects of Great Britain.

At length a rumor reached our shores that the Prince of Orange had ventured on an enterprise, the success of which would be the triumph of civil and religious rights and the salvation of New England. It was but a doubtful whisper: it might be false, or the attempt might fail; and, in either case, the man that stirred against King James would lose his head. Still the intelligence produced a marked effect. The people smiled mysteriously in the streets, and threw bold glances at their oppressors; while far and wide there was a subdued and silent agitation, as if the slightest signal would rouse the whole land from its sluggish despondency. Aware of their danger, the rulers resolved to avert it by an imposing display of strength, and perhaps to confirm their despotism by yet harsher measures. One afternoon in April, 1689, Sir Edmund Andros and his favorite councillors, being warm with wine, assembled the red-coats of the Governor's Guard, and made their appearance in the streets of Boston. The sun was near setting when the march commenced.

The roll of the drum at that unquiet crisis seemed to go through the streets, less as the martial music of the soldiers, than as a muster-call to the inhabitants themselves. A multitude, by various avenues, assembled in King Street, which was destined to be the scene, nearly a century afterwards, of another encounter between the troops of Britain, and a people struggling against her tyranny. Though more than sixty years had elapsed since the pilgrims came, this crowd of their descendants still showed the strong and sombre features of their character perhaps more strikingly in such a stern emergency than on happier occasions. There were the sober garb, the general severity of mien, the gloomy but un-dismayed expression, the scriptural forms of speech, and the confidence in Heaven's blessing on a righteous cause, which would have marked a band of the original Puritans, when threatened by some peril of the wil-derness. Indeed, it was not yet time for the old spirit to be extinct; since there were men in the street that day who had worshipped there beneath the trees, before a house was reared to the God for whom they had become exiles. Old soldiers of the Parliament were here, too, smiling grimly at the thought that their aged arms might strike another blow against the house of Stuart. Here, also, were the veterans of King Philip's war, who had burned villages and slaughtered young and old, with pious fierceness, while the godly souls throughout the land were helping them with prayer. Several ministers were scattered among the crowd, which, unlike all other mobs, regarded them with such reverence, as if there were sanctity in their very garments. These holy men exerted their influence to quiet the people, but not to disperse them. Meantime, the purpose of the Governor, in disturbing the peace of the town at a period when the slightest com-motion might throw the country into a ferment, was almost the universal subject of inquiry, and variously explained.

"Satan will strike his master-stroke presently," cried some, "because he knoweth that his time is short. All our godly pastors are to be dragged to prison! We shall see them at a Smithfield fire in King Street!"

Hereupon the people of each parish gathered closer round their min-ister, who looked calmly upwards and assumed a more apostolic dignity, as well befitted a candidate for the highest honor of his profession, the crown of martyrdom. It was actually fancied, at that period, that New England might have a John Rogers of her own to take the place of that worthy in the Primer.

"The Pope of Rome has given orders for a new St. Bartholomew!" cried others. "We are to be massacred, man and male child!"

Neither was this rumor wholly discredited, although the wiser class be-lieved the Governor's object somewhat less atrocious. His predecessor under the old charter, Bradstreet, a venerable companion of the first set-tlers, was known to be in town. There were grounds for conjecturing, that Sir Edmund Andros intended at once to strike terror by a parade of mili-tary force, and to confound the opposite faction by possessing himself of their chief.

"Stand firm for the old charter Governor!" shouted the crowd, seizing upon the idea. "The good old Governor Bradstreet!"

While this cry was at the loudest, the people were surprised by the well-known figure of Governor Bradstreet himself, a patriarch of nearly ninety, who appeared on the elevated steps of a door, and, with characteristic mildness, besought them to submit to the constituted authorities.

"My children," concluded this venerable person, "do nothing rashly. Cry not aloud, but pray for the welfare of New England, and expect patiently what the Lord will do in this matter!"

The event was soon to be decided. All this time, the roll of the drum had been approaching through Cornhill, louder and deeper, till with reverberations from house to house, and the regular tramp of martial footsteps, it burst into the street. A double rank of soldiers made their appearance, occupying the whole breadth of the passage, with shouldered matchlocks, and matches burning, so as to present a row of fires in the dusk. Their steady march was like the progress of a machine, that would roll irresistibly over everything in its way. Next, moving slowly, with a confused clatter of hoofs on the pavement, rode a party of mounted gentlemen, the central figure being Sir Edmund Andros, elderly, but erect and soldier-like. Those around him were his favorite councillors, and the bitterest foes of New England. At his right hand rode Edward Randolph, our arch-enemy, that "blasted wretch," as Cotton Mather calls him, who achieved the downfall of our ancient government, and was followed with a sensible curse, through life and to his grave. On the other side was Bullivant, scattering jests and mockery as he rode along. Dudley came behind, with a downcast look, dreading, as well he might, to meet the indignant gaze of the people, who beheld him, their only countryman by birth, among the oppressors of his native land. The captain of a frigate in the harbor, and two or three civil officers under the Crown, were also there. But the figure which most attracted the public eye, and stirred up the deepest feeling, was the Episcopal clergyman of King's Chapel, riding haughtily among the magistrates in his priestly vestments, the fitting representatives of prelacy and persecution, the union of church and state, and all those abominations which had driven the Puritans to the wilderness. Another guard of soldiers, in double rank, brought up the rear.

The whole scene was a picture of the condition of New England, and its moral, the deformity of any government that does not grow out of the nature of things and the character of the people. On one side the religious multitude, with their sad visages and dark attire, and on the other, the group of despotic rulers, with the high churchman in the midst, and here and there a crucifix at their bosoms, all magnificently clad, flushed with wine, proud of unjust authority, and scoffing at the universal groan. And the mercenary soldiers, waiting but the word to deluge the street with blood, showed the only means by which obedience could be secured.

"O Lord of Hosts," cried a voice among the crowd, "provide a Champion for thy people!"

This ejaculation was loudly uttered, and served as a herald's cry, to introduce a remarkable personage. The crowd had rolled back, and were now huddled together nearly at the extremity of the street, while the soldiers had advanced no more than a third of its length. The intervening space was empty—a paved solitude, between lofty edifices, which threw almost a twilight shadow over it. Suddenly, there was seen the figure of an ancient man, who seemed to have emerged from among the people, and was walking by himself along the centre of the street, to confront the armed band. He wore the old Puritan dress, a dark cloak and a steeple-crowned hat, in the fashion of at least fifty years before, with a heavy sword upon his thigh, but a staff in his hand to assist the tremulous gait of age.

When at some distance from the multitude, the old man turned slowly round, displaying a face of antique majesty, rendered doubly venerable by the hoary beard that descended on his breast. He made a gesture at once of encouragement and warning, then turned again, and resumed his way.

"Who is this gray patriarch?" asked the young men of their sires.

"Who is this venerable brother?" asked the old men among themselves.

But none could make reply. The fathers of the people, those of four-score years and upwards, were disturbed, deeming it strange that they should forget one of such evident authority, whom they must have known in their early days, the associate of Winthrop, and all the old councillors, giving laws, and making prayers, and leading them against the savage. The elderly men ought to have remembered him, too, with locks as gray in their youth, as their own were now. And the young! How could he have passed so utterly from their memories—that hoary sire, the relic of long-departed times, whose awful benediction had surely been bestowed on their uncovered heads, in childhood?

"Whence did he come? What is his purpose? Who can this old man be?" whispered the wondering crowd.

Meanwhile, the venerable stranger, staff in hand, was pursuing his solitary walk along the centre of the street. As he drew near the advancing soldiers, and as the roll of their drum came full upon his ears, the old man raised himself to a loftier mien, while the decrepitude of age seemed to fall from his shoulders, leaving him in gray but unbroken dignity. Now, he marched onward with a warrior's step, keeping time to the military music. Thus the aged form advanced on one side, and the whole parade of soldiers and magistrates on the other, till, when scarcely twenty yards remained between, the old man grasped his staff by the middle, and held it before him like a leader's truncheon.

"Stand!" cried he.

The eye, the face, and attitude of command; the solemn, yet warlike peal of that voice, fit either to rule a host in the battle-field or be raised to God in prayer, were irresistible. At the old man's word and outstretched arm, the roll of the drum was hushed at once, and the advancing line stood still. A tremulous enthusiasm seized upon the multitude. That state-ly form, combining the leader and the saint, so gray, so dimly seen, in such an ancient garb, could only belong to some old champion of the righteous cause, whom the oppressor's drum had summoned from his

grave. They raised a shout of awe and exultation, and looked for the deliverance of New England.

The Governor, and the gentlemen of his party, perceiving themselves
brought to an unexpected stand, rode hastily forward, as if they would
have pressed their snorting and affrighted horses right against the hoary
apparition. He, however, blenched not a step, but glancing his severe eye
round the group, which half encompassed him, at last bent it sternly on
Sir Edmund Andros. One would have thought that the dark old man was
chief ruler there, and that the Governor and Council, with soldiers at their
back, representing the whole power and authority of the Crown, had no
alternative but obedience.

"What does this old fellow here?" cried Edward Randolph, fiercely.
"On, Sir Edmund! Bid the soldiers forward, and give the dotard the same
choice that you give all his countrymen—to stand aside or be trampled
on!"

"Nay, nay, let us show respect to the good grandsire," said Bullivant,
laughing. "See you not, he is some old round-headed dignitary, who hath
lain asleep these thirty years, and knows nothing of the change of times?
Doubtless, he thinks to put us down with a proclamation in Old Noll's
name!"

"Are you mad, old man?" demanded Sir Edmund Andros, in loud and
harsh tones. "How dare you stay the march of King James's Governor?"

"I have stayed the march of a King himself, ere now," replied the gray
figure, with stern composure. "I am here, Sir Governor, because the cry
of an oppressed people hath disturbed me in my secret place; and beseeching this favor earnestly of the Lord, it was vouchsafed me to appear
once again on earth, in the good old cause of his saints. And what speak
ye of James? There is no longer a Popish tyrant on the throne of England, and by to-morrow noon, his name shall be a byword in this very
street, where ye would make it a word of terror. Back, thou wast a Governor, back! With this night thy power is ended—to-morrow, the prison!—
back, lest I foretell the scaffold!"

The people had been drawing nearer and nearer, and drinking in the
words of their champion, who spoke in accents long disused, like one unaccustomed to converse, except with the dead of many years ago. But his
voice stirred their souls. They confronted the soldiers, not wholly without arms, and ready to convert the very stones of the street into deadly
weapons. Sir Edmund Andros looked at the old man; then he cast his
hard and cruel eye over the multitude, and beheld them burning with that
lurid wrath, so difficult to kindle or to quench; and again he fixed his gaze
on the aged form, which stood obscurely in an open space, where neither
friend nor foe had thrust himself. What were his thoughts, he uttered no
word which might discover. But whether the oppressor were overawed by
the Gray Champion's look, or perceived his peril in the threatening attitude of the people, it is certain that he gave back, and ordered his soldiers
to commence a slow and guarded retreat. Before another sunset, the

Governor, and all that rode so proudly with him, were prisoners, and long ere it was known that James had abdicated, King William was proclaimed throughout New England.

But where was the Gray Champion? Some reported that, when the troops had gone from King Street, and the people were thronging tumultuously in their rear, Bradstreet, the aged Governor, was seen to embrace a form more aged than his own. Others soberly affirmed, that while they marvelled at the venerable grandeur of his aspect, the old man had faded from their eyes, melting slowly into the hues of twilight, till, where he stood, there was an empty space. But all agreed that the hoary shape was gone. The men of that generation watched for his reappearance, in sunshine and in twilight, but never saw him more, nor knew when his funeral passed, nor where his gravestone was.

And who was the Gray Champion? Perhaps his name might be found in the records of that stern Court of Justice, which passed a sentence, too mighty for the age, but glorious in all after-times, for its humbling lesson to the monarch and its high example to the subject. I have heard, that whenever the descendants of the Puritans are to show the spirit of their sires, the old man appears again. When eighty years had passed, he walked once more in King Street. Five years later, in the twilight of an April morning, he stood on the green, beside the meeting-house, at Lexington, where now the obelisk of granite, with a slab of slate inlaid, commemorates the first fallen of the Revolution. And when our fathers were toiling at the breastwork on Bunker's Hill, all through that night the old warrior walked his rounds. Long, long may it be, ere he comes again! His hour is one of darkness, and adversity, and peril. But should domestic tyranny oppress us, or the invader's step pollute our soil, still may the Gray Champion come, for he is the type of New England's hereditary spirit; and his shadowy march, on the eve of danger, must ever be the pledge, that New England's sons will vindicate their ancestry.


## THE WEDDING KNELL


THERE is a certain church in the city of New York which I have always regarded with peculiar interest, on account of a marriage there solemnized, under very singular circumstances, in my grandmother's girlhood. That venerable lady chanced to be a spectator of the scene, and ever after made it her favorite narrative. Whether the edifice now standing on the same site be the identical one to which she referred, I am not antiquarian enough to know; nor would it be worth while to correct myself, perhaps, of an agreeable error, by reading the date of its erection on the tablet over the door. It is a stately church, surrounded by an inclosure of the loveliest green, within which appear urns, pillars, obelisks, and other forms of monumental marble, the tributes of private affection, or more splendid memorials of historic dust. With such a place, though the tumult of the city rolls beneath its tower, one would be willing to connect some legendary interest.

The marriage might be considered as the result of an early engagement, though there had been two intermediate weddings on the lady's part, and forty years of celibacy on that of the gentleman. At sixty-five, Mr. Ellenwood was a shy, but not quite a secluded man; selfish, like all men who brood over their own hearts, yet manifesting on rare occasions a vein of generous sentiment; a scholar throughout life, though always an indolent one, because his studies had no definite object, either of public advantage or personal ambition; a gentleman, high bred and fastidiously delicate, yet sometimes requiring a considerable relaxation, in his behalf, of the common rules of society. In truth, there were so many anomalies in his character, and though shrinking with diseased sensibility from public notice, it had been his fatality so often to become the topic of the day, by some wild eccentricity of conduct, that people searched his lineage for an hereditary taint of insanity. But there was no need of this. His caprices had their origin in a mind that lacked the support of an engrossing purpose, and in feelings that preyed upon themselves for want of other food. If he were mad, it was the consequence, and not the cause, of an aimless and abortive life.

The widow was as complete a contrast to her third bridegroom, in everything but age, as can well be conceived. Compelled to relinquish her first engagement, she had been united to a man of twice her own years, to whom she became an exemplary wife, and by whose death she was left in possession of a splendid fortune. A southern gentleman, considerably younger than herself, succeeded to her hand, and carried her to Charleston, where, after many uncomfortable years, she found herself again a widow. It would have been singular, if any uncommon delicacy of feeling had survived through such a life as Mrs. Dabney's; it could not but be crushed and killed by her early disappointment, the cold duty of her first marriage, the dislocation of the heart's principles, consequent on a second union, and the unkindness of her southern husband, which had inevitably driven her to connect the idea of his death with that of her comfort. To be brief, she was that wisest, but unloveliest, variety of woman, a philosopher, bearing troubles of the heart with equanimity, dispensing with all that should have been her happiness, and making the best of what remained. Sage in most matters, the widow was perhaps the more amiable for the one frailty that made her ridiculous. Being childless, she could not remain beautiful by proxy, in the person of a daughter; she therefore refused to grow old and ugly, on any consideration; she struggled with Time, and held fast her roses in spite of him, till the venerable thief appeared to have relinquished the spoil, as not worth the trouble of acquiring it.

The approaching marriage of this woman of the world with such an unworldly man as Mr. Ellenwood was announced soon after Mrs. Dabney's return to her native city. Superficial observers, and deeper ones, seemed to concur in supposing that the lady must have borne no inactive part in arranging the affair; there were considerations of expediency which she would be far more likely to appreciate than Mr. Ellenwood; and there was just the specious phantom of sentiment and romance in this late union of two early lovers which sometimes makes a fool of a woman who has lost her true feelings among the accidents of life. All the wonder was, how the gentleman, with his lack of worldly wisdom and agonizing consciousness of ridicule, could have been induced to take a measure at once so prudent and so laughable. But while people talked the wedding-day arrived. The ceremony was to be solemnized according to the Episcopalian forms, and in open church, with a degree of publicity that attracted many spectators, who occupied the front seats of the galleries, and the pews near the altar and along the broad aisle. It had been arranged, or possibly it was the custom of the day, that the parties should proceed separately to church. By some accident the bridegroom was a little less punctual than the widow and her bridal attendants; with whose arrival, after this tedious, but necessary preface, the action of our tale may be said to commence.

The clumsy wheels of several old-fashioned coaches were heard, and the gentlemen and ladies composing the bridal party came through the church door with the sudden and gladsome effect of a burst of sunshine. The whole group, except the principal figure, was made up of youth and gayety. As they streamed up the broad aisle, while the pews and pillars seemed to brighten on either side, their steps were as buoyant as if they mistook the church for a ball-room, and were ready to dance hand in hand to the altar. So brilliant was the spectacle that few took notice of a singular phenomenon that had marked its entrance. At the moment when the bride's foot touched the threshold the bell swung heavily in the tower above her, and sent forth its deepest knell. The vibrations died away and returned with prolonged solemnity, as she entered the body of the church.

"Good heavens! what an omen," whispered a young lady to her lover.

"On my honor," replied the gentleman, "I believe the bell has the good taste to toll of its own accord. What has she to do with weddings? If you, dearest Julia, were approaching the altar the bell would ring out its merriest peal. It has only a funeral knell for her."

The bride and most of her company had been too much occupied with the bustle of entrance to hear the first boding stroke of the bell, or at least to reflect on the singularity of such a welcome to the altar. They therefore continued to advance with undiminished gayety. The gorgeous dresses of the time, the crimson velvet coats, the gold-laced hats, the hoop petticoats, the silk, satin, brocade, and embroidery, the buckles, canes, and swords, all displayed to the best advantage on persons suited to such finery, made the group appear more like a bright-colored picture than anything real. But by what perversity of taste had the artist represented his principal figure as so wrinkled and decayed, while yet he had decked her out in the brightest splendor of attire, as if the loveliest maiden had suddenly withered into age, and become a moral to the beautiful around her! On they went, however, and had glittered along about a third of the aisle, when another stroke of the bell seemed to fill the church with a visible gloom, dimming and obscuring the bright pageant, till it shone forth again as from a mist.

This time the party wavered, stopped, and huddled closer together, while a slight scream was heard from some of the ladies, and a confused whispering among the gentlemen. Thus tossing to and fro, they might have been fancifully compared to a splendid bunch of flowers, suddenly shaken by a puff of wind, which threatened to scatter the leaves of an old, brown, withered rose, on the same stalk with two dewy buds,—such being the emblem of the widow between her fair young bridesmaids. But her heroism was admirable. She had started with an irrepressible shudder, as if the stroke of the bell had fallen directly on her heart; then, recovering herself, while her attendants were yet in dismay, she took the lead, and paced calmly up the aisle. The bell continued to swing, strike, and vibrate, with the same doleful regularity as when a corpse is on its way to the tomb.

"My young friends here have their nerves a little shaken," said the widow, with a smile, to the clergyman at the altar. "But so many weddings have been ushered in with the merriest peal of the bells, and yet turned out unhappily, that I shall hope for better fortune under such different auspices."

"Madam," answered the rector, in great perplexity, "this strange occurrence brings to my mind a marriage sermon of the famous Bishop Taylor, wherein he mingles so many thoughts of mortality and future woe, that, to speak somewhat after his own rich style, he seems to hang the bridal chamber in black, and cut the wedding garment out of a coffin pall. And it has been the custom of divers nations to infuse something of sadness into their marriage ceremonies, so to keep death in mind while contracting that engagement which is life's chiefest business. Thus we may draw a sad but profitable moral from this funeral knell."

But, though the clergyman might have given his moral even a keener point, he did not fail to dispatch an attendant to inquire into the mystery, and stop those sounds, so dismally appropriate to such a marriage. A brief space elapsed, during which the silence was broken only by whispers, and a few suppressed titterings, among the wedding party and the spectators, who, after the first shock, were disposed to draw an ill-natured merriment from the affair. The young have less charity for aged follies than the old for those of youth. The widow's glance was observed to wander, for an instant, towards a window of the church, as if searching for the time-worn marble that she had dedicated to her first husband; then her eyelids dropped over their faded orbs, and her thoughts were drawn irresistibly to another grave. Two buried men, with a voice at her ear, and a cry afar off, were calling her to lie down beside them. Perhaps, with momentary truth of feeling, she thought how much happier had been her fate, if, after years of bliss, the bell were now tolling for her funeral, and she were followed to the grave by the old affection of her earliest lover, long her husband. But why had she returned to him, when their cold hearts shrank from each other's embrace?

Still the death-bell tolled so mournfully, that the sunshine seemed to fade in the air. A whisper, communicated from those who stood nearest the windows, now spread through the church; a hearse, with a train of several coaches, was creeping along the street, conveying some dead man to the churchyard, while the bride awaited a living one at the altar. Immediately after, the footsteps of the bridegroom and his friends were heard at the door. The widow looked down the aisle, and clinched the arm of one of her bridemaids in her bony hand with such unconscious violence, that the fair girl trembled.

"You frighten me, my dear madam!" cried she. "For Heaven's sake, what is the matter?"

"Nothing, my dear, nothing," said the widow; then, whispering close to her ear, "There is a foolish fancy that I cannot get rid of. I am expecting my bridegroom to come into the church, with my first two husbands for groomsmen!"

"Look, look!" screamed the bridemaid. "What is here? The funeral!"

As she spoke, a dark procession paced into the church. First came an old man and women, like chief mourners at a funeral, attired from head to foot in the deepest black, all but their pale features and hoary hair; he leaning on a staff, and supporting her decrepit form with his nerveless arm. Behind appeared another, and another pair, as aged, as black, and mournful as the first. As they drew near, the widow recognized in every face some trait of former friends, long forgotten, but now returning, as if from their old graves, to warn her to prepare a shroud; or, with purpose almost as unwelcome, to exhibit their wrinkles and infirmity, and claim her as their companion by the tokens of her own decay. Many a merry night had she danced with them, in youth. And now, in joyless age, she felt that some withered partner should request her hand, and all unite, in a dance of death, to the music of the funeral bell.

While these aged mourners were passing up the aisle, it was observed that, from pew to pew, the spectators shuddered with irrepressible awe, as some object, hitherto concealed by the intervening figures, came full in sight. Many turned away their faces; others kept a fixed and rigid stare; and a young girl giggled hysterically, and fainted with the laughter on her lips. When the spectral procession approached the altar, each couple separated, and slowly diverged, till, in the centre, appeared a form, that had been worthily ushered in with all this gloomy pomp, the death knell, and the funeral. It was the bridegroom in his shroud!

No garb but that of the grave could have befitted such a deathlike aspect; the eyes, indeed, had the wild gleam of a sepulchral lamp; all else was fixed in the stern calmness which old men wear in the coffin. The corpse stood motionless, but addressed the widow in accents that seemed to melt into the clang of the bell, which fell heavily on the air while he spoke.

"Come, my bride!" said those pale lips, "the hearse is ready. The sexton stands waiting for us at the door of the tomb. Let us be married; and then to our coffins!"

How shall the widow's horror be represented? It gave her the ghastliness of a dead man's bride. Her youthful friends stood apart, shuddering at the mourners, the shrouded bridegroom, and herself; the whole scene expressed, by the strongest imagery, the vain struggle of the gilded vanities of this world, when opposed to age, infirmity, sorrow, and death. The awe-struck silence was first broken by the clergyman.

"Mr. Ellenwood," said he, soothingly, yet with somewhat of authority, "you are not well. Your mind has been agitated by the unusual circumstances in which you are placed. The ceremony must be deferred. As an old friend, let me entreat you to return home."

"Home! yes, but not without my bride," answered he, in the same hollow accents. "You deem this mockery; perhaps madness. Had I bedizened my aged and broken frame with scarlet and embroidery—had I forced my withered lips to smile at my dead heart—that might have been mockery, or madness. But now, let young and old declare, which of us has come hither without a wedding garment, the bridegroom or the bride!"

He stepped forward at a ghostly pace, and stood beside the widow, contrasting the awful simplicity of his shroud with the glare and glitter in which she had arrayed herself for this unhappy scene. None, that beheld them, could deny the terrible strength of the moral which his disordered intellect had contrived to draw.

"Cruel! cruel!" groaned the heart-stricken bride.

"Cruel!" repeated he; then, losing his deathlike composure in a wild bitterness: "Heaven judge which of us has been cruel to the other! In youth you deprived me of my happiness, my hopes, my aims; you took away all the substance of my life, and made it a dream without reality enough even to grieve at—with only a pervading gloom, through which I walked wearily, and cared not whither. But after forty years, when I have built my tomb, and would not give up the thought of resting there—no, not for such a life as we once pictured—you call me to the altar. At your summons I am here. But other husbands have enjoyed your youth, your beauty, your warmth of heart, and all that could be termed your life. What is there for me but your decay and death? And therefore I have bidden these funeral friends, and bespoken the sexton's deepest knell, and am come, in my shroud, to wed you, as with a burial service, that we may join our hands at the door of the sepulchre, and enter it together."

It was not frenzy; it was not merely the drunkenness of strong emotion, in a heart unused to it, that now wrought upon the bride. The stern lesson of the day had done its work; her worldliness was gone. She seized the bridegroom's hand.

"Yes!" cried she. "Let us wed, even at the door of the sepulchre! My life is gone in vanity and emptiness. But at its close there is one true feeling. It has made me what I was in youth; it makes me worthy of you. Time is no more for both of us. Let us wed for Eternity!"

With a long and deep regard, the bridegroom looked into her eyes, while a tear was gathering in his own. How strange that gush of human feeling from the frozen bosom of a corpse! He wiped away the tears even with his shroud.

"Beloved of my youth," said he, "I have been wild. The despair of my whole lifetime had returned at once, and maddened me. Forgive; and be forgiven. Yes; it is evening with us now; and we have realized none of our morning dreams of happiness. But let us join our hands before the altar, as lovers whom adverse circumstances have separated through life, yet who meet again as they are leaving it, and find their earthly affection changed into something holy as religion. And what is Time, to the married of Eternity?"

Amid the tears of many, and a swell of exalted sentiment, in those who felt aright, was solemnized the union of two immortal souls. The train of withered mourners, the hoary bridegroom in his shroud, the pale features of the aged bride, and the death-bell tolling through the whole, till its deep voice overpowered the marriage words, all marked the funeral of earthly hopes. But as the ceremony proceeded, the organ, as if stirred by the sympathies of this impressive scene, poured forth an anthem, first mingling with the dismal knell, then rising to a loftier strain, till the soul looked down upon its woe. And when the awful rite was finished, and with cold hand in cold hand, the Married of Eternity withdrew, the organ's peal of solemn triumph drowned the Wedding Knell.

# THE MINISTER'S BLACK VEIL

### A PARABLE [1]

THE sexton stood in the porch of Milford meeting-house, pulling busily at the bell-rope. The old people of the village came stooping along the street. Children, with bright faces, tripped merrily beside their parents, or mimicked a graver gait, in the conscious dignity of their Sunday clothes. Spruce bachelors looked sidelong at the pretty maidens, and fancied that the Sabbath sunshine made them prettier than on week days. When the

---

[1] Another clergyman in New England, Mr. Joseph Moody, of York, Maine, who died about eighty years since, made himself remarkable by the same eccentricity that is here related of the Reverend Mr. Hooper. In his case, however, the symbol had a different import. In early life he had accidentally killed a beloved friend; and from that day till the hour of his own death, he hid his face from men.

throng had mostly streamed into the porch, the sexton began to toll the bell, keeping his eye on the Reverend Mr. Hooper's door. The first glimpse of the clergyman's figure was the signal for the bell to cease its summons.

"But what has good Parson Hooper got upon his face?" cried the sexton in astonishment.

All within hearing immediately turned about, and beheld the semblance of Mr. Hooper, pacing slowly his meditative way towards the meeting-house. With one accord they started, expressing more wonder than if some strange minister were coming to dust the cushions of Mr. Hooper's pulpit.

"Are you sure it is our parson?" inquired Goodman Gray of the sexton.

"Of a certainty it is good Mr. Hooper," replied the sexton. "He was to have exchanged pulpits with Parson Shute, of Westbury; but Parson Shute sent to excuse himself yesterday, being to preach a funeral sermon."

The cause of so much amazement may appear sufficiently slight. Mr. Hooper, a gentlemanly person, of about thirty, though still a bachelor, was dressed with due clerical neatness, as if a careful wife had starched his band, and brushed the weekly dust from his Sunday's garb. There was but one thing remarkable in his appearance. Swathed about his forehead, and hanging down over his face, so low as to be shaken by his breath, Mr. Hooper had on a black veil. On a nearer view it seemed to consist of two folds of crape, which entirely concealed his features, except the mouth and chin, but probably did not intercept his sight, further than to give a darkened aspect to all living and inanimate things. With this gloomy shade before him, good Mr. Hooper walked onward, at a slow and quiet pace, stooping somewhat, and looking on the ground, as is customary with abstracted men, yet nodding kindly to those of his parishioners who still waited on the meeting-house steps. But so wonder-struck were they that his greeting hardly met with a return.

"I can't really feel as if good Mr. Hooper's face was behind that piece of crape," said the sexton.

"I don't like it," muttered an old woman, as she hobbled into the meeting-house. "He has changed himself into something awful, only by hiding his face."

"Our parson has gone mad!" cried Goodman Gray, following him across the threshold.

A rumor of some unaccountable phenomenon had preceded Mr. Hooper into the meeting-house, and set all the congregation astir. Few could refrain from twisting their heads towards the door; many stood upright, and turned directly about; while several little boys clambered upon the seats, and came down again with a terrible racket. There was a general bustle, a rustling of the women's gowns and shuffling of the men's feet, greatly at variance with that hushed repose which should attend the entrance of the minister. But Mr. Hooper appeared not to notice the perturbation of his people. He entered with an almost noiseless step, bent his head mildly to the pews on each side, and bowed as he passed his oldest parishioner, a white-haired great grandsire, who occupied an arm-chair in the centre of the aisle. It was strange to observe how slowly this venerable man became conscious of something singular in the appearance of his pastor. He seemed not fully to partake of the prevailing wonder, till Mr. Hooper had ascended the stairs, and showed himself in the pulpit, face to face with his congregation, except for the black veil. That mysterious emblem was never once withdrawn. It shook with his measured breath, as he gave out the psalm; it threw its obscurity between him and the holy page, as he read the Scriptures; and while he prayed, the veil lay heavily on his uplifted countenance. Did he seek to hide it from the dread Being whom he was addressing?

Such was the effect of this simple piece of crape, that more than one woman of delicate nerves was forced to leave the meeting-house. Yet perhaps the pale-faced congregation was almost as fearful a sight to the minister, as his black veil to them.

Mr. Hooper had the reputation of a good preacher, but not an energetic one: he strove to win his people heavenward by mild, persuasive influences, rather than to drive them thither by the thunders of the Word. The sermon which he now delivered was marked by the same characteristics of style and manner as the general series of his pulpit oratory. But there was something, either in the sentiment of the discourse itself, or in the imagination of the auditors, which made it greatly the most powerful effort that they had ever heard from their pastor's lips. It was tinged, rather more darkly than usual, with the gentle gloom of Mr. Hooper's temperament. The subject had reference to secret sin, and those sad mysteries which we hide from our nearest and dearest, and would fain conceal from our own consciousness, even forgetting that the Omniscient can detect them. A subtle power was breathed into his words. Each member of the congregation, the most innocent girl, and the man of hardened breast, felt as if the preacher had crept upon them, behind his awful veil, and discovered their hoarded iniquity of deed or thought. Many spread their clasped hands on their bosoms. There was nothing terrible in what Mr. Hooper said, at least, no violence; and yet, with every tremor of his melancholy voice, the hearers quaked. An unsought pathos came hand in hand with awe. So sensible were the audience of some unwonted attribute in their minister, that they longed for a breath of wind to blow aside the veil, almost believing that a stranger's visage would be discovered, though the form, gesture, and voice were those of Mr. Hooper.

At the close of the services, the people hurried out with indecorous confusion, eager to communicate their pent-up amazement, and conscious of lighter spirits the moment they lost sight of the black veil. Some gathered in little circles, huddled closely together, with their mouths all whispering in the centre; some went homeward alone, wrapt in silent meditation; some talked loudly, and profaned the Sabbath day with ostentatious laughter. A few shook their sagacious heads, intimating that they could penetrate the mystery; while one or two affirmed that there was no mystery at all, but only that Mr. Hooper's eyes were so weakened by the midnight lamp, as to require a shade. After a brief interval, forth came good Mr. Hooper also, in the rear of his flock. Turning his veiled face from one group to another, he paid due reverence to the hoary heads, saluted the middle aged with kind dignity as their friend and spiritual guide, greeted the young with mingled authority and love, and laid his hands on the little children's heads to bless them. Such was always his custom on the Sabbath day. Strange and bewildered looks repaid him for his courtesy. None, as on former occasions, aspired to the honor of walking by their pastor's side. Old Squire Saunders, doubtless by an accidental lapse of memory, neglected to invite Mr. Hooper to his table, where the good clergyman had been wont to bless the food, almost every Sunday since his settlement. He returned, therefore, to the parsonage, and, at the moment of closing the door, was observed to look back upon the people, all of whom had their eyes fixed upon the minister. A sad smile gleamed faintly from beneath the black veil, and flickered about his mouth, glimmering as he disappeared.

"How strange," said a lady, "that a simple black veil, such as any woman might wear on her bonnet, should become such a terrible thing on Mr. Hooper's face!"

"Something must surely be amiss with Mr. Hooper's intellects," observed her husband, the physician of the village. "But the strangest part of the affair is the effect of this vagary, even on a sober-minded man like myself. The black veil, though it covers only our pastor's face, throws its influence over his whole person, and makes him ghostlike from head to foot. Do you not feel it so?"

"Truly do I," replied the lady; "and I would not be alone with him for the world. I wonder he is not afraid to be alone with himself!"

"Men sometimes are so," said her husband.

The afternoon service was attended with similar circumstances. At its conclusion, the bell tolled for the funeral of a young lady. The relatives and friends were assembled in the house, and the more distant acquaintances stood about the door, speaking of the good qualities of the deceased, when their talk was interrupted by the appearance of Mr. Hooper, still covered with his black veil. It was now an appropriate emblem. The clergyman stepped into the room where the corpse was laid, and bent over the coffin, to take a last farewell of his deceased parishioner. As he stooped, the veil hung straight down from his forehead, so that, if her eyelids had not been closed forever, the dead maiden might have seen his face. Could Mr. Hooper be fearful of her glance, that he so hastily caught back the black veil? A person who watched the interview between the dead and living, scrupled not to affirm, that, at the instant when the clergyman's features were disclosed, the corpse had slightly shuddered, rustling the shroud and muslin cap, though the countenance retained the composure of death. A superstitious old woman was the only witness of this prodigy. From the coffin Mr. Hooper passed into the chamber of the mourners, and thence to the head of the staircase, to make the funeral prayer. It was a tender and heart-dissolving prayer, full of sorrow, yet so imbued with celestial hopes, that the music of a heavenly harp, swept by the fingers of the dead, seemed faintly to be heard among the saddest accents of the minister. The people trembled, though they but darkly understood him when he prayed that they, and himself, and all of mortal race, might be ready, as he trusted this young maiden had been, for the dreadful hour that should snatch the veil from their faces. The bearers went heavily forth, and the mourners followed, saddening all the street, with the dead before them, and Mr. Hooper in his black veil behind.

"Why do you look back?" said one in the procession to his partner.

"I had a fancy," replied she, "that the minister and the maiden's spirit were walking hand in hand."

"And so had I, at the same moment," said the other.

That night, the handsomest couple in Milford village were to be joined in wedlock. Though reckoned a melancholy man, Mr. Hooper had a placid cheerfulness for such occasions, which often excited a sympathetic smile where livelier merriment would have been thrown away. There was no quality of his disposition which made him more beloved than this. The company at the wedding awaited his arrival with impatience, trusting that the strange awe, which had gathered over him throughout the day, would now be dispelled. But such was not the result. When Mr. Hooper came, the first thing that their eyes rested on was the same horrible black veil, which had added deeper gloom to the funeral, and could portend nothing but evil to the wedding. Such was its immediate effect on the guests that a cloud seemed to have rolled duskily from beneath the black crape, and dimmed the light of the candles. The bridal pair stood up before the minister. But the bride's cold fingers quivered in the tremulous hand of the bridegroom, and her deathlike paleness caused a whisper that the maiden who had been buried a few hours before was come from her grave to be married. If ever another wedding were so dismal, it was that famous one where they tolled the wedding knell. After performing the ceremony, Mr. Hooper raised a glass of wine to his lips, wishing happiness to the new-married couple in a strain of mild pleasantry that ought to have brightened the features of the guests, like a cheerful gleam from the hearth. At that instant, catching a glimpse of his figure in the looking-glass, the black veil involved his own spirit in the horror with which it overwhelmed all others. His frame shuddered, his lips grew white, he spilt the untasted wine upon the carpet, and rushed forth into the darkness. For the Earth, too, had on her Black Veil.

The next day, the whole village of Milford talked of little else than Parson Hooper's black veil. That, and the mystery concealed beind it, supplied a topic for discussion between acquaintances meeting in the street, and good women gossiping at their open windows. It was the first item of news that the tavern-keeper told to his guests. The children babbled of it on their way to school. One imitative little imp covered his face with an old black handkerchief, thereby so affrighting his playmates that the panic seized himself, and he well-nigh lost his wits by his own waggery.

It was remarkable that all of the busybodies and impertinent people in the parish, not one ventured to put the plain question to Mr. Hooper, wherefore he did this thing. Hitherto, whenever there appeared the slightest call for such interference, he had never lacked advisers, nor shown himself averse to be guided by their judgment. If he erred at all, it was by so painful a degree of self-distrust, that even the mildest censure would lead him to consider an indifferent action as a crime. Yet, though so well acquainted with this amiable weakness, no individual among his parishioners chose to make the black veil a subject of friendly remonstrance. There was a feeling of dread, neither plainly confessed nor carefully concealed, which caused each to shift the responsibility upon another, till at length it was found expedient to send a deputation of the church, in order to deal with Mr. Hooper about the mystery, before it should grow into a scandal. Never did an embassy so ill discharge its duties. The minister received then with friendly courtesy, but became silent, after they were seated, leaving to his visitors the whole burden of introducing their important business. The topic, it might be supposed, was obvious enough. There was the black veil swathed round Mr. Hooper's forehead, and concealing every feature above his placid mouth, on which, at times, they could perceive the glimmering of a melancholy smile. But that piece of crape, to their imagination, seemed to hang down before his heart, the symbol of a fearful secret between him and them. Were the veil but cast aside, they might speak freely of it, but not till then. Thus they sat a considerable time, speechless, confused, and shrinking uneasily from Mr. Hooper's eye, which they felt to be fixed upon them with an invisible glance. Finally, the deputies returned abashed to their constituents, pronouncing the matter too weighty to be handled, except by a council of the churches, if, indeed, it might not require a general synod.

But there was one person in the village unappalled by the awe with which the black veil had impressed all beside herself. When the deputies returned without an explanation, or even venturing to demand one, she, with the calm energy of her character, determined to chase away the strange cloud that appeared to be settling round Mr. Hooper, every moment more darkly than before. As his plighted wife, it should be her privilege to know what the black veil concealed. At the minister's first visit, therefore, she entered upon the subject with a direct simplicity, which made the task easier both for him and her. After he had seated himself, she fixed her eyes steadfastly upon the veil, but could discern nothing of the dreadful gloom that had so overawed the multitude: it was but a double fold of crape, hanging down from his forehead to his mouth, and slightly stirring with his breath.

"No," said she aloud, and smiling, "there is nothing terrible in this piece of crape, except that it hides a face which I am always glad to look upon. Come, good sir, let the sun shine from behind the cloud. First lay aside your black veil: then tell me why you put it on."

Mr. Hooper's smile glimmered faintly.

"There is an hour to come," said he, "when all of us shall cast aside our veils. Take it not amiss, beloved friend, if I wear this piece of crape till then."

"Your words are a mystery, too," returned the young lady. "Take away the veil from them, at least."

"Elizabeth, I will," said he, "so far as my vow may suffer me. Know, then, this veil is a type and a symbol, and I am bound to wear it ever, both in light and darkness, in solitude and before the gaze of multitudes, and as with strangers, so with my familiar friends. No mortal eye will see it withdrawn. This dismal shade must separate me from the world: even you, Elizabeth, can never come behind it!"

"What grievous affliction hath befallen you," she earnestly inquired, "that you should thus darken your eyes forever?"

"If it be a sign of mourning," replied Mr. Hooper, "I, perhaps, like most other mortals, have sorrows dark enough to be typified by a black veil."

"But what if the world will not believe that it is the type of an innocent sorrow?" urged Elizabeth. "Beloved and respected as you are, there may be whispers that you hide your face under the consciousness of secret sin. For the sake of your holy office, do away this scandal!"

The color rose into her cheeks as she intimated the nature of the rumors that were already abroad in the village. But Mr. Hooper's mildness did not forsake him. He even smiled again—that same sad smile, which always appeared like a faint glimmering of light, proceeding from the obscurity beneath the veil.

"If I hide my face for sorrow, there is cause enough," he merely replied; "and if I cover it for secret sin, what mortal might not do the same?"

And with this gentle, but unconquerable obstinacy did he resist all her entreaties. At length Elizabeth sat silent. For a few moments she appeared lost in thought, considering, probably, what new methods might be tried to withdraw her lover from so dark a fantasy, which, if it had no other meaning, was perhaps a symptom of mental disease. Though of a firmer character than his own, the tears rolled down her cheeks. But, in an instant, as it were, a new feeling took the place of sorrow: her eyes were fixed insensibly on the black veil, when, like a sudden twilight in the air, its terrors fell around her. She arose, and stood trembling before him.

"And do you feel it then, at last?" said he mournfully.

She made no reply, but covered her eyes with her hand, and turned to leave the room. He rushed forward and caught her arm.

"Have patience with me, Elizabeth!" cried he, passionately. "Do not desert me, though this veil must be between us here on earth. Be mine, and hereafter there shall be no veil over my face, no darkness between our souls! It is but a mortal veil—it is not for eternity! O! you know not how lonely I am, and how frightened, to be alone behind my black veil. Do not leave me in this miserable obscurity forever!"

"Lift the veil but once, and look me in the face," said she.

"Never! It cannot be!" replied Mr. Hooper.

"Then farewell!" said Elizabeth.

She withdrew her arm from his grasp, and slowly departed, pausing at the door, to give one long shuddering gaze, that seemed almost to penetrate the mystery of the black veil. But, even amid his grief, Mr. Hooper smiled to think that only a material emblem had separated him from happiness, though the horrors, which it shadowed forth, must be drawn darkly between the fondest of lovers.

From that time no attempts were made to remove Mr. Hooper's black veil, or, by a direct appeal, to discover the secret which it was supposed to hide. By persons who claimed a superiority to popular prejudice, it was reckoned merely an eccentric whim, such as often mingles with the sober actions of men otherwise rational, and tinges them all with its own semblance of insanity. But with the multitude, good Mr. Hooper was irreparably a bugbear. He could not walk the street with any peace of mind, so conscious was he that the gentle and timid would turn aside to avoid him, and that others would make it a point of hardihood to throw themselves in his way. The impertinence of the latter class compelled him to give up his customary walk at sunset to the burial ground; for when he leaned pensively over the gate, there would always be faces behind the gravestones, peeping at his black veil. A fable went the rounds that the stare of the dead people drove him thence. It grieved him, to the very depth of his kind heart, to observe how the children fled from his approach, breaking up their merriest sports, while his melancholy figure was yet afar off. Their instinctive dread caused him to feel more strongly than aught else, that a preternatural horror was interwoven with the threads of the black crape. In truth, his own antipathy to the veil was known to be so great, that he never willingly passed before a mirror, nor stooped to drink at a still fountain, lest, in its peaceful bosom, he should be affrighted by himself. This was what gave plausibility to the whispers, that Mr. Hooper's conscience tortured him for some great crime too horrible to be entirely concealed, or otherwise than so obscurely intimated. Thus, from beneath the black veil, there rolled a cloud into the sunshine, an ambiguity of sin or sorrow, which enveloped the poor minister, so that love or sympathy could never reach him. It was said that ghost and fiend consorted with him there. With self-shudderings and outward terrors, he walked continually in its shadow, groping darkly within his own soul, or gazing through a medium that saddened the whole world. Even the lawless wind, it was believed, respected his dreadful secret, and never blew aside the veil. But still good Mr. Hooper sadly smiled at the pale visages of the worldly throng as he passed by.

Among all its bad influences, the black veil had the one desirable effect, of making its wearer a very efficient clergyman. By the aid of his mysterious emblem—for there was no other apparent cause—he became a man of awful power over souls that were in agony for sin. His converts always regarded him with a dread peculiar to themselves, affirming, though but figuratively, that, before he brought them to celestial light, they had been with him behind the black veil. Its gloom, indeed, enabled him to sympathize with all dark affections. Dying sinners cried aloud for Mr. Hooper, and would not yield their breath till he appeared; though ever, as he stooped to whisper consolation, they shuddered at the veiled face so near their own. Such were the terrors of the black veil, even when Death had bared his visage! Strangers came long distances to attend service at his church, with the mere idle purpose of gazing at his figure, because it was forbidden them to behold his face. But many were made to quake ere they departed! Once, during Governor Belcher's administration, Mr. Hooper was appointed to preach the election sermon. Covered with his black veil, he stood before the chief magistrate, the council, and the representatives, and wrought so deep an impression, that the legislative measures of that year were characterized by all the gloom and piety of our earliest ancestral sway.

In this manner Mr. Hooper spent a long life, irreproachable in outward act, yet shrouded in dismal suspicions; kind and loving, though unloved, and dimly feared; a man apart from men, shunned in their health and joy, but ever summoned to their aid in mortal anguish. As years wore on, shedding their snows above his sable veil, he acquired a name throughout the New England churches, and they called him Father Hooper. Nearly all his parishioners, who were of mature age when he was settled, had been borne away by many a funeral: he had one congregation in the church, and a more crowded one in the churchyard; and having wrought so late into the evening, and done his work so well, it was now good Father Hooper's turn to rest.

Several persons were visible by the shaded candlelight, in the death chamber of the old clergyman. Natural connections he had none. But there was the decorously grave, though unmoved physician, seeking only to mitigate the last pangs of the patient whom he could not save. There were the deacons, and other eminently pious members of his church. There, also, was the Reverend Mr. Clark, of Westbury, a young and zealous divine, who had ridden in haste to pray by the bedside of the expiring minister. There was the nurse, no hired handmaiden of death, but one whose calm affection had endured thus long in secrecy, in solitude, amid the chill of age, and would not perish, even at the dying hour. Who, but Elizabeth! And there lay the hoary head of good Father Hooper upon the death pillow, with the black veil still swathed about his brow, and reaching down over his face, so that each more difficult gasp of his faint breath caused it to stir. All through life that piece of crape had hung between him and the world: it had separated him from cheerful brotherhood and woman's love, and kept him in that saddest of all prisons, his own heart; and still it lay upon his face, as if to deepen the gloom of his darksome chamber, and shade him from the sunshine of eternity.

For some time previous, his mind had been confused, wavering doubtfully between the past and the present, and hovering forward, as it were, at intervals, into the indistinctness of the world to come. There had been feverish turns, which tossed him from side to side, and wore away what little strength he had. But in his most convulsive struggles, and in the wildest vagaries of his intellect, when no other thought retained its sober influence, he still showed an awful solicitude lest the black veil should slip aside. Even if his bewildered soul could have forgotten, there was a faithful woman at this pillow, who, with averted eyes, would have covered that aged face, which she had last beheld in the comeliness of manhood. At length the death-stricken old man lay quietly in the torpor of mental and bodily exhaustion, with an imperceptible pulse, and breath that grew fainter and fainter, except when a long, deep, and irregular inspiration seemed to prelude the flight of his spirit.

The minister of Westbury approached the bedside.

"Venerable Father Hooper," said he, "the moment of your release is at hand. Are you ready for the lifting of the veil that shuts in time from eternity?"

Father Hooper at first replied merely by a feeble motion of his head; then, apprehensive, perhaps, that his meaning might be doubted, he exerted himself to speak.

"Yea," said he, in faint accents, "my soul hath a patient weariness until that veil be lifted."

"And is it fitting," resumed the Reverend Mr. Clark, "that a man so given to prayer, of such a blameless example, holy in deed and thought, so far as mortal judgment may pronounce; is it fitting that a father in the church should leave a shadow on his memory, that may seem to blacken a life so pure? I pray you, my venerable brother, let not this thing be! Suffer us to be gladdened by your triumphant aspect as you go to your reward. Before the veil of eternity be lifted, let me cast aside this black veil from your face!"

And thus speaking, the Reverend Mr. Clark bent forward to reveal the mystery of so many years. But, exerting a sudden energy, that made all the beholders stand aghast, Father Hooper snatched both his hands from beneath the bedclothes, and pressed them strongly on the black veil, resolute to struggle, if the minister of Westbury would contend with a dying man.

"Never!" cried the veiled clergyman. "On earth, never!"

"Dark old man!" exclaimed the affrighted minister, "with what horrible crime upon your soul are you now passing to the judgment?"

Father Hooper's breath heaved; it rattled in his throat; but, with a mighty effort, grasping forward with his hands, he caught hold of life, and held it back till he should speak. He even raised himself in bed; and there he sat, shivering with the arms of death around him, while the black veil hung down, awful, at that last moment, in the gathered terrors of a lifetime. And yet the faint, sad smile, so often there, now seemed to glimmer from its obscurity, and linger on Father Hooper's lips.

"Why do you tremble at me alone?" cried he, turning his veiled face round the circle of pale spectators. "Tremble also at each other! Have men avoided me, and women shown no pity, and children screamed and fled, only for my black veil? What, but the mystery which it obscurely typifies, has made this piece of crape so awful? When the friend shows his inmost heart to his friend; the lover to his best beloved; when man does not vainly shrink from the eye of his Creator, loathsomely treasuring up the secret of his sin; then deem me a monster, for the symbol beneath which I have lived, and die! I look around me, and, lo! on every visage a Black Veil!"

While his auditors shrank from one another, in mutual affright, Father Hooper fell back upon his pillow, a veiled corpse, with a faint smile lingering on the lips. Still veiled, they laid him in his coffin, and a veiled corpse they bore him to the grave. The grass of many years has sprung up and withered on that grave, the burial stone is moss-grown, and good Mr. Hooper's face is dust; but awful is still the thought that it mouldered beneath the Black Veil!

# THE MAYPOLE OF MERRY MOUNT

There is an admirable foundation for a philosophic romance in the curious history of the early settlement of Mount Wollaston, or Merry Mount. In the slight sketch here attempted, the facts, recorded on the grave pages of our New England annalists, have wrought themselves, almost spontaneously, into a sort of allegory. The masques, mummeries, and festive customs, described in the text, are in accordance with the manners of the age. Authority on these points may be found in Strutt's Book of English Sports and Pastimes.

BRIGHT were the days at Merry Mount, when the Maypole was the banner staff of that gay colony! They who reared it, should their banner be triumphant, were to pour sunshine over New England's rugged hills, and scatter flower seeds throughout the soil. Jollity and gloom were contending for an empire. Midsummer eve had come, bringing deep verdure to the forest, and roses in her lap, of a more vivid hue than the tender buds of Spring. But May, or her mirthful spirit, dwelt all the year round at Merry Mount, sporting with the Summer months, and revelling with Autumn, and basking in the glow of Winter's fireside. Through a world of toil and care she flitted with a dreamlike smile, and came hither to find a home among the lightsome hearts of Merry Mount.

Never had the Maypole been so gayly decked as at sunset on midsummer eve. This venerated emblem was a pine-tree, which had preserved the slender grace of youth, while it equalled the loftiest height of the old wood monarchs. From its top streamed a silken banner, colored like the rainbow. Down nearly to the ground the pole was dressed with birchen boughs, and others of the liveliest green, and some with silvery leaves, fastened by ribbons that fluttered in fantastic knots of twenty different colors, but no sad ones. Garden flowers, and blossoms of the wilderness, laughed gladly forth amid the verdure, so fresh and dewy that they must have grown by

magic on that happy pine-tree. Where this green and flowery splendor terminated, the shaft of the Maypole was stained with the seven brilliant
hues of the banner at its top. On the lowest green bough hung an abundant wreath of roses, some that had been gathered in the sunniest spots of
the forest, and others, of still richer blush, which the colonists had reared
from English seed. O, people of the Golden Age, the chief of your husbandry was to raise flowers!

But what was the wild throng that stood hand in hand about the Maypole? It could not be that the fauns and nymphs, when driven from their
classic groves and homes of ancient fable, had sought refuge, as all the
persecuted did, in the fresh woods of the West. These were Gothic monsters, though perhaps of Grecian ancestry. On the shoulders of a comely
youth uprose the head and branching antlers of a stag; a second, human
in all other points, had the grim visage of a wolf; a third, still with the
trunk and limbs of a mortal man, showed the beard and horns of a venerable he-goat. There was the likeness of a bear erect, brute in all but his
hind legs, which were adorned with pink silk stockings. And here again,
almost as wondrous, stood a real bear of the dark forest, lending each of
his fore paws to the grasp of a human hand, and as ready for the dance as
any in that circle. His inferior nature rose half way, to meet his companions as they stooped. Other faces wore the similitude of man or woman,
but distorted or extravagant, with red noses pendulous before their
mouths, which seemed of awful depth, and stretched from ear to ear in an
eternal fit of laughter. Here might be seen the Savage Man, well known
in heraldry, hairy as a baboon, and girdled with green leaves. By his side,
a noble figure, but still a counterfeit, appeared an Indian hunter, with
feathery crest and wampum belt. Many of this strange company wore
foolscaps, and had little bells appended to their garments, tinkling with a
silvery sound, responsive to the inaudible music of their gleesome spirits.
Some youths and maidens were of soberer garb, yet well maintained their
places in the irregular throng by the expression of wild revelry upon their
features. Such were the colonists of Merry Mount, as they stood in the
broad smile of sunset round their venerated Maypole.

Had a wanderer, bewildered in the melancholy forest, heard their
mirth, and stolen a half-affrighted glance, he might have fancied them the
crew of Comus, some already transformed to brutes, some midway between man and beast, and the others rioting in the flow of tipsy jollity
that foreran the change. But a band of Puritans, who watched the scene,
invisible themselves, compared the masques to those devils and ruined
souls with whom their superstition peopled the black wilderness.

Within the ring of monsters appeared the two airiest forms that had
ever trodden on any more solid footing than a purple and golden cloud.
One was a youth in glistening apparel, with a scarf of the rainbow pattern crosswise on his breast. His right hand held a gilded staff, the ensign
of high dignity among the revellers, and his left grasped the slender fingers of a fair maiden, not less gayly decorated than himself. Bright roses
glowed in contrast with the dark and glossy curls of each, and were scat-

tered round their feet, or had sprung up spontaneously there. Behind this lightsome couple, so close to the Maypole that its boughs shaded his jovial face, stood the figure of an English priest, canonically dressed, yet decked with flowers, in heathen fashion, and wearing a chaplet of the native vine leaves. By the riot of his rolling eye, and the pagan decorations of his holy garb, he seemed the wildest monster there, and the very Comus of the crew.

"Votaries of the Maypole," cried the flower-decked priest, "merrily, all day long, have the woods echoed to your mirth. But be this your merriest hour, my hearts! Lo, here stand the Lord and Lady of the May, whom I, a clerk of Oxford, and high priest of Merry Mount, am presently to join in holy matrimony. Up with your nimble spirits, ye morris-dancers, green men, and glee maidens, bears and wolves, and horned gentlemen! Come; a chorus now, rich with the old mirth of Merry England, and the wilder glee of this fresh forest; and then a dance, to show the youthful pair what life is made of, and how airily they should go through it! All ye that love the Maypole, lend your voices to the nuptial song of the Lord and Lady of the May!"

This wedlock was more serious than most affairs of Merry Mount, where jest and delusion, trick and fantasy, kept up a continual carnival. The Lord and Lady of the May, though their titles must be laid down at sunset, were really and truly to be partners for the dance of life, beginning the measure that same bright eve. The wreath of roses, that hung from the lowest green bough of the Maypole, had been twined for them, and would be thrown over both their heads, in symbol of their flowery union. When the priest had spoken, therefore, a riotous uproar burst from the rout of monstrous figures.

"Begin you the stave, reverend Sir," cried they all; "and never did the woods ring to such a merry peal as we of the Maypole shall send up!"

Immediately a prelude of pipe, cithern, and viol, touched with practised minstrelsy, began to play from a neighboring thicket, in such a mirthful cadence that the boughs of the Maypole quivered to the sound. But the May Lord, he of the gilded staff, chancing to look into his Lady's eyes, was wonder struck at the almost pensive glance that met his own.

"Edith, sweet Lady of the May," whispered he reproachfully, "is yon wreath of roses a garland to hang above our graves, that you look so sad? O, Edith, this is our golden time! Tarnish it not by any pensive shadow of the mind; for it may be that nothing of futurity will be brighter than the mere remembrance of what is now passing."

"That was the very thought that saddened me! How came it in your mind too?" said Edith, in a still lower tone than he, for it was high treason to be sad at Merry Mount. "Therefore do I sigh amid this festive music. And besides, dear Edgar, I struggle as with a dream, and fancy that these shapes of our jovial friends are visionary, and their mirth unreal, and that we are no true Lord and Lady of the May. What is the mystery in my heart?"

Just then, as if a spell had loosened them, down came a little shower of withering rose leaves from the Maypole. Alas, for the young lovers! No sooner had their hearts glowed with real passion than they were sensible of something vague and unsubstantial in their former pleasures, and felt a dreary presentiment of inevitable change. From the moment that they truly loved, they had subjected themselves to earth's doom of care and sorrow, and troubled joy, and had no more a home at Merry Mount. That was Edith's mystery. Now leave we the priest to marry them, and the masquers to sport round the Maypole, till the last sunbeam be withdrawn from its summit, and the shadows of the forest mingle gloomily in the dance. Meanwhile, we may discover who these gay people were.

Two hundred years ago, and more, the old world and its inhabitants became mutually weary of each other. Men voyaged by thousands to the West: some to barter glass beads, and such like jewels, for the furs of the Indian hunter; some to conquer virgin empires; and one stern band to pray. But none of these motives had much weight with the colonists of Merry Mount. Their leaders were men who had sported so long with life, that when Thought and Wisdom came, even these unwelcome guests were led astray by the crowd of vanities which they should have put to flight. Erring Thought and perverted Wisdom were made to put on masques, and play the fool. The men of whom we speak, after losing the heart's fresh gayety, imagined a wild philosophy of pleasure, and came hither to act out their latest day-dream. They gathered followers from all that giddy tribe whose whole life is like the festal days of soberer men. In their train were minstrels, not unknown in London streets; wandering players, whose theatres had been the halls of noblemen; mummers, rope-dancers, and mountebanks, who would long be missed at wakes, church ales, and fairs; in a word, mirth makers of every sort, such as abounded in that age, but now began to be discountenanced by the rapid growth of Puritanism. Light had their footsteps been on land, and as lightly they came across the sea. Many had been maddened by their previous troubles into a gay despair; others were as madly gay in the flush of youth, like the May Lord and his Lady; but whatever might be the quality of their mirth, old and young were gay at Merry Mount. The young deemed themselves happy. The elder spirits, if they knew that mirth was but the counterfeit of happiness, yet followed the false shadow wilfully, because at least her garments glittered brightest. Sworn triflers of a lifetime, they would not venture among the sober truths of life not even to be truly blest.

All the hereditary pastimes of Old England were transplanted hither. The King of Christmas was duly crowned, and the Lord of Misrule bore potent sway. On the Eve of St. John, they felled whole acres of the forest to make bonfires, and danced by the blaze all night, crowned with garlands, and throwing flowers into the flame. At harvest time, though their crop was of the smallest, they made an image with the sheaves of Indian corn, and wreathed it with autumnal garlands, and bore it home triumphantly. But what chiefly characterized the colonists of Merry Mount was their veneration for the Maypole. It has made their true history a poet's tale. Spring decked the hallowed emblem with young blossoms and fresh green boughs; Summer brought roses of the deepest blush, and the perfected foliage of the forest; Autumn enriched it with that red and yellow gorgeousness which converts each wildwood leaf into a painted flower; and Winter silvered it with sleet, and hung it round with icicles, till it flashed in the cold sunshine, itself a frozen sunbeam. Thus each alternate season did homage to the Maypole, and paid it a tribute of its own richest splendor. Its votaries danced round it, once, at least, in every month; sometimes they called it their religion, or their altar; but always, it was the banner staff of Merry Mount.

Unfortunately, there were men in the new world of a sterner faith than those Maypole worshippers. Not far from Merry Mount was a settlement of Puritans, most dismal wretches, who said their prayers before daylight, and then wrought in the forest or the cornfield till evening made it prayer time again. Their weapons were always at hand to shoot down the straggling savage. When they met in conclave, it was never to keep up the old English mirth, but to hear sermons three hours long, or to proclaim bounties on the heads of wolves and the scalps of Indians. Their festivals were fast days, and their chief pastime the singing of psalms. Woe to the youth or maiden who did but dream of a dance! The selectman nodded to the constable; and there sat the light-heeled reprobate in the stocks; or if he danced, it was round the whipping-post, which might be termed the Puritan Maypole.

A party of these grim Puritans, toiling through the difficult woods, each with a horseload of iron armor to burden his footsteps, would sometimes draw near the sunny precincts of Merry Mount. There were the silken colonists, sporting round their Maypole; perhaps teaching a bear to dance, or striving to communicate their mirth to the grave Indian; or masquerading in the skins of deer and wolves, which they had hunted for that especial purpose. Often, the whole colony were playing at blindman's buff, magistrates and all, with their eyes bandaged, except a single scapegoat, whom the blinded sinners pursued by the tinkling of the bells at his garments. Once, it is said, they were seen following a flower-decked corpse, with merriment and festive music, to his grave. But did the dead man laugh? In their quietest times, they sang ballads and told tales, for the edification of their pious visitors; or perplexed them with juggling tricks; or grinned at them through horse collars; and when sport itself grew wearisome, they made game of their own stupidity, and began a yawning match. At the very least of these enormities, the men of iron shook their heads and frowned so darkly that the revellers looked up imagining that a momentary cloud had overcast the sunshine, which was to be perpetual there. On the other hand, the Puritans affirmed that, when a psalm was pealing from their place of worship, the echo which the forest sent them back seemed often like the chorus of a jolly catch, closing with a roar of laughter. Who but the fiend, and his bond slaves, the crew of Merry Mount, had thus disturbed them? In due time, a feud arose, stern and bitter on one side, and as serious on the other as anything could be among such light spirits as had sworn allegiance to the Maypole. The future complexion of New England was involved in this important quarrel. Should the grizzly saints establish their jurisdiction over the gay sinners, then would their spirits darken all the clime, and make it a land of clouded visages, of hard toil, of sermon and psalm forever. But should the banner staff of Merry Mount be fortunate, sunshine would break upon the hills, and flowers would beautify the forest, and late posterity do homage to the Maypole.

After these authentic passages from history, we return to the nuptials of the Lord and Lady of the May. Alas! we have delayed too long, and must darken our tale too suddenly. As we glance again at the Maypole, a solitary sunbeam is fading from the summit, and leaves only a faint, golden tinge blended with the hues of the rainbow banner. Even that dim light is now withdrawn, relinquishing the whole domain of Merry Mount to the evening gloom, which has rushed so instantaneously from the black surrounding woods. But some of these black shadows have rushed forth in human shape.

Yes, with the setting sun, the last day of mirth had passed from Merry Mount. The ring of gay masquers was disordered and broken; the stag lowered his antlers in dismay; the wolf grew weaker than a lamb; the bells of the morris-dancers tinkled with tremulous affright. The Puritans had played a characteristic part in the Maypole mummeries. Their darksome figures were intermixed with the wild shapes of their foes, and made the scene a picture of the moment, when waking thoughts start up amid the scattered fantasies of a dream. The leader of the hostile party stood in the centre of the circle, while the route of monsters cowered around him, like evil spirits in the presence of a dread magician. No fantastic foolery could look him in the face. So stern was the energy of his aspect, that the whole man, visage, frame, and soul, seemed wrought of iron, gifted with life and thought, yet all of one substance with his headpiece and breastplate. It was the Puritan of Puritans; it was Endicott himself!

"Stand off, priest of Baal!" said he, with a grim frown, and laying no reverent hand upon the surplice. "I know thee, Blackstone! [1] Thou art the man who couldst not abide the rule even of thine own corrupted church, and hast come hither to preach iniquity, and to give example of it in thy life. But now shall it be seen that the Lord hath sanctified this wilderness for his peculiar people. Woe unto them that would defile it! And first, for this flower-decked abomination, the altar of thy worship!"

And with his keen sword Endicott assaulted the hallowed Maypole. Nor long did it resist his arm. It groaned with a dismal sound; it showered leaves and rosebuds upon the remorseless enthusiast; and finally, with all its green boughs and ribbons and flowers, symbolic of departed pleasures, down fell the banner staff of Merry Mount. As it sank, tradition says, the evening sky grew darker, and the woods threw forth a more sombre shadow.

[1] Did Governor Endicott speak less positively, we should suspect a mistake here. The Rev. Mr. Blackstone, though an eccentric, is not known to have been an immoral man. We rather doubt his identity with the priest of Merry Mount.

"There," cried Endicott, looking triumphantly on his work, "there lies the only Maypole in New England! The thought is strong within me that, by its fall, is shadowed forth the fate of light and idle mirth makers, amongst us and our posterity. Amen, saith John Endicott."

"Amen!" echoed his followers.

But the votaries of the Maypole gave one groan for their idol. At the sound, the Puritan leader glanced at the crew of Comus, each a figure of broad mirth, yet, at this moment, strangely expressive of sorrow and dismay.

"Valiant captain," quoth Peter Palfrey, the Ancient of the band, "what order shall be taken with the prisoners?"

"I thought not to repent me of cutting down a Maypole," replied Endicott, "yet now I could find in my heart to plant it again, and give each of these bestial pagans one other dance round their idol. It would have served rarely for a whipping-post!"

"But there are pine-trees enow," suggested the lieutenant.

"True, good Ancient," said the leader. "Wherefore, bind the heathen crew, and bestow on them a small matter of stripes apiece, as earnest of our future justice. Set some of the rogues in the stocks to rest themselves, so soon as Providence shall bring us to one of our own well-ordered settlements where such accommodations may be found. Further penalties, such as branding and cropping of ears, shall be thought of hereafter."

"How many stripes for the priest?" inquired Ancient Palfrey.

"None as yet," answered Endicott, bending his iron frown upon the culprit. "It must be for the Great and General Court to determine, whether stripes and long imprisonment, and other grievous penalty, may atone for his transgressions. Let him look to himself! For such as violate our civil order, it may be permitted us to show mercy. But woe to the wretch that troubleth our religion."

"And this dancing bear," resumed the officer. "Must he share the stripes of his fellows?"

"Shoot him through the head!" said the energetic Puritan. "I suspect witchcraft in the beast."

"Here be a couple of shining ones," continued Peter Palfrey, pointing his weapon at the Lord and Lady of the May. "They seem to be of high station among these misdoers. Methinks their dignity will not be fitted with less than a double share of stripes."

Endicott rested on his sword, and closely surveyed the dress and aspect of the hapless pair. There they stood, pale, downcast, and apprehensive. Yet there was an air of mutual support and of pure affection, seeking aid and giving it, that showed them to be man and wife, with the sanction of a priest upon their love. The youth, in the peril of the moment, had dropped his gilded staff, and thrown his arm about the Lady of the May, who leaned against his breast, too lightly to burden him, but with weight enough to express that their destinies were linked together, for good or evil. They looked first at each other, and then into the grim captain's face.

There they stood, in the first hour of wedlock, while the idle pleasures, of which their companions were the emblems, had given place to the sternest cares of life, personified by the dark Puritans. But never had their youthful beauty seemed so pure and high as when its glow was chastened by adversity.

"Youth," said Endicott, "ye stand in an evil case thou and thy maiden wife. Make ready presently, for I am minded that ye shall both have a token to remember your wedding day!"

"Stern man," cried the May Lord, "how can I move thee? Were the means at hand, I would resist to the death. Being powerless, I entreat! Do with me as thou wilt, but let Edith go untouched!"

"Not so," replied the immitigable zealot. "We are not wont to show an idle courtesy to that sex, which requireth the stricter discipline. What sayest thou, maid? Shall thy silken bridegroom suffer thy share of the penalty, besides his own?"

"Be it death," said Edith, "and lay it all on me!"

Truly, as Endicott had said, the poor lovers stood in a woful case. Their foes were triumphant, their friends captive and abased, their home desolate, the benighted wilderness around them, and a rigorous destiny, in the shape of the Puritan leader, their only guide. Yet the deepening twilight could not altogether conceal that the iron man was softened; he smiled at the fair spectacle of early love; he almost sighed for the inevitable blight of early hopes.

"The troubles of life have come hastily on this young couple," observed Endicott. "We will see how they comport themselves under their present trials ere we burden them with greater. If, among the spoil, there be any garments of a more decent fashion, let them be put upon this May Lord and his Lady, instead of their glistening vanities. Look to it, some of you."

"And shall not the youth's hair be cut?" asked Peter Palfrey, looking with abhorrence at the lovelock and long glossy curls of the young man.

"Crop it forthwith, and that in the true pumpkin-shell fashion," answered the captain. "Then bring them along with us, but more gently than their fellows. There be qualities in the youth, which may make him valiant to fight, and sober to toil, and pious to pray; and in the maiden, that may fit her to become a mother in our Israel, bringing up babes in better nurture than her own hath been. Nor think ye, young ones, that they are the happiest, even in our lifetime of a moment, who misspend it in dancing round a Maypole!"

And Endicott, the severest Puritan of all who laid the rock foundation of New England, lifted the wreath of roses from the ruin of the Maypole, and threw it, with his own gauntleted hand, over the heads of the Lord and Lady of the May. It was a deed of prophecy. As the moral gloom of the world overpowers all systematic gayety, even so was their home of wild mirth made desolate amid the sad forest. They returned to it no more. But as their flowery garland was wreathed of the brightest roses that had grown there, so, in the tie that united them, were intertwined all the purest and best of their early joys. They went heavenward, supporting each other along the difficult path which it was their lot to tread, and never wasted one regretful thought on the vanities of Merry Mount.

# THE GENTLE BOY

In the course of the year 1656, several of the people called Quakers, led, as they professed, by the inward movement of the spirit, made their appearance in New England. Their reputation, as holders of mystic and pernicious principles, having spread before them, the Puritans early endeavored to banish, and to prevent the further intrusion of the rising sect. But the measures by which it was intended to purge the land of heresy, though more than sufficiently vigorous, were entirely unsuccessful. The Quakers, esteeming persecution as a divine call to the post of danger, laid claim to a holy courage, unknown to the Puritans themselves, who had shunned the cross, by providing for the peaceable exercise of their religion in a distant wilderness. Though it was the singular fact, that every nation of the earth rejected the wandering enthusiasts who practised peace towards all men, the place of greatest uneasiness and peril, and therefore, in their eyes the most eligible, was the province of Massachusetts Bay.

The fines, imprisonments, and stripes, liberally distributed by our pious forefathers; the popular antipathy, so strong that it endured nearly a hundred years after actual persecution had ceased, were attractions as powerful for the Quakers, as peace, honor, and reward, would have been for the worldly minded. Every European vessel brought new cargoes of the sect, eager to testify against the oppression which they hoped to share; and when shipmasters were restrained by heavy fines from affording them passage, they made long and circuitous journeys through the Indian country, and appeared in the province as if conveyed by a supernatural power. Their enthusiasm, heightened almost to madness by the treatment which they received, produced actions contrary to the rules of decency, as well as of rational religion, and presented a singular contrast to the calm and staid deportment of their sectarian successors of the present day. The command of the spirit, inaudible except to the soul, and not to be controverted on grounds of human wisdom, was made a plea for most indecorous exhibitions, which, abstractedly considered, well deserved the moderate chastisement of the rod. These extravagances, and the persecution which was at once their cause and consequence, continued to increase, till, in the year 1659, the government of Massachusetts Bay indulged two members of the Quaker sect with a crown of martyrdom.

An indelible stain of blood is upon the hands of all who consented to this act, but a large share of the awful responsibility must rest upon the person then at the head of the government. He was a man of narrow mind and imperfect education, and his uncompromising bigotry was made hot and mischievous by violent and hasty passions; he exerted his influence indecorously and unjustifiably to compass the death of the enthusiasts; and his whole conduct, in respect to them, was marked by brutal cruelty. The Quakers, whose revengeful feelings were not less deep because they were inactive, remembered this man and his associates in after times. The historian of the sect affirms that, by the wrath of Heaven, a blight fell upon the land in the vicinity of the "bloody town" of Boston, so that no wheat would grow there; and he takes his stand, as it were, among the graves of the ancient persecutors, and triumphantly recounts the judgments that overtook them, in old age or at the parting hour. He tells us that they died suddenly and violently and in madness; but nothing can exceed the bitter mockery with which he records the loathsome disease, and "death by rottenness," of the fierce and cruel governor.

.        .        .        .        .        .        .        .        .

On the evening of the autumn day that had witnessed the martyrdom of two men of the Quaker persuasion, a Puritan settler was returning from the metropolis to the neighboring country town in which he resided. The air was cool, the sky clear, and the lingering twilight was made brighter by the rays of a young moon, which had now nearly reached the verge of the horizon. The traveller, a man of middle age, wrapped in a gray frieze cloak, quickened his pace when he had reached the outskirts of the town, for a gloomy extent of nearly four miles lay between him and his home. The low, straw-thatched houses were scattered at considerable intervals along the road, and the country having been settled but about thirty years, the tracts of original forest still bore no small proportion to the cultivated ground. The autumn wind wandered among the branches, whirling away the leaves from all except the pine-trees, and moaning as if it lamented the desolation of which it was the instrument. The road had penetrated the mass of woods that lay nearest to the town, and was just emerging into an open space, when the traveller's ears were saluted by a sound more mournful than even that of the wind. It was like the wailing of someone in distress, and it seemed to proceed from beneath a tall and lonely fir-tree, in the centre of a cleared but uninclosed and uncultivated field. The Puritan could not but remember that this was the very spot which had been made accursed a few hours before by the execution of the Quakers whose bodies had been thrown together into one hasty grave, beneath the tree on which they suffered. He struggled however, against the superstitious fears which belonged to the age, and compelled himself to pause and listen.

"The voice is most likely mortal, nor have I cause to tremble if it be otherwise," thought he, straining his eyes through the dim moonlight. "Methinks it is like the wailing of a child; some infant, it may be, which has strayed from its mother, and chanced upon this place of death. For the ease of mine own conscience I must search this matter out."

He therefore left the path, and walked somewhat fearfully across the field. Though now so desolate, its soil was pressed down and trampled by the thousand footsteps of those who had witnessed the spectacle of that day, all of whom had now retired, leaving the dead to their loneliness. The traveller, at length reached the fir-tree, which from the middle upward was covered with living branches, although a scaffold had been erected beneath, and other preparations made for the work of death. Under this unhappy tree, which in after times was believed to drop poison with its dew, sat the one solitary mourner for innocent blood. It was a slender and light clad little boy, who leaned his face upon a hillock of fresh-turned and half-frozen earth, and wailed bitterly, yet in a suppressed tone, as if his grief might receive the punishment of crime. The Puritan, whose approach had been unperceived, laid his hand upon the child's shoulder, and addressed him compassionately.

"You have chosen a dreary lodging, my poor boy, and no wonder that you weep," said he. "But dry your eyes, and tell me where your mother dwells. I promise you, if the journey be not too far, I will leave you in her arms to-night."

The boy had hushed his wailing at once, and turned his face upward to the stranger. It was a pale, bright-eyed countenance, certainly not more than six years old, but sorrow, fear, and want had destroyed much of its infantile expression. The Puritan seeing the boy's frightened gaze, and feeling that he trembled under his hand, endeavored to reassure him.

"Nay, if I intended to do you harm, little lad, the readiest way were to leave you here. What! you do not fear to sit beneath the gallows on a new-made grave, and yet you tremble at a friend's touch. Take heart, child, and tell me what is your name and where is your home?"

"Friend," replied the little boy, in a sweet though faltering voice, "they call me Ilbrahim, and my home is here."

The pale, spiritual face, the eyes that seemed to mingle with the moonlight, the sweet, airy voice, and the outlandish name, almost made the Puritan believe that the boy was in truth a being which had sprung up out of the grave on which he sat. But perceiving that the apparition stood the test of a short mental prayer, and remembering that the arm which he had touched was lifelike, he adopted a more rational supposition. "The poor child is stricken in his intellect," thought he, "but verily his words are fearful in a place like this." He then spoke soothingly, intending to humor the boy's fantasy.

"Your home will scarce be comfortable, Ilbrahim, this cold autumn night, and I fear you are ill-provided with food. I am hastening to a warm supper and bed, and if you will go with me you shall share them!"

"I thank thee, friend, but though I be hungry, and shivering with cold, thou wilt not give me food nor lodging," replied the boy, in the quiet tone which despair had taught him, even so young. "My father was of the people whom all men hate. They have laid him under this heap of earth, and here is my home."

The Puritan, who had laid hold of little Ilbrahim's hand, relinquished it as if he were touching a loathsome reptile. But he possessed a compassionate heart, which not even religious prejudice could harden into stone.

"God forbid that I should leave this child to perish, though he comes of the accursed sect," said he to himself. "Do we not all spring from an evil root? Are we not all in darkness till the light doth shine upon us? He shall not perish, neither in body, nor, if prayer and instruction may avail for him, in soul." He then spoke aloud and kindly to Ilbrahim, who had again hid his face in the cold earth of the grave. "Was every door in the land shut against you, my child, that you have wandered to this unhallowed spot?"

"They drove me forth from the prison when they took my father thence," said the boy, "and I stood afar off watching the crowd of people, and when they were gone I came hither, and found only his grave. I knew that my father was sleeping here, and I said this shall be my home."

"No, child, no; not while I have a roof over my head, or a morsel to share with you!" exclaimed the Puritan, whose sympathies were now fully excited. "Rise up and come with me, and fear not any harm."

The boy wept afresh, and clung to the heap of earth as if the cold heart beneath it were warmer to him than any in a living breast. The traveller, however, continued to entreat him tenderly, and seeming to acquire some degree of confidence, he at length arose. But his slender limbs tottered with weakness, his little head grew dizzy, and he leaned against the tree of death for support.

"My poor boy, are you so feeble?" said the Puritan. "When did you taste food last?"

"I ate of bread and water with my father in the prison," replied Ilbrahim, "but they brought him none neither yesterday nor to-day, saying that he had eaten enough to bear him to his journey's end. Trouble not thyself for my hunger, kind friend, for I have lacked food many times ere now."

The traveller took the child in his arms and wrapped his cloak about him, while his heart stirred with shame and anger against the gratuitous cruelty of the instruments in this persecution. In the awakened warmth of his feelings he resolved that, at whatever risk, he would not forsake the poor little defenceless being whom Heaven had confided to his care. With this determination he left the accursed field, and resumed the homeward path from which the wailing of the boy had called him. The light and motionless burden scarcely impeded his progress, and he soon beheld the fire rays from the windows of the cottage which he, a native of a distant clime, had built in the western wilderness. It was surrounded by a considerable extent of cultivated ground, and the dwelling was situated in the nook of a wood-covered hill, whither it seemed to have crept for protection.

"Look up, child," said the Puritan to Ilbrahim, whose faint head had sunk upon his shoulder, "there is our home."

At the word "home," a thrill passed through the child's frame, but he continued silent. A few moments brought them to a cottage door, at which the owner knocked; for at that early period, when savages were wandering everywhere among the settlers, bolt and bar were indispensable to the security of a dwelling. The summons was answered by a bond-servant, a coarse-clad and dull-featured piece of humanity, who, after ascertaining that his master was the applicant, undid the door, and held a flaring pine-knot torch to light him in. Farther back in the passage-way, the red blaze discovered a matronly woman, but no little crowd of children came bounding forth to greet their father's return. As the Puritan entered, he thrust aside his cloak, and displayed Ilbrahim's face to the female.

"Dorothy, here is a little outcast, whom Providence hath put into our hands," observed he. "Be kind to him, even as if he were of those dear ones who have departed from us."

"What pale and bright-eyed little boy is this, Tobias?" she inquired. "Is he one whom the wilderness folk have ravished from some Christian mother?"

"No, Dorothy, this poor child is no captive from the wilderness," he replied. "The heathen savage would have given him to eat of his scanty morsel, and to drink of his birchen cup; but Christian men, alas, had cast him out to die."

Then he told her how he had found him beneath the gallows, upon his father's grave; and how his heart had prompted him, like the speaking of an inward voice, to take the little outcast home, and be kind unto him. He acknowledged his resolution to feed and clothe him, as if he were his own child, and to afford him the instruction which should counteract the pernicious errors hitherto instilled into his infant mind. Dorothy was gifted with even a quicker tenderness than her husband, and she approved of all his doings and intentions.

"Have you a mother, dear child?" she inquired.

The tears burst forth from his full heart as he attempted to reply; but Dorothy at length understood that he had a mother, who, like the rest of her sect, was a persecuted wanderer. She had been taken from the prison a short time before, carried into the uninhabited wilderness, and left to perish there by hunger or wild beasts. This was no uncommon method of disposing of the Quakers, and they were accustomed to boast that the inhabitants of the desert were more hospitable to them than civilized man.

"Fear not, little boy, you shall not need a mother, and a kind one," said Dorothy, when she had gathered this information. "Dry your tears, Ilbrahim, and be my child, as I will be your mother."

The good woman prepared the little bed, from which her own children had successively been borne to another resting-place. Before Ilbrahim would consent to occupy it, he knelt down, and as Dorothy listened to his simple and affecting prayer, she marvelled how the parents that had taught it to him could have been judged worthy of death. When the boy had fallen asleep, she bent over his pale and spiritual countenance, pressed a kiss upon his white brow, drew the bedclothes up about his neck, and went away with a pensive gladness in her heart.

Tobias Pearson was not among the earliest emigrants from the old country. He had remained in England during the first years of the civil war, in which he had borne some share as a cornet of dragoons, under Cromwell. But when the ambitious designs of his leader began to develop themselves, he quitted the army of the Parliament, and sought a refuge from the strife, which was no longer holy, among the people of his persuasion in the colony of Massachusetts. A more worldly consideration had perhaps an influence in drawing him thither; for New England offered advantages to men of unprosperous fortunes, as well as to dissatisfied religionists, and Pearson had hitherto found it difficult to provide for a wife and increasing family. To this supposed impurity of motive the more bigoted Puritans were inclined to impute the removal by death of all the children, for whose earthly good the father had been over-thoughtful. They had left their native country blooming like roses, and like roses they had perished in a foreign soil. Those expounders of the ways of Providence, who had thus judged their brother, and attributed his domestic sorrows to his sin, were not more charitable when they saw him and Dorothy endeavoring to fill up the void in their hearts by the adoption of an infant of the accursed sect. Nor did they fail to communicate their disapprobation to Tobias; but the latter, in reply, merely pointed at the little, quiet, lovely boy, whose appearance and deportment were indeed as powerful arguments as could possibly have been adduced in his own favor. Even his beauty, however, and his winning manners, sometimes produced an effect ultimately unfavorable; for the bigots, when the outer surfaces of their iron hearts had been softened and again grew hard, affirmed that no merely natural cause could have so worked upon them.

Their antipathy to the poor infant was also increased by the ill success of divers theological discussions, in which it was attempted to convince him of the errors of his sect. Ilbrahim, it is true, was not a skilful controversialist; but the feeling of his religion was strong as instinct in him, and he could neither be enticed nor driven from the faith which his father had died for. The odium of this stubbornness was shared in a great measure by the child's protectors, insomuch that Tobias and Dorothy very shortly began to experience a most bitter species of persecution, in the cold regards of many a friend whom they had valued. The common people manifested their opinions more openly. Pearson was a man of some consideration, being a representative to the General Court and an approved lieutenant in the trainbands, yet within a week after his adoption of Ilbrahim he had been both hissed and hooted. Once, also, when walking through a solitary piece of woods, he heard a loud voice from some invisible speaker; and it cried, "What shall be done to the backslider? Lo! the scourge is knotted for him, even the whip of nine cords, and every cord three knots!" These insults irritated Pearson's temper for the moment; they entered also into his heart, and became imperceptible but powerful workers towards an end which his most secret thought had not yet whispered.

. . . . . . . . . .

On the second Sabbath after Ilbrahim became a member of their family, Pearson and his wife deemed it proper that he should appear with them at public worship. They had anticipated some opposition to this measure from the boy, but he prepared himself in silence, and at the appointed hour was clad in the new mourning suit which Dorothy had wrought for him. As the parish was then, and during many subsequent years, unprovided with a bell, the signal for the commencement of religious exercises was the beat of a drum. At the first sound of that martial call to the place of holy and quiet thoughts, Tobias and Dorothy set forth, each holding a hand of little Ilbrahim, like two parents linked together by the infant of their love. On their path through the leafless woods they were overtaken by many persons of their acquaintance, all of whom avoided them, and passed by on the other side; but a severer trial awaited their constancy when they had descended the hill, and drew near the pine-built and undecorated house of prayer. Around the door, from which the drummer still sent forth his thundering summons, was drawn up a formidable phalanx, including several of the oldest members of the congregation, many of the middle aged, and nearly all the younger males. Pearson found it difficult to sustain their united and disapproving gaze, but Dorothy, whose mind was differently circumstanced, merely drew the boy closer to her, and faltered not in her approach. As they entered the door, they overheard the muttered sentiments of the assemblage, and when the reviling voices of the little children smote Ilbrahim's ear, he wept.

The interior aspect of the meeting-house was rude. The low ceiling, the unplastered walls, the naked wood work, and the undraperied pulpit, offered nothing to excite the devotion, which, without such external aids, often remains latent in the heart. The floor of the building was occupied by rows of long, cushionless benches, supplying the place of pews, and the broad aisle formed a sexual division, impassable except by children beneath a certain age.

Pearson and Dorothy separated at the door of the meeting-house, and Ilbrahim, being within the years of infancy, was retained under the care of the latter. The wrinkled beldams involved themselves in their rusty cloaks as he passed by; even the mild-featured maidens seemed to dread contamination; and many a stern old man arose, and turned his repulsive and unheavenly countenance upon the gentle boy, as if the sanctuary were polluted by his presence. He was a sweet infant of the skies that had strayed away from his home, and all the inhabitants of this miserable world closed up their impure hearts against him, drew back their earth-soiled garments from his touch, and said, "We are holier than thou."

Ilbrahim, seated by the side of his adopted mother, and retaining fast hold of her hand, assumed a grave and decorous demeanor, such as might befit a person of matured taste and understanding, who should find him-

self in a temple dedicated to some worship which he did not recognize, but
felt himself bound to respect. The exercises had not yet commenced, however, when the boy's attention was arrested by an event, apparently of
trifling interest. A woman, having her face muffled in a hood, and a cloak
drawn completely about her form, advanced slowly up the broad aisle and
took a place upon the foremost bench. Ilbrahim's faint color varied, his
nerves fluttered, he was unable to turn his eyes from the muffled female.

When the preliminary prayer and hymn were over, the minister arose,
and having turned the hour-glass which stood by the great Bible, commenced his discourse. He was now well stricken in years, a man of pale,
thin countenance, and his gray hairs were closely covered by a black velvet skullcap. In his younger days he had practically learned the meaning
of persecution from Archbishop Laud, and he was not now disposed to
forget the lesson against which he had murmured then. Introducing the
often discussed subject of the Quakers, he gave a history of that sect, and
a description of their tenets, in which error predominated, and prejudice
distorted the aspect of what was true. He adverted to the recent measures
in the province, and cautioned his hearers of weaker parts against calling
in question the just severity which God-fearing magistrates had at length
been compelled to exercise. He spoke of the danger of pity, in some cases
a commendable and Christian virtue, but inapplicable to this pernicious
sect. He observed that such was their devilish obstinacy in error, that
even the little children, the sucking babes, were hardened and desperate
heretics. He affirmed that no man, without Heaven's especial warrant,
should attempt their conversion, lest while he lent his hand to draw them
from the slough, he should himself be precipitated into its lowest depths.

The sands of the second hour were principally in the lower half of the
glass when the sermon concluded. An approving murmur followed, and
the clergyman, having given out a hymn, took his seat with much self-
congratulation, and endeavored to read the effect of his eloquence in the
visages of the people. But while voices from all parts of the house were
tuning themselves to sing, a scene occurred, which, though not very unusual at that period in the province, happened to be without precedent in
this parish.

The muffled female, who had hitherto sat motionless in the front rank
of the audience, now arose, and with slow, stately, and unwavering step,
ascended the pulpit stairs. The quiverings of incipient harmony were
hushed, and the divine sat in speechless and almost terrified astonishment, while she undid the door, and stood up in the sacred desk from
which his maledictions had just been thundered. She then divested herself of the cloak and hood, and appeared in a most singular array. A
shapeless robe of sackcloth was girded about her waist with a knotted
cord; her raven hair fell down upon her shoulders, and its blackness was
defiled by pale streaks of ashes, which she had strown upon her head. Her
eyebrows, dark and strongly defined, added to the deathly whiteness of a
countenance, which, emaciated with want, and wild with enthusiasm and
strange sorrows, retained no trace of earlier beauty. This figure stood gaz-

ing earnestly on the audience, and there was no sound, nor any movement, except a faint shuddering which every man observed in his neighbor, but was scarcely conscious of in himself. At length, when her fit of
inspiration came, she spoke, for the first few moments, in a low voice, and
not invariably distinct utterance. Her discourse gave evidence of an imagination hopelessly entangled with her reason; it was a vague and incomprehensible rhapsody, which, however, seemed to spread its own atmosphere round the hearer's soul, and to move his feelings by some influence
unconnected with the words. As she proceeded, beautiful but shadowy
images would sometimes be seen, like bright things moving in a turbid
river; or a strong and singularly-shaped idea leaped forth, and seized at
once on the understanding or the heart. But the course of her unearthly
eloquence soon led her to the persecutions of her sect, and from thence
the step was short to her own peculiar sorrows. She was naturally a
woman of mighty passions, and hatred and revenge now wrapped themselves in the garb of piety; the character of her speech was changed, her
images became distinct though wild, and her denunciations had an almost
hellish bitterness.

"The Governor and his mighty men," she said, "have gathered together, taking counsel among themselves and saying, 'What shall we do unto
this people—even unto the people that have come into this land to put
our iniquity to the blush?' And lo! the devil entereth into the council
chamber, like a lame man of low stature and gravely apparelled, with a
dark and twisted countenance, and a bright, downcast eye. And he stand-
eth up among the rulers; yea, he goeth to and fro, whispering to each;
and every man lends his ear, for his word is 'Slay, slay!' But I say unto
ye, Woe to them that slay! Woe to them that shed the blood of saints!
Woe to them that have slain the husband, and cast forth the child, the
tender infant, to wander homeless and hungry and cold, till he die; and
have saved the mother alive, in the cruelty of their tender mercies! Woe
to them in their lifetime! cursed are they in the delight and pleasure of
their hearts! Woe to them in their death hour, whether it come swiftly
with blood and violence, or after long and lingering pain! Woe, in the
dark house, in the rottenness of the grave, when the children's children
shall revile the ashes of the fathers! Woe, woe, woe, at the judgment,
when all the persecuted and all the slain in this bloody land, and the
father, the mother, and the child, shall await them in a day that they cannot escape! Seed of the faith, seed of the faith, ye whose hearts are moving with a power that ye know not, arise, wash your hands of this innocent
blood! Lift your voices, chosen ones; cry aloud, and call down a woe and
a judgment with me!"

Having thus given vent to the flood of malignity which she mistook for
inspiration, the speaker was silent. Her voice was succeeded by the hysteric shrieks of several women, but the feelings of the audience generally
had not been drawn onward in the current with her own. They remained
stupefied, stranded as it were, in the midst of a torrent, which deafened
them by its roaring, but might not move them by its violence. The clergy-

man, who could not hitherto have ejected the usurper of his pulpit otherwise than by bodily force, now addressed her in the tone of just indignation and legitimate authority.

"Get you down, woman, from the holy place which you profane," he said. "Is it to the Lord's house that you come to pour forth the foulness of your heart and the inspiration of the devil? Get you down, and remember that the sentence of death is on you; yea, and shall be executed, were it but for this day's work!"

"I go, friend, I go, for the voice hath had its utterance," replied she, in a depressed and even mild tone. "I have done my mission unto thee and to thy people. Reward me with stripes, imprisonment, or death, as ye shall be permitted."

The weakness of exhausted passion caused her steps to totter as she descended the pulpit stairs. The people, in the mean while, were stirring to and fro on the floor of the house, whispering among themselves, and glancing towards the intruder. Many of them now recognized her as the woman who had assaulted the Governor with frightful language as he passed by the window of her prison; they knew, also, that she was adjudged to suffer death, and had been preserved only by an involuntary banishment into the wilderness. The new outrage, by which she had provoked her fate, seemed to render further lenity impossible; and a gentleman in military dress, with a stout man of inferior rank, drew towards the door of the meeting-house, and awaited her approach.

Scarcely did her feet press the floor, however, when an unexpected scene occurred. In that moment of her peril, when every eye frowned with death, a little timid boy pressed forth, and threw his arms round his mother.

"I am here, mother; it is I, and I will go with thee to prison," he exclaimed.

She gazed at him with a doubtful and almost frightened expression, for she knew that the boy had been cast out to perish, and she had not hoped to see his face again. She feared, perhaps, that it was but one of the happy visions with which her excited fancy had often deceived her, in the solitude of the desert or in prison. But when she felt his hand warm within her own, and heard his little eloquence of childish love, she began to know that she was yet a mother.

"Blessed art thou, my son," she sobbed. "My heart was withered; yea, dead with thee and with thy father; and now it leaps as in the first moment when I pressed thee to my bosom."

She knelt down and embraced him again and again, while the joy that could find no words expressed itself in broken accents, like the bubbles gushing up to vanish at the surface of a deep fountain. The sorrows of past years, and the darker peril that was nigh, cast not a shadow on the brightness of that fleeting moment. Soon, however, the spectators saw a change upon her face, as the consciousness of her sad estate returned, and grief supplied the fount of tears which joy had opened. By the words she uttered, it would seem that the indulgence of natural love had given her mind a momentary sense of its errors, and made her know how far she had strayed from duty in following the dictates of a wild fanaticism.

"In a doleful hour art thou returned to me, poor boy," she said, "for thy mother's path has gone darkening onward, till now the end is death. Son, son, I have borne thee in my arms when my limbs were tottering, and I have fed thee with the food that I was fainting for; yet I have ill performed a mother's part by thee in life, and now I leave thee no inheritance but woe and shame. Thou wilt go seeking through the world, and find all hearts closed against thee and their sweet affections turned to bitterness for my sake. My child, my child, how many a pang awaits thy gentle spirit, and I the cause of all!"

She hid her face on Ilbrahim's head, and her long, raven hair, discolored with the ashes of her mourning, fell down about him like a veil. A low and interrupted moan was the voice of her heart's anguish, and it did not fail to move the sympathies of many who mistook their involuntary virtue for a sin. Sobs were audible in the female section of the house, and every man who was a father drew his hand across his eyes. Tobias Pearson was agitated and uneasy, but a certain feeling like the consciousness of guilt oppressed him, so that he could not go forth and offer himself as the protector of the child. Dorothy, however, had watched her husband's eye. Her mind was free from the influence that had begun to work on his, and she drew near the Quaker woman, and addressed her in the hearing of all the congregation.

"Stranger, trust this boy to me, and I will be his mother," she said, taking Ilbrahim's hand. "Providence has signally marked out my husband to protect him, and he has fed at our table and lodged under our roof now many days, till our hearts have grown very strongly unto him. Leave the tender child with us, and be at ease concerning his welfare."

The Quaker rose from the ground, but drew the boy closer to her, while she gazed earnestly in Dorothy's face. Her mild but saddened features, and neat matronly attire, harmonized together, and were like a verse of fireside poetry. Her very aspect proved that she was blameless, so far as mortal could be so, in respect to God and man; while the enthusiast, in her robe of sackcloth and girdle of knotted cord, had as evidently violated the duties of the present life and the future, by fixing her attention wholly on the latter. The two females, as they held each a hand of Ilbrahim, formed a practical allegory; it was rational piety and unbridled fanaticism contending for the empire of a young heart.

"Thou art not of our people," said the Quaker, mournfully.

"No, we are not of your people," replied Dorothy, with mildness, "but we are Christians, looking upward to the same heaven with you. Doubt not that your boy shall meet you there, if there be a blessing on our tender and prayerful guidance of him. Thither, I trust, my own children have gone before me, for I also have been a mother; I am no longer so," she added, in a faltering tone, "and your son will have all my care."

"But will ye lead him in the path which his parents have trodden?" demanded the Quaker. "Can ye teach him the enlightened faith which his

father has died for, and for which I, even I, am soon to become an unworthy martyr? The boy has been baptized in blood; will ye keep the
mark fresh and ruddy upon his forehead?"

"I will not deceive you," answered Dorothy. "If your child become our
child, we must breed him up in the instruction which Heaven has imparted to us; we must pray for him the prayers of our own faith; we must do
towards him according to the dictates of our own consciences, and not of
yours. Were we to act otherwise, we should abuse your trust, even in com-
plying with your wishes."

The mother looked down upon her boy with a troubled countenance,
and then turned her eyes upward to heaven. She seemed to pray internally, and the contention of her soul was evident.

"Friend," she said at length to Dorothy, "I doubt not that my son shall
receive all earthly tenderness at thy hands. Nay, I will believe that even
thy imperfect lights may guide him to a better world, for surely thou art
on the path thither. But thou hast spoken of a husband. Doth he stand
here among this multitude of people? Let him come forth, for I must
know to whom I commit this most precious trust."

She turned her face upon the male auditors, and after a momentary delay, Tobias Pearson came forth from among them. The Quaker saw the
dress which marked his military rank, and shook her head; but then she
noted the hesitating air, the eyes that struggled with her own, and were
vanquished; the color that went and came, and could find no resting-
place. As she gazed, an unmirthful smile spread over her features, like
sunshine that grows melancholy in some desolate spot. Her lips moved
inaudibly, but at length she spake.

"I hear it, I hear it. The voice speaketh within me and saith, 'Leave thy
child, Catharine, for his place is here, and go hence, for I have other work
for thee. Break the bonds of natural affection, martyr thy love, and know
that in all these things eternal wisdom hath its ends.' I go, friends; I go.
Take ye my boy, my precious jewel. I go hence, trusting that all shall be
well, and that even for his infant hands there is a labor in the vineyard."

She knelt down and whispered to Ilbrahim, who at first struggled and
clung to his mother, with sobs and tears, but remained passive when she
had kissed his cheek and arisen from the ground. Having held her hands
over his head in mental prayer, she was ready to depart.

"Farewell, friends in mine extremity," she said to Pearson and his
wife; "the good deed ye have done me is a treasure laid up in heaven, to
be returned a thousand-fold hereafter. And farewell ye, mine enemies, to
whom it is not permitted to harm so much as a hair of my head, nor to stay
my footsteps even for a moment. The day is coming when ye shall call
upon me to witness for ye to this one sin uncommitted, and I will rise up
and answer."

She turned her steps towards the door, and the men, who had stationed
themselves to guard it, withdrew, and suffered her to pass. A general sentiment of pity overcame the virulence of religious hatred. Sanctified by
her love and her affliction, she went forth, and all the people gazed after

her till she had journeyed up the hill, and was lost behind its brow. She went, the apostle of her own unquiet heart, to renew the wanderings of past years. For her voice had been already heard in many lands of Christendom; and she had pined in the cells of a Catholic Inquisition before she felt the lash and lay in the dungeons of the Puritans. Her mission had extended also to the followers of the Prophet, and from them she had received the courtesy and kindness which all the contending sects of our purer religion united to deny her. Her husband and herself had resided many months in Turkey, where even the Sultan's countenance was gracious to them; in that pagan land, too, was Ilbrahim's birthplace, and his oriental name was a mark of gratitude for the good deeds of an unbeliever.

.    .    .    .    .    .    .    .    .

When Pearson and his wife had thus acquired all the rights over Ilbrahim that could be delegated, their affection for him became like the memory of their native land, or their mild sorrow for the dead, a piece of the immovable furniture of their hearts. The boy, also, after a week or two of mental disquiet, began to gratify his protectors by many inadvertent proofs that he considered them as parents, and their house as home. Before the winter snows were melted, the persecuted infant, the little wanderer from a remote and heathen country, seemed native in the New England cottage, and inseparable from the warmth and security of its hearth. Under the influence of kind treatment, and in the consciousness that he was loved, Ilbrahim's demeanor lost a premature manliness, which had resulted from his earlier situation; he became more childlike, and his natural character displayed itself with freedom. It was in many respects a beautiful one, yet the disordered imaginations of both his father and mother had perhaps propagated a certain unhealthiness in the mind of the boy. In his general state, Ilbrahim would derive enjoyment from the most trifling events, and from every object about him; he seemed to discover rich treasures of happiness, by a faculty analogous to that of the witch hazel, which points to hidden gold where all is barren to the eye. His airy gayety, coming to him from a thousand sources, communicated itself to the family, and Ilbrahim was like a domesticated sunbeam, brightening moody countenances, and chasing away the gloom from the dark corners of the cottage.

On the other hand, as the susceptibility of pleasure is also that of pain, the exuberant cheerfulness of the boy's prevailing temper sometimes yielded to moments of deep depression. His sorrows could not always be followed up to their original source, but most frequently they appeared to flow, though Ilbrahim was young to be sad for such a cause, from wounded love. The flightiness of his mirth rendered him often guilty of offences against the decorum of a Puritan household, and on these occasions he did not invariably escape rebuke. But the slightest word of real bitterness, which he was infallible in distinguishing from pretended anger, seemed to sink into his heart and poison all his enjoyments, till he became sensible that he was entirely forgiven. Of the malice, which generally accompanies a superfluity of sensitiveness, Ilbrahim was altogether destitute: when trodden upon, he would not turn; when wounded, he could but die. His mind was wanting in the stamina for self-support; it was a plant that would twine beautifully round something stronger than itself, but if repulsed, or torn away, it had no choice but to wither on the ground. Dorothy's acuteness taught her that severity would crush the spirit of the child, and she nurtured him with the gentle care of one who handles a butterfly. Her husband manifested an equal affection, although it grew daily less productive of familiar caresses.

The feelings of the neighboring people, in regard to the Quaker infant and his protectors, had not undergone a favorable change, in spite of the momentary triumph which the desolate mother had obtained over their sympathies. The scorn and bitterness, of which he was the object, were very grievous to Ilbrahim, especially when any circumstance made him sensible that the children, his equals in age, partook of the enmity of their parents. His tender and social nature had already overflowed in attachments to everything about him, and still there was a residue of unappropriated love, which he yearned to bestow upon the little ones who were taught to hate him. As the warm days of spring came on, Ilbrahim was accustomed to remain for hours, silent and inactive, within hearing of the children's voices at their play; yet, with his usual delicacy of feeling, he avoided their notice, and would flee and hide himself from the smallest individual among them. Chance, however, at length seemed to open a medium of communication between his heart and theirs; it was by means of a boy about two years older than Ilbrahim, who was injured by a fall from a tree in the vicinity of Pearson's habitation. As the sufferer's own home was at some distance, Dorothy willingly received him under her roof, and became his tender and careful nurse.

Ilbrahim was the unconscious possessor of much skill in physiognomy, and it would have deterred him, in other circumstances, from attempting to make a friend of this boy. The countenance of the latter immediately impressed a beholder disagreeably, but it required some examination to discover that the cause was a very slight distortion of the mouth, and the irregular, broken line, and near approach of the eyebrows. Analogous, perhaps, to these trifling deformities, was an almost imperceptible twist of every joint, and the uneven prominence of the breast; forming a body, regular in its general outline, but faulty in almost all its details. The disposition of the boy was sullen and reserved, and the village schoolmaster stigmatized him as obtuse in intellect; although, at a later period of life, he evinced ambition and very peculiar talents. But whatever might be his personal or moral irregularities, Ilbrahim's heart seized upon, and clung to him, from the moment that he was brought wounded into the cottage; the child of persecution seemed to compare his own fate with that of the sufferer, and to feel that even different modes of misfortune had created a sort of relationship between them. Food, rest, and the fresh air, for which he languished, were neglected; he nestled continually by the bedside of the little stranger, and, with a fond jealousy, endeavored to be the medium of all the cares that were bestowed upon him. As the boy became convalescent, Ilbrahim contrived games suitable to his situation, or amused him by a faculty which he had perhaps breathed in with the air of his barbaric birthplace. It was that of reciting imaginary adventures, on the spur of the moment, and apparently in inexhaustible succession. His tales were of course monstrous, disjointed, and without aim; but they were curious on account of a vein of human tenderness which ran through them all, and was like a sweet, familiar face, encountered in the midst of wild and unearthly scenery. The auditor paid much attention to these romances, and sometimes interrupted them by brief remarks upon the incidents, displaying shrewdness above his years, mingled with a moral obliquity which grated very harshly against Ilbrahim's instinctive rectitude. Nothing, however, could arrest the progress of the latter's affection, and there were many proofs that it met with a response from the dark and stubborn nature on which it was lavished. The boy's parents at length removed him, to complete his cure under their own roof.

Ilbrahim did not visit his new friend after his departure; but he made anxious and continual inquiries respecting him, and informed himself of the day when he was to reappear among his playmates. On a pleasant summer afternoon, the children of the neighborhood had assembled in the little forest-crowned amphitheatre behind the meeting-house, and the recovering invalid was there, leaning on a staff. The glee of a score of untainted bosoms was heard in light and airy voices, which danced among the trees like sunshine become audible; the grown men of this weary world, as they journeyed by the spot, marvelled why life, beginning in such brightness, should proceed in gloom; and their hearts, or their imaginations, answered them and said, that the bliss of childhood gushes from its innocence. But it happened that an unexpected addition was made to the heavenly little band. It was Ilbrahim, who came towards the children with a look of sweet confidence on his fair and spiritual face, as if, having manifested his love to one of them, he had no longer to fear a repulse from their society. A hush came over their mirth the moment they beheld him, and they stood whispering to each other while he drew nigh; but, all at once, the devil of their fathers entered into the unbreeched fanatics, and sending up a fierce, shrill cry, they rushed upon the poor Quaker child. In an instant, he was the centre of a brood of baby-fiends, who lifted sticks against him, pelted him with stones, and displayed an instinct of destruction far more loathsome than the bloodthirstiness of manhood.

The invalid, in the meanwhile, stood apart from the tumult, crying out with a loud voice, "Fear not, Ilbrahim, come hither and take my hand;" and his unhappy friend endeavored to obey him. After watching the victim's struggling approach with a calm smile and unabashed eye, the foulhearted little villain lifted his staff and struck Ilbrahim on the mouth, so forcibly that the blood issued in a stream. The poor child's arms had been raised to guard his head from the storm of blows; but now he dropped them at once. His persecutors beat him down, trampled upon him, dragged him by his long, fair locks, and Ilbrahim was on the point of becoming as veritable a martyr as ever entered bleeding into heaven. The uproar, however, attracted the notice of a few neighbors, who put themselves to the trouble of rescuing the little heretic, and of conveying him to Pearson's door.

Ilbrahim's bodily harm was severe, but long and careful nursing accomplished his recovery; the injury done to his sensitive spirit was more serious, though not so visible. Its signs were principally of a negative character, and to be discovered only by those who had previously known him. His gait was thenceforth slow, even, and unvaried by the sudden bursts of sprightlier motion, which had once corresponded to his overflowing gladness; his countenance was heavier, and its former play of expression, the dance of sunshine reflected from moving water, was destroyed by the cloud over his existence; his notice was attracted in a far less degree by passing events, and he appeared to find greater difficulty in comprehending what was new to him than at a happier period. A stranger, founding his judgment upon these circumstances, would have said that the dulness of the child's intellect widely contradicted the promise of his features; but the secret was in the direction of Ilbrahim's thoughts, which were brooding within him when they should naturally have been wandering abroad. An attempt of Dorothy to revive his former sportiveness was the single occasion on which his quiet demeanor yielded to a violent display of grief; he burst into passionate weeping, and ran and hid himself, for his heart had become so miserably sore that even the hand of kindness tortured it like fire. Sometimes, at night and probably in his dreams, he was heard to cry "Mother! Mother!" as if her place, which a stranger had supplied while Ilbrahim was happy, admitted of no substitute in his extreme affliction. Perhaps, among the many life-weary wretches then upon the earth, there was not one who combined innocence and misery like this poor, broken-hearted infant, so soon the victim of his own heavenly nature.

While this melancholy change had taken place in Ilbrahim, one of an earlier origin and of different character had come to its perfection in his adopted father. The incident with which this tale commences found Pearson in a state of religious dulness, yet mentally disquieted, and longing for a more fervid faith than he possessed. The first effect of his kindness to Ilbrahim was to produce a softened feeling, and incipient love for the child's whole sect; but joined to this, and resulting perhaps from self-suspicion, was a proud and ostentatious contempt of all their tenets and practical extravagances. In the course of much thought, however, for the subject struggled irresistibly into his mind, the foolishness of the doctrine began to be less evident, and the points which had particularly offended his reason assumed another aspect, or vanished entirely away. The work within him appeared to go on even while he slept, and that which had been a doubt, when he lay down to rest, would often hold the place of a truth, confirmed by some forgotten demonstration, when he recalled his thoughts in the morning. But while he was thus becoming assimilated to the enthusiasts, his contempt, in nowise decreasing towards them, grew very fierce against himself; he imagined, also, that every face of his acquaintance wore a sneer, and that every word addressed to him was a gibe. Such was his state of mind at the period of Ilbrahim's misfortune; and the emotions consequent upon that event completed the change, of which the child had been the original instrument.

In the mean time, neither the fierceness of the persecutors, nor the infatuation of their victims, had decreased. The dungeons were never empty; the streets of almost every village echoed daily with the lash; the life of a woman, whose mild and Christian spirit no cruelty could embitter, had been sacrificed; and more innocent blood was yet to pollute the hands that were so often raised in prayer. Early after the Restoration, the English Quakers represented to Charles II. that a "vein of blood was open in his dominions;" but though the displeasure of the voluptuous king was roused, his interference was not prompt. And now the tale must stride forward over many months, leaving Pearson to encounter ignominy and misfortune; his wife to a firm endurance of a thousand sorrows; poor Ilbrahim to pine and droop like a cankered rosebud; his mother to wander on a mistaken errand, neglectful of the holiest trust which can be committed to a woman.

.     .     .     .     .     .     .     .     .

A winter evening, a night of storm, had darkened over Pearson's habitation, and there were no cheerful faces to drive the gloom from his broad hearth. The fire, it is true, sent forth a glowing heat and a ruddy light, and large logs, dripping with half-melted snow, lay ready to be cast upon the embers. But the apartment was saddened in its aspect by the absence of much of the homely wealth which had once adorned it; for the exaction of repeated fines, and his own neglect of temporal affairs, had greatly impoverished the owner. And with the furniture of peace, the implements of war had likewise disappeared; the sword was broken, the helm and cuirass were cast away forever; the soldier had done with battles, and might not lift so much as his naked hand to guard his head. But the Holy Book remained, and the table on which it rested was drawn before the fire, while two of the persecuted sect sought comfort from its pages.

He who listened, while the other read, was the master of the house, now emaciated in form, and altered as to the expression and healthiness of his countenance; for his mind had dwelt too long among visionary thoughts, and his body had been worn by imprisonment and stripes. The hale and weather-beaten old man who sat beside him had sustained less injury from a far longer course of the same mode of life. In person he was tall and dignified, and, which alone would have made him hateful to the Puritans, his gray locks fell from beneath the broad-brimmed hat, and rested on his shoulders. As the old man read the sacred page the snow drifted against the windows, or eddied in at the crevices of the door, while a blast kept laughing in the chimney, and the blaze leaped fiercely up to seek it. And sometimes, when the wind struck the hill at a certain angle, and swept down by the cottage across the wintry plain, its voice was the most doleful that can be conceived; it came as if the Past were speaking, as if the Dead had contributed each a whisper, as if the Desolation of Ages were breathed in that one lamenting sound.

The Quaker at length closed the book, retaining however his hand between the pages which he had been reading, while he looked steadfastly at Pearson. The attitude and features of the latter might have indicated the endurance of bodily pain; he leaned his forehead on his hands, his teeth were firmly closed, and his frame was tremulous at intervals with a nervous agitation.

"Friend Tobias," inquired the old man, compassionately, "hast thou found no comfort in these many blessed passages of Scripture?"

"Thy voice has fallen on my ear like a sound afar off and indistinct," replied Pearson without lifting his eyes. "Yea, and when I have hearkened carefully the words seemed cold and lifeless, and intended for another and a lesser grief than mine. Remove the book," he added, in a tone of sullen bitterness. "I have no part in its consolations, and they do but fret my sorrow the more."

"Nay, feeble brother, be not as one who hath never known the light," said the elder Quaker earnestly, but with mildness. "Art thou he that wouldst be content to give all, and endure all, for conscience' sake; desiring even peculiar trials, that thy faith might be purified and thy heart weaned from worldly desires? And wilt thou sink beneath an affliction which happens alike to them that have their portion here below, and to them that lay up treasure in heaven? Faint not, for thy burden is yet light."

"It is heavy! It is heavier than I can bear!" exclaimed Pearson, with the impatience of a variable spirit. "From my youth upward I have been a man marked out for wrath; and year by year, yea, day after day, I have endured sorrows such as others know not in their lifetime. And now I speak not of the love that has been turned to hatred, the honor to ignominy, the ease and plentifulness of all things to danger, want, and nakedness. All this I could have borne, and counted myself blessed. But when my heart was desolate with many losses I fixed it upon the child of a stranger, and he became dearer to me than all my buried ones; and now he too must die as if my love were poison. Verily, I am an accursed man, and I will lay me down in the dust and lift up my head no more."

"Thou sinnest, brother, but it is not for me to rebuke thee; for I also have had my hours of darkness, wherein I have murmured against the cross," said the old Quaker. He continued, perhaps in the hope of distracting his companion's thoughts from his own sorrows. "Even of late was the light obscured within me, when the men of blood had banished me on pain of death, and the constables led me onward from village to village towards the wilderness. A strong and cruel hand was wielding the knotted cords; they sunk deep into the flesh, and thou mightst have tracked every reel and totter of my footsteps by the blood that followed. As we went on"—

"Have I not borne all this; and have I murmured?" interrupted Pearson impatiently.

"Nay, friend, but hear me," continued the other. "As we journeyed on, night darkened on our path, so that no man could see the rage of the persecutors or the constancy of my endurance, though Heaven forbid that I should glory therein. The lights began to glimmer in the cottage windows, and I could discern the inmates as they gathered in comfort and security, every man with his wife and children by their own evening hearth. At length we came to a tract of fertile land; in the dim light, the forest was not visible around it; and behold! there was a straw-thatched dwelling, which bore the very aspect of my home, far over the wild ocean, far in our own England. Then came bitter thoughts upon me; yea, remembrances that were like death to my soul. The happiness of my early days was painted to me; the disquiet of my manhood, the altered faith of my declining years. I remembered how I had been moved to go forth a wanderer when my daughter, the youngest, the dearest of my flock, lay on her dying bed, and"—

"Couldst thou obey the command at such a moment?" exclaimed Pearson, shuddering.

"Yea, yea," replied the old man hurriedly. "I was kneeling by her bedside when the voice spoke loud within me; but immediately I rose, and took my staff, and gat me gone. Oh! that it were permitted me to forget her woful look when I thus withdrew my arm, and left her journeying through the dark valley alone! for her soul was faint, and she had leaned upon my prayers. Now in that night of horror I was assailed by the thought that I had been an erring Christian and a cruel parent; yea, even my daughter, with her pale, dying features, seemed to stand by me and whisper, 'Father, you are deceived; go home and shelter your gray head.' O Thou, to whom I have looked in my farthest wanderings," continued the Quaker, raising his agitated eyes to heaven, "inflict not upon the bloodiest of our persecutors the unmitigated agony of my soul, when I believed that all I had done and suffered for Thee was at the instigation of a mocking fiend! But I yielded not; I knelt down and wrestled with the tempter, while the scourge bit more fiercely into the flesh. My prayer was heard, and I went on in peace and joy towards the wilderness."

The old man, though his fanaticism had generally all the calmness of reason, was deeply moved while reciting this tale; and his unwonted emotion seemed to rebuke and keep down that of his companion. They sat in silence, with their faces to the fire, imagining, perhaps, in its red embers new scenes of persecution yet to be encountered. The snow still drifted hard against the windows, and sometimes, as the blaze of the logs had gradually sunk, came down the spacious chimney and hissed upon the hearth. A cautious footstep might now and then be heard in a neighboring apartment, and the sound invariably drew the eyes of both Quakers to the door which led thither. When a fierce and riotous gust of wind had led his thoughts, by a natural association, to homeless travellers on such a night, Pearson resumed the conversation.

"I have well-nigh sunk under my own share of this trial," observed he, sighing heavily; "yet I would that it might be doubled to me, if so the child's mother could be spared. Her wounds have been deep and many, but this will be the sorest of all."

"Fear not for Catharine," replied the old Quaker, "for I know that valiant woman, and have seen how she can bear the cross. A mother's heart, indeed, is strong in her, and may seem to contend mightily with her faith; but soon she will stand up and give thanks that her son has been thus early an accepted sacrifice. The boy hath done his work, and she will feel that he is taken hence in kindness both to him and her. Blessed, blessed are they that with so little suffering can enter into peace!"

The fitful rush of the wind was now disturbed by a portentous sound; it was a quick and heavy knocking at the outer door. Pearson's wan countenance grew paler, for many a visit of persecution had taught him what to dread; the old man, on the other hand, stood up erect, and his glance was firm as that of the tried soldier who awaits his enemy.

"The men of blood have come to seek me," he observed with calmness. "They have heard how I was moved to return from banishment; and now am I to be led to prison, and thence to death. It is an end I have long looked for. I will open unto them, lest they say, 'Lo, he feareth!'"

"Nay, I will present myself before them," said Pearson, with recovered fortitude. "It may be that they seek me alone, and know not that thou abidest with me."

"Let us go boldly, both one and the other," rejoined his companion. "It is not fitting that thou or I should shrink."

They therefore proceeded through the entry to the door, which they opened, bidding the applicant "Come in, in God's name!" A furious blast of wind drove the storm into their faces, and extinguished the lamp; they had barely time to discern a figure, so white from head to foot with the drifted snow that it seemed like Winter's self, come in human shape, to seek refuge from its own desolation.

"Enter, friend, and do thy errand, be it what it may," said Pearson. "It must needs be pressing, since thou comest on such a bitter night."

"Peace be with this household," said the stranger, when they stood on the floor of the inner apartment.

Pearson started, the elder Quaker stirred the slumbering embers of the fire till they sent up a clear and lofty blaze; it was a female voice that had spoken; it was a female form that shone out, cold and wintry, in that comfortable light.

"Catharine, blessed woman!" exclaimed the old man, "art thou come to this darkened land again? art thou come to bear a valiant testimony as in former years? The scourge hath not prevailed against thee, and from the dungeon hast thou come forth triumphant; but strengthen, strengthen now thy heart, Catharine, for Heaven will prove thee yet this once, ere thou go to thy reward."

"Rejoice, friends!" she replied. "Thou who hast long been of our people, and thou whom a little child hath led to us, rejoice! Lo! I come, the messenger of glad tidings, for the day of persecution is overpast. The heart of the king, even Charles, hath been moved in gentleness towards us, and he hath sent forth his letters to stay the hands of the men of blood. A ship's company of our friends hath arrived at yonder town, and I also sailed joyfully among them."

As Catharine spoke, her eyes were roaming about the room, in search of him for whose sake security was dear to her. Pearson made a silent appeal to the old man, nor did the latter shrink from the painful task assigned him.

"Sister," he began, in a softened yet perfectly calm tone, "thou tellest us of His love, manifested in temporal good; and now must we speak to thee of that selfsame love, displayed in chastenings. Hitherto, Catharine, thou hast been as one journeying in a darksome and difficult path, and leading an infant by the hand; fain wouldst thou have looked heavenward continually, but still the cares of that little child have drawn thine eyes and thy affections to the earth. Sister! go on rejoicing, for his tottering footsteps shall impede thine own no more."

But the unhappy mother was not thus to be consoled; she shook like a leaf, she turned white as the very snow that hung drifted into her hair. The firm old man extended his hand and held her up, keeping his eye upon hers, as if to repress any outbreak of passion.

"I am a woman, I am but a woman; will He try me above my strength?" said Catharine very quickly, and almost in a whisper. "I have been wounded sore; I have suffered much; many things in the body; many in the mind; crucified in myself, and in them that were dearest to me. Surely," added she, with a long shudder, "He hath spared me in this one thing." She broke forth with sudden and irrepressible violence. "Tell me, man of cold heart, what has God done to me? Hath He cast me down, never to rise again? Hath He crushed my very heart in his hand? And thou, to whom I committed my child, how hast thou fulfilled thy trust? Give me back the boy, well, sound, alive, alive; or earth and Heaven shall avenge me!"

The agonized shriek of Catharine was answered by the faint, the very faint, voice of a child.

On this day it had become evident to Pearson, to his aged guest, and to Dorothy, that Ilbrahim's brief and troubled pilgrimage drew near its close. The two former would willingly have remained by him, to make use of the prayers and pious discourses which they deemed appropriate to the time, and which, if they be impotent as to the departing traveller's reception in the world whither he goes, may at least sustain him in bidding adieu to earth. But though Ilbrahim uttered no complaint, he was disturbed by the faces that looked upon him; so that Dorothy's entreaties, and their own conviction that the child's feet might tread heaven's pavement and not soil it, had induced the two Quakers to remove. Ilbrahim then closed his eyes and grew calm, and, except for now and then a kind and low word to his nurse, might have been thought to slumber. As nightfall came on, however, and the storm began to rise, something seemed to trouble the repose of the boy's mind, and to render his sense of hearing active and acute. If a passing wind lingered to shake the casement, he strove to turn his head towards it; if the door jarred to and fro upon its hinges, he looked long and anxiously thitherward; if the heavy voice of the old man, as he read the Scriptures, rose but a little higher, the child almost held his dying breath to listen; if a snow-drift swept by the cottage, with a sound like the trailing of a garment, Ilbrahim seemed to watch that some visitant should enter.

But, after a little time, he relinquished whatever secret hope had agitated him, and with one low, complaining whisper, turned his cheek upon the pillow. He then addressed Dorothy with his usual sweetness, and besought her to draw near him; she did so, and Ilbrahim took her hand in both of his, grasping it with a gentle pressure, as if to assure himself that he retained it. At intervals, and without disturbing the repose of his countenance, a very faint trembling passed over him from head to foot, as if a mild but somewhat cool wind had breathed upon him, and made him shiver. As the boy thus led her by the hand, in his quiet progress over the borders of eternity, Dorothy almost imagined that she could discern the near, though dim, delightfulness of the home he was about to reach; she would not have enticed the little wanderer back, though she bemoaned herself that she must leave him and return. But just when Ilbrahim's feet were pressing on the soil of Paradise he heard a voice behind him, and it recalled him a few, few paces of the weary path which he had travelled. As Dorothy looked upon his features, she perceived that their placid expression was again disturbed; her own thoughts had been so wrapped in him, that all sounds of the storm, and of human speech, were lost to her; but when Catharine's shriek pierced through the room, the boy strove to raise himself.

"Friend, she is come! Open unto her!" cried he.

In a moment his mother was kneeling by the bedside; she drew Ilbrahim to her bosom, and he nestled there, with no violence of joy, but contentedly, as if he were hushing himself to sleep. He looked into her face, and reading its agony, said, with feeble earnestness, "Mourn not, dearest mother. I am happy now." And with these words the gentle boy was dead.

.    .    .    .    .    .    .    .    .

The king's mandate to stay the New England persecutors was effectual in preventing further martyrdoms; but the colonial authorities, trusting in the remoteness of their situation, and perhaps in the supposed instability of the royal government, shortly renewed their severities in all other respects. Catharine's fanaticism had become wilder by the sundering of all human ties; and wherever a scourge was lifted there was she to receive the blow; and whenever a dungeon was unbarred thither she came, to cast herself upon the floor. But in process of time a more Christian spirit —a spirit of forbearance, though not of cordiality or approbation—began to pervade the land in regard to the persecuted sect. And then, when the rigid old Pilgrims eyed her rather in pity than in wrath; when the matrons fed her with the fragments of their children's food, and offered her a lodging on a hard and lowly bed; when no little crowd of schoolboys left their sports to cast stones after the roving enthusiast; then did Catherine return to Pearson's dwelling and made that her home.

As if Ilbrahim's sweetness yet lingered round his ashes; as if his gentle spirit came down from heaven to teach his parent a true religion, her fierce and vindictive nature was softened by the same griefs which had once irritated it. When the course of years had made the features of the unobtrusive mourner familiar in the settlement, she became a subject of not deep, but general, interest; a being on whom the otherwise superfluous sympathies of all might be bestowed. Every one spoke of her with that degree of pity which it is pleasant to experience; every one was ready to do her the little kindnesses which are not costly, yet manifest good will; and when at last she died, a long train of her once bitter persecutors followed her, with decent sadness and tears that were not painful, to her place by Ilbrahim's green and sunken grave.

## MR. HIGGINBOTHAM'S CATASTROPHE

A YOUNG fellow, a tobacco pedlar by trade, was on his way from Morristown, where he had dealt largely with the Deacon of the Shaker settlement, to the village of Parker's Falls, on Salmon River. He had a neat little cart, painted green, with a box of cigars depicted on each side panel, and an Indian chief, holding a pipe and a golden tobacco stalk, on the rear. The pedlar drove a smart little mare, and was a young man of excellent character, keen at a bargain, but none the worse liked by the Yankees; who, as I have heard them say, would rather be shaved with a sharp razor than a dull one. Especially was he beloved by the pretty girls along the Connecticut, whose favor he used to court by presents of the best smoking tobacco in his stock; knowing well that the country lasses of New England are generally great performers on pipes. Moreover, as will be seen in the course of my story, the pedlar was inquisitive, and something of a tattler, always itching to hear the news and anxious to tell it again.

After an early breakfast at Morristown, the tobacco pedlar, whose name was Dominicus Pike, had travelled seven miles through a solitary piece of woods, without speaking a word to anybody but himself and his little gray mare. It being nearly seven o'clock, he was as eager to hold a morning gossip as a city shopkeeper to read the morning paper. An opportunity seemed at hand when, after lighting a cigar with a sun-glass, he looked up, and perceived a man coming over the brow of the hill, at the foot of which the pedlar had stopped his green cart. Dominicus watched him as he descended, and noticed that he carried a bundle over his shoulder on the end of a stick, and travelled with a weary, yet determined pace. He did not look as if he had started in the freshness of the morning, but had footed it all night, and meant to do the same all day.

"Good morning, mister," said Dominicus, when within speaking distance. "You go a pretty good jog. What's the latest news at Parker's Falls?"

The man pulled the broad brim of a gray hat over his eyes, and answered, rather sullenly, that he did not come from Parker's Falls, which, as being the limit of his own day's journey, the pedlar had naturally mentioned in his inquiry.

"Well then," rejoined Dominicus Pike, "let's have the latest news where you did come from. I'm not particular about Parker's Falls. Any place will answer."

Being thus importuned, the traveller—who was as ill looking a fellow as one would desire to meet in a solitary piece of woods—appeared to hesitate a little, as if he was either searching his memory for news, or weighing the expediency of telling it. At last, mounting on the step of the cart, he whispered in the ear of Dominicus, though he might have shouted aloud and no other mortal would have heard him.

"I do remember one little trifle of news," said he. "Old Mr. Higginbotham, of Kimballton, was murdered in his orchard, at eight o'clock last night, by an Irishman and a nigger. They strung him up to the branch of a St. Michael's pear-tree, where nobody would find him till the morning."

As soon as this horrible intelligence was communicated, the stranger betook himself to his journey again, with more speed than ever, not even turning his head when Dominicus invited him to smoke a Spanish cigar and relate all the particulars. The pedlar whistled to his mare and went up the hill, pondering on the doleful fate of Mr. Higginbotham whom he had known in the way of trade, having sold him many a bunch of long nines, and a great deal of pigtail, lady's twist, and fig tobacco. He was rather astonished at the rapidity with which the news had spread. Kimballton was nearly sixty miles distant in a straight line; the murder had been perpetrated only at eight o'clock the preceding night; yet Dominicus had heard of it at seven in the morning, when, in all probability, poor Mr. Higginbotham's own family had but just discovered his corpse, hanging on the St. Michael's pear-tree. The stranger on foot must have worn seven-league boots to travel at such a rate.

"Ill news flies fast, they say," thought Dominicus Pike; "but this beats railroads. The fellow ought to be hired to go express with the President's Message."

The difficulty was solved by supposing that the narrator had made a mistake of one day in the date of the occurrence; so that our friend did not hesitate to introduce the story at every tavern and country store along the road, expending a whole bunch of Spanish wrappers among at least twenty horrified audiences. He found himself invariably the first bearer of the intelligence, and was so pestered with questions that he could not avoid filling up the outline, till it became quite a respectable narrative. He met with one piece of corroborative evidence. Mr. Higginbotham was a trader; and a former clerk of his, to whom Dominicus related the facts, testified that the old gentleman was accustomed to return home through the orchard about nightfall, with the money and valuable papers of the store in his pocket. The clerk manifested but little grief at Mr. Higginbotham's catastrophe, hinting, what the pedlar had discovered in his own dealings with him, that he was a crusty old fellow, as close as a vice. His property would descend to a pretty niece who was now keeping school in Kimballton.

What with telling the news for the public good, and driving bargains for his own, Dominicus was so much delayed on the road that he chose to put up at a tavern, about five miles short of Parker's Falls. After supper, lighting one of his prime cigars, he seated himself in the bar-room, and went through the story of the murder, which had grown so fast that it took him half an hour to tell. There were as many as twenty people in the room, nineteen of whom received it all for gospel. But the twentieth was an elderly farmer, who had arrived on horseback a short time before, and was now seated in a corner smoking his pipe. When the story was concluded, he rose up very deliberately, brought his chair right in front of Dominicus, and stared him full in the face, puffing out the vilest tobacco smoke the pedlar had ever smelt.

"Will you make affidavit," demanded he, in the tone of a country justice taking an examination, "that old Squire Higginbotham of Kimballton was murdered in his orchard the night before last, and found hanging on his great pear-tree yesterday morning?"

"I tell the story as I heard it, mister," answered Dominicus, dropping his half-burnt cigar; "I don't say that I saw the thing done. So I can't take my oath that he was murdered exactly in that way."

"But I can take mine," said the farmer, "that if Squire Higginbotham was murdered night before last, I drank a glass of bitters with his ghost this morning. Being a neighbor of mine, he called me into his store, as I was riding by, and treated me, and then asked me to do a little business for him on the road. He didn't seem to know any more about his own murder than I did."

"Why, then, it can't be a fact!" exclaimed Dominicus Pike.

"I guess he'd have mentioned, if it was," said the old farmer; and he removed his chair back to the corner, leaving Dominicus quite down in the mouth.

Here was a sad resurrection of old Mr. Higginbotham! The pedlar had no heart to mingle in the conversation any more, but comforted himself with a glass of gin and water, and went to bed where, all night long, he dreamed of hanging on the St. Michael's pear-tree. To avoid the old farmer (whom he so detested that his suspension would have pleased him better than Mr. Higginbotham's), Dominicus rose in the gray of the morning, put the little mare into the green cart, and trotted swiftly away towards Parker's Falls. The fresh breeze, the dewy road, and the pleasant summer dawn, revived his spirits, and might have encouraged him to repeat the old story had there been anybody awake to hear it. But he met neither ox team, light wagon chaise, horseman, nor foot traveller, till, just as he crossed Salmon River, a man came trudging down to the bridge with a bundle over his shoulder, on the end of a stick.

"Good morning, mister," said the pedlar, reining in his mare. "If you come from Kimballton or that neighborhood, may be you can tell me the real fact about this affair of old Mr. Higginbotham. Was the old fellow actually murdered two or three nights ago, by an Irishman and a nigger?"

Dominicus had spoken in too great a hurry to observe, at first, that the stranger himself had a deep tinge of negro blood. On hearing this sudden question, the Ethiopian appeared to change his skin, its yellow hue becoming a ghastly white, while, shaking and stammering, he thus replied:—

"No! no! There was no colored man! It was an Irishman that hanged him last night, at eight o'clock. I came away at seven! His folks can't have looked for him in the orchard yet."

Scarcely had the yellow man spoken, when he interrupted himself, and though he seemed weary enough before, continued his journey at a pace which would have kept the pedlar's mare on a smart trot. Dominicus stared after him in great perplexity. If the murder had not been committed till Tuesday night, who was the prophet that had foretold it, in all its circumstances, on Tuesday morning? If Mr. Higginbotham's corpse were not yet discovered by his own family, how came the mulatto, at above thirty miles' distance, to know that he was hanging in the orchard, especially as he had left Kimballton before the unfortunate man was hanged at all? These ambiguous circumstances, with the stranger's surprise and terror, made Dominicus think of raising a hue and cry after him, as an accomplice in the murder; since a murder, it seemed, had really been perpetrated.

"But let the poor devil go," thought the pedlar. "I don't want his black blood on my head; and hanging the nigger wouldn't unhang Mr. Higginbotham. Unhang the old gentleman; It's a sin, I know; but I should hate to have him come to life a second time, and give me the lie!"

With these meditations, Dominicus Pike drove into the street of Parker's Falls, which, as everybody knows, is as thriving a village as three cotton factories and a slitting mill can make it. The machinery was not in motion, and but a few of the shop doors unbarred, when he alighted in the stable yard of the tavern, and made it his first business to order the mare four quarts of oats. His second duty, of course, was to impart Mr. Higginbotham's catastrophe to the hostler. He deemed it advisable, however, not to be too positive as to the date of the direful fact, and also to be uncertain whether it were perpetrated by an Irishman and a mulatto, or by the son of Erin alone. Neither did he profess to relate it on his own authority, or that of any one person; but mentioned it as a report generally diffused.

The story ran through the town like fire among girdled trees, and became so much the universal talk that nobody could tell whence it had originated. Mr. Higginbotham was as well known at Parker's Falls as any citizen of the place, being part owner of the slitting mill, and a considerable stockholder in the cotton factories. The inhabitants felt their own prosperity interested in his fate. Such was the excitement, that the Parker's Falls Gazette anticipated its regular day of publication, and came out with half a form of blank paper and a column of double pica emphasized with capitals, and headed HORRID MURDER OF MR. HIGGINBOTHAM! Among other dreadful details, the printed account described the mark of the cord round the dead man's neck, and stated the number of thousand dollars of which he had been robbed; there was much pathos also about the affliction of his niece, who had gone from one fainting fit to another, ever since her uncle was found hanging on the St. Michael's pear-tree with his pockets inside out. The village poet likewise commemorated the young lady's grief in seventeen stanzas of a ballad. The selectmen held a meeting, and, in consideration of Mr. Higginbotham's claims on the town, determined to issue handbills, offering a reward of five hundred dollars for the apprehension of his murderers, and the recovery of the stolen property.

Meanwhile the whole population of Parker's Falls, consisting of shopkeepers, mistresses of boarding-houses, factory girls, millmen, and schoolboys, rushed into the street and kept up such a terrible loquacity as more than compensated for the silence of the cotton machines, which refrained from their usual din out of respect to the deceased. Had Mr. Higginbotham cared about posthumous renown, his untimely ghost would have exulted in this tumult. Our friend Dominicus, in his vanity of heart, forgot his intended precautions, and mounting on the town pump, announced himself as the bearer of the authentic intelligence which had caused so wonderful a sensation. He immediately became the great man of the moment, and had just begun a new edition of the narrative, with a voice like a field preacher, when the mail stage drove into the village street. It had travelled all night, and must have shifted horses at Kimballton, at three in the morning.

"Now we shall hear all the particulars," shouted the crowd.

The coach rumbled up to the piazza of the tavern, followed by a thousand people; for if any man had been minding his own business till then, he now left it at sixes and sevens, to hear the news. The pedlar, foremost in the race, discovered two passengers, both of whom had been startled from a comfortable nap to find themselves in the centre of a mob. Every man assailing them with separate questions, all propounded at once, the couple were struck speechless, though one was a lawyer and the other a young lady.

"Mr. Higginbotham! Mr. Higginbotham! Tell us the particulars about old Mr. Higginbotham!" bawled the mob. "What is the coroner's verdict? Are the murderers apprehended? Is Mr. Higginbotham's niece come out of her fainting fits? Mr. Higginbotham! Mr. Higginbotham!!"

The coachman said not a word, except to swear awfully at the hostler for not bringing him a fresh team of horses. The lawyer inside had generally his wits about him even when asleep; the first thing he did, after learning the cause of the excitement, was to produce a large, red pocketbook. Meantime Dominicus Pike, being an extremely polite young man, and also suspecting that a female tongue would tell the story as glibly as a lawyer's, had handed the lady out of the coach. She was a fine, smart girl, now wide awake and bright as a button, and had such a sweet pretty mouth, that Dominicus would almost as lief have heard a love tale from it as a tale of murder.

"Gentlemen and ladies," said the lawyer to the shopkeepers, the millmen, and the factory girls, "I can assure you that some unaccountable mistake, or, more probably, a wilful falsehood, maliciously contrived to injure Mr. Higginbotham's credit, has excited this singular uproar. We passed through Kimballton at three o'clock this morning, and most certainly should have been informed of the murder had any been perpetrated. But I have proof nearly as strong as Mr. Higginbotham's own oral testimony, in the negative. Here is a note relating to a suit of his in the Connecticut courts, which was delivered me from that gentleman himself. I find it dated at ten o'clock last evening."

So saying, the lawyer exhibited the date and signature of the note, which irrefragably proved, either that this perverse Mr. Higginbotham was alive when he wrote it, or—as some deemed the more probable case, of two doubtful ones—that he was so absorbed in worldly business as to continue to transact it even after his death. But unexpected evidence was forthcoming. The young lady, after listening to the pedlar's explanation, merely seized a moment to smooth her gown and put her curls in order, and then appeared at the tavern door, making a modest signal to be heard.

"Good people," said she, "I am Mr. Higginbotham's niece."

A wondering murmur passed through the crowd on beholding her so rosy and bright; that same unhappy niece, whom they had supposed, on the authority of the Parker's Falls Gazette, to be lying at death's door in a fainting fit. But some shrewd fellows had doubted, all along, whether a young lady would be quite so desperate at the hanging of a rich old uncle.

"You see," continued Miss Higginbotham, with a smile, "that this strange story is quite unfounded as to myself; and I believe I may affirm it to be equally so in regard to my dear uncle Higginbotham  He has the kindness to give me a home in his house, though I contribute to my own support by teaching a school. I left Kimballton this morning to spend the vacation of commencement week with a friend, about five miles from Parker's Falls. My generous uncle, when he heard me on the stairs, called me to his bedside, and gave me two dollars and fifty cents to pay my stage fare, and another dollar for my extra expenses. He then laid his pocketbook under his pillow, shook hands with me, and advised me to take some biscuit in my bag, instead of breakfasting on the road. I feel confident, therefore, that I left my beloved relative alive, and trust that I shall find him so on my return."

The young lady courtesied at the close of her speech, which was so sensible and well worded, and delivered with such grace and propriety, that everybody thought her fit to be preceptress of the·best academy in the State. But a stranger would have supposed that Mr. Higginbotham was an object of abhorrence at Parker's Falls, and that a thanksgiving had been proclaimed for his murder; so excessive was the wrath of the inhabitants on learning their mistake. The millmen resolved to bestow public honors on Dominicus Pike, only hesitating whether to tar and feather him, ride him on a rail, or refresh him with an ablution at the town pump, on the top of which he had declared himself the bearer of the news. The selectmen, by advice of the lawyer, spoke of prosecuting him for a misdemeanor, in circulating unfounded reports, to the great disturbance of the peace of the Commonwealth. Nothing saved Dominicus, either from mob law or a court of justice, but an eloquent appeal made by the young lady in his behalf. Addressing a few words of heartfelt gratitude to his benefactress, he mounted the green cart and rode out of town, under a discharge of artillery from the school-boys, who found plenty of ammunition in the neighboring clay-pits and mud holes. As he turned his head to exchange a farewell glance with Mr. Higginbotham's niece, a ball, of the consistence of hasty pudding, hit him slap in the mouth, giving him a most grim aspect. His whole person was so bespattered with the like filthy missiles, that he had almost a mind to ride back, and supplicate for the threatened ablution at the town pump; for, though not meant in kindness, it would now have been a deed of charity.

However, the sun shone bright on poor Dominicus, and the mud, an emblem of all stains of undeserved opprobrium, was easily brushed off when dry. Being a funny rogue, his heart soon cheered up; nor could he refrain from a hearty laugh at the uproar which his story had excited. The handbills of the selectmen would cause the commitment of all the vagabonds in the State; the paragraph in the Parker's Falls Gazette would be reprinted from Maine to Florida, and perhaps form an item in the London newspapers; and many a miser would tremble for his money bags and life, on learning the catastrophe of Mr. Higginbotham. The pedlar meditated with much fervor on the charms of the young schoolmistress, and swore that Daniel Webster never spoke nor looked so like an angel as Miss Higginbotham, while defending him from the wrathful populace at Parker's Falls.

Dominicus was now on the Kimballton turnpike, having all along determined to visit that place, though business had drawn him out of the most direct road from Morristown. As he approached the scene of the supposed murder, he continued to revolve the circumstances in his mind, and was astonished at the aspect which the whole case assumed. Had nothing occurred to corroborate the story of the first traveller, it might now have been considered as a hoax; but the yellow man was evidently acquainted either with the report or the fact; and there was a mystery in his dismayed and guilty look on being abruptly questioned. When, to this singular combination of incidents, it was added that the rumor tallied exactly with Mr. Higginbotham's character and habits of life; and that he had an orchard, and a St. Michael's pear-tree, near which he always passed at nightfall: the circumstantial evidence appeared so strong that Dominicus doubted whether the autograph produced by the lawyer, or even the niece's direct testimony, ought to be equivalent. Making cautious inquiries along the road, the pedlar further learned that Mr. Higginbotham had in his service an Irishman of doubtful character, whom he had hired without a recommendation, on the score of economy.

"May I be hanged myself," exclaimed Dominicus Pike aloud, on reaching the top of a lonely hill, "if I'll believe old Higginbotham is unhanged till I see him with my own eyes, and hear it from his own mouth! And as he's a real shaver, I'll have the minister or some other responsible man for an indorser."

It was growing dusk when he reached the toll-house on Kimballton turnpike, about a quarter of a mile from the village of this name. His little mare was fast bringing him up with a man on horseback, who trotted through the gate a few rods in advance of him, nodded to the toll-gatherer, and kept on towards the village. Dominicus was acquainted with the tollman, and, while making change, the usual remarks on the weather passed between them.

"I suppose," said the pedlar, throwing back his whiplash, to bring it down like a feather on the mare's flank, "you have not seen anything of old Mr. Higginbotham within a day or two?"

"Yes," answered the toll-gatherer. "He passed the gate just before you drove up, and yonder he rides now, if you can see him through the dusk. He's been to Woodfield this afternoon, attending a sheriff's sale there. The old man generally shakes hands and has a little chat with me; but to-night, he nodded,—as if to say, 'Charge my toll,' and jogged on; for wherever he goes, he must always be at home by eight o'clock."

"So they tell me," said Dominicus.

"I never saw a man look so yellow and thin as the squire does," continued the toll-gatherer. "Says I to myself, to-night, he's more like a ghost or an old mummy than good flesh and blood."

The pedlar strained his eyes through the twilight, and could just discern the horseman now far ahead on the village road. He seemed to recognize the rear of Mr. Higginbotham; but through the evening shadows, and amid the dust from the horse's feet, the figure appeared dim and unsubstantial; as if the shape of the mysterious old man were faintly moulded of darkness and gray light. Dominicus shivered.

"Mr. Higginbotham has come back from the other world, by way of the Kimballton turnpike," thought he.

He shook the reins and rode forward, keeping about the same distance in the rear of the gray old shadow, till the latter was concealed by a bend of the road. On reaching this point, the pedlar no longer saw the man on horseback, but found himself at the head of the village street, not far from a number of stores and two taverns, clustered round the meeting-house steeple. On his left were a stone wall and a gate, the boundary of a wood-lot, beyond which lay an orchard, farther still, a mowing field, and last of all, a house. These were the premises of Mr. Higginbotham, whose dwelling stood beside the old highway, but had been left in the background by the Kimballton turnpike. Dominicus knew the place; and the little mare stopped short by instinct; for he was not conscious of tightening the reins.

"For the soul of me, I cannot get by this gate!" said he, trembling. "I never shall be my own man again, till I see whether Mr. Higginbotham is hanging on the St. Michael's pear-tree!"

He leaped from the cart, gave the rein a turn round the gate post, and ran along the green path of the wood-lot as if Old Nick were chasing behind. Just then the village clock tolled eight, and as each deep stroke fell, Dominicus gave a fresh bound and flew faster than before, till, dim in the solitary centre of the orchard, he saw the fated pear-tree. One great branch stretched from the old contorted trunk across the path, and threw the darkest shadow on that one spot. But something seemed to struggle beneath the branch!

The pedlar had never pretended to more courage than befits a man of peaceful occupation, nor could he account for his valor on this awful emergency. Certain it is, however, that he rushed forward, prostrated a sturdy Irishman with the butt end of his whip, and found—not indeed hanging on the St. Michael's pear-tree, but trembling beneath it, with a halter round his neck—the old, identical Mr. Higginbotham!

"Mr. Higginbotham," said Dominicus tremulously, "you're an honest man, and I'll take your word for it. Have you been hanged or not?"

If the riddle be not already guessed, a few words will explain the simple machinery by which this "coming event" was made to "cast its shadow before." Three men had plotted the robbery and murder of Mr. Higginbotham; two of them, successively, lost courage and fled, each delaying the crime one night by their disappearance; the third was in the act of perpetration, when a champion, blindly obeying the call of fate, like the heroes of old romance, appeared in the person of Dominicus Pike.

It only remains to say, that Mr. Higginbotham took the pedlar into high favor, sanctioned his addresses to the pretty schoolmistress, and settled his whole property on their children, allowing themselves the interest. In due time, the old gentleman capped the climax of his favors, by dying a Christian death, in bed, since which melancholy event Dominicus Pike has removed from Kimballton, and established a large tobacco manufactory in my native village.

# WAKEFIELD

In some old magazine or newspaper I recollect a story, told as truth, of a man—let us call him Wakefield—who absented himself for a long time from his wife. The fact, thus abstractedly stated, is not very uncommon, nor—without a proper distinction of circumstances—to be condemned either as naughty or nonsensical. Howbeit, this, though far from the most aggravated, is perhaps the strangest, instance on record, of marital delinquency; and, moreover, as remarkable a freak as may be found in the whole list of human oddities. The wedded couple lived in London. The man, under pretence of going a journey, took lodgings in the next street to his own house, and there, unheard of by his wife or friends, and without the shadow of a reason for such self-banishment, dwelt upwards of twenty years. During that period, he beheld his home every day, and frequently the forlorn Mrs. Wakefield. And after so great a gap in his matrimonial felicity—when his death was reckoned certain, his estate settled, his name dismissed from memory, and his wife, long, long ago, resigned to her autumnal widowhood—he entered the door one evening, quietly, as from a day's absence, and became a loving spouse till death.

This outline is all that I remember. But the incident, though of the purest originality, unexampled, and probably never to be repeated, is one, I think, which appeals to the generous sympathies of mankind. We know, each for himself, that none of us would perpetrate such a folly, yet feel as if some other might. To my own contemplations, at least, it has often recurred, always exciting wonder, but with a sense that the story must be true, and a conception of its hero's character. Whenever any subject so forcibly affects the mind, time is well spent in thinking of it. If the reader choose, let him do his own meditation; or if he prefer to ramble with me through the twenty years of Wakefield's vagary, I bid him welcome; trusting that there will be a pervading spirit and a moral, even should we fail to find them, done up neatly, and condensed into the final sentence. Thought has always its efficacy, and every striking incident its moral.

What sort of a man was Wakefield? We are free to shape out our own idea, and call it by his name. He was now in the meridian of life; his matrimonial affections, never violent, were sobered into a calm, habitual sentiment; of all husbands, he was likely to be the most constant, because a certain sluggishness would keep his heart at rest, wherever it might be placed. He was intellectual, but not actively so; his mind occupied itself in long and lazy musings, that ended to no purpose, or had not vigor to attain it; his thoughts were seldom so energetic as to seize hold of words. Imagination, in the proper meaning of the term, made no part of Wakefield's gifts. With a cold but not depraved nor wandering heart, and a mind never feverish with riotous thoughts, nor perplexed with originality, who could have anticipated that our friend would entitle himself to a foremost place among the doers of eccentric deeds? Had his acquaintances been asked, who was the man in London the surest to perform nothing today which should be remembered on the morrow, they would have thought of Wakefield. Only the wife of his bosom might have hesitated. She, without having analyzed his character, was partly aware of a quiet selfishness, that had rusted into his inactive mind; of a peculiar sort of vanity, the most uneasy attribute about him; of a disposition to craft, which had seldom produced more positive effects than the keeping of petty secrets, hardly worth revealing; and, lastly, of what she called a little strangeness, sometimes, in the good man. This latter quality is indefinable, and perhaps non-existent.

Let us now imagine Wakefield bidding adieu to his wife. It is the dusk of an October evening. His equipment is a drab great-coat, a hat covered with an oilcloth, top-boots, an umbrella in one hand and a small portmanteau in the other. He has informed Mrs. Wakefield that he is to take the night coach into the country. She would fain inquire the length of his journey, its object, and the probable time of his return; but, indulgent to his harmless love of mystery, interrogates him only by a look. He tells her not to expect him positively by the return coach, nor to be alarmed should he tarry three or four days; but, at all events, to look for him at supper on Friday evening. Wakefield himself, be it considered, has no suspicion of what is before him. He holds out his hand, she gives her own, and meets his parting kiss in the matter-of-course way of a ten years' matrimony; and forth goes the middle-aged Mr. Wakefield, almost resolved to perplex his good lady by a whole week's absence. After the door has closed behind him, she perceives it thrust partly open, and a vision of her husband's face, through the aperture, smiling on her, and gone in a moment. For the time, this little incident is dismissed without a thought. But, long afterwards, when she has been more years a widow than a wife, that smile recurs, and flickers across all her reminiscences of Wakefield's visage. In her many musings, she surrounds the original smile with a multitude of fantasies, which make it strange and awful: as, for instance, if she imagines him in a coffin, that parting look is frozen on his pale features; or, if she dreams of him in heaven, still his blessed spirit wears a quiet and crafty smile. Yet, for its sake, when all others have given him up for dead, she sometimes doubts whether she is a widow.

But our business is with the husband. We must hurry after him along the street, ere he lose his individuality, and melt into the great mass of London life. It would be vain searching for him there. Let us follow close at his heels, therefore, until, after several superfluous turns and doublings, we find him comfortably established by the fireside of a small apartment, previously bespoken. He is in the next street to his own, and at his journey's end. He can scarcely trust his good fortune, in having got thither unperceived—recollecting that, at one time, he was delayed by the throng, in the very focus of a lighted lantern; and, again, there were footsteps that seemed to tread behind his own, distinct from the multitudinous tramp around him; and, anon, he heard a voice shouting afar, and fancied that it called his name. Doubtless, a dozen busybodies had been watching him, and told his wife the whole affair. Poor Wakefield! Little knowest thou thine own insignificance in this great world! No mortal eye but mine has traced thee. Go quietly to thy bed, foolish man; and, on the morrow, if thou wilt be wise, get thee home to good Mrs. Wakefield, and tell her the truth. Remove not thyself, even for a little week, from thy place in her chaste bosom. Were she, for a single moment, to deem thee dead, or lost, or lastingly divided from her, thou wouldst be wofully conscious of a change in thy true wife forever after. It is perilous to make a chasm in human affections; not that they gape so long and wide—but so quickly close again!

Almost repenting of his frolic, or whatever it may be termed, Wakefield lies down betimes, and starting from his first nap, spreads forth his arms into the wide and solitary waste of the unaccustomed bed. "No,"—thinks he, gathering the bedclothes about him,—"I will not sleep alone another night."

In the morning he rises earlier than usual, and sets himself to consider what he really means to do. Such are his loose and rambling modes of thought that he has taken this very singular step with the consciousness of a purpose, indeed, but without being able to define it sufficiently for his own contemplation. The vagueness of the project, and the convulsive effort with which he plunges into the execution of it, are equally characteristic of a feeble-minded man. Wakefield sifts his ideas, however, as minutely as he may, and finds himself curious to know the progress of matters at home—how his exemplary wife will endure her widowhood of a week; and, briefly, how the little sphere of creatures and circumstances, in which he was a central object, will be affected by his removal. A morbid vanity, therefore, lies nearest the bottom of the affair. But, how is he to attain his ends? Not, certainly, by keeping close in this comfortable lodging, where, though he slept and awoke in the next street to his home, he is as effectually abroad as if the stage-coach had been whirling him away all night. Yet, should he reappear, the whole project is knocked in the head. His poor brains being hopelessly puzzled with this dilemma, he at length ventures out, partly resolving to cross the head of the street, and send one hasty glance towards his forsaken domicile. Habit—for he is a man of habits—takes him by the hand, and guides him, wholly unaware, to his own door, where, just at the critical moment, he is aroused by the scraping of his foot upon the step. Wakefield! whither are you going?

At that instant his fate was turning on the pivot. Little dreaming of the doom to which his first backward step devotes him, he hurries away, breathless with agitation hitherto unfelt, and hardly dares turn his head at the distant corner. Can it be that nobody caught sight of him? Will not the whole household—the decent Mrs. Wakefield, the smart maid servant, and the dirty little footboy—raise a hue and cry, through London streets, in pursuit of their fugitive lord and master? Wonderful escape! He gathers courage to pause and look homeward, but is perplexed with a sense of change about the familiar edifice, such as affects us all, when, after a separation of months or years, we again see some hill or lake, or work of art, with which we were friends of old. In ordinary cases, this indescribable impression is caused by the comparison and contrast between our imperfect reminiscences and the reality. In Wakefield, the magic of a single night has wrought a similar transformation, because, in that brief period, a great moral change has been effected. But this is a secret from himself. Before leaving the spot, he catches a far and momentary glimpse of his wife, passing athwart the front window, with her face turned towards the head of the street. The crafty nincompoop takes to his heels, scared with the idea that, among a thousand such atoms of mortality, her eye must have detected him. Right glad is his heart, though his brain be somewhat dizzy, when he finds himself by the coal fire of his lodgings.

So much for the commencement of this long whimwham. After the initial conception, and the stirring up of the man's sluggish temperament to put it in practice, the whole matter evolves itself in a natural train. We may suppose him, as the result of deep deliberation, buying a new wig, of reddish hair, and selecting sundry garments, in a fashion unlike his customary suit of brown, from a Jew's old-clothes bag. It is accomplished. Wakefield is another man. The new system being now established, a retrograde movement to the old would be almost as difficult as the step that placed him in his unparalleled position. Furthermore, he is rendered obstinate by a sulkiness occasionally incident to his temper, and brought on at present by the inadequate sensation which he conceives to have been produced in the bosom of Mrs. Wakefield. He will not go back until she be frightened half to death. Well; twice or thrice has she passed before his sight, each time with a heavier step, a paler cheek, and more anxious brow; and in the third week of his non-appearance he detects a portent of evil entering the house, in the guise of an apothecary. Next day the knocker is muffled. Towards nightfall comes the chariot of a physician, and deposits its big-wigged and solemn burden at Wakefield's door, whence, after a quarter of an hour's visit, he emerges, perchance the herald of a funeral. Dear woman! Will she die? By this time, Wakefield is excited to something like energy of feeling, but still lingers away from his wife's bedside, pleading with his conscience that she must not be disturbed at such a juncture. If aught else restrains him, he does not know it. In the course of a few weeks she gradually recovers; the crisis is over; her heart is sad, perhaps, but quiet; and, let him return soon or late, it will never be feverish for him again. Such ideas glimmer through the midst of Wakefield's mind, and render him indistinctly conscious that an almost impassable gulf divides his hired apartment from his former home. "It is but in the next street!" he sometimes says. Fool! it is in another world. Hitherto, he has put off his return from one particular day to another; henceforward, he leaves the precise time undetermined. Not tomorrow—probably next week—pretty soon. Poor man! The dead have nearly as much chance of revisiting their earthly homes as the self-banished Wakefield.

Would that I had a folio to write, instead of an article of a dozen pages! Then might I exemplify how an influence beyond our control lays its strong hand on every deed which we do, and weaves its consequences into an iron tissue of necessity. Wakefield is spell-bound. We must leave him, for ten years or so, to haunt around his house, without once crossing the threshold, and to be faithful to his wife, with all the affection of which his heart is capable, while he is slowly fading out of hers. Long since, it must be remarked, he had lost the perception of singularity in his conduct.

Now for a scene! Amind the throng of a London street we distinguish a man, now waxing elderly, with few characteristics to attract careless observers, yet bearing, in his whole aspect, the handwriting of no common fate, for such as have the skill to read it. He is meagre; his low and narrow forehead is deeply wrinkled; his eyes, small and lustreless, sometimes wander apprehensively about him, but oftener seem to look inward. He bends his head, and moves with an indescribable obliquity of gait, as if unwilling to display his full front to the world. Watch him long enough to see what we have described, and you will allow that circumstances— which often produce remarkable men from nature's ordinary handiwork —have produced one such here. Next, leaving him to sidle along the footwalk, cast your eyes in the opposite direction, where a portly female, considerably in the wane of life, with a prayer-book in her hand, is proceeding to yonder church. She has the placid mien of settled widowhood. Her regrets have either died away, or have become so essential to her heart, that they would be poorly exchanged for joy. Just as the lean man and well-conditioned woman are passing, a slight obstruction occurs, and brings these two figures directly in contact. Their hands touch; the pressure of the crowd forces her bosom against his shoulder; they stand, face to face, staring into each other's eyes. After a ten years' separation, thus Wakefield meets his wife!

The throng eddies away, and carries them asunder. The sober widow, resuming her former pace, proceeds to church, but pauses in the portal, and throws a perplexed glance along the street. She passes in, however, opening her prayer-book as she goes. And the man! with so wild a face that busy and selfish London stands to gaze after him, he hurries to his lodgings, bolts the door, and throws himself upon the bed. The latent feelings of years break out; his feeble mind acquires a brief energy from their strength; all the miserable strangeness of his life is revealed to him at a glance: and he cries out, passionately, "Wakefield! Wakefield! You are mad!"

Perhaps he was so. The singularity of his situation must have so moulded him to himself, that, considered in regard to his fellow-creatures and the business of life, he could not be said to possess his right mind. He had contrived, or rather he had happened, to dissever himself from the world—to vanish—to give up his place and privileges with living men, without being admitted among the dead. The life of a hermit is nowise parallel to his. He was in the bustle of the city, as of old; but the crowd swept by and saw him not; he was, we may figuratively say, always beside his wife and at his hearth, yet must never feel the warmth of the one nor the affection of the other. It was Wakefield's unprecedented fate to retain his original share of human sympathies, and to be still involved in human interests, while he had lost his reciprocal influence on them. It would be a most curious speculation to trace out the effect of such circumstances on his heart and intellect, separately, and in unison. Yet, changed as he was, he would seldom be conscious of it, but deem himself the same man as ever; glimpses of the truth, indeed, would come, but only for the moment; and still he would keep saying, "I shall soon go back!"—nor reflect that he had been saying so for twenty years.

I conceive, also, that these twenty years would appear, in the retrospect, scarcely longer than the week to which Wakefield had at first limited his absence. He would look on the affair as no more than an interlude in the main business of his life. When, after a little while more, he should deem it time to reënter his parlor, his wife would clap her hands for joy, on beholding the middle-aged Mr. Wakefield. Alas, what a mistake! Would Time but await the close of our favorite follies, we should be young men, all of us, and till Doomsday.

One evening, in the twentieth year since he vanished, Wakefield is taking his customary walk towards the dwelling which he still calls his own. It is a gusty night of autumn, with frequent showers that patter down upon the pavement, and are gone before a man can put up his umbrella. Pausing near the house, Wakefield discerns, through the parlor windows of the second floor, the red glow and the glimmer and fitful flash of a comfortable fire. On the ceiling appears a grotesque shadow of good Mrs. Wakefield. The cap, the nose and chin, and the broad waist, form an admirable caricature, which dances, moreover, with the up-flickering and down-sinking blaze, almost too merrily for the shade of an elderly widow. At this instant a shower chances to fall, and is driven, by the unmannerly gust, full into Wakefield's face and bosom. He is quite penetrated with its autumnal chill. Shall he stand, wet and shivering here, when his own hearth has a good fire to warm him, and his own wife will run to fetch the gray coat and small-clothes, which, doubtless, she has kept carefully in the closet of their bed chamber? No! Wakefield is no such fool. He ascends the steps—heavily!—for twenty years have stiffened his legs since he came down—but he knows it not. Stay, Wakefield! Would you go to the sole home that is left you? Then step into your grave! The door opens. As he passes in, we have a parting glimpse of his visage, and recognize the crafty smile, which was the precursor of the little joke that he has ever since been playing off at his wife's expense. How unmercifully has he quizzed the poor woman! Well, a good night's rest to Wakefield!

This happy event—supposing it to be such—could only have occurred at an unpremeditated moment. We will not follow our friend across the threshold. He has left us much food for thought, a portion of which shall lend its wisdom to a moral, and be shaped into a figure. Amid the seeming confusion of our mysterious world, individuals are so nicely adjusted to a system, and systems to one another and to a whole, that, by stepping aside for a moment, a man exposes himself to a fearful risk of losing his place forever. Like Wakefield, he may become, as it were, the Outcast of the Universe.

# THE GREAT CARBUNCLE[1]

## A MYSTERY OF THE WHITE MOUNTAINS

AT nightfall, once in the olden time, on the rugged side of one of the Crystal Hills, a party of adventurers were refreshing themselves, after a toilsome and fruitless quest for the Great Carbuncle. They had come thither, not as friends nor partners in the enterprise, but each, save one youthful pair, impelled by his own selfish and solitary longing for this wondrous gem. Their feeling of brotherhood, however, was strong enough to induce them to contribute a mutual aid in building a rude hut of branches, and kindling a great fire of shattered pines, that had drifted down the headlong current of the Amonoosuck, on the lower bank of which they were to pass the night. There was but one of their number, perhaps, who had become so estranged from natural sympathies, by the absorbing spell of the pursuit, as to acknowledge no satisfaction at the sight of human faces, in the remote and solitary region whither they had ascended. A vast extent of wilderness lay between them and the nearest settlement, while a scant mile above their heads was that black verge where the hills throw off their shaggy mantle of forest trees, and either robe themselves in clouds or tower naked into the sky. The roar of the Amonoosuck would have been too awful for endurance if only a solitary man had listened, while the mountain stream talked with the wind.

The adventurers, therefore, exchanged hospitable greetings, and welcomed one another to the hut, where each man was the host, and all were the guests of the whole company. They spread their individual supplies of food on the flat surface of a rock, and partook of a general repast; at the close of which, a sentiment of good fellowship was perceptible among the party, though repressed by the idea, that the renewed search for the Great Carbuncle must make them strangers again in the morning. Seven men and one young woman, they warmed themselves together at the fire, which extended its bright wall along the whole front of their wigwam. As they observed the various and contrasted figures that made up the assemblage, each man looking like a caricature of himself, in the unsteady light that flickered over him, they came mutually to the conclusion, that an odder society had never met, in city or wilderness, on mountain or plain.

The eldest of the group, a tall, lean, weather-beaten man, some sixty years of age, was clad in the skins of wild animals, whose fashion of dress he did well to imitate, since the deer, the wolf, and the bear, had long been

[1] The Indian tradition, on which this somewhat extravagant tale is founded, is both too wild and too beautiful to be adequately wrought up in prose. Sullivan, in his History of Maine, written since the Revolution, remarks, that even then the existence of the Great Carbuncle was not entirely discredited.

his most intimate companions. He was one of those ill-fated mortals, such as the Indians told of, whom, in their early youth, the Great Carbuncle smote with a peculiar madness, and became the passionate dream of their existence. All who visited that region knew him as the Seeker, and by no other name. As none could remember when he first took up the search, there went a fable in the valley of the Saco, that for his inordinate lust after the Great Carbuncle, he had been condemned to wander among the mountains till the end of time, still with the same feverish hopes at sunrise—the same despair at eve. Near this miserable Seeker sat a little elderly personage, wearing a high-crowned hat, shaped somewhat like a crucible. He was from beyond the sea, a Doctor Cacaphodel, who had wilted and dried himself into a mummy by continually stooping over charcoal furnaces, and inhaling unwholesome fumes during his researches in chemistry and alchemy. It was told of him, whether truly or not, that, at the commencement of his studies, he had drained his body of all its richest blood, and wasted it, with other inestimable ingredients, in an unsuccessful experiment—and had never been a well man since. Another of the adventurers was Master Ichabod Pigsnort, a weighty merchant and selectman of Boston, and an elder of the famous Mr. Norton's church. His enemies had a ridiculous story that Master Pigsnort was accustomed to spend a whole hour after prayer time, every morning and evening, in wallowing naked among an immense quantity of pine-tree shillings, which were the earliest silver coinage of Massachusetts. The fourth whom we shall notice had no name that his companions knew of, and was chiefly distinguished by a sneer that always contorted his thin visage, and by a prodigious pair of spectacles, which were supposed to deform and discolor the whole face of nature, to this gentleman's perception. The fifth adventurer likewise lacked a name, which was the greater pity, as he appeared to be a poet. He was a bright-eyed man, but wofully pined away, which was no more than natural, if, as some people affirmed, his ordinary diet was fog, morning mist, and a slice of the densest cloud within his reach, sauced with moonshine, whenever he could get it. Certain it is, that the poetry which flowed from him had a smack of all these dainties. The sixth of the party was a young man of haughty mien, and sat somewhat apart from the rest, wearing his plumed hat loftily among his elders, while the fire glittered on the rich embroidery of his dress, and gleamed intensely on the jewelled pommel of his sword. This was the Lord de Vere, who, when at home, was said to spend much of his time in the burial vault of his dead progenitors, rummaging their mouldy coffins in search of all the earthly pride and vainglory that was hidden among bones and dust; so that, besides his own share, he had the collected haughtiness of his whole line of ancestry.

Lastly, there was a handsome youth in rustic garb, and by his side a blooming little person, in whom a delicate shade of maiden reserve was just melting into the rich glow of a young wife's affection. Her name was Hannah, and her husband's Matthew; two homely names, yet well enough adapted to the simple pair, who seemed strangely out of place among the whimsical fraternity whose wits had been set agog by the Great Carbuncle.

Beneath the shelter of one hut, in the bright blaze of the same fire, sat this varied group of adventurers, all so intent upon a single object, that, of whatever else they began to speak, their closing words were sure to be illuminated with the Great Carbuncle. Several related the circumstances that brought them thither. One had listened to a traveller's tale of this marvellous stone in his own distant country, and had immediately been seized with such a thirst for beholding it as could only be quenched in its intensest lustre. Another, so long ago as when the famous Captain Smith visited these coasts, had seen it blazing far at sea, and had felt no rest in all the intervening years till now that he took up the search. A third, being encamped on a hunting expedition full forty miles south of the White Mountains, awoke at midnight, and beheld the Great Carbuncle gleaming like a meteor, so that the shadows of the trees fell backward from it. They spoke of the innumerable attempts which had been made to reach the spot, and of the singular fatality which had hitherto withheld success from all adventurers, though it might seem so easy to follow to its source a light that overpowered the moon, and almost matched the sun. It was observable that each smiled scornfully at the madness of every other in anticipating better fortune than the past, yet nourished a scarcely hidden conviction that he would himself be the favored one. As if to allay their too sanguine hopes, they recurred to the Indian traditions that a spirit kept watch about the gem, and bewildered those who sought it either by removing it from peak to peak of the higher hills, or by calling up a mist from the enchanted lake over which it hung. But these tales were deemed unworthy of credit, all professing to believe that the search had been baffled by want of sagacity or perseverance in the adventurers, or such other causes as might naturally obstruct the passage to any given point among the intricacies of forest, valley, and mountain.

In a pause of the conversation the wearer of the prodigious spectacles looked round upon the party, making each individual, in turn, the object of the sneer which invariably dwelt upon his countenance.

"So, fellow-pilgrims," said he, "here we are, seven wise men, and one fair damsel—who, doubtless, is as wise as any graybeard of the company: here we are, I say, all bound on the same goodly enterprise. Methinks, now, it were not amiss that each of us declare what he proposes to do with the Great Carbuncle, provided he have the good hap to clutch it. What says our friend in the bear skin? How mean you, good sir, to enjoy the prize which you have been seeking, the Lord knows how long, among the Crystal Hills?"

"How enjoy it!" exclaimed the aged Seeker, bitterly. "I hope for no enjoyment from it; that folly has passed long ago! I keep up the search for this accursed stone because the vain ambition of my youth has become a fate upon me in old age. The pursuit alone is my strength,—the energy of my soul,—the warmth of my blood,—and the pith and marrow of my bones! Were I to turn my back upon it I should fall down dead on the hither side of the Notch, which is the gateway of this mountain region. Yet not to have my wasted lifetime back again would I give up my hopes of the Great Carbuncle! Having found it, I shall bear it to a certain cavern that I wot of, and there, grasping it in my arms, lie down and die, and keep it buried with me forever."

"O wretch, regardless of the interests of science!" cried Doctor Cacaphodel, with philosophic indignation. "Thou art not worthy to behold, even from afar off, the lustre of this most precious gem that ever was concocted in the laboratory of Nature. Mine is the sole purpose for which a wise man may desire the possession of the Great Carbuncle. Immediately on obtaining it—for I have a presentiment, good people that the prize is reserved to crown my scientific reputation—I shall return to Europe, and employ my remaining years in reducing it to its first elements. A portion of the stone will I grind to impalpable powder; other parts shall be dissolved in acids, or whatever solvents will act upon so admirable a composition; and the remainder I design to melt in the crucible, or set on fire with the blow-pipe. By these various methods I shall gain an accurate analysis, and finally bestow the result of my labors upon the world in a folio volume."

"Excellent!" quoth the man with the spectacles. "Nor need you hesitate, learned sir, on account of the necessary destruction of the gem; since the perusal of your folio may teach every mother's son of us to concoct a Great Carbuncle of his own."

"But, verily," said Master Ichabod Pigsnort, "for mine own part I object to the making of these counterfeits, as being calculated to reduce the marketable value of the true gem. I tell ye frankly, sirs, I have an interest in keeping up the price. Here have I quitted my regular traffic, leaving my warehouse in the care of my clerks, and putting my credit to great hazard, and, furthermore, have put myself in peril of death or captivity by the accursed heathen savages—and all this without daring to ask the prayers of the congregation, because the quest for the Great Carbuncle is deemed little better than a traffic with the Evil One. Now think ye that I would have done this grievous wrong to my soul, body, reputation, and estate, without a reasonable chance of profit?"

"Not I, pious Master Pigsnort," said the man with the spectacles. "I never laid such a great folly to thy charge."

"Truly, I hope not," said the merchant. "Now, as touching this Great Carbuncle, I am free to own that I have never had a glimpse of it; but be it only the hundredth part so bright as people tell, it will surely outvalue the Great Mogul's best diamond, which he holds at an incalculable sum. Wherefore, I am minded to put the Great Carbuncle on shipboard, and voyage with it to England, France, Spain, Italy, or into Heathendom, if Providence should send me thither, and, in a word, dispose of the gem to the best bidder among the potentates of the earth, that he may place it among his crown jewels. If any of ye have a wiser plan, let him expound it."

"That have I, thou sordid man!" exclaimed the poet. "Dost thou desire nothing brighter than gold that thou wouldst transmute all this ethereal lustre into such dross as thou wallowest in already? For myself, hiding the jewel under my cloak, I shall hie me back to my attic chamber, in one of the darksome alleys of London. There, night and day, will I gaze upon it; my soul shall drink its radiance; it shall be diffused throughout my intellectual powers, and gleam brightly in every line of poesy that I indite. Thus, long ages after I am gone, the splendor of the Great Carbuncle will blaze around my name!"

"Well said, Master Poet!" cried he of the spectacles. "Hide it under thy cloak, sayest thou? Why, it will gleam through the holes, and make thee look like a jack-o'-lantern!"

"To think!" ejaculated the Lord de Vere, rather to himself than his companions, the best of whom he held utterly unworthy of his intercourse —"to think that a fellow in a tattered cloak should talk of conveying the Great Carbuncle to a garret in Grub Street! Have not I resolved within myself that the whole earth contains no fitter ornament for the great hall of my ancestral castle? There shall it flame for ages, making a noonday of midnight, glittering on the suits of armor, the banners, and escutcheons, that hang around the wall, and keeping bright the memory of heroes. Wherefore have all other adventurers sought the prize in vain but that I might win it, and make it a symbol of the glories of our lofty line? And never, on the diadem of the White Mountains, did the Great Carbuncle hold a place half so honored as is reserved for it in the hall of the De Veres!"

"It is a noble thought," said the Cynic, with an obsequious sneer. "Yet, might I presume to say so, the gem would make a rare sepulchral lamp, and would display the glories of your lordship's progenitors more truly in the ancestral vault than in the castle hall."

"Nay, forsooth," observed Matthew, the young rustic, who sat hand in hand with his bride, "the gentleman has bethought himself of a profitable use for this bright stone. Hannah here and I are seeking it for a like purpose."

"How, fellow!" exclaimed his lordship, in surprise. "What castle hall hast thou to hang it in?"

"No castle," replied Matthew, "but as neat a cottage as any within sight of the Crystal Hills. Ye must know, friends, that Hannah and I, being wedded the last week, have taken up the search of the Great Carbuncle, because we shall need its light in the long winter evenings; and it will be such a pretty thing to show the neighbors when they visit us. It will shine through the house so that we may pick up a pin in any corner, and will set all the windows aglowing as if there were a great fire of pine knots in the chimney. And then how pleasant, when we awake in the night, to be able to see one another's faces!"

There was a general smile among the adventurers at the simplicity of the young couple's project in regard to this wondrous and invaluable stone, with which the greatest monarch on earth might have been proud to adorn his palace. Especially the man with spectacles, who had sneered at all the company in turn, now twisted his visage into such an expression of ill-natured mirth, that Matthew asked him, rather peevishly, what he himself meant to do with the Great Carbuncle.

"The Great Carbuncle!" answered the Cynic, with ineffable scorn. "Why, you blockhead, there is no such thing in *rerum natura*. I have come three thousand miles, and am resolved to set my foot on every peak of these mountains, and poke my head into every chasm, for the sole purpose of demonstrating to the satisfaction of any man one whit less an ass than thyself that the Great Carbuncle is all a humbug!"

Vain and foolish were the motives that had brought most of the adventurers to the Crystal Hills; but none so vain, so foolish, and so impious too, as that of the scoffer with the prodigious spectacles. He was one of those wretched and evil men whose yearnings are downward to the darkness, instead of heavenward, and who, could they but extinguish the lights which God hath kindled for us, would count the midnight gloom their chiefest glory. As the Cynic spoke, several of the party were startled by a gleam of red splendor, that showed the huge shapes of the surrounding mountains and the rock-bestrewn bed of the turbulent river with an illumination unlike that of their fire on the trunks and black boughs of the forest trees. They listened for the roll of thunder, but heard nothing, and were glad that the tempest came not near them. The stars, those dial points of heaven, now warned the adventurers to close their eyes on the blazing logs, and open them, in dreams, to the glow of the Great Carbuncle.

The young married couple had taken their lodgings in the farthest corner of the wigwam, and were separated from the rest of the party by a curtain of curiously-woven twigs, such as might have hung, in deep festoons, around the bridal-bower of Eve. The modest little wife had wrought this piece of tapestry while the other guests were talking. She and her husband fell asleep with hands tenderly clasped, and awoke from visions of unearthly radiance to meet the more blessed light of one another's eyes. They awoke at the same instant, and with one happy smile beaming over their two faces, which grew brighter with their consciousness of the reality of life and love. But no sooner did she recollect where they were, than the bride peeped through the interstices of the leafy curtain, and saw that the outer room of the hut was deserted.

"Up, dear Matthew!" cried she, in haste. "The strange folk are all gone! Up, this very minute, or we shall lose the Great Carbuncle!"

In truth, so little did these poor young people deserve the mighty prize which had lured them thither, that they had slept peacefully all night, and till the summits of the hills were glittering with sunshine; while the other adventurers had tossed their limbs in feverish wakefulness, or dreamed of climbing precipices, and set off to realize their dreams with the earliest peep of dawn. But Matthew and Hannah, after their calm rest, were as light as two young deer, and merely stopped to say their prayers and wash themselves in a cold pool of the Amonoosuck, and then to taste a morsel of food, ere they turned their faces to the mountain-side. It was a sweet emblem of conjugal affection, as they toiled up the difficult ascent, gathering strength from the mutual aid which they afforded. After several little accidents, such as a torn robe, a lost shoe, and the entanglement of Hannah's hair in a bough, they reached the upper verge of the forest, and were now to pursue a more adventurous course. The innumerable trunks and heavy foliage of the trees had hitherto shut in their thoughts, which now shrank affrighted from the region of wind and cloud and naked rocks and desolate sunshine, that rose immeasurably above them. They gazed back at the obscure wilderness which they had traversed, and longed to be buried again in its depths rather than trust themselves to so vast and visible a solitude.

"Shall we go on?" said Matthew, throwing his arm round Hannah's waist, both to protect her and to comfort his heart by drawing her close to it.

But the little bride, simple as she was, had a woman's love of jewels, and could not forego the hope of possessing the very brightest in the world, in spite of the perils with which it must be won.

"Let us climb a little higher," whispered she, yet tremulously, as she turned her face upward to the lonely sky.

"Come, then," said Matthew, mustering his manly courage and drawing her along with him, for she became timid again the moment that he grew bold.

And upward, accordingly, went the pilgrims of the Great Carbuncle, now treading upon the tops and thickly-interwoven branches of dwarf pines, which, by the growth of centuries, though mossy with age, had barely reached three feet in altitude. Next, they came to masses and fragments of naked rock heaped confusedly together, like a cairn reared by giants in memory of a giant chief. In this bleak realm of upper air nothing breathed, nothing grew; there was no life but what was concentrated in their two hearts; they had climbed so high that Nature herself seemed no longer to keep them company. She lingered beneath them, within the verge of the forest trees, and sent a farewell glance after her children as they strayed where her own green footprints had never been. But soon they were to be hidden from her eye  Densely and dark the mists began to gather below, casting black spots of shadow on the vast landscape, and sailing heavily to one centre, as if the loftiest mountain peak had summoned a council of its kindred clouds. Finally, the vapors welded themselves, as it were, into a mass, presenting the appearance of a pavement over which the wanderers might have trodden, but where they would vainly have sought an avenue to the blessed earth which they had lost. And the lovers yearned to behold that green earth again, more intensely, alas! than, beneath a clouded sky, they had ever desired a glimpse of heaven. They even felt it a relief to their desolation when the mists, creeping gradually up the mountain, concealed its lonely peak, and thus annihilated, at least for them, the whole region of visible space. But they drew closer together, with a fond and melancholy gaze, dreading lest the universal cloud should snatch them from each other's sight.

Still, perhaps, they would have been resolute to climb as far and as high, between earth and heaven, as they could find foothold, if Hannah's strength had not begun to fail, and with that, her courage also. Her breath grew short. She refused to burden her husband with her weight, but often tottered against his side, and recovered herself each time by a feebler effort. At last, she sank down on one of the rocky steps of the acclivity.

"We are lost, dear Matthew," said she, mournfully. "We shall never find our way to the earth again. And oh how happy we might have been in our cottage!"

"Dear heart!—we will yet be happy there," answered Matthew. "Look! In this direction, the sunshine penetrates the dismal mist. By its aid, I can direct our course to the passage of the Notch. Let us go back, love, and dream no more of the Great Carbuncle!"

"The sun cannot be yonder," said Hannah, with despondence. "By this time it must be noon. If there could ever be any sunshine here, it would come from above our heads."

"But look!" repeated Matthew, in a somewhat altered tone. "It is brightening every moment. If not sunshine, what can it be?"

Nor could the young bride any longer deny that a radiance was breaking through the mist, and changing its dim hue to a dusky red, which continually grew more vivid, as if brilliant particles were interfused with the gloom. Now, also, the cloud began to roll away from the mountain, while, as it heavily withdrew, one object after another started out of its impenetrable obscurity into sight, with precisely the effect of a new creation, before the indistinctness of the old chaos had been completely swallowed up. As the process went on, they saw the gleaming of water close at their feet, and found themselves on the very border of a mountain lake, deep, bright, clear, and calmly beautiful, spreading from brim to brim of a basin that had been scooped out of the solid rock. A ray of glory flashed across its surface. The pilgrims looked whence it should proceed, but closed their eyes with a thrill of awful admiration, to exclude the fervid splendor that glowed from the brow of a cliff impending over the enchanted lake. For the simple pair had reached that lake of mystery, and found the long-sought shrine of the Great Carbuncle!

They threw their arms around each other, and trembled at their own success; for, as the legends of this wondrous gem rushed thick upon their memory, they felt themselves marked out by fate—and the consciousness was fearful. Often, from childhood upward, they had seen it shining like a distant star. And now that star was throwing its intensest lustre on their hearts. They seemed changed to one another's eyes, in the red brilliancy that flamed upon their cheeks, while it lent the same fire to the lake, the rocks, and sky, and to the mists which had rolled back before its power. But, with their next glance, they beheld an object that drew their attention even from the mighty stone. At the base of the cliff, directly beneath the Great Carbuncle, appeared the figure of a man, with his arms extended in the act of climbing, and his face turned upward, as if to drink the full gush of splendor. But he stirred not, no more than if changed to marble.

"It is the Seeker," whispered Hannah, convulsively grasping her husband's arm. "Matthew, he is dead."

"The joy of success has killed him," replied Matthew, trembling violently. "Or, perhaps, the very light of the Great Carbuncle was death!"

"The Great Carbuncle," cried a peevish voice behind them. "The Great Humbug! If you have found it, prithee point it out to me."

They turned their heads, and there was the Cynic, with his prodigious spectacles set carefully on his nose, staring now at the lake, now at the rocks, now at the distant masses of vapor, now right at the Great Carbuncle itself, yet seemingly as unconscious of its light as if all the scattered clouds were condensed about his person. Though its radiance actually threw the shadow of the unbeliever at his own feet, as he turned his back upon the glorious jewel, he would not be convinced that there was the least glimmer there.

"Where is your Great Humbug?" he repeated. "I challenge you to make me see it!"

"There," said Matthew, incensed at such perverse blindness, and turning the Cynic round towards the illuminated cliff. "Take off those abominable spectacles, and you cannot help seeing it!"

Now these colored spectacles probably darkened the Cynic's sight, in at least as great a degree as the smoked glasses through which people gaze at an eclipse. With resolute bravado, however, he snatched them from his nose, and fixed a bold stare full upon the ruddy blaze of the Great Carbuncle. But scarcely had he encountered it, when, with a deep, shuddering groan, he dropped his head, and pressed both hands across his miserable eyes. Thenceforth there was, in very truth, no light of the Great Carbuncle, nor any other light on earth, nor light of heaven itself, for the poor Cynic. So long accustomed to view all objects through a medium that deprived them of every glimpse of brightness, a single flash of so glorious a phenomenon, striking upon his naked vision, had blinded him forever.

"Matthew," said Hannah, clinging to him, "let us go hence!"

Matthew saw that she was faint, and kneeling down, supported her in his arms, while he threw some of the thrillingly cold water of the enchanted lake upon her face and bosom. It revived her, but could not renovate her courage.

"Yes, dearest!" cried Matthew, pressing her tremulous form to his breast,—"we will go hence, and return to our humble cottage. The blessed sunshine and the quiet moonlight shall come through our window. We will kindle the cheerful glow of our hearth, at eventide, and be happy in its light. But never again will we desire more light than all the world may share with us."

"No," said his bride, "for how could we live by day, or sleep by night, in this awful blaze of the Great Carbuncle!"

Out of the hollow of their hands, they drank each a draught from the lake, which presented them its waters uncontaminated by an earthly lip. Then, lending their guidance to the blinded Cynic, who uttered not a word, and even stifled his groans in his own most wretched heart, they began to descend the mountain. Yet, as they left the shore, till then untrodden, of the spirit's lake, they threw a farewell glance towards the cliff, and beheld the vapors gathering in dense volumes, through which the gem burned duskily.

As touching the other pilgrims of the Great Carbuncle, the legend goes on to tell, that the worshipful Master Ichabod Pigsnort soon gave up the quest as a desperate speculation, and wisely resolved to betake himself again to his warehouse, near the town dock, in Boston. But, as he passed through the Notch of the mountains, a war party of Indians captured our unlucky merchant, and carried him to Montreal, there holding him in bondage, till, by the payment of a heavy ransom, he had wofully subtracted from his hoard of pine-tree shillings. By his long absence, moreover, his affairs had become so disordered that, for the rest of his life, instead of wallowing in silver, he had seldom a sixpence worth of copper. Doctor Cacaphodel, the alchemist, returned to his laboratory with a prodigious fragment of granite, which he ground to powder, dissolved in acids, melted in the crucible, and burned with the blow-pipe, and published the result of his experiments in one of the heaviest folios of the day. And, for all these purposes, the gem itself could not have answered better than the granite. The poet, by a somewhat similar mistake, made prize of a great piece of ice, which he found in a sunless chasm of the mountains, and swore that it corresponded, in all points, with his idea of the Great Carbuncle. The critics say, that, if his poetry lacked the splendor of the gem, it retained all the coldness of the ice. The Lord de Vere went back to his ancestral hall, where he contented himself with a wax-lighted chandelier, and filled, in due course of time, another coffin in the ancestral vault. As the funeral torches gleamed within that dark receptacle, there was no need of the Great Carbuncle to show the vanity of earthly pomp.

The Cynic, having cast aside his spectacles, wandered about the world, a miserable object, and was punished with an agonizing desire of light, for the wilful blindness of his former life. The whole night long, he would lift his splendor-blasted orbs to the moon and stars; he turned his face eastward, at sunrise, as duly as a Perisan idolater; he made a pilgrimage to Rome, to witness the magnificent illumination of St. Peter's Church; and finally perished in the great fire of London, into the midst of which he had thrust himself, with the desperate idea of catching one feeble ray from the blaze that was kindling earth and heaven.

Matthew and his bride spent many peaceful years, and were fond of telling the legend of the Great Carbuncle. The tale, however, towards the close of their lengthened lives, did not meet with the full credence that had been accorded to it by those who remembered the ancient lustre of the gem. For it is affirmed that, from the hour when two mortals had shown themselves so simply wise as to reject a jewel which would have dimmed all earthly things, its splendor waned. When other pilgrims reached the cliff, they found only an opaque stone, with particles of mica glittering on its surface. There is also a tradition that, as the youthful pair departed, the gem was loosened from the forehead of the cliff, and fell into the enchanted lake, and that, at noontide, the Seeker's form may still be seen to bend over its quenchless gleam.

Some few believe that this inestimable stone is blazing as of old, and say that they have caught its radiance, like a flash of summer lightning, far down the valley of the Saco. And be it owned that, many a mile from the Crystal Hills, I saw a wondrous light around their summits, and was lured, by the faith of poesy, to be the latest pilgrim of the GREAT CARBUNCLE.

# DAVID SWAN

### A FANTASY

WE can be but partially acquainted even with the events which actually influence our course through life, and our final destiny. There are innumerable other events—if such they may be called—which come close upon us, yet pass away without actual results, or even betraying their near approach, by the reflection of any light or shadow across our minds. Could we know all the vicissitudes of our fortunes, life would be too full of hope and fear, exultation or disappointment, to afford us a single hour of true serenity. This idea may be illustrated by a page from the secret history of David Swan.

We have nothing to do with David until we find him, at the age of twenty, on the high road from his native place to the city of Boston, where his uncle, a small dealer in the grocery line, was to take him behind the counter. Be it enough to say that he was a native of New Hampshire, born of respectacle parents, and had received an ordinary school education, with a classic finish by a year at Gilmanton Academy. After journeying on foot from sunrise till nearly noon of a summer's day, his weariness and the increasing heat determined him to sit down in the first convenient shade, and await the coming up of the stage-coach. As if planted on purpose for him, there soon appeared a little tuft of maples, with a delightful recess in the midst, and such a fresh bubbling spring that it seemed never to have sparkled for any wayfarer but David Swan. Virgin or not, he kissed it with his thirsty lips, and then flung himself along the brink, pillowing his head upon some shirts and a pair of pantaloons, tied up in a striped cotton handkerchief. The sunbeams could not reach him; the dust did not yet rise from the road after the heavy rain of yesterday; and his grassy lair suited the young man better than a bed of down. The spring murmured drowsily beside him; the branches waved dreamily across the blue sky overhead; and a deep sleep, perchance hiding dreams within its depths, fell upon David Swan. But we are to relate events which he did not dream of.

While he lay sound asleep in the shade, other people were wide awake, and passed to and fro, afoot, on horseback, and in all sorts of vehicles, along the sunny road by his bedchamber. Some looked neither to the right hand nor the left, and knew not that he was there; some merely glanced that way, without admitting the slumberer among their busy thoughts; some laughed to see how soundly he slept; and several, whose hearts were brimming full of scorn, ejected their venomous superfluity on David Swan. A middle-aged widow, when nobody else was near, thrust her head a little way into the recess, and vowed that the young fellow looked charming in his sleep. A temperance lecturer saw him, and wrought poor David into the texture of his evening's discourse, as an awful instance of dead drunkenness by the roadside. But censure, praise, merriment, scorn, and indifference were all one, or rather all nothing, to David Swan.

He had slept only a few moments when a brown carriage, drawn by a handsome pair of horses, bowled easily along, and was brought to a stand-still nearly in front of David's resting-place. A linchpin had fallen out, and permitted one of the wheels to slide off. The damage was slight, and occasioned merely a momentary alarm to an elderly merchant and his wife, who were returning to Boston in the carriage. While the coachman and a servant were replacing the wheel, the lady and gentleman sheltered themselves beneath the maple-trees, and there espied the bubbling fountain, and David Swan asleep beside it. Impressed with the awe which the humblest sleeped usually sheds around him, the merchant trod as lightly as the gout would allow; and his spouse took good heed not to rustle her silk gown, lest David should start up all of a sudden.

"How soundly he sleeps!" whispered the old gentleman. "From what a depth he draws that easy breath! Such sleep as that, brought on without an opiate, would be worth more to me than half my income; for it would suppose health and an untroubled mind."

"And youth, besides," said the lady. "Healthy and quiet age does not sleep thus. Our slumber is no more like his than our wakefulness."

The longer they looked the more did this elderly couple feel interested in the unknown youth, to whom the wayside and the maple shade were as a secret chamber, with the rich gloom of damask curtains brooding over him. Perceiving that a stray sunbeam glimmered down upon his face, the lady contrived to twist a branch aside, so as to intercept it. And having done this little act of kindness, she began to feel like a mother to him.

"Providence seems to have laid him here," whispered she to her husband, "and to have brought us hither to find him, after our disappointment in our cousin's son. Methinks I can see a likeness to our departed Henry. Shall we waken him?"

"To what purpose?" said the merchant, hesitating. "We know nothing of the youth's character."

"That open countenance!" replied his wife, in the same hushed voice, yet earnestly. "This innocent sleep!"

While these whispers were passing, the sleeper's heart did not throb, nor his breath become agitated, nor his features betray the least token of interest. Yet Fortune was bending over him, just ready to let fall a burden of gold. The old merchant had lost his only son, and had no heir to his wealth except a distant relative, with whose conduct he was dissatisfied. In such cases, people sometimes do stranger things than to act the magician, and awaken a young man to splendor who fell asleep in poverty.

"Shall we not waken him?" repeated the lady persuasively.

"The coach is ready, sir," said the servant, behind.

The old couple started, reddened, and hurried away, mutually wondering that they should ever have dreamed of doing anything so very ridiculous. The merchant threw himself back in the carriage, and occupied his mind with the plan of a magnificent asylum for unfortunate men of business. Meanwhile, David Swan enjoyed his nap.

The carriage could not have gone above a mile or two, when a pretty young girl came along, with a tripping pace, which showed precisely how her little heart was dancing in her bosom. Perhaps it was this merry kind of motion that caused—is there any harm in saying it?—her garter to slip its knot. Conscious that the silken girth—if silk it were—was relaxing its hold, she turned aside into the shelter of the maple-trees, and there found a young man asleep by the spring! Blushing as red as any rose that she should have intruded into a gentleman's bedchamber, and for such a purpose, too, she was about to make her escape on tiptoe. But there was peril near the sleeper. A monster of a bee had been wandering overhead—buzz, buzz, buzz—now among the leaves, now flashing through the strips of sunshine, and now lost in the dark shade, till finally he appeared to be settling on the eyelid of David Swan. The sting of a bee is sometimes deadly. As free hearted as she was innocent, the girl attacked the intruder with her handkerchief, brushed him soundly, and drove him from beneath the mapleshade. How sweet a picture! This good deed accomplished, with quickened breath, and a deeper blush, she stole a glance at the youthful stranger for whom she had been battling with a dragon in the air.

"He is handsome!" thought she, and blushed redder yet.

How could it be that no dream of bliss grew so strong within him, that, shattered by its very strength, it should part asunder, and allow him to perceive the girl among its phantoms? Why, at least, did no smile of welcome brighten upon his face? She was come, the maid whose soul, according to the old and beautiful idea, had been severed from his own, and whom, in all his vague but passionate desires, he yearned to meet. Her, only, could he love with a perfect love; him, only, could she receive into the depths of her heart; and now her image was faintly blushing in the fountain, by his side; should it pass away, its happy lustre would never gleam upon his life again.

"How sound he sleeps!" murmured the girl.

She departed, but did not trip along the road so lightly as when she came.

Now, this girl's father was a thriving country merchant in the neighborhood, and happened, at that identical time, to be looking out for just such a young man as David Swan. Had David formed a wayside acquaintance with the daughter, he would have become the father's clerk, and all else in natural succession. So here, again, had good fortune—the best of fortunes —stolen so near that her garments brushed against him; and he knew nothing of the matter.

The girl was hardly out of sight when two men turned aside beneath the maple shade. Both had dark faces, set off by cloth caps, which were drawn down aslant over their brows. Their dresses were shabby, yet had a certain smartness. These were a couple of rascals who got their living by whatever the devil sent them, and now, in the interim of other business, had staked the joint profits of their next piece of villany on a game of cards, which was to have been decided here under the trees. But, finding David asleep by the spring, one of the rogues whispered to his fellow,—

"Hist!—Do you see that bundle under his head?"

The other villain nodded, winked, and leered.

"I'll bet you a horn of brandy," said the first, "that the chap has either a pocket-book, or a snug little hoard of small change, stowed away amongst his shirts. And if not there, we shall find it in his pantaloons pocket."

"But how if he wakes?" said the other.

His companion thrust aside his waistcoat, pointed to the handle of a dirk, and nodded.

"So be it!" muttered the second villain.

They approached the unconscious David, and, while one pointed the dagger towards his heart, the other began to search the bundle beneath his head. Their two faces, grim, wrinkled, and ghastly with guilt and fear, bent over their victim, looking horrible enough to be mistaken for fiends, should he suddenly awake. Nay, had the villains glanced aside into the spring, even they would hardly have known themselves as reflected there. But David Swan had never worn a more tranquil aspect, even when asleep on his mother's breast.

"I must take away the bundle," whispered one.

"If he stirs, I'll strike," muttered the other.

But, at this moment, a dog scenting along the ground, came in beneath the maple-trees, and gazed alternately at each of these wicked men, and then at the quiet sleeper. He then lapped out of the fountain.

"Pshaw!" said one villain. "We can do nothing now. The dog's master must be close behind."

"Let's take a drink and be off," said the other.

The man with the dagger thrust back the weapon into his bosom, and drew forth a pocket pistol, but not of that kind which kills by a single discharge. It was a flask of liquor, with a block-tin tumbler screwed upon the mouth. Each drank a comfortable dram, and left the spot, with so many jests, and such laughter at their unaccomplished wickedness, that they might be said to have gone on their way rejoicing. In a few hours they had forgotten the whole affair, nor once imagined that the recording angel had written down the crime of murder against their souls, in letters as durable as eternity. As for David Swan, he still slept quietly, neither conscious of the shadow of death when it hung over him, nor of the glow of renewed life when that shadow was withdrawn.

He slept, but no longer so quietly as at first. An hour's repose had snatched, from his elastic frame, the weariness with which many hours of toil had burdened it. Now he stirred—now, moved his lips, without a sound—now, talked, in an inward tone, to the noonday spectres of his dream. But a noise of wheels came rattling louder and louder along the road, until it dashed through the dispersing mist of David's slumber— and there was the stage-coach. He started up with all his ideas about him.

"Halloo, driver!—Take a passenger?" shouted he.

"Room on top!" answered the driver.

Up mounted David, and bowled away merrily towards Boston, without so much as a parting glance at that fountain of dreamlike vicissitude. He knew not that a phantom of Wealth had thrown a golden hue upon its waters—nor that one of Love had sighed softly to their murmur—nor that one of Death had threatened to crimson them with his blood—all, in the brief hour since he lay down to sleep. Sleeping or waking, we hear not the airy footsteps of the strange things that almost happen. Does it not argue a superintending Providence that, while viewless and unexpected events thrust themselves continually athwart our path, there should still be regularity enough in mortal life to render foresight even partially available?

## THE HOLLOW OF THE THREE HILLS

IN those strange old times, when fantastic dreams and madmen's reveries were realized among the actual circumstances of life, two persons met together at an appointed hour and place. One was a lady, graceful in form and fair of feature, though pale and troubled, and smitten with an untimely blight in what should have been the fullest bloom of her years; the other was an ancient and meanly-dressed woman, of ill-favored aspect, and so withered, shrunken, and decrepit, that even the space since she began to decay must have exceeded the ordinary term of human existence. In the spot where they encountered, no mortal could observe them. Three little hills stood near each other, and down in the midst of them sunk a hollow basin, almost mathematically circular, two or three hundred feet in breadth, and of such depth that a stately cedar might but just be vis-

ible above the sides. Dwarf pines were numerous upon the hills, and partly fringed the outer verge of the intermediate hollow, within which there
was nothing but the brown grass of October, and here and there a tree
trunk that had fallen long ago, and lay mouldering with no green success-
or from its roots. One of these masses of decaying wood, formerly a majestic oak, rested close beside a pool of green and sluggish water at the
bottom of the basin. Such scenes as this (so gray tradition tells) were
once the resort of the Power of Evil and his plighted subjects; and here,
at midnight or on the dim verge of evening, they were said to stand round
the mantling pool, disturbing its putrid waters in the performance of an
impious baptismal rite. The chill beauty of an autumnal sunset was now
gilding the three hill-tops, whence a paler tint stole down their sides into
the hollow.

"Here is our pleasant meeting come to pass," said the aged crone, "according as thou hast desired. Say quickly what thou wouldst have of me,
for there is but a short hour that we may tarry here."

As the old withered woman spoke, a smile glimmered on her countenance, like lamplight on the wall of a sepulchre. The lady trembled, and
cast her eyes upward to the verge of the basin, as if meditating to return
with her purpose unaccomplished. But it was not so ordained.

"I am a stranger in this land, as you know," said she at length.
"Whence I come it matters not; but I have left those behind me with
whom my fate was intimately bound, and from whom I am cut off forever.
There is a weight in my bosom that I cannot away with, and I have come
hither to inquire of their welfare."

"And who is there by this green pool that can bring thee news from the
ends of the earth?" cried the old woman, peering into the lady's face.
"Not from my lips mayst thou hear these tidings; yet, be thou bold, and
the daylight shall not pass away from yonder hill-top before thy wish be
granted."

"I will do your bidding though I die," replied the lady desperately.

The old woman seated herself on the trunk of the fallen tree, threw
aside the hood that shrouded her gray locks, and beckoned her companion to draw near.

"Kneel down," she said, "and lay your forehead on my knees."

She hesitated a moment, but the anxiety that had long been kindling
burned fiercely up within her. As she knelt down, the border of her garment was dipped into the pool; she laid her forehead on the old woman's
knees, and the latter drew a cloak about the lady's face, so that she was in
darkness. Then she heard the muttered words of prayer, in the midst of
which she started, and would have arisen.

"Let me flee,—let me flee and hide myself, that they may not look upon
me!" she cried. But, with returning recollection, she hushed herself, and
was still as death.

For it seemed as if other voices—familiar in infancy, and unforgotten
through many wanderings, and in all the vicissitudes of her heart and fortune—were mingling with the accents of the prayer. At first the words

were faint and indistinct, not rendered so by distance, but rather resembling the dim pages of a book which we strive to read by an imperfect and gradually brightening light. In such a manner, as the prayer proceeded, did those voices strengthen upon the ear; till at length the petition ended, and the conversation of an aged man, and of a woman broken and decayed like himself, became distinctly audible to the lady as she knelt. But those strangers appeared not to stand in the hollow depth between the three hills. Their voices were encompassed and reëchoed by the walls of a chamber, the windows of which were rattling in the breeze; the regular vibration of a clock, the crackling of a fire, and the tinkling of the embers as they fell among the ashes, rendered the scene almost as vivid as if painted to the eye. By a melancholy hearth sat these two old people, the man calmly despondent, the woman querulous and tearful, and their words were all of sorrow. They spoke of a daughter, a wanderer they knew not where, bearing dishonor along with her, and leaving shame and affliction to bring their gray heads to the grave. They alluded also to other and more recent woe, but in the midst of their talk their voices seemed to melt into the sound of the wind sweeping mournfully among the autumn leaves; and when the lady lifted her eyes, there was she kneeling in the hollow between three hills.

"A weary and lonesome time yonder old couple have of it," remarked the old woman, smiling in the lady's face.

"And did you also hear them?" exclaimed she, a sense of intolerable humiliation triumphing over her agony and fear.

"Yea; and we have yet more to hear," replied the old woman. "Wherefore, cover thy face quickly."

Again the withered hag poured forth the monotonous words of a prayer that was not meant to be acceptable in heaven; and soon, in the pauses of her breath, strange murmurings began to thicken, gradually increasing so as to drown and overpower the charm by which they grew. Shrieks pierced through the obscurity of sound, and were succeeded by the singing of sweet female voices, which, in their turn, gave way to a wild roar of laughter, broken suddenly by groanings and sobs, forming altogether a ghastly confusion of terror and mourning and mirth. Chains were rattling, fierce and stern voices uttered threats, and the scourge resounded at their command. All these noises deepened and became substantial to the listener's ear, till she could distinguish every soft and dreamy accent of the love songs that died causelessly into funeral hymns. She shuddered at the unprovoked wrath which blazed up like the spontaneous kindling of flame, and she grew faint at the fearful merriment raging miserably around her. In the midst of this wild scene, where unbound passions jostled each other in a drunken career, there was one solemn voice of a man, and a manly and melodious voice it might once have been. He went to and fro continually, and his feet sounded upon the floor. In each member of that frenzied company, whose own burning thoughts had become their exclusive world, he sought an auditor for the story of his individual wrong, and interpreted their laughter and tears as his reward of scorn or pity. He spoke of woman's perfidy, of a wife who had broken her holiest vows, of a home and heart made desolate. Even as he went on, the shout, the laugh, the shriek, the sob, rose up in unison, till they changed into the hollow, fitful, and uneven sound of the wind, as it fought among the pine-trees on those three lonely hills. The lady looked up, and there was the withered woman smiling in her face.

"Couldst thou have thought there were such merry times in a madhouse?" inquired the latter.

"True, true," said the lady to herself; "there is mirth within its walls, but misery, misery without."

"Wouldst thou hear more?" demanded the old woman.

"There is one other voice I would fain listen to again," replied the lady, faintly.

"Then, lay down thy head speedily upon my knees, that thou mayst get thee hence before the hour be past."

The golden skirts of day were yet lingering upon the hills, but deep shades obscured the hollow and the pool, as if sombre night were rising thence to overspread the world. Again that evil woman began to weave her spell. Long did it proceed unanswered, till the knolling of a bell stole in among the intervals of her words, like a clang that had travelled far over valley and rising ground, and was just ready to die in the air. The lady shook upon her companion's knees as she heard that boding sound. Stronger it grew and sadder, and deepened into the tone of a death bell, knolling dolefully from some ivy-mantled tower, and bearing tidings of mortality and woe to the cottage, to the hall, and to the solitary wayfarer, that all might weep for the doom appointed in turn to them. Then came a measured tread, passing slowly, slowly on, as of mourners with a coffin, their garments trailing on the ground, so that the ear could measure the length of their melancholy array. Before them went the priest, reading the burial service, while the leaves of his book were rustling in the breeze. And though no voice but his was heard to speak aloud, still there were revilings and anathemas, whispered but distinct, from women and from men, breathed against the daughter who had wrung the aged hearts of her parents,—the wife who had betrayed the trusting fondness of her husband,—the mother who had sinned against natural affection, and left her child to die. The sweeping sound of the funeral train faded away like a thin vapor, and the wind, that just before had seemed to shake the coffin pall, moaned sadly round the verge of the Hollow between three Hills. But when the old woman stirred the kneeling lady, she lifted not her head.

"Here has been a sweet hour's sport!" said the withered crone, chuckling to herself.

# DR. HEIDEGGER'S EXPERIMENT

THAT very singular man, old Dr. Heidegger, once invited four venerable friends to meet him in his study. There were three white-bearded gentlemen, Mr. Medbourne, Colonel Killigrew, and Mr. Gascoigne, and a withered gentlewoman, whose name was the Widow Wycherly. They were all melancholy old creatures, who had been unfortunate in life, and whose greatest misfortune it was that they were not long ago in their graves. Mr. Medbourne, in the vigor of his age, had been a prosperous merchant, but had lost his all by a frantic speculation, and was now little better than a mendicant. Colonel Killigrew had wasted his best years, and his health and substance, in the pursuit of sinful pleasures, which had given birth to a brood of pains, such as the gout, and divers other torments of soul and body. Mr. Gascoigne was a ruined politician, a man of evil fame, or at least had been so till time had buried him from the knowledge of the present generation, and made him obscure instead of infamous. As for the Widow Wycherly, tradition tells us that she was a great beauty in her day; but, for a long while past, she had lived in deep seclusion, on account of certain scandalous stories which had prejudiced the gentry of the town against her. It is a circumstance worth mentioning that each of these three old gentlemen, Mr. Medbourne, Colonel Killigrew, and Mr. Gascoigne, were early lovers of the Widow Wycherly, and had once been on the point of cutting each other's throats for her sake. And, before proceeding further, I will merely hint that Dr. Heidegger and all his four guests were sometimes thought to be a little beside themselves,—as is not unfrequently the case with old people, when worried either by present troubles or woful recollections.

"My dear old friends," said Dr. Heidegger, motioning them to be seated, "I am desirous of your assistance in one of those little experiments with which I amuse myself here in my study."

If all stories were true, Dr. Heidegger's study must have been a very curious place. It was a dim, old-fashioned chamber, festooned with cobwebs, and besprinkled with antique dust. Around the walls stood several oaken bookcases, the lower shelves of which were filled with rows of gigantic folios and black-letter quartos, and the upper with little parchment-covered duodecimos. Over the central bookcase was a bronze bust of Hippocrates, with which, according to some authorities, Dr. Heidegger was accustomed to hold consultations in all difficult cases of his practice. In the obscurest corner of the room stood a tall and narrow oaken closet, with its door ajar, within which doubtfully appeared a skeleton. Between two of the bookcases hung a looking-glass, presenting its high and dusty plate within a tarnished gilt frame. Among many wonderful stories related of this mirror, it was fabled that the spirits of all the doctor's deceased patients dwelt within its verge, and would stare him in the face whenever he looked thitherward. The opposite side of the chamber was ornamented with the full-length portrait of a young lady, arrayed in the faded magnificence of silk, satin, and brocade, and with a visage as faded as her dress. Above half a century ago, Dr. Heidegger had been on the point of marriage with this young lady; but, being affected with some slight disorder, she had swallowed one of her lover's prescriptions, and died on the bridal evening. The greatest curiosity of the study remains to be mentioned; it was a ponderous folio volume, bound in black leather, with massive silver clasps. There were no letters on the back, and nobody could tell the title of the book. But it was well known to be a book of magic; and once, when a chambermaid had lifted it, merely to brush away the dust, the skeleton had rattled in its closet, the picture of the young lady had stepped one foot upon the floor, and several ghastly faces had peeped forth from the mirror; while the brazen head of Hippocrates frowned, and said,—"Forbear!"

Such was Dr. Heidegger's study. On the summer afternoon of our tale a small round table, as black as ebony, stood in the centre of the room, sustaining a cut-glass vase of beautiful form and elaborate workmanship. The sunshine came through the window, between the heavy festoons of two faded damask curtains, and fell directly across this vase; so that a mild splendor was reflected from it on the ashen visages of the five old people who sat around. Four champagne glasses were also on the table.

"My dear old friends," repeated Dr. Heidegger, "may I reckon on your aid in performing an exceedingly curious experiment?"

Now Dr. Heidegger was a very strange old gentleman, whose eccentricity had become the nucleus for a thousand fantastic stories. Some of these fables, to my shame be it spoken, might possibly be traced back to my own veracious self; and if any passages of the present tale should startle the reader's faith, I must be content to bear the stigma of a fiction monger.

When the doctor's four guests heard him talk of his proposed experiment, they anticipated nothing more wonderful than the murder of a mouse in an air pump, or the examination of a cobweb by the microscope, or some similar nonsense, with which he was constantly in the habit of pestering his intimates. But without waiting for a reply, Dr. Heidegger hobbled across the chamber, and returned with the same ponderous folio, bound in black leather, which common report affirmed to be a book of magic. Undoing the silver clasps, he opened the volume, and took from among its black-letter pages a rose, or what was once a rose, though now the green leaves and crimson petals had assumed one brownish hue, and the ancient flower seemed ready to crumble to dust in the doctor's hands.

"This rose,"-said Dr. Heidegger, with a sigh, "this same withered and crumbling flower, blossomed five and fifty years ago. It was given me by Sylvia Ward, whose portrait hangs yonder; and I meant to wear it in my bosom at our wedding. Five and fifty years it has been treasured between the leaves of this old volume. Now, would you deem it possible that this rose of half a century could ever bloom again?"

"Nonsense!" said the Widow Wycherly, with a peevish toss of her head. "You might as well ask whether an old woman's wrinkled face could ever bloom again."

"See!" answered Dr. Heidegger.

He uncovered the vase, and threw the faded rose into the water which it contained. At first, it lay lightly on the surface of the fluid, appearing to imbibe none of its moisture. Soon, however, a singular change began to be visible. The crushed and dried petals stirred, and assumed a deepening tinge of crimson, as if the flower were reviving from a deathlike slumber; the slender stalk and twigs of foliage became green; and there was the rose of half a century, looking as fresh as when Sylvia Ward had first given it to her lover. It was scarcely full blown; for some of its delicate red leaves curled modestly around its moist bosom, within which two or three dewdrops were sparkling.

"That is certainly a very pretty deception," said the doctor's friends; carelessly, however, for they had witnessed greater miracles at a conjurer's show; "pray how was it effected?"

"Did you never hear of the 'Fountain of Youth?' " asked Dr. Heidegger, "which Ponce De Leon, the Spanish adventurer, went in search of two or three centuries ago?"

"But did Ponce De Leon ever find it?" said the Widow Wycherly.

"No," answered Dr. Heidegger, "for he never sought it in the right place. The famous Fountain of Youth, if I am rightly informed, is situated in the southern part of the Floridian peninsula, not far from Lake Macaco. Its source is overshadowed by several gigantic magnolias, which, though numberless centuries old, have been kept as fresh as violets by the virtues of this wonderful water. An acquaintance of mine, knowing my curiosity in such matters, has sent me what you see in the vase."

"Ahem!" said Colonel Killigrew, who believed not a word of the doctor's story; "and what may be the effect of this fluid on the human frame?"

"You shall judge for yourself, my dear colonel," replied Dr. Heidegger; "and all of you, my respected friends, are welcome to so much of this admirable fluid as may restore to you the bloom of youth. For my own part, having had much trouble in growing old, I am in no hurry to grow young again. With your permission, therefore, I will merely watch the progress of the experiment."

While he spoke, Dr. Heidegger had been filling the four champagne glasses with the water of the Fountain of Youth. It was apparently impregnated with an effervescent gas, for little bubbles were continually ascending from the depths of the glasses, and bursting in silvery spray at the surface. As the liquor diffused a pleasant perfume, the old people doubted not that it possessed cordial and comfortable properties; and though utter sceptics as to its rejuvenescent power, they were inclined to swallow it at once. But Dr. Heidegger besought them to stay a moment.

"Before you drink, my respectable old friends," said he, "it would be well that, with the experience of a lifetime to direct you, you should draw up a few general rules for your guidance, in passing a second time through the perils of youth. Think what a sin and shame it would be, if, with your peculiar advantages, you should not become patterns of virtue and wisdom to all the young people of the age!"

The doctor's four venerable friends made him no answer, except by a feeble and tremulous laugh; so very ridiculous was the idea that, knowing how closely repentance treads behind the steps of error, they should ever go astray again.

"Drink, then," said the doctor, bowing: "I rejoice that I have so well selected the subjects of my experiment."

With palsied hands, they raised the glasses to their lips. The liquor, if it really possessed such virtues as Dr. Heidegger imputed to it, could not have been bestowed on four human beings who needed it more wofully. They looked as if they had never known what youth or pleasure was, but had been the offspring of Nature's dotage, and always the gray, decrepit, sapless, miserable creatures, who now sat stooping round the doctor's table, without life enough in their souls or bodies to be animated even by the prospect of growing young again. They drank off the water, and replaced their glasses on the table.

Assuredly there was an almost immediate improvement in the aspect of the party, not unlike what might have been produced by a glass of generous wine, together with a sudden glow of cheerful sunshine brightening over all their visages at once. There was a healthful suffusion on their cheeks, instead of the ashen hue that had made them look so corpse-like. They gazed at one another, and fancied that some magic power had really begun to smooth away the deep and sad inscriptions which Father Time had been so long engraving on their brows. The Widow Wycherly adjusted her cap, for she felt almost like a woman again.

"Give us more of this wondrous water!" cried they, eagerly. "We are younger—but we are still too old! Quick—give us more!"

"Patience, patience!" quoth Dr. Heidegger, who sat watching the experiment with philosophic coolness. "You have been a long time growing old. Surely, you might be content to grow young in half an hour! But the water is at your service."

Again he filled their glasses with the liquor of youth, enough of which still remained in the vase to turn half the old people in the city to the age of their own grandchildren. While the bubbles were yet sparkling on the brim, the doctor's four guests snatched their glasses from the table, and swallowed the contents at a single gulp. Was it delusion? even while the draught was passing down their throats, it seemed to have wrought a change on their whole systems. Their eyes grew clear and bright; a dark shade deepened among their silvery locks, they sat around the table, three gentlemen of middle age, and a woman, hardly beyond her buxom prime.

"My dear widow, you are charming!" cried Colonel Killigrew, whose eyes had been fixed upon her face, while the shadows of age were flitting from it like darkness from the crimson daybreak.

The fair widow knew, of old, that Colonel Killigrew's compliments were not always measured by sober truth; so she started up and ran to the mirror, still dreading that the ugly visage of an old woman would meet her gaze. Meanwhile, the three gentlemen behaved in such a manner as proved that the water of the Fountain of Youth possessed some intoxicating qualities; unless, indeed, their exhilaration of spirits were merely a lightsome dizziness caused by the sudden removal of the weight of years. Mr. Gascoigne's mind seemed to run on political topics, but whether relating to the past, present, or future, could not easily be determined, since the same ideas and phrases have been in vogue these fifty years. Now he rattled forth full-throated sentences about patriotism, national glory, and the people's right; now he muttered some perilous stuff or other, in a sly and doubtful whisper, so cautiously that even his own conscience could scarcely catch the secret; and now, again, he spoke in measured accents, and a deeply deferential tone, as if a royal ear were listening to his well-turned periods. Colonel Killigrew all this time had been trolling forth a jolly bottle song, and ringing his glass in symphony with the chorus, while his eyes wandered toward the buxom figure of the Widow Wycherly. On the other side of the table, Mr. Medbourne was involved in a calculation of dollars and cents, with which was strangely intermingled a project for supplying the East Indies with ice, by harnessing a team of whales to the polar icebergs.

As for the Widow Wycherly, she stood before the mirror courtesying and simpering to her own image, and greeting it as the friend whom she loved better than all the world beside. She thrust her face close to the glass, to see whether some long-remembered wrinkle or crow's foot had indeed vanished. She examined whether the snow had so entirely melted from her hair that the venerable cap could be safely thrown aside. At last, turning briskly away, she came with a sort of dancing step to the table.

"My dear old doctor," cried she, "pray favor me with another glass!"

"Certainly, my dear madam, certainly!" replied the complaisant doctor; "see! I have already filled the glasses."

There, in fact, stood the four glasses, brimful of this wonderful water, the delicate spray of which, as it effervesced from the surface, resembled the tremulous glitter of diamonds. It was now so nearly sunset that the chamber had grown duskier than ever; but a mild and moonlike splendor gleamed from within the vase, and rested alike on the four guests and on the doctor's venerable figure. He sat in a high-backed, elaborately-carved, oaken arm-chair, with a gray dignity of aspect that might have well befitted that very Father Time, whose power had never been disputed, save by this fortunate company. Even while quaffing the third draught of the Fountain of Youth, they were almost awed by the expression of his mysterious visage.

But, the next moment, the exhilarating gush of young life shot through their veins. They were now in the happy prime of youth. Age, with its miserable train of cares and sorrows and diseases, was remembered only as the trouble of a dream, from which they had joyously awoke. The fresh gloss of the soul, so early lost, and without which the world's successive scenes had been but a gallery of faded pictures, again threw its enchantment over all their prospects. They felt like new-created beings in a new-created universe.

"We are young! We are young!" they cried exultingly.

Youth, like the extremity of age, had effaced the strongly-marked characteristics of middle life, and mutually assimilated them all. They were a group of merry youngsters, almost maddened with the exuberant frolicsomeness of their years. The most singular effect of their gayety was an impulse to mock the infirmity and decrepitude of which they had so lately been the victims. They laughed loudly at their old-fashioned attire, the wide-skirted coats and flapped waistcoats of the young men, and the ancient cap and gown of the blooming girl. One limped across the floor like a gouty grandfather; one set a pair of spectacles astride of his nose, and pretended to pore over the black-letter pages of the book of magic; a third seated himself in an arm-chair, and strove to imitate the venerable dignity of Dr. Heidegger. Then all shouted mirthfully, and leaped about the room. The Widow Wycherly—if so fresh a damsel could be called a widow—tripped up to the doctor's chair, with a mischievous merriment in her rosy face.

"Doctor, you dear old soul," cried she, "get up and dance with me!" And then the four young people laughed louder than ever, to think what a queer figure the poor old doctor would cut.

"Pray excuse me," answered the doctor quietly. "I am old and rheumatic, and my dancing days were over long ago. But either of these gay young gentlemen will be glad of so pretty a partner."

"Dance with me, Clara!" cried Colonel Killigrew.

"No, no, I will be her partner!" shouted Mr. Gascoigne.

"She promised me her hand, fifty years ago!" exclaimed Mr. Medbourne.

They all gathered round her. One caught both her hands in his passionate grasp—another threw his arm about her waist—the third buried his hand among the glossy curls that clustered beneath the widow's cap. Blushing, panting, struggling, chiding, laughing, her warm breath fanning each of their faces by turns, she strove to disengage herself, yet still remained in their triple embrace. Never was there a livelier picture of youthful rivalship, with bewitching beauty for the prize. Yet, by a strange deception, owing to the duskiness of the chamber, and the antique dresses which they still wore, the tall mirror is said to have reflected the figures of the three old, gray, withered grandsires, ridiculously contending for the skinny ugliness of a shrivelled grandam.

But they were young: their burning passions proved them so. Inflamed to madness by the coquetry of the girl-widow, who neither granted nor quite withheld her favors, the three rivals began to interchange threatening glances. Still keeping hold of the fair prize, they grappled fiercely at one another's throats. As they struggled to and fro, the table was overturned, and the vase dashed into a thousand fragments. The precious Water of Youth flowed in a bright stream across the floor, moistening the wings of a butterfly, which, grown old in the decline of summer, had alighted there to die. The insect fluttered lightly through the chamber, and settled on the snowy head of Dr. Heidegger.

"Come, come, gentlemen!—come, Madam Wycherly," exclaimed the doctor, "I really must protest against this riot."

They stood still and shivered; for it seemed as if gray Time were calling them back from their sunny youth, far down into the chill and darksome vale of years. They looked at old Dr. Heidegger, who sat in his carved arm-chair, holding the rose of half a century, which he had rescued from among the fragments of the shattered vase. At the motion of his hand, the four rioters resumed their seats; the more readily, because their violent exertions had wearied them, youthful though they were.

"My poor Sylvia's rose!" ejaculated Dr. Heidegger, holding it in the light of the sunset clouds; "it appears to be fading again."

And so it was. Even while the party were looking at it, the flower continued to shrivel up, till it became as dry and fragile as when the doctor had first thrown it into the vase. He shook off the few drops of moisture which clung to its petals.

"I love it as well thus as in its dewy freshness," observed he, pressing the withered rose to his withered lips. While he spoke, the butterfly fluttered down from the doctor's snowy head, and fell upon the floor.

His guests shivered again. A strange chillness, whether of the body or spirit they could not tell, was creeping gradually over them all. They gazed at one another, and fancied that each fleeting moment snatched away a charm, and left a deepening furrow where none had been before. Was it an illusion? Had the changes of a lifetime been crowded into so brief a space, and were they now four aged people, sitting with their old friend, Dr. Heidegger?

"Are we grown old again, so soon?" cried they, dolefully.

In truth they had. The Water of Youth possessed merely a virtue more transient than that of wine. The delirium which it created had effervesced away. Yes! they were old again. With a shuddering impulse, that showed her a woman still, the widow clasped her skinny hands before her face, and wished that the coffin lid were over it, since it could be no longer beautiful.

"Yes, friends, ye are old again," said Dr. Heidegger, "and lo! the Water of Youth is all lavished on the ground. Well—I bemoan it not; for if the fountain gushed at my very doorstep, I would not stoop to bathe my lips in it—no, though its delirium were for years instead of moments. Such is the lesson ye have taught me!"

But the doctor's four friends had taught no such lesson to themselves. They resolved forthwith to make a pilgrimage to Florida, and quaff at morning, noon, and night, from the Fountain of Youth.

NOTE.—In an English review, not long since, I have been accused of plagiarizing the idea of this story from a chapter in one of the novels of Alexandre Dumas. There has undoubtedly been a plagiarism on one side or the other; but as my story was written a good deal more than twenty years ago, and as the novel is of considerably more recent date, I take pleasure in thinking that M. Dumas has done me the honor to appropriate one of the fanciful conceptions of my earlier days. He is heartily welcome to it; nor is it the only instance, by many, in which the great French romancer has exercised the privilege of commanding genius by confiscating the intellectual property of less famous people to his own use and behoof.

*September,* 1860.

# LEGENDS OF THE PROVINCE HOUSE

## I

### HOWE'S MASQUERADE

ONE afternoon, last summer, while walking along Washington Street, my eye was attracted by a signboard protruding over a narrow archway, nearly opposite the Old South Church. The sign represented the front of a stately edifice, which was designated as the "OLD PROVINCE HOUSE, kept by Thomas Waite." I was glad to be thus reminded of a purpose, long entertained, of visiting and rambling over the mansion of the old royal governors of Massachusetts; and entering the arched passage, which penetrated through the middle of a brick row of shops, a few steps transported me from the busy heart of modern Boston into a small and secluded courtyard. One side of this space was occupied by the square front of the Province House, three stories high, and surmounted by a cupola, on the top of which a gilded Indian was discernible, with his bow bent and his arrow on the string, as if aiming at the weathercock on the spire of the Old South. The figure has kept this attitude for seventy years or more, ever since good Deacon Drowne, a cunning carver of wood, first stationed him on his long sentinel's watch over the city.

The Province House is constructed of brick, which seems recently to have been overlaid with a coat of light-colored paint. A flight of red freestone steps, fenced in by a balustrade of curiously wrought iron, ascends from the court-yard to the spacious porch, over which is a balcony, with an iron balustrade of similar pattern and workmanship to that beneath. These letters and figures—16 P. S. 79—are wrought into the iron work of the balcony, and probably express the date of the edifice, with the initials of its founder's name. A wide door with double leaves admitted me into the hall or entry, on the right of which is the entrance to the bar-room.

It was in this apartment, I presume, that the ancient governors held their levees, with vice-regal pomp, surrounded by the military men, the councillors, the judges, and other officers of the crown, while all the loyalty of the province thronged to do them honor. But the room, in its present condition, cannot boast even of faded magnificence. The panelled wainscot is covered with dingy paint, and acquires a duskier hue from the deep shadow into which the Province House is thrown by the brick block that shuts it in from Washington Street. A ray of sunshine never visits this apartment any more than the glare of the festal torches, which have been extinguished from the era of the Revolution. The most venerable and ornamental object is a chimney-piece set round with Dutch tiles of blue-figured China, representing scenes from Scripture; and, for aught I know, the lady of Pownall or Bernard may have sat beside this fireplace, and told her children the story of each blue tile. A bar in modern style, well replenished with decanters, bottles, cigar boxes, and net-work bags of lemons, and provided with a beer pump, and a soda fount, extends along one side of the room. At my entrance, an elderly person was smacking his lips with a zest which satisfied me that the cellars of the Province House still hold good liquor, though doubtless of other vintages than were quaffed by the old governors. After sipping a glass of port sangaree, prepared by the skilful hands of Mr. Thomas Waite, I besought that worthy successor and representative of so many historic personages to conduct me over their time honored mansion.

He readily complied; but, to confess the truth, I was forced to draw strenuously upon my imagination, in order to find aught that was interesting in a house which, without its historic associations, would have seemed merely such a tavern as is usually favored by the custom of decent city boarders, and old-fashioned country gentlemen. The chambers, which were probably spacious in former times, are now cut up by partitions, and subdivided into little nooks, each affording scanty room for the narrow bed and chair and dressing-table of a single lodger. The great staircase, however, may be termed, without much hyperbole, a feature of grandeur and magnificence. It winds through the midst of the house by flights of broad steps, each flight terminating in a square landing-place, whence the ascent is continued towards the cupola. A carved balustrade, freshly painted in the lower stories, but growing dingier as we ascend, borders the staircase with its quaintly twisted and intertwined pillars, from top to bottom. Up these stairs the military boots, or perchance the gouty shoes, of many a governor have trodden, as the wearers mounted to the cupola, which afforded them so wide a view over their metropolis and the surrounding country. The cupola is an octagon, with several windows, and a door opening upon the roof. From this station, as I pleased myself with imagining, Gage may have beheld his disastrous victory on Bunker Hill (unless one of the tri-mountains intervened), and Howe have marked the approaches of Washington's besieging army; although the buildings since erected in the vicinity have shut out almost every object, save the steeple of the Old South, which seems almost within arm's length. Descending from the cupola, I paused in the garret to observe the ponderous white-oak framework, so much more massive than the frames of modern houses, and thereby resembling an antique skeleton. The brick walls, the materials of which were imported from Holland, and the timbers of the mansion, are still as sound as ever; but the floors and other interior parts being greatly decayed, it is contemplated to gut the whole, and build a new house within the ancient frame and brick work. Among other inconveniences of the present edifice, mine host mentioned that any jar or motion was apt to shake down the dust of ages out of the ceiling of one chamber upon the floor of that beneath it.

We stepped forth from the great front window into the balcony, where, in old times, it was doubtless the custom of the king's representative to show himself to a loyal populace, requiting their huzzas and tossed-up hats with stately bendings of his dignified person. In those days the front of the Province House looked upon the street; and the whole site now occupied by the brick range of stores, as well as the present court-yard, was laid out in grass plats, overshadowed by trees and bordered by a wrought-iron fence. Now, the old aristocratic edifice hides its time-worn visage behind an upstart modern building; at one of the back windows I observed some pretty tailoresses, sewing and chatting and laughing, with now and then a careless glance towards the balcony. Descending thence, we again entered the bar-room, where the elderly gentleman above mentioned, the smack of whose lips had spoken so favorably for Mr. Waite's good liquor, was still lounging in his chair. He seemed to be, if not a lodger, at least a familiar visitor of the house, who might be supposed to have his regular score at the bar, his summer seat at the open window, and his prescriptive corner at the winter's fireside. Being of a sociable aspect, I ventured to address him with a remark calculated to draw forth his historical reminiscences, if any such were in his mind; and it gratified me to discover, that, between memory and tradition, the old gentleman was really possessed of some very pleasant gossip about the Province House. The portion of his talk which chiefly interested me was the outline of the following legend. He professed to have received it at one or two removes from an eye-witness; but this derivation, together with the lapse of time, must have afforded opportunities for many variations of the narrative; so that despairing of literal and absolute truth, I have not scrupled to make such further changes as seemed conducive to the reader's profit and delight.

———————

At one of the entertainments given at the Province House, during the latter part of the siege of Boston, there passed a scene which has never yet been satisfactorily explained. The officers of the British army, and the loyal gentry of the province, most of whom were collected within the beleaguered town, had been invited to a masked ball; for it was the policy of Sir William Howe to hide the distress and danger of the period, and the desperate aspect of the siege, under an ostentation of festivity. The spectacle of this evening, if the oldest members of the provincial court circle might be believed, was the most gay and gorgeous affair that had occurred in the annals of the government. The brilliantly-lighted apartments were thronged with figures that seemed to have stepped from the dark canvas of historic portraits, or to have flitted forth from the magic pages of romance, or at least to have flown hither from one of the London theatres, without a change of garments. Steeled knights of the Conquest, bearded statesmen of Queen Elizabeth, and high-ruffled ladies of her court, were mingled with characters of comedy, such as a party-colored Merry Andrew, jingling his cap and bells; a Falstaff, almost as provocative of laughter as his prototype; and a Don Quixote, with a bean pole for a lance, and a pot lid for a shield.

But the broadest merriment was excited by a group of figures ridiculously dressed in old regimentals, which seemed to have been purchased at a military rag fair, or pilfered from some receptacle of the cast-off clothes of both the French and British armies. Portions of their attire had probably been worn at the siege of Louisburg, and the coats of most recent cut might have been rent and tattered by sword, ball, or bayonet, as long ago as Wolfe's victory. One of these worthies—a tall, lank figure, brandishing a rusty sword of immense longitude—purported to be no less a personage than General George Washington; and the other principal officers of the American army, such as Gates, Lee, Putnam, Schuyler, Ward and Heath, were represented by similar scarecrows. An interview in the mock heroic style, between the rebel warriors and the British commander-in-chief, was received with immense applause, which came loudest of all from the loyalists of the colony. There was one of the guests, however, who stood apart, eyeing these antics sternly and scornfully, at once with a frown and a bitter smile.

It was an old man, formerly of high station and great repute in the province, and who had been a very famous soldier in his day. Some surprise had been expressed that a person of Colonel Joliffe's known whig principles, though now too old to take an active part in the contest, should have remained in Boston during the siege, and especially that he should consent to show himself in the mansion of Sir William Howe. But thither he had come, with a fair granddaughter under his arm; and there, amid all the mirth and buffoonery, stood this stern old figure, the best sustained character in the masquerade, because so well representing the antique spirit of his native land. The other guests affirmed that Colonel Joliffe's black puritanical scowl threw a shadow round about him; although in spite of his sombre influence their gayety continued to blaze higher, like—(an ominous comparison)—the flickering brilliancy of a lamp which has but a little while to burn. Eleven strokes, full half an hour ago, had pealed from the clock of the Old South, when a rumor was circulated among the company that some new spectacle or pageant was about to be exhibited, which should put a fitting close to the splendid festivities of the night.

"What new jest has your Excellency in hand?" asked the Rev. Mather Byles, whose Presbyterian scruples had not kept him from the entertainment. "Trust me, sir, I have already laughed more than beseems my cloth at your Homeric confabulation with yonder ragamuffin General of the rebels. One other such fit of merriment, and I must throw off my clerical wig and band."

"Not so, good Doctor Byles," answered Sir William Howe; "if mirth were a crime, you had never gained your doctorate in divinity. As to this new foolery, I know no more about it than yourself; perhaps not so much. Honestly now, Doctor, have you not stirred up the sober brains of some of your countrymen to enact a scene in our masquerade?"

"Perhaps," slyly remarked the granddaughter of Colonel Joliffe, whose high spirit had been stung by many taunts against New England,—"perhaps we are to have a mask of allegorical figures. Victory, with trophies from Lexington and Bunker Hill—Plenty, with her overflowing horn, to typify the present abundance in this good town—and Glory, with a wreath for his Excellency's brow."

Sir William Howe smiled at words which he would have answered with one of his darkest frowns had they been uttered by lips that wore a beard. He was spared the necessity of a retort, by a singular interruption. A sound of music was heard without the house, as if proceeding from a full band of military instruments stationed in the street, playing not such a festal strain as was suited to the occasion, but a slow funeral march. The drums appeared to be muffled, and the trumpets poured forth a wailing breath, which at once hushed the merriment of the auditors, filling all with wonder, and some with apprehension. The idea occurred to many that either the funeral procession of some great personage had halted in front of the Province House, or that a corpse, in a velvet-covered and gorgeously-decorated coffin, was about to be borne from the portal. After listening a moment, Sir William Howe called, in a stern voice, to the leader of the musicians, who had hitherto enlivened the entertainment with gay and lightsome melodies. The man was drum-major to one of the British regiments.

"Dighton," demanded the general, "what means this foolery? Bid your band silence that dead march—or, by my word, they shall have sufficient cause for their lugubrious strains! Silence it, sirrah!"

"Please your honor," answered the drum-major, whose rubicund visage had lost all its color, "the fault is none of mine. I and my band are all here together, and I question whether there be a man of us that could play that march without book. I never heard it but once before, and that was at the funeral of his late Majesty, King George the Second."

"Well, well!" said Sir William Howe, recovering his composure—"it is the prelude to some masquerading antic. Let it pass."

A figure now presented itself, but among the many fantastic masks that were dispersed through the apartments none could tell precisely from whence it came. It was a man in an old-fashioned dress of black serge, and having the aspect of a steward or principal domestic in the household of a nobleman or great English landholder. This figure advanced to the outer door of the mansion, and throwing both its leaves wide open, withdrew a little to one side and looked back towards the grand staircase as if expecting some person to descend. At the same time the music in the street sounded a loud and doleful summons. The eyes of Sir William Howe and his guests being directed to the staircase, there appeared, on the uppermost landing-place that was discernible from the bottom, several personages descending towards the door. The foremost was a man of stern visage, wearing a steeple-crowned hat and a skull-cap beneath it; a dark cloak, and huge wrinkled boots that came half-way up his legs. Under his arm was a rolled-up banner, which seemed to be the banner of England, but strangely rent and torn; he had a sword in his right hand, and grasped a Bible in his left. The next figure was of milder aspect, yet full of dignity, wearing a broad ruff, over which descended a beard, a gown of wrought velvet, and a doublet and hose of black satin. He carried a roll of manuscript in his hand. Close behind these two came a young man of very striking countenance and demeanor, with deep thought and contemplation on his brow, and perhaps a flash of enthusiasm in his eye. His garb, like that of his predecessors, was of an antique fashion, and there was a stain of blood upon his ruff. In the same group with these were three or four others, all men of dignity and evident command, and bearing themselves like personages who were accustomed to the gaze of the multitude. It was the idea of the beholders that these figures went to join the mysterious funeral that had halted in front of the Province House; yet that supposition seemed to be contradicted by the air of triumph with which they waved their hands, as they crossed the threshold and vanished through the portal.

"In the devil's name what is this?" muttered Sir William Howe to a gentleman beside him; "a procession of the regicide judges of King Charles the martyr?"

"These," said Colonel Joliffe, breaking silence almost for the first time that evening,—"these, if I interpret them aright, are the Puritan governors—the rulers of the old original Democracy of Massachusetts. Endicott, with the banner from which he had torn the symbol of subjection, and Winthrop, and Sir Henry Vane, and Dudley, Haynes, Bellingham, and Leverett."

"Why had that young man a stain of blood upon his ruff?" asked Miss Joliffe.

"Because, in after years," answered her grandfather, "he laid down the wisest head in England upon the block for the principles of liberty."

"Will not your Excellency order out the guard?" whispered Lord Percy, who, with other British officers, had now assembled round the General. "There may be a plot under this mummery."

"Tush! we have nothing to fear," carelessly replied Sir William Howe. "There can be no worse treason in the matter than a jest, and that somewhat of the dullest. Even were it a sharp and bitter one, our best policy would be to laugh it off. See—here come more of these gentry."

Another group of characters had now partly descended the staircase. The first was a venerable and white-bearded patriarch, who cautiously felt his way downward with a staff. Treading hastily behind him, and stretching forth his gauntleted hand as if to grasp the old man's shoulder, came a tall, soldier-like figure, equipped with a plumed cap of steel, a bright breastplate, and a long sword, which rattled against the stairs. Next was seen a stout man, dressed in rich and courtly attire, but not of courtly demeanor; his gait had the swinging motion of a seaman's walk, and chancing to stumble on the staircase, he suddenly grew wrathful, and was heard to mutter an oath. He was followed by a noble-looking personage in a curled wig, such as are represented in the portraits of Queen Anne's time and earlier; and the breast of his coat was decorated with an embroidered star. While advancing to the door, he bowed to the right hand and to the left, in a very gracious and insinuating style; but as he crossed the threshold, unlike the early Puritan governors, he seemed to wring his hands with sorrow.

"Prithee, play the part of a chorus, good Doctor Byles," said Sir William Howe. "What worthies are these?"

"If it please your Excellency they lived somewhat before my day," answered the doctor; "but doubtless our friend, the Colonel, has been hand and glove with them."

"Their living faces I never looked upon," said Colonel Joliffe, gravely; "although I have spoken face to face with many rulers of this land, and shall greet yet another with an old man's blessing ere I die. But we talk of these figures. I take the venerable patriarch to be Bradstreet, the last of the Puritans, who was governor at ninety, or thereabouts. The next is Sir Edmund Andros, a tyrant, as any New England school-boy will tell you; and therefore the people cast him down from his high seat into a dungeon. Then comes Sir William Phipps, shepherd, cooper, sea-captain, and governor—may many of his countrymen rise as high from as low an origin! Lastly, you saw the gracious Earl of Bellamont, who ruled us under King William."

"But what is the meaning of it all?" asked Lord Percy.

"Now, were I a rebel," said Miss Joliffe, half aloud, "I might fancy that the ghosts of these ancient governors had been summoned to form the funeral procession of royal authority in New England."

Several other figures were now seen at the turn of the staircase. The one in advance had a thoughtful, anxious, and somewhat crafty expression of face, and in spite of his loftiness of manner, which was evidently the result both of an ambitious spirit and of long continuance in high stations, he seemed not incapable of cringing to a greater than himself. A few steps behind came an officer in a scarlet and embroidered uniform, cut in a fashion old enough to have been worn by the Duke of Marlborough. His nose had a rubicund tinge, which, together with the twinkle of his eye, might have marked him as a lover of the wine cup and good fellowship; notwithstanding which tokens he appeared ill at ease, and often glanced around him as if apprehensive of some secret mischief. Next came a portly gentleman, wearing a coat of shaggy cloth, lined with silken velvet; he had sense, shrewdness, and humor in his face, and a folio volume under his arm; but his aspect was that of a man vexed and tormented beyond all patience, and harassed almost to death. He went hastily down, and was followed by a dignified person, dressed in a purple velvet suit, with very rich embroidery; his demeanor would have possessed much stateliness, only that a grievous fit of the gout compelled him to hobble from stair to stair, with contortions of face and body. When Dr. Byles beheld this figure on the staircase, he shivered as with an ague, but continued to watch him steadfastly, until the gouty gentleman had reached the threshold, made a gesture of anguish and despair, and vanished into the outer gloom, whither the funeral music summoned him.

"Governor Belcher!—my old patron!—in his very shape and dress!" gasped Doctor Byles. "This is an awful mockery!"

"A tedious foolery, rather," said Sir William Howe, with an air of indifference. "But who were the three that preceded him?"

"Governor Dudley, a cunning politician—yet his craft once brought him to a prison," replied Colonel Joliffe. "Governor Shute, formerly a Colonel under Marlborough, and whom the people frightened out of the province; and learned Governor Burnet, whom the legislature tormented into a mortal fever."

"Methinks they were miserable men, these royal governors of Massachusetts," observed Miss Joliffe. "Heavens, how dim the light grows!"

It was certainly a fact that the large lamp which illuminated the staircase now burned dim and duskily: so that several figures, which passed hastily down the stairs and went forth from the porch, appeared rather like shadows than persons of fleshly substance. Sir William Howe and his guests stood at the doors of the contiguous apartments, watching the progress of this singular pageant, with various emotions of anger, contempt, or half-acknowledged fear, but still with an anxious curiosity. The shapes which now seemed hastening to join the mysterious procession were recognized rather by striking peculiarities of dress, or broad characteristics of manner, than by any perceptible resemblance of features to their prototypes. Their faces, indeed, were invariably kept in deep shadow. But Doctor Byles, and other gentlemen who had long been familiar with the successive rulers of the province, were heard to whisper the names of Shirley, of Pownall, of Sir Francis Bernard, and of the well-remembered Hutchinson; thereby confessing that the actors, whoever they might be, in this spectral march of governors, had succeeded in putting on some distant portraiture of the real personages. As they vanished from the door, still did these shadows toss their arms into the gloom of night, with a dread expression of woe. Following the mimic representative of Hutchinson came a military figure, holding before his face the cocked hat which he had taken from his powdered head; but his epaulettes and other insignia of rank were those of a general officer, and something in his mien reminded the beholders of one who had recently been master of the Province House, and chief of all the land.

"The shape of Gage, as true as in a looking-glass," exclaimed Lord Percy, turning pale.

"No, surely," cried Miss Joliffe, laughing hysterically; "it could not be Gage, or Sir William would have greeted his old comrade in arms! Perhaps he will not suffer the next to pass unchallenged."

"Of that be assured, young lady," answered Sir William Howe, fixing his eyes, with a very marked expression, upon the immovable visage of her grandfather. "I have long enough delayed to pay the ceremonies of a host to these departing guests. The next that takes his leave shall receive due courtesy."

A wild and dreary burst of music came through the open door. It seemed as if the procession, which had been gradually filling up its ranks, were now about to move, and that this loud peal of the wailing trumpets, and roll of the muffled drums, were a call to some loiterer to make haste. Many eyes, by an irresistible impulse, were turned upon Sir William Howe, as if it were he whom the dreary music summoned to the funeral of departed power.

"See!—here comes the last!" whispered Miss Joliffe, pointing her tremulous finger to the staircase.

A figure had come into view as if descending the stairs; although so dusky was the region whence it emerged, some of the spectators fancied that they had seen this human shape suddenly moulding itself amid the gloom. Downward the figure came, with a stately and martial tread, and reaching the lowest stair was observed to be a tall man, booted and wrapped in a military cloak, which was drawn up around the face so as to meet the flapped brim of a laced hat. The features, therefore, were completely hidden. But the British officers deemed that they had seen that military cloak before, and even recognized the frayed embroidery on the collar, as well as the gilded scabbard of a sword which protruded from the folds of the cloak, and glittered in a vivid gleam of light. Apart from these trifling particulars, there were characteristics of gait and bearing which impelled the wondering guests to glance from the shrouded figure to Sir William Howe, as if to satisfy themselves that their host had not suddenly vanished from the midst of them.

With a dark flush of wrath upon his brow they saw the General draw his sword and advance to meet the figure in the cloak before the latter had stepped one pace upon the floor.

"Villain, unmuffle yourself!" cried he. "You pass no farther!"

The figure, without blenching a hair's breadth from the sword which was pointed at his breast, made a solemn pause and lowered the cape of the cloak from about his face, yet not sufficiently for the spectators to catch a glimpse of it. But Sir William Howe had evidently seen enough. The sternness of his countenance gave place to a look of wild amazement, if not horror, while he recoiled several steps from the figure, and let fall his sword upon the floor. The martial shape again drew the cloak about his features and passed on; but reaching the threshold, with his back towards the spectators, he was seen to stamp his foot and shake his clinched hands in the air. It was afterwards affirmed that Sir William Howe had repeated that selfsame gesture of rage and sorrow, when, for the last time, and as the last royal governor, he passed through the portal of the Province House.

"Hark!—the procession moves," said Miss Joliffe.

The music was dying away along the street, and its dismal strains were mingled with the knell of midnight from the steeple of the Old South, and with the roar of artillery, which announced that the beleaguering army of Washington had intrenched itself upon a nearer height than before. As the deep boom of the cannon smote upon his ear, Colonel Joliffe raised himself to the full height of his aged form, and smiled sternly on the British General.

"Would your Excellency inquire further into the mystery of the pageant?" said he.

"Take care of your gray head!" cried Sir William Howe, fiercely, though with a quivering lip. "It has stood too long on a traitor's shoulders!"

"You must make haste to chop it off, then," calmly replied the Colonel; "for a few hours longer, and not all the power of Sir William Howe, nor of his master, shall cause one of these gray hairs to fall. The empire of Britain in this ancient province is at its last gasp to-night;—almost while I speak it is a dead corpse;—and methinks the shadows of the old governors are fit mourners at its funeral!"

With these words Colonel Joliffe threw on his cloak, and drawing his granddaughter's arm within his own, retired from the last festival that a British ruler ever held in the old province of Massachusetts Bay. It was supposed that the Colonel and the young lady possessed some secret intelligence in regard to the mysterious pageant of that night. However this might be, such knowledge has never become general. The actors in the scene have vanished into deeper obscurity than even that wild Indian band who scattered the cargoes of the tea ships on the waves, and gained a place in history, yet left no names. But superstition, among other legends of this mansion, repeats the wondrous tale, that on the anniversary night of Britain's discomfiture the ghosts of the ancient governors of Massachusetts still glide through the portal of the Province House. And, last of all, comes a figure shrouded in a military cloak, tossing his clinched hands into the air, and stamping his iron-shod boots upon the broad freestone steps, with a semblance of feverish despair, but without the sound of a foot-tramp.

————————

When the truth-telling accents of the elderly gentleman were hushed, I drew a long breath and looked round the room, striving, with the best energy of my imagination, to throw a tinge of romance and historic grandeur over the realities of the scene. But my nostrils snuffed up a scent of cigar smoke, clouds of which the narrator had emitted by way of visible emblem, I suppose, of the nebulous obscurity of his tale. Moreover, my gorgeous fantasies were wofully disturbed by the rattling of the spoon in a tumbler of whiskey punch, which Mr. Thomas Waite was mingling for a customer. Nor did it add to the picturesque appearance of the panelled walls that the slate of the Brookline stage was suspended against them, instead of the armorial escutcheon of some far-descended governor. A stage-driver sat at one of the windows, reading a penny paper of the day

—the Boston Times—and presenting a figure which could nowise be brought into any picture of "Times in Boston" seventy or a hundred years ago. On the window seat lay a bundle, neatly done up in brown paper, the direction of which I had the idle curiosity to read. "Miss Susan Huggins, at the Province House." A pretty chambermaid, no doubt. In truth, it is desperately hard work, when we attempt to throw the spell of hoar antiquity over localities with which the living world, and the day that is passing over us, have aught to do. Yet, as I glanced at the stately staircase down which the procession of the old governors had descended, and as I emerged through the venerable portal whence their figures had preceded me, it gladdened me to be conscious of a thrill of awe. Then, diving through the narrow archway, a few strides transported me into the densest throng of Washington Street.

# LEGENDS OF THE PROVINCE HOUSE

## II

### Edward Randolph's Portrait

The old legendary guest of the Province House abode in my remembrance from midsummer till January. One idle evening last winter, confident that he would be found in the snuggest corner of the bar-room, I resolved to pay him another visit, hoping to deserve well of my country by snatching from oblivion some else unheard-of fact of history. The night was chill and raw, and rendered boisterous by almost a gale of wind, which whistled along Washington Street, causing the gas-lights to flare and flicker within the lamps. As I hurried onward, my fancy was busy with a comparison between the present aspect of the street and that which it probably wore when the British governors inhabited the mansion whither I was now going. Brick edifices in those times were few, till a succession of destructive fires had swept, and swept again, the wooden dwellings and warehouses from the most populous quarters of the town. The buildings stood insulated and independent, not, as now, merging their separate existences into connected ranges, with a front of tiresome identity,—but each possessing features of its own, as if the owner's individual taste had shaped it,—and the whole presenting a picturesque irregularity, the absence of which is hardly compensated by any beauties of our modern architecture. Such a scene, dimly vanishing from the eye by the ray of here and there a tallow candle, glimmering through the small panes of scattered windows, would form a sombre contrast to the street as I beheld it, with the gas-lights blazing from corner to corner, flaming within the shops, and throwing a noonday brightness through the huge plates of glass.

But the black, lowering sky, as I turned my eyes upward, wore, doubtless, the same visage as when it frowned upon the ante-revolutionary New Englanders. The wintry blast had the same shriek that was familiar to their ears. The Old South Church, too, still pointed its antique spire into the darkness, and was lost between earth and heaven; and as I passed, its clock, which had warned so many generations how transitory was their lifetime, spoke heavily and slow the same unregarded moral to myself. "Only seven o'clock," thought I. "My old friend's legends will scarcely kill the hours 'twixt this and bedtime."

Passing through the narrow arch, I crossed the court-yard, the confined precincts of which were made visible by a lantern over the portal of the Province House. On entering the bar-room, I found, as I expected, the old tradition monger seated by a special good fire of anthracite, compelling clouds of smoke from a corpulent cigar. He recognized me with evident pleasure; for my rare properties as a patient listener invariably make me a favorite with elderly gentlemen and ladies of narrative propensities. Drawing a chair to the fire, I desired mine host to favor us with a glass apiece of whiskey punch, which was speedily prepared, steaming hot, with a slice of lemon at the bottom, a dark-red stratum of port wine upon the surface, and a sprinkling of nutmeg strewn over all. As we touched our glasses together, my legendary friend made himself known to me as Mr. Bela Tiffany; and I rejoiced at the oddity of the name, because it gave his image and character a sort of individuality in my conception. The old gentleman's draught acted as a solvent upon his memory, so that it overflowed with tales, traditions, anecdotes of famous dead people, and traits of ancient manners, some of which were childish as a nurse's lullaby, while others might have been worth the notice of the grave historian. Nothing impressed me more than a story of a black mysterious picture, which used to hang in one of the chambers of the Province House, directly above the room where we were now sitting. The following is as correct a version of the fact as the reader would be likely to obtain from any other source, although, assuredly, it has a tinge of romance approaching to the marvellous.

---

In one of the apartments of the Province House there was long preserved an ancient picture, the frame of which was as black as ebony, and the canvas itself so dark with age, damp, and smoke, that not a touch of the painter's art could be discerned. Time had thrown an impenetrable veil over it, and left to tradition and fable and conjecture to say what had once been there portrayed. During the rule of many successive governors, it had hung, by prescriptive and undisputed right, over the mantel-piece of the same chamber; and it still kept its place when Lieutenant-Governor Hutchinson assumed the administration of the province, on the departure of Sir Francis Bernard.

The Lieutenant-Governor sat, one afternoon, resting his head against the carved back of his stately armchair, and gazing up thoughtfully at the void blackness of the picture. It was scarcely a time for such inactive musing, when affairs of the deepest moment required the ruler's decision; for, within that very hour Hutchinson had received intelligence of the arrival of a British fleet, bringing three regiments from Halifax to overawe the insubordination of the people. These troops awaited his permission to occupy the fortress of Castle William, and the town itself. Yet, instead of affixing his signature to an official order, there sat the Lieutenant-Governor, so carefully scrutinizing the black waste of canvas that his demeanor attracted the notice of two young persons who attended him. One, wearing a military dress of buff, was his kinsman, Francis Lincoln, the Provincial Captain of Castle William; the other, who sat on a low stool beside his chair, was Alice Vane, his favorite niece.

She was clad entirely in white, a pale, ethereal creature, who, though a native of New England, had been educated abroad, and seemed not merely a stranger from another clime, but almost a being from another world. For several years, until left an orphan, she had dwelt with her father in sunny Italy, and there had acquired a taste and enthusiasm for sculpture and painting which she found few opportunities of gratifying in the undecorated dwellings of the colonial gentry. It was said that the early productions of her own pencil exhibited no inferior genius, though, perhaps, the rude atmosphere of New England had cramped her hand, and dimmed the glowing colors of her fancy. But observing her uncle's steadfast gaze, which appeared to search through the mist of years to discover the subject of the picture, her curiosity was excited.

"Is it known, my dear uncle," inquired she, "what this old picture once represented? Possibly, could it be made visible, it might prove a masterpiece of some great artist—else, why has it so long held such a conspicuous place?"

As her uncle, contrary to his usual custom (for he was as attentive to all the humors and caprices of Alice as if she had been his own best-beloved child), did not immediately reply, the young Captain of Castle William took that office upon himself.

"This dark old square of canvas, my fair cousin," said he, "has been an heirloom in the Province House from time immemorial. As to the painter, I can tell you nothing; but, if half the stories told of it be true, not one of the great Italian masters has ever produced so marvellous a piece of work as that before you."

Captain Lincoln proceeded to relate some of the strange fables and fantasies which, as it was impossible to refute them by ocular demonstration, had grown to be articles of popular belief, in reference to this old picture. One of the wildest, and at the same time the best accredited, accounts, stated it to be an original and authentic portrait of the Evil One, taken at a witch meeting near Salem; and that its strong and terrible resemblance had been confirmed by several of the confessing wizards and witches, at their trial, in open court. It was likewise affirmed that a familiar spirit or demon abode behind the blackness of the picture, and had shown himself, at seasons of public calamity, to more than one of the royal governors. Shirley, for instance, had beheld this ominous apparition, on the eve of General Abercrombie's shameful and bloody defeat under the walls of Ticonderoga. Many of the servants of the Province House had caught glimpses of a visage frowning down upon them, at morning or evening twilight,—or in the depths of night, while raking up the fire that glimmered on the hearth beneath; although, if any were bold enough to hold a torch before the picture, it would appear as black and undistinguishable as ever. The oldest inhabitant of Boston recollected that his father, in whose days the portrait had not wholly faded out of sight, had once looked upon it, but would never suffer himself to be questioned as to the face which was there represented. In connection with such stories, it was remarkable that over the top of the frame there were some ragged remnants of black silk, indicating that a veil had formerly hung down before the picture, until the duskiness of time had so effectually concealed it. But, after all, it was the most singular part of the affair that so many of the pompous governors of Massachusetts had allowed the obliterated picture to remain in the state chamber of the Province House.

"Some of these fables are really awful," observed Alice Vane, who had occasionally shuddered, as well as smiled, while her cousin spoke. "It would be almost worth while to wipe away the black surface of the canvas, since the original picture can hardly be so formidable as those which fancy paints instead of it."

"But would it be possible," inquired her cousin, "to restore this dark picture to its pristine hues?"

"Such arts are known in Italy," said Alice.

The Lieutenant-Governor had roused himself from his abstracted mood, and listened with a smile to the conversation of his young relatives. Yet his voice had something peculiar in its tones when he undertook the explanation of the mystery.

"I am sorry, Alice, to destroy your faith in the legends of which you are so fond," remarked he; "but my antiquarian researches have long since made me acquainted with the subject of this picture—if picture it can be called—which is no more visible, nor ever will be, than the face of the long buried man whom it once represented. It was the portrait of Edward Randolph, the founder of this house, a person famous in the history of New England."

"Of that Edward Randolph," exclaimed Captain Lincoln, "who obtained the repeal of the first provincial charter, under which our forefathers had enjoyed almost democratic privileges! He that was styled the arch-enemy of New England, and whose memory is still held in detestation as the destroyer of our liberties!"

"It was the same Randolph," answered Hutchinson, moving uneasily in his chair. "It was his lot to taste the bitterness of popular odium."

"Our annals tell us," continued the Captain of Castle William, "that the curse of the people followed this Randolph where he went, and wrought evil in all the subsequent events of his life, and that its effect was seen likewise in the manner of his death. They say, too, that the inward misery of that curse worked itself outward, and was visible on the wretched man's countenance, making it too horrible to be looked upon. If so, and if this picture truly represented his aspect, it was in mercy that the cloud of blackness has gathered over it."

"These traditions are folly to one who has proved, as I have, how little of historic truth lies at the bottom," said the Lieutenant-Governor. "As regards the life and character of Edward Randolph, too implicit credence has been given to Dr. Cotton Mather, who—I must say it, though some of his blood runs in my veins—has filled our early history with old women's tales, as fanciful and extravagant as those of Greece or Rome."

"And yet," whispered Alice Vane, "may not such fables have a moral? And, methinks, if the visage of this portrait be so dreadful, it is not without a cause that it has hung so long in a chamber of the Province House. When the rulers feel themselves irresponsible, it were well that they should be reminded of the awful weight of a people's curse."

The Lieutenant-Governor started, and gazed for a moment at his niece, as if her girlish fantasies had struck upon some feeling in his own breast, which all his policy or principles could not entirely subdue. He knew, indeed, that Alice, in spite of her foreign education, retained the native sympathies of a New England girl.

"Peace, silly child," cried he, at last, more harshly than he had ever before addressed the gentle Alice. "The rebuke of a king is more to be dreaded than the clamor of a wild, misguided multitude. Captain Lincoln, it is decided. The fortress of Castle William must be occupied by the royal troops. The two remaining regiments shall be billeted in the town, or encamped upon the Common. It is time, after years of tumult, and almost rebellion, that his majesty's government should have a wall of strength about it."

"Trust, sir—trust yet awhile to the loyalty of the people," said Captain Lincoln; "nor teach them that they can ever be on other terms with British soldiers than those of brotherhood, as when they fought side by side through the French War. Do not convert the streets of your native town into a camp. Think twice before you give up old Castle William, the key of the province, into other keeping than that of true-born New Englanders."

"Young man, it is decided," repeated Hutchinson, rising from his chair. "A British officer will be in attendance this evening, to receive the necessary instructions for the disposal of the troops. Your presence also will be required. Till then, farewell."

With these words the Lieutenant-Governor hastily left the room, while Alice and her cousin more slowly followed, whispering together, and once pausing to glance back at the mysterious picture. The Captain of Castle William fancied that the girl's air and mien were such as might have belonged to one of those spirits of fable—fairies, or creatures of a more antique mythology—who sometimes mingled their agency with mortal affairs, half in caprice, yet with a sensibility to human weal or woe. As he held the door for her to pass, Alice beckoned to the picture and smiled.

"Come forth, dark and evil Shape!" cried she. "It is thine hour!"

In the evening, Lieutenant-Governor Hutchinson sat in the same chamber where the foregoing scene had occurred, surrounded by several persons whose various interests had summoned them together. There were the Selectmen of Boston, plain, patriarchal fathers of the people, excellent representatives of the old puritanical founders, whose sombre strength had stamped so deep an impress upon the New England character. Contrasting with these were one or two members of Council, richly dressed in the white wigs, the embroidered waistcoats and other magnificence of the time, and making a somewhat ostentatious display of courtier-like ceremonial. In attendance, likewise, was a major of the British army, awaiting the Lieutenant-Governor's orders for the landing of the troops, which still remained on board the transports. The Captain of Castle William stood beside Hutchinson's chair with folded arms, glancing rather haughtily at the British officer, by whom he was soon to be superseded in his command. On a table, in the centre of the chamber, stood a branched silver candlestick, throwing down the glow of half a dozen wax-lights upon a paper apparently ready for the Lieutenant-Governor's signature.

Partly shrouded in the voluminous folds of one of the window curtains, which fell from the ceiling to the floor, was seen the white drapery of a lady's robe. It may appear strange that Alice Vane should have been there at such a time; but there was something so childlike, so wayward, in her singular character, so apart from ordinary rules, that her presence did not surprise the few who noticed it. Meantime, the chairman of the Selectmen was addressing to the Lieutenant-Governor a long and solemn protest against the reception of the British troops into the town.

"And if your Honor," concluded this excellent but somewhat prosy old gentleman, "shall see fit to persist in bringing these mercenary sworders and musketeers into our quiet streets, not on our heads be the responsibility. Think, sir, while there is yet time, that if one drop of blood be shed, that blood shall be an eternal stain upon your Honor's memory. You, sir, have written with an able pen the deeds of our forefathers. The more to be desired is it, therefore, that yourself should deserve honorable mention, as a true patriot and upright ruler, when your own doings shall be written down in history."

"I am not insensible, my good sir, to the natural desire to stand well in the annals of my country," replied Hutchinson, controlling his impatience into courtesy, "nor know I any better method of attaining that end than by withstanding the merely temporary spirit of mischief, which, with your pardon, seems to have infected elder men than myself. Would you have me wait till the mob shall sack the Province House, as they did my private mansion? Trust me, sir, the time may come when you will be glad to flee for protection to the king's banner, the raising of which is now so distasteful to you."

"Yes," said the British major, who was impatiently expecting the Lieu-tenant-Governor's orders. "The demagogues of this Province have raised the devil and cannot lay him again. We will exorcise him, in God's name and the king's."

"If you meddle with the devil, take care of his claws!" answered the Captain of Castle William, stirred by the taunt against his countrymen.

"Craving your pardon, young sir," said the venerable Selectman, "let not an evil spirit enter into your words. We will strive against the oppres-sor with prayer and fasting, as our forefathers would have done. Like them, moreover, we will submit to whatever lot a wise Providence may send us,—always, after our own best exertions to amend it."

"And there peep forth the devil's claws!" muttered Hutchinson, who well understood the nature of Puritan submission. "This matter shall be expedited forthwith. When there shall be a sentinel at every corner, and a court of guard before the town house, a loyal gentleman may venture to walk abroad. What to me is the outcry of a mob, in this remote province of the realm? The king is my master, and England is my country! Upheld by their armed strength, I set my foot upon the rabble, and defy them!"

He snatched a pen, and was about to affix his signature to the paper that lay on the table, when the Captain of Castle William placed his hand upon his shoulder. The freedom of the action, so contrary to the cere-monious respect which was then considered due to rank and dignity, awakened general surprise, and in none more than in the Lieutenant-Gov-ernor himself. Looking angrily up, he perceived that his young relative was pointing his finger to the opposite wall. Hutchinson's eye followed the signal; and he saw, what had hitherto been unobserved, that a black silk curtain was suspended before the mysterious picture, so as completely to conceal it. His thoughts immediately recurred to the scene of the preced-ing afternoon; and, in his surprise, confused by indistinct emotions, yet sensible that his niece must have had an agency in this phenomenon, he called loudly upon her.

"Alice!—come hither, Alice!"

No sooner had he spoken than Alice Vane glided from her station, and pressing one hand across her eyes, with the other snatched away the sable curtain that concealed the portrait. An exclamation of surprise burst from every beholder; but the Lieutenant-Governor's voice had a tone of horror.

"By Heaven!" said he, in a low, inward murmur, speaking rather to himself than to those around him, "if the spirit of Edward Randolph were to appear among us from the place of torment, he could not wear more of the terrors of hell upon his face!"

"For some wise end," said the aged Selectman, solemnly, "hath Provi-dence scattered away the mist of years that had so long hid this dreadful effigy. Until this hour no living man hath seen what we behold!"

Within the antique frame, which so recently had inclosed a sable waste of canvas, now appeared a visible picture, still dark, indeed, in its hues and shadings, but thrown forward in strong relief. It was a half-length figure of a gentleman in a rich but very old-fashioned dress of embroidered velvet, with a broad ruff and a beard, and wearing a hat, the brim of which overshadowed his forehead. Beneath this cloud the eyes had a peculiar glare, which was almost lifelike. The whole portrait started so distinctly out of the background, that it had the effect of a person looking down from the wall at the astonished and awe-stricken spectators. The expression of the face, if any words can convey an idea of it, was that of a wretch detected in some hideous guilt, and exposed to the bitter hatred and laughter and withering scorn of a vast surrounding multitude. There was the struggle of defiance, beaten down and overwhelmed by the crushing weight of ignominy. The torture of the soul had come forth upon the countenance. It seemed as if the picture, while hidden behind the cloud of immemorial years, had been all the time acquiring an intenser depth and darkness of expression, till now it gloomed forth again, and threw its evil omen over the present hour. Such, if the wild legend may be credited, was the portrait of Edward Randolph, as he appeared when a people's curse had wrought its influence upon his nature.

" 'T would drive me mad—that awful face!" said Hutchinson, who seemed fascinated by the contemplation of it.

"Be warned, then!" whispered Alice. "He trampled on a people's rights. Behold his punishment—and avoid a crime like his!"

The Lieutenant-Governor actually trembled for an instant; but, exerting his energy—which was not, however, his most characteristic feature —he strove to shake off the spell of Randolph's countenance.

"Girl!" cried he, laughing bitterly as he turned to Alice, "have you brought hither your painter's art—your Italian spirit of intrigue—your tricks of stage effect—and think to influence the councils of rulers and the affairs of nations by such shallow contrivances? See here!"

"Stay yet a while," said the Selectman, as Hutchinson again snatched the pen; "for if ever mortal man received a warning from a tormented soul, your Honor is that man!"

"Away!" answered Hutchinson fiercely. "Though yonder senseless picture cried 'Forbear!'—it should not move me!"

Casting a scowl of defiance at the pictured face (which seemed at that moment to intensify the horror of its miserable and wicked look), he scrawled on the paper, in characters that betokened it a deed of desperation, the name of Thomas Hutchinson. Then, it is said, he shuddered, as if that signature had granted away his salvation.

"It is done," said he; and placed his hand upon his brow.

"May Heaven forgive the deed," said the soft, sad accents of Alice Vane, like the voice of a good spirit flitting away.

When morning came there was a stifled whisper through the household, and spreading thence about the town, that the dark, mysterious picture had started from the wall, and spoken face to face with Lieutenant-Governor Hutchinson. If such a miracle had been wrought, however, no traces of it remained behind, for within the antique frame nothing could be discerned save the impenetrable cloud, which had covered the canvas since the memory of man. If the figure had, indeed, stepped forth, it had fled back, spirit-like, at the daydawn, and hidden itself behind a century's obscurity. The truth probably was, that Alice Vane's secret for restoring the hues of the picture had merely effected a temporary renovation. But those who, in that brief interval, had beheld the awful visage of Edward Randolph, desired no second glance, and ever afterwards trembled at the recollection of the scene, as if an evil spirit had appeared visibly among them. And as for Hutchinson, when, far over the ocean, his dying hour drew on, he gasped for breath, and complained that he was choking with the blood of the Boston Massacre; and Francis Lincoln, the former Captain of Castle William, who was standing at his bedside, perceived a likeness in his frenzied look to that of Edward Randolph. Did his broken spirit feel, at that dread hour, the tremendous burden of a People's curse?

---

At the conclusion of this miraculous legend, I inquired of mine host whether the picture still remained in the chamber over our heads; but Mr. Tiffany informed me that it had long since been removed, and was supposed to be hidden in some out-of-the-way corner of the New England Museum. Perchance some curious antiquary may light upon it there, and, with the assistance of Mr. Howorth, the picture cleaner, may supply a not unnecessary proof of the authenticity of the facts here set down. During the progress of the story a storm had been gathering abroad, and raging and rattling so loudly in the upper regions of the Province House, that it seemed as if all the old governors and great men were running riot above stairs while Mr. Bela Tiffany babbled of them below. In the course of generations, when many people have lived and died in an ancient house, the whistling of the wind through its crannies, and the creaking of its beams and rafters, become strangely like the tones of the human voice, or thundering laughter, or heavy footsteps treading the deserted chambers. It is as if the echoes of half a century were revived. Such were the ghostly sounds that roared and murmured in our ears when I took leave of the circle round the fireside of the Province House, and plunging down the door steps, fought my way homeward against a drifting snow-storm.

## LEGENDS OF THE PROVINCE HOUSE

### III

#### LADY ELEANORE'S MANTLE

MINE excellent friend, the landlord of the Province House, was pleased, the other evening, to invite Mr. Tiffany and myself to an oyster supper. This slight mark of respect and gratitude, as he handsomely observed, was far less than the ingenious tale-teller, and I, the humble note-taker of his narratives, had fairly earned, by the public notice which our joint lucubrations had attracted to his establishment. Many a cigar had been smoked within his premises—many a glass of wine, or more potent aqua vitæ, had been quaffed—many a dinner had been eaten by curious strangers, who, save for the fortunate conjunction of Mr. Tiffany and me, would never have ventured through that darksome avenue which gives access to the historic precincts of the Province House. In short, if any credit be due to the courteous assurances of Mr. Thomas Waite, we had brought his forgotten mansion almost as effectually into public view as if we had thrown down the vulgar range of shoe shops and dry goods stores, which hides its aristocratic front from Washington Street. It may be unadvisable, however, to speak too loudly of the increased custom of the house, lest Mr. Waite should find it difficult to renew the lease on so favorable terms as heretofore.

Being thus welcomed as benefactors, neither Mr. Tiffany nor myself felt any scruple in doing full justice to the good things that were set before us. If the feast were less magnificent than those same panelled walls had witnessed in a by-gone century,—if mine host presided with somewhat less of state than might have befitted a successor of the royal Governors,—if the guests made a less imposing show than the bewigged and powdered and embroidered dignitaries, who erst banqueted at the gubernatorial table, and now sleep, within their armorial tombs on Copp's Hill, or round King's Chapel,—yet never, I may boldly say, did a more comfortable little party assemble in the Province House, from Queen Anne's days to the Revolution. The occasion was rendered more interesting by the presence of a venerable personage, whose own actual reminiscences went back to the epoch of Gage and Howe, and even supplied him with a doubtful anecdote or two of Hutchinson. He was one of that small, and now all but extinguished, class, whose attachment to royalty, and to the colonial institutions and customs that were connected with it, had never yielded to the democratic heresies of after times. The young queen of Britain has not a more loyal subject in her realm—perhaps not one who would kneel before her throne with such reverential love—as this old grandsire, whose head has whitened beneath the mild sway of the Republic, which still, in his mellower moments, he terms a usurpation. Yet prejudices so obstinate have not made him an ungentle or impracticable companion. If the truth must be told, the life of the aged loyalist has been of such a scrambling and unsettled character,—he has had so little choice of friends and been so often destitute of any,—that I doubt whether he would refuse a cup of kindness with either Oliver Cromwell or John Hancock,—to say nothing of any democrat now upon the stage. In another paper of this series I may perhaps give the reader a closer glimpse of his portrait.

Our host, in due season, uncorked a bottle of Madeira, of such exquisite perfume and admirable flavor that he surely must have discovered it in an ancient bin, down deep beneath the deepest cellar, where some jolly old butler stored away the Governor's choicest wine, and forgot to reveal the secret on his death-bed. Peace to his red-nosed ghost, and a libation to his memory! This precious liquor was imbibed by Mr. Tiffany with peculiar zest; and after sipping the third glass, it was his pleasure to give us one of the oddest legends which he had yet raked from the storehouse where he keeps such matters. With some suitable adornments from my own fancy, it ran pretty much as follows.

---

Not long after Colonel Shute had assumed the government of Massachusetts Bay, now nearly a hundred and twenty years ago, a young lady of rank and fortune arrived from England, to claim his protection as her guardian. He was her distant relative, but the nearest who had survived the gradual extinction of her family; so that no more eligible shelter could be found for the rich and high-born Lady Eleanore Rochcliffe than within the Province House of a transatlantic colony. The consort of Governor Shute, moreover, had been as a mother to her childhood, and was now anxious to receive her, in the hope that a beautiful young woman would be exposed to infinitely less peril from the primitive society of New England than amid the artifices and corruptions of a court. If either the Governor or his lady had especially consulted their own comfort, they would probably have sought to devolve the responsibility on other hands; since, with some noble and splendid traits of character, Lady Eleanore was remarkable for a harsh, unyielding pride, a haughty consciousness of her hereditary and personal advantages, which made her almost incapable of control. Judging from many traditionary anecdotes, this peculiar temper was hardly less than a monomania; or, if the acts which it inspired were those of a sane person, it seemed due from Providence that pride so sinful should be followed by as severe a retribution. That tinge of the marvellous, which is thrown over so many of these half-forgotten legends, has probably imparted an additional wildness to the strange story of Lady Eleanore Rochcliffe.

The ship in which she came passenger had arrived at Newport, whence Lady Eleanore was conveyed to Boston in the Governor's coach, attended by a small escort of gentlemen on horseback. The ponderous equipage, with its four black horses, attracted much notice as it rumbled through Cornhill, surrounded by the prancing steeds of half a dozen cavaliers, with swords dangling to their stirrups and pistols at their holsters. Through the large glass windows of the coach, as it rolled along, the people could discern the figure of Lady Eleanore, strangely combining an almost queenly stateliness with the grace and beauty of a maiden in her teens. A singular tale had gone abroad among the ladies of the province, that their fair rival was indebted for much of the irresistible charm of her appearance to a certain article of dress—an embroidered mantle—which had been wrought by the most skilful artist in London, and possessed even magical properties of adornment. On the present occasion, however, she owed nothing to the witchery of dress, being clad in a riding habit of velvet, which would have appeared stiff and ungraceful on any other form.

The coachman reined in his four black steeds, and the whole cavalcade came to a pause in front of the contorted iron balustrade that fenced the Province House from the public street. It was an awkward coincidence that the bell of the Old South was just then tolling for a funeral; so that, instead of a gladsome peal with which it was customary to announce the arrival of distinguished strangers, Lady Eleanore Rochcliffe was ushered by a doleful clang, as if calamity had come embodied in her beautiful person.

"A very great disrespect!" exclaimed Captain Langford, an English officer, who had recently brought dispatches to Governor Shute. "The funeral should have been deferred, lest Lady Eleanore's spirits be affected by such a dismal welcome."

"With your pardon, sir," replied Doctor Clarke, a physician, and a famous champion of the popular party, "whatever the heralds may pretend, a dead beggar must have precedence of a living queen. King Death confers high privileges."

These remarks were interchanged while the speakers waited a passage through the crowd, which had gathered on each side of the gateway, leaving an open avenue to the portal of the Province House. A black slave in livery now leaped from behind the coach, and threw open the door; while at the same moment Governor Shute descended the flight of steps from his mansion, to assist Lady Eleanore in alighting. But the Governor's stately approach was anticipated in a manner that excited general astonishment. A pale young man, with his black hair all in disorder, rushed from the throng, and prostrated himself beside the coach, thus offering his person as a footstool for Lady Eleanore Rochcliffe to tread upon. She held back an instant, yet with an expression as if doubting whether the young man were worthy to bear the weight of her footstep, rather than dissatisfied to receive such awful reverence from a fellow-mortal.

"Up, sir," said the Governor, sternly, at the same time lifting his cane over the intruder. "What means the Bedlamite by this freak?"

"Nay," answered Lady Eleanore playfully, but with more scorn than pity in her tone, "your Excellency shall not strike him. When men seek only to be trampled upon, it were a pity to deny them a favor so easily granted—and so well deserved!"

Then, though as lightly as a sunbeam on a cloud, she placed her foot upon the cowering form, and extended her hand to meet that of the Governor. There was a brief interval, during which Lady Eleanore retained this attitude; and never, surely, was there an apter emblem of aristocracy and hereditary pride trampling on human sympathies and the kindred of nature, than these two figures presented at that moment. Yet the spectators were so smitten with her beauty, and so essential did pride seem to the existence of such a creature, that they gave a simultaneous acclamation of applause.

"Who is this insolent young fellow?" inquired Captain Langford, who still remained beside Doctor Clarke. "If he be in his senses, his impertinence demands the bastinado. If mad, Lady Eleanore should be secured from further inconvenience, by his confinement."

"His name is Jervase Helwyse," answered the Doctor; "a youth of no birth or fortune, or other advantages, save the mind and soul that nature gave him; and being secretary to our colonial agent in London, it was his misfortune to meet this Lady Eleanore Rochcliffe. He loved her—and her scorn has driven him mad."

"He was mad so to aspire," observed the English officer.

"It may be so," said Doctor Clarke, frowning as he spoke. "But I tell you, sir, I could well-nigh doubt the justice of the Heaven above us if no signal humiliation overtake this lady, who now treads so haughtily into yonder mansion. She seeks to place herself above the sympathies of our common nature, which envelops all human souls. See, if that nature do not assert its claim over her in some mode that shall bring her level with the lowest!"

"Never!" cried Captain Langford indignantly—"neither in life, nor when they lay her with her ancestors."

Not many days afterwards the Governor gave a ball in honor of Lady Eleanore Rochcliffe. The principal gentry of the colony received invitations, which were distributed to their residences, far and near, by messengers on horseback, bearing missives sealed with all the formality of official dispatches. In obedience to the summons, there was a general gathering of rank, wealth, and beauty; and the wide door of the Province House had seldom given admittance to more numerous and honorable guests than on the evening of Lady Eleanore's ball. Without much extravagance of eulogy, the spectacle might even be termed splendid; for, according to the fashion of the times, the ladies shone in rich silks and satins, outspread over wide-projecting hoops; and the gentlemen glittered in gold embroidery, laid unsparingly upon the purple, or scarlet, or sky-blue velvet, which was the material of their coats and waistcoats. The latter article of dress was of great importance, since it enveloped the wearer's body nearly to the knees, and was perhaps bedizened with the amount of his whole year's income, in golden flowers and foliage. The altered taste of the present day—a taste symbolic of a deep change in the whole system of society—would look upon almost any of those gorgeous figures as ridiculous; although that evening the guests sought their reflections in the pier-glasses, and rejoiced to catch their own glitter amid the glittering crowd. What a pity that one of the stately mirrors has not preserved a picture of the scene, which, by the very traits that were so transitory, might have taught us much that would be worth knowing and remembering!

Would, at least, that either painter or mirror could convey to us some faint idea of a garment, already noticed in this legend,—the Lady Eleanore's embroidered mantle,—which the gossips whispered was invested with magic properties, so as to lend a new and untried grace to her figure each time that she put it on! Idle fancy as it is, this mysterious mantle has thrown an awe around my image of her, partly from its fabled virtues, and partly because it was the handiwork of a dying woman, and, perchance, owed the fantastic grace of its conception to the delirium of approaching death.

After the ceremonial greetings had been paid, Lady Eleanore Rochcliffe stood apart from the mob of guests, insulating herself within a small and distinguished circle, to whom she accorded a more cordial favor than to the general throng. The waxen torches threw their radiance vividly over the scene, bringing out its brilliant points in strong relief; but she gazed carelessly, and with now and then an expression of weariness or scorn, tempered with such feminine grace that her auditors scarcely perceived the moral deformity of which it was the utterance. She beheld the spectacle not with vulgar ridicule, as disdaining to be pleased with the provincial mockery of a court festival, but with the deeper scorn of one whose spirit held itself too high to participate in the enjoyment of other human souls. Whether or no the recollections of those who saw her that evening were influenced by the strange events with which she was subsequently connected, so it was that her figure ever after recurred to them as marked by something wild and unnatural,—although, at the time, the general whisper was of her exceeding beauty, and of the indescribable charm which her mantle threw around her. Some close observers, indeed, detected a feverish flush and alternate paleness of countenance, with corresponding flow and revulsion of spirits, and once or twice a painful and helpless betrayal of lassitude, as if she were on the point of sinking to the ground. Then, with a nervous shudder, she seemed to arouse her energies and threw some bright and playful yet half-wicked sarcasm into the conversation. There was so strange a characteristic in her manners and sentiments that it astonished every right-minded listener; till looking in her face, a lurking and incomprehensible glance and smile perplexed them with doubts both as to her seriousness and sanity. Gradually, Lady Eleanore Rochcliffe's circle grew smaller, till only four gentlemen remained in it. These were Captain Langford, the English officer before mentioned; a Virginian planter, who had come to Massachusetts on some political errand; a young Episcopal clergyman, the grandson of a British earl; and, lastly, the private secretary of Governor Shute, whose obsequiousness had won a sort of tolerance from Lady Eleanore.

At different periods of the evening the liveried servants of the Province House passed among the guests, bearing huge trays of refreshments and French and Spanish wines. Lady Eleanore Rochcliffe, who refused to wet her beautiful lips even with a bubble of Champagne, had sunk back into a large damask chair, apparently overwearied either with the excitement of the scene or its tedium, and while, for an instant, she was unconscious of voices, laughter and music, a young man stole forward, and knelt down at her feet. He bore a salver in his hand, on which was a chased silver goblet, filled to the brim with wine, which he offered as reverentially as to a crowned queen, or rather with the awful devotion of a priest doing sacrifice to his idol. Conscious that some one touched her robe, Lady Eleanore started, and unclosed her eyes upon the pale, wild features and dishevelled hair of Jervase Helwyse.

"Why do you haunt me thus?" said she, in a languid tone, but with a kindlier feeling than she ordinarily permitted herself to express. "They tell me that I have done you harm."

"Heaven knows if that be so," replied the young man solemnly. "But, Lady Eleanore, in requital of that harm, if such there be, and for your own earthly and heavenly welfare, I pray you to take one sip of this holy wine, and then to pass the goblet round among the guests. And this shall be a symbol that you have not sought to withdraw yourself from the chain of human sympathies—which whoso would shake off must keep company with fallen angels."

"Where has this mad fellow stolen that sacramental vessel?" exclaimed the Episcopal clergyman.

This question drew the notice of the guests to the silver cup, which was recognized as appertaining to the communion plate of the Old South Church; and, for aught that could be known, it was brimming over with the consecrated wine.

"Perhaps it is poisoned," half whispered the Governor's secretary.

"Pour it down the villain's throat!" cried the Virginian fiercely.

"Turn him out of the house!" cried Captain Langford, seizing Jervase Helwyse so roughly by the shoulder that the sacramental cup was overturned, and its contents sprinkled upon Lady Eleanore's mantle. "Whether knave, fool, or Bedlamite, it is intolerable that the fellow should go at large."

"Pray, gentlemen, do my poor admirer no harm," said Lady Eleanore, with a faint and weary smile. "Take him out of my sight, if such be your pleasure; for I can find in my heart to do nothing but laugh at him; whereas, in all decency and conscience, it would become me to weep for the mischief I have wrought!"

But while the by-standers were attempting to lead away the unfortunate young man, he broke from them, and with a wild, impassioned earnestness, offered a new and equally strange petition to Lady Eleanore. It was no other than that she should throw off the mantle, which, while he pressed the silver cup of wine upon her, she had drawn more closely around her form, so as almost to shroud herself within it.

"Cast it from you!" exclaimed Jervase Helwyse, clasping his hands in an agony of entreaty. "It may not yet be too late! Give the accursed garment to the flames!"

But Lady Eleanore, with a laugh of scorn, drew the rich folds of the embroidered mantle over her head, in such a fashion as to give a completely new aspect to her beautiful face, which—half hidden, half revealed—seemed to belong to some being of mysterious character and purposes.

"Farewell, Jervase Helwyse!" said she. "Keep my image in your remembrance, as you behold it now."

"Alas, lady!" he replied, in a tone no longer wild, but sad as a funeral bell. "We must meet shortly, when your face may wear another aspect— and that shall be the image that must abide within me."

He made no more resistance to the violent efforts of the gentlemen and servants, who almost dragged him out of the apartment, and dismissed him roughly from the iron gate of the Province House. Captain Langford, who had been very active in this affair, was returning to the presence of Lady Eleanore Rochcliffe, when he encountered the physician, Doctor Clarke, with whom he had held some casual talk on the day of her arrival. The Doctor stood apart, separated from Lady Eleanore by the width of the room, but eying her with such keen sagacity that Captain Langford involuntarily gave him credit for the discovery of some deep secret.

"You appear to be smitten, after all, with the charms of this queenly maiden," said he, hoping thus to draw forth the physician's hidden knowledge.

"God forbid!" answered Doctor Clarke, with a grave smile; "and if you be wise you will put up the same prayer for yourself. Woe to those who shall be smitten by this beautiful Lady Eleanore! But yonder stands the Governor—and I have a word or two for his private ear. Good night!"

He accordingly advanced to Governor Shute, and addressed him in so low a tone that none of the by-standers could catch a word of what he said, although the sudden change of his Excellency's hitherto cheerful visage betokened that the communication could be of no agreeable import. A very few moments afterwards it was announced to the guests that an unforeseen circumstance rendered it necessary to put a premature close to the festival.

The ball at the Province House supplied a topic of conversation for the colonial metropolis for some days after its occurrence, and might still longer have been the general theme, only that a subject of all-engrossing interest thrust it, for a time, from the public recollection. This was the appearance of a dreadful epidemic, which, in that age and long before and afterwards, was wont to slay its hundreds and thousands on both sides of the Atlantic. On the occasion of which we speak, it was distinguished by a peculiar virulence, insomuch that it has left its traces—its pit-marks, to use an appropriate figure—on the history of the country, the affairs of which were thrown into confusion by its ravages. At first, unlike its ordinary course, the disease seemed to confine itself to the higher circles of society, selecting its victims from among the proud, the well-born, and the wealthy, entering unabashed into stately chambers, and lying down with the slumberers in silken beds. Some of the most distinguished guests of the Province House—even those whom the haughty Lady Eleanore Rochcliffe had deemed not unworthy of her favor—were stricken by this fatal scourge. It was noticed, with an ungenerous bitterness of feeling, that the four gentlemen—the Virginian, the British officer, the young clergyman, and the Governor's secretary—who had been her most devoted attendants on the evening of the ball, were the foremost on whom the plague stroke fell. But the disease, pursuing its onward progress, soon ceased to be exclusively a prerogative of aristocracy. Its red brand was no longer conferred like a noble's star, or an order of knighthood. It threaded its way through the narrow and crooked streets, and entered the low, mean, darksome dwellings, and laid its hand of death upon the artisans and laboring classes of the town. It compelled rich and poor to feel themselves brethren then; and stalking to and fro across the Three Hills, with a fierceness which made it almost a new pestilence, there was that mighty conqueror—that scourge and horror of our forefathers—the Small-Pox!

We cannot estimate the affright which this plague inspired of yore, by contemplating it as the fangless monster of the present day. We must remember, rather, with what awe we watched the gigantic footsteps of the Asiatic cholera, striding from shore to shore of the Atlantic, and marching like destiny upon cities far remote which flight had already half depopulated. There is no other fear so horrible and unhumanizing as that which makes man dread to breathe heaven's vital air lest it be poison, or to grasp the hand of a brother or friend lest the gripe of the pestilence should clutch him. Such was the dismay that now followed in the track of the disease, or ran before it throughout the town. Graves were hastily dug, and the pestilential relics as hastily covered, because the dead were enemies of the living, and strove to draw them headlong, as it were, into their own dismal pit. The public councils were suspended, as if mortal wisdom might relinquish its devices, now that an unearthly usurper had found his way into the ruler's mansion. Had an enemy's fleet been hovering on the coast, or his armies trampling on our soil, the people would probably have committed their defence to that same direful conqueror who had wrought their own calamity, and would permit no interference with his sway. This conquerer had a symbol of his triumphs. It was a blood-red flag, that fluttered in the tainted air, over the door of every dwelling into which the Small-Pox had entered.

Such a banner was long since waving over the portal of the Province House; for thence, as was proved by tracking its footsteps back, had all this dreadful mischief issued. It had been traced back to a lady's luxurious chamber—to the proudest of the proud—to her that was so delicate, and hardly owned herself of earthly mould—to the haughty one, who took her stand above human sympathies—to Lady Eleanore! There remained no room for doubt that the contagion had lurked in that gorgeous mantle, which threw so strange a grace around her at the festival. Its fantastic splendor had been conceived in the delirious brain of a woman on her death-bed, and was the last toil of her stiffening fingers, which had interwoven fate and misery with its golden threads. This dark tale, whispered at first, was now bruited far and wide. The people raved against the Lady Eleanore, and cried out that her pride and scorn had evoked a fiend, and that, between them both, this monstrous evil had been born. At times, their rage and despair took the semblance of grinning mirth; and whenever the red flag of the pestilence was hoisted over another and yet another door, they clapped their hands and shouted through the streets, in bitter mockery: "Behold a new triumph for the Lady Eleanore!"

One day, in the midst of these dismal times, a wild figure approached the portal of the Province House, and folding his arms, stood contemplating the scarlet banner which a passing breeze shook fitfully, as if to fling abroad the contagion that it typified. At length, climbing one of the pillars by means of the iron balustrade, he took down the flag and entered the mansion, waving it above his head. At the foot of the staircase he met the Governor, booted and spurred, with his cloak drawn around him, evidently on the point of setting forth upon a journey.

"Wretched lunatic, what do you seek here?" exclaimed Shute, extending his cane to guard himself from contact. "There is nothing here but Death. Back—or you will meet him!"

"Death will not touch me, the banner-bearer of the pestilence!" cried Jervase Helwyse, shaking the red flag aloft. "Death, and the Pestilence, who wears the aspect of the Lady Eleanore, will walk through the streets to-night, and I must march before them with this banner!"

"Why do I waste words on the fellow?" muttered the Governor, drawing his cloak across his mouth. "What matters his miserable life, when none of us are sure of twelve hours' breath? On, fool, to your own destruction!"

He made way for Jervase Helwyse, who immediately ascended the staircase, but, on the first landing place, was arrested by the firm grasp of a hand upon his shoulder. Looking fiercely up, with a madman's impulse to struggle with and rend asunder his opponent, he found himself powerless beneath a calm, stern eye, which possessed the mysterious property of quelling frenzy at its height. The person whom he had now encountered was the physician, Doctor Clarke, the duties of whose sad profession had led him to the Province House, where he was an infrequent guest in more prosperous times.

"Young man, what is your purpose?" demanded he.

"I seek the Lady Eleanore," answered Jervase Helwyse, submissively.

"All have fled from her," said the physician. "Why do you seek her now? I tell you, youth, her nurse fell death-stricken on the threshold of that fatal chamber. Know ye not, that never came such a curse to our shores as this lovely Lady Eleanore?—that her breath has filled the air with poison?—that she has shaken pestilence and death upon the land, from the folds of her accursed mantle?"

"Let me look upon her!" rejoined the mad youth, more wildly. "Let me behold her, in her awful beauty, clad in the regal garments of the pestilence! She and Death sit on a throne together. Let me kneel down before them!"

"Poor youth!" said Doctor Clarke; and, moved by a deep sense of human weakness, a smile of caustic humor curled his lip even then. "Wilt thou still worship the destroyer and surround her image with fantasies the more magnificent, the more evil she has wrought? Thus man doth ever to his tyrants. Approach, then! Madness, as I have noted, has that good efficacy, that it will guard you from contagion—and perchance its own cure may be found in yonder chamber."

Ascending another flight of stairs, he threw open a door and signed to Jervase Helwyse that he should enter. The poor lunatic, it seems probable, had cherished a delusion that his haughty mistress sat in state, unharmed herself by the pestilential influence, which, as by enchantment, she scattered round about her. He dreamed, no doubt, that her beauty was not dimmed, but brightened into superhuman splendor. With such anticipations, he stole reverentially to the door at which the physician stood, but paused upon the threshold, gazing fearfully into the gloom of the darkened chamber.

"Where is the Lady Eleanore?" whispered he.

"Call her," replied the physician.

"Lady Eleanore!—Princess!—Queen of Death!" cried Jervase Helwyse, advancing three steps into the chamber. "She is not here! There, on yonder table, I behold the sparkle of a diamond which once she wore upon her bosom. There"—and he shuddered—"there hangs her mantle, on which a dead woman embroidered a spell of dreadful potency. But where is the Lady Eleanore?"

Something stirred within the silken curtains of a canopied bed; and a low moan was uttered, which, listening intently, Jervase Helwyse began to distinguish as a woman's voice, complaining dolefully of thirst. He fancied, even, that he recognized its tones.

"My throat!—my throat is scorched," murmured the voice. "A drop of water!"

"What thing art thou?" said the brain-stricken youth, drawing near the bed and tearing asunder its curtains. "Whose voice hast thou stolen for thy murmurs and miserable petitions, as if Lady Eleanore could be conscious of mortal infirmity? Fie! Heap of diseased mortality, why lurkest thou in my lady's chamber?"

"O Jervase Helwyse," said the voice—and as it spoke the figure contorted itself, struggling to hide its blasted face—"look not now on the woman you once loved! The curse of Heaven hath stricken me, because I would not call man my brother, nor woman sister. I wrapped myself in PRIDE as in a MANTLE, and scorned the sympathies of nature; and therefore has nature made this wretched body the medium of a dreadful sympathy. You are avenged—they are all avenged—Nature is avenged—for I am Eleanore Rochcliffe!"

The malice of his mental disease, the bitterness lurking at the bottom of his heart, mad as he was, for a blighted and ruined life, and love that had been paid with cruel scorn, awoke within the breast of Jervase Helwyse. He shook his finger at the wretched girl, and the chamber echoed, the curtains of the bed were shaken, with his outburst of insane merriment.

"Another triumph for the Lady Eleanore!" he cried. "All have been her victims! Who so worthy to be the final victim as herself?"

Impelled by some new fantasy of his crazed intellect, he snatched the fatal mantle and rushed from the chamber and the house. That night a procession passed, by torchlight, through the streets, bearing in the midst the figure of a woman, enveloped with a richly embroidered mantle; while in advance stalked Jervase Helwyse, waving the red flag of the pestilence. Arriving opposite the Province House, the mob burned the effigy, and a strong wind came and swept away the ashes. It was said that, from that very hour, the pestilence abated, as if its sway had some mysterious connection, from the first plague stroke to the last, with Lady Eleanore's Mantle. A remarkable uncertainty broods over that unhappy lady's fate. There is a belief, however, that in a certain chamber of this mansion a female form may sometimes be duskily discerned, shrinking into the darkest corner and muffling her face within an embroidered mantle. Supposing the legend true, can this be other than the once proud Lady Eleanore?

Mine host and the old loyalist and I bestowed no little warmth of applause upon this narrative, in which we had all been deeply interested; for the reader can scarcely conceive how unspeakably the effect of such a tale is heightened when, as in the present case, we may repose perfect confidence in the veracity of him who tells it. For my own part, knowing how scrupulous is Mr. Tiffany to settle the foundation of his facts, I could not have believed him one whit the more faithfully had he professed himself an eye-witness of the doings and sufferings of poor Lady Eleanore. Some sceptics, it is true, might demand documentary evidence, or even require him to produce the embroidered mantle, forgetting that—Heaven be praised—it was consumed to ashes. But now the old loyalist, whose blood was warmed by the good cheer, began to talk, in his turn, about the traditions of the Province House, and hinted that he, if it were agreeable, might add a few reminiscences to our legendary stock. Mr. Tiffany, having no cause to dread a rival, immediately besought him to favor us with a specimen; my own entreaties, of course, were urged to the same effect; and our venerable guest, well pleased to find willing auditors, awaited only the return of Mr. Thomas Waite, who had been summoned forth to provide accommodations for several new arrivals. Perchance the public— but be this as its own caprice and ours shall settle the matter—may read the result in another Tale of the Province House.

## LEGENDS OF THE PROVINCE HOUSE

### IV

#### OLD ESTHER DUDLEY

OUR host having resumed the chair, he, as well as Mr. Tiffany and myself, expressed much eagerness to be made acquainted with the story to which the loyalist had alluded. That venerable man first of all saw fit to moisten his throat with another glass of wine, and then, turning his face towards our coal fire, looked steadfastly for a few moments into the depths of its cheerful glow. Finally, he poured forth a great fluency of speech. The generous liquid that he had imbibed, while it warmed his age-chilled blood, likewise took off the chill from his heart and mind, and gave him an energy to think and feel, which we could hardly have expected to find beneath the snows of fourscore winters. His feelings, indeed, appeared to me more excitable than those of a younger man; or at least, the same degree of feeling manifested itself by more visible effects than if his judgment and will had possessed the potency of meridian life. At the pathetic passages of his narrative he readily melted into tears. When a breath of indignation swept across his spirit the blood flushed his withered visage even to the roots of his white hair; and he shook his clinched fist at the trio of peaceful auditors, seeming to fancy enemies in those who felt very kindly towards the desolate old soul. But ever and anon, sometimes in the midst of his most earnest talk, this ancient person's intellect would wander vaguely, losing its hold of the matter in hand, and groping for it amid misty shadows. Then would he cackle forth a feeble laugh, and express a doubt whether his wits—for by that phrase it pleased our ancient friend to signify his mental powers—were not getting a little the worse for wear.

Under these disadvantages, the old loyalist's story required more revision to render it fit for the public eye than those of the series which have preceded it; nor should it be concealed that the sentiment and tone of the affair may have undergone some slight, or perchance more than slight, metamorphosis, in its transmission to the reader through the medium of a thorough-going democrat. The tale itself is a mere sketch, with no involution of plot, nor any great interest of events, yet possessing, if I have rehearsed it aright, that pensive influence over the mind which the shadow of the old Province House flings upon the loiterer in its court-yard.

---

The hour had come—the hour of defeat and humiliation—when Sir William Howe was to pass over the threshold of the Province House, and embark, with no such triumphal ceremonies as he once promised himself, on board the British fleet. He bade his servants and military attendants go before him, and lingered a moment in the loneliness of the mansion, to quell the fierce emotions that struggled in his bosom as with a death throb. Preferable, then, would he have deemed his fate, had a warrior's death left him a claim to the narrow territory of a grave within the soil which the King had given him to defend. With an ominous perception that, as his departing footsteps echoed adown the staircase, the sway of Britain was passing forever from New England, he smote his clinched hand on his brow, and cursed the destiny that had flung the shame of a dismembered empire upon him.

"Would to God," cried he, hardly repressing his tears of rage, "that the rebels were even now at the doorstep! A blood-stain upon the floor should then bear testimony that the last British ruler was faithful to his trust."

The tremulous voice of a woman replied to his exclamation.

"Heaven's cause and the King's are one," it said. "Go forth, Sir William Howe, and trust in Heaven to bring back a Royal Governor in triumph."

Subduing, at once, the passion to which he had yielded only in the faith that it was unwitnessed, Sir William Howe became conscious that an aged woman, leaning on a gold-headed staff, was standing betwixt him and the door. It was old Esther Dudley, who had dwelt almost immemorial years in this mansion, until her presence seemed as inseparable from it as the recollections of its history. She was the daughter of an ancient and once eminent family, which had fallen into poverty and decay, and left its last descendant no resource save the bounty of the King, nor any shelter except within the walls of the Province House. An office in the household, with merely nominal duties, had been assigned to her as a pretext for the payment of a small pension, the greater part of which she expended in adorning herself with an antique magnificence of attire. The claims of Esther Dudley's gentle blood were acknowledged by all the successive Governors; and they treated her with the punctilious courtesy which it was her foible to demand, not always with success, from a neglectful world. The only actual share which she assumed in the business of the mansion was to glide through its passages and public chambers, late at night, to see that the servants had dropped no fire from their flaring torches, nor left embers crackling and blazing on the hearths. Perhaps it was this invariable custom of walking her rounds in the hush of midnight that caused the superstition of the times to invest the old woman with attributes of awe and mystery; fabling that she had entered the portal of the Province House, none knew whence, in the train of the first Royal Governor, and that it was her fate to dwell there till the last should have departed. But Sir William Howe, if he ever heard this legend, had forgotten it.

"Mistress Dudley, why are you loitering here?" asked he, with some severity of tone. "It is my pleasure to be the last in this mansion of the King."

"Not so, if it please your Excellency," answered the time-stricken woman. "This roof has sheltered me long. I will not pass from it until they bear me to the tomb of my forefathers. What other shelter is there for old Esther Dudley, save the Province House or the grave?"

"Now Heaven forgive me!" said Sir William Howe to himself. "I was about to leave this wretched old creature to starve or beg. Take this, good Mistress Dudley," he added, putting a purse into her hands. "King George's head on these golden guineas is sterling yet, and will continue so, I warrant you, even should the rebels crown John Hancock their king. That purse will buy a better shelter than the Province House can now afford."

"While the burden of life remains upon me, I will have no other shelter than this roof," persisted Esther Dudley, striking her staff upon the floor with a gesture that expressed immovable resolve. "And when your Excellency returns in triumph, I will totter into the porch to welcome you."

"My poor old friend!" answered the British General,—and all his manly and martial pride could no longer restrain a gush of bitter tears. "This is an evil hour for you and me. The Province which the King intrusted to my charge is lost. I go hence in misfortune—perchance in disgrace—to return no more. And you, whose present being is incorporated with the past—who have seen Governor after Governor, in stately pageantry, ascend these steps—whose whole life has been an observance of majestic ceremonies, and a worship of the King—how will you endure the change? Come with us! Bid farewell to a land that has shaken off its allegiance, and live still under a royal government, at Halifax."

"Never, never!" said the pertinacious old dame. "Here will I abide; and King George shall still have one true subject in his disloyal Province."

"Beshrew the old fool!" muttered Sir William Howe, growing impatient of her obstinacy, and ashamed of the emotion into which he had been betrayed. "She is the very moral of old-fashioned prejudice, and could exist nowhere but in this musty edifice. Well, then, Mistress Dudley, since you will needs tarry, I give the Province House in charge to you. Take this key, and keep it safe until myself, or some other Royal Governor, shall demand it of you."

Smiling bitterly at himself and her, he took the heavy key of the Province House, and delivering it into the old lady's hands, drew his cloak around him for departure. As the General glanced back at Esther Dudley's antique figure, he deemed her well fitted for such a charge, as being so perfect a representative of the decayed past—of an age gone by, with its manners, opinions, faith and feelings, all fallen into oblivion or scorn —of what had once been a reality, but was now merely a vision of faded magnificence. Then Sir William Howe strode forth, smiting his clinched hands together, in the fierce anguish of his spirit; and old Esther Dudley was left to keep watch in the lonely Province House, dwelling there with memory; and if Hope ever seemed to flit around her, still was it Memory in disguise.

The total change of affairs that ensued on the departure of the British troops did not drive the venerable lady from her stronghold. There was not, for many years afterwards, a Governor of Massachusetts; and the magistrates, who had charge of such matters, saw no objection to Esther Dudley's residence in the Province House, especially as they must otherwise have paid a hireling for taking care of the premises, which with her was a labor of love. And so they left her the undisturbed mistress of the old historic edifice. Many and strange were the fables which the gossips whispered about her, in all the chimney corners of the town. Among the time-worn articles of furniture that had been left in the mansion there was a tall, antique mirror, which was well worthy of a tale by itself, and perhaps may hereafter be the theme of one. The gold of its heavily-wrought frame was tarnished, and its surface so blurred, that the old woman's figure, whenever she paused before it, looked indistinct and ghost-like. But it was the general belief that Esther could cause the Governors of the overthrown dynasty, with the beautiful ladies who had once adorned their festivals, the Indian chiefs who had come up to the Province House to hold council or swear allegiance, the grim Provincial warriors, the severe clergymen—in short, all the pageantry of gone days—all the figures that ever swept across the broad plate of glass in former times—she could cause the whole to reappear, and people the inner world of the mirror with shadows of old life. Such legends as these, together with the singularity of her isolated existence, her age, and the infirmity that each added winter flung upon her, made Mistress Dudley the object both of fear and pity; and it was partly the result of either sentiment that, amid all the angry license of the times, neither wrong nor insult ever fell upon her unprotected head. Indeed, there was so much haughtiness in her demeanor towards intruders, among whom she reckoned all persons acting under the new authorities, that it was really an affair of no small nerve to look her in the face. And to do the people justice, stern republicans as they had now become, they were well content that the old gentlewoman, in her hoop petticoat and faded embroidery, should still haunt the palace of ruined pride and overthrown power, the symbol of a departed system, embodying a history in her person. So Esther Dudley dwelt year after year in the Province House, still reverencing all that others had flung aside, still faithful to her King, who, so long as the venerable dame yet held her post, might be said to retain one true subject in New England, and one spot of the empire that had been wrested from him.

And did she dwell there in utter loneliness? Rumor said, not so. Whenever her chill and withered heart desired warmth, she was wont to summon a black slave of Governor Shirley's from the blurred mirror, and send him in search of guests who had long ago been familiar in those deserted chambers. Forth went the sable messenger, with the starlight or the moonshine gleaming through him, and did his errand in the burial ground, knocking at the iron doors of tombs, or upon the marble slabs that covered them, and whispering to those within: "My mistress, old Esther Dudley, bids you to the Province House at midnight." And punctually as the clock of the Old South told twelve came the shadows of the Olivers, the Hutchinsons, the Dudleys, all the grandees of a by-gone generation, gliding beneath the portal into the well-known mansion, where Esther mingled with them as if she likewise were a shade. Without vouching for the truth of such traditions, it is certain that Mistress Dudley sometimes assembled a few of the stanch, though crestfallen, old tories, who had lingered in the rebel town during those days of wrath and tribulation. Out of a cobwebbed bottle, containing liquor that a royal Governor might have smacked his lips over, they quaffed healths to the King, and babbled treason to the Republic, feeling as if the protecting shadow of the throne were still flung around them. But, draining the last drops of their liquor, they stole timorously homeward, and answered not again if the rude mob reviled them in the street.

Yet Esther Dudley's most frequent and favored guests were the children of the town. Towards them she was never stern. A kindly and loving nature, hindered elsewhere from its free course by a thousand rocky prejudices, lavished itself upon these little ones. By bribes of gingerbread of her own making, stamped with a royal crown, she tempted their sunny sportiveness beneath the gloomy portal of the Province House, and would often beguile them to spend a whole play-day there, sitting in a circle round the verge of her hoop petticoat, greedily attentive to her stories of a dead world. And when these little boys and girls stole forth again from the dark, mysterious mansion, they went bewildered, full of old feelings that graver people had long ago forgotten, rubbing their eyes at the world around them as if they had gone astray into ancient times, and become children of the past. At home, when their parents asked where they had loitered such a weary while, and with whom they had been at play, the children would talk of all the departed worthies of the Province, as far back as Governor Belcher and the haughty dame of Sir William Phipps. It would seem as though they had been sitting on the knees of these famous personages, whom the grave had hidden for half a century, and had toyed with the embroidery of their rich waistcoats, or roguishly pulled the long curls of their flowing wigs. "But Governor Belcher has been dead this many a year," would the mother say to her little boy. "And did you really see him at the Province House?" "Oh yes, dear mother! yes!" the half-dreaming child would answer. "But when old Esther had done speaking about him he faded away out of his chair." Thus, without affrighting her little guests, she led them by the hand into the chambers of her own desolate heart, and made childhood's fancy discern the ghosts that haunted there.

Living so continually in her own circle of ideas, and never regulating her mind by a proper reference to present things, Esther Dudley appears to have grown partially crazed. It was found that she had no right sense of the progress and true state of the Revolutionary War, but held a constant faith that the armies of Britain were victorious on every field, and destined to be ultimately triumphant. Whenever the town rejoiced for a battle won by Washington, or Gates, or Morgan, or Greene, the news, in passing through the door of the Province House, as through the ivory gate of dreams, became metamorphosed into a strange tale of the prowess of Howe, Clinton, or Cornwallis. Sooner or later it was her invincible belief the colonies would be prostrate at the footstool of the King. Sometimes she seemed to take for granted that such was already the case. On one occasion, she startled the towns-people by a brilliant illumination of the Province House, with candles at every pane of glass, and a transparency of the King's initials and a crown of light in the great balcony window. The figure of the aged woman in the most gorgeous of her mildewed velvets and brocades was seen passing from casement to casement, until she paused before the balcony, and flourished a huge key above her head. Her wrinkled visage actually gleamed with triumph, as if the soul within her were a festal lamp.

"What means this blaze of light? What does old Esther's joy portend?" whispered a spectator. "It is frightful to see her gliding about the chambers, and rejoicing there without a soul to bear her company."

"It is as if she were making merry in a tomb," said another.

"Pshaw! It is no such mystery," observed an old man, after some brief exercise of memory. "Mistress Dudley is keeping jubilee for the King of England's birthday."

Then the people laughed aloud, and would have thrown mud against the blazing transparency of the King's crown and initials, only that they pitied the poor old dame, who was so dismally triumphant amid the wreck and ruin of the system to which she appertained.

Oftentimes it was her custom to climb the weary staircase that wound upward to the cupola, and thence strain her dimmed eyesight seaward and countryward, watching for a British fleet, or for the march of a grand procession, with the King's banner floating over it. The passengers in the street below would discern her anxious visage, and send up a shout, "When the golden Indian on the Province House shall shoot his arrow, and when the cock on the Old South spire shall crow, then look for a Royal Governor again!"—for this had grown a byword through the town. And at last, after long, long years, old Esther Dudley knew, or perchance she only dreamed, that a Royal Governor was on the eve of returning to the Province House, to receive the heavy key which Sir William Howe had committed to her charge. Now it was the fact that intelligence bearing some faint analogy to Esther's version of it was current among the townspeople. She set the mansion in the best order that her means allowed, and, arraying herself in silks and tarnished gold, stood long before the blurred mirror to admire her own magnificence. As she gazed, the gray and withered lady moved her ashen lips, murmuring half aloud, talking to shapes that she saw within the mirror, to shadows of her own fantasies, to the household friends of memory, and bidding them rejoice with her and come forth to meet the Governor. And while absorbed in this communion, Mistress Dudley heard the tramp of many footsteps in the street, and, looking out at the window, beheld what she construed as the Royal Governor's arrival.

"O happy day! O blessed, blessed hour!" she exclaimed. "Let me but bid him welcome within the portal, and my task in the Province House, and on earth, is done!"

Then with tottering feet, which age and tremulous joy caused to tread amiss, she hurried down the grand staircase, her silks sweeping and rustling as she went, so that the sound was as if a train of spectral courtiers were thronging from the dim mirror. And Esther Dudley fancied that as soon as the wide door should be flung open, all the pomp and splendor of by-gone times would pace majestically into the Province House, and the gilded tapestry of the past would be brightened by the sunshine of the present. She turned the key—withdrew it from the lock—unclosed the door—and stepped across the threshold. Advancing up the court-yard appeared a person of most dignified mien, with tokens, as Esther interpreted them, of gentle blood, high rank, and long-accustomed authority, even in his walk and every gesture. He was richly dressed, but wore a gouty shoe, which, however, did not lessen the stateliness of his gait. Around and behind him were people in plain civic dresses, and two or three war-worn veterans, evidently officers of rank, arrayed in a uniform of blue and buff. But Esther Dudley, firm in the belief that had fastened its roots about her heart, beheld only the principal personage, and never doubted that this was the long-looked-for Governor, to whom she was to surrender up her charge. As he approached, she involuntary sank down on her knees and tremblingly held forth the heavy key.

"Receive my trust! take it quickly!" cried she, "for methinks Death is striving to snatch away my triumph. But he comes too late. Thank Heaven for this blessed hour! God save King George!"

"That, Madam, is a strange prayer to be offered up at such a moment," replied the unknown guest of the Province House, and courteously removing his hat, he offered his arm to raise the aged woman. "Yet, in reverence for your gray hairs and long-kept faith, Heaven forbid that any here should say you nay. Over the realms which still acknowledge his sceptre, God save King George!"

Esther Dudley started to her feet, and hastily clutching back the key, gazed with fearful earnestness at the stranger; and dimly and doubtfully, as if suddenly awakened from a dream, her bewildered eyes half recognized his face. Years ago she had known him among the gentry of the province. But the ban of the King had fallen upon him! How, then, came the doomed victim here? Proscribed, excluded from mercy, the monarch's most dreaded and hated foe, this New England merchant had stood triumphantly against a kingdom's strength; and his foot now trod upon humbled Royalty, as he ascended the steps of the Province House, the people's chosen Governor of Massachusetts.

"Wretch, wretch that I am!" muttered the old woman, with such a heart-broken expression that the tears gushed from the stranger's eyes. "Have I bidden a traitor welcome? Come, Death! come quickly!"

"Alas, venerable lady!" said Governor Hancock, tending her his support with all the reverence that a courtier would have shown to a queen.

"Your life has been prolonged until the world has changed around you. You have treasured up all that time has rendered worthless—the principles, feelings, manners, modes of being and acting, which another generation has flung aside—and you are a symbol of the past. And I, and these around me—we represent a new race of men—living no longer in the past, scarcely in the present—but projecting our lives forward into the future. Ceasing to model ourselves on ancestral superstitions, it is our faith and principle to press onward, onward! Yet," continued he, turning to his attendants, "let us reverence, for the last time, the stately and gorgeous prejudices of the tottering Past!"

While the Republican Governor spoke, he had continued to support the helpless form of Esther Dudley; her weight grew heavier against his arm; but at last, with a sudden effort to free herself, the ancient woman sank down beside one of the pillars of the portal. The key of the Province House fell from her grasp, and clanked against the stone.

"I have been faithful unto death," murmured she. "God save the King!"

"She hath done her office!" said Hancock solemnly. "We will follow her reverently to the tomb of her ancestors; and then, my fellow-citizens, onward—onward! We are no longer children of the Past!"

---

As the old loyalist concluded his narrative, the enthusiasm which had been fitfully flashing within his sunken eyes, and quivering across his wrinkled visage, faded away, as if all the lingering fire of his soul were extinguished. Just then, too, a lamp upon the mantel-piece threw out a dying gleam, which vanished as speedily as it shot upward, compelling our eyes to grope for one another's features by the dim glow of the hearth. With such a lingering fire, methought, with such a dying gleam, had the glory of the ancient system vanished from the Province House, when the spirit of old Esther Dudley took its flight. And now, again, the clock of the Old South threw its voice of ages on the breeze, knolling the hourly knell of the Past, crying out far and wide through the multitudinous city, and filling our ears, as we sat in the dusky chamber, with its reverberating depth of tone. In that same mansion—in that very chamber—what a volume of history had been told off into hours, by the same voice that was now trembling in the air. Many a Governor had heard those midnight accents, and longed to exchange his stately cares for slumber. And as for mine host and Mr. Bela Tiffany and the old loyalist and me, we had babbled about dreams of the past, until we almost fancied that the clock was still striking in a bygone century. Neither of us would have wondered, had a hoop-petticoated phantom of Esther Dudley tottered into the chamber, walking her rounds in the hush of midnight, as of yore, and motioned us to quench the fading embers of the fire, and leave the historic precincts to herself and her kindred shades. But as no such vision was vouchsafed, I retired unbidden, and would advise Mr. Tiffany to lay hold of another auditor, being resolved not to show my face in the Province House for a good while hence—if ever.

## THE AMBITIOUS GUEST

ONE September night a family had gathered round their hearth, and piled it high with the driftwood of mountain streams, the dry cones of the pine, and the splintered ruins of great trees that had come crashing down the precipice. Up the chimney roared the fire, and brightened the room with its broad blaze. The faces of the father and mother had a sober gladness; the children laughed; the eldest daughter was the image of Happiness at seventeen; and the aged grandmother, who sat knitting in the warmest place, was the image of Happiness grown old. They had found the "herb, heart's-ease," in the bleakest spot of all New England. This family were situated in the Notch of the White Hills, where the wind was sharp throughout the year, and pitilessly cold in the winter,—giving their cottage all its fresh inclemency before it descended on the valley of the Saco. They dwelt in a cold spot and a dangerous one; for a mountain towered above their heads, so steep, that the stones would often rumble down its sides and startle them at midnight.

The daughter had just uttered some simple jest that filled them all with mirth, when the wind came through the Notch and seemed to pause before their cottage—rattling the door, with a sound of wailing and lamentation, before it passed into the valley. For a moment it saddened them, though there was nothing unusual in the tones. But the family were glad again when they perceived that the latch was lifted by some traveller, whose footsteps had been unheard amid the dreary blast which heralded his approach, and wailed as he was entering, and went moaning away from the door.

Though they dwelt in such a solitude, these people held daily converse with the world. The romantic pass of the Notch is a great artery, through which the life-blood of internal commerce is continually throbbing between Maine, on one side, and the Green Mountains and the shores of the St. Lawrence, on the other. The stage-coach always drew up before the door of the cottage. The wayfarer, with no companion but his staff, paused here to exchange a word, that the sense of loneliness might not utterly overcome him ere he could pass through the cleft of the mountain, or reach the first house in the valley. And here the teamster, on his way to Portland market, would put up for the night; and, if a bachelor, might sit an hour beyond the usual bedtime, and steal a kiss from the mountain maid at parting. It was one of those primitive taverns where the traveller pays only for food and lodging, but meets with a homely kindness beyond all price. When the footsteps were heard, therefore, between the outer door and the inner one, the whole family rose up, grandmother, children, and all, as if about to welcome some one who belonged to them, and whose fate was linked with theirs.

The door was opened by a young man. His face at first wore the melancholy expression, almost despondency, of one who travels a wild and bleak road, at nightfall and alone, but soon brightened up when he saw the kindly warmth of his reception. He felt his heart spring forward to meet them all, from the old woman, who wiped a chair with her apron, to the little child that held out its arms to him. One glance and smile placed the stranger on a footing of innocent familiarity with the eldest daughter.

"Ah, this fire is the right thing!" cried he; "especially when there is such a pleasant circle round it. I am quite benumbed; for the Notch is just like the pipe of a great pair of bellows; it has blown a terrible blast in my face all the way from Bartlett."

"Then you are going towards Vermont?" said the master of the house, as he helped to take a light knapsack off the young man's shoulders.

"Yes; to Burlington, and far enough beyond," replied he. "I meant to have been at Ethan Crawford's to-night; but a pedestrian lingers along such a road as this. It is no matter; for, when I saw this good fire, and all your cheerful faces, I felt as if you had kindled it on purpose for me, and were waiting my arrival. So I shall sit down among you, and make myself at home."

The frank-hearted stranger had just drawn his chair to the fire when something like a heavy footstep was heard without, rushing down the steep side of the mountain, as with long and rapid strides, and taking such a leap in passing the cottage as to strike the opposite precipice. The family held their breath, because they knew the sound, and their guest held his by instinct.

"The old mountain has thrown a stone at us, for fear we should forget him," said the landlord, recovering himself. "He sometimes nods his head and threatens to come down; but we are old neighbors, and agree together pretty well upon the whole. Besides we have a sure place of refuge hard by if he should be coming in good earnest."

Let us now suppose the stranger to have finished his supper of bear's meat; and, by his natural felicity of manner, to have placed himself on a footing of kindness with the whole family, so that they talked as freely together as if he belonged to their mountain brood. He was of a proud, yet gentle spirit—haughty and reserved among the rich and great; but ever ready to stoop his head to the lowly cottage door, and be like a brother or a son at the poor man's fireside. In the household of the Notch he found warmth and simplicity of feeling, the pervading intelligence of New England, and a poetry of native growth, which they had gathered when they little thought of it from the mountain peaks and chasms, and at the very threshold of their romantic and dangerous abode. He had travelled far and alone; his whole life, indeed, had been a solitary path; for, with the lofty caution of his nature, he had kept himself apart from those who might otherwise have been his companions. The family, too, though so kind and hospitable, had that consciousness of unity among themselves, and separation from the world at large, which, in every domestic circle, should still keep a holy place where no stranger may intrude. But this evening a prophetic sympathy impelled the refined and educated youth to pour out his heart before the simple mountaineers, and constrained them to answer him with the same free confidence. And thus it should have been. Is not the kindred of a common fate a closer tie than that of birth?

The secret of the young man's character was a high and abstracted ambition. He could have borne to live an undistinguished life, but not to be forgotten in the grave. Yearning desire had been transformed to hope; and hope, long cherished, had become like certainty, that, obscurely as he journeyed now, a glory was to beam on all his pathway,—though not, perhaps, while he was treading it. But when posterity should gaze back into the gloom of what was now the present, they would trace the brightness of his footsteps, brightening as meaner glories faded, and confess that a gifted one had passed from his cradle to his tomb with none to recognize him.

"As yet," cried the stranger—his cheek glowing and his eye flashing with enthusiasm—"as yet, I have done nothing. Were I to vanish from the earth to-morrow, none would know so much of me as you: that a nameless youth came up at nightfall from the valley of the Saco, and opened his heart to you in the evening, and passed through the Notch by sunrise, and was seen no more. Not a soul would ask, 'Who was he? Whither did the wanderer go?' But I cannot die till I have achieved my destiny. Then, let Death come! I shall have built my monument!"

There was a continual flow of natural emotion, gushing forth amid abstracted reverie, which enabled the family to understand this young man's sentiments, though so foreign from their own. With quick sensibility of the ludicrous, he blushed at the ardor into which he had been betrayed.

"You laugh at me," said he, taking the eldest daughter's hand, and laughing himself. "You think my ambition as nonsensical as if I were to freeze myself to death on the top of Mount Washington, only that people might spy at me from the country round about. And, truly, that would be a noble pedestal for a man's statue!"

"It is better to sit here by this fire," answered the girl, blushing, "and be comfortable and contented, though nobody thinks about us."

"I suppose," said her father, after a fit of musing, "there is something natural in what the young man says; and if my mind had been turned that way, I might have felt just the same. It is strange, wife, how his talk has set my head running on things that are pretty certain never to come to pass."

"Perhaps they may," observed the wife. "Is the man thinking what he will do when he is a widower?"

"No, no!" cried he, repelling the idea with reproachful kindness. "When I think of your death, Esther, I think of mine, too. But I was wishing we had a good farm in Bartlett, or Bethlehem, or Littleton, or some other township round the White Mountains; but not where they could tumble on our heads. I should want to stand well with my neighbors and be called Squire, and sent to General Court for a term or two; for a plain, honest man may do as much good there as a lawyer. And when I should be grown quite an old man, and you an old woman, so as not to be long apart, I might die happy enough in my bed, and leave you all crying around me. A slate gravestone would suit me as well as a marble one—with just my name and age, and a verse of a hymn, and something to let people know that I lived an honest man and died a Christian."

"There now!" exclaimed the stranger; "it is our nature to desire a monument, be it slate or marble, or a pillar of granite, or a glorious memory in the universal heart of man."

"We're in a strange way, to-night," said the wife, with tears in her eyes. "They say it's a sign of something, when folks' minds go a wandering so. Hark to the children!"

They listened accordingly. The younger children had been put to bed in another room, but with an open door between, so that they could be heard talking busily among themselves. One and all seemed to have caught the infection from the fireside circle, and were outvying each other in wild wishes, and childish projects of what they would do when they came to be men and women. At length a little boy, instead of addressing his brothers and sisters, called out to his mother.

"I'll tell you what I wish, mother," cried he. "I want you and father and grandma'm, and all of us, and the stranger too, to start right away, and go and take a drink out of the basin of the Flume!"

Nobody could help laughing at the child's notion of leaving a warm bed, and dragging them from a cheerful fire, to visit the basin of the Flume,—a brook, which tumbles over the precipice, deep within the Notch. The boy had hardly spoken when a wagon rattled along the road, and stopped a moment before the door. It appeared to contain two or three men, who were cheering their hearts with the rough chorus of a song, which resounded, in broken notes, between the cliffs, while the singers hesitated whether to continue their journey or put up here for the night."

"Father," said the girl, "they are calling you by name."

But the good man doubted whether they had really called him, and was unwilling to show himself too solicitous of gain by inviting people to patronize his house. He therefore did not hurry to the door; and the lash being soon applied, the travellers plunged into the Notch, still singing and laughing, though their music and mirth came back drearily from the heart of the mountain.

"There, mother!" cried the boy, again. "They'd have given us a ride to the Flume."

Again they laughed at the child's pertinacious fancy for a night ramble. But it happened that a light cloud passed over the daughter's spirit; she looked gravely into the fire, and drew a breath that was almost a sigh. It forced its way, in spite of a little struggle to repress it. Then starting and blushing, she looked quickly round the circle, as if they had caught a glimpse into her bosom. The stranger asked what she had been thinking of.

"Nothing," answered she, with a downcast smile. "Only I felt lonesome just then."

"Oh, I have always had a gift of feeling what is in other people's hearts," said he, half seriously. "Shall I tell the secrets of yours? For I know what to think when a young girl shivers by a warm hearth, and complains of lonesomeness at her mother's side. Shall I put these feelings into words?"

"They would not be a girl's feelings any longer if they could be put into words," replied the mountain nymph, laughing, but avoiding his eye.

All this was said apart. Perhaps a germ of love was springing in their hearts, so pure that it might blossom in Paradise, since it could not be matured on earth; for women worship such gentle dignity as his; and the proud, contemplative, yet kindly soul is oftenest captivated by simplicity like hers. But while they spoke softly, and he was watching the happy sadness, the lightsome shadows, the shy yearnings of a maiden's nature, the wind through the Notch took a deeper and drearier sound. It seemed, as the fanciful stranger said, like the choral strain of the spirits of the blast, who in old Indian times had their dwelling among these mountains, and made their heights and recesses a sacred region. There was a wail along the road, as if a funeral were passing. To chase away the gloom, the family threw pine branches on their fire, till the dry leaves crackled and the flame arose, discovering once again a scene of peace and humble happiness. The light hovered about them fondly, and caressed them all. There were the little faces of the children, peeping from their bed apart, and here the father's frame of strength, the mother's subdued and careful mien, the high-browed youth, the budding girl, and the good old grandam, still knitting in the warmest place. The aged woman looked up from her task, and, with fingers ever busy, was the next to speak.

"Old folks have their notions," said she, "as well as young ones. You've been wishing and planning; and letting your heads run on one thing and another, till you've set my mind a wandering too. Now what should an old woman wish for, when she can go but a step or two before she comes to her grave? Children, it will haunt me night and day till I tell you."

"What is it, mother?" cried the husband and wife at once.

Then the old woman, with an air of mystery which drew the circle closer round the fire, informed them that she had provided her grave-clothes some years before,—a nice linen shroud, a cap with a muslin ruff, and everything of a finer sort than she had worn since her wedding day. But this evening an old superstition had strangely recurred to her. It used to be said, in her younger days, that if anything were amiss with a corpse, if only the ruff were not smooth, or the cap did not set right, the corpse in the coffin and beneath the clods would strive to put up its cold hands and arrange it. The bare thought made her nervous.

"Don't talk so, grandmother!" said the girl, shuddering.

"Now,"—continued the old woman, with singular earnestness, yet smiling strangely at her own folly,—"I want one of you, my children—when your mother is dressed and in the coffin—I want one of you to hold a looking-glass over my face. Who knows but I may take a glimpse at myself, and see whether all 's right?"

"Old and young, we dream of graves and monuments," murmured the stranger youth. "I wonder how mariners feel when the ship is sinking, and they, unknown and undistinguished, are to be buried together in the ocean—that wide and nameless sepulchre?"

For a moment, the old woman's ghastly conception so engrossed the minds of her hearers that a sound abroad in the night, rising like the roar of a blast, had grown broad, deep, and terrible, before the fated group were conscious of it. The house and all within it trembled; the foundations of the earth seemed to be shaken, as if this awful sound were the peal of the last trump. Young and old exchanged one wild glance, and remained an instant, pale, affrighted, without utterance, or power to move. Then the same shriek burst simultaneously from all their lips.

"The Slide! The Slide!"

The simplest words must intimate, but not portray, the unutterable horror of the catastrophe. The victims rushed from their cottage, and sought refuge in what they deemed a safer spot—where, in contemplation of such an emergency, a sort of barrier had been reared. Alas! they had quitted their security, and fled right into the pathway of destruction. Down came the whole side of the mountain, in a cataract of ruin. Just before it reached the house, the stream broke into two branches—shivered not a window there, but overwhelmed the whole vicinity, blocked up the road, and annihilated everything in its dreadful course. Long ere the thunder of the great Slide had ceased to roar among the mountains, the mortal agony had been endured, and the victims were at peace. Their bodies were never found.

The next morning, the light smoke was seen stealing from the cottage chimney up the mountain side. Within, the fire was yet smouldering on the hearth, and the chairs in a circle round it, as if the inhabitants had but gone forth to view the devastation of the Slide, and would shortly return, to thank Heaven for their miraculous escape. All had left separate tokens, by which those who had known the family were made to shed a tear for each. Who has not heard their name? The story has been told far and wide, and will forever be a legend of these mountains. Poets have sung their fate.

There were circumstances which led some to suppose that a stranger had been received into the cottage on this awful night, and had shared the catastrophe of all its inmates. Others denied that there were sufficient grounds for such a conjecture. Woe for the high-souled youth, with his dream of Earthly Immortality! His name and person utterly unknown;

his history, his way of life, his plans, a mystery never to be solved, his death and his existence equally a doubt! Whose was the agony of that death moment?


# PETER GOLDTHWAITE'S TREASURE

"AND SO, Peter, you won't even consider of the business?" said Mr. John Brown, buttoning his surtout over the snug rotundity of his person, and drawing on his gloves. "You positively refuse to let me have this crazy old house, and the land under and adjoining, at the price named?"

"Neither at that, nor treble the sum," responded the gaunt, grizzled, and threadbare Peter Goldthwaite. "The fact is, Mr. Brown, you must find another site for your brick block, and be content to leave my estate with the present owner. Next summer, I intend to put a splendid new mansion over the cellar of the old house."

"Pho, Peter!" cried Mr. Brown, as he opened the kitchen door; "content yourself with building castles in the air, where house-lots are cheaper than on earth, to say nothing of the cost of bricks and mortar. Such foundations are solid enough for your edifices, while this underneath us is just the thing for mine; and so we may both be suited. What say you again?"

"Precisely what I said before, Mr. Brown," answered Peter Goldthwaite. "And as for castles in the air, mine may not be as magnificent as that sort of architecture, but perhaps as substantial, Mr. Brown, as the very respectable brick block with dry goods stores, tailors' shops, and banking rooms on the lower floor, and lawyers' offices in the second story, which you are so anxious to substitute."

"And the cost, Peter, eh?" said Mr. Brown, as he withdrew, in something of a pet. "That, I suppose, will be provided for, off-hand, by drawing a check on Bubble Bank!"

John Brown and Peter Goldthwaite had been jointly known to the commercial world between twenty and thirty years before, under the firm of Goldthwaite & Brown; which copartnership, however, was speedily dissolved by the natural incongruity of its constituent parts. Since that event, John Brown, with exactly the qualities of a thousand other John Browns, and by just such plodding methods as they used, had prospered wonderfully, and become one of the wealthiest John Browns on earth. Peter Goldthwaite, on the contrary, after innumerable schemes, which ought to have collected all the coin and paper currency of the country into his coffers, was as needy a gentleman as ever wore a patch upon his elbow. The contrast between him and his former partner may be briefly marked; for Brown never reckoned upon luck, yet always had it; while

Peter made luck the main condition of his projects, and always missed it. While the means held out, his speculations had been magnificent, but were chiefly confined, of late years, to such small business as adventures in the lottery. Once he had gone on a gold-gathering expedition some-where to the South, and ingeniously contrived to empty his pockets more thoroughly than ever; while others, doubtless, were filling theirs with native bullion by the handful. More recently he had expended a legacy of a thousand or two of dollars in purchasing Mexican scrip, and thereby became the proprietor of a province; which, however, so far as Peter could find out, was situated where he might have had an empire for the same money,—in the clouds. From a search after this valuable real estate Peter returned so gaunt and threadbare that, on reaching New England, the scarecrows in the cornfields beckoned to him, as he passed by. "They did but flutter in the wind," quoth Peter Goldthwaite. No, Peter, they beckoned, for the scarecrows knew their brother!

At the period of our story his whole visible income would not have paid the tax of the old mansion in which we find him. It was one of those rusty, moss-grown, many-peaked wooden houses, which are scattered about the streets of our elder towns, with a beetle-browed second story projecting over the foundation, as if it frowned at the novelty around it. This old pa-ternal edifice, needy as he was, and though, being centrally situated on the principal street of the town, it would have brought him a handsome sum, the sagacious Peter had his own reasons for never parting with, eith-er by auction or private sale. There seemed, indeed, to be a fatality that connected him with his birthplace; for, often as he had stood on the verge of ruin, and standing there even now, he had not yet taken the step be-yond it which would have compelled him to surrender the house to his creditors. So here he dwelt with bad luck till good should come.

Here then in his kitchen, the only room where a spark of fire took off the chill of a November evening, poor Peter Goldthwaite had just been visited by his rich old partner. At the close of their interview, Peter, with rather a mortified look, glanced downwards at his dress, parts of which appeared as ancient as the days of Goldthwaite & Brown. His upper gar-ment was a mixed surtout, wofully faded, and patched with newer stuff on each elbow; beneath this he wore a threadbare black coat, some of the silk buttons of which had been replaced with others of a different pattern; and lastly, though he lacked not a pair of gray pantaloons, they were very shabby ones, and had been partially turned brown by the frequent toast-ing of Peter's shins before a scanty fire. Peter's person was in keeping with his goodly apparel. Gray-headed, hollow-eyed, pale-cheeked, and lean-bodied, he was the perfect picture of a man who had fed on windy schemes and empty hopes, till he could neither live on such unwholesome trash, nor stomach more substantial food. But, withal, this Peter Gold-thwaite, crack-brained simpleton as, perhaps, he was, might have cut a very brilliant figure in the world, had he employed his imagination in the airy business of poetry, instead of making it a demon of mischief in mer-cantile pursuits. After all, he was no bad fellow, but as harmless as a child, and as honest and honorable, and as much of the gentleman which nature meant him for, as an irregular life and depressed circumstances will permit any man to be.

As Peter stood on the uneven bricks of his hearth, looking round at the disconsolate old kitchen, his eyes began to kindle with the illumination of an enthusiasm that never long deserted him. He raised his hand, clinched it, and smote it energetically against the smoky panel over the fireplace.

"The time is come!" said he. "With such a treasure at command, it were folly to be a poor man any longer. To-morrow morning I will begin with the garret, nor desist till I have torn the house down!"

Deep in the chimney-corner, like a witch in a dark cavern, sat a little old woman, mending one of the two pairs of stockings wherewith Peter Goldthwaite kept his toes from being frostbitten. As the feet were ragged past all darning, she had cut pieces out of a cast-off flannel petticoat, to make new soles. Tabitha Porter was an old maid, upwards of sixty years of age, fifty-five of which she had sat in that same chimney-corner, such being the length of time since Peter's grandfather had taken her from the almshouse. She had no friend but Peter, nor Peter any friend but Tabitha; so long as Peter might have a shelter for his own head, Tabitha would know where to shelter hers; or, being homeless elsewhere, she would take her master by the hand and bring him to her native home, the almshouse. Should it ever be necessary, she loved him well enough to feed him with her last morsel, and clothe him with her under petticoat. But Tabitha was a queer old woman, and, though never infected with Peter's flightiness, had become so accustomed to his freaks and follies that she viewed them all as matters of course. Hearing him threaten to tear the house down, she looked quietly up from her work.

"Best leave the kitchen till the last, Mr. Peter," said she.

"The sooner we have it all down the better," said Peter Goldthwaite. "I am tired to death of living in this cold, dark, windy, smoky, creaking, groaning, dismal old house. I shall feel like a younger man when we get into my splendid brick mansion, as, please Heaven, we shall by this time next autumn. You shall have a room on the sunny side, old Tabby, finished and furnished as best may suit your own notions."

"I should like it pretty much such a room as this kitchen," answered Tabitha. "It will never be like home to me till the chimney-corner gets as black with smoke as this; and that won't be these hundred years. How much do you mean to lay out on the house, Mr. Peter?"

"What is that to the purpose?" exclaimed Peter, loftily. "Did not my great-granduncle, Peter Goldthwaite, who died seventy years ago, and whose namesake I am, leave treasure enough to build twenty such?"

"I can't say but he did, Mr. Peter," said Tabitha, threading her needle.

Tabitha well understood that Peter had reference to an immense hoard of the precious metals, which was said to exist somewhere in the cellar or walls, or under the floors, or in some concealed closet, or other out-of-the-way nook of the house. This wealth, according to tradition, had been accumulated by a former Peter Goldthwaite, whose character seems to have borne a remarkable similitude to that of the Peter of our story. Like him he was a wild projector, seeking to heap up gold by the bushel and the cartload, instead of scraping it together, coin by coin. Like Peter the second, too, his projects had almost invariably failed, and, but for the magnificent success of the final one, would have left him with hardly a coat and pair of breeches to his gaunt and grizzled person. Reports were various as to the nature of his fortunate speculation: one intimating that the ancient Peter had made the gold by alchemy; another, that he had conjured it out of people's pockets by the black art; and a third, still more unaccountable, that the devil had given him free access to the old provincial treasury. It was affirmed, however, that some secret impediment had debarred him from the enjoyment of his riches, and that he had a motive for concealing them from his heir, or at any rate had died without disclosing the place of deposit. The present Peter's father had faith enough in the story to cause the cellar to be dug over. Peter himself chose to consider the legend as an indisputable truth, and, amid his many troubles, had this one consolation that, should all other resources fail, he might build up his fortunes by tearing his house down. Yet, unless he felt a lurking distrust of the golden tale, it is difficult to account for his permitting the paternal roof to stand so long, since he had never yet seen the moment when his predecessor's treasure would not have found plenty of room in his own strong box. But now was the crisis. Should he delay the search a little longer, the house would pass from the lineal heir, and with it the vast heap of gold, to remain in its burial-place, till the ruin of the aged walls should discover it to strangers of a future generation.

"Yes!" cried Peter Goldthwaite, again, "to-morrow I will set about it."

The deeper he looked at the matter the more certain of success grew Peter. His spirits were naturally so elastic that even now, in the blasted autumn of his age, he could often compete with the spring-time gayety of other people. Enlivened by his brightening prospects, he began to caper about the kitchen like a hobgoblin, with the queerest antics of his lean limbs, and gesticulations of his starved features. Nay, in the exuberance of his feelings, he seized both of Tabitha's hands, and danced the old lady across the floor, till the oddity of her rheumatic motions set him into a roar of laughter, which was echoed back from the rooms and chambers, as if Peter Goldthwaite were laughing in every one. Finally he bounded upward almost out of sight, into the smoke that clouded the roof of the kitchen, and, alighting safely on the floor again, endeavored to resume his customary gravity.

"To-morrow, at sunrise," he repeated, taking his lamp to retire to bed, "I'll see whether this treasure be hid in the wall of the garret."

"And as we're out of wood, Mr. Peter," said Tabitha, puffing and panting with her late gymnastics, "as fast as you tear the house down, I'll make a fire with the pieces."

Gorgeous that night were the dreams of Peter Goldthwaite! At one time he was turning a ponderous key in an iron door not unlike the door of a sepulchre, but which, being opened, disclosed a vault heaped up with gold coin, as plentifully as golden corn in a granary. There were chased goblets, also, and tureens, salvers, dinner dishes, and dish covers of gold, or silver gilt, besides chains and other jewels, incalculably rich, though tarnished with the damps of the vault; for, of all the wealth that was irrevocably lost to the man, whether buried in the earth or sunken in the sea, Peter Goldthwaite had found it in this one treasure-place. Anon, he had returned to the old house as poor as ever, and was received at the door by the gaunt and grizzled figure of a man whom he might have mistaken for himself, only that his garments were of a much elder fashion. But the house, without losing its former aspect, had been changed into a palace of the precious metals. The floors, walls, and ceiling were of burnished silver; the doors, the window frames, the cornices, the balustrades, and the steps of the staircase, of pure gold; and silver, with gold bottoms, were the chairs, and gold, standing on silver legs, the high chests of drawers, and silver the bedsteads, with blankets of woven gold, and sheets of silver tissue. The house had evidently been transmuted by a single touch; for it retained all the marks that Peter remembered, but in gold or silver instead of wood; and the initials of his name, which, when a boy, he had cut in the wooden door-post, remained as deep in the pillar of gold. A happy man would have been Peter Goldthwaite except for a certain ocular deception, which, whenever he glanced backwards, caused the house to darken from its glittering magnificence into the sordid gloom of yesterday.

Up, betimes, rose Peter, seized an axe, hammer, and saw, which he had placed by his bedside, and hied him to the garret. It was but scantily lighted up, as yet, by the frosty fragments of a sunbeam, which began to glimmer through the almost opaque bull's-eyes of the window. A moralizer might find abundant themes for his speculative and impracticable wisdom in a garret. There is the limbo of departed fashions, aged trifles of a day, and whatever was valuable only to one generation of men, and which passed to the garret when that generation passed to the grave, not for safe keeping, but to be out of the way. Peter saw piles of yellow and musty account-books, in parchment covers, wherein creditors, long dead and buried, had written the names of dead and buried debtors in ink now so faded that their moss-grown tombstones were more legible. He found old moth-eaten garments all in rags and tatters, or Peter would have put them on. Here was a naked and rusty sword, not a sword of service, but a gentleman's small French rapier, which had never left its scabbard till it lost it. Here were canes of twenty different sorts, but no gold-headed ones, and shoe-buckles of various pattern and material, but not silver nor set with precious stones. Here was a large box full of shoes, with high heels and peaked toes. Here, on a shelf, were a multitude of phials, half-filled with old apothecaries' stuff, which, when the other half had done its business on Peter's ancestors, had been brought hither from the death chamber. Here—not to give a longer inventory of articles that will never be put up at auction—was the fragment of a full-length looking-glass, which, by the dust and dimness of its surface, made the picture of these old things look older than the reality. When Peter, not knowing that there was a mirror there, caught the faint traces of his own figure, he partly imagined that the former Peter Goldthwaite had come back, either to assist or impede his search for the hidden wealth. And at that moment a strange notion glimmered through his brain that he was the identical Peter who had concealed the gold, and ought to know whereabout it lay. This, however, he had unaccountably forgotten.

"Well, Mr. Peter!" cried Tabitha, on the garret stairs. "Have you torn the house down enough to heat the teakettle?"

"Not yet, old Tabby," answered Peter; "but that's soon done—as you shall see."

With the word in his mouth, he uplifted the axe, and laid about him so vigorously that the dust flew, the boards crashed, and, in a twinkling, the old woman had an apron full of broken rubbish.

"We shall get our winter's wood cheap," quoth Tabitha.

The good work being thus commenced, Peter beat down all before him, smiting and hewing at the joists and timbers, unclinching spike-nails, ripping and tearing away boards, with a tremendous racket, from morning till night. He took care, however, to leave the outside shell of the house untouched, so that the neighbors might not suspect what was going on.

Never, in any of his vagaries, though each had made him happy while it lasted, had Peter been happier than now. Perhaps, after all, there was something in Peter Goldthwaite's turn of mind, which brought him an inward recompense for all the external evil that it caused. If he were poor, ill-clad, even hungry, and exposed, as it were, to be utterly annihilated by a precipice of impending ruin, yet only his body remained in these miserable circumstances, while his aspiring soul enjoyed the sunshine of a bright futurity. It was his nature to be always young, and the tendency of his mode of life to keep him so. Gray hairs were nothing, no, nor wrinkles, nor infirmity; he might look old, indeed, and be somewhat disagreeably connected with a gaunt old figure, much the worse for wear; but the true, the essential Peter was a young man of high hopes, just entering on the world. At the kindling of each new fire, his burnt-out youth rose afresh from the old embers and ashes. It rose exulting now. Having lived thus long—not too long, but just to the right age—a susceptible bachelor, with warm and tender dreams, he resolved, so soon as the hidden gold should flash to light, to go a-wooing, and win the love of the fairest maid in town. What heart could resist him? Happy Peter Goldthwaite!

Every evening—as Peter had long absented himself from his former lounging-places, at insurance offices, news-rooms, and bookstores, and as the honor of his company was seldom requested in private circles—he and Tabitha used to sit down sociably by the kitchen hearth. This was always heaped plentifully with the rubbish of his day's labor. As the foundation of the fire, there would be a goodly-sized backlog of red oak, which, after being sheltered from rain or damp above a century, still hissed with the heat, and distilled streams of water from each end, as if the tree had been cut down within a week or two. Next these were large sticks, sound, black, and heavy, which had lost the principle of decay, and were indestructible except by fire, wherein they glowed like red-hot bars of iron. On this solid basis, Tabitha would rear a lighter structure, composed of the splinters of door panels, ornamented mouldings, and such quick combustibles, which caught like straw, and threw a brilliant blaze high up the spacious flue, making its sooty sides visible almost to the chimney-top. Meantime, the gleam of the old kitchen would be chased out of the cobwebbed corners, and away from the dusky cross-beams overhead, and driven nobody could tell whither, while Peter smiled like a gladsome man, and Tabitha seemed a picture of comfortable age. All this, of course, was but an emblem of the bright fortune which the destruction of the house would shed upon its occupants.

While the dry pine was flaming and crackling, like an irregular discharge of fairy musketry, Peter sat looking and listening, in a pleasant state of excitement. But, when the brief blaze and uproar were succeeded by the dark-red glow, the substantial heat, and the deep singing sound, which were to last throughout the evening, his humor became talkative. One night, the hundredth time, he teased Tabitha to tell him something new about his great-granduncle.

"You have been sitting in that chimney-corner fifty-five years, old Tabby, and must have heard many a tradition about him," said Peter. "Did not you tell me that, when you first came to the house, there was an old woman sitting where you sit now, who had been housekeeper to the famous Peter Goldthwaite?"

"So there was, Mr. Peter," answered Tabitha, "and she was near about a hundred years old. She used to say that she and old Peter Goldthwaite had often spent a sociable evening by the kitchen fire—pretty much as you and I are doing now, Mr. Peter."

"The old fellow must have resembled me in more points than one," said Peter, complacently, "or he never would have grown so rich. But, methinks, he might have invested the money better than he did—no interest!—nothing but good security!—and the house to be torn down to come at it! What made him hide it so snug, Tabby?"

"Because he could not spend it," said Tabitha; "for as often as he went to unlock the chest, the Old Scratch came behind and caught his arm. The money, they say, was paid Peter out of his purse; and he wanted Peter to give him a deed of this house and land, which Peter swore he would not do."

"Just as I swore to John Brown, my old partner," remarked Peter. "But this is all nonsense, Tabby! I don't believe the story."

"Well, it may not be just the truth," said Tabitha; "for some folks say that Peter did make over the house to the Old Scratch, and that's the reason it has always been so unlucky to them that lived in it. And as soon as Peter had given him the deed, the chest flew open, and Peter caught up a handful of the gold. But, lo and behold!—there was nothing in his fist but a parcel of old rags."

"Hold your tongue, you silly old Tabby!" cried Peter in great wrath. "They were as good golden guineas as ever bore the effigies of the king of

England. It seems as if I could recollect the whole circumstance, and how I, or old Peter, or whoever it was, thrust in my hand, or his hand, and drew it out all of a blaze with gold. Old rags, indeed!"

But it was not an old woman's legend that would discourage Peter Goldthwaite. All night long he slept among pleasant dreams, and awoke at daylight with a joyous throb of the heart, which few are fortunate enough to feel beyond their boyhood. Day after day he labored hard without wasting a moment, except at meal times, when Tabitha summoned him to the pork and cabbage, or such other sustenance as she had picked up, or Providence had sent them. Being a truly pious man, Peter never failed to ask a blessing; if the food were none of the best, then so much the more earnestly, as it was more needed;—nor to return thanks, if the dinner had been scanty, yet for the good appetite, which was better than a sick stomach at a feast. Then did he hurry back to his toil, and, in a moment, was lost to sight in a cloud of dust from the old walls, though sufficiently perceptible to the ear by the clatter which he raised in the midst of it. How enviable is the consciousness of being usefully employed! Nothing troubled Peter; or nothing but those phantoms of the mind which seem like vague recollections, yet have also the aspect of presentiments. He often paused, with his axe uplifted in the air, and said to himself,—"Peter Goldthwaite, did you never strike this blow before?"—or, "Peter, what need of tearing the whole house down? Think a little while, and you will remember where the gold is hidden." Days and weeks passed on, however, without any remarkable discovery. Sometimes, indeed, a lean, gray rat peeped forth at the lean, gray man, wondering what devil had got into the old house, which had always been so peaceable till now. And, occasionally, Peter sympathized with the sorrows of a female mouse, who had brought five or six pretty, little, soft and delicate young ones into the world just in time to see them crushed by its ruin. But, as yet, no treasure!

By this time, Peter, being as determined as Fate and as diligent as Time, had made an end with the uppermost regions, and got down to the second story, where he was busy in one of the front chambers. It had formerly been the state bed-chamber; and was honored by tradition as the sleeping apartment of Governor Dudley, and many other eminent guests. The furniture was gone. There were remnants of faded and tattered paper-hangings, but larger spaces of bare wall ornamented with charcoal sketches, chiefly of people's heads in profile. These being specimens of Peter's youthful genius, it went more to his heart to obliterate them than if they had been pictures on a church wall by Michael Angelo. One sketch, however, and that the best one, affected him differently. It represented a ragged man, partly supporting himself on a spade, and bending his lean body over a hole in the earth, with one hand extended to grasp something that he had found. But close behind him, with a fiendish laugh on his features, appeared a figure with horns, a tufted tail, and a cloven hoof.

"Avaunt, Satan!" cried Peter. "The man shall have his gold!"

Uplifting his axe, he hit the horned gentleman such a blow on the head as not only demolished him, but the treasure-seeker also, and caused the whole scene to vanish like magic. Moreover, his axe broke quite through the plaster and laths, and discovered a cavity.

"Mercy on us, Mr. Peter, are you quarrelling with the Old Scratch?" said Tabitha, who was seeking some fuel to put under the pot.

Without answering the old woman, Peter broke down a further space of the wall, and laid open a small closet or cupboard, on one side of the fireplace, about breast high from the ground. It contained nothing but a brass lamp, covered with verdigris, and a dusty piece of parchment. While Peter inspected the latter, Tabitha seized the lamp, and began to rub it with her apron.

"There is no use in rubbing it, Tabitha," said Peter. "It is not Aladdin's lamp, though I take it to be a token of as much luck. Look here, Tabby!"

Tabitha took the parchment and held it close to her nose, which was saddled with a pair of iron-bound spectacles. But no sooner had she began to puzzle over it than she burst into a chuckling laugh, holding both her hands against her sides.

"You can't make a fool of the old woman!" cried she. "This is your own handwriting, Mr. Peter! the same as in the letter you sent me from Mexico."

"There is certainly a considerable resemblance," said Peter, again examining the parchment. "But you know yourself, Tabby, that this closet must have been plastered up before you came to the house, or I came into the world. No, this is old Peter Goldthwaite's writing; these columns of pounds, shillings, and pence are his figures, denoting the amount of the treasure; and this at the bottom is, doubtless, a reference to the place of concealment. But the ink has either faded or peeled off, so that it is absolutely illegible. What a pity!"

"Well, this lamp is as good as new. That's some comfort," said Tabitha.

"A lamp!" thought Peter. "That indicates light on my researches."

For the present, Peter felt more inclined to ponder on this discovery than to resume his labors. After Tabitha had gone down stairs, he stood poring over the parchment, at one of the front windows, which was so obscured with dust that the sun could barely throw an uncertain shadow of the casement across the floor. Peter forced it open, and looked out upon the great street of the town, while the sun looked in at his old house. The air, though mild, and even warm, thrilled Peter as with a dash of water.

It was the first day of the January thaw. The snow lay deep upon the house-tops, but was rapidly dissolving into millions of water-drops, which sparkled downwards through the sunshine, with the noise of a summer shower beneath the eaves. Along the street, the trodden snow was as hard and solid as a pavement of white marble, and had not yet grown moist in the spring-like temperature. But when Peter thrust forth his head, he saw that the inhabitants, if not the town, were already thawed out by this warm day, after two or three weeks of winter weather. It gladdened him —a gladness with a sigh breathing through it—to see the stream of ladies, gliding along the slippery sidewalks, with their red cheeks set off by quilted hoods, boas, and sable capes, like roses amidst a new kind of foliage. The sleigh-bells jingled to and fro continually: sometimes announcing the arrival of a sleigh from Vermont, laden with the frozen bodies of porkers, or sheep, and perhaps a deer or two; sometimes of a regular market-man, with chickens, geese, and turkeys, comprising the whole colony of a barn yard; and sometimes of a farmer and his dame, who had come to town partly for the ride, partly to go a-shopping, and partly for the sale of some eggs and butter. This couple rode in an old-fashioned square sleigh, which had served them twenty winters, and stood twenty summers in the sun beside their door. Now, a gentleman and lady skimmed the snow in an elegant car, shaped somewhat like a cockle-shell. Now, a stage-sleigh, with its cloth curtains thrust aside to admit the sun, dashed rapidly down the street, whirling in and out among the vehicles that obstructed its passage. Now came, round a corner, the similitude of Noah's ark on runners, being an immense open sleigh with seats for fifty people, and drawn by a dozen horses. This spacious receptacle was populous with merry maids and merry bachelors, merry girls and boys, and merry old folks, all alive with fun, and grinning to the full width of their mouths. They kept up a buzz of babbling voices and low laughter, and sometimes burst into a deep, joyous shout, which the spectators answered with three cheers, while a gang of roguish boys let drive their snowballs right among the pleasure party. The sleigh passed on, and, when concealed by a bend of the street, was still audible by a distant cry of merriment.

Never had Peter beheld a livelier scene than was constituted by all these accessories: the bright sun, the flashing water-drops, the gleaming snow, the cheerful multitude, the variety of rapid vehicles, and the jingle jangle of merry bells which made the heart dance to their music. Nothing dismal was to be seen, except that peaked piece of antiquity, Peter Goldthwaite's house, which might well look sad externally, since such a terrible consumption was preying on its insides. And Peter's gaunt figure, half visible in the projecting second story, was worthy of his house.

"Peter! How goes it, friend Peter?" cried a voice across the street, as Peter was drawing in his head. "Look out here, Peter!"

Peter looked, and saw his old partner, Mr. John Brown, on the opposite sidewalk, portly and comfortable, with his furred cloak thrown open, disclosing a handsome surtout beneath. His voice had directed the attention of the whole town to Peter Goldthwaite's window, and to the dusty scarecrow which appeared at it.

"I say, Peter," cried Mr. Brown again, "what the devil are you about there, that I hear such a racket whenever I pass by? You are repairing the old house, I suppose,—making a new one of it,—eh?"

"Too late for that, I am afraid, Mr. Brown," replied Peter. "If I make it new, it will be new inside and out, from the cellar upwards."

"Had not you better let me take the job?" said Mr. Brown, significantly.

"Not yet!" answered Peter, hastily shutting the window; for, ever since he had been in search of the treasure, he hated to have people stare at him.

As he drew back, ashamed of his outward poverty, yet proud of the secret wealth within his grasp, a haughty smile shone out on Peter's visage, with precisely the effect of the dim sunbeams in the squalid chamber. He endeavored to assume such a mien as his ancestor had probably worn, when he gloried in the building of a strong house for a home to many generations of his posterity. But the chamber was very dark to his snow-dazzled eyes, and very dismal too, in contrast with the living scene that he had just looked upon. His brief glimpse into the street had given him a forcible impression of the manner in which the world kept itself cheerful and prosperous, by social pleasures and an intercourse of business, while he, in seclusion, was pursuing an object that might possibly be a phantasm, by a method which most people would call madness. It is one great advantage of a gregarious mode of life that each person rectifies his mind by other minds, and squares his conduct to that of his neighbors, so as seldom to be lost in eccentricity. Peter Goldthwaite had exposed himself to this influence by merely looking out of the window. For a while, he doubted whether there were any hidden chest of gold, and, in that case, whether he was so exceedingly wise to tear the house down, only to be convinced of its non-existence.

But this was momentary. Peter, the Destroyer, resumed the task which fate had assigned him, nor faltered again till it was accomplished. In the course of his search, he met with many things that are usually found in the ruins of an old house, and also with some that are not. What seemed most to the purpose was a rusty key, which had been thrust into a chink of the wall, with a wooden label appended to the handle, bearing the initials, P. G. Another singular discovery was that of a bottle of wine, walled up in an old oven. A tradition ran in the family, that Peter's grandfather, a jovial officer in the old French War, had set aside many dozens of the precious liquor for the benefit of topers then unborn. Peter needed no cordial to sustain his hopes, and therefore kept the wine to gladden his success. Many halfpence did he pick up, that had been lost through the cracks of the floor, and some few Spanish coins, and the half of a broken sixpence, which had doubtless been a love token. There was likewise a silver coronation medal of George the Third. But old Peter Goldthwaite's strong box fled from one dark corner to another, or otherwise eluded the second Peter's clutches, till, should he seek much farther, he must burrow into the earth.

We will not follow him in his triumphant progress, step by step. Suffice it that Peter worked like a steam-engine, and finished, in that one winter, the job which all the former inhabitants of the house, with time and the elements to aid them, had only half done in a century. Except the kitchen, every room and chamber was now gutted. The house was nothing but a shell,—the apparition of a house,—as unreal as the painted edifices of a theatre. It was like the perfect rind of a great cheese, in which a mouse had dwelt and nibbled till it was a cheese no more. And Peter was the mouse.

What Peter had torn down, Tabitha had burned up; for she wisely considered that, without a house, they should need no wood to warm it; and therefore economy was nonsense. Thus the whole house might be said to have dissolved in smoke, and flown up among the clouds, through the great black flue of the kitchen chimney. It was an admirable parallel to the feat of the man who jumped down his own throat.

On the night between the last day of winter and the first of spring, every chink and cranny had been ransacked, except within the precincts of the kitchen. This fated evening was an ugly one. A snow-storm had set in some hours before, and was still driven and tossed about the atmosphere by a real hurricane, which fought against the house as if the prince of the air, in person, were putting the final stroke to Peter's labors. The framework being so much weakened, and the inward props removed, it would have been no marvel if, in some stronger wrestle of the blast, the rotten walls of the edifice, and all the peaked roofs, had come crushing down upon the owner's head. He, however, was careless of the peril, but as wild and restless as the night itself, or as the flame that quivered up the chimney at each roar of the tempestuous wind.

"The wine, Tabitha!" he cried. "My grandfather's rich old wine! We will drink it now!"

Tabitha arose from her smoke-blackened bench in the chimney-corner, and placed the bottle before Peter, close beside the old brass lamp, which had likewise been the prize of his researches. Peter held it before his eyes, and, looking through the liquid medium, beheld the kitchen illuminated with a golden glory, which also enveloped Tabitha and gilded her silver hair, and converted her mean garments into robes of queenly splendor. It reminded him of his golden dream.

"Mr. Peter," remarked Tabitha, "must the wine be drunk before the money is found?"

"The money *is* found!" exclaimed Peter, with a sort of fierceness. "The chest is within my reach. I will not sleep, till I have turned this key in the rusty lock. But, first of all, let us drink!"

There being no corkscrew in the house, he smote the neck of the bottle with old Peter Goldthwaite's rusty key, and decapitated the sealed cork at a single blow. He then filled two little china teacups, which Tabitha had brought from the cupboard. So clear and brilliant was this aged wine that it shone within the cups, and rendered the sprig of scarlet flowers, at the bottom of each, more distinctly visible than when there had been no wine there. Its rich and delicate perfume wasted itself round the kitchen.

"Drink, Tabitha!" cried Peter. "Blessings on the honest old fellow who set aside this good liquor for you and me! And here's to Peter Goldthwaite's memory!"

"And good cause have we to remember him," quoth Tabitha, as she drank.

How many years, and through what changes of fortune and various calamity, had that bottle hoarded up its effervescent joy, to be quaffed at last by two such boon companions! A portion of the happiness of the former age had been kept for them, and was now set free, in a crowd of rejoicing visions, to sport amid the storm and desolation of the present time. Until they have finished the bottle, we must turn our eyes elsewhere.

It so chanced that, on this stormy night, Mr. John Brown found himself ill at ease in his wire-cushioned arm-chair, by the glowing grate of anthracite which heated his handsome parlor. He was naturally a good sort of a man, and kind and pitiful whenever the misfortunes of others happened to reach his heart through the padded vest of his own prosperity. This evening he had thought much about his old partner, Peter Goldthwaite, his strange vagaries, and continual ill luck, the poverty of his dwelling, at Mr. Brown's last visit, and Peter's crazed and haggard aspect when he had talked with him at the window.

"Poor fellow!" thought Mr. John Brown. "Poor, crackbrained Peter Goldthwaite! For old acquaintance' sake, I ought to have taken care that he was comfortable this rough winter."

These feelings grew so powerful that, in spite of the inclement weather, he resolved to visit Peter Goldthwaite immediately. The strength of the impulse was really singular. Every shriek of the blast seemed a summons, or would have seemed so, had Mr. Brown been accustomed to hear the echoes of his own fancy in the wind. Much amazed at such active benevolence, he huddled himself in his cloak, muffled his throat and ears in comforters and handkerchiefs, and, thus fortified, bade defiance to the tempest. But the powers of the air had rather the best of the battle. Mr. Brown was just weathering the corner, by Peter Goldthwaite's house, when the hurricane caught him off his feet, tossed him face downward into a snow bank, and proceeded to bury his protuberant part beneath fresh drifts. There seemed little hope of his reappearance earlier than the next thaw. At the same moment his hat was snatched away, and whirled aloft into some far distant region, whence no tidings have as yet returned.

Nevertheless Mr. Brown contrived to burrow a passage through the snow-drift, and, with his bare head bent against the storm, floundered onward to Peter's door. There was such a creaking and groaning and rattling, and such an ominous shaking throughout the crazy edifice, that the loudest rap would have been inaudible to those within. He therefore entered, without ceremony, and groped his way to the kitchen.

His intrusion, even there, was unnoticed. Peter and Tabitha stood with their backs to the door, stooping over a large chest, which, apparently, they had just dragged from a cavity, or concealed closet, on the left side of the chimney. By the lamp in the old woman's hand, Mr. Brown saw that the chest was barred and clamped with iron, strengthened with iron plates and studded with iron nails, so as to be a fit receptacle in which the wealth of one century might be hoarded up for the wants of another. Peter Goldthwaite was inserting a key into the lock.

"O Tabitha!" cried he, with tremulous rapture, "how shall I endure the effulgence? The gold!—the bright, bright gold! Methinks I can remember my last glance at it, just as the iron-plated lid fell down. And ever since, being seventy years, it has been blazing in secret, and gathering its splendor against this glorious moment! It will flash upon us like the noonday sun!"

"Then shade your eyes, Mr. Peter!" said Tabitha, with somewhat less patience than usual. "But, for mercy's sake, do turn the key!"

And, with a strong effort of both hands, Peter did force the rusty key through the intricacies of the rusty lock. Mr. Brown, in the mean time, had drawn near, and thrust his eager visage between those of the other two, at the instant that Peter threw up the lid. No sudden blaze illuminated the kitchen.

"What's here?" exclaimed Tabitha, adjusting her spectacles, and holding the lamp over the open chest. "Old Peter Goldthwaite's hoard of old rags."

"Pretty much so, Tabby," said Mr. Brown, lifting a handful of the treasure.

Oh, what a ghost of dead and buried wealth had Peter Goldthwaite raised, to scare himself out of his scanty wits withal! Here was the semblance of an incalculable sum, enough to purchase the whole town, and build every street anew, but which, vast as it was, no sane man would have given a solid sixpence for. What then, in sober earnest, were the delusive treasures of the chest? Why, here were old provincial bills of credit, and treasury notes, and bills of land, banks, and all other bubbles of the sort, from the first issue, above a century and a half ago, down nearly to the Revolution. Bills of a thousand pounds were intermixed with parchment pennies, and worth no more than they.

"And this, then, is old Peter Goldthwaite's treasure!" said John Brown. "Your namesake, Peter, was something like yourself; and, when the provincial currency had depreciated fifty or seventy-five per cent., he bought it up in expectation of a rise. I have heard my grandfather say that old Peter gave his father a mortgage of this very house and land, to raise cash for his silly project. But the currency kept sinking, till nobody would take it as a gift; and there was old Peter Goldthwaite, like Peter the second, with thousands in his strong box and hardly a coat to his back. He went mad upon the strength of it. But, never mind, Peter! It is just the sort of capital for building castles in the air."

"The house will be down about our ears!" cried Tabitha, as the wind shook it with increasing violence.

"Let it fall!" said Peter, folding his arms, as he seated himself upon the chest.

"No, no, my old friend Peter," said John Brown. "I have house room for you and Tabby, and a safe vault for the chest of treasure. To-morrow we will try to come to an agreement about the sale of this old house. Real estate is well up, and I could afford you a pretty handsome price."

"And I," observed Peter Goldthwaite, with reviving spirits, "have a plan for laying out the cash to great advantage."

"Why, as to that," muttered John Brown to himself, "we must apply to the next court for a guardian to take care of the solid cash; and if Peter insists upon speculating, he may do it, to his heart's content, with old PETER GOLDTHWAITE'S TREASURE."

# THE SHAKER BRIDAL

ONE day, in the sick chamber of Father Ephraim, who had been forty years the presiding elder over the Shaker settlement at Goshen, there was an assemblage of several of the chief men of the sect. Individuals had come from the rich establishment at Lebanon, from Canterbury, Harvard, and Alfred, and from all the other localities where this strange people have fertilized the rugged hills of New England by their systematic industry. An elder was likewise there, who had made a pilgrimage of a thousand miles from a village of the faithful in Kentucky, to visit his spiritual kindred, the children of the sainted mother Ann. He had partaken of the homely abundance of their tables, had quaffed the far-famed Shaker cider, and had joined in the sacred dance, every step of which is believed to alienate the enthusiast from earth, and bear him onward to heavenly purity and bliss. His brethren of the north had now courteously invited him to be present on an occasion, when the concurrence of every eminent member of their community was peculiarly desirable.

The venerable Father Ephraim sat in his easy chair, not only hoary headed and infirm with age, but worn down by a lingering disease, which, it was evident, would very soon transfer his patriarchal staff to other hands. At his footstool stood a man and woman, both clad in the Shaker garb.

"My brethren," said Father Ephraim to the surrounding elders, feebly exerting himself to utter these few words, "here are the son and daughter to whom I would commit the trust of which Providence is about to lighten my weary shoulders. Read their faces, I pray you, and say whether the inward movement of the spirit hath guided my choice aright."

Accordingly, each elder looked at the two candidates with a most scrutinizing gaze. The man, whose name was Adam Colburn, had a face sunburnt with labor in the fields, yet intelligent, thoughtful, and traced with cares enough for a whole lifetime, though he had barely reached middle age. There was something severe in his aspect, and a rigidity throughout his person, characteristics that caused him generally to be taken for a school-master, which vocation, in fact, he had formerly exercised for several years. The woman, Martha Pierson, was somewhat above thirty, thin and pale, as a Shaker sister almost invariably is, and not entirely free from that corpse-like appearance which the garb of the sisterhood is so well calculated to impart.

"This pair are still in the summer of their years," observed the elder from Harvard, a shrewd old man. "I would like better to see the hoar-frost of autumn on their heads. Methinks, also, they will be exposed to peculiar temptations, on account of the carnal desires which have here-tofore subsisted between them."

"Nay, brother," said the elder from Canterbury, "the hoar-frost and the black-frost hath donè its work on Brother Adam and Sister Martha, even as we sometimes discern its traces in our cornfields, while they are yet green. And why should we question the wisdom of our venerable Fath-er's purpose although this pair, in their early youth, have loved one an-other as the world's people love? Are there not many brethren and sisters among us, who have lived long together in wedlock, yet, adopting our faith, find their hearts purified from all but spiritual affection?"

Whether or no the early loves of Adam and Martha had rendered it in-expedient that they should now preside together over a Shaker village, it was certainly most singular that such should be the final result of many warm and tender hopes. Children of neighboring families, their affection was older even than their school-days; it seemed an innate principle, in-terfused among all their sentiments and feelings, and not so much a dis-tinct remembrance, as connected with their whole volume of remem-brances. But, just as they reached a proper age for their union, misfor-tunes had fallen heavily on both, and made it necessary that they should resort to personal labor for a bare subsistence. Even under these circum-stances, Martha Pierson would probably have consented to unite her fate with Adam Colburn's, and, secure of the bliss of mutual love, would pa-tiently have awaited the less important gifts of fortune. But Adam, being of a calm and cautious character, was loath to relinquish the advantages which a single man possesses for raising himself in the world. Year after year, therefore, their marriage had been deferred. Adam Colburn had fol-lowed many vocations, had travelled far, and seen much of the world and of life. Martha had earned her bread sometimes as a seamstress, some-times as help to a farmer's wife, sometimes as school-mistress of the vil-lage children, sometimes as a nurse or watcher of the sick, thus acquiring a varied experience, the ultimate use of which she little anticipated. But nothing had gone prosperously with either of the lovers; at no subsequent moment would matrimony have been so prudent a measure as when they had first parted, in the opening bloom of life, to seek a better fortune. Still they had held fast their mutual faith. Martha might have been the wife of a man who sat among the senators of his native state, and Adam could have won the hand, as he had unintentionally won the heart, of a rich and comely widow. But neither of them desired good fortune save to share it with the other.

At length that calm despair which occurs only in a strong and some-what stubborn character, and yields to no second spring of hope, settled down on the spirit of Adam Colburn. He sought an interview with Mar-tha, and proposed that they should join the Society of Shakers. The con-verts of this sect are oftener driven within its hospitable gates by worldly misfortune than drawn thither by fanaticism, and are received without inquisition as to their motives. Martha, faithful still, had placed her hand in that of her lover, and accompanied him to the Shaker village. Here the natural capacity of each, cultivated and strengthened by the difficulties of their previous lives, had soon gained them an important rank in the Society, whose members are generally below the ordinary standard of intelligence. Their faith and feelings had, in some degree, become assimilated to those of their fellow-worshippers. Adam Colburn gradually acquired reputation, not only in the management of the temporal affairs of the Society, but as a clear and efficient preacher of their doctrines. Martha was not less distinguished in the duties proper to her sex. Finally, when the infirmities of Father Ephraim had admonished him to seek a successor in his patriarchal office, he thought of Adam and Martha, and proposed to renew, in their persons, the primitive form of Shaker government, as established by Mother Ann. They were to be the Father and Mother of the village. The simple ceremony, which would constitute them such, was now to be performed.

"Son Adam, and daughter Martha," said the venerable Father Ephraim, fixing his aged eyes piercingly upon them, "if ye can conscientiously undertake this charge, speak, that the brethren may not doubt of your fitness."

"Father," replied Adam, speaking with the calmness of his character, "I came to your village a disappointed man, weary of the world, worn out with continual trouble, seeking only a security against evil fortune, as I had no hope of good. Even my wishes of worldly success were almost dead within me. I came hither as a man might come to a tomb, willing to lie down in its gloom and coldness, for the sake of its peace and quiet. There was but one earthly affection in my breast, and it had grown calmer since my youth; so that I was satisfied to bring Martha to be my sister, in our new abode. We are brother and sister; nor would I have it otherwise. And in this peaceful village I have found all that I hoped for,—all that I desire. I will strive, with my best strength, for the spiritual and temporal good of our community. My conscience is not doubtful in this matter. I am ready to receive the trust."

"Thou hast spoken well, son Adam," said the Father. "God will bless thee in the office which I am about to resign."

"But our sister!" observed the elder from Harvard, "hath she not likewise a gift to declare her sentiments?"

Martha started, and moved her lips, as if she would have made a formal reply to this appeal. But, had she attempted it, perhaps the old recollections, the long-repressed feelings of childhood, youth, and womanhood, might have gushed from her heart, in words that it would have been profanation to utter there.

"Adam has spoken," said she hurriedly; "his sentiments are likewise mine."

But while speaking these few words, Martha grew so pale that she looked fitter to be laid in her coffin than to stand in the presence of Father Ephraim and the elders; she shuddered, also, as if there were something awful or horrible in her situation and destiny. It required, indeed, a more than feminine strength of nerve, to sustain the fixed observance of men so exalted and famous throughout the sect as these were. They had overcome their natural sympathy with human frailties and affections. One, when he joined the Society, had brought with him his wife and children, but never, from that hour, had spoken a fond word to the former, or taken his best-loved child upon his knee. Another, whose family refused to follow him, had been enabled—such was his gift of holy fortitude—to leave them to the mercy of the world. The youngest of the elders, a man of about fifty, had been bred from infancy in a Shaker village, and was said never to have clasped a woman's hand in his own, and to have no conception of a closer tie than the cold fraternal one of the sect. Old Father Ephraim was the most awful character of all. In his youth he had been a dissolute libertine, but was converted by Mother Ann herself, and had partaken of the wild fanaticism of the early Shakers. Tradition whispered, at the firesides of the village, that Mother Ann had been compelled to sear his heart of flesh with a red-hot iron before it could be purified from earthly passions.

However that might be, poor Martha had a woman's heart, and a tender one, and it quailed within her, as she looked round at those strange old men, and from them to the calm features of Adam Colburn. But perceiving that the elders eyed her doubtfully, she gasped for breath, and again spoke.

"With what strength is left me by my many troubles," said she, "I am ready to undertake this charge, and to do my best in it."

"My children, join your hands," said Father Ephraim.

They did so. The elders stood up around, and the Father feebly raised himself to a more erect position, but continued sitting in his great chair.

"I have bidden you to join your hands," said he, "not in earthly affection, for ye have cast off its chains forever; but as brother and sister in spiritual love, and helpers of one another in your allotted task. Teach unto others the faith which ye have received. Open wide your gates,—I deliver you the keys thereof,—open them wide to all who will give up the iniquities of the world, and come hither to lead lives of purity and peace. Receive the weary ones, who have known the vanity of earth,—receive the little children, that they may never learn that miserable lesson. And a blessing be upon your labors; so that the time may hasten on, when the mission of Mother Ann shall have wrought its full effect,—when children shall no more be born and die, and the last survivor of mortal race, some old and weary man like me, shall see the sun go down, nevermore to rise on a world of sin and sorrow!"

The aged Father sank back exhausted, and the surrounding elders deemed, with good reason, that the hour was come when the new heads of the village must enter on their patriarchal duties. In their attention to Father Ephraim, their eyes were turned from Martha Pierson, who grew paler and paler, unnoticed even by Adam Colburn. He, indeed, had withdrawn his hand from hers, and folded his arms with a sense of satisfied ambition. But paler and paler grew Martha by his side, till, like a corpse in its burial clothes, she sank down at the feet of her early lover; for, after many trials firmly borne, her heart could endure the weight of its desolate agony no longer.

## ENDICOTT AND THE RED CROSS

AT noon of on autumnal day, more than two centuries ago, the English colors were displayed by the standard-bearer of the Salem trainband, which had mustered for martial exercise under the orders of John Endicott. It was a period when the religious exiles were accustomed often to buckle on their armor, and practise the handling of their weapons of war. Since the first settlement of New England, its prospects had never been so dismal. The dissensions between Charles the First and his subjects were then, and for several years afterwards, confined to the floor of Parliament. The measures of the King and ministry were rendered more tyrannically violent by an opposition, which had not yet acquired sufficient confidence in its own strength to resist royal injustice with the sword. The bigoted and haughty primate, Laud, Archbishop of Canterbury, controlled the religious affairs of the realm, and was consequently invested with powers which might have wrought the utter ruin of the two Puritan colonies, Plymouth and Massachusetts. There is evidence on record that our forefathers perceived their danger, but were resolved that their infant country should not fall without a struggle, even beneath the giant strength of the King's right arm.

Such was the aspect of the times when the folds of the English banner, with the Red Cross in its field, were flung out over a company of Puritans. Their leader, the famous Endicott, was a man of stern and resolute countenance, the effect of which was heightened by a grizzled beard that swept the upper portion of his breastplate. This piece of armor was so highly polished that the whole surrounding scene had its image in the glittering steel. The central object in the mirrored picture was an edifice of humble architecture with neither steeple nor bell to proclaim it—what nevertheless it was—the house of prayer. A token of the perils of the wilderness was seen in the grim head of a wolf, which had just been slain within the precincts of the town, and according to the regular mode of claiming the bounty, was nailed on the porch of the meeting-house. The blood was still plashing on the doorstep. There happened to be visible, at the same noontide hour, so many other characteristics of the times and manners of the Puritans, that we must endeavor to represent them in a sketch, though far less vividly than they were reflected in the polished breastplate of John Endicott.

In close vicinity to the sacred edifice appeared that important engine of Puritanic authority, the whipping-post—with the soil around it well trodden by the feet of evil doers, who had there been disciplined. At one corner of the meeting-house was the pillory, and at the other the stocks; and, by a singular good fortune for our sketch, the head of an Episcopalian and suspected Catholic was grotesquely incased in the former machine; while a fellow-criminal, who had boisterously quaffed a health to the king, was confined by the legs in the latter. Side by side, on the meeting-house steps, stood a male and a female figure. The man was a tall, lean, haggard personification of fanaticism, bearing on his breast this label,—A WANTON GOSPELLER,—which betokened that he had dared to give interpretations of Holy Writ unsanctioned by the infallible judgment of the civil and religious rulers. His aspect showed no lack of zeal to maintain his heterodoxies, even at the stake. The woman wore a cleft stick on her tongue, in appropriate retribution for having wagged that unruly member against the elders of the church; and her countenance and gestures gave much cause to apprehend that, the moment the stick should be removed, a repetition of the offence would demand new ingenuity in chastising it.

The above-mentioned individuals had been sentenced to undergo their various modes of ignominy, for the space of one hour at noonday. But among the crowd were several whose punishment would be life-long; some, whose ears had been cropped, like those of puppy dogs; others, whose cheeks had been branded with the initials of their misdemeanors; one, with his nostrils slit and seared; and another, with a halter about his neck, which he was forbidden ever to take off, or to conceal beneath his garments. Methinks he must have been grievously tempted to affix the other end of the rope to some convenient beam or bough. There was likewise a young woman, with no mean share of beauty, whose doom it was to wear the letter A on the breast of her gown, in the eyes of all the world and her own children. And even her own children knew what that initial signified. Sporting with her infamy, the lost and desperate creature had embroidered the fatal token in scarlet cloth, with golden thread and the nicest art of needlework; so that the capital A might have been thought to mean Admirable, or anything rather than Adulteress.

Let not the reader argue, from any of these evidences of iniquity, that the times of the Puritans were more vicious than our own, when, as we pass along the very street of this sketch, we discern no badge of infamy on man or woman. It was the policy of our ancestors to search out even the most secret sins, and expose them to shame, without fear or favor, in the broadest light of the noonday sun. Were such the custom now, perchance we might find materials for a no less piquant sketch than the above.

Except the malefactors whom we have described, and the diseased or infirm persons, the whole male population of the town, between sixteen years and sixty, were seen in the ranks of the trainband. A few stately savages, in all the pomp and dignity of the primeval Indian, stood gazing at the spectacle. Their flint-headed arrows were but childish weapons compared with the matchlocks of the Puritans, and would have rattled harmlessly against the steel caps and hammered iron breastplates which inclosed each soldier in an individual fortress. The valiant John Endicott glanced with an eye of pride at his sturdy followers, and prepared to renew the martial toils of the day.

"Come, my stout hearts!" quoth he, drawing his sword. "Let us show these poor heathen that we can handle our weapons like men of might. Well for them, if they put us not to prove it in earnest!"

The iron-breasted company straightened their line, and each man drew the heavy butt of his matchlock close to his left foot, thus awaiting the orders of the captain. But, as Endicott glanced right and left along the front, he discovered a personage at some little distance with whom it behooved him to hold a parley. It was an elderly gentleman, wearing a black cloak and band, and a high-crowned hat, beneath which was a velvet skull-cap, the whole being the garb of a Puritan minister. This reverend person bore a staff which seemed to have been recently cut in the forest, and his shoes were bemired as if he had been travelling on foot through the swamps of the wilderness. His aspect was perfectly that of a pilgrim, heightened also by an apostolic dignity. Just as Endicott perceived him he laid aside his staff, and stooped to drink at a bubbling fountain which gushed into the sunshine about a score of yards from the corner of the meeting-house. But, ere the good man drank, he turned his face heavenward in thankfulness, and then, holding back his gray beard with one hand, he scooped up his simple draught in the hollow of the other.

"What, ho! good Mr. Williams," shouted Endicott. "You are welcome back again to our town of peace. How does our worthy Governor Winthrop? And what news from Boston?"

"The Governor hath his health, worshipful Sir," answered Roger Williams, now resuming his staff, and drawing near. "And for the news, here is a letter, which, knowing I was to travel hitherward to-day, his Excellency committed to my charge. Belike it contains tidings of much import; for a ship arrived yesterday from England."

Mr. Williams, the minister of Salem and of course known to all the spectators, had now reached the spot where Endicott was standing under the banner of his company, and put the Governor's epistle into his hand. The broad seal was impressed with Winthrop's coat of arms. Endicott hastily unclosed the letter and began to read, while, as his eye passed down the page, a wrathful change came over his manly countenance. The blood glowed through it, till it seemed to be kindling with an internal heat; nor was it unnatural to suppose that his breastplate would likewise become red-hot with the angry fire of the bosom which it covered. Arriving at the conclusion, he shook the letter fiercely in his hand, so that it rustled as loud as the flag above his head.

"Black tidings these, Mr. Williams," said he; "blacker never came to New England. Doubtless you know their purport?"

"Yea, truly," replied Roger Williams; "for the Governor consulted, respecting this matter, with my brethren in the ministry at Boston; and my opinion was likewise asked. And his Excellency entreats you by me, that the news be not suddenly noised abroad, lest the people be stirred up unto some outbreak, and thereby give the King and the Archbishop a handle against us."

"The Governor is a wise man—a wise man, and a meek and moderate," said Endicott, setting his teeth grimly. "Nevertheless, I must do according to my own best judgment. There is neither man, woman, nor child in New England, but has a concern as dear as life in these tidings; and if John Endicott's voice be loud enough, man, woman, and child shall hear them. Soldiers, wheel into a hollow square! Ho, good people! Here are news for one and all of you."

The soldiers closed in around their captain; and he and Roger Williams stood together under the banner of the Red Cross; while the women and the aged men pressed forward, and the mothers held up their children to look Endicott in the face. A few taps of the drum gave signal for silence and attention.

"Fellow-soldiers—fellow-exiles," began Endicott, speaking under strong excitement, yet powerfully restraining it, "wherefore did ye leave your native country? Wherefore, I say, have we left the green and fertile fields, the cottages, or, perchance, the old gray halls, where we were born and bred, the churchyards where our forefathers lie buried? Wherefore have we come hither to set up our own tombstones in a wilderness? A howling wilderness it is! The wolf and the bear meet us within halloo of our dwellings. The savage lieth in wait for us in the dismal shadow of the woods. The stubborn roots of the trees break our ploughshares, when we would till the earth. Our children cry for bread, and we must dig in the sands of the sea-shore to satisfy them. Wherefore, I say again, have we sought this country of a rugged soil and wintry sky? Was it not for the enjoyment of our civil rights? Was it not for liberty to worship God according to our conscience?"

"Call you this liberty of conscience?" interrupted a voice on the steps of the meeting-house.

It was the Wanton Gospeller. A sad and quiet smile flitted across the mild visage of Roger Williams. But Endicott, in the excitement of the moment, shook his sword wrathfully at the culprit—an ominous gesture from a man like him.

"What hast thou to do with conscience, thou knave?" cried he. "I said liberty to worship God, not license to profane and ridicule him. Break not in upon my speech, or I will lay thee neck and heels till this time tomorrow! Hearken to me, friends, nor heed that accursed rhapsodist. As I was saying, we have sacrificed all things, and have come to a land whereof the old world hath scarcely heard, that we might make a new world unto ourselves, and painfully seek a path from hence to heaven. But what think ye now? This son of a Scotch tyrant—this grandson of a Papistical and adulterous Scotch woman, whose death proved that a golden crown doth not always save an anointed head from the block"—

"Nay, brother, nay," interposed Mr. Williams; "thy words are not meet for a secret chamber, far less for a public street."

"Hold thy peace, Roger Williams!" answered Endicott, imperiously. "My spirit is wiser than thine for the business now in hand. I tell ye, fellow-exiles, that Charles of England, and Laud, our bitterest persecutor, arch-priest of Canterbury, are resolute to pursue us even hither. They are taking counsel, saith this letter, to send over a governor-general, in whose breast shall be deposited all the law and equity of the land. They are minded, also, to establish the idolatrous forms of English Episcopacy; so that, when Laud shall kiss the Pope's toe, as cardinal of Rome, he may deliver New England, bound hand and foot, into the power of his master!"

A deep groan from the auditors,—a sound of wrath, as well as fear and sorrow,—responded to this intelligence.

"Look ye to it, brethren," resumed Endicott, with increasing energy. "If this king and this arch-prelate have their will, we shall briefly behold a cross on the spire of this tabernacle which we have builded, and a high altar within its walls, with wax tapers burning round it at noonday. We shall hear the sacring bell, and the voices of the Romish priests saying the mass. But think ye, Christian men, that these abominations may be suffered without a sword drawn? without a shot fired? without blood spilt, yea, on the very stairs of the pulpit? No,—be ye strong of hand and stout of heart! Here we stand on our own soil, which we have bought with our goods, which we have won with our swords, which we have cleared with our axes, which we have tilled with the sweat of our brows, which we have sanctified with our prayers to the God that brought us hither! Who shall enslave us here? What have we to do with this mitred prelate,—with this crowned king? What have we to do with England?"

Endicott gazed round at the excited countenances of the people, now full of his own spirit, and then turned suddenly to the standard-bearer, who stood close behind him.

"Officer, lower your banner!" said he.

The officer obeyed; and, brandishing his sword, Endicott thrust it through the cloth, and, with his left hand, rent the Red Cross completely out of the banner. He then waved the tattered ensign above his head.

"Sacrilegious wretch!" cried the high-churchman in the pillory, unable longer to restrain himself, "thou hast rejected the symbol of our holy religion!"

"Treason, treason!" roared the royalist in the stocks. "He hath defaced the King's banner!"

"Before God and man, I will avouch the deed," answered Endicott. "Beat a flourish, drummer!—shout, soldiers and people!—in honor of the ensign of New England. Neither Pope nor Tyrant hath part in it now!"

With a cry of triumph, the people gave their sanction to one of the boldest exploits which our history records. And forever honored be the name of Endicott! We look back through the mist of ages, and recognize in the rending of the Red Cross from New England's banner the first omen of that deliverance which our fathers consummated after the bones of the stern Puritan had lain more than a century in the dust.

FROM MOSSES FROM AN OLD MANSE

# THE BIRTHMARK

In the latter part of the last century there lived a man of science, an eminent proficient in every branch of natural philosophy, who not long before our story opens had made experience of a spiritual affinity more attractive than any chemical one. He had left his laboratory to the care of an assistant, cleared his fine countenance from the furnace smoke, washed the stain of acids from his fingers, and persuaded a beautiful woman to become his wife. In those days when the comparatively recent discovery of electricity and other kindred mysteries of Nature seemed to open paths into the region of miracle, it was not unusual for the love of science to rival the love of woman in its depth and absorbing energy. The higher intellect, the imagination, the spirit, and even the heart might all find their congenial aliment in pursuits which, as some of their ardent votaries believed, would ascend from one step of powerful intelligence to another, until the philosopher should lay his hand on the secret of creative force and perhaps make new worlds for himself. We know not whether Aylmer possessed this degree of faith in man's ultimate control over Nature. He had devoted himself, however, too unreservedly to scientific studies ever to be weaned from them by any second passion. His love for his young wife might prove the stronger of the two; but it could only be by intertwining itself with his love of science, and uniting the strength of the latter to his own.

Such a union accordingly took place, and was attended with truly remarkable consequences and a deeply impressive moral. One day, very soon after their marriage, Aylmer sat gazing at his wife with a trouble in his countenance that grew stronger until he spoke.

"Georgiana," said he, "has it never occurred to you that the mark upon your cheek might be removed?"

"No, indeed," said she, smiling; but perceiving the seriousness of his manner, she blushed deeply. "To tell you the truth it has been so often called a charm that I was simple enough to imagine it might be so."

"Ah, upon another face perhaps it might," replied her husband; "but never on yours. No, dearest Georgiana, you came so nearly perfect from the hand of Nature that this slightest possible defect, which we hesitate whether to term a defect or a beauty, shocks me, as being the visible mark of earthly imperfection."

"Shocks you, my husband!" cried Georgiana, deeply hurt; at first reddening with momentary anger, but then bursting into tears. "Then why did you take me from my mother's side? You cannot love what shocks you!"

To explain this conversation it must be mentioned that in the centre of Georgiana's left cheek there was a singular mark, deeply interwoven, as it were, with the texture and substance of her face. In the usual state of her complexion—a healthy though delicate bloom—the mark wore a tint of deeper crimson, which imperfectly defined its shape amid the surrounding rosiness. When she blushed it gradually became more indistinct, and finally vanished amid the triumphant rush of blood that bathed the whole cheek with its brilliant glow. But if any shifting motion caused her to turn pale there was the mark again, a crimson stain upon the snow, in what Aylmer sometimes deemed an almost fearful distinctness. Its shape bore not a little similarity to the human hand, though of the smallest pygmy size. Georgiana's lovers were wont to say that some fairy at her birth hour had laid her tiny hand upon the infant's cheek, and left this impress there in token of the magic endowments that were to give her such sway over all hearts. Many a desperate swain would have risked life for the privilege of pressing his lips to the mysterious hand. It must not be concealed, however, that the impression wrought by this fairy sign manual varied exceedingly, according to the difference of temperament in the beholders. Some fastidious persons—but they were exclusively of her own sex—affirmed that the bloody hand, as they chose to call it, quite destroyed the effect of Georgiana's beauty, and rendered her countenance even hideous. But it would be as reasonable to say that one of those small blue stains which sometimes occur in the purest statuary marble would convert the Eve of Powers to a monster. Masculine observers, if the birthmark did not heighten their admiration, contented themselves with wishing it away, that the world might possess one living specimen of ideal loveliness without the semblance of a flaw. After his marriage,—for he thought little or nothing of the matter before,—Aylmer discovered that this was the case with himself.

Had she been less beautiful,—if Envy's self could have found aught else to sneer at,—he might have felt his affection heightened by the prettiness of this mimic hand, now vaguely portrayed, now lost, now stealing forth again and glimmering to and fro with every pulse of emotion that throbbed within her heart; but seeing her otherwise so perfect, he found this one defect grow more and more intolerable with every moment of their united lives. It was the fatal flaw of humanity which Nature, in one shape or another, stamps ineffaceably on all her productions, either to imply that they are temporary and finite, or that their perfection must be wrought by toil and pain. The crimson hand expressed the ineludible gripe in which mortality clutches the highest and purest of earthly mould, degrading them into kindred with the lowest, and even with the very brutes, like whom their visible frames return to dust. In this manner, selecting it as the symbol of his wife's liability to sin, sorrow, decay, and death, Aylmer's sombre imagination was not long in rendering the birthmark a frightful object, causing him more trouble and horror than ever Georgiana's beauty, whether of soul or sense, had given him delight.

At all the seasons which should have been their happiest, he invariably and without intending it, nay, in spite of a purpose to the contrary, reverted to this one disastrous topic. Trifling as it at first appeared, it so connected itself with innumerable trains of thought and modes of feeling that it became the central point of all. With the morning twilight Aylmer opened his eyes upon his wife's face and recognized the symbol of imperfection; and when they sat together at the evening hearth his eyes wandered stealthily to her cheek, and beheld, flickering with the blaze of the wood fire, the spectral hand that wrote mortality where he would fain have worshipped. Georgiana soon learned to shudder at his gaze. It needed but a glance with the peculiar expression that his face often wore to change the roses of her cheek into a deathlike paleness, amid which the crimson hand was brought strongly out, like a bass-relief of ruby on the whitest marble.

Late one night when the lights were growing dim, so as hardly to betray the stain on the poor wife's cheek, she herself, for the first time, voluntarily took up the subject.

"Do you remember, my dear Aylmer," said she, with a feeble attempt at a smile, "have you any recollection of a dream last night about this odious hand?"

"None! none whatever!" replied Aylmer, starting; but then he added, in a dry, cold tone, affected for the sake of concealing the real depth of his emotion, "I might well dream of it; for before I fell asleep it had taken a pretty firm hold of my fancy."

"And you did dream of it?" continued Georgiana, hastily; for she dreaded lest a gush of tears should interrupt what she had to say. "A terrible dream! I wonder that you can forget it. Is it possible to forget this one expression?—'It is in her heart now; we must have it out!' Reflect, my husband; for by all means I would have you recall that dream."

The mind is in a sad state when Sleep, the all-involving, cannot confine her spectres within the dim region of her sway, but suffers them to break forth, affrighting this actual life with secrets that perchance belong to a deeper one. Aylmer now remembered his dream. He had fancied himself with his servant Aminadab, attempting an operation for the removal of the birthmark; but the deeper went the knife, the deeper sank the hand, until at length its tiny grasp appeared to have caught hold of Georgiana's heart; whence, however, her husband was inexorably resolved to cut or wrench it away.

When the dream had shaped itself perfectly in his memory, Aylmer sat in his wife's presence with a guilty feeling. Truth often finds its way to the mind close muffled in robes of sleep, and then speaks with uncompromising directness of matters in regard to which we practise an unconscious self-deception during our waking moments. Until now he had not been aware of the tyrannizing influence acquired by one idea over his mind, and of the lengths which he might find in his heart to go for the sake of giving himself peace.

"Aylmer," resumed Georgiana, solemnly, "I know not what may be the cost to both of us to rid me of this fatal birthmark. Perhaps its removal may cause cureless deformity; or it may be the stain goes as deep as life itself. Again: do we know that there is a possibility, on any terms, of unclasping the firm gripe of this little hand which was laid upon me before I came into the world?"

"Dearest Georgiana, I have spent much thought upon the subject," hastily interrupted Aylmer. "I am convinced of the perfect practicability of its removal."

"If there be the remotest possibility of it," continued Georgiana, "let the attempt be made at whatever risk. Danger is nothing to me; for life, while this hateful mark makes me the object of your horror and disgust,— life is a burden which I would fling down with joy. Either remove this dreadful hand, or take my wretched life! You have deep science. All the world bears witness of it. You have achieved great wonders. Cannot you remove this little, little mark, which I cover with the tips of two small fingers? Is this beyond your power, for the sake of your own peace, and to save your poor wife from madness?"

"Noblest, dearest, tenderest wife," cried Aylmer, rapturously, "doubt not my power. I have already given this matter the deepest thought— thought which might almost have enlightened me to create a being less perfect than yourself. Georgiana, you have led me deeper than ever into the heart of science. I feel myself fully competent to render this dear cheek as faultless as its fellow; and then, most beloved, what will be my triumph when I shall have corrected what Nature left imperfect in her fairest work! Even Pygmalion, when his sculptured woman assumed life, felt not greater ecstasy than mine will be."

"It is resolved, then," said Georgiana, faintly smiling. "And, Aylmer, spare me not, though you should find the birthmark take refuge in my heart at last."

Her husband tenderly kissed her cheek—her right cheek—not that which bore the impress of the crimson hand.

The next day Aylmer apprised his wife of a plan that he had formed whereby he might have opportunity for the intense thought and constant watchfulness which the proposed operation would require; while Georgiana, likewise, would enjoy the perfect repose essential to its success. They were to seclude themselves in the extensive apartments occupied by Aylmer as a laboratory, and where, during his toilsome youth, he had made discoveries in the elemental powers of Nature that had roused the admiration of all the learned societies in Europe. Seated calmly in this laboratory, the pale philosopher had investigated the secrets of the highest cloud region and of the profoundest mines; he had satisfied himself of the causes that kindled and kept alive the fires of the volcano; and had explained the mystery of fountains, and how it is that they gush forth, some so bright and pure, and others with such rich medicinal virtues, from the dark bosom of the earth. Here, too, at an earlier period, he had studied the wonders of the human frame, and attempted to fathom the very process by which Nature assimilates all her precious influences from earth and air, and from the spiritual world, to create and foster man, her masterpiece. The latter pursuit, however, Aylmer had long laid aside in unwilling recognition of the truth—against which all seekers sooner or later stumble—that our great creative Mother, while she amuses us with apparently working in the broadest sunshine, is yet severely careful to keep her own secrets, and, in spite of her pretended openness, shows us nothing but results. She permits us, indeed, to mar, but seldom to mend, and, like a jealous patentee, on no account to make. Now, however, Aylmer resumed these half-forgotten investigations; not, of course, with such hopes or wishes as first suggested them; but because they involved much physiological truth and lay in the path of his proposed scheme for the treatment of Georgiana.

As he led her over the threshold of the laboratory, Georgiana was cold and tremulous. Aylmer looked cheerfully into her face, with intent to reassure her, but was so startled with the intense glow of the birthmark upon the whiteness of her cheek that he could not restrain a strong convulsive shudder. His wife fainted.

"Aminadab! Aminadab!" shouted Aylmer, stamping violently on the floor.

Forthwith there issued from an inner apartment a man of low stature, but bulky frame, with shaggy hair hanging about his visage, which was grimed with the vapors of the furnace. This personage had been Aylmer's underworker during his whole scientific career, and was admirably fitted for that office by his great mechanical readiness, and the skill with which, while incapable of comprehending a single principle, he executed all the details of his master's experiments. With his vast strength, his shaggy hair, his smoky aspect, and the indescribable earthiness that incrusted him, he seemed to represent man's physical nature; while Aylmer's slender figure, and pale, intellectual face, were no less apt a type of the spiritual element.

"Throw open the door of the boudoir, Aminadab," said Aylmer, "and burn a pastil."

"Yes, master," answered Aminadab, looking intently at the lifeless form of Georgiana; and then he muttered to himself, "If she were my wife, I'd never part with that birthmark."

When Georgiana recovered consciousness she found herself breathing an atmosphere of penetrating fragrance, the gentle potency of which had recalled her from her deathlike faintness. The scene around her looked like enchantment. Aylmer had converted those smoky, dingy, sombre rooms, where he had spent his brightest years in recondite pursuits, into a series of beautiful apartments not unfit to be the secluded abode of a lovely woman. The walls were hung with gorgeous curtains, which imparted the combination of grandeur and grace that no other species of adornment can achieve; and as they fell from the ceiling to the floor, their rich and ponderous folds, concealing all angles and straight lines, appeared to shut in the scene from infinite space. For aught Georgiana knew, it might be a pavilion among the clouds. And Aylmer, excluding the sunshine, which would have interfered with his chemical processes, had supplied its place with perfumed lamps, emitting flames of various hue, but all uniting in a soft, impurpled radiance. He now knelt by his wife's side, watching her earnestly, but without alarm; for he was confident in his science, and felt that he could draw a magic circle round her within which no evil might intrude.

"Where am I? Ah, I remember," said Georgiana, faintly; and she placed her hand over her cheek to hide the terrible mark from her husband's eyes.

"Fear not, dearest!" exclaimed he. "Do not shrink from me! Believe me, Georgiana, I even rejoice in this single imperfection, since it will be such a rapture to remove it."

"Oh, spare me!" sadly replied his wife. "Pray do not look at it again. I never can forget that convulsive shudder."

In order to soothe Georgiana, and, as it were, to release her mind from the burden of actual things, Aylmer now put in practice some of the light and playful secrets which science had taught him among its profounder lore. Airy figures, absolutely bodiless ideas, and forms of unsubstantial beauty came and danced before her, imprinting their momentary footsteps on beams of light. Though she had some indistinct idea of the method of these optical phenomena, still the illusion was almost perfect enough to warrant the belief that her husband possessed sway over the spiritual world. Then again, when she felt a wish to look forth from her seclusion, immediately, as if her thoughts were answered, the procession of external existence flitted across a screen. The scenery and the figures of actual life were perfectly represented, but with that bewitching, yet indescribable difference which always makes a picture, an image, or a shadow so much more attractive than the original. When wearied of this, Aylmer bade her cast her eyes upon a vessel containing a quantity of earth. She did so, with little interest at first; but was soon startled to perceive the germ of a plant shooting upward from the soil. Then came the slender stalk; the leaves gradually unfolded themselves; and amid them was a perfect and lovely flower.

"It is magical!" cried Georgiana. "I dare not touch it."

"Nay, pluck it," answered Aylmer,—"pluck it, and inhale its brief perfume while you may. The flower will wither in a few moments and leave nothing save its brown seed vessels; but thence may be perpetuated a race as ephemeral as itself."

But Georgiana had no sooner touched the flower than the whole plant suffered a blight, its leaves turning coal-black as if by the agency of fire.

"There was too powerful a stimulus," said Aylmer, thoughtfully.

To make up for this abortive experiment, he proposed to take her portrait by a scientific process of his own invention. It was to be effected by rays of light striking upon a polished plate of metal. Georgiana assented; but, on looking at the result, was affrighted to find the features of the portrait blurred and indefinable; while the minute figure of a hand appeared where the cheek should have been. Aylmer snatched the metallic plate and threw it into a jar of corrosive acid.

Soon, however, he forgot these mortifying failures. In the intervals of study and chemical experiment he came to her flushed and exhausted, but seemed invigorated by her presence, and spoke in glowing language of the resources of his art. He gave a history of the long dynasty of the alchemists, who spent so many ages in quest of the universal solvent by which the golden principle might be elicited from all things vile and base. Aylmer appeared to believe that, by the plainest scientific logic, it was altogether within the limits of possibility to discover this long-sought medium; "but," he added, "a philosopher who should go deep enough to acquire the power would attain too lofty a wisdom to stoop to the exercise of it." Not less singular were his opinions in regard to the elixir vitæ. He more than intimated that it was at his option to concoct a liquid that should prolong life for years, perhaps interminably; but that it would produce a discord in Nature which all the world, and chiefly the quaffer of the immortal nostrum, would find cause to curse.

"Aylmer, are you in earnest?" asked Georgiana, looking at him with amazement and fear. "It is terrible to possess such power, or even to dream of possessing it."

"Oh, do not tremble, my love," said her husband. "I would not wrong either you or myself by working such inharmonious effects upon our lives; but I would have you consider how trifling, in comparison, is the skill requisite to remove this little hand."

At the mention of the birthmark, Georgiana, as usual, shrank as if a redhot iron had touched her cheek.

Again Aylmer applied himself to his labors. She could hear his voice in the distant furnace room giving directions to Aminadab, whose harsh, uncouth, misshapen tones were audible in response, more like the grunt or growl of a brute than human speech. After hours of absence, Aylmer reappeared and proposed that she should now examine his cabinet of chemical products and natural treasures of the earth. Among the former he showed her a small vial, in which, he remarked, was contained a gentle yet most powerful fragrance, capable of impregnating all the breezes that blow across a kingdom. They were of inestimable value, the contents of that little vial; and, as he said so, he threw some of the perfume into the air and filled the room with piercing and invigorating delight.

"And what is this?" asked Georgiana, pointing to a small crystal globe containing a gold-colored liquid. "It is so beautiful to the eye that I could imagine it the elixir of life."

"In one sense it is," replied Aylmer; "or, rather, the elixir of immortality. It is the most precious poison that ever was concocted in this world. By its aid I could apportion the lifetime of any mortal at whom you might point your finger. The strength of the dose would determine whether he were to linger out years, or drop dead in the midst of a breath. No king on his guarded throne could keep his life if I, in my private station, should deem that the welfare of millions justified me in depriving him of it."

"Why do you keep such a terrific drug?" inquired Georgiana in horror.

"Do not mistrust me, dearest," said her husband, smiling; "its virtuous potency is yet greater than its harmful one. But see! here is a powerful cosmetic. With a few drops of this in a vase of water, freckles may be washed away as easily as the hands are cleansed. A stronger infusion would take the blood out of the cheek, and leave the rosiest beauty a pale ghost."

"Is it with this lotion that you intend to bathe my cheek?" asked Georgiana, anxiously.

"Oh, no," hastily replied her husband; "this is merely superficial. Your case demands a remedy that shall go deeper."

In his interviews with Georgiana, Aylmer generally made minute inquiries as to her sensations and whether the confinement of the rooms and the temperature of the atmosphere agreed with her. These questions had such a particular drift that Georgiana began to conjecture that she was already subjected to certain physical influences, either breathed in with the fragrant air or taken with her food. She fancied likewise, but it might be altogether fancy, that there was a stirring up of her system—a strange, indefinite sensation creeping through her veins, and tingling, half painfully, half pleasurably, at her heart. Still, whenever she dared to look into the mirror, there she beheld herself pale as a white rose and with the crimson birthmark stamped upon her cheek. Not even Aylmer now hated it so much as she.

To dispel the tedium of the hours which her husband found it necessary to devote to the processes of combination and analysis, Georgiana turned over the volumes of his scientific library. In many dark old tomes she met with chapters full of romance and poetry. They were the works of philosophers of the middle ages, such as Albertus Magnus, Cornelius Agrippa, Paracelsus, and the famous friar who created the prophetic Brazen Head. All these antique naturalists stood in advance of their centuries, yet were imbued with some of their credulity, and therefore were believed, and perhaps imagined themselves to have acquired from the investigation of Nature a power above Nature, and from physics a sway over the spiritual world. Hardly less curious and imaginative were the early volumes of the Transactions of the Royal Society, in which the members, knowing little of the limits of natural possibility, were continually recording wonders or proposing methods whereby wonders might be wrought.

But to Georgiana the most engrossing volume was a large folio from her husband's own hand, in which he had recorded every experiment of his scientific career, its original aim, the methods adopted for its development, and its final success or failure, with the circumstances to which either event was attributable. The book, in truth, was both the history and emblem of his ardent, ambitious, imaginative, yet practical and laborious life. He handled physical details as if there were nothing beyond them; yet spiritualized them all, and redeemed himself from materialism by his strong and eager aspiration towards the infinite. In his grasp the veriest clod of earth assumed a soul. Georgiana, as she read, reverenced Aylmer and loved him more profoundly than ever, but with a less entire dependence on his judgment than heretofore. Much as he had accomplished, she could not but observe that his most splendid successes were almost invariably failures, if compared with the ideal at which he aimed. His brightest diamonds were the merest pebbles, and felt to be so by himself, in comparison with the inestimable gems which lay hidden beyond his reach. The volume, rich with achievements that had won renown for its author, was yet as melancholy a record as ever mortal hand had penned. It was the sad confession and continual exemplification of the shortcomings of the composite man, the spirit burdened with clay and working in matter, and of the despair that assails the higher nature at finding itself so miserably thwarted by the earthly part. Perhaps every man of genius in whatever sphere might recognize the image of his own experience in Aylmer's journal.

So deeply did these reflections affect Georgiana that she laid her face upon the open volume and burst into tears. In this situation she was found by her husband.

"It is dangerous to read in a sorcerer's books," said he with a smile, though his countenance was uneasy and displeased. "Georgiana, there are pages in that volume which I can scarcely glance over and keep my senses. Take heed lest it prove as detrimental to you."

"It has made me worship you more than ever," said she.

"Ah, wait for this one success," rejoined he, "then worship me if you will. I shall deem myself hardly unworthy of it. But come, I have sought you for the luxury of your voice. Sing to me, dearest."

So she poured out the liquid music of her voice to quench the thirst of his spirit. He then took his leave with a boyish exuberance of gayety, assuring her that her seclusion would endure but a little longer, and that the result was already certain. Scarcely had he departed when Georgiana felt irresistibly impelled to follow him. She had forgotten to inform Aylmer of a symptom which for two or three hours past had begun to excite her attention. It was a sensation in the fatal birthmark, not painful, but which induced a restlessness throughout her system. Hastening after her husband, she intruded for the first time into the laboratory.

The first thing that struck her eye was the furnace, that hot and feverish worker, with the intense glow of its fire, which by the quantities of soot clustered above it seemed to have been burning for ages. There was a distilling apparatus in full operation. Around the room were retorts, tubes, cylinders, crucibles, and other apparatus of chemical research. An electrical machine stood ready for immediate use. The atmosphere felt oppressively close, and was tainted with gaseous odors which had been tormented forth by the processes of science. The severe and homely simplicity of the apartment, with its naked walls and brick pavement, looked strange, accustomed as Georgiana had become to the fantastic elegance of her boudoir. But what chiefly, indeed almost solely, drew her attention, was the aspect of Aylmer himself.

He was pale as death, anxious and absorbed, and hung over the furnace as if it depended upon his utmost watchfulness whether the liquid which it was distilling should be the draught of immortal happiness or misery.

How different from the sanguine and joyous mien that he had assumed for Georgiana's encouragement!

"Carefully now, Aminadab; carefully, thou human machine; carefully, thou man of clay!" muttered Aylmer, more to himself than his assistant. "Now, if there be a thought too much or too little, it is all over."

"Ho! ho!" mumbled Aminadab. "Look, master! look!"

Aylmer raised his eyes hastily, and at first reddened, then grew paler than ever, on beholding Georgiana. He rushed towards her and seized her arm with a gripe that left the print of his fingers upon it.

"Why do you come hither? Have you no trust in your husband?" cried he, impetuously. "Would you throw the blight of that fatal birthmark over my labors? It is not well done. Go, prying woman, go!"

"Nay, Aylmer," said Georgiana with the firmness of which she possessed no stinted endowment, "it is not you that have a right to complain. You mistrust your wife; you have concealed the anxiety with which you watch the development of this experiment. Think not so unworthily of me, my husband. Tell me all the risk we run, and fear not that I shall shrink; for my share in it is far less than your own."

"No, no, Georgiana!" said Aylmer, impatiently; "it must not be."

"I submit," replied she calmly. "And, Aylmer, I shall quaff whatever draught you bring me; but it will be on the same principle that would induce me to take a dose of poison if offered by your hand."

"My noble wife," said Aylmer, deeply moved, "I knew not the height and depth of your nature until now. Nothing shall be concealed. Know, then, that this crimson hand, superficial as it seems, has clutched its grasp into your being with a strength of which I had no previous conception. I have already administered agents powerful enough to do aught except to change your entire physical system. Only one thing remains to be tried. If that fail us we are ruined."

"Why did you hesitate to tell me this?" asked she.

"Because, Georgiana," said Aylmer, in a low voice, "there is danger."

"Danger? There is but one danger—that this horrible stigma shall be left upon my cheek!" cried Georgiana. "Remove it, remove it, whatever be the cost, or we shall both go mad!"

"Heaven knows your words are too true," said Aylmer, sadly. "And now, dearest, return to your boudoir. In a little while all will be tested."

He conducted her back and took leave of her with a solemn tenderness which spoke far more than his words how much was now at stake. After his departure Georgiana became rapt in musings. She considered the character of Aylmer, and did it completer justice than at any previous moment. Her heart exulted, while it trembled, at his honorable love—so pure and lofty that it would accept nothing less than perfection nor miserably make itself contented with an earthlier nature than he had dreamed of. She felt how much more precious was such a sentiment than that meaner kind which would have borne with the imperfection for her sake, and have been guilty of treason to holy love by degrading its perfect idea to the level of the actual; and with her whole spirit she prayed that, for a single moment, she might satisfy his highest and deepest conception. Longer than one moment she well knew it could not be; for his spirit was ever on the march, ever ascending, and each instant required something that was beyond the scope of the instant before.

The sound of her husband's footsteps aroused her. He bore a crystal goblet containing a liquor colorless as water, but bright enough to be the draught of immortality. Aylmer was pale; but it seemed rather the consequence of a highly-wrought state of mind and tension of spirit than of fear or doubt.

"The concoction of the draught has been perfect," said he, in answer to Georgiana's look. "Unless all my science have deceived me, it cannot fail."

"Save on your account, my dearest Aylmer," observed his wife, "I might wish to put off this birthmark of mortality by relinquishing mortality itself in preference to any other mode. Life is but a sad possession to those who have attained precisely the degree of moral advancement at which I stand. Were I weaker and blinder it might be happiness. Were I stronger, it might be endured hopefully. But, being what I find myself, methinks I am of all mortals the most fit to die."

"You are fit for heaven without tasting death!" replied her husband. "But why do we speak of dying? The draught cannot fail. Behold its effect upon this plant."

On the window seat there stood a geranium diseased with yellow blotches, which had overspread all its leaves. Aylmer poured a small quantity of the liquid upon the soil in which it grew. In a little time, when the roots of the plant had taken up the moisture, the unsightly blotches began to be extinguished in a living verdure.

"There needed no proof," said Georgiana, quietly. "Give me the goblet. I joyfully stake all upon your word."

"Drink, then, thou lofty creature!" exclaimed Aylmer, with fervid admiration. "There is no taint of imperfection on thy spirit. Thy sensible frame, too, shall soon be all perfect."

She quaffed the liquid and returned the goblet to his hand.

"It is grateful," said she with a placid smile. "Methinks it is like water from a heavenly fountain; for it contains I know not what of unobtrusive fragrance and deliciousness. It allays a feverish thirst that had parched me for many days. Now, dearest, let me sleep. My earthly senses are closing over my spirit like the leaves around the heart of a rose at sunset."

She spoke the last words with a gentle reluctance, as if it required almost more energy than she could command to pronounce the faint and lingering syllables. Scarcely had they loitered through her lips ere she was lost in slumber. Aylmer sat by her side, watching her aspect with the emotions proper to a man the whole value of whose existence was involved in the process now to be tested. Mingled with this mood, however, was the philosophic investigation characteristic of the man of science. Not the minutest symptom escaped him. A heightened flush of the cheek, a slight irregularity of breath, a quiver of the eyelid, a hardly perceptible tremor through the frame,—such were the details which, as the moments passed, he wrote down in his folio volume. Intense thought had set its stamp upon every previous page of that volume, but the thoughts of years were all concentrated upon the last.

While thus employed, he failed not to gaze often at the fatal hand, and not without a shudder. Yet once, by a strange and unaccountable impulse, he pressed it with his lips. His spirit recoiled, however, in the very act; and Georgiana, out of the midst of her deep sleep, moved uneasily and murmured as if in remonstrance. Again Aylmer resumed his watch. Nor was it without avail. The crimson hand, which at first had been strongly visible upon the marble paleness of Georgiana's cheek, now grew more faintly outlined. She remained not less pale than ever; but the birthmark, with every breath that came and went, lost somewhat of its former distinctness. Its presence had been awful; its departure was more awful still. Watch the stain of the rainbow fading out the sky, and you will know how that mysterious symbol passed away.

"By Heaven! it is well-nigh gone!" said Aylmer to himself, in almost irrepressible ecstasy. "I can scarcely trace it now. Success! success! And now it is like the faintest rose color. The lightest flush of blood across her cheek would overcome it. But she is so pale!"

He drew aside the window curtain and suffered the light of natural day to fall into the room and rest upon her cheek. At the same time he heard a gross, hoarse chuckle, which he had long known as his servant Aminadab's expression of delight.

"Ah, clod! ah, earthly mass!" cried Aylmer, laughing in a sort of frenzy, "you have served me well! Matter and spirit—earth and heaven —have both done their part in this! Laugh, thing of the senses! You have earned the right to laugh."

These exclamations broke Georgiana's sleep. She slowly unclosed her eyes and gazed into the mirror which her husband had arranged for that purpose. A faint smile flitted over her lips when she recognized how barely perceptible was now that crimson hand which had once blazed forth with such disastrous brilliancy as to scare away all their happiness. But then her eyes sought Aylmer's face with a trouble and anxiety that he could by no means account for.

"My poor Aylmer!" murmured she.

"Poor? Nay, richest, happiest, most favored!" exclaimed he. "My peerless bride, it is successful! You are perfect!"

"My poor Aylmer," she repeated, with a more than human tenderness, "you have aimed loftily; you have done nobly. Do not repent that with so high and pure a feeling, you have rejected the best the earth could offer. Aylmer, dearest Aylmer, I am dying!"

Alas! it was too true! The fatal hand had grappled with the mystery of life, and was the bond by which an angelic spirit kept itself in union with a mortal frame. As the last crimson tint of the birthmark—that sole token of human imperfection—faded from her cheek, the parting breath of the now perfect woman passed into the atmosphere, and her soul, lingering a moment near her husband, took its heavenward flight. Then a hoarse, chuckling laugh was heard again! Thus ever does the gross fatality of earth exult in its invariable triumph over the immortal essence which, in this dim sphere of half development, demands the completeness of a higher state. Yet, had Alymer reached a profounder wisdom, he need not thus have flung away the happiness which would have woven his mortal life of the selfsame texture with the celestial. The momentary circumstance was too strong for him; he failed to look beyond the shadowy scope of time, and, living once for all in eternity, to find the perfect future in the present.

# YOUNG GOODMAN BROWN

YOUNG Goodman Brown came forth at sunset into the street at Salem village; but put his head back, after crossing the threshold, to exchange a parting kiss with his young wife. And Faith, as the wife was aptly named, thrust her own pretty head into the street, letting the wind play with the pink ribbons of her cap while she called to Goodman Brown.

"Dearest heart," whispered she, softly and rather sadly, when her lips were close to his ear, "prithee put off your journey until sunrise and sleep in your own bed to-night. A lone woman is troubled with such dreams and such thoughts that she's afeard of herself sometimes. Pray tarry with me this night, dear husband, of all nights in the year."

"My love and my Faith," replied young Goodman Brown, "of all nights in the year, this one night must I tarry away from thee. My journey, as thou callest it, forth and back again, must needs be done 'twixt now and sunrise. What, my sweet, pretty wife, dost thou doubt me already, and we but three months married?"

"Then God bless you!" said Faith, with the pink ribbons; "and may you find all well when you come back."

"Amen!" cried Goodman Brown. "Say thy prayers, dear Faith, and go to bed at dusk, and no harm will come to thee."

So they parted; and the young man pursued his way until, being about to turn the corner by the meeting-house, he looked back and saw the head of Faith still peeping after him with a melancholy air, in spite of her pink ribbons.

"Poor little Faith!" thought he, for his heart smote him. "What a wretch am I to leave her on such an errand! She talks of dreams, too. Methought as she spoke there was trouble in her face, as if a dream had warned her what work is to be done tonight. But no, no; 't would kill her to think it. Well, she's a blessed angel on earth; and after this one night I'll cling to her skirts and follow her to heaven."

With this excellent resolve for the future, Goodman Brown felt himself justified in making more haste on his present evil purpose. He had taken a

dreary road, darkened by all the gloomiest trees of the forest, which barely stood aside to let the narrow path creep through, and closed immediately behind. It was all as lonely as could be; and there is this peculiarity in
such a solitude, that the traveller knows not who may be concealed by the
innumerable trunks and the thick boughs overhead; so that with lonely
footsteps he may yet be passing through an unseen multitude.

"There may be a devilish Indian behind every tree," said Goodman
Brown to himself; and he glanced fearfully behind him as he added,
"What if the devil himself should be at my very elbow!"

His head being turned back, he passed a crook of the road, and, looking
forward again, beheld the figure of a man, in grave and decent attire,
seated at the foot of an old tree. He arose at Goodman Brown's approach
and walked onward side by side with him.

"You are late, Goodman Brown," said he. "The clock of the Old South
was striking as I came through Boston, and that is full fifteen minutes
agone."

"Faith kept me back a while," replied the young man, with a tremor in
his voice, caused by the sudden appearance of his companion, though not
wholly unexpected.

It was now deep dusk in the forest, and deepest in that part of it where
these two were journeying. As nearly as could be discerned, the second
traveller was about fifty years old, apparently in the same rank of life as
Goodman Brown, and bearing a considerable resemblance to him, though
perhaps more in expression than features. Still they might have been tak-
en for father and son. And yet, though the elder person was as simply clad
as the younger, and as simple in manner too, he had an indescribable air
of one who knew the world, and who would not have felt abashed at the
governor's dinner table or in King William's court, were it possible that
his affairs should call him thither. But the only thing about him that could
be fixed upon as remarkable was his staff, which bore the likeness of a
great black snake, so curiously wrought that it might almost be seen to
twist and wriggle itself like a living serpent. This, of course, must have
been an ocular deception, assisted by the uncertain light.

"Come, Goodman Brown," cried his fellow-traveller, "this is a dull pace
for the beginning of a journey. Take my staff, if you are so soon weary."

"Friend," said the other, exchanging his slow pace for a full stop, "having kept covenant by meeting thee here, it is my purpose now to return
whence I came. I have scruples touching the matter thou wot'st of."

"Sayest thou so?" replied he of the serpent, smiling apart. "Let us walk
on, nevertheless, reasoning as we go; and if I convince thee not thou shalt
turn back. We are but a little way in the forest yet."

"Too far! too far!" exclaimed the goodman, unconsciously resuming
his walk. "My father never went into the woods on such an errand, nor
his father before him. We have been a race of honest men and good Christians since the days of the martyrs; and shall I be the first of the name of
Brown that ever took this path and kept"—

"Such company, thou wouldst say," observed the elder person, interpreting his pause. "Well said, Goodman Brown! I have been as well acquainted with your family as with ever a one among the Puritans; and that's no trifle to say. I helped your grandfather, the constable, when he lashed the Quaker woman so smartly through the streets of Salem; and it was I that brought your father a pitch-pine knot, kindled at my own hearth, to set fire to an Indian village, in King Philip's war. They were my good friends, both; and many a pleasant walk have we had along this path, and returned merrily after midnight. I would fain be friends with you for their sake."

"If it be as thou sayest," replied Goodman Brown, "I marvel they never spoke of these matters; or, verily, I marvel not, seeing that the least rumor of the sort would have driven them from New England. We are a people of prayer, and good works to boot, and abide no such wickedness."

"Wickedness or not," said the traveller with the twisted staff, "I have a very general acquaintance here in New England. The deacons of many a church have drunk the communion wine with me; the selectmen of divers towns make me their chairman; and a majority of the Great and General Court are firm supporters of my interest. The governor and I, too—But these are state secrets."

"Can this be so?" cried Goodman Brown, with a stare of amazement at his undisturbed companion. "Howbeit, I have nothing to do with the governor and council; they have their own ways, and are no rule for a simple husbandman like me. But, were I to go on with thee, how should I meet the eye of that good old man, our minister, at Salem village? Oh, his voice would make me tremble both Sabbath day and lecture day."

Thus far the elder traveller had listened with due gravity; but now burst into a fit of irrepressible mirth, shaking himself so violently that his snake-like staff actually seemed to wriggle in sympathy.

"Ha! ha! ha!" shouted he again and again; then composing himself, "Well, go on, Goodman Brown, go on; but, prithee, don't kill me with laughing."

"Well, then, to end the matter at once," said Goodman Brown, considerably nettled, "there is my wife, Faith. It would break her dear little heart; and I'd rather break my own."

"Nay, if that be the case," answered the other, "e'en go thy ways, Goodman Brown. I would not for twenty old women like the one hobbling before us that Faith should come to any harm."

As he spoke he pointed his staff at a female figure on the path, in whom Goodman Brown recognized a very pious and exemplary dame, who had taught him his catechism in youth, and was still his moral and spiritual adviser, jointly with the minister and Deacon Gookin.

"A marvel, truly, that Goody Cloyse should be so far in the wilderness at nightfall," said he. "But with your leave, friend, I shall take a cut through the woods until we have left this Christian woman behind. Being a stranger to you, she might ask whom I was consorting with and whither I was going."

"Be it so," said his fellow-traveller. "Betake you to the woods, and let me keep the path."

Accordingly the young man turned aside, but took care to watch his companion, who advanced softly along the road until he had come within a staff's length of the old dame. She, meanwhile, was making the best of her way, with singular speed for so aged a woman, and mumbling some indistinct words—a prayer, doubtless—as she went. The traveller put forth his staff and touched her withered neck with what seemed the serpent's tail.

"The devil!" screamed the pious old lady.

"Then Goody Cloyse knows her old friend?" observed the traveller, confronting her and leaning on his writhing stick.

"Ah, forsooth, and is it your worship indeed?" cried the good dame. "Yea, truly is it, and in the very image of my old gossip, Goodman Brown, the grandfather of the silly fellow that now is. But—would your worship believe it?—my broomstick hath strangely disappeared, stolen, as I suspect, by that unhanged witch, Goody Cory, and that, too, when I was all anointed with the juice of smallage, and cinquefoil, and wolf's bane"—

"Mingled with fine wheat and the fat of a new-born babe," said the shape of old Goodman Brown.

"Ah, your worship knows the recipe," cried the old lady, cackling aloud. "So, as I was saying, being all ready for the meeting, and no horse to ride on, I made up my mind to foot it; for they tell me there is a nice young man to be taken into communion to-night. But now your good worship will lend me your arm, and we shall be there in a twinkling."

"That can hardly be," answered her friend. "I may not spare you my arm, Goody Cloyse; but here is my staff, if you will."

So saying, he threw it down at her feet, where, perhaps, it assumed life, being one of the rods which its owner had formerly lent to the Egyptian magi. Of this fact, however, Goodman Brown could not take cognizance. He had cast up his eyes in astonishment, and, looking down again, beheld neither Goody Cloyse nor the serpentine staff, but his fellow-traveller alone, who waited for him as calmly as if nothing had happened.

"That old woman taught me my catechism," said the young man; and there was a world of meaning in this simple comment.

They continued to walk onward, while the elder traveller exhorted his companion to make good speed and persevere in the path, discoursing so aptly that his arguments seemed rather to spring up in the bosom of his auditor than to be suggested by himself. As they went, he plucked a branch of maple to serve for a walking stick, and began to strip it of the twigs and little boughs, which were wet with evening dew. The moment his fingers touched them they became strangely withered and dried up as with a week's sunshine. Thus the pair proceeded, at a good free pace, until suddenly, in a gloomy hollow of the road, Goodman Brown sat himself down on the stump of a tree and refused to go any farther.

"Friend," said he, stubbornly, "my mind is made up. Not another step will I budge on this errand. What if a wretched old woman do choose to go to the devil when I thought she was going to heaven: is that any reason why I should quit my dear Faith and go after her?"

"You will think better of this by and by," said his acquaintance, composedly. "Sit here and rest yourself a while; and when you feel like moving again, there is my staff to help you along."

Without more words, he threw his companion the maple stick, and was as speedily out of sight as if he had vanished into the deepening gloom. The young man sat a few moments by the roadside, applauding himself greatly, and thinking with how clear a conscience he should meet the minister in his morning walk, nor shrink from the eye of good old Deacon Gookin. And what calm sleep would be his that very night, which was to have been spent so wickedly, but so purely and sweetly now, in the arms of Faith! Amidst these pleasant and praiseworthy meditations, Goodman Brown heard the tramp of horses along the road, and deemed it advisable to conceal himself within the verge of the forest, conscious of the guilty purpose that had brought him thither, though now so happily turned from it.

On came the hoof tramps and the voices of the riders, two grave old voices, conversing soberly as they drew near. These mingled sounds appeared to pass along the road, within a few yards of the young man's hiding-place; but, owing doubtless to the depth of the gloom at that particular spot, neither the travellers nor their steeds were visible. Though their figures brushed the small boughs by the wayside, it could not be seen that they intercepted, even for a moment, the faint gleam from the strip of bright sky athwart which they must have passed. Goodman Brown alternately crouched and stood on tiptoe, pulling aside the branches and thrusting forth his head as far as he durst without discerning so much as a shadow. It vexed him the more, because he could have sworn, were such a thing possible, that he recognized the voices of the minister and Deacon Gookin, jogging along quietly, as they were wont to do, when bound to some ordination or ecclesiastical council. While yet within hearing, one of the riders stopped to pluck a switch.

"Of the two, reverend sir," said the voice like the deacon's, "I had rather miss an ordination dinner than to-night's meeting. They tell me that some of our community are to be here from Falmouth and beyond, and others from Connecticut and Rhode Island, besides several of the Indian powwows, who, after their fashion, know almost as much deviltry as the best of us. Moreover, there is a goodly young woman to be taken into communion."

"Mighty well, Deacon Gookin!" replied the solemn old tones of the minister. "Spur up, or we shall be late. Nothing can be done, you know, until I get on the ground."

The hoofs clattered again; and the voices, talking so strangely in the empty air, passed on through the forest, where no church had ever been gathered or solitary Christian prayed. Whither, then, could these holy men be journeying so deep into the heathen wilderness? Young Goodman Brown caught hold of a tree for support, being ready to sink down on the ground, faint and overburdened with the heavy sickness of his heart. He looked up to the sky, doubting whether there really was a heaven above him. Yet there was the blue arch, and the stars brightening in it.

"With heaven above and Faith below, I will yet stand firm against the devil!" cried Goodman Brown.

While he still gazed upward into the deep arch of the firmament and had lifted his hands to pray, a cloud, though no wind was stirring, hurried across the zenith and hid the brightening stars. The blue sky was still visible, except directly overhead, where this black mass of cloud was sweeping swiftly northward. Aloft in the air, as if from the depths of the cloud, came a confused and doubtful sound of voices. Once the listener fancied that he could distinguish the accents of towns-people of his own, men and women, both pious and ungodly, many of whom he had met at the communion table, and had seen others rioting at the tavern. The next moment, so indistinct were the sounds, he doubted whether he had heard aught but the murmur of the old forest, whispering without a wind. Then came a stronger swell of those familiar tones, heard daily in the sunshine at Salem village, but never until now from a cloud of night. There was one voice of a young woman, uttering lamentations, yet with an uncertain sorrow, and entreating for some favor, which, perhaps, it would grieve her to obtain; and all the unseen multitude, both saints and sinners, seemed to encourage her onward.

"Faith!" shouted Goodman Brown, in a voice of agony and desperation; and the echoes of the forest mocked him, crying, "Faith! Faith!" as if bewildered wretches were seeking her all through the wilderness.

The cry of grief, rage, and terror was yet piercing the night, when the unhappy husband held his breath for a response. There was a scream, drowned immediately in a louder murmur of voices, fading into far-off laughter, as the dark cloud swept away, leaving the clear and silent sky above Goodman Brown. But something fluttered lightly down through the air and caught on the branch of a tree. The young man seized it, and beheld a pink ribbon.

"My Faith is gone!" cried he, after one stupefied moment. "There is no good on earth; and sin is but a name. Come, devil; for to thee is this world given."

And, maddened with despair, so that he laughed loud and long, did Goodman Brown grasp his staff and set forth again, at such a rate that he seemed to fly along the forest path rather than to walk or run. The road grew wilder and drearier and more faintly traced, and vanished at length, leaving him in the heart of the dark wilderness, still rushing onward with the instinct that guides mortal man to evil. The whole forest was peopled with frightful sounds—the creaking of the trees, the howling of wild beasts, and the yell of Indians; while sometimes the wind tolled like a distant church bell, and sometimes gave a broad roar around the traveller, as if all Nature were laughing him to scorn. But he was himself the chief horror of the scene, and shrank not from its other horrors.

"Ha! ha! ha!" roared Goodman Brown when the wind laughed at him.

"Let us hear which will laugh loudest. Think not to frighten me with your deviltry. Come witch, come wizard, come Indian powwow, come devil himself, and here comes Goodman Brown. You may as well fear him as he fear you."

In truth, all through the haunted forest there could be nothing more frightful than the figure of Goodman Brown. On he flew among the black pines, brandishing his staff with frenzied gestures, now giving vent to an inspiration of horrid blasphemy, and now shouting forth such laughter as set all the echoes of the forest laughing like demons around him. The fiend in his own shape is less hideous than when he rages in the breast of man. Thus sped the demoniac on his course, until, quivering among the trees, he saw a red light before him, as when the felled trunks and branches of a clearing have been set on fire, and throw up their lurid blaze against the sky, at the hour of midnight. He paused, in a lull of the tempest that had driven him onward, and heard the swell of what seemed a hymn, rolling solemnly from a distance with the weight of many voices. He knew the tune; it was a familiar one in the choir of the village meeting-house. The verse died heavily away, and was lengthened by a chorus, not of human voices, but of all the sounds of the benighted wilderness pealing in awful harmony together. Goodman Brown cried out, and his cry was lost to his own ear by its unison with the cry of the desert.

In the interval of silence he stole forward until the light glared full upon his eyes. At one extremity of an open space, hemmed in by the dark wall of the forest, arose a rock, bearing some rude, natural resemblance either to an alter or a pulpit, and surrounded by four blazing pines, their tops aflame, their stems untouched, like candles at an evening meeting. The mass of foliage that had overgrown the summit of the rock was all on fire, blazing high into the night and fitfully illuminating the whole field. Each pendent twig and leafy festoon was in a blaze. As the red light arose and fell, a numerous congregation alternately shone forth, then disappeared in shadow, and again grew, as it were, out of the darkness, peopling the heart of the solitary woods at once.

"A grave and dark-clad company," quoth Goodman Brown.

In truth they were such. Among them, quivering to and fro between gloom and splendor, appeared faces that would be seen next day at the council board of the province, and others which, Sabbath after Sabbath, looked devoutly heavenward, and benignantly over the crowded pews, from the holiest pulpits in the land. Some affirm that the lady of the governor was there. At least there were high dames well known to her, and wives of honored husbands, and widows, a great multitude, and ancient maidens, all of excellent repute, and fair young girls, who trembled lest their mothers should espy them. Either the sudden gleams of light flashing over the obscure field bedazzled Goodman Brown, or he recognized a score of the church members of Salem village famous for their especial sanctity. Good old Deacon Gookin had arrived, and waited at the skirts of that venerable saint, his revered pastor. But, irreverently consorting with these grave, reputable, and pious people, these elders of the church, these chaste dames and dewy virgins, there were men of dissolute lives and women of spotted fame, wretches given over to all mean and filthy vice, and suspected even of horrid crimes. It was strange to see that the good shrank not from the wicked, nor were the sinners abashed by the saints. Scattered also among their pale-faced enemies were the Indian priests, or powwows, who had often scared their native forest with more hideous incantations than any known to English witchcraft.

"But where is Faith?" thought Goodman Brown; and, as hope came into his heart, he trembled.

Another verse of the hymn arose, a slow and mournful strain, such as the pious love, but joined to words which expressed all that our nature can conceive of sin, and darkly hinted at far more. Unfathomable to mere mortals is the lore of fiends. Verse after verse was sung; and still the chorus of the desert swelled between like the deepest tone of a mighty organ; and with the final peal of that dreadful anthem there came a sound, as if the roaring wind, the rushing streams, the howling beasts, and every other voice of the unconcerted wilderness were mingling and according with the voice of guilty man in homage to the prince of all. The four blazing pines threw up a loftier flame, and obscurely discovered shapes and visages of horror on the smoke wreaths above the impious assembly. At the same moment the fire on the rock shot redly forth and formed a glowing arch above its base, where now appeared a figure. With reverence be it spoken, the figure bore no slight similitude, both in garb and manner, to some grave divine of the New England churches.

"Bring forth the converts!" cried a voice that echoed through the field and rolled into the forest.

At the word, Goodman Brown stepped forth from the shadow of the trees and approached the congregation, with whom he felt a loathful brotherhood by the sympathy of all that was wicked in his heart. He could have well-nigh sworn that the shape of his own dead father beckoned him to advance, looking downward from a smoke wreath, while a woman, with dim features of despair, threw out her hand to warn him back. Was it his mother? But he had no power to retreat one step, nor to resist, even in thought, when the minister and good old Deacon Gookin seized his arms and led him to the blazing rock. Thither came also the slender form of a veiled female, led between Goody Cloyse, that pious teacher of the catechism, and Martha Carrier, who had received the devil's promise to be queen of hell. A rampant hag was she. And there stood the proselytes beneath the canopy of fire.

"Welcome, my children," said the dark figure, "to the communion of your race. Ye have found thus young your nature and your destiny. My children, look behind you!"

They turned; and flashing forth, as it were, in a sheet of flame, the fiend worshippers were seen; the smile of welcome gleamed darkly on every visage.

"There," resumed the sable form, "are all whom ye have reverenced from youth. Ye deemed them holier than yourselves, and shrank from your own sin, contrasting it with their lives of righteousness and prayerful aspirations heavenward. Yet here are they all in my worshipping assembly. This night it shall be granted you to know their secret deeds: how hoary-bearded elders of the church have whispered wanton words to the young maids of their households; how many a woman, eager for widows' weeds, has given her husband a drink at bedtime and let him sleep his last sleep in her bosom; how beardless youths have made haste to inherit their fathers' wealth; and how fair damsels—blush not, sweet ones—have dug little graves in the garden, and bidden me, the sole guest to an infant's funeral. By the sympathy of your human hearts for sin ye shall scent out all the places—whether in church, bedchamber, street, field, or forest—where crime has been committed, and shall exult to behold the whole earth one stain of guilt, one mighty blood spot. Far more than this. It shall be yours to penetrate, in every bosom, the deep mystery of sin, the fountain of all wicked arts, and which inexhaustibly supplies more evil impulses than human power—than my power at its utmost—can make manifest in deeds. And now, my children, look upon each other."

They did so; and, by the blaze of the hell-kindled torches, the wretched man beheld his Faith, and the wife her husband, trembling before that unhallowed altar.

"Lo, there ye stand, my children," said the figure, in a deep and solemn tone, almost sad with its despairing awfulness, as if his once angelic nature could yet mourn for our miserable race. "Depending upon one another's hearts, ye had still hoped that virtue were not all a dream. Now are ye undeceived. Evil is the nature of mankind. Evil must be your only happiness. Welcome again, my children, to the communion of your race."

"Welcome," repeated the fiend worshippers, in one cry of despair and triumph.

And there they stood, the only pair, as it seemed, who were yet hesitating on the verge of wickedness in this dark world. A basin was hollowed, naturally, in the rock. Did it contain water, reddened by the lurid light? or was it blood? or, perchance, a liquid flame? Herein did the shape of evil dip his hand and prepare to lay the mark of baptism upon their foreheads, that they might be partakers of the mystery of sin, more conscious of the secret guilt of others, both in deed and thought, than they could now be of their own. The husband cast one look at his pale wife, and Faith at him. What polluted wretches would the next glance show them to each other, shuddering alike at what they disclosed and what they saw!

"Faith! Faith!" cried the husband, "look up to heaven, and resist the wicked one."

Whether Faith obeyed he knew not. Hardly had he spoken when he found himself amid calm night and solitude, listening to a roar of the wind which died heavily away through the forest. He staggered against the rock, and felt it chill and damp; while a hanging twig, that had been all on fire, besprinkled his cheek with the coldest dew.

The next morning young Goodman Brown came slowly into the street of Salem village, staring around him like a bewildered man. The good old minister was taking a walk along the graveyard to get an appetite for breakfast and meditate his sermon, and bestowed a blessing, as he passed, on Goodman Brown. He shrank from the venerable saint as if to avoid an anathema. Old Deacon Gookin was at domestic worship, and the holy words of his prayer were heard through the open window. "What God doth the wizard pray to?" quoth Goodman Brown. Goody Cloyse, that excellent old Christian, stood in the early sunshine at her own lattice, catechizing a little girl who had brought her a pint of morning's milk. Goodman Brown snatched away the child as from the grasp of the fiend himself. Turning the corner by the meeting-house, he spied the head of Faith, with the pink ribbons, gazing anxiously forth, and bursting into such joy at sight of him that she skipped along the street and almost kissed her husband before the whole village. But Goodman Brown looked sternly and sadly into her face, and passed on without a greeting.

Had Goodman Brown fallen asleep in the forest and only dreamed a wild dream of a witch-meeting?

Be it so if you will; but, alas! it was a dream of evil omen for young Goodman Brown. A stern, a sad, a darkly meditative, a distrustful, if not a desperate man did he become from the night of that fearful dream. On the Sabbath day, when the congregation were singing a holy psalm, he could not listen because an anthem of sin rushed loudly upon his ear and drowned all the blessed strain. When the minister spoke from the pulpit with power and fervid eloquence, and, with his hand on the open Bible, of the sacred truths of our religion, and of saint-like lives and triumphant deaths, and of future bliss or misery unutterable, then did Goodman Brown turn pale, dreading lest the roof should thunder down upon the gray blasphemer and his hearers. Often, waking suddenly at midnight, he shrank from the bosom of Faith; and at morning or eventide, when the family knelt down at prayer, he scowled and muttered to himself, and gazed sternly at his wife, and turned away. And when he had lived long, and was borne to his grave a hoary corpse, followed by Faith, an aged woman, and children and grandchildren, a goodly procession, besides neighbors not a few, they carved no hopeful verse upon his tombstone, for his dying hour was gloom.

## RAPPACCINI'S DAUGHTER

[From the Writings of Aubépine.]

WE do not remember to have seen any translated specimens of the productions of M. de l'Aubépine—a fact the less to be wondered at, as his very name is unknown to many of his own countrymen as well as to the student of foreign literature. As a writer, he seems to occupy an unfortunate position between the Transcendentalists (who, under one name or another, have their share in all the current literature of the world) and the great body of pen-and-ink men who address the intellect and sympathies of the multitude. If not too refined, at all events too remote, too shadowy, and unsubstantial in his modes of development to suit the taste of the latter class, and yet too popular to satisfy the spiritual or metaphysical requisitions of the former, he must necessarily find himself without an audience, except here and there an individual or possibly an isolated clique. His writings, to do them justice, are not altogether destitute of fancy and originality; they might have won him greater reputation but for an inveterate love of allegory, which is apt to invest his plots and characters with the aspect of scenery and people in the clouds, and to steal away the human warmth out of his conceptions. His fictions are sometimes historical, sometimes of the present day, and sometimes, so far as can be discovered, have little or no reference either to time or space. In any case, he generally contents himself with a very slight embroidery of outward manners,—the faintest possible counterfeit of real life,—and endeavors to create an interest by some less obvious peculiarity of the subject. Occasionally a breath of Nature, a raindrop of pathos and tenderness, or a gleam of humor, will find its way into the midst of his fantastic imagery, and make us feel as if, after all, we were yet within the limits of our native earth. We will only add to this very cursory notice that M. de l'Aubépine's productions, if the reader chance to take them in precisely the proper point of view, may amuse a leisure hour as well as those of a brighter man; if otherwise, they can hardly fail to look excessively like nonsense.

Our author is voluminous; he continues to write and publish with as much praiseworthy and indefatigable prolixity as if his efforts were crowned with the brilliant success that so justly attends those of Eugene Sue. His first appearance was by a collection of stories in a long series of volumes entitled "Contes deux fois racontées." The titles of some of his more recent works (we quote from memory) are as follows: "Le Voyage Céleste à Chemin de Fer," 3 tom., 1838; "Le nouveau Père Adam et la nouvelle Mère Eve," 2 tom., 1839; "Roderic; ou le Serpent à l'estomac," 2 tom., 1840; "Le Culte du Feu," a folio volume of ponderous research into the religion and ritual of the old Persian Ghebers, published in 1841; "La Soirée du Chateau en Espagne," 1 tom., 8vo, 1842; and "L'Artiste du Beau; ou le Papillon Mécanique," 5 tom., 4to, 1843. Our somewhat wearisome perusal of this startling catalogue of volumes has left behind it a certain personal affection and sympathy, though by no means admiration, for M. de l'Aubépine; and we would fain do the little in our power towards introducing him favorably to the American public. The ensuing tale is a translation of his "Beatrice; ou la Belle Empoisonneuse," recently published in "La Revue Anti-Aristocratique." This journal, edited by the Comte de Bearhaven, has for some years past led the defence of liberal principles and popular rights with a faithfulness and ability worthy of all praise.

A young man, named Giovanni Guasconti, came, very long ago, from the more southern region of Italy, to pursue his studies at the University of Padua. Giovanni, who had but a scanty supply of gold ducats in his pocket, took lodgings in a high and gloomy chamber of an old edifice which looked not unworthy to have been the palace of a Paduan noble, and which, in fact, exhibited over its entrance the armorial bearings of a family long since extinct. The young stranger, who was not unstudied in the great poem of his country, recollected that one of the ancestors of this family, and perhaps an occupant of this very mansion, had been pictured by Dante as a partaker of the immortal agonies of his Inferno. These reminiscences and associations, together with the tendency to heartbreak natural to a young man for the first time out of his native sphere, caused Giovanni to sigh heavily as he looked around the desolate and ill-furnished apartment.

"Holy Virgin, signor!" cried old Dame Lisabetta, who, won by the youth's remarkable beauty of person, was kindly endeavoring to give the chamber a habitable air, "what a sigh was that to come out of a young man's heart! Do you find this old mansion gloomy? For the love of Heaven, then, put your head out of the window, and you will see as bright sunshine as you have left in Naples."

Guasconti mechanically did as the old woman advised, but could not quite agree with her that the Paduan sunshine was as cheerful as that of southern Italy. Such as it was, however, it fell upon a garden beneath the window and expended its fostering influences on a variety of plants, which seemed to have been cultivated with exceeding care.

"Does this garden belong to the house?" asked Giovanni.

"Heaven forbid, signor, unless it were fruitful of better pot herbs than any that grow there now," answered old Lisabetta. "No; that garden is cultivated by the own hands of Signor Giacomo Rappaccini, the famous doctor, who, I warrant him, has been heard of as far as Naples. It is said that he distils these plants into medicines that are as potent as a charm. Oftentimes you may see the signor doctor at work, and perchance the signora, his daughter, too, gathering the strange flowers that grow in the garden."

The old woman had now done what she could for the aspect of the chamber; and, commending the young man to the protection of the saints, took her departure.

Giovanni still found no better occupation than to look down into the garden beneath his window. From its appearance, he judged it to be one of those botanic gardens which were of earlier date in Padua than elsewhere in Italy or in the world. Or, not improbably, it might once have been the pleasure-place of an opulent family; for there was the ruin of a marble fountain in the centre, sculptured with rare art, but so wofully shattered that it was impossible to trace the original design from the chaos of remaining fragments. The water, however, continued to gush and sparkle into the sunbeams as cheerfully as ever. A little gurgling sound ascended to the young man's window, and made him feel as if the fountain were an immortal spirit that sung its song unceasingly and without heeding the vicissitudes around it, while one century imbodied it in marble and another scattered the perishable garniture on the soil. All about the pool into which the water subsided grew various plants, that seemed to require a plentiful supply of moisture for the nourishment of gigantic leaves, and in some instances, flowers gorgeously magnificent. There was one shrub in particular, set in a marble vase in the midst of the pool, that bore a profusion of purple blossoms, each of which had the lustre and richness of a gem; and the whole together made a show so resplendent that it seemed enough to illuminate the garden, even had there been no sunshine. Every portion of the soil was peopled with plants and herbs, which, if less beautiful, still bore tokens of assiduous care, as if all had their individual virtues, known to the scientific mind that fostered them. Some were placed in urns, rich with old carving, and others in common garden pots; some crept serpent-like along the ground or climbed on high, using whatever means of ascent was offered them. One plant had wreathed itself round a statue of Vertumnus, which was thus quite veiled and shrouded in a drapery of hanging foliage, so happily arranged that it might have served a sculptor for a study.

While Giovanni stood at the window he heard a rustling behind a screen of leaves, and became aware that a person was at work in the garden. His figure soon emerged into view, and showed itself to be that of no common laborer, but a tall, emaciated, sallow, and sickly-looking man, dressed in a scholar's garb of black. He was beyond the middle term of life, with gray hair, a thin, gray beard, and a face singularly marked with intellect and cultivation, but which could never, even in his more youthful days, have expressed much warmth of heart.

Nothing could exceed the intentness with which this scientific gardener examined every shrub which grew in his path: it seemed as if he was looking into their inmost nature, making observations in regard to their creative essence, and discovering why one leaf grew in this shape and another in that, and wherefore such and such flowers differed among themselves in hue and perfume. Nevertheless, in spite of this deep intelligence on his part, there was no approach to intimacy between himself and these vegetable existences. On the contrary, he avoided their actual touch or the direct inhaling of their odors with a caution that impressed Giovanni most disagreeably; for the man's demeanor was that of one walking among malignant influences, such as savage beasts, or deadly snakes, or evil spirits, which, should he allow them one moment of license, would wreak upon him some terrible fatality. It was strangely frightful to the young man's imagination to see this air of insecurity in a person cultivating a garden, that most simple and innocent of human toils, and which had been alike the joy and labor of the unfallen parents of the race. Was this garden, then, the Eden of the present world? And this man, with such a perception of harm in what his own hands caused to grow,—was he the Adam?

The distrustful gardener, while plucking away the dead leaves or pruning the too luxuriant growth of the shrubs, defended his hands with a pair of thick gloves. Nor were these his only armor. When, in his walk through the garden, he came to the magnificent plant that hung its purple gems beside the marble fountain, he placed a kind of mask over his mouth and nostrils, as if all this beauty did but conceal a deadlier malice; but, finding his task still too dangerous, he drew back, removed the mask, and called loudly, but in the infirm voice of a person affected with inward disease,—

"Beatrice! Beatrice!"

"Here am I, my father. What would you?" cried a rich and youthful voice from the window of the opposite house—a voice as rich as a tropical sunset, and which made Giovanni, though he knew not why, think of deep hues of purple or crimson and of perfumes heavily delectable. "Are you in the garden?"

"Yes, Beatrice," answered the gardener, "and I need your help."

Soon there emerged from under a sculptured portal the figure of a young girl, arrayed with as much richness of taste as the most splendid of the flowers, beautiful as the day, and with a bloom so deep and vivid that one shade more would have been too much. She looked redundant with life, health, and energy; all of which attributes were bound down and compressed, as it were, and girdled tensely, in their luxuriance, by her virgin zone. Yet Giovanni's fancy must have grown morbid while he looked down into the garden; for the impression which the fair stranger made upon him was as if here were another flower, the human sister of those vegetable ones, as beautiful as they, more beautiful than the richest of them, but still to be touched only with a glove, nor to be approached without a mask. As Beatrice came down the garden path, it was observable that she handled and inhaled the odor of several of the plants which her father had most sedulously avoided.

"Here, Beatrice," said the latter, "see how many needful offices require to be done to our chief treasure. Yet, shattered as I am, my life might pay the penalty of approaching it so closely as circumstances demand. Henceforth, I fear, this plant must be consigned to your sole charge."

"And gladly will I undertake it," cried again the rich tones of the young lady, as she bent towards the magnificent plant and opened her arms as if to embrace it. "Yes, my sister, my splendour, it shall be Beatrice's task to nurse and serve thee; and thou shalt reward her with thy kisses and perfumed breath, which to her is as the breath of life."

Then, with all the tenderness in her manner that was so strikingly expressed in her words, she busied herself with such attentions as the plant seemed to require; and Giovanni, at his lofty window, rubbed his eyes and almost doubted whether it were a girl tending her favorite flower, or one sister performing the duties of affection to another. The scene soon terminated. Whether Dr. Rappaccini had finished his labors in the garden, or that his watchful eye had caught the stranger's face, he now took his daughter's arm and retired. Night was already closing in; oppressive exhalations seemed to proceed from the plants and steal upward past the open window; and Giovanni, closing the lattice, went to his couch and dreamed of a rich flower and beautiful girl. Flower and maiden were different, and yet the same, and fraught with some strange peril in either shape.

But there is an influence in the light of morning that tends to rectify whatever errors of fancy, or even of judgment, we may have incurred during the sun's decline, or among the shadows of the night, or in the less wholesome glow of moonshine. Giovanni's first movement, on starting from sleep, was to throw open the window and gaze down into the garden which his dreams had made so fertile of mysteries. He was surprised and a little ashamed to find how real and matter-of-fact an affair it proved to be, in the first rays of the sun which gilded the dew-drops that hung upon leaf and blossom, and, while giving a brighter beauty to each rare flower, brought everything within the limits of ordinary experience. The young man rejoiced that, in the heart of the barren city, he had the privilege of overlooking this spot of lovely and luxuriant vegetation. It would serve, he said to himself, as a symbolic language to keep him in communion with Nature. Neither the sickly and thoughtworn Dr. Giacomo Rappaccini, it is true, nor his brilliant daughter, were now visible; so that Giovanni could not determine how much of the singularity which he attributed to both was due to their own qualities and how much to his wonder-working fancy; but he was inclined to take a most rational view of the whole matter.

In the course of the day he paid his respects to Signor Pietro Baglioni, professor of medicine in the university, a physician of eminent repute to whom Giovanni had brought a letter of introduction. The professor was an elderly personage, apparently of genial nature, and habits that might almost be called jovial. He kept the young man to dinner, and made himself very agreeable by the freedom and liveliness of his conversation, especially when warmed by a flask or two of Tuscan wine. Giovanni, conceiving that men of science, inhabitants of the same city, must needs be on familiar terms with one another, took an opportunity to mention the name of Dr. Rappaccini. But the professor did not respond with so much cordiality as he had anticipated.

"Ill would it become a teacher of the divine art of medicine," said Professor Pietro Baglioni, in answer to a question of Giovanni, "to withhold due and well-considered praise of a physician so eminently skilled as Rappaccini; but, on the other hand, I should answer it but scantily to my conscience were I to permit a worthy youth like yourself, Signor Giovanni, the son of an ancient friend, to imbibe erroneous ideas respecting a man who might hereafter chance to hold your life and death in his hands. The truth is, our worshipful Dr. Rappaccini has as much science as any member of the faculty—with perhaps one single exception—in Padua, or all Italy; but there are certain grave objections to his professional character."

"And what are they?" asked the young man.

"Has my friend Giovanni any disease of body or heart, that he is so inquisitive about physicians?" said the professor, with a smile. "But as for Rappaccini, it is said of him—and I, who know the man well, can answer for its truth—that he cares infinitely more for science than for mankind. His patients are interesting to him only as subjects for some new experiment. He would sacrifice human life, his own among the rest, or whatever else was dearest to him, for the sake of adding so much as a grain of mustard seed to the great heap of his accumulated knowledge."

"Methinks he is an awful man indeed," remarked Guasconti, mentally recalling the cold and purely intellectual aspect of Rappaccini. "And yet, worshipful professor, is it not a noble spirit? Are there many men capable of so spiritual a love of science?"

"God forbid," answered the professor, somewhat testily; "at least, unless they take sounder views of the healing art than those adopted by Rappaccini. It is his theory that all medicinal virtues are comprised within those substances which we term vegetable poisons. These he cultivates with his own hands, and is said even to have produced new varieties of poison, more horribly deleterious than Nature, without the assistance of this learned person, would ever have plagued the world withal. That the signor doctor does less mischief than might be expected with such dangerous substances is undeniable. Now and then, it must be owned, he has effected, or seemed to effect, a marvellous cure; but, to tell you my private mind, Signor Giovanni, he should receive little credit for such instances of success,—they being probably the work of chance, —but should be held strictly accountable for his failures, which may justly be considered his own work."

The youth might have taken Baglioni's opinions with many grains of allowance had he known that there was a professional warfare of long continuance between him and Dr. Rappaccini, in which the latter was generally thought to have gained the advantage. If the reader be inclined to judge for himself, we refer him to certain black-letter tracts on both sides, preserved in the medical department of the University of Padua.

"I know not, most learned professor," returned Giovanni, after musing on what had been said of Rappaccini's exclusive zeal for science,—"I know not how dearly this physician may love his art; but surely there is one object more dear to him. He has a daughter."

"Aha!" cried the professor, with a laugh. "So now our friend Giovanni's secret is out. You have heard of this daughter, whom all the young men in Padua are wild about, though not half a dozen have ever had the good hap to see her face. I know little of the Signora Beatrice save that Rappaccini is said to have instructed her deeply in his science, and that, young and beautiful as fame reports her, she is already qualified to fill a professor's chair. Perchance her father destines her for mine! Other absurd rumors there be, not worth talking about or listening to. So now, Signor Giovanni, drink off your glass of lachryma."

Guasconti returned to his lodgings somewhat heated with the wine he had quaffed, and which caused his brain to swim with strange fantasies in reference to Dr. Rappaccini and the beautiful Beatrice. On his way, happening to pass by a florist's, he bought a fresh bouquet of flowers.

Ascending to his chamber, he seated himself near the window, but within the shadow thrown by the depth of the wall, so that he could look down into the garden with little risk of being discovered. All beneath his eye was a solitude. The strange plants were basking in the sunshine, and now and then nodding gently to one another, as if in acknowledgment of sympathy and kindred. In the midst, by the shattered fountain, grew the magnificent shrub, with its purple gems clustering all over it; they glowed in the air, and gleamed back again out of the depths of the pool, which thus seemed to overflow with colored radiance from the rich reflection that was steeped in it. At first, as we have said, the garden was a solitude. Soon, however,—as Giovanni had half hoped, half feared, would be the case,—a figure appeared beneath the antique sculptured portal, and came down between the rows of plants, inhaling their various prefumes as if she were one of those beings of old classic fable that lived upon sweet odors. On again beholding Beatrice, the young man was even startled to perceive how much her beauty exceeded his recollection of it; so brilliant, so vivid, was its character, that she glowed amid the sunlight, and, as Giovanni whispered to himself, positively illuminated the more shadowy intervals of the garden path. Her face being now more revealed than on the former occasion, he was struck by its expression of simplicity and sweetness,—qualities that had not entered into his idea of her character, and which made him ask anew what manner of mortal she might be. Nor did he fail again to observe, or imagine, an analogy between the beautiful girl and the gorgeous shrub that hung its gemlike flowers over the fountain,—a resemblance which Beatrice seemed to have indulged a fantastic humor in heightening, both by the arrangement of her dress and the selection of its hues.

Approaching the shrub, she threw open her arms, as with a passionate ardor, and drew its branches into an intimate embrace—so intimate that her features were hidden in its leafy bosom and her glistening ringlets all intermingled with the flowers.

"Give me thy breath, my sister," exclaimed Beatrice; "for I am faint with common air. And give me this flower of thine, which I separate with gentlest fingers from the stem and place it close beside my heart."

With these words the beautiful daughter of Rappaccini plucked one of the richest blossoms of the shrub, and was about to fasten it in her bosom. But now, unless Giovanni's draughts of wine had bewildered his senses, a singular incident occurred. A small orange-colored reptile, of the lizard or chameleon species, chanced to be creeping along the path, just at the feet of Beatrice. It appeared to Giovanni,—but, at the distance from which he gazed, he could scarcely have seen anything so minute,—it appeared to him, however, that a drop or two of moisture from the broken stem of the flower descended upon the lizard's head. For an instant the reptile contorted itself violently, and then lay motionless in the sunshine. Beatrice observed this remarkable phenomenon, and crossed herself, sadly, but without surprise; nor did she therefore hesitate to arrange the fatal flower in her bosom. There it blushed, and almost glimmered with the dazzling effect of a precious stone, adding to her dress and aspect the one appropriate charm which nothing else in the world could have supplied. But Giovanni, out of the shadow of his window, bent forward and shrank back, and murmured and trembled.

"Am I awake? Have I my senses?" said he to himself. "What is this being? Beautiful shall I call her, or inexpressibly terrible?"

Beatrice now strayed carelessly through the garden, approaching closer beneath Giovanni's window, so that he was compelled to thrust his head quite out of its concealment in order to gratify the intense and painful curiosity which she excited. At this moment there came a beautiful insect over the garden wall; it had, perhaps, wandered through the city, and found no flowers or verdure among those antique haunts of men until the heavy perfumes of Dr. Rappaccini's shrubs had lured it from afar. Without alighting on the flowers, this winged brightness seemed to be attracted by Beatrice, and lingered in the air and fluttered about her head. Now, here it could not be but that Giovanni Guasconti's eyes deceived him. Be that as it might, he fancied that, while Beatrice was gazing at the insect with childish delight, it grew faint and fell at her feet; its bright wings shivered; it was dead—from no cause that he could discern, unless it were the atmosphere of her breath. Again Beatrice crossed herself and sighed heavily as she bent over the dead insect.

An impulsive movement of Giovanni drew her eyes to the window. There she beheld the beautiful head of the young man—rather a Grecian than an Italian head, with fair, regular features, and a glistening of gold among his ringlets—gazing down upon her like a being that hovered in mid air. Scarcely knowing what he did, Giovanni threw down the bouquet which he had hitherto held in his hand.

"Signora," said he, "there are pure and healthful flowers. Wear them for the sake of Giovanni Guasconti."

"Thanks, signor," replied Beatrice, with her rich voice, that came forth as it were like a gush of music, and with a mirthful expression half childish and half woman-like. "I accept your gift, and would fain recompense it with this precious purple flower; but if I toss it into the air it will not reach you. So Signor Guasconti must even content himself with my thanks."

She lifted the bouquet from the ground, and then, as if inwardly ashamed at having stepped aside from her maidenly reserve to respond to a stranger's greeting, passed swiftly homeward through the garden. But few as the moments were, it seemed to Giovanni, when she was on the point of vanishing beneath the sculptured portal, that his beautiful bouquet was already beginning to wither in her grasp. It was an idle thought; there could be no possibility of distinguishing a faded flower from a fresh one at so great a distance.

For many days after this incident the young man avoided the window that looked into Dr. Rappaccini's garden, as if something ugly and monstrous would have blasted his eyesight had he been betrayed into a glance. He felt conscious of having put himself, to a certain extent, within the influence of an unintelligible power by the communication which he had opened with Beatrice. The wisest course would have been, if his heart were in any real danger, to quit his lodgings and Padua itself at once; the next wiser, to have accustomed himself, as far as possible, to the familiar and daylight view of Beatrice—thus bringing her rigidly and systematically within the limits of ordinary experience. Least of all, while avoiding her sight, ought Giovanni to have remained so near this extraordinary being that the proximity and possibility even of intercourse should give a kind of substance and reality to the wild vagaries which his imagination ran riot continually in producing. Guasconti had not a deep heart—or, at all events, its depths were not sounded now; but he had a quick fancy, and an ardent southern temperament, which rose every instant to a higher fever pitch. Whether or no Beatrice possessed those terrible attributes, that fatal breath, the affinity with those so beautiful and deadly flowers which were indicated by what Giovanni had witnessed, she had at least instilled a fierce and subtle poison into his system. It was not love, although her rich beauty was a madness to him; nor horror, even while he fancied her spirit to be imbued with the same baneful essence that seemed to pervade her physical frame; but a wild offspring of both love and horror that had each parent in it, and burned like one and shivered like the other. Giovanni knew not what to dread; still less did he know what to hope; yet hope and dread kept a continual warfare in his breast, alternately vanquishing one another and starting up afresh to renew the contest. Blessed are all simple emotions, be they dark or bright! It is the lurid intermixture of the two that produces the illuminating blaze of the infernal regions.

Sometimes he endeavored to assuage the fever of his spirit by a rapid walk through the streets of Padua or beyond its gates: his footsteps kept time with the throbbings of his brain, so that the walk was apt to accelerate itself to a race. One day he found himself arrested; his arm was seized by a portly personage, who had turned back on recognizing the young man and expended much breath in overtaking him.

"Signor Giovanni! Stay, my young friend!" cried he. "Have you forgotten me? That might well be the case if I were as much altered as yourself."

It was Baglioni, whom Giovanni had avoided ever since their first meeting, from a doubt that the professor's sagacity would look too deeply into his secrets. Endeavoring to recover himself, he stared forth wildly from his inner world into the outer one and spoke like a man in a dream.

"Yes; I am Giovanni Guasconti. You are Professor Pietro Baglioni. Now let me pass!"

"Not yet, not yet, Signor Giovanni Guasconti," said the professor, smiling, but at the same time scrutinizing the youth with an earnest glance. "What! did I grow up side by side with your father? and shall his son pass me like a stranger in these old streets of Padua? Stand still, Signor Giovanni; for we must have a word or two before we part."

"Speedily, then, most worshipful professor, speedily," said Giovanni, with feverish impatience. "Does not your worship see that I am in haste?"

Now, while he was speaking there came a man in black along the street, stooping and moving feebly like a person in inferior health. His face was all overspread with a most sickly and sallow hue, but yet so pervaded with an expression of piercing and active intellect that an observer might easily have overlooked the merely physical attributes and have seen only this wonderful energy. As he passed, this person exchanged a cold and distant salutation with Baglioni, but fixed his eyes upon Giovanni with an intentness that seemed to bring out whatever was within him worthy of notice. Nevertheless, there was a peculiar quietness in the look, as if taking merely a speculative, not a human interest, in the young man.

"It is Dr. Rappaccini!" whispered the professor when the stranger had passed. "Has he ever seen your face before?"

"Not that I know," answered Giovanni, starting at the name.

"He *has* seen you! he must have seen you!" said Baglioni, hastily. "For some purpose or other, this man of science is making a study of you. I know that look of his! It is the same that coldly illuminates his face as he bends over a bird, a mouse, or a butterfly, which, in pursuance of some experiment, he has killed by the perfume of a flower; a look as deep as Nature itself, but without Nature's warmth of love. Signor Giovanni, I will stake my life upon it, you are the subject of one of Rappaccini's experiments!"

"Will you make a fool of me?" cried Giovanni, passionately. "*That*, signor professor, were an untoward experiment."

"Patience! patience!" replied the imperturbable professor. "I tell thee, my poor Giovanni, that Rappaccini has a scientific interest in thee.

Thou hast fallen into fearful hands! And the Signora Beatrice,—what part does she act in this mystery?"

But Guasconti, finding Baglioni's pertinacity intolerable, here broke away, and was gone before the professor could again seize his arm. He looked after the young man intently and shook his head.

"This must not be," said Baglioni to himself. "The youth is the son of my old friend, and shall not come to any harm from which the arcana of medical science can preserve him. Besides, it is too insufferable an impertinence in Rappaccini, thus to snatch the lad out of my own hands, as I may say, and make use of him for his infernal experiments. This daughter of his! It shall be looked to. Perchance, most learned Rappaccini, I may foil you where you little dream of it!"

Meanwhile Giovanni had pursued a circuitous route, and at length found himself at the door of his lodgings. As he crossed the threshold he was met by old Lisabetta, who smirked and smiled, and was evidently desirous to attract his attention; vainly, however, as the ebullition of his feelings had momentarily subsided into a cold and dull vacuity. He turned his eyes full upon the withered face that was puckering itself into a smile, but seemed to behold it not. The old dame, therefore, laid her grasp upon his cloak.

"Signor! signor!" whispered she, still with a smile over the whole breadth of her visage, so that it looked not unlike a grotesque carving in wood, darkened by centuries. "Listen, signor! There is a private entrance into the garden!"

"What do you say?" exclaimed Giovanni, turning quickly about, as if an inanimate thing should start into feverish life. "A private entrance into Dr. Rappaccini's garden?"

"Hush! hush! not so loud!" whispered Lisabetta, putting her hand over his mouth. "Yes; into the worshipful doctor's garden, where you may see all his fine shrubbery. Many a young man in Padua would give gold to be admitted among those flowers."

Giovanni put a piece of gold into her hand.

"Show me the way," said he.

A surmise, probably excited by his conversation with Baglioni, crossed his mind, that this interposition of old Lisabetta might perchance be connected with the intrigue, whatever were its nature, in which the professor seemed to suppose that Dr. Rappaccini was involving him. But such a suspicion, though it disturbed Giovanni, was inadequate to restrain him. The instant that he was aware of the possibility of approaching Beatrice, it seemed an absolute necessity of his existence to do so. It mattered not whether she were angel or demon; he was irrevocably within her sphere, and must obey the law that whirled him onward, in ever-lessening circles, towards a result which he did not attempt to foreshadow; and yet, strange to say, there came across him a sudden doubt whether this intense interest on his part were not delusory; whether it were really of so deep and positive a nature as to justify him in now thrusting himself into an incalculable position; whether it were not merely the fantasy of a young man's brain, only slightly or not at all connected with his heart.

He paused, hesitated, turned half about, but again went on. His withered guide led him along several obscure passages, and finally undid a door, through which, as it was opened, there came the sight and sound of rustling leaves, with the broken sunshine glimmering among them. Giovanni stepped forth, and, forcing himself through the entanglement of a shrub that wreathed its tendrils over the hidden entrance, stood beneath his own window in the open area of Dr. Rappaccini's garden.

How often is it the case that, when impossibilities have come to pass and dreams have condensed their misty substance into tangible realities, we find ourselves calm, and even coldly self-possessed, amid circumstances which it would have been a delirium of joy or agony to anticipate! Fate delights to thwart us thus. Passion will choose his own time to rush upon the scene, and lingers sluggishly behind when an appropriate adjustment of events would seem to summon his appearance. So was it now with Giovanni. Day after day his pulses had throbbed with feverish blood at the improbable idea of an interview with Beatrice, and of standing with her, face to face, in this very garden, basking in the Oriental sunshine of her beauty, and snatching from her full gaze the mystery which he deemed the riddle of his own existence. But now there was a singular and untimely equanimity within his breast. He threw a glance around the garden to discover if Beatrice or her father were present, and, perceiving that he was alone, began a critical observation of the plants.

The aspect of one and all of them dissatisfied him; their gorgeousness seemed fierce, passionate, and even unnatural. There was hardly an individual shrub which a wanderer, straying by himself through a forest, would not have been startled to find growing wild, as if an unearthly face had glared at him out of the thicket. Several also would have shocked a delicate instinct by an appearance of artificialness indicating that there had been such commixture, and, as it were, adultery, of various vegetable species, that the production was no longer of God's making, but the monstrous offspring of man's depraved fancy, glowing with only an evil mockery of beauty. They were probably the result of experiment, which in one or two cases had succeeded in mingling plants individually lovely into a compound possessing the questionable and ominous character that distinguished the whole growth of the garden. In fine, Giovanni recognized but two or three plants in the collection, and those of a kind that he well knew to be poisonous. While busy with these contemplations he heard the rustling of a silken garment, and, turning, beheld Beatrice emerging from beneath the sculptured portal.

Giovanni had not considered with himself what should be his deportment; whether he should apologize for his intrusion into the garden, or assume that he was there with the privity at least, if not by the desire, of Dr. Rappaccini or his daughter; but Beatrice's manner placed him at his ease, though leaving him still in doubt by what agency he had gained admittance. She came lightly along the path and met him near the broken fountain. There was surprise in her face, but brightened by a simple and kind expression of pleasure.

"You are a connoisseur in flowers, signor," said Beatrice, with a smile, alluding to the bouquet which he had flung her from the window. "It is no marvel, therefore, if the sight of my father's rare collection has tempted you to take a nearer view. If he were here, he could tell you many strange and interesting facts as to the nature and habits of these shrubs; for he has spent a lifetime in such studies, and this garden is his world."

"And yourself, lady," observed Giovanni, "if fame says true,—you likewise are deeply skilled in the virtues indicated by these rich blossoms and these spicy perfumes. Would you deign to be my instructress, I should prove an apter scholar than if taught by Signor Rappaccini himself."

"Are there such idle rumors?" asked Beatrice, with the music of a pleasant laugh. "Do people say that I am skilled in my father's science of plants? What a jest is there! No; though I have grown up among these flowers, I know no more of them than their hues and perfume; and sometimes methinks I would fain rid myself of even that small knowledge. There are many flowers here, and those not the least brilliant, that shock and offend me when they meet my eye. But pray, signor, do not believe these stories about my science. Believe nothing of me save what you see with your own eyes."

"And must I believe all that I have seen with my own eyes?" asked Giovanni, pointedly, while the recollection of former scenes made him shrink. "No, signora; you demand too little of me. Bid me believe nothing save what comes from your own lips."

It would appear that Beatrice understood him. There came a deep flush to her cheek; but she looked full into Giovanni's eyes, and responded to his gaze of uneasy suspicion with a queenlike haughtiness.

"I do so bid you, signor," she replied. "Forget whatever you may have fancied in regard to me. If true to the outward senses, still it may be false in its essence; but the words of Beatrice Rappaccini's lips are true from the depths of the heart outward. Those you may believe."

A fervor glowed in her whole aspect and beamed upon Giovanni's consciousness like the light of truth itself; but while she spoke there was a fragrance in the atmosphere around her, rich and delightful, though evanescent, yet which the young man, from an indefinable reluctance, scarcely dared to draw into his lungs. It might be the odor of the flowers. Could it be Beatrice's breath which thus embalmed her words with a strange richness, as if by steeping them in her heart? A faintness passed like a shadow over Giovanni and flitted away; he seemed to gaze through the beautiful girl's eyes into her transparent soul, and felt no more doubt or fear.

The tinge of passion that had colored Beatrice's manner vanished; she became gay, and appeared to derive a pure delight from her communion with the youth not unlike what the maiden of a lonely island might have felt conversing with a voyager from the civilized world. Evidently her experience of life had been confined within the limits of that garden. She talked now about matters as simple as the daylight or summer clouds, and now asked questions in reference to the city, or Giovanni's distant home, his friends, his mother, and his sisters—questions indicating such seclusion, and such lack of familiarity with modes and forms, that Giovanni responded as if to an infant. Her spirit gushed out before him like a fresh rill that was just catching its first glimpse of the sunlight and wondering at the reflections of earth and sky which were flung into its bosom. There came thoughts, too, from a deep source, and fantasies of a gemlike brilliancy, as if diamonds and rubies sparkled upward among the bubbles of the fountain. Ever and anon there gleamed across the young man's mind a sense of wonder that he should be walking side by side with the being who had so wrought upon his imagination, whom he had idealized in such hues of terror, in whom he had positively witnessed such manifestations of dreadful attributes,—that he should be conversing with Beatrice like a brother, and should find her so human and so maidenlike. But such reflections were only momentary; the effect of her character was too real not to make itself familiar at once.

In this free intercourse they had strayed through the garden, and now, after many turns among its avenues, were come to the shattered fountain, beside which grew the magnificent shrub, with its treasury of glowing blossoms. A fragrance was diffused from it which Giovanni recognized as identical with that which he had attributed to Beatrice's breath, but incomparably more powerful. As her eyes fell upon it, Giovanni beheld her press her hand to her bosom as if her heart were throbbing suddenly and painfully.

"For the first time in my life," murmured she, addressing the shrub, "I had forgotten thee."

"I remember, signora," said Giovanni, "that you once promised to reward me with one of these living gems for the bouquet which I had the happy boldness to fling to your feet. Permit me now to pluck it as a memorial of this interview."

He made a step towards the shrub with extended hand; but Beatrice darted forward, uttering a shriek that went through his heart like a dagger. She caught his hand and drew it back with the whole force of her slender figure. Giovanni felt her touch thrilling through his fibres.

"Touch it not!" exclaimed she, in a voice of agony. "Not for thy life! It is fatal!"

Then, hiding her face, she fled from him and vanished beneath the sculptured portal. As Giovanni followed her with his eyes, he beheld the emaciated figure and pale intelligence of Dr. Rappaccini, who had been watching the scene, he knew not how long, within the shadow of the entrance.

No sooner was Guasconti alone in his chamber than the image of Beatrice came back to his passionate musings, invested with all the witchery that had been gathering around it ever since his first glimpse of her, and now likewise imbued with a tender warmth of girlish womanhood. She was human; her nature was endowed with all gentle and feminine qualities; she was worthiest to be worshipped; she was capable, surely, on her part, of the height and heroism of love. Those tokens which he had hitherto considered as proofs of a frightful peculiarity in her physical and moral system were now either forgotten, or, by the subtle sophistry of passion transmitted into a golden crown of enchantment, rendering Beatrice the more admirable by so much as she was the more unique. Whatever had looked ugly was now beautiful; or, if incapable of such a change, it stole away and hid itself among those shapeless half ideas which throng the dim region beyond the daylight of our perfect consciousness. Thus did he spend the night, nor fell asleep until the dawn had begun to awake the slumbering flowers in Dr. Rappaccini's garden, whither Giovanni's dreams doubtless led him. Up rose the sun in his due season, and, flinging his beams upon the young man's eyelids, awoke him to a sense of pain. When thoroughly aroused, he became sensible of a burning and tingling agony in his hand—in his right hand—the very hand which Beatrice had grasped in her own when he was on the point of plucking one of the gemlike flowers. On the back of that hand there was now a purple print like that of four small fingers, and the likeness of a slender thumb upon his wrist.

Oh, how stubbornly does love,—or even that cunning semblance of love which flourishes in the imagination, but strikes no depth of root into the heart,—how stubbornly does it hold its faith until the moment comes when it is doomed to vanish into thin mist! Giovanni wrapped a handkerchief about his hand and wondered what evil thing had stung him, and soon forgot his pain in a reverie of Beatrice.

After the first interview, a second was in the inevitable course of what we call fate. A third; a fourth; and a meeting with Beatrice in the garden was no longer an incident in Giovanni's daily life, but the whole space in which he might be said to live; for the anticipation and memory of that ecstatic hour made up the remainder. Nor was it otherwise with the daughter of Rappaccini. She watched for the youth's appearance, and flew to his side with confidence as unreserved as if they had been playmates from early infancy—as if they were such playmates still. If, by any unwonted chance, he failed to come at the appointed moment, she stood beneath the window and sent up the rich sweetness of her tones to float around him in his chamber and echo and reverberate throughout his heart: "Giovanni! Giovanni! Why tarriest thou? Come down!" And down he hastened into that Eden of poisonous flowers.

But, with all this intimate familiarity, there was still a reserve in Beatrice's demeanor, so rigidly and invariably sustained that the idea of infringing it scarcely occurred to his imagination. By all appreciable signs, they loved; they had looked love with eyes that conveyed the holy secret from the depths of one soul into the depths of the other, as if it were too sacred to be whispered by the way; they had even spoken love in those gushes of passion when their spirits darted forth in articulated breath like tongues of long-hidden flame; and yet there had been no seal of lips, no clasp of hands, nor any slightest caress such as love claims and hallows. He had never touched one of the gleaming ringlets of her hair; her garment—so marked was the physical barrier between them—had never been waved against him by a breeze. On the few occasions when Giovanni had seemed tempted to overstep the limit, Beatrice grew so sad, so stern, and withal wore such a look of desolate separation, shuddering at itself, that not a spoken word was requisite to repel him. At such times he was startled at the horrible suspicions that rose, monster-like, out of the caverns of his heart and stared him in the face; his love grew thin and faint as the morning mist, his doubts alone had substance. But, when Beatrice's face brightened again after the momentary shadow, she was transformed at once from the mysterious, questionable being whom he had watched with so much awe and horror; she was now the beautiful and unsophisticated girl whom he felt that his spirit knew with a certainty beyond all other knowledge.

A considerable time had now passed since Giovanni's last meeting with Baglioni. One morning, however, he was disagreeably surprised by a visit from the professor, whom he had scarcely thought of for whole weeks, and would willingly have forgotten still longer. Given up as he had long been to a pervading excitement, he could tolerate no companions except upon condition of their perfect sympathy with his present state of feeling. Such sympathy was not to be expected from Professor Baglioni.

The visitor chatted carelessly for a few moments about the gossip of the city and the university, and then took up another topic.

"I have been reading an old classic author lately," said he, "and met with a story that strangely interested me. Possibly you may remember it. It is of an Indian prince, who sent a beautiful woman as a present to Alexander the Great. She was as lovely as the dawn and gorgeous as the sunset; but what especially distinguished her was a certain rich perfume in her breath—richer than a garden of Persian roses. Alexander, as was natural to a youthful conqueror, fell in love at first sight with this magnificent stranger; but a certain sage physician, happening to be present, discovered a terrible secret in regard to her."

"And what was that?" asked Giovanni, turning his eyes downward to avoid those of the professor.

"That this lovely woman," continued Baglioni, with emphasis, "had been nourished with poisons from her birth upward, until her whole nature was so imbued with them that she herself had become the deadliest poison in existence. Poison was her element of life. With that rich perfume of her breath she blasted the very air. Her love would have been poison—her embrace death. Is not this a marvellous tale?"

"A childish fable," answered Giovanni, nervously starting from his chair. "I marvel how your worship finds time to read such nonsense among your graver studies."

"By the by," said the professor, looking uneasily about him, "what singular fragrance is this in your apartment? Is it the perfume of your gloves? It is faint, but delicious; and yet, after all, by no means agreeable. Were I to breathe it long, methinks it would make me ill. It is like the breath of a flower; but I see no flowers in the chamber."

"Nor are there any," replied Giovanni, who had turned pale as the professor spoke; "nor, I think, is there any fragrance except in your worship's imagination. Odors, being a sort of element combined of the sensual and the spiritual, are apt to deceive us in this manner. The recollection of a perfume, the bare idea of it, may easily be mistaken for a present reality."

"Ay; but my sober imagination does not often play such tricks," said Baglioni; "and, were I to fancy any kind of odor, it would be that of some vile apothecary drug, wherewith my fingers are likely enough to be imbued. Our worshipful friend Rappaccini, as I have heard, tinctures his medicaments with odors richer than those of Araby. Doubtless, likewise, the fair and learned Signora Beatrice would minister to her patients with draughts as sweet as a maiden's breath; but woe to him that sips them!"

Giovanni's face evinced many contending emotions. The tone in which the professor alluded to the pure and lovely daughter of Rappaccini was a torture to his soul; and yet the intimation of a view of her character, opposite to his own, gave instantaneous distinctness to a thousand dim suspicions, which now grinned at him like so many demons. But he strove hard to quell them and to respond to Baglioni with a true lover's perfect faith.

"Signor professor," said he, "you were my father's friend; perchance, too, it is your purpose to act a friendly part towards his son. I would fain feel nothing towards you save respect and deference; but I pray you to observe, signor, that there is one subject on which we must not speak. You know not the Signora Beatrice. You cannot, therefore, estimate the wrong—the blasphemy, I may even say—that is offered to her character by a light or injurious word."

"Giovanni! my poor Giovanni!" answered the professor, with a calm expression of pity, "I know this wretched girl far better than yourself. You shall hear the truth in respect to the poisoner Rappaccini and his poisonous daughter; yes, poisonous as she is beautiful. Listen; for, even should you do violence to my gray hairs, it shall not silence me. That old fable of the Indian woman has become a truth by the deep and deadly science of Rappaccini and in the person of the lovely Beatrice."

Giovanni groaned and hid his face.

"Her father," continued Baglioni, "was not restrained by natural affection from offering up his child in this horrible manner as the victim of his insane zeal for science; for, let us do him justice, he is as true a man of science as ever distilled his own heart in an alembic. What, then, will be your fate? Beyond a doubt you are selected as the material of some new experiment. Perhaps the result is to be death; perhaps a fate more awful still. Rappaccini, with what he calls the interest of science before his eyes, will hesitate at nothing."

"It is a dream," muttered Giovanni to himself; "surely it is a dream."

"But," resumed the professor, "be of good cheer, son of my friend. It is not yet too late for the rescue. Possibly we may even succeed in bringing back this miserable child within the limits of ordinary nature, from which her father's madness has estranged her. Behold this little silver vase! It was wrought by the hands of the renowned Benvenuto Cellini, and is well worthy to be a love gift to the fairest dame in Italy. But its contents are invaluable. One little sip of this antidote would have rendered the most virulent poisons of the Borgias innocuous. Doubt not that it will be as efficacious against those of Rappaccini. Bestow the vase, and the precious liquid within it, on your Beatrice, and hopefully await the result."

Baglioni laid a small, exquisitely wrought silver vial on the table and withdrew, leaving what he had said to produce its effect upon the young man's mind.

"We will thwart Rappaccini yet," thought he, chuckling to himself, as he descended the stairs; "but, let us confess the truth of him, he is a wonderful man—a wonderful man indeed; a vile empiric, however, in his practice, and therefore not to be tolerated by those who respect the good old rules of the medical profession."

Throughout Giovanni's whole acquaintance with Beatrice, he had occasionally, as we have said, been haunted by dark surmises as to her character; yet so thoroughly had she made herself felt by him as a simple, natural, most affectionate, and guileless creature, that the image now held up by Professor Baglioni looked as strange and incredible as if it were not in accordance with his own original conception. True, there were ugly recollections connected with his first glimpses of the beautiful girl; he could not quite forget the bouquet that withered in her grasp, and the insect that perished amid the sunny air, by no ostensible agency save the fragrance of her breath. These incidents, however, dissolving in the pure light of her character, had no longer the efficacy of facts, but were acknowledged as mistaken fantasies, by whatever testimony of the senses they might appear to be substantiated. There is something truer and more real than what we can see with the eyes and touch with the finger. On such better evidence had Giovanni founded his confidence in Beatrice, though rather by the necessary force of her high attributes than by any deep and generous faith on his part. But now his spirit was incapable of sustaining itself at the height to which the early enthusiasm of passion had exalted it; he fell down, grovelling among earthly doubts, and defiled therewith the pure whiteness of Beatrice's image. Not that he gave her up; he did but distrust. He resolved to institute some decisive test that should satisfy him, once for all, whether there were those dreadful peculiarities in her physical nature which could not be supposed to exist without some corresponding monstrosity of soul. His eyes, gazing down afar, might have deceived him as to the lizard, the insect, and the flowers; but if he could witness, at the distance of a few paces, the sudden blight of one fresh and healthful flower in Beatrice's hand, there would be room for no further question. With this idea he hastened to the florist's and purchased a bouquet that was still gemmed with the morning dew-drops.

It was now the customary hour of his daily interview with Beatrice. Before descending into the garden, Giovanni failed not to look at his figure in the mirror,—a vanity to be expected in a beautiful young man, yet, as displaying itself at that troubled and feverish moment, the token of a certain shallowness of feeling and insincerity of character. He did gaze, however, and said to himself that his features had never before possessed so rich a grace, nor his eyes such vivacity, nor his cheeks so warm a hue of superabundant life.

"At least," thought he, "her poison has not yet insinuated itself into my system. I am no flower to perish in her grasp."

With that thought he turned his eyes on the bouquet, which he had never once laid aside from his hand. A thrill of indefinable horror shot through his frame on perceiving that those dewy flowers were already beginning to droop; they wore the aspect of things that had been fresh and lovely yesterday. Giovanni grew white as marble, and stood motionless before the mirror, staring at his own reflection there as at the likeness of something frightful. He remembered Baglioni's remark about the fragrance that seemed to pervade the chamber. It must have been the poison in his breath! Then he shuddered—shuddered at himself. Recovering from his stupor, he began to watch with curious eye a spider that was busily at work hanging its web from the antique cornice of the apartment, crossing and recrossing the artful system of interwoven lines—as vigorous and active a spider as ever dangled from an old ceiling. Giovanni bent towards the insect, and emitted a deep, long breath. The spider suddenly ceased its toil; the web vibrated with a tremor originating in the body of the small artisan. Again Giovanni sent forth a breath, deeper, longer, and imbued with a venomous feeling out of his heart: he knew not whether he were wicked, or only desperate. The spider made a convulsive gripe with his limbs and hung dead across the window.

"Accursed! accursed!" muttered Giovanni, addressing himself. "Hast thou grown so poisonous that this deadly insect perishes by thy breath?"

At that moment a rich, sweet voice came floating up from the garden.

"Giovanni! Giovanni! It is past the hour! Why tarriest thou? Come down!"

"Yes," muttered Giovanni again. "She is the only being whom my breath may not slay! Would that it might!"

He rushed down, and in an instant was standing before the bright and loving eyes of Beatrice. A moment ago his wrath and despair had been so fierce that he could have desired nothing so much as to wither her by a glance; but with her actual presence there came influences which had too real an existence to be at once shaken off: recollections of the delicate and benign power of her feminine nature, which had so often enveloped him in a religious calm; recollections of many a holy and passionate outgush of her heart, when the pure fountain had been unsealed from its depths and made visible in its transparency to his mental eye; recollections which, had Giovanni known how to estimate them, would have assured him that all this ugly mystery was but an earthly illusion, and that, whatever mist of evil might seem to have gathered over her, the real Beatrice was a heavenly angel. Incapable as he was of such high faith, still her presence had not utterly lost its magic. Giovanni's rage was quelled into an aspect of sullen insensibility. Beatrice, with a quick spiritual sense, immediately felt that there was a gulf of blackness between them which neither he nor she could pass. They walked on together, sad and silent, and came thus to the marble fountain and to its pool of water on the ground, in the midst of which grew the shrub that bore gem-like blossoms. Giovanni was affrighted at the eager enjoyment—the appetite, as it were—with which he found himself inhaling the fragrance of the flowers.

"Beatrice," asked he, abruptly, "whence came this shrub?"

"My father created it," answered she, with simplicity.

"Created it! created it!" repeated Giovanni. "What mean you, Beatrice?"

"He is a man fearfully acquainted with the secrets of Nature," replied Beatrice; "and, at the hour when I first drew breath, this plant sprang from the soil, the offspring of his science, of his intellect, while I was but his earthly child. Approach it not!" continued she, observing with terror that Giovanni was drawing nearer to the shrub. "It has qualities that you little dream of. But I, dearest Giovanni,—I grew up and blossomed with the plant and was nourished with its breath. It was my sister, and I loved it with a human affection; for, alas!—hast thou not suspected it?—there was an awful doom."

Here Giovanni frowned so darkly upon her that Beatrice paused and trembled. But her faith in his tenderness reassured her, and made her blush that she had doubted for an instant.

"There was an awful doom," she continued, "the effect of my father's fatal love of science, which estranged me from all society of my kind. Until Heaven sent thee, dearest Giovanni, oh, how lonely was thy poor Beatrice!"

"Was it a hard doom?" asked Giovanni, fixing his eyes upon her.

"Only of late have I known how hard it was," answered she, tenderly. "Oh, yes; but my heart was torpid, and therefore quiet."

Giovanni's rage broke forth from his sullen gloom like a lightning flash out of a dark cloud.

"Accursed one!" cried he, with venomous scorn and anger. "And, finding thy solitude wearisome, thou hast severed me likewise from all the warmth of life and enticed me into thy region of unspeakable horror!"

"Giovanni!" exclaimed Beatrice, turning her large bright eyes upon his face. The force of his words had not found its way into her mind; she was merely thunderstruck.

"Yes, poisonous thing!" repeated Giovanni, beside himself with passion. "Thou hast done it! Thou hast blasted me! Thou hast filled my veins with poison! Thou hast made me as hateful, as ugly, as loathsome and deadly a creature as thyself—a world's wonder of hideous monstrosity! Now, if our breath be happily as fatal to ourselves as to all others, let us join our lips in one kiss of unutterable hatred, and so die!"

"What has befallen me?" murmured Beatrice, with a low moan out of her heart. "Holy Virgin, pity me, a poor heart-broken child!"

"Thou,—dost thou pray?" cried Giovanni, still with the same fiendish scorn. "Thy very prayers, as they come from thy lips, taint the atmosphere with death. Yes, yes; let us pray! Let us to church and dip our fingers in the holy water at the portal! They that come after us will perish as by a pestilence! Let us sign crosses in the air! It will be scattering curses abroad in the likeness of holy symbols!"

"Giovanni," said Beatrice, calmly, for her grief was beyond passion, "why dost thou join thyself with me thus in those terrible words? I, it is true, am the horrible thing thou namest me. But thou,—what hast thou to do, save with one other shudder at my hideous misery to go forth out of the garden and mingle with thy race, and forget there ever crawled on earth such a monster as poor Beatrice?"

"Dost thou pretend ignorance?" asked Giovanni, scowling upon her. "Behold! this power have I gained from the pure daughter of Rappaccini."

There was a swarm of summer insects flitting through the air in search of the food promised by the flower odors of the fatal garden. They circled round Giovanni's head, and were evidently attracted towards him by the same influence which had drawn them for an instant within the sphere of several of the shrubs. He sent forth a breath among them, and smiled bitterly at Beatrice as at least a score of the insects fell dead upon the ground.

"I see it! I see it!" shrieked Beatrice. "It is my father's fatal science! No, no, Giovanni; it was not I! Never! never! I dreamed only to love thee and be with thee a little time, and so to let thee pass away, leaving but thine image in mine heart; for, Giovanni, believe it, though my body be nourished with poison, my spirit is God's creature, and craves love as its daily food. But my father,—he has united us in this fearful sympathy. Yes; spurn me, tread upon me, kill me! Oh, what is death after such words as thine? But it was not I. Not for a world of bliss would I have done it."

Giovanni's passion had exhausted itself in its outburst from his lips. There now came across him a sense, mournful, and not without tenderness, of the intimate and peculiar relationship between Beatrice and himself. They stood, as it were, in an utter solitude, which would be made none the less solitary by the densest throng of human life. Ought not, then, the desert of humanity around them to press this insulated pair closer together? If they should be cruel to one another, who was there to be kind to them? Besides, thought Giovanni, might there not still be a hope of his returning within the limits of ordinary nature, and leading Beatrice, the redeemed Beatrice, by the hand? O, weak, and selfish, and unworthy spirit, that could dream of an earthly union and earthly happiness as possible, after such deep love had been so bitterly wronged as was Beatrice's love by Giovanni's blighting words! No, no; there could be no such hope. She must pass heavily, with that broken heart, across the borders of Time—she must bathe her hurts in some fount of paradise, and forget her grief in the light of immortality, and *there* be well.

But Giovanni did not know it.

"Dear Beatrice," said he, approaching her, while she shrank away as always at his approach, but now with a different impulse, "dearest Beatrice our fate is not yet so desperate. Behold! there is a medicine, potent, as a wise physician has assured me, and almost divine in its efficacy. It is composed of ingredients the most opposite to those by which thy awful father has brought this calamity upon thee and me. It is distilled of blessed herbs. Shall we not quaff it together, and thus be purified from evil?"

"Give it me!" said Beatrice, extending her hand to receive the little silver vial which Giovanni took from his bosom. She added, with a peculiar emphasis, "I will drink; but do thou await the result."

She put Baglioni's antidote to her lips; and, at the same moment, the figure of Rappaccini emerged from the portal and came slowly towards the marble fountain. As he drew near, the pale man of science seemed to gaze with a triumphant expression at the beautiful youth and maiden, as might an artist who should spend his life in achieving a picture or a group of statuary and finally be satisfied with his success. He paused; his bent form grew erect with conscious power; he spread out his hands over them in the attitude of a father imploring a blessing upon his children; but those were the same hands that had thrown poison into the stream of their lives. Giovanni trembled. Beatrice shuddered nervously, and pressed her hand upon her heart.

"My daughter," said Rappaccini, "thou art no longer lonely in the world. Pluck one of those precious gems from thy sister shrub and bid thy bridegroom wear it in his bosom. It will not harm him now. My science and the sympathy between thee and him have so wrought within his system that he now stands apart from common men, as thou dost, daughter of my pride and triumph, from ordinary women. Pass on, then, through the world, most dear to one another and dreadful to all besides!"

"My father," said Beatrice, feebly,—and still as she spoke she kept her hand upon her heart,—"wherefore didst thou inflict this miserable doom upon thy child?"

"Miserable!" exclaimed Rappaccini. "What mean you, foolish girl? Dost thou deem it misery to be endowed with marvellous gifts against which no power nor strength could avail an enemy—misery, to be able to quell the mightiest with a breath—misery, to be as terrible as thou art beautiful? Wouldst thou, then, have preferred the condition of a weak woman, exposed to all evil and capable of none?"

"I would fain have been loved, not feared," murmured Beatrice, sinking down upon the ground. "But now it matters not. I am going, father, where the evil which thou hast striven to mingle with my being will pass away like a dream—like the fragrance of these poisonous flowers, which will no longer taint my breath among the flowers of Eden. Farewell, Giovanni! Thy words of hatred are like lead within my heart; but they, too, will fall away as I ascend. Oh, was there not, from the first, more poison in thy nature than in mine?"

To Beatrice,—so radically had her earthly part been wrought upon by Rappaccini's skill,—as poison had been life, so the powerful antidote was death; and thus the poor victim of man's ingenuity and of thwarted nature, and of the fatality that attends all such efforts of perverted wisdom, perished there, at the feet of her father and Giovanni. Just at that moment Professor Pietro Baglioni looked forth from the window, and called loudly, in a tone of triumph mixed with horror, to the thunderstricken man of science,—

"Rappaccini! Rappaccini! and is *this* the upshot of your experiment!"

# MRS. BULLFROG

IT makes me melancholy to see how like fools some very sensible people act in the matter of choosing wives. They perplex their judgments by a most undue attention to little niceties of personal appearance, habits, disposition, and other trifles which concern nobody but the lady herself. An unhappy gentleman, resolving to wed nothing short of perfection, keeps his heart and hand till both get so old and withered that no tolerable woman will accept them. Now this is the very height of absurdity. A kind Providence has so skilfully adapted sex to sex and the mass of individuals to each other, that, with certain obvious exceptions, any male and female may be moderately happy in the married state. The true rule is to ascertain that the match is fundamentally a good one, and then to take it for granted that all minor objections, should there be such, will vanish, if you let them alone. Only put yourself beyond hazard as to the real basis of matrimonial bliss, and it is scarcely to be imagined what miracles, in the way of recognizing smaller incongruities, connubial love will effect.

For my own part I freely confess that, in my bachelorship, I was precisely such an over-curious simpleton as I now advise the reader not to be. My early habits had gifted me with a feminine sensibility and too exquisite refinement. I was the accomplished graduate of a dry goods store, where, by dint of ministering to the whims of fine ladies, and suiting silken hose to delicate limbs, and handling satins, ribbons, chintzes, calicoes, tapes, gauze, and cambric needles, I grew up a very ladylike sort of a gentleman. It is not assuming too much to affirm that the ladies themselves were hardly so ladylike as Thomas Bullfrog. So painfully acute was my sense of female imperfection, and such varied excellence did I require in the woman whom I could love, that there was an awful risk of my getting no wife at all, or of being driven to perpetrate matrimony with my own image in the looking-glass. Besides the fundamental principle already hinted at, I demanded the fresh bloom of youth, pearly teeth, glossy ringlets, and the whole list of lovely items, with the utmost delicacy of habits and sentiments, a silken texture of mind, and, above all, a virgin heart. In a word, if a young angel just from paradise, yet dressed in earthly fashion, had come and offered me her hand, it is by no means certain that I should have taken it. There was every chance of my becoming a most miserable old bachelor, when, by the best luck in the world, I made a journey into another state, and was smitten by, and smote again, and wooed, won, and married, the present Mrs. Bullfrog, all in the space of a fortnight. Owing to these extempore measures, I not only gave my bride credit for certain perfections which have not as yet come to light, but also overlooked a few trifling defects, which, however, glimmered on my perception long before the close of the honeymoon. Yet, as there was no mistake about the fundamental principle aforesaid, I soon learned, as will be seen, to estimate Mrs. Bullfrog's deficiencies and superfluities at exactly their proper value.

The same morning that Mrs. Bullfrog and I came together as a unit, we took two seats in the stage-coach and began our journey towards my place of business. There being no other passengers, we were as much alone and as free to give vent to our raptures as if I had hired a hack for the matrimonial jaunt. My bride looked charmingly in a green silk calash and riding habit of pelisse cloth; and whenever her red lips parted with a smile, each tooth appeared like an inestimable pearl. Such was my passionate warmth that—we had rattled out of the village, gentle reader, and were lonely as Adam and Eve in paradise—I plead guilty to no less freedom than a kiss. The gentle eye of Mrs. Bullfrog scarcely rebuked me for the profanation. Emboldened by her indulgence, I threw back the calash from her polished brow, and suffered my fingers, white and delicate as her own, to stray among those dark and glossy curls which realized my daydreams of rich hair.

"My love," said Mrs. Bullfrog tenderly, "you will disarrange my curls."

"Oh, no, my sweet Laura!" replied I, still playing with the glossy ringlet. "Even your fair hand could not manage a curl more delicately than mine. I propose myself the pleasure of doing up your hair in papers every evening at the same time with my own."

"Mr. Bullfrog," repeated she, "you must not disarrange my curls."

This was spoken in a more decided tone than I had happened to hear, until then, from my gentlest of all gentle brides. At the same time she put up her hand and took mine prisoner; but merely drew it away from the forbidden ringlet, and then immediately released it. Now, I am a fidgety little man, and always love to have something in my fingers; so that, being debarred from my wife's curls, I looked about me for any other plaything. On the front seat of the coach there was one of those small baskets in which travelling ladies who are too delicate to appear at a public table generally carry a supply of gingerbread, biscuits and cheese, cold ham, and other light refreshments, merely to sustain nature to the journey's end. Such airy diet will sometimes keep them in pretty good flesh for a week together. Laying hold of this same little basket, I thrust my hand under the newspaper with which it was carefully covered.

"What's this, my dear?" cried I; for the black neck of a bottle had popped out of the basket.

"A bottle of Kalydor, Mr. Bullfrog," said my wife, coolly taking the basket from my hands and replacing it on the front seat.

There was no possibility of doubting my wife's word; but I never knew genuine Kalydor, such as I use for my own complexion, to smell so much like cherry brandy. I was about to express my fears that the lotion would injure her skin, when an accident occurred which threatened more than a skin-deep injury. Our Jehu had carelessly driven over a heap of gravel and fairly capsized the coach, with the wheels in the air and our heels where our heads should have been. What became of my wits I cannot imagine; they have always had a perverse trick of deserting me just when they were most needed; but so it chanced, that in the confusion of our overthrow I quite forgot that there was a Mrs. Bullfrog in the world. Like many men's wives, the good lady served her husband as a stepping-stone. I had scrambled out of the coach and was instinctively settling my cravat, when somebody brushed roughly by me, and I heard a smart thwack upon the coachman's ear.

"Take that, you villain!" cried a strange, hoarse voice. "You have ruined me, you blackguard! I shall never be the woman I have been!"

And then came a second thwack, aimed at the driver's other ear; but which missed it, and hit him on the nose, causing a terrible effusion of blood. Now, who or what fearful apparition was inflicting this punishment on the poor fellow remained an impenetrable mystery to me. The blows were given by a person of grisly aspect, with a head almost bald, and sunken cheeks, apparently of the feminine gender, though hardly to be classed in the gentler sex. There being no teeth to modulate the voice, it had a mumbled fierceness, not passionate, but stern, which absolutely made me quiver like calf's-foot jelly. Who could the phantom be? The most awful circumstance of the affair is yet to be told: for this ogre, or whatever it was, had a riding habit like Mrs. Bullfrog's, and also a green silk calash dangling down her back by the strings. In my terror and turmoil of mind I could imagine nothing less than that the Old Nick, at the moment of our overturn, had annihilated my wife and jumped into her petticoats. This idea seemed the most probable, since I could nowhere perceive Mrs. Bullfrog alive, nor, though I looked very sharply about the coach, could I detect any traces of that beloved woman's dead body. There would have been a comfort in giving her Christian burial.

"Come, sir, bestir yourself! Help this rascal to set up the coach," said the hobgoblin to me; then, with a terrific screech at three countrymen at a distance, "Here, you fellows, ain't you ashamed to stand off when a poor woman is in distress?"

The countrymen, instead of fleeing for their lives, came running at full speed, and laid hold of the topsy-turvy coach. I, also, though a small-sized man, went to work like a son of Anak. The coachman, too, with the blood still streaming from his nose, tugged and toiled most manfully, dreading, doubtless, that the next blow might break his head. And yet, bemauled as the poor fellow had been, he seemed to glance at me with an eye of pity, as if my case were more deplorable than his. But I cherished a hope that all would turn out a dream, and seized the opportunity, as we raised the coach, to jam two of my fingers under the wheel, trusting that the pain would awaken me.

"Why, here we are, all to rights again!" exclaimed a sweet voice behind. "Thank you for your assistance, gentlemen. My dear Mr. Bullfrog, how you perspire! Do let me wipe your face. Don't take this little accident too much to heart, good driver. We ought to be thankful that none of our necks are broken."

"We might have spared one neck out of the three," muttered the driver, rubbing his ear and pulling his nose, to ascertain whether he had been cuffed or not. "Why, the woman's a witch!"

I fear that the reader will not believe, yet it is positively a fact, that there stood Mrs. Bullfrog, with her glossy ringlets curling on her brow, and two rows of orient pearls gleaming between her parted lips, which wore a most angelic smile. She had regained her riding habit and calash from the grisly phantom, and was, in all respects, the lovely woman who had been sitting by my side at the instant of our overturn. How she had happened to disappear, and who had supplied her place, and whence she did now return, were problems too knotty for me to solve. There stood my wife. That was the one thing certain among a heap of mysteries. Nothing remained but to help her into the coach, and plod on, through the journey of the day and the journey of life, as comfortably as we could. As the driver closed the door upon us, I heard him whisper to the three countrymen,—

"How do you suppose a fellow feels shut up in the cage with a she tiger?"

Of course this query could have no reference to my situation. Yet, unreasonable as it may appear, I confess that my feelings were not altogether so ecstatic as when I first called Mrs. Bullfrog mine. True, she was a sweet woman and an angel of a wife; but what if a Gorgon should return, amid the transports of our connubial bliss, and take the angel's place. I recollected the tale of a fairy, who half the time was a beautiful woman and half the time a hideous monster. Had I taken that very fairy to be the wife of my bosom? While such whims and chimeras were flitting across my fancy I began to look askance at Mrs. Bullfrog, almost expecting that the transformation would be wrought before my eyes.

To divert my mind, I took up the newspaper which had covered the little basket of refreshments, and which now lay at the bottom of the coach, blushing with a deep-red stain and emitting a potent spirituous fume from the contents of the broken bottle of Kalydor. The paper was two or three years old, but contained an article of several columns, in which I soon grew wonderfully interested. It was the report of a trial for breach of promise of marriage, giving the testimony in full, with fervid extracts from both the gentleman's and lady's amatory correspondence. The deserted damsel had personally appeared in court, and had borne energetic evidence to her lover's perfidy and the strength of her blighted affections. On the defendant's part there had been an attempt, though insufficiently sustained, to blast the plaintiff's character, and a plea, in mitigation of damages, on account of her unamiable temper. A horrible idea was suggested by the lady's name.

"Madam," said I, holding the newspaper before Mrs. Bullfrog's eyes, —and, though a small, delicate, and thin-visaged man, I feel assured that I looked very terrific,—"madam," repeated I, through my shut teeth, "were you the plaintiff in this cause?"

"Oh, my dear Mr. Bullfrog," replied my wife, sweetly, "I thought all the world knew that!"

"Horror! horror!" exclaimed I, sinking back on the seat.

Covering my face with both hands, I emitted a deep and deathlike groan, as if my tormented soul were rending me asunder—I, the most exquisitely fastidious of men, and whose wife was to have been the most delicate and refined of women, with all the fresh dew-drops glittering on her virgin rosebud of a heart!

I thought of the glossy ringlets and pearly teeth; I thought of the Kalydor; I thought of the coachman's bruised ear and bloody nose; I thought of the tender love secrets which she had whispered to the judge and jury and a thousand tittering auditors,—and gave another groan!

"Mr. Bullfrog," said my wife.

As I made no reply, she gently took my hands within her own, removed them from my face, and fixed her eyes steadfastly on mine.

"Mr. Bullfrog," said she, not unkindly, yet with all the decision of her strong character, "let me advise you to overcome this foolish weakness, and prove yourself, to the best of your ability, as good a husband as I will be a wife. You have discovered, perhaps, some little imperfections in your bride. Well, what did you expect? Women are not angels. If they were, they would go to heaven for husbands; or, at least, be more difficult in their choice on earth."

"But why conceal those imperfections?" interposed I, tremulously.

"Now, my love, are not you a most unreasonable little man?" said Mrs. Bullfrog, patting me on the cheek. "Ought a woman to disclose her frailties earlier than the wedding day? Few husbands, I assure you, make the discovery in such good season, and still fewer complain that these trifles are concealed too long. Well, what a strange man you are! Poh! you are joking."

"But the suit for breach of promise!" groaned I.

"Ah, and is that the rub?" exclaimed my wife. "Is it possible that you view that affair in an objectionable light? Mr. Bullfrog, I never could have dreamed it! Is it an objection that I have triumphantly defended myself against slander and vindicated my purity in a court of justice? Or do you complain because your wife has shown the proper spirit of a woman, and punished the villain who trifled with her affections?"

"But," persisted I, shrinking into a corner of the coach, however,—for I did not know precisely how much contradiction the proper spirit of a woman would endure,—"but, my love, would it not have been more dignified to treat the villain with the silent contempt he merited?"

"That is all very well, Mr. Bullfrog," said my wife, slyly; "but, in that case, where would have been the five thousand dollars which are to stock your dry goods store?"

"Mrs. Bullfrog, upon your honor," demanded I, as if my life hung upon her words, "is there no mistake about those five thousand dollars?"

"Upon my word and honor there is none," replied she. "The jury gave me every cent the rascal had; and I have kept it all for my dear Bullfrog."

"Then, thou dear woman," cried I, with an overwhelming gush of tenderness, "let me fold thee to my heart. The basis of matrimonial bliss is secure, and all thy little defects and frailties are forgiven. Nay, since the result has been so fortunate, I rejoice at the wrongs which drove thee to this blessed lawsuit. Happy Bullfrog that I am!"

# THE CELESTIAL RAILROAD

Not a great while ago, passing through the gate of dreams, I visited that region of the earth in which lies the famous City of Destruction. It interested me much to learn that by the public spirit of some of the inhabitants a railroad has recently been established between this populous and flourishing town and the Celestial City. Having a little time upon my hands, I resolved to gratify a liberal curiosity by making a trip thither. Accordingly, one fine morning after paying my bill at the hotel, and directing the porter to stow my luggage behind a coach, I took my seat in the vehicle and set out for the station-house. It was my good fortune to enjoy the company of a gentleman—one Mr. Smooth-it-away—who, though he had never actually visited the Celestial City, yet seemed as well acquainted with its laws, customs, policy, and statistics, as with those of the City of Destruction, of which he was a native townsman. Being, moreover, a director of the railroad corporation and one of its largest stockholders, he had it in his power to give me all desirable information respecting that praiseworthy enterprise.

Our coach rattled out of the city, and at a short distance from its out-skirts passed over a bridge of elegant construction, but somewhat too slight, as I imagined, to sustain any considerable weight. On both sides lay an extensive quagmire, which could not have been more disagreeable, either to sight or smell, had all the kennels of the earth emptied their pol-lution there.

"This," remarked Mr. Smooth-it-away, "is the famous Slough of De-spond—a disgrace to all the neighborhood; and the greater that it might so easily be converted into firm ground."

"I have understood," said I, "that efforts have been made for that pur-pose from time immemorial. Bunyan mentions that above twenty thou-cand cartloads of wholesome instructions had been thrown in here with-out effect."

"Very probably! And what effect could be anticipated from such un-substantial stuff?" cried Mr. Smooth-it-away. "You observe this conven-ient bridge. We obtained a sufficient foundation for it by throwing into the slough some editions of books of morality; volumes of French phil-osophy and German rationalism; tracts, sermons, and essays of modern clergymen; extracts from Plato, Confucius, and various Hindoo sages, together with a few ingenious commentaries upon texts of Scripture,—all of which by some scientific process, have been converted into a mass like granite. The whole bog might be filled up with similar matter."

It really seemed to me, however, that the bridge vibrated and heaved up and down in a very formidable manner; and, in spite of Mr. Smooth-it-away's testimony to the solidity of its foundation, I should be loath to cross it in a crowded omnibus, especially if each passenger were encum-bered with as heavy luggage as that gentleman and myself. Nevertheless we got over without accident, and soon found ourselves at the station-house. This very neat and spacious edifice is erected on the site of the little wicket gate, which formerly, as all old pilgrims will recollect, stood directly across the highway, and, by its inconvenient narrowness, was a great obstruction to the traveller of liberal mind and expansive stomach. The reader of John Bunyan will be glad to know that Christian's old friend Evangelist, who was accustomed to supply each pilgrim with a mystic roll, now presides at the ticket office. Some malicious persons it is true deny the identity of this reputable character with the Evangelist of old times, and even pretend to bring competent evidence of an imposture. Without involving myself in a dispute I shall merely observe that, so far as my experience goes, the square pieces of pasteboard now delivered to passengers are much more convenient and useful along the road than the antique roll of parchment. Whether they will be as readily received at the gate of the Celestial City I decline giving an opinion.

A large number of passengers were already at the station-house await-ing the departure of the cars. By the aspect and demeanor of these per-sons it was easy to judge that the feelings of the community had under-gone a very favorable change in reference to the celestial pilgrimage. It would have done Bunyan's heart good to see it. Instead of a lonely and ragged man with a huge burden on his back, plodding along sorrowfully on foot while the whole city hooted after him, here were parties of the first gentry and most respectable people in the neighborhood setting forth towards the Celestial City as cheerfully as if the pilgrimage were merely a summer tour. Among the gentlemen were characters of deserved eminence—magistrates, politicians, and men of wealth, by whose example religion could not but be greatly recommended to their meaner brethren. In the ladies' apartment, too, I rejoiced to distinguish some of those flowers of fashionable society who are so well fitted to adorn the most elevated circles of the Celestial City. There was much pleasant conversation about the news of the day, topics of business and politics, or the lighter matters of amusement; while religion, though indubitably the main thing at heart, was thrown tastefully into the background. Even an infidel would have heard little or nothing to shock his sensibility.

One great convenience of the new method of going on pilgrimage I must not forget to mention. Our enormous burdens, instead of being carried on our shoulders as had been the custom of old, were all snugly deposited in the baggage car, and, as I was assured, would be delivered to their respective owners at the journey's end. Another thing, likewise, the benevolent reader will be delighted to understand. It may be remembered that there was an ancient feud between Prince Beelzebub and the keeper of the wicket gate, and that the adherents of the former distinguished personage were accustomed to shoot deadly arrows at honest pilgrims while knocking at the door. This dispute, much to the credit as well of the illustrious potentate above mentioned as of the worthy and enlightened directors of the railroad, has been pacifically arranged on the principle of mutual compromise. The prince's subjects are now pretty numerously employed about the station-house, some in taking care of the baggage, others in collecting fuel, feeding the engines, and such congenial occupations; and I can conscientiously affirm that persons more attentive to their business, more willing to accommodate, or more generally agreeable to the passengers, are not to be found on any railroad. Every good heart must surely exult at so satisfactory an arrangement of an immemorial difficulty.

"Where is Mr. Greatheart?" inquired I. "Beyond a doubt the directors have engaged that famous old champion to be chief conductor on the railroad?"

"Why, no," said Mr. Smooth-it-away, with a dry cough. "He was offered the situation of brakeman; but, to tell you the truth, our friend Greatheart has grown preposterously stiff and narrow in his old age. He has so often guided pilgrims over the road on foot that he considers it a sin to travel in any other fashion. Besides, the old fellow had entered so heartily into the ancient feud with Prince Beelzebub that he would have been perpetually at blows or ill language with some of the prince's subjects, and thus have embroiled us anew. So, on the whole, we were not sorry when honest Greatheart went off to the Celestial City in a huff and left us at liberty to choose a more suitable and accommodating man. Yonder comes the engineer of the train. You will probably recognize him at once."

The engine at this moment took its station in advance of the cars, looking, I must confess, much more like a sort of mechanical demon that would hurry us to the infernal regions than a laudable contrivance for smoothing our way to the Celestial City. On its top sat a personage almost enveloped in smoke and flame, which, not to startle the reader, appeared to gush from his own mouth and stomach as well as from the engine's brazen abdomen.

"Do my eyes deceive me?" cried I. "What on earth is this! A living creature? If so, he is own brother to the engine he rides upon!"

"Poh, poh, you are obtuse!" said Mr. Smooth-it-away, with a hearty laugh. "Don't you know Apollyon, Christian's old enemy, with whom he fought so fierce a battle in the Valley of Humiliation? He was the very fellow to manage the engine; and so we have reconciled him to the custom of going on pilgrimage, and engaged him as chief engineer."

"Bravo, bravo!" exclaimed I, with irrepressible enthusiasm; "this shows the liberality of the age; this proves, if anything can, that all musty prejudices are in a fair way to be obliterated. And how will Christian rejoice to hear of this happy transformation of his old antagonist! I promise myself great pleasure in informing him of it when we reach the Celestial City."

The passengers being all comfortably seated, we now rattled away merrily, accomplishing a greater distance in ten minutes than Christian probably trudged over in a day. It was laughable, while we glanced along, as it were, at the tail of a thunderbolt, to observe two dusty foot travellers in the old pilgrim guise, with cockle shell and staff, their mystic rolls of parchment in their hands and their intolerable burdens on their backs. The preposterous obstinacy of these honest people in persisting to groan and stumble along the difficult pathway rather than take advantage of modern improvements, excited great mirth among our wiser brotherhood. We greeted the two pilgrims with many pleasant gibes and a roar of laughter; whereupon they gazed at us with such woful and absurdly compassionate visages that our merriment grew tenfold more obstreperous. Apollyon also entered heartily into the fun, and contrived to flirt the smoke and flame of the engine, or of his own breath, into their faces, and envelop them in an atmosphere of scalding steam. These little practical jokes amused us mightily, and doubtless afforded the pilgrims the gratification of considering themselves martyrs.

At some distance from the railroad Mr. Smooth-it-away pointed to a large, antique edifice, which, he observed, was a tavern of long standing, and had formerly been a noted stopping-place for pilgrims. In Bunyan's road-book it is mentioned as the Interpreter's House.

"I have long had a curiosity to visit that old mansion," remarked I.

"It is not one of our stations, as you perceive," said my companion "The keeper was violently opposed to the railroad; and well he might be, as the track left his house of entertainment on one side, and thus was pretty certain to deprive him of all his reputable customers. But the footpath still passes his door, and the old gentleman now and then receives a call from some simple traveller, and entertains him with fare as oldfashioned as himself."

Before our talk on this subject came to a conclusion we were rushing by the place where Christian's burden fell from his shoulders at the sight of the Cross. This served as a theme for Mr. Smooth-it-away, Mr. Livefor-the-world, Mr. Hide-sin-in-the-heart, Mr. Scaly-conscience, and a knot of gentlemen from the town of Shun-repentance, to descant upon the inestimable advantages resulting from the safety of our baggage. Myself, and all the passengers indeed, joined with great unanimity in this view of the matter; for our burdens were rich in many things esteemed precious throughout the world; and, especially, we each of us possessed a great variety of favorite Habits, which we trusted would not be out of fashion even in the polite circles of the Celestial City. It would have been a sad spectacle to see such an assortment of valuable articles tumbling into the sepulchre. Thus pleasantly conversing on the favorable circumstances of our position as compared with those of past pilgrims and of narrow-minded ones at the present day, we soon found ourselves at the foot of the Hill Difficulty. Through the very heart of this rocky mountain a tunnel has been constructed of most admirable architecture, with a lofty arch and a spacious double track; so that, unless the earth and rocks should chance to crumble down, it will remain an eternal monument of the builder's skill and enterprise. It is a great though incidental advantage that the materials from the heart of the Hill Difficulty have been employed in filling up the Valley of Humiliation, thus obviating the necessity of descending into that disagreeable and unwholesome hollow.

"This is a wonderful improvement, indeed," said I. "Yet I should have been glad of an opportunity to visit the Palace Beautiful and be introduced to the charming young ladies—Miss Prudence, Miss Piety, Miss Charity, and the rest—who have the kindness to entertain pilgrims there."

"Young ladies!" cried Mr. Smooth-it-away, as soon as he could speak for laughing. "And charming young ladies! Why, my dear fellow, they are old maids, every soul of them—prim, starched, dry, and angular; and not one of them, I will venture to say, has altered so much as the fashion of her gown since the days of Christian's pilgrimage."

"Ah, well," said I, much comforted, "then I can very readily dispense with their acquaintance."

The respectable Apollyon was now putting on the steam at a prodigious rate, anxious, perhaps, to get rid of the unpleasant reminiscences connected with the spot where he had so disastrously encountered Christian. Consulting Mr. Bunyan's road-book, I perceived that we must now be within a few miles of the Valley of the Shadow of Death, into which doleful region, at our present speed, we should plunge much sooner than seemed at all desirable. In truth, I expected nothing better than to find myself in the ditch on one side or the quag on the other; but on communicating my apprehensions to Mr. Smooth-it-away, he assured me that the difficulties of this passage, even in its worst condition, had been vastly exaggerated, and that, in its present state of improvement, I might consider myself as safe as on any railroad in Christendom.

Even while we were speaking the train shot into the entrance of this dreaded Valley. Though I plead guilty to some foolish palpitations of the heart during our headlong rush over the causeway here constructed, yet it were unjust to withhold the highest encomiums on the boldness of its original conception and the ingenuity of those who executed it. It was gratifying, likewise, to observe how much care had been taken to dispel the everlasting gloom and supply the defect of cheerful sunshine, not a ray of which has ever penetrated among these awful shadows. For this purpose, the inflammable gas which exudes plentifully from the soil is collected by means of pipes, and thence communicated to a quadruple row of lamps along the whole extent of the passage. Thus a radiance has been created even out of the fiery and sulphurous curse that rests forever upon the valley—a radiance hurtful, however, to the eyes, and somewhat bewildering, as I discovered by the changes which it wrought in the visages of my companions. In this respect, as compared with natural daylight, there is the same difference as between truth and falsehood; but if the reader have ever travelled through the dark Valley, he will have learned to be thankful for any light that he could get—if not from the sky above, then from the blasted soil beneath. Such was the red brilliancy of these lamps that they appeared to build walls of fire on both sides of the track, between which we held our course at lightning speed, while a reverberating thunder filled the Valley with its echoes. Had the engine run off the track,—a catastrophe, it is whispered, by no means unprecedented,—the bottomless pit, if there be any such place, would undoubtedly have received us. Just as some dismal fooleries of this nature had made my heart quake there came a tremendous shriek, careering along the valley as if a thousand devils had burst their lungs to utter it, but which proved to be merely the whistle of the engine on arriving at a stopping-place.

The spot where we had now paused is the same that our friend Bunyan —a truthful man, but infected with many fantastic notions—has designated, in terms plainer than I like to repeat, as the mouth of the infernal region. This, however, must be a mistake, inasmuch as Mr. Smooth-it-away, while we remained in the smoky and lurid cavern, took occasion to prove that Tophet has not even a metaphorical existence. The place, he assured us, is no other than the crater of a half-extinct volcano, in which the directors had caused forges to be set up for the manufacture of railroad iron. Hence, also, is obtained a plentiful supply of fuel for the use of the engines. Whoever had gazed into the dismal obscurity of the broad cavern mouth, whence ever and anon darted huge tongues of dusky flame, and had seen the strange, half-shaped monsters, and visions of faces horribly grotesque, into which the smoke seemed to wreathe itself, and had heard the awful murmurs, and shrieks, and deep, shuddering whispers of the blast, sometimes forming themselves into words almost articulate, would have seized upon Mr. Smooth-it-away's comfortable explanation as greedily as we did. The inhabitants of the cavern, moreover, were unlovely personages, dark, smoke-begrimed, generally deformed, with misshapen feet, and a glow of dusky redness in their eyes as if their hearts had caught fire and were blazing out of the upper windows. It struck me as a peculiarity that the laborers at the forge and those who brought fuel to the engine, when they began to draw short breath, positively emitted smoke from their mouth and nostrils.

Among the idlers about the train, most of whom were puffing cigars which they had lighted at the flame of the crater, I was perplexed to notice several who, to my certain knowledge, had heretofore set forth by railroad for the Celestial City. They looked dark, wild, and smoky, with a singular resemblance, indeed, to the native inhabitants, like whom, also, they had a disagreeable propensity to ill-natured gibes and sneers, the habit of which had wrought a settled contortion of their visages. Having been on speaking terms with one of these persons,—an indolent, good-for-nothing fellow, who went by the name of Take-it-easy,—I called him, and inquired what was his business there.

"Did you not start," said I, "for the Celestial City?"

"That's a fact," said Mr. Take-it-easy, carelessly puffing some smoke into my eyes. "But I heard such bad accounts that I never took pains to climb the hill on which the city stands. No business doing, no fun going on, nothing to drink, and no smoking allowed, and a thrumming of church music from morning till night. I would not stay in such a place if they offered me house room and living free."

"But, my good Mr. Take-it-easy," cried I, "why take up your residence here, of all places in the world?"

"Oh," said the loafer, with a grin, "it is very warm hereabouts, and I meet with plenty of old acquaintances, and altogether the place suits me. I hope to see you back again some day soon. A pleasant journey to you."

While he was speaking the bell of the engine rang, and we dashed away after dropping a few passengers, but receiving no new ones. Rattling onward through the Valley, we were dazzled with the fiercely gleaming gas lamps, as before. But sometimes, in the dark of intense brightness, grim faces, that bore the aspect and expression of individual sins, or evil passions, seemed to thrust themselves through the veil of light, glaring upon us, and stretching forth a great, dusky hand, as if to impede our progress. I almost thought that they were my own sins that appalled me there. These were freaks of imagination—nothing more, certainly—mere delusions, which I ought to be heartily ashamed of; but all through the Dark Valley I was tormented, and pestered, and dolefully bewildered with the same kind of waking dreams. The mephitic gases of that region intoxicate the brain. As the light of natural day, however, began to struggle with the glow of the lanterns, these vain imaginations lost their vividness, and finally vanished from the first ray of sunshine that greeted our escape from the Valley of the Shadow of Death. Ere we had gone a mile beyond it I could wellnigh have taken my oath that this whole gloomy passage was a dream.

At the end of the valley, as John Bunyan mentions, is a cavern, where, in his days, dwelt two cruel giants, Pope and Pagan, who had strown the ground about their residence with the bones of slaughtered pilgrims. These vile old troglodytes are no longer there; but into their deserted cave another terrible giant has thrust himself, and makes it his business to seize upon honest travellers and fatten them for his table with plentiful meals of smoke, mist, moonshine, raw potatoes, and sawdust. He is a German by birth, and is called Giant Transcendentalist; but as to his form, his features, his substance, and his nature generally, it is the chief peculiarity of this huge miscreant that neither he for himself, nor anybody for him, has ever been able to describe them. As we rushed by the cavern's mouth we caught a hasty glimpse of him, looking somewhat like an ill-proportioned figure, but considerably more like a heap of fog and duskiness. He shouted after us, but in so strange a phraseology that we knew not what he meant, nor whether to be encouraged or affrighted.

It was late in the day when the train thundered into the ancient city of Vanity, where Vanity Fair is still at the height of prosperity, and exhibits an epitome of whatever is brilliant, gay, and fascinating beneath the sun. As I purposed to make a considerable stay here, it gratified me to learn that there is no longer the want of harmony between the town's-people and pilgrims, which impelled the former to such lamentably mistaken measures as the persecution of Christian and the fiery martyrdom of Faithful. On the contrary, as the new railroad brings with it great trade and a constant influx of strangers, the lord of Vanity Fair is its chief patron, and the capitalists of the city are among the largest stockholders. Many passengers stop to take their pleasure or make their profit in the Fair, instead of going onward to the Celestial City. Indeed, such are the charms of the place that people often affirm it to be the true and only heaven; stoutly contending that there is no other, that those who seek further are mere dreamers, and that, if the fabled brightness of the Celestial City lay but a bare mile beyond the gates of Vanity, they would not be fools enough to go thither. Without subscribing to these perhaps exaggerated encomiums, I can truly say that my abode in the city was mainly agreeable, and my intercourse with the inhabitants productive of much amusement and instruction.

Being naturally of a serious turn, my attention was directed to the solid advantages derivable from a residence here, rather than to the effervescent pleasures which are the grand object with too many visitants. The Christian reader, if he have had no accounts of the city later than Bunyan's time, will be surprised to hear that almost every street has its church, and that the reverend clergy are nowhere held in higher respect than at Vanity Fair. And well do they deserve such honorable estimation; for the maxims of wisdom and virtue which fall from their lips come from as deep a spiritual source, and tend to as lofty a religious aim, as those of the sagest philosophers of old. In justification of this high praise I need only mention the names of the Rev. Mr. Shallow-deep, the Rev. Mr. Stumble-at-truth, that fine old clerical character the Rev. Mr. This-to-day, who expects shortly to resign his pulpit to the Rev. Mr. That-to-morrow; together with the Rev. Mr. Bewilderment, the Rev. Mr. Clog-the-spirit, and, last and greatest, the Rev. Dr. Wind-of-doctrine. The labors of these eminent divines are aided by those of innumerable lecturers, who diffuse such a various profundity, in all subjects of human or celestial science, that any man may acquire an omnigenous erudition without the trouble of even learning to read. Thus literature is etherealized by assuming for its medium the human voice; and knowledge, depositing all its heavier particles, except, doubtless, its gold, becomes exhaled into a sound, which forthwith steals into the ever-open ear of the community. These ingenious methods constitute a sort of machinery, by which thought and study are done to every person's hand without his putting himself to the slightest inconvenience in the matter. There is another species of machine for the wholesale manufacture of individual morality. This excellent result is effected by societies for all manner of virtuous purposes, with which a man has merely to connect himself, throwing, as it were, his quota of virtue into the common stock, and the president and directors will take care that the aggregate amount be well applied. All these, and other wonderful improvements in ethics, religion, and literature, being made plain to my comprehension by the ingenious Mr. Smooth-it-away, inspired me with a vast admiration of Vanity Fair.

It would fill a volume, in an age of pamphlets, were I to record all my observations in this great capital of human business and pleasure. There was an unlimited range of society—the powerful, the wise, the witty, and the famous in every walk of life; princes, presidents, poets, generals, artists, actors, and philanthropists,—all making their own market at the fair, and deeming no price too exorbitant for such commodities as hit their fancy. It was well worth one's while, even if he had no idea of buying or selling, to loiter through the bazaars and observe the various sorts of traffic that were going forward.

Some of the purchasers, I thought, made very foolish bargains. For instance, a young man having inherited a splendid fortune, laid out a considerable portion of it in the purchase of diseases, and finally spent all the rest for a heavy lot of repentance and a suit of rags. A very pretty girl bartered a heart as clear as crystal, and which seemed her most valuable possession, for another jewel of the same kind, but so worn and defaced as to be utterly worthless. In one shop there were a great many crowns of laurel and myrtle, which soldiers, authors, statesmen, and various other people pressed eagerly to buy; some purchased these paltry wreaths with their lives, others by a toilsome servitude of years, and many sacrificed whatever was most valuable, yet finally slunk away without the crown. There was a sort of stock or scrip, called Conscience, which seemed to be in great demand, and would purchase almost anything. Indeed, few rich commodities were to be obtained without paying a heavy sum in this particular stock, and a man's business was seldom very lucrative unless he knew precisely when and how to throw his hoard of conscience into the market. Yet as this stock was the only thing of permanent value, whoever parted with it was sure to find himself a loser in the long run. Several of the speculations were of a questionable character. Occasionally a member of Congress recruited his pocket by the sale of his constituents; and I was assured that public officers have often sold their country at very moderate prices. Thousands sold their happiness for a whim. Gilded chains were in great demand, and purchased with almost any sacrifice. In truth, those who desired, according to the old adage, to sell anything valuable for a song, might find customers all over the Fair; and there were innumerable messes of pottage, piping hot, for such as chose to buy them with their birthrights. A few articles, however, could not be found genuine at Vanity Fair. If a customer wished to renew his stock of youth the dealers offered him a set of false teeth and an auburn wig; if he demanded peace of mind, they recommended opium or a brandy bottle.

Tracts of land and golden mansions, situate in the Celestial City, were often exchanged, at very disadvantageous rates, for a few years' lease of small, dismal, inconvenient tenements in Vanity Fair. Prince Beelzebub himself took great interest in this sort of traffic, and sometimes condescended to meddle with smaller matters. I once had the pleasure to see him bargaining with a miser for his soul, which, after much ingenious skirmishing on both sides, his highness succeeded in obtaining at about the value of sixpence. The prince remarked with a smile, that he was a loser by the transaction.

Day after day, as I walked the streets of Vanity, my manners and deportment became more and more like those of the inhabitants. The place began to seem like home; the idea of pursuing my travels to the Celestial City was almost obliterated from my mind. I was reminded of it, however, by the sight of the same pair of simple pilgrims at whom we had laughed so heartily when Apollyon puffed smoke and steam into their faces at the commencement of our journey. There they stood amidst the densest bustle of Vanity; the dealers offering them their purple and fine linen and jewels, the men of wit and humor gibing at them, a pair of buxom ladies ogling them askance, while the benevolent Mr. Smooth-it-away whispered some of his wisdom at their elbows, and pointed to a newly-erected temple; but there were these worthy simpletons, making the scene look wild and monstrous, merely by their sturdy repudiation of all part in its business or pleasures.

One of them—his name was Stick-to-the-right—perceived in my face, I suppose, a species of sympathy and almost admiration, which, to my own great surprise, I could not help feeling for this pragmatic couple. It prompted him to address me.

"Sir," inquired he, with a sad, yet mild and kindly voice. "do you call yourself a pilgrim?"

"Yes," I replied, "my right to that appellation is indubitable. I am merely a sojourner here in Vanity Fair, being bound to the Celestial City by the new railroad."

"Alas, friend," rejoined Mr. Stick-to-the-truth, "I do assure you, and beseech you to receive the truth of my words, that that whole concern is a bubble. You may travel on it all your lifetime, were you to live thousands of years, and yet never get beyond the limits of Vanity Fair. Yea, though you should deem yourself entering the gates of the blessed city, it will be nothing but a miserable delusion."

"The Lord of the Celestial City," began the other pilgrim, whose name was Mr. Foot-it-to-heaven, "has refused, and will ever refuse, to grant an act of incorporation for this railroad; and unless that be obtained, no passenger can ever hope to enter his dominions. Wherefore every man who buys a ticket must lay his account with losing the purchase money, which is the value of his own soul."

"Poh, nonsense!" said Mr. Smooth-it-away, taking my arm and leading me off, "these fellows ought to be indicted for a libel. If the law stood as it once did in Vanity Fair we should see them grinning through the iron bars of the prison window."

This incident made a considerable impression on my mind, and contributed with other circumstances to indispose me to a permanent residence in the city of Vanity; although, of course, I was not simple enough to give up my original plan of gliding along easily and commodiously by railroad. Still, I grew anxious to be gone. There was one strange thing that troubled me. Amid the occupations or amusements of the Fair, nothing was more common than for a person—whether at feast, theatre, or church, or trafficking for wealth and honors, or whatever he might be doing, to vanish like a soap bubble, and be never more seen of his fellows; and so accustomed were the latter to such little accidents that they went on with their business as quietly as if nothing had happened. But it was otherwise with me.

Finally, after a pretty long residence at the Fair, I resumed my journey towards the Celestial City, still with Mr. Smooth-it-away at my side. At a short distance beyond the suburbs of Vanity we passed the ancient silver mine, of which Demas was the first discoverer, and which is now wrought to great advantage, supplying nearly all the coined currency of the world. A little further onward was the spot where Lot's wife had stood forever under the semblance of a pillar of salt. Curious travellers have long since carried it away piecemeal. Had all regrets been punished as rigorously as this poor dame's were, my yearning for the relinquished delights of Vanity Fair might have produced a similar change in my own corporeal substance, and left me a warning to future pilgrims.

The next remarkable object was a large edifice, constructed of moss-grown stone, but in a modern and airy style of architecture. The engine came to a pause in its vicinity, with the usual tremendous shriek.

"This was formerly the castle of the redoubted giant Despair," observed Mr. Smooth-it-away; "but since his death Mr. Flimsy-faith has repaired it, and keeps an excellent house of entertainment here. It is one of our stopping-places."

"It seems but slightly put together," remarked I, looking at the frail yet ponderous walls. "I do not envy Mr. Flimsy-faith his habitation. Some day it will thunder down upon the heads of the occupants."

"We shall escape at all events," said Mr. Smooth-it-away, "for Apollyon is putting on the steam again."

The road now plunged into a gorge of the Delectable Mountains, and traversed the field where in former ages the blind men wandered and stumbled among the tombs. One of these ancient tombstones had been thrust across the track by some malicious person, and gave the train of cars a terrible jolt. Far up the rugged side of a mountain I perceived a rusty iron door, half overgrown with bushes and creeping plants, but with smoke issuing from its crevices.

"Is that," inquired I, "the very door in the hill-side which the shepherds assured Christian was a by-way to hell?"

"That was a joke on the part of the shepherds," said Mr. Smooth-it-away, with a smile. "It is neither more nor less than the door of a cavern which they use as a smoke-house for the preparation of mutton hams."

My recollections of the journey are now, for a little space, dim and confused, inasmuch as a singular drowsiness here overcame me, owing to the fact that we were passing over the enchanted ground, the air of which encourages a disposition to sleep. I awoke, however, as soon as we crossed the borders of the pleasant land of Beulah. All the passengers were rubbing their eyes, comparing watches, and congratulating one another on the prospect of arriving so seasonably at the journey's end. The sweet breezes of this happy clime came refreshingly to our nostrils; we beheld the glimmering gush of silver fountains, overhung by trees of beautiful foliage and delicious fruit, which were propagated by grafts from the celestial gardens. Once, as we dashed onward like a hurricane, there was a flutter of wings and the bright appearance of an angel in the air, speeding forth on some heavenly mission. The engine now announced the close vicinity of the final station-house by one last and horrible scream, in which there seemed to be distinguishable every kind of wailing and woe, and bitter fierceness of wrath, all mixed up with the wild laughter of a devil or a madman. Throughout our journey, at every stopping-place, Apollyon had exercised his ingenuity in screwing the most abominable sounds out of the whistle of the steam-engine; but in this closing effort he outdid himself and created an infernal uproar, which, besides disturbing the peaceful inhabitants of Beulah, must have sent its discord even through the celestial gates.

While the horrid clamor was still ringing in our ears we heard an exulting strain, as if a thousand instruments of music, with height and depth and sweetness in their tones, at once tender and triumphant, were struck in unison, to greet the approach of some illustrious hero, who had fought the good fight and won a glorious victory, and was come to lay aside his battered arms forever. Looking to ascertain what might be the occasion of this glad harmony, I perceived, on alighting from the cars, that a multitude of shining ones had assembled on the other side of the river, to welcome two poor pilgrims, who were just emerging from its

depths. They were the same whom Apollyon and ourselves had persecuted with taunts, and gibes, and scalding steam, at the commencement
of our journey—the same whose unworldly aspect and impressive words
had stirred my conscience amid the wild revellers of Vanity Fair.

"How amazingly well those men have got on," cried I to Mr. Smooth-
it-away. "I wish we were secure of as good a reception."

"Never fear, never fear!" answered my friend. "Come, make haste;
the ferry boat will be off directly, and in three minutes you will be on the
other side of the river. No doubt you will find coaches to carry you up to
the city gates."

A steam ferry boat, the last improvement on this important route, lay
at the river side, puffing, snorting, and emitting all those other disagreeable utterances which betoken the departure to be immediate. I hurried
on board with the rest of the passengers, most of whom were in great perturbation: some bawling out for their baggage; some tearing their hair
and exclaiming that the boat would explode or sink; some already pale
with the heaving of the stream; some gazing affrighted at the ugly aspect
of the steersman; and some still dizzy with the slumberous influences of
the Enchanted Ground. Looking back to the shore, I was amazed to discern Mr. Smooth-it-away waving his hand in token of farewell.

"Don't you go over to the Celestial City?" exclaimed I.

"Oh, no!" answered he with a queer smile, and that same disagreeable
contortion of visage which I had remarked in the inhabitants of the Dark
Valley. "Oh, no! I have come thus far only for the sake of your pleasant
company. Good-by! We shall meet again."

And then did my excellent friend Mr. Smooth-it-away laugh outright,
in the midst of which cachinnation a smoke-wreath issued from his mouth
and nostrils, while a twinkle of lurid flame darted out of either eye, proving indubitably that his heart was all of a red blaze. The impudent fiend!
To deny the existence of Tophet, when he felt its fiery tortures raging
within his breast. I rushed to the side of the boat, intending to fling myself on shore; but the wheels, as they began their revolutions, threw a
dash of spray over me so cold—so deadly cold, with the chill that will
never leave those waters until Death be drowned in his own river—that
with a shiver and a heartquake I awoke. Thank Heaven it was a Dream!

# THE PROCESSION OF LIFE

LIFE figures itself to me as a festal or funereal procession. All of us have
our places, and are to move onward under the direction of the Chief Marshal. The grand difficulty results from the invariably mistaken principles
on which the deputy marshals seek to arrange this immense concourse of

people, so much more numerous than those that train their interminable length through streets and highways in times of political excitement. Their scheme is ancient, far beyond the memory of man or even the record of history, and has hitherto been very little modified by the innate sense of something wrong, and the dim perception of better methods, that have disquieted all the ages through which the procession has taken its march. Its members are classified by the merest external circumstances, and thus are more certain to be thrown out of their true positions than if no principle of arrangement were attempted. In one part of the procession we see men of landed estate or moneyed capital gravely keeping each other company, for the preposterous reason that they chance to have a similar standing in the tax-gatherer's book. Trades and professions march together with scarcely a more real bond of union. In this manner, it cannot be denied, people are disentangled from the mass and separated into various classes according to certain apparent relations; all have some artificial badge which the world, and themselves among the first, learn to consider as a genuine characteristic. Fixing our attention on such outside shows of similarity or difference, we lose sight of those realities by which nature, fortune, fate, or Providence has constituted for every man a brotherhood, wherein it is one great office of human wisdom to classify him. When the mind has once accustomed itself to a proper arrangement of the Procession of Life, or a true classification of society, even though merely speculative, there is thenceforth a satisfaction which pretty well suffices for itself without the aid of any actual reformation in the order of march.

For instance, assuming to myself the power of marshalling the aforesaid procession, I direct a trumpeter to send forth a blast loud enough to be heard from hence to China; and a herald, with world-pervading voice, to make proclamation for a certain class of mortals to take their places. What shall be their principle of union? After all, an external one, in comparison with many that might be found, yet far more real than those which the world has selected for a similar purpose. Let all who are afflicted with like physical diseases form themselves into ranks.

Our first attempt at classification is not very successful. It may gratify the pride of aristocracy to reflect that disease, more than any other circumstance of human life, pays due observance to the distinctions which rank and wealth, and poverty and lowliness, have established among mankind. Some maladies are rich and precious, and only to be acquired by the right of inheritance or purchased with gold. Of this kind is the gout, which serves as a bond of brotherhood to the purple-visaged gentry, who obey the herald's voice, and painfully hobble from all civilized regions of the globe to take their post in the grand procession. In mercy to their toes, let us hope that the march may not be long. The Dyspeptics, too, are people of good standing in the world. For them the earliest salmon is caught in our eastern rivers, and the shy woodcock stains the dry leaves with his blood in his remotest haunts, and the turtle comes from the far Pacific Islands to be gobbled up in soup. They can afford to flavor all their dishes with indolence, which, in spite of the general opinion, is a sauce more exquisitely piquant than appetite won by exercise. Apoplexy is another highly respectable disease. We will rank together all who have the symptom of dizziness in the brain, and as fast as any drop by the way supply their places with new members of the board of aldermen.

On the other hand, here come whole tribes of people whose physical lives are but a deteriorated variety of life, and themselves a meaner species of mankind; so sad an effect has been wrought by the tainted breath of cities, scanty and unwholesome food, destructive modes of labor, and the lack of those moral supports that might partially have counteracted such bad influences. Behold here a train of house painters, all afflicted with a peculiar sort of colic. Next in place we will marshal those workmen in cutlery, who have breathed a fatal disorder into their lungs with the impalpable dust of steel. Tailors and shoemakers, being sedentary men, will chiefly congregate into one part of the procession and march under similar banners of disease; but among them we may observe here and there a sickly student, who has left his health between the leaves of classic volumes; and clerks, likewise, who have caught their deaths on high official stools; and men of genius too, who have written sheet after sheet with pens dipped in their heart's blood. These are a wretched, quaking, short-breathed set. But what is this cloud of pale-cheeked, slender girls, who disturb the ear with the multiplicity of their short, dry coughs? They are seamstresses, who have plied the daily and nightly needle in the service of master tailors and close-fisted contractors, until now it is almost time for each to hem the borders of her own shroud. Consumption points their place in the procession. With their sad sisterhood are intermingled many youthful maidens who have sickened in aristocratic mansions, and for whose aid science has unavailingly searched its volumes, and whom breathless love has watched. In our ranks the rich maiden and the poor seamstress may walk arm in arm. We might find innumerable other instances, where the bond of mutual disease—not to speak of nation-sweeping pestilence—embraces high and low, and makes the king a brother of the clown. But it is not hard to own that disease is the natural aristocrat. Let him keep his state, and have his established orders of rank, and wear his royal mantle of the color of a fever flush; and let the noble and wealthy boast their own physical infirmities, and display their symptoms as the badges of high station. All things considered, these are as proper subjects of human pride as any relations of human rank that men can fix upon.

Sound again, thou deep-breathed trumpeter! and herald, with thy voice of might, shout forth another summons that shall reach the old baronial castles of Europe, and the rudest cabin of our western wilderness! What class is next to take its place in the procession of mortal life? Let it be those whom the gifts of intellect have united in a noble brotherhood.

Ay, this is a reality, before which the conventional distinctions of society melt away like a vapor when we would grasp it with the hand. Were

Byron now alive, and Burns, the first would come from his ancestral abbey, flinging aside, although unwillingly, the inherited honors of a thousand years, to take the arm of the mighty peasant who grew immortal while he stooped behind his plough. These are gone; but the hall, the farmer's fireside, the hut, perhaps the palace, the counting-room, the workshop, the village, the city, life's high places and low ones, may all produce their poets, whom a common temperament pervades like an electric sympathy. Peer or ploughman, we will muster them pair by pair and shoulder to shoulder. Even society, in its most artificial state, consents to this arrangement. These factory girls from Lowell shall mate themselves with the pride of drawing-rooms and literary circles, the bluebells in fashion's nosegay, the Sapphos, and Montagues, and Nortons of the age. Other modes of intellect bring together as strange companies. Silk-gowned professor of languages, give your arm to this sturdy blacksmith, and deem yourself honored by the conjunction, though you behold him grimy from the anvil. All varieties of human speech are like his mother tongue to this rare man. Indiscriminately let those take their places, of whatever rank they come, who possess the kingly gifts to lead armies or to sway a people—Nature's generals, her lawgivers, her kings, and with them also the deep philosophers who think the thought in one generation that is to revolutionize society in the next. With the hereditary legislator in whom eloquence is a far-descended attainment—a rich echo repeated by powerful voices from Cicero downward—we will match some wondrous backwoodsman, who has caught a wild power of language from the breeze among his native forest boughs. But we may safely leave these brethren and sisterhood to settle their own congenialities. Our ordinary distinctions become so trifling, so impalpable, so ridiculously visionary, in comparison with a classification founded on truth, that all talk about the matter is immediately a common place.

Yet the longer I reflect the less am I satisfied with the idea of forming a separate class of mankind on the basis of high intellectual power. At best it is but a higher development of innate gifts common to all. Perhaps, moreover, he whose genius appears deepest and truest excels his fellows in nothing save the knack of expression; he throws out occasionally a lucky hint at truths of which every human soul is profoundly, though unutterably, conscious. Therefore, though we suffer the brotherhood of intellect to march onward together, it may be doubted whether their peculiar relation will not begin to vanish as soon as the procession shall have passed beyond the circle of this present world. But we do not classify for eternity.

And next, let the trumpet pour forth a funereal wail, and the herald's voice give breath in one vast cry to all the groans and grievous utterances that are audible throughout the earth. We appeal now to the sacred bond of sorrow, and summon the great multitude who labor under similar afflictions to take their places in the march.

How many a heart that would have been insensible to any other call has responded to the doleful accents of that voice! It has gone far and wide, and high and low, and left scarcely a mortal roof unvisited. Indeed, the principle is only too universal for our purpose, and, unless we limit it, will quite break up our classification of mankind, and convert the whole procession into a funeral train. We will therefore be at some pains to discriminate. Here comes a lonely rich man: he has built a noble fabric for his dwelling-house, with a front of stately architecture and marble floors and doors of precious woods; the whole structure is as beautiful as a dream and as substantial as the native rock. But the visionary shapes of a long posterity, for whose home this mansion was intended, have faded into nothingness since the death of the founder's only son. The rich man gives a glance at his sable garb in one of the splendid mirrors of his drawing-room, and descending a flight of lofty steps instinctively offers his arm to yonder poverty stricken widow in the rusty black bonnet, and with a check apron over her patched gown. The sailor boy, who was her sole earthly stay, was washed overboard in a late tempest. This couple from the palace and the almshouse are but the types of thousands more who represent the dark tragedy of life and seldom quarrel for the upper parts. Grief is such a leveller, with its own dignity and its own humility, that the noble and the peasant, the beggar and the monarch, will waive their pretensions to external rank without the officiousness of interference on our part. If pride—the influence of the world's false distinctions—remain in the heart, then sorrow lacks the earnestness which makes it holy and reverend. It loses its reality and becomes a miserable shadow. On this ground we have an opportunity to assign over multitudes who would willingly claim places here to other parts of the procession. If the mourner have anything dearer than his grief he must seek his true position elsewhere. There are so many unsubstantial sorrows which the necessity of our mortal state begets on idleness, that an observer, casting aside sentiment, is sometimes led to question whether there be any real woe, except absolute physical suffering and the loss of closest friends. A crowd who exhibit what they deem to be broken hearts—and among them many lovelorn maids and bachelors, and men of disappointed ambition in arts or politics, and the poor who were once rich, or who have sought to be rich in vain—the great majority of these may ask admittance into some other fraternity. There is no room here. Perhaps we may institute a separate class where such unfortunates will naturally fall into the procession. Meanwhile let them stand aside and patiently await their time.

If our trumpeter can borrow a note from the doomsday trumpet blast, let him sound it now. The dread alarum should make the earth quake to its centre, for the herald is about to address mankind with a summons to which even the purest mortal may be sensible of some faint responding echo in his breast. In many bosoms it will awaken a still small voice more terrible than its own reverberating uproar.

The hideous appeal has swept around the globe. Come, all ye guilty ones, and rank yourselves in accordance with the brotherhood of crime. This, indeed, is an awful summons. I almost tremble to look at the strange partnerships that begin to be formed, reluctantly, but by the invincible necessity of like to like in this part of the procession. A forger from the state prison seizes the arm of a distinguished financier. How indignantly does the latter plead his fair reputation upon 'Change, and insist that his operations, by their magnificence of scope, were removed into quite another sphere of morality than those of his pitiful companion! But let him cut the connection if he can. Here comes a murderer with his clanking chains, and pairs himself—horrible to tell—with as pure and upright a man, in all observable respects, as ever partook of the consecrated bread and wine. He is one of those, perchance the most hopeless of all sinners, who practise such an exemplary system of outward duties, that even a deadly crime may be hidden from their own sight and remembrance, under this unreal frostwork. Yet he now finds his place. Why do that pair of flaunting girls, with the pert, affected laugh and the sly leer at the by-standers, intrude themselves into the same rank with yonder decorous matron, and that somewhat prudish maiden? Surely these poor creatures, born to vice as their sole and natural inheritance, can be no fit associates for women who have been guarded round about by all the proprieties of domestic life, and who could not err unless they first created the opportunity. Oh no; it must be merely the impertinence of those unblushing hussies; and we can only wonder how such respectable ladies should have responded to a summons that was not meant for them.

We shall make short work of this miserable class, each member of which is entitled to grasp any other member's hand, by that vile degradation wherein guilty error has buried all alike. The foul fiend to whom it properly belongs must relieve us of our loathsome task. Let the bond servants of sin pass on. But neither man nor woman, in whom good predominates, will smile or sneer, nor bid the Rogues' March be played, in derision of their array. Feeling within their breasts a shuddering sympathy, which at least gives token of the sin that might have been, they will thank God for any place in the grand procession of human existence, save among those most wretched ones. Many, however, will be astonished at the fatal impulse that drags them thitherward. Nothing is more remarkable than the various deceptions by which guilt conceals itself from the perpetrator's conscience, and oftenest, perhaps, by the splendor of its garments. Statesmen, rulers, generals, and all men who act over an extensive sphere, are most liable to be deluded in this way; they commit wrong, devastation, and murder, on so grand a scale, that it impresses them as speculative rather than actual; but in our procession we find them linked in detestable conjunction with the meanest criminals whose deeds have the vulgarity of petty details. Here the effect of circumstance and accident is done away, and a man finds his rank according to the spirit of his crime, in whatever shape it may have been developed.

We have called the Evil; now let us call the Good. The trumpet's brazen throat should pour heavenly music over the earth, and the herald's voice go forth with the sweetness of an angel's accents, as if to summon each upright man to his reward. But how is this? Does none answer to the call? Not one: for the just, the pure, the true, and all who might most worthily obey it, shrink sadly back, as most conscious of error and imperfection. Then let the summons be to those whose pervading principle is Love. This classification will embrace all the truly good, and none in whose souls there exists not something that may expand itself into a heaven, both of well-doing and felicity.

The first that presents himself is a man of wealth, who has bequeathed the bulk of his property to a hospital; his ghost, methinks, would have a better right here than his living body. But here they come, the genuine benefactors of their race. Some have wandered about the earth with pictures of bliss in their imagination, and with hearts that shrank sensitively from the idea of pain and woe, yet have studied all varieties of misery that human nature can endure. The prison, the insane asylum, the squalid chamber of the almshouse, the manufactory where the demon of machinery annihilates the human soul, and the cotton field where God's image becomes a beast of burden; to these and every other scene where man wrongs or neglects his brother, the apostles of humanity have penetrated. This missionary, black with India's burning sunshine, shall give his arm to a pale-faced brother who has made himself familiar with the infected alleys and loathsome haunts of vice in one of our own cities. The generous founder of a college shall be the partner of a maiden lady of narrow substance, one of whose good deeds it has been to gather a little school of orphan children. If the mighty merchant whose benefactions are reckoned by thousands of dollars deem himself worthy, let him join the procession with her whose love has proved itself by watchings at the sick-bed, and all those lowly offices which bring her into actual contact with disease and wretchedness. And with those whose impulses have guided them to benevolent actions, we will rank others to whom Providence has assigned a different tendency and different powers. Men who have spent their lives in generous and holy contemplation for the human race; those who, by a certain heavenliness of spirit, have purified the atmosphere around them, and thus supplied a medium in which good and high things may be projected and performed—give to these a lofty place among the benefactors of mankind, although no deed, such as the world calls deeds, may be recorded of them. There are some individuals of whom we cannot conceive it proper that they should apply their hands to any earthly instrument, or work out any definite act; and others, perhaps not less high, to whom it is an essential attribute to labor in body as well as spirit for the welfare of their brethren. Thus, if we find a spiritual sage whose unseen, inestimable influence has exalted the moral standard of mankind, we will choose for his companion some poor laborer who has wrought for love in the potato field of a neighbor poorer than himself.

We have summoned this various multitude—and, to the credit of our nature, it is a large one—on the principle of Love. It is singular, nevertheless, to remark the shyness that exists among many members of the present class, all of whom we might expect to recognize one another by the freemasonry of mutual goodness, and to embrace like brethren, giving God thanks for such various specimens of human excellence. But it is far otherwise. Each sect surrounds its own righteousness with a hedge of thorns. It is difficult for the good Christian to acknowledge the good Pagan; almost impossible for the good Orthodox to grasp the hand of the good Unitarian, leaving to their Creator to settle the matters in dispute, and giving their mutual efforts strongly and trustingly to whatever right thing is too evident to be mistaken. Then again, though the heart be large, yet the mind is often of such moderate dimensions as to be exclusively filled up with one idea. When a good man has long devoted himself to a particular kind of beneficence—to one species of reform—he is apt to become narrowed into the limits of the path wherein he treads, and to fancy that there is no other good to be done on earth but that selfsame good to which he has put his hand, and in the very mode that best suits his own conceptions. All else is worthless. His scheme must be wrought out by the united strength of the whole world's stock of love, or the world is no longer worthy of a position in the universe. Moreover, powerful Truth, being the rich grape juice expressed from the vineyard of the ages, has an intoxicating quality, when imbibed by any save a powerful intellect, and often, as it were, impels the quaffer to quarrel in his cups. For such reasons, strange to say, it is harder to contrive a friendly arrangement of these brethren of love and righteousness, in the procession of life, than to unite even the wicked, who, indeed, are chained together by their crimes. The fact is too preposterous for tears, too lugubrious for laughter.

But, let good men push and elbow one another as they may during their earthly march, all will be peace among them when the honorable array of their procession shall tread on heavenly ground. There they will doubtless find that they have been working each for the other's cause, and that every well-delivered stroke, which, with an honest purpose any mortal struck, even for a narrow object, was indeed stricken for the universal cause of good. Their own view may be bounded by country, creed, profession, the diversities of individual character—but above them all is the breadth of Providence. How many who have deemed themselves antagonists will smile hereafter, when they look back upon the world's wide harvest field, and perceive that, in unconscious brotherhood, they were helping to bind the selfsame sheaf!

But, come! The sun is hastening westward, while the march of human life, that never paused before, is delayed by our attempt to rearrange its order. It is desirable to find some comprehensive principle, that shall render our task easier by bringing thousands into the ranks where hitherto we have brought one. Therefore let the trumpet, if possible, split its brazen throat with a louder note than ever, and the herald summon all mortals, who, from whatever cause, have lost, or never found, their proper places in the wold.

Obedient to this call, a great multitude come together, most of them with a listless gait, betokening weariness of soul, yet with a gleam of satisfaction in their faces, at a prospect of at length reaching those positions which, hitherto, they have vainly sought. But here will be another disappointment; for we can attempt no more than merely to associate in one fraternity all who are afflicted with the same vague trouble. Some great mistake in life is the chief condition of admittance into this class. Here are members of the learned professions, whom Providence endowed with special gifts for the plough, the forge, and the wheelbarrow, or for the routine of unintellectual business. We will assign to them, as partners in the march, those lowly laborers and handicraftsmen, who have pined, as with a dying thirst, after the unattainable fountains of knowledge. The latter have lost less than their companions; yet more, because they deem it infinite. Perchance the two species of unfortunates may comfort one another. Here are Quakers with the instinct of battle in them; and men of war who should have worn the broad brim. Authors shall be ranked here whom some freak of Nature, making game of her poor children, had imbued with the confidence of genius and strong desire of fame, but has favored with no corresponding power; and others, whose lofty gifts were unaccompanied with the faculty of expression, or any of that earthly machinery by which ethereal endowments must be manifested to mankind. All these, therefore, are melancholy laughing-stocks. Next, here are honest and well intentioned persons, who by a want of tact—by inaccurate perceptions—by a distorting imagination—have been kept continually at cross purposes with the world and bewildered upon the path of life. Let us see if they can confine themselves within the line of our procession. In this class, likewise, we must assign places to those who have encountered that worst of ill success, a higher fortune than their abilities could vindicate; writers, actors, painters, the pets of a day, but whose laurels wither unrenewed amid their hoary hair; politicians, whom some malicious contingency of affairs has thrust into conspicuous station, where, while the world stands gazing at them, the dreary consciousness of imbecility makes them curse their birth hour. To such men, we give for a companion him whose rare talents, which perhaps require a Revolution for their exercise, are buried in the tomb of sluggish circumstances.

Not far from these, we must find room for one whose success has been of the wrong kind; the man who should have lingered in the cloisters of a university, digging new treasures out of the Herculaneum of antique lore, diffusing depth and accuracy of literature throughout his country, and thus making for himself a great and quiet fame. But the outward tendencies around him have proved too powerful for his inward nature, and have drawn him into the arena of political tumult, there to contend at disadvantage, whether front to front, or side by side, with the brawny giants of actual life. He becomes, it may be, a name for brawling parties to bandy to and fro, a legislator of the Union; a governor of his native state; an ambassador to the courts of kings or queens; and the world may deem him a man of happy stars. But not so the wise; and not so himself, when he looks through his experience, and sighs to miss that fitness, the one invaluable touch which makes all things true and real. So much achieved, yet how abortive is his life! Whom shall we choose for his companion? Some weak framed blacksmith, perhaps, whose delicacy of muscle might have suited a tailor's shopboard better than the anvil.

Shall we bid the trumpet sound again? It is hardly worth the while. There remain a few idle men of fortune, tavern and grog-shop loungers, lazzaroni, old bachelors, decaying maidens, and people of crooked intellect or temper, all of whom may find their like, or some tolerable approach to it, in the plentiful diversity of our latter class. There too, as his ultimate destiny, must we rank the dreamer, who, all his life long, has cherished the idea that he was peculiarly apt for something, but never could determine what it was; and there the most unfortunate of men, whose purpose it has been to enjoy life's pleasures, but to avoid a manful struggle with its toil and sorrow. The remainder, if any, may connect themselves with whatever rank of the procession they shall find best adapted to their tastes and consciences. The worst possible fate would be to remain behind, shivering in the solitude of time, while all the world is on the move towards eternity. Our attempt to classify society is now complete. The result may be anything but perfect; yet better—to give it the very lowest praise—than the antique rule of the herald's office, or the modern one of the tax-gatherer, whereby the accidents and superficial attributes, with which the real nature of individuals has least to do, are acted upon as the deepest characteristics of mankind. Our task is done! Now let the grand procession move!

Yet pause a while! We had forgotten the Chief Marshal.

Hark! That world-wide swell of solemn music, with the clang of a mighty bell breaking forth through its regulated uproar, announces his approach. He comes; a severe, sedate, immovable, dark rider, waving his truncheon of universal sway, as he passes along the lengthened line, on the pale horse of the Revelation. It is Death! Who else could assume the guidance of a procession that comprehends all humanity? And if some, among these many millions, should deem themselves classed amiss, yet let them take to their hearts the comfortable truth that Death levels us all into one great brotherhood, and that another state of being will surely rectify the wrong of this. Then breathe thy wail upon the earth's wailing wind, thou band of melancholy music, made up of every sigh that the human heart, unsatisfied, has uttered! There is yet triumph in thy tones. And now we move! Beggars in their rags, and Kings trailing the regal purple in the dust; the Warrior's gleaming helmet; the Priest in his sable robe; the hoary Grandsire, who has run life's circle and come back to childhood; the ruddy School-boy with his golden curls, frisking along the march; the Artisan's stuff jacket; the Noble's star-decorated coat;—the whole presenting a motley spectacle, yet with a dusky grandeur brooding over it. Onward, onward, into that dimness where the lights of Time, which have blazed along the procession, are flickering in their sockets! And whither! We know not; and Death, hitherto our leader, deserts us by the wayside, as the tramp of our innumerable footsteps echoes beyond his sphere. He knows not, more than we, our destined goal. But God, who made us, knows, and will not leave us on our toilsome and doubtful march, either to wander in infinite uncertainty, or perish by the way!

## FEATHERTOP: A MORALIZED LEGEND

"DICKON," cried Mother Rigby, "a coal for my pipe!"

The pipe was in the old dame's mouth when she said these words. She had thrust it there after filling it with tobacco, but without stooping to light it at the hearth, where indeed there was no appearance of a fire having been kindled that morning. Forthwith, however, as soon as the order was given, there was an intense red glow out of the bowl of the pipe, and a whiff of smoke came from Mother Rigby's lips. Whence the coal came, and how brought thither by an invisible hand, I have never been able to discover.

"Good!" quoth Mother Rigby, with a nod of her head. "Thank ye, Dickon! And now for making this scarecrow. Be within call, Dickon, in case I need you again."

The good woman had risen thus early (for as yet it was scarcely sunrise) in order to set about making a scarecrow, which she intended to put in the middle of her corn-patch. It was now the latter week of May, and the crows and blackbirds had already discovered the little, green, rolled-up leaf of the Indian corn just peeping out of the soil. She was determined, therefore, to contrive as lifelike a scarecrow as ever was seen, and to finish it immediately, from top to toe, so that it should begin its sentinel's duty that very morning. Now Mother Rigby (as everybody must have heard) was one of the most cunning and potent witches in New England, and might, with very little trouble, have made a scarecrow ugly enough to frighten the minister himself. But on this occasion, as she had awakened in an uncommonly pleasant humor, and was further dulcified by her pipe tobacco, she resolved to produce something fine, beautiful, and splendid, rather than hideous and horrible.

"I don't want to set up a hobgoblin in my own corn-patch, and almost at my own doorstep," said Mother Rigby to herself, puffing out a whiff of smoke; "I could do it if I pleased, but I'm tired of doing marvellous things, and so I'll keep within the bounds of every-day business just for variety's sake. Besides, there is no use in scaring the little children for a mile roundabout, though 't is true I'm a witch."

It was settled, therefore, in her own mind, that the scarecrow should represent a fine gentleman of the period, so far as the materials at hand would allow. Perhaps it may be as well to enumerate the chief of the articles that went to the composition of this figure.

The most important item of all, probably, although it made so little show, was a certain broomstick, on which Mother Rigby had taken many an airy gallop at midnight, and which now served the scarecrow by way of a spinal column, or, as the unlearned phrase it, a backbone. One of its arms was a disabled flail which used to be wielded by Goodman Rigby, before his spouse worried him out of this troublesome world; the other, if

I mistake not, was composed of the pudding stick and a broken rung of a chair, tied loosely together at the elbow. As for its legs, the right was a hoe handle, and the left an undistinguished and miscellaneous stick from the woodpile. Its lungs, stomach, and other affairs of that kind were nothing better than a meal bag stuffed with straw. Thus we have made out the skeleton and entire corporosity of the scarecrow, with the exception of its head; and this was admirably supplied by a somewhat withered and shrivelled pumpkin, in which Mother Rigby cut two holes for the eyes, and a slit for the mouth, leaving a bluish-colored knob in the middle to pass for a nose. It was really quite a respectable face.

"I've seen worse ones on human shoulders, at any rate," said Mother Rigby. "And many a fine gentleman has a pumpkin head, as well as my scarecrow."

But the clothes, in this case, were to be the making of the man. So the good old woman took down from a peg an ancient plum-colored coat of London make, and with relics of embroidery on its seams, cuffs, pocket-flaps, and button-holes, but lamentably worn and faded, patched at the elbows, tattered at the skirts, and threadbare all over. On the left breast was a round hole, whence either a star of nobility had been rent away, or else the hot heart of some former wearer had scorched it through and through. The neighbors said that this rich garment belonged to the Black Man's wardrobe, and that he kept it at Mother Rigby's cottage for the convenience of slipping it on whenever he wished to make a grand appearance at the governor's table. To match the coat there was a velvet waistcoat of very ample size, and formerly embroidered with foliage that had been as brightly golden as the maple leaves in October, but which had now quite vanished out of the substance of the velvet. Next came a pair of scarlet breeches, once worn by the French governor of Louisbourg, and the knees of which had touched the lower step of the throne of Louis le Grand. The Frenchman had given these smallclothes to an Indian pow-wow, who parted with them to the old witch for a gill of strong waters, at one of their dances in the forest. Furthermore, Mother Rigby produced a pair of silk stockings and put them on the figure's legs, where they showed as unsubstantial as a dream, with the wooden reality of the two sticks making itself miserably apparent through the holes. Lastly, she put her dead husband's wig on the bare scalp of the pumpkin, and surmounted the whole with a dusty three-cornered hat, in which was stuck the longest tail feather of a rooster.

Then the old dame stood the figure up in a corner of her cottage and chuckled to behold its yellow semblance of a visage, with its nobby little nose thrust into the air. It had a strangely self-satisfied aspect, and seemed to say, "Come look at me!"

"And you are well worth looking at, that's a fact!" quoth Mother Rigby, in admiration at her own handiwork. "I've made many a puppet since I've been a witch, but methinks this is the finest of them all. 'Tis almost too good for a scarecrow. And, by the by, I'll just fill a fresh pipe of tobacco and then take him out to the corn-patch."

While filling her pipe the old woman continued to gaze with almost motherly affection at the figure in the corner. To say the truth, whether it were chance, or skill, or downright witchcraft, there was something wonderfully human in this ridiculous shape, bedizened with its tattered finery; and as for the countenance, it appeared to shrivel its yellow surface into a grin—a funny kind of expression betwixt scorn and merriment, as if it understood itself to be a jest at mankind. The more Mother Rigby looked the better she was pleased.

"Dickon," cried she sharply, "another coal for my pipe!"

Hardly had she spoken, than, just as before, there was a red-glowing coal on the top of the tobacco. She drew in a long whiff and puffed it forth again into the bar of morning sunshine which struggled through the one dusty pane of her cottage window. Mother Rigby always liked to flavor her pipe with a coal of fire from the particular chimney corner whence this had been brought. But where that chimney corner might be, or who brought the coal from it,—further than that the invisible messenger seemed to respond to the name of Dickon,—I cannot tell.

"That puppet yonder," thought Mother Rigby, still with her eyes fixed on the scarecrow, "is too good a piece of work to stand all summer in a corn-patch, frightening away the crows and blackbirds. He's capable of better things. Why, I've danced with a worse one, when partners happened to be scarce, at our witch meetings in the forest! What if I should let him take his chance among the other men of straw and empty fellows who go bustling about the world?"

The old witch took three or four more whiffs of her pipe and smiled.

"He'll meet plenty of his brethren at every street corner!" continued she. "Well; I didn't mean to dabble in witchcraft to-day, further than the lighting of my pipe, but a witch I am, and a witch I'm likely to be, and there's no use trying to shirk it. I'll make a man of my scarecrow, were it only for the joke's sake!"

While muttering these words, Mother Rigby took the pipe from her own mouth and thrust it into the crevice which represented the same feature in the pumpkin visage of the scarecrow.

"Puff, darling, puff!" said she. "Puff away, my fine fellow! your life depends on it!"

This was a strange exhortation, undoubtedly, to be addressed to a mere thing of sticks, straw, and old clothes, with nothing better than a shrivelled pumpkin for a head,—as we know to have been the scarecrow's case. Nevertheless, as we must carefully hold in remembrance, Mother Rigby was a witch of singular power and dexterity; and, keeping this fact duly before our minds, we shall see nothing beyond credibility in the remarkable incidents of our story. Indeed, the great difficulty will be at once got over, if we can only bring ourselves to believe that, as soon as the old dame bade him puff, there came a whiff of smoke from the scarecrow's mouth. It was the very feeblest of whiffs, to be sure; but it was followed by another and another, each more decided than the preceding one.

"Puff away, my pet! puff away, my pretty one!" Mother Rigby kept repeating, with her pleasantest smile. "It is the breath of life to ye; and that you may take my word for."

Beyond all question the pipe was bewitched. There must have been a spell either in the tobacco or in the fiercely-glowing coal that so mysteriously burned on top of it, or in the pungently-aromatic smoke which exhaled from the kindled weed. The figure, after a few doubtful attempts, at length blew forth a volley of smoke extending all the way from the obscure corner into the bar of sunshine. There it eddied and melted away among the motes of dust. It seemed a convulsive effort; for the two or three next whiffs were fainter, although the coal still glowed and threw a gleam over the scarecrow's visage. The old witch clapped her skinny hands together, and smiled encouragingly upon her handiwork. She saw that the charm worked well. The shrivelled, yellow face, which heretofore had been no face at all, had already a thin, fantastic haze, as it were of human likeness, shifting to and fro across it; sometimes vanishing entirely, but growing more perceptible than ever with the next whiff from the pipe. The whole figure, in like manner, assumed a show of life, such as we impart to ill-defined shapes among the clouds, and half deceive ourselves with the pastime of our own fancy.

If we must needs pry closely into the matter, it may be doubted whether there was any real change, after all, in the sordid, wornout, worthless, and ill-jointed substance of the scarecrow; but merely a spectral illusion, and a cunning effect of light and shade so colored and contrived as to delude the eyes of most men. The miracles of witchcraft seem always to have had a very shallow subtlety; and, at least, if the above explanation do not hit the truth of the process, I can suggest no better.

"Well puffed, my pretty lad!" still cried old Mother Rigby. "Come, another good stout whiff, and let it be with might and main. Puff for thy life, I tell thee! Puff out of the very bottom of thy heart, if any heart thou hast, or any bottom to it! Well done, again! Thou didst suck in that mouthful as if for the pure love of it."

And then the witch beckoned to the scarecrow, throwing so much magnetic potency into her gesture that it seemed as if it must inevitably be obeyed, like the mystic call of the loadstone when it summons the iron.

"Why lurkest thou in the corner, lazy one?" said she. "Step forth! Thou hast the world before thee!"

Upon my word, if the legend were not one which I heard on my grandmother's knee, and which had established its place among things credible before my childish judgment could analyze its probability, I question whether I should have the face to tell it now.

In obedience to Mother Rigby's word, and extending its arm as if to reach her outstretched hand, the figure made a step forward—a kind of hitch and jerk, however, rather than a step—then tottered and almost lost its balance. What could the witch expect? It was nothing, after all, but a scarecrow stuck upon two sticks. But the strong-willed old beldam scowled, and beckoned, and flung the energy of her purpose so forcibly at this poor combination of rotten wood, and musty straw, and ragged garments, that it was compelled to show itself a man, in spite of the reality of things. So it stepped into the bar of sunshine. There it stood— poor devil of a contrivance that it was!—with only the thinnest vesture of human similitude about it, through which was evident the stiff, rickety, incongruous, faded, tattered, good-for-nothing patchwork of its substance, ready to sink in a heap upon the floor, as conscious of its own unworthiness to be erect. Shall I confess the truth? At its present point of vivification, the scarecrow reminds me of some of the lukewarm and abortive characters, composed of heterogeneous materials, used for the thousandth time, and never worth using, with which romance writers (and myself, no doubt, among the rest) have so overpeopled the world of fiction.

But the fierce old hag began to get angry and show a glimpse of her diabolic nature (like a snake's head, peeping with a hiss out of her bosom), at this pusillanimous behavior of the thing which she had taken the trouble to put together.

"Puff away, wretch!" cried she, wrathfully. "Puff, puff, puff, thou thing of straw and emptiness! thou rag or two! thou meal bag! thou pumpkin head! thou nothing! Where shall I find a name vile enough to call thee by? Puff, I say, and suck in thy fantastic life with the smoke! else I snatch the pipe from thy mouth and hurl thee where that red coal came from."

Thus threatened, the unhappy scarecrow had nothing for it but to puff away for dear life. As need was, therefore, it applied itself lustily to the pipe, and sent forth such abundant volleys of tobacco smoke that the small cottage kitchen became all vaporous. The one sunbeam struggled mistily through, and could but imperfectly define the image of the cracked and dusty window pane on the opposite wall. Mother Rigby, meanwhile, with one brown arm akimbo and the other stretched towards the figure, loomed grimly amid the obscurity with such port and expression as when she was wont to heave a ponderous nightmare on her victims and stand at the bedside to enjoy their agony. In fear and trembling did this poor scarecrow puff. But its efforts, it must be acknowledged, served an excellent purpose; for, with each successive whiff, the figure lost more and more of its dizzy and perplexing tenuity and seemed to take denser substance. Its very garments, moreover, partook of the magical change, and shone with the gloss of novelty and glistened with the skilfully embroidered gold that had long ago been rent away. And, half revealed among the smoke, a yellow visage bent its lustreless eyes on Mother Rigby.

At last the old witch clinched her fist and shook it at the figure. Not that she was positively angry, but merely acting on the principle—perhaps untrue, or not the only truth, though as high a one as Mother Rigby could be expected to attain—that feeble and torpid natures, being incapable of better inspiration, must be stirred up by fear. But here was the crisis. Should she fail in what she now sought to effect, it was her ruthless purpose to scatter the miserable simulacre into its original elements.

"Thou hast a man's aspect," said she, sternly. "Have also the echo and mockery of a voice! I bid thee speak!"

The scarecrow gasped, struggled, and at length emitted a murmur, which was so incorporated with its smoky breath that you could scarcely tell whether it were indeed a voice or only a whiff of tobacco. Some narrators of this legend hold the opinion that Mother Rigby's conjurations and the fierceness of her will had compelled a familiar spirit into the figure, and that the voice was his.

"Mother," mumbled the poor stifled voice, "be not so awful with me! I would fain speak; but being without wits, what can I say?"

"Thou canst speak, darling, canst thou?" cried Mother Rigby, relaxing her grim countenance into a smile. "And what shalt thou say, quotha! Say, indeed! Art thou of the brotherhood of the empty skull, and demandest of me what thou shalt say? Thou shalt say a thousand things, and saying them a thousand times over, thou shalt still have said nothing! Be not afraid, I tell thee! When thou comest into the world (whither I purpose sending thee forthwith) thou shalt not lack the wherewithal to talk. Talk! Why, thou shall babble like a mill-stream, if thou wilt. Thou hast brains enough for that, I trow!"

"At your service, mother," responded the figure.

"And that was well said, my pretty one," answered Mother Rigby. "Then thou speakest like thyself, and meant nothing. Thou shalt have a hundred such set phrases, and five hundred to the boot of them. And now, darling, I have taken so much pains with thee and thou art so beautiful, that, by my troth, I love thee better than any witch's puppet in the world; and I've made them of all sorts—clay, wax, straw, sticks, night fog, morning mist, sea foam, and chimney smoke. But thou art the very best. So give heed to what I say."

"Yes, kind mother," said the figure, "with all my heart!"

"With all thy heart!" cried the old witch, setting her hands to her sides and laughing loudly. "Thou hast such a pretty way of speaking. With all thy heart! And thou didst put thy hand to the left side of thy waistcoat as if thou really hadst one!"

So now, in high good humor with this fantastic contrivance of hers, Mother Rigby told the scarecrow that it must go and play its part in the great world, where not one man in a hundred, she affirmed, was gifted with more real substance than itself. And, that he might hold up his head with the best of them, she endowed him, on the spot, with an unreckonable amount of wealth. It consisted partly of a gold mine in Eldorado, and of ten thousand shares in a broken bubble, and of half a million acres of vineyard at the North Pole, and of a castle in the air, and a chateau in Spain, together with all the rents and income therefrom accruing. She further made over to him the cargo of a certain ship, laden with salt of Cadiz, which she herself, by her necromantic arts, had caused to founder, ten years before, in the deepest part of mid-ocean. If the salt were not dissolved, and could be brought to market, it would fetch a pretty penny among the fishermen. That he might not lack ready money, she gave him a copper farthing of Birmingham manufacture, being all the coin she had about her, and likewise a great deal of brass, which she applied to his forehead, thus making it yellower than ever.

"With that brass alone," quoth Mother Rigby, "thou canst pay thy way all over the earth. Kiss me, pretty darling! I have done my best for thee."

Furthermore, that the adventurer might lack no possible advantage towards a fair start in life, this excellent old dame gave him a token by which he was to introduce himself to a certain magistrate, member of the council, merchant, and elder of the church (the four capacities constituting but one man), who stood at the head of society in the neighboring metropolis. The token was neither more nor less than a single word, which Mother Rigby whispered to the scarecrow, and which the scarecrow was to whisper to the merchant.

"Gouty as the old fellow is, he'll run thy errands for thee, when once thou hast given him that word in his ear," said the old witch. "Mother Rigby knows the worshipful Justice Gookin, and the worshipful Justice knows Mother Rigby!"

Here the witch thrust her wrinkled face close to the puppet's, chuckling irrepressibly, and fidgeting all through her system, with delight at the idea which she meant to communicate.

"The worshipful Master Gookin," whispered she, "hath a comely maiden to his daughter. And hark ye, my pet! Thou hast a fair outside, and a pretty wit enough of thine own. Yea, a pretty wit enough! Thou wilt think better of it when thou hast seen more of other people's wits. Now, with thy outside and thy inside, thou art the very man to win a young girl's heart. Never doubt it! I tell thee it shall be so. Put but a bold face on the matter, sigh, smile, flourish thy hat, thrust forth thy leg like a dancing-master, put thy right hand to the left side of thy waistcoat, and pretty Polly Gookin is thine own!"

All this while the new creature had been sucking in and exhaling the vapory fragrance of his pipe, and seemed now to continue this occupation as much for the enjoyment it afforded as because it was an essential condition of his existence. It was wonderful to see how exceedingly like a human being it behaved. Its eyes (for it appeared to possess a pair) were bent on Mother Rigby, and at suitable junctures it nodded or shook its head. Neither did it lack words proper for the occasion: "Really! Indeed! Pray tell me! Is it possible! Upon my word! By no means! Oh! Ah! Hem!" and other such weighty utterances as imply attention, inquiry, acquiescence, or dissent on the part of the auditor. Even had you stood by and seen the scarecrow made, you could scarcely have resisted the conviction that it perfectly understood the cunning counsels which the old witch poured into its counterfeit of an ear. The more earnestly it applied its lips to the pipe, the more distinctly was its human likeness stamped among visible realities, the more sagacious grew its expression, the more lifelike its gestures and movements, and the more intelligibly audible its voice. Its garments, too, glistened so much the brighter with an illusory magnificence. The very pipe, in which burned the spell of all this wonderwork, ceased to appear as a smoke-blackened earthen stump, and became a meerschaum, with painted bowl and amber mouthpiece.

It might be apprehended, however, that as the life of the illusion seemed identical with the vapor of the pipe, it would terminate simultaneously with the reduction of the tobacco to ashes. But the beldam foresaw the difficulty.

"Hold thou the pipe, my precious one," said she, "while I fill it for thee again."

It was sorrowful to behold how the fine gentleman began to fade back into a scarecrow while Mother Rigby shook the ashes out of the pipe and proceeded to replenish it from her tobacco-box.

"Dickon," cried she, in her high, sharp tone, "another coal for this pipe!"

No sooner said than the intensely red speck of fire was glowing within the pipe-bowl; and the scarecrow, without waiting for the witch's bidding, applied the tube to his lips and drew in a few short, convulsive whiffs, which soon, however, became regular and equable.

"Now, mine own heart's darling," quoth Mother Rigby, "whatever may happen to thee, thou must stick to thy pipe. Thy life is in it; and that, at least, thou knowest well, if thou knowest nought besides. Stick to thy pipe, I say! Smoke, puff, blow thy cloud; and tell the people, if any question be made, that it is for thy health, and that so the physician orders thee to do. And, sweet one, when thou shalt find thy pipe getting low, go apart into some corner, and (first filling thyself with smoke) cry sharply, 'Dickon, a fresh pipe of tobacco!' and, 'Dickon, another coal for my pipe!' and have it into thy pretty mouth as speedily as may be. Else, instead of a gallant gentleman in a gold-laced coat, thou wilt be but a jumble of sticks and tattered clothes, and a bag of straw, and a withered pumpkin! Now depart, my treasure, and good luck go with thee!"

"Never fear, mother!" said the figure, in a stout voice, and sending forth a courageous whiff of smoke, "I will thrive, if an honest man and a gentleman may!"

"Oh, thou wilt be the death of me!" cried the old witch, convulsed with laughter. "That was well said. If an honest man and a gentleman may! Thou playest thy part to perfection. Get along with thee for a smart fellow; and I will wager on thy head, as a man of pith and substance, with a brain and what they call a heart, and all else that a man should have, against any other thing on two legs. I hold myself a better witch than yesterday, for thy sake. Did not I make thee? And I defy any witch in New England to make such another! Here; take my staff along with thee!"

The staff, though it was but a plain oaken stick, immediately took the aspect of a gold-headed cane.

"That gold head has as much sense in it as thine own," said Mother Rigby, "and it will guide thee straight to worshipful Master Gookin's door. Get thee gone, my pretty pet, my darling, my precious one, my treasure; and if any ask thy name, it is Feathertop. For thou hast a feather in thy hat, and I have thrust a handful of feathers into the hollow of thy head, and thy wig, too, is of the fashion they call Feathertop,—so be Feathertop thy name!"

And, issuing from the cottage, Feathertop strode manfully towards town. Mother Rigby stood at the threshold, well pleased to see how the sunbeams glistened on him, as if all his magnificence were real, and how diligently and lovingly he smoked his pipe, and how handsomely he walked, in spite of a little stiffness of his legs. She watched him until out of sight, and threw a witch benediction after her darling, when a turn of the road snatched him from her view.

Betimes in the forenoon, when the principal street of the neighboring town was just at its acme of life and bustle, a stranger of very distinguished figure was seen on the sidewalk. His port as well as his garments betokened nothing short of nobility. He wore a richly-embroidered plum-colored coat, a waistcoat of costly velvet, magnificently adorned with golden foliage, a pair of splendid scarlet breeches, and the finest and glossiest of white silk stockings. His head was covered with a peruke, so daintily powdered and adjusted that it would have been sacrilege to disorder it with a hat; which, therefore (and it was a gold-laced hat, set off with a snowy feather), he carried beneath his arm. On the breast of his coat glistened a star. He managed his gold-headed cane with an airy grace, peculiar to the fine gentlemen of the period; and, to give the highest possible finish to his equipment, he had lace ruffles at his wrist, of a most ethereal delicacy, sufficiently avouching how idle and aristocratic must be the hands which they half concealed.

It was a remarkable point in the accoutrement of this brilliant personage that he held in his left hand a fantastic kind of a pipe, with an exquisitely painted bowl and an amber mouthpiece. This he applied to his lips as often as every five or six paces, and inhaled a deep whiff of smoke, which, after being retained a moment in his lungs, might be seen to eddy gracefully from his mouth and nostrils.

As may well be supposed, the street was all astir to find out the stranger's name.

"It is some great nobleman, beyond question," said one of the townspeople. "Do you see the star at his breast?"

"Nay; it is too bright to be seen," said another. "Yes; he must needs be a nobleman, as you say. But by what conveyance, think you, can his lordship have voyaged or travelled hither? There has been no vessel from the old country for a month past; and if he have arrived overland from the southward, pray where are his attendants and equipage?"

"He needs no equipage to set off his rank," remarked a third. "If he came among us in rags, nobility would shine through a hole in his elbow. I never saw such dignity of aspect. He has the old Norman blood in his veins, I warrant him."

"I rather take him to be a Dutchman, or one of your high Germans," said another citizen. "The men of those countries have always the pipe at their mouths."

"And so has a Turk," answered his companion. "But, in my judgment, this stranger hath been bred at the French court, and hath there learned politeness and grace of manner, which none understand so well as the nobility of France. That gait, now! A vulgar spectator might deem it stiff—he might call it a hitch and jerk—but, to my eye, it hath an unspeakable majesty, and must have been acquired by constant observation of the deportment of the Grand Monarque. The stranger's character and office are evident enough. He is a French ambassador, come to treat with our rulers about the cession of Canada."

"More probably a Spaniard," said another, "and hence his yellow complexion; or, most likely, he is from the Havana, or from some port on the Spanish main, and comes to make investigation about the piracies which our government is thought to connive at. Those settlers in Peru and Mexico have skins as yellow as the gold which they dig out of their mines."

"Yellow or not," cried a lady, "he is a beautiful man!—so tall, so slender! such a fine, noble face, with so well-shaped a nose, and all that delicacy of expression about the mouth! And, bless me, how bright his star is! It positively shoots out flames!"

"So do your eyes, fair lady," said the stranger, with a bow and a flourish of his pipe; for he was just passing at the instant. "Upon my honor, they have quite dazzled me."

"Was ever so original and exquisite a compliment?" murmured the lady, in an ecstasy of delight.

Amid the general admiration excited by the stranger's appearance, there were only two dissenting voices. One was that of an impertinent cur, which, after snuffing at the heels of the glistening figure, put its tail between its legs and skulked into its master's back yard, vociferating an execrable howl. The other dissentient was a young child, who squalled at the fullest stretch of his lungs, and babbled some unintelligible nonsense about a pumpkin.

Feathertop meanwhile pursued his way along the street. Except for the few complimentary words to the lady, and now and then a slight inclination of the head in requital of the profound reverences of the bystanders, he seemed wholly absorbed in his pipe. There needed no other proof of his rank and consequence than the perfect equanimity with which he comported himself, while the curiosity and admiration of the town swelled almost into clamor around him. With a crowd gathering behind his footsteps, he finally reached the mansion-house of the worshipful Justice Gookin, entered the gate, ascended the steps of the front door, and knocked. In the interim, before his summons was answered, the stranger was observed to shake the ashes out of his pipe.

"What did he say in that sharp voice?" inquired one of the spectators.

"Nay, I know not," answered his friend. "But the sun dazzles my eyes strangely. How dim and faded his lordship looks all of a sudden! Bless my wits, what is the matter with me?"

"The wonder is," said the other, "that his pipe, which was out only an instant ago, should be all alight again, and with the reddest coal I ever saw. There is something mysterious about this stranger. What a whiff of smoke was that! Dim and faded did you call him? Why, as he turns about the star on his breast is all ablaze."

"It is, indeed," said his companion; "and it will go near to dazzle pretty Polly Gookin, whom I see peeping at it out of the chamber window."

The door being now opened, Feathertop turned to the crowd, made a stately bend of his body like a great man acknowledging the reverence of the meaner sort, and vanished into the house. There was a mysterious kind of a smile, if it might not better be called a grin or grimace, upon his visage; but, of all the throng that beheld him, not an individual appears to have possessed insight enough to detect the illusive character of the stranger except a little child and a cur dog.

Our legend here loses somewhat of its continuity, and, passing over the preliminary explanation between Feathertop and the merchant, goes in quest of the pretty Polly Gookin. She was a damsel of a soft, round figure, with light hair and blue eyes, and a fair, rosy face, which seemed neither very shrewd nor very simple. This young lady had caught a glimpse of the glistening stranger while standing on the threshold, and had forthwith put on a laced cap, a string of beads, her finest kerchief, and her stiffest damask petticoat in preparation for the interview. Hurrying from her chamber to the parlor, she had ever since been viewing herself in the large looking-glass and practising pretty airs— now a smile, now a ceremonious dignity of aspect, and now a softer smile than the former, kissing her hand likewise, tossing her head, and managing her fan; while within the mirror an unsubstantial little maid repeated every gesture and did all the foolish things that Polly did, but without making her ashamed of them. In short, it was the fault of pretty Polly's ability rather than her will if she failed to be as complete an artifice as the illustrious Feathertop himself; and, when she thus tampered with her own simplicity, the witch's phantom might well hope to win her.

No sooner did Polly hear her father's gouty footsteps approaching the parlor door, accompanied with the stiff clatter of Feathertop's high-heeled shoes, than she seated herself bolt upright and innocently began warbling a song.

"Polly! daughter Polly!" cried the old merchant. "Come hither, child."

Master Gookin's aspect, as he opened the door, was doubtful and troubled.

"This gentleman," continued he, presenting the stranger, "is the Chevalier Feathertop,—nay, I beg his pardon, my Lord Feathertop, —who hath brought me a token of remembrance from an ancient friend of mine. Pay your duty to his lordship, child, and honor him as his quality deserves."

After these few words of introduction, the worshipful magistrate immediately quitted the room. But, even in that brief moment, had the fair Polly glanced aside at her father instead of devoting herself wholly to the brilliant guest, she might have taken warning of some mischief nigh at hand. The old man was nervous, fidgety, and very pale. Purposing a smile of courtesy, he had deformed his face with a sort of galvanic grin, which, when Feathertop's back was turned, he exchanged for a scowl, at the same time shaking his fist and stamping his gouty foot—an incivility which brought its retribution along with it. The truth appears to have been that Mother Rigby's word of introduction, whatever it might be, had operated far more on the rich merchants fears than on his good will. Moreover, being a man of wonderfully acute observation, he had noticed that these painted figures on the bowl of Feathertop's pipe were in motion. Looking more closely, he became convinced that these figures were a party of little demons, each duly provided with horns and a tail, and dancing hand in hand, with gestures of diabolical merriment, round the circumference of the pipe bowl. As if to confirm his suspicions, while Master Gookin ushered his guest along a dusky passage from his private room to the parlor, the star on Feathertop's breast had scintillated actual flames, and threw a flickering gleam upon the wall, the ceiling, and the floor.

With such sinister prognostics manifesting themselves on all hands, it is not to be marvelled at that the merchant should have felt that he was committing his daughter to a very questionable acquaintance. He cursed, in his secret soul, the insinuating elegance of Feathertop's manners, as this brilliant personage bowed, smiled, put his hand on his heart, inhaled a long whiff from his pipe, and enriched the atmosphere with the smoky vapor of a fragrant and visible sigh. Gladly would poor Master Gookin have thrust his dangerous guest into the street; but there was a constraint and terror within him. This respectable old gentleman, we fear, at an earlier period of life, had given some pledge or other to the evil principle, and perhaps was now to redeem it by the sacrifice of his daughter.

It so happened that the parlor door was partly of glass, shaded by a silken curtain, the folds of which hung a little awry. So strong was the merchant's interest in witnessing what was to ensue between the fair Polly and the gallant Feathertop that, after quitting the room, he could by no means refrain from peeping through the crevice of the curtain.

But there was nothing very miraculous to be seen; nothing—except the trifles previously noticed—to confirm the idea of a supernatural peril environing the pretty Polly. The stranger it is true was evidently a thorough and practised man of the world, systematic and self-possessed, and therefore the sort of a person to whom a parent ought not to confide a simple, young girl without due watchfulness for the result. The worthy magistrate, who had been conversant with all degrees and qualities of mankind, could not but perceive every motion and gesture of the distinguished Feathertop came in its proper place; nothing had been left rude or native in him; a well-digested conventionalism had incorporated itself thoroughly with his substance and transformed him into a work of art. Perhaps it was this peculiarity that invested him with a species of ghastliness and awe. It is the effect of anything completely and consummately artificial, in human shape, that the person impresses us as an unreality and as having hardly pith enough to cast a shadow upon the floor. As regarded Feathertop, all this resulted in a wild, extravagant, and fantastical impression, as if his life and being were akin to the smoke that curled upward from his pipe.

But pretty Polly Gookin felt not thus. The pair were now promenading the room: Feathertop with his dainty stride and no less dainty grimace: the girl with a native maidenly grace, just touched, not spoiled, by a slightly affected manner, which seemed caught from the perfect artifice of her companion. The longer the interview continued, the more charmed was pretty Polly, until, within the first quarter of an hour (as the old magistrate noted by his watch), she was evidently beginning to be in love. Nor need it have been witchcraft that subdued her in such a hurry; the poor child's heart, it may be, was so very fervent that it melted her with its own warmth as reflected from the hollow semblance of a lover. No matter what Feathertop said, his words found depth and reverberation in her ear; no matter what he did, his action was heroic to her eye. And by this time it is to be supposed there was a blush on Polly's cheek, a tender smile about her mouth, and a liquid softness in her glance; while the star kept coruscating on Feathertop's breast, and the little demons careered with more frantic merriment than ever about the circumference of his pipe bowl. O pretty Polly Gookin, why should these imps rejoice so madly that a silly maiden's heart was about to be given to a shadow! Is it so unusual a misfortune, so rare a triumph?

By and by Feathertop paused, and throwing himself into an imposing attitude, seemed to summon the fair girl to survey his figure and resist him longer if she could. His star, his embroidery, his buckles glowed at that instant with unutterable splendor; the picturesque hues of his attire took a richer depth of coloring; there was a gleam and polish over his whole presence betokening the perfect witchery of well-ordered manners. The maiden raised her eyes and suffered them to linger upon her companion with a bashful and admiring gaze. Then, as if desirous of judging what value her own simple comeliness might have side by side with so much brilliancy, she cast a glance towards the full-length looking-glass in front of which they happened to be standing. It was one of the truest plates in the world and incapable of flattery. No sooner did the images therein reflected meet Polly's eye than she shrieked, shrank from the stranger's side, gazed at him for a moment in the wildest dismay, and sank insensible upon the floor. Feathertop likewise had looked towards the mirror, and there beheld, not the glittering mockery of his outside show, but a picture of the sordid patchwork of his real composition, stripped of all witchcraft.

The wretched simulacrum! We almost pity him. He threw up his arms with an expression of despair that went further than any of his previous manifestations towards vindicating his claims to be reckoned human; for, perchance the only time since this so often empty and deceptive life of mortals began its course, an illusion had seen and fully recognized itself.

Mother Rigby was seated by her kitchen hearth in the twilight of this eventful day, and had just shaken the ashes out of a new pipe, when she heard a hurried tramp along the road. Yet it did not seem so much the tramp of human footsteps as the clatter of sticks or the rattling of dry bones.

"Ha!" thought the old witch, "what step is that? Whose skeleton is out of its grave now, I wonder?"

A figure burst headlong into the cottage door. It was Feathertop! His pipe was still alight; the star still flamed upon his breast; the embroidery still glowed upon his garments; nor had he lost, in any degree or manner that could be estimated, the aspect that assimilated him with our mortal brotherhood. But yet, in some indescribable way (as is the case with all that has deluded us when once found out), the poor reality was felt beneath the cunning artifice.

"What has gone wrong?" demanded the witch. "Did yonder sniffling hypocrite thrust my darling from his door? The villain! I'll set twenty fiends to torment him till he offer thee his daughter on his bended knees!"

"No, mother," said Feathertop despondingly; "it was not that."

"Did the girl scorn my precious one?" asked Mother Rigby, her fierce eyes glowing like two coals of Tophet. "I'll cover her face with pimples! Her nose shall be as red as the coal in thy pipe! Her front teeth shall drop out! In a week hence she shall not be worth thy having!"

"Let her alone, mother," answered poor Feathertop; "the girl was half won; and methinks a kiss from her sweet lips might have made me altogether human. But," he added, after a brief pause and then a howl of self-contempt, "I've seen myself, mother! I've seen myself for the wretched, ragged, empty thing I am! I'll exist no longer!"

Snatching the pipe from his mouth, he flung it with all his might against the chimney, and at the same instant sank upon the floor, a medley of straw and tattered garments, with some sticks protruding from the heap, and a shrivelled pumpkin in the midst. The eyeholes were now lustreless; but the rudely-carved gap, that just before had been a mouth, still seemed to twist itself into a despairing grin, and was so far human.

"Poor fellow!" quoth Mother Rigby, with a rueful glance at the relics of her ill-fated contrivance. "My poor, dear, pretty Feathertop! There are thousands upon thousands of coxcombs and charlatans in the world, made up of just such a jumble of wornout, forgotten, and good-for-nothing trash as he was! Yet they live in fair repute, and never see themselves for what they are. And why should my poor puppet be the only one to know himself and perish for it?"

While thus muttering, the witch had filled a fresh pipe of tobacco, and held the stem between her fingers, as doubtful whether to thrust it into her own mouth or Feathertop's.

"Poor Feathertop!" she continued. "I could easily give him another chance and send him forth again tomorrow. But no; his feelings are too tender, his sensibilities too deep. He seems to have too much heart to bustle for his own advantage in such an empty and heartless world. Well! well! I'll make a scarecrow of him after all. 'Tis an innocent and useful vocation, and will suit my darling well; and, if each of his human brethren had as fit a one, 't would be the better for mankind; and as for this pipe of tobacco, I need it more than he."

So saying, Mother Rigby put the stem between her lips. "Dickon!" cried she, in her high, sharp tone, "another coal for my pipe!"

# EGOTISM;[1] OR, THE BOSOM SERPENT

## [From the Unpublished "Allegories of the Heart."]

"HERE he comes!" shouted the boys along the street. "Here comes the man with a snake in his bosom!"

This outcry, saluting Herkimer's ears as he was about to enter the iron gate of the Elliston mansion, made him pause. It was not without a shudder that he found himself on the point of meeting his former acquaintance, whom he had known in the glory of youth, and whom now after an interval of five eyars, he was to find the victim either of a diseased fancy or a horrible physical misfortune.

"A snake in his bosom!" repeated the young sculptor to himself. "It must be he. No second man on earth has such a bosom friend. And now, my poor Rosina, Heaven grant me wisdom to discharge my errand aright! Woman's faith must be strong indeed since thine has not yet failed."

Thus musing, he took his stand at the entrance of the gate and waited until the personage so singularly announced should make his appearance. After an instant or two he beheld the figure of a lean man, of unwhole-

---

[1] The physical fact, to which it is here attempted to give a moral signification, has been known to occur in more than one instance.

some look, with glittering eyes and long black hair, who seemed to imitate the motion of a snake; for, instead of walking straight forward with open front, he undulated along the pavement in a curved line. It may be too fanciful to say that something, either in his moral or material aspect, suggested the idea that a miracle had been wrought by transforming a serpent into a man, but so imperfectly that the snaky nature was yet hidden, and scarcely hidden, under the mere outward guise of humanity. Herkimer remarked that his complexion had a greenish tinge over its sickly white, reminding him of a species of marble out of which he had once wrought a head of Envy, with her snaky locks.

The wretched being approached the gate, but, instead of entering, stopped short and fixed the glitter of his eye full upon the compassionate yet steady countenance of the sculptor.

"It gnaws me! It gnaws me!" he exclaimed.

And then there was an audible hiss, but whether it came from the apparent lunatic's own lips, or was the real hiss of a serpent, might admit of a discussion. At all events, it made Herkimer shudder to his heart's core.

"Do you know me, George Herkimer?" asked the snake-possessed.

Herkimer did know him; but it demanded all the intimate and practical acquaintance with the human face, acquired by modelling actual likenesses in clay, to recognize the features of Roderick Elliston in the visage that now met the sculptor's gaze. Yet it was he. It added nothing to the wonder to reflect that the once brilliant young man had undergone this odious and fearful change during the no more than five brief years of Herkimer's abode at Florence. The possibility of such a transformation being granted, it was as easy to conceive it effected in a moment as in an age. Inexpressibly shocked and startled, it was still the keenest pang when Herkimer remembered that the fate of his cousin Rosina, the ideal of gentle womanhood, was indissolubly interwoven with that of a being whom Providence seemed to have unhumanized.

"Elliston! Roderick!" cried he, "I had heard of this; but my conception came far short of the truth. What has befallen you? Why do I find you thus?"

"Oh, 'tis a mere nothing! A snake! A snake! The commonest thing in the world. A snake in the bosom—that's all," answered Roderick Elliston. "But how is your own breast?" continued he, looking the sculptor in the eye with the most acute and penetrating glance that it had ever been his fortune to encounter. "All pure and wholesome? No reptile there? By my faith and conscience, and by the devil within me, here is a wonder! A man without a serpent in his bosom!"

"Be calm, Elliston," whispered George Herkimer, laying his hand upon the shoulder of the snake-possessed. "I have crossed the ocean to meet you. Listen! Let us be private. I bring a message from Rosina—from your wife!"

"It gnaws me! It gnaws me!" muttered Roderick.

With this exclamation, the most frequent in his mouth, the unfortunate man clutched both hands upon his breast as if an intolerable sting or torture impelled him to rend it open and let out the living mischief, even should it be intertwined with his own life. He then freed himself from Herkimer's grasp by a subtle motion, and, gliding through the gate, took refuge in his antiquated family residence. The sculptor did not pursue him. He saw that no available intercourse could be expected at such a moment, and was desirous, before another meeting, to inquire closely into the nature of Roderick's disease and the circumstances that had reduced him to so lamentable a condition. He succeeded in obtaining the necessary information from an eminent medical gentleman.

Shortly after Elliston's separation from his wife—now nearly four years ago—his associates had observed a singular gloom spreading over his daily life, like those chill, gray mists that sometimes steal away the sunshine from a summer's morning. The symptoms caused them endless perplexity. They knew not whether ill health were robbing his spirits of elasticity, or whether a canker of the mind was gradually eating, as such cankers do, from his moral system into the physical frame, which is but the shadow of the former. They looked for the root of this trouble in his shattered schemes of domestic bliss,—wilfully shattered by himself,—but could not be satisfied of its existence there. Some thought that their once brilliant friend was in an incipient stage of insanity, of which his passionate impulses had perhaps been the forerunners; others prognosticated a general blight and gradual decline. From Roderick's own lips they could learn nothing. More than once, it is true, he had been heard to say, clutching his hands convulsively upon his breast,—"It gnaws me! It gnaws me!"—but, by different auditors, a great diversity of explanation was assigned to this ominous expression. What could it be that gnawed the breast of Roderick Elliston? Was it sorrow? Was it merely the tooth of physical disease? Or, in his reckless course, often verging upon profligacy, if not plunging into its depths, had he been guilty of some deed which made his bosom a prey to the deadlier fangs of remorse? There was plausible ground for each of these conjectures; but it must not be concealed that more than one elderly gentleman, the victim of good cheer and slothful habits, magisterially pronounced the secret of the whole matter to be Dyspepsia!

Meanwhile, Roderick seemed aware how generally he had become the subject of curiosity and conjecture, and, with a morbid repugnance to such notice, or to any notice whatsoever, estranged himself from all companionship. Not merely the eye of man was a horror to him; not merely the light of a friend's countenance; but even the blessed sunshine, likewise, which in its universal beneficence typifies the radiance of the Creator's face, expressing his love for all the creatures of his hand. The dusky twilight was now too transparent for Roderick Elliston; the blackest midnight was his chosen hour to steal abroad; and if ever he were seen, it was when the watchman's lantern gleamed upon his figure, gliding along the street, with his hands clutched upon his bosom, still muttering, "It gnaws me! It gnaws me!" What could it be that gnawed him?

After a time, it became known that Elliston was in the habit of resorting to all the noted quacks that infested the city, or whom money would tempt to journey thither from a distance. By one of these persons, in the exultation of a supposed cure, it was proclaimed far and wide, by dint of handbills and little pamphlets on dingy paper, that a distinguished gentleman, Roderick Elliston, Esq., had been relieved of a SNAKE in his stomach! So here was the monstrous secret, ejected from its lurking place into public view, in all its horrible deformity. The mystery was out; but not so the bosom serpent. He, if it were anything but a delusion, still lay coiled in his living den. The empiric's cure had been a sham, the effect, it was supposed, of some stupefying drug which more nearly caused the death of the patient than of the odious reptile that possessed him. When Roderick Elliston regained entire sensibility, it was to find his misfortune the town talk—the more than nine days' wonder and horror—while, at his bosom, he felt the sickening motion of a thing alive, and the gnawing of that restless fang which seemed to gratify at once a physical appetite and a fiendish spite.

He summoned the old black servant, who had been bred up in his father's house, and was a middle-aged man while Roderick lay in his cradle.

"Scipio!" he began; and then paused, with his arms folded over his heart. "What do people say of me, Scipio."

"Sir! my poor master! that you had a serpent in your bosom," answered the servant with hesitation.

"And what else?" asked Roderick, with a ghastly look at the man.

"Nothing else, dear master," replied Scipio, "only that the doctor gave you a powder, and that the snake leaped out upon the floor."

"No, no!" muttered Roderick to himself, as he shook his head, and pressed his hands with a more convulsive force upon his breast, "I feel him still. It gnaws me! It gnaws me!"

From this time the miserable sufferer ceased to shun the world, but rather solicited and forced himself upon the notice of acquaintances and strangers. It was partly the result of desperation on finding that the cavern of his own bosom had not proved deep and dark enough to hide the secret, even while it was so secure a fortress for the loathsome fiend that had crept into it. But still more, this craving for notoriety was a symptom of the intense morbidness which now pervaded his nature. All persons chronically diseased are egotists, whether the disease be of the mind or body; whether it be sin, sorrow, or merely the more tolerable calamity of some endless pain, or mischief among the cords of mortal life. Such individuals are made acutely conscious of a self, by the torture in which it dwells. Self, therefore, grows to be so prominent an object with them that they cannot but present it to the face of every casual passer-by. There is a pleasure—perhaps the greatest of which the sufferer is susceptible—in displaying the wasted or ulcerated limb, or the cancer in the breast; and the fouler the crime, with so much the more difficulty does the perpetrator prevent it from thrusting up its snake-like head to frighten the world; for it is that cancer, or that crime, which constitutes their respective individuality. Roderick Elliston, who, a little while before, had held himself so scornfully above the common lot of men, now paid full allegiance to this humiliating law. The snake in his bosom seemed the symbol of a monstrous egotism to which everything was referred, and which he pampered, night and day, with a continual and exclusive sacrifice of devil worship.

He soon exhibited what most people considered indubitable tokens of insanity. In some of his moods, strange to say, he prided and gloried himself on being marked out from the ordinary experience of mankind, by the possession of a double nature, and a life within a life. He appeared to imagine that the snake was a divinity,—not celestial, it is true, but darkly infernal,—and that he thence derived an eminence and a sanctity, horrid, indeed, yet more desirable than whatever ambition aims at. Thus he drew his misery around him like a regal mantle, and looked down triumphantly upon those whose vitals nourished no deadly monster. Oftener, however, his human nature asserted its empire over him in the shape of a yearning for fellowship. It grew to be his custom to spend the whole day in wandering about the streets, aimlessly, unless it might be called an aim to establish a species of brotherhood between himself and the world. With cankered ingenuity, he sought out his own disease in every breast. Whether insane or not, he showed so keen a perception of frailty, error, and vice, that many persons gave him credit for being possessed not merely with a serpent, but with an actual fiend, who imparted this evil faculty of recognizing whatever was ugliest in man's heart.

For instance, he met an individual, who, for thirty years, had cherished a hatred against his own brother. Roderick, amidst the throng of the street, laid his hand on this man's chest, and looking full into his forbidding face,—

"How is the snake to-day?" he inquired, with a mock expression of sympathy.

"The snake!" exclaimed the brother hater—"what do you mean?"

"The snake! The snake! Does it gnaw you?" persisted Roderick. "Did you take counsel with him this morning when you should have been saying your prayers? Did he sting, when you thought of your brother's health, wealth, and good repute? Did he caper for joy, when you remembered the profligacy of his only son? And whether he stung, or whether he frolicked, did you feel his poison throughout your body and soul, converting everything to sourness and bitterness? That is the way of such serpents. I have learned the whole nature of them from my own!"

"Where is the police?" roared the object of Roderick's persecution, at the same time giving an instinctive clutch to his breast. "Why is this lunatic allowed to go at large?"

"Ha, ha!" chuckled Roderick, releasing his grasp of the man. "His bosom serpent has stung him then!"

Often it pleased the unfortunate young man to vex people with a lighter satire, yet still characterized by somewhat of snakelike virulence. One day he encountered an ambitious statesman, and gravely inquired after the welfare of his boa constrictor; for of that species, Roderick affirmed, this gentleman's serpent must needs be, since its appetite was enormous enough to devour the whole country and constitution. At another time, he stopped a close-fisted old fellow, of great wealth, but who skulked about the city in the guise of a scarecrow, with a patched blue surtout, brown hat, and mouldy boots, scraping pence together, and picking up rusty nails. Pretending to look earnestly at this respectable person's stomach, Roderick assured him that his snake was a copper-head, and had been generated by the immense quantities of that base metal, with which he daily defiled his fingers. Again, he assaulted a man of rubicund visage, and told him that few bosom serpents had more of the devil in them than those that breed in the vats of a distillery. The next whom Roderick honored with his attention was a distinguished clergyman, who happened just then to be engaged in a theological controversy, where human wrath was more perceptible than divine inspiration.

"You have swallowed a snake in a cup of sacramental wine," quoth he.

"Profane wretch!" exclaimed the divine; but, nevertheless, his hand stole to his breast.

He met a person of sickly sensibility, who, on some early disappointment, had retired from the world, and thereafter held no intercourse with his fellow-men, but brooded sullenly or passionately over the irrevocable past. This man's very heart, if Roderick might be believed, had been changed into a serpent, which would finally torment both him and itself to death. Observing a married couple, whose domestic troubles were matter of notoriety, he condoled with both on having mutually taken a house adder to their bosoms. To an envious author, who depreciated works which he could never equal, he said that his snake was the slimiest and filthiest of all the reptile tribe, but was fortunately without a sting. A man of impure life, and a brazen face, asking Roderick if there were any serpent in his breast, he told him that there was, and of the same species that once tortured Don Rodrigo, the Goth. He took a fair young girl by the hand, and gazing sadly into her eyes, warned her that she cherished a serpent of the deadliest kind within her gentle breast; and the world found the truth of those ominous words, when, a few months afterwards, the poor girl died of love and shame. Two ladies, rivals in fashionable life, who tormented one another with a thousand little stings of womanish spite, were given to understand that each of their hearts was a nest of diminutive snakes, which did quite as much mischief as one great one.

But nothing seemed to please Roderick better than to lay hold of a person infected with jealousy, which he represented as an enormous green reptile, with an ice-cold length of body, and the sharpest sting of any snake save one.

"And what one is that?" asked a by-stander, overhearing him.

It was a dark-browed man who put the question; he had an evasive eye, which in the course of a dozen years had looked no mortal directly in the face. There was an ambiguity about this person's character,—a stain upon his reputation,—yet none could tell precisely of what nature, although the city gossips, male and female, whispered the most atrocious surmises. Until a recent period he had followed the sea, and was, in fact, the very shipmaster whom George Herkimer had encountered, under such singular circumstances, in the Grecian Archipelago.

"What bosom serpent has the sharpest sting?" repeated this man; but he put the question as if by a reluctant necessity, and grew pale while he was uttering it.

"Why need you ask?" replied Roderick, with a look of dark intelligence. "Look into your own breast. Hark! my serpent bestirs himself! He acknowledges the presence of a master fiend!"

And then, as the by-standers afterwards affirmed, a hissing sound was heard, apparently in Roderick Elliston's breast. It was said, too, that an answering hiss came from the vitals of the shipmaster, as if a snake were actually lurking there and had been aroused by the call of its brother reptile. If there were in fact any such sound, it might have been caused by a malicious exercise of ventriloquism on the part of Roderick.

Thus making his own actual serpent—if a serpent there actually was in his bosom—the type of each man's fatal error, or hoarded sin, or unquiet conscience, and striking his sting so unremorsefully into the sorest spot, we may well imagine that Roderick became the pest of the city. Nobody could elude him—none could withstand him. He grappled with the ugliest truth that he could lay his hand on, and compelled his adversary to do the same. Strange spectacle in human life where it is the instinctive effort of one and all to hide those sad realities, and leave them undisturbed beneath a heap of superficial topics which constitute the materials of intercourse between man and man! It was not to be tolerated that Roderick Elliston should break through the tacit compact by which the world has done its best to secure repose without relinquishing evil. The victims of his malicious remarks, it is true, had brothers enough to keep them in countenance; for, by Roderick's theory, every mortal bosom harbored either a brood of small serpents or one overgrown monster that had devoured all the rest. Still the city could not bear this new apostle. It was demanded by nearly all, and particularly by the most respectable inhabitants, that Roderick should no longer be permitted to violate the received rules of decorum by obtruding his own bosom serpent to the public gaze, and dragging those of decent people from their lurking places.

Accordingly, his relatives interfered and placed him in a private asylum for the insane. When the news was noised abroad, it was observed that many persons walked the streets with freer countenances and covered their breasts less carefully with their hands.

His confinement, however, although it contributed not a little to the peace of the town, operated unfavorably upon Roderick himself. In solitude his melancholy grew more black and sullen. He spent whole days— indeed, it was his sole occupation—in communing with the serpent. A conversation was sustained, in which, as it seemed, the hidden monster bore a part, though unintelligibly to the listeners, and inaudible except in a hiss. Singular as it may appear, the sufferer had now contracted a sort of affection for his tormentor, mingled, however, with the intensest loathing and horror. Nor were such discordant emotions incompatible. Each, on the contrary, imparted strength and poignancy to its opposite. Horrible love—horrible antipathy—embracing one another in his bosom, and both concentrating themselves upon a being that had crept into his vitals or been engendered there, and which was nourished with his food, and lived upon his life, and was as intimate with him as his own heart, and yet was the foulest of all created things! But not the less was it the true type of a morbid nature.

Sometimes, in his moments of rage and bitter hatred against the snake and himself, Roderick determined to be the death of him, even at the expense of his own life. Once he attempted it by starvation; but, while the wretched man was on the point of famishing, the monster seemed to feed upon his heart, and to thrive and wax gamesome, as if it were his sweetest and most congenial diet. Then he privily took a dose of active poison, imagining that it would not fail to kill either himself or the devil that possessed him, or both together. Another mistake; for if Roderick had not yet been destroyed by his own poisoned heart nor the snake by gnawing it, they had little to fear from arsenic or corrosive sublimate. Indeed, the venomous pest appeared to operate as an antidote against all other poisons. The physicians tried to suffocate the fiend with tobacco smoke. He breathed it as freely as if it were his native atmosphere. Again, they drugged their patient with opium and drenched him with intoxicating liquors, hoping that the snake might thus be reduced to stupor and perhaps be ejected from the stomach. They succeeded in rendering Roderick insensible; but, placing their hands upon his breast, they were inexpressibly horror stricken to feel the monster wriggling, twining, and darting to and fro within his narrow limits, evidently enlivened by the opium or alcohol, and incited to unusual feats of activity. Thenceforth they gave up all attempts at cure or palliation. The doomed sufferer submitted to his fate, resumed his former loathsome affection for the bosom fiend, and spent whole miserable days before a looking-glass, with his mouth wide open, watching, in hope and horror, to catch a glimpse of the snake's head far down within his throat. It is supposed that he succeeded; for the attendants once heard a frenzied shout, and, rushing into the room, found Roderick lifeless upon the floor.

He was kept but little longer under restraint. After minute investigation, the medical directors of the asylum decided that his mental disease did not amount to insanity, nor would warrant his confinement, especially as its influence upon his spirits was unfavorable, and might produce the evil which it was meant to remedy. His eccentricities were doubtless great; he had habitually violated many of the customs and prejudices of society; but the world was not, without surer ground, entitled to treat him as a madman. On this decision of such competent authority Roderick was released, and had returned to his native city the very day before his encounter with George Herkimer.

As soon as possible after learning these particulars the sculptor, together with a sad and tremulous companion, sought Elliston at his own house. It was a large, sombre edifice of wood, with pilasters and a balcony, and was divided from one of the principal streets by a terrace of three elevations, which was ascended by successive flights of stone steps. Some immense old elms almost concealed the front of the mansion. This spacious and once magnificent family residence was built by a grandee of the race early in the past century, at which epoch, land being of small comparative value, the garden and other grounds had formed quite an extensive domain. Although a portion of the ancestral heritage had been alienated, there was still a shadowy enclosure in the rear of the mansion where a student, or a dreamer, or a man of stricken heart might lie all day upon the grass, amid the solitude of murmuring boughs, and forget that a city had grown up around him.

Into this retirement the sculptor and his companion were ushered by Scipio, the old black servant, whose wrinkled visage grew almost sunny with intelligence and joy as he paid his humble greetings to one of the two visitors.

"Remain in the arbor," whispered the sculptor to the figure that leaned upon his arm. "You will know whether, and when, to make your appearance."

"God will teach me," was the reply. "May He support me too!"

Roderick was reclining on the margin of a fountain which gushed into the fleckered sunshine with the same clear sparkle and the same voice of airy quietude as when trees of primeval growth flung their shadows across its bosom. How strange is the life of a fountain!—born at every moment, yet of an age coeval with the rocks, and far surpassing the venerable antiquity of a forest.

"You are come! I have expected you," said Elliston, when he became aware of the sculptor's presence.

His manner was very different from that of the preceding day—quiet, courteous, and, as Herkimer thought, watchful both over his guest and himself. This unnatural restraint was almost the only trait that betokened anything amiss. He had just thrown a book upon the grass, where it lay half opened, thus disclosing itself to be a natural history of the serpent tribe, illustrated by lifelike plates. Near it lay that bulky volume, the Ductor Dubitantium of Jeremy Taylor, full of cases of conscience, and in which most men, possessed of a conscience, may find something applicable to their purpose.

"You see," observed Elliston, pointing to the book of serpents, while a smile gleamed upon his lips, "I am making an effort to become better acquainted with my bosom friend; but I find nothing satisfactory in this volume. If I mistake not, he will prove to be *sui generis,* and akin to no other reptile in creation."

"Whence came this strange calamity?" inquired the sculptor.

"My sable friend Scipio has a story," replied Roderick, "of a snake that had lurked in this fountain—pure and innocent as it looks—ever since it was known to the first settlers. This insinuating personage once crept into the vitals of my great grandfather and dwelt there many years, tormenting the old gentleman beyond mortal endurance. In short it is a family peculiarity. But, to tell you the truth, I have no faith in this idea of the snake's being an heirloom. He is my own snake, and no man's else."

"But what was his origin?" demanded Herkimer.

"Oh, there is poisonous stuff in any man's heart sufficient to generate a brood of serpents," said Elliston with a hollow laugh. "You should have heard my homilies to the good town's-people. Positively, I deem myself fortunate in having bred but a single serpent. You, however, have none in your bosom, and therefore cannot sympathize with the rest of the world. It gnaws me! It gnaws me!"

With this exclamation Roderick lost his self-control and threw himself upon the grass, testifying his agony by intricate writhings, in which Herkimer could not but fancy a resemblance to the motions of a snake. Then, likewise, was heard that frightful hiss, which often ran through the sufferer's speech, and crept between the words and syllables without interrupting their succession.

"This is awful indeed!" exclaimed the sculptor—"an awful infliction, whether it be actual or imaginary. Tell me, Roderick Elliston, is there any remedy for this loathsome evil?"

"Yes, but an impossible one," muttered Roderick, as he lay wallowing with his face in the grass. "Could I for one moment forget myself, the serpent might not abide within me. It is my diseased self-contemplation that has engendered and nourished him."

"Then forget yourself, my husband," said a gentle voice above him; "forget yourself in the idea of another!"

Rosina had emerged from the arbor, and was bending over him with the shadow of his anguish reflected in her countenance, yet so mingled with hope and unselfish love that all anguish seemed but an earthly shadow and a dream. She touched Roderick with her hand. A tremor shivered through his frame. At that moment, if report be trustworthy, the sculptor beheld a waving motion through the grass, and heard a tinkling sound, as if something had plunged into the fountain. Be the truth as it might, it is certain that Roderick Elliston sat up like a man renewed, restored to his right mind, and rescued from the fiend which had so miserably overcome him in the battle-field of his own breast.

"Rosina!" cried he, in broken and passionate tones, but with nothing of the wild wail that had haunted his voice so long, "forgive! forgive!"

Her happy tears bedewed his face.

"The punishment has been severe," observed the sculptor. "Even Justice might now forgive; how much more a woman's tenderness! Roderick Elliston, whether the serpent was a physical reptile, or whether the morbidness of your nature suggested that symbol to your fancy, the moral of the story is not the less true and strong. A tremendous Egotism, manifesting itself in your case in the form of jealousy, is as fearful a fiend as ever stole into the human heart. Can a breast, where it has dwelt so long, be purified?"

"Oh yes," said Rosina with a heavenly smile. "The serpent was but a dark fantasy, and what it typified was as shadowy as itself. The past, dismal as it seems, shall fling no gloom upon the future. To give it its due importance we must think of it but as an anecdote in our Eternity."

## DROWNE'S WOODEN IMAGE

ONE sunshiny morning, in the good old times of the town of Boston, a young carver in wood, well known by the name of Drowne, stood contemplating a large oaken log, which it was his purpose to convert into the figure-head of a vessel. And while he discussed within his own mind what sort of shape or similitude it were well to bestow upon this excellent piece of timber, there came into Drowne's workshop a certain Captain Hunnewell, owner and commander of the good brig called the Cynosure, which had just returned from her first voyage to Fayal.

"Ah! that will do, Drowne, that will do!" cried the jolly captain, tapping the log with his rattan. "I bespeak this very piece of oak for the figure-head of the Cynosure. She has shown herself the sweetest craft that ever floated, and I mean to decorate her prow with the handsomest image that the skill of man can cut out of timber. And, Drowne, you are the fellow to execute it."

"You give me more credit than I deserve, Captain Hunnewell," said the carver, modestly, yet as one conscious of eminence in his art. "But, for the sake of the good brig, I stand ready to do my best. And which of these designs do you prefer? Here,"—pointing to a staring, half-length figure, in a white wig and scarlet coat,—"here is an excellent model, the likeness of our gracious king. Here is the valiant Admiral Vernon. Or, if you prefer a female figure, what say you to Britannia with the trident?"

"All very fine, Drowne; all very fine," answered the mariner. "But as nothing like the brig ever swam the ocean, so I am determined she shall have such a figure-head as old Neptune never saw in his life. And what is more, as there is a secret in the matter, you must pledge your credit not to betray it."

"Certainly," said Drowne, marvelling, however, what possible mystery there could be in reference to an affair so open, of necessity, to the inspection of all the world as the figure-head of a vessel. "You may depend, captain, on my being as secret as the nature of the case will permit."

Captain Hunnewell then took Drowne by the button, and communicated his wishes in so low a tone that it would be unmannerly to repeat what was evidently intended for the carver's private ear. We shall, therefore, take the opportunity to give the reader a few desirable particulars about Drowne himself.

He was the first American who is known to have attempted—in a very humble line, it is true—that art in which we can now reckon so many names already distinguished, or rising to distinction. From his earliest boyhood he had exhibited a knack—for it would be too proud a word to call it genius—a knack, therefore, for the imitation of the human figure in whatever material came most readily to hand. The snows of a New England winter had often supplied him with a species of marble as dazzingly white, at least, as the Parian or the Carrara, and if less durable, yet sufficiently so to correspond with any claims to permanent existence possessed by the boy's frozen statues. Yet they won admiration from maturer judges than his school-fellows, and were indeed, remarkably clever, though destitute of the native warmth that might have made the snow melt beneath his hand. As he advanced in life, the young man adopted pine and oak as eligible materials for the display of his skill, which now began to bring him a return of solid silver as well as the empty praise that had been an apt reward enough for his productions of evanescent snow. He became noted for carving ornamental pump heads, and wooden urns for gate posts, and decorations, more grotesque than fanciful, for mantelpieces. No apothecary would have deemed himself in the way of obtaining custom without setting up a gilded mortar, if not a head of Galen or Hippocrates, from the skilful hand of Drowne.

But the great scope of his business lay in the manufacture of figureheads for vessels. Whether it were the monarch himself, or some famous British admiral or general, or the governor of the province, or perchance the favorite daughter of the ship-owner, there the image stood above the prow, decked out in gorgeous colors, magnificently gilded, and staring the whole world out of countenance, as if from an innate consciousness of its own superiority. These specimens of native sculpture had crossed the sea in all directions, and been not ignobly noticed among the crowded shipping of the Thames and wherever else the hardy mariners of New England had pushed their adventures. It must be confessed that a family likeness pervaded these respectable progeny of Drowne's skill; that the benign countenance of the king resembled those of his subjects, and that Miss Peggy Hobart, the merchant's daughter, bore a remarkable similitude to Britannia, Victory, and other ladies of the allegoric sisterhood; and, finally, that they all had a kind of wooden aspect which proved an intimate relationship with the unshaped blocks of timber in the carver's workshop. But at least there was no inconsiderable skill of hand, nor a deficiency of any attribute to render them really works of art, except that deep quality, be it of soul or intellect, which bestows life upon the lifeless and warmth upon the cold, and which, had it been present, would have made Drowne's wooden image instinct with spirit.

The captain of the Cynosure had now finished his instructions.

"And Drowne," said he, impressively, "you must lay aside all other business and set about this forthwith. And as to the price, only do the job in first-rate style, and you shall settle that point yourself."

"Very well, captain," answered the carver, who looked grave and somewhat perplexed, yet had a sort of smile upon his visage; "depend upon it, I'll do my utmost to satisfy you."

From that moment the men of taste about Long Wharf and the Town Dock who were wont to show their love for the arts by frequent visits to Drowne's workshop, and admiration of his wooden images, began to be sensible of a mystery in the carver's conduct. Often he was absent in the daytime. Sometimes, as might be judged by gleams of light from the shop windows, he was at work until a late hour of the evening; although neither knock nor voice, on such occasions, could gain admittance for a visitor, or elicit any word of response. Nothing remarkable, however, was observed in the shop at those late hours when it was thrown open. A fine piece of timber, indeed, which Drowne was known to have reserved for some work of especial dignity, was seen to be gradually assuming shape. What shape it was destined ultimately to take was a problem to his friends and a point on which the carver himself preserved a rigid silence. But day after day, though Drowne was seldom noticed in the act of working upon it, this rude form began to be developed until it became evident to all observers that a female figure was growing into mimic life. At each new visit they beheld a larger pile of wooden chips and a nearer approximation to something beautiful. It seemed as if the hamadryad of the oak had sheltered herself from the unimaginative world within the heart of her native tree, and that it was only necessary to remove the strange shapelessness that had incrusted her, and reveal the grace and loveliness of a divinity. Imperfect as the design, the attitude, the costume, and especially the face of the image still remained, there was already an effect that drew the eye from the wooden cleverness of Drowne's earlier productions and fixed it upon the tantalizing mystery of this new project.

Copley, the celebrated painter, then a young man and a resident of Boston, came one day to visit Drowne; for he had recognized so much of moderate ability in the carver as to induce him, in the dearth of professional sympathy, to cultivate his acquaintance. On entering the shop, the artist glanced at the inflexible image of king, commander, dame, and allegory, that stood around, on the best of which might have been bestowed the questionable praise that it looked as if a living man had here been changed to wood, and that not only the physical, but the intellectual and spiritual part, partook of the stolid transformation. But in not a single instance did it seem as if the wood were imbibing the ethereal essence of humanity. What a wide distinction is here! and how far the slightest portion of the latter merit have outvalued the utmost degree of the former!

"My friend Drowne," said Copley, smiling to himself, but alluding to the mechanical and wooden cleverness that so invariably distinguished the images, "you are really a remarkable person! I have seldom met with a man in your line of business that could do so much; for one other touch might make this figure of General Wolfe, for instance, a breathing and intelligent human creature."

"You would have me think that you are praising me highly, Mr. Copley," answered Drowne, turning his back upon Wolfe's image in apparent disgust. "But there has come a light into my mind. I know, what you know as well, that the one touch which you speak of as deficient is the only one that would be truly valuable, and that without it these works of mine are no better than worthless abortions. There is the same difference between them and the works of an inspired artist as between a sign-post daub and one of your best pictures."

"This is strange," cried Copley, looking him in the face, which now, as the painter fancied, had a singular depth of intelligence, though hitherto it had not given him greatly the advantage over his own family of wooden images. "What has come over you? How is it that, possessing the idea which you have now uttered, you should produce only such works as these?"

The carver smiled, but made no reply. Copley turned again to the images, conceiving that the sense of deficiency which Drowne had just expressed, and which is so rare in a merely mechanical character, must surely imply a genius, the tokens of which had heretofore been overlooked. But no; there was not a trace of it. He was about to withdraw when his eyes chanced to fall upon a half-developed figure which lay in a corner of the workshop, surrounded by scattered chips of oak. It arrested him at once.

"What is here? Who has done this?" he broke out, after contemplating it in speechless astonishment for an instant. "Here is the divine, the lifegiving touch. What inspired hand is beckoning this wood to arise and live? Whose work is this?"

"No man's work," replied Drowne. "The figure lies within that block of oak, and it is my business to find it."

"Drowne," said the true artist, grasping the carver fervently by the hand, "you are a man of genius!"

As Copley departed, happening to glance backward from the threshold, he beheld Drowne bending over the half-created shape, and stretching forth his arms as if he would have embraced and drawn it to his heart; while, had such a miracle been possible, his countenance expressed passion enough to communicate warmth and sensibility to the lifeless oak.

"Strange enough!" said the artist to himself. "Who would have looked for a modern Pygmalion in the person of a Yankee mechanic!"

As yet, the image was but vague in its outward presentment; so that, as in the cloud shapes around the western sun, the observer rather felt, or was led to imagine, than really saw what was intended by it. Day by day, however, the work assumed greater precision, and settled its irregular and misty outline into distincter grace and beauty. The general design was now obvious to the common eye. It was a female figure, in what appeared to be a foreign dress; the gown being laced over the bosom, and opening in front so as to disclose a skirt or petticoat, the folds and inequalities of which were admirably represented in the oaken substance. She wore a hat of singular gracefulness, and abundantly laden with flowers, such as never grew in the rude soil of New England, but which, with all their fanciful luxuriance, had a natural truth that it seemed impossible for the most fertile imagination to have attained without copying from real prototypes. There were several little appendages to this dress, such as a fan, a pair of earrings, a chain about the neck, a watch in the bosom, and a ring upon the finger, all of which would have been deemed beneath the dignity of sculpture. They were put on, however, with as much taste as a lovely woman might have shown in her attire, and could therefore have shocked none but a judgment spoiled by artistic rules.

The face was still imperfect; but gradually, by a magic touch, intelligence and sensibility brightened through the features, with all the effect of light gleaming forth from within the solid oak. The face became alive. It was a beautiful, though not precisely regular and somewhat haughty aspect, but with a certain piquancy about the eyes and mouth, which, of all expressions, would have seemed the most impossible to throw over a wooden countenance. And now, so far as carving went, this wonderful production was complete.

"Drowne," said Copley, who had hardly missed a single day in his visits to the carver's workshop, "if this work were in marble it would make you famous at once; nay, I would almost affirm that it would make an era in the art. It is as ideal as an antique statue, and yet as real as any lovely woman whom one meets at a fireside or in the street. But I trust you do not mean to desecrate this exquisite creature with paint, like those staring kings and admirals yonder?"

"Not paint her!" exclaimed Captain Hunnewell, who stood by; "not paint the figure-head of the Cynosure! And what sort of a figure should I cut in a foreign port with such an unpainted oaken stick as this over my prow! She must, and she shall, be painted to the life, from the topmost flower in her hat down to the silver spangles on her slippers."

"Mr. Copley," said Drowne, quietly, "I know nothing of marble statuary, and nothing of the sculptor's rules of art; but of this wooden image, this work of my hands, this creature of my heart,"—and here his voice faltered and choked in a very singular manner,—"of this—of her —I may say that I know something. A well-spring of inward wisdom gushed within me as I wrought upon the oak with my whole strength, and soul, and faith. Let others do what they may with marble, and adopt what rules they choose. If I can produce my desired effect by painted wood, those rules are not for me, and I have a right to disregard them."

"The very spirit of genius," muttered Copley to himself. "How otherwise should this carver feel himself entitled to transcend all rules, and make me ashamed of quoting them?"

He looked earnestly at Drowne, and again saw that expression of human love which, in a spiritual sense, as the artist could not help imagining, was the secret of the life that had been breathed into this block of wood.

The carver, still in the same secrecy that marked all his operations upon this mysterious image, proceeded to paint the habiliments in their proper colors, and the countenance with Nature's red and white. When all was finished he threw open his workshop, and admitted the townspeople to behold what he had done. Most persons, at their first entrance, felt impelled to remove their hats, and pay such reverence as was due to the richly-dressed and beautiful young lady who seemed to stand in a corner of the room, with oaken chips and shavings scattered at her feet. Then came a sensation of fear; as if, not being actually human, yet so like humanity, she must therefore be something preternatural. There was, in truth, an indefinable air and expression that might reasonably induce the query, Who and from what sphere this daughter of the oak should be? The strange, rich flowers of Eden on her head; the complexion, so much deeper and more brilliant than those of our native beauties; the foreign, as it seemed, and fantastic garb, yet not too fantastic to be worn decorously in the street; the delicately-wrought embroidery of the skirt; the broad gold chain about her neck; the curious ring upon her finger; the fan, so exquisitely sculptured in open work, and painted to resemble pearl and ebony;—where could Drowne, in his sober walk of life, have beheld the vision here so matchlessly embodied! And then her face! In the dark eyes, and around the voluptuous mouth, there played a look made up of pride, coquetry, and a gleam of mirthfulness, which impressed Copley with the idea that the image was secretly enjoying the perplexing admiration of himself and other beholders.

"And will you," said he to the carver, "permit this masterpiece to become the figure-head of a vessel? Give the honest captain yonder figure of Britannia—it will answer his purpose far better—and send this fairy queen to England, where, for aught I know, it may bring you a thousand pounds."

"I have not wrought it for money," said Drowne.

"What sort of a fellow is this!" thought Copley. "A Yankee, and throw away the chance of making his fortune! He has gone mad; and thence has come this gleam of genius."

There was still further proof of Drowne's lunacy, if credit were due to the rumor that he had been seen kneeling at the feet of the oaken lady, and gazing with a lover's passionate ardor into the face that his own hands had created. The bigots of the day hinted that it would be no matter of surprise if an evil spirit were allowed to enter this beautiful form, and seduce the carver to destruction.

The fame of the image spread far and wide. The inhabitants visited it so universally, that after a few days of exhibition there was hardly an old man or a child who had not become minutely familiar with its aspect. Even had the story of Drowne's wooden image ended here, its celebrity might have been prolonged for many years by the reminiscences of those who looked upon it in their childhood, and saw nothing else so beautiful in after life. But the town was now astounded by an event, the narrative of which has formed itself into one of the most singular legends that are yet to be met with in the traditionary chimney corners of the New England metropolis, where old men and women sit dreaming of the past, and wag their heads at the dreamers of the present and the future.

One fine morning, just before the departure of the Cynosure on her second voyage to Fayal, the commander of that gallant vessel was seen to issue from his residence in Hanover Street. He was stylishly dressed in a blue broadcloth coat, with gold lace at the seams and button-holes, an embroidered scarlet waistcoat, a triangular hat, with a loop and broad binding of gold, and wore a silver-hilted.hanger at his side. But the good captain might have been arrayed in the robes of a prince or the rags of a beggar, without in either case attracting notice, while obscured by such a companion as now leaned on his arm. The people in the street started, rubbed their eyes, and either leaped aside from their path, or stood as if transfixed to wood or marble in astonishment.

"Do you see it?—do you see it?" cried one, with tremulous eagerness. "It is the very same!"

"The same?" answered another, who had arrived in town only the night before. "Who do you mean? I see only a sea-captain in his shore-going clothes, and a young lady in a foreign habit, with a bunch of beautiful flowers in her hat. On my word, she is as fair and bright a damsel as my eyes have looked on this many a day!"

"Yes; the same!—the very same!" repeated the other. "Drowne's wooden image has come to life!"

Here was a miracle indeed! Yet, illuminated by the sunshine, or darkened by the alternate shade of the houses, and with its garments fluttering lightly in the morning breeze, there passed the image along the street. It was exactly and minutely the shape, the garb, and the face which the towns-people had so recently thronged to see and admire. Not a rich flower upon her head, not a single leaf, but had had its prototype in Drowne's wooden workmanship, although now their fragile grace had become flexible, and was shaken by every footstep that the wearer made. The broad gold chain upon the neck was identical with the one represented on the image, and glistened with the motion imparted by the rise and fall of the bosom which it decorated. A real diamond sparkled on her finger. In her right hand she bore a pearl and ebony fan, which she flourished with a fantastic and bewitching coquetry, that was likewise expressed in all her movements as well as in the style of her beauty and the attire that so well harmonized with it. The face with its brilliant depth of complexion had the same piquancy of mirthful mischief that was fixed upon the countenance of the image, but which was here varied and continually shifting, yet always essentially the same, like the sunny gleam upon a bubbling fountain. On the whole, there was something so airy and yet so real in the figure, and withal so perfectly did it represent Drowne's image, that people knew not whether to suppose the magic wood etherealized into a spirit or warmed and softened into an actual woman.

"One thing is certain," muttered a Puritan of the old stamp, "Drowne has sold himself to the devil; and doubtless this gay Captain Hunnewell is a party to the bargain."

"And I," said a young man who overheard him, "would almost consent to be the third victim, for the liberty of saluting those lovely lips."

"And so would I," said Copley, the painter, "for the privilege of taking her picture."

The image, or the apparition, whichever it might be, still escorted by the bold captain, proceeded from Hanover Street through some of the cross lanes that make this portion of the town so intricate, to Ann Street, thence into Dock Square, and so downward to Drowne's shop, which stood just on the water's edge. The crowd still followed, gathering volume as it rolled along. Never had a modern miracle occurred in such broad daylight, nor in the presence of such a multitude of witnesses. The airy image, as if conscious that she was the object of the murmurs and disturbance that swelled behind her, appeared slightly vexed and flustered, yet still in a manner consistent with the light vivacity and sportive mischief that were written in her countenance. She was observed to flutter her fan with such vehement rapidity that the elaborate delicacy of its workmanship gave way, and it remained broken in her hand.

Arriving at Drowne's door, while the captain threw it open, the marvellous apparition paused an instant on the threshold, assuming the very attitude of the image, and casting over the crowd that glance of sunny coquetry which all remembered on the face of the oaken lady. She and her cavalier then disappeared.

"Ah!" murmured the crowd, drawing a deep breath, as with one vast pair of lungs.

"The world looks darker now that she has vanished," said some of the young men.

But the aged, whose recollections dated as far back as witch times, shook their heads, and hinted that our forefathers would have thought it a pious deed to burn the daughter of the oak with fire.

"If she be other than a bubble of the elements," exclaimed Copley, "I must look upon her face again."

He accordingly entered the shop; and there, in her usual corner, stood the image, gazing at him, as it might seem, with the very same expression of mirthful mischief that had been the farewell look of the apparition when, but a moment before, she turned her face towards the crowd. The carver stood beside his creation mending the beautiful fan, which by some accident was broken in her hand. But there was no longer any motion in the lifelike image, nor any real woman in the workshop, nor even the witchcraft of a sunny shadow, that might have deluded people's eyes as it flitted along the street. Captain Hunnewell, too, had vanished. His hoarse sea-breezy tones, however, were audible on the other side of a door that opened upon the water.

"Sit down in the stern sheets, my lady," said the gallant captain. "Come, bear a hand, you lubbers, and set us on board in the turning of a minute-glass."

And then was heard the stroke of oars.

"Drowne," said Copley with a smile of intelligence, "you have been a truly fortunate man. What painter or statuary ever had such a subject!

No wonder that she inspired a genius into you, and first created the artist who afterwards created her image."

Drowne looked at him with a visage that bore the traces of tears, but from which the light of imagination and sensibility, so recently illuminating it, had departed. He was again the mechanical carver that he had been known to be all his lifetime.

"I hardly understand what you mean, Mr. Copley," said he, putting his hand to his brow. "This image! Can it have been my work? Well, I have wrought it in a kind of dream; and now that I am broad awake I must set about finishing yonder figure of Admiral Vernon."

And forthwith he employed himself on the stolid countenance of one of his wooden progeny, and completed it in his own mechanical style, from which he was never known afterwards to deviate. He followed his business industriously for many years, acquired a competence, and in the latter part of his life attained to a dignified station in the church, being remembered in records and traditions as Deacon Drowne, the carver. One of his productions, an Indian chief, gilded all over, stood during the better part of a century on the cupola of the Province House, bedazzling the eyes of those who looked upward, like an angel of the sun. Another work of the good deacon's hand—a reduced likeness of his friend Captain Hunnewell, holding a telescope and quadrant—may be seen to this day, at the corner of Broad and State streets, serving in the useful capacity of sign to the shop of a nautical instrument maker. We know not how to account for the inferiority of this quaint old figure, as compared with the recorded excellence of the Oaken Lady, unless on the supposition that in every human spirit there is imagination, sensibility, creative power, genius, which, according to circumstances, may either be developed in this world, or shrouded in a mask of dulness until another state of being. To our friend Drowne there came a brief season of excitement, kindled by love. It rendered him a genius for that one occasion, but, quenched in disappointment, left him again the mechanical carver in wood, without the power even of appreciating the work that his own hands had wrought. Yet who can doubt that the very highest state to which a human spirit can attain, in its loftiest aspirations, is its truest and most natural state, and that Drowne was more consistent with himself when he wrought the admirable figure of the mysterious lady, than when he perpetrated a whole progeny of blockheads?

There was a rumor in Boston, about this period, that a young Portuguese lady of rank, on some occasion of political or domestic disquietude, had fled from her home in Fayal and put herself under the protection of Captain Hunnewell, on board of whose vessel, and at whose residence, she was sheltered until a change of affairs. This fair stranger must have been the original of Drowne's Wooden Image.

# ROGER MALVIN'S BURIAL

ONE of the few incidents of Indian warfare naturally susceptible of the moonlight of romance was that expedition undertaken for the defence of the frontiers in the year 1725, which resulted in the well-remembered "Lovell's Fight." Imagination, by casting certain circumstances judicially into the shade, may see much to admire in the heroism of a little band who gave battle to twice their number in the heart of the enemy's country. The open bravery displayed by both parties was in accordance with civilized ideas of valor; and chivalry itself might not blush to record the deeds of one or two individuals. The battle, though so fatal to those who fought, was not unfortunate in its consequences to the country; for it broke the strength of a tribe and conduced to the peace which subsisted during several ensuing years. History and tradition are unusually minute in their memorials of their affair; and the captain of a scouting party of frontier men has acquired as actual a military renown as many a victorious leader of thousands. Some of the incidents contained in the following pages will be recognized, notwithstanding the substitution of fictitious names, by such as have heard, from old men's lips, the fate of the few combatants who were in a condition to retreat after "Lovell's Fight."

.       .       .       .       .       .       .       .

The early sunbeams hovered cheerfully upon the tree-tops, beneath which two weary and wounded men had stretched their limbs the night before. Their bed of withered oak leaves was strewn upon the small level space, at the foot of a rock, situated near the summit of one of the gentle swells by which the face of the country is there diversified. The mass of granite, rearing its smooth, flat surface fifteen or twenty feet above their heads, was not unlike a gigantic gravestone, upon which the veins seemed to form an inscription in forgotten characters. On a tract of several acres around this rock, oaks and other hard-wood trees had supplied the place of the pines, which were the usual growth of the land; and a young and vigorous sapling stood close beside the travellers.

The severe wound of the elder man had probably deprived him of sleep; for, so soon as the first ray of sunshine rested on the top of the highest tree, he reared himself painfully from his recumbent posture and sat erect. The deep lines of his countenance and the scattered gray of his hair marked him as past the middle age; but his muscular frame would, but for the effect of his wound, have been as capable of sustaining fatigue as in the early vigor of life. Languor and exhaustion now sat upon his haggard features; and the despairing glance which he sent forward through the depths of the forest proved his own conviction that his pilgrimage was at an end. He next turned his eyes to the companion who reclined by his side. The youth—for he had scarcely attained the years of manhood—lay, with his head upon his arm, in the embrace of an unquiet sleep, which a thrill of pain from his wounds seemed each moment on the point of breaking. His right hand grasped a musket; and, to judge from the violent action of his features, his slumbers were bringing back a vision of the conflict of which he was one of the few survivors. A shout—deep and loud in his dreaming fancy—found its way in an imperfect murmur to his lips; and, starting even at the slight sound of his own voice, he suddenly awoke. The first act of reviving recollection was to make anxious inquiries respecting the condition of his wounded fellow-traveller. The latter shook his head.

"Reuben, my boy," said he, "this rock beneath which we sit will serve for an old hunter's gravestone. There is many and many a long mile of howling wilderness before us yet; nor would it avail me anything if the smoke of my own chimney were but on the other side of that swell of land. The Indian bullet was deadlier than I thought."

"You are weary with our three days' travel," replied the youth, "and a little longer rest will recruit you. Sit you here while I search the woods for the herbs and roots that must be our sustenance; and, having eaten, you shall lean on me, and we will turn our faces homeward. I doubt not that, with my help, you can attain to some one of the frontier garrisons."

"There is not two days' life in me, Reuben," said the other, calmly, "and I will no longer burden you with my useless body, when you can scarcely support your own. Your wounds are deep and your strength is failing fast; yet, if you hasten onward alone, you may be preserved. For me there is no hope, and I will await death here."

"If it must be so, I will remain and watch by you," said Reuben, resolutely.

"No, my son, no," rejoined his companion. "Let the wish of a dying man have weight with you; give me one grasp of your hand, and get you hence. Think you that my last moments will be eased by the thought that I leave you to die a more lingering death? I have loved you like a father, Reuben; and at a time like this I should have something of a father's authority. I charge you to be gone that I may die in peace."

"And because you have been a father to me, should I therefore leave you to perish and to lie unburied in the wilderness?" exclaimed the youth. "No; if your end be in truth approaching, I will watch by you and receive your parting words. I will dig a grave here by the rock, in which, if my weakness overcome me, we will rest together; or, if Heaven gives me strength, I will seek my way home."

"In the cities and wherever men dwell," replied the other, "they bury their dead in the earth; they hide them from the sight of the living; but here, where no step may pass perhaps for a hundred years, wherefore should I not rest beneath the open sky, covered only by the oak leaves when the autumn winds shall strew them? And for a monument, here is this gray rock, on which my dying hand shall carve the name of Roger Malvin; and the traveller in days to come will know that here sleeps a hunter and a warrior. Tarry not, then, for a folly like this, but hasten away, if not for your own sake, for hers who will else be desolate."

Malvin spoke the last few words in a faltering voice, and their effect upon his companion was strongly visible. They reminded him that there were other and less questionable duties than that of sharing the fate of a man whom his death could not benefit. Nor can it be affirmed that no selfish feeling strove to enter Reuben's heart, though the consciousness made him more earnestly resist his companion's entreaties.

"How terrible to wait the slow approach of death in this solitude!" exclaimed he. "A brave man does not shrink in the battle; and, when friends stand round the bed, even women may die composedly; but here"—

"I shall not shrink even here, Reuben Bourne," interrupted Malvin. "I am a man of no weak heart, and, if I were, there is a surer support than that of earthly friends. You are young, and life is dear to you. Your last moments will need comfort far more than mine; and when you have laid me in the earth, and are alone, and night is settling on the forest, you will feel all the bitterness of the death that may now be escaped. But I will urge no selfish motive to your generous nature. Leave me for my sake, that, having said a prayer for your safety, I may have space to settle my account undisturbed by worldly sorrows."

"And your daughter,—how shall I dare to meet her eye?" exclaimed Reuben. "She will ask the fate of her father, whose life I vowed to defend with my own. Must I tell her that he travelled three days' march with me from the field of battle and that then I left him to perish in the wilderness? Were it not better to lie down and die by your side than to return safe and say this to Dorcas?"

"Tell my daughter," said Roger Malvin, "that, though yourself sore wounded, and weak, and weary, you led my tottering footsteps many a mile, and left me only at my earnest entreaty, because I would not have your blood upon my soul. Tell her that through pain and danger you were faithful, and that, if your lifeblood could have saved me, it would have flowed to its last drop; and tell her that you will be something dearer than a father, and that my blessing is with you both, and that my dying eyes can see a long and pleasant path in which you will journey together."

As Malvin spoke he almost raised himself from the ground, and the energy of his concluding words seemed to fill the wild and lonely forest with a vision of happiness; but, when he sank exhausted upon his bed of oak leaves, the light which had kindled in Reuben's eye was quenched. He felt as if it were both sin and folly to think of happiness at such a moment. His companion watched his changing countenance, and sought with generous art to wile him to his own good.

"Perhaps I deceive myself in regard to the time I have to live," he resumed. "It may be that, with speedy assistance, I might recover of my wound. The foremost fugitives must, ere this, have carried tidings of our fatal battle to the frontiers, and parties will be out to succor those in like condition with ourselves. Should you meet one of these and guide them hither, who can tell but that I may sit by my own fireside again?"

A mournful smile strayed across the features of the dying man as he insinuated that unfounded hope,—which, however, was not without its effect on Reuben. No merely selfish motive, nor even the desolate condition of Dorcas, could have induced him to desert his companion at such a moment—but his wishes seized on the thought that Malvin's life might be preserved, and his sanguine nature heightened almost to certainty the remote possibility of procuring human aid.

"Surely there is reason, weighty reason, to hope that friends are not far distant," he said, half aloud. "There fled one coward, unwounded, in the beginning of the fight, and most probably he made good speed. Every true man on the frontier would shoulder his musket at the news; and, though no party may range so far into the woods as this, I shall perhaps encounter them in one day's march. Counsel me faithfully," he added, turning to Malvin, in distrust of his own motives. "Were your situation mine, would you desert me while life remained?"

"It is now twenty years," replied Roger Malvin,—sighing, however, as he secretly acknowledged the wide dissimilarity between the two cases,— "it is now twenty years since I escaped with one dear friend from Indian captivity near Montreal. We journeyed many days through the woods, till at length overcome with hunger and weariness, my friend lay down and besought me to leave him; for he knew that, if I remained, we both must perish; and, with but little hope of obtaining succor, I heaped a pillow of dry leaves beneath his head and hastened on."

"And did you return in time to save him?" asked Reuben, hanging on Malvin's words as if they were to be prophetic of his own success.

"I did," answered the other. "I came upon the camp of a hunting party before sunset of the same day. I guided them to the spot where my comrade was expecting death; and he is now a hale and hearty man upon his own farm, far within the frontiers, while I lie wounded here in the depths of the wilderness."

This example, powerful in affecting Reuben's decision, was aided, unconsciously to himself, by the hidden strength of many another motive. Roger Malvin perceived that the victory was nearly won.

"Now, go, my son, and Heaven prosper you!" he said. "Turn not back with your friends when you meet them, lest your wounds and weariness overcome you; but send hitherward two or three, that may be spared, to search for me; and believe me, Reuben, my heart will be lighter with every step you take towards home." Yet there was, perhaps, a change both in his countenance and voice as he spoke thus; for, after all, it was a ghastly fate to be left expiring in the wilderness.

Reuben Bourne, but half convinced that he was acting rightly, at length raised himself from the ground and prepared himself for his departure. And first, though contrary to Malvin's wishes, he collected a stock of roots and herbs, which had been their only food during the last two days. This useless supply he placed within reach of the dying man, for whom, also, he swept together a bed of dry oak leaves. Then climbing to the summit of the rock, which on one side was rough and broken, he bent the oak sapling downward, and bound his handkerchief to the topmost branch. This precaution was not unnecessary to direct any who might come in search of Malvin; for every part of the rock, except its broad, smooth front, was concealed at a little distance by the dense undergrowth of the forest. The handkerchief had been the bandage of a wound upon Reuben's arm; and, as he bound it to the tree, he vowed by the blood that stained it that he would return, either to save his companion's life or to lay his body in the grave. He then descended, and stood, with downcast eyes, to receive Roger Malvin's parting words.

The experience of the latter suggested much and minute advice respecting the youth's journey through the trackless forest. Upon this subject he spoke with calm earnestness, as if he were sending Reuben to the battle or the chase while he himself remained secure at home, and not as if the human countenance that was about to leave him were the last he would ever behold. But his firmness was shaken before he concluded.

"Carry my blessing to Dorcas, and say that my last prayer shall be for her and you. Bid her to have no hard thoughts because you left me here," —Reuben's heart smote him,—"for that your life would not have weighed with you if its sacrifice could have done me good. She will marry you after she has mourned a little while for her father; and Heaven grant you long and happy days, and may your children's children stand round your death bed! And, Reuben," added he, as the weakness of mortality made its way at last, "return, when your wounds are healed and your weariness refreshed,—return to this wild rock, and lay my bones in the grave, and say a prayer over them."

An almost superstitious regard, arising perhaps from the customs of the Indians, whose war was with the dead as well as the living, was paid by the frontier inhabitants to the rites of sepulture; and there are many instances of the sacrifice of life in the attempt to bury those who had fallen by the "sword of the wilderness." Reuben, therefore, felt the full importance of the promise which he most solemnly made to return and perform Roger Malvin's obsequies. It was remarkable that the latter, speaking his whole heart in his parting words, no longer endeavored to persuade the youth that even the speediest succor might avail to the preservation of his life. Reuben was internally convinced that he should see Malvin's living face no more. His generous nature would fain have delayed him, at whatever risk, till the dying scene were past; but the desire of existence and the hope of happiness had strengthened in his heart, and he was unable to resist them.

"It is enough," said Roger Malvin, having listened to Reuben's promise. "Go, and God speed you!"

The youth pressed his hand in silence, turned, and was departing. His slow and faltering steps, however, had borne him but a little way before Malvin's voice recalled him.

"Reuben, Reuben," said he, faintly; and Reuben returned and knelt down by the dying man.

"Raise me, and let me lean against the rock," was his last request. "My face will be turned towards home, and I shall see you a moment longer as you pass among the trees."

Reuben, having made the desired alteration in his companion's posture, again began his solitary pilgrimage. He walked more hastily at first than was consistent with his strength; for a sort of guilty feeling, which sometimes torments men in their most justifiable acts, caused him to seek concealment from Malvin's eyes; but after he had trodden far upon the rustling forest leaves he crept back, impelled by a wild and painful curiosity, and, sheltered by the earthy roots of an uptorn tree, gazed earnestly at the desolate man. The morning sun was unclouded, and the trees and shrubs imbibed the sweet air of the month of May; yet there seemed a gloom on Nature's face, as if she sympathized with mortal pain and sorrow. Roger Malvin's hands were uplifted in a fervent prayer, some of the words of which stole through the stillness of the woods and entered Reuben's heart, torturing it with an unutterable pang. They were the broken accents of a petition for his own happiness and that of Dorcas; and, as the youth listened, conscience, or something in its similitude, pleaded strongly with him to return and lie down again by the rock. He felt how hard was the doom of the kind and generous being whom he had deserted in his extremity. Death would come like the slow approach of a corpse, stealing gradually towards him through the forest, and showing its ghastly and motionless features from behind a nearer and yet a nearer tree. But such must have been Reuben's own fate had he tarried another sunset; and who shall impute blame to him if he shrink from so useless a sacrifice? As he gave a parting look, a breeze waved the little banner upon the sapling oak and reminded Reuben of his vow.

.     .     .     .     .     .     .     .     .     .

Many circumstances combined to retard the wounded traveller in his way to the frontiers. On the second day the clouds, gathering densely over the sky, precluded the possibility of regulating his course by the position of the sun; and he knew not but that every effort of his almost exhausted strength was removing him farther from the home he sought. His scanty sustenance was supplied by the berries and other spontaneous products of the forest. Herds of deer, it is true, sometimes bounded past him, and partridges frequently whirred up before his footsteps; but his ammunition had been expended in the fight, and he had no means of slaying them. His wounds, irritated by the constant exertion in which lay the only hope of life, wore away his strength and at intervals confused his reason. But, even in the wanderings of intellect, Reuben's young heart clung strongly to existence; and it was only through absolute incapacity of motion that he at last sank down beneath a tree, compelled there to await death.

In this situation he was discovered by a party who, upon the first intelligence of the fight, had been despatched to the relief of the survivors. They conveyed him to the nearest settlement, which chanced to be that of his own residence.

Dorcas, in the simplicity of the olden time, watched by the bedside of her wounded lover, and administered all those comforts that are in the sole gift of woman's heart and hand. During several days Reuben's recollection strayed drowsily among the perils and hardships through which he had passed, and he was incapable of returning definite answers to the inquiries with which many were eager to harass him. No authentic particulars of the battle had yet been circulated; nor could mothers, wives, and children tell whether their loved ones were detained by captivity or by the stronger chain of death. Dorcas nourished her apprehensions in silence till one afternoon when Reuben awoke from an unquiet sleep, and seemed to recognize her more perfectly than at any previous time. She saw that his intellect had become composed, and she could no longer restrain her filial anxiety.

"My father, Reuben?" she began; but the change in her lover's countenance made her pause.

The youth shrank as if with a bitter pain, and the blood gushed vividly into his wan and hollow cheeks. His first impulse was to cover his face; but, apparently with a desperate effort, he half raised himself and spoke vehemently, defending himself against an imaginary accusation.

"Your father was sore wounded in the battle, Dorcas; and he bade me not burden myself with him, but only to lead him to the lakeside, that he might quench his thirst and die. But I would not desert the old man in his extremity, and, though bleeding myself, I supported him; I gave him half my strength, and led him away with me. For three days we journeyed on together, and your father was sustained beyond my hopes, but, awaking at sunrise on the fourth day, I found him faint and exhausted; he was unable to proceed; his life had ebbed away fast; and"——

"He died!" exclaimed Dorcas, faintly.

Reuben felt it impossible to acknowledge that his selfish love of life had hurried him away before her father's fate was decided. He spoke not; he only bowed his head; and, between shame and exhaustion, sank back and hid his face in the pillow. Dorcas wept when her fears were thus confirmed; but the shock, as it had been long anticipated. was on that account the less violent.

"You dug a grave for my poor father in the wilderness, Reuben?" was the question by which her filial piety manifested itself.

"My hands were weak; but I did what I could," replied the youth in a smothered tone. "There stands a noble tombstone above his head; and I would to Heaven I slept as soundly as he!"

Dorcas, perceiving the wildness of his latter words, inquired no further at the time; but her heart found ease in the thought that Roger Malvin had not lacked such funeral rites as it was possible to bestow. The tale of Reuben's courage and fidelity lost nothing when she communicated it to her friends; and the poor youth, tottering from his sick chamber to breathe the sunny air, experienced from every tongue the miserable and humiliating torture of unmerited praise. All acknowledged that he might worthily demand the hand of the fair maiden to whose father he had been "faithful unto death;" and, as my tale is not of love, it shall suffice to say that in the space of a few months Reuben became the husband of Dorcas Malvin. During the marriage ceremony the bride was covered with blushes, but the bridegroom's face was pale.

There was now in the breast of Reuben Bourne an incommunicable thought—something which he was to conceal most heedfully from her whom he most loved and trusted. He regretted, deeply and bitterly, the moral cowardice that had restrained his words when he was about to disclose the truth to Dorcas; but pride, the fear of losing her affection, the dread of universal scorn, forbade him to rectify this falsehood. He felt that for leaving Roger Malvin he deserved no censure. His presence, the gratuitous sacrifice of his own life, would have added only another and a needless agony to the last moments of the dying man; but concealment had imparted to a justifiable act much of the secret effect of guilt; and Reuben, while reason told him that he had done right, experienced in no small degree the mental horrors which punish the perpetrator of undiscovered crime. By a certain association of ideas, he at times almost imagined himself a murderer. For years, also, a thought would occasionally recur, which, though he perceived all its folly and extravagance, he had not power to banish from his mind. It was a haunting and torturing fancy that his father-in-law was yet sitting at the foot of the rock, on the withered forest leaves, alive, and awaiting his pledged assistance. These mental deceptions, however, came and went, nor did he ever mistake them for realities; but in the calmest and clearest moods of his mind he was conscious that he had a deep vow unredeemed, and that an unburied corpse was calling to him out of the wilderness. Yet such was the consequence of his prevarication that he could not obey the call. It was now too late to require the assistance of Roger Malvin's friends in performing his long-deferred sepulture; and superstitious fears, of which none were more susceptible than the people of the outward settlements, forbade Reuben to go alone. Neither did he know where in the pathless and illimitable forest to seek that smooth and lettered rock at the base of which the body lay: his remembrance of every portion of his travel thence was indistinct, and the latter part had left no impression upon his mind. There was, however, a continual impulse, a voice audible only to himself, commanding him to go forth and redeem his vow; and he had a strange impression that, were he to make the trial, he would be led straight to Malvin's bones. But year after year that summons, unheard but felt, was disobeyed. His one secret thought became like a chain binding down his spirit and like a serpent gnawing into his heart; and he was transformed into a sad and downcast yet irritable man.

In the course of a few years after their marriage changes began to be visible in the external prosperity of Reuben and Dorcas. The only riches of the former had been his stout heart and strong arm; but the latter, her father's sole heiress, had made her husband master of a farm, under older cultivation, larger, and better stocked than most of the frontier establishments. Reuben Bourne, however, was a neglectful husbandman; and, while the lands of the other settlers became annually more fruitful, his deteriorated in the same proportion. The discouragements to agriculture were greatly lessened by the cessation of Indian war, during which men held the plough in one hand and the musket in the other, and were fortunate if the products of their dangerous labor were not destroyed, either in the field or in the barn, by the savage enemy. But Reuben did not profit by the altered condition of the country; nor can it be denied that his intervals of industrious attention to his affairs were but scantily rewarded with success. The irritability by which he had recently become distinguished was another cause of his declining prosperity, as it occasioned frequent quarrels in his unavoidable intercourse with the neighboring settlers. The results of these were innumerable lawsuits; for the people of New England, in the earliest stages and wildest circumstances of the country, adopted, whenever attainable, the legal mode of deciding their differences. To be brief, the world did not go well with Reuben Bourne; and, though not till many years after his marriage, he was finally a ruined man, with but one remaining expedient against the evil fate that had pursued him. He was to throw sunlight into some deep recess of the forest, and seek subsistence from the virgin bosom of the wilderness.

The only child of Reuben and Dorcas was a son, now arrived at the age of fifteen years, beautiful in youth, and giving promise of a glorious manhood. He was peculiarly qualified for, and already began to excel in, the wild accomplishments of frontier life. His foot was fleet, his aim true, his apprehension quick, his heart glad and high; and all who anticipated the return of Indian war spoke of Cyrus Bourne as a future leader in the land. The boy was loved by his father with a deep and silent strength, as if whatever was good and happy in his own nature had been transferred to his child, carrying his affections with it. Even Dorcas, though loving and beloved, was far less dear to him; for Reuben's secret thoughts and insulated emotions had gradually made him a selfish man, and he could no longer love deeply except where he saw or imagined some reflection or likeness of his own mind. In Cyrus he recognized what he had himself been in other days; and at intervals he seemed to partake of the boy's spirit, and to be revived with a fresh and happy life. Reuben was accompanied by his son in the expedition, for the purpose of selecting a tract of land and felling and burning the timber, which necessarily preceded the removal of the household gods. Two months of autumn were thus occupied, after which Reuben Bourne and his young hunter returned to spend their last winter in the settlements.

.     .     .     .     .     .     .     .     .

It was early in the month of May that the little family snapped asunder whatever tendrils of affections had clung to inanimate objects, and bade farewell to the few who, in the blight of fortune, called themselves their friends. The sadness of the parting moment had, to each of the pilgrims, its peculiar alleviations. Reuben, a moody man, and misanthropic because unhappy, strode onward with his usual stern brow and downcast eye, feeling few regrets and disdaining to acknowledge any. Dorcas, while she wept abundantly over the broken ties by which her simple and affectionate nature had bound itself to everything, felt that the inhabitants of her inmost heart moved on with her, and that all else would be supplied wherever she might go. And the boy dashed one tear-drop from his eye, and thought of the adventurous pleasures of the untrodden forest.

Oh, who, in the enthusiasm of a daydream, has not wished that he were a wanderer in a world of summer wilderness, with one fair and gentle being hanging lightly on his arm? In youth his free and exulting step would know no barrier but the rolling ocean or the snow-topped mountains; calmer manhood would choose a home where Nature had strewn a double wealth in the vale of some transparent stream; and when hoary age, after long, long years of that pure life, stole on and found him there, it would find him the father of a race, the patriarch of a people, the founder of a mighty nation yet to be. When death, like the sweet sleep which we welcome after a day of happiness, came over him, his far descendants would mourn over the venerated dust. Enveloped by tradition in mysterious attributes, the men of future generations would call him godlike; and remote posterity would see him standing, dimly glorious, far up the valley of a hundred centuries.

The tangled and gloomy forest through which the personages of my tale were wandering differed widely from the dreamer's land of fantasy; yet there was something in their way of life that Nature asserted as her own, and the gnawing cares which went with them from the world were all that now obstructed their happiness. One stout and shaggy steed, the bearer of all their wealth, did not shrink from the added weight of Dorcas; although her hardy breeding sustained her, during the latter part of each day's journey, by her husband's side. Reuben and his son, their muskets on their shoulders and their axes slung behind them, kept an unwearied pace, each watching with a hunter's eye for the game that supplied their food. When hunger bade, they halted and prepared their meal on the bank of some unpolluted forest brook, which, as they knelt down with thirsty lips to drink, murmured a sweet unwillingness, like a maiden at love's first kiss. They slept beneath a hut of branches, and awoke at peep of light refreshed for the toils of another day. Dorcas and the boy went on joyously, and even Reuben's spirit shone at intervals with an outward gladness; but inwardly there was a cold, cold sorrow, which he compared to the snowdrifts lying deep in the glens and hollows of the rivulets while the leaves were brightly green above.

Cyrus Bourne was sufficiently skilled in the travel of the woods to observe that his father did not adhere to the course they had pursued in their expedition of the preceding autumn. They were now keeping farther to the north, striking out more directly from the settlements, and into a region of which savage beasts and savage men were as yet the sole possessors. The boy sometimes hinted his opinions upon the subject, and Reuben listened attentively, and once or twice altered the direction of their march in accordance with his son's counsel; but, having so done, he seemed ill at ease. His quick and wandering glances were sent forward, apparently in search of enemies lurking behind the tree trunks; and, seeing nothing there, he would cast his eyes backwards as if in fear of some pursuer. Cyrus, perceiving that his father gradually resumed the old direction, forbore to interfere; nor, though something began to weigh upon his heart, did his adventurous nature permit him to regret the increased length and the mystery of their way.

On the afternoon of the fifth day they halted, and made their simple encampment nearly an hour before sunset. The face of the country, for the last few miles, had been diversified by swells of land resembling huge waves of a petrified sea; and in one of the corresponding hollows, a wild and romantic spot, had the family reared their hut and kindled their fire. There is something chilling, and yet heart-warming, in the thought of these three, united by strong bands of love and insulated from all that breathe beside. The dark and gloomy pines looked down upon them, and, as the wind swept through their tops, a pitying sound was heard in the forest; or did those old trees groan in fear that men were come to lay the axe to their roots at last? Reuben and his son, while Dorcas made ready their meal, proposed to wander out in search of game, of which that day's march had afforded no supply. The boy, promising not to quit the vicinity of the encampment, bounded off with a step as light and elastic as that of the deer he hoped to slay; while his father, feeling a transient happiness as he gazed after him, was about to pursue an opposite direction. Dorcas, in the meanwhile, had seated herself near their fire of fallen branches, upon the mossgrown and mouldering trunk of a tree uprooted years before. Her employment, diversified by an occasional glance at the pot, now beginning to simmer over the blaze, was the perusal of the current year's Massachusetts Almanac, which, with the exception of an old black-letter Bible, comprised all the literary wealth of the family. None pay a greater regard to arbitrary·divisions of time than those who are excluded from ·society; and Dorcas mentioned, as if the information were of importance, that it was now the twelfth of May. Her husband started.

"The twelfth of May! I should remember it well," muttered he, while many thoughts occasioned a momentary confusion in his mind. "Where am I? Whither am I wandering? Where did I leave him?"

Dorcas, too well accustomed to her husband's wayward moods to note any peculiarity of demeanor, now laid aside the almanac and addressed him in that mournful tone which the tender hearted appropriate to griefs long cold and dead.

"It was near this time of the month, eighteen years ago, that my poor father left this world for a better. He had a kind arm to hold his head and a kind voice to cheer him, Reuben, in his last moments; and the thought of the faithful care you took of him has comforted me many a time since. Oh, death would have been awful to a solitary man in a wild place like this!"

"Pray Heaven, Dorcas," said Reuben, in a broken voice,—"pray

Heaven that neither of us three dies solitary and lies unburied in this howling wilderness!" And he hastened away, leaving her to watch the fire beneath the gloomy pines.

Reuben Bourne's rapid pace gradually slackened as the pang, unintentionally inflicted by the words of Dorcas, became less acute. Many strange reflections, however, thronged upon him; and, straying onward rather like a sleep walker than a hunter, it was attributable to no care of his own that his devious course kept him in the vicinity of the encampment. His steps were imperceptibly led almost in a circle; nor did he observe that he was on the verge of a tract of land heavily timbered, but not with pine-trees. The place of the latter was here supplied by oaks and other of the harder woods; and around their roots clustered a dense and bushy under-growth, leaving, however, barren spaces between the trees, thick strewn with withered leaves. Whenever the rustling of the branches or the creaking of the trunks made a sound, as if the forest were waking from slumber, Reuben instinctively raised the musket that rested on his arm, and cast a quick, sharp glance on every side; but, convinced by a partial observation that no animal was near, he would again give himself up to his thoughts. He was musing on the strange influence that had led him away from his premeditated course, and so far into the depths of the wilderness. Unable to penetrate to the secret place of his soul where his motives lay hidden, he believed that a supernatural voice had called him onward, and that a supernatural power had obstructed his retreat. He trusted that it was Heaven's intent to afford him an opportunity of expiating his sin; he hoped that he might find the bones so long unburied; and that, having laid the earth over them, peace would throw its sunlight into the sepulchre of his heart. From these thoughts he was aroused by a rustling in the forest at some distance from the spot to which he had wandered. Perceiving the motion of some object behind a thick veil of undergrowth, he fired, with the instinct of a hunter and the aim of a practised marksman. A low moan, which told his success, and by which even animals can express their dying agony, was unheeded by Reuben Bourne. What were the recollections now breaking upon him?

The thicket into which Reuben had fired was near the summit of a swell of land, and was clustered around the base of a rock, which, in the shape and smoothness of one of its surfaces, was not unlike a gigantic gravestone. As if reflected in a mirror, its likeness was in Reuben's memory. He even recognized the veins which seemed to form an inscription in forgotten characters: everything remained the same, except that a thick covert of bushes shrouded the lower part of the rock, and would have hidden Roger Malvin had he still been sitting there. Yet in the next moment Reuben's eye was caught by another change that time had effected since he last stood where he was now standing again behind the earthy roots of the uptorn tree. The sapling to which he had bound the bloodstained symbol of his vow had increased and strengthened into an oak, far indeed from its maturity, but with no mean spread of shadowy branches. There was one singularity observable in this tree which made Reuben tremble.

The middle and lower branches were in luxuriant life, and an excess of vegetation had fringed the trunk almost to the ground; but a blight had apparently stricken the upper part of the oak, and the very topmost bough was withered, sapless, and utterly dead. Reuben remembered how the little banner had fluttered on that topmost bough, when it was green and lovely, eighteen years before. Whose guilt had blasted it?

. . . . . . . . . .

Dorcas, after the departure of the two hunters, continued her preparations for their evening repast. Her sylvan table was the moss-covered trunk of a large fallen tree, on the broadest part of which she had spread a snow-white cloth and arranged what were left of the bright pewter vessels that had been her pride in the settlements. It had a strange aspect, that one little spot of homely comfort in the desolate heart of Nature. The sunshine yet lingered upon the higher branches of the trees that grew on rising ground; but the shadows of evening had deepened into the hollow where the encampment was made, and the firelight began to redden as it gleamed up the tall trunks of the pines or hovered on the dense and obscure mass of foliage that circled round the spot. The heart of Dorcas was not sad; for she felt that it was better to journey in the wilderness with two whom she loved than to be a lonely woman in a crowd that cared not for her. As she busied herself in arranging seats of mouldering wood, covered with leaves, for Reuben and her son, her voice danced through the gloomy forest in the measure of a song that she had learned in youth. The rude melody, the production of a bard who won no name, was descriptive of a winter evening in a frontier cottage, when, secured from savage inroad by the high-piled snow-drifts, the family rejoiced by their own fireside. The whole song possessed the nameless charm peculiar to unborrowed thought, but four continually-recurring lines shone out from the rest like the blaze of the hearth whose joys they celebrated. Into them, working magic with a few simple words, the poet had instilled the very essence of domestic love and household happiness, and they were poetry and picture joined in one. As Dorcas sang, the walls of her forsaken home seemed to encircle her; she no longer saw the gloomy pines, nor heard the wind which still, as she began each verse, sent a heavy breath through the branches, and died away in a hollow moan from the burden of the song. She was aroused by the report of a gun in the vicinity of the encampment; and either the sudden sound, or her loneliness by the glowing fire, caused her to tremble violently. The next moment she laughed in the pride of a mother's heart.

"My beautiful young hunter! My boy has slain a deer!" she exclaimed, recollecting that in the direction whence the shot proceeded Cyrus had gone to the chase.

She waited a reasonable time to hear her son's light step bounding over the rustling leaves to tell of his success. But he did not immediately appear; and she sent her cheerful voice among the trees in search of him.

"Cyrus! Cyrus!"

His coming was still delayed; and she determined, as the report had apparently been very near, to seek for him in person. Her assistance, also, might be necessary in bringing home the venison which she flattered herself he had obtained. She therefore set forward, directing her steps by the long-past sound, and singing as she went, in order that the boy might be aware of her approach and run to meet her. From behind the trunk of every tree, and from every hiding-place in the thick foliage of the undergrowth, she hoped to discover the countenance of her son, laughing with the sportive mischief that is born of affection. The sun was now beneath the horizon, and the light that came down among the leaves was sufficiently dim to create many illusions in her expecting fancy. Several times she seemed indistinctly to see his face gazing out from among the leaves; and once she imagined that he stood beckoning to her at the base of a craggy rock. Keeping her eyes on this object, however, it proved to be no more than the trunk of an oak fringed to the very ground with little branches, one of which, thrust out farther than the rest, was shaken by the breeze. Making her way round the foot of the rock, she suddenly found herself close to her husband, who had approached in another direction. Leaning upon the butt of his gun, the muzzle of which rested upon the withered leaves, he was apparently absorbed in the contemplation of some object at his feet.

"How is this, Reuben? Have you slain the deer and fallen asleep over him?" exclaimed Dorcas, laughing cheerfully, on her first slight observation of his posture and appearance.

He stirred not, neither did he turn his eyes towards her; and a cold, shuddering fear, indefinite in its source and object, began to creep into her blood. She now perceived that her husband's face was ghastly pale, and his features were rigid, as if incapable of assuming any other expression than the strong despair which had hardened upon them. He gave not the slightest evidence that he was aware of her approach.

"For the love of Heaven, Reuben, speak to me!" cried Dorcas; and the strange sound of her own voice affrighted her even more than the dead silence.

Her husband started, stared into her face, drew her to the front of the rock, and pointed with his finger.

Oh, there lay the boy, asleep, but dreamless, upon the fallen forest leaves! His cheek rested upon his arm—his curled locks were thrown back from his brow—his limbs were slightly relaxed. Had a sudden weariness overcome the youthful hunter? Would his mother's voice arouse him? She knew that it was death.

"This broad rock is the gravestone of your near kindred, Dorcas," said her husband. "Your tears will fall at once over your father and your son."

She heard him not. With one wild shriek, that seemed to force its way from the sufferer's inmost soul, she sank insensible by the side of her dead boy. At that moment the withered topmost bough of the oak loosened itself in the stilly air, and fell in soft, light fragments upon the rock, upon the leaves, upon Reuben, upon his wife and child, and upon Roger Malvin's bones. Then Reuben's heart was stricken, and the tears gushed out like water from a rock. The vow that the wounded youth had made the blighted man had come to redeem. His sin was expiated,—the curse was gone from him; and in the hour when he had shed blood dearer to him than his own, a prayer, the first for years, went up to Heaven from the lips of Reuben Bourne.


# THE ARTIST OF THE BEAUTIFUL


AN elderly man, with his pretty daughter on his arm, was passing along the street, and emerged from the gloom of the cloudy evening into the light that fell across the pavement from the window of a small shop. It was a projecting window; and on the inside were suspended a variety of watches, pinchbeck, silver, and one or two of gold, all with their faces turned from the streets, as if churlishly disinclined to inform the wayfarers what o'clock it was. Seated within the shop, sidelong to the window, with his pale face bent earnestly over some delicate piece of mechanism on which was thrown the concentrated lustre of a shade lamp, appeared a young man.

"What can Owen Warland be about?" muttered old Peter Hovenden, himself a retired watchmaker, and the former master of this same young man whose occupation he was now wondering at. "What can the fellow be about? These six months past I have never come by his shop without seeing him just as steadily at work as now. It would be a flight beyond his usual foolery to seek for the perpetual motion; and yet I know enough of my old business to be certain that what he is now so busy with is no part of the machinery of a watch."

"Perhaps, father," said Annie, without showing much interest in the question, "Owen is inventing a new kind of timekeeper. I am sure he has ingenuity enough."

"Poh, child! He has not the sort of ingenuity to invent anything better than a Dutch toy," answered her father, who had formerly been put to much vexation by Owen Warland's irregular genius. "A plague on such ingenuity! All the effect that ever I knew of it was to spoil the accuracy of some of the best watches in my shop. He would turn the sun out of its orbit and derange the whole course of time, if, as I said before, his ingenuity could grasp anything bigger than a child's toy!"

"Hush, father! He hears you!" whispered Annie, pressing the old man's arm. "His ears are as delicate as his feelings; and you know how easily disturbed they are. Do let us move on."

So Peter Hovenden and his daughter Annie plodded on without further conversation, until in a by-street of the town they found themselves passing the open door of a blacksmith's shop. Within was seen the forge, now blazing up and illuminating the high and dusky roof, and now confining its lustre to a narrow precinct of the coal-strewn floor, according as the breath of the bellows was puffed forth or again inhaled into its vast leathern lungs. In the intervals of brightness it was easy to distinguish objects in remote corners of the shop and the horseshoes that hung upon the wall; in the momentary gloom the fire seemed to be glimmering amidst the vagueness of unenclosed space. Moving about in this red glare and alternate dusk was the figure of the blacksmith, well worthy to be viewed in so picturesque an aspect of light and shade, where the bright blaze struggled with the black night, as if each would have snatched his comely strength from the other. Anon he drew a white-hot bar of iron from the coals, laid it on the anvil, uplifted his arm of might, and was soon enveloped in the myriads of sparks which the strokes of his hammer scattered into the surrounding gloom.

"Now, that is a pleasant sight," said the old watchmaker. "I know what it is to work in gold; but give me the worker in iron after all is said and done. He spends his labor upon a reality. What say you, daughter Annie?"

"Pray don't speak so loud, father," whispered Annie, "Robert Danforth will hear you."

"And what if he should hear me?" said Peter Hovenden. "I say again, it is a good and a wholesome thing to depend upon main strength and reality, and to earn one's bread with the bare and brawny arm of a blacksmith. A watchmaker gets his brain puzzled by his wheels within a wheel, or loses his health or the nicety of his eyesight, as was my case, and finds himself at middle age, or a little after, past labor at his own trade and fit for nothing else, yet too poor to live at his ease. So I say once again, give me main strength for my money. And then, how it takes the nonsense out of a man! Did you ever hear of a blacksmith being such a fool as Owen Warland yonder?"

"Well said, uncle Hovenden!" shouted Robert Danforth from the forge, in a full, deep, merry voice, that made the roof reëcho. "And what says Miss Annie to that doctrine? She, I suppose, will think it a genteeler business to tinker up a lady's watch than to forge a horseshoe or make a gridiron."

Annie drew her father onward without giving him time for reply.

But we must return to Owen Warland's shop, and spend more meditation upon his history and character than either Peter Hovenden, or probably his daughter Annie, or Owen's old school-fellow, Robert Danforth, would have thought due to so slight a subject. From the time that his little fingers could grasp a penknife, Owen had been remarkable for a delicate ingenuity, which sometimes produced pretty shapes in wood, principally figures of flowers and birds, and sometimes seemed to aim at the hidden mysteries of mechanism. But it was always for purposes of grace, and never with any mockery of the useful. He did not, like the crowd of school-boy artisans, construct little windmills on the angle of a barn or

watermills across the neighboring brook. Those who discovered such peculiarity in the boy as to think it worth their while to observe him closely,
sometimes saw reason to suppose that he was attempting to imitate the
beautiful movements of Nature as exemplified in the flight of birds or the
activity of little animals. It seemed, in fact, a new development of the
love of the beautiful, such as might have made him a poet, a painter, or a
sculptor, and which was as completely refined from all utilitarian coarseness as it could have been in either of the fine arts. He looked with singular distaste at the stiff and regular processes of ordinary machinery. Being once carried to see a steam-engine, in the expectation that his intuitive comprehension of mechanical principles would be gratified, he turned
pale and grew sick, as if something monstrous and unnatural had been
presented to him. This horror was partly owing to the size and terrible
energy of the iron laborer; for the character of Owen's mind was microscopic, and tended naturally to the minute, in accordance with his diminutive frame and the marvellous smallness and delicate power of his fingers. Not that his sense of beauty was thereby diminished into a sense of
prettiness. The beautiful idea has no relation to size, and may be as perfectly developed in a space too minute for any but microscopic investigation as within the ample verge that is measured by the arc of the rainbow.
But, at all events, this characteristic minuteness in his objects and accomplishments made the world even more incapable than it might otherwise
have been of appreciating Owen Warland's genius. The boy's relatives
saw nothing better to be done—as perhaps there was not—than to bind
him apprentice to a watchmaker, hoping that his strange ingenuity
might thus be regulated and put to utilitarian purposes.

Peter Hovenden's opinion of his apprentice has already been expressed. He could make nothing of the lad. Owen's apprehension, of the
professional mysteries, it is true, was inconceivably quick; but he altogether forgot or despised the grand object of a watchmaker's business,
and cared no more for the measurement of time than if it had been
merged into eternity. So long, however, as he remained under his old master's care, Owen's lack of sturdiness made it possible, by strict injunctions
and sharp oversight, to restrain his creative eccentricity within bounds;
but when his apprenticeship was served out, and he had taken the little
shop which Peter Hovenden's failing eyesight compelled him to relinquish, then did people recognize how unfit a person was Owen Warland
to lead old blind Father Time along his daily course. One of his most rational projects was to connect a musical operation with the machinery of
his watches, so that all the harsh dissonances of life might be rendered
tuneful, and each flitting moment fall into the abyss of the past in golden
drops of harmony. If a family clock was intrusted to him for repair,—
one of those tall, ancient clocks that have grown nearly allied to human
nature by measuring out the lifetime of many generations,—he would
take upon himself to arrange a dance or funeral procession of figures
across its venerable face, representing twelve mirthful or melancholy
hours. Several freaks of this kind quite destroyed the young watchmak-

er's credit with that steady and matter-of-fact class of people who hold the opinion that time is not to be trifled with, whether considered as the medium of advancement and prosperity in this world or preparation for the next. His custom rapidly diminished—a misfortune, however, that was probably reckoned among his better accidents by Owen Warland, who was becoming more and more absorbed in a secret occupation which drew all his science and manual dexterity into itself, and likewise gave full employment to the characteristic tendencies of his genius. This pursuit had already consumed many months.

After the old watchmaker and his pretty daughter had gazed at him out of the obscurity of the street, Owen Warland was seized with a fluttering of the nerves, which made his hand tremble too violently to proceed with such delicate labor as he was now engaged upon.

"It was Annie herself!" murmured he. "I should have known it, by this throbbing of my heart, before I heard her father's voice. Ah, how it throbs! I shall scarcely be able to work again on this exquisite mechanism to-night. Annie! dearest Annie! thou shouldst give firmness to my heart and hand, and not shake them thus; for if I strive to put the very spirit of beauty into form and give it motion, it is for thy sake alone. O throbbing heart, be quiet! If my labor be thus thwarted, there will come vague and unsatisfied dreams which will leave me spiritless to-morrow."

As he was endeavoring to settle himself again to his task, the shop door opened and gave admittance to no other than the stalwart figure which Peter Hovenden had paused to admire, as seen amid the light and shadow of the blacksmith's shop. Robert Danforth had brought a little anvil of his own manufacture, and peculiarly constructed, which the young artist had recently bespoken. Owen examined the article and pronounced it fashioned according to his wish.

"Why, yes," said Robert Danforth, his strong voice filling the shop as with the sound of a bass viol, "I consider myself equal to anything in the way of my own trade; though I should have made but a poor figure at yours with such a fist as this," added he, laughing, as he laid his vast hand beside the delicate one of Owen. "But what then? I put more main strength into one blow of my sledge hammer than all that you have expended since you were a 'prentice. Is not that the truth?"

"Very probably," answered the low and slender voice of Owen. "Strength is an earthly monster. I make no pretensions to it. My force, whatever there may be of it, is altogether spiritual."

"Well, but, Owen, what are you about?" asked his old school-fellow, still in such a hearty volume of tone that it made the artist shrink, especially as the question related to a subject so sacred as the absorbing dream of his imagination. "Folks do say that you are trying to discover the perpetual motion."

"The perpetual motion? Nonsense!" replied Owen Warland, with a movement of disgust; for he was full of little petulances. "It can never be discovered. It is a dream that may delude men whose brains are mystified with matter, but not me. Besides, if such a discovery were possible, it would not be worth my while to make it only to have the secret turned to such purposes as are now effected by steam and water power. I am not ambitious to be honored with the paternity of a new kind of cotton machine."

"That would be droll enough!" cried the blacksmith, breaking out into such an uproar of laughter that Owen himself and the bell glasses on his work-board quivered in unison. "No, no, Owen! No child of yours will have iron joints and sinews. Well, I won't hinder you any more. Good night, Owen, and success, and if you need any assistance, so far as a downright blow of hammer upon anvil will answer the purpose, I'm your man."

And with another laugh the man of main strength left the shop.

"How strange it is," whispered Owen Warland to himself, leaning his head upon his hand, "that all my musings, my purposes, my passion for the beautiful, my consciousness of power to create it,—a finer, more ethereal power, of which this earthly giant can have no conception,—all, all, look so vain and idle whenever my path is crossed by Robert Danforth! He would drive me mad were I to meet him often. His hard, brute force darkens and confuses the spiritual element within me; but I, too, will be strong in my own way. I will not yield to him."

He took from beneath a glass a piece of minute machinery, which he set in the condensed light of his lamp, and, looking intently at it through a magnifying glass, proceeded to operate with a delicate instrument of steel. In an instant, however, he fell back in his chair and clasped his hands, with a look of horror on his face that made its small features as impressive as those of a giant would have been.

"Heaven! What have I done?" exclaimed he. "The vapor, the influence of that brute force,—it has bewildered me and obscured my perception. I have made the very stroke—the fatal stroke—that I have dreaded from the first. It is all over—the toil of months, the object of my life. I am ruined!"

And there he sat, in strange despair, until his lamp flickered in the socket and left the Artist of the Beautiful in darkness.

Thus it is that ideas, which grow up within the imagination and appear so lovely to it and of a value beyond whatever men call valuable, are exposed to be shattered and annihilated by contact with the practical. It is requisite for the ideal artist to possess a force of character that seems hardly compatible with its delicacy; he must keep his faith in himself while the incredulous world assails him with its utter disbelief; he must stand up against mankind and be his own sole disciple, both as respects his genius and the objects to which it is directed.

For a time Owen Warland succumbed to this severe but inevitable test. He spent a few sluggish weeks with his head so continually resting in his hands that the towns-people had scarcely an opportunity to see his countenance. When at last it was again uplifted to the light of day, a cold, dull, nameless change was perceptible upon it. In the opinion of Peter Hovenden, however, and that order of sagacious understandings. who think that life should be regulated, like clockwork, with leaden weights, the alteration was entirely for the better. Owen now, indeed, applied himself to business with dogged industry. It was marvellous to witness the obtuse gravity with which he would inspect the wheels of a great old silver watch; thereby delighting the owner, in whose fob it had been worn till he deemed it a portion of his own life, and was accordingly jealous of its treatment. In consequence of the good report thus acquired, Owen Warland was invited by the proper authorities to regulate the clock in the church steeple. He succeeded so admirably in this matter of public interest that the merchants gruffly acknowledged his merits on 'Change; the nurse whispered his praises as she gave the potion in the sick-chamber; the lover blessed him at the hour of appointed interview; and the town in general thanked Owen for the punctuality of dinner time. In a word, the heavy weight upon his spirits kept everything in order, not merely within his own system, but wheresoever the iron accents of the church clock were audible. It was a circumstance, though minute, yet characteristic of his present state, that, when employed to engrave names or initials on silver spoons, he now wrote the requisite letters in the plainest possible style, omitting a variety of fanciful flourishes that had heretofore distinguished his work in this kind.

One day, during the era of this happy transformation, old Peter Hovenden came to visit his former apprentice.

"Well, Owen," said he, "I am glad to hear such good accounts of you from all quarters, and especially from the town clock yonder, which speaks in your commendation every hour of the twenty-four. Only get rid altogether of your nonsensical trash about the beautiful, which I nor nobody else, nor yourself to boot, could ever understand,—only free yourself of that, and your success in life is as sure as daylight. Why, if you go on in this way, I should even venture to let you doctor this precious old watch of mine; though, except my daughter Annie, I have nothing else so valuable in the world."

"I should hardly dare touch it, sir," replied Owen, in a depressed tone; for he was weighed down by his old master's presence.

"In time," said the latter,—"In time, you will be capable of it."

The old watchmaker, with the freedom naturally consequent on his former authority, went on inspecting the work which Owen had in hand at the moment, together with other matters that were in progress. The artist, meanwhile, could scarcely lift his head. There was nothing so antipodal to his nature as this man's cold, unimaginative sagacity, by contact with which everything was converted into a dream except the densest matter of the physical world. Owen groaned in spirit and prayed fervently to be delivered from him.

"But what is this?" cried Peter Hovenden abruptly, taking up a dusty bell glass, beneath which appeared a mechanical something, as delicate and minute as the system of a butterfly's anatomy. "What have we here? Owen! Owen! there is witchcraft in these little chains, and wheels, and paddles. See! with one pinch of my finger and thumb I am going to deliver you from all future peril."

"For Heaven's sake," screamed Owen Warland, springing up with wonderful energy, "as you would not drive me mad, do not touch it! The slightest pressure of your finger would ruin me forever."

"Aha, young man! And is it so?" said the old watchmaker, looking at him with just enough penetration to torture Owen's soul with the bitterness of worldly criticism. "Well, take your own course; but I warn you again that in this small piece of mechanism lives your evil spirit. Shall I exorcise him?"

"You are my evil spirit," answered Owen, much excited,—"you and the hard, coarse world! The leaden thoughts and the despondency that you fling upon me are my clogs, else I should long ago have achieved the task that I was created for."

Peter Hovenden shook his head, with the mixture of contempt and indignation which mankind, of whom he was partly a representative, deem themselves entitled to feel towards all simpletons who seek other prizes than the dusty one along the highway. He then took his leave, with an uplifted finger and a sneer upon his face that haunted the artist's dreams for many a night afterwards. At the time of his old master's visit, Owen was probably on the point of taking up the relinquished task; but, by this sinister event, he was thrown back into the state whence he had been slowly emerging.

But the innate tendency of his soul had only been accumulating fresh vigor during its apparent sluggishness. As the summer advanced he almost totally relinquished his business, and permitted Father Time, so far as the old gentleman was represented by the clocks and watches under his control, to stray at random through human life, making infinite confusion among the train of bewildered hours. He wasted the sunshine, as people said, in wandering through the woods and fields and along the banks of streams. There, like a child, he found amusement in chasing butterflies or watching the motions of water insects. There was something truly mysterious in the intentness with which he contemplated these living playthings as they sported on the breeze or examined the structure of an imperial insect whom he had imprisoned. The chase of butterflies was an apt emblem of the ideal pursuit in which he had spent so many golden hours; but would the beautiful idea ever be yielded to his hand like the butterfly that symbolized it? Sweet, doubtless, were these days, and congenial to the artist's soul. They were full of bright conceptions, which gleamed through his intellectual world as the butterflies gleamed through the outward atmosphere, and were real to him, for the instant, without the toil, and perplexity, and many disappointments of attempting to make them visible to the sensual eye. Alas that the artist, whether in poetry, or whatever other material, may not content himself with the inward enjoyment of the beautiful, but must chase the flitting mystery beyond the verge of his ethereal domain, and crush its frail being in seizing it with a material grasp. Owen Warland felt the impulse to give external reality to his ideas as irresistibly as any of the poets or painters who have arrayed the world in a dimmer and fainter beauty, imperfectly copied from the richness of their visions.

The night was now his time for the slow progress of re-creating the one idea to which all his intellectual activity referred itself. Always at the approach of dusk he stole into the town, locked himself within his shop, and wrought with patient delicacy of touch for many hours. Sometimes he was startled by the rap of the watchman, who, when all the world should be asleep, had caught the gleam of lamplight through the crevices of Owen Warland's shutters. Daylight, to the morbid sensibility of his mind, seemed to have an intrusiveness that interfered with his pursuits. On cloudy and inclement days, therefore, he sat with his head upon his hands, muffling, as it were, his sensitive brain in a mist of indefinite musings; for it was a relief to escape from the sharp distinctness with which he was compelled to shape out his thoughts during his nightly toil.

From one of these fits of torpor he was aroused by the entrance of Annie Hovenden, who came into the shop with the freedom of a customer, and also with something of the familiarity of a childish friend. She had worn a hole through her silver thimble, and wanted Owen to repair it.

"But I don't know whether you will condescend to such a task," said she, laughing, "now that you are so taken up with the notion of putting spirit into machinery."

"Where did you get that idea, Annie?" said Owen, starting in surprise.

"Oh, out of my own head," answered she, "and from something that I heard you say, long ago, when you were but a boy and I a little child. But come; will you mend this poor thimble of mine?"

"Anything for your sake, Annie," said Owen Warland,—"anything, even were it to work at Robert Danforth's forge."

"And that would be a pretty sight!" retorted Annie, glancing with imperceptible slightness at the artist's small and slender frame. "Well; here is the thimble."

"But that is a strange idea of yours," said Owen, "about the spiritualization of matter."

And then the thought stole into his mind that this young girl possessed the gift to comprehend him better than all the world besides. And what a help and strength would it be to him in his lonely toil if he could gain the sympathy of the only being whom he loved! To persons whose pursuits are insulated from the common business of life—who are either in advance of mankind or apart from it—there often comes a sensation of moral cold that makes the spirit shiver as if it had reached the frozen solitudes around the pole. What the prophet, the poet, the reformer, the criminal, or any other man with human yearnings, but separated from the multitude by a peculiar lot, might feel, poor Owen felt.

"Annie," cried he, growing pale as death at the thought, "how gladly would I tell you the secret of my pursuit! You, methinks, would estimate it rightly. You, I know, would hear it with a reverence that I must not expect from the harsh, material world."

"Would I not? to be sure I would!" replied Annie Hovenden, lightly laughing. "Come; explain to me quickly what is the meaning of this little whirligig, so delicately wrought that it might be a plaything for Queen Mab. See! I will put it in motion."

"Hold!" exclaimed Owen, "hold!"

Annie had but given the slightest possible touch, with the point of a needle, to the same minute portion of complicated machinery which has been more than once mentioned, when the artist seized her by the wrist with a force that made her scream aloud. She was affrighted at the convulsion of intense rage and anguish that writhed across his features. The next instant he let his head sink upon his hands.

"Go, Annie," murmured he; "I have deceived myself, and must suffer for it. I yearned for sympathy, and thought, and fancied, and dreamed that you might give it me; but you lack the talisman, Annie, that should admit you into my secrets. That touch has undone the toil of months and the thought of a lifetime! It was not your fault, Annie; but you have ruined me!"

Poor Owen Warland! He had indeed erred, yet pardonably; for if any human spirit could have sufficiently reverenced the processes so sacred in his eyes, it must have been a woman's. Even Annie Hovenden, possibly, might not have disappointed him had she been enlightened by the deep intelligence of love.

The artist spent the ensuing winter in a way that satisfied any persons who had hitherto retained a hopeful opinion of him that he was, in truth, irrevocably doomed to unutility as regarded the world, and to an evil destiny on his own part. The decease of a relative had put him in possession of a small inheritance. Thus freed from the necessity of toil, and having lost the steadfast influence of a great purpose,—great, at least, to him,—he abandoned himself to habits from which it might have been supposed the mere delicacy of his organization would have availed to secure him. But when the ethereal portion of a man of genius is obscured, the earthly part assumes an influence the more uncontrollable, because the character is now thrown off the balance to which Providence had so nicely adjusted it, and which, in coarser natures, is adjusted by some other method. Owen Warland made proof of whatever show of bliss may be found in riot. He looked at the world through the golden medium of wine, and contemplated the visions that bubble up so gayly around the brim of the glass, and that people the air with shapes of pleasant madness, which so soon grow ghostly and forlorn. Even when this dismal and inevitable change had taken place, the young man might still have continued to quaff the cup of enchantments, though its vapor did but shroud life in gloom and fill the gloom with spectres that mocked at him. There was a certain irksomeness of spirit, which, being real, and the deepest sensation of which the artist was now conscious, was more intolerable than any fantastic miseries and horrors that the abuse of wine could summon up. In the latter case he could remember, even out of the midst of his trouble, that all was but a delusion; in the former, the heavy anguish was his actual life.

From this perilous state he was redeemed by an incident which more than one person witnessed, but of which the shrewdest could not explain or conjecture the operation on Owen Warland's mind. It was very simple. On a warm afternoon of spring, as the artist sat among his riotous companions with a glass of wine before him, a splendid butterfly flew in at the open window and fluttered about his head.

"Ah," exclaimed Owen, who had drank freely, "are you alive again, child of the sun and playmate of the summer breeze, after your dismal winter's nap? Then it is time for me to be at work!"

And, leaving his unemptied glass upon the table, he departed and was never known to sip another drop of wine.

And now, again, he resumed his wanderings in the woods and fields. It might be fancied that the bright butterfly, which had come so spirit-like into the window as Owen sat with the rude revellers, was indeed a spirit commissioned to recall him to the pure, ideal life that had so etheralized him among men. It might be fancied that he went forth to seek this spirit in its sunny haunts; for still, as in the summer time gone by, he was seen to steal gently up wherever a butterfly had alighted, and lose himself in contemplation of it. When it took flight his eyes followed the winged vision, as if its airy track would show the path to heaven. But what could be the purpose of the unseasonable toil, which was again resumed, as the watchman knew by the lines of lamplight through the crevices of Owen Warland's shutters? The towns-people had one comprehensive explanation of all these singularities. Owen Warland had gone mad! How universally efficacious—how satisfactory, too, and soothing to the injured sensibility of narrowness and dulness—is this easy method of accounting for whatever lies beyond the world's most ordinary scope! From St. Paul's days down to our poor little Artist of the Beautiful, the same talisman had been applied to the elucidation of all mysteries in the words or deeds of men who spoke or acted too wisely or too well. In Owen Warland's case the judgment of his towns-people may have been correct. Perhaps he was mad. The lack of sympathy—that contrast between himself and his neighbors which took away the restraint of example—was enough to make him so. Or possibly he had caught just so much of ethereal radiance as served to bewilder him, in an earthly sense, by its intermixture with the common daylight.

One evening, when the artist had returned from a customary ramble and had just thrown the lustre of his lamp on the delicate piece of work so often interrupted, but still taken up again, as if his fate were embodied in its mechanism, he was surprised by the entrance of old Peter Hovenden. Owen never met this man without a shrinking of the heart. Of all the world he was most terrible, by reason of a keen understanding which saw so distinctly what it did see, and disbelieved so uncompromisingly in what it could not see. On this occasion the old watchmaker had merely a gracious word or two to say.

"Owen, my lad," said he, "we must see you at my house to-morrow night."

The artist began to mutter some excuse.

"Oh, but it must be so," quoth Peter Hovenden, "for the sake of the days when you were one of the household. What, my boy! don't you know that my daughter Annie is engaged to Robert Danforth? We are making an entertainment, in our humble way, to celebrate the event."

"Ah!" said Owen.

That little monosyllable was all he uttered; its tone seemed cold and unconcerned to an ear like Peter Hovenden's; and yet there was in it the stifled outcry of the poor artist's heart, which he compressed within him like a man holding down an evil spirit. One slight outbreak, however, imperceptible to the old watchmaker, he allowed himself. Raising the instrument with which he was about to begin his work, he let it fall upon the little system of machinery that had, anew, cost him months of thought and toil. It was shattered by the stroke!

Owen Warland's story would have been no tolerable representation of the troubled life of those who strive to create the beautiful, if, amid all other thwarting influences, love had not interposed to steal the cunning from his hand. Outwardly he had been no ardent or enterprising lover; the career of his passion had confined its tumults and vicissitudes so entirely within the artist's imagination that Annie herself had scarcely more than a woman's intuitive perception of it; but, in Owen's view, it covered the whole field of his life. Forgetful of the time when she had shown herself incapable of any deep response, he had persisted in connecting all his dreams of artistical success with Annie's image; she was the visible shape in which the spiritual power that he worshipped, and on whose altar he hoped to lay a not unworthy offering, was made manifest to him. Of course he had deceived himself; there were no such attributes in Annie Hovenden as his imagination had endowed her with. She, in the aspect which she wore to his inward vision, was as much a creature of his own as the mysterious piece of mechanism would be were it ever realized. Had he become convinced of his mistake through the medium of successful love,—had he won Annie to his bosom, and there beheld her fade from angel into ordinary woman,—the disappointment might have driven him back, with concentrated energy, upon his sole remaining object. On the other hand, had he found Annie what he fancied, his lot would have been so rich in beauty that out of its mere redundancy he might have wrought the beautiful into many a worthier type than he had toiled for; but the guise in which his sorrow came to him, the sense that the angel of his life had been snatched away and given to a rude man of earth and iron, who could neither need nor appreciate her ministrations,—this was the very perversity of fate that makes human existence appear too absurd and contradictory to be the scene of one other hope or one other fear. There was nothing left for Owen Warland but to sit down like a man that had been stunned.

He went through a fit of illness. After his recovery his small and slender frame assumed an obtuser garniture of flesh than it had ever before worn. His thin cheeks became round; his delicate little hand, so spiritually fashioned to achieve fairy task-work, grew plumper than the hand of a thriving infant. His aspect had a childishness such as might have induced a stranger to pat him on the head—pausing, however, in the act, to wonder what manner of child was here. It was as if the spirit had gone out of him, leaving the body to flourish in a sort of vegetable existence. Not that Owen Warland was idiotic. He could talk, and not irrationally. Somewhat of a babbler, indeed, did people begin to think him; for he was apt to discourse at wearisome length of marvels of mechanism that he had read about in books, but which he had learned to consider as absolutely fabulous. Among them he enumerated the Man of Brass, constructed by Albertus Magnus, and the Brazen Head of Friar Bacon; and, coming down to later times, the automata of a little coach and horses, which it was pretended had been manufactured for the Dauphin of France; together with an insect that buzzed about the ear like a living fly, and yet was but a contrivance of minute steel springs. There was a story, too, of a duck that waddled, and quacked, and ate; though, had any honest citizen purchased it for dinner, he would have found himself cheated with the mere mechanical apparition of a duck.

"But all these accounts," said Owen Warland, "I am now satisfied are mere impositions."

Then, in a mysterious way, he would confess that he once thought differently. In his idle and dreamy days he had considered it possible, in a certain sense, to spiritualize machinery, and to combine with the new species of life and motion thus produced a beauty that should attain to the ideal which Nature has proposed to herself in all her creatures, but has never taken pains to realize. He seemed, however, to retain no very distinct perception either of the process of achieving this object or of the design itself.

"I have thrown it all aside now," he would say. "It was a dream such as young men are always mystifying themselves with. Now that I have acquired a little common sense, it makes me laugh to think of it."

Poor, poor and fallen Owen Warland! These were the symptoms that he had ceased to be an inhabitant of the better sphere that lies unseen around us. He had lost his faith in the invisible, and now prided himself, as such unfortunates invariably do, in the wisdom which rejected much that even his eye could see, and trusted confidently in nothing but what his hand could touch. This is the calamity of men whose spiritual part dies out of them and leaves the grosser understanding to assimilate them more and more to the things of which alone it can take cognizance; but in Owen Warland the spirit was not dead nor passed away; it only slept.

How it awoke again is not recorded. Perhaps the torpid slumber was broken by a convulsive pain. Perhaps, as in a former instance, the butterfly came and hovered about his head and reinspired him,—as indeed this creature of the sunshine had always a mysterious mission for the artist,—reinspired him with the former purpose of his life. Whether it were pain or happiness that thrilled through his veins, his first impulse was to thank Heaven for rendering him again the being of thought, imagination, and keenest sensibility that he had long ceased to be.

"Now for my task," said he. "Never did I feel such strength for it as now."

Yet, strong as he felt himself, he was incited to toil the more diligently by an anxiety lest death should surprise him in the midst of his labors. This anxiety, perhaps, is common to all men who set their hearts upon anything so high, in their own view of it, that life becomes of importance only as conditional to its accomplishment. So long as we love life for itself, we seldom dread the losing it. When we desire life for the attainment of an object, we recognize the frailty of its texture. But, side by side with this sense of insecurity, there is a vital faith in our invulnerability to the shaft of death while engaged in any task that seems assigned by Providence as our proper thing to do, and which the world would have cause to mourn for should we leave it unaccomplished. Can the philosopher, big with the inspiration of an idea that is to reform mankind, believe that he is to be beckoned from this sensible existence at the very instant when he is mustering his breath to speak the word of light? Should he perish so, the weary ages may pass away—the world's, whose life sand may fall, drop by drop—before another intellect is prepared to develop the truth that might have been uttered then. But history affords many an example where the most precious spirit, at any particular epoch manifested in human shape, has gone hence untimely, without space allowed him, so far as mortal judgment could discern, to perform his mission on the earth. The prophet dies, and the man of torpid heart and sluggish brain lives on. The poet leaves his song half sung, or finishes it, beyond the scope of mortal ears, in a celestial choir. The painter—as Allston did—leaves half his conception on the canvas to sadden us with its imperfect beauty, and goes to picture forth the whole, if it be no irreverence to say so, in the hues of heaven. But rather such incomplete designs of this life will be perfected nowhere. This so frequent abortion of man's dearest projects must be taken as a proof that the deeds of earth, however etherealized by piety or genius, are without value, except as exercises and manifestations of the spirit. In heaven, all ordinary thought is higher and more melodious than Milton's song. Then, would he add another verse to any strain that he had left unfinished here?

But to return to Owen Warland. It was his fortune, good or ill, to achieve the purpose of his life. Pass we over a long space of intense thought, yearning effort, minute toil, and wasting anxiety, succeeded by an instant of solitary triumph: let all this be imagined; and then behold the artist, on a winter evening, seeking admittance to Robert Danforth's fireside circle. There he found the man of iron, with his massive substance thoroughly warmed and attempered by domestic influences. And there was Annie, too, now transformed into a matron, with much of her husband's plain and sturdy nature, but imbued, as Owen Warland still believed, with a finer grace, that might enable her to be the interpreter between strength and beauty. It happened, likewise, that old Peter Hovenden was a guest this evening at his daughter's fireside, and it was his well-remembered expression of keen, cold criticism that first encountered the artist's glance.

"My old friend Owen!" cried Robert Danforth, starting up, and compressing the artist's delicate fingers within a hand that was accustomed to gripe bars of iron. "This is kind and neighborly to come to us at last. I was afraid your perpetual motion had bewitched you out of the remembrance of old times."

"We are glad to see you," said Annie, while a blush reddened her matronly cheek. "It was not like a friend to stay from us so long."

"Well, Owen," inquired the old watchmaker, as his first greeting, "how comes on the beautiful? Have you created it at last?"

The artist did not immediately reply, being startled by the apparition of a young child of strength that was tumbling about on the carpet,—a little personage who had come mysteriously out of the infinite, but with something so sturdy and real in his composition that he seemed moulded out of the densest substance which earth could supply. This hopeful infant crawled towards the new-comer, and setting himself on end, as Robert Danforth expressed the posture, stared at Owen with a look of such sagacious observation that the mother could not help exchanging a proud glance with her husband. But the artist was disturbed by the child's look, as imagining a resemblance between it and Peter Hovenden's habitual expression. He could have fancied that the old watchmaker was compressed into this baby shape, and looking out of those baby eyes, and repeating, as he now did, the malicious question:—

"The beautiful, Owen! How comes on the beautiful? Have you succeeded in creating the beautiful?"

"I have succeeded," replied the artist, with a momentary light of triumph in his eyes and a smile of sunshine, yet steeped in such depth of thought that it was almost sadness. "Yes, my friends, it is the truth. I have succeeded."

"Indeed!" cried Annie, a look of maiden mirthfulness peeping out of her face again. "And is it lawful, now, to inquire what the secret is?"

"Surely; it is to disclose it that I have come," answered Owen Warland. "You shall know, and see, and touch, and possess the secret! For, Annie,—if by that name I may still address the friend of my boyish years,—Annie, it is for your bridal gift that I have wrought this spiritualized mechanism, this harmony of motion, this mystery of beauty. It comes late, indeed; but it is as we go onward in life, when objects begin to lose their freshness of hue and our souls their delicacy of perception, that the spirit of beauty is most needed. If,—forgive me, Annie,—if you know how to value this gift, it can never come too late."

He produced, as he spoke, what seemed a jewel box. It was carved richly out of ebony by his own hand, and inlaid with a fanciful tracery of
pearl, representing a boy in pursuit of a butterfly, which, elsewhere, had
become a winged spirit, and was flying heavenward; while the boy, or
youth, had found such efficacy in his strong desire that he ascended from
earth to cloud, and from cloud to celestial atmosphere, to win the beautiful. This case of ebony the artist opened, and bade Annie place her fingers on its edge. She did so, but almost screamed as a butterfly fluttered
forth, and, alighting on her finger's tip, sat waving the ample magnificence of its purple and gold-speckled wings, as if in prelude to a flight. It
is impossible to express by words the glory, the splendor, the delicate gorgeousness which were softened into the beauty of this object. Nature's
ideal butterfly was here realized in all its perfection; not in the pattern
of such faded insects as flit among earthly flowers, but of those which
hover across the meads of paradise for child-angels and the spirits of departed infants to disport themselves with. The rich down was visible upon
its wings; the lustre of its eyes seemed instinct with spirit. The firelight
glimmered around this wonder—the candles gleamed upon it; but it glistened apparently by its own radiance, and illuminated the finger and outstretched hand on which it rested with a white gleam like that of precious
stones. In its perfect beauty, the consideration of size was entirely lost.
Had its wings overreached the firmament, the mind could not have been
more filled or satisfied.

"Beautiful! beautiful!" exclaimed Annie. "Is it alive? Is it alive?"

"Alive? To be sure it is," answered her husband. "Do you suppose any
mortal has skill enough to make a butterfly, or would put himself to the
trouble of making one, when any child may catch a score of them in a
summer's afternoon? Alive? Certainly! But this pretty box is undoubtedly of our friend Owen's manufacture; and really it does him credit."

At this moment the butterfly waved its wings anew, with a motion so
absolutely lifelike that Annie was startled, and even awestricken; for, in
spite of her husband's opinion, she could not satisfy herself whether it was
indeed a living creature or a piece of wondrous mechanism.

"Is it alive?" she repeated, more earnestly than before.

"Judge for yourself," said Owen Warland, who stood gazing in her face
with fixed attention.

The butterfly now flung itself upon the air, fluttered round Annie's
head, and soared into a distant region of the parlor, still making itself
perceptible to sight by the starry gleam in which the motion of its wings
enveloped it. The infant on the floor followed its course with his sagacious little eyes. After flying about the room, it returned in a spiral curve
and settled again on Annie's finger.

"But is it alive?" exclaimed she again; and the finger on which the
gorgeous mystery had alighted was so tremulous that the butterfly was
forced to balance himself with his wings. "Tell me if it be alive, or whether you created it."

"Wherefore ask who created it, so it be beautiful?" replied Owen Warland. "Alive? Yes, Annie; it may well be said to possess life, for it has absorbed my own being into itself; and in the secret of that butterfly, and in its beauty,—which is not merely outward, but deep as its whole system,—is represented the intellect, the imagination, the sensibility, the soul of an Artist of the Beautiful! Yes; I created it. But"—and here his countenance somewhat changed—"this butterfly is not now to me what it was when I beheld it afar off in the daydreams of my youth."

"Be it what it may, it is a pretty plaything," said the blacksmith, grinning with childlike delight. "I wonder whether it would condescend to alight on such a great clumsy finger as mine? Hold it hither, Annie."

By the artist's direction, Annie touched her finger's tip to that of her husband; and, after a momentary delay, the butterfly fluttered from one to the other. It preluded a second flight by a similar, yet not precisely the same, waving of wings as in the first experiment; then, ascending from the blacksmith's stalwart finger, it rose in a gradually enlarging curve to the ceiling, made one wide sweep around the room, and returned with an undulating movement to the point whence it had started.

"Well, that does beat all nature!" cried Robert Danforth, bestowing the heartiest praise that he could find expression for; and, indeed, had he paused there, a man of finer words and nicer perception could not easily have said more. "That goes beyond me, I confess. But what then? There is more real use in one downright blow of my sledge hammer than in the whole five years' labor that our friend Owen has wasted on this butterfly."

Here the child clapped his hands and made a great babble of indistinct utterance, apparently demanding that the butterfly should be given him for a plaything.

Owen Warland, meanwhile, glanced sidelong at Annie, to discover whether she sympathized in her husband's estimate of the comparative value of the beautiful and the practical. There was, amid all her kindness towards himself, amid all the wonder and admiration with which she contemplated the marvellous work of his hands and incarnation of his idea, a secret scorn—too secret, perhaps, for her own consciousness, and perceptible only to such intuitive discernment as that of the artist. But Owen, in the latter stages of his pursuit, had risen out of the region in which such a discovery might have been torture. He knew that the world, and Annie as the representative of the world, whatever praise might be bestowed, could never say the fitting word nor feel the fitting sentiment which should be the perfect recompense of an artist who, symbolizing a lofty moral by a material trifle,—converting what was earthly to spiritual gold,—had won the beautiful into his handiwork. Not at this latest moment was he to learn that the reward of all high performance must be sought within itself, or sought in vain. There was, however, a view of the matter which Annie and her husband, and even Peter Hovenden, might fully have understood, and which would have satisfied them that the toil of years had here been worthily bestowed. Owen Warland might have told them that this butterfly, this plaything, this bridal gift of a poor watchmaker to a blacksmith's wife, was, in truth, a gem of art that a monarch would have purchased with honors and abundant wealth, and have treasured it among the jewels of his kingdom as the most unique and wondrous of them all. But the artist smiled and kept the secret to himself.

"Father," said Annie, thinking that a word of praise from the old watchmaker might gratify his former apprentice, "do come and admire this pretty butterfly."

"Let us see," said Peter Hovenden, rising from his chair, with a sneer upon his face that always made people doubt, as he himself did, in everything but a material existence. "Here is my finger for it to alight upon. I shall understand it better when once I have touched it."

But, to the increased astonishment of Annie, when the tip of her father's finger was pressed against that of her husband, on which the butterfly still rested, the insect drooped its wings and seemed on the point of falling to the floor. Even the bright spots of gold upon its wings and body, unless her eyes deceived her, grew dim, and the glowing purple took a dusky hue, and the starry lustre that gleamed around the blacksmith's hand became faint and vanished.

"It is dying! it is dying!" cried Annie, in alarm.

"It has been delicately wrought," said the artist, calmly. "As I told you, it has imbibed a spiritual essence—call it magnetism, or what you will. In an atmosphere of doubt and mockery its exquisite susceptibility suffers torture, as does the soul of him who instilled his own life into it. It has already lost its beauty; in a few moments more its mechanism would be irreparably injured."

"Take away your hand, father!" entreated Annie, turning pale. "Here is my child; let it rest on his innocent hand. There, perhaps, its life will revive and its colors grow brighter than ever."

Her father, with an acrid smile, withdrew his finger. The butterfly then appeared to recover the power of voluntary motion, while its hues assumed much of their original lustre, and the gleam of starlight, which was its most ethereal attribute, again formed a halo round about it. At first, when transferred from Robert Danforth's hand to the small finger of the child, this radiance grew so powerful that it positively threw the little fellow's shadow back against the wall. He, meanwhile, extended his plump hand as he had seen his father and mother do, and watched the waving of the insect's wings with infantine delight. Nevertheless, there was a certain odd expression of sagacity that made Owen Warland feel as if here were old Pete Hovenden, partially, and but partially, redeemed from his hard scepticism into childish faith.

"How wise the little monkey looks!" whispered Robert Danforth to his wife.

"I never saw such a look on a child's face," answered Annie, admiring her own infant, and with good reason, far more than the artistic butterfly. "The darling knows more of the mystery than we do."

As if the butterfly, like the artist, were conscious of something not entirely congenial in the child's nature, it alternately sparkled and grew dim. At length it arose from the small hand of the infant with an airy motion that seemed to bear it upward without an effort, as if the ethereal instincts with which its master's spirit had endowed it impelled this fair vision involuntarily to a higher sphere. Had there been no obstruction, it might have soared into the sky and grown immortal. But its lustre gleamed upon the ceiling; the exquisite texture of its wings brushed against that earthly medium; and a sparkle or two, as of stardust, floated downward and lay glimmering on the carpet. Then the butterfly came fluttering down, and, instead of returning to the infant, was apparently attracted towards the artist's hand.

"Not so! not so!" murmured Owen Warland, as if his handiwork could have understood him. "Thou has gone forth out of thy master's heart. There is no return for thee."

With a wavering movement, and emitting a tremulous radiance, the butterfly struggled, as it were, towards the infant, and was about to alight upon his finger; but while it still hovered in the air, the little child of strength, with his grandsire's sharp and shrewd expression in his face, made a snatch at the marvellous insect and compressed it in his hand. Annie screamed. Old Peter Hovenden burst into a cold and scornful laugh. The blacksmith, by main force, unclosed the infant's hand, and found within the palm a small heap of glittering fragments, whence the mystery of beauty had fled forever. And as for Owen Warland, he looked placidly at what seemed the ruin of his life's labor, and which was yet no ruin. He had caught a far other butterfly than this. When the artist rose high enough to achieve the beautiful, the symbol by which he made it perceptible to mortal senses became of little value in his eyes while his spirit possessed itself in the enjoyment of the reality.

# FROM THE SNOW-IMAGE

## AND

# OTHER TWICE-TOLD TALES

# THE SNOW-IMAGE:

## A Childish Miracle

One afternoon of a cold winter's day, when the sun shone forth with chilly brightness, after a long storm, two children asked leave of their mother to run out and play in the new-fallen snow. The elder child was a little girl, whom, because she was of a tender and modest disposition, and was thought to be very beautiful, her parents, and other people who were familiar with her, used to call Violet. But her brother was known by the style and title of Peony, on account of the ruddiness of his broad and round little phiz, which made everybody think of sunshine and great scarlet flowers. The father of these two children, a certain Mr. Lindsey, it is important to say, was an excellent but exceedingly matter-of-fact sort of man, a dealer in hardware, and was sturdily accustomed to take what is called the common-sense view of all matters that came under his consideration. With a heart about as tender as other people's, he had a head as hard and impenetrable, and therefore, perhaps, as empty, as one of the iron pots which it was a part of his business to sell. The mother's character, on the other hand, had a strain of poetry in it, a trait of unworldly beauty,—a delicate and dewy flower, as it were, that had survived out of her imaginative youth, and still kept itself alive amid the dusty realities of matrimony and motherhood.

So, Violet and Peony, as I began with saying, besought their mother to let them run out and play in the new snow; for, though it had looked so dreary and dismal, drifting downward out of the gray sky, it had a very cheerful aspect, now that the sun was shining on it. The children dwelt in a city, and had no wider play-place than a little garden before the house, divided by a white fence from the street, and with a pear-tree and two or three plum-trees overshadowing it, and some rose-bushes just in front of the parlor-windows. The trees and shrubs, however, were now leafless, and their twigs were enveloped in the light snow, which thus made a kind of wintry foliage, with here and there a pendent icicle for the fruit.

"Yes, Violet,—yes, my little Peony," said their kind mother, "you may go out and play in the new snow."

Accordingly, the good lady bundled up her darlings in woollen jackets and wadded sacks, and put comforters round their necks, and a pair of striped gaiters on each little pair of legs, and worsted mittens on their hands, and gave them a kiss apiece, by way of a spell to keep away Jack Frost. Forth sallied the two children, with a hop-skip-and-jump, that carried them at once into the very heart of a huge snow-drift, whence Violet emerged like a snow-bunting, while little Peony floundered out with his round face in full bloom. Then what a merry time had they! To look at them, frolicking in the wintry garden, you would have thought that the dark and pitiless storm had been sent for no other purpose but to provide a new plaything for Violet and Peony; and that they themselves had been created, as the snow-birds were, to take delight only in the tempest, and in the white mantle which it spread over the earth.

At last, when they had frosted one another all over with handfuls of snow, Violet, after laughing heartily at little Peony's figure, was struck with a new idea.

"You look exactly like a snow-image, Peony," said she, "if your cheeks were not so red. And that puts me in mind! Let us make an image out of snow,—an image of a little girl,—and it shall be our sister, and shall run about and play with us all winter long. Won't it be nice?"

"Oh yes!" cried Peony, as plainly as he could speak, for he was but a little boy. "That will be nice! And mamma shall see it!"

"Yes," answered Violet; "mamma shall see the new little girl. But she must not make her come into the warm parlor; for, you know, our little snow-sister will not love the warmth."

And forthwith the children began this great business of making a snow-image that should run about; while their mother, who was sitting at the window and overheard some of their talk, could not help smiling at the gravity with which they set about it. They really seemed to imagine that there would be no difficulty whatever in creating a live little girl out of the snow. And, to say the truth, if miracles are ever to be wrought, it will be by putting our hands to the work in precisely such a simple and un-doubting frame of mind as that in which Violet and Peony now under-took to perform one, without so much as knowing that it was a miracle. So thought the mother; and so thought, likewise, that the new snow, just fallen from heaven, would be excellent material to make new beings of, if it were not so very cold. She gazed at the children a moment longer, de-lighting to watch their little figures,—the girl, tall for her age, graceful and agile, and so delicately colored that she looked like a cheerful thought more than a physical reality; while Peony expanded in breadth rather than height, and rolled along on his short and sturdy legs as substantial as an elephant, though not quite so big. Then the mother resumed her work. What it was I forget; but she was either trimming a silken bonnet for Violet, or darning a pair of stockings for little Peony's short legs. Again, however, and again, and yet other agains, she could not help turn-ing her head to the window to see how the children got on with their snow-image.

Indeed, it was an exceedingly pleasant sight, those bright little souls at their task! Moreover, it was really wonderful to observe how know-ingly and skilfully they managed the matter. Violet assumed the chief direction, and told Peony what to do, while, with her own delicate fingers, she shaped out all the nicer parts of the snow-figure. It seemed, in fact, not so much to be made by the children, as to grow up under their hands, while they were playing and prattling about it. Their mother was quite surprised at this; and the longer she looked, the more and more surprised she grew.

"What remarkable children mine are!" thought she, smiling with a mother's pride; and, smiling at herself, too, for being so proud of them. "What other children could have made anything so like a little girl's figure out of snow at the first trial? Well; but now I must finish Peony's new frock, for his grandfather is coming to-morrow, and I want the little fellow to look handsome."

So she took up the frock, and was soon as busily at work again with her needle as the two children with their snow-image. But still, as the needle travelled hither and thither through the seams of the dress, the mother made her toil light and happy by listening to the airy voices of Violet and Peony. They kept talking to one another all the time, their tongues being quite as active as their feet and hands. Except at intervals, she could not distinctly hear what was said, but had merely a sweet impression that they were in a most loving mood, and were enjoying themselves highly, and that the business of making the snow-image went prosperously on. Now and then, however, when Violet and Peony happened to raise their voices, the words were as audible as if they had been spoken in the very parlor where the mother sat. Oh how delightfully those words echoed in her heart, even though they meant nothing so very wise or wonderful, after all!

But you must know a mother listens with her heart much more than with her ears; and thus she is often delighted with the trills of celestial music, when other people can hear nothing of the kind.

"Peony, Peony!" cried Violet to her brother, who had gone to another part of the garden, "bring me some of that fresh snow, Peony, from the very farthest corner, where we have not been trampling. I want it to shape our little snow-sister's bosom with. You know that part must be quite pure, just as it came out of the sky!"

"Here it is, Violet!" answered Peony, in his bluff tone,—but a very sweet tone, too,—as he came floundering through the half-trodden drifts. "Here is the snow for her little bosom. O Violet, how beau-ti-ful she begins to look!"

"Yes," said Violet, thoughtfully and quietly; "our snow-sister does look very lovely. I did not quite know, Peony, that we could make such a sweet little girl as this."

The mother, as she listened, thought how fit and delightful an incident it would be, if fairies, or still better, if angel-children were to come from paradise, and play invisibly with her own darlings, and help them to make their snow-image, giving it the features of celestial babyhood! Violet and Peony would not be aware of their immortal playmates,—only they would see that the image grew very beautiful while they worked at it, and would think that they themselves had done it all.

"My little girl and boy deserve such playmates, if mortal children ever did!" said the mother to herself; and then she smiled again at her own motherly pride.

Nevertheless, the idea seized upon her imagination; and, ever and anon, she took a glimpse out of the window, half dreaming that she might see the golden-haired children of paradise sporting with her own golden-haired Violet and bright-cheeked Peony.

Now, for a few moments, there was a busy and earnest, but indistinct hum of the two children's voices, as Violet and Peony wrought together with one happy consent. Violet still seemed to be the guiding spirit, while Peony acted rather as a laborer, and brought her the snow from far and near. And yet the little urchin evidently had a proper understanding of the matter, too!

"Peony, Peony!" cried Violet; for her brother was again at the other side of the garden. "Bring me those light wreaths of snow that have rested on the lower branches of the pear-tree. You can clamber on the snow-drift, Peony, and reach them easily. I must have them to make some ringlets for our snow-sister's head!"

"Here they are, Violet!" answered the little boy. "Take care you do not break them. Well done! Well done! How pretty!"

"Does she not look sweetly?" said Violet, with a very satisfied tone; "and now we must have some little shining bits of ice, to make the brightness of her eyes. She is not finished yet. Mamma will see how very beautiful she is; but papa will say, 'Tush! nonsense!—come in out of the cold!'"

"Let us call mamma to look out," said Peony; and then he shouted lustily, "Mamma! mamma!! mamma!!! Look out, and see what a nice 'ittle girl we are making!"

The mother put down her work for an instant, and looked out of the window. But it so happened that the sun—for this was one of the shortest days of the whole year—had sunken so nearly to the edge of the world that his setting shine came obliquely into the lady's eyes. So she was dazzled, you must understand, and could not very distinctly observe what was in the garden. Still, however, through all that bright, blinding dazzle of the sun and the new snow, she beheld a small white figure in the garden, that seemed to have a wonderful deal of human likeness about it. And she saw Violet and Peony,—indeed, she looked more at them than at the image,—she saw the two children still at work; Peony bringing fresh snow, and Violet applying it to the figure as scientifically as a sculptor adds clay to his model. Indistinctly as she discerned the snow-child, the mother thought to herself that never before was there a snow-figure so cunningly made, nor ever such a dear little girl and boy to make it.

"They do everything better than other children," said she, very complacently. "No wonder they make better snow-images!"

She sat down again to her work, and made as much haste with it as possible; because twilight would soon come, and Peony's frock was not yet finished, and grandfather was expected, by railroad, pretty early in the morning. Faster and faster, therefore, went her flying fingers. The children, likewise, kept busily at work in the garden, and still the mother listened, whenever she could catch a word. She was amused to observe how their little imaginations had got mixed up with what they were doing, and carried away by it. They seemed positively to think that the snow-child would run about and play with them.

"What a nice playmate she will be for us, all winter long!" said Violet. "I hope papa will not be afraid of her giving us a cold! Sha'n't you love her dearly, Peony?"

"Oh yes!" cried Peony. "And I will hug her, and she shall sit down close by me, and drink some of my warm milk!"

"Oh no, Peony!" answered Violet, with grave wisdom. "That will not do at all. Warm milk will not be wholesome for our little snow-sister. Little snow people, like her, eat nothing but icicles. No, no, Peony; we must not give her anything warm to drink!"

There was a minute or two of silence; for Peony, whose short legs were never weary, had gone on a pilgrimage again to the other side of the garden. All of a sudden, Violet cried out, loudly and joyfully,——

"Look here, Peony! Come quickly! A light has been shining on her cheek out of that rose-colored cloud! and the color does not go away! Is not that beautiful!"

"Yes; it is beau-ti-ful," answered Peony, pronouncing the three syllables with deliberate accuracy. "O Violet, only look at her hair! It is all like gold!"

"Oh certainly," said Violet, with tranquillity, as if it were very much a matter of course. "That color, you know, comes from the golden clouds, that we see up there in the sky. She is almost finished now. But her lips must be made very red,—redder than her cheeks. Perhaps, Peony, it will make them red if we both kiss them!"

Accordingly, the mother heard two smart little smacks, as if both her children were kissing the snow-image on its frozen mouth. But, as this did not seem to make the lips quite red enough, Violet next proposed that the snow-child should be invited to kiss Peony's scarlet cheek.

"Come, 'ittle snow-sister, kiss me!" cried Peony.

"There! she has kissed you," added Violet, "and now her lips are very red. And she blushed a little, too!"

"Oh, what a cold kiss!" cried Peony.

Just then, there came a breeze of the pure west-wind, sweeping through the garden and rattling the parlor-windows. It sounded so wintry cold, that the mother was about to tap on the window-pane with her thimbled finger, to summon the two children in, when they both cried out to her with one voice. The tone was not a tone of surprise, although they were evidently a good deal excited; it appeared rather as· if they were very much rejoiced at some event that had now happened, but which they had been looking for, and had reckoned upon all along.

"Mamma! mamma! We have finished our little snow-sister, and she is running about the garden with us!"

"What imaginative little beings my children are!" thought the mother, putting the last few stitches into Peony's frock. "And it is strange, too, that they make me almost as much a child as they themselves are! I can hardly help believing, now, that the snow-image has really come to life!"

"Dear mamma!" cried Violet, "pray look out and see what a sweet playmate we have!"

The mother, being thus entreated, could no longer delay to look forth from the window. The sun was now gone out of the sky, leaving, however, a rich inheritance of his brightness among those purple and golden clouds which make the sunsets of winter so magnificent. But there was not the slightest gleam or dazzle, either on the window or on the snow; so that the good lady could look all over the garden, and see everything and everybody in it. And what do you think she saw there? Violet and Peony, of course, her own two darling children. Ah, but whom or what did she see besides? Why, if you will believe me, there was a small figure of a girl, dressed all in white, with rose-tinged cheeks and ringlets of golden hue, playing about the garden with the two children! A stranger though she was, the child seemed to be on as familiar terms with Violet and Peony, and they with her, as if all the three had been playmates during the whole of their little lives. The mother thought to herself that it must certainly be the daughter of one of the neighbors, and that, seeing Violet and Peony in the garden, the child had run across the street to play with them. So this kind lady went to the door, intending to invite the little runaway into her comfortable parlor; for, now that the sunshine was withdrawn, the atmosphere, out of doors, was already growing very cold.

But, after opening the house-door, she stood an instant on the threshold, hesitating whether she ought to ask the child to come in, or whether she should even speak to her. Indeed, she almost doubted whether it were a real child after all, or only a light wreath of the new-fallen snow, blown hither and thither about the garden by the intensely cold west-wind. There was certainly something very singular in the aspect of the little stranger. Among all the children of the neighborhood, the lady could remember no such face, with its pure white, and delicate rose-color, and the golden ringlets tossing about the forehead and cheeks. And as for her dress, which was entirely of white, and fluttering in the breeze, it was such as no reasonable woman would put upon a little girl, when sending her out to play, in the depth of winter. It made this kind and careful mother shiver only to look at those small feet, with nothing in the world on them, except a very thin pair of white slippers. Nevertheless, airily as she was clad, the child seemed to feel not the slightest inconvenience from the cold, but danced so lightly over the snow that the tips of her toes left hardly a print in its surface; while Violet could but just keep pace with her, and Peony's short legs compelled him to lag behind.

Once, in the course of their play, the strange child placed herself between Violet and Peony, and taking a hand of each, skipped merrily forward, and they along with her. Almost immediately, however, Peony pulled away his little fist, and began to rub it as if the fingers were tingling with cold; while Violet also released herself, though with less abruptness, gravely remarking that it was better not to take hold of hands. The white-robed damsel said not a word, but danced about, just as merrily as before. If Violet and Peony did not choose to play with her, she could make just as good a playmate of the brisk and cold west-wind, which kept blowing her all about the garden, and took such liberties with her, that they seemed to have been friends for a long time. All this while, the mother stood on the threshold, wondering how a little girl could look so much like a flying snow-drift, or how a snow-drift could look so very like a little girl.

She called Violet, and whispered to her.

"Violet my darling, what is this child's name?" asked she. "Does she live near us?"

"Why, dearest mamma," answered Violet, laughing to think that her mother did not comprehend so very plain an affair, "this is our little snow-sister whom we have just been making!"

"Yes, dear mamma," cried Peony, running to his mother, and looking up simply into her face. "This is our snow-image! Is it not a nice 'ittle child?"

At this instant a flock of snow-birds came flitting through the air. As was very natural, they avoided Violet and Peony. But—and this looked strange—they flew at once to the white-robed child, fluttered eagerly about her head, alighted on her shoulders, and seemed to claim her as an old acquaintance. She, on her part, was evidently as glad to see these little birds, old Winter's grandchildren, as they were to see her, and welcomed them by holding out both her hands. Hereupon, they each and all tried to alight on her two palms and ten small fingers and thumbs, crowding one another off, with an immense fluttering of their tiny wings. One dear little bird nestled tenderly in her bosom; another put its bill to her lips. They were as joyous, all the while, and seemed as much in their element, as you may have seen them when sporting with a snow-storm.

Violet and Peony stood laughing at this pretty sight; for they enjoyed the merry time which their new playmate was having with these small-winged visitants, almost as much as if they themselves took part in it.

"Violet," said her mother, greatly perplexed, "tell me the truth, without any jest. Who is this little girl?"

"My darling mamma," answered Violet, looking seriously into her mother's face, and apparently surprised that she should need any further explanation, "I have told you truly who she is. It is our little snow-image, which Peony and I have been making. Peony will tell you so, as well as I."

"Yes, mamma," asseverated Peony, with much gravity in his crimson little phiz; "this is 'ittle snow-child. Is not she a nice one? But, mamma, her hand is, oh, so very cold!"

While mamma still hesitated what to think and what to do, the street-gate was thrown open, and the father of Violet and Peony appeared, wrapped in a pilot-cloth sack, with a fur cap drawn down over his ears, and the thickest of gloves upon his hands. Mr. Lindsey was a middle-aged man, with a weary and yet a happy look in his wind-flushed and frost-pinched face, as if he had been busy all the day long, and was glad to get back to his quiet home. His eyes brightened at the sight of his wife and children, although he could not help uttering a word or two of surprise, at finding the whole family in the open air, on so bleak a day, and after sunset too. He soon perceived the little white stranger sporting to and fro in the garden, like a dancing snow-wreath, and the flock of snow-birds fluttering about her head.

"Pray, what little girl may that be?" inquired this very sensible man. "Surely her mother must be crazy to let her go out in such bitter weather as it has been to-day, with only that flimsy white gown and those thin slippers!"

"My dear husband," said his wife, "I know no more about the little thing than you do. Some neighbor's child, I suppose. Our Violet and Peony," she added, laughing at herself for repeating so absurd a story, "insist that she is nothing but a snow-image, which they have been busy about in the garden, almost all the afternoon."

As she said this, the mother glanced her eyes toward the spot where the children's snow-image had been made. What was her surprise, on perceiving that there was not the slightest trace of so much labor!—no image at all!—no piled up heap of snow!—nothing whatever, save the prints of little footsteps around a vacant space!

"This is very strange!" said she.

"What is strange, dear mother?" asked Violet. "Dear father, do not you see how it is? This is our snow-image, which Peony and I have made, because we wanted another playmate. Did not we, Peony?"

"Yes, papa," said crimson Peony. "This be our 'ittle snow-sister. Is she not beau-ti-ful? But she gave me such a cold kiss!"

"Poh, nonsense, children!" cried their good, honest father, who, as we have already intimated, had an exceedingly common-sensible way of looking at matters. "Do not tell me of making live figures out of snow. Come, wife; this little stranger must not stay out in the bleak air a moment longer. We will bring her into the parlor; and you shall give her a supper of warm bread and milk, and make her as comfortable as you can. Meanwhile, I will inquire among the neighbors; or, if necessary, send the city-crier about the streets, to give notice of a lost child."

So saying, this honest and very kind-hearted man was going toward the little white damsel, with the best intentions in the world. But Violet and Peony, each seizing their father by the hand, earnestly besought him not to make her come in.

"Dear father," cried Violet, putting herself before him, "it is true what I have been telling you! This is our little snow-girl, and she cannot live any longer than while she breathes the cold west-wind. Do not make her come into the hot room!"

"Yes, father," shouted Peony, stamping his little foot, so mightily was he in earnest, "this be nothing but our 'ittle snow-child! She will not love the hot fire!"

"Nonsense, children, nonsense, nonsense!" cried the father, half vexed, half laughing at what he considered their foolish obstinacy. "Run into the house, this moment! It is too late to play any longer, now. I must take care of this little girl immediately, or she will catch her death-a-cold!"

"Husband! dear husband!" said his wife, in a low voice,—for she had been looking narrowly at the snow-child, and was more perplexed than ever,—"there is something very singular in all this. You will think me foolish,—but—but—may it not be that some invisible angel has been attracted by the simplicity and good faith with which our children set about their undertaking? May he not have spent an hour of his immortality in playing with those dear little souls? and so the result is what we call a miracle. No, no! Do not laugh at me; I see what a foolish thought it is!"

"My dear wife," replied the husband, laughing heartily, "you are as much a child as Violet and Peony."

And in one sense so she was, for all through life she had kept her heart full of childlike simplicity and faith, which was as pure and clear as crystal; and, looking at all matters through this transparent medium, she sometimes saw truths so profound that other people laughed at them as nonsense and absurdity.

But now kind Mr. Lindsey had entered the garden, breaking away from his two children, who still sent their shrill voices after him, beseeching him to let the snow-child stay and enjoy herself in the cold west-wind. As he approached, the snow-birds took to flight. The little white damsel, also, fled backward, shaking her head, as if to say, "Pray, do not touch me!" and roguishly, as it appeared, leading him through the deepest of the snow. Once, the good man stumbled, and floundered down upon his face, so that, gathering himself up again, with the snow sticking to his rough pilot-cloth sack, he looked as white and wintry as a snow-image of the largest size. Some of the neighbors, meanwhile, seeing him from their windows, wondered what could possess poor Mr. Lindsey to be running about his garden in pursuit of a snow-drift, which the west-wind was driving hither and thither! At length, after a vast deal of trouble, he chased the little stranger into a corner, where she could not possibly escape him. His wife had been looking on, and, it being nearly twilight, was wonder-struck to observe how the snow-child gleamed and sparkled, and how she seemed to shed a glow all round about her; and when driven into the corner, she positively glistened like a star! It was a frosty kind of brightness, too, like that of an icicle in the moonlight. The wife thought it strange that good Mr. Lindsey should see nothing remarkable in the snow-child's appearance.

"Come, you odd little thing!" cried the honest man, seizing her by the hand, "I have caught you at last, and will make you comfortable in spite of yourself. We will put a nice warm pair of worsted stockings on your frozen little feet, and you shall have a good thick shawl to wrap yourself in. Your poor white nose, I am afraid, is actually frost-bitten. But we will make it all right. Come along in."

And so, with a most benevolent smile on his sagacious visage, all purple as it was with the cold, this very well-meaning gentleman took the snow-child by the hand and led her towards the house. She followed him, droopingly and reluctant; for all the glow and sparkle was gone out of her figure; and whereas just before she had resembled a bright, frosty, star-gemmed evening, with a crimson gleam on the cold horizon, she now looked as dull and languid as a thaw. As kind Mr. Lindsey led her up the steps of the door, Violet and Peony looked into his face,—their eyes full of tears, which froze before they could run down their cheeks,—and again entreated him not to bring their snow-image into the house.

"Not bring her in!" exclaimed the kind-hearted man. "Why, you are crazy, my little Violet!—quite crazy, my small Peony! She is so cold, already, that her hand has almost frozen mine, in spite of my thick gloves. Would you have her freeze to death?"

His wife, as he came up the steps, had been taking another long, earnest, almost awe-stricken gaze at the little white stranger. She hardly knew whether it was a dream or no; but she could not help fancying that she saw the delicate print of Violet's fingers on the child's neck. It looked just as if, while Violet was shaping out the image, she had given it a gentle pat with her hand, and had neglected to smooth the impression quite away.

"After all, husband," said the mother, recurring to her idea that the angels would be as much delighted to play with Violet and Peony as she herself was,—"after all, she does look strangely like a snow-image! I do believe she is made of snow!"

A puff of the west-wind blew against the snow-child, and again she sparkled like a star.

"Snow!" repeated good Mr. Lindsey, drawing the reluctant guest over his hospitable threshold. "No wonder she looks like snow. She is half frozen, poor little thing! But a good fire will put everything to rights!"

Without further talk, and always with the same best intentions, this highly benevolent and common-sensible individual led the little white damsel—drooping, drooping, drooping, more and more—out of the frosty air, and into his comfortable parlor. A Heidenberg stove, filled to the brim with intensely burning anthracite, was sending a bright gleam through the isinglass of its iron door, and causing the vase of water on its top to fume and bubble with excitement. A warm, sultry smell was diffused throughout the room. A thermometer on the wall farthest from the stove stood at eighty degrees. The parlor was hung with red curtains, and covered with a red carpet, and looked just as warm as it felt. The difference betwixt the atmosphere here and the cold, wintry twilight out of doors, was like stepping at once from Nova Zembla to the hottest part of India, or from the North Pole into an oven. Oh, this was a fine place for the little white stranger!

The common-sensible man placed the snow-child on the hearth-rug, right in front of the hissing and fuming stove.

"Now she will be comfortable!" cried Mr. Lindsey, rubbing his hands and looking about him, with the pleasantest smile you ever saw. "Make yourself at home, my child."

Sad, sad and drooping, looked the little white maiden, as she stood on the hearth-rug, with the hot blast of the stove striking through her like a pestilence. Once, she threw a glance wistfully toward the windows, and caught a glimpse, through its red curtains, of the snow-covered roofs, and the stars glimmering frostily, and all the delicious intensity of the cold night. The bleak wind rattled the window-panes, as if it were summoning her to come forth. But there stood the snow-child, drooping, before the hot stove!

But the common-sensible man saw nothing amiss.

"Come wife," said he, "let her have a pair of thick stockings and a woollen shawl or blanket directly; and tell Dora to give her some warm supper as soon as the milk boils. You, Violet and Peony, amuse your little friend. She is out of spirits, you see, at finding herself in a strange place. For my part, I will go around among the neighbors, and find out where she belongs."

The mother, meanwhile, had gone in search of the shawl and stockings; for her own view of the matter, however subtle and delicate, had given way, as it always did, to the stubborn materialism of her husband. Without heeding the remonstrances of his two children, who still kept murmuring that their little snow-sister did not love the warmth, good Mr. Lindsey took his departure, shutting the parlor-door carefully behind him. Turning up the collar of his sack over his ears, he emerged from the house, and had barely reached the street-gate, when he was recalled by the screams of Violet and Peony, and the rapping of a thimbled finger against the parlor window.

"Husband! husband!" cried his wife, showing her horror-stricken face through the window-panes. "There is no need of going for the child's parents!"

"We told you so, father!" screamed Violet and Peony, as he re-entered the parlor. "You would bring her in; and now our poor—dear—beau-ti-ful little snow-sister is thawed!"

And their own sweet little faces were already dissolved in tears; so that their father, seeing what strange things occasionally happen in this every-day world, felt not a little anxious lest his children might be going to thaw too! In the utmost perplexity, he demanded an explanation of his wife. She could only reply, that, being summoned to the parlor by the cries of Violet and Peony, she found no trace of the little white maiden, unless it were the remains of a heap of snow, which, while she was gazing at it, melted quite away upon the hearth-rug.

"And there you see all that is left of it!" added she, pointing to a pool of water in front of the stove.

"Yes, father," said Violet looking reproachfully at him, through her tears, "there is all that is left of our dear little snow-sister!"

"Naughty father!" cried Peony, stamping his foot, and—I shudder to say—shaking his little fist at the common-sensible man. "We told you how it would be! What for did you bring her in?"

And the Heidenberg stove, through the isinglass of its door, seemed to glare at good Mr. Lindsey, like a red-eyed demon, triumphing in the mischief which it had done!

This, you will observe, was one of those rare cases, which yet will occasionally happen, where common-sense finds itself at fault. The remarkable story of the snow-image, though to that sagacious class of people to whom good Mr. Lindsey belongs it may seem but a childish affair, is, nevertheless, capable of being moralized in various methods, greatly for their edification. One of its lessons, for instance, might be, that it behooves men, and especially men of benevolence, to consider well what they are about, and, before acting on their philanthropic purposes, to be quite sure that they comprehend the nature and all the relations of the business in hand. What has been established as an element of good to one being may prove absolute mischief to another; even as the warmth of the parlor was proper enough for children of flesh and blood, like Violet and Peony,—though by no means very wholesome, even for them,—but involved nothing short of annihilation to the unfortunate snow-image.

But, after all, there is no teaching anything to wise men of good Mr. Lindsey's stamp. They know everything,—oh, to be sure!—everything that has been, and everything that is, and everything that, by any future possibility, can be. And, should some phenomenon of nature or providence transcend their system, they will not recognize it, even if it come to pass under their very noses.

"Wife," said Mr. Lindsey, after a fit of silence, "see what a quantity of snow the children have brought in on their feet! It has made quite a puddle here before the stove. Pray tell Dora to bring some towels and sop it up!"

## THE GREAT STONE FACE

ONE afternoon, when the sun was going down, a mother and her little boy sat at the door of their cottage, talking about the Great Stone Face. They had but to lift their eyes, and there it was plainly to be seen, though miles away, with the sunshine brightening all its features.

And what was the Great Stone Face?

Embosomed amongst a family of lofty mountains, there was a valley so spacious that it contained many thousand inhabitants. Some of these good people dwelt in log-huts, with the black forest all around them, on the steep and difficult hill-sides. Others had their homes in comfortable farm-houses, and cultivated the rich soil on the gentle slopes or level surfaces of the valley. Others, again, were congregated into populous villages, where some wild, highland rivulet, tumbling down from its birthplace in the upper mountain region, had been caught and tamed by human cunning, and compelled to turn the machinery of cotton-factories. The inhabitants of this valley, in short, were numerous, and of many modes of life. But all of them, grown people and children, had a kind of familiarity with the Great Stone Face, although some possessed the gift of distinguishing this grand natural phenomenon more perfectly than many of their neighbors.

The Great Stone Face, then, was a work of Nature in her mood of majestic playfulness, formed on the perpendicular side of a mountain by some immense rocks, which had been thrown together in such a position as, when viewed at a proper distance, precisely to resemble the features of the human countenance. It seemed as if an enormous giant, or a Titan, had sculptured his own likeness on the precipice. There was the broad arch of the forehead, a hundred feet in height; the nose, with its long bridge; and the vast lips, which, if they could have spoken, would have rolled their thunder accents from one end of the valley to the other. True it is, that if the spectator approached too near, he lost the outline of the gigantic visage, and could discern only a heap of ponderous and gigantic rocks, piled in chaotic ruin one upon another. Retracing his steps, however, the wondrous features would again be seen; and the farther he withdrew from them, the more like a human face, with all its original divinity intact, did they appear; until, as it grew dim in the distance, with the clouds and glorified vapor of the mountains clustering about it, the Great Stone Face seemed positively to be alive.

It was a happy lot for children to grow up to manhood or womanhood with the Great Stone Face before their eyes, for all the features were noble, and the expression was at once grand and sweet, as if it were the glow of a vast, warm heart, that embraced all mankind in its affections, and had room for more. It was an education only to look at it. According to the belief of many people, the valley owed much of its fertility to this benign aspect that was continually beaming over it, illuminating the clouds, and infusing its tenderness into the sunshine.

As we began with saying, a mother and her little boy sat at their cottage-door, gazing at the Great Stone Face, and talking about it. The child's name was Ernest.

"Mother," said he, while the Titanic visage smiled on him, "I wish that it could speak, for it looks so very kindly that its voice must needs be pleasant. If I were to see a man with such a face, I should love him dearly."

"If an old prophecy should come to pass," answered his mother, "we may see a man, some time or other, with exactly such a face as that."

"What prophecy do you mean, dear mother?" eagerly inquired Ernest. "Pray tell me about it!"

So his mother told him a story that her own mother had told to her, when she herself was younger than little Ernest; a story, not of things that were past, but of what was yet to come; a story, nevertheless, so very old, that even the Indians, who formerly inhabited this valley, had heard it from their forefathers, to whom, as they affirmed, it had been murmured by the mountain streams, and whispered by the wind among the tree-tops. The purport was, that, at some future day, a child should be born hereabouts, who was destined to become the greatest and noblest personage of his time, and whose countenance, in manhood, should bear an exact resemblance to the Great Stone Face. Not a few old-fashioned people, and young ones likewise, in the ardor of their hopes, still cherished an enduring faith in this old prophecy. But others, who had seen more of the world, had watched and waited till they were weary, and had beheld no man with such a face, nor any man that proved to be much greater or nobler than his neighbors, concluded it to be nothing but an idle tale. At all events, the great man of the prophecy had not yet appeared.

"O mother, dear mother!" cried Ernest, clapping his hands above his head, "I do hope that I shall live to see him!"

His mother was an affectionate and thoughtful woman, and felt that it was wisest not to discourage the generous hopes of her little boy. So she only said to him, "Perhaps you may."

And Ernest never forgot the story that his mother told him. It was always in his mind, whenever he looked upon the Great Stone Face. He spent his childhood in the log-cottage where he was born, and was dutiful to his mother, and helpful to her in many things, assisting her much with his little hands, and more with his loving heart. In this manner, from a happy yet often pensive child, he grew up to be a mild, quiet, unobtrusive boy, and sun-browned with labor in the fields, but with more intelligence brightening his aspect than is seen in many lads who have been taught at famous schools. Yet Ernest had had no teacher, save only that the Great Stone Face became one to him. When the toil of the day was over, he would gaze at it for hours, until he began to imagine that those vast features recognized him, and gave him a smile of kindness and encouragement, responsive to his own look of veneration. We must not take upon us to affirm that this was a mistake, although the Face may have looked no more kindly at Ernest than at all the world besides. But the secret was that the boy's tender and confiding simplicity discerned what other people could not see; and thus the love, which was meant for all, became his peculiar portion.

About this time there went a rumor throughout the valley, that the great man, foretold from ages long ago, who was to bear a resemblance to the Great Stone Face, had appeared at last. It seems that, many years before, a young man had migrated from the valley and settled at a distant seaport, where, after getting together a little money, he had set up as a shopkeeper. His name—but I could never learn whether it was his real one, or a nickname that had grown out of his habits and success in life—was Gathergold. Being shrewd and active, and endowed by Providence with that inscrutable faculty which develops itself in what the world calls luck, he became an exceedingly rich merchant, and owner of a whole fleet of bulky-bottomed ships. All the countries of the globe appeared to join hands for the mere purpose of adding heap after heap to the mountainous accumulation of this one man's wealth. The cold regions of the north, almost within the gloom and shadow of the Arctic Circle, sent him their tribute in the shape of furs; hot Africa sifted for him the golden sands of her rivers, and gathered up the ivory tusks of her great elephants out of the forests; the East came bringing him the rich shawls, and spices, and teas, and the effulgence of diamonds, and the gleaming purity of large pearls. The ocean, not to be behindhand with the earth, yielded up her mighty whales, that Mr. Gathergold might sell their oil, and make a profit of it. Be the original commodity what it might, it was gold within his grasp. It might be said of him, as of Midas in the fable, that whatever he touched with his finger immediately glistened, and grew yellow, and was changed at once into sterling metal, or, which suited him still better, into piles of coin. And, when Mr. Gathergold had become so very rich that it would have taken him a hundred years only to count his wealth, he bethought himself of his native valley, and resolved to go back thither, and end his days where he was born. With this purpose in view, he sent a skilful architect to build him such a palace as should be fit for a man of his vast wealth to live in.

As I have said above, it had already been rumored in the valley that Mr. Gathergold had turned out to be the prophetic personage so long and vainly looked for, and that his visage was the perfect and undeniable similitude of the Great Stone Face. People were the more ready to believe that this must needs be the fact, when they beheld the splendid edifice that rose, as if by enchantment, on the site of his father's old weatherbeaten farm-house. The exterior was of marble, so dazzlingly white that it seemed as though the whole structure might melt away in the sunshine, like those humbler ones which Mr. Gathergold, in his young play-days, before his fingers were gifted with the touch of transmutation, had been accustomed to build of snow. It had a richly ornamented portico, supported by tall pillars, beneath which was a lofty door, studded with silver knobs, and made of a kind of variegated wood that had been brought from beyond the sea. The windows, from the floor to the ceiling of each stately apartment, were composed, respectively, of but one enormous pane of glass, so transparently pure that it was said to be a finer medium than even the vacant atmosphere. Hardly anybody had been permitted to see the interior of this palace; but it was reported, and with good semblance of truth, to be far more gorgeous than the outside, insomuch that whatever was iron or brass in other houses was silver or gold in this; and Mr. Gathergold's bedchamber, especially, made such a glittering appearance that no ordinary man would have been able to close his eyes there. But, on the other hand, Mr. Gathergold was now so inured to wealth, that perhaps he could not have closed his eyes unless where the gleam of it was certain to find its way beneath his eyelids.

In due time, the mansion was finished; next came the upholsterers, with magnificent furniture; then, a whole troop of black and white servants, the harbingers of Mr. Gathergold, who, in his own majestic person, was expected to arrive at sunset. Our friend Ernest, meanwhile, had been deeply stirred by the idea that the great man, the noble man, the man of prophecy, after so many ages of delay, was at length to be made manifest to his native valley. He knew, boy as he was, that there were a thousand ways in which Mr. Gathergold, with his vast wealth, might transform himself into an angel of beneficence, and assume a control over human affairs as wide and benignant as the smile of the Great Stone Face. Full of faith and hope, Ernest doubted not that what the people said was true, and that now he was to behold the living likeness of those wondrous features on the mountain-side. While the boy was still gazing up the valley, and fancying, as he always did, that the Great Stone Face returned his gaze and looked kindly at him, the rumbling of wheels was heard, approaching swiftly along the winding road.

"Here he comes!" cried a group of people who were assembled to witness the arrival. "Here comes the great Mr. Gathergold!"

A carriage, drawn by four horses, dashed round the turn of the road. Within it, thrust partly out of the window, appeared the physiognomy of the old man, with a skin as yellow as if his own Midas-hand had transmuted it. He had a low forehead, small, sharp eyes, puckered about with innumerable wrinkles, and very thin lips, which he made still thinner by pressing them forcibly together.

"The very image of the Great Stone Face!" shouted the people. "Sure enough, the old prophecy is true; and here we have the great man come, at last!"

And, what greatly perplexed Ernest, they seemed actually to believe that here was the likeness which they spoke of. By the roadside there chanced to be an old beggar-woman and two little beggar-children, stragglers from some far-off region, who, as the carriage rolled onward, held out their hands and lifted up their doleful voices, most piteously beseeching charity. A yellow claw—the very same that had clawed together so much wealth—poked itself out of the coach-window, and dropt some copper coins upon the ground; so that, though the great man's name seems to have been Gathergold, he might just as suitably have been nicknamed Scattercopper. Still, nevertheless, with an earnest shout, and evidently with as much good faith as ever, the people bellowed,—

"He is the very image of the Great Stone Face!"

But Ernest turned sadly from the wrinkled shrewdness of that sordid visage, and gazed up the valley, where, amid a gathering mist, gilded by the last sunbeams, he could still distinguish those glorious features which had impressed themselves into his soul. Their aspect cheered him. What did the benign lips seem to say?

"He will come! Fear not, Ernest; the man will come!"

The years went on, and Ernest ceased to be a boy. He had grown to be a young man now. He attracted little notice from the other inhabitants of the valley; for they saw nothing remarkable in his way of life, save that, when the labor of the day was over, he still loved to go apart and gaze and meditate upon the Great Stone Face. According to their idea of the matter, it was a folly, indeed, but pardonable, inasmuch as Ernest was industrious, kind, and neighborly, and neglected no duty for the sake of indulging this idle habit. They knew not that the Great Stone Face had become a teacher to him, and that the sentiment which was expressed in it would enlarge the young man's heart, and fill it with wider and deeper sympathies than other hearts. They knew not that thence would come a better wisdom than could be learned from books, and a better life than could be moulded on the defaced example of other human lives. Neither did Ernest know that the thoughts and affections which came to him so naturally, in the fields and at the fireside, and wherever he communed with himself, were of a higher tone than those which all men shared with him. A simple soul,—simple as when his mother first taught him the old prophecy,—he beheld the marvellous features beaming adown the valley, and still wondered that their human counterpart was so long in making his appearance.

By this time poor Mr. Gathergold was dead and buried; and the oddest part of the matter was, that his wealth, which was the body and spirit of his existence, had disappeared before his death, leaving nothing of him but a living skeleton, covered over with a wrinkled yellow skin. Since the melting away of his gold, it had been very generally conceded that there was no such striking resemblance, after all, betwixt the ignoble features of the ruined merchant and that majestic face upon the mountain-side. So the people ceased to honor him during his lifetime, and quietly consigned him to forgetfulness after his decease. Once in a while, it is true, his memory was brought up in connection with the magnificent palace which he had built, and which had long ago been turned into a hotel for the accommodation of strangers, multitudes of whom came, every summer, to visit that famous natural curiosity, the Great Stone Face. Thus, Mr. Gathergold being discredited and thrown into the shade, the man of prophecy was yet to come.

It so happened that a native-born son of the valley, many years before, had enlisted as a soldier, and, after a great deal of hard fighting, had now become an illustrious commander. Whatever he may be called in history, he was known in camps and on the battle-field under the nickname of Old Blood-and-Thunder. This war-worn veteran being now infirm with age and wounds, and weary of the turmoil of a military life, and of the roll of the drum and the clangor of the trumpet, that had so long been ringing in his ears, had lately signified a purpose of returning to his native valley, hoping to find repose where he remembered to have left it. The inhabitants, his old neighbors and their grown-up children, were resolved to welcome the renowned warrior with a salute of cannon and a public dinner; and all the more enthusiastically, it being affirmed that now, at last, the likeness of the Great Stone Face had actually appeared. An aid-de-camp of Old Blood-and-Thunder, travelling through the valley, was said to have been struck with the resemblance. Moreover the schoolmates and early acquaintances of the general were ready to testify, on oath, that, to the best of their recollection, the aforesaid general had been exceedingly like the majestic image, even when a boy, only the idea had never occurred to them at that period. Great, therefore, was the excitement throughout the valley; and many people, who had never once thought of glancing at the Great Stone Face for years before, now spent their time in gazing at it, for the sake of knowing exactly how General Blood-and-Thunder looked.

On the day of the great festival, Ernest, with all the other people of the valley, left their work, and proceeded to the spot where the sylvan banquet was prepared. As he approached, the loud voice of the Rev. Dr. Battleblast was heard, beseeching a blessing on the good things set before them, and on the distinguished friend of peace in whose honor they were assembled. The tables were arranged in a cleared space of the woods, shut in by the surrounding trees, except where a vista opened eastward, and afforded a distant view of the Great Stone Face. Over the general's chair, which was a relic from the home of Washington, there was an arch of verdant boughs, with the laurel profusely intermixed, and surmounted by his country's banner, beneath which he had won his victories. Our friend Ernest raised himself on his tiptoes, in hopes to get a glimpse of the celebrated guest; but there was a mighty crowd about the tables anxious to hear the toasts and speeches, and to catch any word that might fall from the general in reply; and a volunteer company, doing duty as a guard, pricked ruthlessly with their bayonets at any particularly quiet person among the throng. So Ernest, being of an unobtrusive character, was thrust quite into the background, where he could see no more of Old Blood-and-Thunder's physiognomy than if it had been still blazing on the battle-field. To console himself, he turned towards the Great Stone Face, which, like a faithful and long-remembered friend, looked back and smiled upon him through the vista of the forest. Meantime, however, he could overhear the remarks of various individuals, who were comparing the features of the hero with the face on the distant mountain-side.

" 'Tis the same face, to a hair!" cried one man, cutting a caper for joy.

"Wonderfully like, that's a fact!" responded another.

"Like! why, I call it Old Blood-and-Thunder himself, in a monstrous looking-glass!" cried a third. "And why not? He's the greatest man of this or any other age, beyond a doubt."

And then all three of the speakers gave a great shout, which communicated electricity to the crowd, and called forth a roar from a thousand voices, that went reverberating for miles among the mountains, until you might have supposed that the Great Stone Face had poured its thunder-breath into the cry. All these comments, and this vast enthusiasm, served the more to interest our friend; nor did he think of questioning that now, at length, the mountain-visage had found its human counterpart. It is true, Ernest had imagined that this long-looked-for personage would appear in the character of a man of peace, uttering wisdom, and doing good, and making people happy. But, taking an habitual breadth of view, with all his simplicity, he contended that Providence should choose its own method of blessing mankind, and could conceive that this great end might be effected even by a warrior and a bloody sword, should inscrutable wisdom see fit to order matters so.

"The general! the general!" was now the cry. "Hush! silence! Old Blood-and-Thunder's going to make a speech."

Even so; for, the cloth being removed, the general's health had been drunk, amid shouts of applause, and he now stood upon his feet to thank the company. Ernest saw him. There he was, over the shoulders of the crowd, from the two glittering epaulets and embroidered collar upward, beneath the arch of green boughs with intertwined laurel, and the banner drooping as if to shade his brow! And there, too, visible in the same glance, through the vista of the forest, appeared the Great Stone Face! And was there, indeed, such a resemblance as the crowd had testified? Alas, Ernest could not recognize it! He beheld a war-worn and weather-beaten countenance, full of energy, and expressive of an iron will; but the gentle wisdom, the deep, broad, tender sympathies, were altogether wanting in Old Blood-and-Thunder's visage; and even if the Great Stone Face had assumed his look of stern command, the milder traits would still have tempered it.

"This is not the man of prophecy," sighed Ernest to himself, as he made his way out of the throng. "And must the world wait longer yet?"

The mists had congregated about the distant mountain-side, and there were seen the grand and awful features of the Great Stone Face, awful but benignant, as if a mighty angel were sitting among the hills, and enrobing himself in a cloud-vesture of gold and purple. As he looked, Ernest could hardly believe but that a smile beamed over the whole visage, with a radiance still brightening, although without motion of the lips. It was probably the effect of the western sunshine, melting through the thinly diffused vapors that had swept between him and the object that he gazed at. But—as it always did—the aspect of his marvellous friend made Ernest as hopeful as if he had never hoped in vain.

"Fear not, Ernest," said his heart, even as if the Great Face were whispering him,—fear not, Ernest; he will come."

More years sped swiftly and tranquilly away. Ernest still dwelt in his native valley, and was now a man of middle age. By imperceptible degrees, he had become known among the people. Now, as heretofore, he labored for his bread, and was the same simple-hearted man that he had always been. But he had thought and felt so much, he had given so many of the best hours of his life to unworldly hopes for some great good to mankind, that it seemed as though he had been talking with the angels, and had imbibed a portion of their wisdom unawares. It was visible in the calm and well-considered beneficence of his daily life, the quiet stream of which had made a wide green margin all along its course. Not a day passed by, that the world was not the better because this man, humble as he was, had lived. He never stepped aside from his own path, yet would always reach a blessing to his neighbor. Almost involuntarily, too, he had become a preacher. The pure and high simplicity of his thought, which, as one of its manifestations, took shape in the good deeds that dropped silently from his hand, flowed also forth in speech. He uttered truths that wrought upon and moulded the lives of those who heard him. His auditors, it may be, never suspected that Ernest, their own neighbor and familiar friend, was more than an ordinary man; least of all did Ernest himself suspect it; but, inevitably as the murmur of a rivulet, came thoughts out of his mouth that no other human lips had spoken.

When the people's minds had had a little time to cool, they were ready enough to acknowledge their mistake in imagining a similarity between General Blood-and-Thunder's truculent physiognomy and the benign visage on the mountain-side. But now, again, there were reports and many paragraphs in the newspapers, affirming that the likeness of the Great Stone Face had appeared upon the broad shoulders of a certain eminent statesman. He, like Mr. Gathergold and Old Blood-and-Thunder, was a native of the valley, but had left it in his early days, and taken up the trades of law and politics. Instead of the rich man's wealth and the warrior's sword, he had but a tongue, and it was mightier than both together. So wonderfully eloquent was he, that whatever he might choose to say, his auditors had no choice but to believe him; wrong looked like right, and right like wrong; for when it pleased him, he could make a kind of illuminated fog with his mere breath, and obscure the natural daylight with it. His tongue, indeed, was a magic instrument: sometimes it rumbled like the thunder; sometimes it warbled like the sweetest music. It was the blast of war, the song of peace; and it seemed to have a heart in it, when there was no such matter. In good truth, he was a wondrous man; and when his tongue had acquired him all other imaginable success,—when it had been heard in halls of state, and in the courts of princes and potentates,—after it had made him known all over the world, even as a voice crying from shore to shore,—it finally persuaded his countrymen to select him for the Presidency. Before this time,— indeed, as soon as he began to grow celebrated,—his admirers had found out the resemblance between him and the Great Stone Face; and so much were they struck by it, that throughout the country this distinguished gentleman was known by the name of Old Stony Phiz. The phrase was considered as giving a highly favorable aspect to his political prospects; for, as is likewise the case with the Popedom, nobody ever becomes President without taking a name other than his own.

While his friends were doing their best to make him President, Old Stony Phiz, as he was called, set out on a visit to the valley where he was born. Of course, he had no other object than to shake hands with his fellow-citizens and neither thought nor cared about any effect which his progress through the country might have upon the election. Magnificent preparations were made to receive the illustrious statesman; a cavalcade of horsemen set forth to meet him at the boundary line of the State, and all the people left their business and gathered along the wayside to see him pass. Among these was Ernest. Though more than once disappointed, as we have seen, he had such a hopeful and confiding nature, that he was always ready to believe in whatever seemed beautiful and good. He kept his heart continually open, and thus was sure to catch the blessing from on high when it should come. So now again, as buoyantly as ever, he went forth to behold the likeness of the Great Stone Face.

The cavalcade came prancing along the road, with a great clattering of hoofs and a mighty cloud of dust, which rose up so dense and high that the visage of the mountain-side was completely hidden from Ernest's eyes. All the great men of the neighborhood were there on horseback; militia officers, in uniform; the member of Congress; the sheriff of the county; the editors of newspapers; and many a farmer, too, had mounted his patient steed, with his Sunday coat upon his back. It really was a very brilliant spectacle, especially as there were numerous banners flaunting over the cavalcade, on some of which were gorgeous portraits of the illustrious statesman and the Great Stone Face, smiling familiarly at one another, like two brothers. If the pictures were to be trusted, the mutual resemblance, it must be confessed, was marvellous. We must not forget to mention that there was a band of music, which made the echoes of the mountains ring and reverberate with the loud triumph of its strains; so that airy and soul-thrilling melodies broke out among all the heights and hollows, as if every nook of his native valley had found a voice, to welcome the distinguished guest. But the grandest effect was when the far-off mountain precipice flung back the music; for then the Great Stone Face itself seemed to be swelling the triumphant chorus, in acknowledgment that, at length, the man of prophecy was come.

All this while the people were throwing up their hats and shouting, with enthusiasm so contagious that the heart of Ernest kindled up, and he likewise threw up his hat, and shouted, as loudly as the loudest, "Huzza for the great man! Huzza for Old Stony Phiz!" But as yet he had not seen him.

"Here he is, now!" cried those who stood near Ernest. "There! There! Look at Old Stony Phiz and then at the Old Man of the Mountain, and see if they are not as like as two twin-brothers!"

In the midst of all this gallant array came an open barouche, drawn by four white horses; and in the barouche, with his massive head uncovered, sat the illustrious statesman, Old Stony Phiz himself.

"Confess it," said one of Ernest's neighbors to him, "the Great Stone Face has met its match at last!"

Now, it must be owned that, at his first glimpse of the countenance which was bowing and smiling from the barouche, Ernest did fancy that there was a resemblance between it and the old familiar face upon the mountain-side. The brow, with its massive depth and loftiness, and all the other features, indeed, were boldly and strongly hewn, as if in emulation of a more than heroic, of a Titanic model. But the sublimity and stateliness, the grand expresson of a divine sympathy, that illuminated the mountain visage and etherealized its ponderous granite substance into spirit, might here be sought in vain. Something had been originally left out, or had departed. And therefore the marvellously gifted statesman had always a weary gloom in the deep caverns of his eyes, as of a child that has outgrown its playthings or a man of mighty faculties and little aims, whose life, with all its high performances, was vague and empty, because no high purpose had endowed it with reality.

Still, Ernest's neighbor was thrusting his elbow into his side, and pressing him for an answer.

"Confess! confess! Is not he the very picture of your Old Man of the Mountain?"

"No!" said Ernest bluntly, "I see little or no likeness."

"Then so much the worse for the Great Stone Face!" answered his neighbor; and again he set up a shout for Old Stony Phiz.

But Ernest turned away, melancholy, and almost despondent: for this was the saddest of his disappointments, to behold a man who might have fulfilled the prophecy, and had not willed to do so. Meantime, the cavalcade, the banners, the music, and the barouches swept past him, with the vociferous crowd in the rear, leaving the dust to settle down, and the Great Stone Face to be revealed again, with the grandeur that it had worn for untold centuries.

"Lo, here I am, Ernest!" the benign lips seemed to say. "I have waited longer than thou, and am not yet weary. Fear not; the man will come."

The years hurried onward, treading in their haste on one another's heels. And now they began to bring white hairs, and scatter them over the head of Ernest; they made reverend wrinkles across his forehead, and furrows in his cheeks. He was an aged man. But not in vain had he grown old: more than the white hairs on his head were the sage thoughts in his mind; his wrinkles and furrows were inscriptions that Time had graved, and in which he had written legends of wisdom that had been tested by the tenor of a life. And Ernest had ceased to be obscure. Unsought for, undesired, had come the fame which so many seek, and made him known in the great world, beyond the limits of the valley in which he had dwelt so quietly. College professors, and even the active men of cities, came from far to see and converse with Ernest; for the report had gone abroad that this simple husbandman had ideas unlike those of other men, not gained from books, but of a higher tone,—a tranquil and familiar majesty, as if he had been talking with the angels as his daily friends. Whether it were sage, statesman, or philanthropist, Ernest received these visitors with the gentle sincerity that had characterized him from boyhood, and spoke freely with them of whatever came uppermost, or lay deepest in his heart or their own. While they talked together, his face would kindle, unawares, and shine upon them, as with a mild evening light. Pensive with the fulness of such discourse, his guests took leave and went their way; and passing up the valley, paused to look at the Great Stone Face, imagining that they had seen its likeness in a human countenance, but could not remember where.

While Ernest had been growing up and growing old, a bountiful Providence had granted a new poet to this earth. He likewise, was a native of the valley, but had spent the greater part of his life at a distance from that romantic region, pouring out his sweet music amid the bustle and din of cities. Often, however, did the mountains which had been familiar to him in his childhood lift their snowy peaks into the clear atmosphere of his poetry. Neither was the Great Stone Face forgotten, for the poet had celebrated it in an ode, which was grand enough to have been uttered by its own majestic lips. This man of genius, we may say, had come down from heaven with wonderful endowments. If he sang of a mountain, the eyes of all mankind beheld a mightier grandeur reposing on its breast, or soaring to its summit, than had before been seen there. If his theme were a lovely lake, a celestial smile had now been thrown over it, to gleam forever on its surface. If it were the vast old sea, even the deep immensity of its dread bosom seemed to swell the higher, as if moved by the emotions of the song. Thus the world assumed another and a better aspect from the hour that the poet blessed it with his happy eyes. The Creator had bestowed him, as the last best touch to his own handiwork. Creation was not finished till the poet came to interpret, and so complete it.

The effect was no less high and beautiful, when his human brethren were the subject of his verse. The man or woman, sordid with the common dust of life, who crossed his daily path, and the little child who played in it, were glorified if he beheld them in his mood of poetic faith. He showed the golden links of the great chain that intertwined them with an angelic kindred; he brought out the hidden traits of a celestial birth that made them worthy of such kin. Some, indeed, there were, who thought to show the soundness of their judgment by affirming that all the beauty and dignity of the natural world existed only in the poet's fancy. Let such men speak for themselves, who undoubtedly appear to have been spawned forth by Nature with a contemptuous bitterness; she having plastered them up out of her refuse stuff, after all the swine were made. As respects all things else, the poet's ideal was the truest truth.

The songs of this poet found their way to Ernest. He read them after his customary toil, seated on the bench before his cottage-door, where for such a length of time he had filled his repose with thought, by gazing at the Great Stone Face. And now as he read stanzas that caused the soul to thrill within him, he lifted his eyes to the vast countenance beaming on him so benignantly.

"O majestic friend," he murmured, addressing the Great Stone Face, "is not this man worthy to resemble thee?"

The Face seemed to smile, but answered not a word.

Now it happened that the poet, though he dwelt so far away, had not only heard of Ernest, but had meditated much upon his character, until he deemed nothing so desirable as to meet this man, whose untaught wisdom walked hand in hand with the noble simplicity of his life. One summer morning, therefore, he took passage by the railroad, and, in the decline of the afternoon, alighted from the cars at no great distance from Ernest's cottage. The great hotel, which had formerly been the palace of Mr. Gathergold, was close at hand, but the poet, with his carpet-bag on his arm, inquired at once where Ernest dwelt, and was resolved to be accepted as his guest.

Approaching the door, he there found the good old man, holding a volume in his hand, which alternately he read, and then, with a finger between the leaves, looked lovingly at the Great Stone Face.

"Good evening," said the poet. "Can you give a traveller a night's lodging?"

"Willingly," answered Ernest; and then he added, smiling, "Methinks I never saw the Great Stone Face look so hospitably at a stranger."

The poet sat down on the bench beside him, and he and Ernest talked together. Often had the poet held intercourse with the wittiest and the wisest, but never before with a man like Ernest, whose thoughts and feelings gushed up with such a natural freedom, and who made great truths so familiar by his simple utterance of them. Angels, as had been so often said, seemed to have wrought with him at his labor in the fields; angels seemed to have sat with him by the fireside; and, dwelling with angels as friend with friends, he had imbibed the sublimity of their ideas, and imbued it with the sweet and lowly charm of household words. So thought the poet. And Ernest, on the other hand, was moved and agitated by the living images which the poet flung out of his mind, and which peopled all the air about the cottage-door with shapes of beauty, both gay and pensive. The sympathies of these two men instructed them with a profounder sense than either could have attained alone. Their minds accorded into one strain, and made delightful music which neither of them could have claimed as all his own, nor distinguished his own share from the other's. They led one another, as it were, into a high pavilion of their thoughts, so remote, and hitherto so dim, that they had never entered it before, and so beautiful that they desired to be there always.

As Ernest listened to the poet, he imagined that the Great Stone Face was bending forward to listen too. He gazed earnestly into the poet's glowing eyes.

"Who are you, my strangely gifted guest?" he said.

The poet laid his finger on the volume that Ernest had been reading. "You have read these poems," said he. "You know me, then,—for I wrote them."

Again, and still more earnestly than before, Ernest examined the poet's features; then turned towards the Great Stone Face; then back, with an uncertain aspect, to his guest. But his countenance fell; he shook his head, and sighed.

"Wherefore are you sad?" inquired the poet.

"Because," replied Ernest, "all through life I have awaited the fulfilment of a prophecy; and, when I read these poems, I hoped that it might be fulfilled in you."

"You hoped," answered the poet, faintly smiling, "to find in me the likeness of the Great Stone Face. And you are disappointed, as formerly with Mr. Gathergold, and Old Blood-and-Thunder, and Old Stony Phiz. Yes, Ernest, it is my doom. You must add my name to the illustrious three, and record another failure of your hopes. For—in shame and sadness do I speak it, Ernest—I am not worthy to be typified by yonder benign and majestic image."

"And why?" asked Ernest. He pointed to the volume. "Are not those thoughts divine?"

"They have a strain of the Divinity," replied the poet. "You can hear in them the far-off echo of a heavenly song. But my life, dear Ernest, has not corresponded with my thought. I have had grand dreams, but they have been only dreams, because I have lived—and that, too, by my own choice—among poor and mean realities. Sometimes even—shall I dare to say it?—I lack faith in the grandeur, the beauty, and the goodness, which my own words are said to have made more evident in nature and in human life. Why, then, pure seeker of the good and true, shouldst thou hope to find me, in yonder image of the divine?"

The poet spoke sadly, and his eyes were dim with tears. So, likewise, were those of Ernest.

At the hour of sunset, as had long been his frequent custom, Ernest was to discourse to an assemblage of the neighboring inhabitants in the open air. He and the poet, arm in arm, still talking together as they went along, proceeded to the spot. It was a small nook among the hills, with a gray precipice behind, the stern front of which was relieved by the pleasant foliage of many creeping plants that made a tapestry for the naked rock, by hanging their festoons from all its rugged angles. At a small elevation above the ground, set in a rich framework of verdure, there appeared a niche, spacious enough to admit a human figure, with freedom for such gestures as spontaneously accompany earnest thought and genuine emotion. Into this natural pulpit Ernest ascended, and threw a look of familiar kindness around upon his audience. They stood, or sat, or reclined upon the grass, as seemed good to each, with the departing sunshine falling obliquely over them, and mingling its subdued cheerfulness with the solemnity of a grove of ancient trees, beneath and amid the boughs of which the golden rays were constrained to pass. In another direction was seen the Great Stone Face, with the same cheer, combined with the same solemnity, in its benignant aspect.

Ernest began to speak, giving to the people of what was in his heart and mind. His words had power, because they accorded with his thoughts; and his thoughts had reality and depth, because they harmonized with the life which he had always lived. It was not mere breath that this preacher uttered; they were the words of life, because a life of good deeds and holy love was melted into them. Pearls, pure and rich, had been dissolved into this precious draught. The poet, as he listened, felt that the being and character of Ernest were a nobler strain of poetry than he had ever written. His eyes glistening with tears, he gazed reverentially at the venerable man, and said within himself that never was there an aspect so worthy of a prophet and a sage as that mild, sweet, thoughtful countenance, with the glory of white hair diffused about it. At a distance, but distinctly to be seen, high up in the golden light of the setting sun, appeared the Great Stone Face, with hoary mists around it, like the white hairs around the brow of Ernest. Its look of grand beneficence seemed to embrace the world.

At that moment, in sympathy with a thought which he was about to utter, the face of Ernest assumed a grandeur of expression, so imbued with benevolence, that the poet, by an irresistible impulse, threw his arms aloft and shouted,—

"Behold! Behold! Ernest is himself the likeness of the Great Stone Face!"

Then all the people looked, and saw that what the deep-sighted poet said was true. The prophecy was fulfilled. But Ernest, having finished what he had to say, took the poet's arm, and walked slowly homeward, still hoping that some wiser and better man than himself would by and by appear, bearing a resemblance to the GREAT STONE FACE.

# ETHAN BRAND:

## A CHAPTER FROM AN ABORTIVE ROMANCE

BARTRAM the lime-burner, a rough, heavy-looking man, begrimed with charcoal, sat watching his kiln at nightfall, while his little son played at building houses with the scattered fragments of marble, when, on the hill-side below them, they heard a roar of laughter, not mirthful, but slow, and even solemn, like a wind shaking the boughs of the forest.

"Father, what is that?" asked the little boy, leaving his play, and pressing betwixt his father's knees.

"Oh, some drunken man, I suppose," answered the lime-burner; "some

merry fellow from the bar-room in the village, who dared not laugh loud
enough within doors lest he should blow the roof of the house off. So here
he is, shaking his jolly sides at the foot of Graylock."

"But, father," said the child, more sensitive than the obtuse, middle-
aged clown, "he does not laugh like a man that is glad. So the noise fright-
ens me!"

"Don't be a fool, child!" cried his father, gruffly. "You will never make
a man, I do believe; there is too much of your mother in you. I have
known the rustling of a leaf startle you. Hark! Here comes the merry fellow now. You shall see that there is no harm in him."

Bartram and his little son, while they were talking thus, sat watching
the same lime-kiln that had been the scene of Ethan Brand's solitary and
meditative life, before he began his search for the Unpardonable Sin.
Many years, as we have seen, had now elapsed, since that portentous
night when the IDEA was first developed. The kiln, however, on the mountain-side, stood unimpaired, and was in nothing changed since he had
thrown his dark thoughts into the intense glow of its furnace, and melted
them, as it were, into the one thought that took possession of his life. It
was a rude, round, tower-like structure about twenty feet high, heavily
built of rough stones, and with a hillock of earth heaped about the larger
part of its circumference; so that the blocks and fragments of marble
might be drawn by cart-loads, and thrown in at the top. There was an
opening at the bottom of the tower, like an over-mouth, but large enough
to admit a man in a stooping posture, and provided with a massive iron
door. With the smoke and jets of flame issuing from the chinks and crevices of this door, which seemed to give admittance into the hill-side, it
resembled nothing so much as the private entrance to the infernal regions,
which the shepherds of the Delectable Mountains were accustomed to
show to pilgrims.

There are many such lime-kilns in that tract of country, for the purpose of burning the white marble which composes a large part of the
substance of the hills. Some of them, built years ago, and long deserted,
with weeds growing in the vacant round of the interior, which is open to
the sky, and grass and wild-flowers rooting themselves into the chinks of
the stones, look already like relics of antiquity, and may yet be overspread with the lichens of centuries to come. Others, where the lime-
burner still feeds his daily and night-long fire, afford points of interest to
the wanderer among the hills, who seats himself on a log of wood or a
fragment of marble, to hold a chat with the solitary man. It is a lonesome,
and, when the character is inclined to thought, may be an intensely
thoughtful occupation; as it proved in the case of Ethan Brand, who had
mused to such strange purpose, in days gone by, while the fire in this
very kiln was burning.

The man who now watched the fire was of a different order, and
troubled himself with no thoughts save the very few that were requisite to
his business. At frequent intervals, he flung back the clashing weight of
the iron door, and, turning his face from the insufferable glare, thrust in

huge logs of oak, or stirred the immense brands with a long pole. Within the furnace were seen the curling and riotous flames, and the burning marble, almost molten with the intensity of heat; while without, the reflection of the fire quivered on the dark intricacy of the surrounding forest, and showed in the foreground a bright and ruddy little picture of the hut, the spring beside its door, the athletic and coal-begrimed figure of the lime-burner, and the half-frightened child, shrinking into the protection of his father's shadow. And when, again, the iron door was closed, then reappeared the tender light of the half-full moon, which vainly strove to trace out the indistinct shapes of the neighboring mountains; and, in the upper sky, there was a flitting congregation of clouds, still faintly tinged with the rosy sunset, though thus far down into the valley the sunshine had vanished long and long ago.

The little boy now crept still closer to his father, as footsteps were heard ascending the hill-side, and a human form thrust aside the bushes that clustered beneath the trees.

"Halloo! who is it?" cried the lime-burner, vexed at his son's timidity, yet half infected by it. "Come forward, and show yourself, like a man, or I'll fling this chunk of marble at your head!"

"You offer me a rough welcome," said a gloomy voice, as the unknown man drew nigh. "Yet I neither claim nor desire a kinder one, even at my own fireside."

To obtain a distincter view, Bartram threw open the iron door of the kiln, whence immediately issued a gush of fierce light, that smote full upon the stranger's face and figure. To a careless eye there appeared nothing very remarkable in his aspect, which was that of a man in a coarse, brown, country-made suit of clothes, tall and thin, with the staff and heavy shoes of a wayfarer. As he advanced, he fixed his eyes—which were very bright—intently upon the brightness of the furnace, as if he beheld, or expected to behold, some object worthy of note within it.

"Good evening, stranger," said the lime-burner; "whence come you, so late in the day?"

"I come from my search," answered the wayfarer; "for, at last, it is finished."

"Drunk!—or crazy!" muttered Bartram to himself. "I shall have trouble with the fellow. The sooner I drive him away, the better."

The little boy, all in a tremble, whispered to his father, and begged him to shut the door of the kiln, so that there might not be so much light; for that there was something in the man's face which he was afraid to look at, yet could not look away from. And, indeed, even the lime-burner's dull and torpid sense began to be impressed by an indescribable something in that thin, rugged, thoughtful visage, with the grizzled hair hanging wildly about it, and those deeply sunken eyes, which gleamed like fires within the entrance of a mysterious cavern. But, as he closed the door, the stranger turned towards him, and spoke in a quiet, familiar way, that made Bartram feel as if he were a sane and sensible man, after all.

"Your task draws to an end, I see," said he. "This marble has already been burning three days. A few hours more will convert the stone to lime."

"Why, who are you?" exclaimed the lime-burner. "You seem as well acquainted with my business as I am myself."

"And well I may be," said the stranger; "for I followed the same craft many a long year, and here, too, on this very spot. But you are a new-comer in these parts. Did you never hear of Ethan Brand?"

"The man that went in search of the Unpardonable Sin?" asked Bartram, with a laugh.

"The same," answered the stranger. "He has found what he sought, and therefore he comes back again."

"What! then you are Ethan Brand himself?" cried the lime-burner, in amazement. "I am a new-comer here, as you say, and they call it eight-een years since you left the foot of Graylock. But, I can tell you, the good folks still talk about Ethan Brand, in the village yonder, and what a strange errand took him away from his lime-kiln. Well, and so you have found the Unpardonable Sin?"

"Even so!" said the stranger, calmly.

"If the question is a fair one," proceeded Bartram, "where might it be?"

Ethan Brand laid his finger on his own heart.

"Here!" replied he.

And then, without mirth in his countenance, but as if moved by an involuntary recognition of the infinite absurdity of seeking throughout the world for what was the closest of all things to himself, and looking into every heart, save his own, for what was hidden in no other breast, he broke into a laugh of scorn. It was the same slow, heavy laugh, that had almost appalled the lime-burner when it heralded the wayfarer's approach.

The solitary mountain-side was made dismal by it. Laughter, when out of place, mistimed, or bursting forth from a disordered state of feel-ing, may be the most terrible modulation of the human voice. The laugh-ter of one asleep, even if it be a little child,—the madman's laugh,—the wild, screaming laugh of a born idiot,—are sounds that we sometimes tremble to hear, and would always willingly forget. Poets have imagined no utterance of fiends or hobgoblins so fearfully appropriate as a laugh. And even the obtuse lime-burner felt his nerves shaken, as this strange man looked inward at his own heart, and burst into laughter that rolled away into the night, and was indistinctly reverberated among the hills.

"Joe," said he to his little son, "scamper down to the tavern in the village, and tell the jolly fellows there that Ethan Brand has come back, and that he has found the Unpardonable Sin!"

The boy darted away on his errand, to which Ethan Brand made no ob-jection, nor seemed hardly to notice it. He sat on a log of wood, looking steadfastly at the iron door of the kiln. When the child was out of sight, and his swift and light footsteps ceased to be heard treading first on the

fallen leaves and then on the rocky mountain-path, the lime-burner began to regret his departure. He felt that the little fellow's presence had
been a barrier between his guest and himself, and that he must now deal,
heart to heart, with a man who, on his own confession, had committed the
one only crime for which Heaven could afford no mercy. That crime, in
its indistinct blackness, seemed to overshadow him, and made his memory
riotous with a throng of evil shapes that asserted their kindred with the
Master Sin, whatever it might be, which it was within the scope of man's
corrupted nature to conceive and cherish. They were all of one family;
they went to and fro between his breast and Ethan Brand's, and carried
dark greetings from one to the other.

Then Bartram remembered the stories which had grown traditionary
in reference to this strange man, who had come upon him like a shadow
of the night, and was making himself at home in his old place, after so
long absence, that the dead people, dead and buried for years, would
have had more right to be at home, in any familiar spot, than he. Ethan
Brand, it was said, had conversed with Satan himself in the lurid blaze of
this very kiln. The legend had been matter of mirth heretofore, but looked
grisly now. According to this tale, before Ethan Brand departed on his
search, he had been accustomed to evoke a fiend from the hot furnace of
the lime-kiln, night after night, in order to confer with him about the
Unpardonable Sin; the man and the fiend each laboring to frame the
image of some mode of guilt which could neither be atoned for nor forgiven. And, with the first gleam of light upon the mountain-top, the fiend
crept in at the iron door, there to abide the intensest element of fire until
again summoned forth to share in the dreadful task of extending man's
possible guilt beyond the scope of Heaven's else infinite mercy.

While the lime-burner was struggling with the horror of these thoughts,
Ethan Brand rose from the log, and flung open the door of the kiln. The
action was in such accordance with the idea in Bartram's mind, that he
almost expected to see the Evil One issue forth, red-hot, from the raging
furnace.

"Hold! hold!" cried he, with a tremulous attempt to laugh; for he
was ashamed of his fears, although they overmastered him. "Don't, for
mercy's sake, bring out your Devil now!"

"Man!" sternly replied Ethan Brand, "what need have I of the Devil?
I have left him behind me, on my track. It is with such half-way sinners
as you that he busies himself. Fear not, because I open the door. I do but
act by old custom, and am going to trim your fire, like a lime-burner, as
I was once."

He stirred the vast coals, thrust in more wood, and bent forward to
gaze into the hollow prison-house of the fire, regardless of the fierce glow
that reddened upon his face. The lime-burner sat watching him, and half
suspected this strange guest of a purpose, if not to evoke a fiend, at least
to plunge into the flames, and thus vanish from the sight of man. Ethan
Brand, however, drew quietly back, and closed the door of the kiln.

"I have looked," said he, "into many a human heart that was seven times hotter with sinful passions than yonder furnace is with fire. But I found not there what I sought. No, not the Unpardonable Sin!"

"What is the Unpardonable Sin?" asked the lime-burner; and then he shrank farther from his companion, trembling lest his question should be answered.

"It is a sin that grew within my own breast," replied Ethan Brand, standing erect with a pride that distinguishes all enthusiasts of his stamp. "A sin that grew nowhere else! The sin of an intellect that triumphed over the sense of brotherhood with man and reverence for God, and sacrificed everything to its own mighty claims! The only sin that deserves a recompense of immortal agony! Freely, were it to do again, would I incur the guilt. Unshrinkingly I accept the retribution!"

"The man's head is turned," muttered the lime-burner to himself. "He may be a sinner like the rest of us,—nothing more likely,—but, I'll be sworn, he is a madman too."

Nevertheless, he felt uncomfortable at his situation, alone with Ethan Brand on the wild mountain-side, and was right glad to hear the rough murmur of tongues, and the footsteps of what seemed a pretty numerous party, stumbling over the stones and rustling through the underbrush. Soon appeared the whole lazy regiment that was wont to infest the village tavern, comprehending three or four individuals who had drunk flip beside the bar-room fire through all the winters, and smoked their pipes beneath the stoop through all the summers, since Ethan Brand's departure. Laughing boisterously, and mingling all their voices together in unceremonious talk, they now burst into the moonshine and narrow streaks of firelight that illuminated the open space before the lime-kiln. Bartram set the door ajar again, flooding the spot with light, that the whole company might get a fair view of Ethan Brand, and he of them.

There, among other old acquaintances, was a once ubiquitous man, now almost extinct, but whom we were formerly sure to encounter at the hotel of every thriving village throughout the country. It was the stage-agent. The present specimen of the genus was a wilted and smoke-dried man, wrinkled and red-nosed, in a smartly cut, brown, bobtailed coat, with brass buttons, who, for a length of time unknown, had kept his desk and corner in the bar-room, and was still puffing what seemed to be the same cigar that he had lighted twenty years before. He had great fame as a dry joker, though, perhaps, less on account of any intrinsic humor than from a certain flavor of brandy-toddy and tobacco-smoke, which impregnated all his ideas and expressions, as well as his person. Another well-remembered, though strangely altered, face was that of Lawyer Giles, as people still called him in courtesy; an elderly ragamuffin, in his soiled shirtsleeves and tow-cloth trousers. This poor fellow had been an attorney, in what he called his better days, a sharp practitioner, and in great vogue among the village litigants; but flip, and sling, and toddy, and cocktails, imbibed at all hours, morning, noon, and night, had caused him to slide from intellectual to various kinds and degrees of bodily labor, till at last, to adopt his own phrase, he slid into a soap-vat.

In other words, Giles was now a soap-boiler, in a small way. He had come to be but the fragment of a human being, a part of one foot having been chopped off by an axe, and an entire hand torn away by the devilish grip of a steam-engine. Yet, though the corporeal hand was gone, a spiritual member remained; for, stretching forth the stump, Giles steadfastly averred that he felt an invisible thumb and fingers with as vivid a sensation as before the real ones were amputated. A maimed and miserable wretch he was; but one, nevertheless, whom the world could not trample on, and had no right to scorn, either in this or any previous stage of his misfortunes, since he had still kept up the courage and spirit of a man, asked nothing in charity, and with his one hand—and that the left one—fought a stern battle against want and hostile circumstances.

Among the throng, too, came another personage, who, with certain points of similarity to Lawyer Giles, had many more of difference. It was the village doctor; a man of some fifty years, whom, at an earlier period of his life, we introduced as paying a professional visit to Ethan Brand during the latter's supposed insanity. He was now a purple-visaged, rude, and brutal, yet half-gentlemanly figure, with something wild, ruined, and desperate in his talk, and in all the details of his gesture and manners. Brandy possessed this man like an evil spirit, and made him as surly and savage as a wild beast, and as miserable as a lost soul; but there was supposed to be in him such wonderful skill, such native gifts of healing, beyond any which medical science could impart, that society caught hold of him, and would not let him sink out of its reach. So, swaying to and fro upon his horse, and grumbling thick accents at the bedside, he visited all the sick-chambers for miles about among the mountain towns, and sometimes raised a dying man, as it were, by miracle, or quite as often, no doubt, sent his patient to a grave that was dug many a year too soon. The doctor had an everlasting pipe in his mouth, and, as somebody said, in allusion to his habit of swearing, it was always alight with hell-fire.

These three worthies pressed forward, and greeted Ethan Brand each after his own fashion, earnestly inviting him to partake of the contents of a certain black bottle, in which, as they averred, he would find something far better worth seeking than the Unpardonable Sin. No mind, which has wrought itself by intense and solitary meditation into a high state of enthusiasm, can endure the kind of contact with low and vulgar modes of thought and feeling to which Ethan Brand was now subjected. It made him doubt—and, strange to say, it was a painful doubt—whether he had indeed found the Unpardonable Sin, and found it within himself. The whole question on which he had exhausted life, and more than life, looked like a delusion.

"Leave me," he said bitterly, "ye brute beasts, that have made yourselves so, shrivelling up your souls with fiery liquors! I have done with you. Years and years ago, I groped into your hearts and found nothing there for my purpose. Get ye gone!"

"Why, you uncivil scoundrel," cried the fierce doctor, "is that the way you respond to the kindness of your best friends? Then let me tell you the truth. You have no more found the Unpardonable Sin than yonder boy Joe has. You are but a crazy fellow,—I told you so twenty years ago,—neither better nor worse than a crazy fellow, and the fit companion of old Humphrey, here!"

He pointed to an old man, shabbily dressed, with long white hair, thin visage, and unsteady eyes. For some years past this aged person had been wandering about among the hills, inquiring of all travellers whom he met for his daughter. The girl, it seemed, had gone off with a company of circus-performers, and occasionally tidings of her came to the village, and fine stories were told of her glittering appearance as she rode on horseback in the ring, or performed marvellous feats on the tight-rope.

The white-haired father now approached Ethan Brand, and gazed unsteadily into his face.

"They tell me you have been all over the earth," said he, wringing his hands with earnestness. "You must have seen my daughter, for she makes a grand figure in the world, and everybody goes to see her. Did she send any word to her old father, or say when she was coming back?"

Ethan Brand's eye quailed beneath the old man's. That daughter, from whom he so earnestly desired a word of greeting, was the Esther of our tale, the very girl whom, with such cold and remorseless purpose, Ethan Brand had made the subject of a psychological experiment, and wasted, absorbed, and perhaps annihilated her soul, in the process.

"Yes," he murmured, turning away from the hoary wanderer, "it is no delusion. There is an Unpardonable Sin!"

While these things were passing, a merry scene was going forward in the area of cheerful light, beside the spring and before the door of the hut. A number of the youth of the village, young men and girls, had hurried up the hill-side, impelled by curiosity to see Ethan Brand, the hero of so many a legend familiar to their childhood. Finding nothing, however, very remarkable in his aspect,—nothing but a sunburnt wayfarer, in plain garb and dusty shoes, who sat looking into the fire as if he fancied pictures among the coals,—these young people speedily grew tired of observing him. As it happened, there was other amusement at hand. An old German Jew travelling with a diorama on his back, was passing down the mountain-road towards the village just as the party turned aside from it, and, in hopes of eking out the profits of the day, the showman had kept them company to the lime-kiln.

"Come, old Dutchman," cried one of the young men, "let us see your pictures, if you can swear they are worth looking at!"

"Oh yes, Captain," answered the Jew,—whether as a matter of courtesy or craft, he styled everybody Captain,—"I shall show you, indeed, some very superb pictures!"

So, placing his box in a proper position, he invited the young men and girls to look through the glass orifices of the machine, and proceeded to exhibit a series of the most outrageous scratchings and daubings, as specimens of the fine arts, that ever an itinerant showman had the face to impose upon his circle of spectators. The pictures were worn out, moreover, tattered, full of cracks and wrinkles, dingy with tobacco-smoke, and otherwise in a most pitiable condition. Some purported to be cities, public edifices, and ruined castles in Europe; others represented Napoleon's battles and Nelson's sea-fights; and in the midst of these would be seen a gigantic, brown, hairy hand,—which might have been mistaken for the Hand of Destiny, though, in truth, it was only the showman's,—pointing its forefinger to various scenes of the conflict, while its owner gave historical illustrations. When, with much merriment at its abominable deficiency of merit, the exhibition was concluded, the German bade little Joe put his head into the box. Viewed through the magnifying-glasses, the boy's round, rosy visage assumed the strangest imaginable aspect of an immense Titanic child, the mouth grinning broadly, and the eyes and every other feature overflowing with fun at the joke. Suddenly, however, that merry face turned pale, and its expression changed to horror, for this easily impressed and excitable child had become sensible that the eye of Ethan Brand was fixed upon him through the glass.

"You make the little man to be afraid, Captain," said the German Jew, turning up the dark and strong outline of his visage from his stooping posture. "But look again, and, by chance, I shall cause you to see somewhat that is very fine, upon my word!"

Ethan Brand gazed into the box for an instant, and then starting back, looked fixedly at the German. What had he seen? Nothing, apparently; for a curious youth, who had peeped in almost at the same moment, beheld only a vacant space of canvas.

"I remember you now," muttered Ethan Brand to the showman.

"Ah, Captain," whispered the Jew of Nuremberg, with a dark smile, "I find it to be a heavy matter in my show-box,—this Unpardonable Sin! By my faith, Captain, it has wearied my shoulders, this long day, to carry it over the mountain."

"Peace," answered Ethan Brand, sternly, "or get thee into the furnace yonder!"

The Jew's exhibition had scarcely concluded, when a great, elderly dog —who seemed to be his own master, as no person in the company laid claim to him—saw fit to render himself the object of public notice. Hitherto, he had shown himself a very quiet, well-disposed old dog, going round from one to another, and, by way of being sociable, offering his rough head to be patted by any kindly hand that would take so much trouble. But now, all of a sudden, this grave and venerable quadruped, of his own mere motion, and without the slightest suggestion from anybody else, began to run round after his tail, which, to heighten the absurdity of the proceeding, was a great deal shorter than it should have been. Never was seen such headlong eagerness in pursuit of an object that could not possibly be attained; never was heard such a tremendous outbreak of growling, snarling, barking, and snapping,—as if one end of the ridiculous brute's body were at deadly and most unforgivable enmity with the other. Faster and faster, round about went the cur; and faster and still faster fled the unapproachable brevity of his tail; and louder and fiercer grew his yells of rage and animosity; until, utterly exhausted, and as far from the goal as ever, the foolish old dog ceased his perform- ance as suddenly as he had begun it. The next moment he was as mild, quiet, sensible, and respectable in his deportment, as when he first scraped acquaintance with the company.

As may be supposed, the exhibition was greeted with universal laugh- ter, clapping of hands, and shouts of encore, to which the canine per- former responded by wagging all that there was to wag of his tail, but appeared totally unable to repeat his very successful effort to amuse the spectators.

Meanwhile, Ethan Brand had resumed his seat upon the log, and moved, as it might be, by a perception of some remote analogy between his own case and that of this self-pursuing cur, he broke into the awful laugh, which, more than any other token, expressed the condition of his inward being. From that moment, the merriment of the party was at an end; they stood aghast, dreading lest the inauspicious sound should be reverberated around the horizon, and that mountain would thunder it to mountain, and so the horror be prolonged upon their ears. Then, whisper- ing one to another that it was late,—that the moon was almost down,— that the August night was growing chill,—they hurried homewards, leav- ing the lime-burner and little Joe to deal as they might with their unwel- come guest. Save for these three human beings, the open space on the hill-side was a solitude, set in a vast gloom of forest. Beyond that dark- some verge, the firelight glimmered on the stately trunks and almost black foliage of pines, intermixed with the lighter verdure of sapling oaks, maples, and poplars, while here and there lay the gigantic corpses of dead trees, decaying on the leaf-strewn soil. And it seemed to little Joe —a timorous and imaginative child—that the silent forest was holding its breath until some fearful thing should happen.

Ethan Brand thrust more wood into the fire, and closed the door of the kiln; then looking over his shoulder at the lime-burner and his son, he bade, rather than advised, them to retire to rest.

"For myself, I cannot sleep," said he. "I have matters that it concerns me to meditate upon. I will watch the fire, as I used to do in the old time."

"And call the Devil out of the furnace to keep you company, I sup- pose," muttered Bartram, who had been making intimate acquaintance with the black bottle above mentioned. "But watch, if you like, and call as many devils as you like! For my part, I shall be all the better for a snooze. Come, Joe!"

As the boy followed his father into the hut, he looked back at the way- farer, and the tears came into his eyes, for his tender spirit had an intui- tion of the bleak and terrible loneliness in which this man had enveloped himself.

When they had gone, Ethan Brand sat listening to the crackling of the kindled wood, and looking at the little spirts of fire that issued through the chinks of the door. These trifles, however, once so familiar, had but the slightest hold of his attention, while deep within his mind he was reviewing the gradual but marvellous change that had been wrought upon him by the search to which he had devoted himself. He remembered how the night dew had fallen upon him,—how the dark forest had whispered to him,—how the stars had gleamed upon him,—a simple and loving man, watching his fire in the years gone by, and ever musing as it burned. He remembered with what tenderness, with what love and sympathy for mankind, and what pity for human guilt and woe, he had first begun to contemplate those ideas which afterwards became the inspiration of his life; with what reverence he had then looked into the heart of man, viewing it as a temple originally divine, and, however desecrated, still to be held sacred by a brother; with what awful fear he had deprecated the success of his pursuit, and prayed that the Unpardonable Sin might never be revealed to him. Then ensued that vast intellectual development, which, in its progress, disturbed the counterpoise between his mind and heart. The Idea that possessed his life had operated as a means of education; it had gone on cultivating his powers to the highest point of which they were susceptible; it had raised him from the level of an unlettered laborer to stand on a star-lit eminence, whither the philosophers of the earth, laden with the lore of universities, might vainly strive to clamber after him. So much for the intellect! But where was the heart? That, indeed, had withered,—had contracted,—had hardened,—had perished! It had ceased to partake of the universal throb. He had lost his hold of the magnetic chain of humanity. He was no longer a brother-man, opening the chambers or the dungeons of our common nature by the key of holy sympathy, which gave him a right to share in all its secrets; he was now a cold observer, looking on mankind as the subject of his experiment, and, at length, converting man and woman to be his puppets, and pulling the wires that moved them to such degrees of crime as were demanded for his study.

Thus Ethan Brand became a fiend. He began to be so from the moment that his moral nature had ceased to keep the pace of improvement with his intellect. And now, as his highest effort and inevitable development,—as the bright and gorgeous flower, and rich, delicious fruit of his life's labor,—he had produced the Unpardonable Sin!

"What more have I to seek? what more to achieve?" said Ethan Brand to himself. "My task is done, and well done!"

Starting from the log with a certain alacrity in his gait and ascending the hillock of earth that was raised against the stone circumference of the lime-kiln, he thus reached the top of the structure. It was a space of perhaps ten feet across, from edge to edge, presenting a view of the upper surface of the immense mass of broken marble with which the kiln was heaped. All these innumerable blocks and fragments of marble were red-hot and vividly on fire, sending up great spouts of blue flame, which quivered aloft and danced madly, as within a magic circle, and sank and rose again, with continual and multitudinous activity. As the lonely man bent forward over this terrible body of fire, the blasting heat smote up against his person with a breath that, it might be supposed, would have scorched and shrivelled him up in a moment.

Ethan Brand stood erect, and raised his arms on high. The blue flames played upon his face, and imparted the wild and ghastly light which alone could have suited its expression; it was that of a fiend on the verge of plunging into his gulf of intensest torment.

"O Mother Earth," cried he, "who art no more my Mother, and into whose bosom this frame shall never be resolved! O mankind, whose brotherhood I have cast off, and trampled thy great heart beneath my feet! O stars of heaven, that shone on me of old, as if to light me onward and upward!—farewell all, and forever. Come, deadly element of Fire,—henceforth my familiar friend! Embrace me, as I do thee!"

That night the sound of a fearful peal of laughter rolled heavily through the sleep of the lime-burner and his little son; dim shapes of horror and anguish haunted their dreams, and seemed still present in the rude hovel, when they opened their eyes to the daylight.

"Up, boy, up!" cried the lime-burner, staring about him. "Thank Heaven, the night is gone, at last; and rather than pass such another, I would watch my lime-kiln, wide awake, for a twelvemonth. This Ethan Brand, with his humbug of an Unpardonable Sin, has done me no such mighty favor, in taking my place!"

He issued from the hut, followed by little Joe, who kept fast hold of his father's hand. The early sunshine was already pouring its gold upon the mountain-tops, and though the valleys were still in shadow, they smiled cheerfully in the promise of the bright day that was hastening onward. The village, completely shut in by hills, which swelled away gently about it, looked as if it had rested peacefully in the hollow of the great hand of Providence. Every dwelling was distinctly visible; the little spires of the two churches pointed upwards, and caught a fore-glimmering of brightness from the sun-gilt skies upon their gilded weather-cocks. The tavern was astir, and the figure of the old, smoke-dried stage-agent, cigar in mouth, was seen beneath the stoop. Old Graylock was glorified with a golden cloud upon his head. Scattered likewise over the breasts of the surrounding mountains, there were heaps of hoary mist, in fantastic shapes, some of them far down into the valley, others high up towards the summits, and still others, of the same family of mist or cloud, hovering in the gold radiance of the upper atmosphere. Stepping from one to another of the clouds that rested on the hills, and thence to the loftier brotherhood that sailed in air, it seemed almost as if a mortal man might thus ascend into the heavenly regions. Earth was so mingled with sky that it was a day-dream to look at it.

To supply that charm of the familiar and homely, which Nature so readily adopts into a scene like this, the stage-coach was rattling down the mountain-road, and the driver sounded his horn, while Echo caught up the notes, and intertwined them into a rich and varied and elaborate harmony, of which the original performer could lay claim to little share. The great hills played a concert among themselves, each contributing a strain of airy sweetness.

Little Joe's face brightened at once.

"Dear father," cried he, skipping cheerily to and fro, "that strange man is gone, and the sky and the mountains all seem glad of it!"

"Yes," growled the lime-burner, with an oath, "but he has let the fire go down, and no thanks to him if five hundred bushels of lime are not spoiled. If I catch the fellow hereabouts again, I shall feel like tossing him into the furnace!"

With his long pole in his hand, he ascended to the top of the kiln. After a moment's pause, he called to his son.

"Come up here, Joe!" said he.

So little Joe ran up the hillock, and stood by his father's side. The marble was all burnt into perfect, snow-white lime. But on its surface, in the midst of the circle,—snow-white too, and thoroughly converted into lime,—lay a human skeleton, in the attitude of a person who, after long toil, lies down to long repose. Within the ribs—strange to say—was the shape of a human heart.

"Was the fellow's heart made of marble?" cried Bartram, in some perplexity at this phenomenon. "At any rate, it is burnt into what looks like special good lime; and, taking all the bones together, my kiln is half a bushel the richer for him."

So saying, the rude lime-burner lifted his pole, and, letting it fall upon the skeleton, the relics of Ethan Brand were crumbled into fragments.

# THE CANTERBURY PILGRIMS

THE summer moon, which shines in so many a tale, was beaming over a broad extent of uneven country. Some of its brightest rays were flung into a spring of water, where no traveller, toiling, as the writer has, up the hilly road beside which it gushes, ever failed to quench his thirst. The work of neat hands and considerate art was visible about this blessed fountain. An open cistern, hewn and hollowed out of solid stone, was placed above the waters, which filled it to the brim, but by some invisible outlet were conveyed away without dripping down its sides. Though the basin had not room for another drop, and the continual gush of water made a tremor on the surface, there was a secret charm that forbade it to overflow. I remember, that when I had slaked my summer thirst, and sat panting by the cistern, it was my fanciful theory that Nature could not afford to lavish so pure a liquid, as she does the waters of all meaner fountains.

While the moon was hanging almost perpendicularly over this spot, two figures appeared on the summit of the hill, and came with noiseless footsteps down towards the spring. They were then in the first freshness of youth; nor is there a wrinkle now on either of their brows, and yet they wore a strange, old-fashioned garb. One, a young man with ruddy cheeks, walked beneath the canopy of a broad-brimmed gray hat; he seemed to have inherited his great-grandsire's square-skirted coat, and a waistcoat that extended its immense flaps to his knees; his brown locks, also, hung down behind, in a mode unknown to our times. By his side was a sweet young damsel, her fair features sheltered by a prim little bonnet, within which appeared the vestal muslin of a cap; her close, long-waisted gown, and indeed her whole attire, might have been worn by some rustic beauty who had faded half a century before. But that there was something too warm and life-like in them, I would here have compared this couple to the ghosts of two young lovers who had died long since in the glow of passion, and now were straying out of their graves, to renew the old vows, and shadow forth the unforgotten kiss of their earthly lips, beside the moonlit spring.

"Thee and I will rest here a moment, Miriam," said the young man, as they drew near the stone cistern, "for there is no fear that the elders know what we have done; and this may be the last time we shall ever taste this water."

Thus speaking, with a little sadness in his face, which was also visible in that of his companion, he made her sit down on a stone, and was about to place himself very close to her side; she, however, repelled him, though not unkindly.

"Nay, Josiah," said she, giving him a timid push with her maiden hand, "thee must sit farther off, on that other stone, with the spring between us. What would the sisters say, if thee were to sit so close to me?"

"But we are of the world's people now, Miriam," answered Josiah.

The girl persisted in her prudery, nor did the youth, in fact, seem altogether free from a similar sort of shyness; so they sat apart from each other, gazing up the hill, where the moonlight discovered the tops of a group of buildings. While their attention was thus occupied, a party of travellers, who had come wearily up the long ascent, made a halt to refresh themselves at the spring. There were three men, a woman, and a little girl and boy. Their attire was mean, covered with the dust of the summer's day, and damp with the night-dew; they all looked woebegone, as if the cares and sorrows of the world had made their steps heavier as they climbed the hill; even the two little children appeared older in evil days than the young man and maiden who had first approached the spring.

"Good evening to you, young folks," was the salutation of the travellers; and "Good evening, friends," replied the youth and damsel.

"Is that white building the Shaker meeting-house?" asked one of the strangers. "And are those the red roofs of the Shaker village?"

"Friend, it is the Shaker village," answered Josiah, after some hesitation.

The travellers, who, from the first, had looked suspiciously at the garb of these young people, now taxed them with an intention which all the circumstances, indeed, rendered too obvious to be mistaken.

"It is true, friends," replied the young man, summoning up his courage. "Miriam and I have a gift to love each other, and we are going among the world's people, to live after their fashion. And ye know that we do not transgress the law of the land; and neither ye, nor the elders themselves, have a right to hinder us."

"Yet you think it expedient to depart without leave-taking," remarked one of the travellers.

"Yea, ye-a," said Josiah, reluctantly, "because father Job is a very awful man to speak with; and being aged himself, he has but little charity for what he calls the iniquities of the flesh."

"Well," said the stranger, "we will neither use force to bring you back to the village, nor will we betray you to the elders. But sit you here awhile, and when you have heard what we shall tell you of the world which we have left, and into which you are going, perhaps you will turn back with us of your own accord. What say you?" added he, turning to his companions. "We have travelled thus far without becoming known to each other. Shall we tell our stories, here by this pleasant spring, for our own pastime, and the benefit of these misguided young lovers?"

In accordance with this proposal, the whole party stationed themselves round the stone cistern; the two children, being very weary, fell asleep upon the damp earth, and the pretty Shaker girl, whose feelings were those of a nun or a Turkish lady, crept as close as possible to the female traveller, and as far as she well could from the unknown men. The same person who had hitherto been the chief spokesman now stood up, waving his hat in his hand, and suffered the moonlight to fall full upon his front.

"In me," said he, with a certain majesty of utterance,—"in me, you behold a poet."

Though a lithographic print of this gentleman is extant, it may be well to notice that he was now nearly forty, a thin and stooping figure, in a black coat, out at elbows; notwithstanding the ill condition of his attire, there were about him several tokens of a peculiar sort of foppery, unworthy of a mature man, particularly in the arrangement of his hair, which was so disposed as to give all possible loftiness and breadth to his forehead. However, he had an intelligent eye, and, on the whole, a marked countenance.

"A poet!" repeated the young Shaker, a little puzzled how to understand such a designation, seldom heard in the utilitarian community where he had spent his life. "Oh, ay, Miriam, he means a varse-maker, thee must know."

This remark jarred upon the susceptible nerves of the poet; nor could he help wondering what strange fatality had put into this young man's mouth an epithet, which ill-natured people had affirmed to be more proper to his merit than the one assumed by himself.

"True, I am a verse-maker," he resumed, "but my verse is no more than the material body into which I breathe the celestial soul of thought. Alas! how many a pang has it cost me, this same insensibility to the ethereal essence of poetry, with which you have here tortured me again, at the moment when I am to relinquish my profession forever! O Fate! why hast thou warred with Nature, turning all her higher and more perfect gifts to the ruin of me, their possessor? What is the voice of song, when the world lacks the ear of taste? How can I rejoice in my strength and delicacy of feeling, when they have but made great sorrows out of little ones? Have I dreaded scorn like death, and yearned for fame as others pant for vital air, only to find myself in a middle state between obscurity and infamy? But I have my revenge! I could have given existence to a thousand bright creations. I crush them into my heart, and there let them putrefy! I shake off the dust of my feet against my countrymen! But posterity, tracing my footsteps up this weary hill, will cry shame upon the unworthy age that drove one of the fathers of American song to end his days in a Shaker village!"

During this harangue, the speaker gesticulated with great energy, and, as poetry is the natural language of passion, there appeared reason to apprehend his final explosion into an ode extempore. The reader must understand that, for all these bitter words, he was a kind, gentle, harmless, poor fellow enough, whom Nature, tossing her ingredients together without looking at her recipe, had sent into the world with too much of one sort of brain, and hardly any of another.

"Friend," said the young Shaker, in some perplexity, "thee seemest to have met with great troubles; and, doubtless, I should pity them, if—if I could but understand what they were."

"Happy in your ignorance!" replied the poet, with an air of sublime superiority. "To your coarser mind, perhaps, I may seem to speak of more important griefs when I add, what I had wellnigh forgotten, that I am out at elbows, and almost starved to death. At any rate, you have the advice and example of one individual to warn you back; for I am come hither, a disappointed man, flinging aside the fragments of my hopes, and seeking shelter in the calm retreat which you are so anxious to leave."

"I thank thee, friend," rejoined the youth, "but I do not mean to be a poet, nor, Heaven be praised! do I think Miriam ever made a varse in her life. So we need not fear thy disappointments. But, Miriam," he added, with real concern, "thee knowest that the elders admit nobody that has not a gift to be useful. Now, what under the sun can they do with this poor varse-maker?"

"Nay, Josiah, do not thee discourage the poor man," said the girl, in all simplicity and kindness. "Our hymns are very rough, and perhaps they may trust him to smooth them."

Without noticing this hint of professional employment, the poet turned away, and gave himself up to a sort of vague reverie, which he called thought. Sometimes he watched the moon, pouring a silvery liquid on the clouds, through which it slowly melted till they became all bright; then he saw the same sweet radiance dancing on the leafy trees which rustled as if to shake it off, or sleeping on the high tops of hills, or hovering down in distant valleys, like the material of unshaped dreams; lastly, he looked into the spring, and there the light was mingling with the water. In its crystal bosom, too, beholding all heaven reflected there, he found an emblem of a pure and tranquil breast. He listened to that most ethereal of all sounds, the song of crickets, coming in full choir upon the wind, and fancied that, if moonlight could be heard, it would sound just like that. Finally, he took a draught at the Shaker spring, and, as if it were the true Castalia, was forthwith moved to compose a lyric, a Farewell to his Harp, which he swore should be its closing strain, the last verse that an ungrateful world should have from him. This effusion, with two or three other little pieces, subsequently written, he took the first opportunity to send, by one of the Shaker brethren, to Concord, where they were published in the New Hampshire Patriot.

Meantime, another of the Canterbury pilgrims, one so different from the poet that the delicate fancy of the latter could hardly have conceived of him, began to relate his sad experience. He was a small man, of quick and unquiet gestures, about fifty years old, with a narrow forehead, all wrinkled and drawn together. He held in his hand a pencil, and a card of some commission-merchant in foreign parts, on the back of which, for there was light enough to read or write by, he seemed ready to figure out a calculation.

"Young man," said he, abruptly, "what quantity of land do the Shakers own here, in Canterbury?"

"That is more than I can tell thee, friend," answered Josiah, "but it is a very rich establishment, and for a long way by the roadside thee may guess the land to be ours, by the neatness of the fences."

"And what may be the value of the whole," continued the stranger, "with all the buildings and improvements, pretty nearly, in round numbers?"

"Oh, a monstrous sum,—more than I can reckon," replied the young Shaker.

"Well, sir," said the pilgrim, "there was a day, and not very long ago, neither, when I stood at my counting-room window, and watched the signal flags of three of my own ships entering the harbor, from the East Indies, from Liverpool, and from up the Straits, and I would not have given the invoice of the least of them for the title-deeds of this whole Shaker settlement. You stare. Perhaps, now, you won't believe that I could have put more value on a little piece of paper, no bigger than the palm of your hand, than all these solid acres of grain, grass, and pasture-land would sell for?"

"I won't dispute it, friend," answered Josiah, "but I know I had rather have fifty acres of this good land than a whole sheet of thy paper."

"You may say so now," said the ruined merchant, bitterly, "for my name would not be worth the paper I should write it on. Of course, you must have heard of my failure?"

And the stranger mentioned his name, which, however mighty it might have been in the commercial world, the young Shaker had never heard of among the Canterbury hills.

"Not heard of my failure!" exclaimed the merchant, considerably piqued. "Why, it was spoken of on 'Change in London, and from Boston to New Orleans men trembled in their shoes. At all events, I did fail, and you see me here on my road to the Shaker village, where, doubtless (for the Shakers are a shrewd sect), they will have a due respect for my experience, and give me the management of the trading part of the concern, in which case I think I can pledge myself to double their capital in four or five years. Turn back with me, young man; for though you will never meet with my good luck, you can hardly escape my bad."

"I will not turn back for this," replied Josiah, calmly, "any more than for the advice of the varse-maker, between whom and thee, friend, I see a sort of likeness, though I can't justly say where it lies. But Miriam and I can earn our daily bread among the world's people as well as in the Shaker village. And do we want anything more, Miriam?"

"Nothing more, Josiah," said the girl, quietly.

"Yea, Miriam, and daily bread for some other little mouths, if God send them," observed the simple Shaker lad.

Miriam did not reply, but looked down into the spring, where she encountered the image of her own pretty face, blushing within the prim little bonnet. The third pilgrim now took up the conversation. He was a sunburnt countryman, of tall frame and bony strength, on whose rude and manly face there appeared a darker, more sullen and obstinate despondency, than on those of either the poet or the merchant.

"Well, now, youngster," he began, "these folks have had their say, so I'll take my turn. My story will cut but a poor figure by the side of theirs; for I never supposed that I could have a right to meat and drink, and great praise besides, only for tagging rhymes together, as it seems this man does; nor ever tried to get the substance of hundreds into my own hands, like the trader there. When I was about of your years, I married me a wife,—just such a neat and pretty young woman as Miriam, if that's her name,—and all I asked of Providence was an ordinary blessing on the sweat of my brow, so that we might be decent and comfortable, and have daily bread for ourselves, and for some other little mouths that we soon had to feed. We had no very great prospects before us; but I never wanted to be idle; and I thought it a matter of course that the Lord would help me, because I was willing to help myself."

"And didn't He help thee, friend?" demanded Josiah, with some eagerness.

"No," said the yeoman, sullenly; "for then you would not have seen me here. I have labored hard for years; and my means have been growing narrower, and my living poorer, and my heart colder and heavier, all the time; till at last I could bear it no longer. I set my self down to calculate whether I had best go on the Oregon expedition, or come here to the Shaker village; but I had not hope enough left in me to begin the world over again; and, to make my story short, here I am. And now, youngster, take my advice, and turn back; or else, some few years hence, you'll have to climb this hill, with as heavy a heart as mine."

This simple story had a strong effect on the young fugitives. The misfortunes of the poet and merchant had won little sympathy from their plain good sense and unworldly feelings, qualities which made them such unprejudiced and inflexible judges, that few men would have chosen to take the opinion of this youth and maiden as to the wisdom or folly of their pursuits. But here was one whose simple wishes had resembled their own, and who, after efforts which almost gave him a right to claim success from fate, had failed in accomplishing them.

"But thy wife, friend?" exclaimed the younger man. "What became of the pretty girl, like Miriam? Oh, I am afraid she is dead!"

"Yea, poor man, she must be dead,—she and the children, too," sobbed Miriam.

The female pilgrim had been leaning over the spring, wherein latterly a tear or two might have been seen to fall, and form its little circle on the surface of the water. She now looked up, disclosing features still comely, but which had acquired an expression of fretfulness, in the same long course of evil fortune that had thrown a sullen gloom over the temper of the unprosperous yeoman.

"I am his wife," said she, a shade of irritability just perceptible in the sadness of her tone. "These poor little things, asleep on the ground, are two of our children. We had two more, but God has provided better for them than we could, by taking them to Himself."

"And what would thee advise Josiah and me to do?" asked Miriam, this being the first question which she had put to either of the strangers.

" 'Tis a thing almost against nature for a woman to try to part true lovers," answered the yeoman's wife, after a pause; "but I'll speak as truly to you as if these were my dying words. Though my husband told you some of our troubles, he didn't mention the greatest, and that which makes all the rest so hard to bear. If you and your sweetheart marry, you'll be kind and pleasant to each other for a year or two, and while that's the case, you never will repent; but, by and by, he'll grow gloomy, rough, and hard to please, and you'll be peevish, and full of little angry fits, and apt to be complaining by the fireside, when he comes to rest himself from his troubles out of doors; so your love will wear away by little and little, and leave you miserable at last. It has been so with us; and yet my husband and I were true lovers once, if ever two young folks were."

As she ceased, the yeoman and his wife exchanged a glance, in which there was more and warmer affection than they had supposed to have escaped the frost of a wintry fate, in either of their breasts. At that moment, when they stood on the utmost verge of married life, one word fitly spoken, or perhaps one peculiar look, had they had mutual confidence enough to reciprocate it, might have renewed all their old feelings, and sent them back, resolved to sustain each other amid the struggles of the world. But the crisis passed and never came again. Just then, also, the children, roused by their mother's voice, looked up, and added their wailing accents to the testimony borne by all the Canterbury pilgrims against the world from which they fled.

"We are tired and hungry!" cried they. "Is it far to the Shaker village?"

The Shaker youth and maiden looked mournfully into each other's eyes. They had but stepped across the threshold of their homes, when lo! the dark array of cares and sorrows that rose up to warn them back. The varied narratives of the strangers had arranged themselves into a parable; they seemed not merely instances of woful fate that had befallen others, but shadowy omens of disappointed hope and unavailing toil, domestic grief and estranged affection, that would cloud the onward path of these poor fugitives. But after one instant's hesitation, they opened their arms, and sealed their resolve with as pure and fond an embrace as ever youthful love had hallowed.

"We will not go back," said they. "The world never can be dark to us, for we will always love one another."

Then the Canterbury pilgrims went up the hill, while the poet chanted a drear and desperate stanza of the Farewell to his Harp, fitting music for that melancholy band. They sought a home where all former ties of nature or society would be sundered, and all old distinctions levelled, and a cold and passionless security be substituted for mortal hope and fear, as in that other refuge of the world's weary outcasts, the grave. The lovers drank at the Shaker spring, and then, with chastened hopes, but more confiding affections, went on to mingle in an untried life.

# THE DEVIL IN MANUSCRIPT

ON a bitter evening of December, I arrived by mail in a large town, which was then the residence of an intimate friend, one of those gifted youths who cultivate poetry and the belles-lettres, and call themselves students at law. My first business, after supper, was to visit him at the office of his distinguished instructor. As I have said, it was a bitter night, clear starlight, but cold as Nova Zembla,—the shop-windows along the street being frosted, so as almost to hide the lights, while the wheels of coaches thundered equally loud over frozen earth and pavements of stone. There was no snow, either on the ground or the roofs of the houses. The wind blew so violently, that I had but to spread my cloak like a main-sail, and scud along the street at the rate of ten knots, greatly envied by other navigators, who were beating slowly up, with the gale right in their teeth. One of these I capsized, but was gone on the wings of the wind before he could even vociferate an oath.

After this picture of an inclement night, behold us seated by a great blazing fire, which looked so comfortable and delicious that I felt inclined to lie down and roll among the hot coals. The usual furniture of a lawyer's office was around us,—rows of volumes in sheepskin, and a multitude of writs, summonses, and other legal papers, scattered over the desks and tables. But there were certain objects which seemed to intimate that we had little dread of the intrusion of clients, or of the learned counsellor himself, who, indeed, was attending court in a distant town. A tall, decanter-shaped bottle stood on the table, between two tumblers, and beside a pile of blotted manuscripts, altogether dissimilar to any law documents recognized in our courts. My friend, whom I shall call Oberon,—it was a name of fancy and friendship between him and me,—my friend Oberon looked at these papers with a peculiar expression of disquietude.

"I do believe," said he, soberly, "or, at least, I could believe, if I chose, that there is a devil in this pile of blotted papers. You have read them, and know what I mean,—that conception in which I endeavored to embody the character of a fiend, as represented in our traditions and the written records of witchcraft. Oh, I have a horror of what was created in my own brain, and shudder at the manuscripts in which I gave that dark idea a sort of material existence! Would they were out of my sight!"

"And of mine, too," thought I.

"You remember," continued Oberon, "how the hellish thing used to suck away the happiness of those who, by a simple concession that seemed almost innocent, subjected themselves to his power. Just so my peace is gone, and all by these accursed manuscripts. Have you felt nothing of the same influence?"

"Nothing," replied I, "unless the spell be hid in a desire to turn novelist, after reading your delightful tales."

"Novelist!" exclaimed Oberon, half seriously. "Then, indeed, my devil has his claw on you! You are gone! You cannot even pray for deliverance! But we will be the last and only victims; for this night I mean to burn the manuscripts, and commit the fiend to his retribution in the flames."

"Burn your tales!" repeated I, startled at the desperation of the idea.

"Even so," said the author, despondingly. "You cannot conceive what an effect the composition of these tales has had on me. I have become ambitious of a bubble, and careless of solid reputation. I am surrounding myself with shadows, which bewilder me, by aping the realities of life. They have drawn me aside from the beaten path of the world, and led me into a strange sort of solitude,—a solitude in the midst of men,—where nobody wishes for what I do, nor thinks nor feels as I do. The tales have done all this. When they are ashes, perhaps I shall be as I was before they had existence. Moreover, the sacrifice is less than you may suppose, since nobody will publish them."

"That does make a difference, indeed," said I.

"They have been offered, by letter," continued Oberon, reddening with vexation, "to some seventeen booksellers. It would make you stare to read their answers; and read them you should, only that I burnt them as fast as they arrived. One man publishes nothing but school-books; another has five novels already under examination."

"What a voluminous mass the unpublished literature of America must be!" cried I.

"Oh, the Alexandrian manuscripts were nothing to it!" said my friend. "Well, another gentleman is just giving up business, on purpose, I verily believe, to escape publishing my book. Several, however, would not absolutely decline the agency, on my advancing half the cost of an edition, and giving bonds for the remainder, besides a high percentage to themselves, whether the book sells or not. Another advises a subscription."

"The villain!" exclaimed I.

"A fact!" said Oberon. "In short, of all the seventeen booksellers, only one has vouchsafed even to read my tales; and he—a literary dabbler himself, I should judge—has the impertinence to criticise them, proposing what he calls vast improvements, and concluding, after a general sentence of condemnation, with the definitive assurance that he will not be concerned on any terms."

"It might not be amiss to pull that fellow's nose," remarked I.

"If the whole 'trade' had one common nose, there would be some satisfaction in pulling it," answered the author. "But, there does seem to be one honest man among these seventeen unrighteous ones; and he tells me fairly, that no American publisher will meddle with an American work,—seldom if by a known writer, and never if by a new one,—unless at the writer's risk."

"The paltry rogues!" cried I. "Will they live by literature, and yet risk nothing for its sake? But, after all, you might publish on your own account."

"And so I might," replied Oberon. "But the devil of the business is this. These people have put me so out of conceit with the tales, that I loathe the very thought of them, and actually experience a physical sickness of the stomach, whenever I glance at them on the table. I tell you there is a demon in them! I anticipate a wild enjoyment in seeing them in the blaze; such as I should feel in taking vengeance on an enemy, or destroying something noxious."

I did not very strenuously oppose this determination, being privately of opinion, in spite of my partiality for the author, that his tales would make a more brilliant appearance in the fire than anywhere else. Before proceeding to execution, we broached the bottle of champagne, which Oberon had provided for keeping up his spirits in this doleful business. We swallowed each a tumblerful, in sparkling commotion; it went bubbling down our throats, and brightened my eyes at once, but left my friend sad and heavy as before. He drew the tales towards him, with a mixture of natural affection and natural disgust, like a father taking a deformed infant into his arms.

"Pooh! Pish! Pshaw!" exclaimed he, holding them at arm's-length. "It was Gray's idea of heaven, to lounge on a sofa and read new novels. Now, what more appropriate torture would Dante himself have contrived, for the sinner who perpetrates a bad book, than to be continually turning over the manuscript?"

"It would fail of effect," said I, "because a bad author is always his own great admirer."

"I lack that one characteristic of my tribe,—the only desirable one," observed Oberon. "But how many recollections throng upon me, as I turn over these leaves! This scene came into my fancy as I walked along a hilly road, on a starlight October evening; in the pure and bracing air, I became all soul, and felt as if I could climb the sky, and run a race along the Milky-Way. Here is another tale, in which I wrapt myself during a dark and dreary night-ride in the month of March, till the rattling of the wheels and the voices of my companions seemed like faint sounds of a dream, and my visions a bright reality. That scribbled page describes shadows which I summoned to my bedside at midnight: they would not depart when I bade them; the gray dawn came, and found me wide awake and feverish, the victim of my own enchantments!"

"There must have been a sort of happiness in all this," said I, smitten with a strange longing to make proof of it.

"There may be happiness in a fever fit," replied the author. "And then the various moods in which I wrote! Sometimes my ideas were like precious stones under the earth, requiring toil to dig them up, and care to polish and brighten them; but often a delicious stream of thought would gush out upon the page at once, like water sparkling up suddenly in the desert; and when it had passed, I gnawed my pen hopelessly, or blundered on with cold and miserable toil, as if there were a wall of ice between me and my subject."

"Do you now perceive a corresponding difference," inquired I, "between the passages which you wrote so coldly, and those fervid flashes of the mind?"

"No," said Oberon, tossing the manuscripts on the table. "I find no traces of the golden pen with which I wrote in characters of fire. My treasure of fairy coin is changed to worthless dross. My picture, painted in what seemed the loveliest hues, presents nothing but a faded and indistinguishable surface. I have been eloquent and poetical and humorous in a dream,—and behold! it is all nonsense, now that I am awake."

My friend now threw sticks of wood and dry chips upon the fire, and seeing it blaze like Nebuchadnezzar's furnace, seized the champagne-bottle, and drank two or three brimming bumpers, successively. The heady liquor combined with his agitation to throw him into a species of rage. He laid violent hands on the tales. In one instant more, their faults and beauties would alike have vanished in a glowing purgatory. But, all at once, I remembered passages of high imagination, deep pathos, original thoughts, and points of such varied excellence, that the vastness of the sacrifice struck me most forcibly. I caught his arm.

"Surely, you do not mean to burn them!" I exclaimed.

"Let me alone!" cried Oberon, his eyes flashing fire. "I will burn them! Not a scorched syllable shall escape! Would you have me a damned author?—To undergo sneers, taunts, abuse, and cold neglect, and faint praise, bestowed, for pity's sake, against the giver's con-science! A hissing and a laughing-stock to my own traitorous thoughts! An outlaw from the protection of the grave,—one whose ashes every careless foot might spurn, unhonored in life, and remembered scornfully in death! Am I to bear all this, when yonder fire will insure me from the whole? No! There go the tales! May my hand wither when it would write another!"

The deed was done. He had thrown the manuscripts into the hottest of the fire, which at first seemed to shrink away, but soon curled around them, and made them a part of its own fervent brightness. Oberon stood gazing at the conflagration, and shortly began to soliloquize, in the wildest strain, as if Fancy resisted and became riotous, at the moment when he would have compelled her to ascend that funeral pile. His words described objects which he appeared to discern in the fire, fed by his own precious thoughts; perhaps the thousand visions which the writer's magic had incorporated with these pages became visible to him in the dissolving heat, brightening forth ere they vanished forever; while the smoke, the vivid sheets of flame, the ruddy and whitening coals, caught the aspect of a varied scenery.

"They blaze," said he, "as if I had steeped them in the intensest spirit of genius. There I see my lovers clasped in each other's arms. How pure the flame that bursts from their glowing hearts! And yonder the features of a villain writhing in the fire that shall torment him to eter-nity. My holy men, my pious and angelic women, stand like martyrs amid the flames, their mild eyes lifted heavenward. Ring out the bells! A city is on fire. See!—destruction roars through my dark forests, while the lakes boil up in steaming billows, and the mountains are volcanoes, and the sky kindles with a lurid brightness! All elements are but one pervading flame! Ha! The fiend!"

I was somewhat startled by this latter exclamation. The tales were almost consumed, but just then threw forth a broad sheet of fire, which flickered as with laughter, making the whole room dance in its bright-ness, and then roared portentously up the chimney.

"You saw him? You must have seen him!" cried Oberon. "How he glared at me and laughed, in that last sheet of flame, with just the features that I imagined for him! Well! The tales are gone."

The papers were indeed reduced to a heap of black cinders, with a multitude of sparks hurrying confusedly among them, the traces of the pen being now represented by white lines, and the whole mass fluttering to and fro in the draughts of air. The destroyer knelt down to look at them.

"What is more potent than fire!" said he, in his gloomiest tone. "Even thought, invisible and incorporeal as it is, cannot escape it. In this little time, it has annihilated the creations of long nights and days, which I could no more reproduce, in their first glow and freshness, than cause ashes and whitened bones to rise up and live. There, too, I sacrificed the unborn children of my mind. All that I had accomplished—all that I planned for future years—has perished by one common ruin, and left only this heap of embers! The deed has been my fate. And what remains? A weary and aimless life,—a long repentance of this hour,—and at last an obscure grave, where they will bury and forget me!"

As the author concluded his dolorous moan, the extinguished embers arose and settled down and arose again, and finally flew up the chimney, like a demon with sable wings. Just as they disappeared, there was a loud and solitary cry in the street below us. "Fire!" Fire! Other voices caught up that terrible word, and it speedily became the shout of a multitude. Oberon started to his feet, in fresh excitement.

"A fire on such a night!" cried he. "The wind blows a gale, and wherever it whirls the flames, the roofs will flash up like gunpowder. Every pump is frozen up, and boiling water would turn to ice the moment it was flung from the engine. In an hour, this wooden town will be one great bonfire! What a glorious scene for my next— Pshaw!"

The street was now all alive with footsteps, and the air full of voices. We heard one engine thundering round a corner, and another rattling from a distance over the pavements. The bells of three steeples clanged out at once, spreading the alarm to many a neighboring town, and expressing hurry, confusion, and terror, so inimitably that I could almost distinguish in their peal the burden of the universal cry,—"Fire! Fire! Fire!"

"What is so eloquent as their iron tongues!" exclaimed Oberon. "My heart leaps and trembles, but not with fear. And that other sound, too, —deep and awful as a mighty organ,—the roar and thunder of the multitude on the pavement below! Come! We are losing time. I will cry out in the loudest of the uproar, and mingle my spirit with the wildest of the confusion, and be a bubble on the top of the ferment!"

From the first outcry, my forebodings had warned me of the true object and centre of alarm. There was nothing now but uproar, above, beneath, and around us; footsteps stumbling pell-mell up the public staircase, eager shouts and heavy thumps at the door, the whiz and dash of water from the engines, and the crash of furniture thrown upon the pavement. At once, the truth flashed upon my friend. His frenzy took

the hue of joy, and, with a wild gesture of exultation, he leaped almost
to the ceiling of the chamber.

"My tales!" cried Oberon. "The chimney! The roof! The Fiend has
gone forth by night, and startled thousands in fear and wonder from
their beds! Here I stand,—a triumphant author! Huzza! Huzza! My
brain has set the town on fire! Huzza!"

# MY KINSMAN, MAJOR MOLINEUX

AFTER the kings of Great Britain had assumed the right of appointing
the colonial governors, the measures of the latter seldom met with the
ready and generous approbation which had been paid to those of their
predecessors, under the original charters. The people looked with most
jealous scrutiny to the exercise of power which did not emanate from
themselves, and they usually rewarded their rulers with slender gratitude for the compliances by which, in softening their instructions from
beyond the sea, they had incurred the reprehension of those who gave
them. The annals of Massachusetts Bay will inform us, that of six governors in the space of about forty years from the surrender of the old
charter, under James II., two were imprisoned by a popular insurrec-
tion; a third, as Hutchinson inclines to believe, was driven from the
province by the whizzing of a musket-ball; a fourth, in the opinion of
the same historian, was hastened to his grave by continual bickerings
with the House of Representatives; and the remaining two, as well as
their successors, till the Revolution, were favored with few and brief intervals of peaceful sway. The inferior members of the court party, in
times of high political excitement, led scarcely a more desirable life.
These remarks may serve as a preface to the following adventures,
which chanced upon a summer night, not far from a hundred years ago.
The reader, in order to avoid a long and dry detail of colonial affairs, is
requested to dispense with an account of the train of circumstances that
had caused much temporary inflammation of the popular mind.

It was near nine o'clock of a moonlight evening, when a boat crossed
the ferry with a single passenger, who had obtained his conveyance at
that unusual hour by the promise of an extra fare. While he stood on
the landing-place, searching in either pocket for the means of fulfilling
his agreement, the ferryman lifted a lantern, by the aid of which, and
the newly risen moon, he took a very accurate survey of the stranger's
figure. He was a youth of barely eighteen years, evidently country-bred,
and now, as it should seem, upon his first visit to town. He was clad in
a coarse gray coat, well worn, but in excellent repair; his under garments were durably constructed of leather, and fitted tight to a pair of

serviceable and well-shaped limbs; his stockings of blue yarn were the incontrovertible work of a mother or a sister; and on his head was a three-cornered hat, which in its better days had perhaps sheltered the graver brow of the lad's father. Under his left arm was a heavy cudgel formed of an oak sapling, and retaining a part of the hardened root; and his equipment was completed by a wallet, not so abundantly stocked as to incommode the vigorous shoulders on which it hung. Brown, curly hair, well-shaped features, and bright, cheerful eyes were nature's gifts, and worth all that art could have done for his adornment.

The youth, one of whose names was Robin, finally drew from his pocket the half of a little province bill of five shillings, which, in the depreciation in that sort of currency, did but satisfy the ferryman's demand, with the surplus of a sexangular piece of parchment, valued at three pence. He then walked forward into the town, with as light a step as if his day's journey had not already exceeded thirty miles, and with as eager an eye as if he were entering London city, instead of the little metropolis of a New England colony. Before Robin had proceeded far, however, it occurred to him that he knew not whither to direct his steps; so he paused, and looked up and down the narrow street, scrutinizing the small and mean wooden buildings that were scattered on either side.

"This low hovel cannot be my kinsman's dwelling," thought he, "nor yonder old house, where the moonlight enters at the broken casement; and truly I see none hereabouts that might be worthy of him. It would have been wise to inquire my way of the ferryman, and doubtless he would have gone with me, and earned a shilling from the Major for his pains. But the next man I meet will do as well."

He resumed his walk, and was glad to perceive that the street now became wider, and the houses more respectable in their appearance. He soon discerned a figure moving on moderately in advance, and hastened his steps to overtake it. As Robin drew nigh, he saw that the passenger was a man in years, with a full periwig of gray hair, a wide-skirted coat of dark cloth, and silk stockings rolled above his knees. He carried a long and polished cane, which he struck down perpendicularly before him at every step; and at regular intervals he uttered two successive hems, of a peculiarly solemn and sepulchral intonation. Having made these observations, Robin laid hold of the skirt of the old man's coat, just when the light from the open door and windows of a barber's shop fell upon both their figures.

"Good evening to you, honored sir," said he, making a low bow, and still retaining his hold of the skirt. "I pray you tell me whereabouts is the dwelling of my kinsman, Major Molineux."

The youth's question was uttered very loudly; and one of the barbers, whose razor was descending on a well-soaped chin, and another who was dressing a Ramillies wig, left their occupations, and came to the door. The citizen, in the mean time, turned a long-favored countenance upon Robin, and answered him in a tone of excessive anger and annoyance. His two sepulchral hems, however, broke into the very centre of his rebuke, with most singular effect, like a thought of the cold grave obtruding among wrathful passions.

"Let go my garment, fellow! I tell you, I know not the man you speak of. What! I have authority, I have—hem, hem—authority; and if this be the respect you show for your betters, your feet shall be brought acquainted with the stocks by daylight, tomorrow morning!"

Robin released the old man's skirt, and hastened away, pursued by an ill-mannered roar of laughter from the barber's shop. He was at first considerably surprised by the result of his question, but, being a shrewd youth, soon thought himself able to account for the mystery.

"This is some country representative," was his conclusion, "who has never seen the inside of my kinsman's door, and lacks the breeding to answer a stranger civilly. The man is old, or verily—I might be tempted to turn back and smite him on the nose. Ah, Robin, Robin! even the barber's boys laugh at you for choosing such a guide! You will be wiser in time, friend Robin."

He now became entangled in a succession of crooked and narrow streets, which crossed each other, and meandered at no great distance from the water-side. The smell of tar was obvious to his nostrils, the masts of vessels pierced the moonlight above the tops of the buildings, and the numerous signs, which Robin paused to read, informed him that he was near the centre of business. But the streets were empty, the shops were closed, and lights were visible only in the second stories of a few dwelling-houses. At length, on the corner of a narrow lane, through which he was passing, he beheld the broad countenance of a British hero swinging before the door of an inn, whence proceeded the voices of many guests. The casement of one of the lower windows was thrown back, and a very thin curtain permitted Robin to distinguish a party at supper, round a well-furnished table. The fragrance of the good cheer steamed forth into the outer air, and the youth could not fail to recollect that the last remnant of his travelling stock of provision had yielded to his morning appetite, and that noon had found and left him dinnerless.

"Oh, that a parchment three-penny might give me a right to sit down at yonder table!" said Robin, with a sigh. "But the Major will make me welcome to the best of his victuals; so I will even step boldly in, and inquire my way to his dwelling."

He entered the tavern, and was guided by the murmur of voices and the fumes of tobacco to the public-room. It was a long and low apartment, with oaken walls, grown dark in the continual smoke, and a floor which was thickly sanded, but of no immaculate purity. A number of persons—the larger part of whom appeared to be mariners, or in some way connected with the sea—occupied the wooden benches, or leather-bottomed chairs, conversing on various matters, and occasionally lending their attention to some topic of general interest. Three or four little groups were draining as many bowls of punch, which the West India trade had long since made a familiar drink in the colony. Others, who had the appearance of men who lived by regular and laborious handicraft, preferred the insulated bliss of an unshared potation, and became more taciturn under its influence. Nearly all, in short, evinced a predilection for the Good Creature in some of its various shapes, for this is a vice to which, as Fast Day sermons of a hundred years ago will testify, we have a long hereditary claim. The only guests to whom Robin's sympathies inclined him were two or three sheepish countrymen, who were using the inn somewhat after the fashion of a Turkish caravansary; they had gotten themselves into the darkest corner of the room, and heedless of the Nicotian atmosphere, were supping on the bread of their own ovens, and the bacon cured in their own chimney-smoke. But though Robin felt a sort of brotherhood with these strangers, his eyes were attracted from them to a person who stood near the door, holding whispered conversation with a group of ill-dressed associates. His features were separately striking almost to grotesqueness, and the whole face left a deep impression on the memory. The forehead bulged out into a double prominence, with a vale between; the nose came boldly forth in an irregular curve, and its bridge was of more than a finger's breadth; the eyebrows were deep and shaggy, and the eyes glowed beneath them like fire in a cave.

While Robin deliberated of whom to inquire respecting his kinsman's dwelling, he was accosted by the innkeeper, a little man in a stained white apron, who had come to pay his professional welcome to the stranger. Being in the second generation from a French Protestant, he seemed to have inherited the courtesy of his parent nation; but no variety of circumstances was ever known to change his voice from the one shrill note in which he now addressed Robin.

"From the country, I presume, sir?" said he, with a profound bow. "Beg leave to congratulate you on your arrival, and trust you intend a long stay with us. Fine town here, sir, beautiful buildings, and much that may interest a stranger. May I hope for the honor of your commands in respect to supper?"

"The man sees a family likeness! the rogue has guessed that I am related to the Major!" thought Robin, who had hitherto experienced little superfluous civility.

All eyes were now turned on the country lad, standing at the door, in his worn three-cornered hat, gray coat, leather breeches, and blue yarn stockings, leaning on an oaken cudgel, and bearing a wallet on his back.

Robin replied to the courteous innkeeper, with such an assumption of confidence as befitted the Major's relative. "My honest friend," he said, "I shall make it a point to patronize your house on some occasion, when"—here he could not help lowering his voice—"when I may have more than a parchment three-pence in my pocket. My present business," continued he, speaking with lofty confidence, "is merely to inquire my way to the dwelling of my kinsman, Major Molineux."

There was a sudden and general movement in the room, which Robin interpreted as expressing the eagerness of each individual to become his guide. But the innkeeper turned his eyes to a written paper on the wall, which he read, or seemed to read, with occasional recurrences to the young man's figure.

"What have we here?" said he, breaking his speech into little dry fragments. " 'Left the house of the subscriber, bounden servant, Hezekiah Mudge,—had on, when he went away, gray coat, leather breeches, master's third-best hat. One pound currency reward to whosoever shall lodge him in any jail of the providence.' Better trudge, boy; better trudge!"

Robin had begun to draw his hand towards the lighter end of the oak cudgel, but a strange hostility in every countenance induced him to relinquish his purpose of breaking the courteous innkeeper's head. As he turned to leave the room, he encountered a sneering glance from the bold-featured personage whom he had before noticed; and no sooner was he beyond the door, than he heard a general laugh, in which the innkeeper's voice might be distinguished, like the dropping of small stones into a kettle.

"Now, is it not strange," thought Robin, with his usual shrewdness,— "is it not strange that the confession of an empty pocket should outweigh the name of my kinsman, Major Molineux? Oh, if I had one of those grinning rascals in the woods, where I and my oak sapling grew up together, I would teach him that my arm is heavy though my purse be light!"

On turning the corner of the narrow lane, Robin found himself in a spacious street, with an unbroken line of lofty houses on each side, and a steepled building at the upper end, whence the ringing of a bell announced the hour of nine. The light of the moon, and the lamps from the numerous shop-windows, discovered people promenading on the pavement, and amongst them Robin had hoped to recognize his hitherto inscrutable relative. The result of his former inquiries made him unwilling to hazard another, in a scene of such publicity, and he determined to walk slowly and silently up the street, thrusting his face close to that of every elderly gentleman, in search of the Major's lineaments. In his progress, Robin encountered many gay and gallant figures. Embroidered garments of showy colors, enormous periwigs, gold-laced hats, and silver-hilted swords glided past him and dazzled his optics. Travelled youths, imitators of the European fine gentlemen of the period, trod jauntily along, half dancing to the fashionable tunes which they hummed, and making poor Robin ashamed of his quiet and natural gait. At length, after many pauses to examine the gorgeous display of goods in the shop-windows, and after suffering some rebukes for the impertinence of his scrutiny into people's faces, the Major's kinsman found himself near the steepled building, still unsuccessful in his search. As yet, however, he had seen only one side of the thronged street; so Robin crossed, and continued the same sort of inquisition down the opposite pavement, with stronger hopes than the philosopher seeking an honest man, but with no better fortune. He had arrived about midway towards the lower end, from which his course began, when he overheard the approach of some one who struck down a cane on the flag-stones at every step, uttering at regular intervals, two sepulchral hems.

"Mercy on us!" quoth Robin, recognizing the sound.

Turning a corner, which chanced to be close at his right hand, he hastened to pursue his researches in some other part of the town. His patience now was wearing low, and he seemed to feel more fatigue from his rambles since he crossed the ferry, than from his journey of several days on the other side. Hunger also pleaded loudly within him, and Robin began to balance the propriety of demanding, violently, and with lifted cudgel, the necessary guidance from the first solitary passenger whom he should meet. While a resolution to this effect was gaining strength, he entered a street of mean appearance, on either side of which a row of ill-built houses was straggling towards the harbor. The moonlight fell upon no passenger along the whole extent, but in the third domicile which Robin passed there was a half-opened door, and his keen glance detected a woman's garment within.

"My luck may be better here," said he to himself.

Accordingly, he approached the door, and beheld it shut closer as he did so; yet an open space remained, sufficing for the fair occupant to observe the stranger, without a corresponding display on her part. All that Robin could discern was a strip of scarlet petticoat, and the occasional sparkle of an eye, as if the moonbeams were trembling on some bright thing.

"Pretty mistress," for I may call her so with a good conscience, thought the shrewd youth, since I know nothing to the contrary,—"my sweet pretty mistress, will you be kind enough to tell me whereabouts I must seek the dwelling of my kinsman, Major Molineux?"

Robin's voice was plaintive and winning, and the female, seeing nothing to be shunned in the handsome country youth, thrust open the door, and came forth into the moonlight. She was a dainty little figure, with a white neck, round arms, and a slender waist, at the extremity of which her scarlet petticoat jutted out over a hoop, as if she were standing in a balloon. Moreover, her face was oval and pretty, her hair dark beneath the little cap, and her bright eyes possessed a sly freedom, which triumphed over those of Robin.

"Major Molineux dwells here," said this fair woman.

Now, her voice was the sweetest Robin had heard that night, yet he could not help doubting whether that sweet voice spoke Gospel truth. He looked up and down the mean street, and then surveyed the house before which they stood. It was a small, dark edifice of two stories, the second of which projected over the lower floor, and the front apartment had the aspect of a shop for petty commodities.

"Now, truly, I am in luck," replied Robin, cunningly, "and so indeed is my kinsman, the Major, in having so pretty a housekeeper. But I prithee trouble him to step to the door; I will deliver him a message from his friends in the country, and then go back to my lodgings at the inn."

"Nay, the Major has been abed this hour or more," said the lady of the scarlet petticoat; "and it would be to little purpose to disturb him to-night, seeing his evening draught was of the strongest. But he is a kind-hearted man, and it would be as much as my life's worth to let a kinsman of his turn away from the door. You are the good old gentleman's very picture, and I could swear that was his rainy-weather hat. Also he has garments very much resembling those leather small-clothes. But come in, I pray, for I bid you hearty welcome in his name."

So saying, the fair and hospitable dame took our hero by the hand; and the touch was light, and the force was gentleness, and though Robin read in her eyes what he did not hear in her words, yet the slender-waisted woman in the scarlet petticoat proved stronger than the athletic country youth. She had drawn his half-willing footsteps nearly to the threshold, when the opening of a door in the neighborhood startled the Major's housekeeper, and, leaving the Major's kinsman, she vanished speedily into her own domicile. A heavy yawn preceded the appearance of a man, who, like the Moonshine of Pyramus and Thisbe, carried a lantern, needlessly aiding his sister luminary in the heavens. As he walked sleepily up the street, he turned his broad, dull face on Robin, and displayed a long staff, spiked at the end.

"Home, vagabond, home!" said the watchman, in accents that seemed to fall asleep as soon as they were uttered. "Home, or we'll set you in the stocks by peep of day!"

"This is the second hint of the kind," thought Robin. "I wish they would end my difficulties, by setting me there to-night."

Nevertheless, the youth felt an instinctive antipathy towards the guardian of midnight order, which at first prevented him from asking his usual question. But just when the man was about to vanish behind the corner, Robin resolved not to lose the opportunity, and shouted lustily after him,—

"I say, friend! will you guide me to the house of my kinsman, Major Molineux?"

The watchman made no reply, but turned the corner and was gone; yet Robin seemed to hear the sound of drowsy laughter stealing along the solitary street. At that moment, also, a pleasant titter saluted him from the open window above his head; he looked up, and caught the sparkle of a saucy eye; a round arm beckoned to him, and next he heard light footsteps descending the staircase within. But Robin, being of the household of a New England clergyman, was a good youth, as well as a shrewd one; so he resisted temptation, and fled away.

He now roamed desperately, and at random, through the town, almost ready to believe that a spell was on him, like that by which a wizard of his country had once kept three pursuers wandering, a whole winter night, within twenty paces of the cottage which they sought. The streets lay before him, strange and desolate, and the lights were extinguished in almost every house. Twice, however, little parties of men, among whom Robin distinguished individuals in outlandish attire, came hurrying along; but, though on both occasions, they paused to address him, such intercourse did not at all enlighten his perplexity. They did but utter a few words in some language of which Robin knew nothing, and perceiving his inability to answer, bestowed a curse upon him in plain English and hastened away. Finally, the lad determined to knock at the door of every mansion that might appear worthy to be occupied by his kinsman, trusting that perseverance would overcome the fatality that had hitherto thwarted him. Firm in this resolve, he was passing beneath the walls of a church, which formed the corner of two streets, when, as he turned into the shade of its steeple, he encountered a bulky stranger, muffled in a cloak. The man was proceeding with the speed of earnest business, but Robin planted himself full before him, holding the oak cudgel with both hands across his body as a bar to further passage.

"Halt, honest man, and answer me a question," said he, very resolutely. "Tell me, this instant, whereabouts is the dwelling of my kinsman, Major Molineux!"

"Keep your tongue between your teeth, fool, and let me pass!" said a deep, gruff voice, which Robin partly remembered. "Let me pass, or I'll strike you to the earth!"

"No, no, neighbor!" cried Robin, flourishing his cudgel, and then thrusting its larger end close to the man's muffled face. "No, no, I'm not the fool you take me for, nor do you pass till I have an answer to my question. Whereabouts is the dwelling of my kinsman, Major Molineux?"

The stranger, instead of attempting to force his passage, stepped back into the moonlight, unmuffled his face, and stared full into that of Robin.

"Watch here an hour, and Major Molineux will pass by," said he.

Robin gazed with dismay and astonishment on the unprecedented physiognomy of the speaker. The forehead with its double prominence, the broad hooked nose, the shaggy eyebrows, and fiery eyes were those which he had noticed at the inn, but the man's complexion had undergone a singular, or, more properly, a twofold change. One side of the face blazed an intense red, while the other was black as midnight, the division line being in the broad bridge of the nose; and a mouth which seemed to extend from ear to ear was black or red, in contrast to the color of the cheek. The effect was as if two individual devils, a fiend of fire and a fiend of darkness, had united themselves to form this infernal visage. The stranger grinned in Robin's face, muffled his party-colored features, and was out of sight in a moment.

"Strange things we travellers see!" ejaculated Robin.

He seated himself, however, upon the steps of the church-door, resolving to wait the appointed time for his kinsman. A few moments were consumed in philosophical speculations upon the species of man who had just left him; but having settled this point shrewdly, rationally, and satisfactorily, he was compelled to look elsewhere for his amusement. And first he threw his eyes along the street. It was of more respectable appearance than most of those into which he had wandered; and the moon, creating, like the imaginative power, a beautiful strangeness in familiar objects, gave something of romance to a scene that might not have possessed it in the light of day. The irregular and often quaint architecture of the houses, some of whose roofs were broken into numerous little peaks, while others ascended, steep and narrow, into a single point, and others again were square; the pure snow-white of some of their complexions, the aged darkness of others, and the thousand sparklings, reflected from bright substances in the walls of many; these matters engaged Robin's attention for a while, and then began to grow wearisome. Next he endeavored to define the forms of distant objects, starting away, with almost ghostly indistinctness, just as his eye appeared to grasp them; and finally he took a minute survey of an edifice which stood on the opposite side of the street, directly in front of the church-door, where he was stationed. It was a large, square mansion, distinguished from its neighbors by a balcony, which rested on tall pillars, and by an elaborate Gothic window, communicating therewith.

"Perhaps this is the very house I have been seeking," thought Robin.

Then he strove to speed away the time, by listening to a murmur which swept continually along the street, yet was scarcely audible, except to an unaccustomed ear like his; it was a low, dull, dreamy sound, compounded of many noises, each of which was at too great a distance to be separately heard. Robin marvelled at this snore of a sleeping town, and marvelled more whenever its continuity was broken by now and then a distant shout, apparently loud where it originated. But altogether it was a sleep-inspiring sound, and, to shake off its drowsy influence, Robin arose, and climbed a window-frame, that he might view the interior of the church. There the moonbeams came trembling in, and fell down upon the deserted pews, and extended along the quiet aisles. A fainter yet more awful radiance was hovering around the pulpit, and one solitary ray had dared to rest upon the open page of the great Bible. Had nature, in that deep hour, become a worshipper in the house which man had builded? Or was that heavenly light the visible sanctity of the place,—visible because no earthly and impure feet were within the walls? The scene made Robin's heart shiver with a sensation of loneliness stronger than he had ever felt in the remotest depths of his native woods; so he turned away and sat down again before the door. There were graves around the church, and now an uneasy thought obtruded into Robin's breast. What if the object of his search, which had been so often and so strangely thwarted, were all the time mouldering in his shroud? What if his kinsman should glide through yonder gate, and nod and smile to him in dimly passing by?

"Oh that any breathing thing were here with me!" said Robin.

Recalling his thoughts from this uncomfortable track, he sent them over forest, hill, and stream, and attempted to imagine how that evening of ambiguity and weariness had been spent by his father's household. He pictured them assembled at the door, beneath the tree, the great old tree, which had been spared for its huge twisted trunk and venerable shade, when a thousand leafy brethren fell. There, at the going down of the summer sun, it was his father's custom to perform domestic worship, that the neighbors might come and join with him like brothers of the family, and that the wayfaring man might pause to drink at that fountain, and keep his heart pure by freshening the memory of home. Robin distinguished the seat of every individual of the little audience; he saw the good man in the midst, holding the Scriptures in the golden light that fell from the western clouds; he beheld him close the book and all rise up to pray. He heard the old thanksgivings for daily mercies, the old supplications for their continuance, to which he had so often listened in weariness, but which were now among his dear remembrances. He perceived the slight inequality of his father's voice when he came to speak of the absent one; he noted how his mother turned her face to the broad and knotted trunk; how his elder brother scorned, because the beard was rough upon his upper lip, to permit his features to be moved; how the younger sister drew down a low hanging branch before her eyes; and how the little one of all, whose sports had hitherto broken the decorum of the scene, understood the prayer for her playmate, and burst into clamorous grief. Then he saw them go in at the door; and when Robin would have entered also, the latch tinkled into its place, and he was excluded from his home.

"Am I here, or there?" cried Robin, starting; for all at once, when his thoughts had become visible and audible in a dream, the long, wide, solitary street shone out before him.

He aroused himself, and endeavored to fix his attention steadily upon the large edifice which he had surveyed before. But still his mind kept vibrating between fancy and reality; by turns, the pillars of the balcony lengthened into the tall, bare stems of pines, dwindled down to human figures, settled again into their true shape and size, and then commenced a new succession of changes. For a single moment, when he deemed himself awake, he could have sworn that a visage—one which he seemed to remember, yet could not absolutely name as his kinsman's—was looking towards him from the Gothic window. A deeper sleep wrestled with and nearly overcame him, but fled at the sound of footsteps along the opposite pavement. Robin rubbed his eyes, discerned a man passing at the foot of the balcony, and addressed him in a loud, peevish, and lamentable cry.

"Hallo, friend! must I wait here all night for my kinsman, Major Molineux?"

The sleeping echoes awoke, and answered the voice; and the passenger, barely able to discern a figure sitting in the oblique shade of the steeple, traversed the street to obtain a nearer view. He was himself a gentleman in his prime, of open, intelligent, cheerful, and altogether prepossessing countenance. Perceiving a country youth, apparently homeless and without friends, he accosted him in a tone of real kindness, which had become strange to Robin's ears.

"Well, my good lad, why are you sitting here?" inquired he. "Can I be of service to you in any way?"

"I am afraid not, sir," replied Robin, despondingly; "yet I shall take it kindly, if you'll answer me a single question. I've been searching, half the night, for one Major Molineux; now, sir, is there really such a person in these parts, or am I dreaming?"

"Major Molineux! The name is not altogether strange to me," said the gentleman, smiling. "Have you any objection to telling me the nature of your business with him?"

Then Robin briefly related that his father was a clergyman, settled on a small salary, at a long distance back in the country, and that he and Major Molineux were brothers' children. The Major, having inherited riches, and acquired civil and military rank, had visited his cousin, in great pomp, a year or two before; had manifested much interest in Robin and an elder brother, and, being childless himself, had thrown out hints respecting the future establishment of one of them in life. The elder brother was destined to succeed to the farm which his father cultivated in the interval of sacred duties; it was therefore determined that Robin should profit by his kinsman's generous intentions, especially as he seemed to be rather the favorite, and was thought to possess other necessary endowments.

"For I have the name of being a shrewd youth," observed Robin, in this part of his story.

"I doubt not you deserve it," replied his new friend, good-naturedly; "but pray proceed."

"Well, sir, being nearly eighteen years old, and well grown, as you see," continued Robin, drawing himself up to his full height, "I thought it high time to begin in the world. So my mother and sister put me in handsome trim, and my father gave me half the remnant of his last year's salary, and five days ago I started for this place, to pay the Major a visit. But, would you believe it, sir! I crossed the ferry a little after dark, and have yet found nobody that would show me the way to his dwelling; only, an hour or two since, I was told to wait here, and Major Molineux would pass by."

"Can you describe the man who told you this?" inquired the gentleman.

"Oh, he was a very ill-favored fellow, sir," replied Robin, "with two great bumps on his forehead, a hook nose, fiery eyes; and, what struck me as the strangest, his face was of two different colors. Do you happen to know such a man, sir?"

"Not intimately," answered the stranger, "but I chanced to meet him a little time previous to your stopping me. I believe you may trust his word, and that the Major will very shortly pass through this street. In the mean time, as I have a singular curiosity to witness your meeting, I will sit down here upon the steps and bear you company."

He seated himself accordingly, and soon engaged his companion in animated discourse. It was but of brief continuance, however, for a noise of shouting, which had long been remotely audible, drew so much nearer that Robin inquired its cause.

"What may be the meaning of this uproar?" asked he. "Truly, if your town be always as noisy, I shall find little sleep while I am an inhabitant."

"Why, indeed, friend Robin, there do appear to be three or four riotous fellows abroad to-night," replied the gentleman. "You must not expect all the stillness of your native woods here in our streets. But the watch will shortly be at the heels of these lads and"—

"Ay, and set them in the stocks by peep of day," interrupted Robin, recollecting his own encounter with the drowsy lantern-bearer. "But, dear sir, if I may trust my ears, an army of watchmen would never make head against such a multitude of rioters. There were at least a thousand voices went up to make that one shout."

"May not a man have several voices, Robin, as well as two complexions?" said his friend.

"Perhaps a man may; but Heaven forbid that a woman should!" responded the shrewd youth, thinking of the seductive tones of the Major's housekeeper.

The sounds of a trumpet in some neighboring street now became so evident and continual, that Robin's curiosity was strongly excited. In addition to the shouts, he heard frequent bursts from many instruments of discord, and a wild and confused laughter filled up the intervals. Robin rose from the steps, and looked wistfully towards a point whither people seemed to be hastening.

"Surely some prodigious merry-making is going on," exclaimed he. "I have laughed very little since I left home, sir, and should be sorry to lose an opportunity. Shall we step round the corner by that darkish house, and take our share of the fun?"

"Sit down again, sit down, good Robin," replied the gentleman, laying his hand on the skirt of the gray coat. "You forget that we must wait here for your kinsman; and there is reason to believe that he will pass by, in the course of a very few moments."

The near approach of the uproar had now disturbed the neighborhood; windows flew open on all sides; and many heads, in the attire of the pillow, and confused by sleep suddenly broken, were protruded to the gaze of whoever had leisure to observe them. Eager voices hailed each other from house to house, all demanding the explanation, which not a soul could give. Half-dressed men hurried towards the unknown commotion, stumbling as they went over the stone steps that thrust themselves into the narrow foot-walk. The shouts, the laughter, and the tuneless bray, the antipodes of music, came onwards with increasing din, till scattered individuals, and then denser bodies, began to appear round a corner at the distance of a hundred yards.

"Will you recognize your kinsman, if he passes in this crowd?" inquired the gentleman.

"Indeed, I can't warrant it, sir; but I'll take my stand here, and keep a bright lookout," answered Robin, descending to the outer edge of the pavement.

A mighty stream of people now emptied into the street, and came rolling slowly towards the church. A single horseman wheeled the corner in the midst of them, and close behind him came a band of fearful wind-instruments, sending forth a fresher discord now that no intervening buildings kept it from the ear. Then a redder light disturbed the moon-beams, and a dense multitude of torches shone along the street, concealing, by their glare, whatever object they illuminated. The single horseman, clad in a military dress, and bearing a drawn sword, rode onward as the leader, and, by his fierce and variegated countenance, appeared like war personified; the red of one cheek was an emblem of fire and sword; the blackness of the other betokened the mourning that attends them. In his train were wild figures in the Indian dress, and many fantastic shapes without a model, giving the whole march a visionary air, as if a dream had broken forth from some feverish brain, and were sweeping visibly through the midnight streets. A mass of people, inactive, except as applauding spectators, hemmed the procession in; and several women ran along the sidewalk, piercing the confusion of heavier sounds with their shrill voices of mirth or terror.

"The double-faced fellow has his eye upon me," muttered Robin, with an indefinite but an uncomfortable idea that he was himself to bear a part in the pageantry.

The leader turned himself in the saddle, and fixed his glance full upon the country youth, as the steed went slowly by. When Robin had freed his eyes from those fiery ones, the musicians were passing before him, and the torches were close at hand; but the unsteady brightness of the latter formed a veil which he could not penetrate. The rattling of wheels over the stones sometimes found its way to his ear, and confused traces of a human form appeared at intervals, and then melted into the vivid light. A moment more, and the leader thundered a command to halt: the trumpets vomited a horrid breath, and then held their peace; the shouts and laughter of the people died away, and there remained only a universal hum, allied to silence. Right before Robin's eyes was an uncovered cart. There the torches blazed the brightest, there the moon shone out like day, and there, in tar-and-feathery dignity, sat his kinsman, Major Molineux!

He was an elderly man, of large and majestic person, and strong, square features, betokening a steady soul; but steady as it was, his enemies had found means to shake it. His face was pale as death, and far more ghastly; the broad forehead was contracted in his agony, so that his eyebrows formed one grizzled line; his eyes were red and wild, and the foam hung white upon his quivering lip. His whole frame was agitated by a quick and continual tremor, which his pride strove to quell, even in those circumstances of overwhelming humiliation. But perhaps the bitterest pang of all was when his eyes met those of Robin; for he evidently knew him on the instant, as the youth stood witnessing the foul disgrace of a head grown gray in honor. They stared at each other in silence, and Robin's knees shook, and his hair bristled, with a mixture of pity and terror. Soon, however, a bewildering excitement began to seize upon his mind; the preceding adventures of the night, the unexpected appearance of the crowd, the torches, the confused din and the hush that followed, the spectre of his kinsman reviled by that great multitude,— all this, and, more than all, a perception of tremendous ridicule in the whole scene, affected him with a sort of mental inebriety. At that moment a voice of sluggish merriment saluted Robin's ears; he turned instinctively, and just behind the corner of the church stood the lantern-bearer, rubbing his eyes, and drowsily enjoying the lad's amazement. Then he heard a peal of laughter like the ringing of silvery bells; a woman twitched his arm, a saucy eye met his, and he saw the lady of the scarlet petticoat. A sharp, dry cachinnation appealed to his memory, and, standing on tiptoe in the crowd, with his white apron over his head, he beheld the courteous little innkeeper. And lastly, there sailed over the heads of the multitude a great, broad laugh, broken in the midst by two sepulchral hems; thus, "Haw, haw, haw,—hem, hem,—haw, haw, haw, haw!"

The sound proceeded from the balcony of the opposite edifice, and thither Robin turned his eyes. In front of the Gothic window stood the old citizen, wrapped in a wide gown, his gray periwig exchanged for a nightcap, which was thrust back from his forehead, and his silk stockings hanging about his legs. He supported himself on his polished cane in a fit of convulsive merriment, which manifested itself on his solemn old features like a funny inscription on a tombstone. Then Robin seemed to hear the voices of the barbers, of the guests of the inn, and of all who had made sport of him that night. The contagion was spreading among the multitude, when all at once, it seized upon Robin, and he sent forth a shout of laughter that echoed through the street,—every man shook his sides, every man emptied his lungs, but Robin's shout was the loudest there. The cloud-spirits peeped from their silvery islands, as the congregated mirth went roaring up the sky! The Man in the Moon heard the far bellow. "Oho," quoth he, "the old earth is frolicsome to-night!"

When there was a momentary calm in that tempestuous sea of sound, the leader gave the sign, the procession resumed its march. On they went, like fiends that throng in mockery around some dead potentate, mighty no more, but majestic still in his agony. On they went, in counterfeited pomp, in senseless uproar, in frenzied merriment, trampling all on an old man's heart. On swept the tumult, and left a silent street behind.

. . . . . . . . . .

"Well, Robin, are you dreaming?" inquired the gentleman, laying his hand on the youth's shoulder.

Robin started, and withdrew his arm from the stone post to which he had instinctively clung, as the living stream rolled by him. His cheek was somewhat pale, and his eye not quite as lively as in the earlier part of the evening.

"Will you be kind enough to show me the way to the ferry?" said he, after a moment's pause.

"You have, then, adopted a new subject of inquiry?" observed his companion, with a smile.

"Why, yes, sir," replied Robin, rather dryly. "Thanks to you, and to my other friends, I have at last met my kinsman, and he will scarce desire to see my face again. I begin to grow weary of a town life, sir. Will you show me the way to the ferry?"

"No, my good friend Robin,—not to-night, at least," said the gentleman. "Some few days hence, if you wish it, I will speed you on your journey. Or, if you prefer to remain with us, perhaps, as you are a shrewd youth, you may rise in the world without the help of your kinsman, Major Molineux."

NATHANIEL HAWTHORNE was born in 1804 in Salem, Massachusetts. He attended Bowdoin College in Maine, then returned to
Salem where for more than ten years he did little more than write
short stories, a novel, *Fanshawe* (1828), and extensive entries in
notebooks. His work brought little notice and less money, and he
took a job at a Boston customs house for two years, then partici-
pated briefly at Brook Farm, a Utopian experiment influenced by
the ideas of Robert Owen. In 1842, he married Sophia Peabody
and moved to Concord, where he wrote *Mosses from an Old Manse*.
Still pressed for money and with a growing family, he went to
work at the Salem customs house, but resigned after two years and
within a year completed *The Scarlet Letter*. His fame grew with
the publication of *The House of Seven Gables, The Blithedale Romance* (based on Brook Farm), several collections of short stories,
and *The Life of Franklin Pierce*.

After Pierce, a close college friend of Hawthorne's, was elected
President of the United States in 1852, Hawthorne was appointed
consul at Liverpool. He held the position for four years, then lived
in England and Italy for another four years while writing *The
Marble Fawn*, which appeared in 1860, the year the family returned to America, where Hawthorne continued to write until his
death in 1864.

# MODERN LIBRARY GIANTS

*A series of sturdily bound and handsomely printed, full-sized library editions of books formerly available only in expensive sets. These volumes contain from 600 to 1,400 pages each.*

THE MODERN LIBRARY GIANTS REPRESENT A
SELECTION OF THE WORLD'S GREATEST BOOKS